BEWARE—
THEY'RE SENDING IN THE AUNTS!

"I found Brun and Sirkin," Cecelia informed Heris. "We're all safe." The following pause was eloquent; even over an audio-only link Cecelia could easily imagine Heris searching for a telling phrase.

"You're not *safe*," Heris said finally. "You're square in the midst of a military action. This system is under attack by the Benignity; their ships are in the outer system now, and I need that yacht and its weapons . . . not three useless civilians who were *supposed* to be down on the surface digging in."

Anger flared. "Civilians aren't *always* useless. If you can remember that far back, one of them saved your life on Sirialis."

"True. I'm sorry. It just . . . the question is, what now? I can't get you to safety onplanet . . . . if that's safe."

"So quit worrying about it. Do you think I'm worried about dying?"

"I . . . you just got rejuved."

"So I did. It didn't eliminate my eighty-odd years of experience, or make me timid. If I die, I die . . . but in the meantime, why not let me help?"

A chuckle. She could imagine Heris's face. "Lady Cecelia, you are inimitable. Get yourself up to the bridge; someone will find you a place. I'll let the commander know you're coming."

"Good hunting, Heris," Cecelia said. She felt a pleasant tingle of anticipation.

Baen Books by Elizabeth Moon

Sheepfarmer's Daughter
Divided Allegiance
Oath of Gold
The Deed of Paksenarrion
Liar's Oath
The Legacy of Gird

Hunting Party
Sporting Chance
Winning Colors
Once a Hero
Rules of Engagement
Change of Command
Against the Odds

Remnant Population

Sassinak
(with Anne McCaffrey)
Generation Warriors
(with Anne McCaffrey)
The Planet Pirates
(with Anne McCaffrey & Jody Lynn Nye)

Phases

HERIS SERRANO

ELIZABETH MOON

HERIS SERRANO

This is a work of fiction. All the characters and events portrayed in this book are fictional, and any resemblance to real people or incidents is purely coincidental.

A Baen Books Original Omnibus

Baen Publishing Enterprises
P.O. Box 1403
Riverdale, NY 10471
www.baen.com

ISBN: 0-7434-3552-4

Cover art by Gary Ruddell

First printing, August 2002

Library of Congress Cataloging-in-Publication Data

Moon, Elizabeth.
    Heris Serrano / by Elizabeth Moon.
        p. cm.
    "Heris Serrano has been previously published in parts as Hunting party, Sporting chance and Winning colors."
    ISBN 0-7434-3552-4 (pbk)
    1. Science fiction, American. 2. Serrano, Heris (Ficticious character)—Fiction.
3. Women in astronautics—Fiction. 4. Life on other planets—Fiction.
5. Interstellar travel—Fiction. 6. Space ships—Fiction. I. Title.

PS3563.O557 H47 2002
813'.54—dc21   2002023203

Distributed by Simon & Schuster
1230 Avenue of the Americas
New York, NY 10020

Production by Windhaven Press, Auburn, NH
Printed in the United States of America

10 9 8 7 6 5 4 3 2 1

CONTENTS

HERIS SERRANO

HUNTING PARTY

Acknowledgements

Thanks to those who encourged this project: Alexis and Laurie, who began the chase by saying, "Why *not* fox hunting and spaceships?"; Margaret, who helped retrieve scattered bits after the great computer crash; the several patient friends who read drafts and pointed out logic problems; my husband Richard, who prefers new chapters to hot meals and a neat house; my son Michael, who has finally learned to leave me alone until the oven timer buzzes (as long as it's not more than fifteen minutes). The good people at Vic's Grocery—Vic, Martha, John, Debbie, and Penny— whose interest and support keep the absentminded writer from forgetting milk, bread, and other necessities of life—with special thanks this time to Vic Kysor, Jr., who in a conversation across the meat counter in his father's grocery store created a character and solved a problem for me. Of course the remaining flaws are my fault—even the best helpers can't do it all.

CHAPTER ONE

Heris Serrano went from her room in the small but respectable dockside hotel on Rockhouse Station to the berth of her new command convinced that she looked like an idiot. No one laughed aloud, but that only meant the bystanders had chosen to snicker later rather than risk immediate confrontation with an ex-Regular Space Services officer on the beach.

Heris kept her eyes away from any of those who might be contemplating humor, the dockside traffic of the commercial district. Her ears burned; she could feel the glances raking her back. She would not have changed her military posture even if she could have walked any other way; she had been R.S.S. from birth or before, daughter of officers, admirals' granddaughter and niece, a service family for all the generations anyone bothered to count. Even that miserable first year at the Academy had seemed familiar, almost homey: she had heard the stories from parents, uncles, aunts, all her life.

And here she was, tricked out in enough gold braid and color to satisfy a planet-bound admiral from one of the minor principalities, all because of the whims of a rich old woman with more money than sense. They had to be laughing behind her back, those merchanter officers and crewmen who didn't meet her eyes, who went about their business as if purple and scarlet were normal uniform colors, as if two sleeves covered with gold rings didn't look ridiculous, as if the rim of gold and green striped cord around collar, lapels, and cuffs didn't tell everyone that an R.S.S. officer had descended to the level of carting wealthy eccentrics on pleasure jaunts in something far more like a mansion than a spacefaring ship.

Commercial dockside ended abruptly at a scarred gray wall with a lockgate in it. Heris inserted her card; the barred gate slid aside, then closed behind her, leaving her caged between the bars behind and a steel door with a thick window. Another keyslot, this time her card produced a human door-opener, who swung the door aside and held out his hand for her papers. She handed over the neat packet civilian life required. Master's license, certifications in five specialties, Imperial ID, military record (abbreviated; only the unclassified bones), letters of recommendation, and— what mattered most here—Lady Cecelia de Marktos's seal of employment. The human—Station Security or Garond Family, Heris did not know which—ran a handscanner over this last, and replaced the entire pile in its file cover before handing it back to her.

"Welcome to North, Captain Serrano," the man said, with no inflection of sarcasm. "May I be of assistance?"

Her throat closed a moment, remembering the words she would have heard if she had gone through a similar lockgate on the other side of the commercial docks, where sleek gray R.S.S. cruisers nuzzled the Station side by side. Where her gray uniform with its glowing insignia would have received crisp salutes, and the welcome due a comrade in arms. "Welcome to the Fleet," she would have heard, a greeting used anywhere, anytime, they came together away from civilians. But she could not go back there, back where her entire past would wrap around her. She had resigned her commission. She would never hear those words again.

"No, thank you," she said quietly. "I know where the ship is." She would not say its name yet, though it was her new command. . . . She had grown up with ships named for battles, for monsters, for older ships with long histories. She could not yet say she commanded *Sweet Delight.*

North, on all Stations, defined the environs of aristocracy. Wealth and privilege could be found anywhere, in the R.S.S. as well as the commercial docks, but always near some-thing. Here was nothing but wealth, and its servants. This deck had carpeted walkways, not extruded plastic sheeting;

the shops had no signs, only house emblems. Each docking bay had its own lockgate, enclosing two large rooms: one marked "Service Entrance," lined with racks and shelving for provisions delivered, and the other furnished luxuriously as a reception salon for going-away parties. Heris's card in the slot produced another human door-opener, this time a servant in livery, who ushered her into the salon. Heris made her way between overstuffed sofas and chairs covered in lavender plush and piled with pillows in garish colors, between low black tables and pedestals supporting what were probably priceless works of art, though to her eye, they looked like globs of melted space debris after a battle.

The actual docking tube lay unguarded. Heris frowned. Surely even civilians had someone watching the ship's main hatch, even with the security of a lockgate on the dock itself. She paused before stepping over the line that made the legal division between dock and ship. The lavender plush lining of the access tube hid all the vital umbilicals that connected the ship to Station life support. Unsafe, Heris thought, as she had thought on her earlier interview visit. Those lines should be visible. Surely even civilians had regulations to follow.

Underfoot, the lavender plush carpet felt five centimeters thick. A warm breath of air puffed out of the ship itself, a warm breath flavored not with the spice she remembered from the interview, but with the sour stench of the morning after a very large night before. Her nose wrinkled; she could feel her back stiffening. It might be someone else's ship *in principle,* but she did not allow a dirty mess on any ship she commanded—and would not now. She came out of the access tube into a family row; the tube's privacy shield had kept her from hearing it until she stepped across the barrier. Heris took in the situation at a glance. One tall, angular, gray-haired woman with a loud voice: her employer. Three sulky, overdressed young men that Heris would not have had on her ship, and their obvious girlfriends . . . all rumpled, and one still passed out on a lavender couch that matched the plush carpet and walls. Streaks of vomit stained its smooth velour. As she came through the barrier, the chestnut-haired youth with the ruffled shirt answered a final blast from the older woman with a whined "But, Aunt Cecelia—it's not *fair.*"

What was "not fair" was that rich spoiled brats like him hadn't had the nonsense taken out of them in boot camp, Heris thought. She smiled her normal good-morning-bridge smile at her employer and said, "Good morning, milady."

The youths—all but the unconscious snorer on the couch—stared; Heris could feel her ears going hot and ignored them, still smiling at Cecelia Artemisia Veronica Penelope, heiress of more titles than anyone needed, let alone more money. "Ah," said that lady, restored to instant unruffled calm by the appearance of someone to whom it meant something. "Captain Serrano. How nice to have you aboard. Our departure will be delayed, but only briefly"—here she looked at the chestnut-haired youth—"until my nephew is settled. I presume your things are already aboard?"

"Sent ahead, milady," Heris said.

"Good. Then Bates will show you to your quarters." Bates materialized from some angle of corridor and nodded at Heris. Heris wondered if she would be introduced to the nephew now or later; she was sure she could take that pout from his lips if given the chance. But she wouldn't get the chance. She followed Bates—tall, elegant, so much the butler of the screen and stage it was hard to believe him real—down the carpeted passage to her suite. She would rather have gone to the bridge. Not this bridge, but the bridge of the *Rapier* or even a lowly maintenance tug.

Bates stood aside at her door. "If the captain wishes to rekey the locks now . . . ?"

She looked at that impassive face. Did he mean to imply that they had thieves on board? That someone might violate the privacy of her quarters? The *captain's* quarters? She had thought she knew how far down the scale she'd fallen, to become a rich lady's yacht captain, but she had not conceived of needing to lock her quarters. "Thank you," she said, as if it had been her idea. Bates touched a magnetic wand to the lockfaces; she put her hand on each one. After a moment, the doorcall's pleasant anonymous voice said, "Name, please?" and she gave her name; the doorcall chimed once and said, "Welcome home, Captain Serrano." Bates handed her a fat ring of wands.

"These are the rekeying wands for ship's crew and all the operating compartments. They're all coded; you'll find the full architectural schematics loaded on your desk display.

The crew will await your arrival on the bridge, at your convenience."

She didn't even know if she could ask Bates to tell the crew when to expect her, or if that was something household staff never did. She had already discovered that the house staff and the ship crew had very little to do with each other.

"I could just pass the word to Mr. Gavin, the engineer," Bates said, almost apologetically. "Since Captain Olin left"— Captain Olin, Heris knew, had been fired—"Lady Cecelia has often asked me to speak to Mr. Gavin."

"Thank you," Heris said. "One hour." She glanced at the room's chronometer, a civilian model which she would replace with the one in her luggage.

"Philip will escort you," Bates said.

She opened her mouth to say it was not necessary—even in this perfumed and padded travesty of a ship she could find the bridge by herself—but instead said, "Thank you" once more. She would not challenge their assumptions yet.

Her master's certificate went into the mounting plaque on the wall; her other papers went into the desk. Her luggage—she had asked that it not be unpacked—cluttered one corner of her office. Beyond that was a smaller room, then the bathroom—her mouth quirked as she forced herself to call it that. And beyond that, her bedroom. A cubage larger than an admiral would have on most ships, and far larger than anyone of her rank ever had, even on a Station. A suite, part of the price being paid to lure a real spacer, a real captain, into this kind of work.

In the hour she had unpacked her few necessary clothes, her books, her reference data cubes, and made sure that the desk display would handle them. The chronometer on the wall now showed Service Standard time as well as ship's time and Station time, and had the familiar overlapping segments of color to delineate four-, six-, and eight-hour watches. She had reviewed the crew bios in the desk display. And she had shrugged away her regrets. It was all over now, all those years of service, all her family's traditions; from now on, she was Heris Serrano, captain of a yacht, and she would make the best of it.

And they wouldn't know what hit them.

* * *

Some of them suspected within moments of her arrival on the bridge. Whatever decorator had chosen all the lavender and teal furnishings of the rest of the ship, the bridge remained functional, if almost toylike in its bright, shiny, compactness. The crew had to squeeze in uncomfortably; Heris noticed who squeezed in next to whom, and who wished this were over. They had heard, no doubt. They could see what they could see; she might be wearing purple and scarlet, but she had the look, and knew she had it; all those generations of command came out her eyes.

She met theirs. Blue, gray, brown, black, green, hazel: clear, hazy, worried, frightened, challenging. Mr. Gavin, the engineer—thin, almost wispy, and graying—had announced, "Captain on the bridge" in a voice that squeaked. Navigation First, all too perky, was female, and young, and standing close to Communications First, who had spots and the slightly adenoidal look that Heris had found in the best comm techs on any ship. The moles—environmental techs, so-called everywhere from their need to crawl through pipes—glowered at the back. They must have suspected she'd seen the ship's records already. Moles never believed that strange smells in the air were their fault; they were convinced that other people, careless people, put the wrong things down the wrong pipe and caused the trouble. Gavin's junior engineering techs, distancing themselves from the moles, tried to look squeaky-clean and bright. Heris had read their records; one of them had failed the third-class certificate four times. The other juniors—Navigation's sour-faced paunchy male and Communications' wispy female—were clearly picked up at bargain rates for off-primeshift work.

Heris began, as always on a new ship, with generalities. Let them relax; let them realize she wasn't stupid, crazy, or vicious. Then . . . "Now about emergency drills," she said, when she'd seen the relaxation. "I see you've had no drills since docking here. Why is that, Mr. Gavin?"

"Well, Captain . . . after Captain Olin left, I didn't like to seem—you know—like I was taking liberties above my station."

"I see. And before that, I notice that there had been no drills since the last planetfall. That was Captain Olin's decision, I suppose." From Gavin's expression, that was not the reason, but he went along gratefully.

"Yes, Captain, that would be it. He was the captain, after all." Someone stirred, in the back, but they were so crammed together she couldn't be sure who it was. She would find out. She smiled at them, suddenly happy. It might be only a yacht, but it was a ship, and it was *her* ship.

"We will have drills," she said, and waited a moment for that to sink in. "Emergency drills save lives. I expect all you Firsts to ready your divisions."

"We surely can't have time for a drill before launch!" That was the sour-faced Navigation Second. She stared at him until he blushed and said, "Captain . . . sorry, ma'am."

"It depends," she said, without commenting on his breach of manners. "I know you're all readying for launch, but I would like a word here with the pilot and Nav First."

They edged out of the cramped space; she knew the muttering would start as soon as they cleared the hatch. Ignoring that, she fixed the Navigation First with a firm glance. "Sirkin, isn't it?"

"Yes, Captain." Brisk, bright-eyed . . . Heris hoped she was as good as she looked. "Brigdis Sirkin, Lalos Colony."

"Yes, I saw your file. Impressive qualification exam." Sirkin had topped the list with a perfect score, rare even in R.S.S. trained personnel. The younger woman blushed and grinned. "But what I want to know is whether you plotted the final approach from Dunlin to here." The way she said it could lead either way; she wanted to see Sirkin's reaction.

A deeper blush. "No, Captain. I didn't . . . not entirely, that is."

"Umm. I wondered why someone who'd swept the exam would choose such an inefficient solution. Tell me about it."

"Well . . . ma'am . . . Captain Olin was a good captain, and I'm not saying anything against him, but he liked to . . . to do things a certain way."

Heris glanced at the pilot. Plisson, his tag said; he had been another rich lady's pilot before he came here. "Did you have anything to do with it?" she asked.

The pilot shot Sirkin an angry glance. "She thinks she can shave time to the bone," he said. "It's like she never heard of flux-storms. I guess you could call it efficient, if you're on a warship, but I wasn't hired to kill milady."

"Ah. So you thought Sirkin's original course dangerous, and Captain Olin backed you?"

"Well . . . yes. Captain. And I expect you'll stick with her, being as you're spacefleet trained."

Heris grinned at him; his jaw sagged in surprise. "I don't like getting smeared across space any better than anyone else," she said. "But I've reviewed Sirkin's work only as combined with yours and Captain Olin's. Sirkin, what was your original course here?"

"It's in the NavComp, Captain; shall I direct it to your desktop?"

"If you please. I'll look it over, see if I think you're dangerous or not. Did you ever have any spacefleet time, Plisson?"

"No, Captain." The way he said it, he considered it worse than downside duty. She wasn't sure she wanted a half-hearted first pilot.

"Then I suggest you withdraw your judgment of R.S.S. operations until you see some. War is dangerous enough without adding recklessness to it; I'll expect professional performance from both you and Navigator Sirkin." She turned to go, then turned back, surprising on their faces the expression she had hoped to find. "And by the way, you may expect drills; space is less forgiving than I am of sloppy technique."

Lady Cecelia noticed the shadow in the tube only a moment before her new captain came aboard. She could have wished for less promptness. She would have preferred to finish reaming out her nephew and the residue of his going-away party in the decent privacy afforded by her household staff. Bates knew better than to stick his nose in at a time like this.

But the woman was ex-military, and not very ex- by her carriage and expression. Of course she would not be late; even her hair and toenails probably grew on schedule. Cecelia wanted to throttle the condescension off the dark face that rose serene above the purple and scarlet uniform. No doubt she had no nephews, or if she did they were being lovingly brought up in boot camp somewhere. She probably thought it would be easy to remake Ronnie and his set. Whereas Cecelia had known, from the moment of Ronnie's birth, that he was destined to be a spoiled brat. Charming, bright enough if he bothered, handsome to the point of dangerousness with that thick wavy chestnut hair, those hazel eyes, that remaining dimple—but spoiled rotten by his family and everyone else.

"But it's not *fair*," he whined now. He had expected her to let them all travel with him, all twenty or so of his favorites among his fellow officers and their sweethearts of both sexes. She ignored that, smiled at her new captain, thinking, *Don't you dare laugh at me, you little blot,* and called Bates to take the captain to her quarters. And away she went, impossibly bright-eyed for this hour of the morning (no adolescent partying had disturbed *her* sleep), her trim figure making the girls in the room look like haggard barflies. Which they weren't, really. It was terrible what girls did these days, but these were decent girls, of reasonably nice families. Nothing like hers, or Ronnie's (except Bubbles, the snoring one, and the present cause of dissension), but nice enough.

With a last glance at the captain's retreating form, she turned back to Ronnie. "What is not fair, young man, is that you are intruding on *my* life, taking up space on my yacht, making my staff work harder, and all because you lacked the common sense to keep your mouth shut about things which no gentleman discusses."

Sulky. He had been sulky at one, at two; his parents had doted on his adorable tantrums, his big lower lip. He was sulky now, and she did not dote on the lip or the tongue behind it. "She said I was better. It's not fair that I'm getting sent away, when she's the one who said it. She wanted to be with me—"

"She said it to you, in the confidence of the bedroom." Surely someone had already told him this. Why should she have to explain? "And you don't even know if she *meant* it, or if she says it to everyone."

"Of course she meant it!" Young male pride, stung, flushed his cheeks and drove sulkiness into temper. "I *am* better."

"I won't argue," Cecelia said. "I will only remind you that you may be better in bed with the prince's favorite singer, but you are now on my yacht, by order of your father and the king, and the singer is stuck with the prince." Her pun got through to her a moment before Ronnie caught it, and she shook her finger at him. "Literally and figuratively: you're here, and he's there, and you've gained nothing by blabbing except whatever momentary amusement you shared with your barracks-mates." He chuckled, and the odious George—who had well earned the nickname everyone in society knew—snickered. Cecelia knew the odious George's father fairly well, and dismissed the snicker as an unconscious copy of his father's courtroom manner. She supposed it went over well in the junior mess of the Royal Space Service, where the young sprouts of aristocracy and wealth flaunted their boughten commissions in the intervals of leave and training. "You're the one who talked," she said, ignoring the side glances of her nephew and his crony. "The . . . er . . . lady didn't. Therefore you are in trouble, and you are sent away, and it's my misfortune that I happened to be near enough to serve your father's purpose." He opened his mouth to say something else she was sure she would not want to hear, and she went on, inexorably. "It's better than it could have been, young Ronald, as you will see when you quit feeling sorry for yourself. And I am stretching my generosity to let you bring these"—she waved her hand at the others—"when it crowds my ship and wastes my time. If it weren't that Bubbles and Buttons were going to Bunny's anyway—"

"Well—in fact they don't want to go—"

"Nonsense. I've already sent word I'm bringing them. A season in the field will do you all immense good." She gave him another lengthy stare. "And I don't want any of you sneaking offship to cause trouble on the Station before we launch. It's bad enough having to wait for your luggage; I shall have your father pay the reset fees for changing the launch schedule. I hope he takes it out of your allowance."

"But that's not—" She held up her hand before "fair" could emerge and decided to drop her own bombshell now.

"And by the way, my new captain is ex-*Regular* Space Service, so don't try any of your tricks with *her*. She could probably tie you all in knots without trying." Cecelia turned on her heel and walked out, satisfied that she had given them something besides her hard-heartedness to think about.

It was too bad, really. She lived on her yacht precisely so as to avoid family complications, just as she had avoided marriage and political service. They could have found some other way to keep Ronnie out of the capital for a year or so. They didn't have to use her, as if she were a handy piece of furniture. But that was Berenice all over again: big sisters existed to be of service to the beauty of the family.

Stores. She would have to check with Bates to be sure they had ordered enough additional food—after last night, she suspected they might need more. Young people did *eat* so, when they ate. She reached her own suite with relief. That miserable decorator Berenice had sent her to insisted on doing the whole ship in lavender and teal, with touches of acid green and cream, but she had not let him in here. Perhaps the young people did prefer lavender plush, but she hated it. Here in her own rooms, she could have it her way. Brighter colors, polished wood, carved chairs piled with pillows.

She paused at her desk. Inlaid wood made a pattern of vines and flowers; until she pressed the central blossom, it could have passed for an antique of Old Earth. The desktop cleared, showing the floorplan of that deck, with ghostly shadows of the others. A cluster of dots showed Ronnie and friends, back in the lounge. A dot in her bedroom; that would be Myrtis, her maid. A dot for the captain, in her quarters; a moving dot that must be Bates, coming back. She touched her finger to that one, and his voice came out of the desk speaker.

"Yes, madam?"

"Have Cook check the quantities Ronnie and his friends consumed last night; they seem to eat quite a lot. . . ."

"Cook has estimated an additional fifteen percent over your orders yesterday, madam, and has the purchase order ready for your stamp."

"Thank you, Bates." She might have known. They were usually two steps ahead of her—but that was their duty. She flicked up the lower service deck on the display, found Cook's dot, and touched it. Cook transferred the purchase order to her desktop, and she looked at it. Even with six additional people aboard, it looked like enough to feed them all three times over. It would serve them right, she thought, if she made them eat survival rations until they got to Bunny's. Certainly it would cost less and take up less room. Cook had pointed out that they'd need to air up two more refrigeration units and set out another full section of 'ponics.

That would start another argument between crewside and staffside. The environmental techs were ship's crew, under

the captain's command; Cecelia knew better than to interfere with her captain's crew. But that part of 'ponics
devoted to the kitchen came under the heading of "gardening," which meant staff—her staff. Felix, head gardener, and
two boys (one female), kept her private solarium in fresh
flowers and Cook supplied with fresh vegetables. Felix and
the environmental techs always got into some hassle which
required her decision—one of the things she had not liked
about her former captain was his tendency to let things slide
until she had to quell an incipient riot in staff.

She found Felix's icon, touched it, and told him about
the 'ponics section. He wanted to use half of it for a new
set of exotics he'd bought seedstock for; the pictures of the
so-called vegetables didn't impress her. Felix insisted, though,
that if he could have seed available when they arrived at
Bunny's, he could trade with Bunny's ferocious head gardener
for her favorite (and rarest) mushrooms. Cecelia shrugged;
Ronnie and his pals could eat the things she didn't like.

"And what you tell the moles, eh?" he said finally, having
won his main point. "You got to let them know it's okay,
whatever I grow."

"I will tell Captain Serrano, our new captain, that I've
approved your use of an additional 'ponics section for fresh
produce."

"They bother me, I'll send 'em the halobeets," Felix said.
He would, too. He had done it before, when displeased with
someone. A genius of his type—but like most such geniuses,
a trifle tempery. She put up with him for the luscious fruits
and fresh vegetables, the abundant flowers, which so amazed
those who came to dinner. . . . No other yacht she knew
of was completely self-sufficient in fresh produce.

She looked again for the captain's icon, and found it
moving toward the bridge. Best not interrupt her now; she
would have had the crew assembled. Cecelia's finger hovered over the control. . . . She could easily listen in on
the captain's first briefing . . . but she decided against it.
Instead, she routed a message to the captain's desk about
the 'ponics, and called up a credit status.

The figures meant little to her; the reality was that she could
afford to buy anything for sale on Rockhouse two or three
times over. The desktop offered a bright-colored graphic which
showed how much more she was spending to transport herself

and six young people compared to herself alone. It didn't matter, and Berenice had transferred stock to cover it anyway. She called up Ronnie's status, and pursed her lips. Berenice had put him on the silver family line, and he had already used it. Hardin's Clothiers, Vetris Accessories, Spaulding . . . Cecelia whistled. He had started with two cubes of storage, and at this rate would need another two.

Her desk chimed. "Aunt Cecelia?" came the plaintive voice. "Please—I need to talk to you."

Hardly, she thought. He needed to *listen* to her. "Ah, Ronnie. Very good—I meant to ask you, did you bring your hunting tackle?"

"My . . . uh . . . what?"

"Your riding clothes, your saddles—"

"I—*no!* Of course not. Aunt Cecelia, just because you're crazy enough to ride big stupid animals across rocks and mud—"

"I presumed," said Cecelia, overriding his voice with a surge of glee, "that that was your rather large order at Hardin's and Vetris's and Spaulding's. But since it wasn't, perhaps you'd return some of that foppery, whatever it was, and get yourself some decent riding kit. We are going to Bunny's, as you know, for the season, and since I'm saddled with you, you might as well saddle a horse and learn something useful." She felt good about the pun; puns usually came to her four hours too late, if at all.

The fashion in invective, she was happy to discover, had swung once more from the rough crudities copied from the lower classes to an entertaining polysyllabic baroque style. When Ronnie ran out of breath (which happened more quickly, she noted, with the longer words and phrases), she interrupted again, before he could start another rampage.

"I do not care that you do not like horses, or riding, or that none of your set consider hunting a reasonable or enjoyable pastime. I do not care if you are miserable for the entire year of your exile. You may sulk in your cabin if you like—you will certainly not sulk in mine, or interfere with my pleasure one bit more than I can help. And if you do not order yourself the proper clothes, saddles, and so on, I shall do it for you and charge it to your account." Although it would really make sense to wait until they were at Bunny's—all the really good saddlers came there for the season. But her blood was up. So, it seemed, was his. She could order what she liked, he said angrily, but he was not about to pretend to copy the amusements of a horse-faced old spinster with more money than sense, and he would be damned if she ever found him on a horse chasing some innocent helpless animal across the dripping fields.

"If you think the fox is either innocent or helpless, young Ronald, you are more foolish than I think." She was not sure which of them broke the connection. She did not care. She called her personal assistant at Spaulding's and arranged everything as she wished—of course they knew all his measurements already, and of course they were happy to help a wealthy aunt surprise an almost-as-wealthy nephew. In a final burst of pique, she put the bill on her own account, and not Berenice's. . . . She wanted no questions from the doting mother who had let the brat become so useless.

CHAPTER TWO

Heris led the way into her cabin, wondering if civilians had any concept of shipboard courtesy. Would they know enough to stay on their side of the office? Sirkin did; she stood across the desk as Heris called up the files on the desk display, looking young and earnest.

She looked at the course Sirkin had originally planned. Direct, reasonable flux levels, no abrupt course changes, adequate clearance of the mapped obstacles. It was close to the course she would have selected, although R.S.S. ships could and did shave the clearance margins in the interest of speed.

"And Captain Olin disapproved this course? Why?"

"He said it was too risky. Here—" Sirkin laid her finger on the display, and it enlarged to show finer detail. "He claimed that coming this close to T-77 with a flux of 0.06 was suicidal. I asked him why, and he said he was captain and I'd learn better in time."

"Hmm." Heris leaned over the display. "Did you look up T-77 in the reference library?"

"Yes, ma'am." Heris looked up at the younger woman— then remembered that it might be legitimate civilian usage. The R.S.S. used "sir" for either sex—it meant respect, not recognition of one's chromosome type. Sirkin seemed respectful and attentive. "Baird and Logan said that T-77 is a gravitational anomaly, nothing more. Ciro speculates that it's a burnt-out star. But all the references agree that it's not as dangerous as Gumma's Tangle, and it's perfectly safe to

17

transit that at a flux of 0.2. I *was* being conservative." That
had the bite of old resentment. Heris shook her head.

"Captain Olin must have had some reason. Your relative
velocity would have been quite low, there—did you suggest
boosting your flux and achieving a higher V?"

"No, ma'am. He said it was dangerous at 0.06; boosting
the flux would make it worse—"

"If he meant a flux/mass interaction. That's not the only
danger out there." She chewed her lip, thinking. She hadn't
been in that area for a long time; she wished she had access
to R.S.S. charts and intelligence data.

"But why didn't he say so?" Sirkin had flushed, which
made her look even younger. "I could have redone it for
a higher flux—"

"He didn't want to go anywhere near T-77," Heris said.
"Let's see what else he didn't want to go near." She looked
at the rest of Sirkin's course, comparing it to Olin's, and
calling up references when needed. Slowly, she felt her way
into Olin's logic. "He didn't want to go near any of the low-
danger obstacles, did he? Made you go clear around Cumber's
Finger, instead of taking that short Wedding Ring hop—and
that's a safe hop everyone takes. Made you wander over
here—and why?" She looked up, to meet the same confusion in Sirkin's expression. "Did Lady Cecelia have a preferred arrival time? Did she ask him to be here on a certain
day?"

Sirkin nodded. "She had wanted to be here eight days
before we arrived, for some kind of family party. Olin told
her he couldn't make it; it's one reason she wanted a new
captain. She said he was too slow."

"You heard her?" Heris let her brows rise.

Sirkin turned red. "Well . . . I overheard it. I mean, Tonni
over on the staff side, he told Engineering, and Mr. Gavin
told me."

"Staff side . . ." Heris said.

"You know. There's the household staff, with Bates on
top, and there's the ship's crew, with the captain—with you—
on top. We're not supposed to mix much, but at certain
levels we have to. Our moles are always getting into rows
with milady's gardeners."

Heris felt she'd fallen into a farce of some kind. Gardeners
aboard ship? But she couldn't let this young woman sense

her confusion. "When we say 'staff,' we mean non-line officers," she said, as if it had been a confusion of terms.

"Oh." Sirkin clearly had no idea what that meant, and Heris let it pass. Far more important was getting this ship ready to travel. She could ask Sirkin, but she should learn more about the rest of the crew, and inspections would do just that. She looked back at Olin's chosen route and shook her head.

"I wonder . . . it's as if he knew something about these areas not listed in the references." She wondered what. There were always rumors about "robbers' coasts" and "pirate dens" to excuse ships that showed up late or missing cargo. But those were just rumors . . . weren't they? Olin had chosen to skirt more dangerous—according to the references—points more closely; he had shaved past T-89 inside the line she'd have taken with a cruiser. Of course a cruiser massed more. Slow on the first leg of the trip, hanging about for a long time . . . then racing through the middle section, direct and sure . . . then dodging about again at the end. Smuggling came to mind, but she controlled her expression. Later she could figure out what, and with whom, Captain Olin had been smuggling.

"And you're the newest crew member? What made you decide on this job rather than another?"

Sirkin blushed. "Well . . . it was a . . . friend of mine." From the blush and tone of voice, a lover. Heris looked again: blue eyes, brown hair, slender, unremarkable face. Just very young, and very emotional.

"Aboard this ship?" She kept her fingers crossed.

"No, ma'am. She's back at school—a third-year in ship systems maintenance. If I'd signed with a corporate ship, they'd have expected me to stay with them forever." Not really forever, Heris knew, but to the young even the basic five- and ten-year contracts sounded permanent. "When she graduates— she's not exactly at the top of her class—we wanted to be together, same ship or at least same company. . . ."

"So this is a temporary, until she graduates?"

"Yes, ma'am. But I'm not treating it any less seriously." That in the earnest tone of the very young. Heris allowed herself to smile.

"I should hope not. When are you planning to leave Lady Cecelia?"

"It depends, really. She'll graduate while we're at that fox-hunting place—at Sirialis, I mean." Sirkin's fingers twitched. "Lady Cecelia expects to get back to the Cassian System about six local months after that, and she won't take offplanet work until she hears from me."

You hope, thought Heris. She'd seen more than one juvenile romance collapse when a partner was offplanet for a year or more. "You'll have to keep your mind on your duties," she said. "It's natural to worry about her, but—"

"Oh, I don't worry about her," Sirkin said. "She can take care of herself. And I won't be distracted."

Heris nodded, hoping they hadn't sworn vows of exclusion or anything silly like that. Those were the ones who invariably got an earnest message cube at the next port, with the defaulting lover explaining what happened at excruciating length. In her experience, it always happened to the best of the younglings in her crew. "Good. Now, I plan to have the crew cross-train in other disciplines—would you prefer another bridge assignment, or something more hands-on?"

Sirkin grinned, and Heris was almost afraid she'd say *How fun*—but she didn't. "Anything you wish, Captain. I had two semesters of drive theory and one of maintenance, but I also had a double minor in Communications and computer theory." *Very* bright girl, if she'd topped out in her nav classes and done that as well. Heris approved.

"We'll try you in communications and the more practical side of shipboard computing systems, then. That should keep you busy enough."

"Yes, ma'am."

"That's all, then." With a last respectful nod, Sirkin left. No salute. Heris refused to give in to the wave of nostalgia she felt; she shrugged it away physically and drew a deep steady breath. No more salutes, no more old friends she could call on to find out, for example, what was known about the members of her new crew. She might have that later, as she made friends in the Captains Guild, but not now.

And at the moment, that was her most pressing need: knowledge. According to the ship's record, all the crew but one had been supplied by the same employment agency. A good one: she had chosen to sign with them herself because of their reputation; they supplied crew to major commercial lines and trading corporations. Lady Cecelia was part of an important family; surely they were not sending her their dregs. . . . Yet she had the feeling that at least half these people were below average. She hadn't expected that, not with the wages Lady Cecelia had offered her, and was paying the crew. She should have gotten more for her money. Sirkin was the only really top qualifier, just going by their records—which she didn't. Records only told so much.

She punched up the local office of Usmerdanz, and worked her way up the levels until she found someone she could really talk to. "Captain Serrano . . . yes." The owner of that silky voice had found her reference in the file, she could tell. "We . . . ah . . . placed you with Lady Cecelia—"

"Yes," she said, interrupting. "I notice that Usmerdanz also placed other crew members, and I was wondering if you could give me some details."

"All pertinent details *should* be in the ship files," the voice said, with an edge as if a knife lay under the silk. From their point of view, *she* was the unknown quantity; she had been on their list less than a month, and there would always be questions about someone of her rank who resigned a commission without explanation. "Surely Captain Olin left the files open-keyed . . ."

"I've accessed the ship files," Heris said. "But I find nothing equivalent to our—to the Space Service's fitness reports. Are periodic evaluations handled by the captain aboard or . . . ?"

"Oh." The knife edge receded behind the silk again. "Well . . . there's no established schedule, not really. In the commercial ships, of course, there's always some sort of corporate policy, but not on private yachts. Usually the captain keeps some sort of reports. You found nothing?"

"Nothing," Heris said. "Just the data that might have been in the original applications. I thought perhaps you—"

"Oh, no." The voice interrupted her this time. "We don't keep track of that sort of thing at all." Far from it, the tone said. After all, one could hardly recommend someone known to have problems on a previous vessel; best not to know. Heris had known Service people with the same attitude. "If there's nothing in the ship files," the voice went on, "then I'm afraid we can't help you. We could supply incomplete data on education, background—but nothing more than that. Sorry . . ."

Before the silken-voiced supervisor could disconnect, Heris asked a quick question. "How do you choose which to recommend to which employers?" A long silence followed.

"How do we *what?*" No silk remained; the voice sounded angry.

"I noticed that only Sirkin—the newest crew member— ranked particularly high in her class, and she's told me she was looking for a short-term job on a yacht for personal reasons. The others generally rank in the middle quartiles. Yet Lady Cecelia's paying top wages; I wondered why you weren't recommending these positions to your most qualified applicants."

"Are you accusing us," the voice said, all steel edge now, "of sending Lady Cecelia unqualified crew members?"

"Not at all," said Heris, although she suspected exactly that. "But you aren't sending her your cream, are you?"

"We sent *you*," the voice replied.

"Exactly," Heris said. "I know I'm not on the top of your list of captains . . . and I shouldn't be." As she had hoped, that admission soothed some of the anger in the voice on the com.

"Well. That's true. I suppose." Heris waited through some audible huffing and muttering, and then the voice went on. "It's like this, Captain Serrano. There's good people—qualified people—who aren't right for every opening. You know what I mean; surely you had people even in the R.S.S. who were good, solid, dependable performers in ordinary circumstances, but you wouldn't want to have them in charge of a cruiser in battle."

"That's true," Heris said, as if she'd never thought of it herself.

"We supply crews to all sorts of people. We tend to hold out our best—our cream, as you said—for the positions where it matters most. It's true that Lady Cecelia is a valued client, and her family is important, but . . . it's not like that yacht is the flagship of Geron Corporation, is it?"

"Not at all."

"She's got a fine ship, relatively new, has it refitted at the right intervals, spares no expense in maintenance, travels safe routes at reasonable speeds. . . . She doesn't need someone who can cope with a twenty-thousand-passenger colonial transport, or maneuvering in a convoy of freighters. Other people do. And her requirements dovetail nicely; we suggest for private yachts crew who are stable emotionally, perhaps a little sedate—" Lazy, thought Heris, could be substituted for that euphemism. No initiative. "Obedient, willing to adapt to a variable schedule."

"I see," Heris said, intentionally cheerful. She did see; she did not like what it said about the agency's attitude toward her, or toward her employer. She was sure Lady Cecelia had never been told that her safety was less important than that of a load of frozen embryos or bulk chemicals. She had trusted the agency, and the agency had sent her junk. It had not occurred to Heris before that very rich people could have junk foisted off on them so easily. "Thank you anyway," she said, as if none of that had passed through her mind. "I realize things are different in civilian life; I'll just have to adjust."

"I'm sure you'll do very well," the voice said, once more wrapped in its silken overtones. It wanted to be pleased with her, wanted Lady Cecelia to be pleased with her—wanted everyone to be pleased with everything, for that matter.

Heris herself was not at all pleased by anything at the moment, but she knew she would adjust, though not the way the agency intended. She would pull this crew up to some decent standard; she would exceed the agency's low expectations and make of Lady Cecelia's yacht a ship any captain could take pride in. Even working with the slack crew she'd been given. She knew Lady Cecelia wanted as speedy a departure as possible, but the delay her nephew caused gave Heris just enough time to interview each member of her crew. Those short, five-minute meetings confirmed her original feeling that most of the crew were past whatever prime they'd had. At least the ship was good: a sound hull, components purchased from all the right places. Regular maintenance at the best refitting docks. *Like the crew,* her instincts muttered. Heris blinked at the screen on her desk, fighting off worry. Surely Lady Cecelia hadn't been cheated on everything.

Departure: their slot in the schedule came late in third shift. Lady Cecelia had already sent word that she preferred to sleep through undockings. Heris could understand that;

she did too, on ships she didn't captain. By this time, the ship's own systems were all up and running; by law, a ship must test its own systems for six hours prior to a launch.

Heris arrived on the bridge two hours before undock, having checked all the aired holds herself, and as much of the machinery on which their lives depended as she could. Everywhere she'd looked she'd found gleaming new casings, shiny metal, fresh inspection stickers, their time-bound inks still bright and colorful. It ought to mean everything was all right . . . and the unease she felt must be because this was a civilian ship, tricked out in plush and bright colors, rather than an honest warship.

Her sulky pilot had the helm, his narrow brow furrowed. She put on her own headset and listened in. He was giving voice confirmation to the data already sent by computer: the *Sweet Delight*'s registration, destination, planned route, beacon profiles, insurance coverage. Heris caught his eye, and pointed to herself—she'd take over that tedious chore. The lists of required items came up on her command screen. Why an officer of an outbound vessel had to confirm by voice the closing of each account opened during a Station visit, each time repeating the authorization number of the bank involved, she could not fathom—but so it was, and had been, time out of mind. Even on her own cruiser someone had been required to formally state that each account was paid in full. It could take hours, with a big ship; here it was a minor chore.

"Thank you, *Sweet Delight*," said the Stationmaster's clerk, when she'd finished. "Final mail or deliveries?" Bates had told her that Lady Cecelia had a bag outgoing; the crew's mail had been stacked with it. She sent Sirkin to take it out to the registered Station mail clerk. The furniture and decorations of the outer lobby had already been returned and stowed in one of the holds. When Sirkin returned, the yacht would be sealed from the Station and the final undock sequence would begin.

It seemed to take no time at all, compared to the bigger, more populous ships she was used to. Her own crew closed and locked the outer and inner hatches; the Station's crew did the same on their side of the access tube. The *Sweet Delight*, on her own air now, smelled no different. An hour of final systems checks remained. The crew seemed to be careful, if slow, in working down the last checklists. They didn't skip anything she noticed, although she didn't know all the sequences for this vessel.

"Tug's in position, Captain Serrano," said the pilot. He had been positioning the yacht's "bustle" to protect it from the tug's grapples. Yachts were too small to fit the standard grapple arrangements; they carried special outriggers that gave the tugs a good grip and kept the main hull undamaged. Heris looked at the onboard chronometer: two minutes to their slot. She switched one channel of her com to the tug's frequency.

"Captain Serrano, *Sweet Delight*." There. She'd said it, officially, to another vessel . . . and the stars did not fall.

"Station Tug 34," came the matter-of-fact reply. "Permission to grapple."

"Permission to grapple." Despite the bustle, she was sure she felt the yacht flinch as the tug caught hold. A perfect match of relative motion was rare, even now. Her status lights switched through red, orange, and yellow to green.

"All fast," the tug captain said. "On your signal."

On the other channel of her com, the on-watch Stationmaster waited for her signal. "Captain Serrano of *Sweet Delight*, permission to undock, on your signal. . . ."

"All clear on Station," the voice came back. "Confirm all clear aboard?"

The boards spread emerald before her. "All clear aboard." Fifteen seconds. She, the Stationmaster, and the tug captain all counted together, but the coordinated computers actually broke the yacht's connection with the Station. The tug dragged the yacht—still inert, her drives passive—safely away from the Station and its crowded traffic lanes. Heris used this time to check the accuracy of the yacht's external sensors against Station and tug reports of other traffic. Everything seemed to work as it should. She felt very odd, being towed without even the insystem drive powered up, but civilian vessels routinely launched "cold" and the tug companies preferred it that way. According to them, some idiot was likely to put his finger on the wrong button if he had power.

When they reached their assigned burn sector several hours later, the tug captain called again. "Confirm safe sector Blue Tango 34; permission to release."

"Permission to release grapples," Heris said, with a nod to the pilot and Gavin. The tug retracted its grapples and boosted slowly away. "Mr. Gavin: insystem drive." The pilot, she noticed, was retracting the bustle, and checking with visuals that the lockdown mechanisms secured properly.

"Insystem drive." The yacht's sublight drive lit its own set of boards. "Normal powerup . . ." Heris could see that; she let out the breath she'd been holding. They'd done a powerup as part of the systems check, but that didn't mean it would powerup again as smoothly.

"Engage," she said. The artificial gravity seemed to shiver as the yacht's drive began a determined shove, much stronger than the tug's. Then it adjusted, and the yacht might have been sitting locked onplanet somewhere. "Mr. Plisson, she's yours." The pilot would have the helm until they made the first jump, and during jump sequences thereafter. Heris called back to the tug: *Sweet Delight*, confirmed powerup, confirmed engagement, confirmed oncourse."

"Yo, Sweetie—" The tug captain's formality broke down. "Come and see us again sometime. Tug 34 out." Heris seethed, then, at the pilot's amiable response, realized that "Sweetie" was probably this yacht's nickname, not an insult. After all, even Service tug captains called the *Yorktowne* "Yorkie."

So, she thought, *here I go. Off to someplace I've never been so my employer can chase foxes over the ground on horseback, and I can spend a month at Hospitality Bay making friends with other captains in the Guild.* Somehow the thought did not appeal.

Heris had heard about cruise captains: unlike the captains of scheduled passenger ships, they were expected to hobnob with guests, flattering and charming them. She would not cooperate if that's what Lady Cecelia had in mind. She would make it clear that she was a captain, not an entertainer. She would eat decent spacefaring meals in her own quarters, since the ship offered no separate wardroom for ship's officers.

Cecelia had heard about spacefleet captains from her sisters: cold, mechanical, brutal, insensitive (which meant they had not worshipped at the shrine of her sister Berenice's beauty, she thought). She enjoyed her meals too much to invite a boor to share them.

✳   ✳   ✳

That first evening of the voyage proper, Heris ate in her cabin, working her way through a stack of maintenance and fitness logs. The crew cook provided a surprisingly tasty meal; she had been prepared for bland reconstituted food, but the crisp greens of her salad had never seen a freeze-dry unit, she was sure. She missed having a proper ward-room for the officers' mess, but the officers on *Sweet Delight,* such as they were, were not likely to become rewarding dinner companions.

At least Lady Cecelia had not stinted on fresh food or on the quality of maintenance. Heris nodded at the screenful of data. Not one back-alley refitter in the lot; if the lady was bent on hiring incompetents, as Heris had begun to suspect, she did so from some other motive than mere economy. The bills would have paid for refitting a larg and more dangerous ship than the yacht, but Heris suppo part of it went into cosmetics, like the decor. Which remi her, she must explain to Lady Cecelia the need for t out that plush covering the umbilicals.

She ignored the gooey dessert for another stalk flavored celery, slid her tray into the return bin, a up data from the next refitting. So far—she ref herself contemplate all the future days—nothin very wrong. This life might be bearable after

"I suppose you want us to dress," Ronni sprawled in the massage lounger, his admir body still dripping sweat from his work equipment. Cecelia eyed him sourly; she herself, but not on the clammy cushio behind. When she'd chosen the luy upholstery she'd assumed she'd never saleswoman had mentioned the pote had shrugged it off. Now she felt anyone's fault but hers.

"Yes," she said. "I do. And be improve by sitting."

"Thank you, Lady Cecelia," to be George's companion, sl dark as Captain Serrano. "T dress if you didn't make the

"Why not?" She was in no mood to honor custom; she watched the girls share a glance, then Raffaele tipped her head to one side.

"I feel silly, that's all. My red dress, and the boys in skimps?"

Cecelia chuckled in spite of herself. "If you're going to feel silly just because some lummox doesn't live up to your expectations, you'll have a miserable life. Wear what you want and ignore them."

Another shared glance. One of the girls might have been more tactful, but Ronnie burst out first. "That's what you do—and that's why you never married and live by yourself in a miserable little ship!"

Cecelia stared him down. "That's why I have the money and position I do—independent of any alliance—to do what I want—and that's why I was available to help you when you got yourself into this mess. Or perhaps you don't know that the first suggestion given your father was that you be packed off on an ore-hauler to Versteen?"

"They wouldn't have!" Ronnie looked almost horrified enough.

Cecelia shrugged. "They didn't, but largely because I was available, and could be talked into it. If your mother—well, never mind. But my point is, that if I had been a conventional member of this family, and married to some appropriate spouse, I would hardly have been free to take you on. You persist in regarding this as some kind of lark, but I assure you that most men—grown men, such as your father and his friends—consider your breach of the lady's confidence a disgrace, even apart from its political implications." Ronnie reddened. "Now," she went on. "Go make yourself fit for civilized company at dinner, all of you. That includes you young women. I do not consider the sort of clothes you wear to parties with your own set adequate." She actually had very little idea what kind of clothes they wore to parties with their set, but had a clear memory of herself at nineteen to twenty-three.

When they had left, Cecelia felt the cushions of the lounger and shuddered. Entirely too clammy; she aimed a blow-dryer at it, and decided on a short swim. The privacy screen, a liquid crystal switchable only from within, closed her into a frosted dome, onto which she projected a visual of overhanging forest. She set the pool's sound system, and eased over the edge to the opening bars of Delisande's *Moon Tide.* A choice others would consider trite, but she needed those long rolling phrases, those delicate shadings of strings to ease her tension. The water enfolded her; she let her body and mind merge with water and music, swimming languidly to the music's rhythm, just enough to counter the gentle current.

Just as she felt herself relaxing, the pool's timer beeped, and Myrtis's voice reminded her that it was time to dress.

"Bad words, bad words, bad words." She had gotten away with that in childhood, even before she learned any. Her stomach burned. . . . If it hadn't been for Ronnie and his gang, she could have had dinner held until *she* was ready—and she'd have been ready, because she wouldn't have been interrupted. And her massage lounger wouldn't have been sweaty. She hauled herself out of the pool with a great splash, hit the privacy control without thinking—and only then realized that with guests aboard she would have to be more careful. Luckily they were all off dressing—none of them had straggled back to ask a stupid question. Not that they didn't swim bare, but she had no desire to have them compare her body to their young ones.

She walked into the warmed towelling robe that Myrtis held, and stood still while Myrtis rubbed her hair almost dry. Then she stepped into the warm fleece slippers, took another warmed towel, and headed for her own suite still rubbing at her damp hair. It dried faster these days, being thinner; she hated the blow-dryers and would rather go to dinner a bit damp than use one.

In her cabin, Myrtis had laid out her favorite dinner dress, a rich golden-brown shi-silk accented with ivory lace. Cecelia let herself be dried, oiled, powdered, and helped into the clothes without thinking about it. Myrtis, unlike Aublice, her first maid, had never seen her young body; she treated Cecelia with professional correctness and the mild affection of someone who has worked for the same employer fifteen years and hopes to retire in the same position. Cecelia sat, allowed Myrtis to fluff her short hair, with its odd spatchings of red and gray, and fastened on the elaborate necklace of amber and enamelled copper that made the lace look even more delicate. Those girls might be fifty years younger, but

they would know a Marice Limited design when they saw
it, and it would have its effect. They would not know it
had been designed for her, by the original Marice, or why—
but that didn't matter.

The plump roast fowl sent up a fragrance that made
Cecelia's stomach subside from its tension. She glanced
around the table and nodded to Bates. Service proceeded,
a blend of human and robotic. A human handed her breast
slices of roast, and the gravy boat, but crumbs vanished
without the need of a crumb-brush.

"Do you eat like this all the time, Lady Cecelia?" asked
Bubbles. Sober, cured of her hangover, she was reasonably
pretty, Cecelia thought, except that her gown looked as if
it would burst with her next mouthful. She was not so
plump; the gown was that tight. She wore a warm bright
green; it showed off her white skin and blonde curls
although it clashed with the dark Raffaele's red dress. The
other girl, Sarah, wore a blue that would have been plain
had it not been silk brocade, a design of fishes: d'Albinian
work.

"Yes," said Cecelia. "Why not? Cook is a genius, and I
can afford it, so . . ."

"Tell us about your new captain. Why'd you choose a
spacefleet officer?"

"Why was she available?" added the odious George. Less
handsome than Ronnie, which Cecelia might have approved,
but he had the sort of gloss she distrusted, as if he'd been
coated with varnish.

"I wasn't satisfied with my former captain's performance,"
Cecelia said, as if they had a right to ask. She knew she
mellowed with good food; it was one reason she made sure
to have it. She wasn't going to admit that if Captain Olin
had held to her schedule, she'd have been safely distant
and unavailable when Ronnie was exiled. Why waste good
ammunition? "I wanted more efficiency," she said between
bites, making them wait for it. "Better leadership. Before,
they were always coming to me complaining about this and
that, or getting crossways with staff. I thought an officer
from the Regular Space Service"—she made the emphasis
very distinct—"would know how to maintain discipline and
follow my orders."

"The Regs are crazy for discipline," George said, in the tone of someone who found that ridiculous. "Remember when Currier transferred, Ronnie? He didn't last six weeks. It was all nonsense—it's not as if all that spit and polish and saluting accomplishes anything."

"I don't know . . ." Buttons, Bunny's middle son, looked surprisingly like his father as he ran a thumb down the side of his nose. Gesture, decided Cecelia, and not features; he had his mother's narrow beaky nose and her caramel-colored hair. "You can't get along with *no* discipline. . . ." And his mother's penchant for taking the other side of any argument, Cecelia told herself. In the girl, it had been fun to watch, but as Bunny's wife she had caused any number of social ruptures by choosing exactly the wrong moment to point out that not everyone agreed. The incident of the fish knives still rankled in Cecelia's memory. She wondered which parent Bubbles took after.

"We're not talking about no discipline." George interrupted as if he had the right, and Buttons shrugged as if he were used to it. "We're talking about the ridiculous iron-fisted excuse for discipline in the Regs. I don't mind fitness tests and qualifying exams—even with modern techniques, the best family can throw an occasional brainless wonder." Cecelia thought that he himself could furnish proof of that. "But," George went on, in blissful ignorance of his hostess' opinion, she being too polite to express it, "I really do not see any reason for archaic forms of military courtesy that have no relevance to modern warfare."

This time Buttons shrugged without looking up from his food. He had the blissful expression most of Cecelia's guests wore when they first encountered the products of Cook's genius. George looked around for another source of conversation, and found the others all engaged in their meal; with the faintest echo of Buttons's shrug, he too began to eat.

The rest of the meal passed in relative silence. The roast fowl had been followed by a salad of fresh diced vegetables in an iced sauce strongly flavored with parsley: Cecelia's favorite eccentricity, and one which never failed to startle guests. It awoke, she contended, the sleepy palates which the roast had soothed and satisfied. Crisp rounds of a distant descendant of potato followed, each centered with a rosette of pureed prawns. The trick, which no one but her own cook seemed to manage, was to have the slices of potato boiled slightly before roasting, so that the outer surfaces were almost crunchy but the inside mealy. The young people, she noted, took additional servings of potato as they had of the roast fowl. Finally, Bates brought in tiny flaky pastries stuffed with finely diced fruit in chocolate and cinnamon sauce. One each, although Cecelia knew that a few would be waiting for her later, safely hidden from the young people.

Satiety slowed them down, she noticed, nibbling her own pastry with deliberate care. They looked as if they wanted to throw themselves back in deep chairs and lounge. *Not in my dining room,* she thought, and smiled. The elegant but uncomfortable chairs that Berenice's designer had foisted on her had their purpose after all.

Cecelia neither knew nor cared about the current social fashions of the young. In her young days, the great families had revived (or continued) the custom of a separate withdrawal of each sex with itself for a time after dinner, the women moving to one room and the men to another. She had resented it, and in her own yacht ignored it; either she invited guests (all of them) to continue their discussion in the lounge, or she excused herself and let them do what they would.

Tonight, with a good meal behind her, she felt mellow enough to grant them more of her time. Perhaps well fed, with hangovers behind them, they would be amusing; at least she might hear some interesting gossip, since none of them seemed to have the slightest reticence. "Let's move to the lounge," she said, rising. The young people stood, as they ought, but Ronnie frowned.

"If it's all the same to you, Aunt Cece, I'd rather watch a show. We brought our own cubes." The dark girl, Raffaele, opened her mouth as if to protest, but then shut it.

"Very well." Cecelia could hear the ice in her own voice. Snub her, would they? On her own yacht? She would not stoop to equal their discourtesy, but she would not forget it, either. Buttons again tried to intervene.

"Wait, Ronnie . . . we really should—"

"Never mind," Cecelia said, with a flip of her hand. The quick temper that she'd always blamed on her red hair slipped control. "I'm sure you're quite right, you would only be bored talking with an old lady." She turned on her heel and stalked out, leaving them to find their own way. At least she didn't have to spend more time in that disgusting lavender and teal lounge the designer had left her. She toyed with the idea of having the yacht redone, and charging it to her sister, but the quick humor that always followed her quick temper reminded her how ridiculous that would be. Like the time she and Berenice had quarrelled, only to discover that her brothers had taped the row for the amusement of an entire gang of little boys. A snort escaped her, and she shook her head. This time she was justified in her anger; she wasn't ready to laugh.

Myrtis, recognizing storm signals, had her favorite music playing and stood ready to remove her jewels. Cecelia smiled at her in the mirror as the deft fingers unhooked the necklace. "The young people prefer to watch entertainment cubes," she said. "I'll be reading late, I expect." What she really wanted to do was hook up the system and take a long, strenuous ride, but that would mean another swim to cool off, and she suspected the young people would keep late hours. When Myrtis handed her the brocade robe, she slipped it on and went back to her study. Here, with the door closed, and the evening lights on in the solarium, she could lie back in her favorite chair and watch the nightlife. Two fan-lizards twined around a fern-frond, their erectile fans quivering and shimmering with delicate colors. At the sculpted water fountain, two fine-boned miniature horses dipped their heads to drink. They were not, of course, real horses; other small species had gone into their bioengineering specs. But in the dusky light, they looked real, or magical, depending on her mood.

Something flickered along the shadowy floor of the tiny forest, and a sere-owl swooped. Then it stood, talons clubbed on its prey, and stared at her with silver eyes. Not really *at* her, of course; it saw the windows farside illusion, a net of silvery strands that even an owl would not dare. The little horses had thrown up their heads, muzzles dripping, when the action began; they had shied, but returned to the water as the owl began to feed. Kass and Vikka, Cecelia thought. Her favorite of the little mares, and her yearling. In daytime lighting, the mare was honey-gold dappled with brown on top, with a white belly and striped mane of dark and cream. It was as close as Cecelia had ever found in the miniatures to her performance horse. . . . Most breeders of the tiny animals liked the exotic colors the non-equine species introduced.

When the mare led the young one back into the undergrowth, Cecelia sighed and blanked the window. Now she had the view that in all her memory made her happiest: her study at Orchard Hall, with the window overlooking the stableyard. Across the yard, the open top doors of a dozen stalls, and the horses looking out eagerly for morning feed. If she wanted, she could set the view into motion, in a long loop that covered the entire day's activities. She could include sounds, and even the smell (although Myrtis would sniff, afterwards, and spray everything with mint). But she could not walk out the door over there, the one with the comfortable old-fashioned handle, and step into her former life. She shrugged, angry at herself for indulging even this much self-pity, and called up a new view, a seascape out a lighthouse window. She added the audible and olfactory inputs, and made herself breathe deeply of the salt-tang in the air. She had told Myrtis she would read late: she would read. And not a cube, but a real book, which enforced concentration far better. She allowed herself the indulgence of choosing an old favorite, *The Family of Dialan Seluun,* a wickedly witty attack on the pomposity of noble families four generations past.

"Her sweet young breast roused against the foe, Marilisa noted that it had not hands nor tentacles with which to wield the appropriate weaponry. . . ." As always, it made her laugh. Knowing it was coming, it still made her laugh. By the end of the first chapter, she had finally quit grumbling inside about Ronnie and his friends. She could always hide out in her cabin reading; they would think she was sulking miserably and never know that her sides ached from laughing.

CHAPTER THREE

Heris had had no idea a yacht could be this complicated. It was so small, after all, with so few people aboard . . . but rich civilians did nothing efficiently. As she worked her way through the manuals, the schematics, the overlays, she wished she'd had weeks aboard before the first voyage. Hours were not enough. She wrinkled her nose at the desk screen, muttering. The owner's quarters separate from the household staff's quarters, and both separate from crew quarters. Four complete and separate hydroponics systems: crew support, household support, food, and flowers. *Flowers?* She pushed that aside, to consider later. Ship's crew, *her* people, were responsible for all life support, but not for the household food and flowers. Ship's crew maintained all the physical plant, the wiring, the com connections; in one of the few duties that did overlap, the household kitchen supplied the crew. Not madam's own cook, of course, but her assistants.

Eventually she went in search of further enlightenment, and chose the most senior employee aboard: Bates. She had stayed out of his path, which seemed to be what he expected, but no captain could command without knowledge.

"Who does this in a planetside house?" asked Heris. Bates folded his lip under. She waited him out. He might be a butler, but she was a captain.

"It . . . varies," he said finally. "More than it used to; more than it should, some say. Originally, household staff did it all, unless a wall fell in or something. Then as houses

35

became more technically oriented—plumbing inside, gas laid on, electricity—" Heris had never considered that having indoor plumbing meant someone was technically oriented. "Then," Bates went on, "owners had to resort to outside expertise. Calling in the plumber or the electrician when something went wrong. Some found staff members who could do it, but most of those trades thought themselves too good to be in service. . . ."

"So . . . usually . . . it's outsiders?"

"Mostly, except in the really big households. Where we're going, of course, the staff does it all, but they've a whole planet of homes to care for."

"The whole *planet* is one household?"

"Yes—I thought you understood. Lord Thornbuckle's estate *is* the planet."

She had known it, in an intellectual way, but she had not ever dealt with its implications. Of course the super-rich owned whole planets . . . but not as pleasure-grounds. She had thought of them as owning the land, perhaps—but never as owning everything on the planet—the infrastructure, the houses, the staff to manage it. But it wasn't that impossible, she reminded herself. The R.S.S. owned several planets as well: one for resources, and one for a training base. This would be like a large military installation. At once her first frantic concerns—where do they buy groceries? Where do they educate the kids?—vanished.

"So Lord . . . er . . . Thornbuckle has all the support staff on hand already," she said. "Technicians, moles, all the rest?"

"Yes, Captain. In the off-season, the planet's population is less than two hundred thousand; in the main season, he'll have at least two thousand guests—which means, of course, another ten to twenty thousand of their ships' crews, and ships' staff all rummocking about the Stations or off at Hospitality Bay."

Hospitality Bay sounded like the sort of place Fleet marines went to gamble, wench, and pillage. From Bates's explanation, it was designed as a low-cost recreational base for ships' crews and off-duty house staff . . . in other words, a place to gamble, wench, and pillage. Most of the wealthy guests who arrived in their own yachts left them docked "blind" at one of the Stations (which one depended on the guests' rank). It had proved cheaper and more pleasant, Bates said, for the crews and staff to vacation planetside than to enlarge the Stations enough to hold and entertain idle servants. A largish island, complete with a variety of accommodations, automated service, recreational facilities, and the chance to meet crew and staff from the other yachts. Clubs, bars, entertainment booths, and halls—everything the vacationing staff might want.

"No riots?" asked Heris, remembering the Fleet marines. "No . . ." What would they call shore patrol? "No—security officers?"

"The militia," said Bates, wrinkling his nose in distaste. "Of course there are always those who take advantage, and someone must keep order. It's understood that the usual . . . er . . . structure of command does not apply. I am not held responsible, let's say, if an under-gardener from this ship gets into trouble. Milady would consider that, afterwards, and might say something to me, but not the militia. We each have our own places, you see."

Enlisted bars, NCO bars, and officer bars, Heris thought. She called up a list of the branches of the captains guild, and found one listed for Hospitality Bay . . . so she, too, would be expected to sit out the hunting season entertaining herself with other captains from yachts. Why was that so much worse than spending leave with other Fleet officers? She knew the answer, but pushed it away. She'd joined the Captains Guild; that was all she could do for now. Someday she would belong again . . . or she wouldn't. She'd live with it either way.

"I suppose," she said, looking at Bates carefully, "that if anything . . . arises . . . on the household side that I need to know about, you will inform me?"

"Yes, Captain Serrano." He smiled at her, evidently pleased. She could not imagine why.

"This is *very* different from the Regular Space Service," she said, to see what his reaction would be.

"Yes, it is, Captain." His smile broadened. "It's even different from most civilian households. Lady Cecelia likes to do things her own way."

That, Heris had figured out from the lavender plush. Perhaps servants like Bates took pleasure in their employers' eccentricities, but she didn't. Yet.

"I must warn you," she said, "that I'm planning to run emergency drills just as I would aboard a warship. It's a matter of safety, you understand. Do the . . . er . . . staff have training sessions aboard?"

"Not normally, no, although we do have assigned places and duties for various emergencies. Captain Olin never found it necessary." A faint air of distaste, whether for Captain Olin or her proposal, she couldn't tell.

"Captain Olin, I'm afraid, had eccentricities unsuited to the master of a spacefaring vessel," Heris said, and then realized how odd that sounded. Eccentricities implied activities engaged in with objects obtained from catalogs with names like *Stirrings* and *Imaginations.* The only person she'd ever known thrown out of the Service for "eccentricities" had insisted on sharing his delight in electrical and plumbing lines with those not so inclined. She had sat on the court-martial, and remembered suddenly that he'd also liked having his mouth packed full of feathers. Captain Olin's eccentricities, she was sure, had been ethical and not sensual.

Bates no longer smiled. "And these drills will be . . . unscheduled?"

"Yes. I'm sorry; I realize it's inconvenient, but one never knows when a real emergency will occur, and drills must be a surprise. That way we can find out what didn't work, and prepare for it." She paused. "However, if you would like to arrange training first, I'll delay the drills. At the least, every member of staff should have an emergency station where he or she will be safe and out of the way of crew members with assignments. Ideally, staff would help with things like verifying that emergency hatches have locked, that ventilation systems are working according to specs, and so on."

"What about Lady Cecelia and her guests?"

"They too must have emergency stations where they will be safe. They need to practice evacuation drills just like anyone else. If something should happen—unlikely as that is—we must know where they are to rescue them."

"I see." Bates looked surprisingly grim, as if he had never thought about the dangers inherent in space travel before. "Are there standard ways to do this?"

Heris stared at him, then recovered herself. "You—haven't had any instruction, ever?"

He looked unhappy, but determined. "No, Captain Serrano. To my knowledge, none of Lady Cecelia's captains have ever had drills that involved the staff, owner, or guests."

Heris managed not to sigh aloud, but inwardly she fumed at the incompetence of those captains. Did they have no professional pride at all? "I'd better speak to her, then, hadn't I?" she said gently. "If she doesn't realize the importance of these drills, she might make it very inconvenient for you. And after that, if you have any time . . . perhaps we could work together to decide on the best staff response."

He relaxed, and smiled, and seemed perfectly agreeable. Heris took the list of staff positions, and their listed specialties, and went back to her side of the ship, carefully not muttering.

The yacht's database included, as law required, the complete text of the standard manuals of emergency procedures for crew and passengers. At this point, Heris considered the staff and guests equally passengers. She decided to print out a hard copy—it would be impressively thick, with the Transport Code seal on the cover, and perhaps that would convince Lady Cecelia that it wasn't her own peculiarity.

The last access date for that file was—she stared, though she felt she should not have been surprised—the date the yacht left the builder's. All those years . . . her stomach clenched, as she thought of the past possibilities. No, she could not expect Lady Cecelia, or her woefully ignorant staff, to go through disaster drills until they'd had some instruction. She wondered what the correct procedure was—if there was a correct procedure—for informing a wealthy yacht owner that her ship was, and had been, unsafe for years.

The hard copy thunked into the bin, and she picked it out. The Transport Code seal looked less impressive than she'd expected, but the thing was thick enough. She looked into it, wincing at the bureaucratic prose. It was as bad as Fleet directives. Everything unimportant specified in intricate detail, with requirements to document that it was done, and the important things buried in multisyllabic generality. How far above the deck warning signs must be, and how high the letters, and what color, but—she stopped suddenly. Warning signs? What warning signs?

She flipped to the back sections, headed REQUIRED ITEMS OF COMPLIANCE, and PENALTIES FOR NONCOMPLIANCE.

compartments whose blowers are controlled by box eighteen, and the electrical outlets in the heads—the bathrooms—in all compartments on this passage. And since four boxes are clustered with box seventeen, an electrical fire in that is likely to knock out sixteen, eighteen, and nineteen as well. That means all the blowers in the crew quarters, all the overhead lights, wall sockets, passage lights, and com terminals, since all the compartment desktops take their power from box twenty. It's dark in here, Mr. Gavin, and there's a fire somewhere aboard—do you know if the door will unlock?"

"No . . . no, I didn't . . . I don't . . ."

"And that's why we have emergency drills, Mr. Gavin. To find out, before we find that we're locked in dark, airless boxes while a fire rages somewhere." Before he could say more—and anything he said now would enrage her—she thrust the hard copy of the manual at him. "Here; start learning this. I'll make additional hard copies, and I'll expect you and your section chiefs to have marked necessary modifications within forty-eight hours." He was too stunned to react; he took the manual and backed out. Heris watched the door slide close behind him, and then shook her head. It was much, much worse than she'd thought, to be the captain of a rich lady's yacht.

Lady Cecelia had never thought of herself as an old lady. Age had nothing to do with it, nor the number of rejuvenation treatments. As long as she could ride to hounds, as long as she could go where she wanted, and do what she wanted, and cope with whatever life put on her plate, she was not old. True, she didn't compete in some fields where once she had been at the top, but that she thought of as outgrowing old interests—as developing new ones—as a natural shift from one thing to another. Old people were those who had quit changing, quit growing. Some people quit growing at twenty, most by forty or fifty, and became old within a decade. They would live another thirty to fifty years—longer with rejuv—but they lived those years as old people. Others—her own grandmother Serafina for one—seemed to stay lively and interesting until the last year or so before their deaths.

Staying away from the family kept her from feeling old,

too. Nothing like children growing up and turning into difficult adults to make you feel your age. Particularly if they thought you were an old lady, and treated you as one. She did not look at herself as she dressed in her soft velour exercise suit; she did not want to be reminded of her age. If they were in the gym, she'd throw them out. It was her turn.

But the gym was empty, silent, scented with her favorite aromatics. They had not been here; the cushions of the lounger had dried. Cecelia locked the doors and set up her simulator. She would ride this morning, no matter what anyone said.

An hour later, refreshed after a pleasant but demanding ride over a training field, she stowed the simulator and pocketed the cube. This was not a group she wanted riding over her shoulder, so to speak. She didn't want to hear whatever they might say. She looked at the gym's status board, and saw that they were all still in the guest suites. Fine. She stripped, showered, and let herself into the pool enclosure, blanking the canopy and turning the waterstream up a little. The pool's surface heaved, then steadied, as the current increased. She swam against it vigorously, then climbed out, toweled dry, and wrapped herself in her heated robe. Another check of the board; they were moving now. She grabbed her exercise suit and headed for her own suite; she should be safe.

They did not meet at breakfast. Cecelia ate in her own suite, as she often did anyway, and she paid no attention to the young people. She had her own daily routine—checking with Cook, listening to Bates's report, going over whatever her captain chose to tell her about the ship status. With Olin, that had often been a single bare statement that the ship was proceeding according to plan. She wondered about Serrano. The first day's report had been two pages long, most of it incomprehensible detail about why she'd chosen to move something from one storage hold to another . . . as if Cecelia cared. As long as staff knew, and could find, whatever she wanted, she herself didn't want to worry about something as technical as "center of mass" and "potential resonance interference."

This morning, it was one page, headed with "Emergency Drills." Cecelia blinked. Why should that concern her? The crew would have emergency drills, she assumed, but yachts, unlike liners, did not have to inconvenience their passengers. She read on, already resisting the idea. This Captain Serrano must think she was still a military commander. Her house staff to be given emergency assignments? She and her guests expected to learn and follow emergency procedures? How absurd! She remembered the fire drills, long ago when she had attended the Sorgery School, and how they had all known the drills were useless. If a fire ever did start, it would not wait around for people to get out of bed, find their assigned partner, and "walk down the stairs quietly, without talking, and without pushing or running."

Captain Serrano's reasoning, when she got that far, made somewhat more sense. She had not really thought about the things that could go wrong, barring late meals or illness in a crew member. The vulnerability of a small yacht wandering through interstellar space hadn't occurred to her; everyone she knew traveled in space, and the rare disappearances and accidents were no more frightening than accidents groundside. Sometimes trains and aircraft and limousines crashed; sometimes yachts disappeared. For a moment she almost felt it, the fragility of the ship, the immensity of the universe, but she pushed that away. It was like thinking about the fragility of her skull and the size of a horse and the fence it was approaching. . . . If you thought about it, you'd sit in a padded cocoon forever, and that was ridiculous.

Still . . . perhaps some emergency drills might be a good idea. Not this many, and certainly not without adequate warning (what if she were in the swimming pool?) but some. She called Bates.

"Yes, madam. Captain Serrano has already spoken to me about this matter—she considers it important to your welfare. She would like to help me give your staff instruction, although that would take time—"

"Before these emergency drills?"

"Yes, madam."

"I suppose . . . it's something that should have been done before, though none of the others complained."

"Captain Serrano seems very competent, madam." Which meant that Bates approved. Damn. She had better agree, so it could be her idea, because when Bates approved of something, it happened, owner or no owner. She had wished more than once that he was her captain. He had a talent for command.

"Very well, then. You and the captain see to it, but if she gives you too much trouble, Bates, feel free to let me know."

"I don't think she will, madam. She's not like the others." Whatever that meant. Cecelia didn't ask. She asked how the young people were doing, with no real interest, and Bates reported that they had appeared to enjoy breakfast, and were now viewing old entertainment cubes in the lounge. Cecelia felt an unreasonable irritation that they were happy. They were her guests; they ought to be concerned about her. She went into her garden to play with the miniature equids. . . . They would always come for sugar.

Ronnie watched Raffaele covertly, and wondered if she had heard about the opera singer. He hadn't really noticed before, thinking of her as George's girl, but she had a lovely line of jaw and throat when she lifted her head. Slender without weakness, she seemed hardly aware of her grace. . . . She was chuckling over something Buttons had said. Bubbles, beside him, waved a hand in front of his face.

"Wake up, sweet—you're staring right through Raffa, and it could make me jealous." Bubbles exuded sensuality of a very studied sort, from silver nails to tumbled blonde curls, from the deep-plunging neckline of her clinging jersey to the cutouts on the long black tights. Next to the opera singer, he had always thought of Bubbles as the sexiest girl he knew, but at the moment he was finding her tiresome. She had been singing along with the lyrics from the cube, and the opera singer had spoiled him. Now he could hear the breathiness and the slight errors of pitch.

"Sorry," he said. "I was wondering what we're going to do all that time at your father's. Surely not fox hunting."

"It's not that bad," Buttons said, looking up. "I rather like it, sometimes. If we jiggle the weather-sats, so it's not as cold and wet—"

"Father will find out," Bubbles said. "He likes authenticity."

"I don't see how you can have authenticity when the foxes aren't even foxes," Sarah put in. "Didn't I read somewhere that they're actually reverse-gengineered from cat genes?" Ronnie doubted her interest in bioengineering; she and

Buttons had signed the second-level prenuptials, and this was her first official visit to his family. She would be trying to make points.

"A chimaera," Buttons said, settling into the lecturing tone that made him less than popular in the regiment. Stuffy, in fact, because he couldn't just answer a question: he had to explain all the juice out of it. "Nobody bothered to save Old-Earth red fox genes, so what Dad's people did was go from descriptions, and use what seemed to work. Luckily Hagworth had already done jackals from dogs, and two of the fox species that got publicity. . . . The real problem was getting the color and the bushy tail with a white tip. Our neo-foxes are part kit fox, part jackal, a bit of cat, and raccoon, for the tail."

"I didn't know anyone had saved raccoon genes; I thought they were too common."

"Only to give an outcross for the red panda," Buttons said. Ronnie would not have expected him to know, but after all his father was an enthusiast on many forms of hunting and preservation. Buttons went on to discuss the genetic possibilities at length. Ronnie let his mind drift . . . to the opera singer, in whose bed he had learned about things that before had been only rumors . . . to the prince, whose jealousy he had been glad to arouse . . . to that night in the mess when he had boasted . . . somehow it didn't seem quite as clever now as it had then. Perhaps Aunt Cecelia was right, and he had been a cad. No. The prince should have been a better sport.

He reached up and stroked Bubbles's arm, wondering if anything would come of it. He could not think of anything to say, though, and after a few seconds, she withdrew the arm and stretched herself on the couch across from him. The same couch where she had been so unfortunately sick. . . . He wondered if she remembered. She looked healthy enough now, though her expression of mild sulkiness fit his mood as well as hers.

"I suppose we should get into shape," George said. "Your aunt has that handy little riding-thing. An hour a day, and none of us would have to worry about saddle sores."

"Her simulator?" Ronnie asked. "Do what you like, George, but I have no intention of bouncing around on a mechanical horse. It's bad enough to contemplate bouncing around on a real one. Do you know she had the gall to order me riding attire?"

"Well, you'll need it." Buttons had settled into a pose the male equivalent of Bubbles's sprawl; together they took up both of the couches. Ronnie wondered why he'd thought exile would be more fun with these people than alone. They were looking at him as if he were responsible for entertaining them, when none of it was his fault. Buttons went on. "First of all, my father's head instructor will check you out, before you're assigned your mounts—"

"And he's a terror," Bubbles said. "So far as I know, there's not a military unit in the known universe that still uses horses, but he acts like a cartoon drill instructor. You'll spend at least two hours trotting before he decides what to give you."

"I'd like to see him test Aunt Cecelia," Ronnie said.

"Not her," Buttons said, grinning. "She's an old guest, and he's more likely to ask her to test the horses. 'Pick what you like, milady, not that there's anything here worth your time,' is what he'll tell her."

"Is she really that good?"

Buttons stared at him, eyes wide. "You haven't ever seen her ride?"

"No. The family doesn't think much of her hobby." His father had said that, often enough, and he'd heard his mother talking to his other aunts about "poor dear Cecelia, what a shame she wasted her life on horses."

"It was hardly a hobby, Ron. . . . The woman won the All-Union individual cross-country championship five times, and ranked in the top five for fifteen years." Buttons turned to Bubbles. "Remember when we were just learning to ride, and old Abel was yelling at us, and she stopped him?"

"She got me over my first jump," Bubbles said, sitting upright now. She looked less like a fluffhead than usual. Could she possibly *enjoy* hunting? Ronnie had a brief unpleasant view of himself married to a fox-hunting wife. No. It would not do. "I'd forgotten . . . that was that old gray pony, the one that seemed to like dumping us. She didn't yell at me, just talked me through it."

"Yes, and then she got on one of the good horses and showed us what we were supposed to be doing. Abel fairly purred."

Ronnie felt a knot in his head tightening. It wasn't fair that they knew more about his aunt than he did. That they admired his aunt for things he hadn't known about, and that his family hadn't respected. Things were not going the way he'd planned. He'd expected his friends to rally around him, support him, do what *he* wanted . . . and here they were swapping stories of his old maiden aunt.

"Does everyone hunt together?" he asked Buttons. If he couldn't avoid the topic of horses, at least he could get the conversation away from his aunt. "How many horses does your father have, anyway?"

"To answer your first question, no. There are three hunts out of the main house, where we'll be. Each has its own territory. We'll each be assigned to one of them, depending on riding ability. As for horses . . . many thousands, I suppose, altogether. The main house stables will hold five hundred, though we won't use that many. Hunters, hacks, young horses in training." Ronnie tried to imagine five hundred horses in the same place, and failed. The Academy had had ten, for the training of its young officers, and he had no idea what a "hack" was. He was not about to ask.

"We don't hunt every day," Bubbles put in. "Some people do, but most ride out on alternate days. Particularly in the lower hunts, where they're not as good and get really stiff."

"I'll get really stiff," Raffa and Sarah said together, like a chorus.

"Isn't there anything else but hunting?" Ronnie asked, hoping he didn't sound as desperate as he felt.

"There are other kinds of hunting," Buttons said. "Not all of it's on horseback. You can shoot grouse and pheasant, that sort of thing. It's the wrong season for fishing in the nearby streams. Indoors—well, the things my father assumes were normal indoor sports of the time: billiards, cards, amateur theatricals."

"Oh . . . dear." Worse then he'd imagined. Worse than his mother had imagined, he was sure. Traveling with a wealthy aunt on her private yacht had seemed like a good idea when his mother mentioned it. Perhaps he'd have been better off going to some dull assignment in an out-of-the-way base. At least it wouldn't have had fox hunting, and his work might have kept him busy part of the time.

"There are other places on the planet," Bubbles said. "But we can't possibly get away more than once. We should save that for when you're really desperate. Poor Ronnie."

He wanted to snarl at her. Poor Ronnie, indeed. He needed real sympathy, not the mocking look Bubbles had given him. He needed them to understand that it wasn't his fault—none of it. "I'm not desperate," he said firmly. "For all you know, I may take to hunting as easily as any other sport. I may be leaping over fences and dashing along at a run—"

"Gallop," put in Bubbles.

"Whatever. I mean, I'm naturally athletic, perfectly fit: how hard can it be?" He tried to say it with complete confidence; Bubbles, Buttons, and Raffaele burst into laughter. Raffaele? What did she know about riding? He tried to hide his irritation, and forced himself to laugh with them.

"Better try your aunt's simulator," Buttons said, still chuckling. "You may find a few muscles that aren't quite perfectly fit." Then he sobered. "You should do well, Ronnie, really. You're right: you are a natural athlete; it's quite possible that after a few lessons you'll be up to riding in the field. But it's not like anything else."

Ronnie forced himself to smile, and wondered if he could hide in his stateroom all day and night, watching entertainment cubes, until they got to Buttons's home planet. Probably not. He was going to have to think of something they could do . . . something fun, something to reestablish his leadership of the group. Something mischievous, perhaps. Play a harmless practical joke on the old lady, or the crew.

"You may be right," he said, without meaning it. "I'll see what you look like on the simulator first, and then . . . we'll see."

"We ought to see about some swimming, I think," Raffaele said. "C'mon, girls. Let's go play in the water." Before he quite knew how it happened, the girls had vanished, and his two bosom friends were watching him, bright-eyed.

"Come on," said George. "Tell us more about that opera singer. Is it true they have specially developed muscles?"

CHAPTER FOUR

"I didn't ask you if it was 'going fine,'" Heris said. "I asked you what the sulfur extraction rate was. Do you know, or not?" With each day, her unease about the yacht's basic fabric and systems had grown. Getting answers from the crew had turned out to be harder than she expected.

The moles looked at one another before Timmons answered. "Well . . . pretty much, Cap'n. It's below nom at the moment, but it usually runs that way 'cause that dauber wants a sulf-rich sludge for his veggie plots."

It took Heris a moment to translate civtech slang and decide this meant Lady Cecelia's gardener wanted more sulfur in the first-pass sludge. In the meantime, they still had not answered as she thought they should. She let the steel edge her voice. "Below nom is not what I'm looking for. What, precisely, is the *number* you have for sulfur clearance?" Again, the sidelong look from one mole to another. This time it was Kliegan who answered.

"It's . . . ah . . . zero point three. Of first-sig nom, that is—"

"Which is . . . ?" prompted Heris; she could feel temper edging higher.

"Well, the *book* says one point eight, but this system's never worked any better'n one point six, just under first-sig. Mostly we run about two sigs below, say about point seven or so. System's underutilized, so it's not that important. It's rated for a population of fifty, and we don't have that many aboard."

Heris closed her eyes briefly, running over the relevant equations in her head. Sulfur clearance was only one of the major cycles, but critical to the ship's welfare because errors could not only make people sick, but degrade many ship components as well. Delicate com equipment didn't like active sulfur radicals in the ship's atmosphere. She added ship's crew, house staff, and owner's family. "In case you haven't noticed," she said briskly, "we now have fifty-one humans and a long voyage ahead of us. I presume you flushed the tanks and re-inoculated them while we were in port—?" But the hangdog looks told her they hadn't. "And the last logged maintenance by offship personnel was this— Diklos and Sons, Baklin Station?"

"That's right, ma'am," Timmons said. "They couldn't have done such a good job, fancypants as they are, 'cause the system never did pick up the points, but Captain Olin said never mind—"

"Oh, he did?" Heris struggled to keep her thoughts off her face. First his demand for an odd, inconvenient course that did not meet the owner's needs, and now a tolerance for malfunctioning environmental equipment—something no sane captain would have. Failing to order the tanks flushed and recharged at Rockhouse might have been spite—revenge for being fired—but until then he had risked his own life as well. What could have made the risk worth it? "We'd better see how bad it is," she said briskly. "Suit up and we'll go take a look—"

"You, Captain?" asked Iklind. He almost never spoke, she'd discovered, letting chatty Timmons say anything necessary. But now he looked worried.

Heris let her brows rise. It had worked on other ships; it should work here. "Did you think I wouldn't want to check for myself?"

"Well, it's not that, Captain . . . only . . . these things can smell pretty bad." Pretty bad was an entirely inadequate description of a malfunctioning sulfur loop, and she was sure more than the sulfur scrubbers were in trouble. Once the pH had gone sour, many of the enzymes in other loops worked erratically, as the chemistry fluctuated.

"That's why we'll be suited," she said. When they didn't move she said. "Five minutes, in the number four access bay."

"Complete suits?" asked Timmons. "They're awfully hot—"

"You prefer to risk the consequences?" Heris asked. "With a system you know is malfunctioning?"

"Ah . . . it's just stinks," Timmons said. When she glared at him, he said, "All right, Captain. Suits." But as he left, she heard him mutter, "Damn lot of nonsense. Can't be enough reaction in that loop to give us mor'n a headache at worst."

Quickly, Heris gave Gavin his orders for the next hour: which compartments to seal, which backup crew to have ready, suited, in case of trouble. Then into her own suit— the cost of which had come from the advance on her contract, and which she never begrudged. Whatever else on this gilded cesspool of a yacht did or did not work as designed, her own personal self-contained suit would . . . or her family would enjoy the large sum which Xeniks guaranteed if any of its suits failed. She wasn't worried—only twice in the past fifty years had Xeniks had to pay out.

When she was still a corridor away from the access bay, the alarm went off. For an instant she thought something had gone wrong on the bridge, but then she realized what it must be. One of those fools hadn't waited for her.

"Captain!" Gavin bleated in her ear. She thumbed down the volume of the suit comunit.

"What is it?" she asked. "I'm at E-7, right now." Ahead of her, a gray contamination barrier flapped down from the overhead and snicked tight, its central access closed.

"Computer says dangerous chemical—sulfur something— and the motion sensor said someone was there, but isn't moving. But they're in suits—"

"Get those backups down here," Heris said, mentally cursing civilians in general and the ship's former captain in particular. "Make sure they have their helmets locked on. I'm going in." Despite her faith in Xeniks's legendary suits, she shivered a moment. The gas in there was deadlier than many military weapons, but so familiar throughout human history that people just did not respect it. She wriggled through the access iris, which lengthened into a tube and sealed itself behind her. The suit's own chemical sensors flicked to life, giving the readout she expected: hydrogen sulfide, here in less than life-threatening concentration.

Heris hurried, even though she knew it would almost certainly be too late. Around the corner, she came upon Timmons, who had suited up but not locked on his helmet. Presumably he'd planned to do so when he got to the access bay itself. He lay sprawled on the floor, one arm outstretched toward Iklind, slumped against the open access, wearing no protective gear at all.

She went to Timmons first, locking his helmet in place and turning his oxygen supply to full with the external override. Her suit had all the necessary drugs for standard industrial inhalation accidents—but she'd never used it, nor was she a medic. She'd have to rely on the backup team. Iklind wasn't breathing at all, and no wonder—the hydrogen sulfide concentration in here had peaked at over 1,000 ppm, according to the monitor above the open access hatch. Inside, someone—presumably Iklind—had cracked the seal on a sludge tank. It was brimful, far above the safety line. A black line of filth drooled over its lip.

Heris picked up the wrench on the floor, closed the cover, and tightened the seal, then closed the hatch. Now the monitor indicated the concentration was below 200 ppm, still dangerous but not instantly lethal. They were lucky, she thought, that the agitator hadn't been on in the sludge tank (and why not?) or the concentration could have been a log or so higher.

A shadow moved at the corner of her vision. The backup team—that would be the number two engineering officer and the off-shift senior mole—came around the corner and stopped. Even through their helmets their eyes showed wide and staring.

"Come *on*," Heris said. "Get Timmons to the medbox— he might have a chance." It seemed to her they moved too slowly, but they did wrestle Timmons back up the corridor toward the contamination barrier. Heris called the bridge. "Iklind's dead," she said. "Hydrogen sulfide—apparently he opened the sludge tank without any protective gear—" Gavin started to say something, and she overrode him. "We have three problems here—Timmons first: is that medical AI capable of handling inhalation injuries? Second: we've got to clear up the rest of the contamination, and the system is too overloaded to resorb it unless you can come up with a cargo section full of reactant. And third, of course, is Iklind.

We need medical and legal evaluation; I will take that up with Lady Cecelia. Oh—and another thing—we're not going to continue in this unsafe condition. I want Sirkin to plot a course to the nearest major repair facility, preferably on the way to our destination."

"The medbox ⬩ . . . I don't know, Captain," Gavin said. "It's not—you know—meant for major problems."

Heris managed not to snap at him. "At least you can tell it the problem. All I know is it's a cellular poison, and there's some kind of antidote. Now: send someone down with a recorder, so that I can document Iklind's position and the monitor readings. Then we can bring his body out." Even as she said this, she realized she was straining the crew's resources.

"Milady," said Heris, "we have several problems."

Just what I need, thought Cecelia. Problems with the ship. Now she'll start whining about how different this is from the military. She nodded, trying for a cool distancing expression. That and a straight back usually dissuaded complainers.

"We've had a death among the crew, environmental technician Iklind."

"What! A heart attack? A stroke?" Despite her determination not to react, she felt her heart lurch in her chest, and her voice came out shrill and harsh.

"No, Lady Cecelia." Heris had tried to think of a nonthreatening way to tell her employer—considering how old the woman was—but had not come up with anything better than the bald truth. "He died of hydrogen sulfide poisoning, the result of opening a sludge tank without protective gear. In addition, another crewman is suffering severe inhalation injury from the same source."

"But all we have is a medbox!" Cecelia felt as if she had just fallen off at a gallop. A crewman dead, and another sick . . . was this what came of hiring an ex-military captain? She tried to remember the specifics of the medical unit.

"It's a standard industrial pollutant," Heris said. "The unit has the right medications and the right software to treat him—I checked that, of course, before coming to you."

"Oh—I—" Cecelia realized she'd slumped, and straightened again.

"I'm very sorry to have given you this shock. Perhaps I should call someone?"

Cecelia recognized someone giving her time to pull herself together, and was caught between resentment and gratitude. "I've never lost a crew member before," she said. "Not since I've owned the *Sweet Delight*." She struggled with the mix of emotions, and tried to think clearly. "Poison gas from the sludge tank, you said? Has someone put something in it?"

Heris recognized the attempt for what it was, and masked her amusement that anyone—even a rich old lady—could travel in space and not know the most common and deadly of the environmental by-products. "No, milady. Sludge generates several toxic gases, which are normally converted into harmless chemicals used in your 'ponics sections, when the environmental system is functioning smoothly. This isn't sabotage, just a mishap. . . . Iklind apparently decided to open the tank without proper protective gear, and Timmons tried to rescue him, but hadn't sealed his own helmet."

"Then who saved Timmons?" asked Cecelia.

"I did," Heris said. Cecelia's eyes widened, but she didn't say anything. "I had told them I would inspect the system, and they were to meet me—properly suited—at the access bay. Instead—" She shrugged. "I don't know why Iklind didn't wear his suit, or why Timmons didn't wear his helmet . . . but I will find out."

"Very well, Captain." That was clearly dismissive. "I . . . will expect to hear more from you tomorrow."

"That's not quite all," said Heris carefully.

This time the gaze was direct and challenging. "What? Is something else wrong?"

"I realize," Heris said, "that you just had this vessel redecorated, and it must have been expensive . . ."

"My sister did that," Cecelia said. "What of it?"

"Well . . . your main environmental system is overloaded; that's why I was going to inspect the system: it was not functioning to specifications. Your former captain did not have the system purged and recharged at the correct intervals—"

"He must have! I remember the bills for it." Cecelia called up her accounting software and nodded when the figures came up. "There it is: Diklos and Sons, Refitting General, Baklin Station."

"Sorry, milady," said Heris. "You got the bill, but the work wasn't done. I could see that from the sludge tank Iklind had opened, and since then I've had the other moles—environmental techs—check the filter and culture chambers. It's a mess. The sulfur cycle's in trouble, and that impacts your nitrogen uptake in hydroponics. It isn't presently dangerous, but it will require some caution until we reach a refitting station. My recommendation would be to do that as soon as possible. By choosing a different set of jump points, we can be at your chosen destination only one day after your request."

Cecelia glared. "You didn't find this out before we left."

"No, milady, I didn't." Cecelia waited for the excuse that she herself had rushed their departure, but it didn't come. Her captain had no expression at all, and after a moment went on. "Initially I accepted the log showing that the purge and recharge had been done, and the fresh inspection stickers; you are quite right that I should not have done that. Logs have been faked before, even in the Regular Space Service." A tight smile, which did not reach the captain's eyes. Cecelia wondered if she ever really smiled. "But I noticed an anomaly in the datastream two days ago, and began tracking it down. Your moles—sorry, ma'am, your environmental technicians—claimed it was your gardeners' fault. But the plain fact is, the work wasn't done. I believe it will be possible to document that, and get a refund from Diklos and Sons; your reputation should help."

"Ah . . . yes." Cecelia felt off balance; she had been ready for evasions and excuses, and her captain's forthright acceptance of blame surprised her.

"I realize, milady, that one reason you changed captains is that your former one could not keep to your schedule. But in this instance, I feel that your safety requires an emergency repair of the system."

"I thought," Cecelia said pettishly, "that I had specified an environmental system far larger than I'd ever need, just in case something went wrong."

"Yes, milady, you did. But with your present guests and their personal servants, that limit has been exceeded—and with the degradation of performance of the system, and the lack of refitting capabilities at Lord Thornbuckle's, it would be most unwise to proceed without repair."

"And that will take—?"

"Six days to the nearest refitting facility, I'd trust; two days docked; and with a reasonable course and drive performance, we should be, as I said, just one day late at your destination."

"I suppose that's better than the eight days late I had before—which landed me with young Ronnie, because I wasn't there to argue hard enough and loud enough." Cecelia shrugged and said, "Oh, very well. Do what you think best; you're the captain." But her captain didn't leave, merely stood there. "What else?" she asked.

"I strongly recommend some restrictions in the next six days. At present we have no shipwide emergency, but I would prefer to prevent one."

"But it's only six days—" Cecelia began, then stopped. "You're really worried." To her surprise, her captain smiled slightly.

"Yes, and I cannot justify it by the data alone. But although I've been on this ship only a short time, there's a *feel* of something wrong—"

"Intuition in a Fleet officer?"

"Just so. Intuition I have learned not to ignore. I am instituting quite severe restrictions in crew activities, and strongly recommend them for your staff and guests as well."

"Such as?"

Her captain ticked them off on her fingers. "A change in diet to minimize sulfur and nitrogen loading of the system—for six days, the loss of muscle mass or conditioning from a low-protein diet should not cause any distress, and if you have someone with special needs, that can of course be accommodated. Restrictions in water use, to include the exercise pool since that water is cycled through the same systems, and organic compounds inevitably end up in it. The . . . er . . . gardens will need to be handled as part of the regular environmental system as well . . ."

"The gardeners will love that—!" She thought of her pet equids with a pang. They would have to go—perhaps she could flash-freeze them, but it was always chancy. And the beautiful flowers, the fresh fruits and vegetables—they would have to restock or eat preserved food all the way to Bunny's.

"Sorry, milady, but the environmental tech's excuse for letting the system go outside nominal is that your gardeners had requested a particularly high sulfur effluent for some special crop."

"I see. So we're to arrive at some shipyard hungry, thirsty, dirty, and bored—"

"But healthy and alive. Yes."

Cecelia's heart sank. She could imagine what Ronnie and his friends were going to say about this. It had been bad enough already. For a moment, she was tempted to let go in one of the towering rages of her youth—but she was beyond that now. She had no energy for that kind of explosion. "Very well," she said again. "If you will enter the specifications, I will inform staff and the others."

"Thank you, milady." Her captain's face looked as if it might be intending an apology, but she did not then apologize. She gave a curious stiff nod, and went out quickly. Cecelia blew a long, disgusted breath and called Cook. She might as well get on with it.

Takomin Roads occupied a location that made it ideal for refitting deep-space vessels and little else; not even the most ship-fevered spacer would choose for recreation the bleak cold planet the Station circled. Farther insystem Merice offered sweet shallow oceans, and Golmerrung spectacular peaks and glaciers . . . but Takomin Roads offered reasonable proximity to four mapped jump nodes, one of them apparently bound to the planet. Heris had stopped there with a battle group once, and been impressed by the size of the fixtures and the quality of the crews.

The *Sweet Delight* had communications equipment only just inferior to that of the cruiser Heris had left. She could pop a message just as they left FTL flight, and it would arrive well before them, given the necessary deceleration of the yacht. Mr. Gavin, still gray around the gills from her lecture and Iklind's death, and the very close shave with Timmons, presented her with his estimate of the work to be done, down to the specifications for every component fastener. She took that estimate to the moles themselves, and when they would have initialled it without discussion she insisted on going over every item with them.

"I'm sure Mr. Gavin is right," the junior kept saying, with

nervous glances at the other. She had hardly met Ries before the emergency.

"I'm not." Heris was past worrying about Gavin's reputation with the moles; she was far more concerned with getting the yacht safely to refitting, and back out as quickly as possible.

"I guess you want us to look up this stuff in the manual. . . ." said the senior mole, Kliegan.

"I want you to do your jobs," Heris said. "If you are not sure, of course you must look up the specs."

"Well, I do, but . . ."

"Then is this correct, or not? Don't hedge about, mister." She wondered, not for the first time, how Lady Cecelia had survived so many years with incompetents manning her yacht. Did rich people not even know the difference? She supposed not. A shiny surface would satisfy them, even if it covered decay.

"Yes," he said, after a moment. She nodded; she would hold him to it. At the end of this voyage, she would suggest to Lady Cecelia—no, she would insist—that she replace the least competent of the crew. In fact, with Iklind dead, perhaps they could find someone competent at Takomin Roads.

The refitting specifications all went into the message capsule, along with Lady Cecelia's credit authorization. By the time the *Sweet Delight* had come within a light-hour of the Takomin Roads, the refitters had had time to ready their equipment, unpack the necessary parts, and shift their workload to accommodate a rush job.

Or so they should have, Heris thought. The first message she received began by explaining how impossible it would be to do the work at all, and the next (a day later) argued that it could be done, but not within the time limit she had specified. Heris took none of these to Lady Cecelia; refitting was her responsibility and she knew already that a yacht owner, like an admiral, doesn't want to hear about problems that can be solved at a lower level. Besides, arguing with refitting had been a normal part of her duties as a cruiser captain. Those who didn't argue went to the bottom of the stack and got leftover parts.

She fired back her own messages as fast as the uncooperative ones came in, pointing out Lady Cecelia's holdings in the companies whose ships formed a large part of Velarsin & Co., Ltd.'s work. Alienating a major shareholder could have a negative impact on future contracts . . . she ignored, as beneath her notice, the long list of other work that would run overtime if Lady Cecelia's were done. The refitters capitulated, finally, in the last message received a half-hour before docking, when a Station tug already had a firm grip on the *Sweet Delight*'s bustle. Heris watched the docking critically; she had no real confidence in their pilot, and luckily no need for it—the Station's AI had no glitches as it eased them to Berth 78.

"I hope you're satisfied!" growled the bulky man in a dark gray shipsuit uniform when she called Velarsin & Co. "Shifted a dozen jobs for you, we have. Gonna lose a bonus on one of 'em."

"I shall be satisfied when our work is complete, correct, and prompt," said Heris.

He snorted, half anger and half respect, just like every Fleet Yard superintendent she'd ever known. "I have your specs," he said. "They're as foul as you claim your bilges are."

"I'm not surprised." Heris smiled at him. "We had non-conformance at the last maintenance, before I took this ship; it's my guess it hasn't met the original specs in years. When will your crew board?"

"They're waiting at your access," he said. "And me with 'em. I want to meet the captain of a private yacht that can bend the rules upstairs."

"Fine," said Heris. "I'll be there in five minutes. I have to inform the owner."

The owner, when Heris called her, sounded stiff and resentful. "I still do not understand, Captain Serrano, why we could not have stayed aboard. Surely, with the umbilicals to Station Environmental, we don't need to worry about contamination aboard. . . ."

She had explained before; she explained again, patiently but firmly. "Milady, even the best refitting crews cannot access the system without an occasional leak. It will stink—and worse than that, you might be exposed to hydrogen sulfide or other toxic contaminants. It is safest to seal the crew, staff, and owner's space—the vents themselves—which means no circulation at all. All the working crew will be in protective gear, as I will be while I supervise. It takes only one good lungful of sewer gas, milady, to kill you." She did not need to say more; Lady Cecelia gave a delicate shudder. And she had already arranged for the appropriate law enforcement division to take over Iklind's body, along with the meager evidence. "The crew is waiting, milady, and the sooner they start—"

"Very well." It was crisp and unfriendly, but not an argument. "And where are we staying?" The real problem, Heris thought, was that Lady Cecelia had never been here before and wasn't sure of accommodations. As well, those brats were probably whining and dragging their feet.

"You, milady, have a suite at the Selenor, where the shipping line executives stay. There's limited space, and I had to book the young people into a different hostelry on another level. I realize that's inconvenient—"

This time a trace of warmth in her employer's voice. "I can survive that. Meet me for dinner, then; I'll want a report. Twenty hundred, local time." Six hours; they'd just have started, really. Heris had counted on supervising them closely all through the first shift. But she could come report, and return quickly. She would not have to stay for a meal, she was sure.

"Of course, milady. I'll be at the maintenance access as you leave; please have Bates call when the staff has cleared the ship."

"Very well."

Heris gave her crew a stern look. "Mr. Gavin, you and Environmental will suit and observe the first shift. The rest of you are booked into transient crew quarters less than fifteen minutes from here; I expect you all to stay available. We'll have at least two crew aboard the ship at all times, and you'll rotate." A stir, no more; they knew better than to protest by now. "Have you confirmed Station air supply to every compartment?" she asked Gavin.

"To all but the owner's quarters, ma'am," he said. "I was going to do that as soon as milady left the ship; computer says it's fine, but . . ."

"Do that, then, while I go meet the refitters. Lady Cecelia is debarking now."

She followed the crew off the ship, and met the crew chief of the refitters in the maintenance access. He and his workers already wore pressure suits to protect themselves from contamination and carried helmets tucked under their arms. By the sudden flicker of his eyelids, she saw that he recognized her origins.

"I'm Captain Serrano," she said. "And you're . . ."

"Key Brynear," he said, a slow smile lighting his heavy face. "'Scuse my asking, but you're ex-Regs, aren't you?"

"That's right," said Heris. She wondered if he'd ask more, but he merely nodded.

"Guess that's why you managed to put fear into management. They don't hear command voice real often. Well, Captain, let's see what you've got." He wasted no time asking for details she'd already sent, but ordered his crew into helmets, and nodded sharply to Heris. She suited up, locked her own helmet on, and led him into the ship.

"Let's start from the bottom up," he said over the suit radio. She could hear his voice, but not the clear words, through the helmets; it formed an irritating echo. "Worst first, and then we can give you an estimate."

Heris had always hated suit drill, and even after the suit had saved her life she still disliked it; she hated being closed in with her own breath sounds and the hissing of the air supply. She had two hours of air in her own rebreathing tanks, and the exterior connector allowed her to plug into Station air in any compartment with a vent, but she *felt* smothered.

In the lowest environmental level, her own moles were already suited; they managed to look sheepish even in suits, as well they ought.

"Mr. Brynear," she said to her moles. "He's in charge of this overhaul."

"And here are my shift supervisors," Brynear said "Herak Santana, first shift; Allie Santana, second shift, and Miko Aldovar on third. Any time I'm not here, one of them will be; I expect to be here most of the time, but I may have to goose inventory control if you people are in as bad shape as you said."

The shift supervisors, in bicolored orange and silver suits, stood out from the orange-suited crew, but nonetheless had name and position stenciled on front and back of both suit and helmet. By local time, it was now second shift; the first shift supervisor waved to Brynear, who nodded, and then left. The second shift supervisor's voice came over the radio.

"Captain, would you have your crew secure compartments."

"Certainly." This command she could give herself, direct to the computer; the compartment hatches slid shut. Status lights changed, and they all moved to connect their suits to the compartment's exterior air supply vent. From now on they would have to take care not to tangle each other's umbilicals. "Confirm external air . . ." she said, and waited for each response before nodding to Brynear.

Brynear pointed to one of the ship's moles. "Let's take a look at the scrubber that's looking worst on the computer."

Inside the first protective shell, streaks of black slime marked the joints of the inner cover, and corrosion had frozen the bolts. Heris noticed that the gas sensors had gone red, instantly. One of the refitting techs grunted. "Who'd you say was supposed to have done the refit? And how far back?"

"Never mind, Tare," Brynear said. He moved over to look; when he tapped the scrubber with a wrench, more black goo oozed out. The readouts on the scrubber shell were all offscale. "That's the owner's problem; ours is fixing this mess. And I can tell right off we're going to need more equipment. You were right, Captain, this is an emergency refit if ever I saw one." His orders to his crew were, Heris heard with relief, as decisive as she'd have heard in a Fleet dock, and his explanation to her assumed that she would understand the technicalities.

"We're going to have to vacuum your entire system—and this Yard charges for hazardous storage. On the other hand, if it's this thick it may generate enough methane to pay part of your storage fee. And we've got a repair job in, a big Overhull tanker, that's going to need a whopping inoculation of its hydroponics. . . . I might be able to do a deal with them."

"Safety first, then speed," Heris said. "Money counts, but only third."

"Fine. We suck everything out, sort it, clean and repair, and put back your basic inoculum. . . . How about the living quarters—did you have much contamination up there?"

"No, probably because of the oversized filters; I kept thinking I smelled it the last day or so, but the sensors didn't react."

"Then we'll try a wet flush there—saves time—but the bottom end is going to be a bitch."

"Estimate?"

"Full crews—and it'll depend on whether we replace units or rebuild them—"

"Replace 'em," Heris said. "Anything you can."

"Forty-six hours," he said. "And that's spending your owner's money flat out. Can't be done in less than forty-two, if everything goes right, and it won't. Might be a little longer. . . ."

"Do your best," Heris said.

She had not expected real speed from a civilian refitting firm, but when Brynear's crews moved into high gear, she realized that they made their profit from speed. By mid-shift, four great hoses were draining the muck from *Sweet Delight* into the Yard storage tanks. Half the damaged scrubbers were out; Brynear, she noticed, was meticulous about giving credit for those which could be rebuilt. She and Brynear had documented the condition of scrubbers, chambers, and pipes; Lady Cecelia should have no trouble making a claim on Diklos & Sons. Or for that matter a case against Captain Olin.

In the second half of the shift, new components stacked up in the access bay: scrubbers, environmental chambers, parts, controls. Brynear and Heris inspected them together helmets off.

"We don't have enough to give you a matched set," he said. "You'll get thirteen Shnairsin and Lee 4872's, same as original equipment, and seven Plekhsov 8821's. Personally I prefer the Plekhsovs—we use 'em a lot as replacements and I think they're tougher—but I'd give you a matched set if I could. The performance specs are identical . . . here." Heris looked at the printout and passed it to her moles.

"That's good enough," she said. "What about environmental chambers? And the runs?"

"You'll have to have new chambers—every single culture either overgrew or was contaminated by one that did. Again, we have Shnairsin and Lee, but I recommend Tikman. They've come out with a lining that really is better—we've had about five years' experience with it."

"Go with the Tikman," Heris said. The Regs had seven years experience with the new polymer lining; she hadn't realized it was available on the civilian market. "The runs?"

He frowned. "That depends on whether you want to put

up with a little pitting. We can cut out the worst, and
patch—we have good pipefitters, and I guarantee you won't
have turbulence problems at the joints. Or we can pull them
all and restring the runs. Pitting . . . it's not dangerous,
once we cut out the really bad patches, but you'd want to
replace it within a year or two. It'd get you where you're
going, safe enough. Restringing all the runs will really
squeeze the time I gave you."

"So would finding all the bad places, and being sure of
them," Heris said. He nodded. "I want a safe ship, Mr.
Brynear; I'll take my owner's heat if you run a little over.
But . . ."

"It better be worth it—I understand that. I tell you,
Captain, I'm really shocked at Diklos. They used to be good.
I'd have trusted 'em with my own ship, if I couldn't get
here."

"Mistakes happen," Heris said, somewhat grimly. "But not
on my ship, not again. Now, if you have the hard copy
estimates, I'll go see Lady Cecelia."

CHAPTER FIVE

Even in the garish purple uniform, Heris felt more comfortable on the dockside, with honest ribbed deck-plates and not plush carpet beneath her feet. Everyone here worked on ships, and in that way everyone here was one of her kind, someone she understood. After a walk long enough to make her legs ache, she came out of Velarsin & Co., Ltd.'s docks and into the commercial sectors. She was glad she'd thought to have her luggage taken ahead, with her employer's. Here, sleek transport tubes marked one side of the walkway; fronting the other were shops, hotels, and eating places. None of the great logos bannered here, but often locals were as good. Heris stopped to consult a map display, and decided to take a tram the rest of the way to Lady Cecelia's hotel. As usual, the good hotels were as far as possible from the rumble and clatter of hard work.

She walked through a narrow door, with only the engraved plate with *Selenor* in slightly archaic script to indicate the identity, into a lobby that reached the stars. After one flinching look, she realized it only seemed to. The geometry of this Station allowed those with inside exposure to use the entire interior well as a private display. Those tiny lights were on the far side . . . except for the interior transports, sliding along maglines.

Meanwhile, the concierge was already smiling at her. "You must be Captain Serrano. . . . Lady Cecelia gave us your description."

"Yes—"

"And your room is ready, Captain. In the mauve tower, 2314, adjoining hers. Lady Cecelia said she didn't know when you might be in, but she supposed you'd like something to eat at once."

"How very thoughtful." She was hungry, now that she thought of it, but she needed to see her employer first.

"She said to tell you she would be resting, but—oh, wait. The light's changed. She's up again. I'll let her know you're on your way, shall I?"

"Yes, thank you."

The mauve tower droptubes were scented with a warm flowery fragrance that made Heris think of summer on one of the planets with native grasslands. She emerged into a small lobby splashed with soft color, and felt like a large purple blot. Lady Cecelia's suite unfolded its entrance for her, and a gust of pine fragrance overlay the summer grasslands. Heris felt its carefully engineered stimulants flicking her cortex, and resented it.

"Ah . . . Captain Serrano. And how is the *Sweet Delight*?" Lady Cecelia was not giving a millimeter. She wore a formal dinner gown, cream-colored and drapey, with her graying hair swept up to a peak by a jade clip. Behind her Heris could see a table set for two. Heris wondered who her guest would be. The entire sitting room of the suite seemed to be lined with mauve plush, on which cream-colored furniture floated like clouds in an evening sky.

"Missing a lot of essential equipment," Heris said. "I've authorized replacement rather than repair, since that is quicker and Diklos should reimburse you. They're keeping a complete record of the damage for legal use."

"Ah. And will we be out of here in forty-eight hours?"

"Very likely, but I cannot guarantee that. Sixty is the outside limit." Heris looked around. "If you'll excuse me, milady, I'd like to clean up and eat something before I go back to the ship."

Lady Cecelia's brows raised. "Go back? Surely you're going to rest. . . . I intended you to eat dinner with me. Don't you remember?" Heris had forgotten, but she couldn't say that. Besides, the ship mattered more.

"Considering what happened last time she was in for work—"

"Nonsense. You need sleep the same as anyone else. At least, have dinner here. . . . Go freshen up, get out of that uniform, and relax awhile." Heris wondered if she had correctly interpreted the tone of *that uniform.*

"Umm . . . milady . . . you would prefer that I not wear your uniform here?"

Lady Cecelia's lips pinched; she sighed. "I would prefer that my sister Berenice had not tried to compensate me for Ronnie by insisting that I use her decorator. I would prefer I had had the wit to refuse, but I was already rattled by the change in schedule, by Ronnie, by his friends—"

Mental gears whirled. "You don't . . . ah . . . *like* all that lavender plush?"

"Of course not!" Lady Cecelia glared at her. "Do I look like the kind of silly old woman who would?" That was unanswerable; Heris kept her face blank. Lady Cecelia shook her head and emitted a snort that might have been anger or laughter, either one. "All right. You don't know me; you couldn't tell. But I don't like it, and I'm having it out as soon as I decently can. Your uniform—that's another thing Berenice insisted on. Captain Olin had always worn black, and Berenice thought it was dull and old-fashioned."

"Surely," Heris said carefully, "there's something between black and loud purple with scarlet and teal trim?"

Lady Cecelia snorted again, this time with obvious humor. "You don't know the worst: Berenice wanted me to approve cream with purple and teal trim. She told me the gaudier it was, the more a new captain would be impressed. The purple was the darkest thing offered."

"Ah. Then you wouldn't mind if I . . . modified this a bit?"

"Be my guest." Lady Cecelia scowled again. "Although I don't suppose you can arrange a complete redecoration while we're here?"

Heris grinned, surprising herself as much as her employer. "To be honest, milady, I've wanted to get that lavender plush off the access tube bulkheads—for safety reasons, I assure you—since I first came aboard."

"Safety reasons?" Now Lady Cecelia grinned, more relaxed than Heris had yet seen her. "What a marvelous idea! Is it true?"

"Oh, yes. There's a lot hidden on your ship that shouldn't

be—it's pretty, but it's hard to see trouble in the early stages. We certainly don't have time here for a complete redecoration, but a little *un*decorating won't slow things down."

"Well. Good. Now, about dinner . . ."

"Let me change into something comfortable. Ten minutes?"

Heris returned to her employer's suite in her own off-duty clothes—the first time she'd worn them since leaving the Service. Since Lady Cecelia was wearing a formal dinner gown, she put on her own, and had the satisfaction of seeing her employer truly surprised.

"My dear! I had no idea you looked like that!" Then Lady Cecelia blushed. "I'm sorry. That was unforgivable."

"Not really, although it was your uniform that made me look the other way." Heris knew very well what the close-fitting jet-beaded bodice did for her; the flared black skirt swirled around her ankles as she came to the table. She would never have the advantage of Cecelia's height, but she had learned to use color and line to compensate. "Oh—one last bit of business before dinner . . . what about the inquest on Iklind?"

"Not a problem." Lady Cecelia slipped into her seat and picked up her napkin. "With the documentation you supplied, and the medical evidence from Timmons, this will be treated as an obvious accident."

Heris sat down; she knew she shouldn't continue the subject at table, but questions cluttered her mind. "I wish—"

"Not now," Lady Cecelia interrupted her. "We can discuss this later, if you wish, though I would prefer to wait until tomorrow, local time. By then forensics should have confirmed the cause of death, and I'll know more."

Heris blinked. She had not realized that Lady Cecelia would be dealing with the legal problems of Iklind's death while she worked on the ship; she had thought she would have to do it all herself.

Dinner arrived, with a cluster of attendants. Heris found herself staring at a tiny wedge of something decorated with a sprig of green.

"Lassaferan snailfish fin," Lady Cecelia commented. "The garnish is frilled zillik. We grew that aboard, before—at one time."

Heris tasted the snailfish fin, which had been dipped in

a mustardy sauce; it had an odd but winsome flavor, perfectly complemented by the zillik. She had eaten at places that served this sort of food, usually while on a political assignment, but the Service favored less quixotic cuisine. One rarely had time to spend hours at the table. She hoped she would not have to spend hours at dinner now—with the relaxation induced by comfortable clothes, she had begun to realize how tired she was.

Next came a hot soup, its brilliant reds and golds contrasting with the pallid snailfish fin. Fish and vegetables, flavors well-blended, with enough spice to make her eyes water . . . "Sikander chowder," Lady Cecelia said, smiling. "Good when you're tired. I used to have this a lot when I was competing." Heris wondered what she'd competed at, but didn't ask; she could have eaten two bowls of the chowder, and twice as many of the crisp rolls served alongside it.

"This is delicious," she said, as she finished the chowder.

"I thought you'd like that," Lady Cecelia said. "I'm going to try their roast chicken and rice, but if you want more chowder just say so."

Courtesy and appetite argued, and courtesy won; Heris let the waiter remove her soup plate and accepted the roast chicken—slices of breast meat, marinated and grilled after roasting, formed the wings of a swan; its body was a mound of spiced rice. The graceful head and neck had been artfully formed of curled spicegrass. She took a cautious bite of the rice—ginger? mustard? coriander?—and devoured it with almost indecent haste. She had been hungrier than she knew. . . . The slices of chicken disappeared, then the spicegrass.

The next course seemed out of sequence to Heris, but she realized that Lady Cecelia could set her own standards. Still, the platter of fruit, 'ponics-grown melons and berries, didn't suit her at the moment. She nibbled a jade-green slice of melon, to be polite. Lady Cecelia, too, seemed as ready to talk as eat. She began with a question about the literature studied at the Academy—one of her great-nephews had said no one there read Siilvaas—was that true? Heris recognized this opening and added to her reply (yes, they read Siilvaas, but only the famous trilogy) a comment about a more contemporary writer. For a few minutes they discussed

Kerlskvan's recent work, feeling out each other's knowledge. Lady Cecelia had not read the first novel; Heris had not read the third most recent.

The cheeses came in; the fruit remained. Heris sliced a wafer of orange Jebbilah cheese, and floated a comment about visual arts. Lady Cecelia waved that away. "As for me," she said, "I like pictures of horses. The more accurate it is, the better. Aside from that I know nothing about the visual arts, and don't want to. I was made to study it when I was a girl, but since then—no." She smiled to take the sting out of that. "Now, let me ask you: what do you know about horses?"

"Nothing," Heris said, "except that we had to have riding lessons in the Academy. Officers must be able to sit a horse properly for ceremonial occasions: that's what they said." In her voice was much the same contempt her employer had expressed for visual arts. Anyone who could prefer a horse picture, good or bad, to one of Gorgini's explosive paintings . . .

"You don't like them?" Lady Cecelia asked.

"What—horses? Frankly, milady, to a spacer they're simply large, dirty, smelly animals with an appalling effect on the environmental system. I remember one time having to inspect a commercial hauler which was taking horses somewhere—why, I can't imagine—and it was a mess. I don't blame the animals, of course. They evolved on a planet, and on something the size of a planet there's enough space for them. But in the hold of a starship? No."

"Did you like riding them?" asked Lady Cecelia. She had a mild, vague expression which didn't suit her.

Heris shrugged. "It wasn't as bad as some of the other things we had to learn. I did fairly well, in fact. But it's so useless—when would anyone need to ride a horse anywhere?"

"Only on uncivilized planets where it rains without permission," Lady Cecelia said. Heris was sure she detected an edge to her voice, but the expression stayed mild. Belatedly, she remembered that the reason her employer so wanted to be on time was for the start of the "foxhunting season" which had something to do with horses.

"Of course," she said, "many people do enjoy them. Recreationally."

"Yes." This time the edge was unmistakeable. "Many people do. I, for one. Did your lessons at the Academy ever include riding them in the open—across country?"

"No—we had all our lessons in an enclosed ring."

"So you have no experience of real riding?"

Heris wondered why riding in a ring was not real. The horse had been large and had smelled like a horse. The sore muscles she got from riding had been real enough. But from her employer's face, this was not going to be a popular question. "I haven't ridden anywhere but in those lessons, no," she said cautiously.

"Ah. Then I suggest a wager." This with a bright-eyed glance that made Heris suddenly nervous.

"A wager?"

"Yes. If the refitters are finished, and we clear this station forty-eight hours after we arrived—no, fifty hours, for you will need a little time, I'm sure, to ready for departure—then you win, and I will submit to be lectured by you on visual arts for ten hours. If, however, we are delayed, you lose, and will owe me ten hours, which I shall use in teaching you to ride—really ride—on my simulator."

"An interesting wager," Heris said, nibbling her cheese. "But that assumes that I want to bore you with ten hours of visual arts, which I don't—I'm an admirer of some artists' work, but no expert. What I wish you knew more about was your own ship. Suppose, if I win, you spend ten hours with me learning how to tell if your refitters did a good job?"

"You are that confident that we will be out in fifty hours?"

"I am confident that, either way, we will both learn something worthwhile," said Heris. Lady Cecelia flushed.

"You're mocking me—you don't think riding is worthwhile!"

"No, milady. I am not mocking you, which would be both rude and foolish. You think it is important; I have not, up until now, but perhaps I'm wrong. If I lose, you have the chance to convince me. And I'm very sure that you would have been spared expense and inconvenience both had you known more about the workings of your yacht. Did you always take the horse a . . . ." She struggled for the word, then remembered it. "A groom brought you, and get on and ride away? We were taught to inspect the . . . the tack . . . for ourselves, to look at the animal's feet—"

"Hooves," put in Lady Cecelia, cooler now.

"Hooves, and see if it had any problems."

"I see your point," Lady Cecelia said. "No, certainly I did not take my grooms' word for everything." The quick color had gone from her cheeks, and she seemed to have recovered her earlier good humor. "Very well, then: if you win, I will study my yacht's particulars, and if I win, you will study horsemanship. Is it agreed?"

"Certainly." Heris reached across and shook her employer's hand. How hard could it be, after all? The simulator wasn't a real horse; it couldn't step on her, or bite her, or run away with her.

Whatever else she might have said was interrupted by a chime; Lady Cecelia touched the table's control pad and the concierge's voice announced that her nephew and his friends were on their way up.

"No—I don't want to see them!" Lady Cecelia said. Heris noticed the quick flow and ebb of color to her face.

"I'm sorry, milady; they're already in the tube."

"Blast it!" Lady Cecelia half rose from her chair, and the attendants scurried to help her. She waved them away, reseated herself, and glanced at Heris. "I apologize, Captain, for the past moment and the coming hour. I'll get rid of them as soon as I can."

"Aunt Cecelia, it's unforgivable!" That was Ronnie, first in the door when it opened. "That disgusting captain of yours put us in a cheap place as far from here as you can imagine; they don't even have a—" He stopped abruptly as Heris turned to face him. She was delighted to see how far his jaw dropped before he got it back under control.

"It's the captain," said George unnecessarily. The two young women looked ashamed of themselves and their companions; the blonde one opened her mouth and shut it; the dark one spoke up in a soft voice.

"That's a lovely dress, Captain Serrano." Heris noted that Ronnie gave her a disgusted look, so she smiled at the young woman . . . Raffaele, she thought her name was.

"Thank you," she said sweetly. "I'm glad you appreciate it."

"You might want to know," Lady Cecelia said, in a stiff voice, "that *I* approved your assignment to that hotel. If you want to blame someone, blame me. Captain Serrano has been far too busy saving our lives to spare any energy to make your lives miserable."

Ronnie was a strange color two shades darker than bright pink.

"What is unforgivable," Lady Cecelia went on, "is your rude intrusion into my dinner and private conversation, and your insulting my captain. You will apologize to Captain Serrano, now—or you can find your own way home and take whatever punishment you get, which I am sure you richly deserve."

"Here, now—" began George, but Lady Cecelia quelled him with a glance. Ronnie looked from one to the other, and gave a minute shrug.

"I'm sorry, Aunt Cecelia . . . and Captain Serrano. It was not—I didn't mean to be rude—I just—"

"Wanted your own way. I know. And that is an entirely inadequate apology. You called Captain Serrano 'disgusting'; you will retract that." Heris had not realized that any civilian could sound so much like a flag officer. Suddenly it was easy to imagine Lady Cecelia in full dress uniform with braid up to her shoulders.

Ronnie's flush darkened and his lip curled; the glance he shot Heris was unchastened and furious. "I'm sorry, Captain Serrano," he said between his teeth, "that I referred to you as 'disgusting.' It was ungentlemanly." Heris nodded, dismissing it. She would say nothing that might make things worse between aunt and nephew.

"You may go now," Lady Cecelia said. She picked up her glass and sipped. Heris doubted if she knew whether she had water or wine in it. The girls turned to go at once; George backed up a step, but Ronnie looked as if he were inclined to argue. "Now," Lady Cecelia said. "And don't roam too far from your hotel unless you carry a comunit. I will give you only one hour's notice to reboard, and it would not hurt my feelings to leave you here."

Ronnie gave a stiff bow, turned on his heel and almost pushed the others out of the suite. When the entrance refolded itself, Lady Cecelia shook her head. "I'm truly sorry," she said. "Ronnie suffers from . . . from being the oldest boy in his family, the first grandchild in our branch, and his parents' pride. He was spoiled before he was born, I daresay, if there's a way to indulge an embryo in the tank.

The mess he's in now—" She spread her hands. "Sorry. It's not fair to bore you with this."

Heris smiled, and sipped. Water, for her, while the refitting was going on; she could afford not the slightest haze between her and reality. "Lady Cecelia, nothing that concerns you bores me. Surprises me, perhaps, but don't fear that I'm bored. If you wish to discuss it—"

"I suppose you think you could straighten him out." Lady Cecelia looked grumpy now, in the aftermath of the argument.

Heris shrugged. "It's not my job, straightening out your nephew—unless you request it. And then—I don't know. When I've had someone of his social class to deal with, it's because he or she volunteered; I had leverage based on their own motivation."

"You must despise us," Lady Cecelia said.

"Why? Because you have a bratty nephew? I've seen admirals' children with the same problem."

"Really. I thought military children were born saluting the obstetrician and clicked their heels as soon as they stood up." Although the tone was wry, there was an undertone of real curiosity. Heris laughed.

"Their parents wish! No, milady, we're born squally brats the same as everyone else, and have to be civilized the same way. Your nephew seems to me the logical result of privilege—but no worse than others."

"Thank God for that." Lady Cecelia looked down. "I'd been imagining you all this time turning up your nose at me for having such a nephew." Heris hoped her face didn't reveal that she had thought that, and shook her head.

"Milady, as you said, I've been too busy to give much thought to your nephew. Your crew, now . . ." Was this the time to bring up those problems? No. She smiled and went on. "If you want to talk about your nephew, feel free. I'm listening."

"He got in trouble," Lady Cecelia said, with no more preamble. Heris listened to the story of the prince's singer and the rest with outward calm and inward satisfaction. About what she expected from that sort of young man. She hadn't realized he was in the Royal Aero-Space Service—and wondered why he'd been foisted off on his aunt, when his colonel should have been able to handle the situation. She asked.

"Because my sweet sister wouldn't allow it," Lady Cecelia said grimly. "He certainly could have been posted to . . . say . . . Xingsan, where his regiment has a work depot, for a year. Or someplace where he'd actually do useful work. But Berenice interceded, and got him a year's sabbatical—a sabbatical, in the military—on the promise that he would not show his face in the capital."

"Mmm," said Heris, considering just how Cecelia's sister could have that much influence with the Crown. Her train of thought came out before she censored it. "Does . . . uh . . . Ronnie look much like his father?"

Lady Cecelia snorted. "Yes, but that doesn't answer your real question. Ronnie's an R.E.—" At Heris's blank look she explained. "A Registered Embryo, surely you have them?"

"I've heard of them." It cost more than a year's salary to have an R.E., and what you were paying for was not technology but insurance. In this instance it also meant that Ronnie had not resulted from a casual liaison.

"Anyway," Lady Cecelia went on, "my sister Berenice decided that I should take Ronnie on. She never has approved of the way I live, and I was there, handy."

"Because Captain Olin ran late," Heris said.

"Yes. Normally I'm at the capital only for the family business meeting—in and out as fast as possible. This year I missed the meeting—which meant my proxy voted my shares, and *not* as I would have wished—and arrived just in time for Ronnie's disgrace. These are not unconnected; it was apparently in celebrating his first opportunity to vote his own shares at the meeting that he overindulged, and came to brag about the singer."

"So—your sister had your yacht redecorated—"

"And she is paying for Ronnie's expenses. Up to a point. I'm supposed to be grateful." Lady Cecelia made a face; Heris wondered what had caused the bad feeling in her family in the first place. She waited in attentive silence, in case Lady Cecelia wanted to say more, but the older woman turned to ask the attendants to bring the sweet. Heris was glad to see the last of the fruit and cheese, but not really interested in the sweet. She wanted a few hours' sleep.

"If you'll excuse me," she began. "I really need to check with the refitting crew aboard, and my watch officer."

"Oh—certainly. Go ahead." Lady Cecelia's expression was

carefully neutral. Did she think Heris was disgusted with her? Heris felt a surge of sympathy for the older woman. She grinned.

"I have a wager to win, remember?"

That got the open smile she hoped for, and Lady Cecelia raised her glass in salute. "We shall see," she said. "I have the feeling you'll make an excellent horsewoman."

Heris laughed. "As the luck falls, and my ability to push the refitters succeeds. See you later."

Lady Cecelia watched her captain leave the room, and wondered what the woman really thought. Clearly she had more qualifications than shipboard skills alone: she was well read, she wore good clothes, she knew what to do with the array of eating utensils common to fine dining, and she had surprising tact. On the face of it, she would have made a far more compatible sister than Berenice. She let herself imagine the two of them riding side by side across the training fields . . . relaxing together over dinner. No. This woman never relaxed, not really, while she . . . Lady Cecelia allowed herself a relaxed sigh. Her captain might snatch a few hours' sleep, but would doubtless dream of wiring diagrams and structural steel. She herself would follow this excellent dinner with a relaxing stroll in the hotel's excellent garden, and then sleep as long as she liked in her luxurious bed with all its inventive amenities.

The stroll and the engineered scents in the garden eased the last of the tension her nephew's rudeness had put in her shoulders, and she slipped into the warmed, perfumed bed contentedly. She could hear Myrtis checking all the room's controls, murmured that she'd like it a bit cooler, and was asleep before the cooler draft had time to reach her cheek.

Morning brought complications, as she'd expected. This was not the first time one of her employees had died, just the first on her yacht, and by far the most violent. She had already contacted the legal firm recommended by her family's own solicitors; the bright-eyed young man in formal black had been waiting downstairs by the concierge's desk when she emerged from her bedroom and called for breakfast. She looked at the local time, and whistled. Mid-morning of mainshift, and he had time to wait on her? She checked her captain's whereabouts while he was on the way up, and found, as she expected, that Serrano was back at work on the yacht.

He was talking almost before he got into the room. "Now, Lady Cecelia, I'm sure you're simply devastated by this, but let me assure you that our firm is experienced—"

She stopped him with a gesture. "Wait. I'm going to eat breakfast, and you're welcome to join me. But no business until afterwards, though in fact I'm not devastated, and if you weren't experienced, you wouldn't have been recommended." That stopped him, though he fidgeted all through breakfast, refusing to eat. Finally his nervous twitches got to her, and she gave up on the diced crustaceans in a puree of mixed tubers. . . . It was mediocre anyway, too heavily flavored with dill and some local spice that burnt her tongue without offering a taste worth the pain. She finished with a large pastry, and a silver bowl of some red jam—quite flavorful—and nodded to him. "Go on, now; what's the damage?"

"Your crewman . . . that was killed . . ." He seemed stunned that she wasn't falling apart. What did he think, that older women never saw death?

"Environmental technician Nils Iklind," Lady Cecelia recited. "He disobeyed the captain's orders to wear his protective suit, opened a badly overfull sludge tank, and died of hydrogen sulfide poisoning. You have seen the data cubes?"

"Yes, ma'am . . . Lady Cecelia. Our senior partners reviewed them, and feel that you have a very strong case for accidental death."

"So what is the problem?"

"Well . . ." The young man fidgeted some more, and Lady Cecelia began to compose the memo she would send to the family solicitors explaining why this firm was *not* suitable. "It's the union, ma'am. They think it's the captain's fault for sending him into a dangerous area—for inadequate supervision in allowing him to enter the area without his suit on. Particularly since your other crewman also did not have his suit properly on, and says that all the captain did was tell them to meet there, suited up."

Cecelia sniffed. "And how was the captain to know that he would open the hatch before she got there? Why didn't he wait?"

"That's not the point. They're inclined to argue that the captain should have been there to enforce the order to suit up. Or at least another officer. On larger vessels, of course, there would be a supervisor. Technically, Iklind held a supervisory rating, but he hadn't been acting in that capacity. And the maintenance logs and emergency drills—"

"That was Captain Olin's misconduct; Captain Serrano told me she had begun training crew and reestablishing the correct procedures."

"But she hadn't completed that process yet, and that's what the union is arguing. I'll need to interview the captain—"

"She's aboard the ship, overseeing the refitting. You'd have to suit up." A chime sounded; when she looked, the comunit flashed discreetly. "Excuse me a moment."

"It might be the office for me," he said, but Cecelia waved him to silence as she pressed the button to her ear.

"Sorry to bother you," Captain Serrano said, "but we have a new problem that may help solve an old one."

"What's that?" Cecelia asked. The young man across from her looked as if he were trying to grow his ears longer; it gave him a very odd expression.

"Mr. Brynear has found . . . items . . . in one of the scrubbers. It might explain why Iklind risked going in unsuited, and it might explain why Captain Olin connived at a fake maintenance procedure." Her captain said no more; Cecelia hoped it was because she assumed her employer's innocence and intelligence both.

"Ummm. You would prefer to discuss this someplace else?"

"I would, but it is clearly a matter for law enforcement. Mr. Brynear has documented the discovery." Which meant law enforcement had already been summoned. What, she wondered, could Captain Olin have been up to? Smuggling? But what? She realized she had no idea how large a "scrubber" was, or what would fit into it. But she couldn't ask over an unsecured com line.

"It seems I have a good chance to win our wager," Cecelia said. "Where shall I meet you? I have legal advice with me."

"We could all come there, or you could come to the refitters. . . . Your counsel should know. . . ."

"We'll come." She felt she had to have some refuge from conflict; she would meet trouble elsewhere. In a few brief phrases she explained the little she understood to the young man, who gulped and asked permission to call back to his office. "While I change," she said, and headed for the bedroom and Myrtis. What did one wear when one's crewman had died of an accident that might be related to smuggling, and the goods—whatever they were—had been found aboard one's yacht? What could convey innocence, outrage, and the determination to be a good citizen? She had never been skilled at this sort of thing. . . . Berenice would have known instantly which scarf or pin, which pair of shoes, would give the right impression. Cecelia opted for formal and dark, with a hat, which hid the unruly lock of hair that wanted to stand straight up from her head.

When she emerged, the young man explained that a senior partner would meet her at the refitter's . . . he would escort her there, and hand over the case papers. Cecelia smiled at him, and raged inwardly. They should have sent a senior partner in the first place . . . no doubt they were billing the family at the senior partner's rate.

CHAPTER SIX

"Ah . . . Lady Cecelia?" The gray-haired man flicked a glance at the younger one that made him hand over his briefcomp and then leave.

"Yes, and you're—?"

"Ser Granzia, and you're quite right that we should not have sent a junior partner." He offered his arm; she took it. "We should have known that you would not call in legal help for a minor problem, and the . . . individual who made that decision has been so informed."

"Ah. I had wondered." Cecelia let herself be guided into the front office of the refitters. A respectful secretary murmured that Mr. Desin and Chief Brynear were waiting for them in the conference room. Ser Granzia, it seemed, knew the way; his guidance was subtle but unmistakable. Cecelia noticed that the flat gray tweed carpet of the front office gave way to a flat utilitarian surface dully reflecting the overhead lights. On either side, small offices stood open, cluttered with terminals, parts, schematics. She didn't recognize any of it. Around a corner, carpet reappeared, this time a rich green, much softer. Double doors at the end of the corridor led into a spacious conference room with a wide window to the same sort of view her hotel suite provided. Four people waited there, a tall man in conventional business attire, a shorter one in a rumpled coverall, a nondescript person no doubt representing law and order, and Captain Serrano. On the wide polished table that Cecelia recognized as brasilwood lay a small packet, something lumpy encased in a bag or sack.

"The owner, I presume?" said the tall man. "I'm Eniso Desin, madam. And this is Chief Brynear, the individual in charge of your refitting, and Mr. Files, the local investigator for CenCom."

"Lady Cecelia de Marktos a Bellinveau," said Ser Granzia. Cecelia had not heard herself introduced formally for some time; now she remembered why she disliked it so. It sounded silly. "Of the Aranlake Sept, fides de Barraclough." It could also go on another five lines or so, if she didn't stop him. The complete formality gave the genetic makeup, political affiliations, and social standing of the male and female lines for six generations . . . but was usually reserved for those assumed to be ignorant of it, and in need of awe.

"And yes, I'm the owner," she said, when Granzia paused for breath.

"The ship's registry," Files said, "lists you as Lady Cecelia Marktos. I presume that's equivalent?"

"Yes," Cecelia said. "The registry doesn't have room on the owner's line for all of it. I asked, and they said it would be adequate."

"And you are the same Lady Cecelia to whom the yacht designated SY-00021-38-HOX was originally registered?"

"Yes, of course I am." Who else, her tone said.

His gaze flicked from her to Captain Serrano and back. "Then I regret to inform you that your vessel has apparently been involved in illegal activities of a criminal nature." Cecelia wondered what illegal activities of a non-criminal nature would be, but didn't ask. "How long has this . . . Captain Serrano . . . been your commanding officer?"

"Since I left the Court. I dismissed my former captain for incompetence and refusal to follow my orders, and Captain Serrano had just resigned from the Regular Space Service. She had signed with the employment agency I use and they recommended her highly."

"And that agency is?"

"I don't see what this has to do with anything," Cecelia said, beginning to feel grumpy. Whatever was going on, she was sure Captain Serrano hadn't been involved. The woman might be a stiff-necked military prig, but she wasn't any kind of a criminal. "Perhaps you would be kind enough to explain just what sort of illegal activity you are talking about."

"Do you know what that is?" Files pointed to the packet on the table.

"No." She felt her brows rising, as much irritation as ignorance. She didn't like people playing games with her. "I suppose you are going to explain?"

"In good time, madam. You're sure you've never seen it before?"

"I told you—" she began in an exasperated voice; Ser Granzia intervened.

"Excuse me, but if you are contemplating criminal charges against Lady Cecelia, or her captain, you surely remember that you must inform them."

"I know that," Files said. "But if the lady had nothing to do with it, her answer might help—"

"I think she will answer no further questions until you have explained, to my satisfaction, what you think it is." Ser Granzia's voice, mellow and lush though it was, contained no hint of yielding.

"We believe it to be smuggled goods. It has not yet been subjected to forensic examination, but just glancing at it my guess is proprietary data." From Files's expression, he hoped she wouldn't understand.

"You mean—trade secrets? Something an—an industrial spy might have made off with?"

"Possibly. Because proprietary data is secret—"

"Are secret," Cecelia murmured. She might not know much about industry, but she knew data was a plural noun. Files grimaced.

"Whatever you say, madam. Are secret—anyway, theft is not reported. It may not be known. It's not like jewels in a vault."

"Could it be military?" That from Heris Serrano. Cecelia looked at her captain who looked back with dark, inscrutable eyes.

"Possibly," Files said. "Forensics will tell us." Clearly he had no intention of sharing his turf with anyone. "Then, if it is—"

"Fleet should know." Not even a ridiculous purple uniform could make Heris Serrano look unimportant. Cecelia tried to imagine her former captain in the same garb, and realized that he'd have looked like a purple blimp straining at its tether. This woman, in his black, would have looked dangerous. "Fleet forensics could assist."

"I'll be the judge of that," Files said. Ser Granzia stirred at Cecelia's side; Files shot him a glance. "Did you have *legal* advice, Ser Granzia?"

"That if it is possibly a military secret, the captain is correct: some representative should be present when it is examined in any detail. Otherwise we may all find ourselves compromised. You remember, no doubt, the decision of Army versus Stillinbagh?"

"Very well." Files looked angry. "I will inform the local military attaché."

"Perhaps," Ser Granzia said, "we could wait while you did so?"

Cecelia wondered if she was imagining the threat in his tone. Files flushed, asked for a comlink, and spoke into it. He set it back down with care, as if he really wanted to throw it through the wall, and said the attaché would be along shortly. Cecelia was in no mood to wait for more information. "Captain Serrano," she began, bypassing Files, "can you tell me how this was found?"

Her captain smiled, as if glad to be asked the question. "Yes—you remember that I authorized Velarsin and Co. to exchange all damaged units from the environmental system, rather than repairing them in place?"

"Of course," Cecelia said.

"That was for reasons of both time and safety. You may recall that I also had Mr. Brynear document the condition of those components, to back up your damage claim on Diklos and Sons." When Cecelia nodded, she went on. "Some components could be repaired, and we were to get a refund on those. In the process of examining the components removed, Mr. Brynear's technicians found items secreted in several. Most suggestively, in the scrubber which we were going to examine when Iklind was killed because he didn't have his suit on."

Cecelia felt only confusion. "What does that have to do with it?" Before Serrano could answer, Cecelia realized. "Oh— he *knew* something was there? Something you'd find?"

"We can't know, Lady Cecelia." Heris glanced at Files, who clearly wished she wouldn't explain more, but she went on. "There's a chain of occurrences that makes me suspicious of Iklind and possibly others formerly or presently in the crew. The system flush and recharge that Diklos and Sons didn't do. The curiously inefficient course your former captain set on the way to Court, which made you late. Iklind's apparent haste to get to that scrubber before I did—at the cost of his own life."

"You think he was smuggling something. Iklind and . . . and Captain Olin?" First came anger: how *dare* he? And then fear . . . how had she not known what was happening on her ship? How were the smuggled items transferred if they were? Would Olin have opened the ship to boarders?

"It's possible, madam," said Files, with a sharp glance at Heris. "Ship's crews have been known to do so, without an owner's knowledge. Of course, sometimes the owner is also involved."

"Surely you jest." That was all she could say. The impertinence of the man!

"Are you suggesting the Lady Cecelia was involved in any putative illegal act?" asked Ser Granzia. "Remember—"

"I remember the Sihil-Tomaso ruling, Ser Granzia," said Files. "I made no accusation; I merely answered what seemed to be Lady Cecelia's question." His smile was more of a smirk, she decided. He went on. "Now: procedurally, we must impound the evidence, which includes the location in which it was found; I'm afraid your ship is that location—" Cecelia could hardly believe her ears. Was everything against her?

"Not so, Mr. Files." Her captain's crisp voice interrupted Files. "The scrubbers were not in the ship when the items were found. They had already been removed. All environmental system components are dockside; what's in the *Sweet Delight* is new and empty."

"But that's where they *were*," Files said. "On that ship with the contraband in them. There may be more, hidden somewhere else. It doesn't matter where the scrubbers were when the evidence was actually found—"

"On the contrary." Ser Granzia's honey-smooth voice had an edge to it now. "According to the rules of evidence in a list of rulings going back to Essex versus Jovian Mining Ltd., impoundment of the container does not include impoundment of the vessel in which that container was transported, if the discovery occurred while the container was not aboard."

"But we *know* the contraband was aboard," Files said, more loudly.

"But it doesn't matter, Mr. Files." Ser Granzia did not raise his voice, but Cecelia saw the other man wilt. "The rulings are all clear, and all in favor of my client. I will be glad to get a local ruling, of course, but I'm sure it will uphold my client's position. Now—shall we contact Fleet? I believe it is better for us to do this together."

Files looked angry, but nodded; Ser Granzia turned to Eniso Desin, the senior partner of Velarsin and Co. "May we use your equipment?"

"Of course, Ser Granzia. But I am afraid that we cannot give Lady Cecelia full credit for the reparable elements of the system until they are released from official custody. . . . I am sorry, but—"

"I quite understand," Ser Granzia said. "Indeed, it would be unfair, and my client will be satisfied if you keep account of what was impounded; if it should be released, and still worth repair, perhaps you will bid on it?"

"Oh, certainly," Desin said. "Mr. Brynear assures me that at least sixty percent of the components would be worth working on."

"Excellent." Cecelia wondered if she, too, should say something, but Ser Granzia rolled on. "Now—it seems to me, Mr. Files, that the discovery of items secreted in the scrubber suggests a motive for Iklind to attempt removal at risk of his life. In fact, it strongly suggests his complicity in some illegal activity, and Captain Serrano's innocence. I would suggest that a search warrant, limited to Iklind's personal items and storage spaces, might prove fruitful."

"But—!" Cecelia got that much out before his hand clamped on her wrist.

"It need not," he went on, "inconvenience Lady Cecelia or interfere with her schedule, provided that you act in a timely manner."

"Right." Files seemed sapped of energy. Cecelia wondered if Ser Granzia's voice had a hypnotic overlay. "I'll—get that done as soon as we've contacted the military."

Before she knew how it happened, Cecelia found herself sitting across a table from Heris Serrano in Desin's private office, with a tray of hot pastries and a variety of drinks before her. Ser Granzia was still in conference with Mr. Files and Desin; Desin's assistant had brought the refreshments and now left them alone. Cecelia watched her captain pour herself a cup of something hot from a fluted pot. The woman had a quality Cecelia had not yet defined, but found attractive. She never fidgeted, never seemed divided against herself. Yet she did not seem insensitive . . . someone who had read and enjoyed Siilvaas could not be insensitive.

"You may win our wager, milady," she said now. She offered the steaming cup to Cecelia, who shook her head. She wanted something cold, and chose a bottle of fruit juice from an ice bucket.

"Circumstances have changed," Cecelia said. "Perhaps I should withdraw?"

"No—a wager's a wager." Serrano's short black hair actually moved when she shook her head; Cecelia had begun to wonder if it was a wig. "I shall look forward to my lessons on your mechanical horse." She had an engaging grin, Cecelia decided, which made her look years younger.

"Ummm. I still think the interruption of officialdom makes it unfair: suppose I exchange honors and let you teach me more about my ship? I'm now convinced my own ignorance is both inconvenient and culpable."

The dark eyes measured her; Cecelia felt suddenly as if she had become a novice rider, facing a stern judge in her first event. Why had a woman with such a gift of command given up her commission? Cecelia could not believe it was anything dishonorable . . . not with those eyes. A mistake? A quarrel? She had not seemed quarrelsome so far, even when confronted with Ronnie's rudeness.

"If it is your pleasure," Serrano said. "Then I will be very glad to show you over your ship. But I cannot consider it as your obligation under our wager unless I actually win . . . and despite the best your legal firm can do, I expect we will be late leaving."

Cecelia snorted. "I'm beginning to think this year's season is jinxed. Here I was invited for the opening day—planned to be early for once, planned to attend the first ball, even. Then Olin got me to Court late, and I had young Ronnie foisted on me, and now this. If I'm not careful I'll break a leg or something and miss hunting altogether."

"How long does it last? If it's more than a few days, we should be there for some of it."

The ignorance surprised her again, but she reminded herself that even among her class, not everyone knew much about fox hunting. "The season is just that," she said gently. "A whole season—in this case, a planetary quartile. Ideally, fox hunting is done when it is cool enough so that the horses don't overheat in the long chase, damp enough for hounds to pick up the scent."

"Then—"

"Oh, we'll arrive before it's over, if something else doesn't happen. But it's the opening—the first day—that excitement—" Cecelia stared out the window at the view without seeing it. "You can't understand; you haven't been there. I love it anyway, wet days and dry; I'm one of the last to leave. It's just different, that's all."

"Did you ever do any sailing?" Serrano asked.

"Sailing? You mean on water?" When Serrano nodded, Cecelia went on. "Yes, a little. Bunny has lodges on island groups; I remember sailing little boats, hardly more than floatboards, one afternoon. Why?"

"Because what you describe for hunting reminds me of racing season at my grandparents' place on Lowein. There again there's a season, a weather pattern, that fits the sport, and on the first day all the boats, from the little sailboards up to square-riggers, parade along the coast. Everyone wants to be there."

Cecelia recognized the note of longing. "Did you race sailboats?"

Serrano smiled. "A cousin and I did, before we went in the Academy—it was a Rix-class, which wouldn't mean anything to you, any more than horse terms do to me. And I crewed on a larger yacht one summer."

"And will you do that when you retire? Go back there and sail?"

Serrano's face seemed to close into an impenetrable shell. "No, milady. Lowein is where Fleet officers retire. . . . I wouldn't fit in there, and I've no desire to embarrass my family."

"I hardly think you'd embarrass anyone," Cecelia said. "Is it such a disgrace to captain my yacht?" She was surprised herself at how angry she felt at that thought.

"No—not at all." The voice carried no conviction, though. "Nothing to do with that—this—at all." Serrano managed a forced smile. "Never mind—my retirement plans are far away, and we have a present problem: how to get you to your hunt on time. I'll check with Sirkin, and see if we can't cut some corners."

"With your concern for my safety?" That was meant as a joke, but came out sharper than she had intended.

"Yes—with due concern for your safety." Serrano was serious again. "There's another matter, milady. It's about your crew."

"What—do you think they're all smugglers?" Again, a lightness she couldn't sustain. Cecelia shook her head. "I'm sorry: I am trying to be funny and it's not working."

"No wonder," Serrano said. "You have had your schedule disrupted; you have lost a crewman through a dangerous accident; you have nearly been accused of smuggling; and you had to spend several days of uncomfortable travel under emergency restrictions. Frankly, I think you're holding up surprisingly well."

"You do?"

"Yes. Nonetheless, I must bother you about the crew." Serrano paused to sip from her cup and take a bite of pastry. Cecelia noticed again the dark smudges under her eyes— had she slept enough? Or was it worry? She picked up a pastry herself, and tried it. Leathery, compared to those her own cook turned out. "You hired your crew from one employment agency," Serrano said. "Who recommended that agency to you?"

"I hired you from the same agency," Cecelia said. "What difference does that make?"

"It's a bit of embarrassment, but . . . they don't send you their best. They admitted that to me, when I asked them to forward some information on the crew."

"But—but I'm a *Bellinveau*!" Cecelia's voice rose. "Surely they wouldn't—"

"What they said," Serrano broke in, "was that you did not need the level of expertise that a large ship did. Their top people go to big shipping and passenger lines, where they have a chance to move up—"

"I pay very high salaries," Cecelia said. "That ought to mean something, if my name doesn't." She didn't like being interrupted, and she didn't like the implication that her ship was unimportant compared to a commercial liner.

"It means you get greedy incompetents." Serrano stared her down; Cecelia felt again the power of that dark gaze. Then her face relaxed and she grinned. "Except me, of course. I wasn't so much greedy as desperate to get a civilian job. But they did not recommend me for a commercial ship because of my background—the big corporations like to train their own people their own way, and find a military background a hindrance. You've got a very good navigator in Sirkin—she topped her exams, and I'm very satisfied with her work." Cecelia had the feeling that "very satisfied" from Captain Serrano would have been a dozen flowery adjectives from someone else. "But the others, milady, looked on your yacht as a cushy berth where they would be well paid for doing little, and your previous captains seem to have concurred."

"But everything seemed to run smoothly," Cecelia said, trying to remember if she'd ever noticed anything. Not really. As long as she arrived where she wanted to, when she wanted to, she had assumed the ship was fine. It certainly cost enough. "And I had the regular maintenance and inspections—I don't know what more I could have done." Even as she said it, she realized how she'd feel if someone said that about a stable in which they boarded their horses. She had had contempt for owners who didn't know, who didn't seem to care, about the details of stable management. Apparently she had made the same error with her own ship.

Serrano did not seem surprised, but didn't dwell on the point. "You paid for them, you mean. You had to trust your crew, because you didn't know yourself what to look for. And I think that for some years you had honest, if less than superb, crew members who did their duties fairly well. A good captain would have been enough, to provide the initiative and discipline for crew who were competent but uninspired. But in Massimir Olin, you did not have a good captain. I don't know with any certainty, but I suspect that he was looking for exactly such a ship, a small but fast vessel belonging to someone with no knowledge of ships or space, a vessel whose owner might be expected to visit places closed to commercial trade. You let him choose replacement crew, of course, and when old Titinka had that heart attack, he hired Iklind—from the same agency as the rest."

"But it's quite reputable," Cecelia said. Her mind whirled. She had never thought of herself—independent to the point of eccentricity and with no romantic susceptibilities—as anyone's natural prey. The image of herself as a fat sheep which a wolf might stalk seemed both ridiculous and disgusting. "It's the top agency in its field." Implicit in that was the assumption that no Bellinveau would use less.

"It is reputable," said Serrano. "But no agency is immune from penetration. Where there is blood, the blood-suckers gather: where there is wealth . . ."

"I know the saying," Cecelia said. "But I never expected it to apply to me—I'm old, unattached and intend to remain that way, my money will revert to the family when I die—"

"You are free transportation for your crew," Serrano said. "You pay well enough that they know you must have more—you have everything done by top firms. But I think for Olin it was the places you could go without comment—the places he wanted to go, which you could take him to."

Cecelia thought about that, and set it aside. What Olin's motives had been did not concern her now. "You had a point to make about the crew?" she asked. Serrano's twinkle rewarded her for coming back to that point.

"Yes, I did. I had intended to suggest some replacements of the least effective after your season of hunting; considering what's happened, I think you have both cause and justification for making some changes now. Assuming you don't want to start with me."

"Don't be silly!" Cecelia said. "I don't blame you for any of this."

Serrano shrugged. "You might well have. Good captains don't let such accidents happen. Anyway, you need a replacement for Iklind. I'm seriously concerned about the entire environmental department, and would suggest you also drop the new juniors, retaining only the survivor of the accident. Mr. Gavin I believe to be honest, though totally devoid of initiative, and I think he can be salvaged by some good training. Your pilot . . . actually, besides his manner, I have no complaint of his performance. But he strongly defended Olin's choice of course, in the face of a possible course that would have had you on your schedule. I suspect his complicity. We could do without a pilot, I am licensed for that duty, a separate qualification, and the expense of this refitting would explain your dropping him entirely."

"But can we find good crew out here?" Cecelia asked.

"Yes—in fact I've asked Mr. Brynear about that already. As this is a major repair facility, there are always crews coming through. Someone is sick, and stays behind; someone is unhappy and jumps ship—not that we want that sort. Velarsin and Co., and other firms, hire these temporaries, and their work records here give us something to go on. Also there are people who start in refitting who want to work aboard a ship; if they've taken their exams, and we interview their supervisors, we can find some good ones. But it's up to you, milady."

Exactly what she didn't want, on her ship. She wanted it to function perfectly without her having to make any decisions at all. Just transportation . . . but of course, there were people who looked at horses as just transportation, and she knew what she thought of *them*. "I've always left it up to my captains," Cecelia said slowly. "Are you asking me to interview with you, or—"

"If you wish; it might be helpful to you to understand what I would look for in applicants. But what I meant is that I would not dismiss your employees without gross negligence on their part. You had some input, I assume, in the size of crew when you started out?"

"Well . . . to be honest . . . I took the advice of the employment agency even then. Told them what I had bought, and asked them to arrange a crew." She could see by her captain's expression that this was not the right thing to have done. She shook her head. "I was a fool, wasn't I? Just like people I've known who've gone broke with racing stables. It just never occurred to me that the same things could happen here, in a simple little yacht." Serrano's expression did not change, but her eyes softened.

"You had other things to think about, I'm sure. Why don't you come along to some of the interviews, at least, and begin to pick up some of the terms? It will impress applicants, and it won't bother me."

"Fine. I will." She would learn every screw and bolt on her ship, the way she had once learned the anatomy of horses and every piece of leather and metal on her tack. How could she have left herself unguarded like this?

"And don't be hard on yourself," Serrano said. Cecelia blinked. Was the woman a mind reader as well? "Remember, I still don't know anything about horses."

"Welcome aboard, milady," Heris said. Eight hours late, they would be, undocking, but she felt happy anyway. Better a good job than a fast sloppy one. She had inspected the replacements with Mr. Brynear six hours before, and knew the new system was up to spec. Her new environmental team knew what they were doing, and Timmons was rapidly learning; he wanted to keep his job. The disgruntled pilot had complained bitterly about being dumped in the middle of nowhere; Lady Cecelia had finally paid his passage to one of the inner worlds of the system, even though her legal advisor said it wasn't necessary. Lady Cecelia had told her gleefully about the stormy battle going on between Diklos & Sons, the insurance company, and her lawyers; she thought she would get her money back, at the least, and she had convinced the union that Iklind's death was probably due to the bad work done by Diklos . . . so now Diklos had the union on their backs as well. Lady Cecelia's staff had boarded an hour ago. Heris had given Bates the staff emergency directives, and he'd taken them without comment . . . They would soon begin emergency drills, proper drills, and this would be a proper ship.

"Thank you, Captain Serrano." Lady Cecelia and her maid came aboard serenely, as if nothing had happened; Heris saw her eyes flicker at the change in uniform. Heris had squeezed in a visit to a good tailor, and while it was still purple, it lacked the scarlet, teal, and cream trim and about half its gold braid. The docking access tube still had a thick carpet, but the walls were properly bare for inspection, conduits and tubing color-coded in accordance with Transportation Department directives.

Behind Lady Cecelia, her nephew and his friends straggled in. Heris watched them with contempt behind her motionless features. Rich, spoiled brats, she thought. A waste of talent, if they have any; a waste of the genetic material and wealth it took to rear them this far. She gave a crisp "Welcome aboard," and then walked past them out the tube to the dockside. Bates was waiting in the passage to see to anything more they needed. She would have avoided the greeting altogether except that she wanted to say a last few words to Brynear.

"I hear you had a wager with your owner," he said, grinning at her. "She making you pay up?"

"She'd have let me off, considering the circumstances," Heris said, grinning back. She liked his sort of toughness, his competence. He reminded her of the best she'd known, a memory she didn't want right now. She pushed it out of her mind. "But the forfeit's to learn more about what fascinates her—horses, of all things!—and if I'm to be a good captain for her, I need to understand her."

"If it weren't rude and nosy, I'd ask you a question," Brynear said.

"It is, and I won't answer it," Heris said, with an edge. Then she softened. "I know what you'd ask, and I'm not ready to talk about it. Just wanted to thank you for a good job done well in a hurry. I'm glad we were able to argue our way past your schedule—and sorry to disrupt it."

"You can disrupt my schedule anytime," Brynear said. "As I would have made clear, if you weren't leaving so soon."

"You can repair my ship anytime," Heris said, smiling. He was attractive, but not that attractive. Yet. The other memories were still too clear. "As I did make clear—but I wish we didn't have to leave now. Thanks."

"You're welcome, Captain." He threw her a civilian's version of a salute and turned away. Heris went back to the ship and thoroughly enjoyed showing her crew that she was as good as the former pilot at undock and tug maneuvers.

"You shouldn't have insulted the captain to her face," Raffa said severely. They were two days out of refitting, two days of cool courtesy between Cecelia and the young people. Ronnie pouted, but she did not relent. "Don't put out your lip at me," she said. "It was wrong, and you know it."

"I didn't know she was there. I didn't know Aunt Cecelia had approved it. It's too bad, really. I never asked to come along on this ridiculous cruise; it was all my mother's idea."

"You'd rather be supervising a loading team at Scavell or Xingsan?" asked Buttons. "Come on, now, Ronnie . . . this isn't bad. I admit, I wasn't planning to be home for the season this year—no more than Bubbles—but it's not as if visiting my father were a hardship."

"That's not what I meant," Ronnie said. He looked around for sympathy, and found expressions that told him he was boring, and boring was one thing they would not accept.

"Why don't we swim?" asked Bubbles. "Now that we can use the pool again, a nice swim would be fun." She stretched her long, elegant arms, and wriggled in a way that suggested something other than swimming.

The others agreed; Ronnie knew he should swallow his sulks and go with them, but the sulks were too embedded. "Go ahead," he said, when they turned to look back at him. "I'm going to try Beggarman one more time." That was the computer game they'd been playing until it palled . . . and Ronnie never had gotten above the eighth level.

He had no real intention of playing Beggarman. . . . He wanted to regain the ground he felt he'd lost with the captain. A private apology should do it; he had charmed his way past fiercer dragons than this. No woman of her age could be immune to boyish charm. He showered, put on a fresh jumpsuit, and looked at himself in the mirror. He slicked his hair: innocence? No. It looked as if he were trying for innocence. He tousled it: mischievous waif? Yes. That should do it. He waited until the others had logged into the pool enclosure. Then he strolled down the curving passage, slipped through the hatch between crew and staff areas, and found his way to the bridge. It wasn't that hard; he had memorized the ship plan on his deskcomp.

The bridge did not meet his expectations. He had envisioned something like the bridge of the training cruiser. . . . Aside from that, and the small craft he'd piloted, he'd never been aboard a ship. He stared at the small room crowded with screens and control boards, the watch seats crammed in side by side, the command bench hardly an arm's length from any of them. Something was going on. . . . He sensed the tension, heard it in the low voices that reported values he did not understand. He had expected to find silence, even boredom; he had expected to be a welcome break in a monotonous shift. But no one seemed to notice him. Captain Serrano uttered a series of numbers as if they were important. . . . But how could they be, out here in the middle of nowhere? It must be one of her stupid drills or something.

With all the confidence of youth and privilege, Ronnie strolled into the crowded space.

"Excuse me, but when you've got a moment, Captain, I'd like to speak to you." He spoke with the forthright but courteous tone of someone with a perfect right to be where he was, doing what he was. He expected a prompt response.

He did not expect the smart crack of an open hand across his face; it sent him reeling into the back of someone's chair. He grabbed for a support, and found a handy rail along the bulkhead. His cheek hurt; his mouth burned. Anger raged along his bones, but he was still too shocked to move. Serrano's voice continued, low and even, with one number after another. Someone repeated them, and he saw hands flicker across control boards. Just as he got his breath back, he felt the gut-deep wrench he knew from his one training voyage: the yacht was flicking in and out of a series of jump points.

Anger drained away; fear flooded him now. Jump transitions . . . they'd been near *jump transitions,* and if he'd interfered they might all have been killed. The quick remorse he was never too proud to feel swept over him. He gulped back the apology he wanted to make—he should wait, he should be sure it was safe.

Then Captain Serrano turned to him, anger on her dark face. "Don't you *ever* come on my bridge again, mister," she said. Ronnie's eyes slid around the room; no one looked at him. "Go on—get out."

"But I—I came to say something."

"I don't want to hear it. Get off the bridge."

"But I want to apologize—"

She took a step toward him and he realized that he was afraid of her—afraid of a woman a head shorter—in a way he had not feared anyone since childhood. She took another step, and his hand fell away from the rail; he backed up. "You can apologize to my crew for nearly getting us all killed," she said. "And then you can go away and not come back."

"I'm—I'm sorry," said Ronnie, with a gulp. It was not working the way he'd planned. "I—I really am." She came yet another step closer, and he backed up; she reached out and he flinched . . . but she touched a button on the bulkhead, and a hatch slid closed four inches from his nose.

BRIDGE ACCESS: PRESS FOR PERMISSION appeared on a lightboard above it. Ronnie stood there long enough to realize that his cheek still hurt, and she wasn't going to let him back in. Then he got really angry.

"It wasn't my fault," he told George later. No one else had seemed to notice, but George had asked about the mark on his face. "I mean, it was, in a way, but I didn't mean to interrupt during a jump transition. She didn't have to take it that way. Damned military arrogance. She *hit* me— the owner's *family*—all she had to do was explain. Just you wait—I'll get even with her."

"Are you sure that's a good idea?" But George's eyes had lit up. He loved intrigue, especially vengeance. George had engineered some of their best escapades in school, including the ripely dead rat appearing on the service platter at a banquet for school governors.

"Of course," Ronnie said. "She has other duties; we have nothing to do between here and Bunny's place but get bored and crabby with each other." He felt much better, now that he'd decided. "First thing is, we'll get into the computer and find out more about her."

"You could always give a little kick to one of her drills," George said.

"Exactly." Ronnie grinned. Much better. A good attack beats defense every time; he'd read that someplace.

CHAPTER SEVEN

Heris could have believed the *Sweet Delight* knew it smelled sweeter—or perhaps it responded to the change in the attitude of its crew. Without the sour-faced pilot, and the inept moles, with the addition of two eager, hardworking newcomers, crew alliances shifted and solidified around a new axis. A healthier one, to Heris's mind. They were not yet what she would call sharp, but they were trying, now. No one complained about the emergency drills. No one slouched around with the listless expression that had so worried her before. Perhaps it was only fear of losing their jobs, but she hoped it was something better.

It had been unfortunate that she'd hit the owner's nephew. She knew that; she knew it was her fault from start to finish. She had let them leave the hatch to the bridge open. . . . On such a small ship, with a small crew, where the owner never ventured into the working compartments, it had seemed safe. She had not noticed when he came, and when he startled her she had silenced him in a way that might have been hazardous—would have been, with some people. She was ashamed of herself, even though they'd made it through a fairly tricky set of transition points safely.

She called Cecelia as soon as they were through, and explained. "It was my fault for not securing the bridge—"

"Never mind. He's been insufferable this whole trip; his mother spoiled him rotten."

"But I should have—"

Cecelia interrupted her again. "It's not a problem, I assure you. If you want to feel chastened, schedule your first riding lesson today."

Heris had to laugh at that. "All right. Two hours from now?"

"I'll be there. Regular gymsuit will do for now."

Heris finished the necessary documentation of jump point transition, completed a few more minor chores, and left the bridge to Mr. Gavin.

"This," said Cecelia cheerfully, "is your practice mount." Heris had expected something like a metal or plastic horse shape on some kind of spring arrangement, but the complicated machine in front of her looked nothing at all like a real horse. Except for the saddle—a traditional leather saddle—on a cylindrical section that might have been plastic, it could have been an industrial robot of some sort, with its jointed appendages, power cable connectors, sockets, and dangling wires with ominous little clips. Heris had seen something vaguely like it in one of the wilder bars on Durango. . . . Only that had been, she thought, a mechanical bucking bull.

The jointed extension in the front, Cecelia explained, acted as the horse's neck and head, allowing the rider to use real reins. At the moment, the real reins were looped neatly from a hook on one side. "There are sensors in the head," Cecelia said, "which record how much rein pressure you're using, and feed back to the software. Yank the reins, and this thing will respond very much like a real horse. You'll also get an audible tone, to let you know when your rein pressure is uneven." The VR helmet rose from a cantilevered extension behind the saddle. "It's set now at beginner level," Cecelia said. "I'll control pace and direction; you'll just feel the gaits at first." She stood near a waist-high control panel, which Heris noted had several sockets for plug-in modules as well as the usual array of touchplates.

Heris stared at the thing. She had not enjoyed the obligatory riding lessons at the Academy that much, and this looked like the perfect apparatus for making someone look stupid and clumsy. But a bet was a bet, and she owed Cecelia ten hours. The sooner she mounted, the sooner it would be over.

"You don't have to use the VR helmet at first," Cecelia

said. "Why not just get on and off a few times, and let me start it walking?"

"Fine." Heris tried to remember just how mounting went. Left foot in the stirrup, but her hands . . . ? On the real horse they'd been taught to grip the reins and put a hand on the neck in front of the saddle; here that would have meant on a pair of gray cylinders like slim pipes. She put both hands on the front of the saddle and hauled herself upward. The machine lurched sideways, with a faint hiss of hydraulics, and she slipped back to the deck.

"Sorry," Cecelia said, trying to hide a grin. "I wasn't ready to correct for that kind of mount. You need to be closer, and push off more strongly with your right leg. Straight up, then swing your leg over. If you hang off the side of a real horse like that, it's likely to unbalance, reach out a leg, and step on you."

Heris tried again, this time successfully. She felt around with her right foot until she got the stirrup on. Cecelia came over and moved her feet slightly. "Weight on the balls of your feet, for now. We're going to start with a simple all-around seat. And no reins for now, until you've got the seat right. Just clasp your wrists in front of you. Let me connect the other sensors . . ." This meant clipping a dozen dangling wires to Heris's clothing; she felt she was being restrained by gnats. Cecelia retreated to the control column and touched something. The machine lurched; Heris wondered if she was about to be thrown off, but it settled down to a rhythmic roll and pitch. Her body remembered that it felt quite a bit like riding a real horse.

"It's—strange," she said. She might have to take riding lessons, but she didn't have to refrain from comment.

"It's expensive," Cecelia said. "Most riding sims are limited to three gaits, one speed at each gait, and all you can do is go in a circle or straight. This one can keep me in shape." Heris did not say what she thought this time: keeping one old woman in shape hardly suggested that the simulator had great powers. She didn't have to refrain from comment, but she didn't have to be rude, either.

"Let me try the helmet now," she said instead. If her face was covered by that mass of instrumentation, no sudden expression could give her away.

"Go ahead," Cecelia said. "I think you'll be surprised."

The helmet had all the usual attachments and adjustments; Heris got it on as the sim kept up its movement. As her eyes adapted to the new visual field, she saw in front of her a horse's neck swinging slightly up and down, with two ears . . . and reins lying on that neck, and a long line from the horse's head to someone standing in the center of a white-railed ring. "It doesn't look like you," she said. "Who's the brown-haired man with his arm in a sling?"

"Sorry." Cecelia's voice in the helmet sounded masculine for a moment, then changed. "Someone I used to train with—is that better?" Now it was Cecelia, but a younger Cecelia—her hair flaming red-gold, her tall body dressed in sweater and riding breeches. She looked vibrant and happy and far more attractive than Heris had imagined her.

"Yes—it really does look like a horse." Of course, the simulator for a cruiser really did look like a cruiser, and the simulator for a Station tug really did look like a Station tug. That's what simulators were supposed to do, but maybe Cecelia didn't know that.

"Like *any* horse," Cecelia said, and into the helmet appeared a dizzying array of horse necks and ears: black, brown, white, gray, short, long, thick, thin, with and without manes. Heris blinked.

"I can see that." But after all, how hard could it be to change colors and lengths of neck? It wasn't like going from, say, the bridge of a flagship like *Descant* to the bridge of a tug, or a shuttle. All horses were basically alike, large smelly four-legged mammals that would carry you around if you had no better transportation. The visual settled back to the original neck and ears—light brownish yellow.

"Now—you're going to reverse." Heris expected to halt and back up, but reverse in this case meant making an egg-shaped turn and beginning to circle in the opposite direction, once more facing forward. Different terminology: she filed it away. Next time she would be properly braced for the turn, rather than the halt.

By the end of that first hour, she had walked virtual circles in both directions, halted, reversed, and even done enough trotting to make her thighs ache. She remembered this from her Academy days. There, too, they had walked and trotted back and forth until their legs hurt. It seemed pointless, but harmless, and it might even be good exercise. When she lifted off the helmet, Cecelia smiled up at her.

"And did you find it as bad as you expected?"

"No . . . but is that all there is?"

Cecelia's grin might have warned her, she thought later. "Not at all—I go faster."

"You . . . race?"

"Not racing. Eventing. Do you know what that is?"

Heris racked her memory, and came up with nothing. Event—had to be a sporting event of some kind, she presumed. But what?

"Would you like to see?" Cecelia asked.

"Yes. Of course." Anything her employer cared about that much ought to be important to her.

She had not expected anything like the cube Cecelia showed her, and came up from it breathless. "You—did *that*? That was you on that yellow horse?"

"Chestnut. Yes. That was my last championship ride."

"But those . . . those—obstacles?—were so big. And the horse was running so fast."

Cecelia grinned at her, clearly delighted at her surprise. "I thought you didn't understand. That's what's different about this simulator. You can do all that on it . . . well, all but falling in the actual water, or getting stepped on by the actual horse."

"You mean I could learn to do that—to jump over things like that?"

"Probably not, but you could come close." Cecelia extracted the first cube and fed in another. "This is what fox hunting is like—in fact, this is a cube I made three years ago."

"You made—?"

"Well, I used to be under contract with Yohsi Sports. They'd mount the sim-cam in my helmet, and I wore the wires as well. . . ."

Heris felt that she'd fallen into another layer of mystery. What, she wondered, was "wearing the wires" and what did it have to do with a sports network? But she was tired of asking questions that must sound stupid, so she simply nodded. This time the cube was not *of* Cecelia riding, but from the rider's viewpoint. . . . She saw the green grass blur between the horse's ears, saw a stone wall approaching far too fast . . . and then it was left behind, and another

appeared. Little brown and black and white things were running ahead, yelping, and other horses and riders were all
around.

"Those are the foxes you're chasing?" she asked finally,
as field and wall followed wall and field, apparently without end. There were variations, as some fields were grassy
and others muddy, and some walls were taller or had ditches
on one side, but it seemed fairly monotonous. Not nearly
as interesting as the varied challenges of the cross-country.
Cecelia choked, then laughed until she was breathless.

"Those are *hounds*! The fox is ahead of the dogs; the dogs
find the scent and trail the fox, and the horses follow the
hounds." Then she quit laughing. "I'm sorry. It's not fair,
if you've never been exposed to it, but I thought everyone
knew about foxes and hounds."

"No," Heris said, between gritted teeth. Some of us, she
wanted to say, had better things to do with our time. Some
of us were off fighting wars so that people like you could
bounce around making entertainment cubes for each other.
But that was not entirely fair and she knew it. It probably
did take skill to ride like that, although what the use of
that skill was, once you'd gained it, she still could not figure
out.

"Here." Cecelia handed her yet another cube. "This is the
text of an old book on the subject, and since it's one of
the few left, you might want to look at it. Bunny's designed
his entire hunt around it, even though we know that it
predates the twentieth century, Old Earth, and things must
have changed afterwards."

Heris looked at the cube file labelled "Surtees" with
suspicion. Apparently she would be expected to watch it
on her own time. Historical nonsense about horses struck
her as even more useless than current nonsense about horses.

"And to be fair, I think it's time I schedule my first
lesson in shipboard knowledge, or whatever you want to
call it. Do you have time for a student later today?"

Cecelia was, after all, her employer, and she was making an effort to share an enthusiasm. Heris thought of all
the things she'd rather do, but nodded. "Of course. When
would you like to start?"

"Well . . . after lunch?"

"Fine." Food always came first. But then, it should.

"You could eat with me," Cecelia said, "and give me a
head start. I don't even know what you want me to learn."

Meals with the owner. Heris started to grumble internally,
then remembered that she'd already had meals with the
owner . . . and it hadn't been that bad. "Thank you," she
said. "I am at your service."

Heris had no equivalent of the riding simulator to help
Cecelia, but she used the next best: the computer's three-
dimensional visuals.

"This is a very nice hull," she said. Always start with the
positive. "You've got a fair balance of capacity and speed—"

"But my captains always said it was a slow old barge,
compared to other ships," Cecelia said. "A luxury yacht can't
be expected to compete—"

"You and I both know your former captains had other
reasons," Heris said. "It may be a luxury yacht, but we use
a very similar hull for—" She stopped herself in time from
saying for what, exactly, and managed to finish. "For missions that require a fair turn of speed. And you've got the
right power ratio for it; whoever designed this adaptation
chose well. Now—let me highlight each system in color, and
you can begin to learn how it works."

Cecelia, Heris found, was an apt pupil. She had a surprising ability to grasp 3-D structures, and spotted several
features Heris had meant to mention before she could bring
them up.

"Yes—you do have waste space there; that's a design
compromise, but it's not a bad one. Look at the alternatives. If you ran the coolant this way—see—you get this
undesirable cluster of conduits here—"

"Oh . . . and that's supposed to be at a constant
temperature—"

"Yes. Now, let's add the electricals."

They both lost track of time, and Cecelia's deskunit finally
beeped with a reminder about dinner. She looked surprised.
"I didn't—this isn't really dull at all. I could learn this."

"So you could. I'm glad I didn't bore you." Heris stood,
and stretched. She would need a hot bath, to get the kinks
out this time. "I'll be going—I've got some crew business
to take care of."

"Well . . . thank you. Tomorrow, then?"

"I'll look forward to it," Heris said, hoping that could be taken for both sessions, though she was not in fact looking forward to more riding. But fair was fair, and Cecelia was as diligent a pupil as she could wish.

After a few days, Heris found herself enjoying the riding instruction more than she'd expected. The soreness wore off; she had good natural balance, and a lot of experience with simulators. It was less monotonous than the usual exercise apparatus in the crew gym, or swimming against the current in the pool. And she could not have asked for a more attentive owner. Cecelia had her own way of thinking about the various systems, relating them more often to equestrian matters than Heris thought necessary, but if she could understand better that way, why not? At least she was learning, paying attention . . . and in the future that might save her life.

Still, Heris had not forgotten the need for emergency drills. She herself gave a training session to the house staff and a separate one to Cecelia. Cecelia suggested letting Bates hand out the assignments to the young people, and Heris agreed. She had managed to avoid young Ronnie successfully so far.

That first unannounced shipwide drill would have made a good comedy cube, Heris thought later. She had entered the specs into the main computer the night before, using an event function that kept the time from her as well. It should have been simple: a single small fire, in one of the fire-prone areas. But very little went as planned. The alarm went off at 0400, ship's time. Heris, fairly sure what it was, nonetheless responded as she would to any emergency. Those crew members she thought of as the best arrived at their emergency stations within the time limit; the others straggled in late, in one case three minutes late. ("I was in the head," mumbled the guilty party. "Havin' a bit of a problem, I was.")

Cecelia logged in within the limit, as did Bates and the cook (who, spotting the faked "fire," promptly put an upturned garbage container on it: the right decision). Four of the young people sauntered in to their assigned stations late (but flustered) and two did not appear at all.

"They have to be somewhere," Cecelia said, when Heris told her.

"Oh, they are. They're in the number five storage bay, ignoring the whole thing."

"But they can't—who is it?"

"Ronnie and George," Heris said, having no more patience with them. "Since you gave them their assignments, via Bates—"

"I'll be glad to ream them out, but are you sure they heard the alarm in there?"

"All compartments have a bell. No, they're hiding out, for purposes of their own. One thing I could do is put a scare into them. They think this is just a stupid drill . . . but they don't know what the supposed emergency is. If I dump power in there . . . take off the AG, or lose a little pressure . . ."

"Do it," Cecelia said. Red patches marred her cheeks again. Heris thought to herself that one of the advantages of darker skin was that blushes didn't show. Much. "Do you have sensors in there?"

"Oh, yes." Heris called up the compartment specs. "You have a pretty fair internal security system, probably to let your staff monitor offship loading . . . see?" There were Ronnie and George, looking stubborn, hunched over a hard copy of something. She did not wait to hear what they were saying, but her fingers flicked over the screen controls. The young men suddenly stopped talking, and stared at each other.

"She wouldn't!" George said in a tinny voice.

"Why's he sound like that?"

"Air pressure," Heris said. "Their ears just popped, I'll bet." Her fingers moved again, and both of them looked pale and ill at ease. "You'd better go," Heris said to Cecelia. "You want to be properly angry and upset, and you don't want to know what happened to them . . . not until they tell you. I won't hurt them."

"I know that," Cecelia said, but she left reluctantly.

"If you get into the computer, then you can pull drills on *her*," George said. "She won't know—" He lounged against a burlap sack marked "Fertile seeds: contains mercury: do not use for food."

"Neither will we," Ronnie said. "I don't want to be up all night every night."

"You don't have to be. That's the beauty of it. You just set them up, but cut our bells out of it."

"She'll know who did it," Ronnie said. "I still think I should start with the internal monitors. She's spending a lot of time with Aunt Cecelia now; she's bound to say something I can use." They had a hard copy of the communications board specs, left in an unsecured file from one of Cecelia's training sessions. Getting into the secured files would be harder. Ronnie had the feeling that Captain damn-her-backbone Serrano would not leave *her* files unsecured.

"Yes, but what can she do? You're the owner's nephew—she can hardly throw you out in the void."

"Maybe." Ronnie stared at the specs, trying to remember all that stuff he had had in class. This little squiggle was supposed to mean something about the way that channel and this other channel interacted . . . wasn't it? He put his thumb firmly on the line that came from Cecelia's sitting room, and a finger on the one that came from the gym. He really needed a tap in both. If only Skunkcat had been along. . . . Scatty was the best for this sort of thing.

"Here's the captain's direct line to the bridge," George said, trying to be helpful. George had good ideas, but always managed to get the wrong slant on them. Ronnie did not want to interfere with the captain's communication to the bridge; he wanted them to know how ineffectual she was going to be once he figured out how to sabotage her.

Suddenly his ears popped, then popped again. He saw from George's face that the same unsettling shudder was going through his stomach, too. George said something; he paid no attention. Lower air pressure . . . shifts in the artificial gravity . . . could it have been a *real* emergency? He was suddenly sweaty, and as suddenly cold, the sweat drying on him. No. It had taken too long. That bitch of a captain was doing something to him, doing it on purpose.

"Out!" he said, across the middle of something George was trying to say. "Before the pressure locks engage."

But they had. He could not wrestle the hatch open against the safety locks; he *would* not call for help. His stomach protested, as another shift of AG squashed him, then released . . . and the air pressure dropped again, to another painful pop of his ears.

George looked green. "I . . . I'm going to—"

"Not in variable G—hold it, George." There was nothing to use for a spew-bag. Every storage container in there—bags, boxes, tubes—had a lock-down seal on it. A surge of AG crushed him to the deck, then let up slowly. Air pressure returned; his ears popped just as many times on the way back to ship normal. His stomach tried to crawl out his mouth; George looked as bad as he felt, but had managed not to spew. He swallowed the vile taste in his mouth and rolled over onto his back. He had a sudden pounding headache.

Something banged on the closed hatch. "Anyone inside?"

George croaked, and the hatch opened. A crewman, someone Ronnie did not recognize, in full emergency gear. "My— you weren't in here for the drill, were you?" Without awaiting the obvious answer, the man went on, "It's not anyone's assigned station—you're lucky I found you. We're doing a pressure check on all compartments—"

"Just get us out of here," Ronnie said, staggering to his feet. "That miserable captain—"

"Wasn't her fault," the crewman said, as if surprised at his words. "It's a computer-generated emergency; they all are, you know. Didn't you get your handouts?"

"Yes," George said. "We got our handouts. Thank you. Just let me pass, please." He shoved past and shambled down the passage to the nearest toilet, where Ronnie could hear him being very thoroughly sick.

Ronnie himself hoped to sneak back to his own stateroom, but in the lounge he found a very angry Aunt Cecelia. She said all the things he expected, and didn't want to hear, and he managed not to listen. She had said them all before, and so had others, and it was not really his fault anyway. It was that captain. That arrogant, stiff-necked, conniving bitch of a captain, and he was going to get even with her. If Aunt Cecelia didn't want to see his face for two days, that was fine. He could eat in his room; he would be *glad* to eat in his room. All the more time to figure out how to do what he was going to do. Still, an attempt at patching things up never hurt. He did his best at a contrite apology, but she turned away, ignoring him. Ignoring *him*. No one ignored him.

By the time he reappeared in the dining room, several days later, to all appearances chastened and determined to be a good boy, Ronnie had figured it out. At least the beginning of it. It had been easy, using the specs he had, to get a tap into his aunt's sitting room. And into the gym. He hadn't yet dared try the captain's cabin, but he was hearing a lot as it was. That fool captain actually *liked* his ridiculous aunt, he'd discovered. Enjoyed the riding lessons, enjoyed explaining to Cecelia how her ship worked, enjoyed the relaxed conversations in the evenings, when they explored each others' backgrounds.

A lot of it bored him silly: talk about books he'd never read, and art he'd never seen, and music he avoided. (Opera! He had liked the opera singer's body, and the competition with the prince, but not the music she sang onstage. It was hard to believe even someone like his aunt actually *liked* all that screeching.) No juicy gossip, no political arguments— it was almost like hearing an educational tape, the way they discussed the topics and deferred courteously to each other.

Other bits, though, fascinated him. His aunt's analysis of the workings of the family businesses. . . . His own father hadn't made it that clear. Captain Serrano's version of her resignation from the Fleet, which his aunt teased out of her with surprising delicacy. . . . He had never imagined that someone in the Regular Space Services would dare to dis-obey an order; they were all such stiff-necked prigs. It didn't make sense; she should have known she would lose her ship, one way or the other. He could almost feel guilty listening—he would not have expected to hear that woman so upset, or for that reason—but he loved the sense of power it gave him. She could be shaken from her calm, controlled persona; she was not invincible. He would start with some-thing simple, he decided. Something that might be an acci-dent, that would be hard to trace back to him.

Heris used the reins when she rode now, and the soft tones in her earphones let her know how she managed the tension, even before the simulator responded by swinging one way or the other. If the tones matched, the rein tension was equal; a higher tone meant more tension. She had discovered, as Cecelia gradually enabled the simulator's sensors, just how sluggish that first "mount" had been. Cecelia had shown her a cube of herself at that first lesson, and she was ready to laugh at the novice who couldn't even keep her position for a single circuit. On *this* program, that novice would have been bucked off already. Heris listened to Cecelia's voice, coaching her in the next maneuver, and tried to respond. The brown neck and ears in front of her changed position; she felt the movement in her seat and the lessening tension of the reins in her hand. The simulator lunged; this time Heris was ready, and controlled that with a leg and hand . . . and . . . they were cantering. She liked cantering. Circling. Straight. Circling again. Today she would "jump" for the first time; she was eager, sure she was ready.

A small white fence appeared ahead of her. "Keep your leg on him," Cecelia's voice reminded her. She squeezed, and the fence moved toward her faster. Then the horse's back rose beneath her, and fell again, and she grabbed— and got a handful of metal tubing. The illusion went blank; the simulator beneath her was once more an inert hunk of metal and plastic.

"Not bad," Cecelia said. "You grabbed for the right thing, at least. I had one student who reached for the helmet. And you didn't fall all the way off."

Heris blinked and took a deep breath. "Umm. A real horse wouldn't stop and let me get my breath, would it?"

"No. You can grab for mane like that and stay on, usually, but you were pretty high out of the saddle. I think you need more time in the two-point. Let's go."

The rest of that session, and the next, Heris spent practicing the position she should have taken over the jump. Then she put on the helmet to find the ring full of jumps. "Nothing big," Cecelia said cheerfully. "But if you see more than one, you can't get fixated on it. Now—pick up a trot."

She came out of that lesson a convert to riding. "It's like a boat," she tried to tell Cecelia. "Bouncing over the waves, only in a boat you're *in* it, and this way you're *surrounding* it. Not really like sailing, more like white-water kayaking." Cecelia looked blank. "You never did any?"

"No, just the little bit of sailing I told you about."

"But it's the same thing." Heris ran her hands through her hair, not caring if it stood up in peaks. "You're swooping along between obstacles, only they're rocks making standing waves, not fences."

"If you say so. I always thought of it as music, myself. A choral or orchestral work, where if everything goes well it sounds lovely, and if you get out of time you crash."

"Anyway," Heris said, "I like it. I don't want to quit when my ten hours are up—that is, if you'll let me—"

Cecelia chuckled wickedly. "Your ten hours were up *last* session. Do you think I'd let a potential convert quit before she got hooked? I thought you'd come around. Just wait until you can jump a real course—small, but a real one."

"And you—don't tell me you don't like knowing more about your ship," Heris said.

"That's true." Cecelia rubbed her nose. "I know you think I'm crazy to liken it to stable management, but that's how it makes sense to me."

"Whatever works," Heris said. She would have said more, but Ronnie and the other young people came into the gym.

"Is the pool available, Aunt Cecelia?" He asked politely enough, but his expression showed what he thought of two older women exercising. He did not look at Heris at all.

"Yes—for about an hour," Cecelia said. "But you ought to get in some riding time, Ronnie."

"I'll get enough riding at Bunny's," Ronnie said. It was not quite sulky. "We'll leave you the practice time. . . . Are you enjoying yourself, Captain?"

It was the first time he'd actually spoken to her since the incident on the bridge. His expression was so carefully neutral it could have been either courtesy or insult. "Yes, I am," she said, pleasantly. "Lady Cecelia is an excellent teacher."

"I'm sure." He would have been very handsome, Heris thought, if he'd learned to limit that curl of lip to moments of passion. His voice sharpened. "It's too bad you'll have to let your newfound expertise wither in Hospitality Bay . . . although I understand they have donkey rides along the beach."

Heris would not have answered so childish an insult, but Cecelia did. "On the contrary, Ronnie, I'm taking Captain Serrano with me; she's going to be quite adequate by the time we arrive." Her cheeks flamed, her hair seemed to stand on end. Heris blinked; that was the first she'd heard of this plan.

"You're taking—her—but she—she's just a—" Ronnie looked from one to the other, then to his friends.

"If you'll excuse me, Lady Cecelia," said Heris, giving her employer a covert twinkle, "I have urgent business on the bridge—remember?"

"Oh. Yes, of course," Cecelia dismissed her with a wave, and turned back to her nephew; Heris used the gym's other entrance. It was not all a fake, though she had no desire to watch aunt and nephew sparring—she had in fact scheduled another emergency drill for the crew only, and needed to change. She and the crew would all be wearing full sensor attachments, so that she could analyze the drill in detail later on. She had allowed herself fifteen minutes, originally, but Ronnie's interruption had cost her a couple.

In her cabin, she ripped off her sweaty riding clothes, spent a minute in the 'fresher, and dressed in her uniform with practiced speed. Anyone who couldn't bathe and dress for inspection in eleven minutes would never have survived Academy training. She picked up the sensor patches and placed them on head, shoulders, hands, chest and back of waist, and feet. The recording command unit slipped into her pocket. Three minutes. She picked up the last of her personal emergency gear with one eye on the chronometer's readout. Breather-mask, detox, command wand for hatch-locks, command wands for systems controls . . . the little plastic or foil packets that she had learned to use so long ago, that never left her except in the 'fresher, where she kept them stuck to a wall in their waterproof pouch.

Now. She left her quarters and moved without haste toward the bridge, turning on the recording command unit. Sometime in the next two minutes, something would go wrong—without triggering any alarm on the family side, unless the lockout patch failed. Her skin felt tight. Riding an electronic virtual horse was good exercise, but this was the real thrill: waiting for trouble you knew was coming.

Whatever it was, the crew had just noticed something wrong on the displays when she came onto the bridge at precisely the hour she had set.

"Don't know what that is—" the ranking mole said. "But we'd better find out; cut it off the circulation—"

"Captain on the bridge," said Holloway, with evident relief. "Captain, there's something in environmental—"

Inadequate, even so soon; she switched the command screen to environmental and almost grinned. Pure happenstance, but she'd seen something like this before. She didn't say that; she said, "Isolate that compartment." The mole's hands flickered across his console.

"Captain—the fan blower's stuck on."

Not *quite* the same problem. She hoped it was mostly virtual; the actual compound stank abominably, and would penetrate any porous material. The mole had the sense to cut out the electrical line supplying the blower. Heris said, "Good job," and then the blower cut back in. Something prickled the back of her neck as she watched Gavin override the mole's commands and cut power to the entire section. Having the fan blower stuck on was within the parameters she'd given the computer. Having it come back on after its normal electrical connection was cut pushed the parameters as she remembered them. Had she been imprecise? Could she have forgotten to close a command line somewhere in the problem set? The fan stopped. She listened to Gavin give reasonable orders for clearing the contaminant, based on its presumed identity. Then—and she was not surprised—the fan came back on. Gavin turned to her with an expression between disgust and worry.

"I've got it," she said. From her console, her command set blocked the computer's own, briefly, as she isolated and locked out all executing logic loaded in the past seventy-two hours. That would undo some things that would have to be redone, but it should safely contain the problem. And that second startup took it well beyond the parameters she'd set; someone had interfered. Interfered with her ship, on her drill. . . . Rage filled her, along with the exultation that conflict always brought. This was an enemy she could fight. She knew exactly whom to blame for this one, and he had been ordered off her bridge only sixty-three hours before.

The fan had stopped for good, this time, and she went on with the drill, noting that the crew had responded well even to this more complicated problem.

The question was whether to tell Cecelia. She liked Cecelia, she'd decided, and it wasn't her fault that she had a bratty nephew or even that she'd been stuck with him for this trip. If she could contain Ronnie without bothering Cecelia . . . but on the other hand, she was the owner, and the owner had a right to know what was going on. If it had been an admiral's nephew, she'd have known what to do (not that any admiral's nephew would have gotten so far with mischief still unchecked).

But the first thing to do was find out how he did it, and when.

"Sirkin, you're cross-training in computer systems. I want you to crawl through every trickle in the past . . . oh . . . sixty hours or so, and identify every input." Sirkin blinked, but did not look daunted. The young, Heris thought to herself, believed in miracles.

"Anything in particular, Captain?"

"I entered a problem set for the drill yesterday. What just happened was not within parameters. . . . Someone skunked them. I want to know when, from what terminal, and the details of the hook. Can do?"

"Yes—I think so." Sirkin scowled, in concentration not anger. "Was it that—that young idiot who got himself caught in the storage compartment?"

Heris glanced around; the entire crew was listening. "It might have been," she said. "But when you find out suppose you tell me, not the whole world."

"Yes, ma'am."

Ronnie threw himself back in the heavily padded teal chair in his stateroom and stretched luxuriously. George, in the purple chair, looked ready to burst with curiosity.

"So?"

"So . . ." Ronnie tried to preserve the facade of cool sophistication, but the expression on George's face made him laugh. "All right. I did it, and did it right. You should have seen them, trying to turn off a fan that wouldn't turn off."

"A fan." George was not impressed, and since he'd been decanted looking cool and contained, he could do that look better than Ronnie. The only thing, Ronnie maintained, which he did better.

"Let me explain," Ronnie said, taking a superior tone. That came easily. "The little captain had scheduled another emergency drill, this one for the crew alone. I'd already put my hook into the system—remember?—and had a line out for just this sort of thing. I reeled it in and rewrote it—actually, all I had to do was put a loop in it—and sent it on its way."

"So the fan kept turning back on," George said. "And they couldn't stop it. . . ." A slow grin spread across his face. "How unlike you—it's so gentle. . . ."

"Well," Ronnie said, examining his fingernails, "except for the stink bomb."

"Stink bomb?"

"Didn't I mention? The little captain had put three scenarios in the computer; it would generate one of them, using her parameters. I sort of . . . mixed two. One was a contamination drill . . . and it wasn't that hard to change a canister which would have released colored smoke for one releasing stinks." Ronnie smirked, satisfied with the look on George's face as well as his own brilliance. "The little captain was most upset."

"When she figures it out . . ." George went from gleeful to worried in that phrase.

"She'll never figure it out. She'll think it's her own problem set—even if she calls it up, she'll see that loop. Everyone makes mistakes that way sometimes."

"But that canister?"

"George, I am not stupid. I spent an entire day repainting the drill canisters so they have the wrong color codes. *All* of them. She'll assume it's something left over from the previous captain—like that great mysterious whatever that held us up at Takomin Roads. That's the first thing I did, right after we decided to scrag her. She can look for prints or whatever as much as she likes: she picked that canister up herself, and put it where it went off." Ronnie stretched again. Sometimes he could hardly believe himself just how brilliant he was. "Besides—she thinks I'm a callow foolish youth—that's what Aunt Cecelia keeps telling her—and she won't believe a spoiled young idiot—my dear aunt's favorite terms—could fish in her stream and catch anything." As George continued to look doubtful, Ronnie leaned forward and tried earnestness. If George got nervy, his next intervention would be much harder. "We're safe, I promise you. She can't twig. She can't possibly twig, and if she even thinks of it, Aunt Cecelia's blather will unconvince her."

CHAPTER EIGHT

"We have a slight problem," Heris said to Cecelia. It had not been easy to spirit her employer away along paths she knew were safe, but she managed. They were now in the 'ponics section reserved for fancy gardening. Cecelia had banished the gardeners.

"Again?" But Cecelia said it with a smile.

"Your nephew," Heris said. "I can deal with him, but he may come running to you, if I do. Or I can try to ignore him out of existence, but he may cause the crew some inconvenience."

"Somehow when you say 'inconvenience,' what I hear is much worse." Cecelia looked down her nose as if she were wearing spectacles and had to peer over them. She reminded Heris of one of the portraits of her ancestress.

"Well . . . I can probably keep it to inconvenience." Heris reached out to feel the furry leaf of a plant she didn't recognize. It had odd lavender flowers, and it gave off a sharp fragrance as she touched it.

"I hope you're not allergic to that," Cecelia said. "It makes some people itch for days."

"Sorry." Heris looked at her fingers, which did not seem to be turning any odd color or itching.

"It's got an edible tuber, quite a nice flavor." Cecelia looked at the row of plants as if blessing them with her gaze. "I hope Bunny will trade for this cultivar; that's why we're growing it now. We had to replant, of course, after the . . . mmm . . . problem."

Heris had not considered what, besides convenience, might have been sacrificed. "Did you lose all the garden crops?" she asked. "I thought they'd be unharmed." She also wondered what this had to do with Ronnie, and hoped it meant Cecelia was thinking on two levels at once.

"We lost some . . ." Cecelia's voice trailed away; she was staring at another row of plants, these covered with little yellow fruits. "I don't know what they're thinking of; half those are overripe. And they're not fertile; there's no sense wasting them. . . ." She picked one, sampled it, and picked another for Heris. "You're asking about Ronnie. I've told you before—I'm sick of that boy. If he's done something that deserves response, do what you will, short of permanent injury. I do have to answer to Berenice and his father later; it would be awkward to admit that I sanctioned his death. But aside from that—" She made a chopping motion at her own neck.

Heris ate the yellow fruit, a relative of the tomato, she thought, and watched Cecelia's face. "You're not really happy about that," she observed. "What else?"

"Oh . . . I think what makes me so furious is that he's not all bad. He may seem it to you—"

"Not really," Heris said. "Remember, I told you before that I've seen a lot of young officers, including very wild ones. For that matter, I *was* a wild one."

"You?" That deflected her a moment.

"What—you really thought I was born at attention, with my infant fist on my forehead?" It was so close to what Cecelia had thought, that the expression crossed her face, and Heris laughed, not unkindly. "You should have seen me at sixteen . . . and will you try to tell me you were completely tame?"

"At sixteen? I spent all my time with horses," Cecelia said. Then she blushed, extensively, and Heris waited. "Of course, there was that one young man—"

"Aha!"

"But it didn't interfere with my riding—nothing did— and nothing came of it either." Heris couldn't tell from the tone whether Cecelia was glad or sad about that. "But Ronnie—" Cecelia came back to the point, as she always did, eventually. "He's got brains, and I don't really doubt his courage. He's just spoiled, and it's such a waste—"

"It always is," Heris said. "What he needs is what neither of us can give him—a chance to find out that his own
foolishness can get him in permanent trouble, and only his
own abilities can give him the life he really wants. At his
age, such tests tend to be dangerous—even fatal."

"But you think you can do something?"

"I think I can convince him to play no more tricks on
me. That won't help overall, most likely; he'll blame me,
or you, and not his own idiocy."

"It's that crowd he hangs around with," Cecelia said. "Yes,
his mother spoiled him, but so are they all spoiled."

Heris did not argue; her own opinion was that the influence went both ways. Ronnie was as bad for the others as
they were for him. But it wasn't her nephew, and she didn't
have any remnant guilt feelings. She suspected Cecelia did.
Cecelia had commented more than once on the family's
attempts to make her perform in ways they thought important; some of that must have stuck, even if it didn't change
her behavior.

Cecelia ate another of the yellow fruits. Heris hadn't liked
the first one well enough to pick another; she watched
Cecelia poke about, prodding one plant and sniffing another.
Finally she turned back to Heris. "All right. Do what you
can; I won't expect miracles. And I won't sympathize if he
comes crying to me."

"I don't think he will," Heris said. "He has, as you said,
some virtues."

"Do you want to tell me what you're planning to do, or
do you think I'll let something slip?"

"No—you wouldn't, I'm sure. But my methods are, as
before, not entirely amiable."

"Go on, then. I won't ask. Just see that you're on time
for your lesson—today you get higher jumps and more of
them."

Heris looked at her. "That's one I hadn't thought of . . .
don't use the simulator until I've had a chance to check it,
will you?"

"Ronnie wouldn't touch it—he's being tiresome about
horses."

"No—not for himself or even you—but to get at me. I'll
be on time—in fact, I'll be early, and I'll make sure it hasn't
been tampered with."

* * *

Ronnie had never believed in premonition; he had known himself far too mature and sophisticated for any such superstitions. Thus the results of his first touch of the keyboard, after George left, came as a complete surprise. He had thought of another glorious lark, something harmless to baffle the little captain even further. She liked to go riding on Aunt Cecelia's simulator . . . well . . . what if it turned out to be under his control, and not Cecelia's? He had in mind a mad gallop across enormous fences that would surely have her squealing for mercy—and to Cecelia it could still appear that nothing was wrong and the captain's nerve had broken. He held out for some little time, letting himself imagine all the ramifications: his aunt's scorn of those who couldn't ride well, the captain's fear and then embarrassment, the confusion of both. They would never figure it out, he was sure.

Then he reached for the console. He would just take a preparatory stroll around his battlements, so to speak, making sure that all his hooks were in place. . . . His fingers flicked through the sequence that should have laid all open before him, and the screen blanked.

As anyone who has just entered a fatal command, he first thought it was a simple, reparable error. He reentered the sequence, muttering at himself for carelessness. Something clicked firmly, across his stateroom. It sounded like the door, but when he called, no one answered. Imagination. The screen was still blank. He thumbed Recall, and the screen stayed blank. Odd. Even if he'd hit the wrong sequence, the screen should have showed something. He hit every key on the board, in order, and the screen stayed blank. He felt hot suddenly. Surely not. Surely he hadn't done something as stupid as *that*—there were ways to wipe yourself out of a net, but his sequence had been far from any of the ones he knew.

He stared at the screen, and worry began to nibble on the edge of his concentration. He didn't have to enter the commands here, of course—shifting control to the console in George's or Buttons's suite would do—but he hated to admit he'd been such a fool, whatever it was he'd done. But the screen stayed blank, not so much as a flicker, and he didn't want to lose his good idea. The captain would have her riding lesson not that many hours later, and he wanted to be sure he got the patches in first.

With a final grunt of annoyance, he shut off his screen and went to the door. It didn't open. He yanked hard at the recessed pull, and broke a fingernail; the door didn't move at all. He thumped it with his fist, muttering, with the same effect as thumping a very large boulder: his fist hurt, and the door did not move.

He had flicked the controls of the com to George's cabin when the realization first came. . . . This could not be an accident. The com was dead; no amount of shaking the unit or poking the controls made any sound whatever come out of the speakers. He flung himself at the terminal console again, determined to break through. The screen came on when he pressed the switch, but it responded to nothing he did. No text, no images, no . . . nothing.

"Dammit!" He followed that with a string of everything he knew, and finished, some minutes later, with "It isn't *fair*!"

From the corner of his eye, he saw the screen flicker. Only then did it occur to him that while he might be cut off from the outside, the outside might very well be watching him. He came closer.

ALL'S FAIR IN LOVE AND WAR. The screen's script even seemed to have a nasty expression. DON'T MESS WITH MY SHIP. The meaning was clear enough, though he was in no mood to give in. But the messages stayed, two clear lines, and again nothing he did changed them. Ronnie turned away, furious, and kicked the bulkhead between his room and his private bath. With a *whoosh*, the toilet flushed, and flushed again, and flushed again, three loud and unmistakable raspberries.

"You can't do this to me!" he yelled at the ceiling. "This is *my* aunt's yacht!"

The shower came on; the automatic doors that should have enclosed it had not budged, and he had to wrestle them into place. A dense steam filled his bathroom. He saw with horror that the drain hadn't opened; water rose rapidly, then trickled out between the doors. He yanked towels from the racks, from the cupboards, and threw them at the overflow. . . . If it got into the bedroom, it would stain the carpet. . . . His *mother*, not just Aunt Cecelia, would be furious if he stained new carpet. When every towel was soaked, the drain opened, as if it had eyes to see, the shower stopped, and the water drained peacefully away.

The wet towels squished under his feet; his shoes were soaked, and his trousers to the knees. Ronnie felt the onslaught of a large headache, and glared at the mess. He wrung out the towels into the shower enclosure—better than walking on the wet mess—and hung as many as he could from the racks. The floor was slick; it could be dangerous. He grubbed into the back of the cupboard and found the cleaning equipment he had never used. A sponge—dry, for a wonder—a long-handled brush, a short-handled brush, and two bottles of cleaning solution, one blue and one green. The sponge eventually soaked up most of the damp on the floor, though it still felt clammy.

He had only thought he'd been angry before. Now he experienced the full range of anger . . . anger he had not even suspected he could feel. He was so angry that for once in his life he did not strike out at walls or doors or furniture. Instead, he went back to the terminal and sat before it. As he had expected, the screen had another message line now: YOU ARE CONFINED TO QUARTERS. YOU WILL RECEIVE ADEQUATE RATIONS.

He wasn't hungry; he didn't care about any blankety-blank rations. . . . He filled in all the blanks he usually did not allow himself to fill, forgetting none of the expressions he'd ever heard. But he did so silently. He was not going to give her the satisfaction.

How had she done it? How had she figured it out? She wasn't that smart; she had to be nearly as old as Aunt Cecelia. He fumed, silently, staring at the screen. Suddenly it cleared, and after a moment of blankness, reappeared in almost normal configuration. Almost, because the usual communications icon had been replaced by a black diamond.

Gingerly, as if the screen could bite him, he touched the service icon. A menu appeared: food, linens, clothing, air temperature, water, medical assistance. He thought it had had a few more items the last time he'd noticed it . . . but he hadn't paid much attention. The servants were usually hovering; he hadn't needed to call them. Now he touched linens. The screen blanked and displayed a flashing blue message: NOT IN SERVICE.

"What d'you mean, not in service!" he growled. In the bathroom, the toilet burped: warning. He pressed his lips together, amazed that he could be even angrier than a moment before. He was stuck with wet towels . . . what a *petty* revenge. That captain must come from a very ill-bred family. When he did revenge, he did it with style. He poked the board again; it returned him to the service menu. He thought of trying every single choice, but decided against it. It would only make him angrier to know that the others didn't work either.

He backed out of the service menu and looked at the main screen. Innocent, bland, it looked back. No communications, and missing functions on other icons, he didn't doubt. What else could he try? Information? He almost snarled at the little blue question mark, but controlled himself and put a finger on it.

The screen blanked and gave him a solid ten seconds of GOOD CHOICE before turning up the information menu. He had never tried this one before, since he'd never thought a ship as small as his aunt's could hold serious surprises. Now, he found a choice of items he was sure had not been his aunt's idea.

1. WHAT DID I DO WRONG?
2. WHAT CAN I DO NOW?
3. WHAT ARE YOU GOING TO DO?
4. WHAT DO THE OTHERS KNOW ABOUT ALL THIS?

It looked like someone's bad idea of a strategy game. He was going to have nothing to do with it. . . . It had to be a trap . . . but after sitting there for a long time he realized he was tired, stiff, and hungry. Food had been promised, though it hadn't arrived . . . and he did wonder just how much the little captain knew.

He pressed the first choice. In a cheerful electronic voice, the monitor said, "Good choice." Ronnie jumped. He'd hated the more vocal teaching computers he'd happened across. This one had a particularly chirpy intonation. The screen blanked, then filled with a list which he supposed represented his errors. It was not framed in terms his Aunt Cecelia would use; what hurt particularly was the assumption that he and the captain shared a frame of reference . . . the military. In just the way that his instructors had dissected unfortunate actions of the past, she dissected his action against her. Without, it seemed, the least rancor. That hurt, too. She didn't think of him as a rich spoiled brat—but as an incompetent junior officer, one of many. He did not like being one of many.

He was chagrined to learn that his hooks had been found and rebaited, so to speak; she had the entire conversation with George (it was played back for him) and from his own speech samples had produced com messages to the others telling them he felt like some time alone.

"Of course," the computer voice said brightly, "they think you're in here plotting more mischief against the captain and crew."

"But when am I—" He stopped when he heard the water start to run in the bathroom again. Evidently, he was not meant to do any talking.

"If you have questions," the voice said, "you may choose them from the menu when they appear." As if that captain would know what questions he wanted to ask. But after another paragraph of careful explanation of his faults, he found a list of questions. He chose the one about the canisters, because he really couldn't understand why repainting them had been so bad. They were just disaster-drill fakes anyway. What did it matter if one of them turned out to have red smoke, blue smoke, or a bad smell?

His comunit chimed. Ronnie leaped for it. This time the voice that came out was the captain's.

"You asked about the canisters," she said. "Do you know the chemical compounds in each?"

"You—no." He had caught his first angry response in mid-leap.

"Then you are not aware that some of the compounds are toxic, and some are flammable?"

"They are?" He could not have concealed his surprise if he'd tried. They were for *drills*—the label said so—and things used in drills were harmless, weren't they?

She had a human chuckle, which he didn't want to admit was pleasant. "Tell you what—I'll put the contents up on your screen in detail. Did you have any system in mind when you repainted those canisters, or did you do it at random?"

"Well . . ." Ronnie tried to remember. "Mostly I did them the color of the ones in the next box. That way I always knew which ones I'd done. There were a few, though, that were loose, and I just made 'em all orange with a brown stripe. Most of those were blue and . . . and two green stripes, but one was white and gray."

"Then you switched the box labels?"

"Yeah . . . how'd you know I'd repainted them?" He had been so careful; he could not believe she'd noticed.

"How do you think I knew which storage bay you were in with George?" she asked. He had no idea. He'd assumed she'd messed with all the storage bays. "Think about it," she said. The com went dead. He didn't even bother to try calling out again.

The screen had changed; now it was full of chemical formulas and reaction characteristics. Ronnie fought his way through it. He was actually supposed to know most of this; he remembered having seen it in class. But he had never had a good reason to put it together. He caught himself muttering aloud, and gave the bathroom a nervous look, but the toilet didn't burp. " . . . oxidizes the metallic powder and . . . gosh!" The stuff would really burn. *Really* burn. "I could have built a damn bomb!" he said, almost gleeful for a moment. Silence mocked him. He didn't need a warning roar from the plumbing or a smart remark from the computer to point out that setting off a bomb on a spaceship in deep space was not an intelligent thing to do, and setting one off without even knowing it was, if possible, stupider.

He felt cold, almost as cold as he'd felt when he realized he'd intruded on the bridge during jump transition. If the captain had picked another canister—the gray and white one he'd painted orange and red, rather than the blue and gray he'd painted black and green—it could have been a real emergency. A real disaster. A real—another look at the screen to confirm it—end of the whole trip. For everyone.

"I'm sorry," he said to the silent cabin. "I didn't mean to cause any real trouble."

Instead of an answer, the screen changed yet again, to show a transcript of what he'd said to George, every word. It looked worse, far worse, in glowing script on the screen. It looked as if he had indeed wanted to cause trouble—to harrass and humiliate the captain, to frighten and divide the crew. "I didn't mean it that way," he said, but he knew he had meant it that way, back when he thought it was safe to mean it that way.

The food, when it came, was bland and boring.

Heris climbed off the simulator after a vigorous ride across country on a large black hunter; every time she took the helmet off, the simulator startled her with its metal and plastic parts. Cecelia nodded at her.

"Very good indeed. You'll certainly qualify for one of the mid-level hunts. Depending on who's here, you might even be with me for a run or two."

"Are you sure you want to drag me along?" Heris asked. "I know it's not—"

"It's not common, but it's not unheard of, and anyway I do as I like. It's one of the perks. Bunny won't mind, as long as you can ride decently and don't cause trouble, which you won't. I'll enjoy having you to talk with—there are few enough single women, and I'm past the point where the men want to talk to me."

Heris was not sure she liked the assumption that she herself was also past that point . . . but it was true, she wasn't on the prowl. She wasn't over losing her other ship yet—though she could now think of it as "the other ship" and not the only one—and she would have to get her crew—and certain members of it—out of her mind before she could respond to advances. If anyone made them.

"What's the matter?" Cecelia asked. "Don't you want to go? Would you rather hang around Hospitality Bay with the other captains?"

"No!" She said it more forcefully than she meant to. "I'm sorry—the thought of those other captains has haunted me all along. I hate that. And yes, I would love to see what an estate set up for fox hunting looks like. It's just—I didn't want you to think you had to do it, because you said it in front of Ronnie."

"Nonsense. I said it because I wanted to; Ronnie's opinion is unimportant." Cecelia looked hard at her captain. "And by the way, how is that young man?"

"Perfectly healthy." That was true, if incomplete. He wasn't even that bored, because she had him doing the work he should have done in his basic classes. Math, chemistry, biochemistry, ship systems, military history, tactics. . . . When he kept his mind on it, all his plumbing worked and his food arrived regularly, and the lights worked. When he threw a tantrum—and he hadn't thrown one in the last several days, was he learning?—he found himself dealing with other problems, and the work still to do afterwards. "He may be rejoining you shortly, if you've no objection."

"What have you done, chained him in the 'ponics to dig potatoes?" Then she held up her hands. "No, don't tell me— I don't want to know. But I shall be fascinated to see what happens."

"So shall I," said Heris. She had found him more interesting than she'd expected, in the rare moments she tutored him over the com herself. He had a supple, energetic intelligence that would have rewarded good initial training. It was a shame that no one had ever made him work before. He could have been good enough for the Regular Space Service.

Ronnie reappeared at breakfast one morning, smiling pleasantly. Cecelia, at Heris's suggestion, had begun breakfasting with the young people some days before. This way, Heris had said, the collusion would be marginally less evident. She noticed that Ronnie was clean, dressed neatly, and showed no visible bruises—of which she approved— and the sulky expression she disliked no longer marred his face.

"Well?" George said. "Tell all."

"All of what?" Ronnie looked over the toast rack and chose whole wheat with raisins.

"You said you were up to something." George looked at the others for support, but they weren't playing up. "You said you were—"

Ronnie looked at him, a bland good-humored look. "I've said many things, George, which aren't breakfast conversation. And I'm hungry." He smiled at Cecelia. "Excuse me, Aunt Cecelia—could I have some of that curry?"

Cecelia smiled back. Whatever had happened, she wasn't going to interfere with it. "Certainly. I hope you haven't been ill. . . ."

"Not at all." He engaged himself with the curry, and the variety of other edibles that Cecelia considered appropriate to breakfast with company. George opened and shut his mouth twice, then shrugged and went on eating omelet.

Buttons, never very forthcoming in the morning, finished nibbling toast, excused himself, and went away; the three young women, after glancing several times from Ronnie to his aunt and back, also left. Cecelia ate her usual large breakfast, trying to ignore all the signals they were trying to pass so obviously. Finally only George and Ronnie were left, Ronnie eating steadily, as if to make up for many lost meals, and George in spurts, eyeing Ronnie. Cecelia struggled not to laugh. It was, after all, ridiculous. There was George, trying to protect Ronnie (too little and too late) from whatever horrors an elderly aunt could inflict on him. Finally she decided to intervene, before Ronnie hurt himself over-eating, or George had a stroke.

"I am not planning to harm him, you know," she said to George. George turned bright red and nearly choked on a muffin.

"She's quite right," Ronnie said, in the same pleasant tone he'd used so far. "It's safe to leave us alone."

"But—but you said—"

"It's all right," Ronnie said. "Really it is. I can tell you're not hungry—why not go play something with the others? I'll be along shortly."

George, still red and coughing, managed to say that he hadn't meant to interfere and Ronnie would know where to find him. Then, with a nod to Cecelia, he got out of the room as gracelessly as Cecelia had ever seen him move.

"You are all right. . . ." Cecelia said. Ronnie's clear hazel eyes gazed into hers, a look that combined all the charm and mischief she had seen in him since birth.

"I'm fine," he repeated. "Why shouldn't I be?"

"Well . . ." Cecelia pleated her napkin, a gesture that she knew conveyed feminine indecision to the men in her family. "You were fairly cross about my new captain, and when I wasn't sure your message to me was . . . was quite true, about studying for exams, and I pressured George—"

Ronnie flushed, but managed a smile. "Did he break down and tell you I had planned some mischief? I'm sure he did. Well—so I had, but I—I changed my mind. And I did study for exams, but if I tell George that—"

"Ah. I see." Into Cecelia's mind came the faint glimmer of what Heris must have done. How she had done it still remained a mystery. But she understood this much of the psychology of the younger set. "You don't want George to know you changed your mind, or that you studied—you must have been awfully bored, Ronnie, to decide to study." She hoped her voice didn't tremble with repressed laughter on that . . . or would he think it was a senile tremor?

"It was the only thing I could do in that room without— without letting George know—" That was undoubtedly the truth, Cecelia thought. What a jewel of a captain. What a marvel. She felt like grabbing Heris and dancing her along the passages . . . and at the imagined look on Heris's face she could hardly contain her laughter. Ronnie, she saw, was looking at her with some suspicion.

"My dear, please, I'm just glad you're not sick, and that you didn't do something awful that Captain Serrano would have had to complain to me about, and that you thought better of it and made good use of your time. I have to admit I find the need to placate George amusing . . . but then I'm old, and no longer worry about the opinions of friends. When I was your age, their opinions mattered much more."

"Even you? I thought you never cared about anyone." The tone was more respectful than the words.

"I didn't care about some members of the family—and I'm not bragging about it. But I had friends—others who shared the same interests—and it mattered a great deal to me what they thought. So I will conceal from George your careful study of whatever it was you studied, and pretend to know nothing—which is in fact just what I do know."

"Thank you, Aunt Cecelia," he said. Something in his eyes made her think he was not entirely chastened, but overly polite was easier to live with than whining complaint. "I suppose," he went on, "I should ask you to let me try your simulator." His tone, again, was almost too bland, but she chose not to notice.

"Of course. Some of your friends—Bunny's children, and Raffaele—have been using it; I made up a schedule so that we don't interfere with each other."

"And the captain," he went on. She noticed the tension in his jaw which he probably thought he'd concealed. "Is she coming along well?"

"Oh, yes," Cecelia said. "It's too bad she didn't start earlier; she'd have been competitive in the open circuit. As it is, she'll be a reasonable member of the field once she's had some real experience." She smiled at the look on his face, mingled of mistrust and envy. "You'd be good too, I'm sure, if you spent the time on it she has. You're the right build."

"But I'm not horse-struck," Ronnie said. "Just as well; Mother would say you'd contaminated me."

"Well, make a try at it. You might like it better than you think. The family brought you up to think it was ridiculous, and all because my parents wanted me to marry someone for a commercial alliance, and I wanted to ride professionally. Whether I was right or wrong doesn't affect the nature of the sport."

"All right." He held up his hands, as if in defense, and Cecelia realized her voice had risen. That old quarrel with her parents and her uncles could still make her angry. If they had not been so ridiculously prejudiced, she would not have been that defiant: she would have quit in another year or so, certainly after losing Buccinator, and married someone. If not Pierce-Konstantin, someone reasonable. But they had tried to have her barred from competition, when she was leading for a yearly award; she had rebelled completely.

It occurred to her that she had more in common with Ronnie than she'd imagined.

Most major space stations followed one of three basic, utilitarian designs: the wheel, the cylinder, and the zeez-angle for situations requiring specific rotational effects. When Heris called up the specs for Sirialis, which all her passengers called "Bunny's planet," she felt she'd taken another giant step into irrationality. A blunt-ended castle tumbling slowly in zero-gravity? This time she didn't ponder it alone; she called her employer, and sent along a visual of the Station where Cecelia had said they would dock.

"Is there an explanation, or do I just assume civilian-aristocratic insanity?" she asked.

"Insanity isn't a bad guess," Cecelia admitted. From the tone, she was neither surprised nor insulted by Heris's reaction. "There's been a certain—oh—eccentricity—in that family for some generations. Some of us think that's why they got so rich so fast; they've got monetary instincts where the rest of us keep our common sense. This Station, though—let me see if I can explain it."

"No one," Heris said, watching on her own screen the display of crenellations, towers, stairs, arches, and cloisters, rotating but somehow not making sense, "*no one* could explain this." Her eye tried to follow the progression of one staircase up to a square tower, which was suddenly not where it should have been. . . . The staircase had to be going *down.* Someone, she thought, must have made an error in the display.

"It began with Bunny's great-great-uncle Pirdich," Cecelia went on, ignoring the comment. "They'd just managed to recover the worst the original colonists had done, and the lords of the Grande Caravan had been teasing them about how impossible it was. He wanted to make a statement."

"That Station is a statement?"

"Of sorts, yes. He decided that having overcome what everyone said was an impossible problem in reclamation, he would celebrate it by building an impossible space station. Bunny's family's been overfond of the early modern period of Old Earth all along; this Station is built to look like a design by an artist of that period. I don't know the name; visual arts is not my thing. It is strange, isn't it? And if you think it's impossible, wait until you see the internal configuration and the fountain in the central plaza. Everything in it is taken from the work of the same person, and it's all delightfully skewed."

Delightfully was not the word Heris would have picked. In her experience, design problems in space stations caused everyone grief, especially captains of ships docking there. Creativity should be subordinate to efficiency. "Are all three stations like this one?" she asked. If not, maybe she could talk Cecelia into docking somewhere other than the prestigious but clearly impractical Home Station.

"Of course not. Once they had one unique impossible station, they wanted each one different. Here—" From Cecelia's desktop to Heris's the new visuals flashed: one like a stylized pinecone, in silver and scarlet, and one that looked like a worse mistake than the others, as if someone had dropped a pile of construction material onto a plate with a glob of sticky in the middle. "I think that's the worst," Cecelia said. "It's a Dzanian design, very neo-neo-neo, and the fault of Bunny's aunt Zirip, who married a Dzanian, and insisted that her family's fondness for Old Earth was pathological. You can't take anything very big into it, because the parts that stick out are nonfunctional; the docking bays are all nestled among them. There's only one berth for a decent-sized ship, and that's where they do cargo transfer. Zirip thought it was cute, she told me once, because it made for intimate spaces. But Zirip is also the one who converted the closet in her room into her bed and study, and used the room itself for a dance studio. Up until then, I'd thought the oddness in that family rode the Y chromosome."

Heris pitied the captains of cargo vessels loading and unloading there, but supposed they got used to it. "And the . . . er . . . pinecone?"

"Symbolic. So they told me. I've been there once, on a family shuttle; the docking facilities are lovely, but I got very tired of green and brown and the same aromatics all the time. It has the most capacity, and most guest yachts will dock there." At the end, that had the smug tone of someone who knew she was docking at a more prestigious slot; Heris sighed. She knew what that meant—no hope of talking Cecelia into using another station.

Instead, she looked again at the information for inbound ships. It might look like a peculiar sort of castle in the air, but it had modern, well-designed docking bays. The guidance beacons, the communications and computer links, the lists of standard and on-request equipment and connectors: all perfectly normal, exactly what they'd had at Takomin Roads. She wondered who in the family had had the sense to design the practical part.

"What sort of facilities does it have for off-duty crew?" Heris asked. She knew this was going to cause an explosion, and it did.

"What do you mean, off-duty crew? The crew goes to Hospitality Bay, as I explained earlier." Cecelia sounded annoyed.

"Milady." That formality should get her attention. Cecelia was susceptible, Heris had discovered, to very severe courtesy. "You have an entirely new set of environmental components, and the run here from Takomin Roads was just long enough to break them in—not long enough for this crew to be what I consider well trained. I want a standing watch aboard—"

"The Stationmaster won't like it; everyone sends their crews down to Hospitality Bay, and the ships are secured. What do you think, that rustlers or smugglers or something will come aboard?"

Heris didn't answer that, although she thought that leaving a ship uncrewed at a private station made it very easy for smugglers to do what they'd already done to *Sweet Delight*. She waited. Cecelia was not stupid; she would think of that herself in a few minutes. After a silence, Cecelia's voice came back, unsubdued but no longer angry.

"I see. You do think exactly that. And someone did put whatever it was in my scrubbers." It had now become "my" scrubbers, Heris noted with amusement. At least she knew what scrubbers were. Cecelia went on. "Did you ever find out what that was?"

"No," Heris answered. "And I doubt we will, unless it comes to court. My point is that we need a standing watch aboard; if you authorize it, the Stationmaster will agree."

"But what about the expense? And the crew expects their vacation at Hospitality Bay—won't they be angry?"

"Look—what if a pipe breaks while you're planetside, and floods dirty goo all over this carpet? You don't like the lavender plush any more than I do, but imagine the mess. Imagine what your sister would say. As for the crew, that's my problem; if they're angry, they'll be angry with me. Time they earned what you pay them."

"You're determined, aren't you?" That with a slightly catty edge.

"Where your safety and the integrity of this ship are concerned, yes," Heris said.

The Stationmaster required all the weight of Cecelia's patronage to change his mind. "It is not the usual procedure at all," he said. "We have that procedure for a reason; we can't have idle ships' crews roaming about the Station getting into trouble."

"They won't be," Heris said. "They'll be busy learning the new systems recently installed on this ship. During their shipboard rotation, they will have very little time to roam about—and if you insist, I can confine them to the ship, although I would prefer to allow them a moderate amount of time off. Lady Cecelia expressly requested that the crew be thoroughly trained—there had been incidents—" She didn't specify, and he didn't ask.

"Yes, but—we really don't have facilities . . ."

"Six individuals at a time aboard," Heris said. "No more than three offship—"

"Only three?" the Stationmaster said. Heris smiled to herself. She had won.

"Yes. They'll be standing round-the-clock watches, and they have a lot of work to do; I would prefer, because of that, to let them get their meals on the Station, rather than also detail a cook—"

"Oh . . . I see. Lady Cecelia's credit line?"

"Of course: the ship's account, with a limit—" She had to put a limit, or both the Station vendors and the crew would be likely to cheat.

"I would suggest thirty a day per person," the Stationmaster said. She haggled him down to twenty; she had already called up the vendor ads and knew her people could eat well on fifteen.

Next she had to tell the crew. She did not expect much trouble, and they listened in respectful silence, although she noticed some sideways glances. The new members, who had never been to Hospitality Bay, were glad enough to rotate in and out. Those who were accustomed to idling away a planetary quartile on full pay might have complained, but remembered the departure of the pilot. Heris hoped some of them would decide to quit; she knew she could do better. When she called for volunteers for the first rotation, Sirkin and the newest crew members got their hands up first—exactly what she'd expected. She had planned shorter, more frequent rotations (over the protests of both Cecelia and the Stationmaster) on the grounds that unused skills quickly deteriorated. In fact, there were crew members she didn't want to leave in the ship too long.

By the time they docked—without incident: the peculiar-looking Station turned out to be well designed where it mattered—Heris had the roster settled, and enough work planned to keep the standing watch alert. She had scattered her new and most trusted crew among each rotation . . . and hoped that would keep any remaining smuggler-agents from doing whatever they might otherwise do. Then it was time to pack her own kit, and prepare to accompany Lady Cecelia's entourage to the planet.

"You were right," Heris said to her employer, as she came out of the droptube into the central area of the Station. "I don't believe it." The ornamental object in the middle had as many eye-teasing impossibilities as the station itself, and in addition offered the appearance of a stream of water flowing merrily uphill. That alone wouldn't have been upsetting: everyone had seen inverse fountains or ridden inverse scare rides, since the invention of small artifical gravity generators. But this one flowed uphill without a substrate, burbling from one visible guide channel to another through the empty air. "It's a holo, right?"

"No—it's real, in its own way. You can put your hand into it and find out." Cecelia looked entirely too pleased with herself. Heris argued with her mind, and her stomach, and did not put her hand into the water. She was not going to ask how the illusion had been accomplished. Cecelia grinned. "I can tell you won't ask, so I'll give you a hint: Spirlin membrane."

Heris was very glad she hadn't put her hand in; it could have been embarrassing. Spirlin membranes, suspended in water, increased surface tension dramatically. They were also highly adherent to human skin, which often reacted with the Spirlin chemistry by fluorescing for days after the contact.

"I . . . see." Heris looked around. This area of the Station seemed to consist of gardens designed to the same weird standards as the Station itself and the fountain. Steps, low walls, terraces with seating arrangements that argued visually with each other—that seemed determined to flow from angular to curved, and back to angular, or, in some cases, to suggest by forced perspective the incorrect size or distance. Planters suspended at unnerving angles, all full of strange plants pruned to look like something else. When she looked up, Heris found herself staring into the canopy of another garden, looking down onto the heads of people walking along—she swayed, disoriented for a moment. Cecelia grabbed her arm.

"That one is a holo. I should have warned you—sorry. Almost no one looks up."

After that, Heris had no idea what kind of shuttle they

would find in the bay . . . but although it was more luxurious than commercial or military models, it looked much the same on the outside, and brought them to the surface safely. Lady Cecelia's party had it to themselves; Lady Cecelia and Heris in the forward compartment, the young people in the main compartment, and Lady Cecelia's maid and a few other servants in the aft section. Once well down in the atmosphere, the cabin steward served a full dinner; by the time they landed, shortly before sunset, Heris had almost reconciled herself to being a passenger.

CHAPTER NINE

"We hoped you'd be here for the first day, Lady Cecelia," said the gnarled little man at the entrance to the stable block. They had walked down from the Main House—which Heris had barely seen the night before, after the drive from the shuttle-port—to a set of buildings that looked as large as the house. Pale yellow stone, trimmed with gray stone around windows and doors; a wide, high arch with metal gates folded back . . .

"Things happen," said Cecelia. "Here—I want you to know Heris Serrano, my guest this year. She's a novice at hunting, but she's developing a decent seat."

"Pleased, mum," the man said. Heris felt herself under inspection of some sort, though she wasn't sure what he was looking for. Apparently she passed, for his thin mouth widened to a smile. "Go on in—he'll be waitin' for you."

"Now you'll see," said Cecelia as they came out of the arched entrance into a wide bricked walk that lay between the rows of stalls and a low-fenced dirt enclosure. Beyond was another archway, across which Heris saw a horse and rider move at a trot in yet another enclosure.

"Lady Cecelia!" It was clear from the rearrangement of wrinkles that this man's face seldom found such a smile. Lean, tanned, upright, brisk—this had to be the "Neil" who supervised all the training and the assignment of riders. "About time—I've held back two good prospects for you." He glanced at Heris, and dismissed her, waving for someone to bring a horse forward. Cecelia interrupted him.

136

"First—meet Heris Serrano. She's my guest this year, and I've been giving her preliminary instruction on the simulator—"

He looked at Heris again, this time with attention, and then back at Cecelia. "With full programming?"

"What I use myself. She's a novice, but she's solid as far as she goes. She's taking meter jumps now, but it's only sim; she needs practice before she goes out in the field. . . ."

"And you don't want me to treat her like a boneheaded kid who thinks he can ride because he once stuck on a horse at a gallop, is that it? Did you think I couldn't recognize maturity?"

"No—but I want her to have a good experience. And I want you to supervise, not one of your assistants, unless you've got better than last time."

"No . . . they go away when they get too good." His eyes measured Heris again. "Of course . . . size doesn't matter, and all that, but I'd think to start her on something reasonable. Sixteen?"

"Fine."

"She has to show me in the ring that she has the basics, but I'll shift her to the outside course right away."

"Thanks, Neil."

"No problem." He was still staring at Heris as if she had sprouted scales, then he nodded sharply and called, "Bring me the bay mare in seventeen; size sixteen saddle, and the eggbutt snaffle." To Heris he said, "If Lady Cecelia says you're a promising novice, I'll believe it, and that mare will give you the chance to show it. Honest, can jump, but not fast enough for the field. If you suit, you can use her here until you qualify." Then, to Cecelia, "Now watch this."

A thin girl led up a horse that looked enormous to Heris; it was a brown so dark it looked black except in clear sun. Cecelia nodded. "Is that what you got with the Buccinator sperm?"

"Yep. Off the Cullross mares. Two of 'em; the other's a liver chestnut. This one's five, and before you say anything I know I didn't show him to you last year. . . . Milord said not to, because it's a surprise. Want to try him?"

Heris could see the flush on Cecelia's cheek, the delight and eagerness that made her almost girlish.

"Of course. . . ." She was up in a flash, rising lightly to the hand that gave her a leg up. Heris had, by this time, seen her employer on many horses in the training cubes; she thought she knew how that long, lanky body, almost too stiff at times on the ground, would look astride. Cecelia looked better—as if she and the horse had fused into one.

"Here, sir." That was someone else, with a smaller brown horse for Heris. The man nodded at her, and she mounted without waiting for assistance.

"Come on, the both of you," he said. "You'll need to warm up inside anyway."

Heris, on her first live horse since her time in the Academy, found that coordinating the movement of legs and hands while the horse actually walked—walked toward something—was harder than she expected. She liked the higher viewpoint, but wanted to spend it looking around, not steering. Ahead of her, on the dark horse, Cecelia seemed to be having no problems. Heris lined up behind her and hoped her horse would follow calmly while she tried to remember all the lessons.

The inner training area, a walled oblong, offered fewer distractions. They walked to the right; Neil moved to the center, watching. Heris began to relax, letting her body discover the difference between the simulation and reality. It still felt strange. This was not a mechanical device, or an electronic image: this was an animal, a live thing, that smelled like an animal and felt (when she dared touch the neck) like an animal. The horse blew, a long slobbering breath, and Heris felt that in her legs.

Simulations work, she told herself. They're effective training tools; you learned to pilot a ship off simulators; of course you can ride this animal. The animal was slowing down, she realized, because she wasn't giving enough signal with her legs. The simulation tended to keep a pace more easily; Cecelia had mentioned that some horses required more leg pressure. Heris increased it, and the horse's head came up (just like the VR image!) and it walked faster. Mare. The man had said mare, and mares were females . . . so *she* walked faster.

"Reverse," Neil said. Almost before she thought, Heris had shortened one rein, shifted her legs slightly and the mare was turning smoothly to reverse directions. It worked. Of course it had worked in the simulator, but it worked on a real horse, too. She felt better. Maybe everything would work on the real horse. She looked over at Cecelia, across the circle. Her employer did not look anywhere near her actual age on that horse; she could have been Heris's age or even younger.

"Pick up a nice trot, now," Neil said.

Trotting felt completely different from the simulator. She was off balance at first, and she sensed Neil's disapproval. It took her an entire circuit of the ring to figure out what was wrong; her ship-trained sense of balance had worked on the simulator because it wasn't going anywhere relative to the ship—but the horse was going somewhere on the ground. If she leaned forward a bit more—she experimented—suddenly the movement felt right. Cecelia was right—it could feel like dancing.

With that experience to draw on, she was prepared for the difference in the feel of the canter, and compensated within a few bounds. The rush of cold air on her face was exhilarating; she didn't want to stop.

"She'll do," Neil said to Cecelia. Then, to Heris, "All right, Captain—back to a walk now, and bring 'er in to the center. You can watch Lady Cecelia." Heris slowed, remembering to brace her back, and guided the mare to near Neil. Cecelia's horse was walking again. Heris tried to notice the things she'd been taught to notice, but what struck her most was the horse's size. Even from up here, it looked big. When Heris had settled the mare in a halt, Cecelia nudged her mount to a trot. She hadn't waited for Neil's signal, Heris noticed. Watching the big horse trot, she wondered why Cecelia hadn't overtaken her. It moved so much faster. . . . Cecelia slowed it again; its neck arched and its steps shortened. Then it stretched, then compressed again. Heris was fascinated.

"Let's try you both on a few fences," Neil said. He led the way out of that ring into another, where four small jumps were set up. "You first," he said to Heris. "Just pick up a trot and take the little white one."

Heris collected the mare, pushed her into a trot, and approached the first jump. It seemed to stay in place while she moved, while the simulator had given the illusion of the jump shifting toward her. Even as she thought this, the mare rose to the jump, and Heris leaned into it. It felt the same, though. She turned the mare around, awaiting orders.

"Now try these two," Neil said. That, too, went smoothly; she felt steady and safe, but she knew the jumps were small. At Neil's command, she trotted over all four, then cantered over a pair—an in-and-out, he called it. He yelled, and several husky youths appeared and moved the jumps around. Again she jumped, first at a trot, and then a canter; first one way, then the other, as the fence crew changed distances and heights. Neil said nothing about her performance until it was over, when he called her to him. "Lady Cecelia's right," he said. "You're a solid novice. We'll see later what you do in the open. Walk 'er in circles down there—" He pointed to the far end of the enclosure.

Now it was Lady Cecelia's turn. The big dark horse poured over the jumps at a trot, hardly seeming to lift itself. The jumps were raised, the distances changed. Cecelia had explained the reasons, but even the simulator had not made it clear to Heris just what these changes demanded from a live animal. She watched the dark horse arch, lifting its knees high, as the jumps came up; she watched it compress and lengthen as the jumps were placed closer together or farther apart. And Cecelia, whom she had once considered a rich old eccentric . . . Cecelia flowed with the horse, a part of it.

When they were through, they walked back up to the house together. Cecelia had told Neil she would come back later to ride the other horse. "Now I want to be sure Heris is settled," she said. "She needs to meet a few people, learn where things are."

"Of course," Neil said. "But give me a call just before you come down."

Now Heris looked around her, more at ease than before. Like the house itself, all the surrounding buildings were either built of stone or faced with it. Most had stone or tile roofs as well. It looked remarkably like the cube of Old Earth Europe.

"I suppose it's like the old parts of the Academy," she said, turning to watch someone ride along a narrow cobble street lined with stone buildings. "Nostalgia or something . . ."

"And economy here," Cecelia said. "You have to remember when this was settled—a bare two centuries ago. Bunny's ancestors had money, yes, but it was far cheaper to import workers to build with local stone, than to import an entire factory to create conventional materials. I suspect that the first ones simply copied designs from old books—and then it began to look Old Earthish, and if someone teased them . . . well, that would have done it. They'd have insisted it was intentional." She walked around a circular tub planted with brilliant red flowers. "Of course it had all the usual comforts from the beginning; they didn't start out to build historical reproductions."

"But what about the horses? Have they always had horses here?"

"Probably. Colonial worlds usually have horses; they're cheap local transportation, self-replacing. Horse-based agriculture, too. Have you visited many worlds in the early stages of settlement?"

"No, not on the surface. Except for leave, I've spent my time in ships or offices."

"Mmm. Well, most import draft animals. Which ones depends in part on the world itself, and in part on the settlers. The dominant draft animal can be equine, bovine, or camelid."

"Camels?" asked Heris. She was not sure she knew what a camel looked like.

"And llamas," Cecelia said. "Have you ever seen camels?"

"No." This time she didn't explain.

"I haven't either, except in illustrations. One early Old-Earth breed of horse was used in the same culture that also had camels. Ugly beasts, with humped backs. It was said that they could be ridden, but I don't see how." Heris didn't even want to think how. Tomorrow morning, she would be hunting again. She was sure Heris would graduate into a hunt soon, and perhaps into the greens in a week or so, but for now all she wanted to think about was tomorrow morning.

If it wasn't Opening Day, with its farcical reproductions of ancient ceremonies via Surtees and Kipling, it was a hunting dawn. Cecelia put her head out the window and breathed deeply. Yes. Cool enough, crisp and dry, and she would have a new mount today. A Buccinator son. Sometimes the gods rewarded you for virtues unknown.

Bunny's staff served impeccable, lavish hunt breakfasts— and she enjoyed food—but today she hardly noticed either the traditional dishes or the taste. The green hunt, composed of the most experienced and best riders, talked little at breakfast this early in the season. Later, perhaps. Now they all wanted but one thing—the horses, the cold air, the speed, the chase. They recognized this in each other; glance met glance over the clattering silverware.

Outside, with the low sun gilding the stones, Cecelia walked down to the stable block as happy as she had felt since leaving competition. This is what life was about: a hot breakfast comfortable in one's stomach, and the prospect of a good horse to ride over open country until the day ended. In her saddlebag was her personal choice for a lunch snack—on this, Bunny made no attempt to enforce the more foolish tradition: if you wanted a thermpak of shrimp-in-sweet-sauce, you could have it. Cecelia favored a hot turkey sandwich, pickles and cheese, and hot coffee.

Buccinator's son, powerful and alert, stood waiting, held by a groom. She mounted, picked up her reins, nodded to the groom, and set off at a walk to quarter the yard. Then out the great stone arch to the front of the Main House, where Bunny and the huntsmen would have brought the pack by now. Hooves rang on the stones, riders began to talk, once mounted, in the quiet tones of those who expect to be listened to.

She came around the side of the house. . . . There, in the sunlight, were the hounds, sterns wagging as they swirled in controlled chaos around the hunt staff in scarlet. Bunny grinned as she rode up to him. "You like him, do you?"

"You stinker—you might have let me see him last year."

"He wasn't ready. But you're first to take him into the field; he's been schooled but never hunted."

"You are most generous." And he was. To let a guest take a green horse into the field—with the green hunt, over the most demanding country—she was not sure she would have done it, had it been her horse and her country.

"He couldn't be in better hands," Bunny said. "One concession—we're going to start with the Long Tor foxes today." Which meant less woods riding, more in the open, but the fences were stone walls, unforgiving of mistakes, and in the open they'd be riding faster.

"Sounds like fun," Cecelia said. Other riders came up then, paying their respects to the master, and she circled away.

* * *

The Long Tor foxes cooperated by leading a long, circuitous chase across the open slopes, in and out of difficult ravines, back up and around almost to their beginning. The Buccinator son proved himself, maturing at every wall and ditch, the scope and speed of Buccinator bloodlines keeping him out of trouble and well up. Cecelia didn't push him. There was no reason to race; everyone knew how she could ride, and everyone knew the horse was green. Far more important to give him a good day's work, and the confidence to go on another time. They rode back in a golden afternoon, the young horse still with power to spare, and Neil gave her a thumbs-up when she came through the arch.

"Cool and quiet, and not a mark on him . . . and you're happy with him?"

"He's all you promised. Never shirked, never tried to turn away from anything. He'd have gone faster if I'd asked— actually, I had to hold him back at first."

"Good. That's what I hoped for. He should be ready day after tomorrow; you can have old Gossip tomorrow, if you want."

"Give him two days off," Cecelia said. "It's his first season. Flat work tomorrow, and the day after I'll come do a little schooling on him when I get back from the hunt—"

"You think you'll have the energy?"

Cecelia gave him a mock glare. He was always trying to suggest she was too old, but they both knew it was a joke. "I could school three horses now, as you well know—shall I prove it?"

"No . . . just give Gossip a run tomorrow. I let Cal have him for Opening Day, and he bucked over the first ten fences, Cal said. Your friend Captain Serrano's doing well; I'm going to put her in the blues, for her first run."

Cecelia came back to the house thoroughly satisfied. Now if Heris and young Ronnie would only realize how much fun this was.

Heris had spent several hours riding to Neil's exacting standard, on the flat and over the fences of the outside course. His announcement that she would ride in the blues was, she knew, a reward, though she would just as soon have had something more tangible and immediate. She came back to the house stiff but not really sore, ready for a hot bath, but the house itself fascinated her.

The big stone building was huge, an institution rather than a dwelling place. It had four levels aboveground and one below, and an astounding number of rooms, corridors, staircases, arches, ramps, lifts, balconies, and other architectural bits for which Heris had no name. On the ground floor were rooms devoted to reading, sitting, talking, dancing, dining, lunching, breakfasting, and playing games of chance or billiards. High ceilings and large rooms made Heris think of an overdecorated flight deck on her cruiser. Most of the guest rooms were on the second floor, along with another library and a "withdrawing room" for women, which overlooked a rose garden. The third floor, Cecelia said, had both guest rooms and family suites, while the fourth was (traditionally) the servants' quarters.

Heris had a bedroom the size of her entire suite on the yacht, with a bathroom almost as large as the bedroom. Two windows opened to the east, with a view across a lower roof to scattered buildings on green fields beyond. A white vase filled with fragrant roses stood on the black polished bureau; a deskcomp stood beside it. The bathroom amazed her even more. As big as most rooms, it had every luxury fixture she'd heard of, and two she hadn't. She eyed the nozzles with suspicion and left them alone. She bathed, relaxed for a time in swirling hot water, and dried her hair, half amused at herself for taking so long. It was a very unmilitary situation.

The same dress she had worn that first night at Takomin Roads would do, Cecelia had said, for dinner. She added a simple but elegant silver necklace, then made her way through the maze of corridors to the main stair, and descended its graceful curves. Voices rose toward her; she felt as shy as she had the first night on a new ship, coming to the wardroom.

Cecelia waited at the foot of the stairs, her short hair lifted into a graceful wave of silver and auburn. She wore the amber necklace Heris had admired, and a long, beaded tunic in bronze and ochre over a flowing copper-colored skirt. It was hard to believe she was an old woman, and had spent all day on a horse. She smiled.

"I thought you might like a few introductions."

"Thank you," Heris said. She had tried to form no expectations, but she was surprised. All the men in traditional black and white, all the women in long gowns, looked more like athletes than wealthy layabouts. Yet the surroundings, and the clothes, and the jewelry, were straight out of caricature. She managed not to stare as a dark-haired beauty undulated by in a rustle of silvery silk, its folds seemingly held to her by affection alone.

"That's the Contessa," Cecelia said. Her eyes twinkled. "That's what she likes to be called, rather. It's all a sort of game . . . being a character out of history, or rather out of a story about history. They've read all the fiction of the period, and they take parts. Not formally, in the evenings, but one is expected to recognize a good version of a familiar character."

"Books . . . like the Surtees and Kipling you loaned me?"

"That's a beginning. You'll have to look into Bunny's library. Come along—you need to meet him."

Heris tried to suppress her curiosity in the presence of her host, Lord Thornbuckle. Was he, too, taking a character to portray? Was that long, foolish face his by nature or by design? He murmured a greeting to her, a longer and warmer one to Lady Cecelia, along with his regrets that she had not made the Opening Day.

"We had some delays," Cecelia said.

"So I understand from the children," he said. "How nice of you to have brought them along. Sorry—let's talk after dinner—" And he turned to greet someone else, with a faint shrug that made clear to Heris he'd rather talk to Cecelia.

"And you must meet Miranda," Cecelia said. "His wife, Buttons and Bubbles's mother, though it's hard to believe. She takes rejuv like kittens take cream."

And in fact Heris would not have suspected the sweet-faced blonde to be old enough to have children Bubbles's age . . . let alone older ones. Miranda murmured polite nothings to them, and introduced them to a Colonel Barksly, who eyed Heris warily before wandering off to get something to drink—or so he said. Heris suspected he would go straight to a comp and start looking her up in some index of officers somewhere. She wished him luck. Miranda confided to Cecelia that they were having trouble again with "that Consuela woman" and Cecelia made appropriate sympathetic noises before excusing herself to "introduce Captain Serrano around a bit."

Heris had never been fond of the predinner social hour anyway, and this one seemed to last forever. She felt out of place in these tall, cold rooms with their consciously ancient decorations, surrounded by people whose gowns had cost more than her Fleet salary. But just as she thought how much she would prefer a snack in her room, a sweet-toned bell rang and someone (she couldn't see who) announced dinner. A flurry of movement; she found herself provided with a dinner partner (and felt fortunate to have read the Kipling) and soon sat at the long, polished table beneath the pseudobaronial banners.

Her partner, it seemed, was one of Bunny's distant cousins, and "desperately keen to hunt." Heris had no trouble with the conversation. The cousin wanted only a listener for his tale of the Opening Day hunt, today's hunt, the performance of his horse, the beauty of the weather, the cunning of the fox, and the inept handling of the hounds by the new huntsman.

"—wouldn't pay him any mind at all, and worse all day. Bunny should never have let Cockran retire."

"Nonsense!" huffed a husky man from across the table. "Cockran hasn't been well the last two seasons, and he's due for rejuv. Bunny had no choice. Besides, Drew wasn't that bad. That couple of pups gave him trouble, but the good old 'uns stayed true. And that last run—"

"Well, but you weren't up where you could see the cast in that wood—"

The food that came and went through all this was ample and hearty, not nearly as elegant as the meals Cecelia had served her, but more filling. Heris wondered if Bunny's household adhered to the custom of women leaving the table early, or to the more modern format where the heavy drinkers dispersed to one room, and those preferring stimulants to another. The latter, she found; she went into the "coffee-room" with some relief, for the long-winded cousin had chosen to drown his bruises in brandy.

"You're ex-military aren't you?" asked someone at her elbow. The colonel she'd been introduced to earlier, in fact. Barksly, that was his name. Heris repressed a sigh. Two bores in one evening? But the colonel's brown eyes twinkled at her. "You deserve a medal for that—Laurence Boniface has rarely had such a patient listener; most of the ladies gather their conversational reins at the beginning and try to make a race of it."

"The food was too good," Heris said demurely. He laughed.

"And I thought it was recognition of a hopeless cause. Tell me, though: royals, regulars, or ground forces?" He was not one to give up an inquiry.

"Regulars." She would make it short and firm; would he take the hint?

"Ah," he said. She could almost hear the gears twitching in his brain. "I met an Admiral Serrano once, at an embassy do on Seychartin."

"If he was two meters tall, with a scar from his left ear across his cheek, that was my uncle Sabado. If she was my height, with lots of braids, it was my aunt Vida." Actually there had been eight Admiral Serranos in the past fifteen years, but only two that she knew of had served on Seychartin while holding that rank.

"Your aunt, then. There's a strong family resemblance."

"So I've been told," said Heris. She braced herself for more questions; she knew he was asking them in his mind. But his next words left the questions untouched.

"It's unusual for Regular Fleet officers to have riding as a hobby," he said.

"Lady Cecelia would convert anyone," Heris said, relieved. Maybe she was safe, now, although this sort of colonel had a habit of making oblique attacks later in an acquaintance. "We had a wager, which she won; the forfeit was that I would take instruction from her. In the process, I discovered an interest."

"Ah," he said, this time in a different tone. "Do you know, years ago when I was a small boy, I happened to see her ride, one of her professional events. It was cold and wet, I remember, a nasty blowing mizzling rain that went right through whatever you wore. I had been bored, even though I rather liked horses, because I couldn't see over the grownups. I would see the top of someone's cap flash by, and that was it. People would groan or cheer, and I didn't know why. My feet were cold, my neck was wet; I'd have gone home if I could. Then everyone was saying 'Here she comes!' and someone—I never even knew the man—set me up on his shoulders, and out of the murk came this huge horse with a red-headed woman on it, and they jumped something that looked to my child's eyes to be four meters high and every bit that wide. Of course it wasn't, but I was impressed anyway. For a whole term I wanted to be an event rider."

"Were you ever?" asked Heris. She found she really cared; he had a gift for storytelling that Bunny's poor cousin utterly lacked.

"Oh, no. I was too young to be faithful to dreams; the next thing I wanted to do was play a very rough ball game popular at our school, and since it was available and good horses were not, I learned to play that, and liked it. Real riding came later, and by then I knew I wanted a career in the military or possibly security forces."

"I wish I'd seen her," Heris said. "She's shown me the cubes, of course, but now that I've ridden a real horse I can imagine that the effect is very different if you're actually there, seeing it."

"Magnificent," he said, smiling. "But do you have your hunt assignment yet?"

"Blue," said Heris. "Day after tomorrow, Neil said; tomorrow I'm to have another session over fences."

"Good for you. If he's scheduled you into the blue, you're doing well. Let me introduce you to some of the other blue hunt members." He led her to a cluster of people who were all talking about the day's chase. Heris wondered which hunt he rode with. Cecelia had explained the system, but it still seemed odd. . . . For one thing, she didn't understand why the hunt levels didn't have names taken from the books, instead of colors. If they were all so interested in reproducing history . . .

"Ah," said a tall lanky blond man. "Captain Serrano, Lady Cecelia's new friend—we've heard about you." Heris had no chance to wonder what he meant, for he went on. "Neil's bragging to everyone—of course, she's his pet example of what we should all aspire to, and now as a teacher as well as rider. Is it really true that you had never mounted a live horse until today?"

Heris allowed herself a slow smile. "Not at all. But it's true I had ridden little, many years ago, and hadn't been on a horse since I was . . . oh . . . perhaps twenty-three."

"You'd never jumped?"

"No."

"I told you, Stef, Lady Cecelia's simulator is legendary." That was a red-haired woman about Heris's height, who wore a gown of mossy green with wide sleeves. . . . Heris realized why, when she saw the wrist brace.

"It must be." Stef, the tall man, shook his head. "Maybe it would help me. It took me five seasons to work up from the red hunt to the blue, and I've been stuck in blue for ten." Others chuckled; the red-haired woman turned to Heris.

"Tell me—did you find real horses easy after the simulator?"

"Not exactly easy, but much easier than I would have without it. And after the second ride, it was almost the same, a continuation of the same training."

Cecelia appeared at her shoulder. "I hate to break this up, but you've got that early lesson, and I'm off with the greens at dawn—and there's a message from the Station." She smiled at the group around Heris, and they smiled in a way that let Heris know how much clout Cecelia had. She was almost tempted to refuse the suggestion just to see them react, but that would be cheap, so she said good night and followed Cecelia upstairs.

"Message?" she asked on the way.

"Nothing much—the ones you left aboard—"

"The standing watch," Heris murmured.

"Whatever. Letting you know that the others arrived safely in Hospitality Bay, and that the new equipment is functioning correctly so far. Did you ask for regular reports?"

"Of course," Heris said. "If they didn't report, how would I know whether things are going well?"

"Oh. I'd assume they were—but before you even remind me, if it were a stable and not a ship I would be the way you are. When I was off competing, I spent incredible sums checking back with the home yard to see if they'd remembered things—and they always had."

"Because you checked," Heris said. "I'll call back up—anything else?"

"Well . . . yes. I hope you won't be offended—"

"I won't." Although she wasn't entirely sure. On her home ground—and she treated Lord Thornbuckle's planet as her home ground—Cecelia had some of the very habits Heris had feared when she first hired on with a rich old lady.

"Some of them are terrible gossips," Cecelia said, speaking softly. "It's not just that they'll repeat what you said. . . . They'll embellish it. It'll be worse because you're here as my guest; they've chewed my past to tasteless mush already, and you're something new. I know you can deal with it, but don't be surprised if you hear that we're lovers or something."

"Lovers!" Heris nearly choked. "Us?"

"Predictable gossip," Cecelia said. Her cheeks were very pink.

"I'm sorry," Heris realized that her reaction could be construed as unflattering. "It's just—I mean—"

"We aren't. I know. But since I never married, they've been trying all the theories about why not, one after another until the end and back again. That crowd that rides the blue hunt is the worst—Stef, in particular, would rather talk than ride, as you can tell when you see him mounted."

"You know," Heris said, as they mounted another flight of stairs. "I wouldn't talk about you—or Ronnie."

"I know. It's not that. I just—I want you to enjoy this, Heris. Not as my captain, but as my guest. And it occurred to me that you might not have their sort of gossip in the military."

"Oh, don't we!" Heris chuckled. "Same both places, I expect. Some wouldn't touch it, but others can't wait to guess who's in bed with whom, using what chemicals or gadgets. Don't worry; I can be dense when it suits me."

"Good." Cecelia took a few more steps, then stopped to face Heris. "If you pay attention in the blue hunt, you'll probably be up in green very soon. They're looking for several things—how solid you are over fences, how done the horse comes back, and whether you interfere in the field."

"Do you want me in the green hunt?" Heris asked. It had become clear how much respect the greens had, but not whether Cecelia wanted competition.

"Of course I do! Heavens, girl, I wouldn't have brought you if I'd thought you'd be stuck in a lower hunt the whole season. It wouldn't have been fair to you, or as much fun for me. Go on, now, and get your rest. I'll be interested in hearing about your day."

✳   ✳   ✳

That last visit to the tailor had taken out the slight wrinkle in the back of her jacket. . . . Heris looked at herself in the mirror with a mixture of amusement and pride. Amusement, because the clothing proper to foxhunting still struck her as ludicrous: why wear light-colored tight breeches when you were going to gallop big dirty animals through the mud? And pride, because at over forty she still had the condition to look sixteen or so in those same tight pants, white shirt, and dark jacket.

Despite the training, and Cecelia's assurance that she was ready, Heris found the chaos in the blue hunt's meeting area tingling along her nerves. She looked for Neil but saw only the second level of help. Of course, Neil would be with the green hunt. Surely he'd chosen the mounts, though. . . . She eyed the big red—chestnut, she reminded herself—gelding being led toward her with some concern.

"Tiger II," said the groom, a thickset woman even darker than Heris. "Need a leg?"

"In a moment." Heris went through the drill Cecelia had taught her, checking the bridle and girth herself, then accepted a leg and swung into the saddle. She hoped the beast's name did not reflect his temperament.

"He pulls, sometimes," the groom said. "But he'll answer a sharp check. Keep him back, and calm, and he'll go all day. Get in a fight with him, and you'll wish you hadn't."

Great. She had a problem horse for her first hunt, her first performance in front of everyone. She looked down at the groom, expecting to see sly satisfaction, but the woman's smile was friendly. "Don't worry," the woman said. "He's not a bad 'un for a first time out; he can jump anything, and will—the only thing is don't let him go too strong till he's worked himself down a bit."

"Thank you," Heris said. "Any other advice?"

This time the woman's face creased in a broad grin. "Well—I wouldn't let him slow down in water . . . he likes to roll. If you come to a stream, get him over in a hurry."

The horse snorted and shook his head; Heris firmed her grip on the reins. "I'll be careful," she said. The groom stepped back. Heris looked around and saw that about half the riders were up. She had room to walk the red horse— Tiger—in a small circle, and did so, first one way then the other. As the minutes passed, she calmed down. It was just another horse, and they were going out to ride over just another field. She had told herself that same lie in other situations, and it always helped. So did "tonight this will be over."

CHAPTER TEN

The hounds led the way, their long tails—Heris couldn't make herself call such a biologic ornament a stern; ships had sterns—whipping back and forth or carried high, eager. She got only a glimpse of them before the rest of the field passed out the gate and blocked her view. She intended to make sure Tiger understood who was in charge while they were still at a walk.

As they came around the end of the stable wing, Heris could see both the other hunts moving away to the east and west. The beginners (so Cecelia had called them) would hunt the flat, open country to the east, where the fences were lower and the pseudofoxes lived in brushy thickets. The green hunt had the western hills, with long open slopes and timber at the top and bottom. And they, the blue hunt, had a mixed country, rather like lumpy potatoes in a kettle. Little hills with little creeks between them, little patches of woods and others of brush, odd-shaped fields bordered with stone walls or ditches or both.

Verisimilitude, Cecelia had explained, influenced only some of Lord Thornbuckle's eccentricities. That rather lumpy country had been the first colony settlement on this world, bought out by one of the present owner's ancestors. They had tried to make a quick profit out of open-pit mining to pay off their initial investment, then botched the mid-level terraforming that was supposed to convert the area into something their heirs could live on and from. Instead, they went broke, and left behind ugly pit mines, irregular heaps of spoil, ponds and wandering streams fouled with acid and heavy metals. Now, some hundreds of years later, the area was still unsafe for use in any food chain humans would use, but it could support hardy plants, animals with a tolerance for heavy metals and acid water, and recreation. Wool and leather and sport were its crops.

Tiger yanked on the bit, and Heris brought her mind firmly back to the immediate moment. Someone had trotted past— she found it hard to recognize, in the plain black coats and hats, the people she had met at dinner the night before— and the red horse wanted to follow. She refused, and met his attempt to sidle out from behind the horse in front with a firm leg. He tested her in the next few minutes, as they rode to cover, with a curvet here, and a pretense at a shy there; she was reminded of certain troublemakers she had known, and had no problem keeping him under control.

"Ah—Captain Serrano!" The grinning man next to her was the tall lanky blond Cecelia had said liked talk better than riding. He was on a horse which looked like a stuffed caricature of the animal Neil had shown Cecelia: large, dark brown, but this time coarse and bulgy instead of powerful and sleek. And he rode sloppily; even Heris could tell that. "Lovely morning, isn't it? Are you ready for Tiger? Did they tell you?"

"That he pulls, yes, and to keep him out of the water." Heris glanced around. They were near the tail of the group, and she could tell from the tension in the reins that Tiger wasn't happy about it.

"You don't have to stay back here," the man said. Stef, his name was. "Mid-field's enough; just keep him away from the leaders."

"I'm fine," Heris said. "I like to watch the others." Cecelia had told her to stay well back, even this far back, and she trusted Cecelia's advice more than someone who sat his horse like a jellied custard.

"Come *on*, Stef!" someone called from ahead, and he shrugged and kicked his horse into a trot. Heris anticipated Tiger's attempt to lunge forward, and rehearsed for the hundredth time what Cecelia had told her, and what she had read.

The hounds would be turned loose to find the smell— the scent—of one of the pseudofoxes, and then they would "give tongue." Now that Heris had heard them, from a distance, she agreed that "barked" was inadequate. With the hounds following the scent, the field would follow—cautiously—because pseudofoxes, like their Old Earth predecessors, were tricky beasts. More than once they'd popped into view in the midst or even rear of the field, causing a wild confusion of horses and hounds and usually getting clean away. One had to give the pack time to work the scent, to untangle the maze the prey left, and push the fox into the open. Only when the fox was sighted did things move faster—eventually very fast.

They came to a scrubby wood bordered on one side by a tangle of two-meter brush. Riders gathered in a clump; the few who spoke did so quietly, and most checked girths and stirrup leathers, and kept quiet. Heris put a leg forward cautiously and found that Tiger's girth could come up another notch, just as the groom had said. She drew in a long breath of cold, moist morning air, on which the smell of horse and dog and wet clay hung suspended in a fundamental cleanliness utterly unlike ship's air. Planets felt so spacious; there always seemed to be room, somewhere beyond—although she knew very well they were as tightly limited as any ship, just larger. Somewhere ahead and to the left, she heard the noise of the pack, the busy feet pattering on leaves and twigs, the coarse, eager panting, an occasional muffled yelp. Something small and gray and bouncy—not a pseudofox, but something it probably ate—shot into the clearing and two horses shied away from it. Tiger threw up his head, but Heris held him firmly and the little animal scuttered through the field without causing any real damage. Another animal—Heris got a good look at this one, and it was a small, black tree-climber with a bushy tail—clung to a nearby tree and made angry chattering noises at them, flipping its tail as punctuation.

Heris had just begun to wonder if anything would happen when one of the hounds gave a sobbing moan, and another joined in. She had lost track of their movements; they now sounded ahead and to the right, and she could hear crackling in the brush. Around her, the riders gathered up reins, and edged into position. Some began moving, at a walk, in the direction of the noise. Then a horn blew a signal she didn't know, and everyone set off after it.

For a long time they seemed to move at a walk or slow trot, making their way through the woods and through a lane in the brush beyond it. Tiger tossed his head a lot, but otherwise gave Heris no trouble. At the end of the brush a low stone wall offered the first chance to test jumping skills in the field. Heris, at the end of the field, had to wait a long time while others scrambled over, some with difficulty. By the time it was her turn, stones lay tumbled at the foot, and the wall was scarcely a half-meter high. Tiger bounced over it with contempt, ears flat, and kicked up on the far side. Only those who had had refusals and turned aside to wait were behind her now. She could see the backs of the first riders rising as their horses leaped an obstacle across the field she'd just jumped into.

Tiger fought the bit all the way across the field, took off late for the rail fence on its far side, and whacked it with his forelegs. Heris had no trouble staying on, but she could tell her shoulders would hurt if he was this stubborn all day long. The fence seemed to have settled him, though, for he followed the field along a track through sparse trees without trying to race ahead. Heris couldn't see exactly where they were headed next, but she felt more confidence in her ability to survive this odd ritual.

Tiger's strong trot brought the field back to her, as most of the riders chose to squeeze through a gate at the end of the track rather than jump another, higher wall. Some of those who had tried the jump hadn't made it; Heris saw one woman climbing back onto her horse, and a man stalking a loose horse which was slyly moving off just too fast to be caught. Beyond the gate, they faced a sluggish stream, well-muddied by recent crossings, and a steep slope across it up one of the small irregular hills. Remembering the groom's advice, Heris took a firm contact, and gave Tiger a smart tap in the ribs. With a snort, he plunged into the water, and lurched up the far bank. Heris couldn't remember if she was supposed to avoid trotting up hill or down (someone had said something about it, she thought) so she walked sedately up, trusting that she could see where everyone was from the top. Tiger's ears were no longer back; apparently he'd given up the fight.

She had imagined a hill like an overturned bowl, with a definite top, from which she could see all sides. As soon as the slope flattened, she realized her mistake. She might as well have assumed that being at the top of a loading platform or the flight deck of her carrier would let her see everything going on below. From the irregular and unlevel top of the hill, the downward slopes were mostly invisible. Some fell off steeply, and others were hidden in clumps of trees or brush. She looked around for a clue. The ground had plenty of hoofprints, but she was no tracker to know which were recent. Far off in the distance, tiny horses stretched across the slope of another hill—but that couldn't be the hunt she was following, it was too far away. A fresh breeze made just enough noise in the nearest trees to cover the sound of the hounds . . . although she hadn't heard it for some time, she realized. She'd just been following the tail-end riders.

She felt stupid, and bored, and suddenly very irritated with Lady Cecelia. Surely this was not what riding to hounds was supposed to be like, dawdling along at the end of a group of people who fell off and got lost. How could they call it hunting? Only those in the front of the group were actually hunting, and they were just following the hounds, who were chasing a fake fox, an artificial animal designed to be quarry. The whole thing was a fake—a pretense of historical accuracy, modified for modern convenience.

A quiver beneath her reminded her that she wasn't standing on a machine, or a fake animal, but riding a real, living animal with its own initiative. Tiger's ears were forward, pricked, and he stamped the ground with a forehoof. She looked in the direction of his gaze. The little horses had disappeared into a wood, too far away still, she was sure . . . but Tiger didn't think so.

She muttered a curse that was thoroughly untraditional on the hunting field, being born of things you could do with weapons found only on spaceships, and nudged Tiger into motion. "You like to hunt, they told me," she said to the horse's ears. One of them flicked back, as if he understood. "Find the damned hunt, then." Tiger picked up a trot, and as the downhill slope steepened, he lunged into a gallop. Heris had just time to think she shouldn't have let him do that. Then they were in the trees, and she was too busy keeping her head off limbs to worry about it.

Out of the woods, into a field bounded by more woods:

Tiger took the fence from trees to grass in an easy bound, crossed the field in five strides, and rolled over the wall at the far side into a track Heris had not noticed until they were in it. No trees . . . a long curving ride up and around the shoulder of another hill, through an open gate, down across a grassy field. Tiger, wiser than she, skirted the rock-edged sinkhole in the middle and made for a gap he evidently knew well. A downward rocky slope, where even Tiger slowed to a walk, and Heris got her breath back as they slithered through some spicy-smelling trees toward another creek. That had been fun, if scary: she began to think that whether it counted as hunting or not, it was more fun to ride fast than slow.

By this time Heris had no idea where they were, but the horse's ears still pricked forward. He minced across the little creek and into the woods on the far side. Suddenly Heris heard the hounds again, and from this distance had to admit they sounded almost like horns themselves. They were ahead through the woods, moving left to right. . . . She gathered herself just in time, as Tiger sprang upward, dodging through trees with no regard at all for her legs. She could steer him, she found, and even moderate his speed; she pulled him to a solid canter rather than a headlong gallop.

The belling of hounds rang out nearer; at the top of the wood, they came out of the trees to find the hounds strung out on that hill's bald top, with the field close behind them and the fox in view before. Heris managed to swing Tiger around behind the front runners, though he fought her. Then they were in with others, galloping over short grass toward what looked like a pile of rocks. The leaders swerved around it, and poured over a wall just ahead of Heris. Tiger rose to the wall, and she got a quick glimpse of where they were going—the hounds, the streak of red-brown that must be the fox, the huntsman in red—before they were into the next field, this one draped across the shoulder of its hill like a shawl. Tiger flattened beneath her, passing a gray horse and a black, and jumping the briars and stones that separated that field from another.

"Well ridden!" came from behind her, but she had no attention to spare. His earlier exertions hadn't tired the red horse, and he was pulling her arms out. The leaders were nearer now, as Tiger thundered on, lunging against the reins, and his next jump put him even with the first of the field. Heris knew she should be holding him back . . . but excitement sang the last remnants of doubt out of her bones. She had not felt this exultation since—she pushed that away. Now—this horse, this field, this next jump—was all that mattered. All in a clump they raced, angling across the field after the hounds, to jump a sharp ditch. . . . Someone fell there, but Tiger had carried her over safely.

Ahead was another rockpile, to which the fox sped, and into which it vanished. The hounds swarmed over it, clamoring, but they were not diggers and the fox had found a safe lair. Heris got Tiger slowed, then circled him until he walked; he was wet and breathing hard, but clearly not exhausted. Nor was she; she hoped they'd find another fox and do it again. She could have laughed at her earlier mood: boring? This? No. It was all Cecelia had promised.

The huntsmen set to work to call the hounds back and get them in order. Meanwhile the rest of the blue hunt rode up. Some she had met, and some she hadn't, all now willing to speak to her and tell her how well she'd done.

"I didn't really," she said to the third or fourth person who came up to her. "I got lost, then the horse seemed to hear something—"

"But that's wonderful," the woman said. She had one wrist in a brace, and Heris realized it was the same one she'd seen at dinner. "That's what you're supposed to do, and you actually caught up. Most people, once they're lost, spend the whole day wandering around without a clue, or give up and go home."

"Which hill were you on?" one of the men asked. Heris looked around, but had no idea. The jumbled landscape looked as confused to her as a star chart probably would to these people.

"It was near the beginning," she said slowly. "There was a track through woods, then a creek, then a lot of tracks straight up the hill. . . ."

"The Goosegg? You got here in time for the final run from Goosegg?" Now they seemed even more impressed. Heris wondered why. She thought of asking but shrugged instead.

"Tiger did it," she said. It was true, anyway: he had known where to go, and he'd taken her there without any serious bruises. They liked that, she could see; Cecelia had told her that horse people expect riders to praise horses and take the blame themselves for errors.

For a time, nothing much happened; the hounds stood panting, tongues hanging out; some of them flopped down and rolled. Riders stretched, or took a swallow from flasks in the saddlebag. A few dismounted, and disappeared discreetly behind the rockpile. Horses stood hipshot, or walked slowly around as their riders talked or drank. A few stragglers appeared, one by one, on lathered mounts, but perhaps a third of the field had disappeared. Heris wondered if they were going to look for another fox—it was still morning, by the sun.

When the hunt moved again, it was both calmer and more businesslike than the morning's first action. Heris felt the difference as a sense of purpose, as if a ship's crew steadied to some task. First the huntsman took the hounds down the field, toward a patch of woods near a stream—this one, Heris noted from the hillside, widened to a pond at one point. Riders rechecked girths and stirrups; those who had dismounted got up again, and those who had been chatting stopped. Someone Heris didn't yet know put to her eye a most untraditional military-issue eyepiece; Heris wished she herself had had the wit to get one; that lucky soul would be seeing whatever she looked at in plenty of magnification and perfect lighting. She could see fleas on the fox's coat, if a fox came out.

Then the hounds found another trail. At the first peal of the horn, Tiger trembled; Heris steadied him, but didn't hold him back to the rear of the group this time. Steadily, without haste, the field moved toward the call at a brisk trot. This time no one in front of Heris had a refusal at the low wall and ditch . . . nor did she . . . and they trotted on through the woods, lured by the hound song and the horn. Behind her, the bulk of the field stretched out.

Out of the woods: she could see the scarlet coats ahead, the hounds now fifty meters in the lead across a field. Tiger wasn't pulling as badly, but her sentiments were with him, now; she would like to have charged at the next field as fast as he would go. It had become more than the physical delight of riding over fences at speed; it was a hunt, and she wanted to be part of it. Now she could admit it to herself— she had not felt this completely alive, this exultant, since she'd commanded her own ship in combat. And that had been tempered with grief and worry, knowing that she risked her crew, people who trusted her. Here, she risked only herself; she had no responsibility for the others. No wonder people liked hunting . . . but she had no more time to think about it, and that, too, became part of the pleasure.

That run, her first full run, remained a confusion in her mind, when she tried to tell Cecelia about it. Field and wood and field succeeded each other too rapidly; she had to concentrate on riding, on steering Tiger around trees and readying herself for the fences, walls, ditches, banks that came at her every time she thought she'd caught her breath. It felt as if they'd been riding all day—a lifetime—when she heard the hounds' voices change, heard the huntsman yell at them, and realized that they'd caught the fox, out in the middle of a vast open bowl between the hills, with a little stinking marsh off to one side. This time Tiger was willing to stop; she sat there panting and hoping she would not disgrace herself by slithering off his back to lie in a heap on the ground.

Breath and awareness came back to her even as the rest of the field came up. "You *can* ride," said the woman with the wrist brace, again beside her. "Don't tell me it's all that horse; I've ridden him myself."

In the hunting frenzy of Lord Thornbuckle's establishment, Ronnie saw his companions change. Buttons, who had been growing perceptibly stuffier over the last year, became a proper son of the household, and took over the red hunt without complaint. He seemed almost a parody of his father, despite the difference in looks. Sarah simply vanished; when they asked, Buttons looked down his nose and muttered something about wedding preparations. Ronnie wished he had such a handy excuse. The others had to undergo evaluation by the head trainer—a humiliating experience, Ronnie thought. Raffaele rode better than he'd expected; though the trainer complained about her form, she never fell off, and was passed to the blue hunt after only a week's review. He and George and Bubbles, though, were stuck with two daily lessons.

Ronnie hated the lessons; they spent nearly all the time at a walk or trot, with a sharp-voiced junior trainer nagging them about things Ronnie was sure didn't really matter. The trainer wasn't nearly as hard on Bubbles; he figured that was favoritism toward a family member. Afterwards, on the way back to the house to swim or play chipball, Bubbles would critique his lesson again, in detail. When he finally burst loose and told her she had to be as bad, or she wouldn't still be having lessons too, she slugged him in the arm.

"I could ride to hounds any day of the week, you idiot. I'm babysitting you two. It wouldn't be fair to make you stay in lessons by yourselves, Dad said." She glared at both of them. "You ought to be grateful, but I don't suppose you are."

Ronnie wasn't. That only made it worse, and his arm really hurt. He hadn't asked for this. She was supposed to be his girlfriend, and she'd been acting as if he were a nuisance.

The crisp, clear weather of the first few days ended with a cold front, clouds, and drizzle. It made no difference what the weather was—lessons and hunts went out on schedule. Ronnie hated the cold trickle down the back of his neck, the horrid dankness of wet boots, and he didn't want to get used to it. Tradition be damned; why couldn't they wear proper weather-sensing clothing like the Royal Service did on maneuvers?

At dinner each day, the Main House crowd seemed to divide naturally along hunt lines. The greens, his Aunt Cecelia quite prominent among them, had their favorite rooms and corners, and so did the blues. The reds condescended subtly to those not yet assigned, but knew their place compared to the other hunts. Bubbles left them, pointedly showing off, Ronnie thought, her ability to mingle with ease as well as her white shoulders. The only young women among the unassigned were too young for him, and too gawky—a pair of earnest cousins so obviously overawed by their surroundings that they blushed if anyone came near. Bubbles had introduced them as "Nikki and Snookie; they used to come a lot back when I was a kid" and then walked off.

When Captain Serrano showed up with a foxtail one evening ("Not the tail, stupid, the brush!" Bubbles hissed) after her first hunt with the blues, Ronnie was disgusted. He had spent five hours that day riding three different horses in boring circles, trotting over boring little fences in a boring ring. He'd been told he might be allowed on the outside course in a couple of days, if he concentrated. And she—

twenty years older, if a day—had been allowed to skip the red hunt altogether, go into the blues, and had had a good first hunt. It wasn't fair. For the first time since his lessons on the ship, he thought of revenge, but he resisted. It wasn't worth it.

His only solace in these trying days was Raffaele, of all people. George dragged her away from a group of blues one night, and gave a humorous account of their day's lessons. Ronnie felt humiliated—he didn't fall off that often, and George didn't mention any of his own mistakes—but Raffaele's glance at him was sympathetic. After that she came of her own accord every evening, for a few minutes at least. She asked once where Bubbles was, and Ronnie shrugged. She asked no more, but he noticed that she talked to both of them, not just George. And when George was taken up by a group of older men who knew his father, Raffaele kept coming, chatting quietly with Ronnie in a way he found more and more soothing.

By the time he finally got his pass to hunt with the reds (two days before George, a minor triumph which by then he didn't enjoy), he expected no pleasure. The morning dawned murky and cold with vague clots of mist hiding the low places; Ronnie felt stiff before he even got to the stables. Buttons, spruce and cheerful, grinned at him as he stumped into the yard where the hunt gathered.

"Good for you!" he said, too loudly for Ronnie's taste. "I knew you'd beat George out of the lesson pit. It's a good day for scent, anyway." He wore the red coat and insignia of the M.F.H. of the reds, and looked as if he'd been born in it.

"Oh . . . George will be along soon enough," said Ronnie vaguely, looking around. "Where's Bubbles?"

Buttons laughed. "Taking a vacation. She's riding with the blues today. We decided George could survive without a family member for one lesson."

This reminder of his situation did not help. Ronnie grunted, and looked around again. A groom waved to him, and he went over to get on the dark, heavy animal that was his for the day. "Thumper," he was told, "is good, solid, reliable, and not too fast. Bring him home safe." Ronnie noticed nothing was said about *his* safety.

They rode out into the cold murk. Thumper seemed to

think his place was the back of the field; Ronnie kicked vigorously and got him up to the middle. "Eager, aren't you?" asked someone sarcastically. Ronnie ignored him. They all milled around in a wet meadow while the hounds cast about for a scent. No one spoke to Ronnie, and he knew they were all eyeing him. His neck felt hot. When the hounds began to speak, he urged Thumper in that direction, but the others were faster. He trotted along near the back of the group, getting well spattered with mud the other horses kicked up. Thumper slowed, and Ronnie couldn't blame him. It must be worse for the horse, he thought, getting mud in his face and not just on his legs.

After awhile, the horses ahead of him sped off at a canter. Ronnie followed. Now the mud flew higher; he could see it spattering the ground ahead of him. A hedge appeared from the murk, and Thumper lifted to it. On the far side, a ditch gaped; Thumper stretched, and Ronnie clung, slipping a bit at the rough landing. But he regained his seat and urged Thumper on through a flat field after the others. He wished someone had seen—it was a larger jump than he'd ever taken in a lesson.

After some minutes of this he was breathless and sore. It was much harder than the lessons, even the ones on the outside course. He couldn't tell what kind of obstacle was coming. There never seemed time to plan an approach, to get himself ready for the jump. Thumper had a rough, lumbering stride, and while he jumped safely, never hitting anything, he took off with a lurch and landed hard each time. He was doing better than some (he had seen riders sprawled on the wet ground, loose horses, people remounting) but he couldn't get Thumper to catch up with the field.

Far ahead, the horn rang out again. Thumper knew that signal, and churned ahead faster. Now they passed stragglers, riders whose strained faces showed that they found this as tiring as Ronnie did. He wondered why they bothered. . . . Were there that many bossy aunts in the universe? He saw a rail fence coming up, and braced himself. . . . They were over safely, but another loomed up. With a curse, Ronnie grabbed mane, and survived that one too. Thumper plunged on, into the rear of the slowing field. . . . The dogs had caught the fox, though Ronnie couldn't see it. He pulled on the reins, and Thumper slowed to a walk, then stood, sides heaving.

No one seemed to notice them now; the red-coated hunt staff in the center were doing something, and then everyone laughed and cheered.

The crowd spread out, as the riders walked their horses slowly around. "Made it, did you?" asked someone Ronnie had seen in the red hunt group at dinner. "Must have been pretty far back. Too bad you weren't up. You might've had a chance at the brush, being as it's your first day."

"Well, I made it," Ronnie said. He meant to say it blithely, but it came out sounding disgruntled. The man rode off with a shrug. Thumper heaved a great sigh, and shook his head a little. Ronnie noticed others getting flasks out of their saddlebags. He started to reach for his, and remembered that he'd forgotten to bring it. It seemed suddenly darker, and the first cold drops of the day's rain splashed his hot neck.

By nightfall, he had ridden too many hours, fallen off twice (both times some helpful stranger caught Thumper and brought him back) and was wet to the skin with both sweat and rain. His throat felt raw, his nose was running, and his knees and ankles felt as if he'd played the finals of some dismal professional sport involving large angry men pounding each other to mush. He managed to stay on Thumper until he guided him through the gates of the yard, and then slithered off, staggering as he landed.

"Do you need assistance?" asked the groom, with a quick glance at him. She was already pampering Thumper, he noticed.

"I had a fall," he said, through gritted teeth. "But nothing's broken."

"Good day, then," she said, leading the horse away. "If nothing broke."

He stumped up to the house, hoping to make it to a hot bath without meeting anyone, but of course there was George, dapper and witty, with Raffaele on his arm.

"What did you fall into, the pigpen?" asked George. Ronnie was glad to note that Raffaele did not smirk. She was dry and clean and lovely but she did not smirk.

"Just a muddy ditch," Ronnie said. He hoped it sounded casual, the way he'd heard others speak lightly of problems in the field.

"I haven't fallen off in a week," George said. "Even though it really rained hard during my second lesson today."

"It's different out there." Ronnie shot a glance at Raffaele. She wasn't even smiling; she looked as if she knew that his shoulder and hip hurt, and was sorry.

"I'll bet Bubbles and Raffa didn't fall," George went on. "Did you?"

Raffa turned an enchanting shade of pink; Ronnie had never thought how lovely a blush could look against dark hair. "Almost," she said. "My horse stumbled on landing over a big drop, and I was right up on her neck. . . ."

"But you didn't fall," George brayed. "Now if that had been Ronnie, he'd have gone splat, right?"

"Excuse me," said Ronnie, trying for coolness and achieving only the very tone of wounded dignity he least wanted. "I'd like to take a bath before dinner."

"I should hope so," George said. "You certainly need one."

Ronnie fumed his way to his room. Bad enough to have to spend a wet cold day riding a clumsy horse over mud and rock. Bad enough to fall off and be bruised from head to heel. But to meet the impossibly dapper George on the way back—to be twitted about his muddy state—that was too much. People that thought this was fun must be completely insane . . . except maybe Raffa, because after all women were different.

He simply could not spend the entire winter at this ridiculous sport. He had to get away, somehow, and do something where he didn't feel a complete fool.

CHAPTER ELEVEN

"I'm not sure this is a good idea," Ronnie said.

"Do you really want to spend another day bouncing around on that horse?" asked George. Of course he didn't; that was the point. It had been bad enough before George got into the hunt, and worse afterwards. But sneaking off like this? George went on, "You look ridiculous—"

"I do *not*." Ronnie glared at his friend. George had not fallen off in his first time in the field, and it had gone to his head. He seemed to think a successful maiden appearance made up for later runaways, buckings off, and an inability to keep up with the field on a slow day. "I ride better than you—"

"And not nearly so well as your aged aunt or that demon captain of hers. Honestly, I had no idea the Regs went in for horse riding; I thought they spent all their time polishing weapons and doing drills."

Ronnie snorted. "They do love drills, don't they? At least down here Captain Serrano can't interrupt our sleep."

"No. That's the purview of your aunt, waking us up before daylight to gobble a disgusting breakfast and clamber onto great clumsy, smelly animals. . . ."

Ronnie felt a perverse desire to insist that it wasn't that bad, but Bubbles had already started laughing.

"And you did look so funny, lamb, when you were stuck in that hedge, all red-faced and blubbering." She patted him on the shoulder as she clambered past him. He could see by the dome-light that Raffa was trying to smother her giggles and shush Bubbles.

167

"Fine." Ronnie slid the canopy forward; the others were still giggling and stowing their supplies in the lockers. He was beginning to wish he hadn't agreed to this, but how could he back out now? He called up the preflight checklist on the display and started down it. The computer would have done everything, of course, but he was not as careless as his aunt thought.

"Come on, Ron," George said. "Get this thing off the ground."

"Preflight," Ronnie said. George should know that—or was he so involved with Bubbles that he'd lost the rest of his wits? George heaved a dramatic sigh, which Ronnie ignored. He worked his way down the rest of the preflight list in silence; as usual, everything seemed to be in order. Ronnie inserted the cube and checked the readout: it had accepted his course programming, and calculated fuel consumption based on satellite weather information. "Refuel once," he said. "Anyone care if it's Bandon or Calloo?"

A ragged chorus, which sounded louder for Bandon; Ronnie entered that with the touchpad, cast a glance back to make sure all the loose items were stowed, and pressed the green button. The engines caught, and the computer took over the final preflight power checks. At least he knew what the readouts meant, though he could not, from this point on, override the computer's decisions. Not much like a Royal trainer; these civilian models would fly themselves, given the chance. He laid his hands lightly on the yoke anyway, and punched for manual takeoff. He felt the yoke quiver, and the computer displayed his options. If he stayed within these margins, he could have control—and within those, he could control one axis. For a moment it amused him—for a human to be allowed to fly the machine, he had to fly *like* a machine.

It would be practice, and he had always enjoyed flying. He flicked his fingers over the yoke studs—power, directional focus, attitude—and the computer agreed that he knew what he was doing. He didn't know if the others noticed, but he had manual control until he chose to relinquish it, when the craft was at 5,000 meters and on course to Bandon.

"It's dark outside," Raffaele commented as the craft leveled. "There's nothing but—" She peered back. "Nothing but the House lights. . . ."

"We had to leave before daylight," George pointed out. "Or Ronnie's aunt would have stopped us."

Ronnie tried to see past the reflections on the canopy. Nothing but darkness. . . . He flicked off the interior lights, and looked harder. Nothing ahead but darkness, nothing to either side but darkness. He'd never seen anything quite so black in his life.

"It'll be dawn soon," he said. "And the computer doesn't need daylight." As it came out of his mouth he realized that they knew that—he was comforting himself. Darkness hid his blush. Behind him, ostentatious yawns indicated that the others would pretend to sleep. Someone turned on one of the tiny reading lights, a soft glow in the rear of the cabin; Ronnie left the main cabin lights off.

He found that he kept looking to the right, hoping to see some glimmer of dawn. Just when he had given up hope, and convinced himself that he would have to endure flying down a black drainpipe forever, a sullen glow lit the horizon, more feeling than color. Soon he was sure of it; a dim redness blotched with black—clouds, he realized— and then a curious fuzzy quality to the outside. Still dark, still impenetrable, but somehow seeming larger than it had. As the light strengthened, he saw the sea beneath, oddly brighter than the sky. Away toward sunrise it stretched, and the clouds hung over it in dark columns, their tops flushed pink now with the coming light.

Ronnie had never flown along a coast at sunrise; he had not imagined the impossible combinations of green and blue and purple, the piles of pink and gold, which clouds and sea and sunrise make. He looked down on the dark land slowly coming out of the dark haze of night, the shoreline edged with ruffles of colorless surf that would soon be silver and blue. His quick memory for maps told him they were almost a third of the way to Bandon; the computer would soon change their course away from sunrise, across the narrowing belt of land and out across the ocean to that cluster of islands. He hoped it would not change before he could see the sun lift out of the sea.

"There's nothing down there at all," Raffaele said, in a voice that began sleepy and ended worried. "Where are we?"

"This is the Bottleneck," Bubbles said, yawning. "Gorgeous morning, especially since I don't have to climb on a horse.

Don't worry, Raffa, we can't get lost. The computer on this thing has a direct line to the navsats. If we went down, someone would be there in no time."

"But somebody must live somewhere," Raffa grumbled.

"On up the coast a bit there's a settlement of wildlife biologists," Bubbles said. "They're to keep the stuff we don't want out of the Hunt grounds."

The sun came up and glittered on the surf just as he had imagined, and a few minutes later the computer swung them left, away from the coast, and across the forested Bottleneck. Bubbles served breakfast, pastries and fruit and hot coffee she'd filched from the kitchen before they left. Ronnie stretched, enjoying the comfort of baggy trousers, loose shirt, and low, soft-sided boots after the confines of hunting attire. By the time they'd eaten, they'd crossed the other coast and were headed across a blue wrinkled ocean toward the islands. Ronnie had nothing to do, so he turned his seat around and listened to the girls speculate on when Bunny would send someone after them.

"I hope it's not Aunt Cece," Ronnie said.

"He wouldn't send her; she's a guest," Bubbles said airily. "It'll probably be some boring mid-level administrator."

"We could just *tell* your father," Raffa said. "Once we get there, that is."

Bubbles wrinkled her nose. "You don't know how he is. He'll lecture me. I'll get mad. We'll argue. And then I'll have to make up, or he will, and that takes time I could be enjoying with you."

Ronnie put the landing system on automatic when he thought they were in range of Bandon. It would contact the field, and bring them in without his intervention, though he hoped the computer would allow him a "manual" landing. When the com beeped, and the field-authorization light turned red, he assumed that the field wanted a voice-contact; it seemed a reasonable way to keep out unwanted guests. "Any special code words?" he asked Bubbles. She shook her head.

"No—just give the flitter number. It's on the family list."

"Bandon field," Ronnie said. "Permission to land and refuel, number 002413."

"Permission denied." The flat, almost metallic voice

conveyed no interest in negotiation. Ronnie stared at the computer display. He had never heard of a civilian field refusing permission to land and refuel.

He repeated his original call, and added that they were low on fuel.

"Permission denied," the voice said again.

"Override that," Bubbles said from behind him. "Put in 'Landsman 78342' and see what happens. That's Father's personal code."

Ronnie poked at the screen, and hit the orange override button, but the voice repeated the same statement with the same mechanical lack of expression.

"Can we make Calloo from here?" asked George.

"Just barely," Ronnie said, with a glance at the fuel readout. "And I don't see why we should. This is Bunny's flitter, and Bubbles just gave us the internal authorization number. If it won't accept it, something's wrong."

"We don't want to land if something's wrong," George said. Then, "What could be wrong? What's on this island, anyway?" He turned to Bubbles.

She frowned thoughtfully. "Well . . . the landing field, maintenance station, and the family's lodge—no resident staff, though—"

"There's a lodge here, too?" Ronnie asked. "Then why did you tell me to program for Whitewings?"

"We wanted to be out of everyone's reach. This is too close—it's the first place they'd look."

Ronnie looked out the canopy. Heavily wooded islands lay scattered in odd shapes across the sea. Bandon, the computer readout told him, was a half hour ahead. He could see its distinctive shape beyond the nearest island. Calloo, the northernmost of the chain, lay far to their right. "We ought to find out what's wrong," he said. "We'll go on to Bandon and take a look." They could still make Calloo, he thought, if they had to, and if they found out something important, Bunny might forgive their disappearance. With the vague notion that he was being careful, Ronnie let the flitter drop lower and skimmed just above the forest, following the contours with care, then made a low approach across the sea between that island and Bandon, edging past a smaller island not quite in his path between them. He did not look outside, concentrating instead on his instruments.

If he dipped too low, the flitter's automatic safety overrides would lower the plenum and convert it to an airboat. That could be most embarrassing.

George saw the danger first. "Look out!" he yelled. Ronnie looked back at him, wondering what kind of game they were playing back there; Raffa yelped, peering out the starboard side. Then he saw it, just before it struck, an odd shape trailing a line of orange smoke. The flitter jerked itself out of his control, bouncing up and sideways, and a good half of the readouts went red; something snarled angrily in its power section, a sound that spiralled up into a painful whine and then stopped abruptly.

Ronnie grabbed the controls back, felt the ominous mushiness, and went into the emergency landing sequence he had never expected to use once past his piloting exam. Would they make it to land? The airspeed readout, like all in that bank, was dead; the white beach and green trees ahead moved nearer too slowly. Behind him, no one spoke. George clambered forward, disturbing the flitter's precarious balance, and dropped into the other forward seat.

"I think it was a signal rocket," he said calmly, as if continuing a casual conversation. "All that red smoke . . ."

"She's nose-heavy," Ronnie grunted. "And the hydraulics are shot. Use that big foot on the floor, not your mouth."

Whatever George did made no difference; the flitter sank toward the waves. "Brace up, you girls," George said to the back seats; Raffa was the one who said, "Brace up yourself, Gee—we're trying to get the raft out."

Ronnie tried once more to pull the nose up, but the flitter shivered all over like a nervous dog. *Flitters don't stall,* he remembered being told, *but they crash all the same.* It occurred to him that even if they made it to land, he might simply crash head-on into the lush forest. Could he maneuver at all? *Altitude, then maneuver,* he remembered. But he had no altitude. He tried; the flitter slewed sideways, but answered sluggishly. He could parallel the coastline and those trees. . . .

"George—there—those people—" Ronnie did not look; he had to keep the flitter in the air as long as he could. George leaned to see, then grunted, as if it were a marvel.

"Damn near naked," he said. "But armed. . . . I think that's the launcher he hit us with."

Ronnie put all his strength into willing the flitter not to crash into a lump of trees nearer shore than the rest.

They were down, and not dead—at the moment, that was all he cared about. His hands ached; his ears rang; his whole body hurt. But they were alive, and out of the flitter—which now looked far too small to have held so many people and so much fear. Bubbles and Raffa, with far more gumption than he would have expected, had unloaded everything useful from the flitter. The survival raft and all its provisions, the scuffed but whole duffles.

"Never pays to buy cheap luggage," George said, in the tone that had won him the nickname "Odious," as he brushed the sand off his and hoisted it to his shoulder. "Come on, now, Ronnie—give the girls a hand, can't you?"

Ronnie glared at him. He looked, the odious George, as he always did—fresh, creased, polished to a high gloss. Not a hair of his dark head ruffled, not a smudge. He looked like that on horseback, and even when he fell off he never looked rumpled or dirty. He looked like that on mornings after, and on hot afternoons on parade. It was unfair, and his brother officers had done all sorts of things to ruin that polish—but nothing worked. "Dip the odious George in shit," some senior cadet had said their first year, "and not only wouldn't it stink, it'd take a shine."

Now, on the sandy beach after a flitter wreck, Ronnie thought he knew what *he* looked like. He said nothing, but picked up two of the remaining duffles, staggered a bit, then dropped them.

"What now?" asked George.

"The beacon," Ronnie said, clambering onto the flitter. He wished he could remember how he'd gotten out of it. "We need to signal for a pickup, unless you plan to swim back to the mainland."

"You gave it to me," Bubbles said. She looked worried. "You don't remember?"

He didn't remember. He crouched on the flitter's canopy, suddenly aware that he was not functioning in some important way. He looked around, blinking. The sea, the sand, the trees: he remembered that. They'd crashed the flitter, and whoever owned it would be furious. Who had crashed the flitter? They weren't designed to crash easily and he and George were both good pilots. He looked at the flitter itself, at the large hole in the engine section, the scorchmarks black on the outer skin. "What happened?" he said, knowing it was a stupid question, though it was all that occurred to him.

"Damnation!" George's voice, closer. "He's concussed; he doesn't know what's happened or—c'mon, ladies, we've got to get him away from here."

He heard Raffa ask why, and Bubbles remind George that injured people shouldn't be moved until medical personnel arrived, but someone stronger than Raffa or Bubbles pulled him off the flitter and slung him over a muscular shoulder. That completed his collapse; he spewed the breakfast he'd eaten down George's legs and knew nothing more for a time he could not measure.

Ronnie awoke lying on his back with the sun prying his eyelids apart and someone beating his head with a collection of spoons. At least that's what it felt like. He had no desire to move, though he would have appreciated quiet, darkness, and a cool wet cloth on his forehead. A sympathetic murmur would have been nice too. Instead the only voices he recognized sounded angry and frightened.

"If my father knew—" That had to be Bubbles, pulling off her best daughter-of-greatness act.

"And what makes you think he doesn't?" asked a man's voice, in a tone that meant Bubbles was making no impression at all. Or the wrong one.

An instant's pause, then, "What do you mean, he knows?"

Laughter with no humor in it, the kind of thing Ronnie had heard only a few times in his life; it frightened him then, and now.

"I don't suppose he knows his daughter's involved, no." The man's voice had some familiar tone that Ronnie felt he should know but could not quite recognize. "But something like this, as big as it is, on his favorite resort world: how could he not know?"

"Something like *what*?" That was Raffaele, Ronnie thought. A girl who believed that the facts would explain themselves.

Another man's voice, this one quite different. "Oh, I 'spect you know, little lady." Every hair on Ronnie's body rose at that "little lady." He wanted to leap up and knock that voice into the sea, but he could not move. "It's a hunter's paradise, isn't it? And your dad, or maybe it's her dad, is a famous sportsman, isn't he? And the whole point of sport is you give the prey a chance, eh? Isn't it? That makes it a challenge, see?"

The reiterated questions struck Ronnie as false, theatrical, like something from a storycube. Certain dialects did that, he thought.

"Manhunting," the first voice said. "As you very well know, since you came here for that purpose." Ronnie tried to process that: manhunting? Manhunts were for escaped criminals, or lost children.

"But it can go two ways, see?" the second voice interrupted. "Hunting predators it can always go two ways, and men are the most dangerous. There was a story once—"

"Everyone knows the story, Sid; be quiet." The command in that first voice finally made the connection for Ronnie. It sounded like Captain Serrano. It sounded like Captain Serrano the time she had ordered him off her bridge, or the time he had overheard her talking to Aunt Cece about battle. He struggled to open his eyes and found himself blinking up at a dark unsmiling face. "Well," the man said. "And what have we here, young man? Who are you?"

"Ronald Vertigern Boniface Lucien Carruthers," he heard himself say, as if in one of the practice sessions in the squad. "Royal Aero-Space Stellar Service." He looked around, now that he could see, and there was the odious George, looking remarkably tidy with a gag stuffed in his mouth and an angry expression on the rest of his face. Bubbles looked almost as angry; he wondered if she was going to come out of her usual wild-blonde disguise for the occasion. And Raffa—whom he hoped would someday be *his* Raffaele— had no expression at all. He had never seen her like that, and he hoped he never would again.

The dark face above his did not smile. "Royal ASS, eh? And you probably think that means something here."

Ronnie had heard that version of his service's initials before; he ignored it now, as beneath the notice of a wounded officer. "And you?" he asked, as he wondered which of his limbs still worked. "I have not the honor—"

A snort of contempt, and a growl from others he had not yet noticed. "That's the truth, little boy soldier—you have not the honor indeed. You don't know what honor *is*."

From a little distance, he heard another mirthless chuckle. "Little peep plonks down in a flitter and bumps his poor little head, pukes out his guts, and thinks he has a right to say the H-word. . . ."

"Shut up, Kev. We don't have time for your nonsense any more than *his*." A jerk of the head indicated George. The dark eyes contemplated Ronnie. "But you—you're going to give us the truth, Mister Ronald Vertigern Boniface Lucien Carruthers of the Royal Assholes. You didn't learn to fly with that bunch of old ladies, boy: who are you really from?" Hard hands grabbed his ears and shook his head. He had thought it hurt before; now he knew it had merely been uncomfortable. He felt his eyes water, and hated the man for that. His stomach roiled, and he choked back another wave of nausea.

"I told you," Bubbles said, before he could get any words out. "We're from the Main Lodge; we wanted to get away from the fox hunting—"

"And try other game?" suggested another voice he could not see.

"And just play around," Ronnie said. At the moment he didn't care if he did die; his head might as well have a real axe in it as whatever was causing what he felt. He knew his voice sounded weak and querulous; he *felt* weak and querulous. "My aunt Cece—you wouldn't know her—and that demon captain of hers wanted me to spend all day every day on a horse chasing some miserable little furry thing over fields of cold mud and fences designed to make horses fall down and dump their riders." He took a breath; no one interrupted. "And we got tired of it," he said, closing his eyes against the bright glare of the forest canopy. "We wanted to rest. We wanted to have fun. I asked Bubbles if there wasn't some place on this miserable dirtball that wasn't cold and muddy and full of horses, and she said let's go to the islands."

"Oblo?" The first voice seemed to be addressing someone else; Ronnie gave himself up to contemplation of his headache and the mystery of his stubbornly unhelpful arms and legs. He finally thought he felt something weighing him down, or tying him down, or something of that sort. External, not internal—he was sure he was wiggling his toes. For some reason, the discovery that he probably didn't have a broken neck did not make him feel better.

"No weapons—not with them or on the flitter, 'cept a cateye. That's standard survival gear on flitters, most worlds." Oblo, if that was the speaker, had the same businesslike tone as the first voice. "Food and minor medical supplies in stuff they'd pulled out to take with them. All the IDs check out, as far as we can know without accessing a link. Flitter ID was still in the active comp, no sweat getting it out; it's Lord Thornbuckle's all right."

"And the beacon?" asked the first voice.

"Back aboard, sir, same's you said. Tough to make it look like it hadn't ever been out, though. On the other hand, maybe they'll accept all that cracked casing as why it doesn't work. Did my best."

"I'm sure you did, Oblo."

Ronnie opened his eyes again, to find the dark face he remembered looking across him to someone else. "Why'd you put the beacon *back*?" he asked. "That's stupid—we need rescue here."

"You may need rescue," the dark man said, "but we don't need hunters tracking us by that thing."

"You . . . shot us." He was sure of it, though he saw no weapon that could have served.

"Yep. Thought you were the hunters, and we had a chance to drop you in the water. Not a bad job of work, the way you got that flitter to land." The dark man hawked and spat juicily. "Wasted all the work on you, looks like now, and we've still got them to deal with. And'f they know about you, we've got even more trouble, if that's possible."

"Oh." Ronnie could not think of anything to say, and looked at George—but George, gagged, could not argue for him.

"I'm sure my father doesn't know," Bubbles said, into the brief silence. Her blonde hair looked straggly, coming out of whatever she'd done to keep it in tousled curls. She raked it back with both hands, hooking it behind her ears, and started in again. "This is our special place, the kids' place— even if he did something so horrible, he wouldn't do it here."

"Kids' place?"

"We camped here, every summer until I was fifteen or so. Some of the younger cousins still do." Ronnie let her voice lull him back to sleep; he didn't like being awake any more.

*　　*　　*

When he awoke again, the first thing he heard was George's voice. *Poor idiots* he thought lazily. *You should have left him gagged.* Then he realized what he'd thought, and woke up the rest of the way, ashamed of himself. He was no longer tied (if he had been tied; he found his memory wobbly on that and other points) and when he tried to sit up, someone's arm came behind him, lifting his shoulders. Even under the forest canopy, he could tell that some hours had passed; the bits of sun poking through came at a different angle. Someone had cleaned his face; he couldn't smell the vomit anymore, and was grateful. Without a word, a brown hand came from behind him and offered a flask of water. He took it and drank.

They were all there: Bubbles, Raffa, and George, and the faces he remembered from that nightmarish time when he'd been flat on his back. Now, right side up, he recognized the hostile expressions as exhaustion, fear, uncertainty. He saw only eight or nine, but noises in the thick undergrowth suggested at least as many more.

"The point is, Petris," George was saying, "that Ronnie and I are both commissioned officers of the Royal . . ." His voice trailed away as the snickers began, and he turned red.

"Son," the dark man said, "the point really is that we know how to fight a war and you don't. You'd get us killed; you damn near got yourself and your girls killed. I don't care how many glittery stripes and pretty decorations you've got on your dress uniform, nor how bright your boots shine; you don't know one useful thing about staying alive in this mess, and I do."

George looked around for support, and caught Ronnie's eye. "Good—you're awake now. Tell him—we're officers; we should be in charge."

In charge? In charge of what? The dark man—Petris?—had said something about a manhunt, but he didn't want to hunt anyone. He wanted to wait until he could think straight, and then fly back to the mainland. His mind gave a little jerk, like a toy train jumping to another track. *They* were being hunted, that was it, the men on the island. They were trying to fight back, to hunt the hunters. And George thought he and Ronnie should organize that? Ridiculous. Ronnie shrugged. "He's right, George. We're worse than the girls—they at least know what they don't know. We keep thinking we do know." He hardly knew what he was saying, over a dull pounding in his head, but that made the best sense he could. "You're—Petris, sir? I agree with you."

The dark man gave Ronnie the first friendly look he'd had. "Maybe that knock on the head put your brain right side up after all. Oblo, give this lad a ration bar." The same dark hand that had passed him the water flask held out a greasy, gritty bar that Ronnie recognized as part of the flitter's emergency supplies. He took it and nibbled the end. His body craved the salt/sweet flavor.

"Ronnie, you can't let that—that *person* ignore your seniority."

Ronnie grinned, and his head hardly hurt at all. "I'm not letting *him* ignore my seniority; *I'm* ignoring it. Remember what old Top Jenkins said about tooty young cadets?"

"We aren't cadets any more." George was still bristling; for the first time, Ronnie saw his father in him, the courtroom bully. "We're *officers*."

"We're prisoners, if you want to be precise," Ronnie said. "Come on, George . . . look at it this way. It's an adventure." Petris scowled, but George finally grinned. Ronnie tried to explain to Petris. "It's a saying we have. . . . We started in boarding school together . . . and George would think these things up, or Buttons would, or Dill, and the rest of us would say how crazy it was, and how much trouble we'd get in, and whoever began it would say, 'It's an adventure.'"

George chuckled. "I remember who started it—Arthur whatsisname, remember? Had that streak of pale blue hair he claimed he'd inherited? Got us into some frightful row, and when we were called up said, 'look at it this way, boys—it's an adventure.' And we all went in sniggering like fools and got twice as much punishment as usual."

"I can see why," Petris said, with emphasis that stopped the chuckle in Ronnie's throat. "This is not an adventure. This is a war. The difference is that between whatever punishment you got, and death. Go in sniggering, as you put it, here—play the fool here—and you will be dead. Not charmingly, tidily, prettily dead, either." His gaze encompassed George, who still looked entirely too dapper for the circumstances.

"I know that," George said irritably.

"Then act like it." Petris turned back to Ronnie. "And you, young man, if you're finally getting sense, get enough to live through this and grow up." He glanced sideways at the girls, but said nothing to them directly. Did he think women were nonentities? He must not have known Captain Heris.

He didn't realize he'd said the name aloud until the other man reacted.

"Captain who?" Petris looked dangerous again. Ronnie choked down the rest of the ration bar.

"Serrano. Heris Serrano. She's ex-Regular Space Service, like you."

"So that's where she ended up." A feral gleam lightened his dark eye. Ronnie was startled; it was the first personal emotion he'd seen Petris exhibit. Petris grinned; it was not a nice grin. "She did have a comedown, after all."

"A comedown?"

"To play captain of a rich lady's yacht. Serves her right."

"What for?" asked George. Ronnie was glad; he too wanted to know, but he had already been chewed out for asking too many questions.

Petris glared at him. "None o' your—"

"Tell them," Oblo said. "Why not? You don't want to protect her."

Petris shook his head. "No. That's right enough. But do you think these Royal-ass punks can understand it?"

"Might learn something," Oblo said. Ronnie felt a tension between the two men, not quite conflict, and wondered what it could be.

"All right." Petris wiped his mouth with his hand, and settled back, looking past them. "It started with the Cavinatto campaign, which is too new to have been in your studies, so don't argue with me about it. Scuttlebutt says it was Admiral Lepescu who thought up the lousy plan; from what I know of him I wouldn't doubt it. If our captain had followed his orders, most of us would've died, and it wouldn't have accomplished a damn thing. It was a stupid plan, and a stupid order."

"But—" George began; Petris glared him down.

"Do you want the gag again? Then be quiet. I know what you think—officers that refuse orders are traitors and should be shot—right?"

George nodded and shrugged at the same time, trying not

to offend. Ronnie almost laughed aloud—but not when he saw Petris's face.

"That's what the rules say," Petris went on. "No matter how stupid, how bloody, or how unnecessary, officers obey their seniors and enlisted obey officers. Mostly they do, and mostly it works, because when you're not in combat, a stupid order won't kill you. Usually. But then there's combat. You expect to die someday—it's not a safe profession, after all—" Behind Petris, the others chuckled, but he ignored them. "But what you hope for is that your death will mean something—you'll be expended, as the saying is, in some action that accomplishes something more than just turning you into a bloody mess." He was silent after that so long that George stirred and opened his mouth; Ronnie waved at him, hoping he would keep quiet. Finally Petris looked at both of them and started speaking again.

"It's not that anyone doubted Serrano's courage, you know. She'd been in action before; she had a couple of decorations you don't get for just sitting by a console and pushing the right buttons. No—what she did, refusing a stupid order that would kill a lot of people without accomplishing any objective, that was damn brave, and we all knew it. She was risking her career, maybe her life. When it was over, and she faced the inquiry on it, she didn't try to spread the blame—she took it just the way you'd expect—would have expected—from knowing her before. I'd been with her on three different ships; I knew—I thought I knew—what she was. She was facing a court-martial, dishonorable discharge, maybe prison time or execution, if she couldn't prove that Admiral Lepescu's order was not only stupid but illegal. I was scared for her; I knew she had friends in high places, but not that high, and it's damned hard to prove an admiral is giving bad orders just because he likes to see bloodshed."

He paused again, and drank two long swallows from his flask. "That was the Serrano I thought I knew—the woman who would risk that." His voice slowed, pronouncing every word as if it hurt his mouth. "Not the woman who would take the chance to resign her commission before the court and lay the blame on her crew. Leave *us* to face court-martial, and conviction, and *this*—this sentence." His wave included the place, the people, the situation. "She didn't come to our trial; she didn't offer any testimony, any written

support, nothing. She dumped us, the very crew she'd supposedly risked her career to save. It didn't make sense, unless
her decision to avoid that engagement really was cowardice,
or she saw it as a way to leave the Service. . . ."

Ronnie said nothing. He remembered his first sight of
Captain Serrano, the rigidity with which she had held herself, like someone in great pain who will not admit it. He
remembered the reaming out she'd given him, that time on
the bridge, and what he'd heard her say to his aunt . . .
scathing, both times, and he'd sworn to get his vengeance
someday. She had held him captive, forced his attention,
"tamed" him, as she'd put it. He had had to watch her take
to riding, and hunting, as if she were born to it, while he
loathed every hour on horseback; he had had to hear his
aunt's praise of her captain's ability, and her scorn of him.
That, too, he had sworn to avenge. Now was his chance, and
it required nothing of him but silence.

He met George's eyes. . . . He had told George, he remembered, what Serrano had said about her past. He had been
angry, and he had eavesdropped without shame, and shared
the gossip without shame. Now he felt the shame; he could
feel his ears burning.

"It wasn't that," he heard himself saying. Petris looked
at him, brows raised. "She didn't know," he said.

"How do you know?" asked Oblo, before Petris could.

"I—I heard her talking to my aunt," Ronnie said. He dared
not look at Raffa; she would be ashamed of him. "They told
her—I suppose that admiral you mentioned—that if she stood
trial, the crew would be tried with her, but if she resigned,
no action would be taken against her subordinates."

Petris snorted. "Likely! Of course she'd make up a good story
for later; she wouldn't want to admit she'd sold us—"

"I'm not sure," Oblo said. "It could be. Think, Petris:
which is more like *our* Serrano?"

"She's not *my* Serrano!" Petris said furiously. For a
moment, Ronnie thought he might attack Oblo. "Dammit,
man—she could have—"

"Could have been tricked, same as us." Oblo, Ronnie
realized, had never wanted to believe Serrano guilty of treach-
ery. He turned to Ronnie. "Of course, lad, she's your aunt's
captain—you'd like her and defend her, I daresay. . . ."

"Like her!" That was George, unable to keep quiet any

longer. "That—that puffed-up, arrogant, autocratic, bossy—! No one could like her. Do you know what she did to Ronnie? To Ronnie—on his own aunt's ship? Slapped him in the *face*! Ordered him off the bridge, as if he were any stupid civilian! And me—she told me I was nothing but a popinjay, a pretty face with not the sense to find my left foot—"

"George," said Ronnie, trying not to laugh. "George, never mind—"

"No, Ronnie." George looked as regal as he could, which was almost funnier. "I've had enough of this. Captain Serrano may have been your aunt's choice, but she was not mine. All those ridiculous emergency drills—I've never seen such a thing on a proper yacht. All that fussing about centers of mass, and alternative navigation computer checks, and whatnot. I'm not a bit surprised that woman got herself in trouble somewhere; she's obsessed with rules and regulations. That sort always go bonkers sometime. She drove you—the least mischievous of our set—to eavesdrop on her conversations with your aunt—"

"Enough," said Petris, and George stopped abruptly.

"Let's hear, and briefly, from you, Ronnie. What precisely did you hear, and under what circumstances?"

Ronnie gathered his wits again. "Well . . . she had chewed me out, and waked us up three lateshifts running for drills. I wanted to get back at her—" Put that way, it sounded pretty childish; he realized now it had been. "So I patched into the audio in my aunt's study." He didn't think he needed to tell Petris about the stink bomb, or its consequences. "She and my aunt talked a lot—mostly about books or music or art, sometimes about the ship or riding. But my aunt wanted to know about her time in the Service, why she resigned. I could tell the captain didn't want to answer, but my aunt can be . . . persuasive. So that's what she said, what I told you before. She was offered a chance to resign her commission rather than face a court-martial, and was promised that if she resigned no action would be taken against any of her crew. Otherwise, she was told, her crew would also be charged, and it was more than likely they'd all be condemned. She . . . cried, Petris. I don't think she cries often."

The man's face was closed, tight as a fist; Ronnie wondered what he was thinking. Oblo spoke first.

"That's *our* Serrano, Petris. She didn't know. She did it for us—they probably wouldn't let her come back and explain—"

"Yes," Ronnie put in. "She said that—she had to resign, right then, in that office, and not return to the ship. She said that was the worst of it, that someone might think she'd abandoned her crew, but at least they'd be safe."

"That . . . miserable excuse for an admiral . . ." Petris breathed. Ronnie sensed anger too deep for any common expletives, even in one so accomplished. "He *might* have done that. He might think it was funny."

"Nah," said Sid. Ronnie recognized the nasty voice that had raised the hairs on his arms earlier. "I don't believe that. It's the captain, like you told me at first. Why'd she resign if she wasn't up to something, eh? Stands to reason she has friends to cover for her."

"You weren't in her crew," Oblo said. "You got no right to judge." He looked at Ronnie. "You are telling the truth." It was not so much a statement, as a threat.

Ronnie swallowed before he could answer. "I overheard what I told you—and I told George. I hated her; I hoped to find some way to get back at her. But . . ." His voice trailed away.

"But you couldn't quite let us believe the lie, eh?" said Petris. He smiled, the first genuine friendly smile Ronnie had seen on his face. "Well, son, for a Royal ASS peep, you've got surprising ethics." He sighed, and stretched. "And what would you want to bet," he asked the others, "that Admiral Lepescu planned to let her know later what he'd done? When it was too late; when it would drive her to something he could use. . . ."

"Does he know she's here?" Ronnie asked, surprising himself. "Could he have known who hired her, where she was going?"

"Lepescu? He could know which fork she ate with, if he wanted to."

CHAPTER TWELVE

Heris came out of the shower toweling her hair, to find Cecelia sitting upright in the desk chair, already dressed for the day's hunt.

"I didn't know I was late," Heris said. Her own clothes lay spread on the bed; she had come from the shower bare, as usual, and shrugged when she realized it was too late for modesty. She hoped anger would not make her blush; Cecelia had no right to invade her room.

"You're not," Cecelia said. "I can't find Ronnie. Or George. Or their girlfriends." Then her voice sharpened. "That's a— a scar—"

Heris looked down at the old pale line of it, and shrugged again. "It's old," she said. And then, realizing why Cecelia was so shocked, explained. "No regen tanks aboard light cruisers. If you get cut or burned, you scar." She pulled on her socks, then her riding pants, and grinned at Cecelia. "We consider them decorative."

"Barbaric," said Cecelia.

"True," Heris said. "But necessary. Would you have quit competitive riding if you'd had to live with the scars of your falls?"

"Well . . . of course not. Lots of people did, in the old days. But it's not necessary now, and—"

"Neither is fox hunting," Heris said, buttoning her shirt and tucking in the long tails. "Very few things are really necessary, when you come down to it. You—me—the horses—all the rituals. If you just wanted to exterminate these

185

pseudofoxes, you'd spread a gene-tailored virus and that'd be it. If you just wanted to ride horses across fences, you could design a much safer way to do it—and not involve canids."

"Hounds."

"Whatever." Heris leaned over and pulled on her boots; they had broken in enough to make this easier and she no longer felt her legs were being reshaped as the boots came up. She peered into the mirror and tied the cravat correctly, slicked down her hair, and reached for her jacket. "Ready? I'm starved."

"You didn't hear me," Cecelia said, not moving. "I can't find Ronnie and the others."

"I heard you, but I don't understand your concern. Perhaps they started early—no, I admit that's not likely. Perhaps they're already at breakfast, or not yet up from an orgy in someone else's room—"

"No. I checked."

Heris opened her mouth to say that in a large, complicated building with dozens of bedrooms, near other buildings with dozens of bedrooms, four young people who wanted to sleep in could surely find a place beyond an aunt's sight. Then she saw the tension along Cecelia's jaw. "You're worried, aren't you?"

"Yes. They didn't hunt yesterday; they were supposed to be out with the third pack, and Susannah mentioned she hadn't seen them. The day before, you remember, Ronnie missed a lesson."

"But—"

"I found Buttons, and asked him. He turned red and said Ronnie, George, and the girls had gone picnicking day before yesterday. He didn't know about yesterday, or said he didn't. And there's more." When Cecelia didn't go on, Heris sat on the bench at the foot of her bed. She knew that kind of tension; it would do no good to pressure her. "There's a flitter missing," Cecelia said finally. "I had to . . . to bribe Bunny's staff, to find that out. Apparently Bubbles is something of a tease; it's not the first time she's taken out her father's personal flitter, and the staff doesn't like her to get into trouble. They cover for her, with the spare. So Bunny doesn't know a thing. . . ."

"And they've been gone a day . . . two days? Maybe three?"

"Yes. According to the log—they do keep one, just to be sure Bubbles doesn't get hurt—they left well before dawn day before yesterday. Filed a flight plan for some island lodge called Whitewings. I've never been there, but I've got the map." She handed Heris the data cube; Heris fitted it into the room's display. "The problem is, they aren't at Whitewings, either. It's a casual lodge—no resident staff, although it's fully equipped. There's a satellite beacon on the flitter, of course, and there's been a steady signal here—" Cecelia pointed to an island much nearer than Whitewings. "No distress call, and it's at another lodge. Michaels, who's the flitter-chief, thinks Bubbles just changed her mind and decided to hide out on another island in case I followed the trail this far."

"She'd know about the beacon, though—"

"She'd think I wouldn't."

"Ah." Heris stared at the display. "What's on this other island?"

"Bandon? It's another lodge, more a family place, although it's got a large landing field. Michaels says the family goes there every spring, at least once. When the children were younger, they used to camp on one of the smaller islands, while the adults stayed on Bandon. He says it's lovely: forested islands, clear water, reefs. Imported cetaceans, some of the small ones that Michaels said play with humans. Bubbles has always liked it better than anyplace on the planet, he says. Whitewings is colder, usually stormier."

"That makes sense. So you think they're all sunning themselves, swimming lazily—?"

"No. I can't say why. But I think they're in trouble. And I can't imagine what. This is a safe world; there's nothing on the islands to hurt them—I asked Michaels. Their com links are unbreakable; if they needed help, they'd ask for it. They can't be in any real trouble—not all four of them. But—"

"Tell Bunny," Heris said. When Cecelia's expression changed, she realized she'd used his nickname for the first time. He had always been Lord Thornbuckle to her. She started to apologize, but Cecelia was already talking.

"I don't want to do that. Not yet. He's upset right now with that anti-blood-sports person who got herself invited under an alias. He's not at his best."

"But if his daughter—no, never mind. What do you want me to do?"

"I'm not sure. I don't suppose there's any way the *Sweet Delight* could tell—?"

Heris smacked her forehead with the flat of her hand. Stupid! She'd nearly turned into a dirtsider, all the time she'd spent traveling at the speed of horseflesh. "Of course," she said. Then—"But can I get a closed channel, a secure channel, from the house?"

"Yes, with my authorization. We'd best do it from my room."

Cecelia's room, Heris noted, had even more windows on the morning side of the house—no wonder she woke so early—and was half again as large as her own. The desk-comp looked the same, however, and Cecelia soon had what she considered a secure line to the station. She handed the headset to Heris.

"Captain Serrano; a secure line to the officer on deck, *Sweet Delight*."

"At once, Captain." She thought that was probably the Stationmaster himself, but no visual came up. When the screen lit, it was to show the familiar bridge, warped a bit by the wide-angle lens, and Nav First Sirkin.

"Captain Serrano," the younger woman said. She looked only slightly surprised.

"I'd like a scan report from . . . oh . . . say . . . fifty-five hours back. Did you log a flitter flight from the Main Lodge, this location, to an island group to the west?"

A broad grin answered her. "Yes, ma'am. That was my shift, and I remember it. Let me bring up the log and scan." The log display came online, a narrow stripe along the side of the screen, with time and date displayed in both Standard and Planetary Local. The log entry terse and correct, noted the size of craft, the course, and the recognition code of the flitter beacon. The scan proper, a maze of graphics and numbers, matched the log except in one particular.

"They signalled," Heris said, her finger on the scan. "They called a fixed station—probably the landing field at Bandon. And something responded—"

"Michaels says it's an automatic loop. There's no one at the field unless family's expected."

"Hmmm. And what's this?" Heris pointed to a squiggle

she knew Cecelia could not interpret, and spoke to her Nav First. "Did you log the other traffic?"

"Yes—although since it didn't have a satellite locater signal, I assumed they were just maintenance flights or something."

"Or *something*," said Heris. She felt an unreasoning surge of glee and grinned at Cecelia. "Good instincts: something is definitely going on out there."

"Smugglers, I suppose," Cecelia said with refined distaste. "I never saw a world without some of it. Probably off-duty crews."

"No," the Nav First interrupted. "At least some of them are Space Service. Regular, Captain, like yourself." Heris winced at the pronoun; centuries after overzealous English teachers had tried to stomp out misuse of *me*, the reflexive overcorrection lingered as a class distinction. But that was unimportant now.

"How do you know?" she asked. The younger woman flushed.

"Well, I was sort of . . . listening in to see how good that new scan technology was—"

"And you picked up Fleet traffic?" If she had, Heris would report it, small thanks though she'd get for it.

"No, ma'am. It was a private shuttle from a charter yacht docked at Station Three. Someone groundside asked if Admiral Lepescu was aboard, and the shuttle said yes."

Heris felt as if someone had transplanted icewater into her arteries. She started to ask more, but Cecelia interrupted, with a hand on her arm.

"I want to go after them."

"Why?" Heris's mind had clamped onto the admiral's name; she could not think why Cecelia would want to follow him.

"To bring them back. Before Bunny finds out."

The youngsters. Ronnie and all. Not Lepescu. Heris struggled to keep her mind on the original problem. They had gone off illicitly, and had not signalled, and their craft's locator beacon still functioned. And Cecelia wanted to bring them back. That ought to be simple enough. She forced herself to look closely at all the details Sirkin had displayed. One caught her eye at once.

"Sirkin—that flitter locator beacon—it's not on Bandon."

"No, Captain; there's a whole group of islands, and it's on the one just north of Bandon."

Heris turned to Cecelia. "But the family lodge is on Bandon proper, surely—with the landing field?"

"I think so." Cecelia's face contracted in a thoughtful frown. "I don't really know; I've never been there. Michaels implied it was on the same island."

"Of course they may have decided to camp on the beach. . . ." Heris looked over the rest of the data. "You said Bubbles had camped on one of the other islands. Odd— the flight path of that flitter doesn't look right. You'd think they'd have gone by Bandon to pick up supplies, at least. Did they take off with full camping equipment? Or would Michaels know?"

"I could ask," Cecelia said. "You think they meant to land at Bandon and didn't? They crashed?"

"Could be." Heris felt frustration boiling through her mind. Once she would have had the information she needed; once she would have had trusted subordinates to find out anything she lacked. People she could trust . . . she would not let herself remember more than the trust. At least they were safe, she told herself fiercely. At least they still had each other. She had bought them that much.

And she might have the chance to see Lepescu again. Without Fleet interference. Without witnesses.

"Lepescu," she murmured, hardly aware of saying anything. "You bastard—what are you doing here?"

"I remember," Cecelia said. "He was the admiral who got you in trouble." Heris looked up, startled out of her train of memories.

"He was the admiral who nearly got us all *killed,*" Heris said. "The trouble was negligible, really. . . ." Now she could say that. "The question is, why is he here? To cause me more grief? It would have been easy for him to find out who hired me, and where we were going, but I can't see why—or what he can do worse than he's done. Aside from that—"

"Bunny didn't invite him," Cecelia said smugly. She had the authorization codes for Bunny's personal guestlist database, and had run them on the deskcomp. "Never has, according to this. Let's see . . . no, nor any of Bunny's relatives. He's another crasher."

"Here? No, because Sirkin said that transmission went to a shuttle landing at Bandon."

"Where nobody's supposed to be," Cecelia reminded her. "Where I didn't know there was a landing zone equipped for shuttles."

"Whose ship did he come on?" Heris asked. Cecelia couldn't know, she realized, and asked Sirkin, who had stayed online.

"All I know is it's a charter yacht out of Dismis, the *Prairie Rose.* I'd have to have authorization to find out more. . . ."

"We'll do that," Heris said. "But post the orders to monitor that flitter beacon, and any and all traffic on that island or the ones next to it. I'll want flitter IDs, com transcripts, everything."

"Yes, Captain. Right away."

"And be prepared to patch my signal from a flitter or other light craft. Lady Cecelia and I will be checking on that beacon ourselves." As she said it, she raised her brows at Cecelia, who nodded. It was crazy, really. At the least they ought to tell their host and let him assign his own security forces to it. But the thought that she might come face to face with Lepescu, unwitnessed, slid sweet and poisonous into her mind. With Cecelia's authorization, she could confront him—an uninvited gate-crasher—and demand the answers that had eluded her before. She closed her eyes a moment, imagining his surprise, feeling her hands close around his throat. . . . Her mouth flooded with the imagined taste of victory, and she had to swallow.

"Heris?" Cecelia was looking at her strangely. It was that expression, on the faces of her classmates at the Academy, that had first given her an inkling that she had inherited her parents' gift of command, the essential ruthlessness of decision.

"Just thinking," Heris said, pulling her mind back onto the designated track. It was crazy, she thought again, almost as crazy as the orders she had refused to obey. She and Cecelia had no idea what was going on over there, she knew Lepescu was dangerous in any context, and yet they were preparing to fly off as if it were an afternoon picnic. As if they were safe, protected by the social conventions of Bunny's crowd. But Lepescu wasn't part of Bunny's crowd. Why was he here? What was he doing, and what would he do when he saw her? How many

unauthorized visitors were on this island, and why hadn't
Ronnie and Bubbles called in?

"At worst," Cecelia said, interrupting her thoughts again,
"I suppose we'll find the crashed flitter and they'll all be
dead. Otherwise they'd have called in, if they needed help."
She didn't sound certain of that.

"Um." Heris dug through her daypouch for the notepad
and stylus she carried out of habit. "We need to do a little
planning here. Worst case—all dead. Next worst—injured,
needing evacuation. We really should bring some help. The
local security force, a medic or two—"

Cecelia looked stubborn. "I don't want to. It's my nephew,
after all. If I can get him out of this without Bunny's
knowledge, keep it in the family—"

"Have you considered violence?" asked Heris. At Cecelia's
bewildered expression, she explained. "I told you about
Lepescu. If he's here, uninvited, I would expect some kind
of nastiness going on. There are stories about him and his
cronies—" She could feel her lip curling.

"But what could he be doing?" asked Cecelia. "He doesn't
have any troops to command here—wait—you don't think
he's trying to *invade* or something? Take over Bunny's
holdings?" She looked frightened.

"No . . . I don't think so." It did not make sense that
a mid-list admiral would alienate so powerful a family;
besides, he could not invade without troops, and one shuttle
load would hardly be enough. Heris thought for a moment.
"Wait—remember that Kettlegrave woman?"

"The one blathering on about blood-sports?"

"Yes. She said something—about fox hunting leading to
other things, those who would hunt innocent animals being
just as willing to hunt people—"

"Ridiculous!" Cecelia sniffed. "Bunny's as gentle as his
nickname—"

"Bunny is. But Lepescu is most definitely not. What if
there's some kind of illicit hunting—no, not people of
course, but something *else,* that Bunny wouldn't like, with
the fox hunting season as cover—" Even as she said it,
she remembered that Lepescu belonged to a semi-secret
officers' club. She had not been invited to join, but Perin
Sothanous had. He'd refused, and kept his oath not to
talk of what he'd learned . . . but she had heard him

say it was "—really sick—they think the only true blood-sport is war."

"You have a wicked mind," Cecelia said.

"I know. But it makes sense. You told me that Bunny has some rare and valuable animals that are practically pets. What if they're being hunted? We'll go armed, and expect trouble: it's the only sensible way."

"Armed?"

"Of course. Lepescu is dangerous, and he's not alone. We don't know what those youngsters have gotten into, and we have to be able to get them and ourselves out." Even as she said it, she knew they couldn't possibly do this alone. It was stupid. Militarily, it was suicide. A flitter held eight easily, ten if cramped—could they squeeze in some muscle on the way out? No—she could not command any of Bunny's staff, and she wouldn't trust them anyway. She ached for her lost crew, for Oblo and Petris who would have stood behind her in anything. *Except the trial,* her mind reminded her. She argued back to her memory: They would have, but I wouldn't put them through it.

She shook herself physically, as well as mentally, and signed off with Sirkin, giving the few final orders. She would have to do this alone, because there was no other way. At least she could prepare Cecelia for what they might face.

"Rifles," she said. "At a minimum, and if you can use a bow—"

"Of course," Cecelia said, still looking shocked. "But why—"

"It's quieter." Heris had pulled out her notepad again, and was figuring on it. Supplies: they'd have to assume they couldn't use Bandon, so they'd need food, medical supplies, ammunition for the weapons she intended to take, protective gear, whatever communications and electronic gear she could lay her hands on—she looked at the wall chronometer—in half a standard hour. They'd need to leave before the day's hunt gathered. It was crazy. They should tell Bunny; they should use his staff for this.

"Should we take something larger than a standard flitter?" Cecelia asked.

"Hmm? What else?" Heris computed cubage and mass on her notepad and entered the total. They would have to change from hunting clothes, too, or take along something more suitable and change en route.

"A supply flitter, I was thinking. We could take more supplies, and if one of them is injured . . ."

"Good idea. Will they sign one out to you?"

Cecelia looked affronted. "I've been a family friend for years—of course they will. Michaels will be glad someone's checking on the young people."

"Fine. Then get this list"—Heris handed it to her—"loaded as soon as you can. I'll pack my kit, and what else we need."

"The weapons." Cecelia scowled.

"Yes. The weapons." The weapons were going to be a problem, any way she went at it. Personal weapons were common enough, but Cecelia, as a dedicated fox hunter, had brought none with her, and Heris's own small handgun would not be enough.

That morning the green hunt gathered at Stone Lodge, so the house staff at the Main House seemed less rushed. The housekeeper's eyebrows went up slightly when Heris mentioned weapons, but the brief explanation that Lady Cecelia wanted to find her nephew brought them back down, as if Lady Cecelia could be expected to take after her relatives with firepower.

"Senedor and Clio have a shop here during the season," the housekeeper said, mentioning a firm of weapons dealers as famous in their way as the great fashion houses. "I imagine they would have anything Lady Cecelia might want."

"Thank you," Heris said; once she'd heard the name, she remembered seeing the S&C logo outside one of the little stone buildings that made up the commercial row: saddlers, bootmakers, tailors and bloodstock agents.

Senedor & Clio's local representative welcomed her with a wink and a smile. "Lady Cecelia, eh? What's she doing now, deciding to turn elphoose hunter? You're her captain. . . . You look like regular military."

"I was." Heris did not elaborate. She had thought of a good story on the way over. "Look—I'm buying two lots— they'll need separate accounting. Lady Cecelia's yacht is woefully undergunned; the crew's arms are pitiful." In fact, the crew had no weapons at all. "I finally convinced her that in some of the places she wants to travel, she needs to arm the crew with something more advanced than muzzle-loaders from the family museum."

The man chuckled. "A lot of these aristocrats are like that—they don't expect to need real protection."

"And most of them probably don't," Heris conceded. "The ones who make a safe round from hunting here to deep-sea fishing on Fandro and back to court for the season . . . but you know Lady Cecelia isn't like that." The man nodded. "So . . . I'm going to do my job and see that she isn't hijacked somewhere."

"Umm. We don't carry many of that sort of thing down here," he said. "But let's see . . . here." The holo catalog showed something that looked like the landing troops' rifles and submachine guns. Exactly what Heris had been hoping for. "These are made by Zechard, who as you know supply the fleet marines. Ours, of course, go through additional testing from the factory. We have a gross of each model up at Home Station, and we could deliver anything up to that quantity direct to Lady Cecelia's yacht. The *Sweet Delight,* isn't it?"

Heris wondered if Lepescu knew that somewhere on Home Station were a gross each of military-quality rifles and the stubby-barrelled weapons which had been called OOZ for time out of mind. Heris remembered that one instructor at the Academy had said they were supposed to be 007's, but through a computer glitch they'd been renamed. The landing force's gory jest was that they were called OOZ because that's what they made of anyone foolish enough to get in the way. And how many were on the other Stations? She did not ask, but smiled ruefully at the salesman instead. "That would cause problems," she said. "At least now. You've probably heard that we've a standing watch aboard—?"

"Yes—that's why I thought—"

She shook her head at him. "The Stationmaster was none too pleased about that; Lady Cecelia is sure he will not like having that crew armed with modern weapons. Of course they're harmless—it's only a handful, and most of them don't yet know how to use these—" She tapped the holo catalog and the image shivered. "But she said to gather the weapons here and transport them under her personal seal and responsibility when we leave. She is concerned as well that such weapons look too . . ." Heris's lips pursed and she gave the salesman a look of complicity. "Too real. You know—it would ruin her decorating scheme or something. I wondered if you had a small number of those which could be customized to look more like hunting weapons."

The man's eyes brightened. "Ah . . . yes. Here." The catalog image flicked to something with a stock of burnished wood instead of extruded carbon-fiber/alloy and a civilian-style sighting system and computer socket. "It's the same, exactly, but with add-on about two hundred grams heavier. It does cost more. . . ."

"Perfect," said Heris firmly. "Twenty of the rifles, and five subs. . . ." The OOZ had been prettified with wood and inlay, but less successfully. They would pass, however, for the weapon many explorers carried on pioneer worlds.

"I don't have that many set up," the man said. At her frown, he added quickly, "But it doesn't take long. The hunt's away today, and my techs are both free. A few hours only. . . ."

They didn't have a few hours. "How many do you have ready?" Heris asked. "I wanted to show milady what they would look like."

"If brasilwood and corriwood are acceptable, I've got a couple of beauties already made up." He vanished behind a mesh grill and returned with two of the rifles and a single submachine gun. The rifle stocks had the curly green and blue grain of brasilwood, probably from a plantation on this very planet; the OOZ's wood decoration was in the pale yellow and gray grain of Devian corriwood. Heris ran her fingers over both; the rifles felt silky and the sub a bit tacky, giving a grip that would always hold no matter what. She picked up each weapon to check its balance.

"You'll want to fire them," the man said with certainty. "Our range is back here—"

"Just a moment," Heris said. "This is not all, remember? On Lady Cecelia's personal account, not the yacht account, I will need to select personal weapons for her." She paged through the catalog, and allowed the salesman to lead her toward the items she already knew she wanted. Light hunting rifles with day-and-night optics, IR range finding, and computer links for special purposes, a narrow-beam optical weapon that could also be used to operate ship controls, personal protective gear. . . . The salesman seemed to consider it natural that she ordered for herself as well, but she dared not put vests and helmets for the young people on the list.

Then it was done, and he led her through another mesh grill to the indoor firing range without waiting for her opinion. She forced herself to follow with no sign of hurry. Surely Cecelia wouldn't get the flitter loaded in the time limit she'd given her. And despite her need to hurry her training held—you could not trust a weapon you had not personally tested.

When all the weapons had checked out, as she had been sure they would, she came back to the main showroom and glanced around. "I'll contact you when Lady Cecelia approves the choice of wood for the stocks, and I'm hoping to convince her to buy appropriate armor for the crew as well. We'll be using these in the next few days; I'll need ammunition. . . ."

"Here," he said, stacking boxes of clips. "And I presume a weaponscart?"

Heris nodded, glad that she would not have to pay for this. Cecelia's credit cube went into the reader, and the assembled weaponry stacked neatly into a covered cache on a cart that looked like a miniature flitter and hummed at her.

"Palm-print it," the man said. Heris laid her palm on the membrane set in one side of the thing's bow, and it bleeped. "It won't open the cache to anyone else," he said. "It'll follow you; if you want it to stay somewhere, palm-print and say, 'Stay.' But I'd keep it with you; if it's stolen someone could break in. Local law says those weapons are your responsibility now."

"Thank you," said Heris, and retrieved Cecelia's cube. She hadn't even looked at the total; it was like going into Fleet refitting.

On the way back to the flitter bays, Heris's mind caught up with her again. What she was about to do, with Lady Cecelia and a supply flitter, was exactly what Admiral Lepescu had demanded that she do with her crew and ship . . . what she had refused to do, in fact. Why was she so willing *now* to charge into an obvious trap? If she wouldn't risk a crew of professionals, why would she risk one rich old lady? And what did that say about her loyalty to her employer?

If she tried this, and failed, Lepescu would have beaten her twice—he would have made her play *his* game, something she couldn't avoid as a military officer. . . . But now she had options.

If she could think of them. If she had time. If she could convince her employer who was even more stubborn, if less vicious, than Admiral Lepescu.

Of course, she could try another end play and tell Bunny herself. Let Lady Cecelia fire her, if that's what it came to. That's what she'd done last time, and it hadn't worked. . . . She did *not* have to make the same mistake twice.

This time, if what she suspected was true, Lepescu was in the trap—not her. She could win, using her own strategy, and prove she'd been right.

But she had to convince Cecelia.

CHAPTER THIRTEEN

"This is the island we're on," Petris said, outlining it on the chart. They had survived their first night on the island; Ronnie felt much better, and ignored the dull pain in his head. He had kept that first ration bar down, and another this morning; he was sure he was over his concussion. "About eight kilometers by five," Petris went on, "but most of it's narrower. Relief's about two hundred meters—this hill's given as two-twenty. It's steeper on the west, but nowhere difficult, except for this little ravine here—" He pointed. "Now—the cover is mixed: open forest, on these slopes, and down near the water scrub undergrowth. It's full of trails as a kid's playground in some park—"

"That's what it was," Bubbles said. "I told you; we all camped over here. My cousins, too. About—oh—five years ago was the last time I remember. We'd stay here while the grown-ups were on Bandon. We'd sail over in little boats. My father thought it up—it was out of some old books from England on Old Earth. Kids went camping on an island—"

"Yes, well, this isn't camping." Petris dismissed her memories abruptly. Oblo spoke up.

"Do you remember seeing anything that indicated someone else used the island that way?"

"No." Bubbles wrinkled her nose. "No—in fact, we always had to clear the trails every year. I wanted to have someone do it, but my father insisted we 'have the fun' as he put it."

"So this kind of hunting was either somewhere else, or not going on then," Oblo pointed out. "It would be interesting to know when it started, if your father hired someone new, who could have set it up. It would take connections—someone who knew likely clients—"

Bubbles frowned. "I'm trying to think. Daddy mentioned he'd hired a new outrange supervisor when Vittorio Zelztin retired, but I don't remember what he said. It didn't seem important."

"Not as important as staying alive," Petris said. "And we need to break this up and get moving. Let me finish the briefing." He waited until Ronnie wanted to ask why, then went on, sure of their attention. "They introduce new prey when they have confirmed killing all but two of the old ones. Those are the preeves, the previous survivors. That's how we know some of the things we do, and that's where our few weapons come from. New prey's given two days free, then hunting resumes. They supply basic rations every four days at a single site on the west side of the island, during a non-hunting period. They hunt no more than fourteen Standard hours a day. The problem is, we're not sure *which* fourteen hours. Sometimes they do a split shift. If we don't keep a constant watch, they're over here before we know it.

"What the preeves told us is that the first week they hunt only in daylight. That weeds out the really stupid and incapable, they think. Then they start night-hunting. They have dark gear; we don't. If they hunt all night, they'll leave us alone the following day, but they usually hunt only half a night shift. From sundown to midnight, or midnight to sunrise, say. We've been here a couple weeks, so they're night-hunting almost every night. Last night they didn't— I expect they were waiting to see if you were followed."

"If they have Barstow sensors, why don't they just find us and wipe us out?" asked George.

"They don't use Barstows," Petris said. "Again, that's not 'sporting' in their books. The preeves say if someone eludes them the full month, they'll use a Barstow to find and capture him—but that almost never happens."

"But if they know *we're* here—and they want to eliminate witnesses—won't they use Barstows sooner this time?"

"I was hoping you wouldn't ask that. They might. And

if they do, we're out of luck. We can't build a shelter that will shield us from Barstow scans *and* escape notice in flyovers. The island's not deep enough, and the woods aren't thick enough."

"That other flyover," Raffa said. "That could've been a rescue attempt, but we weren't there." Ronnie had missed the flyover, but they'd told him about the flitter that came, hovered above the wreck, and then departed.

"They'd only want to rescue us if they could do it before we made contact with the prey," Bubbles said. Looking at her now, Ronnie could hardly believe that was her name. None of the fluffhead left, none at all. "They'll think—if we meet them—the secret's out. Either they have to kill us all, and fake an accident somehow, or they have to escape. And even if they do escape, there's the evidence. . . ."

"So the only logical thing for them to do is add our names to the list and go on." Raffa shivered. "I don't like this. Yet—if they kill us, there'll be the evidence then, too. When someone comes to look."

"Unless they try to capture you four," Petris said. "And then kill you in some way that can be explained. They might well try a chemical weapon. Knock you unconscious, take you up in a flitter—even your own—and drop you into the rocks. If we're all dead and gone—or if they can create that accident on another island—it might well pass. Ordinarily, the preeves say, they don't use chemicals, but now they might."

Ronnie lifted his head. Had he really heard something, or . . . Petris was alert too. Something—but he couldn't define it. "Flitter," said Oblo. "I'll see about it."

"We make a plan every day," Petris said, as if nothing had happened. "You have to . . . else it's just running and waiting to be killed. That's what happens to most. Or they make a plan, and run the same one every day. That won't work either. The only hope is to make the hunters work . . . get back at them."

"Attack them?" George asked. "You do have more men, don't you? How many hunters are there?"

"More, but not more firepower. Not more resources. We can't attack in force, but we do feint. We scare them some-times. They like that, the preeves tell us; I hate to give them the satisfaction, but it does make them slow down and be careful. As for how many, it seems to vary. I'm sure we're not seeing the same ones each day; if it's anything like big game hunting, there's a larger party of hunters over on Bandon, and they take turns. I'd like to kill them but so far we haven't."

"Has anyone ever?" Raffa asked.

"So I hear," Petris said. "But you don't know how much to believe. The preeves they send with us are not exactly reliable. They've been known to turn a group that was doing too well. We found a locator on Sid, for instance."

"But you didn't kill him," George said. "Why not?"

"Do you kill everyone who just might hurt you someday?" Petris looked disgusted. "Get some sense, boy. Everyone who's been through this has knowledge we need; we can't afford to lose anyone. He knows we know he might turn; he knows his best chance at survival is with us—at least now."

"So how many do you have, altogether?"

"Never you mind. What you don't know, you can't tell. But we've lost only two, in the time we've been here; the preeves say that's much better than usual. Now—what we're going to do is this. . . ." Petris leaned over the map. "We've got to separate you four, because they need you worst. Can't let them get you in a lump. The longer it takes, the more chance one of you'll be alive to report all this. At the same time, I can't protect you all. My people wouldn't go for it, and I don't have the ability anyway. So you ladies will have to go here"—he pointed to the ravine on the map—"unless you can find those hiding places you think you remember . . . ?" He looked at Bubbles.

"I wish Kell hadn't been so secretive," Bubbles said. "I'm sure there is a cave somewhere—" Petris ignored this; he had not been impressed with a possible cave she had never seen for herself.

"You want me to go somewhere *alone*?" Raffa asked. She looked pale.

"It would be best," Petris said, almost gently. "That ravine's hard to climb; they avoid it except at the ends, and there's a lot of cover—big rocks and so on. They go along the edges, and watch both ends, but they can't see everything. If you tuck yourself under a boulder, that's as safe a place as I can offer."

"I want to *do* something," Raffa said. "Not sit under a rock and shiver."

"We don't have any training," Bubbles said to her. "Not even as much as Ronnie and George. The best we can do is stay out of the way."

"No." Raffa glanced at Ronnie and away; he felt his heart contract. She was thinking about him, he knew it.

"You two," Petris said, with a nod to Ronnie and George, "are another problem. You might be useful, or not—I can't tell until I see you in action. What we're going to do is try to make them think you wandered into the forest north of the stream, maybe heading for the point up there. It's more rugged country. I want you to go up there now, and make some trail. Scuff and scrape as if you're dragging something or someone. Drop something unimportant that might have fallen off your packs. There's no way to disguise what happened to your flitter, but they may not have realized we've met. If you headed that way, and we were keeping watch to the south and east, you could have gotten away from us. Not really, but they might believe it."

In other circumstances, it would have been a pleasant afternoon's hike up the ravine. Bubbles found it hard to remember the danger; the lower forest smelled as fresh as she remembered, and then the scramble up the rocks took her breath away. A clear rivulet still splashed from pool to pool, and red and gold amphibians still hurled themselves into the water as she came near, with agitated squeaks. A few rocks had moved in seasonal floods—she recognized one boulder by an odd inclusion, now upside down from where it had been—but most of the trail was familiar.

Higher on the slope, a breeze stirred, lifting the hair on the back of her head as it rose from the forest canopy below. She could see more of the sky, now, and smell the sea as well as the rock and flowers. Raffa, behind her, scuffed her feet in the dirt but said nothing. Bubbles was glad. She wanted to combine the old memories, once thrust away as too childish, with the present experience. Finally she stopped, winded, on a broad flat outcrop where the ravine angled south, away from the shore. Looking back she could see nothing but billows of green concealing the shape of the land itself. Raffa, panting, dropped to the rock and lifted the hair from her neck.

"You did this every year?" she asked, after a moment.

"Most years, for awhile. When my Uncle Gene would come, and bring the cousins. . . . I suppose, really, Mother wanted us out of the main house, away from more important visitors. All of us together could be noisy." She grinned down at Raffa. "When we camped over here, we'd divide in two groups, at least, and play hunting games. Stuff we'd read about or seen on the old cubes—"

"We used to go to my Aunt Katy's house and ride up in the hills," Raffa said. "On Negaire—no pretty islands there."

Bubbles shivered. "Ugh. Cold and wet all year round, isn't it? You didn't camp out, surely?"

Raffa nodded. "Better than in this heat. We pretended to be steppe nomads and so forth, but mostly we lived in caves. There was a big one, very handy, about a day's ride away, and another smaller one on the other side of the hill. We painted monsters on the walls; one of my cousins tried to paint us, but he couldn't draw."

"Cave." Bubbles glowered at the water. "I wish I knew if Kell told the truth. He said it was big enough for all of us, but he wouldn't share it, the pig. He's like that still, loves secrets and won't share. There's no place else as good, if it's real."

"You're sure you have no idea where it is?"

"Only where it isn't. We did look, but we never found it in the likely places—up here, or in the valley between this hill and the next. And knowing where not to look still leaves a lot of island. Why—you think we should look?"

"If we found it, we'd be a lot safer than hiding under a rock," Raffa pointed out. "And we'd better be going; we certainly aren't safe sitting here chatting."

"We'll climb straight over the spine," Bubbles said, leading the way up the narrowing ravine. "I hope the old trail along the crest is still there. It has a few hidey-holes I know about."

Along the spine of the island, the rock outcrops formed stout pillars, two to three meters tall, in ragged rows that wobbled along parallel to the crest like rotting teeth. Between the rows, the hollows were unevenly filled with soil and overgrown with thorny vines and bushes. A winding thread of trail had been hacked clear at the very crest; Bubbles could not tell if it had been cut by hunters or hunted. It didn't really matter. They would have to get off it quickly, because the hunters certainly knew about it.

She counted the pillars. If only she could remember the pattern . . . three tall ones, a short, two talls and then two— three?—short ones ، . . . there. She squeezed between two of the shorter rocks—had she been that much thinner five years ago, or had the rocks shifted?—and then crouched to wiggle beneath the huge briar that lay over what had always been her own special hiding place. The hooked thorns scraped on her knapsack as she slithered further in, her nose hardly off the dark, dank-smelling soil. It hadn't felt this small the last time. . . . She called back to Raffa. "You have to go under this thing—you can't go through it with anything short of power tools."

"Give me a steppe pony any day," Raffa said, but she gave only one muffled yelp when the thorns caught her hair, and slithered very efficiently for someone who often pretended disdain for physical exertion. "Do you want me to do anything about the way we came in?"

"Nope." Bubbles edged past the cluster of woody stems and felt around the far side of it. She had had a little hole there, once, with a box in it, but she couldn't see. It was dark under the briar's canopy after the brilliant sunlight on the trail, a warm brown gloom lightened by freckles of sun.

"As much as we've shaken it, the outer branches will go back down. I used to do this all the time, and the guys never found me." The little hole in which she'd tucked a boxful of handy items years before had grown into something a handspan across and deeper than her fingers. Burrow. Something was living here. She tried to remember just what did live on this island. Nothing venomous, nothing particularly large or dangerous. Except the hunters. She realized she'd forgotten them for a few minutes, here where her safe childhood was so real, and the hunters hardly believable.

On the far side of the briary tangle, lodged in fallen leaves against another standing stone, Bubbles found her box. She blessed her younger self for insisting she wanted a *real* expedition box, the kind that was supposed to last through anything. She dragged it out of the leaves and scrunched sideways so that Raffa could come up beside her.

"I forgot this the last time we were here," she said. "We were in a hurry to leave—I was going to St. Eleanor's for the first time—and by the time I remembered I'd left it, there was no time to go back." The box had no lock, only an L-shaped catch, now crusted with dirt and time. Bubbles broke a fingernail on it and muttered. Probably nothing in it—a decayed sandwich, some childish bauble—but something drove her to open it.

"Let me try," said Raffa. Bubbles slid the box over to her, and sucked her bruised fingertip. Raffa had picked up a twig, and used that to prod out the caked dirt around the latch, then spit on it. When she pushed, the latch moved with a minute squeak. "Here," she said, handing the box back. "You open it—it's yours."

Bubbles felt a curious reluctance to open it, as odd as the determination a moment ago to make that latch move. Silly, she thought. There could be nothing really useful in this box—not as useful as the things in the survival packs on the flitter. Just junk that would remind her what a silly child she had been. She struggled for a moment, having forgotten the exact movement it took to pry the lid up— the box had a good seal on it. Then it lay open, a time capsule from her childhood, her forgotten treasures rattling a little from the movement of her hand.

A seashell, one of the purple cone-shaped ones. A bracelet woven of dune-grass—she blushed, remembering who had woven it, and why. A little black blob, smooth all over . . . raked from the fire the time Kell had melted the handle from the frying pan. A single sheet of photocells, ready to be spread in the sunlight again . . . if she had anything to recharge. A bit of faded ribbon . . . she remembered clearly the shade of purple it had been. A whistle, a foil-wrapped ration bar, a tube of first-aid ointment and a packet of bandages, a length of fine fish-line, neatly coiled, with two hooks and a handful of differently shaped sinkers. And the compact silvery locator beacon, with the lanyard still looped through the ring on top.

"Isn't that a—?" Raffa started to ask.

"Yes. And it will work." She looked at the charge level on the side; as she'd expected, it had held its charge. . . .

The good ones did, and her dad had always provided them with good ones. Besides, she had the photocells to top it up with. "We can get help," she said, and sat up cheerfully only to ram her head into the nest of thorns close above. Her eyes watered, and she held very still. It was the only way with these island briars: jerk away and she'd lose half her hair and part of her scalp. In the time it took Raffa to work her free, she was able to think why they couldn't use the locator yet. There would be no easy rescue, any more than easy extrication from the briar.

"But if we could get to Bandon," she said. "If we could steal their flitter, maybe, while they're hunting the others . . . this will override anything."

"There's more of them on Bandon," Raffa reminded her. "Hold still, yet. You've got a thorn right in your scalp. Do these things leave the husk in?"

"Sometimes, and it festers if they do. Get it all if you can." She was a little surprised at how deft Raffa's fingers were, and how calm she was staying. Was this the same Raffa who had seemed an obsessive worrier?

"There," Raffa said finally. "I don't think there are any husks, but if you'll hand me that tube of gunk—thanks— I can put a dab on a few places . . . yes . . . they were bleeding a bit. Keep the flies off, eh?"

"How long has it been?" Bubbles asked, putting everything back in the box and latching it. They had left Petris and the others before noon, and she realized they had better think about where to spend the night. Light came to them between the stones, sideways; the slope below, on the west side of the island, would still be in daylight for awhile, but where would the hunters go? Up here, along the high trail? Along the slopes?

"Should we stay here?" Raffa asked, as if she were seeing the thoughts in Bubbles's head. "We're out of sight, but if they have any kind of sensors—"

"I don't know a better place, not without time to look for it." Bubbles peeked out the west side of the tangle; they were high enough that she could see out over the lower forest to the sea. The few clouds drifted past, their shadows sliding up the slope like vast hands caressing the trees. "The main thing is to keep well away from Petris and the others. . . . Someone has to get back. . . ."

"Oh . . ." Raffa's breath came just as Bubbles realized one shadow wasn't sliding upslope. . . . Small, regular, it moved swiftly against the wind, downslope to the south of them, and then ran along parallel to the ridge.

"Eyes down," Bubbles said, taking her own advice. Now that it was upwind, they could hear the faint whine of the flitter. Surely the briar was thick enough—old, tangled, too dense for anyone to see through. But every freckle of light suggested it was as porous as a fishing net. She felt sure she had something shiny on her back, something that would glitter—she should take it off. But her arms had no strength; she lay, hardly breathing, trembling.

The flitter's shadow passed over them, as if a cold hand lay on her back, and went somewhere else. She could hear the whine moving north, she thought, toward the tip of the island, but she dared not move.

"So," Raffa said, hardly louder than a breath. "They're here. And it's not a game."

"No." Immediately below them, on the west slope, the rock nubbins were only sparsely covered. . . . They couldn't count on reaching the cover below without being seen. They would have to stay here until the flitter landed somewhere. What if it didn't? It had not occurred to her that the hunters might well keep someone aloft, especially in this emergency.

"How come people in entertainment cubes never need a bathroom?" asked Raffa.

"Mmm. You're right." Now that Raffa had brought it up, she felt the same desperate need. "We can't leave cover now," she said. She wriggled toward the north side of the briar, where its canopy lay along a lower stub of gray stone. Just beyond that was another hollow; she could see into it by risking another hair-pulling match with the briar's canopy. This one had no handy roof; a small tree had died and collapsed, and the vines that covered it matted the ground.

"We should've found a place before we came in here," Raffa said.

"You're right," Bubbles said, squeezing onward around the briar's central stem and root complex. In the northeast corner of their thorny shelter, she found what she remembered, a niche in the big stone between them and the trail. Here the briar, reaching for light, lifted enough to allow someone to sit upright. And below was the other refinement of her childhood hiding place, a standard expedition one-man composting latrine unit, carefully dug into the soil. Her parents had been, she'd thought then, ridiculously fussy about pollution; one summer they'd all been yanked back to all-day lessons at the Big House for two weeks just because one set of cousins had dug a real latrine in a spurt of enthusiasm for historical authenticity. They had all had to memorize the list of diseases they could have given themselves, and the life cycles of innumerable disgusting parasites, before they could come back. They could have all the prefab units they wanted, her father had said, but they must use them. She scrabbled at the lid, said a brief prayer to some nameless deity that none of the more agile crawlers had gotten into it, and pulled it open. "But here," she said triumphantly. "All the comforts of home, more or less. Deodorizing, too." Since she was in place, she took the first turn, and felt much better. Raffa followed her, gave a sigh of relief, and latched the lid back down.

"Now if you could just excavate us a cave right here . . ."

"Nope. I tried hard enough, but it's solid stone below a few inches of leaf-drift. And I think we'd better get what rest we can. Just at dusk we could move downslope, if we're careful."

Bubbles had not really expected to sleep, cramped under the briar in the hot, sweaty dimness, but she woke at the crunch of footsteps somewhere nearby. It was completely dark, and for a moment she could not think where she was. Then she remembered. The hand on her ankle, a grip hard enough to pinch, must be Raffa's hand. She reached back and touched it, and Raffa gripped her hand instead. Her breath seemed trapped in her lungs. The footsteps came nearer, not hurrying. Panic clogged her ears with her own heartbeat; she could not tell how far away the sound was. A voice murmured something she could not distinguish. A faint crackle followed; her mind raced, suggesting that the crackle was a comunit, which meant the footsteps were a hunter's. *I knew that already,* she argued back at her mind. Raffa's fingers in hers were cold; she shivered, but forced herself to lie still. Another crunch, a boot on the rough path beyond the stone. She heard a scrape and a soft curse as someone found the space between the stones too narrow. Something shook that side of the briar, as if the hunter had taken a stick to it; the branches squeaked overhead. Raffa's fingers tightened suddenly. Could she see something from her side of the briar? But the footsteps went away, the faint scrunching growing fainter. Raffa's fingers relaxed but did not pull away.

Her breath came out all at once; she felt dizzy and faint even lying down. What if she'd been asleep . . . and dreaming . . . and had snored? Her first school roommates said she snored. Just when she thought it might be safe to murmur something to Raffa, she heard another sound. Not nearly so loud as the first, as if the feet wore something softer than boots. Three steps, a pause. Four, and another pause. Two . . . whoever it was was now just outside the cleft they'd come through. Bubbles held herself rigidly still, trying not to breathe.

Then the crack of a weapon echoed along the stones, and the person nearest them gave a soft cry. Bubbles heard the slither and thump as he fell, and the ragged breathing louder than the stifled moans. The other footsteps came back at a run and paused; even from behind the rock, Bubbles could see the glow of light as the hunter turned on a torch.

"Got one," he said, this time loud enough for Bubbles to hear; she assumed he was talking into his comunit. "By the tattoo, it's one of the preeves." The comunit crackled and muttered back to him. "Right," he said. "I'll bring the IDs. No sign of the others." Bubbles heard the click as he shut the comunit cover, and then a grunt and thump as if he bent to set down his weapon and lean over the body.

Then—"Got one too," said the other man, in a harsh voice thick with pain. The hunter squealed, then gasped, and Bubbles heard the fall of another heavy body, the thrashing of limbs, the rattle and clatter of equipment banging on the rocks. The light went out. Then silence, but for a final few noisy gasps.

For the first time in her life, Bubbles envied those of her friends who had a religion: they would have had some deity to swear to, or at, or on. "We can't stay here," she said quietly. Her voice surprised her; it sounded as calm as if she were in her mother's drawing room discussing the weather.

"He touched me," Raffa said. Her voice, too, was quiet. "With a stick or something, when he prodded the briar."

"We have to go," Bubbles said. "They'll send someone." Through the gap in the stones, the smell of blood and something worse rolled as if on a stream of water. Her stomach churned.

"How can we? We can't see anything. . . . ."

"We have to. It won't be so dark out from under this briar. Turn around and let me get past."

"You're not going *that* way?" The calm seeped out of Raffa's voice, leaving honest fear behind.

"I want his weapons," Bubbles said. "And his comunit, and his night goggles."

"But then they'll know someone came after," Raffla said. Bubbles paused. She hadn't thought of that. As it was, they might assume that what it looked like was indeed what happened—a victim not quite dead who killed his careless killer. If she took anything, they'd know someone else had been there. But it didn't matter.

"They know we're here," she said. "They're going to hunt until they find us. His things will give us a better chance. You stay here—we'll go downhill afterwards."

Out from under the briar, starlight gave a faint glow to the standing stones; in the distance, the sea glittered. Bubbles paused in the gap between the stones, listening. She could hear nothing. When she peeked out, she could see the tangle of dark forms that must be the two men's bodies. Quickly, before fear could overwhelm her again, she forced herself to move out onto the path. Her foot slipped, and when she put her hand down it was into warm, wet, stinking slime. She choked down her nausea, and wiped her hand on the nearest body. They were dead; it didn't matter now. She fumbled at the bodies, expecting every moment the shot that would kill her, the hiss of gas that would paralyze her.

The bodies were still warm; she hated the feel of the skin, the stiffening texture of it, as she felt around for the hunter's night gear. Goggles around his neck, on a thong—he would have dropped them before lighting his torch. They felt wet— blood? She cut the thong with her knife, and felt around for the torch. She risked a quick flash of it. The goggles were covered with blood, which she cleaned off with the dead hunter's shirt-tail. There was the comunit which she scooped up, and there the man's rifle with its targeting beam. Her own hands were covered with blood, and one foot would leave bloody footprints until it dried. She flicked off the torch, and called softly to Raffa.

"Come on out—if I go back through, I'll leave a trail. . . . We'll leave the main trail farther down, and have this hidey-hole again later if we need it. Bring my box." She put the comunit in her shirt pocket.

A cautious rustle, and Raffa came out with both knapsacks. Bubbles handed her the rifle, and put on the night goggles. Now she could see well enough without the torch to finish rummaging in the dead hunter's pack. He had carried a backup weapon with a removable stock in his pack; she took that and his needler, and the dead preeve's knife. Unfortunately the hunter had not carried an extra set of night goggles. Finally, she did her best to clean her bloodiest hand and foot, so they'd leave no more traces than necessary.

Then she led Raffa southward down the trail. Neither of them questioned who should lead; it was her island, and her duty to protect Raffa if she could. There had been a series of parallel trails down the west side of the ridge, long ago; as she recalled, you could go down almost anywhere. She ducked between another pair of standing stones, and fought through a tangle of vines, and then found the next gap downhill. To her enhanced vision, the broken slope below was empty of anything but crumbling rock and low scrub; Raffa, behind her, said, "How is it?"

For answer, Bubbles passed her the goggles; she felt suddenly blind when she took them off. "See for yourself. Pick a route, stay low, and don't hurry. We've got to be quiet."

"You need these." Raffa passed the goggles back; Bubbles pushed them away.

"It's your turn, and I'm supposed to know this place. I'll go first; then you can find me. Not too close." Her eyes were adjusting; she squeezed them tightly a moment or two, and when she opened them found she could just make out the larger rocks. Slowly, carefully, she edged downward, placing each foot with precision so that she could test the ground before putting her weight on it. She remembered reading her brother's service manual on this sort of thing; she had found it funny. She had imagined the dapper George crawling about in the dark counting his steps on zigzags and getting dust on his impeccable trousers, or slithering on his stomach. And here she was . . . wishing she knew if crouching was enough, if she should be down flat, crawling, if the zigging and zagging from one rock to another was actually doing any good, or only taking longer. A pebble rolled out from under her foot with a faint clatter. She froze. She could hear nothing now but her own pulse beating. She took another step down, and another. The black line of trees rose toward her, welcoming.

CHAPTER FOURTEEN

"Well, well . . . hello, darlin'." It was not a voice she wanted to hear, that confident male purr. "A gal could get hurt, wanderin' around in the dark like you are. . . . You better let me give you a hand." A blot of nearer darkness rose from the trees and moved toward her, boots scraping on the rock; she could see a narrow gleam that might be starlight on the barrel of his weapon.

"No . . ." She hadn't meant to say anything, but fear left no room for the breath in her lungs.

"C'mon, hon," he said. She couldn't tell quite how far away he was—two meters? Three? "Wasn't that your flitter crashed on the other side of the island? Your dad sent us out to find you. . . ." For a moment relief washed over her, but she couldn't believe in it. Still, if he thought she didn't know, he might not kill her right away. And if he thought she was alone, if he hadn't seen Raffa, perhaps Raffa could still get away.

"You're . . . one of the outrange patrols?" she asked. A confident chuckle came from him.

"That's right, hon. And you're gonna be fine, now. Just come along with me. . . ."

For the third time that night, Bubbles heard death close by. This time she heard the bullet smack into him an instant before the loud crack from upslope, where Raffa was. The impact threw him back, to land with a crash in the low vegetation of the slope. A few loose rocks clattered on downhill. Bubbles doubled up, retching. It was too much.

214

She had little in her stomach to lose, but wanted none of it. She could hear Raffa coming down, much faster than she had, with the aid of the goggles.

"Are you all right?" Raffa's voice, from near the fallen hunter.

"Y-yes." Her body gave a final convulsive heave, then allowed her to lift her head. "I . . . didn't know you knew how to shoot."

"My Aunt Katy. She made us learn. Gave prizes." From the sound of it, Raffa was fighting her own nausea. Bubbles felt shaky and ashamed of herself. She was supposed to be the leader here, and she'd fallen apart. She forced herself to stand, to stumble the few strides in the dark to where Raffa bent over the dying man.

"I thought they died quicker," she said, trying for the calm tone of earlier. "They do on the action cubes." The man's breathing sounded horrible, bubbly and uneven. She was glad she couldn't see his face.

"Here." Raffa pushed a set of goggles into her hands. "Now we can both see. And we'll take his weapons and comunit." She spoke hurriedly and roughly, her voice slightly shaky. "I saw him, after you started down. I didn't dare call. . . ."

"Right," Bubbles said.

"I kept wanting you to go more to the right. Give me space. I was so *scared*—" For a moment they clung to each other, shaking, wanting to cry but knowing they had no time. "Got to go," Raffa said finally, pushing away. "They'll be coming."

Bubbles stood, staggering a little from the weight added to her original pack. They each had two rifles now, and a needler, and a comunit, and more knives than they could possibly use. If they could get some of this back to Petris . . . but they couldn't. Quickly, careless for the moment of the noise, they got themselves into the forest below.

Once or twice, in childhood, they had tried skulking around in the woods at night. With torches, of course. They'd given it up, except for raids along the beach, after someone— she couldn't remember who—had broken an ankle while trying to climb the ridge in a cross-island overnight race. They'd had to call for help, and the adults had been scathing about children who didn't have enough sense to stay off slippery rocks in the dark. Buttons, the acknowledged boss of the campsites, had forbidden night wandering, and they'd mostly obeyed. Bubbles hadn't minded, because she preferred to sleep at night rather than nap in the daytime.

Now, with the night goggles on, she was glad of the covering darkness. She could see well enough to avoid hanging creepers, thornbushes, and other hazards; she knew from her time on the open slope that no one without night goggles could see her. Of course the others had them . . . but so did she.

Soon she slowed, and began listening again. She stopped completely for a moment. Her stomach growled loudly, reminding her it was empty. She heard Raffa scrabbling in her knapsack, then a faint metallic rasp and a gurgle. Water. She realized how thirsty she herself was, and took off her own knapsack, trying for silence. Where was the noisy wind when you needed it? The water eased her throat and washed away the foul taste of her nausea. Now she was hungry. She tapped Raffa's arm, and when she leaned closer murmured to her. "Eat now—while walking." She could see Raffa's nod as clearly as if it were daylight.

They had the survival rations from the flitter, tubes of thick goo that tasted of fat, sugar, and salt. Bubbles swallowed half of hers at once, and tucked the rest into her pocket. She started off again more slowly, trying to remember how the land went on this side of the island. How far south were they, and how near was the swamp? Should they start back north, and hope to work into the more rugged terrain along the north shore?

Nothing moved in the woods around them. She remembered, from those childhood visits, flocks of birds and many small animals—lizards, some nonvenomous snakes, land crabs. Once she'd been frightened by a tortoise big enough to sit on; she'd thought it was a shiny brown rock. There was less undergrowth than she remembered, and she found it easy to walk between the trees. The slope flattened beneath her feet; the forest rose higher overhead, and even with night goggles she couldn't see that much. Whenever she stopped to listen, her legs trembled; she knew they needed to rest.

Raffa tapped her shoulder. Bubbles leaned close to her, and Raffa said, "I think I hear water."

Bubbles tried to filter out the sigh of the breeze in the

leaves . . . yes. A rhythmic rush and silence . . . waves breaking, but gently, in this little wind. "You're right," she said quietly. "And they might have someone on the beach—it's narrow here." Now which way, south or north? Her mind was clogged by exhaustion and fear. She had started out hoping to find her old hiding place, and then thought of Kell's cave, wherever that was . . . but now . . . she wished she knew just where they were, and how far it was to someplace else.

"I'd vote north," Raffa said, as if she'd asked. "Away from their camp." For a moment Bubbles wanted to protest; they had weapons themselves, now, and night gear. They were as dangerous as the hunters. But they weren't, really: they were untrained girls, and very tired. Staying as far from the hunters' camp as possible made sense.

"Good idea," Bubbles said, and turned right, away from the beach. They walked slowly, as quietly as they could manage, stopping every few minutes to look around them. The walk took on a dreamlike character—the eerie landscape in the night goggles, that looked like something meant to be scary but done on a low budget, the silence, their exhaustion that forced concentration on the simplest movements. When a great tree loomed up that Bubbles remembered from her childhood trips, she moved into the dense shadow of its massive bole and stopped.

"We've got to rest," she said, "while one of us can stay awake to watch. You sleep first."

"Right." Raffa's vague shape folded up to sit against the tree. Bubbles leaned, but did not sit. If she sat, she *would* sleep. She could not be scared enough to stay awake, not now. She fished the rest of the ration stick out of her pocket and ate it, and drank more water. Her legs ached; the pack straps seemed to burn along her shoulders, but she was afraid to take the pack off. What if they had to run for it?

She realized then that she hadn't even checked to see if the rifle she carried was loaded. She fumbled at it. It wasn't exactly like the one she'd been taught to use, and she couldn't find the little doohickey—it had a name, but she'd never learned it—to release the clip. She found something sticking out of the stock, and pushed it, and a line of red sprang across the space under the tree to another tree trunk. The rifle hummed; desperately she pushed the knob this way

and that until it moved and the light disappeared and the
hum ceased. She stared around, sure that someone must
have seen that red light, but nothing moved and no sound
disturbed her. After awhile, her heart quit trying to climb
out her mouth, and she tried to think what that had been.
Firearms were not her hobby; she had learned to shoot only
because of the elphoose hunts. Her father had insisted she
must learn.

Red light. A hum. Red light made her think of the vidcams
in the drama department . . . range finders . . . so it might
be a range finder. And the hum . . . like the hum of the
automatic focus adjustments. She felt carefully along the entire
stock. A tiny flap covered a socket—pins inside—a connection for some computer attachment? She found three more
buttons or knobs, and left them alone. The scope . . . she lifted
the rifle to her shoulder and tried to peer through it, but the
goggles interfered. After a quick look around, she slipped them
off and looked through the scope. It gave a brighter image
than the goggles, in crisp grays rather than smudged green-
ish yellow. Her finger found knobs on the scope, too. . . . She
left them alone, and put her goggles back on.

Something flared in her pocket, a small blinking light that
the goggles made into a white beacon. Without goggles—
through her pocket—it was hardly visible. The comunit she'd
taken from the first hunter . . . blinking a two-three sequence.
When she looked at Raffa, asleep against the tree, her pocket
too winked, this one in a two-two sequence. She had not
thought they might be locators, but now it seemed obvious.
If she didn't reply, with some code she could not know, the
hunters would know where to look. . . . They might know
anyway.

"Raffa!" She kept her voice low, but Raffa woke instantly.

"What?" she asked.

"We have to get rid of them—if we leave them here, that's
too close—we don't know how long it will take—" She felt
like crying . . . she was so tired, *she* hadn't had any sleep,
and it was too much. Raffa hugged her.

"We'll throw them in the water. Let 'em think we tried
to swim for it."

"But they might be on the beach!" She could hear the
incipient hysteria in her own voice. Raffa's hand tightened
on her arm.

"We're alive and two of them are dead. Two unarmed, untrained society girls, against trained hunters with night gear, and who has the weapons now? We're going to stay alive, and they're ALL going to be dead, and no you're not going to have hysterics now. Take a deep breath."

Bubbles took a deep breath; her ribs ached. "Right. Sorry."

"No problem—I got some sleep, and you didn't. Now . . . let's get to the shore, and if someone's there we'll blow him away."

"I can't even tell if this thing is loaded," Bubbles said softly. "I tried to find out and got something that made a red light and hummed at me."

"Really? Sounds like a Maseter range finder to me. Here— let me check your status." Raffa took the rifle, did something Bubbles couldn't follow in the dimness, and handed it back. "Full clip, round in the chamber. When you pull that trigger, you'll shoot something."

"Let's go, then." Bubbles angled left, toward the shore. As she remembered, the big tree had been only a couple of hundred meters from the water. She noticed, after a few minutes, that the blinking lights on the comunits had died. It gave her no comfort. . . . A missed signal would rouse them to search, she was sure. At least they had thick cover to the very edge of the beach.

As they neared the water, the night goggles had more light to work with, and brightened once more. At the same time, the undergrowth increased, as it always had near the forest edge, though it was not so thick that they needed to go out of their way. By the time Bubbles peered through the last screen of bushes and vines, she could see up and down the narrow beach at least a hundred meters in each direction. She saw no one . . . although someone could have been hidden in the undergrowth, as they were. A gentle swell out to sea produced small lapping waves that slipped up and back like the strokes of a massage, rolling the little pebbles that made up the beach here so that they clicked and whispered.

"How deep is it?" Raffa asked. "Any chance the things will be too deep for them to find?"

"It's a steep drop-off," Bubbles said. "We used to beach the sailboats on this side of the island sometimes. Give me that one—" Raffa handed over the comunit and Bubbles took another look up and down the beach. Nothing. She shrugged out of her knapsack and left it with Raffa, then moved slowly out of the cover, expecting any moment to hear another shot. The pebbles crunched under her shoes; she thought of wading in a little way, but remembered the times she'd slipped and fallen here. She didn't need to be sopping wet, not on top of everything else.

"Throw it!" muttered Raffa from behind her. Right. As if she were good at throwing. She felt like an idiot as she cocked her arm and threw the first comunit as far into the sea as she could. It wasn't, she thought, all that far; it landed with a juicy splash. With the next she tried harder, and achieved an even noisier splash—it must have been spinning—and no more distance. She found the two uphill steps back to the treeline almost impossible . . . but the impossible, she was discovering, didn't even take longer. It was just harder.

"A little farther," Raffa said, "and it's your turn to rest. Just get back from the edge."

But they actually walked another half hour, by Raffa's watch, before finding another place Bubbles remembered, where a rib of the central ridge ran all the way to the water. From there around the northern end, the island had no beach, but a vertical wall of stone.

When they lay down—this time neither could stand—Bubbles fell asleep at once. She had expected to have frightening dreams, but she woke with no memory of them. When she opened her eyes, she could see Raffa curled into a tidy ball, catlike; her rifle lay across her sleeping hand. Bubbles yawned, stretched, and rubbed the hipbone that had been on the bottom. Her back never hurt after sleeping on the ground, but a hipbone always complained. She had tried all the tricks she'd read about, back in her camping days, and none of them worked. She sat up; Raffa opened one eye and said, "Don't tell me it's morning."

"It's morning." Unless they'd slept all day, and she didn't feel that rested. Besides, the light was brighter; the leaves overhead began to look green, not black. She stretched again, arching her back, then rolled to her feet. Nothing stirred but the leaves overhead, as the dawn breeze strengthened. Her shoulders were stiff and sore from the pack straps. Raffa yawned, and groaned a little, stretching.

"I hate morning," Raffa said. Then her eyes came open all the way, and she sat up. "It's real."

"What?" Bubbles knew what, but she wasn't sure she believed it yet.

"Us. Here. Last night." Raffa was staring at her own hands. "Blood."

"Yeah." Bubbles had already seen the disgusting mess on her own hands. And she'd eaten something held in them. "I guess we should've washed off when we got to the beach." Her slacks were filthy too, and she could smell her own sour smell. Raffa looked as bad, her dark hair in lank dirty strings and the knees of her slacks black with dried blood and dirt.

"They won't have to see us," Raffa said. "They could track us by smell. Without dogs."

"Then we'll get clean." Bubbles had no idea how they would get clean. They certainly could not light a fire and boil a pot of water for washing. For that matter, she needed to think where the nearest drinking water might be. She picked up her knapsack and got it on, wincing as her shoulders complained. "Come on," she said. "It won't help us to sit here and wish."

Raffa stood, shook herself, brushed at the stains, and finally picked up her knapsack and weapons. "I know, I know. What's the boys' regimental motto? 'Onward to glory' or something equally unreasonable?" She got the knapsack onto one shoulder and grunted. "This thing weighs twice what it did yesterday. And don't scold me; I'm getting my complaints out of the way all at once, early, before they can bother you. You notice I didn't complain last night."

"Right. You complain in the morning, and I'll complain at midnight or whenever it was I went bonkers, and between us that'll cover the whole day."

"And leave us time to survive, evade the hunters, kill them all, and save everyone. Tally-ho." Raffa started off, then looked back. "By the way, where are we going now?"

"Water, I thought," Bubbles said. "Water first, then some-place to hide."

"Like last time," Raffa said, but with a grin. "A hiding place convenient to a trail so that we can get weapons and supplies from dead hunters."

For all the banter, they went warily enough once they started. Without talking about it, they began to move apart, so they could just see each other, and take alternate pauses for listening and looking backwards. Nothing disturbed them but the silence, which the wind in the leaves overhead seemed to emphasize. The sky lightened; Bubbles knew that it was now full day, though they were walking in the shadow of the ridge. The slope began to fall away under their feet, and Bubbles turned right, inland; she remembered that there was another, smaller stream in a ravine between the last hill on the main ridge, and the outlier hill at the north end of the island. It rose from a spring on the ridge, and over the years the children had made a series of wading and splashing pools along its path to the sea. Between them, the stream was no more than ankle-deep except after a rainstorm, but they might find enough water in one of the pools to wash their clothes. Even if all the dams had fallen apart since the last campers, there should be enough loose handy stones to let them build one up again. It wouldn't take long.

When she finally saw water, it was one of the larger pools. Someone had repaired the dam—she assumed it was the prisoners—and raised it enough so that the pool looked to be waist-deep. Its surface was littered with fallen leaves and twigs. She started toward it, then waved Raffa back to cover. It looked safe and deserted, but . . . she noticed something glinting at the upper end of the pool. Warily, she worked her way toward it, trying to keep to thicker growth. A foil packet with one end torn off, that's all, discarded by some careless hunter. It could have held rations, candy, a damp wipe to clean with. She relaxed, then saw the first dead amphib, turning slowly in the pool, its legs extended. Another lay by the stream; with a growing sense of horror she realized that the "floating leaves" were in fact a mass of dead amphibs, insects, fish. She backed away, her hands to her mouth.

"What?" said Raffa, from behind her.

"Poison. They've poisoned the stream." And if this stream, then all the streams—and if the streams, probably the springs as well. After horror, anger. This was *her* place, her childhood, and she had spent hours lying belly-down beside one stream or another, watching the brilliant red-and-gold amphibs, the speckled fish, the brilliant blue and green butterflies that came to drink.

"The . . . I can't even find words bad enough. . . ." She had used all the bad words she knew for common things like escorts who got drunk and threw up on her, or girl-friends who told someone else her secrets—she hadn't known there was something worse to save curses for. "How could they—?" How could anyone destroy so carelessly . . . anyone past childhood, that is.

"It would be hard to hide, in an autopsy," Raffa said thoughtfully. Bubbles almost hated her at that moment. Of course it wasn't her island. She had never seen it as Bubbles remembered it. "What I mean is," Raffa went on, "it's probably meant to put us to sleep or something. The . . . the other things are accidents."

"That's what's worst," Bubbles said. "They have a reason to kill us. A bad one, but a reason. To kill all these, just by accident, as a sort of by-product—"

"We shouldn't stay here. They'd check this pretty often, I'd guess."

"Right. Upstream, then." They might have someone stationed upstream, too, but she had to know if they'd poisoned it all. She had to. She wondered when they'd done it—the day before, dropping packets from the flitter? Landing at each small stream? Or had someone been walking the forest that night, someone who might have walked past them as they slept, not seeing them? She shivered; it would do no good to think of that. As she walked, what Raffa said began to make sense. The same things had different effects on humans and animals—she knew that. A drug to make them sleepy might have killed the amphibs by accident, or . . . didn't the fish need to swim for their gills to work? So if they drowsed and didn't swim, they'd die just from that . . . but she was still angry. She felt decades older than the day before, than even the night before.

Upstream, as anywhere, grew steeper and narrower. They came to another pool, with its scum of dead amphibs and fish; she had seen nothing alive along the banks of the rivu-let. Beyond that, the stream forked. To the left, poisoned water gurgled pleasantly in its narrow bed. To the right was the waist-high ledge that formed a miniature waterfall in the wet season. A damp patch of mud in the hollow above it was the only sign that a creek had ever flowed there.

"That way," Bubbles said, heaving herself up and over the rock ledge. "We can't take any water from that stream, and there might be a spring up here they didn't notice."

"You don't know for sure?" Raffa asked, as she sat on the ledge and swung her legs up.

"No . . . my favorite places were the eastern ravine, where I could watch the sunrise, and my bramble. And our camp was on the eastern shore, south of where we crashed. Sometimes we had three or four main camps, depending on how many cousins showed up. Kev and Burlin used to set traps and things up at this end of the ridge—then they'd sit there and snigger."

"Urgh. I wouldn't have wanted to have them along."

"Well . . . Silvia finally told on Burlin, and that was the end of them. But somehow he always made Buttons and me feel like it was our fault. If we'd had a more exciting island, he wouldn't have gotten into mischief."

"Like Stanley, my cousin that always blamed his pony for everything. But he brought it back with whip welts once, and my Aunt Katy wouldn't put up with that."

They followed the dry creekbed upstream, careful not to step in any drying mud. Bubbles looked for any sign that the hunters had been there, but the few scuffmarks could as well have been those of desperate prisoners. Her breath came short; it was hard to climb the steepening slope, and she realized they were close under the ridge. The creekbed turned suddenly, leading them into a narrow cleft roofed with trees; it closed around them, and Raffa exclaimed over the ferns draping the walls. Ahead, the cleft ended in a sheer wall hung with shaggy ferns and vines. At the foot of it, the ground seemed damp, but there was no spring.

"Well," Bubbles said, a little blankly. "That's it. No water here." She sat down; her legs had suddenly given out, and her eyes burned, though she could not cry.

Raffa crouched beside her. "We're hidden, at least. If we stay quiet, and they don't find our trail. They can't come on us from behind."

Bubbles nodded, but could not speak past the lump of misery in her throat. She set her rifle carefully to one side, away from the damp spot, and pushed the knapsack straps off her shoulder.

"We should eat something," Raffa said. "We never did have breakfast."

"Not without water," Bubbles said. "At least, that's what the books say." But at the mention of food, her stomach cramped and rumbled. She felt she could eat three meals at once.

"We have some water," Raffa said. "And what about tropical fruits and things? They have water in them."

"I . . . haven't seen any. It's the wrong season, or the prisoners have eaten them, or something. . . ." Bubbles leaned back against the ferny rock, careless of insects. Her eyes sagged shut.

"Come *on*—you can't give up!"

"I can rest," Bubbles said, not opening her eyes. "Just a little while." She wasn't sure what she felt, except exhaustion and hunger, and right now she didn't care if a whole troop of hunters came up the creek.

"All right," Raffa said, "but I'm not giving up." Bubbles heard Raffa move around her, and the scrape of Raffa's pack on the pebbles. "Although a soft place to rest my aching back may be a good idea. Aahhh—" That relaxed sigh ended in a yelp, quickly muffled. Bubbles opened her eyes. Raffa lay on her back, covered with ferns to the waist; she seemed to have fallen *into* the rock. The mass of ferns and vines had hung over some opening like a shaggy curtain. From the muffled splutters, she was trying to say something. Bubbles grabbed her feet and pulled.

"Are you all right? Need help?"

Raffa undulated, snakelike, and slithered out on her back, spitting dirt out of her mouth. "It's a wonder I didn't crack my skull."

"What is it, a hollow or something?"

"A hollow, yes. A cave!"

"Cave?"

"Yes. And I heard water dripping. Come on. . . ." Raffa grabbed her knapsack and started to shove it through the curtain of ferns.

"Wait—they'd know we went in." Bubbles looked at the broken fronds of fern where she had been resting, the bruised moss. If someone came this way—and they probably would—they'd start looking harder. And they wouldn't miss a cave, she was sure.

"We'll make it look like we rested here, and then went somewhere else," Raffa said. "Come on—shove your pack in, and the rifles. It's the best chance we've seen yet."

Bubbles shrugged and complied. She didn't have any better idea, and if Raffa had found water inside the cave, surely it hadn't been poisoned. She hoped. Raffa went in with their things, and reported that she'd found plenty of room; they could both hide there, with their gear. She crawled back out, as Bubbles lifted the vines cautiously.

"Now for disguise," Raffa said. "A few footprints going in both directions, just in here where we got careless because we figured no one would have tracked us further back. We sat here and rested—that's the squashed ferns on your side. Actually they may not know there *are* two of us, so why don't I make all the footprints?"

"Because we might both have left them somewhere else," Bubbles said. "If we were going to leave here, which way would we go? Back up the ridge, I think—we came here looking for water, didn't find any, and started up to find a spring. . . ." Together, they edged back out of the narrow cleft, and cautiously made a few scuffmarks up a steeper slope. Since they had been careful not to make prints on the way in (and didn't see any) they walked back normally.

The hanging ferns and vines looked undisturbed, Bubbles noticed, even after Raffa had been through twice. Raffa went first, and then Bubbles slid in backwards. They had left marks, sliding in; it looked like someone had dragged bodies over the ground. She was trying to think what to do about it when she heard a shot, from high overhead, and then another. She didn't try to see who it was, or if they'd seen. . . . She jerked backwards under the matted vines and tried not to breathe. Raffa's hand closed on her arm, almost as tightly as the night before. Had it been only one night?

Although it was near midday, inside the cave she could see very little. The thick vines shut out nearly all the light, and it was cool and damp. She lay on level stone thinly coated with damp mud. She could hear the musical plink and plonk of water dripping into deep water, somewhere behind her in the dark. A cold drop hit the back of her neck, and she jumped.

"We should get back from the opening," Raffa said quietly. "Just in case they find it."

"Let's try the night goggles." Bubbles fished hers out and put them on. The nearer part of the cave appeared in shadowy blurs, with stabbing brilliance coming from the entrance. Several meters behind them, a black level surface had to be the water they'd heard. To the left, the cave's inner wall dove directly into the water, but on the right, their flat ledge extended around a buttress and out of sight. Overhead, even the night goggles could not define the roof; when Bubbles reached up, she felt nothing.

Slowly, Raffa got to her knees and crawled away to the right. Bubbles followed, backing up at first so that she could watch the entrance. She had never been one for caves; she had not expected that the light would fade so fast. She slipped the goggles up; the blackness pressed on her face, as if it would invade her skull. Shuddering, she put the goggles back on, and stared at the faint glow from the entrance as if to remember it forever.

"They shot somebody!" George grabbed Ronnie's arm. Ronnie shook it off.

"They shot *at* somebody," he said. "You don't know they hit anyone."

"But the girls are up there—you know that."

He knew that; he could close his eyes and see Raffa's face, smell her hair. "They're in the ravine. They're in cover somewhere. And the hunters wouldn't shoot the girls right off. . . ." He wished he hadn't said it; that thought was no better.

"If Bubbles tried to fight—she's kind of wild sometimes."

"Petris sent one of the preeves up to the high trail, he said. Could have been that. And the hunter might've missed. And we can't even be sure where the shot came from." Although he was sure enough: high on the ridge, south of them. That put it too close to the girls, entirely too close. The hunters were supposed to come this way, and fall into the trap he and George had spent the afternoon constructing. They were just off one of the larger trails, that angled up and over the gap between the main ridge and the outlying northern hill.

Time had gone rubbery; he did not want to trust George's watch. His had not survived the crash. George's could have been damaged. He was aware that not trusting a watch was

as silly and dangerous as not trusting the instruments in
an aircraft; he knew he'd had a concussion. But time felt
wrong; the glowing digits seemed to hang forever or race
past. A vague irritation seized him: *he* had had the concussion, he shouldn't be having to calm George.

Another shot, more distant. His shoulders twitched. He
had thought during Petris's briefing that he understood
exactly where everyone would be, at least to start with. Now
he found he could not remember who might be southward
on the ridge, or on the west side. . . . He felt sick and sleepy
both, and kept wanting to yawn.

"We ought to go find out," George said. "That's got to
be somewhere near them. . . ."

"And if we go crashing up there we'll just lead the hunters
to them." Ronnie tried to sound soothing, but even to him
his voice seemed lusterless and whiny. "Petris said stay here,
and we should stay here."

"He's not even an officer," George said, but he didn't
move.

Ronnie stiffened in the midst of a yawn. A rhythmic noise
flicked the edge of his hearing. Like someone walking, but
walking with an intentionally odd gait. A few steps, a pause:
a few more steps, a pause. The sound of steps—the swish
of leaves, the soft pad of foot—varied in number but not
duration. Despite his fear, Ronnie grinned to himself. They'd
been warned about that mistake. . . . He'd done it himself, counting to himself as he tried to move stealthily, he'd
put four or five or three steps into the same interval, thus
making the sound as periodic as a pendulum. This person
varied his pause intervals, but not the walking ones. Ronnie
reached out to touch George in case he hadn't heard. The
walker might come within reach, if they were lucky.

Ronnie's mind drifted. It had been, he thought, an impossibly bad day, and it had started far too early. Yet he didn't
feel as bad as he should; he knew that, and knew, in some
distant corner of his mind, that it had something to do with
the bump on his head. He wasn't tracking right; he wasn't
feeling what he should feel, whatever that was. The long,
hot afternoon after the girls left, when Petris tried to figure
out what to do with them, where to put them, when the
others tested Petris's command, wanting to kill them,
wanting to leave them anywhere and get away safely

themselves. . . . It had been hell, but a hell from which he felt somewhat remote. As long as he didn't have to talk, as long as he didn't have to do anything, the others could do what they wanted.

CHAPTER FIFTEEN

"We cannot do this alone." Heris put into that all the command voice she'd ever had. Cecelia merely looked exasperated.

"We've been over that. I don't want to bother Bunny."

"Lady Cecelia." The formality got through; Cecelia actually focussed on her. "Do you remember why I lost my commission?"

"Yes, but what's that—"

"This is exactly the same thing. If we go off, the two of us—you with no military experience whatever—with no proper intelligence, no backup, no plan—that is exactly as stupid, in the same way, as what Lepescu proposed. It is frankly suicidal, and I will not cooperate."

Cecelia stared at her. "I thought we settled it; I thought you agreed."

"In anger, yes. At the thought of getting Lepescu's neck between my hands, yes. But I have no right to risk you and your nephew and the others to serve my vengeance. We don't know what we're facing; we don't know what shape they're in; we won't have backup or medical assistance—and if we get killed, what about the youngsters?"

For a moment, Heris thought Cecelia would explode; she turned red, then pale, then stood rigidly still. And finally shook herself slightly and let out a sharp *huff* of air. "I suppose you're right. That's why I came to you; you have the military background. So—you want me to tell Bunny?"

"I think we should both go. He may want confirmation

from Sirkin up in *Sweet Delight*—and besides, I still want to be part of the row."

"Fine." With no more argument, Cecelia called Michaels over. "Michaels, Captain Serrano feels that we should not go alone on this." Heris noticed that Michaels relaxed slightly; he had had more sense than either of them, but not the courage to say so.

"Yes, milady?"

"I'm going to tell Lord Thornbuckle; this will mean telling him that you knew Bubbles took the flitter." Heris had not thought about that—how much trouble would he be in? Not much, she hoped.

"I don't think you should tell anyone else about this," Lady Cecelia went on, as if Michaels were a child to be lectured. "I'm sure you'll be hearing from his lordship very shortly."

"Yes, milady."

"All right," Cecelia said. "Now we have to find Bunny before that damned hunt starts. We're lucky Stone Lodge is at this end of the settlement."

The others were mounted, ready to set out, the hounds swirling around the horses' legs. Heris was sure that only Cecelia could have gotten Bunny off his horse and into the hall of Stone Lodge so quietly and quickly.

"What is it?" he asked, the moment the door had shut out the sound of milling hooves and human chatter. Cecelia explained, giving as clear an account as Heris herself could have done: her discovery that the young people were missing, Michaels's report of where they had gone, and the beacon data and data from *Sweet Delight* which indicated that they were on an island near Bandon. Then she mentioned the uninvited guests, the intruders that Heris suspected might be hunting illegally. Lord Thornbuckle looked at Heris.

"You know this person?" Heris thought she had not heard anyone pronounce "person" with that intonation before; just so did seniors at the Academy refer to incoming cadets.

"Yes, I do," she said. "He cost me my commission; he has a bad reputation—but the relevant point is that he is here without your invitation."

"Yes . . . I see that. Just a moment." He went out the door, leaving Heris and Cecelia staring at one another. In moments, he was back inside. "I told Clem to take over the hunt today; no sense in having them hounding us, as it were. Buttons has already ridden out with the blue hunt; I'll have him brought back—" As he spoke, his fingers tapped on his personal comunit. Heris had seen him only at the hunt, or at leisure after dinner; he had always seemed friendly enough, but not particularly decisive except when some fool rode too close to the hounds. The nickname Bunny had fit him well enough, the long slightly foolish face, the quick movements of his head at dinner, on the lookout for unpleasantness. Now, though, she saw someone used to command responding to an emergency, someone for whom a title made more sense than a nickname.

"Sir, the other thing—" She interrupted him cautiously; he raised an eyebrow but nodded for her to speak. "There must be someone in this household working with them— whoever they are. Someone to give warning if you're headed that way, at least."

He nodded. "And it can't be Michaels, because he knew about Bubbles and whoever was there didn't."

"We hope." Lady Cecelia looked grim. "They haven't called in; their flitter's not at a regular field—"

"Which island?" Lord Thornbuckle asked. "Could your ship make that out?" He called up a map which displayed on the hall wall as thin green lines.

"That one," Heris said, pointing.

"Bubbles's favorite," he said. "The children camped there many summers; she knows every meter of that island. I wonder if she's just camping and hiding out."

"If it weren't for the unauthorized shuttle, and the fact that Lepescu is on Bandon—" Cecelia began.

"We hope on Bandon, and not on this island," Heris put in, tapping the map again.

"Yes. We must assume he is, and that he's up to no good." His focus shifted to her, completely. "You were formerly an officer in the Regular Space Service, isn't that right, Captain Serrano?"

"Yes, sir."

"Then please give me the advantage of your professional assessment. What are we facing here, and what is your recommendation?"

Heris felt like a junior officer caught out at an admiralty briefing. "We are presently lacking important information," she began. "We know, or rather strongly suspect, that. Admiral Lepescu is on Bandon. The shuttlecraft that landed him could have held as many as fifty individuals, but since it came from a chartered yacht, it is reasonable to suppose that it did not. That it was configured for luxury work, with a maximum of perhaps ten. We do not know how many such shuttle flights have been made to and from Bandon, or the number of people on each. However, it's reasonable to assume that an actual invasion force is unlikely."

"Why, Captain?"

"Both practical reasons and the character of Admiral Lepescu, sir. Practically, invading an inhabited planet is difficult, and one like this would require complicity of too many of your employees. You have four orbiting Stations, additional navigation and communications satellites, and a high-tech population scattered around the planet. An invader would have to gain control of communications to prevent an alarm being sent. Your own militia would have to be suborned or defeated in battle, and from what I've heard of your militia, they're loyal and tough, and very well equipped. Right now, you have thousands of legitimate guests, and their crews and servants—and it might be easier to sneak onplanet in the confusion, but it certainly would not be easier to deal with so many . . ." She struggled for a word that expressed what she meant without rudeness.

"Difficult individuals?" suggested Lord Thornbuckle, with a smile.

"Yes, sir. And as well as practicality there's the matter of Lepescu. He's not a man to involve himself in something that blatant; his tastes run otherwise."

"Ummm. You said he cost you your commission?"

"Yes, he did." When Lord Thornbuckle's expression did not change, Heris realized she was going to have to say more. Anger roughened her voice.

"He considers war a noble sport, sir. He considers that putting troops in impossible situations is sporting; his expression is 'see what they're made of.' Until recently, the only way he could do this was by risking his own ship, but two years ago he attained flag rank and was given command of a battle group. You are no doubt aware of the Cavinatto action. In that conflict, he ordered my ship, and the ground forces under my command, to make a frontal attack on a strongly defended lunar complex. The defense could have been breached another way—in fact, several other ways, which I and other captains presented as alternatives. But he insisted that it must be done the one way likely to fail—even the battlecomps said so—and certain to cost the most lives."

"Is that legal?" asked Lord Thornbuckle.

"Perfectly," Heris said. "An admiral's fitness for command is judged afterwards, by results. He is not obliged to take advice from anyone but his own commander, and our group was operating far from anyone more senior. It was something Lepescu had worked toward for years."

"Did his order to you risk the whole operation?"

"No. Most of the group would attack the main objective, and while his orders for that were not what I'd have given, they weren't as reckless. Our diversionary action was important, but it need not have been suicidal."

"Did this admiral have a grudge against you before? It seems he must have. . . ."

"I'm not sure." In her own mind she was sure, but she would not condemn even Lepescu on the basis of her personal belief. "I had not anticipated anything like this. But the point is, that in the event I did not obey his very plain orders. My ship and forces attacked the lunar complex, and gained control of it, but I didn't do it his way." At the change in his expression, Heris nodded grimly. "That's right: I deliberately disobeyed the order of a lawful superior, in combat status. Grounds for court-martial; in fact, that's what I expected. I knew exactly how serious it was; my family's been Service for generations, after all. I had evidence, I thought, that would protect my crew at least, and that seemed better to me than losing several thousand of them because Admiral Lepescu enjoyed 'a good fight.' There was even a chance that a court might see it my way—small, but there it was."

"And then what?"

"Then I was offered the chance to resign my commission, in exchange for immunity for my officers and crew, or a court-martial for all. The scan data had disappeared; accidents happen in combat. I had some junior officers whose careers would be cut short forever by a court-martial now, even if they won . . . the stigma never really goes away. And some hotheads in the crew would, I knew, convict themselves if they got before a court; there are always people who can't keep quiet even to save themselves. So I resigned."

"You didn't tell me all that," Cecelia said. "Not about what he wanted you to do."

"It didn't seem relevant," Heris said. The rest of it boiled up in her mind—what Lepescu had said to her and about her: *Coward. Stupid bitch. Typical woman, only good to lay and lie.* And more, that she would never tell anyone. Who could understand?

"So I judge from your report," Lord Thornbuckle said, "that Admiral Lepescu is more likely to put someone else in danger than to risk his own hide?"

Heris struggled to be fair. "He's not a coward, sir; he had a name for boldness when he commanded his own ship. But he's also ambitious in politics and society. He would enjoy hunting here under your nose, but he would not chance making such a powerful enemy by attempting open invasion."

"What about taking hostages?"

"Possibly. Especially if he found himself in a trap."

"Do you think he's the head of whatever is going on?"

"I don't know. He has other hunting friends—" Quickly, she told him about the club she'd heard of, and the rumors about it.

"And you would recommend?"

"Taking in enough force to make resistance futile—and there's the problem of surprise and collusion. If they find out you're coming in, they might get the shuttle off, and the yacht—"

"Not if their crew's in the Bay," Lord Thornbuckle said. "That'll be easy enough to find out; it's on a routine report." All this time, he had been tapping out orders on his personal comunit. "There's a Crown Minister here—Pathin Divisti—but I hate to involve the Crown if we can avoid it. And he's here for hunting; he brought no staff."

Heris hoped her face didn't reveal her reaction. She thought of Crown Ministers as a particularly bloated form of bureaucratic incompetence, whose internal struggles for power resulted in unexpected budget changes for the Services.

The door chimed; a servant Heris had hardly noticed opened it to a militia squad, uniformed and armed. Lord Thornbuckle smiled at Heris.

"Captain Serrano, if you'd brief my Captain Sigind while I get some more information—"

Heris stepped outside; the hunt had ridden off some time before, and she could just hear the hounds giving tongue somewhere in the distance. Captain Sigind was a lean, tough man a decade younger than she, whose expression hardly wavered when he saw he was to be briefed by an older woman in hunting attire. Heris laid out the situation as far as she knew it, and he nodded.

"I know Bandon, of course, and something of the other islands. Haven't been there in a couple of years, but here's the layout." He pulled out a map display and flicked through the file. Bandon came up in a standard military format, with topo lines and color-codings for vegetation types. "The landing field's here—with shuttle extension into these woods. When they expanded the field, they cleared a little place at the lodge itself for small flitters—right here. It's grass, not paving. It'd be real handy if we knew how many were at the lodge, and how many on this other island—"

"All I know about is one shuttle load, and I don't even know if it was troop-fitted or civilian," Heris said.

"Ah. You're military?" His pale eyes were shrewd, wary.

"I was. Regular Space Service."

"Any ground combat experience?"

"No, not myself. That's—"

"Why you didn't rush into this like a damn fool. Smart." His brisk nod approved. "But you see our problem. . . ."

"Of course. You need to know how many they are, what their resources are, and which of Lord Thornbuckle's employees are on their side."

"The outrange supervisor, for one," he said. "I'm sure of that, because it's his responsibility to know who's on which settlement, and when. They'd have needed his codes to get the Bandon beacon functioning for the shuttle."

"And someone at that Station," Heris said. "Where the charter yacht that launched the shuttle came from, because I understand that the use of private shuttles isn't permitted."

"Right. But back to you—you say this man Lepescu is part of some sporting club? Most sportsmen have self-imposed limits on the weaponry they'll use—or is he a trophy hunter type?"

"I don't know," Heris said. The door opened, and Lord

Thornbuckle came out. The bony face she had once considered amiable but weak now looked anything but amiable.

"Complete shuttle records for the past thirty days," he said. "The same station where that charter's berthed has launched twice its normal quota of shuttles. Cargo and supplies, most of them were said to be, for Bandon lodge. We don't land supplies for Bandon there very often, not offworld supplies. Certainly not at this season. One of my comsats recorded the same conversation your officer picked up, Captain Serrano—as well as these—" He handed over strips of hard copy, which Heris glanced at. She could not read that fast, and he was still talking.

"I've relieved the Stationmaster there, and put old Haugan in charge—I know he's loyal, at least. Suspended all shuttle flights, and all communications, with the explanation of power problems on the Station. If I understand correctly, there are fewer than twenty people who've taken shuttles like the one Lepescu was on. All but one have returned to the Station. You were right, Captain Serrano, that they were fitted for civilian luxury use, with a total capacity of ten passengers—and carried less. Here are the latest satellite images of Bandon and the adjacent islands—there's some cloud interference, apparently a storm overnight—"

Heris and the militia captain leaned over them. Three shots of Bandon, five minutes apart, and two of each adjacent island. They looked at the Bandon pictures first. One atmospheric shuttle stood on the end of the runway; no other vehicles were near it. Three flitters were parked on an apron off to one side in two pictures, and only two in the third and last. A tiny blob the captain identified as an electric groundcar moved along the narrow driveway between the landing field and the lodge. Comparing the three pictures, they could tell that it had left the lodge for the field—and then a flitter had taken off.

On the islands to the east, south, and west—four in all—the captain found nothing remarkable, though heavy clouds still clung to the peaks of the eastern island. But the island to the north—"where the children camped"—Lord Thornbuckle put in—they saw what they were looking for.

A flitter on the east beach, hatch open. A flitter parked on the south end of the island another a few hundred meters offshore, as if approaching. They could see nothing on the visual of the island's center; it, too, was cloaked in cloud.

"We have continuous loops, of course," Lord Thornbuckle said. "And we can get infrared and radar images. But it seems to me that's enough to go on."

"Right, sir." The militia captain closed his eyes a moment, and then said, "We'll need all the Homestead militia, and those at the Neck. Day 'n night gear both, full armor, and riot weapons—" He paused, as the clatter of hooves broke upon them. Heris looked up to see Buttons riding breakneck up the avenue on a lathered horse. Servants ran out to take the horse; he flung himself off and ran up the steps to the portico.

"What happened? Is Bubbles all right?"

His father glared at him. "What do you know about Bubbles?"

"She took a flitter with the others to Whitewings for a few days—she asked me to cover for her—what's happened?"

"We don't know. We know the flitter's down on that small island north of Bandon, the one you youngsters camped on. We haven't been able to contact her, and Cece's Captain Serrano has reason to believe she's in great danger."

"And you want me to do what?"

"Be my representative with the rescue force. We expect some opposition. . . ."

"Opposition?"

"Captain Sigind will brief you fully. You'll need your personal gear—"

"Liftoff in thirty minutes, sir," the militia captain put in.

"Right." Buttons dashed into the hall, as changed as his father from the amiable and rather foolish young man Heris had thought him. Captain Sigind eyed her thoughtfully.

"You want to come along?"

"Of course we're coming—" began Lady Cecelia, but the militia captain's eyes never wavered from Heris's. Heris shrugged.

"It's your operation; I don't know the terrain, the entire situation, or your troops. If you can find a corner where I won't be in your way, yes—but I'm not going to step on your toes."

"Heris!" Lady Cecelia's bony finger poked her in the back. "We have weapons—!"

"We have weapons, milady," said Heris formally, "but you have no training and I have not been on a groundside operation in years. We are superfluous, and we might even be in the way. Captain Sigind must decide."

His earlier indecision came down on the side of respect; she had won that much. "Thank you, Captain Serrano. I'm glad you understand. Now, if you and the lady will agree to act under orders, I'm sure we can fit you in."

"We had a supply shuttle almost loaded," Heris said. "Including personal armor for Lady Cecelia and me, and decent weapons."

"Good. Then I can send a squad with you—expand the standard medical unit—and now if you'll excuse me, I'll be off. Twenty-five minutes, now."

Heris set off for the flitter hangars again, Cecelia in tow. They'd have to change there into whatever clothes Cecelia had packed earlier, or go in hunting attire and look like idiots. It shouldn't bother her, she told herself, after that purple uniform. She knew it wasn't really the clothes that made her feel incompetent. She had never been on a mission as an observer; she had always had a place, a duty. Now her duty was to keep out of the way, stay out of trouble, keep Cecelia out of trouble. It felt wrong.

"'I wish we could take the horses," Cecelia grumbled. Heris looked over at her. Cecelia was not used to being rushed; the bustle and scurry of the militia's preparation, the need to scramble out of her clothes and into others in the cramped restroom at the flitter hangars, had ruffled her composure, and she had reacted with a string of complaints. The personal armor Heris had insisted she wear under her jacket made her look, Cecelia had said, ridiculous.

Heris didn't agree; nothing looked as ridiculous as holes in one's body. She hadn't said that, since it hadn't been necessary. Heris's own armor felt odd, shaped differently than military issue, but she hoped it would be effective. She hoped even more that they wouldn't need it. The supply flitter's cargo compartment held food, weapons, tools, ammunition, clothes, medical supplies, and flexible plastic tanks of water. With them were four trained medics, two of them full-time militia. A saddle wouldn't have fit aboard, let alone a horse.

"Horses? To this island? What good would that do?"

"I've always said war wouldn't be as bad if I could ride into it." Cecelia twitched her shoulders. "Not that I could ride with this thing on—another advantage of riding."

"You'd be dead before the first stride," Heris said. She could feel her own breathing tighten. . . . It always did, until the action began, and here she had no way to work it off. The supply flitter, needing no pilot, stayed in position well behind the troop carriers. The medics talked softly among themselves, eyeing her as if checking her for stress levels. She made herself open her hands, let them rest lightly on her lap as if she were relaxed.

"It's on an island, with a forest," Cecelia said. "Horses are faster over the ground than people."

"Bigger target," Heris said. She didn't want to talk; she never wanted to talk ahead of time. She wanted to pace, to check over the plans she had not made, to see the faces that were not her people look at her the way her people had.

"You're nervous," Cecelia said more quietly. Heris glared at her.

"I am *not* nervous." It came out with more bite than she intended; Cecelia did not flinch, but nodded as if it confirmed her opinion. Heris stretched her hands and shrugged. "Not nervous, exactly . . . just unsettled. It's not the way I'm used to."

"Did it bother you when you had command?"

"Bother me? Yes, and no." She knew what Cecelia was doing, trying to keep her focussed intellectually, but she did not mind. It might help both of them. "I worried—one always does—about the plan. Was it good enough, had I missed something, would people die because of my stupidity? And that includes preparation—had I trained them well enough, often enough? Would they make stupid mistakes because I'd been too lenient? But beyond that, it didn't bother me. There's a . . . a sort of quiet place, between the commitment and the combat itself. In a way you probably felt it, from what you've said of starting a cross-country. Once you're on the course, once the horse is galloping, the time for worry is over. From then on you just deal with it, one fence at a time."

Cecelia nodded slowly. "I hadn't thought of it that way—

but that is what I said, and that's what I did. One fence at a time, but remembering all the ones ahead, too."

"Oh, yes." Heris sat still a moment, remembering. "You don't quit riding the course until it's over—the last fence, or the last opponent, can kill you if you're careless at the end. But the commitment is there. The difference here—I can't begin to explain it."

"I was surprised that you backed away from it," Cecelia said, even more quietly. "Bunny would have let you—"

Heris shook her head vigorously. "It wouldn't work. These aren't my people; they don't know me, and I don't know the local situation well enough. The person who doesn't fit in, who doesn't know the people or the terrain, is going to get someone killed. Other people killed. I'm old enough to let someone else do the job for which they're trained, and simply chew my nails until it's over."

"Umm." Cecelia looked out the canopy, and then back. "A point where riders differ from soldiers, I suppose. I've taken on someone else's mount if they were injured. If you're a good enough—"

"That's different. But I'll bet you didn't drag some first-timer off her horse just because you thought you could ride it better." Cecelia turned red. Heris looked at her. "You did?"

"I didn't think of it that way, but—" She shifted in her seat, and looked away. "Money and influence are another way of dragging someone off a horse—with the coach convinced Ivan would never do for that horse what I could, and the All-Union Challenge coming up in six months—"

Heris knew her expression had said what she thought before she could hide it. Cecelia, still red, did not try to excuse her younger self.

"I shouldn't have done it—and even at the time, I felt a bit guilty. It wasn't until much later that I realized how much even the best riders—even I—depended on finding an outstanding horse; I thought Ivan's failure to stay in the senior circuit after that reflected his ability. Justified the coach's decision, and my . . . influence."

"Was that your . . . your best horse?" Heris hoped not. She wanted to think better of Cecelia.

"No. It was a horse I thought might replace my best horse. A big piebald from Luminaire, that Ivan found on a farm, and bought literally out of harness. Ivan had done all his early work, but I thought—we all thought—the horse was such a natural anyone could have made an eventer out of him. What he needed was a better rider, we thought. After I got him, he slammed his stupid hoof into a stall partition while being shipped to the Challenge, and ripped his leg up. Never jumped sound again. I had another mount qualified, and you'll probably think it justice that she dumped me headfirst in the water—along with the minicam on my helmet."

Heris struggled not to laugh. "A cube they never made, eh?"

"Oh, they made it. You can buy my dive into the water along with a number of other embarrassing incidents, and since it was full-sim pickup, you can program your own simulator to take the same bounce and see if you can stay on. Sometimes I can." She sighed. "It was a stupid mistake— and to be honest, I've never quite forgiven myself for it. It was just the sort of thing I hated to see, and never meant to do. Yet I could never go back and apologize to Ivan— and a few years later, he was killed in a slideway accident, nothing to do with horses at all."

Ahead, Heris saw the lead carriers spread out. She knew— they had been kind enough to tell her—that they planned to land two on Bandon proper, to secure the island, and two on the island where the flitter had crashed. The supply flitter would land on Bandon behind the others. She could see the smudges of islands ahead, distorted by the curve of the canopy, but she couldn't recognize them. Cecelia prodded her side, and pointed. Sunlight glinted off something large and shiny on one of the islands.

"Shuttle on the field," said one of the medics. Their squad leader spoke into his com, then turned to glance at Heris.

"Shuttle's not primed for takeoff; there's nothing on the field with a hot signature. Captain's got the satellite data, and thinks there's fewer than a dozen people on Bandon proper, maybe less."

"Thanks." Heris managed that much before her throat closed. She didn't want to sit back here with Cecelia; she wanted to be up there—not even in this flitter, but the lead one. The flitter droned on; the medics, after a long glance out the canopy, went back to checking their gear, over and over. The squad leader stared ahead, not speaking. Ahead, the islands rose out of the sea, by ones and twos, their forest-clad flanks showing dark against glistening beaches and the glowing blue sea.

CHAPTER SIXTEEN

"We're in luck," Raffa murmured. Even that soft voice woke complex echoes from the water surface, the stone spaces in the cave. Bubbles inched backwards around the corner, fighting her terror of the blackness.

"Light," said Raffa. It flared too brightly in the dark goggles; Bubbles tore them away and stared. Raffa had found an old-fashioned candle lantern, and the striker to light it. Without the goggles, it lit the space around them only dimly, yet it felt so much better . . . that warm flame the color of afternoon sunlight. Bubbles tried to breathe slowly and calmly, and felt her body gradually relax. They were hidden . . . they had light . . . they were, after all, alive.

"D'you think it's safe?" she asked, hoping for reassurance.

"In daylight, certainly—they can't see a little light like this around the corner, not after being out in real daylight. At night—they'd still have to put their heads through that vine curtain, and maybe see sparkles on the water." Raffa put the lantern back on the stone shelf it had come from. Bubbles saw there the other evidence of Kell's occupation: his initials, carved into the stone above the ledge, a row of seashells and colored stones, a tangle of wire leaders, coils of fishing line and some fish hooks, and a pile of wooden blocks, all daubed with white painted numbers, and lengths of twine with lead weights attached.

"I wonder what that's all about," Bubbles said. "They look like bobbers, for fishing, but why so many? And why numbered?" Raffa meanwhile was exploring the space below.

244

"Look at this—a sleeping bag or something—soft, anyway. My aching bones will appreciate that."

"I wish I knew if the water was safe," Bubbles said. "We still have some, but—"

"We could look for dead fish." Raffa picked up the candle lantern again, and carried it to the water's edge. When she held it low, Bubbles could see how clear the water was, how pale and unappealing the bottom. Something almost colorless fled through the edge of the light. "Fish," said Raffa, as if she were sure. "My aunt's caves had some pools with fish like this. No color, shy of light."

"So it's probably not poisoned. If these fish are susceptible to the same poison."

Raffa laughed, softly. "So you *do* pay attention in class sometimes. Maris claimed she had to spoon-feed you all your answers to the exams."

Bubbles snorted. "Maris couldn't tell the truth if she were being interrogated under truth serum by the Imperium. I didn't mind learning things but you know how it is—"

Raffa nodded. "Never show how smart you are, dears, or someone will envy you. And then we're supposed to show how rich and prominent our families are, as if no one would envy *that*." In the faint glow of the lantern, Bubbles could not quite read the expression that Raffa turned to her. "D'you mind if I ask something?"

"No . . . while we're hiding in a cave from people who want to kill us, I think your questions are not going to be that threatening." Nonetheless, Bubbles felt a twinge of anxiety. Surely Raffa wouldn't ask about Cecely's infamous birthday party. . . . She didn't want any more lies between her and death.

"Why *do* you let them call you Bubbles?" The very unexpectedness of it made Bubbles laugh aloud; the cave's echoes laughed back, hollowly. She choked the laughter down.

"That—I'm sorry—that's a long story, well suited to this place, I guess. You have brothers and cousins, though—you'll understand." Raffa gave a soothing murmur that might have been anything. "The fashion for Old-Earth, North-European great names was at its height. . . . You know we're all stuck with things like Cicely and Marilys and Gwenivere—your Raffaele is actually pretty, but some of them—"

"My cousin Boethea Evangeline," said Raffa. "My brother Archibald Ferdinand."

"Right. Well, Mother had finally come over to fashion, after reasonably naming Gari and Tighe; Buttons got stuck with Bertram Harold Scaevola. I really think they made a mistake there: Scaevola doesn't sound British to me, but Mother said it was an important name in history somewhere. Then I came along. You promise you won't tell?"

"Tell whom? The hunters? Don't be ridiculous."

"All right. Brunnhilde Charlotte."

Raffa smothered an obvious bleat of laughter. "What!" Bubbles felt her face go hot.

"Brunnhilde Charlotte. You don't have to make a production out of it. Anyway," she hurried on, "Buttons is only two years older, and when they told him he had a baby sister named Brunnhilde, he could only say 'Buhbuh.' My mother thought it was cute. . . . She liked the idea of a little girl called Bubbles. Then I turned out blonde, and 'Champagne Bubbles' became the family form of Brunnhilde Charlotte. They all thought it was cute. . . . I was only a baby, Raffa. I didn't know what they were setting me up for."

"So you sort of lived out the Bubbles persona, hmmm? Like Dr. Fisher-Wong in psych class says happens."

That cut too near the bone. "Some children are naturally cheerful and . . . and . . ."

"Bubbly. I know. But you're not the fluffhead you act like sometimes." Raffa softened that with a grin. "And you haven't been acting like a pile of bubbles on this little jaunt."

"No. Well . . . to be honest . . . I've been getting tired of Bubbles myself. But look at the alternative. Brunnhilde? What kind of name is that?"

"Brunn isn't bad, as a short form. Wonder what it meant."

"For all I know, Brunnhilde is the Old Earth equivalent of bubblehead. But it sounds better and better the more people snicker at Bubbles. I should've changed years ago, but my cousin Kell—the one who had this cave—was just the sort to make nasty jokes. He gave me so much grief about Bubbles I pretended to like it, just to blunt the point."

"You could use Charlotte. Chara . . . that's not bad. Or Brun."

"Well." Bubbles shrugged. "That decision won't matter if

we don't survive, and we won't survive without water, so I think the next step is to check it out."

"With your portable chemistry kit, of course," said Raffa.

"With Kell's portable chemistry kit," Bubbles said sweetly. "The one on the shelf that you didn't recognize." But the little bottles and tubes were all empty, their contents no more than a few dried grains of unrecognizable grit. "With our brains," Bubbles said, when she discovered that. "We can think it out. It's safe for the cave fish; they're alive."

"Alive now."

"Yes. And that's all we can go on. They're swimming normally, not gasping or floating. And that means—"

"We still don't know. Look—whatever it was had to be pretty quick—not more than a day—because Petris told us they'd never bothered the water. That flyover could've dropped the poison, or set someone down to do it afoot. So if one of us drinks here . . . and nothing happens in a day . . . then this water is safe."

"I'll drink. It's my island." Bubbles scooped up a handful of water and sucked it quickly. It tasted of nothing but water. "I won't drink much," she went on, "just in case. Maybe if it's only a little, it'll put me to sleep or something."

"Or only make you throw up once. You *are* a gutsy wench, and you shouldn't be stuck with Bubbles one day longer. Take your pick: Brun or Chara."

Bubbles sat back on her heels. "I'm used to the B. . . . Let's try Brun. If I hate it tomorrow, no one ever needs to know." If she died of poison no one ever would know. . . . She shoved that thought away.

"Good for you, Brun. Now . . . how can we do the hunters the most harm?"

Ronnie could not tell whether the pounding in his head was from the concussion or excitement. The too-regular uneven footsteps came nearer, and he could just hear George trying to breathe quietly. Then the footsteps turned back toward the little creek; he heard a rock turn, and splash noisily, and a muffled curse. One of the red-and-yellow amphibians gave a tiny bark, and several more answered. George's breath came hot and wet against his ear.

"I *told* you," George murmured. "We should've put our trap on the creek itself."

He wanted to say "Shut up" but the person at the creek might hear. Instead, he touched George's wrist, a sharp tap. He could hear the walker, moving upstream, occasionally tipping a rock, and then the squelch of wet boots on mud.

"Let's follow," George said, tickling his ear again. "Maybe we can take him."

Maybe we can get killed very easily, Ronnie thought. If the hunter had night goggles, if he had a fully equipped night-hunting rifle, they would be easy prey. "Wait," he breathed, as quietly as he could. "The spring's not that far away. . . . He may come back and spring the trap."

Another splash, some ways upstream, and the sound of something large moving through brittle brush. "He ought to be more careful," George said.

"We too," Ronnie said pointedly. George subsided, though his sigh was louder than Ronnie approved. After an interminable period, they heard sounds returning. The same hunter? Another whose planned route had crossed his? One of Petris's men? Ronnie didn't know. His neck prickled; he felt that someone was looking at him, that he was outlined by a spotlight. He blinked, hard. . . . No spotlight, nothing but darkness. Whoever it was coming downslope stayed in the water, for the most part. . . . They could hear the rocks grinding and turning under his boots, and occasional splashes. He moved faster, as most people do going downhill, and as if he could see his way.

He passed their position, still moving downstream, and did not turn aside along his former path. Apparently he was going to follow the stream all the way down.

"This is stupid," George said in Ronnie's ear, all hissing *s*'s. "If we stay here . . ."

Ronnie's control broke; he grabbed George's mouth and dug his fingernails into his lips. "The idea is to stay alive," he muttered. "Be quiet." He let go as quickly as he'd grabbed, and they spent the remaining hours of darkness in icy silence, both furious. An occasional shot rang out at a distance; they heard no cries, nor anything that let them know what was happening.

In the first faint light of dawn, when Ronnie realized he could see his hand in front of his face again, the peaceful gurgle of the creek off to their left seemed to mock their fears. Not even the amphibians were making their usual racket . . . no sound but the faint sigh of a breeze in the leaves far overhead, and the water in the creek, and the sound of waves below, borne on the wind. He had heard no shots for a long time. His head ached dully, an ache he was almost used to now. His eyes burned. He felt stiff, dirty, sore . . . but alive. He looked at George, who had fallen asleep leaning against a tree. Perhaps he should let George sleep a little longer? But as he thought it, George produced a faint noise that ripened into a snore, and woke up, almost falling.

"We survived," Ronnie said, trying for cheerfulness. The sound of his own voice woke painful echoes in his head.

"Survived!" George rubbed his eyes, looking disgusted but still dapper. When he brushed at a smudge on his sleeve, it actually vanished. "We should have gone after that fellow. . . . We haven't done anything useful yet." He gave their trap an angry glance. Even in that early light, the leaves they had cut to conceal it drooped and no longer matched the greenery around them. Ronnie hadn't realized that they'd wilt in only twelve hours or so.

"It was a stupid idea, just the sort of thing you might expect from someone like Petris."

"All he said was stay up in this area, and perhaps we could trap someone. You're the one who had the idea for the trap itself."

George glared, but silently. Ronnie wondered if they should take the now obvious trap apart, or leave it. Moment by moment the light increased, and the trap's outline became clearer. It would take, he thought, a very stupid hunter to step into it now.

George stretched. "We'll have to clear that mess up," he said. "It certainly won't fool anyone."

"I suppose not." Ronnie wanted to lie down and sleep, preferably for two days straight, and wake up in a clean, comfortable bed. He did not look forward to undoing the trap, particularly when he couldn't remember exactly how the lines ran on this side. "Although . . . suppose we left it, and they saw it and sniggered, and then we had another trap they didn't see?"

"Like what?" George asked. It was a reasonable question for which Ronnie had no answer. "Dig a pit trap with our fingernails and disguise it with more wilting greenery?" Ronnie resented the inherited knack for clever phrasing.

"Perhaps a snare sort of thing—you know, where a rock drops on them." Somewhere, in some class, Ronnie remembered seeing something . . . a leaning stick or limb, with something heavy balanced above, and when someone went through—

"A rock . . . and where are we supposed to find more rope and a rock?" Evidently George didn't have the same illustration in mind. Ronnie didn't think his had rope in it.

"I've . . . got to sit down," he said, as his head and stomach renewed yesterday's quarrel. George, after all, had slept standing up. George grabbed his arm as he went down, more a fall than a controlled descent.

"You look awful," he said. Ronnie felt slightly less sick, lying on his back, but his head pounded just the same. George's thumb appeared in front of his face. "Focus on this—can you?" He could, but he didn't really want to let George assess his eyes' ability to focus—George wasn't even a medic, let alone a doctor. He let his eyes close. "I'll get water," George said, and Ronnie heard his footsteps heading toward the creek.

Silence. Aside from the untalented drummer in his head, lovely dark silence lay around him. No buzzing insects, no barking amphibians—he remembered how startled he'd been to find how loud a sound those tiny wet bodies could make. The sea sounds lay at the threshold of hearing, below the headache's contribution most of the time. He wiggled his shoulders in the soft leaves, hoping no biting insects would get him, and felt his stiff muscles relax.

He did not know he was falling asleep until he woke; the sun had speared through a break in the forest canopy, directly into his eyelid. He squinted, twisted, and bit back a groan. He still hurt, though not as badly. He had slept some hours—too many hours; it must be near midday. George should not have let him sleep so long. He forced himself up on one arm and looked around. He couldn't see George.

Silence lay on the forest, heavy and dangerous. It wouldn't be that still if nothing was wrong. Slowly, carefully, Ronnie sat up, then levered himself to one knee, then to his feet. Nothing stirred. No birds, no insects—nothing. His own breath sounded loud to him. His mouth tasted foul, and his lips were dry. Where was George?

He had gone for water. Ronnie remembered that much, and after a short panic remembered which way the stream was. He glanced at the trap—the leaves covering it were now a sickly brown—and eased his way toward the creek, as quietly as possible.

It lay in a steep-sided bed, just here; he could see the glint of water trickling down from a pool above before he could see it right below him. Then he saw George. George sprawled gracelessly, as if he'd simply slumped to the ground while climbing back toward Ronnie. Ronnie looked around for the enemy he assumed had shot him . . . but saw and heard nothing. When he looked again, he saw no blood, no burn mark, no injury at all.

Ronnie sank to his heels and tried to think this out. George down, without a cry, but—he could now see his back move—breathing. Had he just fallen asleep? And why there? He glanced at the creek, and frowned. From here, he could see something floating, a bit of scum or something. He stood, and moved closer to George. George was definitely breathing, and from the new angle he could see that his eyes were closed.

"George," Ronnie said softly. Nothing happened. He reached out and touched George's shoulder. No response. He glanced around again, sure someone was watching, but saw and heard nothing at all. George's slack hand lay atop the water bottle he'd carried to the creek; its cap had come off in the fall, and it held only a scant swallow or two. Ronnie poured it on George's face, hoping to wake him, but aside from a grimace, George did not rouse. Perhaps more would work. With another look around, Ronnie took the bottle to the creek to refill it.

The scum he had seen lay in drifts against the rock. At first he didn't recognize it . . . but when he swished it away to put the bottle in, there were the limp legs and tails of the red and gold amphibians, the motionless fins of tiny fish. Dead . . . beginning to stink. . . . He stared at them, his hand frozen in place, not quite touching the water, the bottle half immersed. Then he moved his arm back, and let the bottle drip on the ground. Thoughts whirled through his mind in odd fragments. The man they'd heard last night. The silence—nothing croaking or barking after he came back downstream. George asleep. The dead things. The water he hadn't touched. . . . He hoped the dizziness he felt suddenly came from his concussion, or even from fear, and not from the touch of that contaminated water.

That unseen hunter had somehow poisoned the water . . . killed everything in it . . . and whatever it was put George to sleep. Or was he dying? Ronnie staggered back to George and felt the pulse at his neck. It beat slowly, but regularly, against his sweaty fingers. He shook George's shoulder. Again no response. A frantic look upstream and down . . . tree trunks, vines, bushes, rocks. No moving figures, no sounds that shouldn't be there.

But if the poison was supposed to put anyone who drank the water to sleep, that meant someone might come to collect them. He couldn't leave George so near the water, out in the open. He grabbed George firmly under the arms and heaved. His headache escalated from dull throbbing to loud rhythmic pounding, and his stiff ribs felt as if someone had dragged sharp knives across them. George, meanwhile, had moved hardly a centimeter, but he did begin to snore, a loud unmistakable snore that Ronnie was sure could be heard a long way.

"A . . . whatchamacallit," Ronnie muttered to himself. "Something to drag him on . . ." He looked around. An older cousin had gone through a period of enthusiastic camping, but Ronnie spent that long vacation at a music school, honing what his mother fondly believed to be superlative talent. After hearing his cousin's stories, most of them involving borderline criminal assaults on the younger campers, he milked the talent he himself knew to be minor, and managed another session of music school. By then, his older cousin had moved on to other amusements, and Ronnie had escaped even one six-week session at his brother's camp. Right now, he would have accepted a few buffets, tosses into ice-cold ponds, burr-pricked mounts, or stinging crawlers in bunks, for some of the practical knowledge Knut had claimed. Ways to drag heavy loads when you didn't have lifters or flitters, ways to make traps that actually worked.

His first version of the travois bound with vines cost Ronnie three blisters, an itchy rash from the vine sap, and most of the hours of afternoon. When he finally rolled George onto the vines and lifted the handles, George's limp body worked quickly through the vines to the ground before

Ronnie had, with great difficulty, pulled it ten meters. Cursing softly, Ronnie untangled George and tried to weave the vines into a more stable configuration. That was when he noticed the itching rash. He had never woven so much as a potholder; he knew in theory how weaving worked, but nothing about fishnets or hammocks or anything else that would hold a sixty kilo body safely between two poles as someone dragged them along.

He did not let himself notice hunger or thirst, but the darkness creeping out from under the trees finally blurred his vision before he had anything that would support George. He had tried dragging three times, and all he had to show for it were the obvious scars in the forest soil.

And now it was almost too dark to see. . . . His hands were itching, burning, shaking; when he tried to stand, cramps seized his legs and arms; he staggered. Now he was thirsty; his mouth burned. He took several steps toward the creek before he remembered.

Don't panic, he told himself. Think. But he could not remember when he had thought last . . . days ago, it seemed. For a moment it was hard to think where he was, or why. . . . Then it came clear. They had had supplies, of course they had. Back where the trap was. He could get water there, and food. He started back, in the near dark, hoping he could recognize which dark blur was the right tree.

The worst thing about being in a cave, Bubbles thought, was how you could lose track of time. They had drunk some of that cool, clean water, eaten a little food, and then, while trying to figure out all the things Kell left, day had turned to night. Even with night goggles on, she could see nothing. If they left the candle burning, anyone who looked in the entrance might see it sparkle on the water . . . and she didn't want to go outside and make sure no gleam showed through the leaves.

Sleep came to them slowly, with many starts and twitches, but they were both still tired from the night before, and finally slept. I'm not Bubbles any more, was her last conscious thought. I'm grown up now—I'm someone else, named Brun.

What woke them was the sound of rock falling someplace. In the echoing darkness, they could not tell how far off it fell, only that it was inside and not outside. Bubbles had slept with the goggles on, and when she woke could just make out a paler smudge beyond the rock buttress. Raffa's hand reaching for hers almost made her squeak, but she managed to stay silent. She squeezed Raffa's hand and then put it aside. She would have to crawl to the edge of the buttress, and look around, to see how near daylight it was.

The pool of water tinkled pleasantly, as if it were being rained on, and when she got to the corner of the buttress, she could see light seeping in from the entrance. Not as bright as the day before (if it was the day before—had they slept the clock around?) but enough to show that no one was in the visible part of the cave. If someone had caused the rockfall, they were now out of sight. She started to creep around the buttress, and realized suddenly that her knees were wet—the pool was rising. Yesterday there'd been at least two meters between the buttress and the pool, and a meter between the pool and the entrance. Now the gleam of light reflecting from water extended to the entrance . . . perhaps even outside. She backed up until her feet bumped into Raffa.

"I think it's raining," Bubbles said softly. The cave felt slightly less resonant, or perhaps the tinkle and chime of dripping water, and its echoes, covered her voice. "The pool's up."

"Can we get out?" Raffa asked.

"For now, yes. . . . It's probably not more than a couple of centimeters at the entrance. And I doubt it goes much higher for long—that's never a large creek out there."

"The creekbed—yes." Raffa sounded pleased. "If it actually flows, it'll take care of our tracks coming in."

"What about our tracks going out? And with water coming out there, it'll be obvious something's inside."

"Maybe we won't have to go out. . . . Let's look." Raffa lighted the candle-lantern again, and they peered at the water, then the cave walls. A pale streak topped by a dark one ran along the wall perhaps knee-high. Farther up, a blurrier mark showed.

"That's common—probably a seasonal flood. And the other is older, and rare. Didn't you say there were seasonal rains?"

"Yes—and this is supposed to be the dry season."

"Well, then: I'll bet it won't get that high." Raffa pointed to the lower mark. Bubbles thought she sounded entirely too cheerful.

"That's our lives you're betting," Bubbles said.

"That sounds like Bubbles and not Brun. It's our lives either way—if we go out now, they'll have nice muddy footsteps to show where we were. How long do the off-season rainstorms last?"

"Only a few hours, usually, but they can drop a lot of rain when they hit." Bubbles sighed. "I'm not used to being Brun, you know. It's going to take some getting used to. You're right—it's not likely to come up even as high as the wet-season floodmark. And even if it does, we can climb—there are ledges. . . ." They looked big and high enough. In the meantime. "We can use Kell's floaters and weights to mark the pool's edge and see how fast it's rising." She took down the pile of floats, and poked the weight tied to one at the edge of the water. Luckily they had a supply of candles for the lantern, and need not sit in the faint light that came from around the buttress.

Several hours passed with only the musical tinkling of water falling into the large pool. A bar of concentrate eased the hunger pangs, but Bubbles would have been very glad of a hot breakfast. The cave's damp coolness no longer seemed a comfortable refuge from the heat outside. Slowly, in tiny lapping ripples, the water rose. Each hour, Bubbles put another weight at the edge of the water. The first one now lay two centimeters under; the last, as the third hour came to an end, was hardly covered by a skim of water.

"Made it," Raffa said, giving Bubbles an affectionate shove. Then they both heard the voices. Raffa reached out and snuffed the candle in the lantern; darkness closed around them. They dared not move, lest they trip on something and make a noise. Bubbles slipped the dark goggles back on, to find her vision just as black.

Then a ray of light flared across. . . . Someone had flashed a light inside. A man's voice, magnified and distorted by the cave's echoes, boomed from the entrance. "Nothing. There's water right up to the entrance; if anyone had come inside, we'd see the marks."

Another voice. "—got here before the rain?"

"Not likely. Nothing—no sounds, no movement—nothing on IR scan." Bubbles blessed the thick rock that lay between

them and the entrance, and the cold cave water that had
covered any mark they'd left. She had thought of the hunters having dark goggles; she'd forgotten the special equipment on the rifles.

"—those weapons?"

"Nah. They'll be basic by now—they don't have any way
to revalidate them. C'mon." The light vanished, and the
voices faded. Bubbles realized she was shaking, and tried
to take deep slow breaths. What had they meant, the
weapons would be "basic" by now? She reached out and
found Raffa's shoulder; Raffa grabbed her back and they
hugged, both of them still trembling. For an unmeasured
time they clung together, until they were both breathing
normally.

"We were stupid," Raffa murmured in Bubbles's ear. "We
didn't even have our weapons within reach."

"It's so hard to believe," Bubbles said. "I keep remembering the old camping trips: we played at chase and
smuggling and capture . . . but it was just play, though we
took it seriously then. Now—it's real, but it's hard to keep
remembering that."

"I'm going to check that rifle." Raffa stood up and reached
for it. "It can't have a locator, or they'd have known it.
Must have been something else." Bubbles heard soft noises,
Raffa handling the weapon, and then a grunt. "Ah. I see.
That socket in the side must be for a computer link—
probably an ID chip. That's what they meant by validation.
None of the good stuff works now—the range finder, IR
scope, all that—but it'll still fire."

"Which means?"

"It can't see in the dark. We have to be better. But if
we avoid them completely, we won't need them anyway."

Bubbles had forgotten the earlier alarm, the sound of
falling rocks, but when it came again, an echoing clatter
and roar, she remembered. *Something* was in the cave with
them. Her mind pictured all the large predators on the planet,
even though she knew none were on the island.

"What was that?" asked Raffa. Her voice sounded shaky
and breathless.

"Rocks," Bubbles said. "I guess." She lifted the rifle,
although she had no target at all. "Maybe the water loosened something, and it just fell."

 *   *   *

Ronnie had found the meager cache of food and water, and a couple of swallows restored some of his wits. He couldn't move George alone. Even if he got the vines woven the right way, dragging the travois alone would leave obvious tracks. He would have to find Petris and the others, even though that had been against his orders. He sucked at a ration bar, letting the surface coating of salt and sugar revive him, then took another swig from the safe bottle. He shouldn't eat much, he remembered, if he was short of water.

A gust of wind stirred the trees overhead, and its warm moist hand brushed his face. If only it weren't dark—if only his head didn't hurt—if only he had someone to help him . . . but reality settled on his shoulders like a cloak of misery. Dark, hurt, alone; either he figured it out, or no one would.

He made his way back to George's unconscious body in the dark, tripping more than once on unseen roots and stones. How long would the drug or poison keep George unconscious? He wished he knew more about drugs. He tried to redo the vines, in the dark, by feel, but his heart wasn't in it. A drop of cold water flicked his hot neck, and he jumped. Then another. Now he could hear the spatter of rain, as well as the rush of wind gusts in the trees.

If it rains, he thought, *if I can pull George along, the rain will wash out our tracks.* He didn't let himself think how much harder it would be to pull the travois through mud. Instead he yanked at the poles, straining, staggering uphill, away from the creek. Suddenly it was easy; he lurched forward, almost jogging, then realized that must mean George had fallen off, or through, the vine webbing. He was almost sobbing as he turned back. It was too much, the pain in his head, the rain, the danger, the uncooperative vines.

He had just found George's body when he saw the lights in the sky. A flitter, its searchlight directed into the forest. . . . He threw himself back, away from George. They had IR sensors, of course, and night-vision goggles. They could see George. They could see him. He crouched, shaking from fear and exertion both, dithering. Above the wind and thickening rain, he could just hear the flitter's drone. Its searchlight flicked among the trees, probing, but the canopy was thick here near the stream, and the light never touched him. It did flick across George, and that garish beltpack he'd refused to bury . . . and it came back, and centered there. Ronnie bit back the groan he wanted to utter. Why hadn't he taken the thing off? He'd known it was stupid . . . too late now.

The flitter sank into the canopy, its searchlight illuminating slanting lines of rain above, and drips below. He heard the squeal and clunk of a hatch opening. They would have a ladder or line, he realized, for dropping hunters directly into the forest. If he stayed here . . .

He took a deep breath and plunged away, into darkness. Upslope, upstream, into the thicker forest and more broken country. If he could get rock between him and the IR scans, they couldn't see him. He picked his way from tree to tree in the dim radiance of the flitter's light. It would do no good to hurry; he must not fall and make a noise. He had a few seconds perhaps, as someone came down the line from the flitter, someone who surely must be concentrating on a safe descent rather than a possible fugitive.

He heard the metallic clatter of someone landing, a weapon (he was sure) rattling against something else, the cable or a ladder. Light brightened behind him; he dared a peek and saw a lightsource at head level. A helmet light, feebler than the flitter's searchlight, but perfectly adequate for close work. It lowered, as if its bearer crouched. Over George, Ronnie was sure; he struggled against the desire to go back and protect his friend. He heard the peculiar squawk of a badly tuned comunit, then another clatter as if someone else had come down. Now two helmet lights glowed back there. The flitter's engine whined—retracting its cable?—and then moved off, to the east. He heard voices, muted by wind and rain.

He had to leave. He had to go now, while they did whatever they were doing to George, because they must not catch all four of them. That was the only chance. But he had never imagined that he might have to leave a friend behind. He made himself move, one slow step after another, away from the lights. *I'm sorry*, he let himself say to George in his mind. *I'm sorry.*

He had covered perhaps fifty meters when he heard the shout behind him. Reflex threw him forward, into a wild panicky run. The shout came again, then a shot smacked into a nearby rock. Ronnie fell over another rock, banging both shins, and scrambled up. Too late for silence, for subtlety; only speed would help him now. Lightning flashed overhead, blinding him momentarily. He tried to move faster through his memory of what it revealed and fell again. He was in the creek, now only a meter wide; rain lashed at him as he climbed, stumbled, climbed again. Another shot rang out, but he never heard it hit anything. Surely, the one rational corner of his mind thought, surely the lightning will blind those in night goggles even worse. . . .

Ronnie struggled on, uphill, ignoring everything but the need to get away. His feet slipped on wet rocks, in mud; rain beat in his face, plastering his hair down, dragging at his shirt and trousers. Flash after flash of lightning revealed a grotesque landscape of wind-whipped foliage, ragged rocks, wind-tossed rain. He followed the creek, no longer worried about the poison in its water, until he reached its source. Behind him, he could see flickering lights . . . the hunters, following what must be an obvious trail. He licked his lips, grateful for the pure rainwater that drenched him. Where now?

The next flash of lightning showed him a narrow black cleft, above and to his right. He clambered over the wet rocks, hoping it was deep enough to hide in, hoping it wasn't just a trick of lightning. Thunder shook the ground, trembled in his breath. Behind him, a shout and a stab of light; his shoulder burned. He plunged to the ground, behind a rock, and tried to see where the cleft had been. Lightning again; there, only a jump and stretch. It still looked deep, a black gash in the rocky slope. Rain poured down, even harder now. He forced himself to stand, to take those few steps, to reach up and haul himself into darker darkness.

When the next lightning came, he saw it as a blue-white flash against dark walls. Limping, staggering, he tried to work his way further in. Water trickled along between his feet, getting deeper; pebbles rolled and he lurched against the rocks, biting his tongue at the pain in his shoulder. Then the ground fell out from under his feet, and he slid down a crumbling slope into black oblivion.

CHAPTER SEVENTEEN

George awoke with a stiff neck and aching head. It was dark. Night, he thought. He tried to stretch, and discovered that his wrists were bound behind his back. This, he thought, will never do. He blinked several times, and drew in a breath that stank of cleaning solution, old wood, and sour water. When he let the breath out in a gusty sigh, the sound seemed small and confined, as if he were in a closet. He felt around with his legs, glad to find that his captors had not tied his ankles. He could sit up, though he felt dizzy.

The mind his father always doubted he had began to work. He couldn't remember how he'd gotten into this, but his friends never pulled tricks this unpleasant. He forced his mind back to the last clear memory, then tried to go forward. The flight to the island—the crash—Ronnie pale and sick—the ragged islanders who claimed to be the victims of a manhunt. He and Ronnie, building a trap of leaves and branches—a sound in the night—dawn—then nothing.

He had not liked capture the first time, with Petris and Oblo; this time, when he was sure it was their enemies, he liked it less. He had been captured somehow—that he could not yet remember—and he was confined in something that sounded and smelled like a closet for cleaning supplies. The others must still be free—or some of them—or he would be dead.

He brushed that thought aside. He, George Starbridge Mahoney, was not going to die. That would not happen; sordid deaths happened to others, not to young men of good family whose trousers never lost their crease. He was going to escape, and warn Lord Thornbuckle, and then go rescue Ronnie and the others. And the first thing to do was find out more about his prison.

With difficulty, he levered himself up to his feet. It was remarkably hard to find his balance in the dark. He backed up slowly, until his hands bumped a wall. His fingers recognized wood, then something papery, then more wood. He edged along, feeling for a corner, and bumped into a shelf that caught him painfully above the elbows. Something rattled on the shelf, and he felt a small bump against his back as whatever it was fell over and rolled.

It occurred to him then that he should not let that object fall off the shelf. It would make noise, and noise might bring his captors, and his captors might think he knew where the others were hiding. His captors might even be unpleasant. He had not enjoyed the classes on interrogation resistance which even the Royals found necessary; he wanted nothing to do with the real thing.

He leaned a little on the shelf, trying to encourage the small item to roll backwards, and the entire shelf fell off its supports. Hard, sharp-edged cans banged against his arms, the backs of his legs, and clattered on the floor; something breakable smashed. Stinging fumes rose, and he choked, then coughed helplessly. His eyes burned, tears rolled down his face; he staggered away from the shelf, tripping over unseen rolling hazards on the floor, and hit his shin on a bucket with a loud clang. He gave a most ungentlemanly curse.

Light stabbed his eyes, and the door opened. He lunged toward it, but the shadowy figures there shoved him back so hard that he could not keep his feet. He fell against the bucket—it hurt just as much on the backs of his legs—and sat down hard in a puddle of whatever it was with the strong smell. He could feel it oozing through his expensive Guilsanme trousers.

"Shut up!" said one of the shadows, before he knew his mouth was open. "Or get another dose."

Another dose. That meant he'd been drugged or poisoned—he had a tiny, shrinking vision of a creek, of a full waterflask coming to his lips. With that memory came thirst, worse even than his headache.

"I'm thirsty," he said, surprised by the rough weakness of his voice.

Someone laughed, unpleasantly. It reminded George of the senior bully, the year he'd started school. "Too bad," someone said; the voice sounded as if it belonged to the laugh. "But not for long."

"No, wait . . . if they autopsy, they'll look for dehydration." The other voice had an undertone of anxiety.

"So?" George tried to squint past the lights aimed at him, but still could not see either figure—or if there were more than two. "Seawater might do that—"

"Nah. The old man said take care of 'em until we got the whole bunch—"

"He didn't say tell 'em the whole plan!" The door slammed; George could hear raised voices, but not the words. He glanced around the closet. In the light of its single fixture, it was as cramped and unpleasant as his experience in the dark suggested. It was about two by three meters, with the door on the middle of one long side, and shelves on either side of the door. Above the shelf he'd broken, two more supported a collection of brushes, cans, and jugs; on the other side of the door, the shelves held bathroom supplies in neatly labelled boxes. Behind him mops and brooms hung from a rack; he had been lucky not to dislodge any of them when he fell over the mop bucket.

It had to be a large house or building, probably on the neighboring island. Bandon, its name was. Bandon where the landing field had signalled that they were unwelcome. Where the hunters, according to Petris, were living in comfort in the lodge, while the victims struggled to survive on the island.

George shook his head at the state of his trousers, which the bright light revealed to have suffered from the island even before the noxious green liquid that still filled his nose with stinging vapor. Never in his life had he been this disheveled. . . . He noticed a rip in one sleeve, and a long greasy stain, as if he'd been thrown in a dirty cargo compartment for the trip here. He probably had. And without the use of his hands, he could not even tidy himself up.

But he could get out of the puddle of smelly green stuff, which he was sure would do his trousers more harm than simple grime. For all he knew it would eat its way through his skin, as well. He braced his back against the wall of mops, and stood. There. He could just grasp the handle of a mop. . . . There ought to be some way of using it as a weapon the next time those persons opened the door. But he couldn't think of one, and the door opened again.

"You weren't supposed to get up," said the voice he associated with the nasty laugh. With the two spotlights trained on his face, he still could see nothing of the men holding them.

"I couldn't breathe," George said. "That stuff chokes me."

He had been right; it was the same laugh. "I wouldn't worry about that," the voice said. "But you said you were thirsty—come on, then."

Was it safe to go out? It wasn't safe to stay here, he knew that much. He tried to step forward with assurance, as if he weren't even worried, but the green liquid was slippery as oil. He staggered, and fell into the door frame. Ungentle hands caught him under the armpits. "What a comedy act you are, aren't you?" He had no time to catch his breath before it was slammed out of him at the end of a hard fist, and he fell back against a wall. Thick cloth muffled his head, blinding him, and he felt hands—large, strong, and gloved, he thought—yank him along.

He tried to judge from the sounds—the scrape of shod feet, the sound of breathing—what sort of space they were in, how far they'd come. A corridor, he thought, but he could not judge distance, not with the hard hands shoving him this way and that, breaking his concentration with slams against the wall or yanks on his bound arms.

Finally he heard a door open—a swing door, he thought— and a final shove sent him forward through it just as the cloth was pulled away from his face. He staggered, and fell onto a hard, cold floor in the dark, and heard the snick of a lock on the door behind him.

For a time he lay there, nursing his new bruises, and wondering what to do now. But thirst drove him to explore. This smelled different, cleaner, colder. Like a bathroom, he decided. He got to his knees, and considered shuffling around like that, but the hard floor hurt his knees after only a few awkward moves, and he realized he would have to stand up. Again.

This exploration, however, ended in success. He found the

door through which he'd been shoved, and beside it the predictable panel of switches to control light and ventilation. Cool white light showed him a bathroom—certainly a staff facility, for it had none of the amenities the family rooms would have had. A row of sinks set into a counter, with mirrors above—he winced away from his image—and a row of plumbing fixtures. The stack of clean glasses on the counter mocked him. How was he supposed to turn the water on? Or get it in the glass?

That struggle occupied him some time. The sinks had watersaving faucets, so that they would not run long without a finger on the control—and the control was mounted at a convenient height for someone with free hands. George had to hitch himself up onto a sink, almost sitting in it, to reach the control. . . . He was sure the entire counter-and-sinks arrangement was going to fall off the wall and cause a flood. He could turn the water on, but he could not drink, not while facing away from the sink. And the sinks had no plugs, so he could not fill one and drink from it. Finally he realized that he would have to take a glass from the stack and position it in a sink—all out of his sight—and then climb up to start the water and hope the glass was in the right position. Then take the glass out of the sink and set it on the counter, close enough to the edge that he could tip it with his mouth, and finally drink.

It took a very long time; he broke two glasses, cut his fingers, and almost decided that thirst was better than this struggle. But his stubbornness forced him on. And the luke-warm water, the half glass of it he managed to drink before the glass tipped over and spilled the rest down his chin and neck, tasted amazingly good. He could almost feel his brain cells soaking it up and going back to work. Now he would think of what to do; now he would get back to his own script for this miserable outing, and come out as he always did: clean, pressed, and in control.

It was not so bad, being locked in a bathroom. Basic bodily functions accounted for . . . he stopped, halfway to the fixture he had planned to use, and realized another problem. How was he supposed to open his trousers with his hands tied behind him? It wouldn't do any good to yank on the waistband from behind, not with these; they were designed to withstand incredible force.

He would think about it later; it was not that big a problem. Yet. On the other hand, he would make do with that one half glass of water, and not waste energy trying to get another.

"You really should consider the legal aspect," George said. His stomach growled; the food the two men were stuffing into their mouths with such indecent haste smelled delicious. He had been given no food, though it was promised for "just before you go swimming." He had, instead, been given the novel experience of cleaning all the plumbing fixtures in the building with a toothbrush held in his teeth. He had not been willing, but the two men had not offered him any alternatives. His bruises throbbed, and his shoulders ached abominably from the strain of his bound arms.

"Like what?" asked the slender one. "You think this will come up in court or something?" He was the bully, George had discovered, when after some hours of jeering and shoving, they had finally helped him lower his trousers to use the toilet; the stocky one who looked meaner, with that scar across his chin, was only rough, not cruel. In the hours since, the slender man had taken every opportunity to cause pain in ways that would not show on an autopsy.

"Probably," said George. It was most inconvenient, having one's hands tied. He had not realized how dependent he was on gesture, a habit learned from his father. "My father gets most things to court, and he will certainly sue someone when I'm dead." He was proud of himself; he said that without a quaver.

The men laughed, and looked at each other. "Poor Lord Thornbuckle," the slender one said. "I'm sure he'll be worried."

George stared into space above them, the closest he could come to the pose he usually achieved at these moments. "Oh—I expect my father will represent him, too. A class action suit, I imagine. Damages, negligence—"

"Nonsense," the slender man said, and took a bite of toast. Through it, he said, "And don't think you can scare us with your father. I've known better lawyers than your father, in my life."

George managed a casual chuckle. "I doubt that. You don't even know who my father is."

"He's not in the same class with . . . oh . . . Kevil Starbridge Mahoney. Now is he?"

George laughed aloud, this time with genuine pleasure. "My dear lads, he *is* Kevil Starbridge Mahoney, and if you know him, you know how surely he will pursue anyone who harms his family. I'm George Starbridge Mahoney."

A pause, during which the slender man chewed steadily, and the stocky one cast nervous glances from George to his companion. Finally the slender man swallowed, and pushed himself away from the table. George felt his heart begin to pound. "I don't believe you," the slender man said. "And I don't like liars." He spoke quietly, but with a studied viciousness that promised pain. George hoped his face didn't show how frightened he was, a sudden burst of fear that made him glad he was in the chair, and not trying to stand up.

"Now wait," the stocky man said. "We aren't supposed to mark 'em up, remember?"

"I won't." The slender man smiled at George. "Now . . . what did you say your name was?"

"George Starbridge Mahoney," George said. He was going to be hurt anyway, just as the bully at school had twisted ears or arms no matter what you said, but one might as well tell the truth. And if they concentrated on asking him about himself and his past, perhaps they wouldn't ask where the others might be hiding on the island. He braced himself for whatever the slender man might do, but he did nothing. Then he slipped a hand into a pocket, and came out with a glove.

"You're sure of that," the man said, putting the glove on, and tapping its fingers on George's head, just hard enough to sting and demonstrate that the fingers were tipped with something hard. "Then I suppose you know all about Viilgas versus Robertson Colony."

"It's against ethics to talk about cases outside professional venues," George quoted. A gloved finger probed behind his ear, and he squirmed away. "But . . . sometimes at home, of course, it did happen." The whole case was over, appeals and all, long ago; what harm could it do to admit that? And, now that he thought about it, there'd been a threat against the family; his father had insisted that none of them go out without an escort. "I remember the threat," he said, as the finger jabbed behind his other ear. "But I was only eight."

"Ah. Which would make you now . . . ?"

"Twenty-three." Had it really been fifteen years? He would never forget the bomb in the vegetable shipment that had destroyed the old kitchen and scared the cook so that she went into early retirement. Of course she hadn't been in danger; none of the servants were even in the house for the duration of the threat. His father had insisted on that.

"And was the threat ever carried out?" The finger prodded beneath his chin, only slightly painful so far.

"A bomb in the vegetables," George said. "It blew all the tiles off the wall." It occurred to him that this man might have been involved, for all that he didn't look old enough. How old did you have to be to send bombs through the food system? Perhaps he'd started young. Perhaps he wanted revenge. . . .

"And what was the outcome—the real outcome?"

That, too, he would not forget, because he had been just old enough to recognize the discrepancy between the public news and what his father said to a colleague in the study. "How did you know about the real outcome?" he asked, and was rewarded by a sharp jab in the neck. It hurt more than he'd have expected.

"Answer the question," the slender man said.

"The Robertson Colony paid an indemnity," George said sulkily. "Enough to keep them working hard for the next fifty years, my father said, with no offplanet travel until it was paid. Slocumb and DeVries got mindwiped. Viilgas died, but they hushed it up, so his heirs could get the profits."

"Mmm. You do know more about it than the average young sprout. Tell me this, then: when your father, assuming he is your father, approaches the bench, what does he do with his hands?"

George's arms strained, trying to reproduce the familiar gesture; he could not say it without doing it. And was it the left hand or the right—? Finally he got it out. "His left hand's in his vest pocket, as if he felt a pain, and his right hand is holding down the tail of the frill."

The slender man turned away a moment, to look at his companion, then turned back to George. "So . . . if you're Mahoney's son, why should we care?"

"You said already—you know what he's like. He'll see money somewhere, and go after it."

"I'm not rich," the man said, and went back to the table. He served himself another plateful of eggs and sausage, and George's stomach growled again. "Why should I worry? He'll go after the deep pockets."

"He'll go after anyone involved," George said. Some tone in the other's voice let him think he'd made an impression. "Deep pockets hire their own lawyers. . . . Will they hire one for you?"

"Don't try to scare me," the slender man said. "It won't work." But he said it without full conviction, and he glanced at his stocky partner a moment too long. George knew what his father must feel, in the courtroom, when some change in his opponent's body or face let him know he had scored. He had always assumed law was dull—all those racks of data cubes, all those hours under the helmet—but he had never felt anything like the rush of excitement that now roared through him.

Then the slender man's eyes came back to his face, and the triumph chilled. . . . This man enjoyed pain too much to give it up, even for safety.

"If I escaped," George said, quickly, against the lust in those eyes, "I could call Lord Thornbuckle. You'd have time to get away, if you wanted, although I would testify that you helped me. The people who thought this up are the real criminals. My father would be on your side then."

"It's a thought," the stocky one said. "I'd rather have Mahoney on my side than cross-examining me."

"If it came to that—" The slender man stared at George in a way that made his insides twitch. "If we can't get it out of this 'un . . ."

George hoped his shrug was casual enough. "I don't know where the others are. You can get me to tell you where I last saw them, but if they were still there they'd have been captured. And I've been here at least a day—" He was sure it was two; why else would they have shoved him back into the closet for a time, and kept him below ground level except for that one foray of bathroom cleaning in the upstairs suites? He tried very hard not to think about the cave Bubbles had mentioned. He didn't know where it was; he was very glad he didn't know where it was . . . and they might not be in it anyway.

"More," said the stocky one, and hushed at the other's gesture.

"Time's going to run out," George said. "Someone will notice that we're gone, and start hunting for us. They can get Michaels to say we went to Whitewings, easily enough, but we aren't at Whitewings, and it'll be obvious we weren't. Besides, that flitter beacon still operates. If anyone checks the satellite logs—"

"He's right," the stocky one said, this time with complete conviction. "They should've pulled out as soon as the flitter crashed there. Someone was bound to come looking; it's a wonder they haven't before now. There wasn't really a chance of catching the passengers—"

"A sporting chance," the slender man said. "That's what our admiral likes, remember? The more chance, the more challenge. But if we can get out from under, while he takes the blame . . . then that's a chance I like." He gave George a smile that was anything but benign. "You do understand that we want to be free and clear?"

"Of course," George said. His father's son could not miss the undertones. But it was a chance. The slender man nodded at the stocky one.

"Go check upstairs," he said. "We don't want to run into the admiral, though he said he wouldn't be back until it was over, or we got something out of this one."

George had hoped for a glimpse of the outside world on his way to the communications setup, but the com shack at Bandon Lodge was in the basement. Two long light-gray corridors and a windowed door . . . he didn't even know if it was day or night outside. The slender man tapped the main board's controls; screens lit and the soft hum of the audio units sharpened.

"Satellite bounce to the Main House?" the slender man asked. "Or up to Home Station?"

"I'd try for Main House," George said. "That'd be quickest; there're people who know me."

"Here, then. You're ready."

George had a moment of panic when he couldn't remember the flitter's number, but it came to him. He pressed the button and spoke.

✳   ✳   ✳

Heris, in the supply flitter with the medical squad only a few minutes from landing, recognized George's voice at once. So did Cecelia.

"Why, then there's nothing—" Cecelia said; Heris grabbed her arm and Cecelia hushed.

"—Captive and in danger," George was saying. "Armed men are hunting them, the condemned criminals and us both. The hunters have poisoned the water. We need assistance; I am at Bandon Lodge; the flitter crashed on . . . on the island north of Bandon. Be prepared for—" His voice stopped, suddenly. Heris found she was holding her breath, and let it out. How had that young fool, of all of them, escaped to Bandon? When he spoke again, his voice sounded different: still clearly George, but a George who had changed in the space of a few moments. "And please recognize the assistance of two men formerly in the employ of the hunters . . . Svaagart Iklind"—Heris stiffened. Another Iklind? A relative?—"and Kursa Dahon. Without them, I could not have made this call."

A moment's silence. Heris could not tell, over the sound of the flitter itself and the stirs of those around her, if the com stayed live or dropped the signal. She closed her eyes. She wondered what the militia captain—Sigind—would do. She knew what she would think of so convenient a signal. Which, of course, Lepescu and his cronies would have heard—if they hadn't arranged it. Her mind began to replay the words she'd heard, even the ones overlain by Cecelia's voice. "Hunters." What had George meant by hunters, by "condemned criminals"?

Hunters . . . she had expected to find Lepescu hunting some rare animal illegally, with a band of cronies; she had expected him to be dangerous to innocent youngsters out for a spree. But . . . criminals? People? She shivered suddenly, and Cecelia laid a hand on her arm.

"Heris? What is it?"

She could not see her own face, but Cecelia's reaction told her what she must look like. The older woman drew back, as if frightened. Heris saw others glance at her; one stared.

"That—!" Words literally failed her; the worst words she knew were not bad enough. She fought to breathe past the knot in her throat, and finally said, "He *is* hunting people. It's a manhunt; he's not hunting animals at all!"

"Who?"

"Lepescu." Her mind raced, fitting it all together. "He's gotten convicts from somewhere—" Could they be R.S.S. convicts? She shivered again, at the thought of shipmates—not her crew, of course, but someone's shipmates—being hunted by Lepescu as if they were only wild beasts. Though it was no better if he had raided other prisons; at least military prisoners would know how to defend themselves, might have a chance. She heard others muttering, the same tones of shock and outrage that she heard in her own voice. "It can't be!" someone said, and someone else said, "Must be crazy—Lord Thornbuckle'll tack his hide up in the kennels." She would have said more, but the flitter swerved, and she lurched against Cecelia's arm. She turned to peer out the forward canopy. Ahead, the first attacking ships had dropped to their final approach.

"I can't believe it," Cecelia said. "Hunting people—he wouldn't do that. I know you hate what he did to you—what he tried to do to your crew in battle—but he couldn't be crazy enough to think he'd get away with . . . with this. Not right under Bunny's nose."

Staring ahead, trying to see what she knew she could not see—how the assault was going—she did her best to answer. "He would think that made it better. More . . . sporting. A risk for him, other than the risk from the people he hunted." Had he given them weapons? Had the young people had weapons? "I told you, he once commented that he considered most hunting demeaning, because it wasn't dangerous enough—that the proper game for a real man was man."

Cecelia considered this silently as their flitter dropped steadily toward the Bandon field, now occupied by the two militia flitters. Heris appreciated the silence, but knew it wouldn't last. She knew her employer too well. "I don't think," Cecelia said at last, in the remote and formal tone Heris had not heard for weeks, "that I want to know this person. A disgrace to his uniform."

"Yes." Heris braced herself for landing. The militia squads already down had vanished except for a single soul waving them in. Then they were down safely, onto a quiet field with no sign of conflict. Heris did not need the squad leader's warning; she knew that silence was deceptive.

The medical squad went through a low-voiced routine of some sort; she supposed they were reminding each other what equipment was in whose pack or something. The air smelled fresh and wet, heavy with fragrances completely different from the woods and fields near the Main House. A comunit squawked, and Heris jumped. She didn't understand; she hated not knowing the local codes, not knowing anything, not having a place in this. The medical squad scrambled back into the supply flitter, and the squad leader said, "They've found the kid; he's hurt," just as the flitter lurched into the air again. Cecelia gasped; Heris grabbed her hand and squeezed until the older woman's color returned.

"George," she reminded her. "It has to be George they mean. He's the one on this island."

At the lodge proper, the supply flitter crowded the parking area; the medics poured out and Heris and Cecelia followed. No one stopped them; Heris saw no sign of trouble until they came to the room where George lay with a medic already working on him. One dead body sprawled across the control board of the communications shack; someone else gasped noisily from another clump of medics. Cecelia leaned against the wall, but pushed Heris forward. "Find out," she said. "For his father."

Heris had no interest in George's father. She picked her way across the floor, blood-spattered and already littered with the detritus of emergency medical care, to a point where she could see George without interfering. He was alive, breathing on his own, with one IV line in. He looked dirty, and pale, and both older and younger than she remembered him. She knew that look, from the youngsters she'd seen in her own ship's sickbay; being flat on their backs in clean pajamas made them look like children, but what they had been through aged them.

"What happened to him?" she asked quietly.

"Caught in crossfire," one of the medics said, without looking up. "Small caliber in the abdomen, missed the big stuff." Which didn't mean it felt good, or even that he would recover, just that he was likely to make it back to a hospital without dying on the way. Caught in crossfire . . . maybe, she thought, and maybe not. Perhaps someone wanted to get rid of witnesses. There must be more than one traitor in Bunny's pay. Heris watched the medics, who seemed to go about their business as quickly and competently as any she'd seen, then met George's gaze.

"Captain . . . where's Ronnie?"

"On the other island, I presume. Militia went there; he'll be fine." He might not be, but George needed to hear the best chance, not the worst.

"Don't talk," said a medic, and put a warning hand on George's shoulder. "You need to lie still."

"Cave," said George, struggling now, his eyes locked on Heris's. "Might be in the cave . . . Bubbles said . . ." and then a groan he tried to bite back, as the medics did something that hurt even more.

"I understand," Heris said, as much to reassure him as because she did. "Bubbles knew about a cave, and they might be in it. All of them?"

"No—Ronnie—hurt—"

The medic's angry face looked up at Heris. "He shouldn't talk; don't bother him. He's got other injuries, too." Heris glanced down and saw that they'd cut George's shirt away now, revealing the deep bruises along his side; broken ribs, maybe.

"He—shot me," George said, struggling against the medic's hands. "He—"

"It's all right, George," she said again. Time enough later to find out which *he* George meant. From the glazed look in his eyes, they had given him some drug, and he wouldn't be thinking clearly now. She hoped he had been right about the cave. "Everything will be fine." The medics lifted George onto a stretcher, and rolled him away. He lay quiet, eyes already closed. Her mind raced. A cave—a cave Bubbles knew about. Did Lepescu? Ronnie hurt, and not in the cave. What kind of hurt? If Ronnie was hurt, why hadn't he been captured? And again: did Lepescu know about the cave? Did the others being hunted? Did the militia captain know about that cave, and if so—

She went back to Cecelia, who looked less pale than when she'd come in. "George has a gunshot wound he should survive, assuming Bunny's got a good trauma center in his hospital."

"Very good," Cecelia said. "Riding horses at speed is hardly a safe hobby." Her voice was a shade brittle, but under control.

"He hasn't lost anything vital yet," Heris said. "Could you hear what he said?"

"No—not really."

"There's a cave on the island where the others are; Bubbles knew about it, and George thinks the others might be hiding in it." She waited to make sure Cecelia understood that. Then she went on, "Would the militia captain know about it? Did you ever hear of it?"

"A cave . . . no. I didn't. I don't know if anyone else would, besides the children who camped there. A big cave?"

"George didn't know, I suspect. But the militia captain needs to. If there's a cave, anyone might be in it: the youngsters, or the hunters, or whoever they're hunting." Heris looked around. Someone had dragged the corpse away, and the other wounded man, whoever he was, and one medic was stuffing medical trash in a sack. "We can't just comcall the militia commander; Lepescu would overhear it. If that's where the youngsters are hiding—"

"We'll go tell him," Cecelia said, and pushed away from the wall.

"Yes, but—" Heris stifled her doubts. They'd been told to stay here, safely out of trouble, and she'd agreed to that. She looked around for the person in charge.

The person in charge, busily arranging transport to a hospital for George and the other wounded man, was in no mood to listen. Heris had no idea what the insignia on his collar meant but he was acting like a harried sergeant.

"The captain said you were to stay here," he said. "And here you'll stay. You don't even know where this cave is, or if the kids are in it, or if anyone else knows about it."

"That's why—" Heris began, but he flapped a hand at her.

"The captain's got good maps of the island; if there's a cave worth worrying about, he'll know. He's got a bloody mess over there—" Then the man shut his mouth and glared at her, as if she had extracted that information unfairly. "Just because you used to be a spaceship commander doesn't give you the right to throw your weight around here. Captain Sigind said to keep you safe here, and that's exactly what I'll do. Now if you'll get out of my way so I can do my job—"

Heris swallowed more years of experience than this

person had age, and said, "Excuse me," very quietly. No use arguing with this sort; she had seen them before. The problem now was working around him, and that was most easily done out of his sight.

CHAPTER EIGHTEEN

It had amused the prince to come hunting with the older men, political cronies of his father. He knew they invited him to curry favor, but still—it was thrilling. Illegal, but thrilling. He had been on this planet before, of course, at the invitation of Lord Thornbuckle. Everyone who was anyone had, at one time or another, spent interminable hours riding large stinking vicious beasts chasing after small stinking vicious beasts. Silly work, on the whole, and he had heard others—including this group—snicker about it privately. Lord Thornbuckle didn't care; he could afford to not care.

But this—this was different. What can be the thrill of chasing a harmless small creature bioengineered to be chased and killed? So the admiral had said, and so he had agreed. Other game—even other animals, large and dangerous in themselves—offer more sporting chances. No, my boy, the admiral had said (he had hated the admiral's arm on his shoulder, but he knew he must endure it), there's only one game worth the trouble. Show your stuff, prove yourself, and in the process finish off some useless criminals. And besides, after that . . . we'll have a party. With lots of girls.

He hadn't expected to feel queasy about it. He had felt queasy when he read the reports on the prison colonies, things his tutor had thought he ought to know. That was cruelty, if you liked, confining someone to dirty, dangerous work and mean, ugly surroundings, for years on end. Killing someone cleanly with a bullet in the head was merciful by comparison. He had agreed, in more than one

276

not-so-casual conversation, that this was so; imagining himself a prisoner, he would rather have died in the open like that than slowly of boredom and overwork. And hence, the invitation to this hunt, which had thrilled him as much with its illicit nature as with its prestige. He was born to prestige; he didn't need it . . . but he found himself craving the respect of Admiral Lepescu and Senator-at-Large Bodin.

Still, the first one he killed himself—that had startled him with his own reaction to it, the nausea and guilt, the feeling of shame for being ashamed, the reluctance of his fingers to touch the tattooed ear which he must hack off and turn in to get credit for his trophy. He had done it, but he had made a private pact with himself to be content with one. That was surely enough to prove his ability, to prove he wasn't just a spoiled wastrel who got into quarrels over opera singers (his father's words).

So after that first kill, he found reasons to hang around Bandon lodge the rest of that day. It was easy to play cards too late, drink too much, and sleep heavily when someone knocked on his door. He roused late on the morning after his "blood party" as they called it . . . and found the lodge quiet and nearly empty. Fine with him; his head ached and the ear, proof of his trophy, looked disgusting in its jar of preservative. He stared at it morosely and rang for medicine and breakfast. After that he went back to bed and slept heavily, having promised himself he would find some way of avoiding more hunting.

But now something had gone wrong. He didn't know what. Lepescu had yanked him out of bed in late afternoon, and insisted that he had to come hunt again, right now, whether he wanted to or not. The habit of obedience to older men got him into the flitter before he could organize his mind to protest, and then it was too late. They were on the island, and Lepescu was telling him where to go and what to do in the rough voice he probably used on his subordinates in the Regular Fleet. Before he could argue, Lepescu was gone.

The prince stumbled around that night, angry and tired, and found nothing but mudholes in the swamp. He measured his length in one, and only his custom hunting suit kept him dry. He heard some shots in the distance, but nothing close enough to startle him. At dawn, Lepescu reappeared, and handed him a mealpack. "Eat this here," he said. "We have to get them all, fast. None of us are going back until we do."

"Why?" the prince asked. The mealpack had a picture of helicberry tarts on it, and he hated helicberries. He wanted puffcakes with sarmony honey, fat sausages, a bone-melon.

"Just do it," Lepescu said. He strode off, looking more military, in the dangerous sense, than the prince had seen before. And the prince, tired and hungry, sat down and ate his excellent breakfast. He did not follow Lepescu afterwards; he did not patrol his allotted section of island. It had ceased to be fun, or exciting, or anything but a deadly bore, and he would insist on returning to his comfortable bed on Bandon as soon as someone else showed up. Long after noon, someone else appeared—one of the servants with vaguely military bearing—and brought him two more mealpacks, coldpacks of water, and warnings. He was to stay on the island; he was not to drink any local water; he was not to call anyone on his comunit; he was to shoot anything that didn't identify itself instantly.

The prince was more than somewhat annoyed. One did not do this to princes. Even powerful political figures—even admirals—did not do this to princes. It was supposed to have been an adventure, with girls to follow, and the chance to reminisce for years to come, and the camaraderie of men who had proved themselves real men. It was not an adventure anymore, and no one had said anything about the promised girls for days. He said nothing to the servant, who strode away almost as purposefully as Lepescu, and ate his excellent lunch, then his excellent supper, and finally lay down where he was (protected by his excellent weatherpack) to sleep as long as he liked. If the criminals got him, so much the better: Lepescu would find his head in a noose.

He woke to hard rain drumming on the shelter and the smell of wet leaves. Good. No one would be skulking around in *this*, and Lepescu would have to let him sleep. Lightning crackled, thunder boomed, but the prince slept on, unconcerned.

The Admiral Lepescu who woke him in the dark dripping aftermath of the storm was someone he had never met. He could now credit the more vivid rumors about the admiral's career, faced with that cold, angry countenance, those still gray eyes with so much hunger in them. The tongue-lashing he got for not having followed orders actually frightened him; the scorn in Lepescu's face shamed him all over again. He wanted to please this man, and only the habits drilled into him from early childhood kept him from cringing apology.

"I don't understand the problem," he said stiffly, when Lepescu paused in his tirade. "These are just criminals. . . ."

"You don't have to understand," the admiral said. "You have to obey." Then, as if suddenly remembering who the prince was, he added, "Your highness."

"But what's the hurry?" the prince asked. "You said we'd be here four or five weeks, and it's only been—"

"Someone knows about the hunt," the admiral said. "You wouldn't want to be compromised. . . . You know what this could do to your future career. And we can't get them all without your help before we're discovered. Someone is bound to recognize Ser Smith."

"But surely—" the prince began, but the expression on Lepescu's face stopped him. "All right," he said, trying to sound decisive rather than scared. "I'll be glad to help out." The moment it was out of his mouth, he realized how silly that sounded; he could feel his ears burn. He still didn't understand why they couldn't just flitter back to Bandon, take the shuttle up to the Station, and find some compliant girls there, but he knew he couldn't ask Lepescu. Not now.

Morning had brought an end to the rain, though clouds still clung to the ridge and mist rose from the sodden ground to meet them. Somewhere on the other side of the ridge, the sun might be spearing through that mist, but not here. The prince sighed, punched the button on his breakfast mealpack, and waited for it to heat. He would get his boots muddy again, and they would drag at his feet. . . . He hated mud. This whole expedition looked more and more like a mistake, rather than high adventure. The invitation had specified that they would be here in the dry season, that it could not possibly be compromised . . . and now he was going to be wet, muddy, and in trouble with his father. Not so much for blowing away a few criminals (or rather, one criminal) as for getting caught doing it.

Nonetheless, he set out to do what he was told, and worked his way up the west side of the island. He left his comunit off; he didn't want to be distracted by whatever might come over it. Twice, he saw something move that wasn't ID'd as hunter, and shot at it. Once, whoever it was shot back. He found two bodies, both criminals, with the ears clipped. Lepescu's plan didn't make sense to him—herding the criminals into the interior ridge and its rough terrain would make a final cleanup harder— but he went along. He couldn't think of anything else to do. He followed the stream uphill because it was easier to walk that way.

The clatter of rocks falling echoed through the cave; Bubbles was sure it was loud enough to be heard outside. Had the hunters found another entrance? Was Petris trying to find them?

"We have to move," she said to Raffa. "We might find a better place to hide, and here we're trapped."

"Good idea," Raffa said. "We'll have to take the candles, and mark our way—"

"We can't mark it; someone could follow."

"How could they tell how long ago the marks were made? We can't just go into the cave and not know how to get out—"

"Right." Bubbles picked up her pack, and stuffed into it everything of Kev's that would fit; Raffa would have to carry the rest. The night goggles gave her a blurry picture of the inside of the cave, and she could see a ledge extending along the left wall. Black water lay still and smooth at its edge. She fumbled at the rifle she'd taken, making sure it had a round in the chamber, and slung it on her shoulder. This is an adventure, she told herself. Just do it like you used to, and it will come out all right.

Raffa followed her lead; Bubbles shuffled along wishing she dared light a candle as her vision dimmed. Even with the goggles, she could see very little by the time she came to the first angle of stone that blocked the entrance. She ducked around it, and leaned against the damp wall. Ahead, all was black, utterly black. Water dripped into the central pool in an unpredictable rhythm. Somewhere in the distance, another rock fell. Raffa touched her arm, and she jumped.

"I think it's safe to light the candles now," Raffa said. "We're out of sight of the entrance."

"But they could reflect on the water," Bubbles said. "And if we're the light source, then anyone hiding back here would see us first."

"Yes, but if we don't have a light, we'll step off a ledge somewhere—we can't just feel our way along."

"I know." She took a long breath. The darkness pressed on her eyes, her face; she could almost feel furry hands clasping her. Ridiculous. She'd never been afraid of the dark before. But then she'd never been in this cave before, either. She pushed the goggles up, so that the sudden flare wouldn't blind her, and scraped the lighter until a spark caught the candle. Dim yellow light flickered around them. She put the candle into its lantern, and four beams made clear the distinction between light and shadow. Raffa's face, underlit, looked strange and dangerous and oddly exciting. Bubbles pushed that thought away—she had no time for anything but the present crisis. She looked around. They had turned a corner into a rough corridor, low, narrow, and twisting. On the opposite wall, a blurred mark showed, one of Kell's she had no doubt. It looked like a cartoon sailboat, she had no idea why. She moved the lantern about, looking on all the rock surfaces nearby. Another mark, this one somewhat resembling a tree, near what might be a niche or another corridor, a black gash in the rock. The central cavern's water extended into all the dark entrances she could see, as if all drained into or from it.

"Boat equals water," Bubbles said finally. "Water flows downhill, meets the sea—"

"A way out?" asked Raffa.

"We know where the trees are," Bubbles said. "On top of this cave, and full of hunters." She turned to continue downward, the way she hoped the boat indicated.

A clatter of rock, clearer now, from the tree-marked gash, and then a splash. And a scream.

"The light!" Raffa said, but Bubbles had snuffed it already. In the darkness, they clung together again, hearts pounding. Bubbles saw red and yellow blotches floating on the darkness, and told herself they were the afterimage of the candle. Irregular splashes continued, coming nearer; Bubbles thought she could hear rough breathing, something that might be boots scraping on stone. She felt Raffa's warm breath tickling her ear, and Raffa said, "He must have seen the light somehow."

They must not move. In the dark, they would make the kind of noise he was making; he would surely hear them; he would have one of the weapons with night-sensing equipment. Bubbles realized she'd left the night-vision goggles hanging around her neck while carrying the candle lantern, and pushed them into place, but there was no ambient light to amplify. Thick darkness pressed in on her again. *I hate caves,* she thought.

"I *hate* caves!" came a male voice from somewhere in the echoing distance, to the accompaniment of a clatter and splash.

She was never sure which word, which intonation, made recognition sure.

"Ronnie!" said Raffa, not quite aloud. "It's Ronnie!"

Bubbles concentrated on relighting the candle in its lantern.

He looked like someone who had been at the tail end of a hunt on a muddy day, Bubbles thought. Wet, his clothes streaked heavily with clay, his face haggard with exhaustion, he stared at them, swaying slightly, in the feeble light of the candle lantern.

"You're not hunters," he said hoarsely. Stupidly.

"Raffa . . . Bubbles," said Raffa, her voice warming to a gentle hum that left Bubbles in no doubt of *her* feelings. "Don't you remember?" She had rushed to him; she hovered now as though he were a fragile ornament she might break with her gaze.

"Yes . . ." His voice trailed away; he stood there, his hands trembling, and seemed to be near collapse. One of his eyes had a dark stain around it. Bubbles saw raw scratches and scrapes on his hands and face.

"You need to be dry and you need food," Bubbles said. "Come on, Raffa—get him to dry ground." He stood in ankle-deep water, with a dry ledge not a stride away—but of course he'd been in the dark the whole time.

It was harder than she had imagined to dry a large, very wet and dirty young man in a damp cave. Once out of the water, he dripped water and mud onto the ledge; she had no dry clothes for him, and nothing to dry him with. Food—

the food she had brought along from the first cache—he held in his hand as if he couldn't remember its purpose.

Finally she and Raffa had to undress him, struggling with the wet fasteners, the uncooperative cloth, and use every scrap of spare clothes to dry him. His skin was cold, as disgusting to touch as meat from a cold locker. He sat huddled, shivering, hardly seeming aware of them. Bubbles heated the food bar over the candle lantern until it sizzled and gave off an oily, heavy smell, then pinched off a bit with her fingers.

"Here," she said firmly. "Eat this." His mouth gaped; she pushed the food in. His jaw moved a little, and he swallowed.

"I'll do that," Raffa said. "You keep watch." She pulled off her shirt and laid it around Ronnie's shoulders. He didn't even glance at her slender nakedness; Bubbles looked away as she stood up.

Keep watch. Fine idea, but how? They needed the candle lantern; it made them visible. They had to talk; it made them audible. Bubbles moved back to the margin of the main cavern, and peeked around. She could just see, with her goggles on, the smudge of light from the entrance, across the water.

An impossible situation. And yet, in the near-silence, with the murmur of Raffa's voice coaxing Ronnie to eat, with the random tinkle and splash of water drops into the lake, in the almost-darkness, she felt secure. Cupped in some great hand, a feeling she remembered from those camping trips, when she had felt the land under her as a benign presence. Silly, her schoolmates would have said. She had said it herself, of younger girls' illusions.

Here she felt like herself again. Her real self. Not the mosaic of consensus she was in public, in society. Here she felt connected to the little girl who learned to swim in the waves with the cetes, who learned to scramble up steep rocks, dig holes. The little girl who had been called Bubbles, and had thought of herself as a great hero out of some tale. . . . She felt her face shifting to a grin, felt the pressure of the goggles change with that grin. Such a tomboy, her mother had said . . . her brothers had said. But tomboys grow up.

Not always, she thought. At least not if it meant changing completely. Ronnie's aunt hadn't.

"Bubbles—he's better. Come—"

It had been long enough that she was stiff, but she thought at once that Raffa had forgotten to use her new name, the name she now felt was really hers. This was no time to worry about that—but she wouldn't forget. She shook herself and retreated to the lantern light, pushing the goggles down. Raffa nestled close to Ronnie; Bubbles thought to herself that he was undoubtedly warm on that side, and suspected that Raffa had done more than lean against him. Ronnie had expression on his face now: misery and worry.

"They got George," he said. "He was alive then, but—"

"How?"

"They poisoned the water—I don't suppose you know—"

"Yes," Bubbles said. "We did. That's how we found the cave, going upstream to look for safe water." Ronnie's voice was still unsteady; she didn't know if they should press him to talk. Whatever had happened to George must be over now. But he pushed aside Raffa's arm, and made himself explain what had happened. . . . She wasn't at all sure he had it straight. How many times had he lost consciousness or fallen asleep? Where had they been, exactly? He had no idea where he had fallen into the cave, except "upstream" from where he'd left George.

"Never mind," Raffa was saying, trying to soothe him. "You couldn't help it, and it'll be all right."

It wouldn't, of course. If Raffa thought about it, she'd know. Ronnie surely knew, though he might let himself be comforted by Raffa. Certainly she, Bubbles, knew that everything would not be all right. The hunters might keep George alive, trying to catch the rest, but too many had died already. Too much had happened. However this turned out, things would not be all right, not the way they had been before.

"We have to help George," Ronnie said, more loudly. He sounded hoarse, as if he were catching cold. "We have to get out of this cave." He tried to stand up, and Raffa pulled him back down.

"Not until the hunters give up," Bubbles said. She knew they wouldn't, but she didn't want Ronnie yelling and charging around making it obvious where they were.

"They probably took him to Bandon," Raffa said. "If they didn't kill him right away." From her tone, she could no more imagine George dead on the ground than Bubbles could. George would be at Bandon, tied up like someone from an adventure cube, to be rescued later and reunited with his friends. In the cube, she would be the designated girlfriend, the blonde who gave him a passionate kiss as the end music came up.

The problem was that she didn't want George to die, but she didn't want to be the designated blonde, either. She was Brun, not Bubbles, and so far Brun wasn't a designated anything. She put that thought aside to think about later, and with a glance at Raffa set to work to cheer Ronnie up and keep him from doing something rash.

Muddy footprints led to a sheer cliff with water seeping out from under a thick mat of ferns. The prince felt safe, enclosed by the rocky, fern-covered walls, although he realized it could be a trap, too. Someone overhead who happened to see him could shoot him easily. He peered up into the overlapping layers of green, and shivered. He was tired, hungry, and confused. What could have happened? Where were the promised girls?

Wet leaves dripped on his head and neck. It made him feel stupid, as well as tired. In the solitude and silence, he had time to track the feeling back and analyze it. Long ago— it seemed long, anyway—he had been at school with boys who had known each other for years while he'd been isolated at court. Someone had thought it would be fun to play a joke on the prince, to make him late for roll-call and incidentally make him look stupid. Ethar Krinesl, that had been. He had been lured from his bed on a dark, rainy night by the promise of a rendezvous with girls from the neighboring school. . . . He had trekked across the campus to crouch in a muddy ditch, while (he learned later) the other boys had sewn his clothes together so that he couldn't possibly dress in the morning. And the shadowy figure that had come in the dark, and with giggles had agreed to kiss him, had been Ethar's older brother Potim. Ethar had had the cube recorder.

Painful as the memory was, it made him feel better. Now he understood what was going on. All the other men were older, and they formed a tight clique. This was a joke; they were testing him. After a time, when they thought he had been sufficiently humiliated, they would come out and take him into the group, as Ethar and his crowd had done. It was annoying, but understandable. The prince was proud of having figured it out, and felt a little superior to the childishness of the older men. They should have realized he would not panic; he had already killed someone and proved himself. They would have swept the criminals from in front of him; they weren't really risking his death. Perhaps the criminals had never been armed with anything lethal. Not very sporting, perhaps, but prudent.

The girl's voice completed his understanding. Soft, hardly audible, it could still be nothing but a girl—a girl some distance away chuckling softly at something. That had to mean the original promise held; girls *were* part of the entertainment here. He looked around carefully. She might be hiding anywhere.

The voice came again, from the rock wall in front of him. He stared, then saw that two big, cleated bootprints lay half under the ferns. He felt himself tingling with excitement. A cave. It must be a cave, full of the girls he'd been promised, hidden away in safety until the dangerous part of the hunt was over. And he'd found them without being shown— perhaps before the other hunters, even. Carefully, he stooped and lifted the mat of ferns, peering into the darkness beyond. Water lapped at his boots; he could see that he stood on the edge of a large pool. He pulled his night goggles out of his pocket and put them on, squinting until he got his head inside where it was darker. A large domed chamber, with smudged reflections off the surface of water as far as he could see. But clearly someone was inside. He smelled cooking food, and again he heard what had to be human voices, distorted by the shape of the cave and the water.

Had they marooned the girls in a lake? No, all that rain had probably made the water rise. They were somewhere inside, dry and safe. He imagined nooks and crannies cushioned with colorful pillows and rugs, rock-walled chambers where naked nymphs bathed in clear subterranean pools or streams. In all likelihood there was a way that wasn't very deep. With his goggles on, he should be able to find his way safely around—ankle-deep water wouldn't bother him, not in his boots.

Now that the hunt was over, or mostly over, he saw no

reason to crawl under the hanging mat of ferns; he was dirty enough already. He kicked at it until most of it fell, revealing a hole large enough to get through if he stooped. That let more light into the entrance; even without goggles he could now see the shape of the first chamber . . . and hear more clearly the distorted murmur of girls' voices. The other hunters would be surprised, he thought, to discover he had found the place himself, ahead of whatever time they planned to start the party. He might even be the first; he could see, now, that the bootprints he'd noticed stopped there, and backed out again. Of course anyone coming after him would know someone had gone in, but he wasn't hiding from anyone—certainly not unarmed criminals.

The light coming from behind him made it hard to see, even with the goggles. Some things were too bright, and others hazed into murky reflections. He had to feel his way along the edge of the cave, so he chose to move to his left, where his right arm was still free to hold his weapon. Not that he'd need it, he was sure. The girls might be startled, but he had the patch that identified him as a hunter, and afterwards . . . He stumbled over something and bit back a curse. It would be much more fun to sneak up on them. The smell of cooked food grew stronger.

The first flicker of light blazed into his vision, and he pulled the goggles off, blinking. Now he could see nothing. Standing still, silent, he heard murmuring voices that might have been nothing more than a trickling stream—but not that smell. After a few moments, his eyes adjusted, and he saw a faint sparkle ahead, where some light source reflected from moving water. He crept through the darkness, smugly certain of what he would find. The light strengthened; he felt his way around a corner of the rock, and saw them at last.

His first thought was disappointment; he wasn't the first to find the girls after all. The dark-haired girl had her arm around the lucky first-comer; the prince wondered why he'd preferred her to the more curvaceous blonde. His second thought stumbled over the first in a wave of righteous rage. Ronnie!

"You unspeakable cad!" he said. "What are you . . ." His voice trailed away as he realized that the two black circles were the bores of hunting rifles like his own. Both girls, blonde and dark, held them steadily. "You're hunters, too?" he asked, with a half-nervous laugh.

Ronnie's head came around, and he saw the dark stain of a black eye and bruised face. "My sainted aunt," Ronnie said, in a voice that didn't sound much like his own. "It's the prince."

"Gerel?" the blonde girl asked. She peered at him, but the rifle did not waver. Her nod, too, came without a move in the weapon's aim. "It is. And you know what? He's not on the list either."

The prince took a deep breath. Whatever was going on here, it had to be irregular. "I demand to know what you're doing here," he said firmly. "I am here at the invitation of—" But that, he suddenly realized, he couldn't finish. Ronnie might mention it; it could be embarrassing. He interrupted himself with an alternate line of reasoning. "You might introduce me to your—uh—young women."

Ronnie gave a harsh bark that might have been intended for laughter but sounded more like pain, and the dark young woman touched him with her shoulder, not removing her hand from her rifle. The blonde one laughed louder.

"Introduce me? Heavens, Gerel, you've been dancing with me since boarding school." He couldn't think of anyone like this at any dance he'd been to. She was blonde, yes, but hardly stylish in rumpled pants and shirt, with her hair yanked back behind her ears. She looked older by five or ten years than he was, someone serious and even dangerous. "Bubbles," she said finally. "Lord Thornbuckle's daughter—surely you remember now."

Bubbles. Ronnie. None of it made sense. If this was Bubbles—and he supposed it was, though he did not recognize her in these clothes, with her hair pulled back—then she could not be one of the girls Lepescu meant. Those girls would be . . . another kind of girl, from another kind of family. Not Bubbles the wild sister of Buttons, and Ronnie the wild son of a cabinet minister, and . . . "Raffaele?" he asked uncertainly.

"Of course," she said. It sounded like her voice. The prince swallowed, and wished very much to sit down.

"I don't understand," he said.

"You're wearing an ID tag," Bubbles said. "What is it?"

He had forgotten the bright-colored tag on his collar, which transmitted a signal to other hunters. "This? It identifies me to other hunters."

"Other . . . hunters." That was Raffaele again. She sounded grim, nothing like the witty girl with the silvery laugh he remembered from the parties last season. "You'd better put your rifle down," she said, using neither name nor title. That made him nervous, and he couldn't think why.

"But if you're one of us . . ." That didn't make sense either. He knew the others; they had all been at the lodge. No women, certainly not these girls, and no Ronnie. He turned to Ronnie. "I thought you'd been shipped off somewhere for punishment."

"Put your rifle down," Bubbles said. When he looked at her, he felt almost assaulted by the anger that radiated from her. "Now," she said, and he felt his arm moving before he thought about it.

"But this is ridiculous," he said, not quite obeying. "I'm the prince. You're friends. Why should I—"

"Because I have the drop on you," Raffaele said. "And so does Bubbles. And you're standing there with the same ID patch as men who tried to kill us."

"Kill *you*? Why?"

"Drop it!" Bubbles yelled suddenly. Her voice rang in the cave, echoing off odd corners and coming back as a confused rumble. Rocks clattered somewhere, as if her voice alone had riven the stone. His hand was empty; he could hear the afterimage of the rifle's thud on the damp floor of the cave. "You idiot, Gerel," she said more quietly. "And I'll bet you've led the rest of them straight here, too."

CHAPTER NINETEEN

Heris seethed inwardly. Of course she had no right of command, but it should have been obvious that knowing where the young people might be was important enough. She led Cecelia outside the room. There had to be some way—perhaps she could get hold of a flitter—

"Excuse me, ma'am." A young, earnest-faced militiaman had followed them out. Heris nodded at him.

"Yes?" she said through gritted teeth.

"You said you might know where the young miss is?"

It took her a moment to untangle that: young miss? Bubbles, of course. "I'm not sure," she said. "Why?"

"I'd take you over there to tell the captain," the man said. "If you wanted. . . ."

Of course that's what she wanted, but why was he being so helpful? "What about your boss?" she asked. He reddened and grinned.

"Well, ma'am . . . that Bortu, he just got promoted, you know. Never been on anything like this before."

That could indeed explain it. On the other hand . . . Heris looked at Cecelia. "What about it? This—what's your name?"

"Dussahral, ma'am."

"This man says he'll fly us over to meet the captain—want to come along?"

"Of course," Cecelia said, looking determined.

"Thanks," Heris said, smiling at him. "Go find us a flitter—we'll need to stop into the . . . ." She nodded at a door down the hall.

"Don't be long," he said. "In case that Bortu figures it out."

"Just a moment, promise." Heris watched him go, then led Cecelia to the bathroom.

"What's that about? I don't need to—"

"Yes, you do. We need a couple of minutes to make plans, and you never go into combat with a full bladder."

"We're not going into combat; we're just going over to tell the militia captain where to look for Ronnie."

Heris caught her employer by a shoulder and turned her around. "Listen. We're going into an unsecured zone where people are shooting at each other—possibly three different sets of people *all* shooting at each other—and if you can think of a better definition of combat, tell me when we're safely back in our hot tubs. Now, I am taking a very dangerous chance here, because there's no reason to trust Dussahral—"

"But he wants to help us."

"So he said. Didn't it occur to you that Lepescu might want to know about that cave just as badly as the captain? And if he had an agent in this batch of militia, that person would be eager to tell him?"

Cecelia frowned. "Why would he be stupid enough to stick with what is obviously a losing side? Any smart agent would clam up and wait to see what happens."

"Not all agents are smart. And Dussahral may be innocent and completely loyal to Bunny. But—" Heris ducked into a cubicle and continued talking through the closed door. "But if he's not, we need a plan. We take our weapons. He will think I'm the dangerous one; I'll let him jump me, and you shoot him if he does."

Cecelia, too, had gone into a cubicle. Heris heard the seat squeak. "Me? I've never shot anyone. Just game—"

"New experiences keep you young. You have to; he won't expect it from you. Just have a round in the chamber, in case, and don't shoot me by mistake." Heris came out and washed her hands. Cecelia, when she emerged, had a strange expression on her face.

"You're trusting me with your life."

Heris shrugged. "You trust me with yours in the ship. Besides, what I'm really doing is taking you into danger. You could get killed too. Remember that, when you're tempted to wonder if you really should shoot." Then she grinned at the older woman. "Now—cheer up. I'm wearing body armor under my clothes; he doesn't know that, and it will help. And don't stare at him as if you suspect him. He's thinking of you as a helpless old woman in a flutter about her nephew."

Cecelia snorted, and the color came back to her cheeks. "I can see," she said, "how you commanded a ship." They walked out side by side, as if they had nothing better to do than sightsee, and the guards now posted in the corridors smiled and nodded at them.

Dussahral, when they reached the parking area, had one of the flitters rolled out where the supply flitter had been. He looked tense and excited, but that was reasonable. Heris smiled, and accepted his hand up into the flitter.

"Lady Cecelia should be in back," she said. "In case of stray rounds." He nodded, and looked at Heris.

"You want to copilot?" There wasn't much copiloting to be done in a flitter, but Heris nodded.

"I'll keep a lookout," she said. "Maybe I can spot the captain." Little chance of that, but he relaxed a bit, as if this evidence of her inexperience in ground operations eased his mind.

The hop across to the other island took only minutes; it looked short enough to swim. Heris noted its narrow spine, higher than Bandon's low rounded hills, the beach along the south and east—and two flitters parked at the south end. A squad of militia there worked on something—she could see what looked like bodies. She hoped Cecelia hadn't spotted them.

"Is that the captain's flitter?" she asked Dussahral, who shook his head. "Should we land there?"

"No . . . that's the number two . . . captain must've gone somewhere else. I'll fly up along the beach." They flew north slowly; Heris tried to see into the thick canopy with no success. Then Dussahral touched her arm and pointed, and Heris saw a flitter sitting lopsided on the beach. Not the command flitter: it had the serial number they'd been told was on the one Bubbles checked out. Heris saw the gaping hole along one flank, something else she hoped Cecelia missed. The flitter hadn't landed, or simply crashed—someone had shot it down. She felt cold.

Dussahral swung the flitter inland, and they rose over the central rocky spine, where tufts and wisps of fog still swirled. Down the other side—and the man waved suddenly. "There— I see something—I'll put us down in that clearing."

That clearing, to Heris, looked entirely too convenient a place for a trap, but she said nothing. She had seen nothing of the captain's flitter, either. But if there were a cave, surely it had to be in the hills somewhere.

Dussahral made a steep approach, dropping the flitter so rapidly that Heris caught her breath. They landed hard; she felt the jolt out the top of her head . . . and let herself act more stunned than she was. Dussahral, she saw through nearly closed eyes, changed the setting of the flitter's comunit and pushed the transmission switch all the way over. With his other hand, he had shoved the canopy back.

"Come on," he urged. "I'm sure I saw the captain's signal over there—" A wave toward the higher ground. "I'll help you. Do you have any idea where the cave might be?" All this in a voice easily loud enough to carry over the comunit.

Heris pushed away his hand, but slowly, as if she almost needed it, and clambered out, intentionally clumsy. She held her rifle loosely. Dussahral waited for Cecelia to clamber out—Heris hoped the jolting landing hadn't jarred Cecelia's reflexes. She also hoped Dussahral was as stupid as he seemed so far. They could get rid of him quickly, and still have a chance to block Lepescu, now that the cave was no longer a secret.

Dussahral led them into the forest, away from the flitter. Upslope, Heris noted, across a streambed with a trickle of water in it. Heris wished she dared jump him now, but there was a chance he was leading her to Lepescu—perhaps he had a real signal to home on—and in that case it would be stupid to strike too soon. He halted soon enough, and pointed to a rocky bluff. "There—the captain's probably up there. I'll go back and keep an eye on the flitter."

"I can't see," Heris said, trying to sound querulous. She felt querulous; it had just occurred to her that he might have wanted an excuse to bring the flitter for Lepescu's escape. Even now the admiral might be flying away to safety, however temporary. "Where?" She pushed past him, giving him every chance. His sudden grasp on her arm was vindication, even as the feel of his weapon prodding her side made her face the next likely outcome. She wondered if her armor would hold against a point-blank shot, but he slid the muzzle of the weapon up, as if he knew she wore it. Of course—he had seen Lady Cecelia's, and guessed that she had armor too. Her mind insisted on showing her, in vivid detail, what would happen if he fired now, with the muzzle where it was at the back of her neck.

"Stop here, ladies," he said, this time in a voice unlike the deferential, pleasant tone he'd used so far. "I think Admiral Lepescu might have something to say to Captain Serrano."

Cecelia let out a terrified squeak, and Heris's heart sank. So much for civilians. Dussahral smirked.

"You're not going to give me any trouble, are you?" he asked. "I know you ladies don't go around with loaded weapons, so don't try to pretend you'll shoot me."

"I won't," said Cecelia, eyes wide. "I—I—don't hurt her."

"Drop the gun," Dussahral said. Heris wondered whether she could reach her bootknife and decided she couldn't. Cecelia stood there, gawky and gray-haired, clinging to the rifle as if it were a child. She probably hadn't chambered a round, Heris thought, so it wasn't really dangerous to be standing here with the bore pointing at her. . . . It shifted a little, and Dussahral sighed. She could feel his disgust; she felt it herself. "Listen, lady," the man said, "you can't shoot me with an unloaded rifle, and I'm not going to be fooled. Either drop it, now, or I'll shoot you, not just your friend." Cecelia said nothing, and looked as if she couldn't; Heris had never seen a better picture of frozen panic. Dussahral shifted his weight; Heris tried to shift her own to take advantage, but his blow to her head came too fast. She didn't quite lose consciousness, but she stumbled, unable to move fast when he let go of her and swung his weapon toward Cecelia.

Then the crack of Cecelia's rifle and the ugly sound of a round hitting bone came together, and Dussahral was flung away from her. Heris stared. Her employer stared back. "You said to pick the right moment," Cecelia said. Bright color patched her cheeks. "I think I did." She held the rifle steady as if she were perfectly calm.

"Damn." Heris felt her head. It hurt, but she was alive, not a scratch, and Dussahral lay dead, the back of his skull and its contents splattered for a meter or more on the forest floor. "Yes—you did. But I thought for a moment—"

"I wanted him away from you—at least his weapon." Cecelia shivered suddenly. "I never—did that before. Not a person."

"You did it perfectly." Heris picked up her own rifle, and walked back to Cecelia. "You saved my life, is what you did." It occurred to her now just how stupid it had been to give Dussahral a chance. If she made the same mistake with Lepescu . . . well, she wouldn't.

"That's what I meant to do—but he's so . . . so ugly."

"They are." Heris turned Cecelia away from it, but Cecelia twisted back.

"No. If I do it, I should see what I did." She walked deliberately up to the body; already a few tiny flies buzzed near it. "So little time between life and death. We think we have years . . ." Heris did not tell her how long it often took men to die of wounds. Not now. Now they had other prey.

"It's amazing," Cecelia went on, "how young men like this think we old people are frail, emotional, likely to fall apart at any emergency." When her eyes met Heris's, it gave Heris a chill; they were the cold gray of frozen oysters. "Because of course," Cecelia continued, "we've done everything they imagine they might do. One time or another."

"But that's crazy," the prince said. He had said it before, and Ronnie thought he would go on saying it until he died. "No one would kill *you*—not like this. Let me call Admiral Lepescu and get you back to civilization." After he'd dropped the rifle, the girls had grudgingly lowered theirs, and let him sit down. He had refused to believe they were really in danger, and continued to defend the hunters.

Had he listened at all? Ronnie thought not. "What about the others?" he asked. "Serrano's crew."

"There's some kind of mistake," the prince said firmly. "Those men are criminals, condemned to life at hard labor; they have this option, risking death against a chance for a lesser sentence on a colony world. This is easier, for some people, than life in prison."

It occurred to Ronnie that he himself would have made that argument not long before. The topic of life sentences versus the death penalty had been a favorite debate in the mess. Of course, none of those debating ever expected to face either alternative.

"They're not criminals," Raffa said hotly. "They're decent people your admiral has a grudge against."

"I know it's fashionable for some people to argue against the justice system," the prince said. "But these people have all been tried and convicted and sentenced; do you think I'd be here if they weren't?"

A long silence. Finally Bubbles said, "I am frankly surprised that you're here even though they are. Does your father condone hunting people for sport? The last time I heard, he was scolding my father for hunting foxes."

Another long silence. "Well . . . he doesn't exactly know," the prince said, staring at his boots. He looked younger than Ronnie remembered, more the schoolboy he had known. "I'm supposed to be at the Royal Aero-Space depot on Naverrn. Admiral Lepescu fixed that for me."

"Mmm. And do you think he'll approve, even if they are convicted criminals? Which they aren't, but just to argue the point." Bubbles, on the other hand, looked older, tougher. She had laid aside her weapon, as if the prince were no longer a threat. Except for his stubbornness, Ronnie thought, he wasn't.

The prince scuffed his boot along the wall. "Probably not. But he doesn't need to know everything I do, and he certainly approved of my association with people like the other men in the club. Men of stature, men with . . . with . . . with . . ."

"Influence," Bubbles said. She made the word sound like something with little legs scuttling along the floor.

"The thing is," Ronnie said, "we've got to get out of here and rescue George."

"George? The odious George Starbridge Mahoney is here too? How fitting." The prince chuckled, leaning back against the stone. "Don't worry—no one will hurt George once they realize who his father is."

"They know who my father is, and they've tried to shoot me," Bubbles said. Ronnie glanced at her. She had changed as much as any of them, he realized, and in a way he could not have predicted. She looked like someone it would be dangerous to cross.

"Of course," the prince went on, ignoring that, "as soon as we *do* get back to civilization, I've a bone to pick with you, Ronnie. We simply can't ignore it; we must duel."

Ronnie stared at him. "A duel? You mean—formally?"

"Yes, of course, formally. It wouldn't have been necessary had we not met, but we did. And I had told them, if I saw you again anytime in the next twelve months, I would insist on it. It's a matter of honor." The prince drew himself up, glanced around at the two girls, and posed. Bubbles burst into giggles; Raffa merely looked scornful. Ronnie could not decide whether to laugh or scream.

"Look," he said, trying for reasonableness, "that whole thing is over. Past. Gone. She's all yours, and I'm sorry I said anything, and I'll never bother you again, but—"

"You're not going to back out of a duel, are you? That's—"

Ronnie felt anger roll up from his gut to the top of his head in one refreshing wave. "I am not going to pretend to stick holes in you with a holographic sword because of a stupid quarrel over a stupid opera singer who is probably sleeping with both our younger brothers right this moment! Can you get it through your skull that we are being *hunted*, by people with *real* weapons who want to kill us *really* dead? We are—Bubbles and Raffa and George and I— and I am not playing your silly games any more."

"Honor," the prince said, "is not a game."

"No," said Ronnie more quietly. "You're right, it's not a game. But my honor doesn't depend any more on the kind of things we got into in the regiment. I have other claims on it now."

"But what will I tell them when I get home?" the prince asked.

"If you get home," Bubbles said, "tell them you grew up. If you did."

The prince shook that off and stroked his moustaches. "Well—if we're to rescue George, we'd better get on our way. If you're convinced Lepescu is dangerous to you, how do you propose to get to Bandon?"

"Now what?" Cecelia asked. "We don't know where the captain is, we don't know where the cave is, and we don't have a flitter any more."

"Now . . . we think." Heris rubbed the knot on her head. She felt stupid, and she didn't like feeling stupid. "We can be reasonably sure Dussahral didn't put us down near the captain, but he might have put us down near Lepescu, if Lepescu needed a flitter to escape in."

"Fine." Cecelia looked thoroughly annoyed. "So now we've provided the villain a *machina* for his *deus* to come out of."

"Not if we get back to it and use it ourselves," Heris said. "Of course, explaining how all this happened might be tricky later—but we can worry about that when the time comes. Nemesis, as well as helpful gods, arrived by air."

She led the way back downslope. The streambed, she noted this time, had a lot of boot tracks in it or alongside. Some went upstream, and some—not as many, she thought— went down. She wasn't enough of a tracker to know when they had been made, though they looked fresh.

Cecelia stopped, and looked more closely. "Expensive boots," she commented. "Look—that pair's Y and R." That meant nothing to Heris, who let her expression speak for her. "Custom, high quality, and even higher prices," Cecelia said. "These won't be the designated victims, nor even Ronnie's. I saw most of his things, and his boots are Pierce-Simons. Also expensive, but not quite as exclusive. Might be George's, but the tracks are too fresh."

"You can tell?" Heris asked.

"I hunt," Cecelia said, not looking up. Her fingers hovered above first one print, then another. "Not the girls' boots, and not Ronnie's—that means a hunter's up there somewhere."

"The way Dussahral was leading us," Heris said. "Lepescu, I would bet."

"You've noticed that two matching sets go that way and back—" Cecelia pointed. Heris hadn't noticed that, exactly, but she didn't explain her own ignorance. "Expensive, from hunting outfitters, but not as unusual as the Y and R pair. One pair of Y and Rs going up, and not coming back, and an even fresher set of Dolstims going up . . . two hunters, but not together. Not long ago, either—within an hour."

"So we go upstream?"

Cecelia pursed her lips. "I'd say so. Assuming that the men who went downstream wanted our flitter, they'd have it before we could get back. And upstream . . . I'm really curious. I thought Y and R put this symbol"—she pointed at what looked to Heris like a squashed bug—"only on boots they made for the royal family. Does your Admiral Lepescu have a habit of stealing shoes from princes? Or does he pretend to be one?"

"It wouldn't surprise me," Heris said. She was past being surprised, she thought; who would have expected someone like Lady Cecelia to know much about tracking? "Let's go find out."

She led the way upstream, weapon ready, all senses alert. Was this another stupid idea, following the tracks so openly? What they should be finding was the cave Ronnie and Bubbles might be in, or the militia captain. But she went on, because after all the hunters were the danger here. Anticipation shivered in her stomach. *Hunters all,* she thought. *We're all dangerous.*

All the hunters but two were safely dead: no threat. He touched the canisters in his pocket lightly, careful not to depress the switches. One only still menaced him, and that the most difficult to kill without reprisal. But it had to be done, unless the man could somehow be made to kill the others; after that, blackmail would be easy. It would be easiest to kill, and not attempt that—but he had always found the most difficult hunts the greatest pleasure. Worth a try, anyway, and if he had to kill even that one, he would have no witnesses.

That broadcast from Bandon had startled him—shaken him, he would even admit to himself. He wondered if the guards he'd left with the boy had turned against him. One of them could be difficult. At least his name had not been mentioned. Perhaps the prisoner didn't know about him. Soon no one would.

The prince led the way back to the cave entrance. They hadn't been able to talk him out of it, although they had tried. The argument had gone on longer than he'd expected. The girls seemed to think their opinion should weigh equally with his own. Bubbles had even threatened to shoot him, but when he pointed out that shooting a member of the royal family could be a serious offense, she had looked at Raffa and shrugged. Of course she would not shoot him, now that she knew who he was, any more than he would have shot her. One did not prey on one's own class. And he was the right one to decide what to do; he was the prince, after all. He felt only slightly nervous with the girls behind him carrying their weapons; he had insisted that they not carry loaded weapons, in case they stumbled. He didn't want them to get in trouble for shooting him by accident, either. Once they were outside, in the light, they could reload—though he hoped to dissuade them. If Ronnie hadn't been so shaken (he felt sure that he, in a similar situation, would not have been a wet, shivering mess) he'd have had Ronnie carry one of the rifles, but as it was the girls were actually less dangerous than Ronnie. As for any danger— he was sure there wouldn't be any real danger, not once he told Lepescu who they were—he could protect them himself.

Light shimmered and bounced from the surface of the pool; already it had gone down a few centimeters. He squinted against what now seemed like glare, and never saw the figure that waited until it stepped out of the shadows to confront him. He stared. Who could that be, in a protective suit almost like a spacesuit, with a hunting rifle in the crook of the right arm, and something clasped in the gloved left hand?

"Ah . . ." a voice said. The prince shivered. Lepescu? "You found them. Congratulations. Very good . . . now shoot them."

"What?" He had misunderstood. He could not have heard the words his memory now replayed to him. Behind him, he heard the girls' indrawn breath, Ronnie's muttered curse.

"Shoot them, I said." When he hesitated, Lepescu gestured with his rifle. "Either you shoot them," Lepescu said, his voice only slightly distorted by his suit's filters, "or I will have to kill you, too. Surely you see the necessity."

"But they're *ours*," the prince said. His voice trembled slightly. "Can't you see? This is Lord Thornbuckle's daughter—you can't kill *her*. And Raffaele, and Ronnie Carruthers—"

"I thought you hated Ronnie," Lepescu said. "Isn't he the one who dishonored you with your—"

"I do, of course, but—but I can't kill them. Not just . . . just shoot them." Silently, he begged someone to shoot

Lepescu . . . but he had insisted on unloaded weapons. The girls could not reload now. If they tried, Lepescu would shoot . . . and he was in the middle. Sweat rolled down his sides, sudden and cold.

"We should never have let him talk us into this—" Bubbles muttered. "We *knew* better. He can see me—can you—?"

"Too late smart, too soon dead," Raffa said. Neither of them had sounded as frightened as the prince felt. He wished he could see them. He wished he could see any help at all.

Lepescu's hand turned, showing a slick gray canister. "It would be a more merciful death," he said. "If you care about that." The prince realized that fear had layers he had never imagined. . . . That had to be a gas canister. Riot gas? Nerve gas? He struggled to stay calm; he had to convince Lepescu.

"But they're my *friends*," the prince said. "You can't expect me to do it; there has to be another way." This could not be happening; it must be some kind of joke or test. He had to find the right thing to say. "We could agree to keep your secret."

"I doubt it," Lepescu said. Even through the gleaming curve of his face mask, his eyes looked distinctly from face to face. "Lord Thornbuckle's daughter is not likely to keep such secrets from her father."

"You're right about that," came Bubbles's voice from behind the prince. "Not that killing us will do any good in the long run. He'll find out, and then he'll find you."

Lepescu lifted the canister in a mock salute. "To your courage, my dear. You may stop that shuffling you're doing; you cannot screen your friend as she reloads; I can shoot the prince, and you, before you shoot me . . . and I'm wearing protection." With a change in tone, he addressed the prince again. "As for your friend Ronnie, a young man who cannot keep from boasting about his amatorial conquests is hardly likely to hold his tongue about this, the next time he gets drunk. The dark girl—well, it's a pity, but many have died already, and so it goes. You choose: kill them, and I know you will not talk. It would not be in your own best interests. I have a flitter; we can escape somehow. I always do. But if you cannot kill them . . . then I'm afraid you, too, must die." After a moment he went on. "Go ahead—it won't be easier for waiting."

* * *

Heris followed the bootprints up the narrowing cleft. Suddenly one pair stopped; whoever it was had shifted around, trampling his own prints, and then completely new prints—larger, with a different tread—set off again. She frowned at them, trying to remember where she'd seen that tread pattern, then shrugged. It really didn't matter.

"He put on overshoes," Cecelia murmured, from behind her. "Why?" Heris waved a hand to hush her. They had to be close; she could tell the slope was closing in ahead of them.

If she hadn't been following the tracks, she might have missed the angle to the cave entrance . . . but the tracks led directly to it. A mat of wilting ferns and moss, a gaping hole into darkness, and a voice—no, more than one voice. She was sure one of the voices was Lepescu's.

She pulled Cecelia close and murmured into her ear. "He's there—ahead of us—and I think it's the youngsters. Stay back; be ready to shoot if I go down. And watch for anyone behind us." Cecelia nodded, eyes hard again. Heris crept nearer to the cave entrance, fighting down a surge of excitement that threatened to send her charging straight at Lepescu, no matter what.

Now she could hear his voice clearly. She knelt in the mud, and peered around the edge of the hole into the dimness. Nothing but water, a pool almost lapping the entrance. She would have to go in. Voices came from her left, around an angle of stone. She gave Cecelia a last look and ducked inside.

Her eyes adjusted quickly; more light came in the entrance than she'd have thought from outside. She flattened herself against the damp stone to her left and edged around it. There. A big, bulky shape in a protective suit, its back to her, and four faces beyond, pale against the black behind them. The suit had to be Lepescu. Could she get him without hitting them? Was he wearing armor under the suit? And why the suit, in this weather? What contamination did he fear? Then she saw the clenched left hand, and caught her breath. If that was a gas grenade—

She edged nearer, hoping none of the youngsters would notice her, although she knew she must be a very visible dark blot against the bright entrance. Lepescu was still talking. . . .

"Go ahead," he was saying. "It won't be easier for waiting."

What did he mean? And why *four* people? Heris stared, just able to make out Ronnie, Bubbles, and Raffa . . . but who was that fourth young man with the extravagant moustache and a gleam of earring? A friend of Lepescu's? She bit her lip; she could not possibly get both of them before someone else got shot. She wondered if Lepescu was wearing armor under the suit; she reset her weapon for the alternate clip of ammunition. This should penetrate personal armor. More danger to bystanders, but not as much danger as a live Lepescu.

But as her eyes adjusted to the dim light, she saw the mysterious young man shift his weight, his expression changing from bewilderment and disbelief to mulish stubborness. "I won't do it," he said, and dropped his weapon. "And I think you'll find it impossible to explain *my* disappearance." Heris aligned her sights, and shifted a little to clear Ronnie. It was at best a tricky shot. . . . The ricochets would be wicked. . . .

"Not really," Lepescu said. "An inconvenience, yes—but not nearly an impossibility. It's a pity, and I'm sorry—this is not a sporting proposition, but—" He rocked forward, blood spraying out the front of his protective suit. Echoes of the shot and the impacts on him and on stone roared through the cave, deafening, confusing. Lepescu dropped his rifle; the canister dropped from his left hand, bounced, and rolled along the stone toward the water. Heris flinched; she was too far away to do anything more. If its seal broke, they were all dead. Ronnie and the prince leaped together and landed on it like two eager players trying to recover a fumbled ball.

"Run!" Ronnie yelled to Raffa and Bubbles; Heris knew it would have been useless. The girls didn't run; after their first startled jerk, both of them seemed to be calmly reloading their weapons. Heris stared at them. They must have known they were in danger; why hadn't they had a round in the chamber? Then the echoes died away . . . and the canister had not fired. . . . It lay under the young men, inert and deadly only in anticipation. They were alive; they were going to stay alive.

Heris rose from her careful crouch, and walked light-footed across the cave to Lepescu's body . . . not body yet, for he was alive though mortally wounded. She looked down at him warily. He might have other weapons.

"You . . ." he began, but pain caught at him, and he could not go on. His breathing sounded loud, now that the echoes of the shot had faded; she could hear the ominous snoring rattle that meant his lungs were filling.

She could not think what to say. All the clever retorts she remembered from history crumbled and blew away in the wind of her anger. "Yes," she said, and it came to her that she did not need to say much, under the circumstances. "Commander Serrano, with all due respect."

Even dying, even in pain, he had a courage she could not deny. Scorn dragged his face into a mask of contempt. "Wait—" he breathed. "Haven't won—yet—"

She wanted to throttle him, finish it with her fingers on his throat, but she could not do that. Instead, she removed, with such control that she felt herself almost a machine, his other weapons; she paid no attention to the bubbling breaths that faded to nothing.

Cecelia could not have stayed out of the cave after the gunshot if someone had chained her to the rock. She scrambled into the darkness, stumbled into the pool and back out, and came up, panting, against the stone buttress that had blocked Heris's vision. Now, shocked and fascinated by her captain's behavior, she had let her attention wander from the cave entrance. When she thought to look around, there was another stranger, this one dirty and ragged, as well as armed. Another stood behind him. He glared at her, his weapon aimed where it could menace all of them.

"What . . . are *you* doing here?" The pause, Cecelia was sure, held a dozen suppressed curses. The man looked dangerous and probably was. He must be one of those the hunters had chased.

"I'm Lady Cecelia—" she began. Then she realized he wasn't even looking at her. He was looking past her, at Heris.

"Petris . . ." Heris said. Her voice wavered.

"Captain Serrano. Heris." His didn't, nor did the muzzle of his weapon.

"*You're* with Admiral Lepescu?" Quiet though it was, that question held a vast pain; it got through to Cecelia, who stared at her captain.

"You know this man? Who is he?"

Heris shook her head; for that instant she could not speak. Petris with Lepescu? Had he always been Lepescu's agent? Was this what Lepescu's dying words had meant?

Cecelia started to reach for her ID packet, but the shift of his weapon stopped her hand. Not her tongue. "I'm Lady Cecelia de Marktos, as I said; we came looking for my nephew Ronnie and his friends. With the militia."

"Ah." Petris still looked past her, to Heris. "The rescue arrives." He glanced briefly at Cecelia. "Tell me what you know about Admiral Lepescu."

Cecelia thought of objecting, but the weapon suggested caution, even cooperation. She had not realized before just how large the bore could look, seen from this angle. "I don't know him," she said.

"She didn't tell you?" he asked, jerking his chin at Heris.

Cecelia's patience snapped. "Whatever she told me is no concern of yours, young man." He laughed, a short ugly sound with little humor in it.

"You're not the best judge of that," he said. Then, to Heris, "And *you* think I'm working with the admiral?"

Cecelia glanced at her, and recognized Heris's expression for what it was, sorrow and despair, a great wound. Even when telling the story of her resignation, she had never looked this shattered.

"I know he organized the hunt, here," Heris said. Her voice had no vigor, as if the words lay dead in her mouth. "And why else would military personnel be here with him—?"

"*With* him." Petris's voice was no louder, but the passion in it would have fuelled a scream. "You—of all people—can believe I might work with that—that—and does it look like I'm *with* him? Is this a uniform?" His voice had risen then, chopped off by a gesture from the other man. "No," he said savagely. "I am not with Lepescu." He turned away, still pale around the mouth. Cecelia stopped him.

"Excuse me, young man, but although you and my captain may be perfectly clear about what is going on, I am not. Heris has told me the admiral is an old enemy she would rather not meet save over a weapon. When my nephew and his friends disappeared, and we found that Lepescu was expected, she became convinced he had something to do with it."

Finally, the man seemed to focus, really focus, on Cecelia. *"Your* captain? You're her . . . uh . . . employer?"

"That's right. Captain Serrano signed a contract with me only two days after resigning her commission."

"And then?" He matched her gaze, as if he could pull answers out through her eyes.

"And then she took command of my yacht, and we came here. Now—"

"Directly?"

Cecelia drew herself up, annoyed. She had questions of her own, and he kept interrupting her. "No," she said, not caring if he realized she was miffed. "No—although I don't quite see what business it is of yours. My former captain had been negligent, if not actually criminal, in maintaining systems, and we had to detour for emergency repair of the environmental system."

The man turned to Heris, the corner of his mouth twitching. *"You* didn't check things yourself before you started?"

"The inspection sheets had been faked," Heris said dully. "Lady Cecelia's schedule had already been set back; she wanted a quick departure, and I—" Her voice trailed off.

"You couldn't wait to escape," Petris said. Sarcasm edged his voice. "You took your bribe and ran off—"

"Bribe!" This time it was Heris's voice that got the silencing gesture from the other man. At least, Cecelia thought, the insult had broken through and forced a live reaction. "Is that what he told you?"

"He told us nothing, except the list of charges."

"Charges? But I resigned so they wouldn't prosecute any of you—"

"Wait." Petris lowered his weapon suddenly. "Then it's true what this youngster heard?" He nodded at Ronnie. "Will you tell *me* you resigned? To save us, without any . . . any reward?"

"Yes. That was the choice. Resignation, and no trouble for you, or courts for all. It wasn't fair to put all of you through that; it had been my decision. What do you mean about charges?"

"That . . . motherless son," Petris said. Cecelia remembered hearing once that on some planets that was still an insult, although most people were now decanted and not birthed. "He got you out of the way, brought us to trial, and then had us here, to play his little games with."

Heris stared, the whites of her eyes showing clearly in the dimness. "You—it was *you* he was hunting?" Petris nodded. Heris shook her head, like someone who has just taken a hard blow, and turned to Lepescu's body with such violence that Cecelia was afraid she would attack it bare-handed. "Damn you! I killed you too soon! If only I could—" She was shaking now, starting to cry. Cecelia gaped, she had never imagined Heris losing control.

Petris strode past Cecelia and grabbed Heris by the shoulders, dragging her away. "He's dead—don't . . . you can't change it now—"

"I'd have—have done *something*—it's not fair—!" She turned a tear-streaked face back to Cecelia. "He took my ship—my career—and then to *kill* them this way—" And then to Petris, suddenly dry-eyed again, a sorrow too deep for tears. "I'm sorry, Petris. I didn't—imagine this. I couldn't. I believed they'd hold to the agreement."

"No," he said soberly. "You couldn't. I'm sorry I misunderstood what you'd done."

"How many—how many died?" Heris asked. Cecelia could hear the fragile control, the tremor in her voice.

"Too many," Petris said. "But it's over now."

"It's not over," Heris said. "It will never be over." But she stood straight, motionless, and Cecelia watched her usual control return, layer by layer.

"Well, it's mostly over," said a cheerful voice from the cave entrance. Petris and the other men whirled, startled, but relaxed when they saw the distinctive uniform of Bunny's militia. The militia captain was grinning at them. "Unless one of you is the wicked Admiral Lepescu?"

"Admiral Lepescu is dead," Heris said. Her voice seemed to hold no emotion at all; it was the simple statement of fact.

Captain Sigind came nearer, glanced at Lepescu's body, and nodded. "You shot him?"

"Yes; he was threatening them—" Heris nodded at the young people. Ronnie and the prince had untangled themselves from each other, the floor, and the quiescent grenade, and now stood more or less at attention. Raffa had gone to Ronnie, Cecelia noticed, as if he were her responsibility.

Bubbles stood a little apart from the group, rifle in hand, watching Heris intently. Cecelia had time to wonder why, when both girls were armed, neither had shot the admiral.

Captain Sigind looked them over.

"And here's Lord Thornbuckle's daughter, and I presume that's your nephew, ma'am, and the other young lady, and who's this—?" The militia captain looked at the prince, and the prince looked confused.

"Mr. Smith," said Ronnie firmly. "A friend of the family."

Captain Sigind allowed a dubious expression on his face, and then shrugged it away. "Mr. Smith, indeed. An invited guest? Pardon, but I'm required to ask."

Bubbles spoke up. "Mr. Smith has often been an invited guest here; my father will confirm it."

"I . . . see." The captain looked as if he would like to pursue that, but again chose discretion. Well trained, Cecelia thought; a quick glance at Heris's face, and she caught another well-trained expression. Heris, however, would certainly pursue the matter later. The captain did not quite shrug before going on. "Well, if everyone will come along, we can get you back to Bandon this evening, and fly you back to the Main House by morning—or you could spend the night on Bandon, and fly back tomorrow, whichever you prefer." He spoke into his comunit; Cecelia heard something about "retrieve the bodies" and "forensics" and then realized she was very, very tired indeed and wanted to sit down.

"What about George?" she heard Ronnie ask. Then she heard nothing.

CHAPTER TWENTY

Cecelia awoke only moments later, thoroughly ashamed of herself, to find Ronnie kneeling beside her. He looked, she thought, far worse than she possibly could, with that colorful pattern of bruises on his head and face, his muddy, still-wet clothes, and the pallor of exhaustion and hunger. She glanced around for Heris. Her captain was talking to the militia captain, who nodded as he keyed information into a wristcomp. Other militia had appeared; Lepescu's body had already been put into a black bag and lifted onto a stretcher. . . . She saw it being carried out.

"Are you all right, Aunt Cecelia?" He sounded genuinely concerned, not annoyed by an aunt who had fainted.

"I'm fine," she said, and pushed herself up on her elbows. She was too old to faint; at her age people took it seriously and talked about medical causes. "Just hungry," she said, which was now true. She was ravenous, and remembered that she had not had breakfast or lunch. Ronnie looked around frantically, as if he thought she expected him to pull a good meal from the rock. "Don't worry," she said, more tartly than she intended. "I forgot to eat, that's all." When she glanced around again, she saw that the two young women were sitting together, doing something to each other's faces, and the other young man stood awkwardly alone. "What's the—"

"Mr. Smith," Ronnie said softly but firmly. "He's Mr. Smith—I don't know if you've met."

"Oh, we've met." She eyed him, then glanced at the prince.

"Mr. Smith, is it? Did you two arrange to meet here and continue your disagreement?"

"No!" Ronnie hushed himself with a shrug. "He was here on . . . other business. Finished business, now."

Cecelia looked at the prince, who seemed to feel her gaze and returned it. In the cave's uncertain light, she could not be sure of his expression, but he approached them.

"Excuse me," he said. "Ronnie, I really do need to talk to you. About the duel—"

"Mr. Smith," said Cecelia, in the voice that had not failed her in fifty years or more. "You do not need to talk to anyone. Under the circumstances, Mr. Smith"—she emphasized the name slightly—"the less you talk to anyone the better. I very much doubt your father knows where you are."

"Well, no, he doesn't, but still—"

"You would be wise, Mr. Smith, to wait until your father explains your situation more fully. There is no question of a duel. Is that quite clear?" Cecelia put her eye upon him, the eye that had quelled many a brash young man even when she herself was young. He subsided; even the stubborn knot along his jaw went away, and the jaunty curl at the tips of his moustache seemed to droop. His voice lowered to a hesitant growl.

"What I was going to say, ma'am, was that your nephew's courage in landing on the gas grenade cancelled out any previous disagreement we might have had."

"You did, too," Ronnie said quickly.

"Wise of both of you," Cecelia said, allowing them to see her smile. "Now if someone can find me something to eat—"

Cecelia had never thought about how long it could take to move a few people across a short stretch of ocean. She had always been, she realized, the one who didn't have to wait. This time, she waited, and heard from both militia and the young people what had happened. Even with her wits restored by hot broth and half a survival bar from Bubbles's pack, it didn't make sense to her.

"Lepescu killed the other hunters? Why?"

Heris rubbed her nose. "My guess would be that he thought he could get away alone. No witnesses on his side, convicted criminals—if any survived—on the other. . . . If he'd killed the young people, gotten into that flitter, and made it away—"

"But he couldn't possibly—"

"I'm not sure. Suppose we had still been on the mainland when George's transmission went out. He'd have had hours, not minutes, to complete his plans. Kill the witnesses, gas the remaining victims from the flitter. Fly back to Bandon, take the shuttle up. A wild gamble, but he liked wild gambles. Better than surrendering tamely to be tried himself."

"But why not get the others to help him?"

"Likely they wouldn't. That Mr. Smith—and by the way, are you and the others going to tell me who Mr. Smith is?"

"Someone who shouldn't be here," Cecelia said. "Later, perhaps—" She glanced around at the militia who might be within earshot.

"Ah. Like someone's son, perhaps? Yes." Heris's eyes twinkled. "Anyway, Mr. Smith explained that there had been a lot of confusion after the flitter crashed here, and the admiral had insisted on continuing the hunt. He might well fear that his allies would turn on him. If he had gotten away—well away—we would have found an island full of dead people and no witnesses to convict him. He would not necessarily know that I was here at all, or that I knew he was onplanet." Heris cocked her head. "A bold plan, typical of him, but as usual wasteful of resources."

"And Raffa told me about what happened after they crashed—although she doesn't know all of Ronnie's story, or George's, or the others'. Were they all your crew?"

"Apparently not. This wasn't the first such hunt, and Petris said some who survived a few weeks of a hunt were kept to seed the next, to keep it 'interesting.'" Her voice flattened on the word. "Too many were, though. I never thought—I *swear* I never imagined any such thing—"

"Of course not." Cecelia leaned against the rock, and smiled at the younger woman. So much older than the younglings, Ronnie and his friends, but still so vulnerable. . . . She clearly needed someone to reassure her. Yet, in Cecelia's experience, no reassurance made up for bad results . . . and this had to be a bad result, no matter how selfless the original decision. She looked away from Heris, and thought about what she could do. Did she know anyone in the admiralty?

✳   ✳   ✳

By the time Heris and Cecelia landed on Bandon again,
the young people—except for Buttons, who remained the
family's representative on Bandon—had been taken to the
mainland along with two wounded militia and three wounded
victims. Ronnie needed medical observation; the girls had
wanted to check on George themselves, and Bubbles had
an appointment with her father. Cecelia relaxed in the luxury
of Bandon Lodge—a full set of servants had been flown out
as soon as the island was secured—and left Heris to her
own devices. Heris, after a bath and change of clothes,
gathered her courage and went to see if her former crew
would even speak to her. They were scattered through the
guest rooms, according to the information in the deskcomp.
She found door after door with its privacy locks engaged,
and didn't try to intrude. Finally she found one door ajar,
and tapped lightly.

Petris looked out at her. "Ah. Captain Serrano." The
formality went to her heart. "I was just about to bathe."

"I'm sorry. I'll—" Wait, she would have said, but she had
no right to force him to speak to her if he didn't want to.

"I'm sorry I yelled at you, back there," he said. "It was
just hard to believe—"

"I'm sorry I thought you could have been with . . . with
Lepescu."

"Look—I'm still stinking filthy—I was checking on Oblo,
and he's fine. Let me get clean, and why don't we go walk
somewhere?"

At least he was willing to talk to her. Heris nodded,
silently, and turned away. Back in her room she tried to
relax, but her eyes kept moving to the window, with its
striking view of the beach and the other island across the
water. The sun slid lower; the colors of sea and sky changed
minute by minute. Flitters came and went; they were, she
supposed, picking up the bodies and taking them away,
bringing more investigators to look for more clues. . . . Her
head ached. She had fallen into a restless doze in her chair
when the tap on her door woke her.

Bathed and dressed in clean clothes, Petris looked more
like the man she remembered—and less. He was not in
uniform, the only clothes she'd seen him wear except for
the rags of the island. He was not in the mental uniform
that had kept them both from acknowledging what they could

feel if they allowed it. His eyes challenged her. "If you need a rest, we could hold this until morning."

A night with issues unsettled would be no rest. "No. I'm ready."

To her surprise, he smiled at her. "My favorite captain. Always ready." He held up a basket. "I've had my first free meal, but thought we should bring something. There are enough cooks here to feed two cruisers. And the young lord, whats-his-name—"

"Buttons," Heris said. "They call him Buttons."

"The staff don't. Anyway, he gave me a map, and suggested something called the 'seabreeze trail.'"

She started to object—she had no idea where such a place might be—but didn't. After what had happened, she had no right to quibble. "How is . . . everyone?"

Petris shrugged. "Most of 'em are asleep, I think. Oblo said to tell you thumbs-up on coming to the rescue, and I said I would. He said there's a nurse in the clinic, there on the mainland, that almost makes the whole thing worthwhile. Remember the time we had to get him out of that rathole on Sekkis?"

Heris grinned, genuinely amused for the first time. "Oh, yes. Purple-dyed skin and all."

Petris led the way down the carpeted hall, hung with soft-toned pictures of flowers and birds, and out to the parking area. "The young man said we could take a flitter or walk—which would you rather?"

It was nearly dark—though why that should matter, she couldn't think. "Let's walk," she said. "If it's not too far."

"Nope. Just down this way." In the gathering dusk, he led the way to a trail edged with white stones. It wound around one wing of the Lodge, skirted a clump of very tall trees, then dipped to the shore. Far off the sun hung in a glowing net of haze; the sea held the light and threw it back at them. The island across the strait showed a pale edge of beach, and a dark hump, but no details.

They walked on, along the beach, to an outcrop of gray rock very like the rock on the other island. It lay across the end of the beach, and beyond it Heris could see a rougher, stony shore where the sea nibbled and sucked hungrily. Here they stopped, as if the rock were a real barrier, although its blunt steps could have been climbed by a child.

Petris set down his basket. "While we still have light, we should see what the cooks came up with. Ah . . . *real* food." He spread the serving containers out. Heris sat down abruptly. It couldn't be this easy. Something had to happen, some further punishment for her mistake. It would be fair, she thought dismally, if he had put poison in the food, if he leapt on her and strangled her. She hadn't meant bad to come of it, but it had—and when had intention ever been justification for causing the deaths of innocents?

He looked at her and shook his head. "Captain— Heris—" It was the first time he had used her first name except to yell at her. "You're about as relaxed as a novice gunner before the first battle. What do you think, I'm going to scold you?"

"You'd have a right," she said.

"Well . . . yes. In one way, I do. In another, I don't." He looked into her eyes. "I think you *want* your scolding, is that it?"

Tears burned her eyes. "I—don't know. I want—what happened to be different. For it to have worked the way it was supposed to. You safe—"

Anger roughened his voice. "By the gods, Heris, do you think we'd have joined the Regs if we'd wanted to be *safe*? And safe at the cost of the best commander we ever had? Keep us from being butchered by that fool and his stupid tactics, yes—but not ruin yourself, and us, into the bargain."

"You're right," she said. No use denying it. "I was wrong." The rest of the pain she had put off feeling stabbed her, the thought of her crew, from that scrawny new kid in Power Systems, who had burst into tears with the first mail from home, to the wizened old senior medical mate, finishing out her last tour before retirement. What had happened to them? Tears spilled over; she could feel the wind chilling them as they ran down her cheeks; she struggled to control her breathing.

Petris moved close, and put his arm around her, a firm but gentle hold.

"You should have trusted us," he said, his breath stirring her hair. "Did you think we'd fail you?" She could hear in that the pain she had dealt them—worse for some than the pain of court-martial and public dishonor.

"I had failed *you*," Heris said. "The scan data were all lost—they told me you'd all be court-martialed along with me, risk discharge at least and probably time in prison."

"So you resigned. Walked out."

"Yes." It all came back, the nightmare she'd relived so often these past months. The Board behind their polished table, the familiar faces as strange as masks, the feel of her dress uniform collar tabs on her throat, a blade no less dangerous for being fabric and not steel. "I was told," she went on, careful to withhold all emotion, "that if I resigned immediately, they would take no action against you—the crew. They would hush it up; it would not have happened. Sorkangh—my father's friend, one I'd counted on to help me argue my case—he said that. And if Sorkangh was against me—" She shook her head. She had said this already; it made no difference. She had had her reasons, she had fought herself to make that decision, and none of her reasons mattered. It had been wrong, as wrong as not anticipating any enemy's position and firepower.

"Well," he said, squeezing her shoulders, "if it helps, not all your crew was as loyal as they should have been. Lepescu had a ringer in, and that's what happened to the scan data."

"How'd you find that out?" She had wondered, but could not have proven her suspicions.

"First transit brig. Friend of a friend of a friend—couldn't do much for us, but did tell us who did it and on whose orders. We took care of *him*."

Heris shuddered; she didn't want to understand, although she did. "How many . . ."

"I'm not sure. They split us up, early on—we were tried in different groups, supposedly determined by our level of responsibility. Some weren't formally charged, I heard—but I couldn't tell you what happened to them. Of those brought to court, the scuttlebutt is that all but three were convicted. Some were discharged, and some had the usual loss of rank, or pay, but no brig time. They decided to make an example of about fifty of us, the senior NCOs and officers, and from that about thirty were brought here. The others are in the prison system somewhere."

"I'll have to do something about that," Heris muttered.

Petris shifted beside her. "I don't see how you can, now," he said. "Maybe if this comes out, their cases can

be reevaluated, but whatever Lepescu was up to, the original charges are still there."

"I'll think of something," she said. "Maybe Lady
Cecelia—"

"Maybe." He didn't sound convinced. "But I had something else to say to you." She braced herself, but he didn't
go on for a long time. Then he sighed. "I wish it was darker.
Thing is . . . you're not my commander now, right?"

"Right." Heris picked up something—it was dark enough
she could hardly see the food—and stuffed it in her mouth.
Cheese and pastry and something; she nearly choked.

"You were always professional . . . you know . . . but
I used to wonder if you felt something . . . something like
I did." He wasn't looking at her, but at the last fading purple
glow in the west. Then up at the stars. Heris had time to
remember times she had not wanted to be professional; she
choked down the food in her mouth.

"Mmm. Yes. Something . . ." How could she have known
it was a mutual feeling? They had both understood professional etiquette; nothing must come of any feelings, and thus
better to leave them unfelt—or at least unsaid.

"So?" The flat, gray light, all that was left of sunset, caught
in his eyes. Heris opened her mouth to say how impossible
it was, then realized it wasn't. Not any more.

"So . . ." She still could not say it. She moved, instead,
into the arc of his arm.

"You should have trusted *me*," he said again, but without
heat. "It hurt, when you went away like that, without a word."

"Yes. It did." She leaned against him; his arm felt good
against her back. Better than good. "It hurt a lot. But I'm here
now, and I'm trusting you."

"About time." Then his grip tightened. She had never
allowed herself to imagine—really imagine—what embracing
him would be like. It would have been too difficult to go
through everyday shipboard life, if she had. Now she was glad
of her former discipline. She had no nagging comparisons to
make, just the experience to savor.

"I fixed it," Cecelia said. She sounded smug. Bright
morning light gilded her hair, and she looked crisp and
refreshed by ample sleep and good food.

"Fixed what?" Heris had bathed and changed, when she

and Petris got back to the Lodge shortly before dawn, but inside her clothes her body felt lush and relaxed. She wondered if Cecelia could tell. She had her own list of things for Cecelia to fix, and hoped her employer hadn't used up her energy on something minor.

"Your resignation," Cecelia said, as if continuing a conversation in progress. "I hate to lose you, but I know how you've grieved. And the evidence is clear. So I just argued my way along, and they've agreed to take you back. Quite willingly, in fact. Everyone knows that George's father will sue Lepescu and his cronies, and the Regular Space Service is anxious to dissociate themselves from any of that."

Heris stared, her brain racing. Cecelia had fixed *that,* in a few hours, from an obscure planet with no real-time communications beyond its own system? Then: Go back? Retrieve her command, her career? She felt her heart begin to hammer, the racing pulse pounding her body, making her hands shake. Exultation flooded her; she could see the look on her father's face, on her mother's. . . . She could imagine how her younger brother, still in the Academy, would react. *Yes,* she thought. *Yes.*

"How?" got out of her mouth first.

Cecelia beamed, clearly glad to be asked. "I'd been afraid it would take weeks, but you remember Bunny said a Crown Minister was here hunting? Bunny asked me to speak to him about Mr. Smith, and of course I told him about you. I pointed out that going through the usual channels would require your complete explanation, and you, as an honest person, could hardly fail to mention Mr. Smith when you justified the killing of Admiral Lepescu."

"Mr. Smith," said Heris blankly. She had almost forgotten that mysterious young man. Then her brain snapped back into focus. "A . . . royal, you said, about the boots." Which, given his age, meant . . . *"Not* the one Ronnie was in trouble for—"

Cecelia grinned. "Quite so. The Minister saw my point, of course, and assured me that no statement from you would be required, under the circumstances. Enough evidence of Lepescu's unfitness existed to overturn the judgment without recalling whatever court or board it was. You can trust him," Cecelia went on, as if anticipating Heris's doubts. "With Mr. Smith's reputation at stake, he would do more than this. Luckily for us, the Minister requires a special communications link—I don't know what you call it, but it's almost instantaneous through some kind of relay back to Court. He was able to contact the necessary officials, and—"

"And the surviving crew?" Heris asked. She felt already like a Spacefleet officer, the purple uniform forgotten along with the past several hours.

Cecelia nodded briskly. "Oh, yes. All rehabilitated, as they called it. I knew you would want that, so I insisted. Wherever they are, if some of them were not on that abominable island." When Heris didn't answer at once she went on. "I *do* understand, you know. We are both aristocrats, even if we aren't in the same aristocracy."

"I—thank you, milady." Only that formality would serve, could possibly express her gratitude.

"I will hate losing you," Cecelia said, more softly. "Not only as a captain, and student of equitation, but as a friend. I like you, and I don't like many people." Then her voice firmed again. "Will it be difficult, for you and Petris?"

Heris stared at her, disoriented by the double-change of direction. "Petris . . . ? Oh." So Cecelia had noticed. At once the exaltation left her, as quickly as if someone had pulled a plug in her heart. She could go back, and he could go back, and they might serve on the same ship . . . but they could not go back to the past hours. Not ever. She tried to imagine him as a civilian . . . husband . . . but that would destroy him. "Oh, my," she said, hardly hearing her own voice. "I didn't think."

"Most people don't, in your position," Cecelia said. "That's why I mentioned it, before you go and tell the others. You can go back . . . but you don't have to."

Didn't she? She could hardly breathe for a moment, in the alternation of possibility and impossibility. She could not give up her chance in the R.S.S. again—she could not give up Petris. She could not ask him to give up his career, as miraculously restored as her own, but if either of them . . .

"Damn," she said. It was all she could say. She sat down suddenly, and Cecelia made a show of turning away, preparing something to drink, offering her a steaming cup of some brown liquid. . . . She should know what it was, but she couldn't recognize anything.

"As a classical maiden aunt," Cecelia said, not looking at her, "I am qualified to give useless advice, which you are free to ignore. You love that man, and he loves you; that was obvious when I first saw you two together. You can't be together in the Service, and neither of you will be happy as a civilian partnering the one who stays in. If you do go back, Heris, be sure you're never on the same ship . . . You know that."

"I know that." Her lips felt numb—was it the drink? Was she going to faint? She never fainted; it was ridiculous. But her skin remembered his touch; her ears remembered his voice, the sound of his breathing, the beat of his heart when her head lay on his chest. She wanted that, wanted it more than anything . . . except her commission, her ship, her crew . . . which she couldn't have, if it meant him.

"I still need a captain," Cecelia went on. "I need new crew members—you told me that. If you choose not to reenter the Service, you would have a place with me."

And Petris would become just a crew member on a rich old lady's yacht—she could not see him being happy with that. He had taken as much pride in his career as she in hers. He would not settle for less.

"You ought to ask him," Cecelia said, as if reading her face. "You didn't ask before, and look where that got you. Give him the chance, now, while you have the chance . . . while you are, for the moment, free."

It was true. She had not thought she had a chance, before; she had taken the commander's way, the solitary way, and had not asked anyone, and because of that Lepescu had been able to ruin her *and* her crew. This time she could ask him. She stood up, nodding to Cecelia without saying a word— she could not have said a word—and went to find Petris.

He was staring out to sea, staring at the island on which he had been hunted. "Looks pretty from here," he said as she came up.

"Yes," she said. Her throat closed on more. He looked at her closely.

"What's happened?"

She couldn't answer; tears flooded her eyes. He reached for her, hugged her close, his lips in her hair. "Heris . . . Heris . . ." he breathed. She gulped, tried to calm herself, and finally choked the lump down.

"Lady Cecelia has intervened," she said finally. Her voice came out thin, unlike herself. "With the Service."

"You're getting your commission? Good." His arms loosened, and she heard the effort in his voice. "I hoped you would—they ought to have that much sense."

"They're reversing all the disciplinary actions," she said. "All the survivors will be reinstated, with all records cleared. It would probably have happened anyway, but Lady Cecelia—"

"Has connections. I'm glad she cares that much—you must have impressed her." His arms dropped from her shoulders, and he stretched. "Well. Back into harness for us, eh? And—"

Heris stared at the sand. "We don't *have* to go."

"Eh? Of course you'll go—you're not meant to be a yacht captain."

"She said I should give you the chance. The chance I didn't give you before."

He stared at her; when she looked up, his gaze was fixed on her face. "What do you mean? Are you saying—?"

"Petris—" She used his first name deliberately. "Petris, there is a choice. If we go back, you know—you know it would be best if we never serve together. But if we don't go back—"

"You love it," he said. "Your family—the Serrano Admiralty—" She had heard that phrase before; it was inevitable for a family that had produced admiral after admiral through many generations. She had never considered how they might look from underneath—from out to sea, like a great cliff wall made of stars and flags, with no safe beach to land on. She felt herself a rock loosed from that cliff, now rolling in the surf, being broken into fragments the cliff would no longer recognize.

"My family," she said slowly, "have already endured the worst: a Serrano resigning under a cloud rather than face a court. They will abide my decision, one way or the other . . . or they will not, and I will abide their decision. I don't know what they'll do, but I don't fear it. Your family?"

"Mine." He stared past her now, at the island again. "Farmers and small merchants on Vonnegar's World; I was the outlaw there, too. Ran off to join the military, like kids have always done. . . . Wouldn't walk behind a plow or pull onions if I could see stars. They wouldn't mind—they gave me up for lost when I told my uncle Eth what I thought of farming. I couldn't go back and ask for land, that's sure. But away—I can do what I want." A quick glance to her, then away again. "I liked my work."

"I know that. You can have it back; that's what Cecelia told me. She's got you all cleared."

"Ah . . . yes, but it can't be the same. Not just us, the whole thing. Some of 'em died, through this; I can't forget that."

Heris felt cold. They had died because of her, because she had left; she already knew that. If he couldn't forget, he probably couldn't forgive either, and last night had been . . . last night.

But he was looking at her again, this time steadily, eye to eye. "But what did you offer as an alternative? You said if we don't go back—"

"We could both work for Lady Cecelia. On her yacht." Of course he had already said *she* wasn't meant to be a yacht captain, and of course he wasn't meant to be on a yacht's crew either, but she had to ask.

"You must like her a lot," he said, "even to consider it. What do you . . . do?"

She could tell he was avoiding the familiar terms, like "mission." "Lady Cecelia travels," she said. "From the existing records of past voyages, she travels widely, and from the events of the first weeks I worked for her, her yacht has harbored smugglers . . . without her knowledge, of course."

"You're sure of that." It was not quite a question.

"Yes. She's stubborn, opinionated, and all the other things you expect from a rich old lady, but she's honest."

"Like you," Petris said, without a smile. "No wonder you get along. So—you'll continue?"

"It depends." Even as she said it, she wondered if it did depend on his decision. Oddly, she now thought of going back to the Service as a kind of defeat. Someone else had fought her battle for her; someone else had bought her commission back. She hated that. Bad as Lepescu was, some would always mistrust her loyalty; she would never be the unflawed Serrano in clear line of succession to an admiralty. Even her family would have reservations. She did not realize she had said some of this aloud until the end. . . .

"—and I would rather take an honest salary from her than a commission restored with her influence. So . . . it's either stay with her, or look for something else, and I have no reason now to leave her. At least not until I've straightened out that crew."

Petris chuckled. "I know that tone. All right, then—I think all of us will have the same problems. Those who don't think so are welcome to go back, but as for me . . . no. D'you think your Lady Cecelia will hire more than one of us, and will we have to bow as she sweeps by?"

"Are you saying yes?"

"No . . . I'm saying yes, *ma'am* . . . since I believe that's the correct civilian usage." The end of that was smothered in a hug, out of which he said finally, "I gather the restriction on fraternization doesn't apply either?"

"No," Heris said firmly. "Not off the bridge." Her thoughts raced, crashing into each other like fox hunters of two hunts in collision. What came out, at last, was the professional ship's officer. "I've got to check in with Sirkin—the standing watch—and let her know there's a sealed weapons cargo coming up to the ship. It's a good thing we had a complete refitting at Takomin Roads. Did you know the sulfur cycle was off by two sigs?"

He released her with a roar of laughter. "Dear heart—Heris—Captain—your owner had better pull up her bloomers or whatever they call them on aristocrats. *Weapons?* Does she know?"

"Of course she knows; I used her credit line." That had been—how long ago? And would Cecelia still authorize those weapons? Better get them aboard before she changed her mind. Somewhere the smugglers that had put that contraband aboard had to be wondering what had happened to it. The rich were no safer, if they didn't bother to defend themselves, than someone on the docks. In the depths of her mind, the final door to her past shut, and she faced the future as a civilian without the old pain. It would return, she knew, as old pains always did, in the dark hours everyone faced . . . but the worst was over.

CHAPTER TWENTY-ONE

Discretion must be served. Two by two, the former prey, Heris's former crew members, left for the mainland hospital, where (Heris was assured) Bunny's excellent medical staff would check them out, and where they would live in privacy and luxury until they decided what they wanted to do. She had spoken to each one, but they were too dazed to talk much. She understood; she felt that way herself. Too many emotions, too much turmoil. Finally, with the lodge empty, it was her turn. She and Cecelia and Petris had a luxurious flitter, with Michaels himself at the controls, for the flight back. No more clouds. . . . The wrinkled ocean lay blank and blue under a clear sky until they reached the mainland. Heris stared at it until she felt the pattern was imprinted forever on her retinas. She wondered why Petris was traveling with them, then wondered why she wondered. And why couldn't they talk? After that first night, she had not expected the awkwardness of the days and nights since, when they could cling together . . . but not complete a sentence.

The flitter delivered them to the wide courtyard before the Main House rather than the flitter hangars. Here it was cold, with low clouds racing across the sky before a sharp wind. Heris sealed the jacket she had not needed on the island and shivered. She was glad she wouldn't have to walk up the hill from the other end of the village. Inside, Petris looked up the great staircase that first time with an odd expression that mingled delight and apprehension.

"This is exactly how I thought a great lord's house would look, and I don't trust it," he said finally. "It's too perfectly what it is, like an entertainment-cube version of a fleet cruiser."

"It's intimidating," said Heris. Now she could admit that. "I couldn't believe anyone actually lived in it. But they do." She wondered where the servants were; usually two or three at least were in the hall at this hour. But the one who had opened the door had vanished, leaving it to Cecelia to lead the way upstairs.

Petris, she found, had the room next to hers, where she remembered someone else having been, but she did not raise her brows to Cecelia, who already looked entirely too smug. How had Cecelia known that?

"Don't forget," Cecelia said, "that Petris will need to check in with Neil. I'll let him know you're coming, shall I?"

Heris looked at Petris. He had not had the benefit of Cecelia's riding simulator. But he grinned. "I can hardly wait to see Heris on horseback, chasing a fox," he said. "Although I'm not looking forward to those early starts."

"Nonetheless. And of course I needn't warn either of you about discussing all this—"

"Not at all." Petris raised and lowered his brows at her, a clear dismissal.

"Dinner at eight," Cecelia said. She strode off down the corridor.

"Your employer—" Petris began.

"Our employer," Heris said. "Unless you change your mind."

"I never change my mind," Petris said. "Come in here—" He led her into his room, a twin of her own. "I don't believe this, either!" He was staring at the furniture, the gleaming expanse of the bathroom and its glittering toys. He walked around the room, opening and closing the doors of wardrobes, looking into drawers in tall polished chests. Heris could see the racks of clothes, and wondered. "I'm sure these all fit—Lady Cecelia would have seen to it. I always knew there was a good reason to leave the onion farm." Then he looked into the bathroom again. "Plenty of room, and warm towels. Shall I scrub your back, my love, or will you scrub mine?"

✳　　✳　　✳

Ronnie was sure they were all making too much fuss about his condition. George had been shot; George might die. He still had that nagging headache, and a collection of bruises and scrapes, but after a night in the hospital he was ready to go back to hunting. Or at least, back to living in the far more comfortable quarters he had enjoyed before.

"Time enough," the nurse said. "You're not leaving until the doctor agrees, and your scans aren't normal yet." It wasn't the same nurse as before, he thought, and wondered how often their shifts changed.

"Nothing's broken," Ronnie said. "You let that fellow in the other bed leave just twenty-four hours after a broken leg—"

"Bones aren't brains," the nurse said. Ronnie closed his eyes, feigning sleep, and was surprised to find dark outside his windows when he opened them again. The next morning (which morning?) he woke without a trace of the headache, and the awareness that he had not been clear-headed before.

"And you're not yet," the doctor said, when she arrived to talk to him before he left. "You think you are, but it's like climbing out of a hole: it's lighter where you are, but you're still in shadow. I know this will disappoint you, but I've already notified Lord Thornbuckle's head groom: you are not to ride for at least ten days, and you'll have to be reevaluated then."

"But I didn't—" Ronnie began, but the doctor smiled and patted his knee as if he were a child. Considering her white hair and wrinkles, she probably thought of him that way. *I didn't want to ride,* he said silently. *And now I don't have to.* "What about George?" he asked. They had told him nothing so far except soothing murmurs. He braced himself to hear that George had died.

"*That* young man," the doctor said. "Do I understand that everyone calls him the odious George?"

"Yes," Ronnie said.

"I can see why," she said. "He can have visitors—in fact, he has visitors all day, now. So if you want to know, just take the lift up one, and it's the third door on the left. He's still on the surgical floor, though really—" She shook her head without finishing that and left. Ronnie pulled on his clothes, hardly wondering where they'd come from, and went to see George.

George lay propped up in bed, looking like an advertisement for a hospital company: dark hair perfectly in place, fading bruises on his face suggesting courage without diminishing his good looks. Ronnie knew that on anyone else the yellow and green and dull purple would have looked hideous, but George's luck seemed to hold.

"Ronnie!" His voice sounded the same, if not quite as loud as usual. "I wondered when you'd make it up here. You missed all the excitement."

Ronnie stared at him. Missed all the excitement? Had no one told George about the admiral and the gas grenade, or the prince, or—

"My father's on the way," George said. He looked exactly as he had always looked, smug. Odious. Ronnie wanted to hit him, but you couldn't hit someone in bed with a gunshot wound. He went in, nonetheless, holding a vague grudge but not sure how to let it go. Should he tell George about the prince? He thought he remembered it was supposed to be a secret.

George's face changed, and his voice softened. "I—was really scared. You passed out on me, then they caught me, and those two—"

"Who?"

"The guards back on Bandon. I never saw the hunters at all, just these two men."

"They're the ones who shot you?"

"Oh, no. One of Bunny's militia shot me, and it wasn't an accident, either. I tried to tell Captain Serrano, but couldn't get it across. . . . He was standing there, eyeing your aunt as if he'd like to kill her right then."

"Did you tell Bunny? When you got back here?" Ronnie had an urge to leap up himself, right then, and go find his aunt.

"It's all right. That's part of what you missed. That's the same man who tried to kill your aunt and Captain Serrano when they went to find you in the cave."

"Oh." Ronnie tried to remember if he'd heard about that man before. He remembered some things vividly: finding George unconscious, trying to build a litter, the storm, Raffa's warmth against him in the cold, dark cave, that moment of sheer terror when he jumped for the gas grenade. But he had no clear mental map of the time . . . how long they'd been on the island, or whether they'd stayed on Bandon overnight or flown straight back.

"Your aunt plugged him," George said, with relish. "He had the captain covered."

"She would," Ronnie said vaguely. He hated not remembering; it was like being very old, he thought. He had probably said things, and done things, without really knowing it. What if he had said something stupid? What if he had said something stupid to Raffa? Was that why he couldn't remember seeing her in the hospital?

George sobered again. "It's not that easy, being a hero. At least, it wasn't for me. You—"

"Not for me, either. There's a lot I can't remember."

"There's a lot I wish I couldn't remember." George scowled. "I have never been so scared, so humiliated, in my life—not even that first term at school." He sounded far more human than usual. "At least you didn't have to scrub any toilets."

"Not that again!" Raffa's voice; Ronnie turned to look. She might never have been off the mainland; she looked like all the other polished young women who had come for the hunting party, and she looked like no one else in the universe. Bubbles, beside her, leaned against the door and grinned broadly.

"Now I can quit holding Raffa's hand every night. You had us all scared, Ronnie."

"Me? George is the one who got shot."

"All George needed was a good surgeon, a day in the regen tank, and a personality transplant; my father could supply the first two, but not the last."

"You'll regret that, Bubbles—" George said, but it had no bite. "My reputation depends on being odious. And wrinkle-free."

"Your reputation depends on your father," Bubbles said. "Or someone would have beaten the odiousness out of you long before."

"Unfair," George said. Then he grinned. "Well—partly unfair. And I do resent the damage to my good trousers."

"I assure you," Bubbles said, in the same dry tone, "that you'll be wrinkle-free and out of here in time for the Hunt Ball. If you promise to keep your mouth shut and cause no trouble about Mr. Smith."

George made an innocent face that would not have fooled anyone. It certainly did not fool Ronnie or the girls.

"If you don't promise—and keep that promise," Bubbles went on, "I'll make sure that someone slips the wrong stuff in the regen tank for your next treatment, and you'll have wrinkles in places you don't think wrinkles can form. *Permanent* wrinkles. Then you can stay in this room until you die of genuine old age."

"And I," Raffa said, coming over to take Ronnie's hand, "will personally ruin every garment you own *and* send your tailor a certified letter giving your new measurements. *Interesting* new measurements." She mimed the anguish of someone in trousers with a short rise, the problems of skimpy sleeves and a baggy, short jacket.

George rolled his eyes dramatically. "You might have trusted me. Lawyers' sons learn *some* discretion." The others snorted. He went on. "All right. I promise. No leading questions, no suggestive remarks, nothing about Mr. Smith or his . . . mmm . . . other identity. But how am I supposed to explain my disappearance from the noble sport of fox hunting?"

"We took the flitter to go picnicking, and we crashed, and you and Ronnie were hurt saving us. Very simple, very—"

"What about Lady Cecelia and Captain Serrano?"

"Unrelated, except that Lady Cecelia is the one who let Bunny know we were missing—just as it happened. We're hoping to get past the Hunt Ball without the whole story coming out."

Neil had pronounced Petris's seat "untidy but effective," and passed him into the blue hunt at once. Heris had little interest in riding to hounds any more, but also little choice; if she stayed home, it would be noticed, and tongues were already wagging. Cecelia, pleading age, could go out only twice a week; Heris had to ride five days out of seven. She knew Cecelia was up to something again—or still—because the Crown Minister stayed in the same days as Cecelia.

"I might just as well go back to the ship," she argued with Cecelia one afternoon. Her horse had stumbled on landing from a wall, fallen heavily, and come up lame; Heris herself had bruised her shoulder. The fox—if there was a fox—had got clean away. She wanted to be back on a decent ship, where large heavy animals didn't dump her off and then roll on her. Her leg wasn't broken, but it felt reshaped.

"You should go by the hospital and spend a few hours in the tank," Cecelia said. "You've had a hard fall, and you're sore. It'll heal."

"We'll have crew changes—"

"You can't go until after the Hunt Dinner and Ball. We have to finish out this much of the season, or it will be suspicious. You notice that no one comments on what happened?"

"But—"

"But Mr. Smith is safely contained; I've offered to take him home since we already officially know. We'll stay until the Hunt Dinner, and leave the next day. I *always* stay for the first Hunt Dinner." Heris found this confusing, since in the books she'd read there was only one official Hunt Dinner per hunt club, but presumably Bunny did things his own way. And with such a long season, perhaps most people didn't stay for the whole thing. Cecelia patted her shoulder; Heris tried not to wince. "Now go spend a few hours in the tank, and ask Sari to give you a good rubdown. Petris will be in the green hunt, Neil says, by the day after tomorrow, and you'll feel much better by then."

Heris didn't want a rubdown from Sari; she wanted a pleasant night with Petris. But with her bruises, it wouldn't be pleasant. "When is this Hunt Dinner?" she asked, resigned to a trip to the hospital. She would remember to look in on everyone.

"End of next week." Cecelia took a few twirling steps that startled Heris. She flushed. "I may be old, and plain, but there's no law that says I can't dance."

Dance. Heris thought of dancing with Petris, and felt her bones begin to melt. She would manage not to hunt in the next week; she didn't want to risk missing that. It might even be worth the hours in the regen tank. She was in the tank, trying to relax as the technicians fussed over her bruised arm and leg, when one of the things Cecelia had said brought her bolt upright, splashing.

"Sorry," she said, to the technician who had contained his own curse but not the expression on his face. "Bad memory." The prince. Cecelia had said they were going to transport the prince home. That meant . . . she squeezed her eyes shut, and thought about it. Would Ronnie stay here? Surely she wouldn't have that pair on her ship at the same time!

The last week passed in a flurry . . . cold blue days, icy nights, glorious rides across the open land the green hunt favored. Heris had come out of the tank with more than her bruises healed, and suspected Cecelia of telling someone to load her IV with mood elevators. Either that, or the old books were right when they described the glow of lovers riding stirrup to stirrup at a gallop.

"Gallop by day, and . . . other gaits by night," Petris said, his arm under her head again. Heris didn't answer, as the gait in question required concentration. They could talk again, she had discovered, but this was not the time. Later, he asked, "And what are you wearing to the ball tomorrow?"

"A dress," Heris said. She could feel herself starting to chuckle in anticipation, a quiver that Petris must surely recognize. He tapped her nose with his finger.

"A dress. Amazing. I thought fox hunters wore skins and furs to a ball. Or horse hides or something equally barbaric. What are you laughing about? Are you wearing a fur dress?"

"No . . . but I won't tell you. You'll have to see it." An extravagance, which she had not intended, but it had made an excuse to miss one day's hunt. It made a sizeable hole in the salary Cecelia had yet to pay her. She could hardly wait to see Petris's face when he saw her in it.

Heris had not meant to wait until the day of the Hunt Dinner to tackle Cecelia about the changes needed in the ship, but there never seemed to be time. But she had made promises to Petris and the others; she had to make sure Cecelia understood before they actually boarded. The argument (she was sure it would be an argument) must be private. She slithered into her own gown, and shook her head at the image in the mirror. The beaded bodice shifted color with every movement, shimmering; the soft pleats of the midnight-blue skirt were spangled with random beads, as if the bodice had dripped fire onto it. And she looked . . . very unmilitary, she decided. *Very* unmilitary.

She found Cecelia almost dressed, and fiddling with the

amber necklace she favored. A flounce of ivory lace refused to lie properly beneath it.

"I need to talk to you about the ship," Heris said.

"What's wrong?"

"Nothing's wrong. . . ."

"So what is it now?"

"Some changes will have to be made." Heris watched Cecelia as she said it. The older woman had looked tired for the last week, and claimed it had nothing to do with the ship. The Minister? Mr. Smith? The Service?

"Such as?" Cecelia's voice was tart. "Oh—I suppose we'll have to have another environmental system, to take care of the extra people?"

"Not really." Heris ignored the tartness, and went on. "You have four crew who have asked for separation. Three want to stay here, and have applied for employment with Lord Thornbuckle's personnel. The other wants to leave at the next major Roads. Then there's a member of your house staff who got pregnant in Hospitality Bay—Bates says he is sure of intent, in this case, because she had pursued even him. And one of your undergardeners—so you see, we won't be overloaded."

"What changes then?"

Heris met the problem head-on. "Weapons," she said. And as Cecelia stared, her mouth opening, she talked on. "You are a very wealthy woman in a very luxurious and capable ship. Remember that you've already been used by smugglers. What if they want their cargo? What if they want the whole ship? What if they want *you*? The places you like to travel are not exactly the safest corners of the universe. We need proper armament—"

"Now that you have gunners, you have to have guns." So, Cecelia had understood—or found someone to translate—the military specialty codes her new crew members carried. Heris cocked her head; Cecelia could hardly claim to be a philosophical pacifist, not after having shot someone herself.

"What's the matter, milady? Do you think I'll deliberately lead you into danger?" Of course, she had done just that, but it was for a good reason.

"No. I don't know." Cecelia moved restlessly, her long fingers tangled together. "Things have changed. Before, I knew what I was doing—yes, I was just cruising around

having fun, but I knew that was it. Now . . . when I think
of leaving here and going off to Roledre for the qualifying
trials, or on to Kabrice for the finals, it's—it's not that
interesting."

Heris smothered a grin. Better than she'd hoped for. "If
it's bothering you, milady, I'm sure we can find *something*
to do with this ship."

Cecelia's eyes narrowed. "Something? You mean you still
consider me an idle old lady?"

"You said it; I didn't. But think; you are healthy and tough,
and yet you had smugglers using your ship. Don't you have
friends, equally old and wealthy—"

"Not really," muttered Cecelia. Heris ignored that.

"—who might have worse parasites aboard than even your
Captain Olin? There are," Heris said, thinking of it in that
moment, "other things to hunt besides foxes, and other
mounts besides horses."

"Which prey is beneath the notice of the Regular Fleet?"

"Or too elusive for the less agile. Consider—"

"How many guns, Heris? What size? And do I get to
mention cost?"

"No more than we need, no bigger than we need, and I
will respect your resources only less than your life." She
didn't remind Cecelia about the weapons already purchased.

"As you did at Takomin Roads—no, don't defend yourself; I knew what you were doing and agreed. But from now
on, I want to be a member of the hunt staff, not just the
owner who pays the fees. You'll have to keep teaching me
about my ship, and let me be part of your plans."

"You have earned that, and more," Heris said, and meant
it. Cecelia grinned back at her.

"Then let us go down and dazzle the Hunt Dinner, and
dance the night away," she said. "And as for the future . . .
a hunting we shall go. . . ." And she grabbed Heris's arm
and led her down the corridor to the main staircase, where
Petris, correct in formal dinner attire, waited below. Heris saw
his expression shift from surprise through amusement to
admiration as she and Cecelia came down arm in arm, singing.
"Tan-tivvy, tan-tivvy, tan-tivvy—a hunting we shall go . . ."

"Ladies, ladies! Such unseemly levity!" But his lips
twitched. He offered an arm to each, and cocked an eyebrow
at Heris. "You settled it, I gather?"

"She was never a military officer, Petris," Cecelia said with a sweet smile. "She was born to be a pirate. Look at her."

"I'll do more than look," Petris said into Heris's ear. "Later . . ."

But the tumult of the others interrupted whatever Heris might have said. Already the tall rooms rang with many voices, and more and more men and women in their formal best came down the stairs. Bunny, looking as foolish tonight as he had at first, chatted with one group after another. Then he caught sight of Cecelia, and came over without obvious haste.

"So glad you could stay for the Ball," he said, including Petris in the greeting with a nod. "We may have a slight inconvenience. . . ."

"Oh?" Cecelia's brows raised.

"Mr. Smith. He's eluded the Minister's manservant again."

Again? Heris stared; she hadn't realized Mr. Smith had been loose before.

"Declared he wasn't going to be sent home like a naughty schoolboy, in an old lady's yacht with a battleaxe for a captain." Bunny's mouth smiled, as if they discussed the day's run, but his eyes were cold and angry. "As you know the Minister had refused to let me place him under a proper guard . . . but as the Minister does not know, I put a tracer-tag on him. He dashed off to the woods, silly twit. Captain Sigind will bring him in, but I'd like to sedate him and send him up in a shuttle right away, if you don't mind. I can isolate him in the Station sickbay—"

Cecelia's expression hardened. "You've got every right to lock him in your local jail. On bread and water. Stupid boy!"

"Since there's a standing watch aboard, milady," Heris said, "we can have him aboard your yacht straight from the shuttle. Fewer eyes to see, fewer mouths to talk."

"Fine. Do it." Cecelia looked angrier than before; Heris couldn't understand why. Then she changed expression, to astonishment and relief. Heris looked over and saw Ronnie, George, Bubbles, and Raffa. With them was a heavier man whose resemblance to George lay more in manner than in feature. Bunny turned, and waved them over.

"Good to see you up and about," he said. And to the older man, "And you, of course, Ser Mahoney."

"I have no quarrel with you, Bunny," the older man said.

"Don't go formal on me, or I'll have to start wondering if I should."

"All right, Kevil. Just so you know I took this very seriously indeed."

"I can see George, and I know what happened; that tells me you took it seriously. Your lovely daughter was in it too, I understand." He patted Bubbles on the shoulder; Heris was surprised at the expression on the girl's face. She had changed, Heris thought, in some way that none of them yet knew—perhaps not even the girl herself. "And of course Cece's nephew. Those two have never been in trouble alone, or out of it together." Kevil Mahoney had a trained voice that could carry conflicting messages with ease; Heris watched both George and Ronnie flush, then subside without saying a word. He leaned closer to Bunny, and let that voice carry another weight of meaning with little volume. "And Mr. Smith? How is that estimable young man?"

"He will go home shortly," Bunny said. His eyelids lowered. "Transportation has already been arranged."

"Ah. Well, to be honest, Mr. Smith's travel arrangements do not concern me, at least not this evening. I'm simply delighted to be here for the festive occasion, with both lads out of the hospital and able to enjoy it." Kevil Mahoney smiled, bowed slightly, and walked off, leaving the young people behind. They heard him call out to someone he knew, and then he had disappeared in the crowd.

"I promised," George said, looking anxious, "but did my father?"

"Enough," Bunny said. "It's almost time for the dinner, and I will not have it ruined by speculation. Captain Serrano, if I might have the honor of your company?"

Heris had not expected this. She glanced at Cecelia, who after all ranked her in every conceivable way these people calculated rank, but Cecelia now looked more relaxed, and simply smiled and nodded. Petris, after one startled look, offered his arm to Cecelia, who accepted it with another smile.

Heris took Bunny's arm and hoped she did not look as confused as she felt. He led her through the crowd, and she could hear the subdued murmurs that must be comments on this unusual occurrence. Just as they reached the entrance to the dining room, a fanfare rang out. Heris jumped, and Bunny chuckled. Under cover of the music, he murmured, "Didn't mean to alarm you, Captain, but this is traditional."

His wife, Heris noted, was standing with Buttons. As they made their way into the dining room, she realized that the participants in the recent adventures had been provided with partners that justified their being seated at the head table. Bunny's wife with Buttons, and George with Bubbles, and Ronnie with an elderly lady, and Raffa with an elderly man of the same vintage.

"That's my aunt Trema," Bunny said, "and my wife's uncle. They're both quite deaf, and they've refused implants. They love coming to a couple of Hunt Dinners a year; they sit together at the ball afterwards and write each other saucy notes on their compads. Eccentric, but harmless." Petris, with Lady Cecelia, certainly had a place at the family table. George's father sat at the far end, with another elderly relation on one side, and one of the gawky cousins on the other.

"You see the advantages," Bunny went on, with a slight smile, "of a reputation for eccentricity and archaicisms?"

"Indeed yes," Heris said. She looked down the long dining hall, to the trumpeters in their beribboned tunics who were ready to lead in the feast. Most of the guests had found their places, but Bunny waited until even the clumsy soul who overturned his chair had safely reseated himself. Then he nodded at the trumpeters, who lifted their instruments once more.

To the blare of trumpets and the shrill wailing of pipes, the feast came in. Cecelia reached around Petris to say, "It's about as authentic as the foxes, but it's fun." Bunny winked at her, and Heris began to relax. It could be worse . . . would have been worse, if Cecelia hadn't told her, if they hadn't told Bunny, if she and Cecelia both had not been good shots. They could all have been dead.

She pulled her mind away from that with an effort, and made herself enjoy the spectacle. Serving trays loaded with exotic foods whose origin she couldn't even guess. Servants in colorful livery. And the music. The food, when she tasted it, drove the last grim thought from her mind.

"I hadn't had a chance to thank you," Bunny said, somewhere between the soup and fish. "It's been hectic since you got back."

"I didn't realize Mr. Smith had been giving trouble," Heris said.

"Mmm. Although that's not the reason I asked you to come in with me, it may prove convenient to have you here when he's found. If you're sure the transfer to Lady Cecelia's yacht poses no problem."

"Not if I have a direct line up."

"Of course. My debt to you continues to grow. I don't know if you actually enjoyed the sport, but please consider yourself welcome here anytime." Under the pleasant tone, the calm expression, Heris sensed tension and even savagery. They ate in silence for some minutes, as the fish course came and went, and slices of roast appeared. Bunny sighed, and resumed as if he had not paused. "Bubbles—says she wants to talk to you."

"To me?"

"An experience like that would change anyone; I understand. But she's been the youngest, the wildest—so of course her change had to be greater."

Heris eyed her host. "Did she tell you about it?"

"Some. Not all. She thinks you—because you were military— will understand her better."

Heris could think of nothing socially acceptable to say. She could imagine the sort of thing Bubbles would think she could understand—and she did understand, but not in the way Bubbles would want. Nor did she wish to interfere in this family, especially not now. "She's almost certainly wrong about that," Heris said. "But of course I'll listen to her."

"I must admit," he went on, cutting a slice of roast into matching slivers, "that before I knew you better, you would not have been my choice of confidante for my daughter."

"The military woman?" Heris asked, lightly.

"Not exactly. The Serrano Admiralty is well known . . ." His voice trailed away, and his gaze slid sideways to meet hers. Heris was surprised, and probably looked it.

"My family? They think *I'm* the disgrace—why should you object to them?"

"I prefer you," Bunny said, and did not answer the rest of the question. He pushed the slivers of meat aside. Something bleeped, beside his plate, and he picked up a silvery button and clipped it to his ear. Moments later, his jaw bunched. Heris tried not to stare, and made inroads on her dinner. Beside her, Petris was chatting with Cecelia, almost pointedly ignoring her. Cecelia winked past him—so she had explained. Or so Heris hoped.

Bunny touched her wrist lightly, and she turned back to him. "We may have a problem," he said. "Mr. Smith divested himself of the tagger. Captain Sigind found it, but not the . . . Mr. Smith. He's already sealed the flitter hangars and other sources of transport, but Mr. Smith is a skilled rider."

Heris spoke before her tact caught up with her tongue: "We are not going out looking for that scamp on horseback in the dark!"

"No. You're right, we aren't. The militia are, and if he founders that mare he stole, I will have his hide on my wall. I don't know how a Registered Embryo could end up this stupid."

"He'll come here," Heris said softly, thinking it through. "He wants in on the fun, that's all. There's a party; he wants to play. He's like Ronnie was before. He'll think of a disguise, or something from—"

A crash from outside the hall interrupted, followed by the obvious clattering of hoofs on a hard floor. Before anyone could get up to investigate, someone outside flung the doors open. There stood a masked man in a costume more bizarre than any in the room. Puffed breeches under a loud tartan kilt, white hose, buckled shoes, a doublet, a wide-sleeved shirt, a short cape, and a curious pile of velvet and feathers on his head: it looked as if he had ransacked a costume shop. He held the reins of a skittish horse, and brandished a sword. Someone whooped nervously; Bunny sat rigid. From the far end of the table, the elderly lady Ronnie had partnered stood up abruptly.

"Now this is ridiculous. Disgraceful mixing of periods. Not one of these young people has any respect for historical reproduction. Imagine wearing a kilt over breeches! Just what century does he think he is, anyway?" She had the loud, off-pitch voice of someone who has not heard herself speak for years. She glared at Bunny. "If this is your surprise, young Branthcome, it is singularly unamusing."

For once Bunny had nothing to say. Heris stared at the masked man with instant certainty. No one else on the planet would do something like this. Were those moustaches sticking

out from behind the mask? And what should she do? They
had to capture him, but also conceal him. Some of the people
here must have met the prince face-to-face. Could she and
Petris subdue him without displacing his mask? She caught
a glimpse of a servant behind the horse, trying to edge
nearer, but the frightened animal plunged and kicked, and
the servant retreated.

"It is traditional, I believe, to have a masked stranger make
away with a beautiful woman at affairs like this. . . ." The
man's voice certainly matched that of Mr. Smith. Heris looked
around the room. The Crown Minister had turned white,
but most people were amused, interested . . . already the
hum of conversation had returned. The servant Heris had
first seen came in sight again; the masked man turned and
handed him the reins. "Here—hold my mount, please." Wide-
eyed, the servant did so. Then the masked man strode into
the dining hall, up the length to the family's table, and
grabbed Raffaele firmly by one wrist. With a bow to Ronnie,
he said, "You stole a singer from me; I but return the
compliment—"

"Imposter!" Ronnie leapt to his feet and yanked the mask
from the man's face and the sword from his hand. Heris heard
the startled gasps. Mr. Smith, without a doubt. But Ronnie's
furious stare down the table denied it. "You would have us
think you're the prince, because everyone knows I quarrelled
with the prince . . . but you're only a common mechanic."

"Let go of my arm," Raffaele said, in the tone she would
have used to a social inferior. Mr. Smith complied, looking
confused.

"But I *am* the prince—"

"You're a . . . a *mole*," Ronnie said. Raffaele rubbed her
wrist and looked away, pointedly ignoring the intruder. Heris
suddenly realized where Ronnie was going with this, and
could hardly believe he had thought so fast. She waited for
the cue she was sure he would give. "Don't think I didn't
see you ogling Raffa on my aunt's yacht. Just because you
are fair-haired and tall, just because you know how to use
makeup, you thought you could pass yourself off as the
prince." He shook the man's shoulder. "Look at you! You're
in a roomful of people who know the prince—didn't you
think of that? Did you really expect to fool people by covering
your face? Did you hear what Lord Thornbuckle's aunt said?

We know how to dress in period costumes—this mess you have on is a—a travesty. Pitiful." He looked down the table at Heris. "I must complain, Captain Serrano, about the actions of your crewman."

Heris stood smoothly. "You're quite right. I regret that I didn't recognize him in his disguise, but he is only the junior environmental tech, and I've never seen him in anything but a shipsuit. I take full responsibility. Petris—" Petris stood, as well. "We'll make sure this—individual—" She could not think of a name to give him. Mr. Smith was too dangerous now. "—doesn't intrude again, and I daresay his working papers will be cancelled permanently."

"But I *am*—and this was all I could find—"

"Silence." Bunny had found his voice at last; when he chose to be loud, he could be heard across an open field in a blowing wind. Here it silenced everyone, even the furtive whisperers in the corners. "I insist that my militia escort this individual to the shuttleport, and all the way into the custody of your yacht, Lady Cecelia. I believe I am correct in saying there may be charges beyond my jurisdiction, involving impersonation of a member of the Royal Family—?" He inclined his head to Kevil Mahoney, who nodded. "Then I would not have him on this planet one hour longer than necessary. Captain Serrano, if you will inform your standing watch?"

"With pleasure."

Still protesting, but uselessly, Mr. Smith found himself overpowered and dragged away by militia, while Heris called the yacht and arranged for his confinement. Ronnie still stood at the end of the table, and when the room quieted, he looked to Bunny for permission to speak. Bunny nodded.

Ronnie rubbed his nose a moment, until he had everyone's attention. "Most of you know that I was exiled for a year after the prince and I had a dispute. Some of you know more. But what you may not know is how I could be so sure the prince had not come here in some disguise or other. When I knew where my aunt was bringing me, I worried about that myself, and looked it up. The prince was posted to the Royal Aero-Space Service depot on Naverrn—" Ronnie was looking at the Crown Minister, who, Heris noted, suddenly looked very alert. "I'm sure any of you can check that posting, and confirm it. And this man—

I don't even know his name—caught my eye on the yacht because he did somewhat resemble the prince, and he was sneaking around Raffaele."

"But are you sure it wasn't the prince *pretending* to be an environmental tech?" asked a woman near one corner.

"Of course it wasn't," Ronnie said. "We had both sworn an oath to duel if we saw each other within the next year—do you think *both* of us would be coward enough to ignore that? That—that *person* didn't even know how to use a sword." He looked angry; Raffa patted his hand, and he sat down again.

Heris could almost hear the collective lurch with which everyone tried to return to the mood of a Hunt Dinner and Ball and ignore the interruption, as Bunny signalled and the servants brought in another course.

George leaned against the mirrored wall of the ballroom feeling sulky again. Ronnie and Raffa hardly seemed to notice the music, but flowed with it like leaves on a stream. Captain Serrano and Petris . . . he would like to have made a jest of them, but could not. They had gone through so much; they deserved their obvious happiness. If only Bubbles had not turned against him . . . they could have made another good match, he was sure. He liked her well enough, now that Raffa had turned to Ronnie. Blondes set off his own dark handsomeness.

It was unfair. He and the prince alone, out of all that crowd, could not enjoy the party. And while he was luckier than the prince, in being here and not under guard somewhere, he had no one to share his evening. He watched the whirling dancers idly for awhile, then stared. His father. His father and Ronnie's aunt. Talking, laughing, obviously enjoying each other. . . . They danced by, and Lady Cecelia winked at him. His father, and that old . . . although she wasn't all that bad, really. She danced remarkably well, in fact. He just didn't want her as a stepmother, or aunt, or whatever she and his father might have in mind. The two of them together were definitely too smart for him; he and Ronnie would never enjoy more pranks. He turned away, ready to take a long walk somewhere, and almost fell over the girl coming his way. Her eyes widened. "You're—you're George Starbridge Mahoney, aren't you? Kevil

Mahoney's son?" He knew what to do with that kind of look, and drew himself up.

"Yes," he said. "I am."

"Somebody told me your nickname was Odious, but I don't believe it. I think you're nice." She had hazel eyes and fluffy hair of a red-brown shade he couldn't have put a name to. Something about her made him feel protective, something more than the slender wrists and hands, he was sure, or the somewhat pointy face. "You don't know me," she said, almost timidly. "I'm just one of the cousins; you've seen me out hunting, but usually covered with mud."

"I should have seen beneath it," he said gallantly. He liked being gallant. "Would you care to dance?" He led her onto the floor.

"I love Hunt Balls," the girl said. They whirled around; she danced as lightly as a fox over a fence on its way to take a chicken from the coop. George drew back a moment, wondering. Was he the hunter, or was she? It didn't matter, he decided; she couldn't be that certain herself.

"So do I," he said, and took her past his father and Ronnie's aunt, enjoying their reaction. "So do I."

SPORTING CHANCE

Dedication

For all the great-aunts—Jessie, Ruth, and Grace—
who showed generations of young people that
age is a rich gift to be savored, not feared.
And for those gifted therapists who recognize
the individual, the person, obscured by disability.

Acknowledgments

Among the people who made this project
possible were the Usual Crew at home . . . the
new horse, who ensured that I didn't waste time
riding by bucking me off and breaking some
ribs . . . Richard and Michael, who know when to
quietly sneak away and come back with pizza . . .
the people on Main Street who tell me to quit
talking about it, and go finish the (ahem) book.
Thanks to Mary Morell, a very old friend who
said the right things at the right time, and also
to Judy D'Albini Tuley for the same reason.
Margaret Ball, for help with names and
references. Nancy McGibbon, for assistance with
the theory and practice of hippotherapy—
especially of controversies in the field and ideas
about its future. The use I've made of them is all
mine; none of it represents her views.

CHAPTER ONE

"Of course there is a minor problem," Lady Cecelia said, as she turned to allow her maid to take her stole. A brisk wind tossed cold rain at the windows; it hissed and rattled alternately.

"Yes?" Heris Serrano eyed her employer with some suspicion. The words "minor problem" had become an all too frequent catch-phrase between them. She resented the niggling delays that prevented their departure; they should have been in space already, two days out on the voyage back to Rockhouse Major. She had begun to long for the ship, and space. Besides, the sooner they got to Rockhouse, the sooner that young troublemaker, the prince, would be off her hands, someone else's responsibility.

"It's our numbers again." Lady Cecelia waved her maid away, and settled herself into a comfortable chair drawn up before a fireplace. A small fire of real wood crackled on the hearth behind an ornate fire screen. Heris settled in the chair opposite and raised her brows. "I thought we'd be fine," Lady Cecelia went on, "since Bunny's children wouldn't be coming, nor Buttons's fiancée. George is still in the hospital, mostly for legal reasons, and I thought I could leave Raffaele and Ronnie here for the rest of the season, under the circumstances." Heris said nothing; her mind busily subtracted the volume and resources needed for those six young people and their servants, and the crew and staff she knew were quitting, and added the same for new crew and the one passenger she knew of. "But that won't work," Lady

Cecelia said. She ran one long hand through her short hair, and left it standing up in peaks.

"Why not?" asked Heris, since it seemed called for.

"Reasons of State, so I was told. I nearly cancelled my invitation, but that might be embarrassing too, so . . . the Crown Minister insists that if I have the young—er—Mr. Smith aboard, I must have an adequate bodyguard, a cabinet-level minister, and of course the servants. And . . . Ronnie."

"Ronnie! Why?" Someone had made a serious mistake. She wondered how that had happened. The whole point of bringing Cecelia's nephew Ronnie here in the first place had been to keep him away from the prince.

"I'm not sure, but it was one of the points made, very firmly. When I added the numbers, it came to fifty-six. That's over our limit, right?"

"Yes—but how many 'bodyguards' are we supposed to have, and who are they?"

"They want to send Royal Security—"

"Blast." Heris suppressed the expletives she'd have liked to use.

"—And they want us to wait until they get here. On the ship, with the prince." That went without saying, since he could not be trusted to stay out of trouble anywhere else.

"And you planned to go where?"

"Well . . . we have to go back to Rockhouse, to take him home, but after that I'd planned on Zenebra. The Wherrin Horse Trials—"

By now Heris knew enough to recognize that name. Of course her horse-crazy employer would want to be there; she had won Wherrin more times than anyone else. "Umm. And waiting for the Royal Security bodyguard would make us late for that, I'll bet. Silly. We've got former Regular Space Service combat troops, and suitable arms now: we can take care of him."

"Are you sure?"

"With Petris and Oblo? We could keep him safe in a small war."

Cecelia shivered. "Don't say that. It's like saying your horse can't possibly miss a fence."

"Still. We'd be safer to leave now. I haven't forgotten that smugglers were using your ship. Somewhere there's a very unhappy criminal waiting for delivery of whatever was in the scrubber. And I'd expect the smugglers to come looking for us, eventually. It's not as if we'd be hard to find; everyone knew where you were going from Takomin Roads, and we've filed the trip to Rockhouse in Bunny's computer—and with the Crown Minister."

"Good point. I'll mention that to the Crown Minister, and of course he already has the names of your crew. I assume that until the courts-martial, they were all considered loyal servants of the Crown?"

"As far as I know. If they weren't, they could have lost us some battles."

"Fine, then. You set up our departure as you wish; I'll deal with the political end later."

Heris looked after her employer and shook her head. She had not expected Cecelia—who had seemed to have a one-track mind firmly aimed at horses—to be so effective politically. Of course, she came from a political family, but every family had its black sheep. Heris shivered suddenly. She was, in her own way, the black sheep of her family. *Two black sheep don't make a white*, she thought, and shivered again.

In the flurry of preparation, it was hard to remember the last few days with Petris. He was now aboard, supervising the resupply, and (at Heris's suggestion) tucking away the new weaponry before Cecelia decided they didn't need it.

"Nothing for the ship, I notice," he'd said to her over a secure comlink.

"No. Not stocked locally. I know; I've already talked to Lady Cecelia about it."

"Um. Crew rotations?"

"Well . . . you'll all be on your secondary specialties. We'll have to reorganize quite a bit. Civilian regulations divide the responsibilities a bit differently. There's a manual on it—"

"I found that one," Petris said. She wished she could see him face-to-face, but she needed to be downside just a few hours longer. "But I haven't had the returning crew list from Hospitality Bay yet. Sirkin's the only one staying from the shift up here. You were right, by the way; she's a nice girl and very competent."

"Glad you agree," said Heris. "About that crew list—it was supposed to have been there yesterday. I wonder what's going on? I'll find out."

When she tried calling the crew hostel at Hospitality Bay, none of her crew answered. That seemed odd; she had sent word several days before that they would be leaving Sirialis shortly. Someone should have been there, ready to take any messages from her. She wished she could dump the whole lot of them and replace them with qualified people. She left an urgent message, and asked the hostel clerk when they were expected back.

"Sometime tonight, I 'spect, ma'am," the clerk said. "They rented a cat and took it out to Shell Island."

"Without a comunit aboard?" Heris asked.

"Well, there is one, but the charge to relay is pretty high. That Mr. Gavin said you might call, and to say they'd be back tonight." Heris grimaced, but it wouldn't help to yell at the hostel clerk.

"Tell Mr. Gavin to call here at once when he gets in, whatever the hour," she said. Should she threaten? No. Wait and see what was really going on, she reminded herself.

Gavin's call, relayed to her in the drawing room the green hunt favored, revealed a plot as spiritless as he himself. On the tiny screen of the drawing-room communications niche, he looked sunburnt and nervous.

"I'm not coming back, Captain," he said. "You'll have to find another chief engineer." It sounded almost smug, but she ignored that. She didn't need him.

"And the others?" she asked.

"They don't want to . . . they're not coming either. Not without Lady Cecelia changing . . . I mean, they're not coming." Now his expression was defiant. Heris took a long breath, conscious of the need to control her expression in a roomful of curious and intelligent observers. They couldn't hear what was said, but they could certainly see her reactions.

"Would you care to explain, Mr. Gavin?" she asked. The edge of steel in her voice cut through his flabby resistance.

"Well, it's just . . . we . . . they . . . we don't want you for our captain." That last phrase came out all in a rush. "We're not coming back. You don't have a crew. We want to talk to Lady Cecelia. She has to find someone else, or we won't come back to her." When Heris said nothing, momentarily silenced by fury, he blundered on. "It's—you're not fair, that's what it is. You got poor Iklind killed, and you're so rigid and all you do is criticize and you don't—you don't *respect* us." It was so outrageous, so ridiculous, that Heris found herself fighting back a sudden incongruous laugh as well as a tirade. The unborn laugh moderated her tone.

"I see you don't know the situation," she said without even a hint of anger. That seemed to make Gavin even more nervous.

"I don't— It doesn't matter," he said, almost stammering. "It doesn't matter what happened—what you say; we're not coming back as long as you're the captain."

"I see," Heris said. "Perhaps I'd better let you speak to Lady Cecelia." She waved her employer over, and stepped away from the comunit, out of its pickup range, for a moment. In brief phrases, she explained Gavin's message, and watched almost amused as Lady Cecelia went white with fury and then red.

"Damn them!"

"No . . . think a moment. They're incompetent, lazy, and we wanted to get rid of them anyway. Now they're also in legal jeopardy—and you have the reins. They don't know what's happened over here—none of it. They don't know you have a crew already. Have fun, milady!" Heris grinned, and after a last glower, Lady Cecelia grinned, too. She beckoned Heris to join her at the comunit niche.

Gavin's self-pitying whine had scarcely begun when Lady Cecelia cut him off with a terse and almost certainly inaccurate description of his ancestry, his progeny, his intellect, and his probable destination. Heris decided that foxhunting offered unique opportunities for invective, and found her own anger draining away as Cecelia continued her tirade.

"And I shall certainly file suits for breach of contract," she wound down, "and I daresay Lord Thornbuckle will be investigating you to see if you're involved in this other affair."

"But Lady Cecelia," whined Gavin. "What other affair? And why—I mean, we've served you—" She cut him off, and turned to face Heris, breathing heavily.

"How was that?"

"Fine. And since we know you had one smuggler in the group, I would carry through on that threat to have them investigated."

"I certainly will," Cecelia said. She stalked off, her tall angularity expressing indignation with every twitch of her formal skirt. Heris excused herself early and went upstairs to contact Petris again.

"So we're going out short-crewed," Heris said. She was not unhappy about it. "By civilian standards, that is. And over-crewed on the house-staff side, considering Lady Cecelia's guests this round." The prince had his own set of servants, and Cecelia insisted on adding another cook.

"Looks adequate to me, Captain," Petris said. He had worked up a crew rotation. "We could use two or three more, but—"

"But you're right, this is adequate. If we don't run into trouble, and if everyone works at Fleet efficiency. Which I expect you will. Something to consider is that we can hire replacements to fill out the list at Rockhouse Major. And we might think of hiring ex-Fleet personnel, while we're about it."

"Are you looking for trouble, Captain?" Petris's dark eyes twinkled.

"No. But I expect it anyway." A tap at her door interrupted. "Oh—that'll be Bunny's daughter Bubbles, I expect." She had forgotten, thanks to Gavin, that she'd agreed to talk to Bubbles after she went up to her room. "She's insisted on talking to me." Petris grinned at her expression.

"What—do you think she wants to come along?"

"Yes, and I can't let her. And I don't like the role she's casting me in."

"You'll do her no harm," Petris said.

"That's what her father told me," Heris said, shaking her head. "I'll get back to you shortly." She closed the uplink, and turned to the door of her suite. The blonde girl she'd first seen passed out drunk on a couch in the yacht had changed beyond recognition, and although being in mortal danger changed most people, this was exceptional.

"Captain Serrano," the young woman said. She stood stiffly, as if in a parody of military formality.

"Yes—do come in. We had a small crisis aboard, and I was just dealing with it."

"I—if this is a bad time—" She had flushed, which made her look younger.

"Not at all. Between crises is an excellent time." Heris led the way to a pair of overstuffed chairs beneath the long windows, and gestured as she sat in one of them. "Have a seat."

The girl sat bolt upright, not her usual posture, and looked like a young officer at a first formal dinner. Heris wondered again what this was about. Her father had refused to give any hints; Heris's own experience was that when young people preferred to talk to a relative stranger, the topic was usually embarrassing—at least for the youngster. But she didn't know what, in the current state of the aristocracy, would be likely to provoke embarrassment. What "rules" could such a girl have broken—or be planning to break— when most of society's rules didn't affect her at all?

"I want to change my name," the girl said, all in a rush, as if it were a great confession. Heris blinked. She would never have allowed herself to be called Bubbles in the first place, and she could understand why the girl would want to change . . . but not why anyone would object. Was this the big problem? Surely there was more.

"Bubbles doesn't really fit you," she said cautiously.

"No, not now." The girl waved that off as if it were trivial—which is what Heris thought it. "My full name's Brunnhilde Charlotte, and Raffa and I thought Brun would be a good version. But that's not the whole problem."

"Oh?"

"No—my parents are willing to give up Bubbles, though Mother would prefer some other variation, but it's the other part . . ."

The other part meaning what, Heris wondered. She sat and waited; youngsters usually told you more if you did.

"It's . . . the family name." Aha. That would cause a row, she could see. "I haven't told them yet, but I know they won't like it." They would more than "not like it" if she wanted to give up her family name; they would, Heris suspected, be furious and hurt. The girl—Brun, she tried to think of her now—went on. "It's just that I've always been Bubbles, Bunny's daughter—Lord Thornbuckle's daughter—and not myself. I feel—different now. When we were in the cave—" Ah, thought Heris. The rapid personal maturation by danger has left behind the social immaturity. "—I realized I didn't feel like who I was. I mean, I felt different, and it didn't match." She took a deep breath and rushed through the rest. "I want to change my name and go into the Regular Space Service and learn how to really do things and find out who I am."

Heris blinked again, remembering her own impulse (quickly squashed) to change her name and apply to the Academy not as a Serrano but purely on her own merits. She had even made up a name and practiced the signature. The silly romanticism of youth—or, if you looked at it another way, the integrity and courage.

"And you thought I could help you?" she said, keeping her reactions to herself.

"Yes. You know how things work—and you could take me to someplace I could enlist."

Now the problem was how to say no without shutting the girl off completely.

"How old are you?" Heris asked. "And what kind of background would you offer the Fleet?" She already suspected the answers. Brun was too old to enlist with the skills she could reasonably claim—having been taught marksmanship by your father didn't count, even if he was a renowned hunter—and lacking any education the Fleet would recognize. At least, under an assumed name. "Which will get you in trouble anyway," Heris explained. "After all, plenty of people the Fleet doesn't want would like to get in. Falsifying one's identity is fairly common—and nearly always detected, and when detected is always justification for rejection."

"But I thought if I explained that I just don't want to use my father's privilege—"

"To whom would you explain? A recruiting officer? That would get you sent for psychiatric and legal evaluation— are you impersonating a member of your father's family? And if not, what's wrong with you that you don't enjoy your privilege? No—" She held up her hand. "I see your point, and I admire you for wanting to make your own way, but you cannot sneak into the Fleet that way. Not with our methods of certifying identity. You'd do better, if you're intent on a dangerous military career, to travel as a tourist outside the Familias Regnant and take service with some planetary ruler. Don't try to be fancy—just say you're running away from family problems. Someplace like Aethar's World or the Compassionate Hand would probably hire you."

"But Aethar's World is all . . . those hulks, isn't it?"

"Soldiers can't afford prejudice," Heris said with an internal grin. She'd thought that would get a reaction. "Aethar's World always needs soldiers. Admittedly, that's because the Fatherland uses them up in bloody and unnecessary battles, but they do give you a glorious funeral, I hear. And yes, they're all big-boned and fair-haired—one reason they might hire you—and they have anachronistic ideas about warrior women—another reason they might hire you. But they do pay on time, if you survive."

"And the . . . the Compassionate Hand?" asked Brun, her brow furrowed.

"Not an accurate name, but you don't want to call them the Black Scratch unless you've got a battle group behind you. A *large* battle group. You may not have heard of them; the Familias discourages trade that way. We have a border incident every few years, though. They would like to control Karyas and the nearby jump points."

"Black Scratch . . . Compassionate Hand?"

"Well, you know about protection rackets, don't you?" Brun nodded, but still looked puzzled. "The motto of the families that settled Corus IV-a was 'You scratch my back, and I'll scratch yours.' They referred to this as being a compassionate hand—a helping hand. But the first colony they raided, on Corus V, called it the 'black scratch.' They now control the Corus system, with heavy influence in two nearby systems, and their official designation is 'The Benignity of the Compassionate Hand.' They hire offworlders for mercenary actions, often against underground groups who still call them the Black Scratch."

"But they're—illegal," said Brun.

"Not by their laws, and they're not part of our legal system. From what I read of Old Earth history, their ancestors ran the same kinds of rackets there and no one ever converted them to what we call law and order. Actually, if you're on an official visit, it looks like a model government. I've known a few people who had served in their military—said it wasn't bad, if you followed the rules exactly, but they have no tolerance for dissent."

"You're saying I can't really do what I was talking about," Brun said. "If my choices run to the barbarians of Aethar's World or the Compassionate Hand—"

"There are others. But I'm not exactly sure what you're looking for. A military career? If so, leading to what? Coming back to your family someday, or retiring on your own independent savings? How much adventure—otherwise known as danger—do you really want? Do you have something against your family which would prevent your adventuring within its canopy?"

"Mmm." Brun looked thoughtful; Heris was glad to see that she could calm down and think. "I suppose—I want change. Change from what I was, and from what people think of me." She looked up at Heris, who said nothing. Let the girl work it out for herself; then she'd believe it. "Lady Cecelia crossed her family—but—she did use her own money—"

"Makes it easier," said Heris. "And there's no reason to do things the hard way if you don't have to."

"I don't know what, really," Brun said. "I guess I just want to serve notice to my family—to others—that I'm not the bubblehead they think—that I'm not the designated blonde sure to marry someone like the odious George." She grinned then. "And you're saying there are easier ways to do that than get myself killed by barbarians with blond braids or a knife in the ribs from the . . . er . . . Compassionate Hand."

"I didn't say it," Heris said. "You did. I'd think you'd had enough adventure for a while . . . although . . . if you liked that, there's training that would help you survive other . . . adventures."

Brun's face lit. "That's what I'd like—what bothered me most wasn't the danger, but not knowing what to do. But I thought you could only get that training in the military."

"No—in fact, not everyone in the military does. There are other sources, if that's what you want. Tell you what, I'll give you a list of skills and places I know you can get training . . . and then you can find a use for that training. How about that?"

"I'd love it. Can't I come to Rockhouse with you? I already know about Mr. Smith, of course."

"No—I'm sorry. We're overloaded, with the required escorts for Mr. Smith. But if you're going back there, you can start to acquire some of the things I'm talking about—"

"Tell me what sorts of things," Brun interrupted, eyes bright.

"Well . . . the more you know about all the technology we use for transportation and communication, the better. Not just classroom theory but practical stuff like being able to maintain and repair the equipment. Lady Cecelia's taken an interest in her yacht now, and she's finding it very helpful. I wish we had time for you to meet Brigdis Sirkin— my Nav First. She's done it all by formal schooling, but she's taken every opportunity to expand her skills and knowledge on the job, too."

From the look on Brun's face, she wanted to *be* Brigdis Sirkin. Heris wondered if Sirkin would return the favor, if she imagined the opulence and privilege of Brun's background. Probably not. That very practical young woman was headed exactly where she wanted to go—perhaps a narrow goal, but one she knew she could attain. Brun had so many choices it must be hard to make them.

"Do you like space travel?" Heris asked.

"Yes—but I don't know if I'd like to spend all my time in space." And this was someone who had thought of joining Fleet! "What I really like—liked—was thinking up elaborate pranks, but of course there's no place for that in the real world."

Was there not! Heris cocked her head. "What kind of pranks?"

"Oh—you know—like when we were kids on that island, and having mock wars." She had flushed again, clearly embarrassed to put her childhood mock wars up against the real thing, even in imagination. "I got pretty good at ambushes. And at school, my first term . . . they never did figure out who had reprogrammed the water supply so all the hot was cold and vice versa. Silly stuff. Except about Lucianne—keeping her away from her uncle when he came to visit was serious enough, but necessary."

It really was too bad that they couldn't take Brun along with them. She might have resources to match the prince's— she might keep Ronnie amused—and it would be fun to find out if she really did have a knack for innovative tactics. In Heris's experience, the people who created interesting pranks for the pranks' sake (not just to inconvenience people) often had good luck in real-life tactical situations. They just needed to be kept busy. For a moment her mind toyed with the idea of Brun as part of her crew—of talking Cecelia into some clandestine adventure somewhere—but she pushed it away. Getting the prince back to his father in one piece, and Ronnie with him, was enough to deal with for the moment.

"Tell you what," she said. "After we finish this mission, you might ask Lady Cecelia if she'd let you come along on a voyage or two. That's *if* you've been working on the things I'll list."

"Yes!" Brun grinned broadly. "I will—and thanks."

And what did I just get myself into? Heris asked herself. The girl's father had asked her to give advice—it wasn't as if she was going behind anyone's back—but she still felt odd about it. She made a note to herself to come up with that list of skills and resources before they left.

Their final head count came to forty-nine. Heris had had to accept a couple of Bunny's militia, and two crew from his personal yacht, to satisfy the Crown Minister that the prince would be travelling safely. When the *Sweet Delight* eased away from the peculiar eye-twisting space station, it had its holds stuffed with supplies enough for a year-long voyage. Heris had had plenty of time to complete her list for Brun while waiting for the last luxuries to be ferried up from Sirialis.

Once the ship was on its way out of the system, Heris released the prince from his suite. She expected a tantrum, but the young man smiled at her, and asked the way to the gym. Heris wondered why he hadn't looked it up on his deskcomp, but perhaps princes didn't ever look things up for themselves.

Dinner that first night surpassed anything Lady Cecelia's cook had produced on the voyage out. Cecelia wore her amber and ivory lace; Ronnie and the prince both appeared in semiformal dress. Heris had to admit they were handsome, as decorative as young roosters. She preferred Ronnie, whose recent adventures seemed to have settled him a bit. At least he never rose to the prince's obvious attempts to tease. The prince . . . she had not really been around him in the days of his captivity, and his brief appearance at the Hunt Dinner had given her no feel for his real personality. Now, at the dinner table, he looked the very picture of a prince, and yet she felt something missing. Not quite the same as Ronnie and George, who had been so difficult on the voyage out, but whose spoilt manners clearly overlay interesting minds. The prince, aside from a hectic energy that emerged as one stale joke after another, was . . . to put it plainly . . . boring. Heris, imagining him as a king in the future, could form only a blurry vision of someone dull and stolid, with an eye for the girls and a taste for wine and game, a stout middle-aged fellow who elbowed his cronies in the ribs but never quite got the point of stories.

Four days into the voyage back to Rockhouse, Ronnie brought up the prince's intellectual gaps in a private conversation with Heris and Cecelia. He looked earnest and worried. "Did you know the prince was stupid?"

Heris nearly choked, and Cecelia let out an unladylike snort before she controlled herself and glared at her nephew. "You are not going to start quarrelling with him. I forbid it."

Ronnie waved that away. "I'm not quarrelling. It's not like that. But I just realized—he's really stupid."

"Perhaps," his aunt said, looking down her longish nose, "you would care to explain that discourteous comment."

"That's why I'm here." Ronnie settled into his chair, leaning forward, hands clasped tensely. "I think something's wrong. We have to do something."

"That is not an explanation," Cecelia said crisply. "Please get to it."

"Yes. All right." He took a deep breath, and began. "We haven't been in the same classes or anything for years, or I'm sure I'd have noticed. He's just not very smart."

Heris repressed a smile. She had never expected royalty to be overburdened with brains. "Probably he never was very smart. Children can't really tell about each other—" But a memory lifted through her mind like a bubble . . . that boy who had been so brilliant in primary: she had known that, and so had all the other kids. She herself had been smart, but he had been something far more.

"He *was*," Ronnie said, with a return of his old sullenly stubborn expression. "He was, and now he's not. If I didn't know it was Gerel, I wouldn't believe it was the same person."

Cecelia sat up suddenly. "If you didn't know—how *do* you know it's the same person?"

Ronnie looked at her blankly. "Well, of course it is—how could it be anyone else? He's too well known."

"Now he is. But a child?"

"Gene types," Heris said, cutting off that wild idea. "It

would be impossible to switch someone else; surely he has annual physicals. And it could be checked so easily . . ."

"That's right. He's a Registered Embryo." Ronnie wrinkled his nose. "And that's odd, too. Registered Embryos are at least one sig above average IQ." Heris looked at him; he turned red. "All right, we don't all act it, but we have the brains, if we learn to use them. Gerel wasn't stupid in childhood, and he's near that now. Something's happened to him."

Heris had an unpleasant crawling sensation in her midsection; she recognized fear of the unknown in the ancient form. Her forebrain didn't like it, either. Something to make princes stupid: it had been done before, and never with good intent.

"Someone must have noticed," she said slowly, wanting it to be false. But already she believed. Despite the physical beauty, the athletic body, the energy, the prince was dull.

"Some people wouldn't notice on principle," Cecelia said. "But his parents, surely . . . Kemtre wasn't that dim the last time I chatted with him. Admittedly that was ten years or so ago; I hate social functions where people expect me to be up on the latest Court gossip and I feel like a fool fresh off the farm. But we had a nice talk about the expansion of agricultural trade into the Loess Sector, and he seemed quite knowledgeable. Velosia, of course, was immersed in the gossip and wondered why I didn't spend more time with my sisters. I could believe this meant she was a dullard, except that she and Monica played dual-triligo and were ranked in the top ten. I never could understand the rules beyond primary level, so if they're stupid, I'm worse."

"Ten or twelve years ago, Gerel was just starting school outside the home for the first time," Ronnie pointed out. "What if something happened there, something that took a while to show up? We were only together for three or four years, then they shifted him to Snowbay and I stayed at Fallowhill." The names meant nothing to Heris, but Cecelia nodded.

"Or it could've started at Snowbay. I remember there was some concern about sending him so far away, to such a strict headmaster. But Nadrel had gotten in all that trouble—" Heris blinked again. She knew—it had been her business to know— the names of the various members of the Royal Family, but she wasn't used to anyone calling them by first names. Nadrel, the second son, had died when he eluded his Security protection and got himself into a brawl with someone who didn't worry about the niceties of aristocratic duelling. Before that, he had been considerably wilder than the current prince.

"I hadn't realized," Ronnie said, looking at his hands. "I feel . . . bad about it. It's sort of indecent, I mean—our quarrel, when he's not—not like he was. Like the time George had that virus or whatever, and nearly flunked everything for a month; we started out teasing him, but it wasn't funny."

"It's indecent that it happened, if you're right. The quarrel's beside the point, although I expect it influenced him." Heris fought her way through Cecelia's logic in that and by the time she had it figured out both aunt and nephew were off on another tangent. Whom to tell, and how, and when.

"Better not tell anyone," she said, interrupting them. "It's dangerous knowledge." They stared back at her.

"But I must," Cecelia said. "He's the only surviving prince. If his father doesn't know—"

"Then someone doesn't want him to know. Someone who will be glad to eliminate you. His father probably does know, after all, and I doubt very much he wants it widely recognized or talked about."

"I'm not a gossip. Everyone knows that." Cecelia looked exasperated. "It's not something I can ignore. If I do, and he knows, then he'll suspect—it will be worse than telling him."

"But it's dangerous," said Heris. Surely Cecelia could see that; it was like taking a light escort straight into a suspicious scanfield. They needed to know more before anyone said anything. Her mind tickled her with something Ronnie had just said about George. George had had a month of being stupid? A virus? Or the same thing that affected the prince? But Cecelia, sticking to her own main interest, was talking again.

"They need to know. Even if it's dangerous, it's more dangerous to have him like this, unrecognized. Dangerous to everyone, not just to me. It can't be hidden much longer anyway; he's getting to an age where he'll be expected to take on some Crown functions. The sooner it's known, the sooner we—" This time the *we* clearly meant those who managed things, the great families of the realm, "—can change our plans and adjust. If it's permanent, for instance, he can't take the throne later. Then there's the Rejuvenant/Ageist split; this could change the balance in Council."

"But it'll be terribly embarrassing, Aunt Cecelia," said Ronnie. "Maybe Captain Serrano is right—"

But Heris could tell from the stubborn set of Cecelia's jaw that they weren't getting anywhere. Maybe later. They were still a long way from Rockhouse. She could talk to Ronnie about George's experience in private.

The ship itself functioned smoothly. Sirkin had looked startled the first time she heard Oblo say "Aye, sir" to Heris, but she soon got used to the preponderance of military backgrounds. Heris thought it improved the tone a lot; it seemed a comfortable compromise between military formality and civilian casualness. Bunny's yacht crew, efficient enough, held themselves slightly aloof from Lady Cecelia's; she didn't mind, since they'd be going back to Bunny's from Rockhouse.

Her relationship with Petris, however, seemed as uneven as the foxhunting fields. She had understood the prohibition of relationships between commanders and their subordinates as preventing both sexual harassment of subordinates and favoritism . . . it had not occurred to her that there was any intrinsic problem with the relationship if both desired it. She learned differently.

"I don't know," Petris said one late watch, when they had expected a pleasant evening in bed, and instead found themselves less interested in bed than talk. "It's not the past, really. I'd been crazy about you for a long time, and once I found a way—but on this ship—"

"It's the teal and lavender," Heris said, trying to make light of it.

"No. It's—how can I say this and not sound like a barbarian?—it's the authority. Here, you're in charge—you have to be. And—" Heris waited out a long silence as he worked his way through it. "When we were back on that island, you weren't. You were hurting, and I could help. I had the choices to make."

"Mmm. An authority block?"

"I suppose. Except I've never resented your authority, you know. Not with the ship. It never has bothered me who captained a ship, so long as they were good at it. I knew early on I never would . . . didn't really want to." That surprised her.

"Didn't you?"

"No. Not all enlisted are lusting for command, you know. Commanders maybe, but not command itself. It's damned scary; I can see that in your eyes. Maybe I feel that way here—it's scary, because I'm stepping out of my role, with the commander. It didn't bother me off the ship . . ."

"And it's not something I can command," Heris said. Some did; she knew that. But she couldn't. "How about we pretend this isn't the ship?"

"I'll try." It seemed to be working—Heris had felt the shifts in her own breathing that went with great pleasure long deferred—when the intercom intruded.

"Captain Serrano—there's something on the screen—" She lunged across Petris to answer it, and he cursed.

By the time she'd been to the bridge, where the image onscreen had vanished, and gotten back to her quarters, Petris was gone. Heris didn't call him back. Later. There would be time enough later.

CHAPTER TWO

Nothing had been settled—not about the prince, not about Petris—when the *Sweet Delight* made its last jump. They came out of the anomalous status of jump space precisely where Sirkin had intended, for which Heris gave her a nod of approval. She wished Sirkin hadn't had a lover waiting at Rockhouse Major—she'd have liked to keep her as crew.

"Somebody flicked our ID beacon," Oblo said. "Stripped it clean and fast: R.S.S., I'd say, remembering the other side . . ."

"We're not fugitive," Heris said. "And they'd be looking for the *Sweet Delight*, considering . . ."

"Mmm. Wish we had better longscans and a decoder that could do the same. Feels all wrong to have someone stripping our beacon when we can't strip theirs."

"Mass sensors show a lot of ships," Sirkin put in. "And the delays are too long to tell me where they are now—"

"That's what I meant," Oblo said. "Now in the Fleet, we've got—" He broke off suddenly as Heris cleared her throat, and looked up at her. "Sorry, Captain. I'm used to being on the inside of security, not outside."

"We'd all best be careful, if we want to stay outside a prison, and not inside," Heris said. The only bad thing about Sirkin—and Bunny's crew—was this tension between what the ex-military crew knew and what they weren't supposed to know and couldn't share with shipmates. It would have been easier if they'd all been her former crew members.

She had sent off a message when they first dropped out of FTL, with the codes given them by the Crown Minister. Now the system's outer beacons blipped the first response.

"Captain, *Sweet Delight*, proceed on R.S.S. escort course—" and the coordinates followed.

Oblo whistled. "They're putting us down the dragon's throat, all right."

"What?" Sirkin asked.

"Escort course is the fastest way insystem; eats power and makes a roil everyone in the whole system can pick up. Hardly what I'd call discreet. All other traffic gives way, and we're snagged by a tug that could stop a heavy cruiser, in a counterburn maneuver. Plus, we go past the heavy guns and damn near every piece of surveillance between us and Rockhouse."

Heris glared at him, and Oblo actually flushed. He knew better, and she had already warned him. Sirkin wasn't military, had never been military, wasn't ever going to be military, and he had no business explaining Fleet procedure to her. But he had a thing for neat-framed dark-haired girls, whether they liked men or not, and he had taken a liking to Sirkin.

They were only halfway home, as Cecelia put it, when the escorts pulled up on either side. R.S.S., both of them; Heris got an exterior visual and grinned. She had once captained one of these stubby, peculiar-looking ships; ridiculously overpowered, designed for fast maneuvers within a single system, their small crews prided themselves on "flair." On distant campaigns, they traveled inside podships, even though they mounted FTL drives.

The voicecom board lit. Heris flicked the lit buttons, and then a sequence which informed the caller that she had no secured channel.

"Ahoy, *Sweet Delight*. R.S.S. Escort *Adrian Channel* calling—"

"Captain Serrano, *Sweet Delight*," Heris said.

"You don't have any kind of secure com?" At least that showed some discretion; she'd been afraid they'd ask in clear if she had the prince aboard.

"Negative."

"Well . . ." A pause, during which Heris amused herself by imagining the comments passing between the two escorts and

their base. Then the voice returned. "We understand you have urgent need for priority docking at Rockhouse Major. Is that correct?"

"Yes, it is," Heris said. "The relevant enabling codes were in my initial transmission—"

"Yes, ma'am. Well, ma'am, we're here just to see you make a safe transit, and chase any boneheaded civvie that doesn't listen to his Traffic Control updates out of your way. Our instruments show you on course—" Oblo scowled at that; with him on the board there was no question of being off course.

The counterburn maneuver, when it came, strained the resources of the *Sweet Delight*'s artificial gravity; dust shimmered in the air and made everyone on the bridge cough. For one moment Heris felt nausea, then her stomach ignored the odd sensations. Others were not so lucky. She saw a medic light go on in the prince's stateroom, and in the galley.

Then the internal gravity stabilized again; the tug's grapple snagged the yacht's bustle, and Petris shut down their drive. Far faster than a commercial tug, the R.S.S. ship shoved them toward Rockhouse Major, and put them in a zero-relative motion less than 100 meters away from the docking bay. Visuals, boosted several magnifications, showed the Royal Seal above their assigned bay, and the gleaming sides of a Royal shuttle and a larger, deepspace yacht twice the size of *Sweet Delight*. Grapples shot out, homing on magnetic patches on the yacht's hull. These would stabilize, but not change, their inward drift under docking thrusters. Heris had always enjoyed docking maneuvers, and the chance to show off at a Royal berth delighted her. She eased the yacht in, with neither haste nor delay, until the grapples were fully retracted and the hull snugged against the access ports.

Until this moment, she had spoken with the Rockhouse Major Sector Landing Control—a professional exactly like any other landing control officer—and their exchanges were limited to the necessary details of bringing the yacht in. Now another channel lit on the board. Heris took a steadying breath. This would be a very different official, she was sure— and even after hours reading everything Cecelia's library had on Royal protocol, she wasn't sure she would get it right. Once, she could have relied on the military equivalent, but as a civilian captain—

"Royal Security to the captain of *Sweet Delight*—"

"Captain Serrano here," she said.

"We need to establish a secure communications link before your passengers debark; we'll need hardwire access. Open the CJ-145 exterior panel next to the cargo access, please."

At least he'd said "please." For a moment she was surprised that they knew which panel to use, but of course they would: the yacht was a standard design, built at a well-known yard. They'd had weeks to get all the specs.

"Just a moment, please," she said. She nodded at Oblo, who put the relevant circuits up on a screen, and cut out all but the communications input. No reason to give them easy access to Cecelia's entire system, just in case they were of a mind to strip that, too. When he grinned at her, she popped the latch and waited while Security set the link up.

And after all that, the formalities were no different than docking at any fairly large Fleet base. Mr. Smith—the prince—had spoken to Security from his suite, she presumed in some code. She herself admitted the Royal Security team (one technician in gray, the others in dress blues, a major commanding) who would escort the prince down to the planet. No one seemed to expect any protocol from her that she didn't already understand.

But when the prince came into the lounge, Lady Cecelia was with him. Her maid followed, with a small travel case in her hand. The prince's servants, behind the maid, filled the passage with luggage.

"I'm going with him," Cecelia said. Heris, who hadn't expected this, stared at her. Cecelia pulled herself to her full height, and looked every millimeter the rich, titled lady she was. "The Crown Minister gave me the responsibility—"

"But madam . . . we're Royal Security." The major looked unhappy, as well he might.

"Very well. Then you can make sure that I also reach groundside safely."

"But our orders were to take . . . er . . . Mr. Smith . . ."

The red patches of incipient temper darkened on Cecelia's cheekbones. "Your sacred charge, young man, is the personal safety, the life itself, of your prince. If you think *I* endanger it, you are sadly mistaken about the source of danger. I suggest you need to have a long talk with the Crown Council. I went out of my way, at my own expense, to bring this young man safely home from a life-threatening situation. It might be asked where you, the Royal Security, were when he was being shot at!"

"Shot at!" Clearly this man had not heard the whole story. Heris wished Cecelia had not said so much; she'd assumed they would know already. "But he was on a training mission, with military guard—"

Cecelia glared. "Perhaps your superior will, if you prove discreet, tell you the full truth later. Suffice it to say that my honor, and my family's honor, are involved in this, and I will witness Mr. Smith's return to his father myself. You will find that his father agrees, should you care to take it that far."

"Yes, madam." The Security man still looked unhappy, but resigned. Exactly what she wanted.

"I will not require my maid's attendance, since I expect to travel directly to my brother's residence once I've spoken to the king. I am ready." She glanced back, to find Gerel and his luggage in the passage behind her, took her small case from her maid, and stepped forward.

The Royal shuttle eased into atmosphere with hardly a shiver in its silken ride. Four Royal Aerospace Service single-seaters flanked it, and another pair led it in. The prince sprawled in a wide seat, looking glum. Cecelia divided her glances between the viewports—she had always liked watching planetfall—and the Security men, who avoided meeting her gaze. She enjoyed the excellent snack a liveried waiter served her. The prince, she noticed, waved it away, and the Security men drank only water.

Two flitters waited on the landing field. Both dark blue, both with the Crown Seal in gold and scarlet. Honor guards stood by both. Cecelia snorted to herself. It wasn't going to work; she would see to that.

Sure enough, Security steered the prince toward one flitter, and attempted to lead her to the other. She strode on after the prince.

"Gerel—wait a moment." He paused, and looked back almost blankly.

"Yes, Lady Cecelia?"

"You're too fast for an old woman," she said, grinning at him. "Ronnie knows to slow down for me."

He smiled. She saw no malice in his smile, but no great

intelligence either. What had gone wrong? How could the king not know? "I'm sorry," he said. "I was just thinking of being home."

"But sir," one of the Security men said. "We're supposed to take you home, and Lady Cecelia to her—"

"I told you," Cecelia said, still smiling, "I'm going with Gerel. It is a matter of honor." To her surprise, Gerel nodded.

"Yes, it is. A matter of honor." And he held out his arm for her. Whatever had blunted his intelligence had not ruined his manners. Here, she saw no sign of the hectic energy, the tension that had led him to such stupid outbreaks at Sirialis. Through the flitter ride, he sat quietly, not fidgeting, and when they arrived at the palace landing field, he gave her his arm again on the way in. Although she had believed Ronnie before, Cecelia found herself even more worried about the prince now.

"So, you see, I felt it necessary to come to you myself," Cecelia said, watching the king's face for any reaction. He had offered her one of the scarlet and gold striped chairs in his informal study, where she was both amused and delighted to see a picture of herself among the many others on one wall. It was one of her favorites, too, one the king had taken himself just as her horse sailed over a big stone wall.

The king looked tired. Rejuv had smoothed his skin, but he still had deep discolored pouches beneath his eyes. "I'm glad you did," he said. "Do you have any idea how many other people have noticed?"

"I'm not sure." Heris had warned her not to answer this question; she felt a warning flutter in her diaphragm. But this was the king; she had known him from boyhood. Surely she could trust him, though not his ministers. "I would guess that plenty of people know he can act like a silly young ass—but then so do many of them, my nephew Ronnie included."

"It's a difficult situation," the king said, toying with a stylus.

"You did . . . know something." Cecelia made that not quite a question. The king looked at her.

"We knew something. But—you will forgive me—it's not something I want to discuss."

Cecelia felt herself reddening. His tone, almost dismissive, irritated her. She was not some old busybody. Just because she hadn't accepted rejuvenation, he shouldn't assume her brain had turned to sand. It was this kind of attitude that made Ageists out of people who simply didn't want rejuv. He smiled, a gentle smile for a man of such power, and interrupted what she might have said.

"I do appreciate your coming to tell me yourself. It was thoughtful of you; I know you won't spread this around. And you're right, we must do something, soon. But at the moment, I'm not ready to discuss it outside the family. In the meantime, let's talk about you. You have a new captain and crew for that yacht of yours, I understand . . . and you've infected the captain with your enthusiasm for horses . . ." Cecelia smiled back, well aware that she had no way to force him to confidences he didn't want to give. They chatted a few more minutes, then she took her leave.

The king stared at the picture of Lady Cecelia he had taken. She was a good fifteen years older than he; he had taken that picture in his youthful enthusiasm for photography, before he realized that kings have no time for hobbies— especially not hobbies that reveal so much about their interests and priorities. He had grown up a lot since then; the adolescent who had admired her so openly, who had taken that picture and sent her a print with a letter whose gushing phrases he still recalled, had learned to mask his feelings—had almost learned to feel only what suited the political reality.

She had not matured the same way, he thought. She still rode her enthusiasms as boldly as she had ridden horses; she said what she thought, and damn the consequences. She felt what she felt, and didn't care who knew it. Immature, really. A slow comfort spread through him, as he finally grasped the label that diminished her concern to a child- ish fretfulness, an undisciplined outburst of the sort he had long learned to forego. Deep inside, his mind nagged: she's not stupid. She's not crazy. She's right. But he smothered that nagging voice with ease; he had quit listening to his conscience a long time ago.

Heris had plenty to do while waiting to hear from her employer, but she could not banish the chill she felt. She had to get all the crew properly identified for Royal Security; not even Bunny's crewmen, who had been there before, and were only passing through on the way downplanet, could leave the Royal Docks without a pass. Heris put them first in the identification queue, and within a few hours they were on their way downplanet to Bunny's estate on Rockhouse. Then there was the usual post-docking business: arranging for tank exchange, for recharging depleted 'ponics vats, for lines to the Station carbon-exchange tanks (waste) and water (supply). It would be hours yet before Cecelia's shuttle would land, before she could reach the king, before whatever would happen could happen.

But the knot in her belly remained; she barely picked at the delicious lunch the two cooks produced. Something would go wrong. She knew it. She just couldn't figure out what it would be.

By the time Cecelia called, Heris had dug herself into a nest of clerical work. She had almost forgotten why she was so tense. Cecelia called up from the surface, with such a cheerful, calm expression that Heris had to believe everything had gone well. She did not, on a commercial communications channel, mention the prince. Instead, she chattered about refitting.

"I've discussed matters with the family, and my sister has agreed not to be offended if I have *Sweet Delight* redecorated to fit my tastes instead of hers. It really was generous of her to do it before, but as you know, lavender and teal are not colors I'm fond of. We've had a dividend payout, from some business, and I can easily afford to redo it. I'll be up in a few days; you'll have to move the ship to a refitting dock over on the far side of Major—at least that's the one I'm leaning toward. Even though I didn't like the colors, they did a good job last time. I'll bring the preliminary plans with me, and if you'd supervise—"

"Of course," Heris said. For a moment her original estimate of rich old ladies resurfaced. How could she think only of redecoration at such a time? But something about Cecelia's eyes reassured her. Something else was going on than changing the color of carpet and upholstery. "Have any idea how long it will take?"

"A few weeks, last time. Presumably about the same this time, although restocking the solarium may take longer. I've missed my miniatures—"

"Ummm . . . but milady, you said you wanted to be at Zenebra for the horse trials . . ."

"I know, but if I have a choice between missing the Trials one time and living with that lavender for the weeks between here and there, and then however long it takes to get to refitting, I'm willing to miss the Trials. And we'll have plenty of time to make the big race meetings after the Trials. A friend has asked me to look for replacement bloodstock."

"Ah. I see. Very well, milady, as you ask. If you could tell me when to expect you back . . . ?"

"Not tomorrow or the next day. Perhaps the day after. I'll put a message on the board for you; I should be able to find my way from the shuttledock to the ship by myself."

Unwise, Heris thought. Very unwise. But she could have an escort there if Cecelia told her which shuttle she was taking. "If you're going to delay for redecoration, milady, there are a few other equipment changes I'd like to suggest."

Cecelia didn't even ask questions. "Quite all right. Whatever you want. This time let's do it all, so there's nothing to worry about for *years.*"

Heris wondered if she'd gotten a refund from Diklos & Sons—or would it be the insurance? She wasn't sure just how the refitters would be made to pay for that fraudulent, almost-fatal job they didn't do, but Cecelia could get solid credits out of them if anyone could. She somehow didn't believe in the dividend payout—not at this odd time of year. Cecelia probably didn't realize that midlevel officers could have investment experience too. When Cecelia cut the link, Heris turned to Petris and Oblo.

"You heard that. You know what we need. Go find me the best deals on it, will you? I spent too much of her money buying those small arms on Sirialis."

"Good weapons, though," Petris said. He had, of course, tried them out. "Fancied up, but quality."

"Well, now I want quality without any fancying up. Whatever's legal—"

"Legal!" That was Oblo, of course. Then he sobered. "You mean, not stolen?"

"I mean legal, as in 'will pass inspection.'" Heris found she could not maintain the severity she wanted. A grin puckered the corner of her mouth. "All right . . . you know what I mean. Don't cause us trouble, but get us what we need."

"Yes, sir." Oblo saluted in the old way, and retreated from her office. Petris stayed.

"Is Lady Cecelia all right?" he asked.

"I hope so. I don't think she half understands the danger she could be in." Heris's uneasiness had not faded, despite Cecelia's assurances.

"Of course," the Crown Minister said, "if someone had to notice, Lady Cecelia de Marktos is the safest . . . she's not a gossip like most of them."

His sister, demure in her long brocaded gown, said nothing. True, Lady Cecelia was not a gossip. Her danger lay in other directions. Perhaps Piercy would figure it out for himself.

"It's a nuisance, though. If she did take it into her head to mention it to someone, they might pay attention, precisely because she's known to be no gossip." Ah. He had realized the danger. "I wonder if that scamp Ronnie knows. The king didn't say—"

"If Ronnie knew, Cecelia would have told the king," his sister said. Always argue the point you oppose; people believe what they think up for themselves.

"I suppose. He might not have told me, though. And the idiot—" Only here, in this carefully shielded study, did the Crown Minister allow himself to speak of the king this way. Here it had begun to seem increasingly natural; his sister radiated neither approval nor disapproval, merely acceptance. "That idiot didn't even record the conversation. Said it would have been a breach of manners and trust. Said of course Lady Cecelia was loyal. And she is, I've no doubt." But people said "I've no doubt" when their doubts were just surfacing. He knew that now. His sister had taught him, gently, over the years.

"It must have been upsetting for her, and yet exciting in a way," she said. At his quizzical expression, she explained, her delicate voice never rising. "Of course she worried— she has a warm heart under her gruff manner, as we all know. Look at the way she took on young Ronnie after his . . . troubles. But at the same time . . . she's always thrived on excitement. To be the one who brings important news—even bad news—must have made her feel important. And it's been so long since she won any of those horse trials."

"Well, but Lorenza, she's over eighty. And she won't take rejuvenation."

"Quite so." Lorenza studied her fingernails, exquisitely patterned in the latest marbleized silver and pale pink. Piercy would, in time, realize the problem and its necessary solution. He wasn't stupid; he just had the soft heart of a man whose every comfort had been arranged for years by a loving and very efficient sister.

Ordinarily, she never intervened; she felt it was important for him to feel, as well as appear, independent of any influence from his family.

She had her own life, her own social activities, which kept her out and about. But in this instance, she might do him a favor, indulge his softheartedness by taking on the task—not in this instance unpleasant at all—of removing the threat of Lady Cecelia de Marktos and her unbridled tongue.

You stupid old bitch, she thought, making sure to smile as she thought it. *I always knew the time would come . . . and now you're mine.* Still smiling, still silent, she poured Piercy a cup of tea and admired the translucency of the cup, the aroma, the grace of her own hand.

"Here you are," she said, handing it to him. He smiled at her, approving. He had never seen her contempt for him; he never would. If necessary he would die, but he would die still believing in her absolute devotion. That small kindness she had promised him. She promised none to Cecelia. Already her mind lingered on possibilities . . . which would be best for her? Which would be worst for that arrogant loud-mouthed old bitch who had humiliated her all those years ago?

"I can't believe you're not taking this more seriously," Piercy said, reaching for a sandwich from the tray.

"Oh, I do, Piercy. But I know you and the king are quite competent to deal with any problems that might arise. Although, perhaps—I could keep my ear to the ground, among the ladies?"

"Bless you, Lorenza." He smiled at her. "If there's any gossip, you'll hear it."

There won't be, she thought. *Until they're all talking about what happened to poor dear Cecelia.*

* * *

"I want you to meet my captain, Heris Serrano," Lady Cecelia said. She wore tawny silk, a flowing gown with a flared collar, low boots, and jewels Heris hadn't seen before. She had arrived at the shuttleport in high good humor, and insisted that they go straight to the most prestigious of the yacht refitters. The woman behind the desk of Spacenhance flicked Heris a glance.

"Pleased, Captain Serrano."

"She's my agent for this project," Lady Cecelia said. "I have too much business groundside to be on call for the questions that always come up." Her puckish grin took the sting out of that. "I've told her what I want, and she knows the ship's capacity. You two settle everything, and let me know when it's done."

"Very well, milady," the woman said. "But we must have your authorization for credit—"

"Of course." Cecelia handed over her cube. "Heris has my power of attorney if you need more."

Heris tried not to stare . . . power of attorney? What was Cecelia up to? Or did rich people typically give power of attorney to ship captains when they didn't want to be bothered?

"Well, then," the woman said. "You're fortunate that you called when you did . . . we happen to have a slot open at the moment. Bay 458-E, North Concourse. Do you have a storage company in mind, Captain Serrano, or shall I schedule removal and storage with one of our regulars?"

Heris had no idea which storage company was reputable; she wished Cecelia had given her more warning of what to expect. "Schedule it, please; if you would just tell me what you require—"

"It's in our brochure. We do ask specifically that the owner remove all valuables, organic and inorganic, under private seal. We ourselves seal all electronics components. Depending on the owner's decisions, some service areas may be sealed off and left intact. Quite often owners choose to leave the galley and food-storage bays the same."

Heris took the datacards, the hardcopies (the cover of one, she noted, showed the *Sweet Delight*'s earlier redecoration, unless teal and lavender and spiky metal sculptures were everyone's taste).

"Let's have lunch at Shimo's," Cecelia said cheerily, as they swept out of the Spacenhance office. The last thing

Heris wanted was a fancy meal at that most expensive and exclusive of Rockhouse Major restaurants. If she was supposed to move the ship, and prepare for storage of all the furniture and personal items, she needed to get back aboard. And where would the crew stay? But from the look on Cecelia's face, she would get no more information until her employer had some food.

Shimo's was just what she feared: fashionably dressed ladies of all ages, and a few obviously wealthy men, all tucked into the intricate alcoves that surrounded a lighted stage on which live musicians played something that made Heris's nerves itch. Cecelia fussed over the menu far more than usual, and finally settled on what Heris thought of as typical ladies' luncheon fare. It was very unlike her. She waited, less patient than she seemed, for Cecelia to explain what was going on.

"The Crown is paying for it; it's my reward for bringing the prince home. That's why there's a berth open at Spacenhance." Cecelia spoke softly, between mouthfuls of the clear soup she had ordered. Heris sipped her own warily, wondering why Cecelia had chosen this public place to talk about it. The alcoves had privacy shields, but she doubted they were effective against anything but the unaided ears of those in the next alcove. "I told them I didn't want a reward, but Council doesn't want an unpaid debt to my family right now. I'm not sure what's going on . . . but Ronnie's father isn't happy. Meanwhile, I'm undoing the damage done during the annual business meeting—changing my registered proxy, moving assets around." She grinned at Heris. "Nothing for you to worry about. I don't walk down dark alleys at night; I'm spending hours in business offices, and then going home to my sister's town house."

"But you don't have anyone with you."

"Only lawyers, accountants, clerks, the odd section head, salespeople when I shop, and the entire staff of the house. And the family." From the sound of Cecelia's voice, these were annoyances.

"Milady." Heris waited until she was sure Cecelia had caught the tone. "Considering what Ronnie said about Mr. Smith—and if anyone should care if it's known, you're the one most likely to have noticed—don't you think some precaution is warranted?"

Cecelia huffed out a lungful of air, and looked thoughtful. Heris waited. In this place where anyone might have
heard what they said, she dared not press her argument.
Finally Cecelia shook her head. "I think not. And if I should
fall dead of a heart attack or even a street assault, I would
prefer you consider that the natural end of a long, eventful life. I am, after all, over eighty—all original parts, no
rejuv. There is no advantage to be gained by killing me.
I'm not political. For all that I grumbled about my proxy,
and made some changes, I have little to do with the family business, and they know it. I have no children whose
plans would change were I a hostage. Besides, if—and I think
it's unlikely, remember—*if* someone has designs on me, there
is no way to tell without awaiting a move."

"You could wear a tagger."

"Detectable, is it not, by anyone with the right equipment?
Which means that the very persons you most fear would be
first to know, and—should they wish—disable it."

That was true. Yet Heris was sure that Cecelia didn't
realize her peril; she had lived her entire life in privilege,
safely sheltered from any violence she didn't herself choose.
That she had chosen a dangerous hobby still did not
prepare her for attack. She could say she wasn't political,
but what else could her report to the king be called?

"You are coming back to the ship this afternoon, aren't
you? Perhaps we can talk—"

"No." That was firm enough; the red patches on her
cheeks gave additional warning. "No . . . I think it best that
I not come aboard right now."

"But—"

"Captain Serrano—" That formality stung; Heris stared and
got back a warning look. "Please. Do this my way. I am not
stupid, and I have my reasons."

Did this mean she was worried about the Crown's response,
or was something else going on? Heris couldn't tell, and she
realized Cecelia was not about to discuss it. They finished
the meal in near silence.

"Captain Serrano?" Heris looked up; she had headed back
to the yacht's berth still concentrating on Lady Cecelia's
odd behavior. The woman who'd spoken had a soft voice
and sleepy green eyes. Her hair, chopped short by some

unpracticed hand, had once been honey gold, and her face might have been attractive before something cut a broad slash down one side. But it was the voice that stopped Heris in her tracks.

"Methlin Meharry—Sergeant Meharry!" Petris had not known what had happened to the women who'd been court-martialed, although he'd heard rumors. And none of them had contacted Heris after the amnesty Cecelia had arranged. Until now.

"Didn't know if you'd remember," the woman said. She held herself with the same pride as always, but she wasn't in uniform, and Heris couldn't read her expression. Did she know that Heris hadn't known about the courts-martial, or was she still as angry as Petris had been? "Arkady Ginese said you would—"

"Of course I do. But—I was told you'd all been reinstated, with back pay and all—"

Meharry spat. "If they can screw us once, they can do it again. I've got sixty days to think about it, and what I think is I never want to see the inside of another Fleet brig, thank you very much. Arkady said you were hiring."

Heris's mind scrambled. She couldn't hire everyone who had suffered on her behalf; not even Cecelia had that much money, or that large a ship. But Meharry—an unusual set of specialties, she'd started with ground troops and gone on to shipboard weapons systems. "I need a weapons specialist, yes. Ideally someone who can do bodyguard work on Stations or onplanet. And ideally a woman, since Lady Cecelia's the one who'll need guarding. Was that what you wanted?"

Meharry shrugged. "Sounds good to me. Anything would, after that. You know, Captain, we were upset with you." Upset was a ludicrously mild expression. Heris nodded.

"So you should have been. I thought I was keeping you out of worse trouble, and all I did was take my protection away from you. Biggest mistake I ever made."

Meharry cocked her head. "Not really, Captain. Biggest was being born a Serrano, begging your pardon. I should know, given my family." The Meharry family was almost as prominent in Fleet enlisted ranks as the Serranos in the officer corps. "Families get your judgment all scrambled sometimes. But that's over with. Point is, I don't want to go back in, and if you trust me, I'll trust you. You're not a bad commander." Heris almost laughed at the impudence. This was the perfect bodyguard for Lady Cecelia, if only she could persuade her employer.

"Right. Why don't you come aboard and look at what we've got. You may not like a yacht once you've seen it."

Meharry grinned; the scar rippled on her cheek and gave her a raffish look. "Why not? It's built on a good hull, Arkady says, and you're giving it some teeth."

"True, but not for publication. Come on, then, and let's see what you think."

On one side of her mind, Heris thought how glad she was to be out of that ridiculous purple uniform—she could just imagine Meharry's reaction to that garish outfit. On the other side, she thought of the balance of her crew. With Methlin Meharry to back Arkady Ginese, she would need only one more person to serve the ship's weapons in a short combat—the only kind she intended to be involved in. Ships the size of *Sweet Delight* didn't get into slugfests with other ships—not if their captains had sense. But she wouldn't have to depend on Bunny's loans, even though they seemed happy enough to be with her. Yet—the ship was becoming more Fleet with every change she made. And she wasn't sure Cecelia would like it.

Back at the ship, Meharry grinned at Petris and Oblo, who just happened to be lurking around the access tube.

"Found her, did you?" Petris said to Heris.

"Was I looking?" Heris asked mildly. She had the feeling she'd been outmaneuvered by all of them, a feeling intensified when Arkady happened to be in the passage between the bridge and the number four storage bay. He grinned at her, too.

"I hope you don't mind, Captain," he began. Courteous always, even when cutting your throat, one of his former commanders had said. "I happened to see Meharry's name on a list of those returning from . . . er . . . confinement—"

"Glad you did," Heris said. "And I remember you two worked well together. Why don't you show her around, and let her find out if she wants to stay."

An hour later, on the bridge, Meharry and Ginese were deep in consultation on the control systems of the weapons already installed. Heris called Petris into her office.

"Suppose you tell me just how many more little surprises you people have cooked up. I'm delighted about Meharry, but there's a limit, you know."

"If we crewed entirely with former R.S.S. personnel, we wouldn't have to worry about the official secrets people jumping on us," he said. Heris frowned; she was always wary when Petris went indirect. It meant he was trying to outflank her somewhere.

"Numbers," she said, flicking her fingers at him. "I'm not objecting to former Fleet personnel, but I do need numbers."

"I was going to ask you that," he said. "What do you think we need, for what Lady Cecelia's going up against? These smugglers—how likely are they to attack and with what force? What kind of protection do we need to be able to give her where she visits? Can't plan the necessary force until we know the mission."

"I wish I knew," Heris said. "One of the things bothering me is lack of good information. I know there are information networks in the civilian world, but I haven't made my connections yet. And I'm used to having Fleet intelligence to work with—bad as it sometimes was."

"Ummm. You might want to switch Oblo over from Navigation to Communications—reorganize the roster that way—and let him poke around. You know his talents."

She did indeed. They did not appear on any official list of occupational skills.

"He wants to put in some . . . er . . . equipment he sort of found the other day."

Heris felt the hair rising on the back of her neck.

"Found?"

"In a manner of speaking. In return for . . . mmm . . . certain services." That could mean anything, up to and including a discreet killing. "Good stuff," Petris went on, with a wicked grin that made her want to clout him. "Navigational aids. Communication enhancements. He'd like to put it in when no civilians—I mean, those who've always been—are aboard. Just in case."

She couldn't ask if it was stolen Fleet equipment, not directly. Petris would have to answer, and she'd have to do something about it—or he'd have to lie, which would be another problem.

"How much is it costing Lady Cecelia?" she asked instead. Might as well find out.

"Nothing. It's between Oblo and . . . er . . . someone who wanted him to do something. A private donation, you might call it. Are you hiring Meharry?"

"If she wants to come. We need another weapons specialist."

"Good. And how are you going to get hooked into the civilian network?"

"By checking in with the Captains' Guild," Heris said. "If that's a hint." She'd spend some time browsing the general databases, too. Her understanding of politics had been limited to what impinged on the military—on funding, on procurement, on what the admirals optimistically called grand strategy. She'd never heard of some of the groups Cecelia and Ronnie had mentioned. Ageists? Rejuvenants? The meanings seemed obvious, but what did these groups actually do?

CHAPTER THREE

Her new uniform clashed with the lavender and teal, but no longer made Heris feel like an exotic bird. Severely plain midnight blue suited her, and the captain's rings on her sleeves were enough proof of her rank. Her pass to the royal docking sector hung from one lapel. She'd been advised to wear it even on the public concourse.

"Isn't that conspicuous?" she'd asked.

"Yes . . . but they'll expect you to be monitored, so they won't ask," the Royal Security officer said. "And by the way, you *are* being monitored. It's in the tag, so don't leave it somewhere or we'll have to do a full investigation, and we hate that." His tone said they'd take it out of her hide somehow.

"Fine with me," Heris said. It wasn't, but it wouldn't do any good to argue. What she intended to do was above-board anyway. She wanted to report her dismissal of some former crew to the employment agency, with her reasons, and find out if Sirkin's friend had registered for employment yet. She would like to keep Sirkin, but that meant hiring her partner. She needed to check in with the Captains' Guild. And she needed to consult her banker; she didn't know if Cecelia had paid her salary yet. It had not seemed a good time to ask Cecelia directly.

Once out of the royal sector, she took the slideway past the exclusive shops and transferred to the tubetram for the ride to the outer rims. It was midshift of the second watch . . . the tram was half-empty, its other occupants a pair of obvious tourists, rich kids, and four quiet middle-aged men who looked like off-duty crew from a royal shuttle. Possibly they were. They got off at Three, the tourists at Four, and she rode out to Six in splendid solitude.

Six, Sector Orange: back where she'd started, when she left Fleet. Now it didn't bother her the same way at all . . . not in the new uniform, not with the new understanding of what being Cecelia's captain meant. She stopped by the Captains' Guild, paid her onstation fee, smiled at the Warden.

"Do you want to list for posting?" he asked, his hand hovering over the board.

"No, I'm still with Lady Cecelia," she said. "Is there much demand?"

"There's always a demand for those with a clean record," he said. "Lots of people want to retire here. Anything to report?"

"No." Guild members were supposed to inform the Guild of unusual occurrences, including those that they might not want to report to the Fleet or other law enforcement. If you paid the pirates off, Fleet would want to be sure it wasn't a plot; the Captains' Guild simply wanted to know where the pirates had been and how they'd trapped you. Heris had considered whether to tell the Guild about the smugglers' operation on *Sweet Delight*—but Olin was a Guild member, too.

The Warden's brow rose, and he stared pointedly at her royal pass. *That* certainly wasn't the Guild's business. Heris smiled until he shrugged. "Want a room here?" he asked then.

"No, thank you. I'm staying aboard. But—can you tell me if Sagamir Olin is listed here?" She didn't expect the *Sweet Delight*'s former captain would cooperate with her, but she would try.

"Olin?" His eyes shifted aside. "You hadn't heard—? No, that's right; you left so fast. Olin . . . died. A . . . er . . . random assault."

"Random assault" didn't get that expression or that mumble. Heris felt her hairs prickling. Olin had been killed . . . why? Because he hadn't delivered the goods, or because he'd lost that handy ship, or both?

"When?" she asked.

"Oh . . . let me see." He muttered at his console, and then

turned to her. "Five weeks after you left. He had been drinking, the militia said. A bar fight spilled over; someone got him on the way home. They said."

And you don't believe it, Heris thought, *but you aren't going to explain it to me.*

"Thanks anyway," she said. "I'd have bought him a drink . . . here, put this in the memorial fund."

His eyes widened, then he relaxed. "Ah . . . ex-Fleet. You people do that, don't you, whether you know someone or not?"

"That's right," Heris said cheerfully. "Hear of a death, put something in . . . there's always someone needs it."

"Well . . . thank you. It's very kind. I suppose we'd do well to follow that habit ourselves, but . . ."

"Never mind. I couldn't do any less." With a wave, she went back out before he could say more. Her mind was working too hard; he would see it on her face if she stayed. Where could she find out what had really happened without making herself conspicuous? She went on toward the banker and the employment agency. Chores first, fun later.

The employment agency turned out to be fun in its own way. Now that she wasn't a suppliant, the gray and white decor merely looked functional, not cold and threatening. The receptionist might have been sniffy, but not once he saw that Royal Sector pass. Ser Bryn could see her in an hour; perhaps she would prefer to come back? No? Then the private lounge . . . Heris accepted this offer, and settled into a comfortable chair to wait. The viewscreen and cube reader were supplemented by glossy hardcopies of periodicals.

"Captain Serrano." She looked up from an article advising prudent investors to be wary of unregistered companies offering investment in heavy-metal mining operations on worlds like Chisholm and Sakati. The article argued pure finance; Heris, who had been to Chisholm once, thought the influence of the Compassionate Hand there was more reason to keep clear of it. The only profits out of Chisholm would go straight to the Black Scratch. But the man standing at the door, she reminded herself, could as easily be a Compassionate Hand agent. Who *were* the smugglers?

"Ser Bryn?" She stood and extended her hand. He shook hers; she did not let herself glance down to see if he had the telltale tattoo on the thumb web. He wouldn't, not in this position. If he'd ever had it, it would have been redone in flesh tones when he was chosen for a position on Rockhouse.

"What can we do for you, Captain?" he asked, his voice cordial and his eyes guarded.

Heris smiled at him. "I needed to speak to you about Lady Cecelia's former employees." His eyes flickered; he didn't like the sound of that. And, of course, with the security measures on the Royal Docks, he wouldn't have heard about the new crew. "It's rather a long story," she said. "Perhaps we could discuss it privately?" The lounge where she'd been waiting had no one else in it, but she knew it would have full monitoring.

"Ah . . . yes, Captain. Do come along to my . . . er . . . private office." He led the way into a spacious, luxurious office, where Heris suspected wealthy clients gave their requirements for employees. It didn't look anything like the office where she'd been interviewed.

"I brought along a data cube with their records and my reports on them," she said. "But for the obvious reasons there are some details which I'd prefer not to have on cube, and which you need to know."

"Ah." That seemed to be his favorite response to possibly upsetting news. Safe enough.

"As you may or may not know, Ser Bryn, before I departed, I asked this office for any additional details on the quali-fications of Lady Cecelia's existing crew. I was told there were none, and furthermore I was told that private employers such as Lady Cecelia were furnished with—I won't say *dregs*, because that would be insulting—but let's say with less quali-fied personnel than, for example, a major commercial employer. The reasons I understood, if I didn't approve them." She paused to see if he had any response. Beyond a tightening around his eyes, he gave none. She continued.

"With that, I had to be content. Unfortunately, events on the voyage revealed how . . . imprudent . . . that policy was. You may have heard from Takomin Roads about the death of one environmental tech, Iklind?" At this he nodded, but still said nothing. "Presumably you also heard that Iklind was considered to be responsible for the contraband found on the ship. I myself am not sure that he alone was responsible. Surely Captain Olin knew that the maintenance had not been performed; I had intended to pursue his responsibility, but the Guild tells me he's dead."

"Er . . . yes. Random assault, the militia said."

"Perhaps." Heris steepled her fingers and waited for the twitch of muscles beside his mouth before she went on. "At Takomin Roads, I found it necessary to relieve the pilot of his duties—no great hardship, since a ship that size doesn't require one, if the captain is qualified." She let that sink in, too—she knew that the agency's recommendation on crewing had cost Lady Cecelia at least two extra salaries. "You, of course, are not responsible for the crew's astonishing lack of training or fitness—that would be the captain's responsibility, and the captain involved is dead. But at Sirialis, most of the remaining employees tried to stage a mutiny."

"What!" That got a reaction. "What did you do to them?"

"I did nothing. They chose not to return to the ship after spending time at Hospitality Bay—need I explain Hospitality Bay?" He shook his head; as she expected, such an elite agency would know all about the amenities of Bunny's planet. "They didn't want to work with an ex-military captain; they felt my precautions were excessive—and this after the death of one crew member and the near death of another. You are probably not aware that a simultaneous crisis on Sirialis made Lord Thornbuckle suspect that they might be politically motivated. Lady Cecelia accepted their applications to terminate employment and they are currently in custody on Sirialis, where they will be tried for conspiracy."

"But—but who's crewing the ship now?" She could see the flicker of greed in his eyes. Surely she'd need more crew, and if she didn't get it here, she would enrich some other employment agency.

"I should mention," she went on, "that I'm extremely pleased with one former employee, Brigdis Sirkin. *That* young woman has what I consider adequate qualifications, and to the extent that Lady Cecelia wishes to make crew changes, that is the level of qualification I shall insist on." She waited until she saw that take effect, and then answered his question. "Presently, the crew consists of former R.S.S. personnel . . . I am not at liberty to discuss the exact way they . . . er . . . became employed. Only that it has both Fleet and Crown approval. However—none of them presently have civilian licenses. I shall be sending them here, where you can arrange for the transfer of skills registration and the appropriate civilian licensure into specialties . . . for your standard fee, of course. Unless you have some objection?"

Ser Bryn gulped. Her meaning was clear to both of them. He could get his firm the minimal profit involved in transferring registered military skills to civilian ones—the paper pushers' fees—in return for a chance to regain some chance of providing Lady Cecelia with employees later. Or, he could be difficult, and see that influence vanish—and possibly, considering who she was, more business vanish at the same time. Heris watched the glisten of perspiration on his forehead.

"We . . . we are always glad to help Lady Cecelia in any way we can," he said finally. "I hope, Captain Serrano, that you do not think *we* had any suspicion whatsoever that any persons we supplied would become involved in . . . er . . . illegal acts of any nature. We do our best to supply only the most qualified and responsible personnel."

Heris gave him her best grin, and watched him flinch from it. "I'm sure you didn't," she said. "But from this time, Lady Cecelia will be understandably more . . . selective . . . in her dealings with you. She may be only one old lady, on one small yacht, but she pays well and deserves to have the best crew. So I've explained to her." She gave a short nod and turned to her second topic. "Now. Do you have a young woman named Yrilan—Amalie Yrilan—registered with the firm?"

"Just a moment." He slid out a drawer that Heris assumed contained a deskcomp link and poked at it. His next glance at her showed honest confusion. "Yrilan—yes, but—but she's not what you're looking for—not if what you just said—"

Heris turned her hands over. "Ser Bryn, even for me there are occasional personal matters that impinge on business. I assume from your statements that she is not as supremely qualified as, say, Sirkin?"

"By no means," he said.

"Would you have sent her to Lady Cecelia a year ago?"

"Well . . ." He had the grace to flush. "We might have. As an entry-level tech. It's not a demanding job, after all—" Not with the ship heavily overcrewed and underutilized.

"Then send me her application file, and send her for an

interview. To the ship. I meant what I said, and I doubt I'll hire her if she's not up to my standards, but I might hear of another slot . . . and of course I would inform you, first." That got a nod of understanding and approval. "Thank you, then, Ser Bryn. I'll have the military personnel report to your office next mainshift—is that convenient?"

"Er . . . yes. And thank you, Captain Serrano."

From there, Heris decided to begin opening contacts with other ships' officers. Some of her former acquaintances in the R.S.S. would still speak to her, she thought, and the sooner she began networking again, the better.

Bryssum had always been a mixed bar, a place respectable officers of both Fleet and civilian ships could eat and drink in proximity if not friendship. Sometimes it was friendship, of sorts. She remembered, as a young officer, being treated to dinner by the captain of a great liner who had owed favors to Fleet. Now she was the civilian, finding a table on the civilian side, but not too near the windows. She didn't recognize any of the Fleet officers. It didn't matter. Her heart pounded, and she argued it back to a normal rhythm. It really did not matter. She had her ship; she had her place.

"Service, Captain?" Bryssum also had human service, unless you requested otherwise. She liked it.

"Yes," she said. "Mainshift menu." She glanced at the display, flinched inwardly at the prices, and chose a simple meal from among the day's specials.

"Heris!" She looked across to the tables kept by tradition for Fleet officers. A woman a few years her junior waved at her; she had clearly just walked in. Constanza D'Altini, she remembered. The man with her gave Heris an uncertain look. Who would that be, she wondered. Constanza always had someone . . . Heris grinned and nodded, but didn't rise. She couldn't appear too eager. Besides, Constanza had curiosity enough for the whole Intelligence department. After a quick conversation with her table partner, she came over to Heris. The man sat down alone, looking grumpy.

"I hate it that you're out," Constanza said. Along with curiosity, she had the tact and directness of a toppling tree. "It had to be a frame-up; rumor says Admiral Lepescu. Was it?"

"I can't talk about it," Heris said. Constanza's black eyes glinted.

"Not even to me?"

"Not even to you. But thanks for coming over."

"Word is you got amnesty, you and all the rest—"

"That are alive," Heris said. Until she said it, she had not expected to say it, or with that bitterness. But that was Constanza's effect on most people.

"Ah." A careful look. "So that's why you're not coming back?"

Heris made herself grin. "Connie, I've got a cushy job working for a very rich old lady in a beautiful yacht—why should I come back and get myself in more trouble?"

Constanza snorted. "You'll get yourself in trouble, Heris, wherever you are. It's your nature, perhaps the one thing you inherited from your family." She leaned closer. "What do you think of him?" *Him* had to be the man at the table, now pointedly ignoring them.

"He's handsome," Heris said. "Not my type, though."

"He's exec on a heavy cruiser," Constanza said. That was explanation enough; Heris could read her insignia and knew from experience what limited facilities escorts had . . . besides, cruiser duty helped more at promotion time than it was supposed to. Constanza still hadn't made Sub-commander and had only one more Board to do it.

"Good luck, Connie," Heris said. She meant it. Constanza was a good officer whose slow promotion had more to do with her tactlessness than anything that mattered. "Don't queer your chances by hanging around with me."

"I'm not. I'll just tell him you're involved in something you can't talk about." And she was gone, with a last grin and wave. Heris wanted to wring her neck, and felt a moment of compassion for those officers who had given her less than stellar fitness reports.

The rest of her meal passed without incident. She reviewed her personal finances with a link to her banker, and discovered that Cecelia had indeed transferred her salary to her account—a quarter's worth. She called up her investment files, and allowed herself to order an expensive dessert in celebration. Her guesses had once more outperformed the market as a whole.

"This is Amalie," Sirkin said with the unmistakable tone that meant *my lover*. Amalie looked nervous, and well she might. Heris had reviewed her records, and she was nowhere near as qualified as Brigdis Sirkin. Moreover, her credentials, such as they were, overlapped an area Heris had filled with her former crewmates. She didn't really need a third-rate engineering technician.

But she did need a superb navigator, if she could keep her. "Amalie Yrilan," she said. "And you're considering small-ship work, too?"

"Since Brigdis found this . . . and she likes it." Amalie, smaller and rounder than Sirkin, had a deeper voice. Heris knew that meant nothing. "But we quite understand if you don't have an opening in engineering."

"You have a minor in environmental systems—"

"Yes, ma'am, but I'm not really—" Her voice trailed away. She didn't have to say that; her test scores showed it. She had barely made the lower limit of certification.

"You've applied to other places, of course," Heris said, wishing that the scores would go up by themselves.

"I . . . talked to the same agency Brig used," Amalie said. "They . . . said to talk to you." They had said, no doubt, that someone with her scores could whistle for a job and she had better start doing it. Linked with Sirkin, she might get a job, but more likely they'd both fail. Heris sighed.

"You do understand that your scores aren't very good."

"Oh . . . yes, but I'm just not very good at tests. I know more than that, really. Brig can tell you."

Sirkin flushed. In the months under Heris's command, she had continued to develop in her field, and contact with other ships' officers at Sirialis had shown her how much more was possible. Whatever she had thought of Amalie's ability earlier, now she knew better. Heris noted the flush, and spoke first. No need to humiliate her in front of a friend.

"Sirkin has been aboard more than a standard year now; your scores are your best witness. Test anxiety, you say? Didn't you ever take the Portland treatments?"

"Well, yes, ma'am, but they . . . but I was just so busy sometimes, you know. Working part-time . . ."

She had not worked part-time for the first two years, and her scores had been no better then. Sirkin, whose record also showed employment during school, had finished in fewer terms with top scores. Either ability or effort was missing here; Heris wasn't sure which.

"Sirkin's an outstanding junior officer, as I'm sure you know; if it weren't for that, I wouldn't be considering your application. I've got a full crew in engineering, and while I could use someone in environmental, I don't want slackers. I won't tolerate anything but excellence."

The tension around the young woman's eyes said it all, as far as Heris was concerned. This one didn't want to work that hard, and would always find excuses for herself. Too bad for Sirkin; irresponsibility made for bad lovers as well as bad shipmates. But she would give it a try, for the time they'd be onstation, just in case.

"I can understand that, ma'am, but—"

Heris held up her hand. "Tell you what. According to the owner, we're going to be here awhile, doing some work on the yacht. I'll hire you as general labor—mostly environmental work, some powerplant engineering—on a thirty-day temp contract. You and Sirkin can job hunt together in your off-shift time. If you satisfy me, and don't find something you like better, I may offer you a longer contract then. But I won't promise anything. How's that?"

That didn't satisfy Amalie, though she forced a smile, but Sirkin was relieved. She had clearly expected refusal.

"We'll be installing quite a bit of replacement electronics," Heris went on. "And a new backup set of powerplant control systems. The environmental system was overhauled thoroughly only a few months ago, but given the state of the former system, I want a complete baseline calibration."

"Yes, ma'am," Amalie said. At least she had that part right. Heris nodded.

"Sirkin, take her over to engineering, and introduce her to Haidar and Kulkul—they're the Environmental first, and Engineering second, Yrilan. I'll post the relevant orders on the comp for them."

Amalie started to open her mouth; Sirkin got there first with "Thank you, ma'am," and pulled her friend along by the arm. Heris shook her head once they were out of sight. What a shame that a brilliant young person like Sirkin had fallen for a loser. She was sure Amalie was a loser; she had seen too many of that type.

Over the next few days, Nasiru Haidar reported that Amalie Yrilan was reasonably willing when supervised, but lacked the expertise she should have had and wouldn't stick to a job without constant supervision. Padoc Kulkul agreed, and added that he would rather have a dumbot—the lowest level of robotic assistant—than a fluffheaded girl who kept humming popular music off-key.

"About what I thought," Heris said. "Can you perk her up? Maybe that school—"

"I can try," Nasiru said. "But how much do you want to risk on her? She'll never go beyond third class on the exams, I'd bet my last credit chip. Half the work would do twice as much with a good candidate." Padoc simply shook his head.

"Well, we're not in the service anymore," Heris said. "We don't have an endless supply of recruits. I was hoping—"

"I'll work on it." Nasiru sounded not quite grumpy. "But I won't promise anything. I know Sirkin's good, but young love doesn't last forever."

Heris snorted. "Don't try to tell them that. We have to remember, we're all a lot older, and with real experience." By real, of course, she meant military.

"That one'll get herself killed, and maybe her friends," Padoc said. "You know we all like young Sirkin, but— Amalie's like that cute little kid back on *Fisk*." Heris raised her brows, but he didn't back down. The cute little kid on *Fisk* had been someone important's nephew, and he had hit the wrong control in combat and—luckily—died along with those his idiocy killed. Turned out his uncle had known about the addiction problem, but concealed it in the hopes that life on a ship would straighten him out.

"Well, if she's that bad, we don't want her," Heris said. "I know that. But as long as we're in dock, she can't hurt us that much, and we just might pull off a miracle."

"There's a slight chance that you may have some trouble dockside," Heris said. She had called the crew together before giving them Station liberty. "Those of you who were aboard at the time know about the smugglers' stash. If they choose to retaliate for its loss—"

"But they've already killed Olin," Petris said.

"Wouldn't they go after Lady Cecelia?" asked Nasiru. "Or the ship itself?"

"They might. But they also might make an example of

a crew member." She knew her ex-military crew would know how to handle any invitations to criminality, but Sirkin and Yrilan were young and vulnerable, bait for everything from gambling sharks to smugglers. "I suggest you travel in pairs, at least, and keep your eyes open. You're not children, to be coddled and watched over, but as long as we don't know what the danger is, you're vulnerable. I'm not sure just how far they'll go to express their displeasure. If you want to indulge in anything mind-altering, be sure you're in a safe place."

"If there's trouble, how about weapons?" Oblo, as usual with a fight even remotely in view, looked both sleepy and happy. The sleepiness was entirely deceptive.

"No. Not on Station. We don't need legal trouble as well as illegal. And given Lady Cecelia's . . . mmm . . . connections, we could even have political trouble. Fight if you have to, but call for the gendarmes right away."

"Yes, ma'am." That with a heavy-lidded look that meant he would interpret it in his own way. Petris gave him a sharp glance, and Heris told herself to talk to Petris about Oblo before he had a shift off. His formidable brawling skills should be reserved for times they needed them, not wasted on casual displays.

CHAPTER FOUR

Under the supervision of Nasiru Haidar, Yrilan earned her pay. Heris had to respect her for coming back, shift after shift, to face the grudging acceptance of the rest of the crew. Sirkin, she noticed, stayed clear of Yrilan during work hours, but she was looking increasingly tense. Heris assumed that meant they hadn't found a joint berth on some other ship. Sirkin would be facing a hard decision soon enough; Heris didn't try to offer advice she was sure the younger woman would resent.

On the day they completed the new installations, which would be sealed again when the yacht entered the refitting docks, Heris gave the crew a half-shift bonus off. She gave Ginese the standing watch, and finished the interminable forms necessary to clear the Royal Docks and transfer the ship around the station on the next mainshift but one. She hated the thought of letting a tug do the shift but those were the rules. She expected all the off-duty crew to be gone by the time she finished, but as it happened she left the ship just behind Sirkin and Yrilan. They were not quite holding hands as they hurried through the Royal sector to the public concourse beyond. She wondered if they'd job hunt or spend the extra time another way.

They seemed to be headed the same direction she was. Once in the transit car, they shared a seat at the far end. Heris hung back at the exit, hoping they wouldn't think she was following them, but traffic was light, just before shiftchange. In another half hour, all transit tubes would be crowded. She dawdled, glancing at a shop window down the concourse from the Captain's Guild, until they were nearly out of sight around the curve.

Heris turned into the Captains' Guild, mentally shaking her head. When she'd been that young, she hadn't been unlucky enough to fall that far in love. Sirkin and Yrilan were together, but it could hardly be called alert awareness of possible danger. Yet it would do no good to suggest anything to them; they might try, but in twenty paces they'd be back to concentrating on each other. At least Sirkin had basic good sense, and they had promised to bunk aboard until the decorators took the ship over. Surely they wouldn't get in much trouble. After all, Oblo had the history of dockside and planetside brawls.

The Captains' Guild rooms had begun to look familiar, and the Warden knew her now. She posted her daily report, and looked over the news. Here again, the different format had begun to make sense. Which ships were in, with which captains, reporting changes they'd noted in their routes. She was looking specifically for anything to suggest what Captain Olin had been doing in the regions where he'd hung about as if looking for a rendezvous. So far, she'd found no comment helpful. After all, if another captain was up to the same game, she could hardly expect an honest report to the Captains' Guild.

"Captain Serrano's following us," Yrilan said. "We're off duty—she doesn't have to—"

"Captains' Guild's down this way," Sirkin said. "Don't get paranoid, Amalie. She isn't bothering us."

"Just wish she'd mind her own—" Yrilan glanced over her shoulder and turned back. "Or catch up. Something."

Sirkin laughed. "What've you done or not done that you think she'll scold you for? You're trying, aren't you?"

Yrilan nodded. "'Course I am, but it's a lot harder than school. That Haidar is so picky. I swear he watches me every second, and he wants everything to be just so."

"But you're learning," Sirkin said. "And we're together." For how long? she asked herself. She had overheard some of Haidar's comments, and even more from Kulkul. They didn't think the captain should hire Yrilan permanently. She forced herself not to think about it. They had a full three-shift off, and for once the money to enjoy it. "Where shall we eat?" she asked. "Why not a dinner-dance place like Califa's?"

Yrilan grinned at her, the grin she had first fallen for, and gave a little skip-step. "Great—but why not Uptop first, to get in the mood?"

"I'm already in the mood," Sirkin said, and ran a finger down Yrilan's arm.

"Patience is a virtue," Yrilan said, tossing her head, and Sirkin had to laugh. They both knew who had the patience. She wished Yrilan didn't like noisy taverns like Uptop, but she'd have put up with worse for the evening to come.

By the time they reached Uptop, it was crammed with mainshift rush hour business, vibrating to the beat of its music. Sirkin saw a sonic cop check her meter from across the corridor, shrug, and go on. Well-bribed, perhaps. She inserted her own filters, and followed Yrilan inside. They stood with a clump of others waiting for space at the bar or booths; Sirkin saw merchant ship patches on some arms, nothing on others. Uptop had never been a favorite of either Fleet or Royals, which made it more popular with other groups. Remembering the captain's warning, she tried to notice anything out of the ordinary, but she didn't like this kind of place anyway. How could she tell if the big, scar-faced man in front of her was really from Pier's Company #35 or not? Against her hip, she felt Yrilan's hip twitch to the music. She wouldn't be wearing sonic filters; she liked it this loud. Sirkin had to admit that the bass resonances dancing up her bones from heel to spine were exciting, but she wished the higher tones didn't tangle her eardrums in the middle of her skull.

Two seats finally opened at a large table. Yrilan nodded before Sirkin had a chance to see everyone clearly, but she shrugged and followed the flashing arrow on the floor. Two women in matching gray with a yellow stripe: Lyons, Inc., but probably not ship crew, since they were hunched over a digipad poking at it with styluses. Probably accountants. A man in rusty black; Sirkin was glad he sat on the far side of the table. A woman and two men in nondescript blue, playing some sort of game on the table's projector. An elegant woman, hair streaked with silver, whose silui-silk suit probably cost more than all the other clothes at the table. The empty seats were between her and the Lyons, Inc. women.

Yrilan edged in beside the older woman. She would, Sirkin thought, amused. She had a passion for jewels, the classic case of champagne tastes on a beer budget, and the woman wore jewelry as costly and elegant as her clothes. Sirkin wondered what she was doing there . . . she wasn't much like the rest of Uptop's clientele. She herself squeezed in beside Yrilan and looked at the table's display. She wanted wine with dinner; she really didn't want anything now.

"Let's have a mixed fry as well," Yrilan said in her ear. "Or will it spoil your appetite?"

The tickle distracted her from the question for a moment. "If we're going to eat a good dinner, why . . . ?"

"Oh . . . there's no hurry, is there? I think I just want to cram it all in, love, all the things we like. I can see the signs as well as you can. Your Captain Serrano isn't going to hire me, and this may be our last chance to celebrate together."

Implicit in that was the understanding that she, Sirkin, wasn't going to quit the *Sweet Delight* to work wherever Yrilan found a berth. Nor would Yrilan wait. Her eyes stung; she hadn't admitted it to herself yet, but it was true. She drew a breath, trying to think how to say what she really felt.

"Don't spoil it, now," Yrilan said, punching her arm lightly. "Let's just party and enjoy it." She reached out and entered an order for both of them. Sirkin didn't cancel it; right then she didn't care.

The mixed fries, hot and spicy, gave her an excuse for watering eyes; the first gulp of her drink took the edge off both spice and emotion. Was Yrilan trying to anesthetize her, or what? She glanced sideways, and saw that Yrilan was smiling at the elegant older woman. Fine. Drag her into a place like this and then ignore her.

"Amalie—" That got a quick sidelong look, a nudge. "Look—maybe we should go somewhere and talk—"

"No . . . talk's the last thing we need." Yrilan shook her head decisively, and reached for more fries. Sirkin shrugged and sat back. Even with filters, her ears hurt. On her right, the conversation between the two women she thought of as accountants consisted of sequences of numbers with exclamations like "But of *course* the rate's pegged to the Green List!" She knew the Green List had something to do with investments, but had no idea what. Glancing that way, she saw their display covered with intersecting lines that flicked from one pattern to another. "All profit," one of them was saying. "See, the first shipment makes up the difference between—"

Yrilan poked her. "Wake *up*, Brig. Kirsya here has asked us to dine with her."

Sirkin peered around Yrilan at the elegant woman, startled out of her mood and into wariness. Had Yrilan known her before? But she was explaining.

"I met Kirsya while waiting for *Sweet Delight* to arrive—I wanted you to meet her before, but we've been so busy—"

Was this her replacement? But she had to say something; Kirsya was reaching around to shake her hand. Sirkin forced herself to smile. "Glad to meet you," she said. At least she didn't have to say how much she'd heard, since she'd heard nothing. Surely Yrilan could have mentioned her.

"And I." Kirsya had a lovely voice, surprisingly clear through the music and the filters. "I asked Amalie to let me be a surprise . . . I hope it doesn't bother you."

Bother was the wrong word. Sirkin felt that she was somehow in the wrong when she hadn't done anything. Yet.

"I'm Amalie's therapist," Kirsya said. Sirkin glanced at Yrilan, whose cheeks were slightly flushed.

"Therapist? What's wrong?" Immediately she knew that was the wrong thing to say, even before both sets of eyebrows went up. "I'm sorry," she said quickly, but too late. "I know—it doesn't mean anything's wrong—it's just—" Just that unless Amalie was going to confront her laziness, there was nothing she really needed to change. Not to please Sirkin, anyway.

"I was really miserable, waiting for you," Yrilan said, not quite apologetically. "I got into a little . . . mess, sort of. And they recommended therapy."

"Who?" asked Sirkin, her heart sinking right to the floor. Mess? She hadn't mentioned any mess, and they'd always shared everything before. What kind of "mess" got a recommendation of therapy, and how had she concealed that from Captain Serrano? Sirkin felt a sudden desire to bolt from the tavern, straight back to *Sweet Delight*.

"The . . . uh . . . Station police. They said no charges might be filed if I agreed to short-term therapy . . ." Yrilan's voice had the pleading tone which had always worked before. Now it sawed on Sirkin's nerves almost like the music. "And . . . Kirsya really helped me. We got to be friends—"

In the short time that Yrilan had had to wait, of course. Friends. Sirkin bit back all she was thinking, and simply nodded. Memories flooded her: the day she'd first seen Amalie Yrilan in the registration line, fumbling with a stack of forms and data cubes. What had it been, the look in her green eyes or the quick toss of her hair? The study dates, the walks by the lake, the long intense discussions of their future.

"It's not what you think," Yrilan was saying now, with a worried look. Kirsya's face was composed. So it well might be, Sirkin thought, finally recognizing her own anger. She with her good clothes and jewels— "Of course I still love you," Yrilan went on. "I always will—" The necessary *but* hung in the air, battered by the music.

"I see," said Sirkin, just to stop the process, whatever it was. She had to have time, space, silence. She couldn't deal with all this now. She made herself meet the older woman's eyes. "Is this meeting your idea?"

Kirsya smiled. It was a very mature smile. "A meeting, certainly. But Uptop was Amalie's idea. In my experience, meetings should take place where the client is comfortable— not that Amalie is my client anymore, of course."

"Of course," Sirkin echoed.

"I certainly wasn't planning to intrude on your . . . evening together." Again, a missing word hung in the air; she had not quite said *last* evening together. "I did want to meet the person who has been so important in Amalie's life. Perhaps we could chat a bit another time, where it's quieter?"

"Of course," Sirkin said, though she couldn't think what about. Perhaps this woman thought she would come for therapy, too. *Never*, she thought, and hoped it didn't show on her face. She struggled for lightness in her tone, and turned to Yrilan. "Well, Amalie, just what kind of mess did you get into? Or is that confidential now?"

"Oh—I was playing Goorlah and I sort of . . . well . . . overdid it."

Gambling again. She'd promised to quit, and since she hadn't shown up broke or in debt, Sirkin thought maybe she'd really reformed. "How bad?" she asked now.

"No worry. I got a temp job with Kirsya's help, and paid it off. And I know, I shouldn't have gambled at all. I promised you. But it was only that once."

It wouldn't have been only that once, Sirkin knew, but it would be useless to argue. She found herself cataloguing the things she had loved about Amalie Yrilan from the beginning, from the color of her hair to the sound of her laugh, as she would have catalogued the attractions of a navigating system she would never use again. Already Amalie belonged to the past, although she sat there, eyes wide and excited. Sirkin felt a cold lump in her belly, and wished she could evaporate like the spilled drinks.

Kirsya, with an understanding look that Sirkin wanted to remove from her face with a blaster, turned to Yrilan. "Well— what have you two planned for the evening?" Yrilan answered eagerly, her voice already showing the effects of the drinks she'd had.

"Califa's for dinner, maybe some dancing, then a party wherever we find one. We're in the mood for fun, aren't we, Brig?"

Sirkin forced a smile to meet Kirsya's. She would not, absolutely not, show that cradle-robbing sleaze what she felt. "Celebration," she said, surprising herself with the sound of her own voice. It held none of the pain she felt, but considerable force. Kirsya looked confused a moment, then smiled widely and pushed back her chair.

"Then I'd better get along and let you enjoy it. By the way—if you didn't happen to see the announcement, they've closed the F-way slides for repair, so if you're going to Califa's, it's shorter from here to use the Number 11 bounce-tube and that shortcut through Avery Park than go all the way back to the G-way slides."

"Thank you," said Sirkin. Shortcut through Avery Park, indeed. She had more sense than that, and she'd bet that Kirsya never went there—not dressed in silk and jewels, anyway. "We're in no hurry," she said. "There's a shop on G-way that I'd like to visit anyway." She had meant to buy Yrilan a certain piece of jewelry there. Now . . . she didn't know, but she certainly didn't want to follow Kirsya's suggestion. The older woman shrugged, gave Yrilan a smile that seemed entirely too warm, and squeezed past other chairs on her way out. She had an elegant back, long and supple, and Sirkin saw how many others noticed it.

"She really helped me," Yrilan said. "I hoped you'd like her."

"I'm glad," Sirkin said to the first part of that. She couldn't deal with the second part. Her throat had closed; she didn't want any more of the spicy fries. "Are you ready?" It sounded churlish even to her.

"Look—" Yrilan glanced around and leaned closer. "I know you're upset, but let's not spoil the evening. Maybe I'm wrong; maybe Serrano will hire me. If she does, I'll do anything I can to stay on her good side. At least we can enjoy this."

"Right." Sirkin tried to push the depression and grumpiness away. "But I'm really not in the mood for more fries— and you're not eating them now—so could we please go somewhere that the music doesn't split my brain?"

"All right." Yrilan twitched her shoulders and pushed away from the table. Sirkin followed her out, sighing internally.

But out in the open, Yrilan seemed to relax, and they walked together as they always had. They stopped to look in shop windows—Yrilan thought a blue-and-violet wrap would look good on Sirkin, and Sirkin shrugged and agreed to try it on. The shop wasn't much out of their spending range, though they both agreed the wrap didn't look that good on. Sirkin felt her own nerves settling as they came out of the shop. Maybe it would be all right this time— maybe. She was still thinking that when Yrilan turned toward the Number 11 bounce-tube entrance.

"Hey—let's go back to G-way slides. There's a place I wanted to show you—"

"Maybe after dinner." Yrilan scowled. "I saw the look on your face—you're just afraid of Avery Park. And that's silly at this time of day. It's not that far past shiftchange rush, and it's only second shift anyway." Sirkin glanced around. Traffic had eased, but it was busy enough; the bounce-tube entrance had a short line. If they waited until after dinner, and then Amalie insisted on testing her courage, the park would be even more dangerous.

✳   ✳   ✳

"Eh, Amalie!" The man wore ordinary spacers' coveralls, but no ship patch. He had appeared suddenly in the park, just when Sirkin had been thinking how empty it was, how silly it had been to object to the shortcut. Sirkin felt the twitch in Yrilan's hand. Someone she knew, then, and someone she didn't really want to see. An ordinary face, perhaps a bit paler than average, with lank gray-brown hair. "That your friend you told us about? Handsome, she is."

"Back off, Curris." Yrilan sounded cross and scared both. "We're not interested in your games."

"Games of your own, eh?" He laughed, and so did his companions. Sirkin did not like the looks of the three men and two women. All, like him, wore spacers' coveralls with not a ship patch among them. Bad sign, that. Station dwellers didn't wear spacers' clothes; they had their own styles that didn't offer as many hiding places for weapons. "She looks a bit nervous, Amalie—didn't you tell her about the party?"

"We're not coming," Yrilan said. "That's why I came up here—to tell you. We've got other plans."

"Now that's not friendly, hon," the man said. "Y'know what we agreed. Just a party, that's all, just a chance to chat with your friend there."

"No." Sirkin realized suddenly that Yrilan was really scared, not just nervous. That the tension of the past hour or so had had little to do with her, and a lot to do with this man and the "party" he mentioned.

"Kirsya knows about it," Yrilan said. She was bluffing, whatever that was supposed to mean. Sirkin had known her too long to be fooled by that tone. And the man must recognize it, too. "She approved the change of plans."

"I don't think so," the man said. "You're as bad at lying as you are at gambling, Amalie."

"You—" Yrilan began. Sirkin touched her arm.

"Let's go, Amalie. No sense talking."

"Now there you're wrong," the man said, switching his gaze to her face. Sirkin tried not to shiver visibly. She had known they shouldn't come this way; now she wondered how far away a Security alarm was. "There's a lot of sense talking, when the alternatives are . . . less pleasant."

A gleam, in his hand. In another hand or two, in that group. All Captain Serrano's warnings came back to her, and everything her former crew had added. But she didn't have that training; she had no idea what to do when faced with people like this in a shadowy corner where she should never have come. Yet she couldn't have let Amalie come this way alone, could she?

"We have nothing to talk about," Sirkin said, hoping her voice didn't sound as scared as she felt. "We're meeting friends—"

"I don't think so," the man said again, in the same tone he'd used to Yrilan. "That's not what we heard from Kirsya. She says you two were planning a quiet little farewell dinner . . . but Amalie really prefers a party, don't you? Quite a party girl, our Amalie." He bared his teeth in an expression nothing at all like a normal smile. "Now we'll have us a nice chat, and you'll find us a friendly bunch."

"No," Sirkin said, before she had time to think how scared she was.

"Brig—" Yrilan's hand closed over hers. "Don't—"

She didn't have to say more. There were the weapons, the bulbous snout of a very illicit sonic pulser, familiar from entertainment cubes, and several plasteel knives. Sirkin felt her mouth go dry. The advice she'd had—never go with the attacker, the place you're accosted is the most dangerous for the attacker, and the place he takes you is safer for him— now seemed impossible to follow. Her imagination leaped ahead to the effects of sonic pulser and knife . . . she saw blood, felt the pain. What could they do? She tried to look around without moving her head, but saw nothing helpful, no one she could call for help.

"Come on," the man said, gesturing with the sonic pulser. "It's party time, girls." Behind him, the others grinned and moved forward.

"You're going to spoil their fun," Methlin Meharry said. Oblo shook his head.

"Not me. If they find a nice room and spend the night together, fine—but that's not the mood Yrilan's in. She's out for trouble of some kind. I know that look."

Methlin gave him a poke. "You should. You're always out for trouble . . ."

"Captain'll be upset if we let Sirkin get trashed because of Yrilan's foolishness. You know what she thinks—and besides, the girl's worth working on; she could have been Fleet." High praise, for Oblo. "And they'll never know we're watching, 'less something goes sour."

"I can think of things I'd rather do on my off shift—"

"Fine. Let me do it."

"Not you alone . . . I know better."

They lounged in the doorway of Uptop, drinking pirate chasers from the outside bar. "Classy one sitting with 'em," Oblo said. "Doesn't fit here."

"Don't like her looks. Actin' like a shill. Let's check 'er out." Methlin pulled out her very illicit Fleet data-capture wand. Oblo grinned.

"Good idea." Methlin pointed it at the overdressed woman for a moment, capturing her image, then looked around for a public dataport. "Go on," said Oblo. "I'll wait here."

Methlin found a 'port two shops down, and it even had a privacy shield. Her wand stabbed into the port and over-rode the usual restriction codes, sucking the data she wanted out of the station computers. When she slid the wand into the 'port of her handcomp, the display showed everything the station personnel files knew about Kirsya, Melotis Davrin.

"A therapist," she murmured to Oblo.

"Wipe your hand," Oblo said. "Never."

"Says. Licensed and all that. Does work for the Station militia, mostly addicts up for minor stuff. Has interesting friends."

"Oh?"

"That agency." They both knew which agency; Heris had told them her suspicions about the employment agency before sending them over to get their civilian licenses and ratings. It had smelled as rotten to them as it had to Heris. "Finds jobs for clients, sometimes."

"Ah." Oblo sucked his teeth noisily, drained the rest of his drink, and grinned. "Sounds whole to me. Got?"

"Got. Who?"

"The kids. We'll stay with the kids, but put a ferret on the tinker." They retreated across the corridor. Methlin slid the wand into another public connection, and trans-mitted both the data on Kirsya and Oblo's request to the *Sweet Delight*.

"Ah—there she goes." Oblo grunted. "Huh. Just passed a signal, too. Wonder who that was?"

"I didn't see . . . oh, yes. Classy rear view the lady has."

"Keep your mind on business."

When Sirkin and Yrilan came out, Oblo could tell that they were at odds. He and Meharry dropped back a little. No need to embarrass Sirkin if she suddenly stormed back this way.

"Just a little chat," the man said. "Just a suggestion your friend wasn't confident enough to take."

"I don't need to chat with you," Sirkin said. "If Amalie didn't want to do it, I don't either."

"Unwise," the man said. "You're smart enough to know she's not. And we're offering an unusual opportunity here. We'd pay well for a contact aboard the *Sweet Delight*. No risk worth mentioning, and a profit—and no harm done your employer, if that bothers you."

"No risk?" Sirkin was glad to find her voice didn't shake. "Like Captain Olin?"

"He didn't follow instructions," the man said. "He upset the old lady, got himself fired—and then we hear that Iklind died and the goods were discovered because he was trying to double his profit with a payoff to the refitters. He double-crossed us . . . we couldn't let that pass."

"I suppose not." Sirkin had been hoping someone would come into the park, but no one did. Had these people somehow cut it off from the corridors? Had they bribed the Station militia?

"Don't hurt her!" Yrilan's voice was shrill.

"Convince her, then," said the man.

"No—let her alone. It's not her fault. She had nothing to do with it, any of it."

"Get out of the way." His voice had flattened, utter menace.

"No." Yrilan, stubborn, was immovable. He lifted the weapon, his finger tightening, and Yrilan launched herself in useless rage and love. Sirkin grabbed for her lover and missed, but it was already too late. Yrilan screamed as the sonic pulser focused its lethal vibrations on her; she curled into the agony, still screaming. Sirkin, on the edge of that cone, felt as if someone had stabbed her brain with a needle; tears burst from her right eye and she lurched sideways. The man strode forward, but somehow Yrilan grabbed at his leg and tripped him. Sirkin, fighting off the dizziness of the sonic attack, managed to knock the weapon out of his hand before he could turn it on Yrilan again.

The others joined the melee then, knives and fists and boots. Sirkin tried to get to Yrilan, but one of them slammed an elbow into her face, and another kicked her legs out from under her. She hit someone hard enough to make him grunt, then a blow in the belly took all her breath. And Yrilan—she couldn't see. She couldn't hear anything but curses, grunts, the slam of boots and fists. A hand came over her mouth, and she twisted her head and bit, hard. A curse, a blow to the head that made her eyes water—someone yanking her arms up behind her—then more yells and the feeling that someone else had arrived.

Gasping, Sirkin tried to break the armhold and find a way to strike back. Another kick, this one in the ribs—she felt something crunch—and then someone fell on top of her, hard knees and elbows and too much weight. She couldn't breathe . . . she couldn't complain about not breathing . . . her vision grayed out, and the next blow sent her into darkness.

"Captain Serrano!" That was the Warden, with quiet urgency. She wondered why he hadn't simply buzzed her carrel until she saw his face. He was gray around the lips, his eyes showing too much white. She came at once, ignoring a few surprised glances from other captains who had noticed the Warden's unusual invasion of the inner rooms.

Heris didn't bother to ask; she simply followed him back to the reception area. He almost scurried. Waiting for them were two uniformed Station Security Police, faces grim. Heris felt her heart begin to pound, a great hammer. If they had come, instead of asking her to visit one of the waitstations, whatever had happened was serious—even fatal.

"Captain Serrano?" asked the shorter one. "I'm Detective Morin Cannibar. We have a problem concerning your crew."

"Who is it?" asked Heris. Oblo came automatically to mind, but he ought to be busy installing that semipirated bit of navigational electronics he had come back with the day before. He had wanted to do it himself, when Sirkin and Yrilan were not aboard. That thought struck a chill in her—those two?

"We aren't sure, Captain Serrano. The—uh—body carried identification as a member of your crew, but—uh—"

Heris felt herself going cold, the protective freeze of emotion that would carry her through any necessary action. "Do you need me to identify the body?"

"It's—it's not going to be easy, ma'am. She's a young woman, that's all we can tell. Hit with a sonic pulser, then . . . pretty well beaten to a pulp."

Let it not be Sirkin, Heris thought, then hated herself for thinking that. Yrilan might be a bit lazy and not over-bright, but she had not deserved anything that would put that expression on the faces of police officers.

She nodded shortly. "I'll come now. I have two young female crew members, and they are both off duty at present. Can you tell me something about it?"

The taller one shrugged. "Someone wanted her dead. Messily. Either of them have enemies you know about?"

Heris looked at him sharply. "You know I filed a report when we arrived that my crew might be the target of retaliation from some criminal organization. And that I had been contacted, subsequently, by someone whose credentials worried me."

"Yes, but you didn't know many details. Made it hard for us to help you."

"True—nonetheless, my guess is this young woman ran afoul of that group, not an enemy of her own. Neither of them had been on this station very long. One arrived with my ship, and the other met her here after finishing her technical training. I don't suppose you know where the other is—"

"No, ma'am. If it's some group like you're thinking of, and they were together, then I'd expect both . . ."

"So would I." She walked along between them, trying not to feel trapped. "Where are we going? The morgue?"

"No, ma'am. We'd like you to see the . . . body . . . in place. In case you can help figure out what happened."

In place meant in a corner of Rockhouse she'd never known about. "It's a park, actually," one of the men said. "Reasonably safe during shiftchanges, because it's a short-cut from a concentration of civilian housing units to two big employers. There's a primary school that uses it during mainshift for recreation and exercise. But it's a bit out of the way—especially midshift on Second. And the usual patrol had a domestic disturbance call and missed two rounds through here."

"Planned?" Heris asked. She could see the cluster of people working ahead, under brilliant lighting.

"Maybe. Can't tell—it's a family with a history. This time they'll be split up for a while, see if that settles them."

Then they were close enough for Heris to see the bodies under the lights.

CHAPTER FIVE

She recognized Yrilan by the hair and clothes. The young woman's face was disfigured by parallel knife slashes, the skin reddened by the sonic pulser wound. "That's mine," she said, pointing. The man beside her nodded.

"Right—do you know which?"

"Amalie Yrilan, on temporary contract. She left the ship today about when I did, and that's what she was wearing. Also the hair—" That ginger-colored hair, once fluffy and now matted with blood.

"You don't seem—that upset by . . . the other . . ." the man said. She could hear the suspicion in his voice.

"My background's Fleet," she said. "Regular Space Service." Let them think she was a coldhearted military bitch . . . easier than explaining that her feelings would come later, when she felt safe. That she would have the right number of nightmares about the ruin of Amalie Yrilan's face, enough to prove her own humanity. She braced herself for criticism, but the man merely nodded.

"Right. You've seen combat trauma, then." It wasn't a question. "This was sonic pulser plus, I suspect, being on the ground in the midst of a major brawl. We think the knife wounds were after death, maybe accidental; the autopsy will check for that."

Heris stared at the parallel wounds across Yrilan's face, and the deep gash between thumb and first finger on both hands. Did the militia not recognize those wounds? Or did they wonder if she did? Better to be honest.

"Those marks—the last time I saw something like that, it was a Compassionate Hand action."

"Ah. I wondered if you'd know."

"We were called to Chisholm once." They could look that up in her service record, the public part. "They had trouble with their ore haulers being hijacked between the insystem Stations and the jump-point insertion." They had had more trouble than that, but the rest was classified.

"Two of the dead bodies had C.H. marks on the thumb web," the man said. "Did Yrilan?"

"Certainly not. Not overt, anyway. But you're right, that hand cut's usually given to traitor members, not stray associates." And where was Sirkin, her mind insisted? Was she, too, a Compassionate Hand victim?

"You recognize any of the others?"

None of the others had mutilated faces, beyond a bruise or two. She knew none of them. But something about the pattern of injuries on two—she frowned. "No. But—" Suddenly it came clear. The time she had had to get Oblo out of trouble . . . the miners he'd felled had exactly the same marks. "But none of them are my crew," she said, finishing smoothly. "We've been staying close to the ship, most of the time, getting it ready to leave the Royal Docks—"

"I know." He had checked, then. "I didn't really think you would recognize them, but it was a chance." He paused, then asked, "And you say this—Yrilan, was it?—usually had a companion?"

"Yes—she did tonight. Brigdis Sirkin, my Navigator First. They'd known each other at school, and Yrilan had hoped I'd hire her. Unfortunately, she wasn't nearly as qualified."

"Was Sirkin going to leave your crew?"

"I'm not sure. I had hoped not, but they were close. She had a tough decision coming up. I hope—" It was stronger than that, a plea to whatever powers ran the universe. "I hope Sirkin's not a prisoner or anything."

"We can't tell." The man frowned. "Five dead, including your crew member. This Sirkin must be some kind of fighter if she didn't have help. Someone badly wounded got away that direction—" He pointed to smears of blood heading to the far end of the little park. "There's all too many ways out down there, though we're looking. But two bounce tubes, and a slideway."

Heris looked again at the dead she already thought of as "enemy." She couldn't see the thumb-web marks from here— probably they were flesh-colored tattoos, designed to fluoresce under UV light. But the pattern—again she thought of Oblo. One of the dead had been hit by someone shorter, she thought, but this wasn't her field of expertise. Shorter than Oblo would be most of her crew, but her mind drifted to her weapons specialists. Arkady Ginese? No; Arkady, even onstation, would have carried something that left distinctive marks. No one had ever broken him of the habit. Besides, he had the standing watch; he wouldn't have been here. Methlin Meharry, perhaps? Those sleepy green eyes had fooled more than one, but her unarmed combat skills topped even Arkady's. And the two of them could have got Sirkin away—somewhere. Where?

"Ah—Captain Serrano?" That was another of the investigating militia. She turned to him. "Urgent message from your ship. Shall I put it on the local tapline?"

She hoped that meant they'd gotten Sirkin back to the ship safely. She nodded, and stepped over to the little communications booth set up for the investigators. The headset they gave her hissed a bit—no doubt from the offtake tape spool—but Petris's voice was clear enough.

"Captain? Hate to bother you, but we've got a problem here."

"Ah, yes, Mr. Petris." That should warn him. "I'm dealing with one here, too. It seems Yrilan has been killed by thugs, and the investigating officers have found no sign of Sirkin."

"Right. I'm at the Royal Security office, at the access. The officer in charge prefers your personal authorization before passing some of our crew members who . . . have had an accident. The scanners picked up bloodstains."

"How many?" Heris asked, mentally crossing her fingers.

"Mr. Vissisuan, Ms. Meharry, and Ms. Sirkin," Petris said. "With injuries." Such formality could only mean trouble. No one had called Oblo "Mr. Vissisuan" since his second tour. At least Sirkin was alive.

"Would it help if I spoke to Royal Security?"

"Maybe," Petris said cautiously. "Here's Major Defrit."

Major Defrit sounded as frosty and formal as Heris would have in his place. She explained that she was on the site of a murder, with the station militia.

"Your crew seems to have a talent for trouble," Major Defrit said.

"I hardly think that justified," Heris said, in the same tone. Actually Oblo had more than a talent for it—genius, more like—but it wasn't something to brag about. "Are any of my crew injured?"

"Ms. Sirkin seems to have some injuries, but I would judge them not serious. She is conscious and her vital signs appear within normal limits." He sounded entirely too certain; Heris trusted the worry in Petris's voice.

"I'd prefer to have Sirkin evaluated by medical personnel. You are not, I gather, a physician?"

"Well no, but—"

"Since one of my crew died from a murderous assault, and Sirkin is injured, it would be prudent to have her examined, don't you think?"

"But that would mean admitting her to this Sector—unless you want her sent to the central clinic—" His resolution wavered; she could hear it in his voice, a faint whine.

"Major, Sirkin has a valid Royal Docks pass, as have my other crew members. You have no real reason to exclude them. I can understand that you might want to escort them to medical care—"

"But—"

"I will be there as soon as possible," Heris interrupted. "And I expect to find my crew members receiving adequate medical treatment." Watching her, the militia communications tech raised his eyebrows; Heris winked, and they went up another notch. "Let me speak to my second in command."

Petris came back on the line. "Yes, Captain?"

"I believe the major understands the need for Sirkin to receive immediate medical evaluation and treatment. I'd like you to stay with her. If Mr. Vissisuan is not injured, I'd like him to meet me at the access area on my return. Ms. Meharry can return to the ship if she needs no medical care, and I'll speak to her there. Clear?"

"Clear, Captain."

Heris came out of the little booth shaking her head. "Well, my other crew member has shown up, wounded apparently, at the Royal Docks access station. I don't know if she was trying to get help or what. I know you'll need to talk to her, but I think her medical care should come first."

"I'll come with you," Cannibar said. "Want to leave now? What about the disposition of your crew member's remains after autopsy?"

"I'm not sure—I'll have to check my files aboard." She would have to ask Sirkin, most likely. Anything but token cremation would be impossibly expensive; most who died aboard went into the carbon-cycle tanks. But it was always possible that Yrilan had taken out a burial insurance policy that would pay for shipping her body to a planet for "real" burial. Heris felt guilty that she had not known even this about the girl.

At the Royal Docks Access, Oblo and the Royal Security major waited in unamiable silence. Oblo had a ripening bruise on his forehead and his hands bore the marks of a good fight. But his expression was that of a large predatory mammal fully fed and satisfied. Heris spared him only a glance, then met the major's angry gaze. Before he could say anything she introduced the Station militia captain.

"—investigating the death of Amalie Yrilan, a temporary-contract crew member."

"I suppose you'll want in to interview the others," the major said sourly, transferring his glare to the militia captain.

"As a matter of fact, yes." Heris had warmed to the captain already, and she liked his tone now. Not a trace of arrogance or obsequiousness either: he simply stated the obvious in a voice that meant to be obeyed. The major shrugged, and handed over a clip-on pass.

"Very well. This is a forty-eight-hour pass; if you need an extension, just give us a call."

"How's Sirkin?" Heris asked Oblo. He looked less smug.

"She caught part of a sonic blast, and a couple of knife slashes. I think she's got some broken ribs, but this officer thinks it's just bruising. Some heavy people landed on her, and she got some hard kicks I know of, one in the head."

"Unconsciousness?"

"Yes, for a bit, but the one that landed on her weighed enough it could have been that."

Heris thought of all she'd like to ask him, but not in front of Royal Security and Station militia officers. Why had he waited so long to come into the fight? Why had he brought

Sirkin back here rather than the nearest militia station? Why had he been on the scene in the first place?

"Could I talk to you now?" said the militia captain. It wasn't really a question.

"Sure, sir," said Oblo, rubbing his hands over his head and trying to look innocent. It didn't work. He had the face and hands of the experienced brawler, and the bruise was like a rose on a rosebush—a fitting decoration.

"I'm going to see Sirkin," Heris said. "Oblo—when you've finished here, I'll see you aboard."

Sirkin had been through the diagnostics when Heris got to the clinic. She lay in a bed, in a bright-patterned gown Heris thought had been chosen to disguise bloodstains and other marks. Her face looked lopsided—she had swollen bruises down one side, and the other was discolored with the sunburn flush of the sonic pulser that had burst small blood vessels. That eye, too, was bloodshot. If Heris hadn't seen the medical report, she'd have worried, but the eye had escaped real damage. She looked drowsy and said nothing when Heris came into the room. That would be the concussion the scans had shown.

Petris rose from a chair at the bedside. "Captain. Meharry's gone back to the ship, as you asked. Oblo?"

"He's talking to the militia captain in charge of the investigation. I still haven't heard what happened. Have you?"

"Sirkin and Yrilan were out for a night, and took a short-cut through that park; they were jumped by a gang. Oblo and Meharry were following them, but trying to be discreet. They tried to deal quietly with someone who tried to keep them from entering the park—maybe part of the gang—and that took enough time that the row had started when they caught up. Yrilan was down, probably dead or dying, and Sirkin was fighting. They both think the gang was trying to capture Sirkin at that point—someone had cuffs out."

"And they brought her out of the park because they weren't sure if more trouble would arrive, or who it was— I can understand that," Heris said. "But they should have called the ship, at least."

"No time, Oblo said. But you know him—he hates to call for help."

"True." Heris looked down at Sirkin. So far she hadn't

spoken; her expression hadn't changed. How badly was she really hurt—not physically, but emotionally? How would she react when she woke fully and realized that her lover was dead? "Brigdis," she said, touching the young woman's bandaged hand. "How are you feeling?"

"Captain?" Her voice was blurred; that could be the injuries or the drugs used to treat them. "You . . . came."

"Yes." No use to explain who had come when, not until her mind cleared. But tears rose in the younger woman's eyes.

"Amalie . . . she screamed . . ."

"I'm sorry, Brigdis," Heris said.

"Is she dead?" That sounded rational enough.

"Yes. I'm sorry. The sonic pulser got her at close range— you barely escaped."

"She—jumped in front of me," Sirkin said. "She—died for me." Her body trembled, as if she were trying to cry but was too exhausted. Probably those ribs, Heris thought. They wouldn't want to put her in the regeneration tank for the ribs until her concussion had stabilized.

"She was very brave," Heris said. It never hurt to praise the dead, and Amalie Yrilan could be brave and foolish both. Many people were.

"But . . . she had gambled." Heris wondered what that was about. Sirkin took a cautious breath. "She got in some trouble. I don't know what. There was this woman." All short sentences, carried on one difficult breath after another.

"You don't have to talk now," Heris said. "You're safe here. We'll stay with you, Petris or I."

"But I want to." Sirkin's face had a stubborn expression now, someone forcing herself past a margin of discomfort for her own reasons. "She died. She saved me. But that woman said go there." What woman? What was Sirkin talking about? Heris glanced at Petris, who shrugged.

"Brigdis, you've had a sonic charge to half your face, and some blows to the other half . . . I really think you shouldn't try to talk now. You're not clearheaded."

"But—I thought she loved me. And then I thought she didn't. And then she died. For me. So she must have—" Sirkin's expression was pleading now. Heris wished she was still small and young enough to pick up and hug—that's what she needed, medicine be damned.

"She did love you," she said firmly. "I could see that.

She loved you enough to try to qualify for deep-space work, to follow you here. Whatever happened, she did love you. And she proved it at the end." She had long suspected that Yrilan would never have chosen a career aboard ships if Sirkin hadn't been so intent on one. That face and attitude belonged somewhere else, though Heris didn't know where.

"You're sure?" Sirkin asked.

"I'm sure." Heris stroked her head. "Now you get some sleep. I know you feel sick and hurt all over, but you're alive, and you have friends to help you." Sirkin closed her eyes, and in a few minutes was snoring delicately. Heris looked at Petris. "I should go back to the ship and check on Meharry and Oblo. Can you stay with her for now, and I'll be back later?"

"Of course. If you'd just speak to the staff here, and let them know—they wanted to throw me out, earlier."

"Right. She shouldn't be alone, and I want to be notified at once if the militia or Royal Security tries to talk to her."

Shiftchange chimed as Heris headed for the *Sweet Delight*. She would be up three shifts running, probably, and she hated to admit that it got harder every year. At her former rank in the R.S.S., she'd have been up for automatic rejuvenation treatment within the next few years, but as a civilian she'd have to pay for it herself. She wondered if she could afford it. Lady Cecelia claimed not to want rejuvenation; would she disapprove of her captain taking it?

In the access tube, Issigai Guar waited for her. "Captain, Oblo's not back yet, but Meharry's here . . . how's Brigdis?"

Heris shook her head. "She's got reparable physical injuries, but Yrilan's death is going to shake her badly. I'm going back there after I debrief Meharry—any messages?"

"No, Captain, not since you've been back to this side of the dock. Station militia called here earlier, and I told 'em you'd headed for the Captains' Guild. But that was hours ago. Ginese is on the bridge, of course."

"Let me know, then. I'm going to talk to Meharry and I may put in a call to Lady Cecelia." Heris went on into the ship. The lavender plush didn't look quite as bad to her now, especially since it was all going to disappear in the next few weeks. Lady Cecelia had chosen crisp blues and greens with white for her new scheme, over the protests

of the decorator, who insisted that the very latest colors were
peach, cream, and something called sandfox. With accents
of hot coral and hunter green. Feminine, the decorator had
said, and flattering to mature complexions. Cecelia's complexion had turned red at that, and she'd muttered that she
could take her business to a place that would do what she
wanted.

Meharry was outside her office, obviously fresh from a
shower and change of clothes. She had a few visible bruises,
but no worse damage.

"Sirkin's in the clinic—the ribs are broken, and she does
have a concussion," Heris said before the other could ask.
"They're trying some new drug on the concussion—supposed
to counter diffuse damage and reduce swelling—and they'll
put her in regen for the ribs when that's done. I'm going
back later; Petris is with her now."

"Tough kid," Meharry said. "We'd been showing her some
things, but I wouldn't have expected her to use them that
well her first time out."

"Tell me about it," Heris said. The story from Meharry's
viewpoint took longer than it had when Petris gave her the
short form, and began with her pointing out to Oblo that
even if Sirkin had been learning how to fight, when she
was with Yrilan she wasn't really alert.

"I thought Oblo was installing that . . . navigational
equipment."

"Well, ma'am, he was. But those two didn't leave right
away—they spent awhile in Sirkin's cabin—and Oblo was
just about nearly finished when they did. We just didn't want
anything to happen . . . like it did."

"I didn't see you," Heris said. "And they were ahead of
me."

Meharry's green eyes twinkled. "You weren't exactly looking,
ma'am. You's looking at them, and we's looking at you . . .
and them. They saw you, didn't see us. . . . Classic, y'know?"

"So?"

"So," Meharry said, with an eloquent shrug, "they went
to this bar." Here she fished out the datawand. Heris felt her
own brows rise. "You might want to read this off, Captain.
We sent the main stuff back here already, but there's a bit
more hasn't gone in the computer yet."

"You have a *Fleet* wand?"

"It's not Fleet now." The green eyes had gone muddy, like stagnant water. "It gives us that edge in networking you were talking about." If no one caught her with it. If it wasn't traced back to Heris.

"Still accesses Fleet nets?"

Meharry cocked her head. "Don't know, really. Haven't tried that yet. Be really risky to try it, if it doesn't." A mild way of putting it. "But it sucks strings out of civilian nets, no problem. Take a look."

Heris brought the data up on her desk screen. The picture of the woman in the silk suit and jewels was clear enough for recognition.

"Enhanced by her database identification," Meharry said, leaning over Heris's shoulder. "That's what she was wearing in the bar, but the face has been cleaned up by the ID subroutines. We didn't have a picmic to overhear what they said—the noise level in there was really bad and there were sonic cops out in the concourse, who'd have detected anything good enough to filter voices."

"Therapist," said Heris thoughtfully. "And Sirkin said something about Yrilan gambling—could the girl have had a gambling problem and seen a therapist?"

"Yrilan got crosswise and got mandatory counseling instead of a hotspot in records," Meharry said. "Pulled that out of this lady's office files, once I knew where. But Oblo and I think she's working for someone else. She definitely—definitely—signalled to these guys—" She pointed to the display again. "—when she came out. Then she fell off our scanners like a rock off a cliff. Had to be counterscan, had to be illegal." Meharry sounded righteous about that.

"Meharry, *your* scans are illegal," Heris said, trying not to laugh.

"Well, sure, but that's how I know her counterscans were. Legal citizen-type scans aren't worth the space in your pockets. Anybody can privacy-shield from them. We had to have something that'd work." Meharry shrugged that off and pointed to the display.

"Her accounts, now . . . look at what she spends just on clothes. Public service therapists don't make that much."

"Investment income, it says," Heris commented, not mentioning that sucking data from the banking nets was even more illegal than the rest of it.

"Yeah, but what investment? I grant you dividend income, but I wonder about the companies. You have investments, don't you? Why don't you check this stuff out, Captain?"

Heris laughed aloud. "In what spare time? I suppose I could ask about—uh—Siritec, since it seems to be paying her the most, but without knowing her initial investment there's no way to tell . . . and no, I'm not about to stick a wire into investment accounts myself. What you've got is interesting—I wish I could figure out a way to let the militia in on it without compromising you."

"You said Sirkin mentioned Yrilan's gambling. Maybe just that?"

"I'll think about it; I don't want her catching any more trouble if we can help it. Now—about the fight itself—"

Meharry grinned. "Like I said, the kid was tough. Yrilan was down when we got around the corner, one of 'em leaning over her—probably making her that C.H. pattern—and Sirkin was fighting hard, but not hard enough. 'Course, she was outnumbered, and they were armed." From the tone, she was making excuses she didn't think would have to be made for her. "They weren't trying to kill her, though. Somebody was on top of her, trying to cuff her, when Oblo 'bout took his head off. After that—" She gave a surprisingly detailed account of the brawl, interspersed with her assessment of the enemy's ability and training. "And it was after they were all down, that we saw Yrilan's face and hands. That's when we figured it was Compassionate Hand business, and we'd better get Sirkin back to safety—"

"Eh, Captain." That was Oblo, free surprisingly early from the militia captain. Heris had thought he'd be much later.

"Well—let's hear it from you." Oblo gave Meharry an oblique glance and settled into a seat. His clothes still had the marks of the fight, though he had daubed at the bloodstains somewhere along the line. His version was even racier than Meharry's. She hadn't bothered to mention the delay at the park entrance; they hadn't wanted to kill any of their opponents at that point, but his description of the action made her wonder why the militia hadn't found more inert bodies. Heris heard him out, then sent them off to rest. She was a little surprised that no more calls had come in for her, but she told Guar to patch them to the clinic if they did come. After a look at the time cycle where Cecelia was, she decided not to wake her.

When she called later, she found that Cecelia was in a mood Heris privately considered ridiculous. She was in a raging fury about some point of family politics, and threatening to throw things. Her reaction to Heris's news was just as strong and no more helpful.

"*Just* what I needed," she snapped. "You can't even keep things straightened out up there. Why I ever thought you were more efficient than the prissy officious managers down here, I cannot now recall." Heris tried not to get angry in return. "Another dead body . . . and that nice girl Sirkin injured . . . and that overpaid lot in the clinic will probably charge me double."

"As a matter of fact, no." Heris broke in with quiet satisfaction. "Since Sirkin is the victim of a crime, and it's quite clear that she bears no responsibility for what happened, no charges apply to your employee accounts, and it will not affect your medical-tax rates in the future."

"Oh. Well." Heris could practically see the boiling temper settling down again. "Well, of course I care most about Sirkin and . . . whoever."

"Sirkin will be fine, they tell me. In fact, while it's a selfish thought at such a time, we're more likely to keep her now. Her lover, Yrilan, wasn't really qualified and I could not have justified offering her a long-term contract. Sirkin might or might not have stayed with us, if it meant separation from Yrilan."

"That's sad." Now Cecelia sounded like herself again. Heris was glad she had the experience to know that the harsh, biting voice was only an expression of mood, not basic personality. "What a price to solve a dilemma."

"True. Now, both Royal Security and the Station militia prefer that we remain docked here until Sirkin is out of the clinic and back aboard. That means we'll be late to the Spacenhance slot, but I've already contacted them and they're holding it for you. I'll be very careful arranging accommodations for the crew during the time the ship won't be habitable."

"Of course," Cecelia said. "And I'm sorry if I sounded off at first. It's just that you haven't been having to deal with the flat-footed *idiots*—" Her voice rose again. "—who messed up my perfectly clear instructions and landed me with a lot of low-grade bonds. These people who rejuvenate too often end up with brains like babies—no sense at all."

Heris shook her head, and tried not to grin. For a woman who claimed to know and care about nothing but horses and good food, Lady Cecelia had strong opinions about the minutiae of investing.

Three days later, Sirkin was finally cleared for the regen tanks, and her broken ribs responded with the alacrity of youth. "She's still not completely recovered from the concussion," the doctors warned Heris. "Don't expect rapid calculations, or long concentration—you're not going to make jump points any time soon, are you?"

"No. We're going in for redecorating—she'll have plenty of time to recover."

"Good. We'll want to see her every ten days until the scans are completely normal. Immediately, of course, if you notice any changes in behavior that might be the result of head injury. I know she's lost a close friend, and grief can produce some of the same symptoms—so be alert."

Heris walked back to the ship access with Sirkin. The sparkle she had enjoyed was gone; the younger woman looked pale and sad. Natural, of course. Heris knew from experience that nothing she said would really help. In time, she'd work through her grief, but right now she needed time and privacy to react. As they came aboard the yacht, Sirkin turned to her.

"Can you tell me what—where Amalie's—where they put . . . her?"

"In the morgue, awaiting instructions. The necropsy's finished; the sonic pulser killed her. Do you know what her wishes would have been?"

Sirkin frowned. "She didn't have burial insurance . . . I suppose it'll have to be the usual. But I wanted to see her."

Heris started to say *Better not*, then thought again. Would she have shielded a military youngster that way? Sirkin had earned a right to choose the difficult.

"Would you like me to come with you?"

"You'd do that?" Naked relief on her face. Heris nodded.

"Of course I will—and so will Petris. Oblo and Meharry, too, if you don't mind."

"I thought—I'd have to go alone," Sirkin said. Heris could see her determination to do just that if necessary, and her relief that she would have friends beside her.

"It's what shipmates are for," she said. "But you're just out of the clinic. If you'll take my advice, you'll get cleaned up, eat a good meal, and then go. By then I'll have called them to schedule a visit."

"Is it all right to wait? They won't . . . do anything?"

"Not without legal clearance."

"Then . . . I think I'd like to lie down a bit . . ." Sirkin looked even paler; Heris got an arm around her before her knees gave way, and helped her to her quarters.

"You'll be better in a few hours," she said. She hoped it would be true.

On the way to the morgue, next mainshift, Sirkin said, "I suppose I should find out about Amalie's things. Or would the militia have done that?"

"They'll have looked in her lodgings. I haven't asked about that, but we can find out. Anything in particular?"

"Not really." It was the tone that meant yes, of course.

"Did she have a will?"

"Not . . . yet. We hadn't thought . . . you know . . . that she could die. Yet." That complicated things, but not too badly. If Sirkin wanted a keepsake, something not too valuable, Heris was sure she could get it.

At the morgue, Heris called in to the militia headquarters to ask about Yrilan's belongings. Cannibar wasn't in; she spoke to his assistant.

"Her stuff's in storage already, Captain Serrano, but if your crew has a legal claim—"

"No—she said Yrilan had made no will. I suspect they'd exchanged gifts, keepsakes—"

A long bored sigh in her ear. "Younglings. I wish she'd thought of this before we sealed the storage cube."

"She had a concussion," Heris said. "She was under medical treatment, remember?"

"Oh. Right. Well . . . she has to come by here for an interview anyway, doesn't she? I suppose, if you're willing to sit in, so I don't have to waste someone else's time—

and it can't be anything of substantive value. Does your—uh—Sirkin have the next-of-kin names and addresses?"

"I'll find out," Heris said. "Right now we're at the morgue."

"Young idiot," said the voice, but with a tinge of humanity this time. "When can we expect you?"

"An hour or so, I expect, from here to there. She's not supposed to ride drop-tubes for a few more days. I'll call back if it's longer."

"If she comes apart," said the voice, this time full of resignation.

"Have you caught the ones who got away?" asked Heris. Time to put the voice on the defensive.

"Not yet. I'd figured from the blood that at least one would show up in some medical facility, but no such luck. Maybe he died and they put the body in the tanks." Heris opened her mouth, but the voice went on. "And before you ask, no, we can't do the kind of analysis you could on a Fleet ship—this Station's too big for that. We've always got some unauthorized recycs garbaging our figures."

"Too bad," Heris said. She glanced over and saw that Sirkin was about to go through a door into the viewing area. "Talk to you later," she said, and punched off.

Oblo and Meharry stood on either side of Sirkin as she waited in the viewing area. It was cold and a sharp odor made Heris's nose itch. A waist-high bar separated them from the polished floor on which the wheeled trays slid out from a wall of doors. Sirkin punched in the numbers she'd been given at the front desk. A door snicked open, and a draped form emerged so smoothly it seemed magical. The tray unfolded wheeled legs as it cleared the door, and rolled along tracks sunk in the floor until it stopped in front of their group. Heris glanced past to see an arrangement of visual baffles and soundproofing that would allow several—she could not tell how many—viewings at once. With a thin buzz, the bar lifted to let them through.

Rituals for the dead varied; Heris had no idea what Sirkin felt necessary for Yrilan. Slowly, the young woman folded back the drape, and stared at the face. Morgues were nothing like the funeral hostels of those religions that thought it important to make the dead look "lifelike." No one had worked on Yrilan's face with paint or powder, with clay or gum or needle to reshape and recolor it. Her dead body looked just that: dead. Heris guessed that under the rest of the sheet the marks of the fight and the autopsy both would be even more shocking. Sirkin had given one sharp gasp, as the reality of it hit her. Heris touched her shoulder, lightly.

"It's so . . . ugly," Sirkin said. Heris saw Oblo's eyelids flicker. This was far from ugly, as they had both seen ugly death . . . but it was Sirkin's first, maybe. "Her hair's all dirty and bloody—" She touched it, her hands shaking.

"She had beautiful hair," Meharry said. Heris glanced at her. She hadn't expected Meharry to notice, or to comment now. But Meharry was watching Sirkin. "Lovely hair it was, and if you cut yourself a lock—over on this side, it's just as clean and lovely as ever . . ."

Sirkin's hand went out again, then she turned and grabbed for a hand, anyone's hand. Heris took it, and put an arm around her shoulders. "I'm sorry," she said, and meant it. "You've seen enough now, haven't you? Do you have a picture, the way she was?"

"I—yes—but that's not the point." Sirkin, trembling, was still trying to stay in control. "She died for me; the least I can do is look."

Heris was surprised in spite of herself. She'd been impressed with Sirkin before, but death spooked a lot of people. Sirkin pushed herself away from Heris, but Oblo intercepted her.

"There's a right way," he said. "You loved her; we all respect her body. You take that corner; let the captain take this."

What lay beneath the drape met Heris's expectations. None of Yrilan's beauty remained, nor any clue to her personality. In slow procession across the inside of Heris's eyelids passed the dead she had seen in all her years, one blank face after another. She, too, always looked—and she had never yet become inured to it. Sirkin, only a fine tremor betraying her, stared blankly at the evidence of a violent death, and then, with Heris's help, stretched the drape across the body once more. A last stroke of the hand on that fire-gold hair, and she turned away, mouth set.

Meharry, Heris noted, had clipped a single curl and folded it into a tissue: Sirkin might want it later. Or might not— she trusted Meharry to know whether to offer it or not.

CHAPTER SIX

Shifting the *Sweet Delight* from the Royal Docks to the decorators took only a few hours, but Heris felt she'd put in a full shift's work by the time they had linked with their new docking site. First there'd been the formalities of leaving the Royal Sector, with a double inventory of all badges issued, and multiple inspections of the access area. That had made them half an hour late in departure. Then the captain of the tug designated to move the yacht, angry because of the delay, took out his frustrations with several abrupt attitude changes that strained *Sweet Delight*'s gravity compensators. Heris had to be almost rude to get him to stop. Finally, even the docking at Spacenhance presented problems. Although Heris had given them the yacht's specifications as soon as the contract was signed, the slot had been left "wide" for the much larger vessel just completed. Heris had to hold the yacht poised, just nuzzling the dock, while the expansion panels eased out to complete the docking seal.

"They probably thought you'd tear up their space if they resized it ahead of time," Petris pointed out. Heris wanted to grumble at him but there was no time. Somewhere on the dock, the moving and storage crews would be racking up time charges. Her crew would supervise the packing and removal of all the yacht's furnishings, and the sealing of essential systems from whatever chemicals the decorators used.

At least the lavender plush was about to disappear. Heris

424

wondered if they'd roll it up and sell it to someone else. Perhaps that's why they'd tried to argue Cecelia into yet another color scheme she didn't like. It would save energy and resources to reuse all that material. She led the crew to the access tube and looked around for the decorator's representative.

The decorator's dockside looked nothing like the luxurious offices in which Cecelia had made her choices of color and texture. A vast noisy space, in which rows of shipping containers looked like children's blocks on the floor of a large room, gaped around them. Machinery clanked and grumbled; something smelled oily and slightly stale. A crew in blue-striped uniforms, presumably from the moving and storage company, lounged near the shipping containers.

"Ah . . . Captain Serrano." That was a tall, gangling man in a formal gray suit. "Are we ready to get started?"

"Quite," said Heris. He had an ID tag dangling from his lapel, with the firm's logo in purple on peach. Typical, she thought. He turned and waved to the moving and storage crew.

"You do understand that everything must be removed or sealed? Not that there's any question of contamination . . ." He laughed, three very artificial ha-ha-has, and Heris wondered what ailed him. "But we want no questions. I am Ser Schwerd, by the way, the director on this project. I suppose the owner is still determined on that . . . unfortunate color scheme?"

"If you mean green and white, yes."

"Pity. We can do so much more when given a free hand. Really, if clients would only realize that we know much more about decorating than they do. However, the client's satisfaction is more important than any other consideration, though if we could strike a blow for artistic integrity—"

"Lady Cecelia," Heris said, "is quite sure what she wants."

He sighed. "They always are, Captain Serrano. All these old ladies are sure they know what they want, and really they have no idea. But let's not waste our time lamenting what can't be changed. Always think positively, that's my motto. If the lady is unsatisfied with this redecoration, perhaps next time she'll trust the judgment of someone with real expertise."

Heris managed not to laugh at him. Anyone who knew

Lady Cecelia knew that she had no doubts about her own desires; she would not likely change her mind because someone else claimed to have better taste. Ser Schwerd introduced the movers' supervisor, a thickset bald man with twinkling brown eyes.

"Gunson," he said. "Quite reliable." Gunson's expression said he could prove that without Schwerd's commentary. Heris liked him at once, and they exchanged handshakes.

A steady stream of packers and movers moved through the ship. Cecelia's belongings disappeared into padded containers, which then fit into the larger storage/shipping containers. With all the crew to help, the inventory checkoffs went more quickly than usual—according to Gunson. Cecelia's own quarters, the guest quarters, the public areas of the ship, crew quarters. Furniture, the contents of built-in storage, clothing, decorations—everything.

"What about this?" Gunson asked, opening the galley door.

"Nothing—seal it off," Heris said. Schwerd grimaced.

"It needs something—"

"No . . . Lady Cecelia has a very exacting cook. He's got it just the way he wants it, and if you'll look at the contract, it specifies absolutely no change in the galley or pantries."

"But foodstuff should be removed—"

"Why?" Heris asked, surprised. "These are staples; they won't deteriorate in the few weeks you'll be working. If the galley's sealed, there's no danger of contamination from any paint fumes or whatever. Besides, we were told initially that there was no need to remove anything from compartments that could be sealed and were not to be worked on."

He looked unhappy, but nodded. The decorators had provided coded seals for compartments not part of the contract. Heris had her crew seal the hatches under his supervision; she wasn't sure she trusted the decorators not to try something fancy where it wasn't wanted. The bridge, for example, and the ships' systems compartments. The garden sections of hydroponics were all empty now, but the gas-exchange tanks remained operational, the bacterial cultures on maintenance nutrients. She didn't want to take the time to recharge them all later.

At last everything was off the ship, and all the crew had their personal gear loaded on carryalls. Heris sent them ahead to the lodgings she'd arranged. She and Ser Schwerd had to do the final inspection, checking both the seals to areas not being worked on and the areas that were supposed to be clear.

"Someone always leaves something," Schwerd said. "Always. Sometimes it's valuable—once, I recall, a distinguished lady's diamond-and-ruby brooch, lying there in the middle of the owner's stateroom. Why someone hadn't stepped on it and broken it, I never knew. More often it's some little thing the movers can't believe is important, but it has sentimental value. A child's soft toy, an unimportant trophy." He strode through the passages with an expression of distaste, glancing quickly into each compartment.

"Ah . . ." This was in Cecelia's quarters, the study which looked so different with its antique books and artwork removed. Sure enough, a squashed and dusty arrangement of faded ribbons, which Heris realized, after Schwerd smoothed it with his hands, had once been a rosette of some sort. "One of Lady Cecelia's earlier triumphs, I would say." He held it out; Heris could just make out " . . . hunter pony . . ." in flaking black letters on the purplish ribbon. "It would have been a first place blue," Schwerd said. "Those letters were originally gold or silver ink. And I'm sure she'd notice if it were gone." He handed it to Heris, ceremoniously, and she brushed off the rest of the dust, folded it, and tucked it into her jacket. Perhaps Cecelia would notice, perhaps not, but she would keep it safe.

Back at the hostel, Heris checked on her crew. Transient crew housing had few amenities; the ship had been far more comfortable. But they had settled in, having arranged adjoining cubicles. She had decided to stay here, with them, rather than at the Captains' Guild. She worried about the next few weeks—how to keep them busy and out of trouble until they could go back aboard. With the Compassionate Hand looking for revenge—and despite the militia's assurances, she knew they would be looking for revenge—all were in danger until something else distracted that organization. Perhaps she could schedule some training in civilian procedures.

Petris signalled her with raised eyebrows. Did she want to—? Of course, though she'd like to have a long uninterrupted

sleep first. With the ship now the responsibility of the decorating firm, she could reasonably sleep late into the next shift.
Surely her crew could cope by themselves for a day. She
posted a crew meeting far enough in the future that she
knew she couldn't sleep that long, no matter what, and
nodded to Petris.

"Dinner first?" he asked. Heris yawned and shook her
head.

"If you're hungry, go ahead—I'm more tired than
anything."

"Umm. Perhaps my suggestion was premature?"

"No. I've missed you. It's amazing how few times we've
managed to be together. Something always happens. I'm
beginning to feel like the heroine in a farce."

"Don't say that." He made a mock-angry face at her.
"You'll bring the bad luck down on us."

"Not this time," she said. "The ship's safe, and Sirkin's
safe with Meharry in the same section. If the rest of them
go wandering, they'll be a match for anything. Besides,
they're too tired right now, just like I am. Maybe I'll nap
a bit, and then—we'll finally have time to enjoy ourselves."

In the quiet dark of her quarters, she lay against his warm
length and felt her muscles unkinking, strand by strand. This
was, indeed, better than dinner . . . she dozed off, aware
of his hand tracing patterns on her back but unable to stay
awake to appreciate them fully. They had time . . . she needed
just a little sleep . . .

She was deep in a dream about sunlit fields and people
dancing in circles when the insistent voice in the intercom
woke her. "Captain Serrano. Captain Serrano. Captain
Serrano . . ."

"Here," she said, blinking into the darkness. A sour taste
came into her mouth.

"There's an urgent message from downside. It's on a
tightlink; you'll have to come to a secure line."

"At once." Petris roused then; she found him looking at
her when she turned on a single dim light to dress by. His
expression was both rueful and grumpy.

"What happened?"

"I don't know." She didn't, but her heart was racing. It
had to be something about Cecelia; the bad feeling she'd
had loomed as close as a storm. "It's a tightlink call from

downside. Not Cecelia calling, I don't think—they'd have told me—but they said it was urgent."

"I told you not to bring bad luck down on us," he said, but his grin took the sting out of it. "I'll get up; you go on."

"I'll be back soon," she said, and kissed him. Now she was awake, she wanted to leap back into bed with him. Why couldn't she have waked from that dream to the sound of his voice, the feel of his hands, with nothing to do but enjoy herself? With a sigh, she pushed herself away, and went out.

It wasn't really that late, she realized once she was out in the public meeting areas. She found a tightlink booth, and entered it. The ID procedure was almost as complete as for Fleet links, and she had several seconds to wait before the screen cleared from the warning message. She put the headset on.

"Captain Serrano?" It was Ronnie, and he sounded as if he'd been crying.

"What's wrong?" she asked. "Is your aunt—?"

"She's—she may die, they said." His voice broke, then steadied. "She—she just fell down. And she was breathing oddly, and the doctors think she's had a massive stroke."

Heris found it hard to think. She had anticipated some trouble, but not this. "Where is she? Where are you?"

"She's at St. Cyril's, and I'm at home—at my parents' house. That's where it happened. Mother's at the hospital; she said to stay here and out of the way." He paused, cleared his throat, and continued. "She didn't tell me to tell you, but I thought you should know."

"Thank you. You're right that I needed to know." Heris tried to think who else would need to know. The redecorators? Probably, although they already had the guarantee on the job. The crew, certainly. She wondered whether Cecelia had told Ronnie about the attack on Yrilan and Sirkin . . . was there any possibility that this was a covert action by the Compassionate Hand? "Did you see it?" she asked.

"No. I was there, but in the next room, talking to my father. We didn't hear her fall, but we heard Mother scream. We called emergency medical help, of course . . ."

"Was anyone else there? Any visitors?"

"Well, yes. It was a reception for the Young Artists' League—Mother's a sponsor—and she had a time convincing Aunt Cecelia to come. Why?"

How much to tell him, even on a tightline. She had to risk it. "Ronnie—did your aunt mention the attack on Sirkin?"

"Something happened to Sirkin? What?"

"She was attacked, with her lover, by the Compassionate Hand—a criminal organization—"

"I know about them," Ronnie said, affronted.

"Fine. Her lover was killed, and Sirkin's alive because Oblo and Meharry came into the fight. But think—is there any chance, any chance at all that your aunt's collapse could have been an attack? I don't know how—you were there—but could it have been?"

"You mean—they'd get after her? Like . . . er . . . poison?"

"They might. Ronnie, listen: you must not, absolutely must not, talk about this to anyone. Anyone. We don't know if it happened, but if it did happen the worst thing you could do is talk about it. Something should give you a clue later on . . . something will happen, or be said . . . but you're the only one available to interpret it. You have to stay alive, well, and free. Is that clear?"

"It's really serious." It was not a question. "You really think—yes. All right. I will keep it quiet, but how do I talk to—wait a minute, someone's here—" The open line hummed gently, rhythmically, with the scrambling effect. She could hear nothing from the far end—she wasn't supposed to. Finally Ronnie came back on, slightly breathless. "Sorry— my father's back. Aunt Cecelia's in a coma; they don't know if she'll come out of it. He thinks not. I—I'll get back to you when I can."

Heris waited for the triple click of the line closing, then the ending sequence on her console. Alongside the shock and fear she felt was a trickle of amusement—once again, something had interrupted her night with Petris. Once again it had been something she couldn't anticipate. She shook her head, and emerged from the booth to find Petris watching her.

"Lady Cecelia?" he asked.

"Yes," she said. "Let's go back—you need to hear about it."

In the little room, both of them glanced at the rumpled bed and away from it again. Heris settled in the chair; Petris pulled the covers back across the bed and sat on its edge.

"She's alive," Heris said. "But I don't know for how long. According to Ronnie, she collapsed suddenly and the doctors are saying it's a stroke."

"She's old," Petris said, answering her doubt, not her words. "And she hasn't had rejuv, has she?"

"No. She told me once she disapproved of it; she had healthy genes, she said, and when her time was up it was only fair to give someone else a chance."

"Silly attitude." Petris scowled. "In a universe this big, there's room for everyone. Besides, she was rich."

"She might have reconsidered—I think she made that decision when she was unhappy, and stuck to it out of stubbornness. I had been seeing signs of change in her."

"But still—in her eighties, even now, without rejuv. It could be a natural stroke." He cocked his head at her. "But you don't think so, do you?"

"It would be a damned convenient stroke, Petris. Coming so soon after the attack on Sirkin and Yrilan, combined with her . . . er . . . revelations to the Royals about Mr. Smith—" Heris didn't want to be any more specific in quarters that might easily be under surveillance.

"And you said she was in a foul temper about something just a few days ago—some family business. Perhaps there's someone else with a reason to put her out of action. Although temper—isn't that a cause of strokes?"

Heris laughed, and surprised herself. "If it were, no Serrano would have survived to take rejuv. I'm one of the mild ones."

"But it *could* have been a stroke, no enemy action."

"Could have been. There's no way we can tell from here. I just worry—"

"Wouldn't the doctors figure out if it's not a real stroke?"

"I don't know. And if they do think someone did something, that doesn't mean they can fix it. At least they can't blame *us*—we're up here, and she's been down there for days."

"Well. Nothing we can do right now, is there?"

"No, but I—"

"You're not in the mood, I understand that, but do you think you could sleep?"

By this time, Heris wasn't sleepy anymore; she and Petris finally went out for an early breakfast, and came back to tell the rest of the crew. Heris wasn't sure what to do about them. She really wanted to take a shuttle downside and see for herself how Cecelia was. But that would leave the crew with nothing to do but fret. As for the future, if Cecelia died, or stayed in a coma, she wouldn't need a yacht and crew . . . at some point Heris would have to look for another job, and hope a few of her crew could find work on the same ship. Not likely, but . . . she scolded herself for thinking of her own convenience, her own desires, when a friend lay comatose. Conflicting loyalties tugged at her.

The crew took the news quietly at first. Sirkin still looked shocky from her own loss and her injuries; she sat pale and silent, not meeting anyone's eyes. The others glanced back and forth and deferred their questions. Heris, knowing them so well, knew they had questions, and would come to her individually.

By the time she thought of sleep again, she and Petris both had little interest in pleasure. He pleaded a headache— "Nontraditional as it is, my love, it's boring a hole in my skull and frying my brain"—and went to his own quarters; she slept badly, waking often to think she'd heard the intercom calling.

The next call finally came from the family legal firm two days later. They had no interest in answering her questions, and had plenty of their own. What was the status of Lady Cecelia's yacht? Heris explained about the redecorating. Couldn't it be halted? She had anticipated this question, and had already contacted the redecorators. No—the ship's existing finishes were already being stripped. They could delay applying the new carpeting and wallcoverings, but they couldn't replace those already removed—not without a surcharge. Heris pointed out that Cecelia had loathed the color scheme, and it would make no sense to replace the same one.

"But her *sister* selected it," said the lawyer, in an outraged tone.

Heris wondered whether to mention who was paying for the new one, and decided better not.

"Lady Cecelia preferred something else," she said. "She was quite firm about it."

"I don't doubt," he said sourly. "The point is, if she is, as seems likely, permanently incapacitated, she will have no need for the yacht and a new color scheme hardly seems worth the price. If it's for sale—"

"Perhaps simply having the decorators delay installing the new—that way, any potential buyer could choose his or her own scheme—"

"Perhaps. Now, about the crew payroll—"

"Lady Cecelia had given me permission to authorize payment from the yacht expenses account. I can transmit all the recent transactions, if you'd like."

"Yes, thank you." He seemed a bit surprised. Heris wondered if he'd expected her to try something dishonest.

"And I would like some idea of when a determination will be made about the yacht, since the crew will need the usual warning before being asked to find new positions." That should convince him she wasn't trying to get them on the family payroll forever.

"Oh. Quite. Well, er . . . no hurry, I should think. In case she recovers, though that seems unlikely . . . there's always the chance . . . and anyway, some legal action would have to be taken to transfer control of the yacht to her heirs. Certainly that won't happen for . . . oh . . . sixty days or more."

Heris chose her words carefully. "You mean, I am authorized to maintain and pay an idle crew for sixty days?"

"Well . . . er . . . yes . . . I suppose so . . ." Unspoken conflicts between parsimony and habit cluttered his words.

"I would prefer to have that in writing," Heris said briskly, with no sympathy for his problems. "It's possible that either Lady Cecelia's bankers or Station personnel could have questions."

"Oh, certainly. I'll see that you get that, and I'll speak to her bankers." Faced with an assignment, his voice picked up energy. This was simply business, a routine he was used to. "Of course, that's limited to . . . er . . . the usual schedule of payments."

"Of course. I'm sure Lady Cecelia's records already contain a pay scale and the account activity, but I'll send those along."

Spacenhance were not pleased to have the redecorating halted midway, but maintained a polite, if frosty, demeanor about it. They could, they admitted, simply leave the ship "bare" for a week or so. Even longer, if no other business came in, though if they needed the dock space the yacht would have to be moved to another site. Heris pointed out that she would have to have legal authorization to move it, since Lady Cecelia's affairs were now in the hands of her legal staff, and might soon be a matter of court decision. They subsided so quickly that Heris was sure another player had made the same point more forcibly. The king? Certainly the Crown could command a berth there as long as it wanted.

After another three days of waiting, she tried to contact Cecelia's sister or brother-in-law. A frosty servant informed her that neither was home, that no family member was home, and that inquiries from employees should be made to the family legal representative. She couldn't tell, from the tone, if that was aimed at her, specifically, or at any low-level employee. She realized she didn't even know what other employees Cecelia might have onplanet, besides her maid Myrtis.

The news media had had nothing to say about it, of course, though it showed up on the hospital admissions list. Heris thought of having Oblo insinuate himself into the hospital datanet, but that could have serious repercussions. The hospital census let her know that Cecelia was alive still.

Ronnie called her a day after she'd tried to reach the family.

"She's alive, still in a coma," he said. "They're talking about moving her to a different facility, which prepares people for long-term care."

"Have you seen her yourself?" Heris asked.

"Only through glass. She's hooked up to so many tubes . . . they say that's temporary, until they've got implanted monitors in her. So far she's breathing on her own—"

"No response?"

"None I can see. Of course, she could be sedated. There's no way for me to tell, but I know the family's very concerned. They've had outside consultants already." He sounded as if he wanted to burst into tears.

"What happens now?" Heris asked. "Who decides what to do?"

"My mother's her nearest relative on this planet. Aunt Cecelia had filed all the . . . er . . . directives old people are supposed to file, and my mother agrees with them, so she's the one to sign the papers."

"When will they move her? Do you know?"

"Not exactly. She's out of the first unit, and into something they call the Stabilization Unit. As I understand it, they'll implant the first sensors and something so they can plug feeding tubes and things in. Then they'll send her to this other place. If she comes out of the coma, fine—they can just take the implants out. If she doesn't, there's some other surgery—I don't know it all yet—and they'll send her somewhere for long-term care."

"For the rest of her life," Heris said, trying to take it in.

"That's what they said." Ronnie sounded uncertain. "They said she might live out her normal life span, even." Heris tried to think what that would be for a woman Cecelia's age. "Oh—" Ronnie broke into her thoughts. "Do you know if she was taking any kind of medicine?"

"Your aunt? Not that I know of. She told me she didn't take anything unless she had an injury."

"That's what I told them when they asked, but I thought— if you knew—maybe it would help."

"I can't even look in her quarters," Heris reminded him. "Everything's in storage for refitting. Have you asked Myrtis?"

"Yes, but she didn't know of any. There's another thing—"

"Yes?"

"I'm not sure why, but my parents are really upset with you. They seem to think you've been a bad influence on Aunt Cecelia. I told them about how you shot that admiral, and all, but they have something against you."

Heris frowned. "I wonder what. Did your aunt talk about me?"

"Yes—she thought you were great, but I would've thought it just bored them—excuse me, but you know what I mean."

"Perhaps she said too much about me; if it bored them, they could decide not to like the boring topic." She said it lightly, but it worried her. Were Cecelia's relatives really that silly?

Several days later, Ronnie called again. "I found out what was upsetting them," he said. "And you need to know."

"What?"

"Aunt Cecelia left you the yacht in her will."

"She *what*? She couldn't have."

"I thought you didn't know," he said, sounding smug. "They think you did. It was one of the first things she did when she got here, apparently. Went to her attorney and had her will changed."

"But she shouldn't have—there's no reason—"

"Well, her attorney argued about it, but she insisted; you know her. And when the doctors said the stroke might have been caused by a drug of some kind, the attorney thought of you, because you would benefit."

"But she's not dead." That popped out; the rest of her mind snagged on "might have been caused by a drug" and hung there, unable to think further.

"She could have died. Besides, you know the law—if she's not competent in law for long enough—I forget how long it is—they open her will and distribute her assets under court guardianship."

"You mean someone can inherit before she's dead?" Heris found she could deal with the lesser curiosity while the greater dread sank deeper into her mind. She had never heard of such a possibility.

"Yes, but with some controls, so if she's suddenly competent again she can regain control." From Ronnie's tone, this was something most people knew about. Most people as rich as his family, at least.

"But—I'm not the sole beneficiary, am I?"

"No, but you're the only one outside family or long-term business associates. She left her forty-seven percent interest in her breeding and training stables to the woman who's owned the other fifty-three percent for the past twenty years, for instance. But that's been expected. The yacht wasn't. And for some reason Mother's really annoyed about it. I think she's still upset with Aunt Cecelia for not liking the decorator she chose. Besides, we don't have a yacht, and Mother's always wanted one."

"You don't?" Keep him talking. Maybe then she could process that dire possibility, figure out what to do.

"No . . . my father always said it made more sense to travel on commercial liners, and if you really needed off-schedule travel you could always charter. We've done that. Of course we have shuttles." To Heris, private deep-space ships made more sense than shuttles, and she said so. Ronnie explained. "If you have your own shuttle, you're never stuck onplanet. And no one knows for sure if you're traveling yourself, which they would in a public shuttle. Aunt Cecelia didn't agree; she'd take the public shuttles as often as not, even if my father offered her the use of ours. Now Bunny's family keeps shuttles on several worlds *and* a yacht. That's the most convenient, but my father says it's far too expensive." Heris gathered her scattered wits and came up with one idea.

"Ronnie, is his daughter—Brun—back here now? Or could you find out?"

"Brun? Oh, Bubbles's new name. Yes, she's here . . . why?"

"Does her father know about Lady Cecelia?"

"Yes, and Bubbles—Brun—says he's upset. Of course he would be; they've been friends all their lives."

"Ask her to call me, will you? I'd like to see her, if possible."

"Of course, but why?"

Heris herself wasn't sure, but something glimmered at the back of her mind, something that might help Cecelia. "We had a long talk before we left Sirialis. I'd just like to chat with her."

"Oh." She could tell from his expression that he thought this was a silly side issue, that she should stick to the problem of Cecelia's coma and the irate family. "Well . . . I'll tell her. Do you want her to come up there?"

"If possible."

Heris wanted to suggest that Brun take some precautions, but she was afraid Ronnie would waste time asking why. And after all, the girl wanted to be an adventurer—give her a chance to show any native talent.

Brun called on an open line, direct to the desk at Heris's hostel. She sounded just like the petulant girl Heris had first met. "Captain Serrano!" Her upper-class accent speared through the conversation in the lounge. Heris sensed others listening to the overspill from the speaker. So much for talent. Brun went on. "Have you seen my blue jewel case?"

"I beg your pardon." It was all Heris could think of, a reflex that meant nothing but bought a few seconds.

"This is Bubbles, Bunny's daughter," the voice went on. "When we were on Lady Cecelia's yacht, I had my blue jewel case and now I can't find it. It's not at Sirialis, and it's not here—it must be on the yacht. Would you please look in the stateroom I was using, and send it to me?"

For a moment Heris wondered if Brun had gone mad. Or if she'd given up the change of name and gone back to being a fluffhead. How could she be worrying about a jewel case with Cecelia in the hospital, in a coma? She could hear the annoyance in her own voice when she answered. "I'm sorry—Lady Cecelia's yacht is empty—everything was removed to storage because the yacht was to be redecorated, but now—"

"But I *need* it!" Brun's voice whined. "I *always* wear that necklace at the family reunion, and it's next week, and if I don't wear it, Mother will want to know why, and—"

"I'm sorry," Heris said. A glimmer of understanding broke through her irritation . . . if Brun was really that devious, she might indeed have talent. "You'd have to get into the storage facility, and I don't know . . ." She let her voice trail away.

"I'll come up there," Brun said, suddenly decisive. "They'll have to let me in—you can introduce me; it's not like I'm a criminal or anything. I just want my own blue jewel case, and I know just where I must have left it, in the second drawer from the bottom in that bedside chest . . ."

"But I'm not sure," Heris said, shaking her head for the benefit of the listeners in the hostel lounge. "I don't think they'll let anyone but Lady Cecelia's agent—"

"But you *are* her agent," Brun said. "You can do it—I know you can. I'll be up there in—let's see—late tonight. I'll call." She broke the connection. Heris looked around and sighed dramatically.

"The rich are different from you and me," said the clerk, with sympathy. Heris shrugged.

"They think they are. Can you believe? She thinks she left something aboard Lady Cecelia's yacht months ago, and expected me to retrieve it. Of course everything's in sealed storage. Of course they aren't going to let her into it."

"Who is she?" the man asked.

"Lord Thornbuckle's youngest daughter. They call her Bubbles."

"Ah—I've heard of her. They *will* let her in, bet you they do. Likely her father owns the company that owns the company that owns them. Might as well cooperate with that kind."

* * *

In person, Brun had indeed reverted to the fluffhead Bubbles. Her blonde hair, brushed into a wild aureole, had been tinted pink at the ends. She wore an outfit of pink and lime green which Heris assumed was an extreme of fashion; bright clattering bracelets covered both arms to the elbow.

"Captain Serrano!" Her greeting almost went too far; Heris recognized the tension around the eyes that didn't fit the wide smile. "I'm simply devastated . . . I have to have that necklace."

"Nice to see you again, miss." Heris couldn't bring herself to call the girl Bubbles, but "Brun" would break the fluffhead cover. "I've checked with the storage company; they will meet with you Mainshift tomorrow. Perhaps you could give me a few more details? They thought the chests in that stateroom had all been empty."

"Oh, of course. Let's go eat somewhere—I'm starved. I'm sure the food's better at my hotel." And Brun turned away, clearly someone who expected flunkies to do as they were told. Heris saw the amused glances of the others in the lounge, and gave them a wry grin as she followed Brun out into the concourse.

CHAPTER SEVEN

Cecelia's first sensory impression was smell: not a pleasant scent, but a sharp, penetrating stink she associated with fear and pain. After a timeless rummage through the back shelves of memory, her mind decided it was medicinal, and that probably meant she was in a doctor's office. Gradually, over time she could not guess, she became aware of pressure. She lay on her back; she could feel the contact between a firm surface and her shoulders and her buttocks. She was less sure of her arms and legs . . . and in trying to feel their position realized in one stab of panic that she could not move.

She did feel the leap her heart gave then, and she heard, as if from a great distance, the voices that chattered above her. Her mind rattled around the vast dark space it sensed, and reminded her of other unpleasant wakenings. The eighteenth fence at Wherrin, that bad drop that she'd misjudged in the mud. The time a new prospect had gone completely berserk under a roofed jump, and nearly killed her. She wondered what it had been this time . . . she couldn't quite remember. An event? Training? Foxhunting? Oddly, she couldn't even remember the horse—even any horse she'd worked recently.

The voices above gave her no clue. No one asked her name or what had happened; no one spoke to her at all. A bad sign, that: she knew it from times she'd sat waiting outside for a hurt friend. A few of the technical terms sounded familiar, BP and cardiac function and perfusion. If she didn't know what they meant, she knew they meant something. But others . . . her mind tried to grasp the unfamiliar syllables, but they slipped away. Demyel-something and something about selective pathways and neuromuscular dis-something. The drug names she didn't expect to know, but she knew the voices discussed things to be put in this line or that. A harder pressure against her arm—at least she knew now that her arm was up there, not down here—might be an injection.

It didn't hurt. Nothing hurt, and that scared her. If you didn't hurt, something really big was wrong. The longer it didn't hurt, the worse it was. If it was really bad—her mind shied away from the idea of spinal cord injury, brain injury— you would never hurt again, but that was worst. Sometimes even regeneration tanks wouldn't work on central nervous system injuries.

If she could move something . . . she struggled, first to decide what to move, and then to move. An eyelid. She felt no movement, and the darkness did not lift.

"A bit of excess activity there," someone said. Had she managed a movement she did not feel? She tried again. "Another tenth cc of motor inhibition," she heard. "And increase the primary decoupler one cc an hour." Inhibition? Decoupler? Just as the additional drugs pushed her beneath the surface of thought again, her mind made all the connections and nearly exploded in panic. No accident at all . . . someone had done this to her. On purpose. And she had no way to summon help. *Damn,* she thought. *I was stupid. Heris was right. Hope she figures it out . . .*

She woke again, to the same medical-ward smells, the same darkness, the same inability to move or speak.

"Hopeless, I'm afraid," she heard. She didn't recognize the voice. "There's been no change at all, nothing in the brain scans . . . look, here's the first. Massive intracranial bleed, typical cerebral accident. Probably all those years of riding, with repeated small concussions, caused significant weakening in the vascular attachments here and here—"

Someone else was here, not a medical person. Someone who wanted to know if she was going to get well. Someone who cared. If she could only make a sound, a small movement, anything.

"You can see the monitors yourself," the voice said, nearer

now. "If we use a strong aversive stimulus—" Acrid fumes stung her nose; her brain screamed danger/poison/run. "—you see a very slight reaction in the brainstem, there. The fourth line. But she doesn't move. I can open an eye—" She felt the pressure on her eyelid, felt the movement across the eye itself, but saw nothing. "No change in pupil size, no response here. Cortical blindness. There's no evidence of auditory response, no indication of higher cortical functions."

"Couldn't you have operated on the bleed?" The voice was male, used to authority, but Cecelia didn't recognize it. Certainly it wasn't her brother-in-law. "With all your facilities—"

"Too diffuse, I'm sorry. We think branches of both cerebral arteries failed at once. As if she'd been repeatedly bludgeoned, but of course that wasn't the cause. I still think the years of riding had something to do with it, but I can't prove it. I've sent for her scans after the previous accidents."

"Could it have been . . . a result of poisoning?" *YES!* Cecelia thought. *Good man. Smart man. Of course it was poisoning.*

"I doubt it," the other voice said. "There are neurotoxins, of course, that mimic natural strokes. But the evidence from her scans is clear: this is bleeding." She heard a finger tap on something—a display, perhaps.

"I didn't mean that it wasn't bleeding," the skeptical voice said. "I wondered if someone had induced the bleeding with a poison, perhaps a blood thinner or something of that sort."

"Ah." The professional voice sounded more relaxed now. Of course it would. "According to her records, she wasn't taking any medication of that sort . . . and I don't know if they analyzed her blood for that in the hospital that first night. They should have, of course; I just presumed that if it were a drug it would be in the records when she was transferred here."

So she had been somewhere else and was now who knew where? She wondered where she'd been when she first woke up. Was that the original hospital? Had it been the big downtown one, or the upper-class clinic near her sister's house?

"The thing is," the skeptical voice said, "the family are concerned that she might have been under . . . er . . . undue influence, as it were, of someone. Until the formal proceedings, we cannot be sure, but the date of her last testamentary revision suggests that something happened recently. If there should be an unforeseen bequest, and if that individual had exerted undue influence, then there would have been . . . er . . ."

"Motivation to cause her harm. I see, precisely."

Damn. The fool. The utter, incompetent fool. Now whoever had done this would have a chance to blame it on the one person it couldn't be, and this stupid lawyer—she was sure it was a lawyer—had given them all they needed.

"But that's another problem, and what we really need from you, doctor, is your assessment of prognosis. Is Lady Cecelia going to recover competency, or not? And if so, when? We have petitions of incompetency . . ."

"As I said originally, we cannot hold out much hope of recovery. I would hate to be hasty, but . . . my professional opinion is that irreversible brain damage has occurred, and I would be willing to present the evidence to a court. Although I see no reason for haste—"

"The statutes prescribe the waiting periods, doctor. It has been thirty days—" Thirty days. Thirty *days*. She had to scream, but she couldn't; she forced rage and panic down and listened. "—and petitions may be presented, although of course no final action will be taken just yet." A pause, during which she *felt* someone's gaze across her face, painful in its lack of caring. "It is curious, isn't it, that with so much damage she requires no life support?"

"Unusual, but quite easily explained," said the doctor. She wanted to know his name, wanted to have some name to curse in the darkness. "See here—on this shot—the bleeds stopped short of areas regulating breathing, for instance. It's quite likely that she will live out her normal span."

"Without rejuvenation treatments."

"Oh, certainly. We couldn't recommend rejuvenation for someone in her condition. No, indeed."

Normal span. Her mind calculated . . . at least another ten years, maybe twenty. If she didn't get pneumonia, if she didn't catch a virus. If whoever had done this didn't simply kill her.

And why hadn't they killed her? Why this? Did someone know she was still alive, aware, inside, and was that person gloating over her suffering? If Heris's wicked admiral had been alive, she could have believed that of him.

·"I thought I saw a movement, a tremor," said the skeptical voice.

"It's nothing," the doctor said. "Random discharges in peripheral nerves—she's due to be turned again, to prevent pressure sores. Even in these special beds . . . and they do have tremors sometimes. Breakdown products, perhaps, of the damage."

"I see." She heard the footsteps, fading away, and the sigh and thud of a door opening, shutting again.

She had heard and understood. If their damned scans were any good, they'd know she could hear and understand. Had they bothered to look lately? Or were they lying, and displaying fake scans for anyone who visited? Thirty days . . . she'd been here for thirty days? Where was Heris? What had happened to the prince?

Time had no meaning. She slept, she supposed, and woke again; it seemed like a moment of inattention rather than normal sleep. Sometimes she heard voices around her, and sometimes they talked about her; more often they talked of other things. She came to know one woman's voice, and built from her gossipy chatter a picture of someone with bright, avid eyes and a pursed mouth. Then another, who never added to the gossip, but had a satisfied chuckle, as if she were glad to hear bad things about others. The doctor who had talked to the lawyer came infrequently, but she always knew him.

Scents merged with sounds, with pressures. She knew the smell of her own body and its output; she hated the wet warmth that turned cold too often before someone came to change her. She hated the hands that turned and moved her as if she were a slab of meat . . . she came to hate with special fervor a flowery perfume one pair of hands wore, hands colder and less deft than the others, belonging to a sharp, whining voice that complained of her incontinence.

Hate blurred thought; she fought it back. She could not afford that, any more than she could afford to go insane from the darkness and immobility. Instead, she scrabbled at her memories, struggling to rip another minute detail from the black fog. Gradually she assembled them in order, like torn scraps of a picture laid out on black velvet. That first awakening, with the terrifying talk about drugs to inhibit, to decouple. It had come after whatever happened, but before—and in another place. Then only the odd glimmer, not even clear memories, until the doctor/lawyer conference. A string of clearer memories, then another lapse, after which she no longer felt the wetness of incontinence. From what she overheard, she had had surgery to implant "controllable sphincters"—however that worked. Since then, more and clearer memories, but still no return of function. She could not move; she could not see; she could not talk.

Her mind slid inexorably sideways to the memory of riders she'd known with broken necks or head injuries. But those were injuries, trauma . . . this was something else. She was still thinking, and if she'd had her head crushed against a tree, she wouldn't be.

Thirty days plus. How many plus? Or was it how much plus? For a moment her mind chased that grammatical hare into a thicket of forgotten rules. She yanked it back out, and slapped its nose. Only one thing mattered . . . and it certainly wasn't a point of grammar. She had to find a way out, a way to make some connection to the world—and yet she had to be sure it was the right connection. Whoever had done this would be watching, she was sure, for any untoward behaviors, any return of speech or movement. And how could she tell who was safe, when she couldn't communicate?

Someone had to know. Unless doctors had never known what they were doing, someone had to know she was still alive inside, still capable of thinking . . . still thinking, in fact. Either someone wanted to torment her—and she couldn't think of a good reason, since apparently she didn't even twitch in ways that would amuse a sadist—or someone was concealing her remaining capacity.

She liked that idea better. She had an ally, somewhere, faking brain scans and whatever other tests the medical system used to determine that her brain wasn't working. It would have been easy to kill her, easy to do the damage that was supposed to have been done . . . easy to do that still. But—they hadn't. She had an ally. If she could stay sane, maybe—just maybe—that someone would figure out a way to rescue her and undo the damage.

✳ ✳ ✳

"You're sure she's aware?" Lorenza had to ask again; she could not hear the answer too often.

"Yes, ma'am. And like I said, the way it's set up, there's a blind feed on her cables; it'll never show up on her scans now that she's got the implants."

Perfect. A delicious shiver fluttered inside her. Cecelia helpless, motionless, blind . . . and knowing it. The only thing that would be better would be a very personal and private way to communicate, to let her know who was responsible. Unfortunately, that wasn't possible, and the original drug would have wiped out her memory of the reception.

"You'll find your investment in Sultan Realty has paid unexpected dividends," Lorenza said to her medical contact. "It will be very profitable, I think you'll agree."

"Yes, ma'am." He cleared his throat. "But I just want to be sure you really understand the maintenance requirements. Because you wanted her aware, she's going to need regular maintenance doses—"

"Are you saying it's reversible? I told you it must not be—"

"It's not reversible, no. Not the main brain damage. But the dose wasn't as massive—it takes tinkering to keep her neuromuscular status where we want it, with normal maintenance at the nursing home feeding her other drugs . . . that's all." He sounded scared, as well he should be. If he crossed her, he knew what to expect.

"Very well." She didn't understand the medical details, and didn't intend to learn. The important thing, all that mattered, was the thought of Cecelia—arrogant, athletic, triumphant Cecelia—reduced to a flaccid blind body that anyone could manipulate. She didn't even have to visit the place herself; it was enough to know that Cecelia inhabited a dark, friendless place where she was utterly helpless, and from which there was no escape. "Your payments will arrive quarterly; that's the normal schedule for dividend payout from Sultan Realty. When it's time for you to invest in another company, your broker will inform you." She cut off the call, and sat poised in her tapestry chair, looking around her exquisite sitting room. All the lovely colors Cecelia would never see again, all the sensual pleasures of silken clothing, savory food and drink, fresh flower-scented air, favorite music, sex . . .

Her brother, the Crown Minister, found her pensive in the firelight, hand pressed to her cheek, and tea cold in the cup beside her on the table.

"What's the matter?" he asked. "Are you ill?"

"It's that poor woman," she said, in a voice that she let tremble a bit. It would seem like regret. "That poor, poor woman, stricken like that . . . I just can't stop thinking about poor dear Cecelia."

Heris faced Brun over the dining table in her suite at the fanciest hotel the Station offered. One waiter hovered, serving expensive food Heris didn't want, but had to pretend to eat. Brun, still playing the spoiled rich girl, gobbled eagerly. Finally she chose the most elaborate of the dessert pastries offered, and waved the cart and waiter away. "We'll ring when we're through, thanks," she said. As they left, she picked up the pastry and bit into it, showering flakes in all directions. When the door closed, she took a small gray wand out of her pocket and handed it to Heris with a grin.

Heris picked it up, and scanned the room. Apparently clean of recorders, spyeyes, and such, and this wand, activated, made as good a privacy shield as civilian life afforded. She turned it on its side and placed it between them.

"So—you've taken my advice in that direction?"

"Of course. I told you I was serious." Brun put her pastry down, wiped her mouth, and leaned forward. "Ronnie said you wanted to see me about his Aunt Cecelia; I thought I should make it easy to explain."

"Good for you."

"You know what they're saying about you?"

"Ronnie told me some of it."

"Ronnie only knows what his parents tell him. His mother's telling all her friends that you're the most dangerous woman since that charlatan that bilked the Kooslin sisters out of their fortune by pretending to contact their dead lovers . . . and then killed them to cover up when their nephew found out about it. She nearly killed him, too."

"I never heard of that."

"No, you wouldn't have. But the thing is, Berenice is telling everyone that you must have had that kind of influence on Lady Cecelia. She even thinks that stuff on the island didn't

really happen—that you hypnotized Aunt Cecelia into thinking
it happened. Dad's not here, or he'd set her straight about
that. She's hinting that you even did something—no one will
say what—to cause the stroke. Ronnie thinks his mother's
upset about the redecorating, but I know it's more than that.
I'm not sure just what."

"I had thought of going down to see her, of course—"

Brun shook her head. "Better not. I don't think Berenice'd
let you see her; you're not family, and she's got a right to
decide who else can visit."

"What about you?"

"Me?" Brun looked startled, then thoughtful. "I'm not
family, or one of Cecelia's friends, but . . . I suppose . . .
I could be Dad's representative, sort of."

"Exactly what I thought," Heris said. She hesitated a
moment, then decided to trust the girl. "Did Ronnie tell you
about the will?"

"Will?"

"I presume he didn't, then; it will come out later, if there's
a competency hearing, or if Lady Cecelia dies. Apparently,
she changed her will almost as soon as she arrived, and
she left me a . . . er . . . substantial legacy. The yacht."

Brun's eyes widened. "So *that's* what—"

"That may be part of it. She didn't tell me she was doing
this, or I'd have talked her out of it, of course. But the point
is, that if there's a chance the stroke was caused by a drug
or something, then I'm the obvious suspect. It's understandable that her family would resent the bequest, and that it
would make them suspicious of me and my motives. They're
not going to listen to anything I say. But I hope you will."

"What else?"

Quickly, Heris outlined the attack on Sirkin and Yrilan,
and what she had found out about its background, including
the dishonesty of Cecelia's former captain and the loot found
aboard the yacht at Takomin Roads. "So you see, I worry
that if her stroke was drug-induced—the guilty parties are
working for the Compassionate Hand—in retaliation for
having their comfortable little smuggling ring disrupted."

"Oh my." Brun's face shifted from one expression to
another, fluffhead to practical young woman, as she thought
about this. "Is that what Ronnie meant when he said his
aunt had been to see the king? Was she complaining to him

about the Regular Space Service, perhaps—it wasn't stopping smugglers, but it had dumped you and promoted that horrible admiral?"

"Perhaps," Heris said. She didn't want to mention the prince if it could be avoided. That was another motive for an attack, but one that she had no way of investigating. "My thought was this: it's not unknown for the Compassionate Hand to suborn medical professionals. There was a case in the Chisholm system where doctors certified that someone was paralyzed when he was only drugged. It was meant to terrorize business associates, which it did, and of course it was also terrifying for the victim." Who had died before he could be rescued, but the evidence had been clear enough; the R.S.S. had found the cube records of the drugging and the results. "If you can visit Lady Cecelia, without arousing suspicions—and without it seeming to be my suggestion—perhaps you can ascertain if she is really brain damaged or not. We can set up a discreet way to keep in touch."

"I see." Brun nibbled on the pastry again. "I suppose you don't have any outrageously handsome young men in your crew, do you, that I could pretend to have fallen for on the voyage?"

"No . . . in fact, all those people quit. The only crew member from the voyage you were on is my navigator, Brigdis Sirkin. And she just suffered a loss herself; her lover was killed in that brawl."

Brun's eyes lit up. "Oh, yes. I remember you telling me about her. I think—I think I'd like to meet her. It would be in my character, even as Bubbles, to be wildly sympathetic."

Heris felt immediately protective of Sirkin. "She's not expendable, Brun. I don't want her hurt."

Brun glared back. "I won't hurt her; I'm not that stupid. I'm sorry she lost someone she cared about—that's true. And I will be careful. But I can call her, or meet her, even though she's your crew, if there's a good reason for me to be interested otherwise."

"Just be careful. She's a good person." Heris forced herself to calm down. "And I'll have to ask her." Not even for Cecelia would she expose Sirkin's pain without her permission. "Let's see. Why not have her escort you to the storage company tomorrow—assuming you really should carry out that errand—and I'll have briefed her on the situation. Then it's up to the two of you to make it understandable that you'd keep in touch."

"It's always understandable when rich young people and not-so-rich young people start spending time together," Brun said.

Brun modified her fluffhead persona just slightly the next Mainshift; she appeared at the crew hostel without the pink-tipped spiky hairstyle, opting for a swept-back pouf instead, all the pink ends hidden under an elaborate ribbon arrangement. She wore a more conservative outfit, something she might have worn a year ago in like circumstance. Her heart was pounding; she hoped that she'd find young Sirkin in the hostel lounge, and not Captain Serrano. She liked Captain Serrano, but it was a strain trying to impress her, knowing she wasn't going to succeed, having to try anyway.

Sirkin and another crew member, a blonde woman with sleepy green eyes, waited at the desk. Brun barely remembered Sirkin; the slender dark-haired figure was only vaguely familiar. The other she didn't know at all.

"Captain Serrano had other things to do this morning," the blonde woman said. "I'm Methlin Meharry, and this is Brig Sirkin. Captain said we should escort you to the storage company."

"Yes—well—" She had planned to ask Sirkin to call her Brun, but what about this Meharry? She didn't feel like using her title, and she was getting very tired of Bubbles. The older woman's sleepy green eyes seemed to wake, like a cat's.

"It's all right," she said. "I have the paperwork."

Brun shrugged. "Fine, then. Let's go." If you couldn't figure out what else to do, you could always be rude. On the way, she said to Sirkin, "Captain Serrano told me you had been hurt in a brawl, and your friend was killed—I'm sorry."

"Thank you." Sirkin's voice was low; her eyes clouded. Brun felt like an idiot, a cruel one. This was much harder with Meharry along. She glared at Meharry. Meharry gave her a lazy smile.

"She was damn near killed herself. Don't suppose you rich girls ever have to worry about things like that. Always got protection."

Brun couldn't think what to say—was this Heris's idea of briefing?—but Sirkin spoke up. "That's not fair, Methlin! She was nearly killed in that mess at Sirialis—" Sirkin looked at Brun, who suddenly realized Heris had used her own trick on her. Of course they had set up this quarrel on purpose. Now, what was she supposed to say? Methlin had already given the next line, in a contemptuous drawl.

"Nonsense—it was her Dad's place—how much danger could she be in?"

"Quite enough, thank you." Brun put as much contempt into her own voice. "Sirkin was there; she knows."

"An' you call her like a servant, 'Sir-kin.' She has a name, you know, Miss Priss."

"Methlin!" Was Sirkin really shocked, or was that part of the game? Brun warmed to it.

"It would be impolite of me to use her first name without her permission," she said. "And I don't think much of you, either."

"Captain said I was to come; you can't make me leave," said Meharry, in a dangerous whine that got attention from others on the slideway.

"I'm not trying to make you leave," Brun said. "I'm merely trying to make you observe the rudiments of polite behavior." She hoped Meharry realized she, too, was playing the role; the woman scared her.

"Damned snob," muttered Meharry. Brun pretended not to hear it; she smiled unctuously at Sirkin.

"I'm so sorry, truly. It must have been terrible for you. Captain Serrano always praised you so highly."

"It was . . . she . . . she jumped in front of me." Genuine grief and guilt; Brun felt another pang of guilt. All too clearly she remembered how she and Raffa had felt each other's peril as well as their own. She tried to put that into words.

"When . . . when my friend and I were being shot at, we were as scared for each other . . . once she had to shoot the man who had me at gunpoint, and she was afraid she'd hit me . . ."

Sirkin blinked back tears; Brun wanted to hug her. "You do understand. But your friend lived—was that George?"

"George! No, not George, Raffa. She was the dark-haired one, like you." It suddenly occurred to her that Sirkin might misunderstand something here, but it was not the time to clarify the order of events and feelings.

"Our stop's next," Meharry said loudly. Brun looked up, and led the way out into the concourse and then into the storage company's main office. For the next couple of hours, as the bored and contemptuous storage company workers located and unpacked half a dozen boxes from Lady Cecelia's yacht, to no avail, Meharry made sarcastic remarks about the aristocracy, and Sirkin became Brun's natural ally. Finally, Brun agreed that she must have been mistaken. She cheerfully handed over a credit chip to cover the extra work done on her behalf and murmured to Sirkin that she'd really like to take her to lunch if Meharry would let her come.

By then it seemed natural that Meharry, with a few last caustic comments about the aristocracy, would head back to the crew quarters alone. Brun, alone with Sirkin, said, "You know, if you want to talk about it, I really am a safe person to tell. I'm not quite the fluffhead I seem . . ."

"I know," Sirkin said. "Captain Serrano said you had to be pretty tough to survive on the island."

"But if you don't want to, that's fine, too. What's your favorite food?"

After a luxurious lunch, they spent the afternoon showing why not-so-rich girls liked to spend time with rich ones. Brun found it more fun than she expected to take Sirkin to one shop after another, buying her more gifts than she could carry. She had long quit calling her Sirkin: Brig and Brun, they were to each other. Neither mentioned Lady Cecelia that afternoon; neither needed to.

Wakening after wakening . . . time lost all meaning, in the dark, with only ears and nose to accept sensory data and offer meat for Cecelia's thoughts. And the only smells around were artificial, soaps and perfumes and medicines, nothing evocative of her old life. She had read about such things, but never imagined herself so cut off . . . she, who had been a sensualist all her life. She tried to tell herself that at least she felt no pain . . . but she would have traded pain for that nothingness that threatened her mind.

She would not go insane. She would not give whomever had done this the satisfaction. She told herself she was lucky to be old, that the old had more memories to process, more experiences to relive. She worked her way through her own life, trying to be methodical. It was hard; she would like to have spent more time in the good years, on the winning rides, when the jumps flowed by under the flashing hooves. But even in her extraordinary life, those moments were brief compared to the whole. Instead, she tried to concentrate on the duller bits. Just how many tons of hay had she ordered that first winter in Hamley? How many tons of oats, of barley? Which horse had required flaxseed to improve its hooves? What was the name of that farrier who had been found slipping information to the Cosgroves? Had the third groom's name been Alicia or Devra?

Not even the horses were enough. She made herself catalog her wardrobe—not only every garment she owned now, but every garment in every closet since childhood. Had that blue velvet robe been a gift for the Summerfair or Winterfest, and was it Aunt Clarisse or Aunt Jalora? When and where had she bought the raw-silk shirt with the embroidered capelet? What had finally happened to the uzik-skin boots, or the beaded belt from Tallik? She tried to remember every room she'd walked in, placing the furniture and every ornament. She considered every investment, from the first shares of bank stock she'd bought herself (with a Winterfest gift from her grandfather—he had forbidden her to spend the money on horses, or she would have bought a new Kindleflex saddle) to the most recent argument with her proxy.

Visitors came regularly, in this unnamed place. Berenice, first teary and chattery (reminded by the staff that she should not get hysterical, that she could not bring flowers or food), and her husband Gustav (stiff, ponderous, but gentle when he touched her hand), and even young Ronnie. They talked to her, in a way.

"I don't know if you can hear me, but—"

Berenice talked of their childhood. Sometimes she mentioned things Cecelia had forgotten, things she could then use in the empty hours between visits. This birthday party, that incident at school, a long-forgotten playmate or servant. And she explained, at excruciating length, why she thought Cecelia had been a fool to waste all that time on horses instead of getting married or at least working in the

family. She had accepted the idea that years of small head
injuries from riding had led to a massive stroke.

Gustav talked of business and politics, but not in a way
she could use. He would tell her which stocks were up or
down, and who had been elected, as if he were reading a
list from a fairly dimwitted periodical—with none of the meat
behind the facts. What did she care if Ciskan Pharmaceuticals
was up $1/8$ point, and Barhyde Royal was down $3/4$? Or if
the Conservative Social Democrats had won two more seats
in the lower house while the Liberal Royalists had gained
a critical appointment in the Bureau of Education? Of course,
Gustav had never been known for lively repartee, but even
he might have realized that someone in a coma is hardly
likely to understand the nuances of a field they never
mastered while awake.

Ronnie spent the first visit saying what she had hoped
to hear: he could not believe that his vital, strong, healthy
aunt had been stricken like this; he was sure she was alert
inside, listening to him, understanding him. He would never
believe Captain Serrano had done this—how could she?—
and it would all come right in the end. But she could not
communicate anything to him, could not confirm his guess,
and gradually he settled into what she thought of as useless small talk. He was no longer in exile, of course; the
prince was offplanet somewhere; Raffaele had gone to visit
her family before he had actually talked to her about
marriage; the Royals seemed rather slack after his adventures on Sirialis. George was back to being odious in the
regiment, but came out of it when alone with Ronnie.

This was better than Gustav, but it didn't give her much
to work with when he'd gone. And none of them thought
to tell her the date, the weather, or even where she was,
the things that might have kept her oriented.

It wasn't enough. Still she woke into blankness, helpless
and afraid, and at times could not force her mind to work
through another memory. The brilliant colors of blood bay
and golden chestnut, of the sunlight on a cobbled yard, or
a red coat against dark woods, began to gray. She had heard
of that—the deep blindness that follows blinding, when the
memory of color fades. She could still think yellow and red
and blue and green, but the images that came were paler,
almost transparent.

Worst were the nightmares when she seemed to wake to a soft voice she could never quite recognize, a voice that whispered "*I did it*," and a hand cold and smooth as porcelain laid along her cheek. Who, she wondered. Who could be so cruel?

CHAPTER EIGHT

Meharry had returned to the crew quarters spitting fire against Brun for the benefit of anyone in the public lounge. When Sirkin went to lunch with Brun again the next day, and then to a concert, Meharry took it up with Heris in public.

"That spoiled kid is making a fool out of Sirkin—taking her out, buying her expensive presents. And poor Sirkin—she's not over Amalie yet!"

"I know," Heris said. "I don't like her any better than you do, but we have no right to interfere. If it gets Sirkin's mind off her grief, maybe—"

"It's not healthy," growled Meharry. "It's not as if they could have a real relationship—not someone like that, daughter of some guy too rich to know how many planets he owns."

"Now, wait a minute," Heris said, conscious of all the listening ears. "That's not fair; I met Lord Thornbuckle. He's a friend of Lady Cecelia's, our employer, you may recall. I'll admit, this youngest daughter is something of a . . . problem . . . but she may grow out of it."

"Might," Meharry said, and subsided. "Does Sirkin talk to you about it?" she asked in a milder tone.

"No," Heris admitted, "and I wish she did. You're right; she could get in over her head; she's had no experience with that sort of wealth and privilege. But I can't stop her. Her free time is her own."

Finally, after a whirlwind week, Brun went back

456

downplanet. To Meharry's expressed surprise, she kept up almost daily calls or correspondence with Sirkin.

"Could really be love," said one of the men in the lounge one afternoon. He had heard more than he wanted of Meharry's complaints about Brun, and thought he understood the reason behind them. "Maybe you're just jealous."

"The rich don't love," Meharry said. "They buy. 'Course I'm not jealous; I'm too old for her and besides she's not my type. I just don't want to see her get hurt. She's setting up for it."

Sirkin had walked in on that—they had set up this conversation before but had no takers—and now she said, "I wish you'd mind your own business, Meharry. Just because you were nice to me after Amalie died doesn't mean you own me now!" The man gave a satisfied grin as Sirkin stalked on out the door; Meharry cursed and returned to her quarters.

After several weeks, Heris got the first piece of solid news through her pipeline. Brun had permission to visit Cecelia, but it had taken a request from her father, back on Sirialis, to get it. Right now, Cecelia was being prepared for long-term care, which meant a series of small surgeries; she could not visit until Cecelia had been placed in the permanent care facility her family had chosen.

In the meantime, Cecelia's family had begun the first moves against Heris herself. At the hearing to petition for an Order of Guardianship, Cecelia's will had been formally read . . . and the bequest to Heris noted with dismay by those who hadn't already heard. The first notice she got was a call from a court officer, who informed her that she was now the official owner of the *Sweet Delight*, and court documents to that effect were on the way. Scarcely two hours later, a Station militia officer (not the captain she knew from the murder investigation) showed up to question her about "circumstances pursuant to Lady Cecelia's stroke."

"I don't know anything about it except what Ronnie told me — "

"You weren't there?" He peered at a printout she couldn't read upside down and backwards.

"No; I haven't been downplanet since we came back to Rockhouse. Lady Cecelia has been back up only once, some days before her stroke. She seemed fine then."

"Tell me about it."

Heris explained about the redecoration of the yacht, about Cecelia's ability to make quick, firm decisions on matters of color and style, about her cheerful mood.

"You don't think having her yacht redone so soon—and in a style so different from what's in fashion—reveals, perhaps, that her mind was already going?" Heris bit back a sharp retort. A stroke was not "a mind going" but a direct physical insult to the brain, with resulting cognitive problems.

"Not at all. Lady Cecelia was not your average old lady, but she seemed every bit as competent and alert as she was when she first hired me. She had never liked the colors her sister chose before; she'd decided to redo the yacht her way. She could afford it—why not?"

"Was she on any medication?"

"Not that I know of."

"You don't think her . . . er . . . euphoric mood might have been the result of some drug?"

"Hardly. It wasn't euphoric, just happy. She didn't use drugs for mood control; she felt that she was a happy, fit, healthy individual who didn't need them."

"She had refused rejuvenation," the man said, as if that proved insanity. Heris explained Cecelia's position.

"She told me that she thought people went into rejuvenation from either fear of death or vanity; she wasn't afraid of death, and she thought vanity was a silly vice." No need to mention that she didn't agree about rejuvenation; it wouldn't convince the man of her innocence or Cecelia's wit.

His voice was disapproving. "She seems to have told you a lot; you hadn't been working for her that long."

"True, I hadn't. But living alone on that yacht, as she did, perhaps she found another woman, younger but not juvenile, a comfortable companion. So it seemed."

"I see. There's been questions asked, I might as well tell you. Someone down there is setting up to make trouble for you. I hope you know what you're doing."

If there had been the least scrap of evidence that she had had any physical contact with Cecelia in the days before her stroke, or any way to get drugs to her, she would have been arrested for attempted murder. That became clear in the next few days, when the militia asked for repeated interviews, and Cecelia's family's lawyers and the court officers descended. Luckily, the medical evidence suggested that if (it could not be proven) Cecelia's stroke had resulted from poison, the poison would have to have been administered shortly before her collapse. Repeated questioning of her maid and her sister revealed nothing into which Heris could have put such a drug—no medicines taken regularly, no foodstuffs brought down from the ship. Records at the Royal Docks access showed that Lady Cecelia had not even been to her ship on her last visit to the space station; Heris remembered her protest and wondered if Cecelia had had some sort of intuitive knowledge.

Against the animosity of Cecelia's sister and the rest of the family, however, evidence meant little. They had petitioned the court at once to set aside the bequest to Heris on the grounds of undue influence. Perhaps they couldn't prove an assault, but they were sure of the undue influence. Ronnie sent word through Brun that he dared not call Heris directly; they were already recommending treatment for him on the grounds that he, too, might have been under her supposed spell.

It would have been funny, in a story about someone else. Heris found it infuriating and painful. How could anyone think she would hurt Cecelia? She had begun to love the old woman as if she were her own aunt. No—as a friend. She felt hollow inside at the thought of losing her forever. She tried to explain to Petris.

"They think I did this to her," Heris said, looking up from the cube reader with the latest communication from the family's legal staff. "To get the ship. They think I influenced her to change her will—I didn't even *know* she'd changed her will!"

"I know that. Don't bristle at me."

"They think that I did it all for the ship. Which is why they're insisting that I can't have it."

"Well . . . screw the ship. We can go back to the Service—"

"I'm not so sure. We refused their kind invitation; they may not be willing to have us now. And to find a berth, all of us, somewhere else—" Heris shook her head. It had all seemed to be coming together, a new direction not only possible but rewarding, and now—!

"Well, we're still Lady Cecelia's employees," Oblo put in. He was demonstrating one of his less social abilities with a sharp knife. "As long as we're her employees, we have a right to work on her ship, eh?"

"That's another thing." Heris thumped the hardcopy on her desk. "Since she's believed to be permanently impaired, they say there's no reason to maintain an expensive and useless ship crew. When the yacht's ownership has been determined in court, then it can be crewed with whomever the new owner wants. We're supposed to get out and stay out."

"But you're the designated owner, aren't you?"

"Were you listening, Oblo? The family's petitioned the court to have that part of the will thrown out; Cecelia's own attorney, who drew up the new will, argues that it is an unreasonable bequest to an employee so recent. Apparently all of them think I did something—what, they don't say—to influence the bequest, and some of them think I then did whatever it was that's happened to her."

"Which we aren't sure about," murmured Petris, his gaze sombre.

"Which *I* am sure isn't just a stroke," Heris agreed. "I *told* her she was going into danger . . . but that's beside the point. This letter says we'll be paid through the end of that sixty days they first promised—be glad I got that in writing— and then we're no longer her employees. They're cancelling the redecoration, permanently. They want the ship in deep storage until final disposition. I'm supposed to present my own petition to the court, at my own expense, of course, if I want to contest the petition. They think I'll walk away . . ."

"What else can you do?" Oblo said, eyeing her. "You don't have the money for an attorney. We've been depending on your lady . . ."

"It will split us up," Petris said. "That's what they want— we'll have to ship out separately, because no one hires ready-made crews, especially not us. I don't like this."

"It's not fair," Sirkin put in. Everyone looked at her.

"Fair?" Oblo raised one scarred eyebrow. "You're a grownup now, Sirkin. Another voyage, and you'll be almost family."

"Except there isn't going to be another voyage." Heris felt her mind slumping even as she held her body erect. "We don't have the resources. The family's offered me a settlement, not to contest . . . it's enough for a couple of months living on Rockhouse Minor, but not for all of us. Not nearly enough for a ship."

"For tickets away?"

"Yes, but where? Besides, I don't want to leave Cecelia down there until I know what happened. Maybe even more if I did know what happened." She took another breath. "I have savings, of course. Investments. Maybe enough to contest it, but not if they bring criminal charges for whatever it was that happened to her. They're powerful enough they might be able to do it even without evidence. Since she didn't tell me about the bequest, I wasn't prepared—I don't even know why she did it." She paused. "But I do have legal help. Remember that young man George?"

"Kevil Mahoney's taking your case?" Petris asked, eyes wide.

"No, not himself, but he's recommended someone, and the fee's not as bad as it could be. The problem is, he thinks the settlement might be reasonable. And in any case, he says we must comply with the court order to vacate. I asked about that old 'Possession is nine points—' you always hear about, and he says it has never applied to space vessels. And of course we're not actually in the yacht; she's sitting over there in Spacenhance, empty." With Spacenhance grumbling almost daily about having one of their slots tied up uselessly. If it hadn't been for the Royal connection, they'd have insisted on having the ship moved long before.

"And it'll cost us to live . . ."

"If we can't get other work."

"Like what? Dockside work on Rockhouse Major's simply not available for ship-certified. They don't want crews spending time here, for political reasons. Downside—who wants to work on a dirtball anyway?"

"You're not looking at this as a tactical problem," Arkady said. "Think of Lady Cecelia. We have to stay mobile if we're to help her at all. If we're trapped, whether it's broke, or working for someone else, or in custody, we can't help her."

"You mean get her out?" Sirkin's eyes sparkled. "I like that. We could get a shuttle, and—" Petris put a hand on hers, and she subsided. Heris shook her head, and explained.

"We don't know for certain that she's a prisoner . . . if

she's really had a massive stroke, if she's really comatose, we can't just snatch her away from medical care. But if she's not—"

"If she's been . . . disabled . . . ?"

"Yes. Then she needs allies who aren't bound by . . . er . . . the usual considerations."

"Rules," Oblo said with satisfaction. "Laws. Even traditions . . ."

"We need a ship," Petris said. Heris felt the challenge in his gaze. She grinned back at him.

"We have a ship." She took a deep breath. "It is highly illegal, and we will be fugitive criminals, the lawful prey of every R.S.S. ship, every planetary militia . . . but we have a ship."

"Not quite," Oblo pointed out. "You haven't forgotten she's over in refitting, with all her pretty carpets and plush walls gutted?"

"And all her new weaponry aboard," Heris said. "What do we care what the decks and bulkheads look like?"

"You're actually going to do it," Petris said. She had, she realized, surprised him. "You, Heris Serrano, are actually going to steal a yacht and set off to rescue a friend in peril. . . . Do you realize how theatrical this is?"

"It will be even more theatrical when the shooting starts," Heris said. "And we can't just leap into it. We need to know exactly what her condition is. *Sweet Delight*'s not a planetary shuttle; we can't use it to snatch her, even if it's safe to do so. We'll have to find someone with a shuttle first."

She remembered Ronnie saying that both his family and Lord Thornbuckle had private shuttles onplanet, but didn't mention it to the crew. Not yet. She would have Sirkin check with Brun at their next encounter.

It's not working, Cecelia thought in the worst moments. No one will ever come; no one will ever figure it out. If they were going to, they'd have gotten me out by now. And I can't go on like this for years and years; it would be better to go mad and not know any more. She fought herself on that, in the motionless silence, screaming curses at her fears as she had never allowed herself to scream in real life. For a short time the discovery that she had remembered so many exple-
~~ that ladies were not supposed to notice amused her. A

fine talent for curses, she thought. But it was useless. No one could hear them. She forced herself back to the dry bones of accounting (tons of hay, price of oats and bran, the cost of bits and saddles) as her hope dwindled. How long?

Then one wakening she found herself flooded with emotion. Not the usual fear, but joy so strong she could hardly believe she did not leap from the bed. What—? A smell, a rich, natural scent, overlay the room's usual sterility. Leather, conditioning oil—not quite the smell of a saddle, but certainly one associated with riding. Horse and dog. Cautiously, afraid to respond now because someone might withdraw that aroma, Cecelia sniffed.

"It's so sad to see her this way," said a voice. A voice she knew from before; she struggled to put a name to it. Young, female, not family—who was this? "She loved the out-of-doors so—"

One of the voices she heard often. "I'm sure they did everything they could."

"Oh, of course." A pressure against her cheek, and the scent grew stronger. Her mind drank it in gratefully. Leather, oil, horse, dog, sweat: a hand that had been outdoors? No, a hand alone wouldn't carry that scent. A glove would, she thought. A young woman wearing gloves? Why? Gloves weren't in fashion, unless she'd been mired here so long that fashion had changed again. "But I don't understand why I couldn't bring flowers. She always loved flowers, especially the aromatic ones. It smells so—so sterile in here."

"Strong scents interfere with the room monitoring," the attendant said.

"Oh, dear." The young woman's voice sounded mischievous. "And here I came straight from the track. Should I have showered?"

"No, because you're just visiting. The blowers will clear it out shortly. Now I'll leave you—just a half hour, please, and check at the main desk on your way out."

"Thank you." As Cecelia listened to the familiar soft noises of the doors, the hand never left her cheek. Then, at the final distant click of the outer door, it did. Into her right ear, the same voice, softened to a murmur. "Cecelia, it's Brun. Bunny's daughter. Dad wanted me to visit you; he couldn't believe what happened."

Bubbles. Brun. For a moment her mind tangled the two

names, then she remembered, with utter clarity, their last conversation.

"If you have anything left at all, it's olfactory. I saw your nose flare with this—" The smell came back, and Cecelia rejoiced. "I'm going to try some things—smells—and see if you can respond. That was my glove—I rubbed it all over two horses and the stable dog today—"

I knew that, Cecelia thought. She could hardly focus on what Brun was saying; she wanted to cry, scream, and laugh all at once. The familiar beloved scents faded, replaced now by a fruity tang.

"Apple," Brun said. "I'm not supposed to have food in here, I think it's because they don't want you to smell it. I think they know you can." Cecelia struggled to move something, anything, and felt a firm pressure on her arm. "You twitched an eyelid," Brun said. "If you can do it again, I'll take that as a 'Yes.'" Cecelia tried; she could not feel if she succeeded, but Brun gave her another squeeze. "Good. Now I'm going to pretend you can hear me, because my aunt said sometimes people in comas could hear—"

Of course I can hear, Cecelia thought angrily. I just did what you asked me to do! Then she realized that Brun might be dealing with another kind of monitoring. She had to make this look like an innocent visit.

"So," Brun went on, "I'm going to tell you about the last hunt, after you left. You know, I've always wondered what it would be like to be the fox—" A sharp stink of fox entered Cecelia's brain like a knife, clearing away the fog of anger. "Foxes are so cunning," Brun continued. "Clever beasts— I'll bet ours are smarter than Old Earth foxes ever were. But it must be scary. Down there in the dark holes, hearing the hounds coming out the gate—" This time a smell of dog, and another squeeze.

Cecelia struggled to comprehend. Brun was trying to tell her something, something important, but she was too old, too tired, too confused. Foxes? Hounds? Foxes in dark holes . . . like I am, she thought suddenly. With the hounds up there somewhere . . . she could almost feel her mind coming alive now, and hoped that no brainwave monitor was on her at this moment.

"Anyway, there was this kid who decided that the hunt was unfair to foxes. Too easy for us, too hard for them.

His first season; he's one of the Delstandon cousins, I think. So he decided to help the fox. He understood that hounds followed the scent, so he figured if he made a false trail, we'd waste our time and the foxes would have a day off." The alternation of fox and dog scent fit with this story; Cecelia wondered where it would lead. "But to get the fox scent, he had to find foxes himself—a den—and you can imagine what happened when Dad's huntsman found him lurking around a den."

Cecelia couldn't, but she concentrated on breaking Brun's code. The huntsman had been signalled with the glove again; she recognized that particular mix now, as well as the constituent scents.

"I thought it was kind of funny, protecting the foxes from someone who wanted to protect them—" Again the stink of fox. "But I guess that happens sometimes." Now a different smell, woodsy and soothing. Change of topic? "I was thinking back to the island—"

Yes. Change of topic indeed. Cecelia found her memory of the island fragmented; she hoped Brun wouldn't depend on something no longer there.

"It was such fun camping there when I was a child. Now I don't know if I'll ever feel the same way about it." This time the smell was oily, dangerous yet attractive. Not leather: metallic plus oil plus some chemical. Abruptly she recognized it. How had Brun smuggled a weapon in here? Or was it just a cloth saturated with the smell of gun oil and ammunition? It meant danger, she was sure of that.

As she realized that, she heard the door opening. "I wish I knew if she even heard me," Brun said, in a different tone, almost petulant. "My aunt says sometimes they can, but she doesn't *do* anything."

"I need to check the monitors," the attendant said. This was the one who liked to gossip.

"Do you think she hears anyone?" Brun asked.

"No, miss. The scans don't show anything; the doctors think she's completely comatose. I just need to check this—" Cecelia felt pressure on her head, then a sparkle ran through her brain, bringing up a vivid picture of her own gloved hands clasped on her knee. Someone was whistling "Showers of Orchids," a song she had not heard or thought of in decades. Then it was gone, and the voice overhead said,

"That's all right then. The supervisor thought I'd better check."

"What?" asked Brun.

"Well . . . I suspect it is all that smell of horse you brought in. It seems to have clogged the monitors or something."

"Sorry," said Brun, not at all contritely. "Mum said to come today, and I almost forgot. Didn't have time to clean up first or anything."

"You're another horsewoman?"

"Not like her. To tell the truth, I'm fonder of the jockeys than the horses." The attendant chortled. "But I always pat the horses; the trainers like that."

"Well, your time's almost up," the attendant said. Cecelia wondered if he'd leave again, but he didn't.

"I know," Brun said. "I don't suppose it matters, really. If she can't hear me—and she certainly doesn't respond— why should I stay the whole time anyway? Is her family visiting?"

"Yes, miss. Her sister and brother-in-law and nephew, every week. Each has a special day. If you're going to visit regularly, you should put yourself on the weekly schedule—that way the receptionist will have your tag ready, and the gate guard will have you on the list—"

"Oh, I don't think so." Brun sounded casual. "I've known her all my life, of course, but she's not my aunt. I mean, I care, but it's not like—you know."

"Yes, miss." The satisfaction in the attendant's voice was unmistakable.

"I mean, I might come again before we go back to Sirialis— I suppose I should—but not every week or anything."

The wonderful smell of horse and dog and leather came back, as Brun laid her hand on Cecelia's cheek again. "Goodbye, Lady Cecelia. I'm so sorry—but your friends haven't forgotten you. You'll always have a place in the hunt." Cecelia felt Brun's warm lips on her face—a goodbye kiss—and then she heard her footsteps leaving the room.

Someone knew, at last. Someone believed. Someone outside, someone free, knew she was still alive inside and would do something about it. What, she could not imagine, or how or when . . . but something. Cecelia wanted to laugh, to cry, to leap and shout for joy. Her immobility hurt worse then than it had for a long time. But hope always hurt, she remembered. Hope gave the chance of failure, as well as the chance of success.

She clung to that hope in the timeless dark that followed, as she replayed her memories again and again. Somewhere, sometime, someone would come and take her away from this, into the smell of horse and dog and fox, the real world.

Brun invited Sirkin to dinner; Sirkin wore—to Meharry's voluble disapproval—an expensive outfit Brun had bought her. Heris paced in her own small room, waiting for Sirkin to return with some word of Cecelia's condition.

"She'll be late," Petris said, lounging as usual on her bed. "We could improve the shining hour."

"And be interrupted again? No, thank you. Afterward . . ."

Afterward didn't happen; Sirkin didn't come back until next Mainshift, arms laden with packages bearing the logos of expensive stores, and her expression clearly that of someone whose needs had been satisfied. Brun came with her, wearing matching earrings, and a smug look.

"Sirkin, you were supposed to be back last midshift," Heris said. She'd begun to wonder if something had happened to them, and she felt almost as irritated as she sounded.

"It's my fault," Brun said airily. "I just—it was easier for her to spend the night, and then we overslept—"

"I see, miss." Very formal, for all the ears and eyes. "Sirkin, if you could get yourself into uniform, we are having crew training this shift."

"Yes, Captain." Sirkin accepted a last squeeze from Brun, and went off to her quarters with the load of presents. Brun waved an irreverent goodbye to Heris.

"I hope," Heris said, "you haven't made promises you aren't prepared to keep."

"Not me," Brun said over her shoulder. "I never make promises at all."

Sirkin handed Heris the scrawled note later. *Yes, she's there. They won't let you near her; I'll work something out. Don't worry. Brun.*

Don't worry? How could she not worry? Yet . . . if she herself couldn't rescue Cecelia—and she had not been able to come up with a viable plan for getting her out of the nursing home and away from the planet—she would bet on

Brun. They'd just have to figure out a way to have the ship where Brun needed it . . . if that meant stealing it and hiding out somewhere in the meantime.

The Crown summons arrived "by hand"—the hand being a member of the Household, in a formal uniform that no one could overlook. Heris took the summons warily— old-fashioned, imprinted paper, the strokes of a real pen having scored the thick, textured paper with black letters—and wondered what now.

Not that it mattered. A Crown summons had the force of law, although no legislation supported it—it was simply inconceivable that someone invited to an audience would refuse. She noted the time, and the clothing required. A shuttle awaited her. She could not help but think of Cecelia riding a royal shuttle down . . . and where Cecelia was now. She suspected she was meant to think of that.

The messenger waited in the private meeting room while she changed into her formal uniform . . . not as formal as the dress uniform of Fleet, but it would have to do . . . and told Petris where she was going and why. His brow furrowed.

"You might be going into trouble. One of us should come."

"If there's trouble that direction, one wouldn't help. No, you stay free. Here's the authorization codes for the bank, the lockboxes . . ." For every power she held that she could transfer that fast. "Take care of them," she said as she left, and his hand lifted in the old salute. *Make no promises you can't keep. Keep the ones you make.* The old words ran through her mind as she walked beside the messenger, and saw how passersby reacted.

"We have a problem," the king said. He looked much like his son Gerel, only older. Was he as foolish? Heris could not let herself think so. If the king had also been damaged, she could see no hope for any but the conspirators who had done it. He paused, and she wasn't sure if it was for her response, or a decision. "You have already, with Lady Cecelia, been of service to the Crown." Considering that her entire adult life had been spent as a Fleet officer, this was, Heris thought, an understatement. "You know Gerel," the king went on. "Both as himself and as Mr. Smith. You know the . . . er . . . problem he has developed."

"Yes, sir," Heris said. It was all she could say, really. She was glad that the Familias had never taken up the full formality of address of past historical periods.

"You are in a position to do the Crown, and the Familias Regnant, a great service, if you will."

"Of course, sir; it would be a privilege." Provided it didn't take too long or take her away from Lady Cecelia. She was still determined to find a way to help.

"It is a very delicate matter, possibly quite dangerous. I would not consider asking you, were it not for your military background, your proven courage and discretion." Which meant it was not just delicate and dangerous, but impossible. Others had been asked and refused, most likely. "And I will understand if you feel you cannot jeopardize your crew, or if the . . . er . . . legal difficulties you face require your immediate presence and participation."

"Perhaps if you could tell me a bit more," Heris murmured. She did not miss the flutter of his eyelid, the outward and visible sign of an inward and secretive nature.

"Let me be frank, Captain Serrano." Which meant he would divulge as little as possible, she thought sourly. Politicians! "I know, of course, your situation vis-a-vis the Bellinveau-Barraclough family. Lady Cecelia left you her yacht in her will; her relatives contest her mental fitness at the time of the bequest, and have charged you with undue influence. They have sufficient standing that the court has agreed to deny you access to the ship while the matter is under adjudication. You turned out to have unexpected resources—though they should have realized that officers of your rank are rarely penniless spendthrifts—and unexpectedly good legal advice, thanks to the debt Kevil Mahoney owes you for the life of his son. You may win in the end, but in the meantime you will have, unless you find other employment, no income—nor will your crew." All this, though Heris knew it, sounded grimmer from his mouth than she'd allowed herself to think.

"They think you're a greedy, sly woman capable of insinuating yourself into the affections of an elderly spinster—and possibly capable of doing her actual harm, by precipitating a stroke." He stared at her a long moment, then held up his hand when she opened her mouth. "No—don't answer that. I disagree with them, in part because I've known Cece all my life, and when she came to talk to me about Gerel I got an earful about you as well. I've known Cece, as I said, and she's never been taken in by anyone charming since she was sixteen or so. She's a superb, if acerbic, judge of character; she's located and remarked on all *my* failings. Cece thought you were a rare find, and I abide by her judgment. That's another reason for my request."

Heris tried not to shift about in her chair. She was glad to know the king trusted Cecelia's judgment, but she wished he would get to the *point*. She distrusted easy compliments and indirection.

"Now—without going into all the historical tangles—we've got a mess, the entire Familias Regnant. You saw Gerel's problem—" Heris wished she dared interrupt to say *You mean his stupidity?* but simply waited. "It's not innate," the king said. "I'm sure you know that many prominent people have doubles."

That startled her, and she tried not to show it. "I . . . had heard of that, sir." And what did that have to do with it?

"No one knows how many of the heads and heirs of prominent families have them, of course. In the military, except for covert operations, regulations prohibit them for any but flag officers in major military actions . . . otherwise, we'd be stumbling all over extra Lieutenants Smith and Brown whenever the real ones wanted to spend an extra thirty days on home leave. You can understand, I hope, that the royal family is well-supplied with doubles, both for convenience and security. In fact, that's how Admiral Lepescu got Gerel away from Naverrn without anyone noticing. One of his doubles was there; we're claiming that it was one of his doubles who went to Sirialis, although I'm afraid Bunny won't believe it."

"I . . . see." Heris wondered for a moment if the foolish young man could have been the prince's double. She didn't know the prince, after all. And the Crown would have had to respond as if he were, even if he weren't. In that case, maybe only the double was stupid. If the king was telling the truth. It shocked her to realize how she doubted him.

The king sighed, and steepled his hands. "Captain Serrano,

I must admit—in confidence—that the person you met as Mr. Smith was in fact the prince. The real prince. He is now back on Naverrn, and his double is safely back in hiding. That's not the problem. As I said, his infirmity is not natural—not inborn—and it was induced in much the same way as I think Cece's stroke was induced. I knew about it, of course, from the beginning. It was the threat. They'd killed Jared, his oldest brother—" Heris remembered that, the assassination of the eldest prince, when she was serving aboard the *Stella Maris*. The whole Fleet had gone on alert, expecting some kind of rebellion, but nothing happened. "Until then I hadn't used doubles much; certainly not for the children. After that—with Gerel—we switched him around quite a bit. They were proving they could still find him—and hurt him—without the public scandal of another death."

"Do you know who?" Heris asked. The king shook his head.

"We have three or four major possibilities. You're not a political fool; you can probably figure them out for yourself."

"What do you want me to do?" asked Heris. She wasn't about to speculate about politics; it wasn't her field. Moreover, it was obvious that the king himself, or his faction, must be among the possibilities. Who else would have more opportunity, both for the act and its later concealment? Despite her distaste for the exercise, motives sprouted in her mind: fear, greed, lust for power.

"I daren't trust any medical facility in the Familias," the king said. "But beyond the Compassionate Hand, there's the Guerni Republic. They have the best medical facilities in known space; they trade in biomedical knowledge and skill. I want you to take Gerel there, and see if his condition can be treated or reversed without killing him. I have his entire medical file—the people responsible actually gave me some of the details, to prove they'd done it. Our specialists say they can't do anything without causing permanent damage, even death. I need you, because I dare not send him by Fleet or commercial vessel. Not only would his condition become known, but those responsible would surely intervene. I had planned to ask Cece if she'd be willing to do it, but then she had her stroke . . . if it was a stroke."

Was that openness a sign that the king hadn't done

whatever was done to Cecelia? Or just an attempt to convince her? Heris chose her words with care. "You want me to steal the yacht out from under the noses of the family, against all law and regulation, and go to Naverrn and take the prince from there to the Guerni Republic—which is some dozen worlds around two or three stars, if I recall—to attempt a treatment you know nothing about? Begging your pardon, but that seems a . . . very strange proposal."

"Of course it does," the king said. "It *is* a strange proposal. Dangerous—"

"Suicidal," Heris said. "We'll be outlaws here, for having taken the ship when it was under legal dispute, and since we've taken it out of the system, the R.S.S. will be after us as well. It is essential for your plan that we not be known as your agents—and thus you cannot keep the wolves off our track. We can circumvent the Compassionate Hand—it just takes longer—but how are we supposed to pick up the prince when every ship will know we're fugitives already?" Actually, that wasn't such a problem; Oblo had already set up an alternate identity for the *Sweet Delight*. But the king needn't know that. "As for the Guerni Republic . . . exactly where did you expect us to deliver the prince? And how long might the treatment take? And suppose it doesn't work? What will happen then?" Before the king could answer any of this, Heris said, "And beyond all that, there's Lady Cecelia. Why should I leave her in peril, among those I cannot trust?"

The king grimaced. "Your oath of service, I could have said once—but I see you do not feel bound at all by that anymore." That stung; Heris felt her teeth grating, but said nothing. She had not broken that oath; others had broken their trust, had failed her. "If I swore to see that Lady Cecelia was protected? That no further harm came to her—assuming that harm has been done?"

"With all due respect, since I do not know what happened, I do not know whom to blame." That came close to accusing the king. At his angry scowl, she added, "I'm sure you intended no harm in the first place, and yet it happened."

"I see." Heris could almost see the ideas shuffling through his head like a pack of cards. She wanted to tell him not to bother coming up with a good story, but one did not interrupt a monarch. It was an impossible mission, and she would be crazy to accept it—except what choice did she have? If she refused it and stayed here, the family would put the yacht in deep storage and her own savings would go to support her and as many of the crew as wanted to stay. She might get other employment, but not with her people, and rumors that she was responsible for Lady Cecelia's condition might keep her unemployed the rest of her life. Without a shuttle—and not even Oblo had found a way to obtain a shuttle secretly—she couldn't get Cecelia offplanet. A ship and a mission—even this mission—was better than nothing.

"You do realize that you cannot help Lady Cecelia yourself," the king said. It was as much threat as bare statement of fact. "She is well-guarded against you in particular. If she has a chance for recovery, it would be with someone else." Heris nodded, dry-mouthed. "If you were gone, perhaps the level of suspicion would drop. Not that that would help her physical condition, but like you I hate to think of her living the rest of her time in what must seem like confinement." The look he gave her then had years of manipulation behind it: was she cowed enough? Had she taken the bait of that implied promise? Heris stared back at him, almost regretting those years of loyal service. But no: it meant something to her, something she still treasured. "I will give you letters patent," the king said finally. "I believe I can trust you not to reveal them except in direst need." When, thought Heris, they wouldn't be worth the elegant old-fashioned paper they were written on, no matter its cost. She could just imagine a Compassionate Hand pirate-merchant holding its fire because of a piece of pressed slush-fiber with writing on it. This, like his assurance that he would protect Cecelia, could not be trusted. But her doubts would do her no good. She made herself smile at the king.

"Sir, I accept your mission." At least it meant a ship, a chance, another short space of freedom. And she might—she *would* find some way to help Cecelia. Perhaps, as the king implied, if she were gone, the family would let down their guard . . . the first glimmer of an idea came to her, but she forced it back. She didn't want anything to show in her face.

*　*　*

The king sat alone with his uncertainties. He would have liked to confide in that captain, explain all the knots in the tangled mess that had led to Gerel's situation, and Cecelia's. He had never meant it to turn out like this. It hadn't been his idea anyway, not the clones or the drugs; he had only wanted to avert another disaster after the deaths of his two older sons. But it was far too late for easy honesty.

CHAPTER NINE

Heris explained the Crown mission with as little expression in her voice as possible. She had assembled the crew in a private lounge of a respectable hotel, as she'd done at weekly intervals all along, and Oblo had turned on one of his gadgets before she started to speak. Sirkin opened her mouth twice, but subsided. The rest of the crew stared at her without expression.

"You realize the whole thing is a trap." Petris sounded almost angry. She wished he wouldn't. Anger with him was next door to passion, and she had no time for that now.

"Of course," she said. She could feel the additional tension. "But we don't have to walk into the trap."

"I thought we just did." Oblo was giving her his look, the one which made ensigns pale and civilians switch to the other side of streets and slideways.

"So does the Crown," Heris said, grinning. "Safer that way—what do you think they'd do if I refused the bait? Kill us off one by one, like Sirkin's friend, and certainly finish Lady Cecelia. I don't like that solution, but we're vulnerable as long as we're tied to a ship in dock, and weak if we separate. No, we're going to take their bait— then we're going to pick up the whole trap and walk off with it."

"How?" Trust Oblo to get to the sticky bit and say it aloud. Petris, shaking his head, grinned at her.

"I don't know yet. But that's the plan."

"All strategy, no tactics," Petris said. Not an angry voice, but behind the neutrality was doubt. "Unless just staying out of whatever trap they've set is tactics."

"I'll work on it," Heris said tartly. "And here's what I need. You each have your list." She handed out the handwritten notes. She sat back and watched their expressions. Oblo's brows rose, and he looked up to give her a short nod. Yes. He'd figured it out.

"But the Crown gave us permission . . . why this?"

"It was indicated to me that they'd rather we looked like outlaws. I have . . . assurance . . . that it will be cleared up later."

"Anything worthwhile?" asked Petris.

"Yes. And not going with us, though they don't know that. I was given letters patent, empowering us to act as one of His Majesty's Fleet in certain matters. To be presented to certain . . . ah . . . personages we are unlikely to find where I was told to meet them."

"Because—?" began Sirkin. Petris gave her his best "civilians are idiots" look. Heris glared at him. Sirkin was their weak point—young, inexperienced, and emotionally vulnerable after Amalie's death. She didn't need any more pressure from any of them. Petris answered Sirkin in a very different tone than his first expression had promised.

"Because either they aren't there, or the captain expects we won't be, or both. And she's not telling us now, because we shouldn't know too much."

"Those letters are staying behind, in what I devoutly hope are secure locations, which I will not divulge even to my crew," Heris said. Kevil Starbridge Mahoney owed her favors; he could jolly well put some unopened documents in his own security files for her.

"Suppose . . . we actually find out who's putting the pressure on the king, and take it off?" That was Sirkin again. Heris was glad Petris hadn't yet squashed her initiative; the girl was young, but she had promise, and her unmilitary background gave her something the others didn't share.

"Fine, if we can do it without having the same pressure land on us," Heris said. "But it's like maneuvers—getting the fire off someone else doesn't make us safe. Our first priority is staying alive, uncaught by the trap we know about and any others."

"And Lady Cecelia?" Sirkin asked. "I thought maybe we

could . . ." Her voice trailed away as the others looked at her.

"We can't help her," Heris said firmly. "We're the ones anyone would expect to do something, and for that very reason we can't."

"But someone has to—"

"Sirkin, we have enough to worry about as it is. Keeping the ship free, and whole, and ourselves alive, in the first place." Heris signalled the others with her eyes. Time to leave, before Sirkin asked more questions Heris didn't want to answer, especially since she could. They stood, and Sirkin followed, still looking stubborn. "That's all . . . see you here next week as usual." The weekly dinner meeting, which she hoped the watchers had given up worrying about. Oblo turned off his gadget, with a wink, and Heris went on without a pause. "The court's agreed to hear the case, at least, which I—" She stopped suddenly, as if realizing the gadget was off. "Well, see you next week, if that stinking lawyer doesn't come up with something to drag me downside."

On her way out, she reserved the same room for the same time the following week, as she had from the beginning.

Sirkin agreed to pass along to Brun a message which made no sense to her, but would, Heris hoped, make sense to that inventive young lady. Brun's answer, relayed through Sirkin, showed she had done her homework. She had also had her visit with Cecelia, and she believed Cecelia's coma was not as deep as the medical records indicated.

"How did she get hold of the medical records?" Heris asked, then shook her head. "Never mind. If she says Lady Cecelia is still alive inside, I'll believe it. And if she thinks she can arrange a rescue, we'll get out of her way and let her at it."

"But it's dangerous." Sirkin was looking better these days, and her sparkle had begun to come back. Heris wondered momentarily if it was just time, or if Brun had anything to do with it. She had to admit the two of them seemed to hit it off well. "If they catch her—" That meant Brun, of course.

"If they catch her, she's young, rich, titled, and will have Kevil Mahoney on her side. I'd bet on her not to get caught, though. You didn't see her on the island. I was impressed."

"I wish I had," Sirkin said. Admiration. And Brun wished she knew as much about ships. Heris wondered what would come of this—she hoped it wouldn't cause them any trouble more serious than young people usually had.

Next, Heris went to find Oblo. "I've got our slot," Heris said, with no preamble. "The family's requested that the yacht be put in deep storage. The court agreed. Spacenhance doesn't want the responsibility of moving it, and I've refused to allow a ferry crew, under provisions of my employment contract with Lady Cecelia *and* my rights as possible heir. The court agreed to that, too. Suspicious, but they did agree. So we're to move her."

"But what about stores? If you're planning to go outsystem at once—"

"Are you telling me that the best thief I ever knew can't manage to get a few cargo cubes aboard a yacht guarded by an interior decorator?"

"Well . . . no. But it won't be easy. Those people are strange."

"Oh? You've been checking?"

"Of course." Oblo looked up at the ceiling. "You said get ready for a quick departure, so I thought I'd . . . ease things. Turns out they have an almighty sticky AI on their dockgate."

"But you can do it."

"Unless you're planning to run a year without stopping anywhere, she's fit." He didn't look at her directly, but she knew his face too well to be fooled. He had begun shifting provisions into the yacht long before. It had probably started simply to prove he could bugger the AI.

"Now?"

"I'd like another three shifts, to sort of finish things off. But we could go now, and not be much shorter."

"Good. You can have three shifts, but not a second more, and you'd better not get caught." Oblo looked insulted at that, as well he might.

"And that includes weaponry."

"No problem." By the tone, he'd installed that first. He would.

"Right, then. We file a flight plan for eight shifts from now—" Oblo scowled, and Heris pointed at him. "Think about it. You're going to be sure they are as stupid as you think. If you've been doing something every shift or so, five blanks will make them show themselves, especially with a plan filed. I'll have reserved our space in Rockhouse Minor's deep storage, and tickets back here on the ferry. Show up in uniform; we're Lady Cecelia's employees, and not a gang of toughs who might go larking off somewhere in her ship. Very formal, very sad. Look as grim as you like—you're miserable about this, and you don't mind saying so. But not in the bars yet, not until the last night."

Heris had no trouble looking grim as she filed the flight plan. Everyone knew about the legal dispute; this would make it clear who was winning.

"Tough luck, Captain," said the Traffic head clerk. He had been on Rockhouse for years; she had filed Fleet plans with him. "It's disgusting the way they've messed up what the old lady intended."

"Lady Cecelia is—was—a fine woman," Heris said. "And I only hope they don't scour the tubes when they shut the main drive down over there."

"Oh—you're not going to Duibly's?"

"No. Lady Cecelia's family insists that it's not cost effective, since they don't foresee the ship being used for several local years—and possibly sold away. As you see, they specified Harrigan's." The clerk would know what that meant, in credits and in skill. Harrigan's was a fine deep-storage yard, if you were planning to send a ship or sell it to someone who would be doing a major overhaul anyway. Duibly's, far more expensive, boasted it could power and air up a ship from deep storage in less than 50 hours.

"A shame. A lovely ship, I've heard."

"It is." He wanted to know more; she could tell. "You know, she had just had it redone when I first took command, and she was having it redone again." His eyes widened; he wanted even more details. "Real wood paneling," Heris said. "Furnishings brought up from the family estate. And it was impressive before."

"I know," he said. "Spacenhance has been using the interiors in their advertising. That was their top designer; I wonder why she wanted to change it."

Heris shrugged. "She could, I suppose. Perhaps it didn't have the effect she expected. But you see what I mean."

The clerk nodded as if that had meant something, and sealed the flight plan with a coded magnetic strip.

On the way back from the Traffic Control office, a short brown-haired young woman stopped her at a slideway entrance.

"Captain Serrano?" Her face and voice were slightly familiar. Heris paused, wary.

"Yes?"

"I don't expect you remember me—I was just a very junior ESR-12." Military: environmental systems technician, enlisted. With the specialty and rank, the name came back to her.

"Yes . . . Vivi Skoterin." Another reminder of her earlier failure, though Skoterin might have been junior enough to escape the courts-martial that devastated the officers and NCOs of her former crew. "How have you been? Did you—?"

"They didn't send me to prison, no ma'am. But—but I didn't re-up." No wonder, Heris thought. The young woman looked thin and depressed; what had she been doing?

"Find a job all right?"

"Well, ma'am . . . I just got in . . . been working on a bulk transport, independent carrier, Oslin Brothers. Maybe you know of them?"

Oslin Brothers meant nothing to Heris, but independent carriers of bulk cargo were marginal profit concerns. She shook her head, and Skoterin went on.

"I . . . was hoping for something better. Scuttlebutt around Station is you have your own ship and are hiring some of your former crew . . . and I was wondering . . ." Damn. Heris didn't need this, not now. But responsibilities didn't come when you needed them. At least she could get this woman a square meal and perhaps a little money to help her find a better berth.

"Scuttlebutt's got it slightly wrong, as usual, but come on—at least have lunch with us. You remember Sergeant Meharry and Oblo?" Something flickered in Skoterin's eyes, but Heris dismissed it as recognition. "They'll be glad to see you. Come on, now." Skoterin climbed onto the slideway with her, and Heris spent the trip back to the hostel thinking furiously. What would she do now? She owed Skoterin, as she owed all her former crew . . . and they were short an environmental tech, as Haidar had reminded her only that week. The others were willing to do the work, but in an emergency, they'd have their own stations to keep.

Haidar remembered Skoterin at once, which relieved Heris: what if the woman had been planted on them somehow? While she went off to freshen up for lunch, he said, "You will bring her along, won't you, Captain? We really need another tech—I could use two more, in fact."

"You're sure of her?"

"Oh, yes. That's Vivi. Kind of dull, except for her work: she's absolutely reliable. She got top reports from Lieutenant Ganaba—" Lieutenant Ganaba, who had been killed on the island even before the hunt started; Heris had heard the story from Petris. The admiral had not liked to leave officers alive as effective leaders. And Ganaba had been tough; if he approved of Skoterin, then she was good.

"Seems a good solution to me," Heris said. "But if we ask her, she has to say yes . . . we can't leave her behind to tell the tale."

"Just tell her we're ferrying the yacht, and not the rest of it."

"But that's like hijacking her—"

"Hell, Captain, we're going to kidnap a prince—why not an environmental tech? Besides, she wants a berth."

And Skoterin, offered a short-time job ferrying the yacht, with "maybe a longer job later" agreed at once. Haidar took her off to lunch himself, waving away Heris's offer of funds.

With the flight plan filed, and the *Sweet Delight* entered into the undock sequencer, time seemed to compress. Heris had her own list to complete. Check out of the hostel, with reservations for herself at another, lower-priced hostel for the end of the week. Consigning the letters patent to Kevil Mahoney's office downside; she sweated out the hours until he called to confirm receipt. The messenger service was supposed to be secure, but one never knew.

She had avoided telling Spacenhance about the new orders, lest they send someone aboard to do something and find what Oblo had stashed. So at the last reasonable time, when she was due aboard to begin the undocking procedures, she stopped by the Spacenhance office and showed her official authorization.

"But you can't—" said the decorative person in the front office.

"Court orders it," Heris said. "Long-term storage has been arranged at Harrigan's, Bay 85; I'm due aboard to begin undock in ten minutes."

"But—"

"I don't see the problem," Heris said. "You had the cease-work order more than 40 days ago; surely the ship's just sitting there empty—isn't it?"

"Well, yes, but—I'll have to check with a manager." Not *the* manager, Heris noted, but *a* manager. Soon the woman Heris had seen before came out of the back rooms.

"Captain Serrano! How nice. Mil tells me you're moving Lady Cecelia's yacht into deep storage . . . does this mean the court has ruled against you?"

"Not yet, just until the case is heard and finally settled. Her family petitioned the court, and the court agreed."

"Well, that's too bad. Such a lovely ship. We can have her ready for you in . . . oh . . . another twenty-four hours. How's that?"

"Sorry. I've got undock starting in eight minutes; we're on the sequencer, and we have a flight plan. The Harrigan's berth is time-logged, and we have passage back to Major on Triamnos. If you'll just give me the access codes—"

"But Captain! The ship isn't—it's not ready. You know we had to stop in the middle—"

Heris shrugged. She had expected Spacenhance to try some kind of delay but this seemed silly. "As I told your assistant, you had the cease-work order weeks ago; surely your people aren't using the ship . . ."

"Well, no, it's not that . . . it's just such a mess. We don't like to let even an unfinished job go out of here in that state—"

"Sorry, but this time you must." Heris stared her down; the woman seemed uncommonly flustered, and Heris wondered if Spacenhance was involved in some kind of smuggling, and had been using the yacht as a storage bay. If so, they were about to be in real trouble. All of them.

"Well. I suppose if you're on the sequencer—" Traffic Control had a reputation for shredding anyone who fouled up the system, including Stationside companies whose failure to comply with ships' orders caused the delay. Heris had never liked Traffic Control's tyranny, but this time she blessed it.

"I'll just come with you," the woman said. Heris didn't argue. Six minutes was cutting it close, even for her.

The crew waited, looking as solemn and grim as Heris could have hoped, in formal dark blue. But the Spacenhance woman hardly glanced at them, opening the gates and hatches one after another. Heris hardly had time to glance at the status board, and see that it was safely green, before the woman opened the access hatch itself and started into it.

"Excuse me," Heris said firmly. "We really don't have much time before undock starts—if you could just get back to the dock—"

"Oh . . . right." The woman still looked nervous; Heris's suspicions went up another notch. She smiled anyway, and led the way past the Spacenhance manager, trusting Oblo to make sure she didn't stay aboard.

The ship smelled funny. She had expected a new smell, cleaning solutions or solvents or something like that, but this was a strange, yeasty odor. Perhaps that's what bothered Spacenhance—maybe whatever they used to strip the carpets and wallcoverings smelled bad, and they didn't want clients to know. The bridge still looked too tiny, especially with the new screens crammed into every spare corner. Before, it had looked like a toy . . . now, it looked like some electronic hobbyist's workbench.

Heris took her seat and called Traffic Control. She could hear the crew moving into position; in her mind's eye she followed them all to their stations.

"*Sweet Delight*, Heris Serrano commanding, initiating undocking procedures."

"Confirm your flight plan to Rockhouse Minor, Harrigan's Long-Term Storage; please accept course burst."

"Accepting." Heris shunted the course to Sirkin's board, and went on with the interminable formalities of undocking from Rockhouse Major. Registration, ownership, insurance, ship's beacon profiles, accounting details. Even though they weren't going outsystem (as far as Traffic Control knew) the rules required long minutes of voice confirmation of details already on file. The cost of pursuing legal remedies against ships that left Stations owing money meant that it was much

easier to insist on clear accounts before they left. If so much
as a single glass of ale were outstanding, the ship could
lose her place in the sequence and be assessed a hefty fine,
to boot.

After the formalities came the systems checks, which she
watched carefully. The ship had been aired up the entire
time, but something might still be wrong. At least she now
had crew she trusted. All boards were green except the
newest: those would stay dark, untouched, until they had
cleared the Station. Those, if detected, could get them in
trouble.

"Tug approaching," said Traffic Control. "Channel 186."

"Thanks." Heris switched to the tug's channel. She would
have preferred a hot start, but no civilian ship left Rockhouse
Major under its own power. She checked to see that the
yacht's bustle had been deployed; Petris gave her a thumb's
up. With no pilot (a rating not used on the Fleet vessels)
he had taken over some of those functions.

"Captain Serrano, *Sweet Delight*," she said on the tug's
channel. The memory of the first time she'd said that,
undocking here long months before, came to her. She felt
very differently now.

"Station Tug 16," came the reply. "Permission to grapple."
She was glad it wasn't the same tug; that would have been
a bit too much coincidence.

"Permission to grapple." She felt the jar; Tug 16 was a
lot clumsier than the earlier one. The status lights switched
through the color sequence, and ended green.

"All fast," the tug captain said. "Your port bustle coupling
is a bit stretchy, though." Excuses. He had come in too fast.
"On your signal."

She called Traffic Control on their channel. "Captain
Serrano of *Sweet Delight*: permission to undock, on your
signal."

"All clear on Station. Confirm all clear aboard?"

Nothing but green on any of the boards; her crew nodded.
"All clear aboard." Twenty seconds. She, the Stationmaster
on watch in Traffic Control, and the tug captain all counted
together, but the computer actually broke the connection to
the Station. She watched the display as the tug dragged them
slowly away from the crowded traffic near Rockhouse Major.
This would be a shorter tug, because they were headed for

Minor, on an insystem route. In fact, the tug could give them the correct vector and let them ride that trajectory most of the way to Minor, but Heris had chosen the more common option of powering up and "hopping" it.

When the tug released them, she called for the insystem drive.

"Insystem drive, sir." Petris, that was. "Normal powerup." The lights flicked once, as the internal power switched from the storage units to the generators working off the drive.

"Engage." Now the artificial gravity shivered momentarily, then steadied, as the insystem drive pushed them along the course handed out by Traffic Control. Not that they would stay on it long. "Turn on the new scanners." Oblo reached up and did so. Now she had almost as much data on traffic in near space as Traffic Control.

Insystem space had no blind corners, no places where the sudden change in acceleration of a yacht would go unnoticed. As soon as they started their move away from assigned course, Traffic Control would be all over them. So might any fast-moving patrol craft, though none showed on the scans. It felt very strange. She had never, in her entire life, done anything intentionally wrong. Even as a child, she had always asked permission, always followed the rules . . . well, most of the rules. She had cut herself off from the Fleet for a good cause, she thought; now she was cut off from all lawful society. She hoped the cause was good enough. She *really* hoped her mathematics was good enough.

What they had was the advantage of small mass and initiative. The longer she waited, the less initiative . . .

Petris reached back and caught her hand. "You don't have to do this, just to impress me," he said. "If you think it's wrong—"

"I think it's all wrong," Heris said. "But this is the least wrong part of it. No. We'll go and scandalize the Fleet, and then get blown away by a smuggler or something—"

"You don't really think that . . ."

"No, not without a fight." *Do it,* she told herself fiercely. And as always, cementing the responsibility, she made the move herself. Flat down on the board: the main drives answered smoothly, and the *Sweet Delight*, bouncing like a leaf in a rapid, skipped out of her plotted course. They needed another 10,000 kilometers . . . She sweated, watching the plots.

It should take a few seconds to register; someone should be tapping the screens, wondering what had happened to the plots. Then it would take time to transmit the message. No one had the right firing angle for missiles; no one could intercept with tractors before they got their critical distance. Optical weapons would fry them—no civilian vessel carried shields—but the overrun could be tricky. She knew there was traffic beyond them, bound on other routes. She had counted on that.

Seconds ticked by. They still had the civilian beacon on; no use to play games with it in a system where their ID was known.

"There," Oblo said, with grim satisfaction, as one of his lights blinked red, then returned to green. "Stripped it, even though they should've known who we were."

"Wondering," Petris said. "They're wondering what happened."

"Not for long," Heris said. Even as she spoke, the Traffic Control blared at them.

Course error! Course error! Contact Traffic Control Officer at once.

Automatically, Heris's finger found the button, but she stopped it before the channel opened. When she glanced around, they were watching her. She pulled her hand back, and shrugged. "Nothing to say. We'll wait it out." At the edge of her vision, in front of Oblo, the counter ran down the long chain of numbers.

General warning! Vessel off course in sector Red Alpha Two! All traffic alert! Do not change course without direct orders! Stand by for Traffic Control override! The words crawled across the navigation near-scan screen, and bellowed from the speakers. The new scanners showed the reaction in color changes, as other traffic dumped velocity or changed course. Heris had counted on that, too. Everyone believed in Traffic Control until something went wrong, at which point at least twenty percent of the captains would use their own judgment. Time after time that had proven deadly, but it happened anyway. Now Traffic Control had more to worry about than one yacht off course, as each panicky ship caused problems for others.

A tight beam obliterated Traffic Control's blare, and the near-scan screen showed a face in Fleet gray, with the insignia of an admiral on his shoulders. Maartens, it must be; he had just taken command of Fleet at Rockhouse Major. He had served with Lepescu, though she didn't know if they'd been friends. "Damn you, Serrano," the man said. Heris stared back, impassive. Of course they knew, but she wasn't going to give him her visual. "I never thought even you would cripple an old woman just to get a free ride. We'll find you." A threat she trusted, as she trusted a knife to be sharp. But it bit deep anyway; she made herself stare into those angry eyes until the beam cut off. Then she cut the link to Traffic Control herself. She didn't need that nonsense blaring at her. They weren't going to impede anyone's course more than another few seconds.

"We're clear in theory," Oblo said. She gave him a tight smile.

"Then let's surprise them." With the new control systems, she had only one button to push; she wished she could have heard the comments from Traffic Control when their abrupt skip into FTL left an unstable bubble in the local space for others to avoid.

They were still alive. She didn't think she'd ever heard of anyone using FTL drive that close to a planet, and she hadn't entirely trusted the theory that said it was possible for something of their mass. But they were alive, the *Sweet Delight* as solid as ever, and presumably they hadn't destroyed anything vital back there. She had gotten as far from the main stations as she could, although there were too many satellites up to avoid them all.

"And now," Oblo said, with his crooked leer, "for a life of piracy and plunder, eh? Gold, girls, adventure—"

"Shut up," Petris said, so that she didn't have to comment. "First we have to find a quiet place to do a little cosmetic work on our friend here."

Heris tried to relax. Nothing could have followed them; not even the escorts could have gone into FTL so close. Pursuit would have hours of boost to get out far enough, by which time they would have nothing to follow. They had slipped their leash. She looked around at her crew. They looked busy and outwardly calm, but she suspected more than one felt the same internal tremors she did. They had not set out in life to become criminals. Those who had been through the disastrous court-martial would be more hardened, but Sirkin—she glanced again at the young navigator. Sirkin had had a promising career before her, and no military background. Now she had lost her lover and her career . . . but the latter had been her own choice. Still she must feel strange, the youngest and the only one without military experience, without years of working with Heris.

But her face, when she turned to face Heris, seemed calm enough. "Captain, the new equipment's working well. It's— I really can pick up navigation points even here." *Here* being that indefinable location into which FTL drives projected. Heris grinned at her.

"Just remember that the apparent motion you'll see isn't right. When we drop out, we won't be where you would expect, but where the charts say." Sirkin looked confused, and Heris didn't blame her. The military navigational gear which Oblo had liberated had counterintuitive properties which Sirkin would learn best by experience. The point of it was not to steer by the detected navigation nodes, but to detect other vessels in FTL state.

They passed two more jump points safely, with no pursuit detected. Heris didn't fool herself that this meant no pursuit—it meant only successful, and very temporary, evasion. Finally they returned to normal space in a region with no known maintenance stations. As Petris had said, they needed to do a bit of work on the yacht.

Better Luck had been built at the same yards, within a year of *Sweet Delight*, the utility version of the same hull. She'd been modified for carrying very low temperature cargo, then rebuilt to handle rough landings, then rebuilt again to return her to a deep-space freighter, reclaiming the cargo space lost to the landing gear. She had been lost to the finance company, which chose to scrap her rather than pay for refitting (the last cargo had rotted when the low-temp compartments failed, and the stench had gone into the deck tiling). Oblo had her registration number, and her papers— or a reasonable facsimile—and the overall hull design matched. Now he was making sure the beacon matched, too . . . and the little tramp freighter had never operated in this region of space.

"I wonder how Lady Cecelia is," Sirkin said one day. "If Brun's been able to do anything . . ."

"We all wonder," Heris said. She knew someone would have let Cecelia know she'd run off with the ship; she hated that, knowing Cecelia would feel betrayed.

Lorenza had listened without interruption to the Crown Minister's version of the theft of the yacht. Now she said, "So—it was that Serrano person after all, eh?"

"I suppose." The Crown Minister seemed more interested in his ham with raisin sauce. "Suppose she got tired of waiting for the court to rule. Silly—it might have ruled in her favor. There are all sorts of precedents for enforcing quite stupid wills."

"Berenice is sure they'd have ruled against her. Even if she didn't poison Cecelia herself, it was clearly a matter of undue influence."

He stopped to put maple-apple-walnut butter on a roll. "You women! I think you were convinced the captain did it just because she's another woman, and one who wears a uniform."

Lorenza raised her eyebrows at him, slowly. "Now, Piercy, you know that's not fair. I have nothing against military women; I have the highest admiration for their courage and their dedication. But this woman was no longer military; she left under a cloud—"

"She was cleared," the Crown Minister said. Lorenza wondered why he was being stubborn. Did he know something she should know?

"I understand that her own family—her own well-known family—didn't stand behind her. That tells me something. Even if she was cleared, they may know something that never came out in court. It wouldn't be the first time."

"True." He was retreating; he had turned his attack to the ham, and then to the rice pilaf.

"Berenice says Bunny's daughter Bubbles started acting odd after spending time with her on Sirialis. Wanted to change her name, or something."

"Bubbles has been acting like a fool since she hit puberty," the Crown Minister said, and took a long swallow of his wine. "It wouldn't take a yacht captain to send her off on another tack." That struck him as funny, and he laughed aloud. Lorenza didn't smile, and he ran down finally. "Sorry—a nautical joke."

"My point is that it's now perfectly clear she did something underhanded to influence poor Cecelia. And now she's stolen the yacht. Just what you'd expect."

"Do you ever visit Cecelia?" the Crown Minister asked. She almost smiled at his transparent attempt to change the subject and make her feel guilty.

"Yes, occasionally. I'm going tomorrow, in fact." She had not been able to resist, after all. Twice now she had sat beside the bed, her soft hand on Cecelia's unresisting cheek, and murmured into her ear. *I did it. I did it.* That was all: no name, only the whisper. It excited her so she could hardly conceal it all the way home. And now she could be the one to tell Cecelia that her precious yacht captain had stolen her yacht . . . that she had been abandoned once more. If she had had any hope left, that should finish it. Lorenza let herself imagine the depths of that despair . . . what it must be like to have one's last hope snuffed out by a voice in the darkness. She was very glad she had specified that Cecelia's auditory mechanisms should be left intact.

CHAPTER TEN

"This is the craziest idea I ever heard." Ronnie glared at Brun. "You want to take a sick, paralyzed old lady up in a hot-air balloon, then bang around in a shuttle, then—and what are you going to do when you get to Rockhouse Major?"

"I'm not going to Rockhouse Major." Brun glared back. "Dad's yacht is at Minor; that's all you need to know."

"A balloon—dammit, you can't fly a balloon like a plane. They just drift. How can you possibly be sure you'll even get there—or do you expect me to chase you across country on foot with Aunt Cecelia over my shoulder?"

"No, of course not. And yes, I can aim a balloon—there are ways. They're clumsier than planes, but quieter and much more difficult to find on scans designed for planes and shuttles. I can be there within fifteen minutes of a set time, and close enough that you won't have to run any races."

"So what do you want me to do?"

"You visit her—you have a regular pass."

"Yeah, but they're still watching me." Less warily since Serrano had run off with his aunt's yacht, but still watching.

"That's fine. They can watch you all they want. What's your regular visiting day?"

"Saturday, of course, when I have a half-day off. You know this already—"

"Yes, but I'm checking my own plans. Your mother visits on Tuesdays, and your father on Thursdays, and you on Saturdays—and you almost never miss—"

"I liked her," Ronnie said. He noticed the past tense, and wished he had said "like" even though it wasn't true. No one could like that limp, unresponsive body in the bed. And he had only Brun's conviction, formed in that one visit, that Cecelia-the-person still lived inside her inert shell, to give him hope.

"So while they watch you, and her, it's just routine. They expect you."

"I still can't walk out with her—"

"You won't have to. All you have to do is get her unhooked from the bed, and outside. Like this—" Brun flipped open her notecomp and showed him the plan. She had it all down, all the medical background, sketches of wires and tubes and things he didn't want to look at. What to do in which order, what he would have to take with him. Suggestions for making sure the bothersome attendants didn't interrupt—he thought of another way himself, and realized he was being drawn in. It still looked ridiculous, but Ronnie didn't argue. He didn't have anything better to offer. He didn't have anything at all. And the longer they left Aunt Cecelia trapped in her helplessness, the worse for her . . . he could hardly believe anyone could stay sane month after month.

"When, then?"

"Festival of the Air, of course." He felt himself flushing. He'd been so miserable he'd forgotten that annual celebration was almost upon them. "Plenty of confusion in the air— for some reason the wilder sorts are thinking of dropping in on the starchier resorts and sanctuaries in the area. Can't think why." She grinned. "And no, it's not traceable to me. Now—let's get busy. You'll have to practice getting a flight suit on me when I'm lying limp."

Oblo had managed to load the yacht with a surprising number of amenities. Toiletries, leisure clothes, entertainment cubes, and a cube reader. Music disks and players. Despite the bare bulkheads and naked decks, the lack of furniture, ample bedding, and bright-colored pillows made comfortable nooks for lounging and sleeping. Heris asked about the pillows—she could not imagine Oblo sneaking through the docks with big puffy orange and puce and turquoise pillows under his arms—and he gave her his best innocent glare.

"Bare decks get cold, Captain. You know that." Then a sheepish grin. "And besides, these pillows . . . they were sort of . . . lying about somewhere . . ."

"Somewhere?" She could feel her eyebrows rising.

Now he stared at the overhead. "To tell you the truth—" which meant it would be his fiction. "They belonged to someone Meharry and I kind of blame for that girl Amalie's death." Possibilities ran through Heris's mind, and she settled on the obvious.

"That therapist?"

He grinned as if he was glad she'd figured it out. "Yeah. Had this big room with lots of pillows in it. Needed cleaning, they did. Cleaners picked them up, delivered them. We sort of . . . liberated them on the way back." As a specimen of Oblo's vengeance, this was mild. Heris decided to let it go.

"You know it was wrong," she said.

"So was getting Amalie killed and Sirkin hurt," he said, with no remorse. "Captain, it was the *least* we could do." About what she'd expected; she managed not to laugh until he was out of her office.

So far the voyage was going well. Skoterin had not protested when she realized they were not, in fact, ferrying the yacht a short distance. She had been glad of a longer job, she said, and she trusted the captain. Heris found that amazing, but then so were the others trusting her. She got along well with the others, though she was younger by some years than anyone but Sirkin. Heris wondered if that would turn into anything. She couldn't remember what Skoterin's preferences had been—if she'd ever known. Not that it mattered, really. As long as they both did their work. Sirkin she saw on the bridge; she was happily absorbing all Oblo and Guar could teach her about the new navigational equipment. Haidar reported that Skoterin was as efficient as he remembered. All she had to worry about was the mission itself.

"I wish there were a way to be sure the Crown offer was faked," Heris grumbled. "Then we wouldn't have to bother with this ridiculous rendezvous. What if the prince doesn't show up?" She had never enjoyed covert ops, and didn't now. Petris ignored that, and kept rubbing her shoulders. Oblo had the bridge, with Arkady Ginese to second him;

nothing would get by those two. She and Petris had retired
to her cabin, where they turned up the thermostat and
lowered the lights so that they could enjoy the rest of the
shift out of uniform. Surely this time nothing could interrupt them, not in FTL space.

"What kind of job do you think we can get as cover if
we need it?" he asked. His hands slid lower; she wondered
if he really meant to continue a serious conversation or if
this was just another form of teasing. She was almost afraid
to try the response she was eager to make; the obstacles
to their pleasure had gone far beyond a joke. What would
happen *this* time if they started something? She felt she
would die of frustration if they didn't.

"Soft side of legal, I expect." Heris did not meet his
eyes, and leaned back against him. Maybe he would take
the hint and continue without talking about it. Petris shifted
her in his arms, and she quit thinking about future problems. Present pleasure was enough for now. Apparently he
thought so too; he quit asking silly questions. And nothing interrupted them, though she didn't think of that for
some time.

But afterwards, they came back to it. A small tramp cargo
ship couldn't simply idle along from place to place; it had
to have cargo, and destinations. Otherwise, as they knew
well, the authorities would have questions, backed up with
force.

"It would be simpler if we had two ships," Heris said
finally. She rolled over and stretched. "We could transfer
cargo from one to the other, as if—*what is that?*" Her
convulsive lurch upset Petris, who had been curled over
watching her stretch; they collided, and then Heris was out
of the bed, clutching the sheet, and pointing at the bulkhead above him.

"What?" Petris glared first at her, then at the bulkhead.
Then his gaze sharpened. "I—don't have any idea." He edged
away from the bulkhead, and got off the bed.

"It's alive," Heris said. She was aware that her voice had
squeaked, and still hadn't returned to normal. The thing was
just lighter than the bulkhead, a dull creamy white, as long
as her hand. It had long antennae; she could just see them
wiggling.

"And there's more than one of them," Petris said. He

pointed. Out of the crack between bulkhead and bunk, two more of the things crept.

Heris had wrapped the sheet tightly around herself; now she leaned closer. "Six legs . . . antennae . . . you know what it looks like? It looks like an albino—" Something skittered down her leg, from under the sheet, and tickled her toes as it ran over them. "COCKROACH!" She was out of the sheet before she knew it, and across the room. Shuddering, she looked back. Petris, on one foot, looked around like someone who had forgotten what the other leg was for. Neither of them had anything handy for whapping a cockroach, because ships didn't have cockroaches. Ships were routinely cleaned out before and after each trip; everyone feared vermin.

"Albino cockroaches?" Petris said, still on one leg like some kind of exotic bird. "Do they . . . I mean, what do they eat?"

Heris headed for the shower. "I don't know, but they're filthy. It's disgusting. On my ship!" She strode into the shower and bounced back out. "They're in there, too!"

"They like warmth, I recall," Petris said. He was back on two feet, but looked anxious. "We turned up the heat in here—"

"And what if they're all over the ship?" Heris asked. She had a nightmare vision of a full-bore inspection arriving to find her and her first officer and lover stark naked amid swarming albino cockroaches. Could she claim they'd eaten her uniform? And would they?

"They probably are," Petris said gloomily. He shook out his shirt before putting it on. "And they probably breed. Where could they have come from? None of us had been out of Station quarantine."

"*That's* why the redecorators didn't want us on the ship," Heris said. She remembered the frightened look on the woman's face. It made sense if she was afraid of being caught with illegal biologicals. "They put them here."

"But why?"

"I . . . don't know. But we had best find out. Perhaps they're used in some stage of the process."

"It can't be legal." Petris shook out his shoes, one by one, before putting them on. "It's against all the regulations I ever heard of to have biologicals on a Station or a ship.

Except for the registered ones, like you told me Lady Cecelia had."

"I wonder." Heris checked her own clothes carefully before getting back into them. "At least we now have a cargo."

"These? They're not cargo—they're a reason to quarantine us." He sounded horrified at the thought. Heris felt the same way but struggled to think past her revulsion.

"Yes, but . . . let's assume the decorators keep them, and put them here. That means they're valuable to the decorators. That might mean they're valuable to another firm doing the same work somewhere else."

He looked dubious. "I don't see how. First we'd have to catch them, confine them somewhere, take care of them. We don't even know what they're *for*."

"Can you catch one?" Heris asked, pointing to the cluster that still clung to the bulkhead over the bunk.

"Me?" He looked at her. She looked back, pointedly. "Oh, all right. If they're poisonous or something, though, you had better figure out how to save my life, or I'll haunt you."

"I should figure out first what to keep it in . . . let me think—something in the galley should hold it. And we'll turn the temperature down, in case they're more active in warmth. If I remember, most insects are."

Once clothed, she found the pale cockroaches just as disgusting, but less frightening. If they attacked, they'd hit her clothes and not her skin. She shuddered, remembering the touch of those legs. With the thermostat down, she had an excuse for shivering.

"I suppose you want me to stay here while you fetch a cage?" Petris didn't sound happy about that.

"I can stay," Heris said. "Get a food container with a tight lid—except we'll have to ventilate it somehow—I wonder what size holes these things can crawl through."

He came back with a canister whose top had a dozen perforations; Heris wondered why, then it occurred to her it looked like a giant salt shaker. Perhaps that was how Cecelia's cook had covered pastry with powdered sugar.

"We had similar things back home," Petris said, as he smacked the open end of the canister down over the nearest cockroach and carefully slid a flat piece of metal under it to trap it. "Farmers hate 'em too—those ate crops, clothing, pillows, rugs—"

"Rugs?" Heris stared at him. "Like—the carpet that used to be here?"

"We didn't have real carpet; we had rugs woven of plant fiber and animal hair. Some handwoven, and some factory-produced. But yes, they ate holes in rugs. And upholstery. Old-fashioned books, too, especially the bindings. My uncle said it was the glue. And they'd make a mess of data cubes left lying around, even though they couldn't eat them. They'd leave their . . . mess . . . on them, which glopped up the cube readers. Why?"

"Because . . . that may be why the decorators have them. I hadn't really thought about it but . . . the stuff the decorators take out of a ship—all the wall coverings and carpet and upholstery—has to go somewhere. They'd pay to have it processed in the Station recycler, and then they'd have to pay to replace that with new material. Imported or fabricated, either one. Let me run the figures . . ."

This was something she could work out, once she thought of it. And the specifications were in the contract she'd brought along. She called them up. "Look—here's an estimate of square meters, times minimum thickness of carpet, of wall covering, of upholstery. Which comes to—" She looked at the volume result. "—And they're required to give chemical composition—organics—so in case anything's volatile, what kind of outgassing the ship's environmentals will have to handle. Interesting."

"What?"

"If they're honest, given the density and composition, the volume of material they'd have to have processed onstation or transport would cost them—" She called in the financial subroutines. "Too much. Plus replacement. I'll figure that both ways, local processing and importation. No, three ways—from planetary sources and importation from more distant sources." The result exceeded the bid on Cecelia's job.

"Can't be," Petris said. "You've made a mistake somewhere."

"I might have," Heris said. "But if I didn't, and if these disgusting insects were put here for a reason—and if they eat rugs and pillows and upholstery—"

"They eat them," Petris said, with distaste. "They certainly don't manufacture their replacements. It might be cheaper to have them gobble up the client's old stuff, but unless they can be cooked into delicious banquet meals, I don't see how that helps." Then his face changed expression. "Unless, of course, they're cooked into something else—the new furnishings."

"That's sick," Heris said. "Besides, how could you get them all back out?"

"It would explain why they risk breaking the vermin laws, if it did work."

"And it gives us something to sell," Heris said. "Both the information and the . . . er . . . samples."

"It certainly establishes us as outlaws," Petris said. "Selling vermin—carrying them loose on a spaceship?"

"Not loose if we can capture them," Heris said. "I don't want any more surprises."

Capturing the clots of pale cockroaches in Heris's cabin turned out to be easy, but everyone soon knew that those had not been the only ones aboard. Although their pale color made them hard to spot in some locations, they were obvious in the galley when someone flipped the lights on and they scuttered for dark corners. They swarmed to every food spill, and for a while food spills were more common. Even Heris, who had convinced herself they were harmless, dropped a mug of soup when one ran up her arm. Eventually the crew learned to tolerate the sight of them—or at least not drop things—but no one liked it.

"What's this thing?" asked Nasiru Haidar one day, carrying the tiny object gingerly between thumb and forefinger. "And I already know it's not a dropping—I've learned to recognize those."

Petris peered at it. "Egg case, and it's already hatched. Or they have. So they're fertile."

"How fast do they reproduce?" Nasiru asked.

Petris shrugged. "I have no idea. Where I grew up, the entire life cycle of some insects was only 20 planetary days— and our days were close to Old Earth days, they said."

"And these insects were mature when introduced—possibly more than ten days before we undocked. So they could have laid eggs immediately they came aboard—"

"It's possible that we undocked with only egg cases," Petris said, "and all the cockroaches on the ship are those who came with us as eggs."

"So I couldn't have seen them," muttered Oblo. Everyone had pointed out that he'd been aboard the ship, stashing supplies. He'd insisted there were no cockroaches then.

"Possible." Heris grimaced. "What doesn't seem possible is getting them all. I wish we knew how long ago that had hatched. Are the ones we see now first or second generation? Or worse?"

Haidar and Skoterin, with their specialty in environmental systems, seemed the logical ones to devise living quarters for the captured cockroaches, and ways of eliminating those still loose. Heris hoped Cecelia would never need to know that she had had cockroaches running loose all over her ship.

Brun waved at her friends as her balloon tugged on the mooring lines. Dozens of other balloons obscured her view of the hills. She signalled her handler, who released the line; she kept a steady burn as the balloon rose. A few were already high above her, bright colors hardly visible; a dozen released within a second of her release, and still more waited for a last passenger. The Festival of the Air . . . she remembered how she'd gasped the first time she saw all the balloons and kites and gliders and parasails. She'd had to learn to pretend disdain, even while learning to pilot a balloon; she'd claimed her father made her do it. But she'd always loved it.

Surface winds pushed her back over the taller hills, away from her goal. She didn't hurry to rise above them. Half a dozen balloons she knew well were drifting as she was, toward the course marker on the highest hill ten kilometers away.

"Racing, are you?" called a Kentworth, from a yellow balloon striped with purple. "I thought you declared non-competitive this year."

"Declarations are secret; the wind doesn't lie!" she yelled back. Every year some people pretended not to be racing until the race itself; it was one of the things she'd counted on. She let the balloon sag as it approached the next ridge of hills; with the wind behind her, she'd gain altitude here anyway, and she didn't want to be pushed into the contrary winds aloft. Not yet.

She was still a couple of kilometers short of the first

marker when she turned on the burner. She had let herself sag below most of the competitors, but that was her style. Now the burner's roar drowned out the sound of others, and the hooting and cheering of watchers below. Slowly at first her balloon steadied, then lifted . . . then surged upward, as if yanked by a string.

"Damn!" she yelled. The nearest balloon might or might not hear her over the burner, but anyone watching or recording her on cube could see her mouth moving. "Burner's stuck on; I'm going to lose my wind—" She hauled herself up onto the basket rim, and banged noisily at the burner with a wrench as the balloon surged upward. Her stomach protested; she ignored it. It was no worse than a fast elevator ride. Around her, then below, the others receded to multicolored blobs. When she felt the wind shift, she whacked the burner control in the right place, which she'd been studiously missing, and turned it off. In the silence, she heard laughter from below, and one bellow asking if she needed help. "No," she yelled back down. "Fine now." The balloon kept rising; it had plenty of heat in it, and the air at this level was cooler.

She leaned out, watching all the other craft in the air. She knew what the winds aloft had been when she launched, but winds changed . . . she was drifting back now, away from the course marker, back past the launch site where balloons just launching looked like overstuffed sofa pillows. Half a dozen balloons were higher and ahead, well on their second race leg, having passed the first course marker before gaining altitude to ride the other wind direction.

The morning's mist had cleared, and now the remnants thickened into clouds defining the boundaries of different air masses. She pulled the burner control and sent the balloon up another several hundred feet. Up here somewhere she should find a current angling in from the approaching low pressure . . . over there where the clouds thickened into murk.

Ronnie craned his head to look over the guardhouse at the first of the balloons. Of course it wasn't time for Brun's yet . . . He looked at the guard, who smirked at him.

"Festival of the Air . . . you like it, sir?"

Ronnie allowed himself to look abashed. He had practiced the expression for two days now. "I know it's childish, but—it's always been my favorite seasonal festival. If I hadn't had to come visiting today, I could've been up there too . . . not that I don't love my Aunt Cecelia, of course." He put on what he hoped was a contrite but haughty look. The man nodded.

"A bit dull, visiting elderly relatives. They tell you all about their childhoods—"

"Well . . . not my aunt," Ronnie said. He was sure the man knew already; he had to assume that. "She . . . she can't speak, actually. She had a stroke."

"Ah." The man nodded again. "Sorry to hear that, sir. Makes it harder to visit, I expect. Although perhaps she can hear you, give some sign that she knows you're there?"

Ronnie felt cold. He wanted to smash the man's head on the ground. Instead, he shook his own head. "No . . . they say not. She's just a vegetable, just lying there. But Mother says . . . I mean, I would come anyway, she's my aunt, but . . ."

"But not today, if you didn't have to? No shame in that, sir; at least you came. It speaks well of your family."

Ronnie nodded without speaking as the man held out a stamped visitor's pass. He could feel the man's eyes watching his back as he walked up the beautifully landscaped lawn. Could the man tell that he had something under his clothes? In his pockets? He glanced up, and walked on with his head thrown back as if he could not resist watching the balloonists.

As required, he checked in at the main desk, where he was told his aunt's room number—the same as always, he was relieved to note. Her condition was unchanged, the receptionist said; he would please observe the rules of the facility, including . . . His mind tuned the voice out. He could have recited them by heart. No smoking, no alcohol, no eating in the room, no tampering with equipment or medication. He was free to use the toilet, or drink from the water fountain; if he required something else, he could ring for an attendant. He could stay two hours, but he would have to leave immediately if his aunt required active medical treatment. He nodded, as always, and exchanged his entrance pass for a unit pass that gave him access only to his aunt's treatment unit. The receptionist, safe behind her counter, hardly looked at him except for a quick glance at his face.

"And no flowers," the receptionist said to his departing back.

Sometimes they offered an escort; if they were busy, they didn't. This time no staff member came to check on him, and he strode along a neat stone pathway edged with flowers, free to think without interruption.

If they failed, his aunt would die. He was sure of that— either they made a clean getaway, or whoever had done this would kill her. Or you, his mind said suddenly, forcing on him an image of himself in Cecelia's state. He shuddered; sweat ran cold down his back. He saw, without registering them, other people walking on other paths: family members of other patients, staff in the cheerful, bright coveralls they wore. The treatment units, low stone-faced buildings scattered among trees and lawns and flowerbeds, looked like expensive apartments. The path led him around one, then another. He saw a terrace outside one, with someone in a hoverchair talking to two people in normal clothes. Off to one side, on a smooth stretch of lawn, a patient struggled to walk from a hoverchair to a picnic table spread with food.

At last he came to the final row of buildings, to Cecelia's treatment unit. Like the others, it was stone-faced and low, with a covered terrace on this side. The terrace on the far side had no roof; that should make it easier. He put his card in the door, which slid open. Inside, the expected staff member, this time the gray-haired man in yellow, who checked his pass, his ID, and reminded him again of the rules.

"She's having a good day," the man said with a wide smile. "And I've just finished toileting and bathing her; she's all fresh and sweet for you." Ronnie wanted to gag, but managed to thank the man. "If she could see," the man went on, "she'd have a perfect view of the Festival . . . at least you can enjoy it."

Ronnie wondered whether a fake sulk or a pretense of boredom would be better. "I wish I could," he said, letting his anger edge that. "If I hadn't—I mean—my regiment's got a contestant up."

"Ah—balloon or glider?"

"Both, of course." Ronnie pulled himself up and tried for pompous. It had been easy last year, when he still thought the regiment's place in the air races mattered.

"Well, you can see them through her window . . . or, if you wish, open the sliding door onto the west terrace. It won't bother her." Again, that faint cynical edge.

Ronnie shook his head. "I'd better not. If Mother found out I was neglecting Aunt Cecelia to look at the Festival, she'd skin me."

The man laughed. "I won't tell. Go ahead."

"I think she gets the tapes or something; she knew last week when I read for half an hour." He had read for half an hour, setting up this situation; his mother hadn't mentioned it, but he was sure tapes were being made, and someone at this level shouldn't know how many people got copies.

Now the man looked uneasy. "Oh . . . ah . . . that's easy to arrange. I can put it on a loop, for . . ."

Ronnie took the bait. "Would you? I'd be terribly grateful. It can't matter to Aunt Cecelia; you're all very tactful about it, but the doctor said her brain was gone. And if I have to spend all today cooped up in here, just looking at her and pretending to talk to her—" He held out his credit chip. "I'd like to buy a fruit punch, too . . ." The man fed the chip into the unit reader, flicking the buttons, and handed it back to Ronnie when it popped free. The cash—how much Ronnie couldn't tell—never actually changed hands.

"What you do," the man said, "is go in there and act normal for about ten minutes. Don't just sit still: pour some water, touch her hand, sit down, stand up, talk to her softly. Then come out, and go to the toilet; I'll loop the tape at that point and only an expert will know you're just repeating things for the rest of your visit. See this button? Push it when you leave, and it'll put the tape back to realtime."

"Thanks," Ronnie said. He had no idea if the man was honest, or honestly dishonest, but it was worth a try.

He went in and for ten minutes that felt like ten years acted like a bumbling, nervous, miserable nephew . . . as near as he could, the same he'd acted in all his visits. The bed's automatic movements still made him nervous; it looked and sounded as if some animal were rolling and twisting under the covers. He stroked Cecelia's cool, dry brow, and her thin, wrinkled, flaccid hands; he murmured to her, then turned away to wipe his eyes and pour himself a glass of water. Finally he left, and went into the toilet in the outer room. When he came out, the man in yellow stood by the outside door, gave him a final thumbs-up, and left.

Ronnie went back to Cecelia and sat there a little longer before letting himself look outside. Behind Cecelia's unit, the clinic land ran down to the river, a meadow mowed just too high for comfortable walking. He could see four or five balloons from inside the room, one quite low . . . but it was the wrong color. A parasail slid across, a long low glide that ended with a landing at the far end of the meadow. Ronnie gave Cecelia a kiss on the brow, and then walked over and opened the glass door to the terrace.

Balloons crowded above him, the whoosh of the burners much louder now. The air smelled fresh, the scent of mown grass mingling with a faint tang of smoke from the burners. He heard laughter, shouts, shrill cries of excitement or dismay. People hung over the edges of baskets and waved; he waved back. Some balloonists could indeed steer, he saw: not all used the same method, but he saw balloons wallowing across the wind with the aid of propellers, compressed-air jets, and even oddly-shaped "rudders." All in brilliant colors, in stripes and stars and plaids . . . he took a quick look at his watch, then tried to peer upwind. She ought to be here soon.

And he had to unhook his aunt from her monitors, praying that the attendant had been honest, that the tape was on a loop, that the loop included her monitors. He ducked back inside, and put on the thin surgical gloves he'd brought. Inside his own shirt and slacks were clothes for her—pants and shirt, socks, soft slippers. Folded flat between his jacket and its lining was a thin balloonist's coverall with garish stripes. Bubbles was supposed to bring something to cover Cecelia's hair.

Quickly, with a murmured apology, he threw back the covers. The sight of her thin white legs, her feet strapped into braces "to prevent contractures" nearly broke his concentration. As gently as he could, he unstrapped them, and struggled to put her socks on. He had never dressed even a child; he had no idea how hard it was to put socks on without cooperation. Then he lifted her legs and worked each foot into one leg of the slacks. She seemed so much heavier than she looked; he was having to tug and yank at her. He hoped it didn't hurt.

Bubbles had warned him what he might find next. The tubes, the bags . . . he didn't want to think about it, let alone look at it or touch it—but he had to. He glanced, feeling the blood rush to his face even though he was alone with an unconscious woman. Nothing. His breath came out in a gasp. She must have had—his mind, avoiding the present, struggled for the phrases—that surgery which implanted a programmable sphincter control. Without really looking, he wrestled the slacks up to her hips, and with a skillful lift he'd practiced on Bubbles, all the way up to her waist. He wouldn't have made it without that practice; he should have practiced all the dressing, but he'd assumed it would be easier. Perhaps the attendants who cared for her did more than guard against intruders.

His eyes registered the scars on her belly, but he refused to stop and stare at them. Now for the rest. He risked another quick glance outside, and saw the rose and silver balloon in the distance. He ducked back inside; he had to work quickly.

The bed sighed and gurgled, arching against his knee. He wished he knew how to turn it off. Of course it had saved Cecelia from pressure sores, but he couldn't lean against it without his skin crawling. Trying not to feel anything at the sight, he pulled open the front of the clinic gown. He had to find the ports through which she was fed, suctioned, medicated. A flat, peach-colored plastic oval on her upper chest must be one; three little caps stuck up like grotesque nipples, one blue, one green, one yellow. Behind her right ear, another plastic oval, this one with a silver nipple.

If the monitors don't use external wires—and most don't these days—they'll have built-in transmitters to either the bed, with relays to a nursing station, or direct to the nursing station. He remembered that, the quiet voice of the specialist. *Either sort can transmit up to thirty meters.* Which meant that nothing should show on the monitors—even if they were being watched—until Cecelia was more than ten meters from the bed. He had that much time to get well away from the unit, before the alarms went off.

No external wires today, and nothing connected to the ports. It should have been simple, but the feel of his aunt's flaccid body, as he pulled her forward, pulled off the gown, and worked her arms into the shirt, made it difficult. Now the coverall . . . this was quicker, since it had been designed to fit loosely over clothes, and since he had practiced how to put it on Brun. Of course, she wasn't as limp, even when she tried to lie still. He rolled Cecelia up on one side, fighting the wavelike motion of the bed, and got foot and hand into the loose sleeves. He worked the coverall close under her, then rolled her back over, tugged—and fitted the second arm and leg in. Then the pressure seals . . . and now she looked like a fallen balloonist, a normal person, a real person.

It must have taken hours; Bubbles would have drifted past. He was vaguely aware of sounds from outside, hoots and cries and angry voices back toward the main buildings, laughter and shouts from the meadow. He picked his aunt up, again surprised at how heavy she was, and moved near the door. The rose and silver balloon blocked his view upwind; he looked up to see Bubbles's white face staring back at him. The balloon sagged heavily, the basket scraping through the ornamental hedge between the next unit and this; it tilted half-over before breaking free. Then it dragged along the ground, and bumped the edge of the terrace.

"Now!" Bubbles said. "I can't stop it—"

Ronnie lunged outside, clumsy with the weight in his arms. He staggered into the side of the basket; Bubbles grabbed his aunt by the shoulders and pulled. Together, they got her over the basket's rim and in, although she landed heavily almost on her head.

"Straighten her out!" Ronnie said urgently, as the balloon pulled the basket along. "Get her head up—"

"Get back inside!" Bubbles snarled. He wanted to protest, but her hand was already on the burner control, and the roaring flame drowned out anything he could say. He looked around. Bubbles's balloon had blocked his view of the meadow and the air overhead; he hoped it had blocked others' view of the basket for that critical few moments. Now that it was past, he could see that the meadow roiled with balloons, parasails, even two gliders being hastily dewinged for transport.

When he went back into the empty room, the open bed seemed to stab his heart; his eyes filled. Forcing himself to be calm, he checked the IV pump and stripped off the medicine label—it might or might not help, but it was worth a try. Then he pulled the covers up and went into the unit's front room. He badly wanted to use the toilet, but didn't dare take the time. Now he had to get out—to be seen leaving, with nothing in his hands, and no aunt slung over his shoulder. He reached for the outer door, and remembered that he still had on those gloves. He was supposed to have put them in the basket for Bubbles to take away. Instead, he'd have to have them in his pocket, along with the medicine label.

On the east terrace, he could see more of the confusion wrought by the Festival of the Air participants. Someone's balloon had caught its basket solidly in a large tree, and attendants and balloonist were having a loud argument about it. Several other balloons had apparently dropped baskets of confetti and party toys, which littered lawns and walkways.

"We're just having a picnic!" he heard someone say—someone over his head, in the tree-trapped basket. "And we thought your old geezers might like to see a little color and life—"

"It's trespass," said a dark-coated man that Ronnie recognized as an administrator.

"Hi, Ronnie!" called a girl in the same basket. He peered up; the administrator, he knew, was watching him. "Come to our picnic."

He made himself laugh. "Picnic? In a tree? What are you idiots doing this time?"

"We're headed down to the shore, but Corey had a bet with George on who could drop a marker square in the middle of the administration building—"

"Why?" Ronnie asked, amused in spite of himself. It was the sort of thing George would think of. All they had told him was that they needed lots of balloons hanging around the nursing home on some ridiculous pretext.

"I don't know." The girl, whom he vaguely remembered from last Season, had dyed her hair in streaks of green and blue, and wore a tan coverall with one blue and one green arm. "Somebody said this would be a good place. Cheer up the patients who couldn't come to the Festival. Anyway, why not climb up and come along?"

"Because you're not going anywhere," Ronnie pointed out. "Not until you get out of that tree. Besides, your balloon is deflating—haven't you noticed?"

"Oh." The girl looked and shrugged, then turned on the young man. "I told you you were too low, Corey. We'll be stuck here for hours, and the others will have all the fun."

"You could ride with me," Ronnie offered. "It's not as much fun as flying there, but more fun than hanging in a tree like an ornament."

"No!" The administrator looked angrier than ever. "Unauthorized persons cannot just wander around unsupervised. You—" He turned on Ronnie. "Where's your pass?"

"Here." Ronnie held it out. "I'm on my way out; couldn't I escort Andalance? It's not her fault."

"She's an intruder. A trespasser—"

"Oh, come on. It's the *Festival*—" Corey sounded both angry and slightly drunk. "She's my date—"

"She didn't trespass intentionally," Ronnie said. The longer he stood here arguing, the more obvious it was that he didn't have his aunt hidden on his person. He told himself that the gloves in his pocket didn't really glow bright yellow, either. "And it would get her out of your tree. Or I could help free the basket—it looks like you've got other problems, too."

"No," the man said again, handing Ronnie's pass back. "It would be most helpful if you would simply check out now. If we clear the property of legitimate guests it will be easier to deal with these—" He glared upward. Corey made a rude noise.

"Well—if that's what you want—" Ronnie shrugged, and turned away, looking he hoped like someone reluctant to leave. He gave a last glance up to the trapped basket. "I'll take your place, shall I, Corey? Sing by the bonfire and all?"

"You can't go; you aren't flying," Corey yelled back.

"I can pick up a parasail at home—there's still enough daylight. Enjoy your treehouse." Ronnie walked on, ignoring the jeers behind him. He made himself walk slowly, looking up when a balloon's burner whooshed overhead, grinning and shaking his head when a shower of glittery confetti covered him in blue and turquoise. At the main desk, a crowd of visitors clustered, complaining about the noise and confusion, about being forced to leave early. Ronnie handed his pass to the harried receptionist with a shrug and smile, and accepted the gate pass she gave him.

Someone tapped his shoulder and said, "Isn't your aunt in that last row?"

"Yes, why?" Ronnie said without flinching.

"All that noise—and I saw one balloon land almost on top of that row, dragging the basket along—"

"Must have been after I left," Ronnie said. "It won't bother her, I'm sorry to say."

"Oh?" The avid curiosity of the other man annoyed Ronnie, but he knew he must answer.

"She's in a coma," he said. "Has been for months."

"Oh, well, that's not so bad. But still. My father nearly had another stroke, when he saw someone fall out of a basket and have to climb back in."

"It's just the Festival," Ronnie said vaguely and turned away. He had to get out of here. He made it out the door, down the long walk to the gatehouse, in a clump of departing visitors. Another low-flying balloon nearly scalped him—someone behind yelled a warning—and the guard at the gatehouse was shaking his head when he collected the gate passes.

"Every year or so they get wild like this. No, madam, I don't know why. The administration sends warnings out to all the Families and the Clubs, but every so often they take it into their heads to ignore the rules. Can't explain it. I don't think it's so bad myself; patients might enjoy a bit more color and excitement, but I can see why it riles the staff. Like this young gentleman here, with that blue confetti—what fell on the ground, someone's got to clean up."

He had made it to his own vehicle; he had started it up. Others crowded the exits; he glanced behind, half-expecting to see someone running to stop him. But nothing. He was on the road home; no one signalled him, no pursuit appeared. At home he faced the tricky part. While his parents had agreed that "something must be done" it had been clear that whatever was done must be done secretly. None of them ever discussed possibilities. For all he knew, they had their own plans to rescue Cecelia, and he had just ruined them. Then again, maybe they'd given up. But they certainly had no idea what he'd been part of. Suddenly the casual self-invitation to the beach party sounded like just the thing.

He left a message on the house board, and went to get his parasail out of storage.

CHAPTER ELEVEN

Brun crouched as the burner roared, and pulled the blanket she'd brought along over Cecelia's crumpled form. Finally— it always seemed to take too long—the balloon rose with a jerk, and the basket hung straight beneath it. "Sorry!" Brun yelled down at someone who had had to dive away from the basket on the terrace behind another unit. "Bad currents." She watched ahead: there. She could continue to ascend between that balloon and the other—and there was just room to use the directional thruster as well. Carefully, while tossing sackfuls of confetti out with one hand, she set the thruster controls and pumped the burner.

The idea had been to rise directly above Cecelia's unit, in hopes of not triggering any alarms when her monitor-transmitters went out of range, and then catch a strong wind home. But the surface breeze, twisting between the units and deflected as well by so many jostling balloons, didn't cooperate. She was already more than thirty meters from the room where Cecelia's bed had been; she needed to gain altitude and start running *now*.

Her balloon rose; she felt the pressure in her boots. Now she could see over the last row of units. Was that Ronnie, walking toward the administration building? Someone had caught a basket in a tree; that balloon, deflating, draped itself over the tree like a discarded party dress. She didn't envy the owner. If they got it out at all, there'd be plenty of rips to repair. A vast green-and-silver surface blocked her view as it slid by, someone else's balloon. Out the other side, she saw yellow striped with light blue. Above, her own balloon blocked her view. She had to hope that she didn't bump into someone from below.

Now she was higher than most of the others—than anyone near. Behind and below, balloons obscured her view of the nursing home and its meadow. Most were still aflight, but some were on the ground, surrounded by clumps of people. Ahead and higher were other balloons headed for the shore, but no one was near her. That in itself was dangerous . . . anyone might notice the color of a balloon that lifted too suddenly from the nursing home. She looked back again, glad to see that five or six others were rising as fast now. They would block a clear view of hers from the ground.

She let go the burner controls. In the sudden silence, she checked her gauges. Still rising, slowly. She knelt beside the crumpled shape, and as gently as she could tugged Cecelia to a half-sitting position. The older woman's skin was cold, but she had a strong regular pulse and she seemed to be breathing normally. Brun stuffed a pillow under her head.

"It's Brun, Lady Cecelia. If you can hear me—we've got you out. Here, smell this." She tugged out her riding gloves, and laid them against Cecelia's face. A nostril fluttered. "That's it. Horse and dog and out-of-doors. I can't talk more—we're in the air."

She stood up again. Behind, the other balloons were gaining altitude on her; the nursing home was now a blur of dark trees and bright meadow, the units scarcely visible. With any luck, the attendants were still too busy with the chaos to be watching her.

From here, at this altitude, the wind would take her straight to the picnic site on the shore. Above, the northbound current of air should be shifting as the front neared, and the southbound current above that would sweep her past the shore, on across the bay to the peninsula where her landing crew waited. She eyed the clouds to the west.

The residual sense of where her body was jolted Cecelia into wakefulness. Something was wrong. Pressures in the wrong place, strange noises—yelling voices in the distance, harsh roars—and then she felt herself falling, and cramped into a position she could not change. She smelled a fuel gas, and something that reminded her of flower baskets without the flowers. And, in great gusts, the fresh green smell of spring she had been kept from. Mown grass, oak trees, the bitter tang of willow. Outside? She was outside?

It must be the rescue she had prayed for. Overhead, the roaring went on and on; she felt a vague nausea. Then the roaring ceased. In the silence, she heard distant roars, distant voices, and the nearby creaking of . . . baskets again? She felt herself being moved. Then the scent of horse and dog and leather, and the girl's voice, reassuring her.

She wanted to cry for joy; she wished she could move a finger, at least. But it was enough, just to be out of that place.

"There's a chance of surveillance," Brun said above her. "I can't talk to you all the time—but don't be afraid."

She wasn't afraid now. She wasn't afraid for the first time since the hospital. If the balloon—she had put together her memories of the roaring burner, the smell of gas, the sound of wicker—fell out of the sky and killed them both, she would not be afraid. Not now.

She busied her mind with interpretation of the smells that rose from below through the basket. That made it easier to ignore the lurch in her stomach every time the burner roared and the balloon lifted abruptly. At some point they flew near enough to a bakery to sail through a gust of aroma from new bread, and she tried to guess which city. She recognized the damp-rot smell of the shore, and wanted desperately to ask which shore . . . because she began to feel she almost knew where they were.

"Heading southeast," Brun said, as if she'd heard the question. "Out over water, and into a little weather. Now that we're farther from shore, I'll put the rain cover on you."

She heard the rustle of it, and later the spat of raindrops. The air smelled rich and clean, heady. She wanted to breathe in, and only in, forever. She would have been glad to have the rain on her face. Her skin felt starved for the moistness, the changing pressures.

The landing, when it came, produced a jolt she could feel. Then the disorienting sensation of being put in all the wrong positions. Hauled out like a sack of grain, she thought. I certainly can't help. Brun said little, only brief phrases to the others—how many others?—who were handling her. Then a familiar position, flat on her back on some surface, but a vibration rumbling the entire surface.

The scents of a spring night still enchanted her. They must be in a vehicle with open windows: she could smell the new grass, a fruit orchard in bloom, all the good smells of open country. No one talked; all she could hear was the windrush outside. When the vehicle stopped, she felt movement again, as her surface (bed? stretcher?) was lifted out and rolled somewhere. She sniffed again. This smelled mechanical, almost industrial. Metal, plastics, pavement . . . something that sounded like a very large door on rollers, with metallic echoes beyond. A warehouse? A factory?

Another lift, and she was in a different set of smells. Almost all plastics and fine oils, like a . . . like a . . . shuttle. A shuttle—she was being shipped offplanet? Still no conversation, just the faint sounds of feet on the floor, and the snick of buckles fastening. If I were making this up, Cecelia thought, I would figure out some way for my heroine to communicate. It's entirely too boring to lie here knowing nothing.

Footsteps moved away, and something went *chunk* with the finality normally associated with hatches closing. She could feel no more vibration—no, there it was, the slightest rhythmic thump that must be tires passing over seams on the runway.

Her mind ran through the private shuttleports, and decided they were at Bunny's Crown residence. She felt the firm pressure of acceleration on her body, and the rhythmic bumps came closer together . . . then ceased. Wherever they were going, they were on the way. Wherever they were going, it had to be better than where she'd been.

"I'm sorry I couldn't talk to you earlier," Brun said. Her hand, smelling of soap lightly pine scented, lay along Cecelia's cheek. "Those who helped me could not know who you were." She chuckled, and went on. "They think you're a drunken friend of mine, who's going to wake up on Station as the result of a Festival wager. You're wearing balloonist gear, and it's fortunate you don't look your age. You probably wonder why we took the risk of taking you offplanet right away."

Cecelia hadn't yet wondered that, but now she did. Why not simply hide her somewhere until she recovered?

"We expect a solid search effort," Brun went on. "We weren't sure if they'd implanted a locator of some kind, and we wanted you out of range of detectors. And they might start checking private shuttle flights after tonight. Luckily, with the Festival, there's sure to be more than one private shuttle up. And . . . we don't know how long your recovery will take."

Behind that, Cecelia caught a concern that it might not come. She wanted to signal, to convince Brun that she was alive inside, but nothing worked.

"We need to get you to good medical care—someone we know is safe, and not part of the plot—in a place where it won't be interrupted."

The questions she could not ask whirled through Cecelia's mind. What about Ronnie? Where were they going? What had happened to her own yacht? And Heris? What kind of medical care, and how did Brun know the doctors were safe, and how long was it going to take to get her life back? She didn't even know exactly how long she'd been like this— months, at least, because the Festival was in spring, but she couldn't remember exactly when *it* had happened. She did remember that rehabilitation took longer the longer someone was down.

"It's going to seem disjointed, I know." Brun's voice had the edge that came from trying to stay calm when it wasn't easy. "First yanking you out of that bed and into the balloon basket, and then into the shuttle—and the transfer at Rockhouse Minor is going to be tricky, too—and we've got a priority undock already filed. We couldn't get most of the equipment Dad's neurologist said we needed onto the yacht, so some things will have to wait until we get where we're going."

Which she still hadn't said. Cecelia wondered if Brun knew, or if she had a reason not to say it aloud. She'd already said enough to make any surveillance tapes dangerous.

"Actually we're still arguing about that." Again, it was as if Brun had read her thoughts. "The specialists want you at a major medical facility, but Dad says that's too dangerous; whoever did this is bound to be checking the

best-known facilities. He wanted you back home, but your
Captain Serrano said the same argument applied to that.
She thinks you ought to be somewhere with horses, some-
where obscure. There's a couple of possibilities—Dad's
been checking them out, and once we get to the yacht,
I'll have his latest advice. But there's the medical problem."

The medical problem. Whatever had been done to her,
whatever might be undone. She wanted to argue her own
case, demand the risks of the top specialists, explain who
might have done this, and why. But that would have to wait
until she could talk—if she ever could.

Cecelia surprised herself by falling asleep in the shuttle.
Real sleep, deep comfortable sleep. She felt safe, with Brun's
hand on her cheek, safer than she had felt in months.

When she woke, the voices overhead sounded medical
again, and for a moment she panicked. But the medicinal
smells interwove with more pleasant ones, and Brun's voice
made up part of the conversation.

"—better strip the programming on those sphincters." A
woman's voice; she sounded as if she were scowling.
"We'll want to keep her hydrated, but we don't want any
distension."

"But let's check the drug port—they may have an implanted
delivery system, and there might still be residuals."

"Just remember that she can hear you," Brun said, from
a little distance. "Talk to her, not just about her." Then,
taking her own advice, she spoke to Cecelia. "You're on the
yacht now; I think you went to sleep for a while, though
it's hard to tell. You've got Dr. Czerda and Dr. Illik with
you, right now."

"I'm Czerda," the woman's voice said. "I'm a geriatric
neurologist, with special interest in pharmacological insults.
I'm checking the ports on your chest: cardiac monitor, venous
access, feeding tube. There's a . . . yes . . . a set of three
miniature pumps in the venous access. I'm going to have
to take these out very carefully . . ." Cecelia could just feel
a faint tug, disconcerting but not painful. "Brun—if you'll
take these over to the bench there—"

"Can you tell what the drugs are?" Brun asked.

"Probably. At least we can tell the class, and if it's refer-
enced we can identify it precisely. If not . . . it may take a
while. What the drugs do is my specialty, but identifying them

isn't. We can get it done, though. Now . . . I'm going to leave the rest of this in; we'll want the cardiac monitor and the venous access, although I hope we can get her—you, sorry— off the feeding tube and back on oral."

"I've got the signals on the implants," the man's voice said. "Standard Zynnis model fives, and we have the manuals." His voice came toward Cecelia's head. "Brun says you're hearing us; I know that's possible. I'm Dr. Illik; you met me at Sirialis when young Ronnie was in the hospital there. I was the tall skinny bald one." Cecelia remembered a pleasant, homely face and jug ears. "We're going to give you the same kind of care that you had, except that we'll be triggering your bladder implant more often. Right now you need that again; it's been over twelve hours." He sounded embarrassed; Cecelia had long given up embarrassment. It wasn't her fault someone else had to operate her once-private functions. She could tell when they changed her body position, although she wasn't sure how much, and she could hear the result when the implant opened. It did feel better, although she'd hardly known what the vague discomfort was.

"We're not going to mess with your cranial access right now," Czerda said. "There's a small chance they put in a lockout circuit that could hurt you if we didn't key in correctly. I want a full readout of everything else first, and we're going to try to get your cranial implant to talk to our monitors. So far it's not. But I would like to see if you can swallow. We did that ultrasound when you first came aboard, and I don't think they bothered to do an esophageal pinch."

Cecelia had no idea what an esophageal pinch was, but assumed it had something to do with whether or not she could eat. The thought of actually tasting food again thrilled her. Her mouth filled with saliva. Surely she had to be able to swallow, or she'd have choked before now.

"Now . . . what I'm going to put at your lips is a soft plastic nipple, on a water bottle. When you feel it, try to suck."

She felt nothing, then a dull bump as something hit a tooth. She tried to suck, but wasn't sure she remembered how. She had not had anything in her mouth in a long time.

"Serious loss of sensation," Czerda said. "Let's see . . ."

A cool wetness tasting faintly of lemon filled her mouth.

Cecelia swallowed without thinking; her tongue felt ungainly and misshapen, but she didn't choke.

"Very good," Czerda said. "That time I squeezed some out; I'd like you to do it this time."

Cecelia struggled with a recalcitrant tongue and cheek muscles that no longer worked willingly. A tiny drip rewarded her, then a trickle.

"That's too much," Illik said. "Look at the cardiac monitor—she's straining."

"But it's something." Czerda sounded angry. "Even a tiny, weak suck, and we know she's still got that. Let's see about something else—"

This time it was cold, and sweet, and smooth . . . a chilled custard, perhaps. The flavor developed in Cecelia's mouth, from the initial sweetness to a rich, fruity taste . . . and she was able to swallow the spoonful, savoring the feel of it all the way down her throat. Date-caramel custard, with a touch of almond essence, she thought.

"Oh, very good," Czerda said. "Brun, do you happen to know what foods she liked best?"

"She had one of the best cooks anywhere," Brun said. "She liked good food, all kinds." Not all kinds, Cecelia thought. Prustocean cuisine is ghastly, and there's no way anyone can cook Abrolc cephalopods so they don't taste like oily rubber. Surely Brun could remember her favorite spices, at least.

"Great. If she can eat custards now, she'll be able to eat solids very soon. I'm glad I insisted on including a dietician in the primary team." Dietician! Cecelia wanted to glare. Dieticians thought more of nutrition than flavor; she imagined herself with a mouthful of pureed halobeets, unmitigated by spices. "We'll leave the feeding tube access in, just in case, but the sooner she's on an oral diet, the sooner we can get her an oral communication system."

"You mean talking?"

"No, not at first." Cecelia hoped she was wrong about the undertone that suggested *Maybe never.* "Her inability to talk could be all neuromuscular—loss of control of voluntary muscles of speech—or it could also involve central language problems. I suspect the latter. But if she can swallow, that means she can control her tongue and breath—and that means she can learn to suck and blow, and that means she can use a mechanical system to signal. Yes and no, at least, and probably a lot more."

"But if she can swallow, then why can't she move her jaw?"

"Good question. It could be a local paralysis, either from an injection into the nerve, or maintained by the drugs we found in that packet. Or, in a woman her age, it could be simple arthritis of the temporomandibular joint. If they kept her jaw immobilized for long enough, muscle atrophy and arthritis together could produce what seemed to be paralysis. At any rate, until she has control of her jaw, she can't chew. We can open and close it—and we will—but that's not really chewing."

Cecelia knew exactly whom she'd bite if she had the chance, these long-winded idiots who blathered on as if she weren't there.

Lorenza grimaced when the light flashed on her deskcomp. Someone wanted her badly enough to override the recorded message explaining that she wasn't available. She hated being interrupted after dinner. It had better be a real emergency. She picked up an impressive-looking pile of documents before flicking the screen on. That way whoever it was would know she had been interrupted in the midst of real work.

On the screen, Berenice's distorted face looked much older, as if her rejuv were failing all at once, and her words at first made no sense. "She's gone! She's gone!"

"Who?" A maid, a cook, even a pregnant cow, thought Lorenza idly. Why did people think she was a mind reader?

"Cecelia!" Berenice said, too loudly. "She disappeared from the home sometime today. After Ronnie's visit, in fact; he says she was certainly there when he was. The attendant who let him in remembers that—"

"Maybe Ronnie's playing a prank." Lorenza's mind raced. Crazy young men did such things. Cecelia gone? What would it mean? She felt cold, and then excited. "Perhaps he took her out for a joyride or something." Perhaps another enemy had abducted her, raped her, killed her.

"No—there was some kind of mixup with the Festival, lots of balloonists coming down in that meadow, and some getting caught in the trees. Lots of people saw Ronnie leave, and he was alone. Besides, he's as confused as I am—I can tell; I'm his mother. Lori, she's *gone*. She'll *die* without care—I can't bear to think of it—" Berenice, who had quarrelled with Cecelia for years, still actually cared about her. Lorenza thought that was stupid, but knew better than to argue that Cecelia was better off dead. Especially for her own purposes.

"Who do you think—could it be that awful yacht captain?"

"Oh, no. She's been gone for weeks—and she couldn't have come back in the system without being caught. It's just—I can't figure out why anyone would do this!" Lorenza made soothing noises. She could think of several reasons, and after a while produced the one she thought most useful.

"There's always kidnapping for ransom, although in her condition most such people would expect you to abandon her. Perhaps . . . someone, some business associate, wants to do something with her assets. If they produced an imposter, and claimed she'd recovered . . ."

"I hadn't thought of that." Berenice's voice had calmed; she might be overemotional, but she wasn't stupid. Not really. "We've had auditors checking things over to be sure that captain hadn't been embezzling—maybe someone else was."

"Or maybe that captain had an ally," Lorenza said.

"I'll tell Gustav," Berenice said firmly, and cut off what Lorenza was about to say.

Surely it would be all right. Someone had kidnapped a helpless old lady—it would be either for ransom or—the idea made more sense the longer she thought about it—to produce an apparently recovered imposter, whose remaining lapses of memory and function could be laid to the injury. Or Cecelia herself, with an AI unit implanted so that she seemed to speak what someone else had chosen. If they had enough time, whoever had done this, they could even produce a clone-Cecelia. Of course, not even a clone-Cecelia would know what had been done to her, or how, or who.

She was, therefore, unprepared for the second call, from her medical agent.

"What do you mean, trouble?" she asked airily. "It's nothing to do with us; I didn't snatch her."

"Have you forgotten what I told you? She needs maintenance doses—and anyone who scans her now will find those implants. If they're removed, a high-level scan will show brain activity."

"You said it was irreversible." She fought the impulse to scowl at the screen. She never scowled; scowling caused wrinkles.

"Under the circumstances we had, yes. But not in a medical facility I can't get into, or send someone to. Oh, she'll never get up and walk off—at least, I don't think so—but once someone suspects she's still cognating, they'll start looking at her old scans and know they were falsified. And then they'll figure out how, and that leads to who. I want out—I want transportation and a lump sum, enough to live on—"

"Wait a minute—you're running out on me? Won't that make it obvious you did it?"

"Not if you set it up right. Do you know what they do to medical professionals who do something like this? I'll be in therapeutic reassignment the rest of my life. No. I want out. You've got to get me out of here."

"But you say she can't really recover . . ."

"Of course not. Not really. But they don't need *her* testimony to put me at risk, I tell you. And if they catch me, I'll tell them who it was—I've no reason to protect you if I'm going to prison. It's to your advantage to keep me safe."

"I see. Well, then . . . it will take me a day or so . . ." To choose which way to eliminate this unstable and most undesirable of accomplices. To make sure it would not be traced to her. To see if it could possibly be done in person . . . she would miss the visits to Cecelia, the chance to savor that triumph. This one could make up for it.

CHAPTER TWELVE

The transfer station at Naverrn had none of the luxury and elegance of Rockhouse Major. It was as large—it had to be, to handle the transfers of entire troopships—but only in the Exchange did any civilians color and brighten the drab corridors and docksides. The *Better Luck* had come in, with its new identity unchallenged—just another scruffy little tramp freighter and her slipshod crew.

"Recognition's supposed to be easy," Heris said, eyeing the material she'd been given. "The prince has seen me; I've seen him."

"But the double," said Petris. "You might mistake the double for the prince."

"The double doesn't know me. He won't approach. It's true, both of them will be there . . . but only one will come aboard."

Like all but the restricted stations, Naverrn Station had no objection to civilian traffic—in moderation—and civilians could shop at the Exchange, paying higher prices. Heris was claiming a subcontract with Outworld Parcel, one of the independent companies transferring small hardcopy documents and packages for individuals who preferred not to use the government mail service. The Crown had provided such documents, and arranged for her to dump any business received at a nearby Outworld Parcel main depot.

Heris checked in at the Outworld Parcel local office, handing the clerk the little strip of platinum-embossed plastic. The clerk glanced at her as he fed the strip into the reader. "You're new on this run, aren't you? What happened to Sal?"

Heris shrugged. "Have no idea. I don't ask questions—they shift me around wherever there's a gap."

"Oh. Maybe that port drive pod finally went sour, and he's in refitting." The clerk touched a keypad and a sign lighted up: *Outgoing Active.* "How long are you here for? There's only a few letters now, but if you'll be here long enough for a shuttle from below, I can guarantee at least a 50-kilo cargo."

"How long's that?" asked Heris, as if she didn't know the shuttle schedule already.

"Let me check our downside office," the clerk said, and vanished into a back room. A few minutes later he came out. "You're in luck. They can add the downside accumulation to the next shuttle, and that's tomorrow's. It'll be up here by 1800, but it won't unload until 2000, at least."

"I suppose," Heris said, feigning reluctance. "They didn't say I'd have to wait; it was supposed to be a scoop and run . . ."

"Are you time-locked for your next destination?" That would make it a legal requirement to keep the schedule.

"No." As if she'd just decided, Heris gave a quick nod. "Fine—we can wait. Let me know the mass and cubage when the shuttle lifts. You have the codes." He would return the identification strip when she signed for the outgoing mail.

The Exchange was next door; Heris glanced in at rows of displayed merchandise. Once such places had been her territory; she had paid the lower, military price; she had felt at home. Now—she made herself enter, with a quick smile at the security guard by the door.

"New onstation?" he asked.

"Right. The *Better Luck*; we have a subcontract with Outworld Parcel."

"About time," the guard said, grinning. "I'm expecting a package from my parents—"

"Sorry," Heris said. "I was sent on pickup—we didn't bring anything." The guard glowered at her.

"Dammit! It's been twice as long as government mail, and it's supposed to be quicker."

"The guy at the office said maybe Sal had a drive out and had to go to refitting," Heris said. Offering gossip would at least make her seem knowledgeable about it. "We weren't told—but if that's true, another ship will have picked up that load and be bringing it." She only hoped Sal himself wouldn't show up in the next day or so.

"Well, enjoy yourself," said the guard, in a tone that implied no one could do that on this station. "Shop your little heart out."

Heris wandered around, picking up an entertainment cube and a box of sweets, for which she paid an outrageous price. Having heard this complaint often from civilians while she was still in the Fleet, she grumbled at the guard on her way out. "Dammit, the prices go up every trip—you expect us to maintain you in luxury, while hardworking taxpayers go short—" The guard gave her the same bored look she had given others, and she almost giggled.

Naverrn Station, according to its listings, had no housing for transient civilians, and no recreational facilities—not even a gym, and only one place to eat, a vast and gloomy cafeteria clearly meant to feed hordes of troops in a hurry. Heris glanced into it and realized that her crew would much rather eat off of Oblo's stolen supplies aboard than the sort of mush they'd get here. She wondered why anyone would come up to the Station on liberty; Naverrn itself was a pleasant planet, and the training base (she'd seen the holograms) looked far more attractive than this empty, boring station.

When the shuttle arrived, Naverrn Station took on a spurious gaiety. Heris cast a critical eye on the young officers, and almost immediately thought better of Ronnie and George at their worst. The Royal Aerospace Service (known to those in the Regular Space Service as the Royal ASS) attracted the wealthy and highborn into its officer corps; its enlisted personnel were recruited mostly from those just below the Regular Space Service cutoffs. The young officers sported a foppish uniform with an abundance of braid and shiny metal: sky-blue tunics with cream facings over dark-blue trousers, cream and scarlet piping on every seam, tall shiny boots. No wonder they seemed as businesslike and military as a gaggle of debutantes. Most of them quickly shed their colorful uniforms for even more outlandish and expensive civilian clothes. Whatever sense they might have shown at their duties onplanet, they shed as quickly, and Heris saw little sign of supervision or discipline. She was glad she had no responsibility for them.

Naverrn stationers wouldn't put themselves out for a small tramp freighter, which could be assumed to have no spending power, but fifty familiar Royal junior officers were another matter. Heris could hardly believe it was the same service area she'd seen before. Suddenly there were dozens of attractive young men and women (far more than one per officer, she suspected) strolling the corridors, bait for even more colorful fish. A door that had presented only a blank gray metal face before now opened on a cozy bar with a live band playing in one corner. The smell of real food wafted out another door that Heris hadn't seen. Two sleek, dripping, naked figures chased each other out a door just in front of her; she heard splashes and yells from inside that argued for the existence of a swimming pool.

But where was the prince? He should have had a message—they had sent one in the code given them—and he was supposed to make the contact. She would have no excuse to hang about once she'd collected the Outworld Parcels cargo. She needed to find him—or have him find her—now. She strolled back toward the OP office, to check the status of the cargo.

"Another shift, at least, even with no more problems," the clerk told her. He looked harried; a line of impatient young officers had hand-carried mail and packages to check through. "Tarash is out with something she ate, and Jivi sprained an ankle, but the clinic is packed. It always is, with this bunch."

"Fine. Let me know."

That still didn't find the prince, she thought, as she walked on back to the docking area. Where could he be lurking? Why hadn't he contacted her? Back aboard *Better Luck*, she checked on the progress of the cockroach egg hunt. They had cleared the bridge, and the galleys, and were working on the owner's quarters. If the prince found cockroaches aboard, Heris knew the news would spread. She took a look at what had been an elegant guest suite, in which the prince had travelled from Sirialis. Bare decking and bulkheads, just as in crew quarters, with the bed platform's framing all too visible. Oblo had installed a bare-bones communications node, nothing like the handsome system Cecelia had had, with its touchscreens and voice-response. Plenty of bedding, though, and towels, and those colorful pillows. Worst, though, the suite still held a faint odor of cockroach. Heris realized she was wrinkling her nose. That would never do; she'd send someone to buy an olfactory screen.

Gradually, Cecelia began to regain a sense of structure in her existence. Brun and the other attendants spoke to her often, telling her what time it was, what watch, who was in the room, what they had done, and were about to do. She could not see the light level change, or the colors they described on the walls, but she could imagine it all. She began to know, when she woke, what shift to expect, who would be in the room. So she knew it was morning—ship's morning, early in the main dayshift—when the doctors both arrived to explain her situation as they then understood it.

"Lady Cecelia, I'm now sure that you are able to hear—and, I hope, understand—what we're saying. I'm going to explain what tests we've done, what more we can do aboard the yacht, and what we'll be trying to do later. You may know more about what happened to you than we do, although we're ready to make an educated guess. The drugs we found in the venous access reservoirs consisted of a perfectly ordinary array of cardiac drugs—which would have been dispensed automatically at signals from the cardiac monitor—and some very unusual neuroactive drugs, one of them not in the data banks at all. I suspect that these drugs were merely for maintenance, not the ones that caused the initial damage. We cannot tell yet how much function will return just because you no longer have the maintenance drugs in your system, or how long it will take. It depends on how the damage was done, and whether the maintenance drugs were considered essential or just a safeguard against spontaneous recovery.

"I can tell you that the maintenance drugs targeted voluntary muscle innervation, motor and sensory both. Thus I expect you to regain some sensation of touch, and some ability to move. How much is impossible to say. It is unusual for someone with your level of deficit to be able to breathe spontaneously—they did a fine job of sparing respiratory function. It's amazing that you can hear, and yet the few medical records we were able to get indicate that you couldn't—that your auditory cortex was inactive in the presence of both speech and sound. Either someone fiddled with the scans, or . . . I can't imagine what."

Cecelia struggled to remember the early days, what everyone had said. She knew the lawyer had been told she could not hear; she had heard that. She remembered hearing about the scans that were supposed to prove it. That suggested intentional deception. But she had no way to let Dr. Czerda know what she had heard.

Over the next few days, sensation returned slowly, in odd patches. One time Cecelia woke, she felt the side of her face as if it were a patch of harsh cloth laid on her skull. She felt the slight pressure of air against it from the ventilator. The nurse's gentle facewashing felt like being scrubbed with a broom. Still she could not move, could not flinch away. Later that day, she had an uncanny sensation in her left arm, as if something were crawling down it from shoulder to elbow, and from there along the outside of her forearm to her little finger. The feeling grew to a tingle, then an itch, then a painful throbbing that subsided gradually over far too long a time. Each time Czerda came in, she touched Cecelia everywhere, explaining the process over and over. The monitors they had, crude as they were compared to those in a major neuro ward, showed Cecelia's response . . . and Czerda was mapping the return of sensation. The nurses and Brun massaged her, too . . . and gradually, fitfully, she remapped the feeling of her own body.

Blank patches remained. Her left upper chest had no sensation: Czerda explained that was where the implanted ports were. They'd probably destroyed the innervation there. That was standard practice. She felt nothing on the insides of both arms . . . where the median nerve should have supplied sensation and controlled movement. One foot regained sensation, in a maddening pins-and-needles form, days before the other. Her nose itched.

The first movement, the first *real* movement, came when the nurse's washcloth dripped cold on her shoulder. She flinched . . . and knew she moved even as the nurse exclaimed. She tried again.

"Again!" said Czerda, who had come at the nurse's call. Cecelia twitched again, as proud as if she'd just taken a big drop jump. "That's great. Now try the other one."

Cecelia tried, but couldn't remember how to move that

shoulder. Someone tickled her, just above the collarbone. Ah. Yes. She struggled again, and felt her skin move against the sheet.

"Not as strong, but something. Good progress . . . keep doing that."

She kept doing that, but it didn't seem to lead anywhere. She tried to imagine what it looked like, the twitch of a shoulder. Not as communicative as a facial expression. And no matter how she struggled, she couldn't move her hands. Surely she would have to move her hands to use sign language. Then, three days later, when Czerda had pulled her lower jaw down, she snapped it closed so hard her teeth hurt. She couldn't open it . . . but she could close it when Czerda opened it again. Czerda chuckled.

"Yes—a good response. Now we start your communication training. I know you're an intelligent adult, and I know there's lots you want to say, but we'll start with what we need to know first. We want you to have a yes and a no. Right now your shoulder jerk is your strongest motion: let's try one jerk for yes, and two for no. Understand?"

Cecelia twitched her shoulder with contemptuous ease. She could have done that three days ago—why hadn't they told her? Why hadn't she thought of it?

"Good. Now . . . did you like your breakfast?" Breakfast had been a bland flavor of custard; she had never liked bland anything. She gave two twitches. "Excellent. You may not realize it, but you've just demonstrated that your higher language functions are still intact: you understood both directions and a question form. Did you like lunch?" One twitch. Lunch had been the date-caramel-almond custard, her favorite of the flavors she'd had.

"Now I've got to ask you a lot of boring questions that are standard on neuro-psych exams. And I'm going to record this, on full video, because it may be used in court to establish your competency."

Cecelia hadn't thought of that. Could someone who only twitched one shoulder be considered competent legally? She had thought she couldn't fight that battle until she was well.

"Is your name Cecelia de Marktos?" One twitch. That wasn't her full name, but she used the short form oftener than the long. "Do you know where you are?" Now that was a hopeless question. She knew she was on a yacht, but she had no idea where the yacht was. She shrugged both shoulders, the right more strongly. Apparently that got through; Czerda muttered, "Bad question" and changed it to, "Are you in a hospital?" Two twitches. "Are you in a spacecraft?" One twitch. "Are you aware of the nature of your disability?" One twitch. "Was this disability the result of natural causes?" Two twitches. No one was going to believe this, Cecelia thought. It might convince Czerda, or Bunny, but she couldn't see it working in court. Czerda proceeded to questions of reasoning and general knowledge, most of them ridiculously easy: "Is a circle a geometric solid?" No, of course not. "Is a horse a mammal?" Yes, dummy. "Did you name Heris Serrano a beneficiary in your will?" Yes. Cecelia came alert again. "Did Heris Serrano unduly influence you to make her a beneficiary in your will?" No! She made that twitch as big as she could, and then a muscle in her back cramped. She gasped. Czerda stopped the questions, and patiently massaged the cramp out.

"I wish we could give you muscle relaxants," she said. "But I don't want to risk any more dissociation between your nerves and your muscles. Things are bad enough."

Cecelia wondered what that meant. She had thought things were going well. If she could move a shoulder now, if she could answer questions . . . she pushed aside her own doubts and refused to pay attention to the doctor's. Whatever the medical agenda, her own would include figuring out a way to ask for specific foods, things with more flavor and more texture.

Now, with even that meagre amount of communication, the days moved more swiftly. Would she like to try something with more texture? *Yes* . . . and a mouthful of something soft but grainy—still too bland—challenged her ability to move her tongue and swallow it. Would she like music? *Yes.* This music? *No.* Trial and error—more error than success, at first— remapped her choices in flavors and music. As she had feared, the dietician could not be persuaded to offer really tasty food, and there was no way to say *More garlic, you idiot!* with a twitch of the shoulder.

She learned to move her knees, one by one, and wished someone would think of using the twitch of her other shoulder and both knees for other useful signals, but no one did. Yet. In her mind she fashioned her own code: more, less, not yet, hurry up, enough, go away, question. The question signal would have been really helpful; she had more to ask them, she thought, than they had to ask her. But she realized, from their talk, that they were fully engaged already in discovering what had been done to her, and what might be done about it. For the urgency they conveyed, she could forgive a lot.

"Captain—two young . . . gentlemen to see you." Petris's voice carried some message, but she wasn't sure what. This had to be the prince, and presumably some necessary companion. Valet, bodyguard, whatever. Heris made her way quickly to the access tube.

The prince all right, just the same as she'd seen in Sirialis, with that smug little smile on his face. Beside him—she blinked as she focused on the other face. The same face, rather. Side by side, two apparent princes, both with that smug little smile. Both in uniform, for a wonder . . . her mind ran headlong into the logical flaw here.

The prince and his double, of course, but the prince and his double were not to be seen together. Certainly not here, not now. If someone saw them both enter *Better Luck* and only one of them left . . .

"Welcome aboard," Heris said, trying to think this out. "Mr. Smith, I believe?" She offered the same bland smile to both of them, no longer sure which was which. It was very *good* plastic surgery, she told herself.

"Yes," they said. "Mr. Smith." Even their voices sounded alike, which might mean vocal training or surgery there, too. Impressive, but still stupid. If they'd both come up on the shuttle with the others, then everyone on the Station knew.

"We don't have a lot of time for games," she said, trying for a combination of sweet reason and firmness. "We'll be departing as soon as the Outworld Parcel cargo comes aboard, and in the meantime we'll need to ensure that your . . . er . . . double has appropriate cover."

"I just came to tell you I'm not going," one of the young men said. "I don't want to spend more time on this yacht, especially since it's not even carpeted." He looked at the bare deck and bulkheads with contempt.

"But your father planned—" Heris began. The other young man interrupted.

"If my father insists, let my double do it."

"Sir, it's extremely important—" Heris began, but the first one interrupted this time.

"Besides, I'm perfectly healthy; there's nothing wrong with me. My own physician checked me out after we arrived at Rockhouse." His voice was petulant; Heris wondered if it was really higher, more childish, than it had been. His blue eyes were guileless as a child's; his expression mildly annoyed. Nothing quite fit.

"Your father told us to take you," Heris said. She softened her voice, speaking as she would to a younger child. This time the prince didn't interrupt. "He really wanted you to go— he said you would—"

"But I don't want to," the second young man said. In exactly the same voice.

"But he'll be mad at me," Heris said, in almost the same tone, with the same quaver. She'd seen that work once, with a hysterical Senior Minister. It didn't work this time.

"So?" They both glanced around, boredom and contempt plain on their features. Heris wanted to smack their heads together.

"We shouldn't discuss this here," she said. "Come along to the bridge—you never saw it before, did you?—and we can settle things there."

"It won't make any difference," said one of them languidly. "I'm not going."

Heris refrained from comment, simply gave them the regulation smile that so often got her way. They shrugged and followed her into the ship, scuffing their boot heels on the deck and commenting on the yacht's ugliness in this state. At least they didn't comment on any odd smells—perhaps the last of the cockroach odor had adhered to the powdery scavengers in the air circulation. She stopped by her office, to show the prince and his double the official authorization from the king himself.

"I didn't doubt you," the prince said. She hoped this was the prince. "I quite understand that you are who you are, and my father told you to come get me. But I'm not going." *Oh yes you are, you little tick,* thought Heris. Aloud, she said nothing then, leading the way to the bridge.

"Pretty," the prince said, as if she'd given him a toy he didn't want, and he felt it necessary to be polite. He was looking at Sirkin, she realized after a moment, not the bridge layout at all. Ginese gave him a look and Heris began to hope the other one was the prince. She'd forgotten the prince's temporary attraction to Raffaele; perhaps he liked dark-haired girls best, and considered Sirkin an adequate substitute.

"If you had more girls like this," the double said—or was it the prince?— "I might reconsider. But it simply won't do."

"Perhaps you should take a look around," Heris said. "Your suite is a little bare now, but we've funds to provide some . . . amenities . . . from the Station sources. Let Mr. Ginese show you around—" She gave Ginese another look; he nodded. The prince and his double shrugged.

"It's terribly dull on Station this time—might as well." And they followed Ginese meekly. Heris allowed herself a brief grin.

"Lambs to the slaughter," she said softly. Meharry grinned, but Sirkin looked shocked.

"What are you going to do?" asked Petris.

"I wish you hadn't asked," Heris said. "If we take him by force, that blows the double's cover—and the king said it was important to have the double to cover for him."

"If we don't take him by force, he won't come," Petris said. He had a plug in his ear, listening to the conversation with Ginese somewhere else in the ship. "He's blathering on about the social calendar on the liner where they will have plenty of girls, he says."

"I knew this was a stupid idea," Heris said. "His father should have known he wouldn't want to come. Unless that was the plan. The possibilities for a double cross on this mission are endless." She drummed her fingers on her console. "I'm afraid we're going to have to do it, though. The only way to help Lady Cecelia is to lead the trouble away from her . . . and if we're believed to have kidnapped the prince, everyone in the Familias will be after us."

"How can we be sure we've snatched the right one?"

"Standard ID scan. We've got the data from his father."

"It won't work," said one of the princes, when she put it to them.

"Of course it will," Heris said. "You can't fool a full-ID scan with plastic surgery."

"Fine. Go ahead." He smirked. So did the other prince.

Heris wanted to hit both of them, but thought better of it. If she did, she'd be sure to hit the real prince—and that wouldn't do.

The ID scans of both young men took only a few minutes, but the results made no sense. "Both of them are the prince," said Heris. She heard the disbelief in her voice. "Or neither, if they're identical twins—clones—"

"Clone doubles are illegal," Petris said. "Not that that would stop the Crown."

Heris felt like pulling her hair. "It's . . . ridiculous. *Why* didn't the king tell us—"

"If he knew."

"He must have known. This is just like the slowness— he, of all people, cannot *not* know." Heris glared at the scan results. "How am I supposed to know which is which? Dammit—it's like something out of an entertainment cube, a joke or something. And it's not funny."

"So—what do we do?"

"We take them both," Heris said. "And we keep them separate—we'll have to use the original guest suites—and surely there'll be something in the real prince's memories of the affair on Sirialis that will make it clear who is which."

"Umm. And the . . . er . . . reaction?"

Heris found herself grinning in spite of everything. "Well, you know what they say—when you haven't any other place to step, it doesn't matter which foot lands in the shit first."

CHAPTER THIRTEEN

Naverrn Station expected ships to arrive and depart on their own power—a fortunate circumstance. With Kulkul and Petris on the boards, the *Better Luck* powerup went smoothly, the displays rising through orange and yellow to the steady green of full insystem power. The FTL drive next—it was only slightly risky to powerup the jump units while docked. Using them was another matter; Heris had no intention of risking another near-planet jump.

"Weapons?" Heris asked. Arkady Ginese flashed her a wicked grin.

"Code Two," he said. "We'll go three once we're outside the near-scans." Bringing their weapons to full readiness might set off the Station's own defensive armament. Too many bloody results had taught Stationmasters to take no chances with ships in dock.

"Nav?"

"Ready, ma'am," Sirkin said. Her voice was steady; she had plotted an unusual course around to the Guerni Republic. They both hoped it would confuse any chance encounter, and avoid any confrontation with ships of the Compassionate Hand.

"Naverrn Station, the *Better Luck* requests permission to undock—" Still formal.

"On the count, *Better Luck* . . ." On the count, the cables and umbilicals detached, some coiling back to the Station and others to the ship. Tiny attitude controls nudged the ship back, away from the rotating Station. With the power

on, the ship's own artificial gravity created their internal
field; they felt none of the change in acceleration so visible
in the external monitors as Heris brought in the main drives
and began the long curve out toward the safe jump radius.
Naverrn shrank visibly, the terminator creeping along its blue-
and-white ball as they swung toward the nightside. An hour
passed, then another and another.

"Station scans faded below detection; no other scans
detected," Ginese said. He glanced at her, brows raised.

Heris had considered whether to wait until they made the
first jump transition to bring the weapons up, but that had
its own risk. If they were unlucky, they could come out of
jumpspace into trouble. "Weapons to Code Three," she said.

"Sir," said Ginese; now his board had a row of scarlet
dots at the top, with green columns below. He grinned. "The
tree's lit, Captain."

"Thank you, Mr. Ginese," said Heris formally; she grinned
back at him. "Now if we—"

"Oh, *shit*." No one had to ask what had happened; all
the boards showed it. A ship—a *large* ship, armed, its
weapons ready, had just dropped into the system and painted
them with its scans. And there they were, their own illicit
weaponry up and active, as detectable as a searchlight on
a dark night. "Douse it?"

"Too late," Heris said. "We'd look even more suspicious
if we blanked. We shouldn't be detecting their scans. What
is it?" Their scans should be as good—and the other ship
wouldn't know they had such accurate scans. She hoped.

"Big—military—armed to the teeth, light cruiser. If we're
lucky it's a Royal ASS ship full of rich playboys. Lemme
see—"

"Dumping vee like anything," Oblo commented. "They
came in really hot, and they don't care who knows it. That
turbulence pattern's a lot like—"

"Corsair class. *Not* Royals. Regs. Standard assortment up—"
Which meant about half the total armament. Heris felt a
pang of longing and pushed it away. She had had the bridge
of a Corsair Class cruiser . . . she knew exactly what that
captain would be seeing. And thinking.

"Time to jump status?" she asked.

Sirkin glanced at her. "Emergency, like at Rockhouse?" She
didn't wait for an answer; her fingers were flying on her

board, calling up the data. "Naverrn's a little more massive, and there's that satellite; we should use their combined center of mass for the calculation . . ." Heris didn't interrupt; she had her eye on the other ship's plot as the data points multiplied.

"She'll have her data coming back from us," Ginese said. "She's still on course for Naverrn."

"The angle isn't wide enough yet," Heris said. "Got a beacon strip?"

"Just—now. Fleet beacon . . . now let me see, what did they say the encryption key was?"

Even in the crisis, that got Heris's attention. "You got the encryption key as well as the other stuff?"

"Wouldn't be near as useful without. Ah. Yes. Regular Space Service, we knew that. Corsair Class light cruiser, we knew that. *Martine Scolare*, we didn't know that, and commanded by Arash Livadhi. Worse luck."

"Too true." Heris stared at the scan, and wished it different. The Livadhi family had as long a history in the Fleet as Serranos; a Markos Livadhi had commanded through most of the campaign that established the Familias Regnant.

"Arash Livadhi," said Petris. "That means Esteban Koutsoudas as scanner one. We are really in a nest of comets." Koutsoudas was himself a legend, known for building up entire ships from the faintest data.

"Fourteen minutes, seventeen seconds," Sirkin said. "At our present acceleration and course."

To run or not to run. With Livadhi commanding, with Koutsoudas on scan, the Fleet vessel could not miss them and would not ignore them. The Fleet vessel had a considerable excess of vee; it might find maneuver difficult. Or it might not; a cruiser was by no means as clumsy as a freighter of the same mass.

"Eleven minutes, twenty six seconds at maximum acceleration," Sirkin said, answering the next question Heris would have asked. *Good for her*, Heris thought. *If we get out of this I'll tell her so.*

If they ran, they'd look guilty. But they looked guilty now—she could easily imagine what Arash Livadhi was thinking, arriving insystem to find an absurdly small freighter lighting up his scans with weapons that belonged on his own cruiser. He'd be asking Naverrn Station about them, and Naverrn Station wouldn't have any answers to satisfy him. His curly red hair would be standing up in peaks already; the incredible Koutsoudas (she remembered coveting Koutsoudas for her own crew) would be checking their signature against his personal memory of tens of thousands of ship signatures. Had he ever scanned Cecelia's ship? If so, he would know who they really were. Or did they already—had they been sent here to intercept?

If they ran, they might reach a safe distance for jump transition before Livadhi's equally trained weapons crews could get them. Especially since he'd have to contact them first. But if they ran, he'd follow. If they didn't run, maybe they could brazen it out.

"They have nothing against us," murmured Petris, not giving advice but stating his knowledge.

They could answer the hail that was surely coming; they could spin out a plausible story long enough to make the jump point . . . maybe. Livadhi had always been one to check every detail; he would want not only code but voice communication; not only voice but visual—and there it would all fall apart. Heris felt cold all over. No mere change of uniform would work with Livadhi: he knew her. They had served together as junior officers on the *Moreno Divide*. Moreover, he knew Petris and Ginese by sight; he had been aboard her ship several times, and they'd both been on the bridge. And if he had followed the courts-martial (or any of his bridge crew had) he would know every face on this ship but Sirkin's. Could Sirkin play the role of captain for the time it would take? No. Heris could not ask that.

"Arash Livadhi knows us," Heris said. She advanced power, pushing the insystem drive to the limit listed for the *Better Luck*. She had another ten gravs of acceleration in reserve, but using them would reveal that the beacon data were false. She saw on every face but Sirkin's the recognition. Then came the hail she expected, as if in response to the change in acceleration, though she knew it had originated before. She sent in reply the standard coded message. Oblo grunted.

"They've stripped our beacon. Took 'em long enough."

"I wish I knew if they'd queried the Station yet." Livadhi tended to do things in order, but he had his own flashes of brilliance. If the delay in stripping their beacon meant he'd tight beamed the Station and waited for a reply, he could have known about the disappearance of the prince and his double . . . although Heris hoped no one had noticed yet. The shuttle to the planet wasn't supposed to leave for another eleven standard hours, and she had expected no real search for him until a few hours before boarding. She'd counted on that delay to get out of reach. But he would have the ship's identity as they'd given it to the station; he would have something to compare that beacon blurt with. Worst case, the station might even have sent visuals of the *Better Luck*'s captain.

Heris stared at the display, which attempted to simplify the complex spatial relationships of both ships and the Station, and the planetary mass. The cruiser decelerating relative to the planet; the *Better Luck* accelerating away; the interlocking rotations of planet and satellite and Station. Once the scan computer had plotted the cruiser's course and decel pattern, it displayed blue; changes would come up highlighted in orange. She hoped to see nothing but blue until they jumped, but she expected at any moment an ominous flare.

"Time?" she asked Sirkin.

"Ten minutes four seconds," Sirkin said. Blast. Livadhi was reacting as quickly as ever. And why was he here, anyway? No R.S.S. presence had been expected; nothing the king had given her showed any planned activity near Naverrn at all. Unless this was the king's double cross. It seemed entirely possible.

There. The blue cone caught fire; the tip burned orange. If she were Livadhi, she'd go ballistic, using the planetary satellite's mass to redevelop velocity and swing around, then push the cruiser's insystem drive to its limit to catch up with the trader. That is, knowing what she wanted him to know; *Better Luck*, as built, could not possibly outrun the cruiser to the standard jump distance. Why stress his ship and waste power, when the easy way would work?

But if he knew all of it—if he knew what ship this really was, and who captained her, and what she'd done leaving Rockhouse Major . . . *I do wish we'd been able to mount really effective screens on a hull this size*, she thought. To Sirkin she said, "Display the remaining time to the closest computed jump distance, and give me thirty-second counts." Then, to Ginese, "I expect pursuit and warning. I prefer not to engage at this time." She preferred not to engage at any time, certainly not with Arash Livadhi's cruiser. By any sensible calculation, he could blow them away easily. The orange-tipped blue cone, she saw, was now leaning drunkenly to one side as the scan computer calculated new possibilities. He wasn't going to do it the easy way; he was wasting considerable power to make the course correction necessary for a direct pursuit. That suggested he knew too much already.

Another hail, this one demanding voice communication. Heris grimaced. "At least he's still calling us *Better Luck*," she said. "There's a chance—"

But there wasn't. The scan display showed a white star where the last fleck of orange had been: a microjump. It lit again to show the cruiser much closer, its vector now approaching theirs. Heris admired the precision and daring of that maneuver, even as she wished his navigator had miscalculated.

"Nine minutes, thirty seconds," Sirkin said.

Heris sent a voiceburst, the reply expected from a ship requested to give voice communication, in a directional beam aimed toward the cruiser's previous course prediction but intersecting the new. Livadhi couldn't know about their new scans; he would expect that. He might pick up the reply, or he might hail again. The seconds crawled past; the displays showed their velocity increasing, the distance to a safe jump point decreasing, and the cruiser coming up behind them with a clear advantage in acceleration. Only five gravs, but enough to cut their margin to the jump point dangerously close. Moreover, he had more in reserve once past the kink of the course change, and onto the flatter curve of their own course.

"Nine minutes," said Sirkin.

If he knew, if he guessed, that the ship he chased was *Sweet Delight*, he'd know she had more acceleration in reserve. He'd account for that. But if he thought he was overhauling a ship already at full power, he might not expect that last burst; she might be able to get into FTL before he got her. Heris weighed possibilities. His aggressive pursuit suggested he knew; his use of their faked identity suggested he didn't . . .

"His communications to the Station should be blurring

out," Oblo said. "Screens are up, half-power, and his own turbulence is in the way."

"He got something," Heris said. "Something he didn't like."

"Yes, but they're not shooting at us." The unspoken *yet* rang in her ears.

"There might be another reason for that," Heris said, putting her worst fears out for them all. "If they've missed the prince, onstation . . . and if they told Livadhi . . . he won't blow us away, but he'll be on our track forever."

"So the good news would be a shot across the bows?" asked Ginese. Sirkin gave a sudden twitch, as if she'd only now realized what was going on.

"In a way. Thing is, if he knows who I am, then he knows how I would've reacted—"

"Would have?"

"I've changed," Heris said. "So have we all." The veterans settled; without a word spoken, she knew she had reassured them about something no one could articulate. Sirkin glanced at the display.

"Eight minutes, thirty seconds."

Another request for voice communications, as if he had not received the first; he might not have, if his shields distorted the angled beam. Heris checked. If she had the standard civilian-quality scans, would she have had time to notice the new position? Yes. She sent the same packaged burst. It didn't sound much like her, she thought, though a comparison to her own voiceprint would show that it was. At the least, the accent suggested someone with years of spacer experience, commercial or military. Heris wondered how long it would take him to react to this. Several seconds to arrive, several seconds to decompress and play—she had made the message longer than strictly necessary. A few seconds for the return . . . any additional time off the clock was his reaction time.

"His optical weapons are just within range," Ginese reported. "They still have active scans on us, and theirs are hot, but I'm not detecting the targeting bursts I'd expect."

Would he wait until he could deliver more firepower, or would he act now? It was harder to deliver a warning shot from behind but easier to blow someone away . . . was he wondering which to do? He would need to be much closer to deliver a warning in front of them; he had to be sure it went off far enough in front. The seconds ran on.

"Eight minutes," said Sirkin.

This time it was a voiceburst hail; Oblo had it running almost as Heris saw the communications board flicker.

"F.R.C.S. *Better Luck*," came the voice. "This is the Familias Regular Space Service frigate *Skyfarer*. You are suspected of carrying contraband. Heave to for inspection." An old term, and not what they would do if they were going to comply . . . and . . . *frigate*? Named the *Skyfarer*? Heris stared across the bridge at Oblo, who shook his head.

"No, sir—ma'am—that's no frigate. But look at the old scan."

On the original scan board, which they'd left in because it was the standard required, the R.S.S. ship's profile did indeed resemble a frigate—half the mass of a cruiser. That made no sense. Why would a captain misrepresent his ship that way? Did he expect her to willingly engage a frigate? Surely in attempting to stop a civilian vessel, it was better to claim all the ship size you had . . . she'd always done so.

"Our weapons profile should look to him about even, if he were a frigate," Ginese pointed out. "If we engaged, then he'd be legally in his rights—"

"To blow us away," Heris said. "I do remember that much. But if that's his game, he can't know the prince is aboard." *Or can he?* she wondered. If the king—or anyone else—wanted to get rid of the inconveniently stupid prince, this would be a way . . . a tragedy of course, but one to be blamed on the unstable Captain Serrano. And perhaps on her employer or the employer's family.

"You're going to tell him?" Petris's eyebrows rose.

"Of course not. We're not supposed to have tight beam capability; it would be telling him and everyone else in this system."

On the tight beam, Livadhi's familiar face had an earnest expression that sat oddly with the rumpled red curls she remembered. Behind his head was the curved wall of the communications booth, which meant he hoped his crew wasn't spiking into this conversation.

"Captain Serrano, it is imperative that we keep this as short as possible." His stubby hands raked his hair again, so that one lock stuck straight up. "You have . . . er . . . the wrong person aboard your ship."

"Four minutes," Sirkin said.

"I know you can make jump inside the usual radius; you did it before. But don't do it now. Please."

Fleet captains rarely said "please" to civilian captains they had already ordered to heave to.

"I don't want to have to fire on you," Livadhi said. "But under the circumstances, it would be necessary. I say again, you have the wrong person aboard. You must not complete your mission."

Great. He knew about the mission and the prince, which meant he'd been sent here to intercept her. So much for the honor of kings, Heris thought, and wondered if he knew the actual radius at which she *would* risk jump. They had the data from her earlier jump, but . . . would that give them the same figures Sirkin was using?

And she had no tight beam for response. Anything she sent would be available to other listeners in time.

Carefully, weighing each word, she composed her response. "All persons aboard this ship have His Majesty's permission to be here."

"Captain Serrano—Heris—you know me!" Livadhi was sweating. And since he could be a coldhearted bastard when he wanted to—he had not been sweating when they'd stood before old Admiral Connaught to answer his questions about the alleged massacre of civilians on Chisholm Station—something about this bothered him. "You have the wrong . . . er . . . individual; it's not Mr. Smith, but a . . . er . . ."

"I have two individuals," Heris said. "Both carry legal identification which matches their descriptions; neither is a fugitive." Captive, yes, but not fugitives. And of course they both fit the description of the same person, but that was another problem, not his. Would he realize from what she said that she meant the prince and his double?

"You have two clones," Livadhi said. "I have the real prince, and we need to get him aboard your ship. Without anyone noticing, although the way you've been behaving, anyone would . . ."

"Captain Livadhi—" Had she ever called him Arash? Had she ever really run her fingers through those rumpled red curls, and felt a thrill? If so, it was the thrill of being noticed by someone slightly senior, the thrill of ambition realized, not the thrill of passion. She could remember *that* bit well enough. "We received departure clearance from Naverrn Station; our course since then has been in accordance with the filed plan. We took on only a single bin of cargo, the Outworld Parcel shipment, for which we hold a legitimate subcontract. All personnel aboard have been identified by legal methods and none is a fugitive from justice." More than that she could not say. Would not say.

"Three minutes," said Sirkin.

"We cannot let you continue with clones in place of the prince," Livadhi said. "It would embarrass the Crown—"

It would more than embarrass the Crown; the illegality of using unmarked clones as royal doubles would throw a political bombshell. Heris could not begin to imagine what would be destroyed.

"They're in easy range now," Ginese put in. "Not just the OR weaponry, but the overboosted missiles, too. Either boost us out of here, or we're dinner on the table."

"Heris, you have to trust me," Livadhi said. "I know it's hard; I know about the . . . er . . . problem you had, but you have to ignore that. You know I wasn't part of that." But did she? Ambitious, hard-driving: how could she know that Livadhi hadn't been part of Lepescu's clique?

"We have to talk," Livadhi said. "Face-to-face—or I'm sorry, but—"

"Meet you at the Tank," Heris said. Would he remember, and understand, that reference? It was worth a try. To her relief, his face relaxed.

"Deep or shallow?" he asked.

"The orange bucket," she said, hoping for the best.

"Two minutes, thirty seconds," Sirkin said.

Livadhi's face constricted in a mass of wrinkles, as he seemed to pry the memory out of some corner of his brain. Then he grinned. "Your honor, Heris?"

"Absolutely." With the word, she called in the last acceleration in reserve, and the *Better Luck* aka *Sweet Delight* skipped forward, momentarily outranging the cruiser. Livadhi's tight beam lost its lock, and before he could reestablish contact, they had reached the jump threshold. Heris held her hand up, waiting precious seconds, until the beam found them, only then chopping a signal to Sirkin. The ship flipped into FTL space.

Petris let out a whoosh of breath. "You cut that fine," he said.

"Should I give them more accurate data?" Heris asked, with relief now that it was over. "He'll assume I jumped as soon as I could—why else accelerate like that? And that's our safe margin now—what I just made for us."

"But how'd you know he'd try to talk again and not shoot?" asked Sirkin.

Heris shrugged. "It was worth a try. Either we have the prince, or just clones, as he said. If we have the prince, I doubt he'd fire *on* us without fire *from* us. That would create a lot of records to be faked. If we don't—if the prince is somewhere else—that's another set of problems. Suppose Livadhi has the prince aboard . . . he must look out for his welfare . . . he will not invite attack. He was in our range by the time we broke the link. If he doesn't have the prince, there's still the clones . . . I would imagine he'd like to bring them back where they came from."

"What's that business about meeting at a tank?" asked Petris.

"Well . . ." Heris rubbed her nose absently. "It's true, in a way. I did promise to meet him, and I do feel bound by that promise, but it should work out all right."

"Care to explain?"

"Don't look down your nose at me. You know perfectly well it's officers' slang; you're about to find out what it means." She put the Reference Quads up on the secondary screen. "In every sector, there's a mapped set of coordinates called the Tank. If one wants to meet somewhere discreet, for any reason, that's where one goes . . ."

"And every Fleet officer knows it, so it's about as secret as how many royals it takes to screw in a lightbulb?"

"Not quite that bad. Not just one set of coordinates, actually, but one for each combination of officers. It starts in training; each class has its own definition. Then once you're out in the Fleet, it's a matter of relationships. If you become friends with someone, you may choose to share your definition of Tank. For one sector, or several, or all. In fact, it's always shifting, because we use it even within a single ship, or on a Station. Lazy people might give the same set to everyone, but neither Livadhi nor I were lazy—not that way. *Orange bucket*, to him, means a particular set of coordinates—" She highlighted them. "In this sector, and not a difficult jump away. Nor out of the way to where we want to go."

"Weapons?" asked Ginese.

"Oh, live of course. Just in case he's got someone with him, or we hit bad luck again. Sirkin—what's our onboard time going to look like to reach those coordinates?"

"Thirty hours, give or take—what insert velocity?"

"I'd like to come in slow, minimal turbulence. We'll be on a similar vector, unless he double-jumps, which will give us even more time. Work out the details." She pushed herself to her feet. "And now, if you'll join me, Petris, we'll have a word with our passengers."

The first passenger had improved the shining hours since they left Naverrn by going to sleep. He snored, curled on his side in the sleepsack. Heris listened awhile, and decided the snore was genuine, not faked. No one could create all those little gurgles for punctuation on purpose, not without giggling.

"Let him complete his slumbers," she said. "We'll have a word with the other one."

The other one glowered at them from the sleepsack he had folded into a seating pad. "This is unconscionable. Not even a bed."

"I know," Heris said. "It's so sad that both of you must suffer. But your father expects you will understand."

"My father!" That with a snarl. "Easy enough for him to send me off without even my servants."

"If either you or your . . . double . . . had been cooperative, we might have been able to improve matters," Heris pointed out. "Now that we're under way, suppose you tell us which you are."

"Which?"

Heris wished she dared smack him. "Whether you are the prince, or he's the fellow down the corridor," she said.

"Oh." He appeared to ponder that much longer than necessary. "I . . . don't think either of us is the prince," he said.

"You don't think," Heris said. Was he trying to be cute, or could he possibly not know?

"No . . . I'm not entirely sure. I mean, I know *I'm* not the prince. But we switch around so much, you know, that I rather lose track."

"All clones?" Heris asked. "All *his* clones?"

"I suppose so," the young man said. "I never really thought."

"And do you have a name? When you aren't using the prince's, I mean?"

"Mr. Smith," he said, with a grin. "Gerald Smith. It's all I've ever been called. We all use it—his name is Gerel, so ours had to be close enough that his would be familiar, and yet not the same. My middle initial's B, and I'm the second one."

Heris wanted to ask him if they were all as stupid as the prince himself, but thought better of it. More important at the moment was the size of her problem. "How many of you clones are there?"

"Three, at least," he said promptly. "I went through the first stages of training with two others; our fourth had a metabolic problem and died early. But we might not have been the only cluster. On the other hand, we're almost never all together, so if one of us died in the line of duty, the others wouldn't know."

If there were three clones—or more—then the putative prince Livadhi had might not be the prince at all. "Why so many? I thought clones were expensive, and the confusion must have been difficult—"

He shrugged. "We're also prone to losses in the early embryonic stages, just as nonclones are. Given the expense, they don't take chances; they bring a cluster along together. If it's absolutely necessary to have a clone in place—as it is here—it's much safer to have a spare or two."

"Or three," Heris said. Where was the prince himself? With Livadhi? Somewhere else? "By any chance, was another clone on Naverrn? Or the prince himself?"

"No—I was primary, this trip, and Gerald C. was secondary. At least, I think that's Gerald C. you've got in the other room. I don't know where Gerald A. or Gerel Prime is."

"Gerel Prime being your code name for the prince?" The clone nodded. Heris could not see any difference between him and the prince she had transported from Sirialis. If that had been the prince—she had a sudden chilling suspicion that maybe her passenger had been one of the other clones, and the prince himself not involved in any of that mess. Yet the king clearly thought that had been the real one.

"How are you briefed about the prince's activities?" Heris

asked. A minor matter now, but it might provide useful information. "Surely all of you must be kept up-to-date on his recent actions—and he on yours. Who monitors your . . . ah . . . personal interactions, and your personality profile?"

"We all carry implanted recorders," the clone said. She had trouble thinking of him as Gerald B., but she made herself repeat it silently. This was Gerald B., an individual, though genetically identical . . . "They're harvested regularly, by a Crown-certified technician, and we're retaped with the others at the same time. Usually takes a couple of hours. I've been told the prince is also equipped for retaping."

"Like training tapes?" Heris asked.

The clone—Gerald B., she reminded herself again— frowned. "I've been told it's like the military training tapes, the ones used before simulator training."

"Ah." With the right drug induction, those were powerful— one could almost believe one had already been through the simulators.

"As for the personality profile, we're evaluated on that at every retaping, as we are for physical parameters." Heris noted that Gerald B. seemed a lot more cooperative now than he had been, and wondered why. Did he have some conditioned response to a phrase she'd used, or was the admission of his clone identity a releaser for more cooperation? "That's why I'm not sure about the others," he went on. "We're not encouraged to concern ourselves with the actual identity of the person presenting himself as the prince. Nor are we encouraged to form independent relationships with each other. We're just doubles; our value lies in being mistaken for the prince, not each other."

What a sad life, Heris thought. But as if he'd read her mind, Gerald B. grinned at her. "Don't pity me," he said. "I see so many singletons trying to be mistaken for a parent, a mentor, a patron . . . they, who could be themselves wholly and freely, choose to copy another almost as closely as I must. So it can't be that bad. Besides—my prime is a wealthy, privileged young man. I enjoy those advantages even when I'm not on."

True, but such a philosophical outlook was nothing like the prince as Heris had known him. Were they as bright as the prince should have been? And if so, how did they feign stupidity? Did they know it was stupidity they were feigning? "Have you been retaped on what happened at Sirialis?" she asked.

"Oh, yes. A courier brought both physician and tapes . . . it was an emergency, such a dramatic break. Actually there was some concern that Gerald A., who had been first doubling right then, should have broken his role to inform the authorities when the prince left, but it was decided once more that our role should be confined to doubling, not surveillance."

Curiouser and curiouser. Gerald B. began to sound more and more intelligent and mature. That alone made it likely he wasn't the prince; he could feign stupidity more easily than a stupid person could feign intelligence. But—again she wondered if the real prince had been the one drugged.

"So . . . you would not know from seeing someone on a ship-to-ship video if it were the prince or another clone?"

"Nor just from seeing him. Only if he broke role, and revealed himself."

Livadhi arrived at the rendezvous an hour after Heris, weapons dark to her scan. A good sign, if he hadn't managed to fox her scans. Nor did his weapons light, though he must have known hers were hot. Slowly, they brought the ships close, cutting the delay in communication so it was hardly noticeable.

"You don't entirely trust me," Livadhi said.

"No—should I?" Heris gestured around her. "You know these people—members of my crew, court-martialed with false evidence, imprisoned. Too many of them died. Where were you, Livadhi? When I needed friends in the Fleet, when I needed someone to testify at my own hearing?"

His eyes fell. "I was . . . convinced you had done what they said. Sorry, Heris, but that's the truth. Your own cousin Marlon—your uncle Sabado—I thought if they spoke against you, with such sorrow and regret, it must be true."

"Yet you had known me." She wasn't as angry as she'd expected to be. His lack of support hurt, but it had melted into the general pain that none of her friends at Fleet had come to her aid. She shrugged, putting aside that aspect of the situation. "You wonder why I don't trust you now? That's the smallest part of it. You've heard about Lepescu?"

"Only that he died, and rumor said discreditably." His

eyes glittered; she could almost see the questions struggling for precedence in his head.

"He was involved in a group that hunted humans for sport," Heris said. His eyes widened; even with what he knew of Lepescu that shocked him. "He was killed, and the surviving victims freed. More than that I should not say."

"You—were there?" A transparent attempt to be indirect. Heris could not contain her laughter. He scowled.

"I was there," she said. "I witnessed it." Let him wonder if she was one of the hunted, or there in some other role. Right now he did not deserve to know more. "He's definitely dead," she went on. "And so are his associates on that trip, while records have been found listing those who accompanied him other times." Livadhi stirred. Heris searched his face, finding nothing certain.

"If you have such experience," she went on, "it's one more reason I should not trust you. Although . . . I myself suspect he sometimes lured officers into it, and then blackmailed them later." Livadhi flushed. Heris simply looked at him until his color returned to normal. So. Now she knew. But what would he do?

"I suppose . . . the Crown knows all about it." His voice was low, hoarse.

"I would imagine so," Heris said carefully. She didn't actually know what the various investigators had turned up, but if Livadhi wanted to think she did, that suited her purpose.

"Nobody said anything—I mean, I haven't heard any rumors."

Heris shrugged. "I suppose the investigations aren't complete, and they're not moving until they are. Besides, why ruin the careers of good officers for one mistake?" That came out a little bitter, and she meant it to. Her one "mistake" had saved lives and won a battle, but still cost her a career.

Livadhi looked at her oddly. "I hope that attitude prevails," he said. "Though I'm surprised to find you so lenient."

"You mistake me," Heris said. "I'm not lenient at all. This is not my fight. Carrying out the king's request is. I will not let any . . . old grievances get in my way."

"I see." Livadhi's face was carefully neutral again. "And

you have no interest in rekindling an old friendship? You would prefer that . . . former shipmate?"

"My former shipmates suffered considerably on my behalf," Heris said, ignoring the implication. If Livadhi had heard about Petris, it was still none of his business. "They proved themselves trustworthy. Can you blame me for wanting to put trust where it's been rewarded before?"

"No, I suppose not. Well, then what about the mission?"

"You tell me what your mission was, and I will decide if you're a potential help or hindrance to mine," Heris said. Livadhi's stare took on new respect.

"You've acquired an even keener edge to your blade," he said. "You know the regulations—"

"And the realities," Heris said. "Come, now—if you are loyal to the Crown and the Familias, you know why I have to hear your mission, and before I tell you of mine."

"All right." Livadhi sighed, and Heris sensed that his resistance had ended. "I was told that you were going to Naverrn Station to take the prince to the Guerni Republic, but that by a mix-up, the prince's double was there instead. I was supposed to transport the prince and intercept you, ensuring that you had the right person aboard. I was to do this not while you were onstation, but in deepspace, to avoid detection. We expected you to be there another day or so, and I was going to hang about insystem—as you know, R.S.S. ships do sometimes observe in that system. My . . . er . . . sources told me that one of your crew had obtained, if that's the right word, a tight beam receiver, so I planned to contact you before you left Naverrn Station, so that we could rendezvous at a distance, making it look like a routine inspection."

"Except that there are no routine inspections out here," Heris said. "As you well know."

"It was all I could think of," Livadhi said.

Heris would like to have made a sharp comeback, but she couldn't think of a better plan herself, not off the top of her head.

"What were you supposed to do with the double I had?"

"Take him to Xavier, where he's booked on a commercial liner, and put him aboard."

"I see." How much to explain? "You're right: we were supposed to impersonate a small independent cargo vessel, and transport the prince to the Guerni Republic." She was not about to explain for what purpose. "I was told his double would take over on Naverrn."

"But you snatched his double—"

"But only because he was refusing to come, and I could not distinguish them . . . since they were clones."

"That should have told you they were fakes, neither of them the prince."

"Not . . . necessarily. After all, they matched the prince's ID specs."

Livadhi looked startled. "They can't. They're clones of each other, not of the prince."

"Let's check that out," Heris said. She spread out the hardcopy of the identification specs in front of the scanner. "Is this what you got?"

Livadhi peered at it. "Yes . . . close, at least. I'll need to check mine." He touched one of his screens, and pointed a wand at the input screen from Heris. After a moment, he blanked his screen. "The same, our computer says. And our man matches. That means—"

"Three clones. One of them the prince."

"Maybe," Livadhi said. "And maybe not."

"There's only one thing to do," Heris said. "Get all three of them where we were supposed to take the prince and let the medical personnel sort it out."

"But that will risk detection," Livadhi said.

"So would taking in a vat-grown clone as the prince," Heris replied. "Do you think they couldn't tell? The clones tell me that there is a technique, not part of the identification scan, but something to do with leftover markers of accelerated growth."

"But I can't take my ship off to the Guerni Republic. I have another assignment."

"Then send your putative prince over here, and I'll take all three of them."

"But—alone?"

"You said it yourself. If you show up there in a Familias R.S.S. cruiser, it'll be an Incident with a capital I. It's safe enough for me; I've never been there, and neither has this ship."

"I don't like it," Livadhi muttered. "But I can't think what else to do. I suppose you have a shuttle lock on that thing?"

"Yes," Heris said. She nodded to Petris and Kulkul, who picked up their weapons and left the bridge. "You can send your pinnace over and swim him through the tube."

"By the way," Livadhi said a few minutes later, when the pinnace was on its way. "I am authorized to tell you that a certain Lady Cecelia disappeared from an extended care medical facility a few weeks after you left Rockhouse Major. Would you like to explain that to me?"

"No," Heris said shortly. "I would not." But that wouldn't do; Livadhi would pursue the mystery eagerly, just to annoy her. "She was my former employer," she said. "You may have heard—she had a stroke, and her family blamed me. That's why the king thought my leaving with the yacht wouldn't be connected to any plan of his." That far she could go.

"But why was I told to tell you?"

Heris shrugged. "I can't imagine. I can't say I think much of her family, keeping her in a place with no better surveillance than that. I hope she's in good hands." What could she say to change direction? The obvious topic came to her. "Who's your new admiral?"

Livadhi grimaced. "Silipu, remember her?" His comments on the changes in command since Lepescu's death filled all the time it took to unload the prince and retrieve the pinnace. When he signed off, she wondered just how much she'd fooled him.

CHAPTER FOURTEEN

"We're almost there," Brun said. Cecelia had come to prefer her hands to others; she had no professional skill, but a very human affection to convey. Amazing how different she was from the girl who had thrown up in the lounge of Cecelia's yacht. It was hard to believe she had ever seemed a shrill-voiced selfish fluffhead. Was it the adventure she'd had on the island, or just normal maturation? She had helped dress Cecelia, this time in clothes Cecelia could feel—soft pants and shirt, a soft tunic, low soft boots. She had helped lift Cecelia into the hoverchair; the inflated supports held Cecelia's head steady and gave her, she hoped, the look of someone disabled but alert. For now, the hoverchair was locked down . . . Cecelia felt a moment's panic, but Brun's hand stroking her hair calmed her. She hated herself for that panic; she could not get used to being helpless, blind, vulnerable. She wanted to be brave and calm. "It's all right," Brun was saying. "You are brave. It's just—no one could be, every single minute."

If this was what children could be like, she should have had children. Ronnie, whom she'd despised, and this girl, whom she had once dismissed as a fluffhead, had rescued her when adults her own age either didn't care or couldn't think what to do. She would have to revise her ideas about young people. Of course, when she herself was young she'd known young people had sense. But looking back at her own idiocies later, she'd forgotten the generosity, the courage . . .

Pressure pushed her back into the chair. They were close,

then, to the landing site. A thud, a rumble that rattled her bones. Landing, rolling along a landing field. Her stomach argued; without sight, she felt nausea and swallowed it nervously.

The chair, unlocked, floated at Brun's push through air that stank of fuels and hot metals and plastics, then into a smell of leather and dust. She heard the clicks that meant the chair was being locked down again. She heard the rustle of clothes, the thump of cases being loaded. A vehicle, filling with people and luggage. Then a jerk and swerve, and more movement she could not see.

A cool current of air blew the hair off her face. Soon it smelled of morning in the country, though a different country than she'd left. A pungent herb tickled her nose, teasing her with a vagrant memory. She should know that smell, and these others that crowded in: pines, dew-wet grass under the sun, plowed fields, horses, cattle, goats. Cecelia breathed it in. Only a few weeks ago, she'd been trapped in the sterile room without even the scent of flowers. Now . . . she could eat, and move a few muscles on her own, and live in a place that smelled good.

Finally it all came together, the sharp smell of the purple-flowered herb, the broader, roasting scent of tall yellow flowers edging the road, the squatty resinous pines of the dry hills and the lush grass of valleys. She knew which planet, of all the planets she'd visited, and she began to suspect the exact place.

She knew when the vehicle turned where she had come. Her body had felt that sequence of swerves and bounces too often to forget it. Into her mind sprang the picture she had had so long on the screen of her study . . . the stable yard, with its rows of stalls . . . the cats sprawled in the sun after a night chasing mice . . . the long house with its high-ceilinged rooms that were cool even in midsummer.

She felt the hot tears running down her face. "Do you know where you are now?" asked Brun. Her shoulder came up, emphatic *yes*. I'm home, she wanted to say. I'm where I should never have left. Home on Rotterdam, at the stable I left to Meredith. The vehicle they were in—the old farm van?—rolled to a bumpy stop. Had no one ever fixed that wet spot in the driveway? She knew within ten centimeters where they were, just far enough past the mud puddle that someone stepping out wouldn't land in it, pulled to one side to let the hay trucks get to the gate.

A horse whickered, down the row, and another answered. Near feeding time, she thought. She heard a door open, heard the clatter of pails, and someone in boots scuffing out of the feed room. She smelled hay, and oats, and molasses, and horses, and leather . . .

But it was going to be worse, in a way. To be here, among horses and the people who cared for them, and be unable to move, to see, to talk, to ride. Pain and longing contended in her mind. Another horse whickered. She recognized that it was not the same as either of the others; at least she had not lost her ear for horse voices. Though what good it would do . . . she argued back at herself. At least it was going to be better than that sterile nursing home. And they thought she had a chance of recovery, at least partial recovery.

She felt the coolness when the hoverchair reached the shadow of the entrance. Up three steps and across the porch. The house smelled different. Someone here had cooked foods she didn't particularly like, and the downstairs hall didn't have the pleasant aroma of leather, but a more formal scent—something floral but artificial. But she recognized the soft rattle of the lift doors, and the machine-oil smell. She had had the lift installed after struggling up the spiral stairs one too many times on crutches . . . that broken ankle, the third one. She wouldn't buy a hoverchair then; only old people used them. Brun pushed her hoverchair into the lift, and slid the doors closed.

The lift jerked, and whined, and they were on their way upstairs. She wished she could see the upstairs passage, with the arched windows on either end, and the shining wood floor—or was it still shining? She could hear Brun's shoes on the floor, and it sounded polished.

"You'll be in your own room," Brun said. "It's not the same, of course. The furnishings—do you want me to describe them?" She waited while Cecelia thought about that. She had such vivid memories of this room, every detail of fabric, every ornament on the shelf above the window. She wanted to sink back into that . . . and yet, the room sounded different, and smelled different. She'd have that discord between the visual memory and the auditory reality if she clung to the past.

Her shoulder jerked *yes*, and Brun squeezed it a moment.

"I'll bet you remember everything, and wish you could keep it that way. But here's what it looks like to me. The walls are dark cream—" They'd aged, Cecelia thought. They needed a new coat of paint every few years to keep the precise tone Cecelia had chosen. "—there's a medbed in place of yours; you'll be on monitoring awhile longer. But the cover is one of those Rekkian handwoven blankets in green and gold and tan, with flecks of orange in the gold. The pattern's more an irregular stripe than anything else. The bed has its head against the far wall; the window over the yard will be on your left as you lie in bed. Is that right?" Cecelia signalled *yes* again. "Good. We didn't put anything on the windows. There's a wooden chest, painted oxblood red, against the wall opposite the bed, and a tall bookcase/chest on the wall to the right, next to that window. A couple of reproduction Derrian side chairs we picked up in the city, and no rug in here at all."

Cecelia wanted to ask about the pictures on the wall. She had taken her Piucci originals, the portraits of her top horses, but had left behind the old hunting scenes. But Brun said nothing about that. She heard other footsteps in the passage, and waited.

"Here are your clothes," Dr. Czerda said. "Your new clothes, I should say. Your friends thought of trying to get your own, clothes you knew by feel and smell, but decided it was too risky. Brun gave us a shopping list, and you're now equipped with the basics, in colors she remembers you wearing. Including riding attire."

Riding attire? She couldn't ride—might never ride again. For all she knew, she was bloated up to the size of Brun's hot air balloon, and no horse could hold her up. She jerked her shoulder *No* and hoped it carried the exclamation point she intended.

"Yes," Brun said. "You've got breeches and boots and helmet for the very good reason that you're going to ride again. You *are*!" In that was the fierceness of the young, who thought wanting something enough made it happen. Cecelia had heard that tone in her own voice, when she'd insisted she would ride again, after this or that accident. Then she had believed it. Now . . . she wasn't sure.

"You're facing a time limit," the doctor said. "One formal— the legal requirement to show competency before your estate is finally distributed—and one informal—before whoever did this to you finds you. So we aren't going to waste any time: you will have a full schedule of rehab work, every day, no vacations."

Cecelia thought about that, and her immediate wish to stretch out on that unseen medbed, and jerked her shoulder *Yes* with as much emphasis as the earlier *No*. She was tired, but better to be tired than forever lost in this helplessness.

"Except tonight," the doctor said. "Most of your therapists are still in transit. We didn't want to make it obvious where you were if someone is keeping track of them, so they've had to take roundabout routes. So tonight you can just rest."

Until that moment, she hadn't thought of pursuit—Brun had mentioned it, but reality itself seemed hardly real. Now, with the familiar smells and sounds around her, the thought of being recaptured, returned to a blank prison existence, terrified her. It was the wrong place; it was the obvious place. Anyone would know where she was. What fools!

Brun recognized her panic somehow. "It's all right," she kept saying. "It's not as obvious as you think."

Why not? she wanted to say. Brun went on to explain. Rotterdam had horses, but no advanced medical facilities. It was far from the logical place for someone in her condition. Moreover, her lifelong investments in Rotterdam— not only money, but time and friendship—meant that few mouths would talk. And even if they did, Rotterdam lay far off the usual networks of transport and communication.

"They'll figure out it was Dad's yacht, eventually. They'll think of Sirialis, and then Corhulm, where most of our pharmaceutical research is done. They may send a query about Rotterdam, but—I'm assured nothing will come of it. At least for months."

Cecelia hoped Brun was right. She would much rather die than go back to that nonlife.

Her earlier experiences in recovering from more minor injuries helped only a little. It had been twenty years since her last broken bone—well, *large* broken bone—and longer than that since the near-fatal headlong crash in the Trials. She had forgotten how infuriating it was to struggle, panting, for what seemed like hours, in order to twitch something slightly—and then have the physical therapist's bright, cheerful voice say, "Pretty good, hon, now do it again." And again and again, until she was a quivering wreck. She had forgotten how much weakened muscles and ligaments hurt when forced to work again; she had forgotten how even the best therapists talked over patients' heads, as if they weren't really there. "There's a spike on that adductus longius" and "Yeah, and isn't that a twitch in the flexor radialis?" and "If she doesn't get something going on these extensors we're going to have to start splinting; the tone's up on the flexors." She hated that; she wanted them to remind her what they were talking about, and what it meant.

And she was tired. Bone-tired, sore, short of sleep—because she woke in a panic, night after night, afraid she was back in the nursing home. With so limited a communication system, she couldn't tell them that, and they'd decided she would sleep better alone. She was too old for this; she didn't have the resilience, the sheer energy, that she had had two decades before. She had not believed she was old—not the woman who could still ride to hounds—but now she believed it. If she had been able to talk, she would have said it; she would have argued, out of exhaustion and despair, that they were wasting their time. She couldn't talk; she could only endure.

But twice a day, between sessions with physical therapists and occupational therapists and massage therapists and tests and all the rest, Brun took her out to the stable yard. That was her reward for a good morning, incentive for a good afternoon. She learned each horse's voice, and the voices of the stablehands only a few days later. Brun poured handfuls of sweet feed into her passive hand, and she felt the soft velvet horse lips mumbling over her palm. Brun lifted her hands, and laid them against satiny necks and shoulders. The first time her fingers really moved, it was along a horse's shoulder; her first strong grasp was of a horse's mane.

And yet she hated the obviousness of it. She did not want her love of horses to be so utilitarian, so selfish. They deserved her love for themselves, not because it could help her therapy. She would have sulked, except how could she sulk when she couldn't talk at all? How could she rage, when her movements were slow and awkward, and she couldn't scream?

* * *

Cecelia free. Heris held that thought in mind as she laid out the roundabout safe course from their present location to the Guerni Republic. It had to be Brun's plan; she told herself that the villains in this piece had no reason to abscond with Cecelia. Only her friends did; only Brun could have put together the resources to do it. She imagined Cecelia in Sirialis; it was easy to imagine her in rooms Heris had seen, around horses and people she knew. Obvious, of course, to the king and anyone else, but—she put it out of her mind. Brun had acted; the first part had gone well. She could do nothing herself until she'd delivered these clones and the prince (if he was one of them). Then, she promised herself, then she would find Cecelia.

Somewhat to Heris's surprise, the rest of the trip to the Guerni Republic went peacefully, jump point after jump point, day after day after day. The three clones, each of whom insisted he was not the prince, were less trouble than Ronnie and George had been at first. They agreed to wear nametags to help the crew avoid the confusion of offering a meal to a clone who had already eaten. This helped, although it occurred to Heris that they might switch the nametags for a lark. Heris could not assess their intelligence, not with the possibility—no, likelihood—that they would not cooperate and perform at their best. Yet they seemed to have more common sense than she'd expected.

"There's no use our pretending, with all three of us here," A. said when she asked. "Our cover's blown, totally, as far as you and the others aboard this ship are concerned. You know we're clones of the prince; you know what that means legally. It wouldn't matter if one of us were the prince; the damage has already been done."

Heris didn't like the sound of that. Cold tickles ran down her spine, as if a frozen cockroach were rousing there. "You mean we're now a danger to the prince, or to the Crown?"

"No—we are." That one wore Gerald B.'s tag. "After all, that cruiser captain knows; some of his crew either know or suspect. There's no way to be sure the secret's safe even if they silenced you. They'll probably dump us."

"Kill you?" asked Petris, putting down his fork.

"No, there are other ways. They can do plastic surgery

to make us no longer doubles, and there's some kind of way to mark our genomes more prominently."

"Look through the microscope and the chromosomes spell CLONE," said one of the others. He sounded perfectly calm about it; Heris wondered if that was part of their act.

"But what will you do?" Petris asked. "Have you had any . . ." He paused, struggling for a tactful way to say it.

"Job training?" asked the one with the C. tag. "No, we just laze around acting like silly-ass rich boys." One of the others snorted, and Heris realized it was supposed to be a joke.

"Some," said the one who had snorted. "Lots of courses in all sorts of things he's supposed to know. Of course, we didn't attend formal classes, or get degrees, but I'm sure they'll cobble up some sort of resume for us."

They seemed remarkably unconcerned, but they were, Heris reminded herself, twenty or more years younger than she. People that age had more confidence than their lack of experience warranted.

Except for Sirkin. Something was wrong, and Heris couldn't quite figure it out. Of course, she would still be grieving for Amalie—that might be it. She had seen violent death up close for the first time in her life, and the victim was someone she loved. But Heris had seen other young people deal with their first serious losses. Usually, they came back to normal in fits and spurts, but with an upward trend. Sirkin had seemed to be recovering normally, but then took a downward turn. Heris didn't expect her to be lively, happy, or full of the sparkle that had first convinced her the girl was a good prospect, but she did expect consistent good work at her job. And that's where Sirkin had begun to fail.

Only little things so far—a missing log entry after a course change, a data cube left out on the counter rather than filed in its case. Heris had been tactful at first, murmuring reminders when she found the data cube, noticed the missing entry. Sirkin had looked appropriately remorseful and made quick corrections. But it went on. The other crew had noticed, and Heris arrived on the bridge one day to find Oblo giving Sirkin a serious scolding.

"I don't care what your problem is, bright eyes, but if you don't shape up, the captain'll kick your tail off this ship the next port we come to. It's not like you can't do better—we know you can. And don't tell me it's grieving over Yrilan, because we could tell you were really falling for Brun." Heris paused, just out of sight. Perhaps Oblo could do better at unkinking Sirkin than she had so far.

"But I tell you, I *did* log the jump coordinates. I entered them shift before last—" Sirkin sounded more defensive than apologetic.

"They're not here. And Issi was on just after you—are you telling me he wiped your log entry?"

"No! I don't know—I know I made that entry; I went over it twice because I know I've been making mistakes somehow . . . it was there, I swear—"

"Don't bother; you don't know how." Oblo in that mood was dangerous; Heris could feel the hostility oozing out of him from here. "See here, girl: you have only two possibilities. Either you didn't enter anything, or someone wiped it. I know damn well Issi wouldn't wipe it, nor would I, nor would the captain. Who are you accusing? You think one of those clones sneaked in here?"

"I don't know!" Sirkin's voice trembled; Heris heard her take a deep breath that was almost a sob. "I don't know what's happening . . . I was so careful . . . and then it's gone . . ."

"I've got to tell the captain; you know that. I can't pretend not to notice something like that. It could kill us all later."

"I know that," Sirkin said. "I—I can't explain it." Heris shook her head, and went on in. Sirkin looked tired and unkempt—that was new. She had always been neatly groomed and bright-eyed. What could be wrong with the girl?

"Ms. Sirkin . . . I'll see you in my office, please." She did not miss the desperate look Sirkin threw at Oblo, who gave her no encouragement at all.

Sirkin's explanation, if one could call it that, made little sense. She was trying to be careful; she didn't understand how these mistakes happened; she was sure she'd logged the course changes and jump points, and had no idea how they had vanished from the log. Her hands trembled, and her eyes were bloodshot.

"Are you taking anything?" Heris asked. Drugs seemed likely, given the combination of physical appearance and

absentmindedness. Sirkin hadn't used before, that she knew
of, but in the stress of Yrilan's death perhaps the girl had
started.

"No, ma'am. Not even the pills the doctor gave me
after . . . after Amalie . . ." Her voice broke. "Things are just
coming undone," she said, tears beginning to slide down
her cheeks. "And . . . and that makes me sound like Amalie.
She used to say things like that . . . I wonder if she felt like
this, trying and trying and nothing seems to work . . ."

Heris had no intention of getting off into that blind alley.
Amalie Yrilan's excuses were no longer anyone's problem.
"Sirkin, we both know you're capable of better. You were
doing extremely well up until we left Rockhouse Major. You
must have some idea what's gone wrong. Is someone . . .
bothering you?" She was sure she could trust her former
crew not to harass a young civilian, but it was only fair
to ask. Skoterin, the newest? She'd have expected one of
the others to notice and straighten out the offender, or tell
her. No, more likely one of the clones, assuming a royal
right to any pretty face and body. She wouldn't put it past
them to bring drugs aboard, either.

"No, ma'am. Nobody's bothered me. I know I . . . still
miss Amalie, but I honestly don't think it's that. It's just—
I do something, or think I do something, and then later it's
not done. I don't understand it. Maybe I'm going crazy."
She looked up with an expression Heris had seen too many
times on youngsters who had somehow gotten out of their
depth and hoped an elder had a magic solution. "Going
crazy" had been a favorite hypothesis in one ship, because
there were medicines for going crazy. Simple inattention and
laziness had no cure.

"I don't think you're going crazy," Heris said. She tried
to sound both calm and firm. "But I do think you can pull
yourself together—and you must. Tell you what. Let's let
another bridge officer sign off on your log entries for a few
days. If *those* entries disappear, we'll know it's not your
fault . . . and you'll have a witness to having made them.
How's that?" It was an insult, but Sirkin took the suggestion as gratefully as if it had been praise. "Now—take the
rest of this shift off—we've no jump points coming up—
and put yourself to bed. You look exhausted."

"Yes, ma'am."

As Heris expected, Sirkin's log entries didn't disappear when someone else countersigned them. So . . . logically . . . Sirkin had never made the earlier entries. It wasn't a computer glitch; it was the far more common human error. Sirkin seemed to be making fewer of them now, in all categories— another data point on the plot of carelessness. Her appearance improved; she looked almost normal, if not the bright-eyed girl she had been. Oblo and Issi reported that she seemed alert, careful, everything she should be.

Just to be sure, Heris asked about conflicts with the crew; as she'd expected, they all insisted they liked the girl. None of them reported conflict with anyone else. And a discreet surveillance indicated that she wasn't sneaking off to one of the clones (or any of them to her) when she was off-duty.

Yet . . . what had made Sirkin suddenly careless? Even in the aftermath of Amalie's death, she had done tedious jobs with her former precision. Why now? Heris worried, unsatisfied. She sensed something wrong and promised herself to pursue it once the clones had been delivered safely for medical attention.

One morning Cecelia lay in her bed and did her best to hate herself to death. She was too old to rage at simple unfairness, but the unfairness of her situation went beyond anything she could accept. When Brun came to dress her and take her to breakfast, she did not respond to the usual morning sallies. The smell of hot bread and sage honey roused no response. She wasn't hungry, and she wouldn't eat. After the necessary rituals of personal care, she waited for her first workout, numb and passive.

"We've got someone new," Dr. Czerda said. Czerda had begun to sound increasingly apologetic; it grated on Cecelia. "A specialist who might help. We had to wait, because she's so well-known—just the person they might be watching."

"Hi," a woman's voice said. "I'm Carly, your new therapist." Another new therapist. Cecelia needed that like she needed a fluorescent bathing suit. She was glad she couldn't say what first came to mind: such a string of obscenity would alienate all of them. "You're very angry," Carly said, in a voice that offered neither blame nor apology. "Did you know you could show that without words?"

Cecelia did not bother to twitch her answer. It was a lucky guess, that was all, or the infuriating certainty that she was in a predicted stage. They couldn't tell; they'd been nagging her because she didn't have control of her facial muscles, so it couldn't be the scowl she would like to have worn.

A warm hand lay on her arm; it radiated comfort. "Here," Carly said. "Anger tenses certain muscle groups, and fear tenses different ones. You're tense in all the anger groups. I don't think the others saw that, because of the overall weakness. Does it make you even more angry that I know you're angry?"

Cecelia thought about it, drawn into the intellectual puzzle despite herself. If it was an observation of her, of her real self, she didn't mind. It was being put into a category that made her want to scream.

"You're not as angry now," Carly said. Her hand moved slowly along Cecelia's arm. "Perhaps because I paid real attention to you, and not a theory?" Her voice, almost as warm as her hand, conveyed honest curiosity, real interest.

Cecelia could feel herself calming, the prickly rage receding.

"You've had good therapists, but they're young," Carly said. "And the enthusiasms of younglings can drive anyone mature to tears or screams. Besides, they've worked you too hard. I think you're tired, more than they've believed. Would you like to sleep?"

Cecelia twitched *yes,* and then shrugged both shoulders.

"You would, but what's the use? Or, you would but then this session is wasted?" Carly waited. Cecelia wondered how she was supposed to answer that with a yes or no, and in the silence—a peaceful, accepting silence—wondered if she could move anything else enough to communicate. She had clamped onto a horse's mane, first with her right hand, and then with both. If the first alternative was one hand, the second could be both. She tried to visualize her hands moving, and felt the fabric under her fingers slide across her fingertips.

"Both hands," Carly said, with approval. "That would be the second choice, I expect. Can you confirm with your shoulder?"

Yes.

"Then I would say this session is not a waste, even if

you sleep the rest of it. You're tense, and angry, and very tired. I'm going to make you comfortable."

Carly's warm hands, steady and firm, kneaded sore muscles and ligaments. Not the massages that Cecelia remembered, but something deeper and more serious. Soon she was drifting, not quite in contact with her aging body, but not in the sensory limbo of the drugs. She felt warm, contented, relaxed, and very sleepy.

When she woke, she felt completely adrift. Someone's hands steadied her back; she was leaning against—over?—something.

"It's all right," Carly said. "You slept well, and now you're resting on a large padded ball. If your arms feel funny, it's because they're hanging free, not at your sides."

It felt worse than funny; it felt ridiculous. Yet it also felt good, and she was rested and comfortable.

"Can you wiggle your hands again?" Carly asked. Something about her voice, her mature, calm voice, maintained the relaxation. Cecelia tried. With her arms resting against the curve of the ball, almost dangling, she could move her fingers. She could feel them shift across the fabric one by one. "Excellent," Carly said. "Some of the things they worried about aren't so. You don't have real spasticity in your fingers; the weakness and the tension in your arms have made it seem so. In this position, when you're rested, you might even tap a keyboard."

A keyboard. A keyboard meant letters, meant words, meant language, meant—she had been told this—a speech synthesizer. Real communication, not just twitches and jerks. She wanted to cry and laugh at once; she felt her shoulders seize, cramping. Carly rubbed the cramps out.

"Right now, the biochemical responses of your limbic system are working against you. Like anyone else, you'll do best when you're relaxed and happy. That's my job."

Why hadn't the others thought of this? Cecelia felt the difference in Carly's hands, as they responded to her muscles rather than trying to overpower them. Her arms twitched, trembled, then finally hung relaxed and heavy. Comfortable. It had been so long since she'd been really comfortable.

"It's been known for a very long time," Carly said. "But it's tricky to do, and a lot of people don't think it's important. If a regen tank will work, if the rehab is expected to be short, they say why bother? I think it's always worth it, for the patient's comfort if nothing else. And in cases like this, it's essential."

Cecelia felt mildly alert, rested, ready to try again. That afternoon, the relentless work with weights seemed less impossible. She was sweating, gasping, sore—but it made sense again. Afterwards, Carly gave her another massage, easing the pains of the exercises, and she slept well that night, waking rested and eager to go on.

Day by day, Carly suggested modifications to the various therapists—a tactile guide that let her get a bit of food to her own mouth, a communication system that used every movement she could make to signal meaning. After that came a communication board, with tactile clues for its segments; Carly promised that work on that would give her the strength and precision to use a real keyboard later. Cecelia began to believe again that she could make it out of this mess, that she would not be a helpless blind victim forever. Now her anger rose from impatience, not despair; she wanted her life back, and she wanted it now.

The Guerni Republic traded widely with a dozen different political entities. On one side, the Compassionate Hand and the Familias Regnant beyond. On the other, Aethar's World and its allies (a confederation so loose it refused the name). On yet another, some solo worlds so scattered that political union had so far been impractical. Like Italy's central protrusion into the Mediterranean on old Earth (back when that body of water was known as Mare Nostrum), the Guerni Republic enjoyed a location both handy for trade and easy to defend.

Astrophysicists had argued the unlikelihood of six stars of the right type, with assorted habitable planets, arriving at such a configuration by chance, but the unanswerable counterargument was that everything—even the taste of chocolate—was inherently unlikely, difficult as it may be to imagine a universe without chocolate in it. The Guernesi preferred to believe their situation had been created for them by a beneficent deity, and shrugged off contrary theories as the envy of those God chose not to favor. In case that envy went further than bad-mannered carping, the Guernesi maintained an alert and quietly competent military, as the

Compassionate Hand had found. As practical in its way as the Guerni Republic, the Benignity declared the Guernesi off-limits to Compassionate Hand activity—at least as long as delicate probes of the defenses showed them to be still alert and effective.

As a result of their location and the resulting trade, the Guernesi had developed efficient and relatively painless entrance protocols. But efficient, painless, and swift did not mean careless.

"While it's no concern of ours, are you aware that your broadcast ID and your ship do not agree?" asked the bright-faced young woman in blue.

"I beg your pardon?"

"According to our database, the *Better Luck* was scrapped over in Jim-dandy eight years ago. I know the Familias records aren't kept that long, but if you bought this ship as the *Better Luck* we could provide the data to sustain a claim of fraud." For a price, of course. The Guernesi, polite and willing to help, did nothing for nothing.

"Uh . . . I don't think that will be necessary." Heris had trouble not looking at Oblo. He would be embarrassed.

"On the other hand, if you reprogrammed the beacon, your tech did an excellent job—even got the warble in the 92 band exactly right. We have people who would pay a bonus for that kind of work, if that individual is here and wants to immigrate—" Another thing about the Guernesi, they were always looking for a profit.

"Now, I notice you have major ship weapons aboard . . ." And how had they figured that out? With the weapons locked down, no scan should have detected them. "Since you've come in past Compassionate Hand space, I'm afraid we'll have to visually inspect and seal them . . . I don't want to insult you, but the Benignity tries our borders at intervals."

"How—!" Oblo couldn't contain himself. "Your scans are—are they for sale?"

The young woman dimpled at him. "Of course, sir. I can give your captain a list of suppliers certified by the government. We have no restrictions on the foreign purchase of military-grade materials."

"Mr. Ginese will accompany you on your inspection of the weapons," Heris said. "What about small arms?"

"May not be taken off the ship; the penalty is death, and

destruction of the ship that brought you." That was clear enough. "If you want to shoot yourselves aboard your own ship, that's your business." She spoke into a communicator hooked to her uniform collar; the language was unfamiliar. "I'm just asking our weapons inspection team to step aboard . . . if your Mr. Ginese will meet them at the access hatch?" Of course. Heris was already impressed. She had never been here—R.S.S. vessels visited only on ambassadorial duty—and the rumors she'd heard didn't begin to match the reality.

"You do not have to state your business here," the young woman went on, "but if you do, it would be my pleasure to advise you on the easiest way to accomplish your purposes."

"Medical technology," Heris said. "I understand that you have superb research and clinical facilities—"

"Yes—can you mention a specialty?"

"Neurology, specifically the treatment of neurochemically induced cognitive dysfunction." That had been in the papers the king had given her.

"Ah, yes." The inspector spoke into her collar mic again, and waited a moment. "According to the current listings, I'd recommend Music—"

"Music?" Heris knew she must have looked and sounded as confused as she felt. The younger woman smiled, but not in mockery.

"Sorry, Captain. It's this translator. All the planets of Guerni's fifth star are named for the artes liberales: music, mathematics, history, and so on. Music is the planet with the largest medical complex devoted to neurology. From here, it's a very short jump, and about two weeks on insystem drive—we do ask, by the way, that you do not jump except at the designated jump points: we have a lot of traffic. By the time you arrive, Music Station will have a list of contacts for you. Do you wish to append any patient data at this time?"

"No," said Heris, feeling slightly overwhelmed. "No, thank you."

"Our pleasure. As soon as my team reports your weapons sealed, you're free to go. By the way, while I'm sure you wouldn't think of doing any such thing, I should warn you that unsealing your weapons will be a cause for retaliation,

even should you manage to frustrate the automatic detona-
tors on the seals which are designed to blow a ship of the
size that usually carries these weapons. Good day!"

Heris had worried about getting three identical young
men named Smith through the Customs Inspection at Music
Station. She had imagined every possible complication, but
when she brought up the problem, all three laughed.

"We're used to this," Gerald A. said. "If we don't wear
the same clothes, or stand together, or go through the same
intake booth too close together, no one will notice. All the
machines care about is whether our physical features match
our formal ID. And of course they do, from blood type and
retinal scan to DNA analysis."

"We can do costuming," Gerald B. said. "But it's not really
necessary here." Heris wondered. She still didn't trust their
judgment; she still suspected that one of them actually was
the prince, concealed by a shell-game with the nametags.
But when they showed up at her office, without the nametags
and in different outfits, she had to admit they no longer
looked so identical. One wore a scruffy set of spacer coveralls he must have gotten from a crew member; he slouched
against the wall looking sullen and grubby. Another displayed
himself with the peacock air of a young man of fashion,
and the third had the earnest, slightly harried look of a
businessman late for a conference. They looked different
enough, but how lax were the Guernesi?

Heris continued to worry until she was through Customs
herself, with her royal letters to the physicians, and found
the three Smiths grinning at her from the shuttle waiting
lounge.

CHAPTER FIFTEEN

Carly's influence on the treatment team extended into the stable as well. Maris Magerston had been Cecelia's hippotherapist from the beginning, when she had been slung over the horse's back like a stuffed doll . . . she knew that wasn't a fair description, but that's what it had felt like to her. Although Maris had patiently explained *why* she was sprawled on a broad pad, facing backwards, she still hated it. In her mind she had composed one furious argument after another, shutting out Maris's description of this and that muscle group doing important things. She didn't want to be this way, an inert load on the horse's back; she felt ridiculous, ugly, flabby, useless, old. She wanted to *ride*, and that meant sitting up and facing forward.

She arrived one day for her session to find an argument going on between Carly and Maris; Brun, pushing her hoverchair, guided it into the tackroom out of sight and let her listen. Maris sounded angry and defensive; Carly, as usual, sounded calm and cheerful, as she said she thought Cecelia was ready to ride properly.

"We start all our clients that way," Maris said. "I've read those articles, thank you—" Carly must have handed her something. "We're not quite as ignorant out here as you seem to think. But it's dangerous to rush clients . . . and she's over eighty . . ."

Carly took her up on the oblique attack. "Are you upset that I've been called in to supervise?"

"Oh, no!" Definite bitterness; Cecelia could imagine Maris's

570

expression. "We're not *bitter*. We're just local therapists on a backwoods planet, all so grateful for a chance to learn from the *great* Dr. Callum-Wolff."

"You sound pretty upset to me . . . I probably would be, too. You've been doing a good job for a lot of people all your career here; you do what you've been taught, and people get better . . . and I come along telling you to change. Is that about it?" Carly's voice held no anger and no defensiveness.

"Well . . ." Maris sounded much calmer. Then she actually chuckled. "Actually, I have your training cubes, up through three years ago. I'd have come to your presentations, if you'd ever come here before." A long pause. "The thing is . . . Lady Cecelia's really special on this planet, to a lot of people. And we were all trained as strict structuralists, Spinvirians. 'When you know the electrochemical scan of a nerve, you know what it can do.' Period. If I let her get hurt—especially doing something new—"

"Ah. Tough choice. I see your problem. Well, I could be bossy and overrule you—that'd give you an out—but I'd rather not. I do wish you'd let us try." That tone restored—at least symbolically—Maris's authority.

"Oh, why not? At worst, she'll just fall off."

Brun pushed her back out, as if they'd just arrived; Cecelia hoped her expression hadn't betrayed a joy she wasn't supposed to feel yet. This time they lifted her up into a proper saddle, facing forward. It felt entirely wrong: her legs were wrong, her back was wrong, her seat was wrong. She couldn't *see*. She felt a warm hand on either leg: Brun, on the right, and the stable girl Driw on the left. They had been to every session; and Brun had told her enough about Driw that she felt she knew the groom well.

"We're going to move, now," said Maris. "Circling to the right." *NO*, she thought, but she didn't move her shoulder. Pride left her that much dignity. She heard Maris cluck; the horse moved under her and she sagged sideways. Brun's firm hands propped her up. She could feel her legs flopping uselessly against the saddle; only the hands of her helpers kept her on the horse.

But she was sitting up, facing forward. Gradually, the saddle beneath her took on a familiar rhythm; she could feel the horse's stride as its barrel bunched and lengthened, swung slightly from side to side. Maris began to talk, again explaining what the horse was doing to enforce movements Cecelia's body must learn to make. Cecelia decided not to listen. Her back began to feel the horse the way it used to; she had no attention left for someone's words.

"Good," Brun murmured. "You're doing better." It didn't feel like balancing better; her spine felt as solid as her luncheon custard. But somewhere between lurches from side to side, she felt for a moment that it was *right* again. Somewhere in each stride, she was riding.

"Think of halting," Maris said. Cecelia tried to let herself sink into the saddle the way she would have, and felt herself slump forward as the horse halted. The helper's hands caught her. "Good for you!" Maris said. "You halted her yourself. Now—think forward."

Cecelia waited a moment, recovering what balance she could from the halt, and tried to remember how. She felt her spine lengthen, the pressure in her seat bones, a rising tension between her and the horse. Then the horse lunged forward into a trot, and for one instant Cecelia's body responded, moving with the beat, just as Maris said "Whoa!" The horse slowed, but already Cecelia was off-balance, sliding gracelessly off the outside into Driw's arms. Both of them fell.

"Are you hurt?" Brun sounded terrified. Cecelia quickly signalled *no*. She wasn't hurt at all. She was exultant. She had stopped a horse. She had compelled it forward. Without the use of her arms or legs, blind, unable to speak, she had nonetheless controlled a horse again.

"That'll be enough for today," Maris said, closer. Cecelia jerked her shoulder, *no*. "We'll have to check for damage. I was afraid of this—"

"She said no," Carly said. "She's not upset by a soft fall like that."

"But she's over eighty! And she shouldn't have been able to get this horse to trot. I'll have to switch to another—"

"Cecelia." That was Carly, grasping her hands now. "Cecelia, you did it! You stopped her; you got her into a trot. Are you happy about it?"

Yes! Of course she was happy about it. She tried to remember their other signals; right now she was too excited to think. "More"—that's what she wanted to say. Was she supposed to jerk her right knee, or her left? "Muhhh," she heard herself say softly. "Muhhh . . ." and then the shoulder jerk for *yes*.

"More, yes? You want to ride more?"

YES! Why hadn't she established a signal for "Dammit, you idiot!" Why hadn't she established a signal for "reins?" She flexed her fingers in Carly's, then pulled slightly.

"She wants to hold the reins, don't you, Lady Cecelia?" That was Brun, bless her, who knew more about riding than Carly.

"Maris, I think she needs to try again."

"All right." Maris was resigned, not hostile.

It was going to work. She knew it. This time Cecelia ignored the need for helpers, ignored the internal voice that told her how ridiculous she must look. The saddle felt familiar this time. The nubbly surface of the reins against her fingers felt better than fine silver or silk. By the end of that session she had halted the horse three more times, and started her into a walk, all with no surprises. She felt as if she had regained herself.

Steadily, both her riding and her other therapies made progress. She could grip the special table tools (she did not consider them flatware) and get most solid foods into her mouth. With someone to remind her where they were on the tray, she could choose for herself whether to follow a bite of ham with a bite of toast, or eat all the fruit first. She could sit in a regular chair, if it had a straight back, and with leg braces on could stand supported, leaning against a chest support, to use a keyboard or scrawl with a crayon. She could push the buttons to control her hoverchair; she could, at last, use a keyboard. Bit by bit, her voice came back, though most words defeated her; she began to spell things out, as she did on the keyboard.

Now, for the first time since the dark months in the nursing home, she began worrying at the problem of what had really happened. Who had done this? Why?

She was dozing one afternoon, after the best ride she had yet had. Maris had taken her out into one of the big fields on a lead line, and they had ridden together in the open. The horse had a lovely long flat walk; she had enjoyed the longer stretches of straight movement, the sound of wind in the trees at the edge of the field and the feel of it on her face. A pleasant lunch, a relaxing nap . . .

In one white-light burst, memory returned. She was at Berenice's dressed for that damned reception; she could feel the ivory silk smooth on her shoulders, the weight of her favorite necklace on her chest. Berenice had worn pale green, and the other ladies were much the same, a gaggle of old women in appropriate pastels, she thought sourly. It didn't matter if some of them had had rejuvenation; they were still old. She remembered them as children; they remembered her the same way. She hated this kind of thing. Gabble, gabble, nibble and sip, sit listening to a mediocre string trio, and then make a donation to whatever cause. Simpler just to make the donation and go do what you wanted, but she was trying to get Berenice to come around on the subject of Heris Serrano, so she had agreed to "be good" at the reception.

At her elbow, that insipid twit Lorenza. Amazing that a man like Piercy could have a sister like Lorenza. Lorenza, of course, had gone for rejuvenation, early and often, but she had always cared more for her complexion than anything else. *I am being nice*, Cecelia reminded herself, and smiled at Lorenza. Smooth gold hair, fair skin looking thirty—but those eyes held all of eighty years of malice. It was unnerving, those wicked old eyes in that young face . . . exactly why Cecelia hated the thought of rejuv for herself.

"Dear Cecelia, I haven't seen you for years," Lorenza said. Cecelia shivered. It was a soft voice, insistently gentle; why did it grate so on her ears?

"Well, I run off a lot," Cecelia said. She felt big and coarse next to Lorenza; she always had. As a child, Lorenza had been picture perfect, the quiet, well-behaved, clean and tidy girl to whom Cecelia had been compared when in disgrace. *Why can't you be more like dear Lorenza?* had come from both her mother and Berenice, every time she'd broken something, or come home dirty and disheveled. "I just got back." Her neck felt hot; she always felt she should say more to Lorenza, but she never could think what.

"I understand you took care of dear Ronnie for Berenice," Lorenza said, smiling up at her. There was nothing overtly wrong with that statement, but Cecelia was sweating.

"Yes . . . he's changed a lot. Fine young man." Too late, she realized that admitted he hadn't been. If Berenice heard, she'd be furious. Cecelia wished she were anyplace else—outside, by preference, and hoped she wouldn't trip over her own feet. Dammit! She was over eighty, rich and famous in her own right; she didn't need to feel like this about Lorenza. *I am being good*, she told herself again.

"You look hot, dear," Lorenza said. "Here—have a glass of juice." She produced a glass, snatched no doubt from some passing waiter, and offered it. Cecelia didn't want juice; she wanted out. But she had promised to be good; she tried not to grimace as she sipped the tangy-sweet juice. Interesting flavor—spiced with cinnamon and something else, she decided. She turned to thank Lorenza, and found to her surprise that the other woman had disappeared.

Cecelia gasped. She was shaking, her heart racing, and someone had hold of her hands. She knew, after a wild moment of panic, where she was, and what had happened. Lorenza. Lorenza had poisoned her. And she knew why, or part of why. It made sense now. And she had to tell them, before Lorenza poisoned Ronnie and Berenice and Bunny's family and the Mahoneys . . . and for that matter Heris and the crew and the prince.

"Cecelia! Tell us . . . try . . ."

Struggling, fighting her uncooperative body, she managed to spell it out. L.o.r.e.n.z.a. D.i.d. I.t. They didn't have to ask her what; they understood that much. Brun's voice cut across the others.

"The Crown Minister's sister? *That* Lorenza?"

Yes. Back to the new signal system; it was faster than spelling.

"Why?" Brun asked, and put the keyboard into her hands.

Dared she tell now? What if Lorenza had an agent here? Panic shook her, but she had to try it. If she died, she had to save the others.

Letter by letter, she got it out; no one interrupted. "P.r.i.n.c.e. m.a.d.e. s.t.u.p.i.d. D.r.u.g.s. K.i.n.g. k.n.o.w.s. G.e.o.r.g.e. d.e.m.o. L.o.r.e.n.z.a. g.a.v.e. d.r.u.g. R.o.n.n.i.e. n.o.t.i.c.e.d. T.o.l.d. m.e."

"And you told the king—Ronnie said that," Brun broke in then. "He didn't tell me about George . . . but I remember a joke about the term George almost flunked out of school. Was that it?"

Bless her wits. *Yes*.

"Lorenza did it because you know—because you told the king, and he must've told the Crown Minister who told her—and that means she might get the others. Ronnie—!"

Yes.

"His family?"

Yes.

"More?"

Yes. Of course, you idiot! When she finally could, she would give Carly an earful about what nonverbal people really wanted to say.

"Right, let me think." Brun thought aloud, either from habit or courtesy to Cecelia; Cecelia could imagine her intent face. "Anyone Ronnie might've talked to. His family. Me. Maybe my family as well. And George! Of course, and George's father. Heris Serrano, she knew, but I don't know if anyone else knows that."

Yes. The king would figure it out; he would already have told the Crown Minister. And didn't Brun say something about Heris having a mission from the king, that apparent theft of the yacht?

"So what do we do?" That was Brun to the others, and the gabble of voices rose. Cecelia began spelling again; that silenced them for the moment.

"G.o. t.e.l.l. R.o.n.n.i.e. G.o. t.o. R.o.c.k.h.o.u.s.e. w.a.r.n. t.h.e.m."

"Me?" Brun asked

Yes. They would listen to Brun; they wouldn't listen to any of the others. "C.a.r.e.f.u.l." she spelled.

"I'll leave now," Brun said in her ear. "I'll be careful, and I'll make sure no one else gets hurt." With a quick hug, she was gone; Cecelia heard her quick steps on the stairs.

It was all very well to say "I'll leave now," but she could hardly walk to the nearest spaceport carrying her clothes in a sack. Brun rummaged through her drawers, trying to think of twenty things at once. She needed her papers, her credit cubes, enough clothes. How long would it take by commercial carriers? What were their schedules? Why hadn't she kept the yacht here? That was easy—it had to go somewhere else and not be obvious about it. She didn't even know where it was.

"I'll drive you to the port." That was Driw, the groom who helped with the hippotherapy. She had ridden out with Driw, times she wasn't with Cecelia; she liked the tough, competent little woman.

"I don't even know when things leave," Brun said. Driw grinned at her.

"Here—the closest thing we have to a schedule." A battered folder, listing every ship that intended to arrive at the port for a year at a time. Which meant not often. "Are you going to travel in that?" *That* being the shorts and pullover Brun had put on as usual that morning. With a startled look at herself in the mirror, Brun dove into the shower, then into something that wouldn't instantly trigger suspicions. She hoped.

On the bumpy road out, she quit trying to read the schedule and instead tried to remember all the things Captain Serrano had told her. Cautions, things to think of—too many. Driw drove the way Cecelia had ridden in the horse trials: flat out, attacking every obstacle (curves, corners, other traffic) with utter concentration. When they reached the paved road that led to the port, Brun dared to say, "Are there any traffic laws?"

Driw chuckled. She had both legs extended, and one arm hanging out the window of the stable feed truck. "Yes . . . but not much enforcement. As long as I don't kill anybody—" She paused, to swerve around a tractor hauling three huge round bales of hay. "—we shouldn't have any problems. The port's on our side of the city."

Brun could just read the fine print of the schedule now; the truck only lurched occasionally. She had lost track of the date and had to ask Driw, who only knew it in local time: they had thirteen thirty-two day months, with names like Ock and Bir and Urg. For a moment her mind drifted to the possible language of the first settlers, then she dragged it back to the important stuff. If this was 14 Urg, then . . . damn. Nothing due for two days; she might as well have stayed at the stable.

"Except that there's other stuff sometimes," Driw said. "You know—casual, unscheduled stuff. It's faster, I hear. Kareem got to the Wherrin Trials in less than eight days, while the shortest scheduled passenger time was twelve. 'Course, it's kind of rough, he said, but I figured you were in a hurry."

Brun nodded. She could always find a room at the port, she supposed. She didn't remember much about it, actually, landing with Cecelia in the shuttle that one time. It had seemed small and bare, compared to the commercial ports she knew, but busier than the home port on Sirialis. She would just have to figure it out herself. That felt scary, but also exciting.

It was more scary and less exciting three hours later, after Driw had dropped her off at the shabby little shuttle terminal. The status board there showed nothing up at the Station but a bulk hauler headed for Romney—the wrong direction. Her schedule was out of date; the next scheduled passenger ship, also to Romney, wouldn't arrive for four days. Unscheduled was, of course, unscheduled. The shuttle . . . *the* shuttle, she realized, meant there was only one . . . was on its way up, and wouldn't be back until the next day. In the meantime, there was nowhere to sleep, because the people who ran the hostel were on vacation.

Brun put her gear in a locker and wandered outside. The shuttleport was also the regional airport; that terminal lay across a half mile or so of paved runways and scrubby grass. She could see aircraft moving over there, and wondered if any other terminal would do better. Probably not: there was only one Station aloft, and what mattered was its traffic. No wonder they hadn't been found yet.

"Hey—you!" She turned to find the shuttleport clerk leaning out the door. He waved, and she strode back in. "You're that friend of Cecelia de Marktos, aren't you?"

"Yes," Brun said, wondering slightly.

"Where you going?"

Should she tell him? She hadn't planned to tell anyone here, and buy her ticket on the Station. "Back home for a bit," she said. "Rockhouse."

"Mmm. Got money?"

"Some."

"If you're in a hurry—a friend of hers, y'know, is a friend of ours—might be there's a fellow could help you."

"Tell me," Brun said, trying not to sound too eager.

"Private shuttle," the clerk said. "Over at E-bay." He pointed at a wall, beyond which was presumably E-bay. "I'll tell him you're coming," the clerk said. Which assumed she would. But otherwise she'd just have to sleep on the floor waiting for the regular shuttle. Brun smiled her thanks, retrieved her duffle from the locker, and walked out again.

E-bay was neither bay nor hangar, but a large angled parking slot off the shuttle runway. On it was something that looked too small to be a shuttle. It looked, in fact, like one of the training planes Ronnie and George flew in the Royals. Its hatch was propped open, and someone stooped by it, tossing bundles inside. Brun walked closer, more uncertain the closer she got. The locals tended toward casual dress and behavior, but the young man in scuffed coveralls with shabby boots and a dirty scarf around his neck looked worse than Cecelia's grooms. He glanced up as she came nearer.

"You're that girl's been over at the lady's—you brought her, right?"

"Yes." No use denying what eager gossips had spread.

"She better?" He had bright black eyes, and rumpled black hair.

"Much better," Brun said.

"She sent you?" The eyes had intelligence, and some real concern for Cecelia. Brun wondered why.

"Uh . . . sort of, yes."

"I'm going up. Then on to Caskar, if that's any use." Brun wasn't sure, and she'd left the schedule in the truck. Her helplessness must have showed, because he sighed and explained. "Caskar—eight days—gets you a bigger port. Should be something going through each way within a few days. Here most everything's going to Romney."

"I noticed," she said, but couldn't help a doubtful look at the shuttle. Travel in *that* for eight days. He interpreted that look correctly.

"She's little, but she's stout. Get us there safely. If you don't mind it being a bit rough."

"No—no, that's fine. How much?"

"Well . . . say . . . eight hundred?" That was ridiculously low; she started to say something and he was already talking. "I hate to say that, but see, I can't afford the fuel myself. Not right now. I know it's for the lady, but . . ."

"No, that's fine," Brun said. "I thought it would be more. Look—why not a round thousand?" He wouldn't take more than the eight hundred, and had her insert the cube herself.

"That way you know I didn't cheat you. Now—they'll release the fuel . . ."

In the end she had to help him drag the fuel hoses over and start the pumps. The little ship held an astonishing load of fuel; Brun wondered if it would get off the ground once it started. Inside, she hardly had room to turn around.

"You fly?" the young man asked.

"A little." Her Rockhouse and Sirialis licenses would be no good here; each world regulated its own pilots since the differences in atmospheres, gravity, and weather made specific knowledge necessary.

"Just sit there, then, and keep an eye out." The copilot's seat, up in the needle nose of the shuttle, gave her a great view of the ground going past as they trundled along the runway. It seemed they had gone a mile or more, and she was wondering if they'd ever get airspeed, when the vibration of the gear died away and they were airborne. With a suddenness she did not expect from the long run, the young man tipped up the nose, did something to the controls, and the craft acted like a real shuttle, shoving her back in her seat for long minutes as the sky darkened from light blue to royal to midnight.

"No . . . traffic control?" Brun asked, aware that she had asked this question in another context only a few hours before.

"Nah . . . not enough traffic." The shuttle had minimal scans, she noticed. Minimal everything. "Do you really need to stop at the Station?" he went on. "I'd just as soon go straight on over—save us a few hours."

"Fine." Brun looked out the little port to see stars beginning to show as they reached the fringes of atmosphere. She could hardly believe she was riding in something like this, with someone whose name she didn't even know yet, to go into deep space and spend eight days . . . she was terrified. She was blissfully happy.

"I'm Brun, by the way." That seemed to have been right; he turned to grin at her and held out a calloused hand.

"I'm Cory. Stefan Orinder's son. The lady helped my dad out a lot when he arrived. Just let me set up the course, here, and get the autopilot locked in . . ."

Eight days later, Brun debarked at Caskar Station in the same outfit she'd started in. Cory's ship had no shower, although it did have a functioning toilet. Mostly functioning. She had had plenty of food (sandwiches, soup, tinned stew) and half as much sleep as she needed, because she stood watch with Cory. She knew all about Cory's family, three generations backwards and out to third cousins by marriage, and why his family would do anything for Lady Cecelia, including forget that she herself had ever existed and taken a ride on Cory's ship. She knew it would be an insult to tuck an extra two hundred credits into one of the cabinets, but she promised to tell Cecelia who had helped her.

Her first stop on Caskar Station was a public restroom, where she paid for a hot shower and sudsed herself thoroughly. She dumped her clothes in a washer and called up the status board on the restroom screen. Ah. A passenger ship headed for Greenland (which she knew from Cory's tutoring was more-or-less the way she wanted to go) would be in the next day. She called up its schedule. Twelve days to Greenland, six more to Okkerland, ten to Baskome. At Baskome she could get direct service to Rockhouse Major, no stops, on a major carrier. That looked good, except that the ship from here got there one day late, and the next Rockhouse connection wasn't for sixteen days. Damn.

Here she couldn't use Cecelia's influence . . . but—she looked at herself in the restroom mirror—maybe she could use her own. Or her wits. After all, even after these months, they might be looking for Lord Thornbuckle's daughter. She didn't want to lead them to Lady Cecelia. Not yet, not until she'd had another competency hearing, and regained her legal identity. Wits, then.

The status board showed five ships at this much busier Station. None were scheduled passenger ships, but Cory had explained that many freighters, scheduled and unscheduled, carried a few passengers. The big shipping firms had the better accommodations, but were pickier about who they took; the smaller firms—or owner-operator tramp freighters— would take anyone but an obvious criminal, especially if he or she were willing to do some of the less favored chores aboard.

Ten hours later, Brun was aboard the *Bucclos Success*, shoveling manure. Though most livestock was shipped as frozen embryos, some travelled "whole," in its mature state. Such a ship was known to crews as a "shit shoveler" for obvious reasons. The oversized environmental system had been built to handle the bulk and nitrogen load, but someone had to get the stuff from the animal pens into the system. A human and a shovel worked as efficiently as anything else, especially when valuable animals had to be coddled. Brun's stable experience got her the job—and a free berth.

A third of the cargo was horses, heavy drafters. Another third was hybrid cattlopes, their long straight horns cut short and tipped with bulky foam knobs for shipment. The rest were mixed medium and small: eight pens of dairy goats, seven of does and one of bucks; sixteen pens of sheep; fifty-eight cages of pedigreed rabbits, some of them carrying embryos of other species; sixty cages of small fowl and thirty cages of large. Brun had expected to be put to work with the horses, but as casual labor she was assigned wherever there was need. She learned to mix feed for goats and sheep, hose down the cattlope pens, change waterers and feeders for rabbits and birds. For sixteen days, she spent twelve-hour shifts caring for noisy demanding smelly critters, and eight hours of her shift off sound asleep in her surprisingly comfortable bunk.

"With all that methane production, we have plenty of onboard power generation," one of the others explained. "And we have to carry extra water anyway." Plenty of hot water for showers, an exercise room used mostly by bridge officers (everyone else got plenty of exercise caring for the animals), even a small swimming pool. And in sixteen days, Brun left the ship at Baskome Station. They would have taken her farther—she was hardworking and stayed out of quarrels and she wasn't afraid of the larger animals—but they weren't going where she wanted to go. She got actual pay—less than her private allowance for the same period, but the first money she had ever earned in her life. She turned in the credit strip the ship's paymaster handed her at the first bankstation she saw, and got back a cube representing her present balance in a newly opened Baskome Station account. It did not escape her notice that if she didn't have to spend more than that in her time here, she would not have to touch her own accounts, which might be under surveillance.

Baskome Station looked like real civilization. Besides the bankstation, which had both automated booths and a couple of windows with live tellers, the first concourse she came to had logos of all the standard travellers' organizations and credit services. She had her cards, of course, but if she used them . . . no. It would be a challenge, as well as prudent, to make it to Rockhouse without alerting any watchers. She wouldn't try to use a fake identity, but "Brunnhilde Charlotte Meager" without her usual wild clothes and credit cubes might be anyone. She didn't think anyone would be looking for her in the hold of a livestock hauler, for instance.

So she bypassed the expensive sectors of Baskome Station, the luxury hotel, the fine restaurants, and got a room at a hostel for transient crew—people who lived on such jobs as shoveling manure and running forklifts in warehouses. She ate at the little cafe two doors down, and washed her clothes in a smelly little laundry where the washing machines overflowed at least once a shift.

The transient crew hostel had its own version of the status board, with listings of crew openings and comments by those who had worked for different ships. Brun discovered she had a reputation which had preceded her (how, she couldn't figure out)—someone on the *Bucclos Success* had spread the word that she was a hard worker and trouble-free, so she had offers posted to her mail slot by the time she thought to check it. The rest of her reputation she didn't know about until later.

She picked what seemed like the fastest way to Rockhouse Major, a bulk hauler carrying fish protein meal. Two shifts out of Baskome Station, she discovered that "nice kid" was not the label to carry among people who thought "nice" meant "naive and helpless." And while she wasn't all that helpless, in proving it she broke the wrist and nose of the permanent crewman who tried to rape her. In a dispute between permanent and transient crew, transients are always wrong. Brun found herself facing an angry captain, while the first mate pored over her identification and other belongings.

"I suppose you can explain why someone named Brun Meager, if that is your real name, would have credit cubes and strips that belong to the Carvineau family? Brunnhilde Charlotte Meager-Carvineau, which according to my database is Lord Thornbuckle's youngest daughter. Or do you want to try to tell me you *are* Lord Thornbuckle's youngest daughter? The one who appears in society papers as

Bubbles Carvineau . . . admittedly she is blonde, and so are you, but that hardly seems adequate . . . did you kill her for her papers, or is she wandering around someplace trying to convince a thickheaded planetary militia that she's not some farmer's daughter?"

None of the answers that came first seemed likely to help the situation. Brun wondered what Captain Serrano would have done if (as seemed most unlikely) she'd ever been in a similar fix. One thing, she wouldn't make any jokes, such as that her father *was* a farmer, among other things. A family saying she'd heard since childhood—*When in doubt, tell the truth*—came to mind. It might work.

"Those are my papers, sir," she said. *Respect costs nothing, and pays a high dividend*, she had heard from her grandmother. She hadn't believed it then, but she had never been at the mercy of someone as angry as the captain looked.

"So you *are* claiming to be this . . . uh . . . Lord Thornbuckle's daughter?"

"Yes, sir."

"Care to explain why you're travelling on a freighter carrying fishmeal and working your passage when you could buy the whole damn freighter, according to your credit rating?" Blast. If they'd done a credit check, then anyone watching might pick up where she was. Nothing to do about it now; she had more urgent problems. The first mate's expression was as forbidding as the captain's, and she'd already heard about his propensities from the relief cook.

The truth, but not the whole truth. "Sir, I . . . I wanted to prove I wasn't just a fluffhead like they said."

A snort, not amused. "The way you broke Slim's wrist—" The nose, it seemed, wasn't worth mentioning— "I wouldn't think anyone would call you a fluffhead. Hothead, maybe. How'd you get a reputation as trouble-free on the *Winter*? I thought Jos Haskins was a better judge of character than that."

Brun felt her ears heating up. "Nobody on that ship tried to drag me into a bunk and rape me."

"What's so bad about Slim? Does he have bad breath, or what?" That was the mate; the captain quelled him with a look.

"The point is, I have trouble believing Lord Thornbuckle would let his daughter go off working transient crew jobs halfway across Familias space. Does he know where you are?"

"Well . . . no, sir." He would have found out from the yacht's crew where she had been, with Lady Cecelia; he had expected her to stay there. She suspected he wouldn't be entirely pleased to know where she was now . . . and as for her mother . . .

"My mother would have a cat," she said, thinking aloud. This time the captain's snort was amusement. She eyed him, wondering if she could take advantage of that momentary lapse in his anger. Probably not.

"Tell you what," the captain said. "We can't afford legal trouble, of any type. I don't really care who you are, but if you're who these papers say, you've no business pretending to be a commoner, and if you're not—" He looked down his nose to read the full thing, "—Brunnhilde Charlotte Meager-Carvineau, then her family needs to know someone else is using her papers. This is something for law enforcement to sort out. I'm confiscating your ID and your credit cubes until we arrive at Rockhouse; I'll turn them over to the Station militia. Do you happen to know the balances of the accounts?"

She hadn't looked at them in some time. "Not really, sir. Why?" That admission, she saw, shook his conviction that she was an imposter.

"Because you and I and my mate are going to certify the balances as of this date, so you can be sure—or the real Brunnhilde Charlotte's family can be sure—that I haven't run off with some of it. And if you're the real Brunnhilde Charlotte, I will allow you to send a message to your family, if you wish. Charged as an advance on your salary."

Did she wish? She tried to think what the date would be on Rockhouse—the local date, not Universal. Her father might be there for the biennial Council meeting—Uncle Serval would be, anyway—and even Buttons might be there. But what could she say? Could she phrase a warning so they would understand it, and not get themselves into worse danger? And she really did not want the Crown Minister or his sister Lorenza to know she was on her way.

She came down finally on the side of caution—both kinds. Caution with the captain (perhaps he'd see that an imposter would hardly send a message to a home that wasn't hers) and with her family (so they couldn't reveal information they didn't have).

"I'd like to send a message, but I don't want to tell them when I'm arriving. As you said, my parents would not approve of my . . . er . . . choice of conveyance."

"I'm not prepared to lie for you, young woman."

"No, sir. Could you send: 'You were right; I'm on my way home,' and then 'Love, Brun'?"

"Tell me one thing—why do the society papers say your name is Carvineau when your papers say it's Meager?"

"My mother's name is Meager; all the children use the maternal last name on identification until we're twenty-five. It's supposed to be safer."

"Ah. Well, Ms. Meager, consider yourself warned against any further brawling; you are confined to quarters except when on duty in the galley—I'm taking you off general duty and making you the cook's assistant—and as I said, your identification and other materials will be turned over to Station militia when we reach Rockhouse. Do you have anything further to say?"

"No, sir."

"Right then. Get to work."

She had plenty of time locked in her tiny cubicle with its blank walls and hard bunk to realize how close she had come to complete disaster. And how close it still was . . . suppose the mate decided to come after her, too? He didn't, but she slept badly the rest of the trip.

CHAPTER SIXTEEN

Brun discovered that Rockhouse Major turned a different face to transient crew suspected of impersonating rich girls. Her captain had contacted Station militia, and she found herself and her papers in a dingy, cluttered office, watched by a bored but obviously capable young person of doubtful gender with a sidearm.

"If I could just make a call," she kept saying. No one answered. People in uniform wandered in and out; voices spoke at a distance that blurred the words but not the emotion: boredom, hostility, defiance, fear.

Finally, a tired-eyed older man appeared, looked at her, shook his head, and said, "Come on." He led her to a proper ID booth, where in only a few minutes her retinal scan, fingerprints, and other data confirmed her papers. He shook his head again. "You really *are* Lord Thornbuckle's daughter. Would you mind explaining what you were doing hiring on as transient crew?"

"It was an adventure," Brun said. She realized now just how silly that sounded, and she didn't seem able to find the insouciant tone she had cultivated in years past. He just stared at her, a tired man who clearly wished spoiled rich kids wouldn't waste his time.

"Do you need anything?" he asked finally.

"No . . . if I can have my things."

"Yes—just sign here." Her credit cubes and strips, itemized, lay on the sheet he pointed to. She started to sign and he pointed, making it clear he wanted no mistakes. She checked then, and found nothing missing. Her battered little duffle, with its few changes of clothes, seemed full enough, and if it wasn't she could buy replacements. "The captain said if you were legal, he'd deposit your pay, less a fine for brawling. What'd you do, if you don't mind my asking?"

Brun shrugged. "Another crewman tried to jump me; I broke his nose and wrist. Stupid—I should've seen it coming."

"I don't know what it is you kids are looking for," the man said, shaking his head yet again. "You've got everything . . . why look for trouble?"

Brun smiled at him. "I'm sorry—I was stupid, and I'm going home to admit it—is that all right?"

This time he really looked at her, and his eyes warmed. "I'm glad you weren't hurt," he said. "We see enough kids getting hurt."

Out in the concourse, she was still a scruffy transient spacer to look at, dirty and shabby, with an ordinary scuffed duffle over her shoulder. She ambled along, relaxing a bit in this familiar territory. First she would get something to eat, then a shower—no, a shower first, then call Ronnie—no, call the estate downside and get someone to send the shuttle up—she slowed, as she came to a bank of public communications booths. She put her duffle on the shelf of an empty booth and started to close the door. Someone leaned across from another, a big bulky man who looked both frustrated and dangerous.

"Hey—you just came out of that militia station, didn't you?"

"Yeah." No sense arguing, if she'd been seen.

"Seen a rich-bitch youngster in there, the kind that throws their weight around?"

Her belly tightened. "No," she said shortly. "All I saw was this fat cop tryin' to make out I was somebody else."

"Dammit." His strong fingers tapped the partition. "I'm supposed to find this girl—loudmouth blonde, they said, real stylish, some mucky-muck lord's daughter. Sure you haven't seen her?"

"Not me. Is that the only militia station?"

"No, worse luck. Where you in from?" His eyes were intent, measuring. "You permcrew or transient?"

"Transient now." Brun tried for a sullen tone. She held

up her well-calloused hand. "Signed onto a shit shoveler as cook's assistant, and they had me down in the stalls three shifts out of four. I didn't leave home to be some cow's personal assistant."

His eyes lost interest after a long look at her hand. "Yeah, well, I guess you didn't meet any daughters of the aristocracy shoveling manure." He moved away, toward the militia station entrance. Brun could not move. She had to move. If he went in, if he talked to that man, he would know . . .

She picked up the headpiece, put it back as if uncertain, and moved on down the concourse. How could someone like that be looking for her already? Had something happened? She lengthened her stride, almost ran into someone pausing to look in a display window, and told herself not to spook. The captain had queried ahead about her . . . anyone who watched the militia regularly might have overheard. As long as she got off Rockhouse Major before that dangerous man could find her, she should be safe.

She took a slideway, then a tram, putting a sector and two levels between her and the militia office before she dared stop at another combooth cluster. This was higher-income territory, though her scruffy clothes weren't that unusual. No used-clothing stores here, but also none of the high-priced places that expected you to know their names. Display windows showed the latest style; she'd been gone long enough for them to change. Thigh boots? Laced socks? Tunics were longer, dresses shorter, and someone had decided to ignore the waistline again. They'd done that when she was twelve, too—but then the top colors had been muted moss greens and browns. Now the fashion seemed to be icy pastels. She stared at a long tunic patterned with zigzags of pale pink on pale green over pink slacks as she waited for her connection to go through. She had decided to start by warning Ronnie.

"Yes?" It sounded like Ronnie's voice, but a very cautious Ronnie. Brun hoped it was; Ronnie she might influence, but anyone else in his family would lecture first and listen afterwards, if then.

"Ronnie?"

"Yes, who is this?"

"It's me. Brun . . . Bubbles . . . you know." Then, as she heard him take a deep breath that would no doubt end in a loud outcry, she went on quickly. "Don't say my name! Don't! I'm up at Rockhouse Major and you're in great danger and so is your family. Don't say anything—pretend I'm someone else. George, maybe."

"I was expecting a call from him—er—from Gerry, that is. I don't really have time to chat right now . . ." He must have done something to the privacy shield; behind him now she could hear high voices chattering, glasses clinking. What was local time down there? She'd completely forgotten to check. "Listen, George," he went on. "Why don't you call me back later?"

"Shield again," Brun said. When the background sound disappeared again, she continued. "Ronnie, you must listen. It's critical—I'm being followed. Your aunt has remembered who did it to her."

"Then she's—" With an abrupt change of voice, "—she's not *pregnant*! I don't believe it. And if she is, it's certainly not *mine*. Who does she think she is?"

Brun grinned. Ronnie had an unexpected gift for this. "Lorenza. You know, the fluffy one with the soft voice, with the important brother . . ."

"Oh, I say. Surely not—harmless as a—and besides, she's here."

"Now?" Brun broke off, appalled at the squeak in her voice. More quietly, she went on. "Ronnie, believe me. Poison. Don't take anything she offers—get out of there, now. Get George—he's in danger, too. I'll explain when I get down—" Though how she was going to do that without using her ID and thus triggering pursuit, she didn't know.

"Well, of course we'll come," Ronnie said brightly, as if agreeing to a party invitation. "Short notice no bother. Anything for the Royals, what?"

"Don't overdo it," Brun said. "Assuming she's listening."

"Read my lips," Ronnie said, in the same bright tone. "It's no problem. We'll be there. Pick a number."

That old game. Now, what were the shuttleslot codes for this Station? The booth had local datanet access; she punched up the information she needed.

"E-19 or 21."

"Be there soonest."

Brun put down the headset. Soonest gave no real idea of how long it would take Ronnie to extricate himself from his house, find George, get to the family shuttle, file flight plans, and get here. Right that moment she wanted him here instantly, someone she knew, someone she could trust. She was getting very, very tired of adventure.

Ronnie closed the satellite circuits carefully and clicked off the privacy shield. It wouldn't have been hard for someone to tap into that unscrambled call, if they'd had a mind to. Had anyone? He'd better assume the worst.

"Ronnie, dear, who was that?" His mother, in her long lace gown, stood at the door of a room full of older women, all similarly dressed. They were talking and eating all at once, stocking up for an evening at the theater.

"Fellow at the Regiment," he said. "Sorry—seems something has come up."

"Oh, no! I was counting on you, dear. Why can't they get George or someone else?"

"I'm supposed to pick George up on the way, actually. Sorry, Mother, it's rather urgent." Curiosity lit her eyes.

"What, dear?"

"Now Mother, you know I'm not supposed to talk about Regimental business." Her face clouded; she opened her mouth. He gave her the old smile, the one that always melted her. "But I will tell you, because I know you won't gossip, that some fellow's gotten in a bit of trouble about this girl— claims she's pregnant, claims she can prove whose . . . you know."

"Ah." Her face cleared. "But you have the implant—and the law doesn't—"

"There's law, and there's family," Ronnie said. "All of us who . . . er . . . knew her, as it were, must confer with the Regimental legal staff. Terribly confidential; you won't tell any of your old cats, will you?"

"It wasn't you!? You and Raffa . . . ?"

"Nothing to do with me and Raffa. A wild party a while back; I know I didn't reverse my implant, or even know the girl, but there could be a claim if I don't go in and have it checked out. And they've got the gene militia or whatever they are standing by. Oh—remember I told you George and a few of us were taking the shuttle up after the opera? I think we'll just go on after this—it's too much trouble to stop back by—" He was appalled at his own invention; the story seemed to be sprouting branches and luxuriant foliage in all directions. He could almost see the young woman he had supposedly partied with, although her motivations wavered: was she trying to claw her way up the social ladder from a not-quite-important family, or was she a muckraking journalist out to expose the foibles of the rich and notorious? She had a sister in entertainment; she had worn purple that night that had never happened; she had a fake diamond collar . . .

"Be careful, Ronnie—"

"Of course, Mother." In ways she would never know, he intended to be very careful. He was already in evening clothes, and he didn't have time to change. As he went toward the door, he heard Lorenza calling to his mother, and shivered in spite of himself. How could he leave her there, in peril? But Brun's was worse, he told himself.

George, dressing for the same evening's entertainment— he had also been snagged as an acceptable young male escort for the party of mothers and aunts attending the theater— was glad enough to hear he wouldn't be seeing a revival of Darwinian grand opera.

"But Lorenza!" he said, buttoning the soft shirt he had grabbed to replace the dress shirt he hadn't fastened yet. "Are you sure?"

"Brun is sure that my aunt is sure. That's enough for me, at least until we talk more to Brun. And she's being hunted, she says."

"Lorenza. Dad needs to know this. He's at the office—"

"Call from the shuttle—we've got to go. I told Mother an incredible lie about a pregnant girl accusing half the Regiment, and all of us having to have genetic scans, and if she calls—even though I told her it was all being kept quiet—"

"The colonel will have cats, and then have us for breakfast. Right. I'm ready." He looked at Ronnie. "But you— you'll stick out like anything, up there." He dug into his closet and bundled up another shirt and pair of casual slacks. "We'll take these along—you can change on the shuttle while I call."

Ronnie reflected that George was a good deal less odious lately. Of course he had been through that mess on Sirialis, and being shot in the gut was, according to the redoubtable Captain Serrano, a specific for youthful idiocy, but still. George had been odious for years; he had not so much turned over a new leaf as uprooted an entire forest.

On the shuttle trip to Rockhouse Major, Ronnie told George all he knew or suspected and had kept from him before. "Brun said if anyone else knew my aunt was conscious inside, her life would be in danger. I couldn't talk to anyone . . . I thought it was because she'd gone to see the king about Gerel—"

"About the prince? Why? Just because he showed up on Sirialis?"

"No . . . because on the trip home I noticed something." Even now he was reluctant to tell George—but if the worst happened, someone had to know. And he had begun to think George was involved, had been from the beginning. "Do you remember that term when you nearly flunked all your subjects?"

George grimaced. "Not as clearly as I should, but I've heard about it often enough. My father insists it proves the need of diligent application—that's his term—that even the brightest boy can't skate by forever on native brilliance. The masters—well, you remember. As far as they were concerned I was a typically lazy, careless, spoiled young brat. I thought I was working harder than I ever had, but nothing came of it—I suppose they were right, and I was fooling myself thinking I was working. Daydreaming, maybe."

"I think you were right, George, and they didn't recognize it. At thirteen, they expect boys to slack off, daydream, hang around making mischief with others. So when your grades dropped, that's what they said. But I think it was something else."

"What, then? Hormones?"

"No—at least not your native hormones . . . George, this is *very* secret."

"Right. I nearly flunk all my courses and it's on my permanent records, and it's now a great secret. Nobody knows except you and every other boy I was at school with, all the masters, my family—" George's talent for being odious had not, Ronnie realized, vanished; it had merely been in hiding.

"Shut up, George," he said cheerfully. He actually felt better knowing George was not abandoning a lifelong habit. "I think someone made you stupid for a while. On purpose."

"Made me stupid! Why?" Then that handsome face changed, became more like his father's. "Oh . . . and you said something about the prince . . . and he changed schools . . ."

"And got a reputation for silly-ass idiocy. Like that quarrel with me—" Ronnie reflected that his own end of that quarrel didn't argue for any great intelligence either, and flushed, but George didn't take that up.

"The prince is stupid. The prince is—he can't be, Ron, someone would've noticed. Someone would have told the king."

"Aunt Cecelia did just that, after we got back. On her usual high horse about it, too."

"And *then* she has that stroke you say wasn't a real stroke. Like my term of being stupid wasn't real stupidity. Like the prince—" George stopped and looked at Ronnie with dawning comprehension.

"Isn't really stupid. Not on his own."

"But mine went away. Why didn't the prince's?" Then he answered his own question. "Because someone wanted him to stay that way. And it had to be—" They stared at each other and said in unison, "The king."

"Oh . . . dear." Ronnie remembered that he had planned to change and began pulling the studs from his dress shirt. "Oh . . . my. We are in trouble."

George, with nothing to occupy his mind but the problem at hand, leaned back in his seat. "If your aunt claims Lorenza poisoned her, and if that's why Lorenza poisoned her, then Lorenza may have done it to the prince."

Ronnie paused, his shirt half-undone. "Remember that scandal a few years ago about the Graham-Scolaris?"

"Of course. Dad defended the old man."

"What if . . . what if Lorenza supplies all sorts of useful poisons—chemicals—not just to the Crown but to others?"

"What, a medieval poisoner in our midst? That's awfully dramatic, Ronnie."

"So is a stupid prince kept that way for years. So was my aunt's collapse."

"Point taken." George frowned at him, and Ronnie remembered he hadn't finished changing. He tore off the dress shirt and shrugged into George's casual one. A bit tight across the shoulders, but not enough to matter. He buttoned it slowly, still thinking.

"Something else I just thought of . . . remember when Gerel's older brothers died? That assassination, and then the duel?"

"Yes—do you think they were stupid, too?"

"No—I remember, though, that was when we were what? Twelve, thirteen, along in there. Before your bad term, anyway. And Jared was almost thirty; there was talk of having the Grand Council Familias agree to his succession in advance."

Now George frowned. "I don't—yes, just a minute. I think they actually did, and then rescinded it after he died, so it wouldn't interfere with Nadrel's or Gerel's succession later."

"I remember Gerel getting lots of visits from his brothers right before that. Picnics and so on. Remember? He'd wanted to ask us along, and his brothers said no, and he was annoyed with them. Then afterwards, he was all excited about something he wouldn't tell us . . . ."

"I don't remember any of that." George tossed Ronnie a tie. "Here—put on this anachronism. That shirt needs a reason to look tight across the shoulders."

"But—" Ronnie stretched his neck, and worked the tie into position. "But I remember—and you and he were thick as anything for a week or so—you were grinning all over your face, and wouldn't tell me—"

"Was that the time you tried to get it out of me by twisting my arm?"

"No—we already knew that wouldn't work. No, we tried bribery—an entire box of chocolate. You scarfed the lot and refused to divulge. You don't remember?"

"No . . . only it was next term I had trouble. You don't suppose someone really did drug me, and it took the memory, too?"

"I know Gerel avoided you that term—you'd gotten involved with those Hampton Reef boys."

George shuddered. "I do remember them. Nasty beasts, and then the next year I couldn't scrape them away. Thank heavens they transferred at midterm."

The shuttle intercom chimed, and the pilot spoke. "We're in the Rockhouse Major approach now, gentlemen. If you'd take your seats, please, and prepare for docking . . ."

✳   ✳   ✳

Brun wanted a shower, food, and sleep, in that order, but ahead of everything else in her personal queue was safety. She changed levels and sectors again, finally choosing a spacers' hostel down the row from the one Heris had used before she left. She didn't dare use that one, in case someone was watching it, or the clerk recognized her—unlikely as that seemed. Cleanliness felt wonderful—better than food, and she'd just as soon sleep, she decided, stretching out on the comfortable bunk. Ronnie couldn't possibly get here for several hours, probably six or seven. She could sleep safely at least two of them.

The buzzing timer woke her from the kind of vaguely unpleasant dream that isn't a nightmare but leaves a dull, foreboding feeling behind the eyes. Another shower cleared most of it from her head. Now she was really hungry. She checked the time. If he really had left home right away, if he had gone straight to the family's shuttle, and if they'd gotten priority clearance, Ronnie might be arriving within the hour. She would head for the shuttle deck and get something to eat there.

The timer informed her it was partway into second shift—aftermain, some called it. Both names were on the timer's dial. That meant the Station equivalent of nightlife, including the nightcrawlers. Brun dug through her duffle for possible outfits that wouldn't be too visible and wouldn't say the wrong things. She didn't want to be transient crew anymore, and she certainly didn't want to stick out as Lord Thornbuckle's daughter out being adventurous. She just hadn't brought the right clothes . . . but she had brought enough makeup.

Down the way, she found a clothing store for people with no imagination. Not the pastels she'd seen before, but good old boring classic beiges and browns and grays and dull blues. Clerks' clothes, maybe. Brun found that even so she was drawn to the most striking outfits in the shop; she kept picking up accessories that screamed "Look at me!" No. Buy what she automatically disdained. The blue slacks, the beige top, the brown belt—not the braided one, not the one with sequins, just plain brown. Sensible brown shoes. In the mirror she looked like a low-income copy of her mother . . . if you were born with those bones, plain looked classic. What could look just plain . . . plain? A different blouse, blue and rose flowers scattered loosely on beige, and a bit too tight. Beige shoes with little gold doodads on them. That helped; they made her feet hurt, so she walked differently. She could do the rest with makeup.

When she reached the shuttle deck, the status boards showed three private shuttles on approach, identified only by registration number. Great. She had never known the registration number of Ronnie's family's shuttle. Then one of the other numbers sank in. That was *her* family's shuttle, the same one she'd taken Cecelia up in. Had Ronnie been crazy enough to borrow that one? The watchers would be looking for it.

Brun ducked quickly into one of the fast-food outlets that opened onto the concourse. She ordered the first thing she saw, and took it to a windowseat. Between bites of something greasy and meaty coated with something doughy, she scanned the area for the man who had spoken to her before. Of course he wouldn't have been alone—and she had no idea what other watchers might look like. The food helped; her stomach gurgled its contentment, and she felt her courage returning. She was clean, and fed, and didn't look anything like her earlier self—either of them.

"Sorry we're having to wait a bit," the shuttle pilot said. "There's quite a crowd of arrivals just now."

"Private shuttles?" Ronnie asked.

"Yes—Lord Thornbuckle's is just ahead of us."

George and Ronnie stared at each other. "Why would she call me, if she was going to call the family shuttle?" Ronnie asked. "Or did I misunderstand—we were trying to talk in a sort of instant code—"

"I suppose it could be another family member, though that's quite a coincidence. And they usually bring the family yacht in over at Minor, to avoid the traffic."

"The yacht's not operational," Ronnie said. "Don't you remember? Some kind of harebrained terrorist attack or something."

"So it could be one of the others, come by commercial passenger service." George peered out the tiny window. Ronnie, looking past his head, could make nothing of the strings of lights. Finally—not that long by the clock on the forward bulkhead—he felt the slight bump of docking. When the status lights turned green, he led George out the access tube to the reception lounge. Across from the access tube was the door into the public corridor that led to the concourse. A status screen above it showed that Lord Thornbuckle's shuttle was docked to their right.

Ronnie headed that way, receiving a polite nod from the man at the door to that lounge. He didn't see Brun anywhere.

Brun saw Ronnie and her brother at the same moment. Buttons, looking happy and relaxed, with his fiancée Sarah on his arm, strolled along the concourse from the commercial gates toward the entrance to the private shuttle bays. Ronnie was just coming out, looking around.

Brun had just had time to notice Sarah's outfit—flowing rose silk, a corsage of fresh white roses—when Sarah staggered, and the corsage blew apart, leaving a single red rose. Buttons threw himself on top of her; the tough-looking man who had spoken to Brun rushed at them, weapon in hand. People in the concourse screamed; some dove for the floor. Brun pushed away from the table and tried to get to her brother, but the people in the doorway were backing away. She pushed and shoved, using elbows and sharp kicks to move them.

Over their heads, she could see Ronnie turn toward the trouble, and then make a flying tackle on the armed man. George erupted from the corridor behind him; the two of them were on the attacker by the time Brun got free of the tangle and staggered across the concourse, cursing her new shoes. In the distance, whistles blew; she hoped someone had had the sense to call Station militia. And medical help.

"Help me!" Buttons was saying. "She's bleeding—!" Brun fell on her knees beside him and unzipped her duffle, pulling out her last clean shirt.

"Here," she said, stuffing it in the wound. The months she'd spent with therapists and doctors gave her more knowledge than she wanted of what lay behind the blood. But Sarah had a pulse, and was breathing. Buttons looked at her and his eyes widened.

"What are *you* doing here?"

"Saving Sarah," Brun said. Sarah opened her eyes.

"That really hurts," she said, and closed them again. Typical of Sarah, Brun thought. No wasted words, no unnecessary fuss.

"It's my fault," Brun said to Buttons. "He thought I was Sarah—I mean, the other way around."

"Who?" But he had already turned toward the continuing tussle between Ronnie and George and the attacker, who had acquired allies from points unknown. Just as it looked like spreading into a wholesale brawl, the militia arrived.

The same tired-eyed man Brun had met before took their statements after Sarah had been taken to the Station clinic. His gaze sharpened when he recognized Brun and the blood on her clothes.

"Did you expect to meet your sister here?" he asked Buttons. "Was that your purpose?"

"No—Sarah and I had legal business to transact before our wedding. Brun's been out of touch quite a while; I frankly didn't know where she was."

"Ah. And you . . . gentlemen . . ." Ronnie and George were attempting to look innocent and noble through their bruises. "You . . . were coming up to meet this young gentleman, perhaps?"

"No . . . actually . . ." Ronnie's eyes slid toward Brun's. She nodded. "We had come up to meet Brun. She called me."

"I see. You are also . . ." He was clearly groping for the word. Brun spoke up.

"We aren't engaged, but we've been friends a long time. I didn't want to call our people until I'd had a chance to clean up and change—"

"Yes," drawled Buttons, looking her up and down. She recognized that tone; he was going to back her, but have his own fun. "I can see why. Mother would have had a fit. Where have you been, anyway?"

"Working as transient crew," Brun said, holding up her calloused hand for him to see. "I was hoping to get my hair done and so on before she knew I was anywhere around. Besides, there was a little trouble when I arrived."

"Do you have any idea why someone shot your fiancée?" The militia officer interrupted.

"No," Buttons said. Brun wondered a moment about that

flat negative, but she didn't challenge him. Instead, she answered.

"I do. I think he meant to shoot me, and didn't have a good description." The man's eyebrows went up. Brun explained. "A man stopped me after I left the militia station earlier and asked if I'd seen a rich young woman in there. He knew my name, and a rough description, but the way I was dressed then, he didn't recognize me. It scared me; it's one reason I called Ronnie."

"Well, then, miss, do you know why someone might want to shoot you?"

"No—but it's clear someone did, and since Sarah and I are both blonde, and about the same height, he probably figured someone heading for our shuttle, with my brother, was the right person."

"I see. If you'll thumbsign this report, then—" With a sideways glance at Buttons, Brun pressed her thumb to the pad, and the man nodded. "That's it for now—I presume you'll be available downside if we need you?"

"Yes, of course."

"I'm staying up here," Buttons said. "Until Sarah's released. I don't know how long it will take—if they'll do the regen here, or ship her down. Brun, since Ronnie's here with their shuttle, could you ride with him?"

"Of course." Something in his voice suggested he needed to talk with her alone. "Do you mind if we come with you to the clinic?"

"No . . . that's fine . . ." He stood, and looked about uncertainly. The militia had dispersed the crowd and the four of them stood alone. Then he looked down at Brun. "The thing is, I'm still worried about you. Did you know Lady Cecelia had filed for reinstatement of competency?"

"What? I thought she'd wait until—"

"She didn't wait; it was on the nets four days ago. There's been an uproar you wouldn't believe in the press and among the Families. Dad's afraid she's in danger—and you, of course. We didn't put a query on your ID because we didn't want to call attention to it, so we haven't known where you were—"

"But somebody did," Brun said. "Or at least they were watching for any word of me."

"Yes. Dad's convinced now that you were right—he's had

his doubts—but that means whoever did it will be moving. You and Ronnie are both prime targets. Frankly I think you'd better get in that shuttle and go—and then stay on the estate. Don't go into town; we don't know just how hard whoever it is will come after you."

"But you and Sarah?" Should she tell him about Lorenza now? Or would it make it more dangerous for him? She was too tired to think.

"We should be safe now that they know she's not you."

"Buttons, there's something we need to tell you—" Ronnie had lowered his voice. "It's really important. George and I think we know—"

"Not here. Take Brun, get down to our place, and *stay there.* I'll be along as soon as Sarah can travel. They'll probably send her down for regen treatment when she's stabilized. Dad's on his way, too."

Buttons turned away with a little wave; Brun suddenly felt the weight of fear and exhaustion settle back on her shoulders. Her feet hurt.

"He's right," she said. "Let's go home."

CHAPTER SEVENTEEN

The grounds of the Institute of Neuroscience had lush green lawns and flowering shrubs. A few low domes protruded through the greenery, and a stubby blocklike building rose from a grove of trees in the distance. Heris rode a silent electric car hardly big enough for her and the driver from the public transit stop to the entrance, and wondered aloud at the spaciousness.

"A bomb attack thirty years ago," the driver said, over his shoulder. "The Benignity, of course. They thought they were getting a manufacturing complex . . . we rebuilt underground, even though that's no real protection against modern munitions. But it was all ugly and crowded before; this way we have something pretty to look at."

At the front desk, Heris handed over her official documents, with the Royal Seal of the Familias Regnant. She had noticed three nondescript men in the waiting room . . . Geralds all, scattered among the other patients.

"Ah—are you the patient, Captain?"

"No. But I would prefer not to explain here."

"Of course. Perhaps you and . . . is the patient here?" The clerk managed, heroically Heris thought, not to peer into the waiting room.

"Yes."

"Then perhaps you and the patient would come this way." Heris gave the hand signal the Geralds had taught her, and one by one they ambled up to the desk, leaned over, and took the colored card the clerk held up. Her eyes widened but she said nothing.

* * *

Doctors Koshinsky and Velun. Male and female, short and tall, thick and thin, dark and fair. Koshinsky's dark beard was only slightly darker than his skin, and he came up to Velun's elegant silk-clad shoulder. Heris wondered what they thought of her and the clones. The clones had shed their disguises, and now wore identical coveralls; they looked like a frieze of tall blond princes, to which she was a short dark punctuation. Or, in the metaphor of music (she still thought it was strange to name a planet Music), "da-da-da-dum."

"Can you describe the problem any more precisely, Captain?" asked Dr. Velun. Height, blonde hair, a glacial beauty . . . she could be mother or aunt to those princes.

"I thought that was in the king's letter."

"Unfortunately not. What it says is that he was given a demonstration of a drug to inhibit higher cognitive processes, and its reversibility, in a person of his son's age. Then that same drug—he thinks—was administered to his son, causing a relative inability to learn and perform cognitive tasks at the level his innate abilities warranted—" She broke off and gave Heris a hostile look. "Quite frankly, Captain Serrano, we would regard such a use of any method of lowering intelligence to be quite unethical. In our culture, intelligence is respected."

"If I understand correctly," Heris said, "the king was given a choice of having his son partially and temporarily incapacitated or assassinated; his older sons had both died, one by assassination and one in . . . er . . . dubious circumstances. It was not an easy choice."

"Even so," Dr. Velun said. "And now, I understand, he wants to see if the effect can be reversed by someone other than the . . . mmm . . . perpetrator?"

"That's right. I should also mention that the use of clone doubles is not only unethical but illegal in our society."

"Not here," Dr. Koshinsky said. "We grow clones all the time; we've nothing against clones. They have full legal identity."

"The problem is, these clones have been trained to be the prince's doubles. Now each of them claims he is not the prince, that the prince is somewhere else. I was twice informed that the person I was taking aboard was the prince, only . . ." Heris nodded at the three. "Only I have no way of telling the difference. And I think it likely that they are somehow programmed or conditioned not to reveal the prince's identity."

"Were the clones also treated to inhibit their intelligence?"

"I don't know. I wasn't even told there were clones."

"Hmm. Then, the first step is to examine these young men—with their permission of course—"

"Certainly," said the three princes, or clones, or Geralds. And, still in unison, "You won't be able to distinguish us from one another." Heris had her doubts. Anyone who could scan weapons an R.S.S. ship would miss might well have new and better ways to tell a prime from its clone.

Two days later, Dr. Velun called Heris in for another conference. She had a stack of data cubes and a cube player already set up.

"Let me tell you what we've found out so far . . . do you have a medical background, by any chance?"

"No, sorry."

"Well—I'll do my best. Do ask questions when they occur, will you? Now. We know that the prince is a Registered Embryo. Now in the Familias Regnant, that means an embryo guaranteed to carry the genetic markers of the certified biological parents. All known flaws eliminated, and enhancements included—"

"Enhancements?"

The doctor was glad to explain. "Legally, all the genes—whole genes—must come from either the certified mother or the certified father. Given a sufficiency of sperm and ova, from almost anyone, it's possible to select desirable—even outstanding—gene fragments. Humans are superbly heterozygous; it's only a question of knowing which sequences correlate with which desired trait. But there are practical limits on the quantity of genetic material . . . time constraints, for instance. By the time you've located the single recessive gene you want, in one of the fifty million sperm you examined, the ovum may be overripe. If it's not to be a gamble, much like the original, you use enhancements."

"And those are?"

"Gene *fragments*, not whole genes, which means they can be substituted—with the usual techniques—" Heris had no idea what the usual techniques were and didn't really care.

"For instance, intelligence. Everyone has known since Old Earth times that intelligence is not a single entity, a single faculty. There are modules, specialized clumps of neurons which preferentially work with certain inputs." That made Heris think of the yacht's scanning computers—this one for detecting one kind of input and interpreting it, and that one for another. She said that and Dr. Velun looked pained. "Not really. Or rather, in a way, but not completely. The human brain has developmental preferences, but it's also remarkably plastic: it responds to experience, so that the more experience in a cognitive domain, the more likely that function is to work well. But more important, to this patient, is what happens when things go wrong."

Heris nodded. She found it hard to concentrate, even though she needed to be able to explain to the king later. What had gone wrong was the prince got stupid: simple, and—if not reparable—the end of the king's hopes. The doctor talked on and on, and Heris felt herself falling more and more behind. What was a dedicated neuron? What did Dr. Velun mean by saying that some of them were supposed to die off?

Dr. Velun began to talk about drugs that might have caused the prince's problem. "One thing that would work is a protein that blocks the production of a given neurotransmitter by tying up the RNA on which the protein would be constructed—I presume you do know something about biochemistry—?"

She must have recognized Heris's glazed incomprehension at last. "Sorry," Heris said. "My specialty lies elsewhere. I know what DNA is—" Sort of, she thought to herself. A spiral molecule of genetic material, that was about it. "But the function of different kinds of RNA—that's beyond me."

Dr. Velun looked pained, started with a chemical description, stopped short, glared at her, and finally shrugged. "You won't get it, not in the time we have."

Perversely, Heris was now determined to understand. "Look—if you'll give me time to read something—even a child's version—I'm sure I can learn. It's just that it's so far from my own background—"

Velun's face contracted in a scowl. "Right. Warfare. I suppose you know how to kill people."

This sort of hostility was familiar; Heris smiled at her. "Well, yes, but so do you. Any medical researcher knows as many lethal tricks as I do. No, my expertise is in the equipment and the personnel—to take just one system, knowing how the environmental system aboard each class of ship works, where the pipes are, how many technicians are needed to service it, and what to look for to be sure it's working correctly. I must know the interactions of all shipboard systems, so that if the electrical system goes down for any reason, I can keep the ship's crew alive without the electrically powered pumps and blowers in the environmental system."

"Engineering," the doctor muttered.

Heris let her smile widen. "Yes, it is. So is clinical medicine, to my view: know the systems, recognize when something's wrong, and know what to do about it."

That coaxed a tiny smile. "Well . . . I suppose. We like to think of ourselves as researchers, too."

"I'm sure you are. So are some of us—spacefleet officers, I mean. A friend of mine solved a century-old problem in oxygen exchange systems. That's never been my talent— I can keep on top of existing systems, but I'm not an innovator. But I know and respect those who are."

"Well." Velun seemed to be considering that fairly. "If you really want to know, then, there's an undergraduate course on cube—I have a copy because my second daughter's going to be taking it next year. Or, if you want a fast take, there's the induction trainer."

The induction trainer gave Heris a headache. Still, it was fast. She agreed.

When she came up from the course, the first thing she thought of was not the prince, but Lady Cecelia. She had a glimmer of what might have been done to her, although she recognized her own inexpertise.

"Could that—the same mechanism—cause a strokelike appearance in an elderly patient?"

This time she talked to Dr. Koshinsky; Dr. Velun was, he said, busily working out sequences . . . and now Heris understood, in principle, what that was and why it was important. Dr. Koshinsky rocked back on his heels, considering her suggestion. "Not by itself, I wouldn't think. It could maintain that appearance, but the onset would be too slow. Why?"

Heris explained all she knew of Cecelia's condition. "One of her visitors described what looked like an implanted delivery system for drugs. That could be the maintenance drug you're talking about."

The doctor's eyebrows went up. "Is this a . . . political person you're speaking of?"

"Heavens no." Heris wondered, even as she said it, if that were completely true. Lady Cecelia did not choose to involve herself in politics much, but she had, after all, pressured the Crown into arranging the pardon and restitution for convicted military personnel. If that wasn't political power, Heris wondered what was. She tried to explain to the puzzled doctor. "She's a very wealthy, very independent elderly lady—my former employer, in fact. In perfect health, so far as anyone knew. She collapsed in what appeared to be a stroke, followed by coma, but we have reason to suspect that's not what really happened. If she was felled by some chemical attack, could you reverse it?"

The doctor pursed his lips. "We'd have to get to her, or her to us. There's no way I'd touch this long distance. Where is she?"

"I have no idea. I can—possibly—get in contact with someone who knows where she is."

"It would be better to intervene as soon as possible. If spontaneous recovery doesn't occur in the absence of the neurotoxins, degeneration can occur from inhibition of response."

"I—don't know how her recovery has gone."

"Find out. You're sure this was an intentional injury?"

"Reasonably sure. She had made some enemies." Heris paused a moment, then added, "In fact, I was suspected of having done it." If their investigation revealed this, better she had been open about it. "Her family, a very prominent one, was upset because she mentioned me in her will." She paused a moment, and realized there was no real advantage to concealing Cecelia's identity. "Lady Cecelia de Marktos . . ." He was nodding before she finished the full thing; he recognized the name.

"I see. But you want her to recover." It was not quite a question. Heris fought back the automatic anger.

"Yes. Not only is she my employer, she's my friend. She's . . . remarkable." There was no way to describe Cecelia to a stranger. Heris's memory presented an image of Cecelia on that special horse at Bunny's, wind whipping back her short grizzled hair, face alight as they galloped down to a stone wall. "You'd have to know her."

"As a matter of fact, I know a little. My niece is horse crazy, and we gave her the complete set of *Great Riders*. So I've seen Lady Cecelia, at least as she was at her peak." He paused, then went on. "If you don't know where she was taken, may I suggest a possibility? She used to own a stud farm and training facility on Rotterdam . . ."

"She wouldn't be there," Heris said quickly. "It's too obvious. She'd have been taken somewhere less . . ."

"The thing is, you could find out without much trouble. She's known and loved in the world of those who breed and train performance horses. They don't care about politics, on the whole, but they do care about each other. They will know where she is, I'm sure, and while they may not tell you, they'll tell her friends you're looking."

It was a chance, the best one she'd had. "Do you need me here while you work on the prince?"

"Not really."

"Then—I think I'll go find her. Bring her back. You have adequate security here . . . ?"

"We hope so."

"Then I can leave the prince and his clones—or the clones without the prince—and, by the way, haven't you found any way yet to distinguish them?"

"Not yet. They claim they were told it was possible, but none of them knows how it worked. Or so they say. It's a pity; I have to say we find their creation and use as mere doubles very bothersome. As I said before, we consider clones to be fully human, with the same rights as other humans. These young men seem to think they have no right to exist without their so-called prime. It is an ethical problem for us, because we would normally attempt to give them the psychological support they need to become independent, fully-functioning adults . . . yet this is not what your king asked for in his contract, and we suspect he will not approve that service. You are only his agent, I realize, but if you're going back to Familias space, I hope you can convey to him our very grave reservations. We would like to have some guarantee that these young men will be granted some sort of citizenship when they return."

✳ ✳ ✳

"Do they need all three clones to untangle them?" Petris asked when she reported this conversation.

"I don't know. Why?"

"Because like you I worry about assassination. If those doctors are so convinced the clones should be treated like everyone else, then they aren't going to confine them. After all, they're healthy, full of energy . . . what do you want to bet they'll decide to give them outpatient privileges or something? I agree that we should try to find Lady Cecelia and bring her here if she wants to come—but even though the king lied to us, we still have that obligation." Petris sounded as if he'd been thinking about this for days.

"So, what do you suggest?"

"Take one or two of the clones with us. Openly. Then if someone tries to wipe them out, they'll get only two—or one—whatever."

"Ah. So which should I take?"

"I don't see that it matters; let them choose."

"Get us ready, then. I want to leave as soon as possible."

"I suppose I should warn you that Oblo's made some new friends." But there was a trickle of amusement in Petris's voice.

"What this time?" Heris asked.

"Well, he got a good deal on a new ship identity that he thinks will hold up better than the last one. . . . we're now the *Harper Valley*, in case you want to know."

CHAPTER EIGHTEEN

"This Court is now ready to record the first session of the competency hearings of Lady Cecelia de Marktos, who is petitioning for the reversal of the Order of Guardianship imposed by the Crown Court after medical certification of irreversible coma. Present in the Court—" Present in the Court were local magistrates, attorneys Bunny had hired on Lady Cecelia's behalf, her medical staff, and attorneys representing those who had originally instituted the Order of Guardianship: her family. Later, if this Court ruled in her favor, she would have to do the same things again, in another court, but for now Bunny thought it should be enough.

First her medical team instructed the Court in her signal system. The shoulder jerks, the knee movements, the hand clasps. They demonstrated the lapcomp she would use, and everyone present got to try it out. Thus her testimony couldn't be programmed into the machine—not overtly, anyway. The synthesized voice had been shaped to sound like hers, from old tapes, but her attorneys recommended that she use both the body movements and the lapcomp, to provide additional evidence of her understanding and competency.

The session began with the same sorts of questions Dr. Czerda had asked months before on the yacht. Did she know her name? Was it Lady Cecelia—this time the magistrate asked using the entire formal string. Did she know the date, the place, the circumstances? She answered yes; she was able, with the lapcomp's help, to give the date in both local and Universal calendars. Did she know the date of her injury, and had she been conscious continually since?

That was trickier. Brun had finally told her the date when she was supposed to have collapsed with the stroke: she could give that. But she had lost weeks in the first drug-induced coma. They had anticipated this question, and had decided that her struggle to answer it honestly, within the limits of her equipment, would stand her in good stead.

Her family's attorney, evidently poorly briefed, seemed most determined to prove she was not Lady Cecelia, and then that she had been unduly influenced by Heris Serrano. Her medical team dealt with the first (at least to the satisfaction of that court) by providing the biochemical profile proving her identity. Since such profiles were the standard way of proving identity, the attorney was reduced to arguing that it might have been faked. His argument about Heris was harder to counter. Bunny's attorneys led her through the questions.

No, Heris Serrano had not known about the bequest. No, she did not think leaving a yacht to a yacht captain was peculiar. The yacht represented only a small percentage of her total estate, and no interest in the businesses which provided the bulk of her—and her family's—wealth. No, she did not think Heris Serrano had had anything to do with her accident. Her attorney spoke.

"Since we have established this lady's identity and her mental alertness, despite a terrible ordeal, we ask a summary judgment in her favor, reversing the Order of Guardianship." Cecelia heard the faint rustle as Bunny's lawyer sat back down, the louder stir of others, the creak and rasp of the opposing lawyer standing, most likely to object.

"Just a moment," the presiding magistrate said. Cecelia heard the hollow thock of the gavel. She wished she could see his face. He sounded reasonable, but she was used to judging people by a combination of their expressions and their actions. "All this court need consider is Lady Cecelia's mental status. And on that point, I wish to state that I am now convinced that the individual seated there—" Cecelia assumed he pointed at her. "—and introduced in this court as Lady Cecelia is in fact Lady Cecelia. Clearly, Lady Cecelia is not comatose; she is oriented in time and place, and knows her own identity. But whether that constitutes adequate mental capacity to require that the guardianship be withdrawn, and her affairs returned to her sole control, remains in doubt—"

"Exactly what we said!" interrupted her family's lawyer.

"It is not," Bunny's lawyer interrupted as quickly. "You claimed this wasn't even Lady Cecelia."

"It seemed reasonable to doubt the identity of someone appearing at so great a distance from Lady Cecelia's last known location, when the management of great assets were at stake," said her family's lawyer frostily. "After Lady Cecelia's disappearance, with all the publicity, anyone could have decided to claim to be her. Any lapses of memory could be attributed to the stroke or subsequent medication . . . it would be very hard to prove in the absence of definitive biochemical identification—"

"Which, Ser, was presented. Now, if you don't mind—" Was that a crumb of humor in the magistrate's voice? Cecelia hoped for it.

"Not at all."

"Very well, then. I am going to address some questions to Lady Cecelia, and I wish you legal gentlemen to keep quiet, and not interfere. If I need interpretation of her signal system, I will ask her medical and rehabilitative staff to assist. But I want *her* answers, indicative of *her* understanding, unaffected by your comments. If you do interfere, I will consider that adversely in rendering my judgment. Do I make myself clear?" He had, of course, made himself very clear. Cecelia braced herself. Now it would come.

"Lady Cecelia . . ." The timbre of his voice changed; Cecelia groaned inwardly. A sort of spurious sweetness oozed from it, the tone of an adult who is trying to communicate with a child believed to be slightly dimwitted. "Let me explain the situation." She already knew the situation; her lawyers had explained it in detail. "If you had come before the first competency hearing as you are now, I am certain that no Order of Guardianship would have been issued. However, you did not represent yourself, and no one challenged the presumption that your condition was completely disabling and permanent. Indeed, I cannot find a precedent for this situation in this jurisdiction's records, and the only similar cases in the entire Familias Regnant are not, in fact, that similar."

He paused. Cecelia realized he was planning to drag everyone through the entire legal history of competency hearings, Orders of Guardianship, and so on. How she wished she could say "Get on with it, dammit!"

"Reversing an Order of Guardianship requires some proof that you are capable of managing your affairs—at least choosing and designating an appropriate representative. Is that clear?"

"Yes." Cecelia used the synthetic voice for that one, and she could tell by the indrawn breaths that it surprised more than one in the court.

"I want you to explain, as well as you are able, what you consider your main business interests," the magistrate said. "Can you tell me something about your affairs, enough that I know you understand the extent of your holdings?"

This they had not expected. Cecelia could hear her lawyers shifting on their seats. She hoped they would keep quiet; she knew, if she could only figure out a way to communicate it. First the easy signal, the "yes" for "Yes, I understand." Then—she formed the list in her mind, and began spelling them into the synthesizer input. "B.e.c.o.n. I.n.v.e.s.t.m.e.n.t.s." Pause. "M.e.t.a.l.s. a.n.d. h.e.a.v.y. i.n.d.u.s.t.r.y." Pause. "Forty-seven point six—" the synthesizer handled numbers more easily than spelled words. "p.e.r.c.e.n.t." Pause. "E.q.w.i.n. f.o.u.n.d.a.t.i.o.n." Pause. "Eighty-five p.e.r.c.e.n.t." Pause. Laboriously, she spelled on and on, seeing in her mind's eye the logos and prospectuses and annual reports of the various corporations, partnerships, limited and unlimited companies, in which she had once (and should still) have an interest.

"Excuse me, Lady Cecelia," the magistrate interrupted, when she was halfway through trying to explain that she had an undivided fifth of an eighth part of the great mining venture on Castila. She stopped short, suddenly aware that her back ached, sweat had glued her blouse to her back, and she had no idea how long she'd been "talking." His voice now held the respect she hoped for. "That's enough; I can see that explaining this is a laborious process with the communication system you now have. Clearly, however, you do know your holdings; I've no doubt you could complete the list, but there's no reason to put you through it."

"Objection!" The opposing lawyer's voice sounded more

resigned than hopeful. "She might have been given the list to memorize; it could even have been programmed in . . ."

"Overruled. This court sees the effort Lady Cecelia is making; this court believes that effort is hers. I have only a few more questions, ma'am. For the record, I want to ask why you willed your yacht to your captain of a short time."

"She . . . saved . . . my . . . life." Those words were in the synthesizer; she had insisted on that phrase, but had chosen to leave it as separate words which she would have to call out one by one. "On . . . Sirialis."

"Ah." Under the magistrate's satisfied word she heard a datacube clattering on the opposition's table. She realized then that Heris must not have mentioned that little escapade. Some of her resentment vanished. If they thought it was just a whim . . . *I have a right to my whims,* she told herself. Still, whims could mean loss of judgment. With no reason given at all—and she had not wanted to embarrass her captain by mentioning the reason in the will—her family had had only the worst reasons to consider. Ronnie should have told them, but perhaps they hadn't listened to the family scapegrace. "And I presume, Lady Cecelia, that you need access to your assets in part to pay for your rehabilitation and further treatment."

"Yes." And to return to her own life, and to control her world again, though she couldn't say it. Yet.

"If you please—" That was her family's lawyer; she recognized a last-ditch strain in his voice. "I'm sure Lady Cecelia's family would be glad to pay whatever medical expenses she has incurred or may incur—"

"Objection!" Bunny's lawyer. "Her family incarcerated Lady Cecelia in a long-term care facility where she was given no effective treatment—"

"They were told there was none!"

"Which turned out to be untrue, as you can see. Lady Cecelia must be free to choose her own treatment, since her choice has already been shown to be better than her family's abuse and neglect."

"Gentlemen!" The magistrate's gavel, twice. "Enough squabbling. It is clear to this court that the individual seated here is in fact Lady Cecelia de Marktos, that she is not comatose, that she is in fact fully oriented as defined by law, that she is aware of her business interests, and capable

of communicating her wishes and orders to her chosen
agents, and that her medical status is not stable, but evolving
toward increasing ability. Moreover, she is capable of giving rational explanations for her actions in the past and
present. She is, quite certainly, legally competent. As you
all know, in this very unusual circumstance, it is not possible to overturn an Order of Guardianship completely with
one hearing. However, as of this date I order that Lady
Cecelia's Order be transferred to Court supervision, pending final revocation. Also as of this date, Lady Cecelia regains
her access to all her accounts, wherever they are; I order
that her family give this Court a complete listing of all such
accounts by the end of this business day. Notification of
financial institutions will begin immediately. Within thirty
days, I expect a complete accounting of the Guardianship
to date; at that time I confidently expect that a subsequent
hearing will restore Lady Cecelia's status in all respects. From
this date, the family is not to make any decisions respect-
ing Lady Cecelia's holdings without her express permission,
given through this court. I will expect Lady Cecelia to name
a legal representative of her choice to whom she will assign
power of attorney for the purpose of transacting business
until her condition improves."

Cecelia felt as if she could float out of her chair and up
to the ceiling. Around her, rustles and scrapes and carefully
muffled mutters indicated the legal actors reacting to the
verdict. She pressed the keyboard and the synthesizer said,
"Thank you, sir."

"Now," her lawyer said on the way back to the house,
"Now you can start living again."

Cecelia let herself sink into the cushioned seat. Living
again? This was far better than a few months ago, but she'd
hardly call it living.

"Of course there's a lot of busywork stacked up," he went
on. She knew what that was—medical and legal bills, that
Bunny had guaranteed for her, but that she would now need
to authorize. "It won't take too long," he said, in the tone
that business people used when they meant less than a week.
"As soon as the accounts are accessible again—tomorrow,
probably, for the local lines, and within a week for the
others. I don't expect the . . . other side . . . to make any

trouble about it." From a firm with long experience in dealing
with prominent families, he was not about to bad-mouth
her relatives, even now. It had all been a matter of business, he had assured her. Nothing personal, just the need
to keep the family assets from evaporating in a crisis.

Now, with her credit restored, with the ability to pay her
own bills, and choose her own medical care, she was surprised to find herself as angry with her family as ever. She
still didn't think it was only a matter of business; there had
been some satisfaction at seeing the renegade brought low . . .
and while Berenice and Gustav had not actually done the
deed, they had consented to the humiliation she'd suffered
far too easily. She longed to stride into Berenice's parlor
and tell her sister exactly what she thought.

With that thought, she realized that in restoring her legal
competence, the magistrate had unwittingly told her attacker
she was alive, dangerous, and—worst of all—where she was.
Panic stiffened her; she fought to reach the keyboard which,
in the car, was out of her reach.

"What? What's wrong?" He was smart enough to hand
it to her, and hit the power switch.

"L.o.r.e.n.z.a. w.i.l.l. k.n.o.w. I.D. w.i.l.l. g.o. a.c.t.i.v.e."

"Oh . . . dear." From the tone of his voice, he understood
the problem. He should. "But—it's automatic when legal
status is restored. At least she won't know where you are;
that's not part of the system . . ." She waited impatiently
for him to figure it out. "Except—she knows your sister. No
doubt your family told everyone about this hearing." Yes,
of course. And worse. She had respected the king's desire
for secrecy; she had not told anyone at all what she knew
about the prince. She was now sure, though she had no
proof, that Lorenza had provided whatever it was that made
the prince stupid. If Lorenza panicked, and started picking
off Cecelia's relatives on the grounds she might have told
them something, she might soon be the only person who
knew about the prince.

It was going to be a working day, not a celebration, and
she wasn't going to waste time on busywork after all.

Heris approached the Rotterdam Station cautiously. She
still didn't think this was where Lady Cecelia had been taken,
but just in case she didn't want to blunder into any R.S.S.

or law enforcement scrutiny. Oblo insisted that *Sweet Delight*'s latest identity would hold up to anyone's checking, but she preferred not to test it if possible.

The Station itself had a scuffed old clunker of a freighter nuzzled into one docking station, and two small chartered passenger vessels spaced around the ring from it. The Stationmaster, who ran Traffic Control herself during mainshift, told Heris to dock four slots down from the freighter.

"That charter's a bunch of high-powered lawyers," she told Heris, while explaining which coupling protocol they used—Rotterdam Station had no tugs. "Couldn't come on the same ship—not them. Ridiculous! Bet it comes out of our taxes, some way."

Two ships full of lawyers? Heris suspected they'd found Cecelia, and so had someone else. Several someones else.

"And now you. We haven't seen so much unexpected traffic in years. I don't suppose you want to declare your business?"

"Bloodstock," said Heris, inspired. After all, Cecelia was supposed to have had a training farm. "We hauled something for Lord Thornbuckle last year—" His children, when Cecelia was aboard, but the Stationmaster didn't need to know that.

"Ah. You're horse people?"

"Well . . . I'd hate to claim that; I've got no land of my own. I ride, of course."

"Over fences?"

"To hounds," Heris said, hoping this would work the miracle the doctor had mentioned.

"Mmm. Better come by my office, Captain."

Heris left everyone aboard when they'd docked, and made her way alone to the Stationmaster's office. There, she found a stout gray-haired woman with only one arm yelling into a vidcom.

"No, you may *not* preempt a scheduled shuttle flight, and I don't care who your employer is! We got people downside depend on that shuttle, people that live here, and you can just wait your turn like anyone else." She glanced at Heris, waved her out of pickup range, and continued the argument. "Or you can charter a plane, fly to the other shuttleport, and see if they've got room for you. Take your pick." She cut off the complainer, and grinned at Heris.

"You know Lady Cecelia. You know Bunny . . . right?"

"Uh . . . yes, Stationmaster."

"Forget that. M'name's Annie. Who told you she was here?"

"Nobody—a doctor over in the Guerni Republic said to start looking here because this was where she'd had the training stable. Frankly, I thought that was too obvious . . ."

"But someone would've heard? Good thinking. Situation now is she just got her legal status back . . . those snobs I was arguing with were her family's lawyers trying to keep her from it. Probably getting fat fees from managing her affairs."

Heris blinked. Cecelia well enough to get a competency hearing and reverse the earlier ruling? Perhaps she didn't need any more medical treatment . . . but surely she'd need her own transportation.

"By the way," the Stationmaster said, "you might want to avoid those lawyers. First thing they did when they arrived is show a holo of you all over this Station asking if anyone had seen you." She grinned. "Of course we hadn't, and we haven't now. You didn't tell me your name was Heris Serrano, and that ship out there isn't the *Sweet Delight*, or even that other name—what was it?—*Better Luck*. Where'd you get the new beacon, Miskrei Refitters over at Golan?"

Heris had to laugh. "Annie, you'd make a good match for one of my crew. Any way I can get transport down without running into those lawyers coming up?"

"Why do you think I told them they couldn't charter a special run of the shuttle? Down shuttle leaves in half an hour; they've found out its return run is fully booked, and with any luck they'll all be on their way over to Suuinen to catch the other one."

"Is there a young woman named Brun with Lady Cecelia?" She hoped so; maybe Brun could figure out what was going wrong with Sirkin.

"That blonde girl? Bunny's daughter, isn't she? No, she took off for Rockhouse a while back with Cory—well, you don't know him."

Heris wondered what that was about, but she had a shuttle to catch. "My second-in-command's Kennvinard Petris, and the other seniors . . ." She gave the Stationmaster the names. She almost named Oblo instead of Sirkin, but that would

insult the girl, and besides she had an awful vision of what
Oblo and the Stationmaster could do in the way of mischief if they put their heads together. She would not be
responsible for that—not until she needed it. "None of my
people should come onto the Station except Skoterin; the
others were known to be part of my crew back at Rockhouse
Major. I'll tell them, too." She called the ship, and explained
quickly. Skoterin, and only Skoterin, could leave the ship
for anything the others wanted or needed.

The down shuttle had only two other passengers, both
obviously Station personnel on regular business. Heris tried
to relax—the shuttle's battered interior did nothing to promote its passengers' confidence—and endured the rough ride
silently. Sure enough, the shuttle station onplanet was almost
empty; the clerk ignored her request for a communications
console, and simply led her out the door. A big green truck
huffed clouds of smelly exhaust at her, and a thin dark-haired
girl leaned out the window. "You for the stable? The . . . uh . . .
captain?"

"Right." If the girl didn't say her name, she wouldn't,
though she could see no watchers. The girl pushed open the
other door, and Heris climbed up. Amazing. She had seen no
sign of customs checks. Did they let anyone on and off the
planet without even checking identification?

"Lady Cecelia's *really* glad you're here," the girl said, as
the truck lurched off in a series of slightly controlled leaps.
"Sorry about that—Cory was supposed to have fixed the
transmission. It's the road, really. It shakes everything loose."
She was already driving at a speed that made Heris nervous,
ignoring the warning signs as she approached the road
beyond the shuttleport. The truck leaped forward, into a gap
between another truck loaded with square bales of hay, and
one hauling livestock. Heris didn't recognize the animals:
dark, large, and hairy.

"I'm Driw," the girl continued, as if she hadn't heard the
squeal of brakes and tires, the bellows of rage from the other
drivers. "I'm one of the grooms, and I always get stuck with
the driving." The truck swayed as she put on speed, and over-
took the hay truck ahead. Heris found herself staring fixedly
out the side window; she didn't want to know about oncoming
traffic. "Because I'm safe," Driw said, taking a sharp curve
on fewer wheels than the vehicle possessed. Heris could hear

its frame protesting. "Everyone else has wrecked the truck at least twice, and Merry—that's Meredith Lunn, Lady Cecelia's partner—said I was to do all the driving." She laughed, the easy laugh of someone who finds it natural, and Heris tried to unclench her own hands from the seat.

"Don't worry," Driw said. "We've got a load of feed back there; it'll keep us on the road."

Heris had a vision of the feedsacks reaching down grainy fingers to grip the road—or perhaps it was molasses in sweet feed—and felt herself relaxing. If she died in a feed truck driven by a crazed groom, it would at least be unique. No Serrano she'd ever heard of had done that. She began to notice the countryside—the gently rolling terrain, the trees edging fields fenced for horses, the horses themselves.

"How is she?" she asked.

"Lady Cecelia? Better . . . when she got here, she couldn't do more than lie in the bed and twitch. Now . . . she can walk a little, with supports. She can spell things out on a keyboard, and there's a voice synthesizer. She's ridden again—"

"Ridden?"

"Well . . . riding therapy, not real riding. On a horse, though. They tried to fit her with some kind of artificial vision things—looked like something out of a monster-adventure entertainment cube, metal contact lenses. She can feed herself, and things like that . . . 'course, I haven't seen all this, it's what I hear. You taking her away?"

"Whatever she wants," Heris said. "If she still needs medical care—"

"She needs to kill the bitch who did it to her," Driw said coldly. Heris was startled. Aside from her driving, she had seemed like such a nice girl, not at all violent. "There we are—see the gates?" Heris didn't pick out the gates, surrounded by a thicker clump of trees, until Driw swerved through them. Heris barely grabbed hold in time, but Driw seemed to think the turn routine.

On the gravelled road, or drive, beyond the gates, Driw slowed down a little and grinned at Heris. "You didn't squeak once—most outsiders do. That girl Brun, for instance."

"Were you testing me, or just being efficient?" Heris asked.

"A little of both," Driw said. "We're very fond of Lady Cecelia. Wanted to know if her friends were tough enough

to do her any good. There's the place." The place: brick
house and brick-and-stone stable yard. Heris recognized it
from the holo in Cecelia's study aboard the yacht. Here, the
horses were real, black and bay and chestnut and gray . . .
here the stable cat lounged on a pile of saddle pads waiting to be washed; a dog sprawled in the sun. Someone
waved to the truck and pointed. Driw swung away from the
stable gate to follow a track around one side. "They want
the feed in the old barn," she explained. "Won't take but
a few minutes. You can walk through to the house."

Heris felt scared, and angry with herself for that. She did
not want to see the ruin of the woman she had come to
respect and even love. She reminded herself that Cecelia,
locked in the dark in a helpless body, must have been more
terrified, with more reason.

She felt her hands cramping and tried to unclench them.
Cecelia was better; she'd been told Cecelia was better. But
that single image she'd seen, of the motionless body, the
expressionless face, stayed in her mind's eye. She could imagine nothing between that and Cecelia well . . . and Cecelia
was a long way from well.

She walked through the stable yard, the forecourt, up to
the graceful little porch on the big house. She felt she knew
it; Cecelia had talked about it enough. But inside, it looked
more like a medical center. Parallel bars and weight machines
surrounded by colored mats to the right. Massive gray cabinets
that might house anything at all to the left. Ahead were the
stairs—and coming down, step by careful step, the tall, lean
figure she had been afraid to see lying flat, helpless.

Over and under her loose shirt and slacks, Heris could see
tubes and wires, the structure and electronic connections that
let her walk. One hand clamped to the rail, and the other lay
atop a boxlike machine attached to the wide belt around her
waist. Her eyes looked odd . . . some kind of contact lenses,
Heris decided, though they looked opaque. A headband flickered, red and green. What was that? Beside her, but not touching her, was a competent-looking woman with dark hair in
a thick braid. She looked up and smiled at Heris.

"You must be Captain Serrano—we heard Driw's truck
go by."

"Yes—I am." For an instant, she didn't know whether to

speak to Cecelia or not; manners won out. "I'm glad to see you up again, milady," Heris said. Cecelia smiled. Clearly it was a struggle to smile; the movement of her face was deliberate. Her left hand moved over the top of the box at her waist.

"I'm glad to see you." A synthesized voice, only vaguely like Cecelia's, came from the box. "I heard you driving in."

Heris couldn't think what to say. She wanted to stare, to figure out what each blinking light, tube, and cable was for, but she didn't want to embarrass Cecelia.

"How . . . is . . . my . . . ship?" asked Cecelia. The voice still didn't sound like her, but Heris accepted it as her speech.

"She's . . . a mess, frankly." Heris shook herself. She could certainly talk about the ship. "I don't know how much you've heard . . . we had to yank her out of the decorators, bare naked, and make a run for it." How much to explain? "The king—asked a favor of me. It was hinted that my taking it would ensure your safety."

"And . . . you . . . did . . . it?"

"I'm working on it. Perhaps you'd like to sit down?" That ungainly figure poised on the stairs made her nervous.

"I . . . want . . . to . . . go." Go? Heris scowled, uncertain what Cecelia meant and unwilling to ask. The other woman on the stairs touched Cecelia's arm lightly.

"May I explain? You said it was urgent."

"Yes." Cecelia continued her slow, difficult progress on down the stairs. The other woman moved with her, but spoke to Heris.

"Lady Cecelia's competency hearing ended yesterday. She has recovered her memory of the incident that started all this some weeks ago, including who administered the drug, but she hasn't told the court yet. She didn't want that person to know she had the memory, because it imperiled her family."

"Back on Rockhouse," said Heris. "Where's Brun?"

"She sent Brun, as soon as she recovered the memory, to warn her family—discreetly—against the individual. Anyway, because of the competency hearing, the person who injured her now knows where she is, and because the magistrates ruled in her favor, her ID is now flagged active on the universal datanets. She has to presume the individual knows that, and will take action. None of us feel that

Rotterdam is safe for her anymore. Passenger service is infrequent, and in her condition she still needs medical attendants. We had thought of sending her off on the same ship that carried her lawyers, but that ship is known—"

"That's easy," Heris said. "The yacht looks terrible right now, but it's roomy and safe—and we're not using its original ID beacon. How many people will she need along?"

"But if they've seen you—at the spaceport—"

"The Stationmaster saw to it that no one did. The only one of my crew who has permission to leave the ship is a woman who joined us the day we left Rockhouse—they won't associate her with me or Lady Cecelia. Let's get things packed and on the way."

"Lady Cecelia," the other woman said. Cecelia had made it to the bottom stair, and the chair beside it. "How soon could you be ready to leave?"

"Now." The synthesized voice had no tone for humor, but Heris was sure Cecelia intended it. "Go . . . pack. Let . . . me . . . talk . . . to . . . Heris."

"We'll need comfort items," Heris said, as the other woman started away. "We have only minimal bedding—you might want to load that sort of thing."

"She told me her yacht had had a swimming pool—is that operational?"

"Yes, though again the walls in the gym are bare. We had the pool filled in the Golan Republic—and that's what I wanted to tell you, milady. The doctors believe that the neurochemical assault you suffered is very similar to what was done to the prince. If so, it may be reversible. However, they will need a detailed history, and your own tissues to work on. I can take you there, if you want to risk it."

"Yes. I . . . trust . . . you . . ." Cecelia said.

The big sprawling house that had seemed to be dozing in the afternoon sun erupted like a kicked anthill. Heris crouched on the bottom step of the stairs, holding Cecelia's hands in hers, until someone fetched another chair for her. Four or five women in blue tunics bustled in and out, up and down stairs. Boxes and suitcases began to accumulate in the front hall, as the sun slanted farther and farther through the windows into the room.

"I . . . knew . . . you . . . would . . . come . . ." Cecelia said.

Her hand squeezed Heris's. "Brun . . . knew . . . you . . . had . . . to . . . leave . . ."

"I'm sorry I couldn't get you out right away," Heris said. "Your family blamed me—and I didn't even know about the bequest."

"No. It's . . . all . . . right . . ."

The lift whirred, and out came two women, a hoverchair, and another stack of boxes. Two men came in from outside and began carrying the growing pile out to the driveway. Heris heard a truck motor grinding up from the stable, and winced at the thought of Cecelia at the mercy of Driw's driving. The lift came down again, this time with what looked like a hospital bed folded up. A woman in a big apron appeared at their side with trays.

"Milady—time for your snack." Heris watched as Cecelia managed to find the food on her plate and get it into her mouth without incident.

"Milady, I'm sorry, but . . . are those artificial eyes?"

"No . . . not . . . exactly. Ask . . . medical." Cecelia went on eating; Heris was suddenly ravenous and found herself engulfing one thick sandwich after another. Where, and how, had Cecelia found another great cook?

"I should see about the shuttle schedule," Heris said finally, around a last bite of fresh bread stuffed with something delicious. She was sure it had celery and herbs and cheese in it, but what else?

"Don't worry about that," said the cheerful woman she had first met on the stairs. "I called Annie, and she'll make sure we've got one. She thinks we should wait until the opposition lawyers have left."

Shadows chased the sun across the driveway, and up the front of the house, leaving the windows clear to a distant blaze of sunset behind trees. Heris stood up to stretch, and walked outside. Fine brushes of cloud high overhead; the sound of buckets and boots and water faucets from the stable yard. A shaggy dog stood up to look at her, then shook itself and wandered away, tail wagging gently. So peaceful here—she wanted to stretch out and sleep the night away.

"Excuse me, ma'am," said someone behind her, and she shifted aside. The folded bed was coming down the front steps, a mattress balanced atop and almost hiding the men carrying it.

* * *

The caravan started for the shuttleport well after dark. Heris, breathing in the fresh damp air, found herself wishing she could stay longer. She rode with Cecelia, two of her medical team, and a lawyer, in a real car; Driw drove the truck with supplies and equipment; another car carried the rest of the medical team. And the cook.

The lawyer had kept Cecelia busy all evening. They could not risk alienating the magistrates with her disappearance; calls and letters had been necessary. Now he was taking notes on her orders for the next few months—who could vote which stock in which company, what to do if Berenice and Gustav tried to interfere further in the recovery of her competent status.

Heris marveled at Cecelia's energy. She looked . . . old, sick, exhausted. But she pushed herself, kept going, stayed alert. Heris dozed, half ashamed of that, but knowing she had a long watch ahead when she must be alert.

CHAPTER NINETEEN

Although it was nighttime, the shuttleport looked dark and almost deserted. Heris wondered what had gone wrong. Then someone came out of the dimly lit terminal and leaned into the driver's side of their car. "Ah—it's you. Just go on out to the runway . . . follow the yellow lights."

In this way, the caravan trundled down a long runway to a dark shape bulked at the end of it. Heris felt she'd fallen into some surrealistic action-adventure. She had never, even in dreams, imagined herself sneaking along a darkened runway toward a clandestine shuttle. And she had a burning curiosity about what Cecelia could possibly have done to generate this level of loyalty on the planet.

She had no time to ask while the truckload of gear was put aboard the shuttle's cargo bay, while she and the medical team carefully eased Cecelia and her attachments into the shuttle's shabby passenger compartment. They were not the only passengers, either. After Cecelia and her party were aboard, half a dozen others climbed up and settled themselves at the back of the passenger space. Perfectly ordinary, the sort of people you'd expect to find taking a shuttle flight up from the surface of any planet . . . except, Heris noticed, they all had remarkably similar bulges in their clothes.

At the Station, Heris noticed that one of the chartered passenger ships had gone, and the corridors were almost deserted. Everyone—including the shuttle's other passengers—helped unload the shuttle and move its cargo to the yacht.

626

There Heris found Annie—offduty, as she explained—and Oblo lounging in the loading area.

"I thought I told you to stay aboard," Heris said to Oblo. He gave her his innocent look, and she winced inwardly. What had he been up to?

"I am aboard," he said. "Legally—there's the line." He stretched. "I was chatting with Annie here on the Station com, and we discovered some mutual interests, so when she got offshift, she came over . . ."

"Right. Fine. Now let's get our owner aboard, and her gear installed." Oblo looked hurt, another of his certified expressions, and vanished up the access tube. Annie gave Heris a cheerful grin, intended to disarm.

"Thought you wouldn't mind if I came around and made sure your lady's ship was secure. Just in case those lawyers snooped, although since all our exterior videos seem to be on the blink right now . . ."

Heris found herself smiling in spite of her annoyance. "Amazing how equipment around here seems to behave," she said. "For instance, the shuttle tonight—"

"Had a block in the hydraulic line to the steering of the nosewheel," Annie said promptly. "They couldn't seem to get it to roll into the usual parking slot, and decided it was safer to keep it on the straight runway."

"And yet they felt it was safe enough to fly . . . ?"

Annie shrugged. "It got you here, didn't it? And if any nosy person was looking for unusual activity, all they saw was a dark field." Heris nodded, not bothering to mention that any decent surveillance gear would pierce the darkness like a needle into wax . . . but Annie must know that.

"It was most convenient," Heris said instead. Annie chuckled.

"We hoped so." Then her expression sobered. "By the way, that tech you had running errands for the ship—Skoterin, isn't it?" Heris nodded. "One of those lawyers stopped her and talked to her a few minutes. I'd given her warning they might be coming through, but I guess she was curious or something—"

"I'll talk to her," Heris said. "They'd been briefed, of course; I'm sure she said something appropriate, but I'll check."

"Do that," Annie said. Then, looking past Heris, her eyes lit up. "Milady—it's good to see you again. And you do look so much better."

To Heris, Cecelia looked pale and exhausted . . . but Annie would have seen her the first time she came through, she realized. She must have looked much worse then. Now Cecelia struggled and achieved a smile.

"Thank . . . you . . . Annie . . ."

Behind Cecelia came the trail of people pushing dollies loaded with equipment, luggage, odds and ends. Heris left Cecelia with her medical people and Annie, and went on into the ship to get the crew ready for departure. To Oblo, who had been hovering in the access tube as if afraid he'd miss something, she gave the task of directing traffic.

"Brigdis, we're going to want a fast, but very safe, course back to the Guerni Republic," she said, coming onto the bridge. She was glad to see that Sirkin looked bright-eyed and capable again; she had done much better on the trip from Guerni, and Heris hoped whatever had been wrong was now over and done with. "We don't want to take any chances with the Benignity, not with our decoy clone and Lady Cecelia aboard." Not ever, but especially not now. "Methlin—" Arkady was offwatch at the moment, "—I want our weapons ready, but not lit. If we do run into trouble, I want to be able to surprise them. Make sure standby mode is really standby."

"I've got this course plotted already, Captain," Sirkin said. She sounded a bit tentative, but presumably her confidence would return in time. Heris looked at the string of numbers, and the display. She realized she was too tired to follow through all the calculations.

"Did you check this with Oblo?"

"No, ma'am, not yet . . . he's not been back to the bridge this watch. Vivi got me the latest data from the Stationmaster's nav file—I thought if she went for it, instead of calling in, nobody could tap the line . . ."

"Good idea." For an instant, Heris wondered why Annie hadn't mentioned that when she was talking about Skoterin . . . but Annie was offwatch now, and might have been when Sirkin requested the data. It didn't really matter. The outside communications board blinked, and Heris reached for it.

"Captain Serrano, this is Stationmaster Tadeuz." His voice sounded as friendly as Annie's. "If Annie's still over there, would you ask her to step 'round the office? I've got a question for her."

"Of course," Heris said, wondering why he hadn't used the Station paging system.

"Sort of a confidential thing," Tadeuz said in her ear. "Nothing to worry you, though. More like a filing problem."

"I'll tell her right away," Heris said. "What about clearance for departure?"

"I'd like five minutes, just to make sure nobody's coming up for a shift change, ten if you can give it to me, otherwise you're cleared." Just like that. Heris had never heard of anything so casual, anywhere.

"I'll tell Annie," she said again, and went off shaking her head.

Annie was still chatting with Cecelia; the tail end of the equipment train was just about to enter the access tube.

"Stationmaster Tadeuz asked me to tell you he'd like to see you in the office," Heris said to Annie.

"Then why didn't he—oh. Sorry, milady, but I'd better scoot. Hope to see you again soon, in even better health. Bye, Captain . . ." And Annie took off down the corridor much faster than her looks suggested.

"I've got to go back aboard, milady," Heris said to Cecelia. "We'll be able to depart once everything is aboard and stowed."

"And how long will that be?" asked the woman with her.

"I'm not sure," Heris said. "I'd guess less than an hour; Lady Cecelia can come aboard now, but there's no place to sit, really. No furniture except what's just come aboard."

"Better . . . there . . . than . . . here . . ." Cecelia's hands moved on the hoverchair controls and the chair lifted, swaying slightly.

"Good idea," Heris said. She felt stupid not to have realized that Cecelia didn't need any other chair to sit on.

Inside, the ship was still in chaos. The woman with Cecelia locked down the hoverchair in the lounge, and went to help the others arrange Cecelia's suite. Heris saw the clone looking out of his quarters and beckoned. "Here—why don't you keep Lady Cecelia company until we're ready to leave. Lady Cecelia, this is Gerald B. Smith, one of the prince's doubles."

She didn't want to explain the clone business now. "Mr. Smith, Lady Cecelia de Marktos."

"Yes, ma'am." Gerald B. smiled at her, and gathered some bright colored pillows to make himself a soft seat on the bare decking. "Lady Cecelia, I'm delighted to meet you again. We've met, though I was at the time impersonating my prime, the prince."

"I . . . shall . . . call . . . you . . . Mr. . . . Smith . . ." Cecelia said. Heris decided they'd do well enough alone, and went back to her own work. Petris had the engineering figures ready for her; Haidar had computed the new load on the environmental system (well within its capabilities) and had a projection for the supplies that would be needed at Guerni. Meharry and Ginese were discussing the exact amount of power necessary to keep the weapons just below scannable levels.

"Not Guerni scans, of course," Meharry said. "We know about *them* now. I think they'd know if the toothpick in your pocket was intended for offensive use . . . maybe they read minds, do you think?"

"I don't think. Mind reading is a myth. I just wish we had their capability," Heris said. "But you think our stuff isn't scannable by normal means?"

"We could ask the Stationmaster to look us over," Meharry said.

"No . . ." Heris thought about it a moment longer, then shook her head. "So far I've seen no sign that anyone on this Station—or this planet—wishes Lady Cecelia ill, but why take chances? I'll trust your judgment."

She reminded herself that she wanted to speak to Skoterin, but Skoterin was busy in the guts of the ship, resetting flow rates to accommodate the larger load on the environmental system. Haidar, on his way to help her, said he'd give her the word once all the chores were finished. No hurry, Heris thought. In fact, it was a duty so low in priority that she didn't put it into her deskcomp for a reminder request.

Getting the *Sweet Delight* back into deepspace and a jump or so away from Rotterdam was all that really concerned her. She did a final walk-through inspection after the last loaders left and Lady Cecelia was settled in her bed in her own suite. Everything looked as it should, her crew alert and at their stations, and nothing lying around where it shouldn't be. Undock had none of the ceremony she was used to . . . no financial records to clear, no lists of regulations to follow . . . she wondered what would happen if any sort of government inspection ventured this far from the center of Familias space. Did they ever? Could Annie or Tadeuz adhere to rules (what rules?) if they found it necessary?

But with the yacht in insystem drive, and the Station receding in the distance, she put that out of her mind. However it was run, by whatever gang of independents, that Station wouldn't be there without some kind of discipline. Its air had been good, its water plentiful, its power supply and gravity controls steady. The docking collars had held pressure—so what was she fretting about? Heris grinned as she realized what it was . . . she had spent so many years putting up with boring, routine double and triple checks, because she had believed them necessary. Without them, stations would fall out of the sky, air would fail, spacecraft would go boom. And here was someone ignoring—or at least seeming to ignore—the usual precautions, and doing very well anyway. She resented the time she'd wasted.

She also resented the return of Sirkin's mysterious problem. Nothing happened on her first shift, but as they were approaching the first jump point, Oblo reported that Sirkin had left an open circuit in the communications control mechanism. Not a fatal error—yet—but a sign of carelessness. Heris was furious when he called her about it. Enough was enough. She'd replace Sirkin when they got to Guerni. She flung off the covers and dressed, thinking how to say it, and how to explain to Lady Cecelia. It was simply too bad to have to bother her now, in her condition.

When she was dressed, she went to the bridge, where the tension needed no words to express. Ginese nodded at her, and Kulkul handed her the log, with Oblo's entry. All three of them looked as upset as she felt. Heris read it, and looked at the circuits herself. Anger and sorrow both—she hated to see someone with potential go bad, but that's what Sirkin was doing.

"Have Sirkin report to my office," she said to Kulkul, the watch officer.

The Sirkin who appeared seemed to be the bright-eyed,

alert Sirkin she had first worked with, the young woman who should have had a successful career ahead of her.

"Yes, ma'am?" She was even smiling, and nothing in voice or manner suggested any concern about her own duties. Heris handed her the log.

"Can you explain that entry, Ms. Sirkin?" The formality wiped the smile from Sirkin's face; she reached for the log with the first signs of uncertainty. As she read it, her face flushed.

"But I—it can't be!"

"I assure you, Ms. Sirkin, that Mr. Vissisuan neither lies nor makes elementary mistakes. You signed off your shift; he found the open circuit. Those are facts; I asked for an explanation."

Now Sirkin looked as miserable as she should. "I—I don't . . . know how it happened, Captain. I didn't—I swear I didn't leave any circuits open, but I know Oblo wouldn't . . . wouldn't make it up. I—I don't know—"

Heris picked up the log Sirkin had dropped. "Ms. Sirkin, my patience has run out. Whatever your problems, I don't want them on my ship. You will be released from contract when we arrive at Golan. Until then, Mr. Vissisuan will serve as Nav First; you will perform such duties as Mr. Vissisuan and Mr. Guar can oversee. You can expect to have your work checked very carefully, and any more lapses will be reflected in my statements to any future employer. You have done good work in the past; I hate to handicap you with a bad reference, but I'm not going to risk lives . . . do you understand?"

Sirkin had gone so pale Heris was afraid she might faint. "Yes, ma'am," she said in a voice empty of all emotion.

"You may go," Heris said. "You're offshift now; see if you can pull yourself together in time to be of some help to Issi Guar next shift."

"Yes, ma'am." Sirkin left with the gait of someone who has just taken a bad wound and hasn't felt it yet. Heris wanted to clobber the girl and cradle her at the same time. What a waste of talent! If she could only clear her head . . . but she'd learned early in her career that you could spend only so much time trying to rehabilitate losers. Get rid of them, and get on with the job—which, right now, meant getting Lady Cecelia and Mr. Smith safely to the Golan Republic.

She went back to the bridge. "Oblo, you're now Nav First

and Issi's your second. I don't want Sirkin standing any watches alone; she's to back up Issi during the jumps next watch, and do any other routine work you and Issi can check."

"Yes, Captain." He looked angry, but she knew it was more with circumstances than either Sirkin or herself. He had liked Sirkin—they all had—and they all felt betrayed by her failures. Padoc Kulkul, who rarely said anything at all, spoke up.

"Good idea, Captain. I know you and Petris both liked her and I had nothing against her before . . . but we can't risk anything now."

"Meharry's really mad," Ginese said without turning around. "She thought a lot of the girl."

"So did I. Now, with Sirkin off any solo watches, Nav's going to be as short as the rest of you—" A general chuckle. Navigation/Communication had had three to the other sections' two, but no one had minded. "If you need help up here, grab Skoterin from Haidar. She's capable of watching a board for a few minutes."

"And she's Fleet," Ginese said, this time looking at Heris. "We know we can trust Fleet—at least our old crew."

"Right. Now—I think whatever's wrong with Sirkin is psychological, personal, but there's the smallest chance it's not. We know her lover was killed by Compassionate Hand bravos. We know her lover may have been recruited by that woman you saw, Oblo—"

"That counselor—"

"Right. It's just barely conceivable that Sirkin was recruited too—then or later, perhaps terrorized after Yrilan's death—and if so, she could be working for the Benignity. I don't want her near the communications—they'll have a hard time finding one little yacht bouncing around jump after jump, but not if someone's got us lighted up for them."

"What about that course she laid out?" Oblo asked. "What if it's wrong—takes us into C.H. space or something?"

"Check it. She said . . . let me think . . . that Skoterin brought her up-to-date chart data from the Stationmaster's office. Let's ask Skoterin."

Skoterin, roused from her offshift sleep, arrived on the bridge looking only mildly puffy around the eyes, and answered Heris's questions readily.

"Yes, ma'am; I did go over to the Stationmaster's office for Ms. Sirkin. Made sense to me we didn't want to use the Station voicecom without knowing if anyone could listen in. That other shuttle had come with the lawyers from Lady Cecelia's competency hearing."

"Ah—yes. Annie mentioned that you'd talked to one of them. What happened?"

Skoterin grinned. "One of 'em stopped me, and wanted to know what ship I was off of. Guess they'd noticed the Station employees' uniform on the way down or something. I told 'em just what you had said was our story. 'We're the *Harper Valley*,' I said, and told 'em we were an independent freighter picking up a load of frozen equine sperm and embryos. Wanted to know where we were bound next, and I said 'Wherever the captain wants, I reckon. I'm just a mole.' They didn't know what that meant, and I told 'em environmental tech, and they said what was our captain's name, and I said he was a sorry sonuvabitch named Livadhi, which was all I could think of at the time. They said did we work for Lord Thornbuckle, and I said I wished! and they said oh never mind, she doesn't know anything we want to know, and I thought to myself, *little you know*, and they went off and so did I."

"I wonder why they asked about Lord Thornbuckle," Heris said. "Unless they've figured out that it was Brun who brought Lady Cecelia here. Good job, Vivi; they may find out that Livadhi is an R.S.S. captain but it won't do them much good. Now—about the charts and things you picked up—"

"Yes, ma'am. Got those from the Stationmaster, and came back without running into any more of those people, and gave the data to Ms. Sirkin." Heris noted that the formality in referring to Sirkin came easily to Skoterin.

"Is this what you gave her?" Heris asked, pointing to the data cube and hardcopy on Oblo's desk.

Skoterin looked. "Yes, ma'am. 'Course, I don't know what it means. Jump points and stuff, but not what."

"That's fine, then. Go on back to bed." When Skoterin had left the bridge, Heris turned to Oblo.

"Check the course Sirkin laid in against those sheets, and make sure she actually used the current data. I don't want us stumbling into Benignity space because of Sirkin's carelessness."

"Yes, ma'am." Oblo went to work. Heris sat there, wishing she were back in bed with Petris, but knowing it was too late. It seemed their jinx had returned. Besides, something nagged at her. Skoterin's story had been plausible—and Skoterin wasn't the problem anyway—so what could Sirkin have been up to, besides getting current data? Had she known the lawyers were aboard the Station just then? Had she wanted Skoterin to be seen and questioned? If—somehow—she had managed to let them know that the ship in dock was Cecelia's yacht, then getting Skoterin out there to be seen was one way of giving the enemy a complete crew list. They already knew about the others; she had counted on Skoterin going unrecognized—and now they knew about Skoterin, too.

That didn't satisfy her either, but she could not reconcile the two Sirkins, the two possible explanations for sending Skoterin out.

Next mainshift, Cecelia sent for her. Heris came into Cecelia's suite to find her sitting up in the hoverchair, an attendant with her.

"We didn't have time to explain all Lady Cecelia's signal system to you," the attendant said, before Heris could even greet her employer.

"Lady Cecelia," Heris said pointedly, "Always good to see you."

"Bev . . . will . . . help . . . you," Cecelia said.

"Fine; I'll be glad to learn whatever I can. Are you interested in what's been happening with your ship?" Cecelia's shoulder jerked. Was that a response?

"That is Lady Cecelia's easiest way to say 'yes,'" the attendant explained. "Lady Cecelia, show her 'no.'" That was the other shoulder. Heris realized that what she had taken for uncontrollable twitching in the shuttle on the way up had been Cecelia "talking."

"Right shoulder for 'yes' and left shoulder for 'no'?" Heris asked. Cecelia gave a quick jerk of her right shoulder. "I got that. What next?"

What next took longer to learn, but an hour later, Heris was a good bit more comfortable with twitches, jerks, hand clenches, and the timbre of the synthesized voice. Cecelia had even allowed her to hear her own voice—distorted, uneven in volume and pitch, but her biological voice.

"I'm amazed," Heris said. "I confess I hadn't imagined anything like this. It's so different from—" From the inert helplessness she'd been told of, or the full recovery of a feisty, healthy woman that she'd hoped for.

"We didn't dare try a regen tank," the attendant said. "Use of regen tanks with neurological problems is tricky at best. You sometimes get good responses, but more often the deficit 'hardens,' as it were. Much safer not to try it until neurochemical repair's been done. Then it's fine for dealing with residual physical deficits."

"I . . . see." Heris remembered that she had more information on the techniques the Guerni Republic doctors had suggested. "I'm going to download everything I got in the Guerni Republic to your deskcomp . . . or . . . ?"

Yes. A firm response. Heris wondered if the visual prosthesis allowed her to read displays, or could be hooked to a computer output, but she didn't like to ask. The attendant seemed to recognize her discomfort.

"I can read it to Lady Cecelia; her visual capacity is fairly blunt at this time."

"Mr. Smith . . . is . . . prince?" Cecelia interrupted. Heris was surprised.

"No . . . he's the prince's double. Didn't I say that? I'm not sure where the prince is."

"Not . . . double. He . . . is . . . prince."

"Lady Cecelia . . ." Even though several dozens of people now knew about the clones, Heris was reluctant to discuss them in front of an attendant she didn't know. She picked her words with care. "Even though I admit he looks like the prince, and sounds like the prince, I have been informed by . . . er . . . reliable sources that he is not the prince."

"C.l.o.n.e.?" That came out spelled, letter by letter, in the synthesized voice; evidently no one had thought she needed the whole word.

"Er . . . milady, clone doubles are, as I'm sure you know, illegal."

"Not . . . my . . . question . . ." Whatever her employer had lost, none of it had been intelligence points. Or the determination to find out what she wanted to find out. Heris mentally threw up her hands and answered.

"Yes, milady, he's a clone. Moreover there are several clone doubles." Quickly, as clearly as she could, she explained the king's mission, her problem with the clones on Naverrn, and the discovery that Livadhi's ship had yet another one. "And we don't know which, if any, is the prime—the prince. They call him their prime. They all have the same memories: they're given deep-conditioning tapes after each separation, so that they're up to date."

"If . . . all . . . alike . . . doesn't . . . matter." Heris had privately thought this for some time; why not just declare one of the capable clones the prince, and quietly retire the damaged prince? The answer, of course, was that someone might have planned just that, and the apparently capable clone could be someone's pawn. So might the prince.

"We left two of them at Guerni, and brought one along as a decoy, for the safety of those in the medical center. If Sirkin hasn't botched our course, we'll have them all back together and then let the doctors sort it out. If they can."

Cecelia scowled, as difficult an operation as her smile. "That . . . nice . . . Sirkin? What . . . is . . . wrong?"

"I don't know. You remember her lover was killed—well, I made allowances for that. She seemed to be coming out of it, doing better, until after we'd left Naverrn. Then she started making careless mistakes, doing sloppy work." Heris paused. She still couldn't reconcile the Sirkin who did the calculations for those emergency jumps with someone who would forget to make necessary log entries, leave switches on the wrong settings and so forth. She took a deep breath. "I'm cancelling her contract when we get to Guerin. I won't risk your life—or mine, for that matter—on someone like that."

No. No mistaking that answer.

"Lady Cecelia, I must. I liked her too; you know I did. But a navigator's error can kill the whole crew. I've talked to her, Oblo's talked to her—we've all tried to help her. She made another serious mistake after we left Rotterdam. I can't take the chance."

No. "Wrong . . . you . . . are . . . wrong." Lady Cecelia's synthesizer had little expression, but there was no way to miss the strong emphasis of that shoulder jerk.

"I wish I were," Heris said. She debated telling Cecelia of her other suspicions about Sirkin and decided against it. If the girl merely had personal problems, she would not want to have planted other ideas. Time would tell. Besides, Cecelia was a fine one to give warnings—she had ignored Heris's warnings, and look what happened. She glanced at the wall display. "I'm sorry, but I need to get back to the bridge. We can discuss Sirkin later. We're coming into a series of critical jumps to circumnavigate Compassionate Hand territory."

When she returned to the bridge, Skoterin smiled at her from the secondary Nav board, and Sirkin was nowhere to be seen. Fine. If Issi and Oblo felt more comfortable with an old crewmate there instead of an unstable civilian, she'd accept that.

The first three jumps went without incident. Here the Benignity had thrust a long arm into former Familias space, but since there were no habitable worlds in the area no response had been made. It was easy enough to jump over the Compassionate Hand corridor; in fact, it set up a nice series of jumps to avoid the rest of the Benignity. The only tricky bit was a rotating gravitational anomaly in the neighborhood of the fourth jump point. After bouncing through the first three jumps, it was necessary to drop into normal space and time the next jump to avoid the rapid G changes of the anomaly's active arm. Current charts—such as those Skoterin had picked up from Rotterdam Station—gave ships the best chance to get through that fourth jump with the least wasted time. A mistake in timing could send a ship directly into the Benignity—and the Benignity was known to take advantage of any such lapses.

Heris reviewed the charts several times before that critical fourth jump to make sure their course would not take them too close to the Benignity. Even if it did, they should be safe: they were small, fast, and it would be sheer bad luck if anyone were patrolling the area where they might emerge. She had Oblo check and recheck the course too, both against the charts and against older references.

"The new one's a bit closer, but the border shifts over there, with the anomaly and all. I'd say this was fine."

"Very well." They dropped back into normal space on the mark; Oblo pulled up scan data at once, and began cursing. Heris didn't have to ask. Something—and she wouldn't wager it was sheer bad luck—had gone wrong.

"We're off course—*way* off course." He threw the display up on the main screen. "We should be there—" A green circle, fairly near the red dashed line that represented the border of the Benignity. "And instead we're *here*." Another green circle, this one not so close to the red dashed line, on the opposite side. "And we're entirely too near a gas giant to play games with jumps out. We'll have to crawl it."

"Just what system are we in?" Heris asked.

"Nothing we want to be in." Oblo was scrolling past entries in the reference library, looking for a chart with more detail. "Ah. Not good. Not good at all. The Benignity has bases on the larger moons of this big lump of gravity we're too close to, and the way we dropped out of jumpspace on their doorstep, they could hardly miss us."

"It can hardly be an accident," Ginese said. Neither he nor Meharry turned from their boards. "Coming out right on top of a Benignity base . . . it has to be . . ."

"I know," Heris said. She swatted down the last of her regrets, and touched the control that would lock Sirkin in her quarters, for all the good that would do now. At least she couldn't cause any more mischief. Then she opened the ship's intercom and explained, as briefly as she could, what had gone wrong. "I want Mr. Smith and Lady Cecelia protected, while we have any options at all." There weren't any options, if the Compassionate Hand responded. She would ask Lady Cecelia, out of courtesy, but was sure she'd prefer death to being a Compassionate Hand captive. As for Mr. Smith, he could not be allowed to fall alive into their hands.

"Captain—" That was Ginese. "Ships are on us, and their weapons are hot."

"How many?" she asked.

"Only two," he said, sounding surprised. So was she. If she'd been that base commander, if she'd known (and he must have known) such a prize was coming, she'd have had a net of every available craft, just in case.

CHAPTER TWENTY

Sirkin, slumped in dull misery on her bunk, heard first the delicate snick of the door lock going home, and then the intercom. She clenched her hands in her quilted coverlet. It was impossible. She had checked and rechecked that course; she had paid attention to every warning in the charts . . . she could *not* have made such an error. But here they were, and of course—she had to admit the logic of it—the captain had decided she was responsible. She was the traitor.

I am not! She wanted to scream that aloud, but what good would it do? No one would believe her. All the miseries of the past months landed on her again. Amalie's weakness and Amalie's betrayal . . . and then Amalie's death, the way that mutilated face and body looked in the morgue. Hot tears rolled down Sirkin's face; she didn't notice. And she had tried, tried so hard to work her way out of it. She had acted cheerful; she had gone on working. She had even enjoyed (and felt guilty for enjoying) those visits with Lord Thornbuckle's daughter. Her hand strayed to the locket Brun had bought her; inside was the lock of Amalie's hair Meharry had snipped. Brun—if Brun were here, *she* wouldn't believe it was Sirkin's fault.

Except it had to be. She knew Oblo and the others couldn't be doing it; they were too loyal to Captain Serrano. Besides, why would they start playing tricks now, when everything had gone so well on the way back from Sirialis? It made no sense. She knew she was no traitor; she knew she had done her work carefully. Yet the work she did came undone somehow, between one watch and the next, and if it wasn't Oblo or Issi Guar, who could it be? Was she going crazy? Was she losing her memory? Had someone planted some kind of mind-control in her? The thought terrified her. She sank into a daze of misery, staring at the opposite bulkhead.

When her door lock clicked again, she thought someone had come to kill her. She didn't really care anymore, she told herself, but her gut churned with fear and she felt icy cold. She watched the door slide open with sick dread.

"I . . . know . . . you . . . didn't . . . do . . . that . . ." Lower than she was looking, in the hoverchair, Lady Cecelia. She had not seen Lady Cecelia since she came aboard, and the shock brought her out of herself. She rolled off the bunk and stood up, instantly dizzy from time she'd spent motionless.

"Sit . . . down . . . don't . . . faint."

Sirkin struggled with her dizziness and finally did what she was told, slumping back to the bunk. Lady Cecelia carried a set of keying wands, and looked as smug as her condition allowed.

"You shouldn't—the captain will be really angry—"

"Let . . . her."

"But she's right—something is wrong, and it must have been my fault, because I know Oblo wouldn't—" She was babbling, and couldn't stop; she wanted to cry and fought not to.

"She . . . is . . . wrong . . . I . . . told . . . her . . ."

"Did she say you could let me out?" Hope rose—maybe the captain had found out what really happened; maybe it wasn't her fault after all. Lady Cecelia's face contorted with what she wanted to say, and couldn't.

"Not . . . that. . . . Earlier . . ." Lady Cecelia guided the hoverchair into the cubicle, crowding the bunk, and closed the door behind her. "She . . . doesn't . . . know . . . I . . . came . . . here. . . . She . . . is . . . wrong . . . about . . . you."

"How do you know?" Rude, she realized a moment later, but she had to know.

"Age . . ." Lady Cecelia said, and grinned a death's head grin. "You . . . are . . . not . . . that . . . kind . . . of . . . girl." She held up her hand, a clear signal for Sirkin to listen without interrupting. "Who . . . joined . . ." Pause. "Ship . . . last?"

That had to mean crew, Sirkin thought. "Vivi Skoterin, just before we left Rockhouse. She's from the ship Captain Serrano had in the R.S.S. She's an environmental tech."

"Where . . . now?"

"On the bridge, I expect. Oblo asked her to stand in for me as navigation second during the jumps."

"No . . . Mistake . . ."

"Well, she's not trained as a navigator, but all she has to do is check the numbers as Oblo enters them."

"No . . . that . . . is . . . the . . . mistake."

She wasn't getting all that Lady Cecelia meant.

"She . . . is . . . problem . . ."

Sirkin stared at the old lady, shocked.

"Skoterin? But she's—she's one of *them*. She served with them before. They trust her—" Even as she said it, she saw the flaw in that. They trusted her; it didn't make her trustworthy. "She couldn't have . . ." she breathed, even as she realized that Skoterin might very well have been able to make Sirkin look incompetent. "She . . . she *brought* me those charts—the ones I used to set up the course . . . the *wrong* course." Inside, a great joyous shout in her head: *Not my fault. It's not my fault. I'm not crazy.*

Lady Cecelia nodded. "She . . . made . . . you . . . look . . . bad . . ." Long pause. "Captain . . . did . . . not . . . look . . . further . . . mistake."

Sirkin's relief rebounded to fear. "It's too late, though. We're going to be attacked—captured—"

"Not . . . captured . . ." Lady Cecelia's head jerked through a slow shake. "It . . . is . . . too . . . convenient . . . if . . . we . . . disappear. Prince . . . me . . . and . . . all."

"We do have weapons; we might fight free," Sirkin said hopefully. "That is, if Vivi hasn't—"

"She . . . would . . . have . . ." Lady Cecelia said. "But . . . prince . . . help . . ." She turned the hoverchair, opened the door again, and started out as Sirkin stood up uncertainly. "Come . . . with . . . me . . ."

*   *   *

Once the enemy ships began their stalk, Heris gave no further thought to her passengers. At the end, if capture seemed likely, she'd make sure they didn't suffer, but now she had a battle to fight. Maybe.

"How far do we have to go before we can jump?" she asked Oblo.

"A long way . . . my first approximation is over seven hours. Thing's got moons as massive as your average planet—we don't want to be wrong . . ."

"Fine—keep an eye on it. Arkady, what are we facing?"

"Right now just two, but of course our scans are skewed at this relative velocity. Looks like they knew what vector to expect for our insertion but not how much vee we'd have on us. They're running parallel and catching up. And no, we can't outrun them, not if they're the usual C.H. cruiser-weight." He paused, and transferred his scan data to her display. "You can see the weaponry—all hot and ready to fire. Want me to bring them up? I don't think it's enough to scare them off, but—"

"No. We can't bluff, but maybe we can surprise them when it counts." Heris glanced over at his boards, where the status lights showed ships' weapons as strings of green lights, each column tipped with one yellow. "I wonder why they didn't take us when we dropped out," she asked, not expecting an answer. "The logical thing for them to do is blow us away—no one knew we would be inside Benignity space—and if they did know, they'd shrug and go 'Oops.' If we quietly disappear, it solves a lot of problems for some powerful people."

"I'd be glad to quietly disappear if I could figure out how," Oblo said, scowling at his board. "Vivi, pull up this section in Shirmer's Atlas, will you? Maybe they've got something—"

"Yessir." Heris watched as Skoterin picked her way around the backup navigation board, punching first one key then another. Slow—of course, she didn't know the board well; it wasn't her specialty. If only Sirkin—the good Sirkin—had been there . . . but no use wishing. Suddenly Ginese and Meharry both cursed and started tapping at their boards.

"What?" Heris asked, though she could see from here that the weapons boards had changed color. Green lights had gone orange; the yellow lights at the top had gone to blue; the system was locked down, nonfunctional.

"Damn her!" Petris turned to glare at Heris. "What do you want to bet she had a control tap to her quarters?"

"No bet. Go down there and—" And what? Kill her? Heris couldn't give that order, not yet. "Get it fixed," she said. "Call Mr. Guar to the bridge, Oblo; you need more experienced help. Skoterin, get back to Mr. Haidar, and tell him to unlock the small arms. Bring us each a weapon, and start stacking the excess in the corridor. Here's the key wand for the weapons locker."

"Yes, Captain." Skoterin hurried away; Petris grabbed a toolkit off the bulkhead and followed her.

"They stripped our beacon," Oblo said. "Maybe they wanted to be sure they had the right ship . . ."

"Maybe." Seconds ticked away.

"Heris, Sirkin isn't in her quarters." Petris, on the open intercom. "And I can't find any control tap. She might have been somewhere else when you locked the doors—" He sounded both angry and uncertain. Heris tried to remember if she'd actually checked the personal monitors to confirm Sirkin's location . . . she didn't know.

"Or she might have gotten out. If she's been planning this, she might have key wands—"

"I'm not finding a hard tap," Ginese said, from the deck under his control boards. "Not one single thread that shouldn't be here. Of course, a directed magnetic pulse could do that, but it would have to be close."

"A control override would work, anywhere between here and the weapons themselves," Meharry said. She, too, was half under her console, prodding at things.

"But not on this ship—it's not like a ship designed for fighting. We had no regional alternative nodes. Remember how we had to route the cables all over the place? To knock the whole board down like that, it'd have to be intercepting signals pretty high up . . . which ought to show as an additional cable . . . or be a pulse signal from somewhere on the bridge." Arkady's voice sounded muffled as he disappeared completely from view. "And I don't see . . ."

Meharry's face popped up from beneath her console.

"Mine's clean. I see what you mean, Arkady. We put in that shielding—if it's pulse, it has to be on the bridge somewhere."

Heris said, "What about a secondary? Something exterior to signal a controller on the bridge, through the regular optical cables, and set off a pulse signal?"

"Might be. Complicated, though. Doesn't always work even on *our* ships." Our ships clearly meant R.S.S. ships. "What's Sirkin's secondary training?"

"She could do it," Heris said, answering the real question. "I had her crawling through all the computer controls on the first voyage—she knows as much about this ship's electrical and electronic layout as I do. The only thing she might not know is the weapons systems you installed when she wasn't aboard."

"INTRUDER. FAMILIAS SHIP *HARPER VALLEY*." That was on the broad band, in their own language—heavily accented, but quite understandable.

"Just in case we didn't know who we were," Oblo said with a shrug. "Now what, Captain?"

"Well, they didn't blow us away straight off," Heris said. "Let's see what they do with this." She thought a moment, then said, "Send them a voiceburst, just as we did with Livadhi." That might buy a few seconds—but they needed hours. She got back on the intercom. "Petris—better link with Skoterin and get yourself a weapon. Wherever Sirkin is, she might be dangerous."

"Right." He had left Sirkin's quarters, she saw on the personnel monitor, and headed toward the main service corridor. She couldn't find Sirkin now, but that made sense; she'd have taken off the tagger, and probably done something to keep the automatic sensors from recognizing her. Heris hadn't yet entered the data for all Cecelia's medical team, so she didn't know who made up that cluster of dots outside Mr. Smith's quarters, the cluster now moving along a corridor toward the service area.

"Lady Cecelia," Heris said over the intercom. "Please stay in your quarters, and get your medical team with you. It is not safe to wander around right now."

"INTRUDER SHIP *HARPER VALLEY* CEASE MANEUVERS OR WE WILL FIRE ON YOU."

"So tactful," Ginese said.

"I've got the last squirt out of her," Oblo said. "Trying to get in the shadow of that moon—"

"Which you hope no one is hiding behind," Heris murmured. "I would be."

"Swing out, then?"

"Costs us vee, gains us space. I hate the feeling we're being driven into a preset trap."

"Fine." He made adjustments on his board. Meharry straightened.

"That's odd."

"What?"

"You touched your board, and mine flickered. Do something on the other one."

Issigai Guar, on the secondary, shrugged, and fed in a query.

"Aha." Meharry reached for her own toolkit and fiddled with it. "So that's—it's controlled from your board, Issi. Let me get at it." He pushed back willingly, and Meharry ran her instruments over it. "She must have set this up with a time delay, so anyone touching the board after a certain time would set off a signal locking up weapons control. Clever. If she'd been better at the patches, my board wouldn't have flickered and we'd never have found it. Glad she was careless about this, too."

"They're targeting," Ginese said. Meaning, *Shut up and fix it.*

"I'm not wasting time," Meharry said. She plucked the overlay off the top of the secondary board and prodded something underneath with delicacy. "This little beauty— I don't want to blow anything if it's wired that way—can just now slip . . . *out*." She slipped the tiny object into her pocket.

Heris saw, before Ginese could speak, his board come live. One by one, the orange lights turned green, one column after another as the weapons ran through self-checks and warmed.

"Code Three as soon as you can, Mr. Ginese," Heris said. Meharry's board began to green up, far slower than Heris wanted. Guar was reassembling his console; Oblo wore an expression of limpid unconcern that Heris knew from earlier battles.

"LAST WARNING. INTRUDER SHIP CEASE MANEUVERING IN TEN SECONDS OR WE WILL FIRE ON YOU." Nicely calculated, that. The transmission lag was down to eight seconds, but the whole—

"Here it goes—" said Ginese. On the large screen, the tracks of the other ships, the analysis of their weaponry, the first white-hot arcs as two missiles lofted toward where they would be, one from each pursuer. His board was almost completely green, the yellow dots lit now halfway across the top.

And in the corridors of the yacht, small-arms fire erupted, short and disastrous. Then silence. Meharry shifted her board's controls to Ginese, and moved to stand by the bridge hatch.

"Lockdown, Captain?"

"No—we've got loyal crew out there . . ."

Oblo was up, too. "Issi, your control. I can go out—"

"No . . . there's only one to worry about, and with any luck she's dead." And with enough luck there's no hole in the hull, and no one else was hit, and Lady Cecelia and Mr. Smith are still safe for the brief length of this uneven fight. All that ran through Heris's mind as she watched on the screen the enemy's missiles coming nearer. On Ginese's board, the yellow dots turned red as the weapons came operational.

"Let's just see . . ." Ginese said. His finger stabbed at the board and the two missiles seemed to stagger in their course, then swerve aside. "Yeah. Still works fine."

Heris let out the breath she had taken. "If they could all be that easy," she said. That hadn't even required their offensive weaponry. Ginese chuckled, a sound to strike any sensible person cold.

"Then I couldn't play with my other little darlings." His shoulders tensed, watching his displays, and he murmured, "Oh, you would . . . idiots."

Heris didn't interrupt with questions. The second wave of missiles had been launched before the enemy would have had time to get scan data back from the yacht's activated weapons. Four, this time, bracketing their expected course. These Arkady dispatched with contemptuous ease. What mattered now was what else they would use . . . their scans revealed optical and ballistic possibilities.

"Response, Captain?" They could of course launch a counterattack—no one was there to remind her it was a bad idea to get into a slugfest with two larger ships.

"Let's try to dodge their bullets and help them run low on ammunition," Heris said. "Why change what's working?" She kept an eye on Oblo's scanning screens . . . if that moon had held a trap, and if the pursuers had realized they weren't going into it, a third ship might come dashing out right about . . . *there.* But they had trusted too much to their trap; the third ship had low relative vee, and though boosting frantically, was caught deep in the well with little maneuverability.

"There's a target, Mr. Ginese, if you just want something to shoot at."

"A bit chancy," he said. "I'd rather save what we've got for these two."

"Just don't forget that third one; if it launches something at us, it could still hurt us."

"Right, Captain." In the tone of teach-your-grandmother-to-suck-eggs. In that long pause, while the enemy realized they had an armed ship and not a helpless victim to subdue, while the enemy commander—Heris imagined—cursed and chose an alternate plan—she had time to wonder why it was so *quiet.* Someone should have reported back by now.

She called up the personnel monitor again, and saw the cluster of green dots in exactly the wrong place, down in the service corridor near the weapons locker. What if Sirkin had attacked Lady Cecelia—shot the clone—was holding Lady Cecelia hostage?

"Meharry."

"Yes, Captain."

Heris pointed to the layout with the little green dots. "Get down there and find out what's going on—and break it up. First priority, secure the ship; next, Lady Cecelia; next, Mr. Smith."

"Yes, sir!" Meharry's sleepy green eyes were wide awake now, and eager. Oblo moved forward but Heris waved him back.

"No—we've got a battle up here, too, and you can do either nav or weapons. Go help Ginese for now."

Sirkin followed Lady Cecelia's chair out of her quarters with a mixture of reluctance and glee. It wasn't her fault; she hadn't made those mistakes, and she knew—she thought she knew—who had. But nobody would believe her, she was sure, and she doubted the captain would have the patience to let Lady Cecelia literally spell it out. If anyone came down here, they'd believe the worst of her . . . especially now that she was out of her quarters.

Lady Cecelia's hoverchair made swift, silent progress along the corridor toward the main lounge. Sirkin looked over her head to see Mr. Smith and several of Lady Cecelia's medical team clumped together there. As she watched, they came forward, and Lady Cecelia reversed the chair, nearly hitting Sirkin.

"Weapons," said Mr. Smith. "Where are the small-arms lockers?" Sirkin knew that, but she wasn't sure what they were doing, or if it was right. He grinned at her, that famous grin she'd seen on many a newscast, and punched her arm lightly. "Come on, we've got to get armed, and keep whoever it is from taking the ship away from your captain."

"Skoterin," she found herself saying as she led the way back into crew country. "Joined the ship just before we left Rockhouse . . . old crewmate . . ."

"One of the group that was court-martialed?"

"No—just demoted afterwards. Some enlisted were, she said."

"What specialty?"

"Environmental systems," Sirkin said, almost jogging to keep up with his long legs.

They came out of that corridor into another, which angled downward; Heris would have recognized it as leading to the place where Iklind had died. Sirkin did not; she only knew they should take the turn to the right. The weapons lockers, filled with all those expensive oddments (as Ginese had called them) on Sirialis, were that way, around a turn or two. Sirkin, sure of the way, went first; Mr. Smith came behind her, and then Lady Cecelia in her chair, surrounded by attendants.

Around the last corner . . . Sirkin stopped abruptly, and almost fell as Lady Cecelia's chair bumped into the back of her legs. The weapons lockers were open, and on the deck lay Nasiru Haidar, facedown and motionless, with blood pooled under his head. Sirkin could not speak; her mind ran over the same words like a hamster in its wheel . . . *I didn't do it, I didn't do it, I didn't do it.* Mr.

Smith pushed past her, and knelt beside the fallen man; Sirkin edged forward, trying to remember to breathe. And one of the medical attendants rushed forward, opening a belt pack.

"Just stop right there," someone said. Sirkin looked up as Skoterin stepped out of an open hatch across from the weapons lockers. Skoterin had one of the weapons—Sirkin wasn't sure what it was, though she knew she'd seen its like in newsclips and adventure cubes. It looked deadly enough, and Skoterin handled it as if it were part of her body. "How very convenient," Skoterin said. "Just the people I wanted to see, and now you're all here together." She had on a black mesh garment over her uniform; Sirkin found her mind wandering to it, wondering what it was.

"Poor Brigdis," Skoterin said, looking right at her. Sirkin felt her heart falter in its beat. "You must continue to be the scapegoat awhile longer, I fear. Pity that you went mad and murdered Lady Cecelia and the prince—or his clone, it doesn't much matter."

"But I didn't do any of it!" That burst out of Sirkin's mouth without any warning.

"Of course you didn't, though I rather hoped you wouldn't figure that out until whatever afterlife you believe in."

"But you were on her ship! How can you do this to her? To the others?"

Skoterin grimaced. "It is distasteful, I'll admit. I have nothing against Captain Serrano, even though she did manage to ruin my career as a deep agent. It's certainly not personal vengeance for having managed to arrange the deaths of two of my relatives—"

"Who?"

"Relatives I didn't particularly like, in fact, though we do take family more seriously than some other cultures. Who scratches my brother—or cousin, as in this case—scratches me. You were there, Brigdis: surely you remember the terrible death by poisoning of poor Iklind."

"But you—"

"Enough. You two by Haidar—move back over there." Mr. Smith and the medical team member—Sirkin had not even had a chance to learn their names or positions—moved back near Lady Cecelia. "You, Brig—you stand by Haidar."

She was moving, under the black unseeing eye of that

weapon, despite herself. She could hardly feel her body; she felt as if she were floating. Her foot bumped something; she looked down to find her shoe pressed against Haidar's head. He was breathing; she felt the warm breath even through the toe of her shoe. Her mind clung to that, like a child clinging to a favorite toy in a storm. One thing was normal: Haidar was alive.

"Take one of those weapons from the rack, and hit him." Sirkin stared at Skoterin. "Go on, girl. They're not loaded; you can't hurt me with it. I want your fingerprints on it, along with his blood. Whack him in the head with it, hard."

"No." It came out very soft, but she had said it. Skoterin's face contracted.

"Do it now, or I'll shoot your precious Lady Cecelia."

"You will anyway." Sirkin felt the uselessness of her argument, but she also felt stubborn. If she was going to die anyway, she wanted to die without her fingerprints on a weapon which had killed someone else. "Why should I help you?"

"I don't have time for this," Skoterin said, and levelled the weapon at Sirkin. Sirkin panicked, grabbed the nearest object in the rack, and threw it at Skoterin, just as Mr. Smith made a dive for her, and Skoterin fired.

The noise was appalling; Sirkin heard screaming as well as the weapon itself. When it was over, she felt very very tired, and only slowly realized that she had been hit . . . that was her blood on the deck now . . . and she had to close her eyes, just for a moment.

Meharry smelled trouble before she got anywhere near the weapons lockers. An earthy, organic stench that had no business wafting out of the air vents. She knew it well, and proceeded with even more caution thereafter, taking a roundabout route she hoped no one would expect. She had her personal weapons, just as Arkady had—hers were the little knives in their sheaths, and the very small but very deadly little automatic tucked into her boot. If Sirkin thought she was going to take Meharry by surprise . . . She paused, listening again. A faint groan, was it? Real or fake? Scuffing feet, difficult breaths . . . really she didn't know why everyone didn't carry a pocket scanner. Much more sensible than sticking your head around corners so that someone could shoot it off. Carefully, she slid out the fiberoptic probe, and eased its tip to the corner . . . then checked her backtrail and overhead before putting her eye to the eyepiece.

Carnage, she'd suspected. Bodies sprawled all over the deck near the weapons lockers. And on his feet, cursing softly as he applied pressure bandages as fast as he could, Petris. Why hadn't he reported? Then she saw the ruin of the nearby pickups. He must have found this and simply set to work to save those he could. She retrieved the visual probe, and hoped she was right in her guess—because if Petris was the problem they were in a mess far too bad for belief.

"Petris—" she called softly, staying out of sight.

"Methlin! Tell Heris to get the rest of the medic team down here fast. Lady Cecelia's still alive."

"You all right?"

"I got here late," Petris said, not really answering the question. Good enough. Meharry backed up to the first undamaged intercom and called in. Multiple casualties, what she'd seen.

"What?"

"Just get the medics down here, he says. I'm going to help unless Arkady needs me—"

"No, we only have three ships after us now." Only three, right. "I've put Oblo with Arkady."

Meharry walked around the corner, still wary, and found a situation that didn't fit her theories.

"Here—" Petris shoved rolls of bandaging material at her. "See what you can do with those three; they're alive. The clone's dead; so is Skoterin, and I think Haidar and Sirkin, but now you're here I can look."

Meharry continued Petris's work, glancing at Lady Cecelia—clearly alive, though bloody, but lying against the wreck of her chair as if stunned. She took a quick look at Skoterin, startled to see her wearing personal armor—it hadn't saved her from a shot to the head.

"Damn Sirkin," Meharry said. "I didn't think she could shoot that straight."

"She didn't," Petris said. "I did. It wasn't Sirkin after all."

"Skoterin?"

"Yep. The dumbass wasted time explaining it to them— if she'd gone on a bit longer, I'd have nailed her without the rest of this. But she started to shoot Sirkin, and the clone jumped her, and that's when I arrived."

Meharry shook her head. "I didn't know *you* could shoot that straight." Whatever else she might have said was cut off by the arrival of the others in Lady Cecelia's medical team.

CHAPTER TWENTY-ONE

On the bridge, Heris heard Meharry's first report with disbelief; she located the rest of Cecelia's staff and sent them down. Meanwhile . . .

Meanwhile the Compassionate Hand ships continued to close, but did not attack.

"What are they waiting for?" Ginese asked. "Do they think we can take them?"

"Nice thought. Let's hope they think so until Meharry gets back up here. Maybe they think we'll surrender if they give us time."

Issi Guar said, "There's something coming into the system—something big."

"Not Labienus and the Tenth Legion again," Heris said. They had been dragged through innumerable ancient texts on warfare in the Academy: ground, sea, air, and space. One of the clubs had put on a skit about Labienus and the Tenth Legion—the way the Tenth Legion kept showing up like an adventure cube hero in the nick of time—which they all thought very funny until one of their professors reminded them of Julius's career stats. Nonetheless, it had become a byword among officers of her class.

"No . . . I doubt it." His fingers flew over the board, trying on one screen after another. "I wish we'd gotten that VX-84 you found, Oblo."

"She said nothing stolen," Oblo said, with a sidelong glance at Heris.

"I said nothing *illegal*," Heris corrected. "But you didn't pay any attention to that—what stopped you this time?"

"Guy wanted more than I wanted to pay . . . I don't like messy jobs." Messy, to Oblo, could have several meanings. "Let him take care of his own family problems," he continued. Heris let it roll over her and tried to figure out what the Compassionate Hand commanders were doing. The yacht was running flat out, on a course that the gas giant and its satellites would curve into a blunt parabola. They had emerged from jump too close to its mass to do anything else. The two larger C.H. vessels paralleled it, slowly catching up; the signal delay from them was down to five seconds. The third had been unable to gain on them.

Meharry appeared at the bridge entrance, bloodstained and breathless. "Captain—it wasn't Sirkin after all. It was Skoterin. Sirkin's been shot; she's alive—"

"INTRUDER YOU HAVE BEEN WARNED. UNDER THE JUSTICE OF THE BENIGNITY OF THE COMPASSIONATE—"

"Now, Arkady!" Heris said.

"—HAND YOU STAND CONDEMNED OF TRESPASS, REFUSAL TO HEAVE TO—"

"They never said 'Heave to'; they said 'don't maneuver'," Oblo said. "Weapons away, Captain. And it's supposed to be 'convicted,' not 'condemned.' "

"—AND OTHER SERIOUS CRIMES FOR WHICH CAPITAL PUNISHMENT IS THE CUSTOMARY SENTENCE. PROTESTS WILL BE REGISTERED WITH YOUR GOVERNMENT AND INDEMNITY DEMANDED FOR YOUR CRIMES. BY THE POWER VESTED IN ME AS AN OFFICER OF THE—"

"Targeting . . . incoming, live warheads, *much* faster than before."

"BENIGNITY OF THE COMPASSIONATE HAND, SENTENCE IS HEREBY CARRIED OUT. JUSTINIAN IKLIND, COMMANDER—"

"I think those little warts were just testing us before—" Ginese sounded more insulted than worried.

"Get off my board, Oblo, and let me at them," Meharry said.

"Spoilsport." They switched places smoothly, and Oblo returned to his own console. His brows rose. "My, my. Look who's come calling."

"Unless it's half a battle group, I don't care," Heris said, her eyes fixed on the main screen. The incoming missiles jinked, but relocked on the yacht; their own seemed to be going in the right direction but—no—she lost them in the static from the incomings, which had just blown up far short of their target.

"If they thought all we had was ECM to unlock targeting, they're going to be annoyed," Ginese said.

"That wasn't a bad guess, Captain," Oblo said. "Although it's only one cruiser."

"Our side?"

"By the beacon, yes. By behavior—we'll have to see when their scans clear. It says it's Livadhi again."

Livadhi's cruiser had arrived with far more residual velocity than the yacht, and more mass as well—it appeared on the scan with its icon already trailing a skewed angle. Livadhi, it seemed, meant to be in on the action.

The Compassionate Hand ships, on the other hand, made it clear what they thought of his interference. One engaged him at once, with a storm of missiles. The other changed course, angling across the yacht's path to come between the yacht and Livadhi's cruiser. The third—

Heris reached out for the tight beam transmitter they weren't supposed to have. "Oblo, get me a lock on Livadhi's ship."

"Why? He's got Koutsoudas on scan one—d'you think he'd miss anything?"

"No, but he's being shot at. Give him a break, can't you?"

"Right." Oblo nodded when he had the lock.

Heris flipped the transmitter switch. "Livadhi—third bogie on your tail—watch it."

As if he'd been waiting for her signal, her own tight beam receiver lit. "We've got to stop meeting like this, Heris. You got bad data at Rotterdam. You've got a traitor aboard. That's why we're here."

"Not for long if you don't watch it," Heris sent back, eyeing her own scans. But Livadhi, in a fully crewed cruiser, had more eyes to watch than she did, and the first attacking missiles died well outside his screens. She wondered what his orders were—if he had any—because his counterattack was already launched. She had never thought of him as a possible rogue commander, but here he was deep in someone else's territory and opening fire.

"Something else I wish we had," Oblo muttered, watching. "Screens that would stop something bigger than a juice can."

"Wouldn't fit, remember?" Military-grade ship screens ate cubage and power both; offensive armament could be crammed into small ships without room for shields.

Both Compassionate Hand cruisers now engaged Livadhi's ship. Heris began to hope everyone would forget about her . . . given enough time, they could continue their swing around the gas giant, reach a safe jump distance, and disappear. That would leave Livadhi in a fix, but he seemed to be doing very well. His first salvo sparkled all over one of the enemy's screens, an indication that he had almost breached them. And if he had come to rescue them, give them a chance, then the smart thing to do was creep away and let the professionals do the fighting. She didn't really like that, but the yacht was no warship.

"Captain—" That was Petris, on the intercom. "Medical report: We've got three dead, two critical, three serious—"

"Lady Cecelia?"

"Alive, conscious, in pain but she'll make it. Skoterin, Mr. Smith, and Haidar are dead. Sirkin and Lady Cecelia's communications therapist are critical—we may lose them without a trauma team, which we don't have. Three others of her medical team are in serious condition. Lady Cecelia's physician is unhurt, but trauma's not her specialty—she's a geriatric neurologist—and she says she's out of her depth with open chest and belly wounds."

Heris fought down her rage and grief. That wouldn't help. She felt her mind slide into the familiar pattern . . . a cool detachment that allowed rapid processing of all alternatives, uncluttered by irrelevant worries. They had dying passengers; they needed medical care. The nearest source of trauma care was . . . right over there, being shot at.

And of course it was the best excuse for getting involved, although she pushed back a niggling suspicion that that carried more weight than it should.

"Thank you, Petris," she said. "We'll do what we can. Livadhi's out there now, and he has a trauma center. Assuming we win the battle."

Silence for a moment, as he digested that, and calculated for himself the probability that the yacht and Livadhi's ship might be in one piece, in one place, able to transfer patients, before they died. "Right. I'm going back down to check the damage—stray shots hit some circuits around there, and now that we've no live environmental specialists—" It was not the time to tell him that one of the things she loved about him was his ability to stick to priorities.

"I think," she said, in a thoughtful tone that made Oblo and Meharry give her a quick look, "I *think* those Compassionate Hand ships have decided we're not worth bothering with. They seem to think the important thing is keeping Livadhi away from us."

"Yes, Captain?" Oblo looked both confused and hopeful.

"Well, they got between us. All of them—" Because the trailing third ship had risked a microjump—a *huge* risk, but it had worked—to catch up to the battle. Dangerous, but it had worked. "And nobody's targeting us. Now speaking as a tactical commander, don't you think that was stupid?" None of them answered, but they all grinned. "I think they just put themselves in our trap. Oblo, how much maneuvering scope do we have?"

"Not much—but we can close the range on them, if you want. It'll cost us another half hour to a safe jump range."

"Jump won't get our wounded to care any sooner," Heris said. "But Livadhi's got a perfectly good sickbay over there, if somebody doesn't blow a hole in it. Let's make sure no one does."

The Compassionate Hand ships clearly thought they had an enemy cruiser locked in their box; for all that Heris's scans could detect, they paid no attention to the yacht's change of course that brought her swinging out toward the warships. They were too busy pounding at Livadhi's ship, and dealing with his salvos. If the yacht had not existed, it would have been a well-conducted attack, almost textbook quality.

"Of course, when we *do* fire, they'll be all over us," Heris said.

"If they don't notice us another minute or so, we'll be close enough to blow one of them completely," Ginese replied.

"One of them . . ." Meharry said softly. "But the other two will have to acquire us, get firing solutions . . . we have time."

That minute passed in taut silence. Livadhi's attack breached one of the enemy ship's shields, but it neither broke up nor pulled away. Major damage, was Oblo's guess, but he couldn't understand the Compassionate Hand transmissions, which were in a foreign language and encoded anyway. "I think they rolled her, though, to put the damaged shields on this side."

"That's your prime target," Heris told Ginese. "You know wounded C.H. commanders—they get suicidal. How much longer?"

"At your word, Captain."

"Now." The yacht shivered as Ginese sent a full third of its ballistic capability down the port tubes and out toward the wounded C.H. ship. Oblo rolled the yacht on its axis to present the remaining loaded tubes to the fight. Seconds ticked by. Then the yacht's missiles slammed into the enemy cruiser, one after another exploding in a carefully timed sequence. The external visual darkened, protecting its lenses from the flare of light as the cruiser itself ruptured and blew apart.

Heris spent no time watching. "Oblo—maximum deceleration, now."

He gave her a startled look but complied. The yacht could not withstand extreme maneuvers, but a course change like this might be enough to surprise the enemy. And avoid any late-arriving missiles that Livadhi had sent at that cruiser. Unfortunately, it would blur their scans just when they needed them clear, but—

"There they go—Livadhi did have a couple on the way."

"I would hate to get blown away by my rescuer," Heris said.

"I have a lock on the second cruiser," Meharry said. "Permission—"

"Do it." Again the yacht shivered; she wasn't built for this kind of stress. But the salvo was away . . . Heris tried to calculate what that did to their gross mass, and what that meant to maneuvering capability, but at the moment the figures wouldn't come.

The scans had adjusted to their new settings; she could see that the other two Compassionate Hand ships were changing course, the trailing one swinging wide now, losing range to take up a safer position, where Heris could not attack it without risking Livadhi in the middle or performing maneuvers beyond the yacht's capacity. The nearer enemy ship and Livadhi continued to exchange fire, and Oblo reported that the nearer ship was trying to get a targeting lock on the yacht.

With their course change, it took seconds longer for their salvo to reach the enemy, and this time someone had been watching. Heris felt a grudging admiration for a crew that could react that quickly to a new menace. Half their missiles detonated outside the ship's shield, and the rest splashed harmlessly against it. Return fire, already on its way . . . but Meharry and Ginese were able to break the target lock of some, and the timers of the rest.

This time it was Livadhi's crew that exploited an opening— or perhaps defending against Heris's attack had taken just that necessary bit from the shields—for Livadhi's salvo blew through, and the enemy cruiser lost power and control. It tumbled end over end, shedding pieces of itself to clutter the scans.

"And that leaves number three," Ginese said.

"And their reinforcements. It may take them a while to get here, but they'll arrive."

The third ship now fell farther back. Heris didn't trust that, but she didn't have the resources to pursue it. Instead, she changed course again, returning to maximum forward acceleration, and put a tight beam on Livadhi's ship.

"We have critical casualties," she said. "Can you accept five patients?"

"How's your ship?"

"Not from that—from a fight inside. That traitor you mentioned."

"I see. Frankly, I don't want to risk docking with you while that other warship's untouched . . . I can send over a pinnace with a trauma team, would that help?"

"Yes." It would help, but would it be enough? She could see Livadhi's point—if she'd commanded the cruiser, she wouldn't want to have some civilian ship nuzzled up close when an attack started. "But we have no supplies for trauma, and just empty space . . . send what you can."

"Right away. Stand by for recognition signals—"

"Why not Fleet Blue—I already know that."

He actually laughed. "Of course—sorry. Fleet Blue it is."

The pinnace should be too small to attract fire from that third ship; Heris could barely find it on scans herself and she was much closer.

Time passed. Heris could not leave the bridge, not with a hostile ship out there; she sent Petris to help the pinnace mate with their docking access tube and reported its safe arrival to Livadhi. Was it too late for their casualties? She heard nothing from the medical team—of course, they would be busy. Better not to interrupt. Another hour, and another. The third Compassionate Hand ship continued to fall behind, though it did not turn away.

"Sorry it took so long." That was Petris, as blood-streaked as Meharry. "I wanted to patch up a few things—near as I can tell, nothing really important got holes in it. I'll have to read up on the systems, though."

"And our casualties?"

He shook his head. "Can't tell yet. They brought two trauma surgeons and their teams; Sirkin's the worst, but they're still working on her. Said if they could stabilize them, a regen tank would do the rest, but there's no way to load a regen tank on a pinnace."

"Lady Cecelia?"

"Is spitting mad, near as I can tell. A fragment got her synthesizer, and her communications specialist died, so she's having a hard time making herself understood. She got a shallow flesh wound—probably the same fragment that ruined her synthesizer—but she's fine. Wants to see you, when you've time, but I explained you wouldn't."

"Where is she?"

"In the thick of things. Insists she wants to stay with Sirkin, and the med teams are too busy to carry her out—her hoverchair got a solid hit and it's down, too."

"Have you found out any more about Skoterin?"

"Only what I heard as I came on the scene. She was a deep agent for the Compassionate Hand, before she joined up, and a relative of that mole who died on your first voyage."

"And perhaps that guard who died on Sirialis, the one who shot young George," Heris said. "Iklind—that was the name. Livadhi claims we got bad chart data from Rotterdam Station, which is why we ended up here . . . and Skoterin is the one who fetched the charts from the Stationmaster."

"And altered them on the way? Could be done. She could've been messing up Sirkin's work, too—we trusted her, old shipmate as she was."

"Lady Cecelia tried to tell me—said it wasn't Sirkin—but I wouldn't believe her. And now three people are dead—"

"One of whom should be." Petris reached out a hand and drew it back. Heris saw the movement, and wished they were not on the bridge in a hostile situation; she needed that touch, some comfort in a bad time. "If it's any comfort, not one of us caught on; we all made the same mistake." The others on the bridge nodded.

"I had liked Sirkin a lot," Meharry said. "So I cut her more slack than the rest of you—kept thinking it was delayed grief reaction or something—but it never occurred to me it could be sabotage. Just like you, and Petris, I trusted Skoterin just because she'd served with us even though I knew some of that crew were Lepescu's agents. I didn't know her before, but—she was military, she'd been a shipmate, that was enough. And that was flat-out stupid."

"That may be," Heris said, "but I'm still at fault."

"That's true." Oblo turned around and grinned. "The great Captain Serrano makes mistakes—what a surprise! We thought you were perfect!"

"I didn't," Guar said. "I always said her nose was too short."

"All right, all right," Heris said, fighting back a chuckle. "I get your point. We're all old friends and we all made a mistake, and we go on from here, sadder but wiser. If Sirkin dies, a *lot* sadder."

"I'd bet on her to make it," Petris said. "With Lady Cecelia sitting there radiating mother-hen protectiveness. She doesn't need speech to convey how much she cares."

Heris's tight beam receiver lit again, and she picked up the headset. "Heris, how close are you to your critical jump distance?"

She looked at Oblo and mouthed, "Jump? How long?" He looked at his plot and punched in some corrections, then looked again.

"Less than an hour, Captain—looks like we might make it. Forty-three minutes and a handful of seconds, to be more precise."

Heris relayed that to Livadhi. "Good," he said. "If nothing

else lights up, I'll expect you to jump out of here as soon as you can—take my medical teams with you for now—and I'll cover your backtrail. Don't tell me your destination, but do you need any coordinates for a safe jump out?"

"Yes," Heris said. "I'd like to clear the Benignity with one jump—possible?"

"Yes—here—" He read off a string of numbers that Heris passed to Oblo. When she read them back, he said, "Fine. Now—I am authorized to say that the situation we both know about is extremely unstable. The Council would like to speak with Lady Cecelia at her earliest convenience; Lord Thornbuckle has filed a Question with the Grand Table; the Crown asks if you can transport a certain Mr. Smith and his friend back home."

"Medical intervention must come first," Heris said, her mind beginning to buzz with the implications of Livadhi's report.

"Of course. I understand. I would urge extreme caution, and suggest that we rendezvous for your return so that we can provide an escort. You might also consider rearming—"

"Thank you," Heris said. "Give me a contact coordinate." Another string of numbers followed. Then Livadhi broke contact. Minute by minute the yacht edged closer to safety. Heris kept expecting something else to go wrong—another Compassionate Hand ship appearing in their path, another crisis aboard—but nothing interrupted them, and at last Oblo was able to put them back into jump mode, into the undefined and chaotic existence that lay between the times and spaces they knew.

Livadhi's trauma teams had turned two of the guest suites into sickbays. In one, Sirkin lay attached to more tubes and wires than she had arms and legs. Beside her, on a stretcher, Lady Cecelia lay on her side holding Sirkin's hand. Across that room, two of the less critically wounded were dozing, their bandages making humps and lumps under the bedclothes.

"Lady Cecelia," Heris said. Her employer looked only slightly better than Sirkin, pale and exhausted.

"I . . . told . . . you . . ." Her own voice, with its cracked and uneven tone, was just understandable.

"You did, and you were right. I'm very sorry. I should have listened to you."

"If . . . I . . . could . . . talk . . . dammit . . ."

"I know—you have so much to say—and your people died, too. Must be much worse for you—"

"Thought . . . we . . . all . . . die . . ."

"So did I, for a while there. Let me tell you what happened." Heris outlined the events, and then waited for Cecelia's response.

"Damn . . . lucky . . ."

"It's not over," Heris said. "We have to get you all to Guerni; we have to get you home safely, and survive whatever's going on. And find out who's doing it, and why."

"Lorenza . . . Tourinos," Cecelia said. "Remember . . ."

"I will. But you're going to be able to give your own testimony."

The Guerni Republic's customs were as quick and capable with incoming medical emergencies as with casual trade. Heris requested the fastest possible incoming lane; customs sent an escort alongside to do a close-up scan.

"You've been here before; your references are good; you're cleared with the usual warnings," the escort officer said.

"Thanks. What about a medical shuttle from the Station?"

"We'll arrange it. Actually, trauma cases may not need to go downside; we have major medical available on all stations. We normally handle everything onstation unless that facility is full—saves transport stress and time."

Heris was impressed all over again. It made sense, but in Familias space, most stations transferred serious trauma down to the planet. She had heard it explained as being more cost-effective, but the Guernesi were supposed to be the galaxy experts on cost-effectiveness.

When they arrived at the Station, medical teams awaited them dockside, and the casualties were transferred quickly to the Station trauma center. Cecelia would be shuttled down to the neuromedical center later; she had agreed to have Meharry and Ginese escort her there. Heris would stay up at the Station until Sirkin was out of danger. As soon as she had arranged a private shuttle for Cecelia, her surviving attendants, and her bodyguards, Heris went to the Station hospital.

"Just barely in time," she was told. "That artificial blood substitute saved her, but you really pushed its limits— should have been using exterior gas exchange as well . . . I'm surprised your doctors didn't."

Heris decided not to explain the limits of transferring medical equipment between ships in deep space while in hostile territory. "When they've finished packing up on our ship, maybe they'll talk to you about it," she said. After all, Livadhi's medical teams had already said they wanted to explore the medical riches of the system.

"And we have a newer substitute with a better performance you might want to consider stocking—a license to manufacture would be available through our medical technology exports office—"

Typical. To the Guernesi, every disaster had the seeds of profit in it. "When can I see our casualties?" she asked. "Especially Brigdis Sirkin . . ."

"The two worst, not for at least two days. They'll have two long sessions in regen, but they need transfusions first. The other three will be out of the regen tanks in another six hours, so any time after that—"

Heris went back to the yacht, and found that Livadhi's teams had scoured the areas they'd been using; these now smelled like any sickbay. But one of them stopped her in the midst of her thanks.

"What's this, Captain?" The woman held up an unmistakable cockroach egg case. Heris had a sudden vision of being detained forever on a charge of importing illegal biologicals.

"An egg case," Heris said, trying to sound unconcerned. Inspiration hit. "We had to evacuate Lady Cecelia from Rotterdam in haste; we had no time for proper disinfection procedures. And she was living at a training stable."

"Ah. I presume you disinfected the ship—?"

"Oh, yes. I can't be sure we got them all, but we'll do it again. It was on my schedule, but then we came out of jump in the wrong place—"

"Oh—of course." The woman's accusing expression relaxed. "I'd forgotten about Lady Cecelia's luggage . . . and from a stable yard . . . it's just that contamination from vermin is a serious problem."

You don't know the half of it, Heris thought. At least

they'd found an egg case, and not one of the albino cock-roaches. She wasn't about to tell this starchy person about the cockroach colonies down in 'ponics.

"They were telling me in the hospital here that they have a newer, more efficient oxygen-exchange fluid for blood replacement," she said. Sure enough, that took the woman's attention off cockroach egg cases.

"Really! Expensive?"

"They said something about a license to manufacture—if you found something the Fleet wanted to use, it might make your time here worthwhile."

"Certainly—thanks. I'll just get the team together—"

Sirkin was asleep, curled on her side like a child, when Heris arrived. She looked perfectly healthy, with color in her cheeks again, and no obvious bandages. Heris had made herself visit Cecelia's attendant first, though she didn't know the man at all . . . now she sat beside the bed and waited for Sirkin to wake. Once an attendant peeked in, jotted down some numbers off the monitor above the bed, smiled at Heris, and went back out. Heris dozed off, waking when Sirkin stirred.

"Captain . . ." Her voice was drowsy.

"You're almost recovered, they tell me," Heris said. "I'm sorry—all of us are. We should have trusted you."

"I—don't know. I didn't trust myself. And I don't know how she could—she had been on your ship—"

"Don't worry about her. Let's talk about you. You know Lady Cecelia stood by you all along?"

"Yes—she came to my cabin and said she knew it wasn't my fault."

"She'd like you to stay with us, Brig, though no one will blame you if you don't. We all want you to."

"You're sure?"

"Of course. I can make stupid mistakes, but I can also admit them. It wasn't your fault; you did good work and someone else messed it up. You'll do good work again. It's more a matter of whether you trust us—if you're sure of us."

"I want to," Sirkin said. "I like you." That almost child-like admission struck Heris to the core. She could have cried. "You were all so . . . so good when Amalie died. Even Lord Thornbuckle's daughter . . ."

"Even? Brun's a remarkable young woman, if she did happen to be born rich. She liked you; I daresay if she'd been aboard she'd have chewed my ears about you, and made a dent in my suspicions."

"I really like her . . ." That was said so softly Heris barely heard it, and Sirkin flushed. Heris mentally rolled her eyes. Youngsters. Meharry had told her privately that Brigdis and Brun were likely to go overboard. Clearly Sirkin had. But they'd have to work that out; she never interfered in her crew members' romantic entanglements unless it endangered the ship. This wouldn't . . . in fact . . .

"Not surprising," she said dryly. "Considering—" Considering what, she didn't say. "One of us will be by every shift, until you're out of here. You're under guard, because we still don't know how much trouble we face, but you can call the ship any time you're concerned. I've got to go down and see how Lady Cecelia's coming along."

"Thank you," Sirkin said. Completely awake now, she had begun to regain that sparkle she'd had at first. Resilience, thought Heris, and wondered again if she would be able to afford rejuvenation someday. And what her employer would think about it.

CHAPTER TWENTY-TWO

Cecelia had had reports sent up to Heris—encouraging reports, on the whole. Heris didn't entirely understand the medical terminology—she skipped whole paragraphs of multisyllabic gibberish and tried to figure out the "prognosis" sections. Here she hoped the percentages referred to functions recovered, and not permanently lost—87% this, and 79% that, and 93% the other thing. Livadhi's medical teams might have helped interpret, except that they were spending all their time in the station hospital. She would do better, she decided, to go down and find out in person.

The receptionist recognized her now, and gave her Cecelia's room number. When she came out of the lift on that floor, Meharry was stretched out in the visitors' lounge.

"How is she?"

"Better you should see her," Meharry said gruffly. "We're taking alternate shifts now; Arkady's in the visitors' hostel."

"Sirkin's doing well," Heris said, anticipating Meharry's question. "She's staying with us."

"She's a sweet kid," Meharry said. "Almost too sweet for her own good. I think that's what made me so mad—I liked her so much, and she was so good, and then—you know, if Skoterin had been anything but a bland nothing, I'd have figured it out."

"So we look out for bland nothings," Heris said. "See you after I talk to Lady Cecelia."

"You'll be surprised," Meharry said. It was an odd tone of voice, not at all encouraging, and Heris worried all the

668

way down the corridor. The bright floral prints and soft carpet did nothing to reassure her.

She found the number and knocked lightly.

"Come in." It didn't sound like Cecelia; perhaps a nurse was with her. Even more worried, Heris pushed the door open.

The large room opened onto an atrium filled with flowering plants and ferns. Across an expanse of apricot carpet, a woman in a green silk robe stood by a table set for a meal.

The woman couldn't be Cecelia, Heris realized after a startled glance. She was only in her forties, and although she was tall and lean, she had not a single strand of gray in her red hair. It must be the wrong room. Heris turned to look at the room number, and the woman chuckled. Heris felt that chuckle as a blow to the heart.

"It *is*—but how—?"

"Do come in and shut the door. That's better." Cecelia gestured to the chairs by the table. "Here—sit down; you look as if you'd seen a ghost."

"I—I'm not sure—"

"Vanity has its uses, you know." Cecelia sat down herself, and grinned at Heris. "I decided to take advantage of it."

"But you—you said you'd never go through rejuv."

"If you'd asked me, I'd have said I'd never be poisoned by that wretched Lorenza. Here, have a cup of broth. They have quite good food here."

Heris opened her mouth to say she wasn't hungry, and realized she was. And her employer was looking at her with a wicked gleam in her eyes. She sipped the broth.

"It was vanity that saved me, actually," Cecelia said. "And now I'll have to confess it, and you'll laugh at me—"

"No, I won't. I'm too glad to have you alive—and by the way, thanks for saving us from that mess on the ship."

"I only wish I'd done a better job of it. But—let me tell you. You remember how smug I was about taking no medicines and refusing rejuv?"

"Yes," Heris said cautiously.

"Well, I was lying. To everyone and to myself. There was this . . . this preparation. Herbal stuff. Lots of women used it, and none of us considered it medicinal exactly. Or cosmetic, exactly. I thought of it as a kind of tonic . . . of course

I knew my skin was smoother, and I felt better, but I didn't consider what it really was."

A pause followed; since a comment seemed to be required, Heris said "And it was . . . ?"

Cecelia laughed. "I was so arrogant about drugs, it never occurred to me that many of them come from herbs—plants. That I was taking quite a solid dose of bioactive chemicals that functioned in some ways like the rejuvenation chemicals." She shook her head. "So there I was, smugly certain that I wasn't like those others—the ones I despised— and in fact I was. I must have known—I didn't tell anyone I took it, not even my maid, and certainly not anyone medical. My doctor just thought I had naturally good genes. Which I do, but not that good." She paused and drank a few swallows of broth herself.

"So when Lorenza poisoned me, she used a dose based on my supposed drug-free biochemistry. It worked, but the damage was not as complete. It required more maintenance drug than expected, which meant that when I came off the maintenance drugs, I could recover with therapy . . . and it also meant that a complete rejuvenation treatment would reverse all the damage."

"And so you thought if vanity had saved you so far, you'd go the whole way?"

"That, and the fact that nothing but rejuv would give me natural eyesight again. That visual prosthesis is good enough for walking around without bumping into things, but it doesn't begin to substitute for real sight." Cecelia looked out at the atrium. "The colors . . . the textures . . . oh, Heris, I thought I would go mad, locked away in that darkness, motionless, helpless."

Heris reached to touch her hand. "Cecelia—milady—I don't know how you did it, but it took incredible courage."

Cecelia gave a harsh laugh, almost a croak. "No—not courage. Pigheaded stubbornness. I simply would not give up. And the advantage of being over eighty when something like that happens is that you have a lot of experience to remember. Not enough—it's never enough—but a lot."

"Do you think this person—Lorenza—intended to kill you?"

"Oh, no. She intended exactly what happened. She used to come visit, you know, and sit by my bed and whisper into my ear. 'I did it,' she would say. She never gave her

name, and at that time I couldn't figure out who it was . . .
but it told me that someone had done it, and that—that
helped. It gave me a target. I didn't remember—the drug I
was given was supposed to knock out short-term memory
for the event—until one day after a long ride in therapy. I
was suddenly there, where it happened, in Berenice's drawing
room, with Lorenza handing me a glass of fruit juice."
Cecelia stared at the ferns and flowers a long moment before
going on. "She said that once, too: *You'll never ride again,
Cecelia. You'll never feel the wind in your face, never smell
the flowers.*"

Heris shivered in spite of herself. "She must be a terrible
woman."

"She's the main reason I refused rejuvenation so long. We
knew each other as children . . . and she began to have rejuv
early, and often. She was obsessed with her appearance—and
I admit, she's a beauty, and always was. But the last time I
saw her . . . that smooth young skin and glossy hair, and those
ancient, evil eyes . . . I didn't want to become that sort of
person."

"You couldn't," Heris said.

Cecelia smiled at her. "Heris, I love your loyalty, but
one thing I have learned in my long eventful life is that
anyone can change into anything. It takes only carelessness. My mistake was in confusing surface behaviors with
the reasons behind them. It wasn't rejuv that made Lorenza
what she is—what she is propelled her to that many rejuv
procedures."

"Still, you would never—"

"I hope not. Certainly nothing that cruel. But if you put
Lorenza and me in the same room? I could kill her. You
know I can kill."

Remembering Cecelia as she had been on Sirialis, when
she shot the man who would have killed them both, Heris
nodded. "For cause, you could. Maybe even in vengeance.
But you would not ever torment someone as she tormented
you—that I'm sure of."

"Good. So far I feel no temptation that way, though I do
have a strong urge to pull her blonde hair out by the roots."

Heris had to laugh then. "So—when do we do just that?"

"I have one more round of neurological testing, and we
want to be sure Sirkin's fully recovered . . ."

"She's younger than both of us, and recovers faster even without rejuv—"

"Good, then. Let's go back and . . . er . . . clean house, shall we?"

Heris said, "There is the problem of the prince and his clone, or the clones and no prince. I accepted a mission from the king, as I explained to you—"

Cecelia scowled. "The medical reports haven't straightened anything out?"

"Not really. All the tissue samples are identical. The clones believe—they told me—that they carry markers somewhere. But if these doctors can't find them, who can? As for the mental limitations, both these clones perform at normal levels on tests. Not as high as you'd expect from a Registered Embryo, but not as low as you'd expect from the prince, judging by what we saw on the way back from Sirialis."

"What do the clones say now? Have you talked to them since you got back?"

"No—have you?"

"Once, yes. Heris, I believe in my heart that the young man with us—Gerald A., as you called him—was the real prince. Their prime. I can't give you any reason that would make sense except an old woman's intuition. But remember how he and Ronnie both fell on that gas grenade?"

"If that was the prince."

"It was. Everything that's happened since proves it. Neither the king—nor Lorenza, I believe—would go so far to protect a mere clone; if a clone fails, you get rid of it. My point is that along with Gerel's undeniable witlessness he had great and generous gallantry. A meaner boy, stupid or bright, would not have done what he did. And when Skoterin threatened Sirkin—the moment the weapon swung toward her and away from me—Gerald A. did the same thing. In the same style. Generous, brave, and incredibly stupid. It provoked her to shoot; she might not have fired, and your Petris might have killed her before anyone else got hurt. I think that was no clone; I think that was the prince himself."

"But he had seemed more sensible at times . . . on the voyage with the others."

"Think, Heris. If they were protecting him, if *they* knew his problem, they would shift about, so that you could not be sure which one you spoke to—you'd have to ask. Couldn't that be it? Or perhaps all that time without the drug began to reverse the dullness."

"But if that's true, then I've failed in the mission the king gave me. And what do we do with the clones?"

"I'll tell you what we *don't* do. We don't take them back to be discarded or killed by someone who would let his own son be ruined. Go talk to them. I told them what I thought; they didn't say much. They may to you. If they are the clones, and Gerel is dead, I will not let you take them on my ship. I don't want their ruin on my conscience."

Brun had no intention of staying safely at home on the family's estates. They knew who had poisoned Lady Cecelia; they had figured out that the prince had also been slowly poisoned, and that the same method had been used on George for a short time. She and Ronnie and George were ready, the moment Buttons and Sarah arrived, to do battle with the minions of evil.

"Whoa," Buttons said. "You haven't thought it all out."

"What's to think?" George said. "The woman's a menace: she poisoned me, and then the prince, and then Lady Cecelia, and maybe a dozen others—"

"Why?"

"Why? I suppose . . . I guess . . . she likes poisoning people."

"George, you're sounding about as intelligent as you did in your bad term. I have some missing links you'd better add to your chain of evidence. You mentioned Gerel being excited after visits from his brothers . . . do you remember any more?"

"No." George sounded grumpy. He hated being interrupted.

"I do." Buttons stood and paced around the big library. "It annoys all of you when I remind you I'm older . . . but it matters. You were in school with each other and Gerel; I was in school with Gerel's older brother, Nadrel."

"Who was killed in a duel; we know that."

"Shut up, Ronnie. That's only part of it. Because I was his friend, I got to know the oldest, and don't bother to tell me you know Jared had been accepted as Successor by the Grand Council. That happened our last year in school; it was terribly exciting, and I got to attend, with Nadrel.

But what I didn't know—because Jared had said I was too stuffy and priggish and would spill the beans—was that Jared had been groomed by some of the Familias to head a rebellion. Nadrel knew, of course . . . and they dragged in poor young Gerel, who worshipped his oldest brother. And it was Gerel who spilled the beans . . . to you, George."

"I—I don't remember." George looked stunned, as if a rock had landed on his head.

"No—you wouldn't, if they drugged you. I don't suppose you told anyone intentionally—you had a certain innate cunning even then—but your father got wind of it, and he told the king. That assassination—"

"The king killed his own son?"

"No. Nor ordered it . . . but one of the other Familias felt it had to be done. No one knew how far the plot had gone; the military was on alert for months. Nadrel . . . Nadrel was a problem, bitter and violent; I couldn't swear his duel was spontaneous."

"And Gerel—?"

Buttons shrugged. "I would guess—I knew nothing about it, until you told me this—I would guess the king wanted to be sure Gerel could not be the same kind of threat. Perhaps you, George, were the experimental subject, to prove the effects reversible. Then Gerel—I would like to believe the king meant no harm by it."

"No harm!" Brun was so angry she felt her hair must be bristling. "Poor Gerel, everyone thinking him a fool—and then Lady Cecelia being poisoned—and Sarah shot—"

"I didn't say there was no harm, only that he may not have intended it. If Lorenza was the king's arm in this, she may have done more than he knew."

"Then it's Lorenza we have to stop. Now." Ronnie was on his feet now. "What if she attacks my mother, thinking I might have said something to her? Or George's parents?"

"Ronnie, we can't simply walk in and seize her. She's a Crown Minister's sister—another complication, because I for one have no idea how much influence she has with him—or he with the king, for that matter. She's got a vote in the Grand Council in her own right. We have no legal standing—"

"Tell my father," George said. "I'll call him—"

"George, will you listen! Your father's already involved—

so is ours. They've filed a Question. But none of us can grab Lorenza; we have no evidence. We need Lady Cecelia alive and well, her competency completely restored so that she can testify; we need the prince alive and well—and both of them are a long way away with a lot of things that can go wrong. Less will go wrong if we all act discreetly."

"Then you didn't need my warning at all—you already knew about Lorenza, and I could have stayed with Lady Cecelia—" Brun felt tired and grumpy.

"No—we didn't know about Lorenza. We knew it had to be someone, but we didn't know who—and that's important. But we can't afford to lose anyone, so I want you all to agree to stay calm and follow orders."

"Whose?" Ronnie asked bluntly.

"Mine, for now, and Dad's when he gets here. George's father will tell him the same. Now will you use sense and act like the adults you are?"

Cecelia looked around the main lounge of her yacht with distaste. "I thought the lavender plush was bad, but I have to admit this is worse." Then she grinned. "Though I must say I'm glad to see it—really see it. Show me everything." Heris glanced at Petris, now their new environmental section head and assistant. "Everything, milady?"

"Every bit of it. I'll be thinking how lovely it will look when Spacenhance has finished with it." She looked from one to the other of them. "Come on! What are you waiting for?"

"Well, we have this little problem," Heris said, leading her down the streaked grayish walls, wondering how Cecelia was going to react when she saw them. She opened the door to the 'ponics section: stacks of mesh cages held an ever-increasing number of cockroaches, filling the air in that compartment with an odd, heavy smell. "This."

"What on—they're *alive.*"

"Yes . . . and I don't want you mentioning this to the medical teams, either."

"Where did they come from?"

"Spacenhance," Heris said.

"The decorators? They put *cockroaches* on my ship? On *my* ship?" Outrage made her voice spike up; Heris grinned.

"We think they put cockroaches on everyone's ship, to eat the old wallcovering and carpeting, and the adhesives.

Illegal, of course. A trade secret, no doubt. We thought we might need to deal in trade secrets, so we trapped the ones we found and let them breed."

"But what did they do with the cockroaches after they ate the stuff?" Cecelia leaned forward to look at the nearest cage.

"We think . . . mind, this is only our speculation . . . that they converted the cockroaches into a sort of organic slurry, which could then be extruded into fiber or other shapes . . . to make carpets or wallcoverings—"

"You mean they put *ground-up cockroaches* on people's floors? Walls? You mean that horrible lavender plush was really nothing but ground-up *cockroaches*?"

"Quite possibly," Heris said, enjoying Cecelia's reaction. "Of course, they would have dyed them—that's why they're white, I'm sure—and they may have added other materials."

Cecelia stepped back. "I have never even imagined anything so . . . so disgusting."

Heris grinned at Petris. "There is something worse . . ."

"What?"

"When they're loose and you haven't noticed them in the sheets." She and Petris both started laughing, and Cecelia glared at them.

"It's not funny. Or—I suppose it is, but—oh, my, have we got a whip hand here."

"That's what I thought," Heris said. "Of course, we're now in violation of half a dozen regulations ourselves, but we've been careful. I would prefer, however, that Commander Livadhi's people not know about the live ones."

"Oh, absolutely," said Cecelia, beginning to smile. "But I suspect that restocking my solarium with miniatures will be well within my budget."

From that beginning, the trip back to Rockhouse Major went smoothly. Heris made the rendezvous with Livadhi's *Martine Scolare*, and his pinnace picked up the medical teams. Heris had braced herself for questions about the clones, but the medical teams were so excited about the new technologies they'd discovered in those few days on the Station that they could talk of nothing else. Livadhi asked, of course, and Heris gave the answer she and Cecelia had worked out. It was not exactly a lie.

"I left the clones behind; neither of them was the prince. As you know, one was killed in the shooting, and tissue analysis at autopsy could neither prove nor disprove that that one was the prince. Perhaps postmortem degradation . . ."

"Or perhaps he's off in a bar somewhere making an idiot of himself," Livadhi said. "I wonder if the king knows how many doubles he had?"

"We may never know," Heris said cautiously. "What's the latest on the uproar?"

"Not quite civil war," Livadhi said. "Fleet's on standby, all the Family Delegates are gathering for an emergency session, and rumor has it the king is considering abdication. The Benignity has filed complaints, and threatens to take action if we don't pay reparations for their two cruisers, which have somehow grown to dreadnoughts; Aethar's World decided this was a great time to try a little piracy . . . oh, yes, and the Stationmaster at Rotterdam says to tell Lady Cecelia that the black mare has foaled. Anything else?"

"No—thank you. What about the Fleet and us?"

"You personally, or you in Lady Cecelia's yacht?"

"Either or both."

"Well, I've had strong representations from senior Familias that my neck is in the noose if Lady Cecelia doesn't get back safely—how is she, by the way?"

"Quite able to take up her duties," Heris said.

"Good. And I've had strong pressure from some . . . er . . . elements in the Fleet that your permanent disappearance would just about guarantee my first star. While others say the opposite. I would suggest the fastest possible course, and I suggest you allow me to escort you in."

"I accept both suggestions." She was not entirely sure of him in all respects, but if he wanted her dead, it would have been easy enough to leave her in Compassionate Hand space without help.

The Familias Grand Council met in a domed hall. High above, painted stars on pale blue echoed the carpet of deep blue patterned with gold stars. Each Family had its Table; each voting member had his or her Chair. On the north wall, opposite the entrance doors, the Speaker's Bench had become the king's throne, and the king, wearing his usual black suit, sat there behind a desk with its crystal pitcher of water, its goblets, its display screens, and the gold-rimmed gavel.

For an hour now, the Members had streamed in past uniformed guards and weapons checks and more guards and more weapons checks. The lines extended across the lobby, out the tall front doors, down the steps, to the sidewalk where yet more limousines disgorged yet more Members. A light rain brushed the steps with one slick layer after another, and those who had not expected a wait got damp and grumpy.

Cecelia watched her sister and brother-in-law climb up the steps. She, Heris, Meharry, and Ginese were part of a thin crowd held back by a chain attached to a movable post. From the chain a little tin sign dangled, with the words "Members Only Past This Point." Across from them, on the far side of the entrance steps, another such chain restrained another small clump of observers.

"When are you going?" Heris asked.

"After Lorenza. I want to be sure she's here."

"What if she doesn't attend?"

"Oh, she will. She may not take her own Chair, but she always attends her brother. There—that's theirs—" Cecelia started to look down, then remembered she didn't look anything like the Cecelia Lorenza would recognize. They had docked the yacht over on Rockhouse Minor, where Bunny's shuttle retrieved them. There would have been gossip, of course, but Livadhi, at Heris's suggestion, had docked at the Fleet terminal at Rockhouse Major, and complained loudly to his fellow officers that "that bitch Serrano" had disappeared again.

Cecelia watched as the portly Crown Minister—when had Piercy gained all that weight?—climbed out and offered his arm to Lorenza. She, at least, had prepared for a wait, in a pretty ice-blue raincoat. Piercy had an umbrella; Cecelia felt her lip curling. If you couldn't stand a bit of rain, then carry a personal shield, not an ostentatious umbrella. That was carrying the fashion for antiquity too far. Piercy held the umbrella over Lorenza's head; she looked out from under it with catlike smugness. Cecelia realized she was trembling only when Heris touched her hand. Rage filled her; she could hear that voice whispering in her ear . . . how had she not known who it was? How could she not leap over the chain and strangle that smug little tramp?

Lorenza looked around, as if for admiration. Cecelia stood straight, watching her; their eyes met. Lorenza frowned a little, shook her head minutely, and went on up the steps to the tail of the line. Half a dozen more Members got in line; Cecelia shifted her feet.

"Let's go."

"It's too close," Meharry said. "She'll see you—she'll start trying to remember—"

"Let her!" Cecelia was breathing deeply as if before a race. Heris gripped her hand.

"Milady, we're with you. You have allies; you know that. Don't let her shake your resolution. Even if she does look like the worst insipid tea biscuit I ever saw."

That got a grim chuckle; Cecelia felt her tension ease. "All right. But not much longer."

"No, not much longer." They waited until Lorenza and her brother were near the top of the steps, when the guards at the door recognized them and swept them inside ahead of the others. "Now," Heris said. They stepped around the barrier, and Cecelia clipped her Member badge to her coat. The others put on the ID tags Bunny had arranged; Members could bring their personal assistants, as long as none carried weapons. Heris wasn't worried; Meharry and Ginese *were* weapons.

Most of the delegates had arrived; the line moved faster. At the door, Cecelia moved into the Members Booth for an ID check. The others, with staff IDs, went through without incident. Cecelia came out of the booth and found them waiting. Now, in the lobby, out of the rain, she could hear the steady sound of all those people talking. She felt weak at the knees. She had been alone so long . . . and then with a few friends . . . and now, to face that crowd . . . she had always hated public speaking. She felt the others close in.

"All right, milady?" Heris asked.

"All right. I just—I'm fine." The line they were in snaked slowly forward. She could see in the door at last . . . it had been decades since she'd attended a Grand Council. When she'd been a young woman, first eligible for a Chair, it had been a thrill . . . later a bore . . . later something she delegated to a proxy without a second thought. Now that earlier awe struck her again. That tall dome spangled with stars, those dark polished Tables, each with its Chairs of red leather, all symbols of power that had kept her safe and wealthy all these years, and then had nearly killed her. Across the chamber, as she came to the door, she saw the king on his throne. He stared out, seeming to see no one.

Her family Table had moved since the last time she'd attended; Tables were drawn by lot every other Council. Now it was midway down the right side of the left aisle, almost directly across from the Speaker's Table. A page led them to it, and checked Cecelia's ID again before handing her to her Chair. The Chair itself required her to insert her Member card . . . a precaution resulting from the behavior of a speedy young man who had once managed to vote two Chairs by flitting from one to another while a long roll-call vote dragged on. With the card in place, the screen before her lit. Only then did she look around. Her sister Berenice, two Chairs down, stared at her, white-faced, then glanced at her companions and turned even whiter. Ronnie, at the foot of the Table, started and then grinned happily. Gustav would be at his family's Table; Cecelia had no idea where it was now.

"Good to see you again," Cecelia said. They had not told Berenice; they had not told anyone. Berenice's shock was almost vengeance enough for her treatment of Heris.

"You're—you had—"

"Rejuv, yes. Just as you did." Cecelia smiled. "Where's Abelard?"

"Probably having a last drink," Berenice said. Abelard, their oldest surviving brother, always came late. Ronnie looked as if he were bursting with glee and news both. Cecelia gave him a look she hoped would quell him. They already knew what he knew; Bunny had told her. She looked around. Kevil Mahoney was in his Chair, with George beside him. Bunny, his brothers, and his sons were already seated; Brun, a year too young for her own Chair, crouched beside her mother at another Table. She was scanning the chamber, looking . . . and she saw Cecelia. A grin spread over her face; Cecelia gave a little nod. Now . . . to find Lorenza. The Crown Ministers sat together, at two Tables to either side of the throne . . . but when she found Piercy, leaning back to hand a file to a page, she did not see Lorenza's gold head anywhere near. She let her eyes rove the chamber, but it was Meharry who spotted her.

A nudge—Cecelia leaned over and Meharry murmured, "Top tier, near the right aisle." Cecelia turned casually. There. The ice-blue raincoat had been slung carelessly over the back of a neighboring Chair—unlike the precise Lorenza. But there she was, leaning over to talk to someone else Cecelia couldn't see. Whose Family was that? Not Lorenza's certainly . . . Lorenza's mother had been a Sturinscough, and her aunt Lucrezia should be heading that Table. So she was, an upright old tyrant in black lace whom no amount of rejuvenation could soften . . . maybe, thought Cecelia, it runs in the family.

So why was Lorenza back with the Buccleigh-Vandormers? True, people sometimes got permission to sit in other Chairs—if they had physical problems, if they planned to leave early—ah. Cecelia felt her smile widening to a dangerous grin. Let her leave . . . let her try to escape. It wouldn't do her any good.

Chimes rang out, and the bustle in the chamber quieted. A last few Members came scurrying in, swiping at their wet clothes. The chimes rang again, and the king picked up the gavel. Grand Council was about to begin.

The king had not recognized Lady Cecelia in the lithe redhead who stalked down the aisle as if she owned it. Not until she sat at that Table, in that Chair, not until her name lit on his screen of Members Present. Then, as if his vision had suddenly cleared, he recognized Heris Serrano with her. Where was the prince? Panic gripped him suddenly; icy sweat broke out all over him; he felt himself trembling. If the prince were alive, she would have brought him; the conclusion was inescapable. Dead.

He could see, as if part of his brain had turned into a tiny viewscreen, the concatenation of errors that had led him to this place. One time after another, he had done the convenient thing, the expedient thing; he had let himself be led from one folly to the next. Jared's assassination, Nadrel's duel, Gerel's drugs, the clones, the secrets and countersecrets, the lies and evasions. He had lost his power; he had lost his sons; worst of all, he had lost the respect of those two women and everyone like them, all the decent men and women in the realm. His former allies would certainly disown him and his policies now, even as they scrambled to save their influence. He had thought Cecelia immature, with her strong enthusiasms, her blunt honesty. Now that immaturity seemed far wiser than the sly counsels he'd convinced himself represented maturity.

He wanted to break into tears; he wanted to throw his gavel down and leave. Tears would not help; he had nowhere to go. If Gerel had come back, he might have stood against the Question already before the meeting, but no longer. He knew what he had to do.

Lorenza could not shake the uneasiness that had become her constant companion. That stupid goon on Rockhouse Major had attacked the wrong girl, and thereby raised suspicion. No one had seen Thornbuckle's daughter; no one had seen Lady Cecelia. Berenice had complained that Ronnie was spending all his time with his regiment; he had run out on the opera party over some ridiculous little chit of a girl, and now he never came home. She knew that George, too, had not been home for weeks. The men she hired could not locate them anywhere.

Piercy had come home with vague stories of great unrest here and there. The Benignity was upset, Aethar's World . . . she had tried to listen, but all she could think of was Lady Cecelia. Lady Cecelia awake, alert, able to walk and see and speak . . . worst of all, Lady Cecelia able to remember. She wasn't supposed to be able to remember, but then she wasn't supposed to be able to achieve legal competency, either. Lorenza found herself seeing Lady Cecelia everywhere when she went out. None of them were, of course. The tall woman in the store had had the wrong face when she turned around; the woman with the short graying-reddish hair had been too short when she stood up at the reception. It was just nerves, she told herself. If she comes, then she comes, and then . . . and then kill her. She began carrying a weapon, a tiny thing that fired darts tipped with poison.

Yet no sign of Lady Cecelia—the real Lady Cecelia—showed up before the Grand Council meeting. One informant tried to tell her that Lady Cecelia's yacht had come into Rockhouse Minor—but the database had an entirely different listing, and a more reliable source on Rockhouse Major reported a conversation between Arash Livadhi and another R.S.S. officer, one known to be hostile to Serrano. She had that recording. It could be, she thought wistfully, that Lady Cecelia was afraid to come, that she and that renegade captain had gone off together somewhere.

She didn't believe that for a moment. She had dressed that morning as if for her last appearance; she had her jewel case hidden in her raincoat; she had her pearls under her dress. If she had to flee, if she couldn't use her credit cubes, she would have something . . .

For a moment, just after getting out of the limousine, she had been sure Cecelia was near. She had looked around, at the little clumps of people who wished they were rich enough to be Familias, to have Chairs and votes. In the rain, it was hard to tell . . . one tall woman with red hair reminded her of Cecelia, but she was forty years younger, at least. And she was prettier than Cecelia had ever been.

Lorenza took precautions anyway. She would sit with the Buccleigh-Vandormers, to whom she was distantly related, claiming an upset stomach. She could leave quickly if she had to; she had a reservation on the noon shuttle to Rockhouse Major under another name, and she knew the number to call when she got there. They owed her plenty of favors.

Even with all her caution, she did not see Lady Cecelia until the king struck for order with his gavel. Her eyes checked the tables: there was Piercy, looking stuffy. There was Abelard, and Berenice, and . . . the back of a red head, a tall woman. The woman turned, and looked her in the eye . . . and smiled, a slow smile of absolute delight. Lorenza almost fainted; her fists clenched on the table before her. Cecelia. The bitch was not only recovered but rejuvenated . . . and she remembered.

She forgot the weapon she carried. She heard nothing the king was saying; in a scramble she grabbed her raincoat and rushed the door, pushing past the row of pages. "Madam!" she heard behind her; she shoved the tall door open and strode across the wide lobby, trying not to run. Behind her she heard the roar of upraised voices, cut off by the closing door. The guards, alert to stop intruders, did not move as she went out the glass doors of the building, down the rain-wet steps. She was on the street, drenched, before she remembered she was carrying a raincoat. She dragged it on over her wet dress and looked for the nearest transportation.

Cecelia half-rose when she saw Lorenza bolt; Heris grabbed her wrist. "Not now—she won't escape." Between Livadhi and Bunny, Lorenza would find no transportation farther than the stations. If she bolted that far, they might find out who her allies were.

"Right." The king was speaking, his voice sounding flat and tired. The ritual welcome, to which he had given some grace and humor in years past, sounded as stilted as it actually was. Piercy, at the Crown Ministers' Table, was staring at the door through which Lorenza had left with a worried expression. The moment the welcome ended, Bunny stood for recognition. He was very much Lord Thornbuckle in his formal suit.

"If you'll wait a moment," the king said. It was more plea than direction, and that lack of control released a buzzing hum of conversation.

"There is a Question before the floor," Bunny said.

"I know that," the king said. "But I have a preemptive announcement."

"May I request the floor when you have made it?" That was not so much question as command; the king nodded. Bunny sat down, stiffly.

"Members of Familias," the king said. A long pause, during which curiosity rose again, expressed as a crisp ruffle of subdued talk. "I wish to announce . . ." another pause. "My resignation. Abdication. I . . . am not able to continue."

"Why?" bellowed someone from the far right corner. "We don't want that."

"Yes, we do!" yelled someone else. Other voices rose, louder and louder, in argument. The king banged his gavel, and the noise subsided.

"I cannot—I have reason to believe . . . my last son is dead. In my grief—I am aware of failings that—" He laid the gavel down, shook his head, then put it down on his desk. Profound silence filled the chamber; Cecelia saw puzzlement, anger, and fear on the faces around her. Bunny stood again.

"I was promised the floor to address the Question, which

all of you have been sent. The king has indeed preempted that Question, which called for his resignation. I move we accept it, without further inquiry."

"How can we vote, without a Chair?" someone asked.

Cecelia spoke up, without having meant to. "By putting your finger on the little button, the way you always do," she said loudly. A ripple of nervous laughter followed, circled the chamber, and returned. She pushed the voting button on her screen; others followed. The vote carried. She felt a sudden burst of compassion for the king. Had he meant any of the harm he had brought to pass? Probably not. She had not meant him any harm either, but she had been the means of destroying his reign.

After the vote, a long silence, and then confusion. The king—no longer the king, but a man whose Familia name nearly all had forgotten—sat immobile, staring at the desk in front of him. Cecelia watched the Crown Ministers' heads swaying from side to side as they whispered among themselves, exactly like pigeons on a roost. The sound of many voices rose, filling the chamber as if a vast river roared through it. Finally Bunny went to the Ministers' Tables and leaned over to speak to them. One of them rose and approached the ex-king. He looked up, then, and in his expression Cecelia saw a new resolution form. Stillness came as swiftly as the earlier noise. He stood.

"I yield the floor," Kemtre said. "To Lord Thornbuckle." He held out the gavel. And Bunny, grave, unsmiling, took the few steps necessary. The gavel passed between them, and Kemtre stepped down to meet Bunny on the level below the throne. Though his voice was quiet, unaugmented by the sound system, most heard what he said next. "I'm going back for Velosia. If she waits. Then home—" That would be the Familia estates, not the Crown ones. "I'm sorry, Bunny—I hope you have better luck. At least this gives you a chance—"

Then he came up the steps toward Cecelia; she felt Meharry and Heris tense on either side of her. "It's all right," she muttered; she might as well have tried to calm a pair of eager hounds with the game in view. If he meant her any harm, he was a dead man.

"I'm sorry, Cecelia," he said to her. "I cannot say how happy I am to see you recovered; it was not my plan, but

I'm sure it was, in some way, my fault. You did me a good service and I did you a bad one."

Cecelia thought of the suffering of the months—almost two years, in local time—and gave him a stare that made him flush, then pale. "I can forgive you for myself," she said then, into the hushed silence of the chamber. "But the boys? I was never a mother, Kemtre, but I could not have done to anyone's child what you did to your own. How could you?" Before he could answer, her gaze swept the Tables. "Still—I don't blame you as much as Lorenza." Below her, Piercy flinched. "She's the one who poisoned me; I daresay she's poisoned others. She's the one I want."

That brought another uproar. Lorenza's aunt Lucrezia gave Cecelia a glare that should have ignited asbestos at a hundred paces. Bunny gavelled the noise down, and called Kevil Mahoney forward. "The king has resigned; we need not fall into disorder for that, Chairholders. We had a government before we had a king; we can have one now, with or without a king. Ser Mahoney has legal advice for us all; I ask your attention." As Kevil's practiced voice compelled the others to listen, Kemtre looked past Cecelia to Heris. She shook her head, offering no details; all he really needed to know was in that negation. Kemtre seemed to sag on his bones, and then turned away. Cecelia returned her attention to Mahoney, but Heris watched the former king climb slowly to the exit. No one greeted him; no one stretched out a hand to comfort him. She was not sure what she felt; she was only sure it was neither triumph nor pity.

The meeting went on for hours, never quite erupting into complete disorder. Piercy resigned. Two other Crown Ministers resigned. Cecelia's brother Abelard proposed a vote to restore the Speaker's position; Cecelia had not imagined he had that much initiative. The vote passed, which surprised her even more. She stayed, when she would rather have pursued Lorenza, caught up despite herself in the excitement, until at last the meeting adjourned for the day. She went home with Bunny, despite Berenice's plea . . . she wasn't ready to forgive Berenice yet, not until she'd had her vengeance on Lorenza.

❊   ❊   ❊

No one on the noon shuttle paid any attention to Lorenza; their attention was on the news being shown on the forward viewscreen. The king's abdication, the surprise vote to abolish the monarchy and restore the Speaker's position, was enough to hold even the most jaded. Lorenza ignored it; she was fingering the pearls hidden beneath her dress and wondering how far they would take her. Although the Benignity owed her favors for her many useful acts, she had no illusions about them. They would do more for pearls or the other jewels than for old times' sake. She slipped into an uneasy doze, missing the interview with Lady Cecelia de Marktos, famous horsewoman and prominent member of her Family, whose miraculous recovery from a coma provided the news program's obligatory "good news" spot.

Rockhouse Major bubbled with rumors and excitement when she arrived. Lorenza put on her most demure expression and made her way to the office whose location she had long ago memorized but had never visited. A lady of her standing did not visit the kind of therapist employed to counsel criminals. Now . . . now she needed to contact the Benignity's senior agent on the station.

She did not like the tall, handsome, self-assured woman in the pale-yellow silk suit. Liking didn't matter, of course, but she felt abraded by the woman's appraising eye, as if she could see through the rejuvenations to her real age, through her carefully groomed exterior to her inner self. She introduced herself with the code words she'd been given long ago. The woman smiled.

"Of course. We'll have to hide you until a suitable ship comes. Come with me, please." She had no choice, really. "Do you have any luggage? Any—I presume you don't want to use your credit cubes—anything to contribute toward expenses?" Lorenza didn't protest.

"Only this." She started to open the jewel case, but the woman took it from her, then smiled.

"You needn't worry—the Benignity is scrupulously honest."

Of course, but why not let her carry her own jewel case? Lorenza had no time to think about it; she was being hurried through back passages, past little cubicles with chairs and mirrors in them, like changing rooms at dress shops.

"This one," the woman said, opening a door at the end of the row. "No one will bother you here. I'll get you something less conspicuous to wear. You might want to take off that raincoat—you must have been seen in it." Under the raincoat, her dress was still damp from the rain. The woman clucked sympathetically. "Get that wet thing off before you catch a chill; I'll get you a warm robe." She went out, the raincoat over her arm, and shut the little door behind her.

Lorenza looked at herself in the mirror: damp, haggard, her gold hair rumpled to one side by that nap on the shuttle. Terrible. She raked at her hair with her fingers. A draft brushed her damp shoulder; she looked up and realized that the walls in this little cubicle went all the way to the ceiling. There shouldn't be any draft . . . but there was, with a whiff of something acrid in it. She grabbed the door handle; it came off in her hand, leaving a slick metal panel. The mirror—as she looked, the upper half blurred, no longer reflective. An image formed; the therapist, with a handful of Lorenza's jewels.

"You ruined it, Lorenza," the woman said, shaking her head. "The Benignity is scrupulously honest, but it doesn't tolerate mistakes."

Lorenza gasped, finding it difficult. "I—please—I still have these—" and she tore at her dress, pulling out the pearls. Their lustrous surface turned a dirty green; she could feel them crumbling.

"Damn!" said the woman. "You had pearls, too! That gas ruins pearls."

"I'm terribly afraid we may have damaged some of your . . . er . . . property," Heris said. She had had no trouble getting an appointment with Spacenhance; at the moment, anything Lady Cecelia wanted was hers to command.

The senior partner looked as if something were crawling over his skin. "Yes . . . ?"

"Some . . . er . . . pets, I suppose."

"Pets?"

"Yes. Unfortunately, they've been somewhat of an embarrassment to us. During a crisis, a medical team member spotted . . . well, let's just say evidence of their presence. They recommended we contact Environmental Control to fumigate the ship—"

He paled; Heris was afraid he might faint. "You told them . . . ?"

"No . . . I decided they represented no present hazard. We could dispose of them appropriately." So they had, she thought with wicked glee. Sirkin, Brun, Meharry, and Oblo had ensured a most unpleasant surprise for a certain therapist they blamed for Yrilan's death. With any luck at all, the discovery of illegal biologicals in her possession would lead to full investigation of all her activities.

His flush was as pronounced as the pallor had been. "Ahhh . . . thank you, Captain."

"No need. It would have benefited neither of us for Environmental Control to come down on *you*." Heris smiled. From his expression, her smile was not reassuring; she hadn't meant it to be.

"Benefited . . . ?"

"Come now—it's clear to me what you do with those . . . er . . . insects. That is, I presume, an industrial secret of some worth to you. So the benefit to you of my silence is obvious. The benefit to me—" She leaned forward, savoring his uneasiness. "You know, the ship still needs redecorating. The deposit paid to you has been earning you interest all this time—I think you owe me—and Lady Cecelia—a very fast, very special redecoration."

"But—but Captain Serrano—"

"Very fast," Heris emphasized. Then she opened her hand, where an egg case lay. "Don't you?"

He gave in, as she had known he would. "As planned before, or do you have something else in mind?"

"Here are the specifications," Heris said, handing him a datacube. She and Cecelia and the crew had discussed it. "Except for one thing." She dropped the egg case on his desk. "This time, make sure you get all the bugs out."

WINNING COLORS

Dedication

This one's for Mary Morell, who introduced me to science fiction in the ninth grade, and then insisted the wonderful (!) stories I wrote in high school were lousy. (She was right.) And for Ellen McLean, who refused to be my friend in the first grade, only to be a better friend later than anyone could ask. And for all the horses, from the horse next door to the little bay mare who presently has her nose in my feed bucket, who enriched my life with everything from (a few) broken bones to the feel of going at speed across country.

CHAPTER ONE

Twoville, Sublevel 3, on the planet Patchcock,
in the Familias Regnant

Conspirators come in two basic flavors, Ottala thought. The bland vanillas, usually wealthy, who meet in comfortably appointed boardrooms or dining rooms, scenting the air with expensive perfumes, liqueurs, and good food. The more complex chocolates, usually impoverished, who meet in dingy back rooms of failing businesses or scruffy warehouses, where the musty air stinks of dangerous chemicals and unwashed bodies. The vanillas, when they cursed, did so with a sense of risk taken, as if the expletives might pop in their mouths like flimsy balloons and sting their tongues. The chocolates cursed without noticing, the familiar phrases embedded in their speech like nuts in candy, lending texture. The vanillas claimed to loathe violence, resorting to it with reluctance, under the lash of stern morality. The chocolates embraced violence and its tools as familiar and comforting rituals. No wonder, since when the vanillas chose violence, they employed chocolates for it.

Ottala much preferred luxury herself; she considered that a long leisurely soak in perfumed water was the only civilized way to begin the day. She too felt the little shock of surprise when she heard the expletives come out of her own mouth with no immediate punishment. Her skin preferred the sensuous touch of silk; her taste buds rejoiced during elaborate dinners created by talented cooks. But she could not confine her sensuality to the bland end of the spectrum. Vanilla was not enough. In her own mind, she considered her taste for chocolate an expression of unusual sensitivity.

What she tasted at the moment was the sour underbite of processed protein extruded into pseudo-sausages nested in pickled neo-cabbage. She sat on a hard bench, elbow-to-elbow with the rest of Cell 571, munching the supper that preceded the evening's entertainment. Or so she called it; she was aware that her fellow conspirators considered it more important than anything else they did with their lives.

Her friends would not have recognized her. Her normally bronze skin had the pallor associated with the underbellies of cave-dwelling amphibians; her dark eyes were masked with blue contact lenses, which also gave her red-rimmed lids, the better to fit in with the locals. She wore the same dark, ill-cut coveralls and had the same fingertip calluses as the others; she had held a real job on the assembly line—with faked papers, which wasn't that unusual—for the past two months.

It was all a great adventure. She knew things about her family's company that she had never imagined; she would have incomparable tales to tell when she went back topside. Meanwhile, she could eat sour pseudo-sausage, drink cheap wine, use words her parents didn't even know, and find out for herself if the reputation of Finnvardian men was deserved. So far she wasn't sure. . . . Enar had ranked only average on her personal scale, but if Sikar would only look at her . . .

She finished her supper, as the others finished theirs. Odd, how the same custom held at tables high and low—everyone tried to finish at the same time. Across the room, Sikar stood, and silence spread around him. He was the contact from higher up, the man whose respect they all wanted. Even in the baggy dark clothing, he had presence. Ottala couldn't analyze it; she only knew that she felt his intensity as a pressure under her rib cage. She wanted that pressure elsewhere.

As usual, Sikar began speaking without preamble. "We, the young, serve the old," he said. "And the old can live forever now, and they expect us to serve forever. We will grow old and die, but they will not. Is this right?"

"NO!" the room vibrated to that angry response.

"No. It was bad before, when the old rich first set their hands against the gate of death, but a hundred fifty years is not forever. That is why our fathers and grandfathers submitted; they hoped to afford that process for themselves, and it was limited. But now—"

"They live forever," a woman's voice interrupted from behind Sikar. "And we work forever, and our children—"

"Forever." Sikar made the word obscene. "Their children will live forever too; our children will DIE forever." An angry rumble, indistinct, shook the room again. "But there is a chance. Now, while the government is shaken by the king's departure." They had discussed this, night after night, what it meant that the king had resigned. Would it help the cause, or hurt it? Rejuvenants littered both sides of the political scene; almost everyone rich and powerful enough to be a force in the government had been rejuvenated at least once. Apparently the hierarchy had decided: it was a good thing, and now they could act. Ottala pulled her mind back from its contemplation of the aesthetics of Sikar's striking coloring—those fire-blue eyes, the pale skin, the black hair with the silver streak—to listen to his speech.

"But before we act," Sikar said, "we must purify ourselves. We must not allow any taint of the Rejuvenant to corrupt our purpose. Are you sure—*sure*—that none among you harbors a sneaking sympathy with those old leeches?"

"No!" growled the crowd, Ottala among them. Her parents weren't old leeches; they were merely idiot fools. When she had to say these things, she always thought of people she didn't like.

"Are you *sure*?" Sikar asked again. "Because I am not. In other cells, we've found those pretending to be with us, and secretly spying on us for the Rejuvenants—"

"Secretly spying" was exactly the kind of rhetoric that Ottala enjoyed. She curled her tongue around it in her mouth, not realizing until Sikar stood in front of her table what he was leading up to. The tool in his hands, though, clenched the breath in her chest. She recognized it; everyone did, who had ever changed fertility implants. It would locate even unexpired implants, and could be used to remove them. But—no one here had implants. She did.

"Put out your arms, brothers and sisters," Sikar said. "For this is how we found the traitors before—they had implants."

She couldn't move. She wanted to jump and run; she wanted to scream, "You don't understand," and she knew that wouldn't work. Sikar smiled directly into her eyes, just as she'd wanted since she'd first seen him, and the people on either side of her forced her arms out flat on the table. The tool hummed; even though she knew she could not really feel anything, she was sure her implant itched. The skin above it fluoresced, a brilliant blue.

"Perhaps she was a manager's favorite—" said Irena, down the table. She had liked Irena.

"Perhaps she's an owner's daughter," said Sikar. "We'll see." He pressed the tool to her arm; she had no doubt of the next sensation. No anesthetic spray, no numbing at all— the tool's logic ignored her pain and sliced into her arm, retrieving the implant, and pressed the incision closed with biological glue. Her arm throbbed; she was surprised that she hadn't screamed, but she was still too scared. Those holding her tightened their grips. Sikar held up the implant. "You see? And this tool will tell us whose it is."

She had forgotten that, if she'd ever known. Implants carried the original prescription codes; that had something to do with proving malpractice. Sikar touched the implant to a flat plate on the tool's side, and laughed harshly.

"As we suspected. This is no Finnvardian assembly worker. This is a Rejuvenant, child of Rejuvenants, our mortal enemies. This is one who would enslave our children to her pleasure, for all time."

"No—" She got that out in a miserable squeak before Sikar slapped her. It hurt more than she had imagined.

"I hate you!" That was Irena, who had come up behind her and now clouted her head. "You lied to me—you were never my friend—"

"I was—" But no one was listening. Shouts, growls, curses, those hands tight on her arms, and Sikar staring at her with utter contempt.

"Rich girl," he said. "This is not a game."

Before she died, she wanted to revise her earlier opinion, and say that some conspirators tasted of neither vanilla nor chocolate, but of blood. But she could not speak, and no one would have listened if she had.

Castle Rock: the former king's offices

Midafternoon already, and they'd hardly made a dent in the day's work. Lord Thornbuckle leaned back in his chair and stretched. "I could be angry with Kemtre about this, too: because he was an idiot, I have to sit here doing his work."

"You wanted the job." Kevil Mahoney, formerly an independent and successful attorney, had agreed to help his friend in the political crisis left by the king's resignation. "Am I supposed to sympathize? I could be in court, showing off—"

"As if you'd miss it. No, we're doing the right thing, if we can pull it off."

"If? The eminent Lord Thornbuckle has doubts?"

"Your old friend Bunny has doubts. Nothing makes a rabbit nervous like the predator who pretends not to see him. We haven't heard anything from the Benignity; by now, I expected at least one raid."

"Don't stare at that fox too long, my friend: there are wolves in the world too."

"As if I didn't—" He paused, as his deskcomp chimed, and flicked the controls. "Yes?"

"Sorry, milord. An urgent signal from Patchcock. Shall I transfer, or bring it in?"

"Bring it," Bunny said. "And the coffee, if it's ready." He would have that, at least, no matter what the trouble was.

One of the senior clerks—Poisson, he thought the name was—came in with a cube, followed by two juniors with a trolley. Poisson waited until they had left before handing over the cube.

"It's partly encrypted, milord, but I read the part that wasn't. It's the same region on Patchcock where the troubles were before, and apparently a Family heir has gone missing."

Family. Bunny could hear the capital letter that elevated mere genetic relationship to political power—not just a family, but *a* Family, one of the Chairholding Families.

"Ottala Morreline, the second oldest but designated heir of—"

"Oscar and Vitille Morreline, Vorey sept of the Consellines. Right." One of his own daughter's schoolmates. He remembered Bubbles—no, she was calling herself Brun now—talking about her. Brun hadn't liked her; he remembered that much, though he didn't remember why. The Consellines . . . that extended family had over a dozen Chairs in Council; the Vorey sept, though the minor branch, had five. The Morrelines held four of them. "Kidnapped?" he asked.

"Ah . . . no. It seems she had disguised herself as a Finnvardian and infiltrated a workers' group—"

"A Morreline?" The Morrelines had, for the past two centuries at least, chosen to emphasize their darker ancestry. And the video of Ottala that came up when he inserted the cube showed a dark-skinned, dark-haired young woman. A beauty, Bunny noted, remembering now that he had seen her at some social function a year or so before. She had matured, as Brun had, showing more bone structure. But how had this girl imitated a pale, blue-eyed Finnvardian?

"The family located the skinsculptor. She bought a four hundred day depigmentation package, bleached her hair, wore blue contact lenses—"

"Why didn't she get an eye job while she was at it? What if she'd dropped a lens?" That was Kevil Mahoney, cross-examining as usual.

Poisson shrugged. "I couldn't say, sir. When she didn't turn up for her younger brother's *seegrin*, the family popped her emergency cache, and found her last report. She included a vid of herself after she adopted the disguise, and said she planned to involve herself in a workers' organization to see what it felt like."

"Ummm." Bunny watched the cube readout. Ottala's disguised self looked very different, he had to admit—if not quite Finnvardian, at least nothing like the Morreline heir. He wondered if she'd had a temporary bone job too—her face seemed to have changed shape as well as color. According to the readout, she had had no trouble buying false IDs, and getting a job in an assembly factory on Patchcock. But she'd dropped out of sight, without notice to her work supervisor or anyone else, some forty days before her family came looking.

"The problem is, milord, that it's Patchcock. . . ." Bunny looked up.

"Yes?"

"I don't know if you knew . . . *all* about Patchcock."

"Not really. It was a nasty situation, is all I know, and

someone in the Regular Space Service messed up in a major way."

"I think perhaps you need to read the background briefs." That was far more assertive than Poisson's usual approach, and Bunny stared.

"Very well. If you'll—"

"Here they are." A stack of cubes it would take him hours to wade through, all marked with the security code that meant they were encrypted and could be read only with all the room's security systems engaged. Bunny glanced at Kevil, and sighed.

"Don't remind me that I volunteered for this job. I could cheerfully strangle his late majesty." Poisson, he noticed, had the look he had always imagined concealed satisfaction at landing responsibility on someone else.

The Patchcock affair, when they finally got it straight late that night, explained a lot of things . . . many more than were explicated in the cubes, revealing as those were.

"That had to be the stupidest thing Ottala could have done," Kevil said, summing up the latest chapter in the story. "Going undercover in a workers' organization would be risky enough right here in Castle Rock—but on Patchcock! Didn't she know any history?"

"We didn't," Bunny pointed out. "If she thought it was just a military blunder, if she didn't know how her family came to gain control of the investments there—"

"She must be dead, you know," Kevil said. "If she were alive, she'd have refreshed her emergency cache."

"Captive? Held for ransom?"

"No. My criminal experience tells me she's dead. They found her out somehow, stripped her of any information they could pry out, and killed her. Eventually the Morrelines will figure that out too, and then—then we'll have real trouble."

"Yes." Bunny thought about the Morrelines: he knew them in the casual way that all the Chairholders knew each other, but they were not really in his set. They didn't hunt, for one thing. But he had dealt with them more than once in business, and in the Council—they were tough, aggressive, and very sore losers. That this could be a self-description he recognized, but that didn't make the prospect of angry Morrelines any more appealing.

"If we send Fleet back in there, it will only make things worse—"

"If she's dead already—" If she was dead already, why bother? But he had to know what Ottala Morreline had found, even if he couldn't bring her back. He sighed, and stretched his back out. The whole situation he'd inherited—*jumped into*, he reminded himself—felt dangerously mushy. Too many things he didn't know, past and present. Too many ways to make mistakes even if he did know everything. And the image of his daughter Brun intruded—Brun had already involved herself in wild adventures, working her way across Familias space as an ordinary spacer. If Brun heard about this, she would insist on going herself to find out about Ottala. Where could he park her safely?

"At least," Kevil said, stretching in turn, "it'll be a change from this stupid bickering about rejuvenation. Those poor bastards in the mines and factories on Patchcock have more substantial concerns."

Bunny nodded, but his thoughts kept running to Brun. Finally he thought of the one thing he might be able to do; in the morning he would place a call to Heris Serrano.

"I must thank you again, for whatever you said to my daughter," Lord Thornbuckle said. He didn't look much like Bunny in his dark formal suit, in the paneled office. He didn't intend to. "She was, I'm sure, about to do something rash. What she told me afterwards was that she'd planned to run away and join the Regular Space Service anonymously—but I expect it was worse than that."

"No—or at least, that's what she told me." Heris Serrano had been aboard the yacht, supervising the last of its refitting. Her office aboard looked nothing like his; on the wall behind her were only a military-grade chronometer and the framed certificates of her rating. She had a new uniform, not the loud purple Lady Cecelia had once used, but the same competent expression, the same intelligent dark eyes. She paused a moment, but he said nothing. "She outgrew herself in a hurry, on the island."

"I know. And she seems to have inherited ancestral temptations to adventure. You know how she got to Rockhouse Major from Rotterdam?" Heris nodded. "Even the unpleasantness she got into didn't dissuade her. And now she wants to use some of her inheritance to finance a small expedition—a small ship, rather, on which she intends to wander around looking for excitement. Responsibly, she assures me. Nothing wild of the sort she did in her youth." Lord Thornbuckle snorted. "Youth. The girl's barely old enough to consider a Seat in Council, and you'd think she was fifty."

"She did come through safely, sir," Heris ventured. He could tell she was being tactful, wondering if he would understand how important that was. Some people, following every rule of prudence, could hardly travel to the corner and back without breaking an ankle. Brun's luck had to be more than luck, perhaps that unconscious intuitive grasp of situation and character which was more valuable than all the education in the world. But not only the military recognized and used that quality.

"Yes, I know, and I know it means she's inherited—no doubt from the same ancestors—the ability to survive adventure. But I'm not sure I can survive her acquisition of the necessary experience. Not without knowing there's someone with more expertise and more . . . er . . . maturity to help her out of the tight spots she's so determined to get into. Even Thornbuckles have limits to their luck; get Cece to tell you about my great-uncle Virgil."

Heris focussed on the comment that might refer to her. "You were thinking that I might know someone with the right skills to accompany her?"

"I thought you might be that person. Not that alone—" He waved off the protest she opened her mouth to make. "I know, you'll be traveling with Cece. But she said she wanted to do more than make the various horse events, and I wondered if you'd let Brun come along. As an employee, or passenger, or whatever you like. I would of course pay her passage. . . ."

"No, sir," Heris said quickly. "Don't pay her passage; if she's set on adventuring, she might as well earn her own way. She's already proved she could. I assume she has an allowance; let her use that, if she wants."

"Right. Fine. Then you'll take her?"

"I . . . don't know." She had liked Brun well enough, he knew, but clearly she was thinking about the difficulties inherent in mixing a girl like Brun into a crew already facing difficult adjustments. She wouldn't want trouble; she had

had enough already. "I'm not sure I'm the right person," she said finally.

Lord Thornbuckle leaned over and touched his desk; he gestured to the row of red lights that came on, and waited for her look of recognition. "Heris, let me tell you something that must remain a secret. A young woman Brun knows—knew—a schoolmate, went off on an adventure, joined a workers' organization over on Patchcock, and got herself killed when she was discovered. Brun doesn't know; we've managed to suppress it. But the girl's family is furious with me. They want me to send the R.S.S. to Patchcock again—"

Heris stared. "That's—not wise, sir." She could easily imagine the carnage; it had been bad enough the first time.

"No, I understand that. I've seen the classified briefings now. The thing is, Brun's the ideal hostage to use against me. Either side might try it. She's too old to send home—she wouldn't stay, and I can't tell her about Ottala. . . . I know she won't be safe, really safe, anywhere, but you might be able to keep her safer than anyone else."

Heris nodded. "All right. I'm willing to have her aboard, if she's willing to come. I'm not about to shanghai her."

"Oh, she's willing. Apparently she made some friends in your crew, didn't she?"

Heris looked puzzled, then her face cleared. "Sirkin, I suppose. At least they went around together for a while, but that was our plan, a way that Brun could pass information about Lady Cecelia to me indirectly. I wouldn't have called it a friendship—Sirkin's lover had just died—but it's something. All right . . . I suppose Brun could have considered it friendship," she said. "I'll list her as unskilled crew, and let them teach her some things, if that's acceptable."

"Good." Lord Thornbuckle smiled at her. "On top of everything else, I'll be glad to have her out of pocket while the political situation is so uncertain."

The country house of Kemtre Lord Altmann, formerly king of the Familias Regnant

"I don't see why you can't understand," Kemtre said, trying not to breathe heavily. "They're your sons as much as mine."

"They're no one's *sons*," his wife said. Although she seemed to lean on the end of the table, elbows on either side of a tray of fancifully carved fruits, that was illusion, a matter of expensive communications equipment synchronizing her image from past breakfasts with her voice from very far away. "Certainly not mine, and not yours either, if you only knew it. They're *clones*, constructs, human only in genome. You were never a father to them; I was never a mother."

He pressed his fingers to his temples, a gesture that had been effective in Council meetings. It had not worked with her for years, and it did not work now, not least because she did not have the visual display on her console turned on . . . he kept hoping to see the telltale red light turn green. He wanted to meet her eyes—her *real* eyes, not those of the construct, and convince her with his sincerity. "They're all we've got," he said. "They could be our sons, if you'd only—"

"They're grown," she said. "They're not little boys. They're bad copies of Gerel . . . was he the only one you cared about?"

Of course not, he wanted to say. He had said it before, just as they had had this argument before in the weeks since his resignation. At first face-to-face, then down the length of that long dining table, then by the various communications devices required by the increasingly great physical distances between them as she removed herself from his demands.

"Please," he said.

"No." The faint hollow noise of a live connection ended; the construct sat immobile, waiting for his finger to extinguish its imitation of life. He put his thumb down and cursed. She wanted him to give it up, deal with the loss of his sons, get on with whatever life was left him. He couldn't do that, not until he had at least tried to get the clones to cooperate. They were the only sons he had now; he couldn't just give them up.

The Boardroom of the Benignity of the Compassionate Hand

"I don't see any reason to butcher the cash cow," said the Senior Accountant. "Breed her, and we'll have more calves to send to market."

"She's a shy breeder," muttered one of the diplomatic

subordinates, who should have kept quiet. It was his last mistake.

When the meeting resumed, several people walked across the damp patch on the carpet as if nothing had happened. It wasn't unusual, and it didn't really reflect on Sasimo, whose protégé had been unwise. Every senior man present had discovered that a first appearance in the Boardroom could unsettle a youngster previously considered promising.

"Still, he had a point," the Chairman said. No one asked who, or what point; those who couldn't figure it out didn't belong there. "The Familias walks like a tart, and talks like a tart, but carries a hatpin in her purse." The hatpin being, as they all knew, the Regular Space Service's unbought fraction, which they knew down to the level of cook's assistants.

After a respectful silence, the Senior Accountant coughed politely and began again. "It is a short hatpin, not long enough to reach the heart of a strong man. A little risk, a prick perhaps, and—better a marriage than a disgrace, eh?"

"Quite so," said the Chairman. "If it is only a flesh wound. Perhaps our admiral would review the situation?"

But indeed, the situation looked good. Not only were so many Fleet personnel on the Compassionate Hand payroll, as it were, but they had been placed into critical positions. Given a good start, with new forward bases increasing the number of jump points they could reach undetected, the Regular Space Service should be immobilized by uncertainty as well as internal problems.

"We start here," the admiral said, pointing out the system on the display. "They're used to neglect from the R.S.S.; Aethar's World raiders took out their stationary defenses last year, and they've been issued nothing to replace them. It's an agricultural world, thinly populated; we'll lose no essential industries if we scorch it lightly."

"Resistance?"

"Negligible. Farmers with hand weapons, even if they scatter and survive the scorch—we can ignore them."

"Principal crop?"

The admiral chuckled, a daring act in that room. "Horses, if you can believe it."

"Horses?"

"And not workhorses. They export sperm and embryos of fancy horses."

The Chairman leaned back, thumbs in his waistcoat pockets. "Show horses . . . I like horses. If they survive the scorch, I'd like a souvenir, Peri." Which meant they had better survive the scorch . . . it was punishment, mild enough, for laughing in the Boardroom.

"Of course," the admiral said, making the best of it.

"My granddaughter, you know," the Chairman said to the others, as if he needed to explain. "She likes pretty horses." He turned back to the admiral. "Be sure to bring one 'Lotta would like. White feet, a long tail, that kind of thing."

"Of course," the admiral said again, tallying in his mind the extra time it would take to scorch selectively, so that the Chairman's granddaughter could have a pretty horse for a souvenir. It shouldn't be too bad, even if their agent betrayed them. He would add another couple of ships to the advance strike force, which would give them the margin for a careful scorch.

"Why not this system?" asked one of the others, pointing. "It has the same advantages."

"Nearly," the admiral admitted. One did not directly contradict one of the Board, not if one wanted to leave the room with breath intact. "But it connects directly to only one jump point, with only three mapped vectors. As well, it's near enough to Guerni space that the Guernesi might take notice. Our chosen target connects directly to two jump points, offering a total of eight mapped vectors, most of them into high-vector points. And of course, its other border is the unstable one with Aethar's World, from which the raiders have come."

"Quite so," said the Chairman. "We have already approved your target, Admiral." That was dismissal, and the admiral saluted, bowed, and left.

When he reached his office, he found that he had been given a final command . . . interesting that the Chairman had not wanted to say that in front of the others. The Chairman would be honored if the admiral would allow the Chairman's great-nephew, now in command of a heavy cruiser, to be part of this expedition. Unmentioned was the young man's record; neither needed to mention it. The young man had risen more by influence than ability, everyone was sure . . . and yet he wasn't stupid or cowardly. Dangerous to both friends and enemies, the admiral thought. Convinced of his ability; convinced he had not been given a chance because of the relationship . . . that his real successes had been overlooked, along with his mistakes. Perhaps it was true.

The admiral considered. Was this the Chairman's way of letting the younger man hang himself, or his way of sabotaging the admiral, whose own grandson might otherwise have been chosen? He couldn't take both—he could afford only one less experienced captain. Of course he must take the Chairman's choice, but he need not make it easy. He would assume—he would document that assumption—that the Chairman wished to test his kinsman, wished him to prove himself.

He grinned suddenly. Let him be the one to find and bring home a pretty horse for Carlotta.

CHAPTER TWO

Uncertain, Heris thought as she closed her end of the secured comlink, was a mild term for the swiftly unraveling tangle of political yarn that had so recently seemed to be a stable web of interlocking interests. All her life—for many hundreds of Standard years—the Familias Regnant had had its Grand Council, and commerce had passed between its worlds and stations as if no other way existed. She knew of course that other ways did—that Familias space was surrounded by other ways of doing things, from the cold efficiency of the Compassionate Hand to the berserker brigandry of Aethar's World. But aside from those whose business it was to keep the borders safe and enforce the laws, most of the Familias worlds and the people on them had behaved as if nothing but fashion would ever change.

And now it had. With the king's resignation, with Lorenza's flight, the founding families looked at each other with far more suspicion than trust. If the king had poisoned his own sons—or if Lorenza had done it for him—if she had attacked the powerful de Marktos family through Cecelia—then who else might have been her target? Her allies? Those who had used her services through the decades tried to cover their tracks, and others worked to uncover them.

What bothered Heris the most, in all this, was the civilians' innocent assumption that "the Fleet" would never let anything bad happen. She had heard it from one and then another—no need to worry about Centrum Rose; the Fleet will see that they stay in the alliance. No need to worry about the Benignity attacking; the Fleet will protect us. Yet she knew—and Bunny should have known—that the Fleet itself was suspect. Lorenza hadn't been the only rat in the woodpile. Admiral Lepescu and whoever cooperated with him . . .

But she could not solve everything, not all at once. She had other work to do before Cecelia came aboard the yacht.

Her personal stack had a message from Arash Livadhi. Now what, she thought. It had been a long enough day already, and she had hoped Petris would get back in time for some extended dalliance. She called Arash.

"How are things going?" he asked brightly, as if she had initiated the contact.

"Fine with me . . . and you?"

"Oh, very well, very well. It's been an interesting few weeks, of course."

So it had, with rumors of entire squadrons of Fleet in mutiny. With one cryptic message from her grandmother, and a very uncryptic message from the cousin who had always hated her.

"Yes," said Heris, drumming her fingers on her desk. "I had a message that you called," she said finally, when the silence had gone on too long.

"Oh. Yes. That. I just . . . I just wondered if you'd like to have dinner sometime. Tonight maybe? There's a new band at Salieri's."

"Sorry," Heris said, not really sorry at all. "There's ship's business to deal with." Certainly the captain's relationship with the First Engineer was ship's business.

"Oh . . . ah . . . another time? Maybe tomorrow?"

Tone and expression both suggested urgency. What was he up to? Heris opened her mouth to tell him to come clean, then remembered the doubtful security of their link. "I . . . should be free then. Why not? What time?"

"Whatever's best for you . . . maybe mid-second shift?" An odd way of giving a time, for either a civilian or a Fleet officer. Heris nodded at the screen, and hoped she could figure out later what kind of signal he was giving her.

"Mid-second indeed. Meet you there?"

"Why not at the shuttle bay concourse? You shouldn't have to dash halfway across the Station by yourself." Odder and odder. Arash had never minded having his dates use up their own resources. Heris entered the time and place in her desktop calendar and grinned at him.

"It's in my beeper. See you tomorrow."

"Yes . . ." He seemed poised to say more, then sighed and said "Tomorrow, then" instead.

"There's a little problem," Arash Livadhi said. He had been waiting when Heris reached the shuttle docks concourse; he wore his uniform with his old dash and attracted more than one admiring glance. Heris wanted to tell the oglers how futile their efforts were, but knew better. Now he walked beside her as courteously as a knight of legend escorting his lady. It made Heris nervous. "Nothing major, just a bit . . . awkward."

"And awkward problem solving is a civilian specialty? Come on, Arash, you have some of the best finaglers in Fleet on your ship."

"It's not that kind of thing, exactly."

"Well what, exactly?"

"It's something you'd be much better at . . . you know you have a talent—"

She knew when she was being conned. "Arash, I'm hungry, and you've promised me a good meal . . . at least wait until I'm softened up before you start trying to put your hooks in."

"Me?" But that wide-eyed look was meant to be seen through. He grinned at her; it no longer put shivers down her spine, but she had to admit the charm. "Greedy lady . . . and yes, I did agree to feed you. Salieri's is still acceptable?"

"Entirely." Expensive and good food, a combination rarer than one might suppose. And whatever Arash thought he was getting from her, it would not include anything more than a dinner companion . . . she wondered if he had any idea of her present situation with Petris. Probably not, and better that he live in blissful ignorance.

Salieri's midway through the second shift had a line out to the concourse, but Arash led her past it. "We have reservations," he said. Sure enough, at his murmur the gold-robed flunky at the door let them pass. Heris felt her spirits lift in the scarlet and gold flamboyance of the main foyer, with the sweet strains of the lilting waltz played by a live orchestra in the main dining room. Whatever Arash wanted, this would be fun.

Two hours later, after a lavish meal, he got down to it. "You do owe me a favor, you know," he said.

"True. That and a fat bank account will get you a dinner at Salieri's."

"Hardhearted woman. I suppose even civilian life couldn't soften your head." He didn't sound surprised.

"I'll take that as a compliment, Captain Livadhi. What's your problem?"

"You mentioned my illustrious crew. My . . . er . . . talented finaglers."

Heris felt her eyebrows going up. "So I did. So they are. What else?"

Livadhi leaned closer. "There's someone I need to get off my ship. Quickly. I was hoping—"

"What's he done?" Heris asked.

"It's not so much that," Livadhi said. "More like something he didn't do, and he needs to spend some time out of contact with Fleet Command."

"Or he'll drag you down with him?" Heris suggested, from a long knowledge of Livadhi. She was not surprised to see the sudden sheen of perspiration on his brow, even in the dim light of their alcove.

"Something like that," he admitted. "It's related to the matter you and I were involved in, but I really don't want to discuss it in detail."

"But you want me to spirit him away for a while, without knowing diddly about him?"

"Not . . . in detail." He gave her a look that had melted several generations of female officers; she simply smiled and shook her head.

"Not without enough detail to keep my head off the block. How do I know that you aren't being pressured to slip an assassin aboard to get rid of Lady Cecelia? Or me?"

"It's nothing like that," he said. In the pause that followed, she could almost see him trying on various stories to see which she might accept. As he opened his mouth, she spoke first.

"The truth, Livadhi." To her satisfaction, he flushed and looked away.

"The truth is . . . it's not like that; it's not an assassin.

It's my best communications tech, who's heard what he shouldn't have, and needs a new berth. He's a danger to himself, and to the ship, where he is."

"On my ship," said Heris. "With my friends . . . are you sure no one's put you up to this to land trouble on me?" This time his flush was anger.

"On my honor," he said stiffly. Which meant that much was true; the Livadhis, crooked as corkscrews in some ways, had never directly given the lie while on their honor. She knew that; he knew she knew that.

"All right," she said. "But if he gives me the wrong kind of trouble, he's dead."

"Agreed. Thank you." From the real gratitude in his voice she knew the size of the trouble his man was in. Then what he'd said earlier caught up with her. Communications tech . . . best? That had to be . . .

"Koutsoudas?" she asked, trying to keep her face still. He just grinned at her, and nodded. "Good heavens, Arash, what is the problem?"

"I can't say. Please. He may tell you, if he wants—I don't think it's a good idea, but the situation may change, and I trust his judgment. Just take care of him. If you can."

"Oh, I think we're capable of that. When do you want him back?"

"Not until things settle down. I'll get word to you, shall I?" Then, before she could say anything, he added, "Well, that's all taken care of . . . would you like to dance?" The orchestra had just launched into another waltz. Heris thought about it. Arash had been a good dancing partner in the old days, but in the meantime she'd danced with Petris at the Hunt Ball.

"No, thank you," she said, smiling at the memory. "I had better get back to work. When shall I expect . . . er . . . your package?"

Arash winced. "Efficient as ever. Or have I lost the touch?"

"I don't think so," Heris said. "You just put the touch on me, if you think about it that way, and I do. But my owner isn't thrilled with the number of ex-military crew we have now, and she's going to have kittens—or, in her case, colts—when she finds out about this. I have some preliminary groundwork to do."

"Ah. Well, then, allow me to escort you at least to the concourse."

"Better not." Heris had been thinking. "This was a very public meeting, and I can understand your reasoning. But why let whomever is interested think you might have convinced me of whatever it is you were after?"

"I thought an open quarrel would be too obvious," Livadhi said. "If we were simply courteous—"

Heris grinned at him. "I am always courteous, Commander, as you well know. Even in a quarrel."

"Ouch. Well, then, since I can't persuade you—" He rose politely, with a certain stiffness, and she nodded. An observant waiter came to her chair, and although they walked out together, they were clearly not a couple.

In the anteroom, she said, "I'm sorry, Commander, but things have changed. It's not just being a civilian . . . I have other . . . commitments. I'm sure you'll understand. It's not wise, at times like these . . ."

"But—"

"I can find my way, Commander. Best wishes, of course." Watching eyes could not have missed that cool, formal, and very unfriendly parting.

The newly refurbished yacht *Sweet Delight* lay one final shift cycle in the Spacenhance docks, as Heris Serrano inspected every millimeter of its interior. Forest green carpet soft underfoot . . . she tried not to think of its origin, nor that of the crisp green/blue/white paisley-patterned wall covering in the dining salon. At least the ship didn't *smell* like cockroaches anymore. The galley and pantries, left in gleaming white and steel by Lady Cecelia's command, had no odd odors. In the recreation section, everything looked perfect: the swimming pool with its new screen programs . . . Heris flicked through them to be sure the night sky had been removed. Lady Cecelia didn't want any sudden darkness to remind her of the months of blindness she'd endured. The massage lounger had its new upholstery; the riding simulator had a new saddle and a whole set of new training cubes, including the two most recent Wherrin Trials recordings.

The crew quarters, while not quite as luxurious as the owner's section, had more amenities than crews could expect anywhere else. Heris's own suite reflected a new comfort with her civilian status; she had installed a larger bed, a comfortable upholstered chair, and chosen more colorful appointments. Down in the holds, she checked for any leftover debris from the renovation. She had already found a narrow triangle of wall covering and two odd-shaped bits of carpet.

"Heris!" That had to be Lady Cecelia herself. Heris grinned and backed out of the number three hold. Cecelia would want to see for herself that every single cockroach cage had been removed.

"Coming," she called. But the quick footsteps didn't wait for her to get back to the owner's territory. Cecelia's rejuvenation had left her with more energy than she could contain; here she was, striding down the corridor at top speed.

"Did you know about this?" Cecelia waved a hardcopy at her; she had bright patches of color on her cheeks and her short red hair seemed to be standing on end.

"What?" Heris couldn't tell what it was, although the blue cover suggested a legal document. Whatever it was had made the owner furious, and Lady Cecelia furious made most people move quickly out of her way. Heris, secure in her status as captain and friend, stood her ground.

"This court decision." The blue-gray eyes bored into hers.

"Court decision? On your competency?" Of course the court would restore full competency to Cecelia; it would be crazy to pretend that this individual was anything but competent.

"No—on the yacht."

For a moment Heris was completely confused. "No—what about it?"

Cecelia bit off each word as if it tasted foul. "The court has decided against the petition of my family to set aside that portion of my will which left you the yacht. Therefore, the yacht belongs to you." Heris stared at her.

"That's . . . ridiculous. You're not comatose; you're competent. That reverses all the bequests—you told me that—"

"Yes . . . it does. It would have, that is, if that idiot Berenice and her fatheaded husband hadn't quarreled with my will and involved the court directly in that instance. Because the matter came under separate adjudication—don't you love this verbiage?—the court's decision is final, and not reversed by my regaining competence. And the court decided in your favor, thank goodness, or otherwise it would've been Berenice's. It's your yacht."

"That's the stupidest thing I ever heard of." Heris raked a hand through her dark hair. She had not even thought about the bequest or the court's decision since Cecelia had been declared competent. "I can't—what am I supposed to do with a yacht—or you, without one?" She came to the obvious decision. "I won't take it. I'll give it back to you."

"You can't give it back. Not unless you're willing to pay the penalty tax—it's within the legal limit for a bequest, but not a gift."

"Oh . . . dear." She had no idea what that tax would be, but her own affairs were somewhat confused at the moment, thanks to the abrupt changes in the government. She didn't know if she had enough to pay the tax or not.

"It's not so bad," Cecelia said. Now that she'd blown her stack, she had calmed back down, and leaned comfortably against the bulkhead. "I suppose you'll run it as a charter, and I suppose you'll let me charter it."

"Of course, if that's what it takes, but—what a mess." Still, she felt a little jolt of delight at the base of her brain. Her own ship. Not even a Fleet captain owned a ship outright. She fought back unseemly glee with little struggle when she realized the other implications of ownership. Docking fees. Repairs. Crew salaries. All her responsibility now.

Cecelia's expression suggested she had already thought of these things and was enjoying Heris's realization. "Don't worry," she said, after a moment in which Heris was trying to remember the last time the crew had been paid, and how much was due. "I'll pay generously. I'll supply my own staff, cook, gardener. . . ."

"Er . . . just so." And there were bound to be legalities associated with running a charter, too. Heris had no idea what kind of contractual agreement owners needed with those who hired them. What permits she might need from whatever government bureaus were still grinding out the daily quota of paperwork.

"Kevil Mahoney," Cecelia said, with a wicked grin, as if she really could read minds. "He can tell you where to go for legal advice, if you don't want the same person who argued your case for the bequest."

"Thanks," Heris said. "It would have been so much easier—"

"I know. And I don't blame you for fighting back when my family acted like such idiots. It's not your fault, though I was mad enough to grind you into powder too. Just when I'd gotten her back to a decent look, instead of that lavender and teal abomination. Berenice will pay for this." She glowered. "I've filed suit against them, and I intend to make up every fee they cost me."

"I'm sorry," Heris said again, this time for the trouble between Cecelia and her family. "It's just that I thought if I had the ship, I could help you."

"And you did. And don't lie to me, Heris Serrano. I may be rejuvenated, but I didn't lose eighty years of experience. One second after you were appalled, you were delighted. You've always wanted your own ship."

Heris felt herself flushing. "Yes. I did. And I tried to fight it down."

"Don't." Her employer—still her employer, even though the terms would be different now—gave her a wicked grin. She had found Lady Cecelia de Marktos to be formidable enough as an unrejuvenant . . . clearly, that had been the mellow form. "Nobody knows what the government's going to do, now; Bunny seems to be running things with the same bureaucrats—except for poor Piercy. I don't myself think it was Piercy's fault, but everyone's afraid he was in it with Lorenza."

Surprising tolerance from someone who had been Lorenza's helpless victim, for someone planning to sue her family . . . family that had, however ineptly, tried to protect her interests. This was no time to argue, though. Heris looked away, and spotted another bit of scrap from the renovation.

"I don't hate Piercy," Cecelia said. "I don't even hate Lorenza, although if she stood in front of me I would kill her without a second thought, as I would kill anyone that vile. I do hate to think of her running around loose somewhere."

"I don't think she is," Heris said, glad to change the subject from the yacht. "A few of my crew—" Oblo, Meharry, Petris, and Sirkin, though she didn't intend to mention names where anyone might have left a sensor. "—had a bone to pick with the individual who gave the orders that led to

Yrilan's death. The . . . er . . . remaining biological contaminants were salted into her quarters. In the ensuing investigation, it was discovered that she had a very efficient lethal chamber built into her counseling booths—"

"I didn't hear about this—"

"Station Security didn't allow it to be newsed. They thought it would cause panic, and they were probably right. Just the discovery of that many illicit biologicals could panic Station dwellers. Anyway, they also found items the lady could not account for, which apparently match with jewels known to the insurance databases as Lorenza's."

"And you found out because—?"

"I found out because I have the best damn datatech in or out of Fleet, milady, and that's all I'll say here and now."

"Ah. Then suppose you come to my suite—if you still consider it my suite—and we'll decide where your ship is headed, and whether I want to tag along."

Cecelia's furniture had been reinstalled, and they settled into her study. Cecelia looked around nodding. "I do like the effect of that striped brocade with the green carpet," she said finally. "Although I'm not sure about the solarium yet."

"I thought you were going to restock it with miniatures," Heris said.

"I was—but I keep thinking that I could go back to riding—" She meant competition, Heris understood, just as she herself would have meant "the Fleet" if she'd said "return to space."

"I like the ferns," Heris said, watching the miniature waterfall in the solarium; she preferred falling water to any sort of fake wildlife.

"One thing I will insist on, if you're to have me for a passenger, is a crew no more than half ex-military." Cecelia leaned back in her chair, with an expression that made it clear she meant what she'd said.

Heris bit back the first thing she could have said, took a deep breath, and asked, "Why?" Skoterin, probably, but surely Cecelia ought to realize that Skoterin had been more than balanced by that crew of civilian layabouts and incompetents she'd had before. This didn't surprise her, but she'd hoped Cecelia would be less blunt about it.

"Not just Skoterin," Cecelia said, as if she'd read Heris's

mind. "I know you can argue that my original civilian crew was just as full of lethal mistakes. Of course not all ex-military are crooks or traitors, nor are all civilians honest and hardworking. But what bothered me was your inability to see past the distinction yourself. You had had superb performance from that girl Sirkin all through the earlier trouble; you had been so happy with her. And you were willing to believe that she went bad when even I, isolated as I then was, could spot sabotage."

Heris nodded slowly. "You're right; I did make a mistake—"

"Not *a* mistake, my dear: a whole series of them. You misjudged her not once but repeatedly. That's my point. You have a pattern, understandable but indefensible, of believing that the military is more loyal, more honorable, than most civilians. You even told me that Sirkin was 'as good as Fleet' more than once. And your inability to see past that pattern nearly got us all killed." She grinned, as if to take the sting out of it. It didn't work. "I'm doing this for your own good, Heris—as one of my early riding instructors used to say when making us post without stirrups by the hour. You have chosen to live in a civilian world; you must learn how to trust those of us who can be trusted, and recognize deceit even in former shipmates."

"And you think the way to do this is to hire civilians." That came out flat, with an edge of sarcasm. She didn't like that "chose to live in a civilian world." If there'd been any other way . . .

"I think the way to do it is to admit what went wrong and work on correcting it. Isn't that what you would do if an admiral pointed out a characteristic error?"

Heris wanted to say that Cecelia was no admiral, but she had to admit the logic of Cecelia's argument. She had mistaken the cause of Sirkin's problem; she had not even looked for sabotage, not seriously. "I don't want to fire any of our present crew," she began, crossing mental fingers as she told herself that Koutsoudas, not yet aboard, still counted as "present crew."

"No need. Just hire civilians for a while. Like Brun." Heris almost glared. Had she set this up with Bunny, as much to force a civilian crew on Heris as to help Brun? Cecelia smiled at her. "I'm sure you can find others, perhaps not as good as Sirkin, but good enough. Think of recruits, if you must, rather than the trained people you had. Surely there were good and bad recruits."

"Oh yes." Heris chuckled in spite of herself, remembering a miserable tour as an officer in charge of basic training. She had hated it, and she hadn't been very good at it. Of course there had been bad recruits—Zitler, for instance, who had come into the Fleet convinced that he could make a fortune manufacturing illicit drugs aboard ship. Or the skinny girl from some mining colony who had gotten all the way through medical screening without anyone noticing she had parasites.

"There you are, then," Cecelia said. "It's just a matter of overcoming your biases."

"Yes, ma'am," said Heris, with enough emphasis that Cecelia should know when to quit. She hoped. It was unnerving to see all those years of experience in the bright eyes across from her. She began to understand why Cecelia had been reluctant to have rejuv treatments before.

"I don't see why it makes the least difference," Ronnie said, into Raffaele's dark hair. "I didn't go along with my family; you know that. I'm the one who got Aunt Cecelia out of that nursing home. Why should your parents take it out on me?"

"They're not taking it out on you," Raffaele said. "They're pulling their investments out of your parents' operations, and they don't think that's a good time to discuss marriage settlements."

"But will they come around later?" He didn't want later; he wanted right this minute. But with Raffaele, pressure wouldn't work.

"I don't know, Ron. They're seriously annoyed with your parents, and they don't see your prospects improving any time soon. They think you'll be under a cloud politically—"

"Hang politics!" Ronnie said. "I have enough; you have enough; we could go off somewhere and just live—"

"But you have a Seat in Council now—"

"As long as that lasts," Ronnie said under his breath. While daily life seemed to be unchanged, the political structure had shifted back and forth dramatically in the past few weeks.

"They don't want trouble between us because you're voting

your family stock, and your Seat, and they're voting against you. And don't say it wouldn't cause trouble, because look how angry you are now."

Unfair. He wasn't angry because they'd voted against him in Council; he was angry because they didn't want Raffa to marry him because he might be upset later if they voted against him. That was too complicated; he fell back on the obvious. "I love you, Raffa," Ronnie said.

"I know. And I love you. But we are both wound up in our families and their rivalries, and I can't see either of us pulling something dramatic and stagey." With her hair in a neat braid behind, and a tailored soft tunic over the blouse and slacks, she looked entirely too rational.

"Brun did," Ronnie said. He could imagine himself running off with Raffa . . . he thought . . . but then again he wanted to have his usual credit line, his usual communications links. . . .

"Brun is a law unto herself," Raffa said. "Even as a fluffhead, she was, and now—we aren't like Brun, either of us. We were born to be respectable."

"We did have one adventure," Ronnie said, almost wistfully. He didn't like thinking of most of their time on the island, but finding Raffa and being comforted . . . *that* he could live with.

"And we'll have each other later, or we won't, and we'll survive either way. Be reasonable, Ronnie: you got your aunt out of the building, but it was Brun who thought up the hot air balloon. Neither of us could have been that crazy."

True, but he wanted to be crazy enough to live with Raffa the rest of his life, starting this moment. He started to say he'd wait for her forever, but he knew she might not. And he might not either, really. "I don't want to leave you," he said fiercely. "I don't want to lose you."

"Nor I." For a moment she clung to him with all the passion he desired, then she pushed herself away and was gone, her light footsteps barely audible on the carpeted hall.

"Damn!" Ronnie wanted to kick the wall, as he would have before the island. He really hated it when she was right. Then he thought who might be able to help. If only he could make her understand how important it was.

✳   ✳   ✳

Cecelia looked up from her desk to see her nephew standing in the doorway. "Ronnie—I'm delighted to see you. I'd hoped you'd come before we left."

He didn't answer, just gave her a sickly smile.

"What? I already thanked you for getting me out of that place—and if you don't think I mean it, just take a look at your stock accounts."

"It's not that, Aunt Cecelia—and I wish you hadn't done that, really."

The boy didn't want money? That was new; that was unbelievable. She looked more closely. The wavy chestnut hair looked dull; he had lavender smudges under his hazel eyes, and a skin tone that would have made her think "hangover" if he hadn't been so obviously sober and miserable.

"What, then?" she asked, without much sympathy. She'd fixed him once; he was supposed to stay fixed; she couldn't provide deadly danger every time he needed pepping up.

He slouched into her room as if his backbone were overcooked asparagus, and slumped into one of her favorite leather chairs. "It's Raffaele," he said.

Of course. Young love. She'd been glad he wasn't still involved with Brun, since that young lady was in no mood for romance, but she'd approved of Raffa. Moreover, she'd thought the girl had more sense than to jilt Ronnie. He wasn't bad, and Raffa was just the sort of girl to keep him in line.

"What did you do?" she asked. It must have been something he did; perhaps he'd had another fling with theatrical personalities.

"Nothing," Ronnie said. His tone held all the bitterness of disillusioned youth. "But my parents did plenty, and her parents told her to break it off."

"Because of—"

"Because of you." He shook his head to stop the protest already halfway out her mouth. "I know—you've got every right to be angry with them—" She had more than a right, she had very viable suits in progress. "But the thing is, Raffa's parents don't want the families involved right now."

"I'm not angry with *you*," Cecelia said. "They shouldn't blame you if I don't."

"She says they do."

"And you're sure it's not that she's found someone else?"

"Yes. I'm sure. She said . . . she said she loves me. But—she won't cross them."

"Idiot." Cecelia opened her mouth to say more, and then realized the other implications, the ones Ronnie hadn't yet seen. Her suits imperiled the holdings of Ronnie's parents—his guarantees of future income—and might imperil any financial settlements made in the course of betrothal, exchange of assets being the normal complement to marriage. And Raffa, the levelheaded Raffa that she considered strong-minded enough to keep Ronnie in check, would not tangle her family in any such trouble either. It all made perfectly good sense, and Cecelia found herself doubly angry that the good sense could not be denied.

"She's not, really," Ronnie said. "She's just loyal, that's all." Greedy, thought Cecelia. Carrying prudence to a ridiculous degree—the girl had money enough of her own; she was of age, she could make her own decisions. As Ronnie went on making Raffa's arguments, as a true lover would, Cecelia found herself countering them, in the courtroom behind her eyes. Ronnie's final declaration caught her off-balance; she'd been imagining herself as the judge, looming over Raffa as incompetent counsel. "So," he was saying, "I thought if I could do something to prove myself . . . and maybe you would let me come along. . . ."

"No!" Cecelia said, even before her mind caught up with what he had actually said. Then more mildly: "No, Ronnie, though you are my favorite nephew and I owe you my life. This is not the place for you."

"But I thought if Raffa's parents knew I was with you, it would change their minds—"

"No, dear." The *dear* slipped out and shocked her. She never called any of her relatives *dear*; had the Guernesi done something to her mind during rejuvenation? The memory of those lawsuits reassured her: she hadn't softened. Not really. "It won't work because you'd still be seen as a boy with a patron. You need them to see you as a man, an independent man with his own property, his own assets." He looked at her as if he had never thought of that. Perhaps he hadn't. He was, after all, some sixty years younger.

"Then what can I do?" he asked. Cecelia wished for a

moment she had been a more conventional aunt. He would not have consulted a more conventional aunt; he would have found someone outrageous, someone who had never been married, or wanted to be, and she could have clucked from the sidelines. She felt like clucking now. Grow up, she wanted to say. Just do something, she wanted to say. But there he was, born charming and even more so with this new and genuine worry upon him. She wanted to smack him, and she wanted to cuddle him, and neither would do any good.

When in doubt, call in the experts. "You might go talk to Captain Serrano," she said. She didn't expect him to agree, but his face lit up.

"Great idea," he said. "Thanks—I will." And he bounced up, suddenly vibrant and eager again. She watched him stride out, with the spring in his step and the sparkle in his eye, and wondered at herself. Rejuvenation was supposed to rejuvenate everything; she had herself made the usual jokes about those of her friends who suddenly acquired young companions. But Ronnie did nothing for her, and she knew it wasn't because he was her nephew. She just didn't feel like it.

"Not that I was ever ridden by that torment much," she muttered, as she ran over the shopping lists on her deskcomp again. She had been too busy, and too aware of the power such a passion would have over her schedule, if nothing else.

Heris saw not the spoiled brat she'd once despised but the handsome, bright young man who had become what she thought of as officer material. "Aunt Cecelia said you might be able to help me," he said.

"If I can, of course," she said, wondering if this was Cecelia's obscure vengeance for Arash's favor.

"It's about Raffaele," he began, and outlined his problem.

Heris recognized the implications as Cecelia had, but unlike her saw no reason not to tell Ronnie about them. She still thought of him as "young officer material," which put her in the teaching role. She led him through the relevant financial bits, and watched his dismay growing.

"But—but Raffa isn't that greedy," Ronnie said at the end.

"I don't know that I'd call it greedy." Heris steepled her

hands. "But you're both Registered Embryos, remember? Smart, educated, trained from birth to consider the welfare of the family as a whole. I don't think it has anything to do with wanting more things than you could give her; I think it has to do with conflicting loyalties."

"But if she loves—"

Hormones, thought Heris. "Ronnie, think: would you have married that opera singer?"

She could see "What opera singer?" forming on his forehead, until his memory caught up. "Oh—her. No, of course not. She was nothing like Raffa."

"Why not? You were besotted with her at the time, I gather. Loved her, didn't you?"

"Oh, but that was—it was different. She'd never have done for a wife."

"And why? Was she personally disgusting in some way? Lacking manners? Stupid?"

"No . . . no, it wasn't anything like that. But—she wouldn't have been a good match . . . for the family. . . ." Finally, he was catching on.

"Whether you really loved her or not—you can imagine someone you did really love, that wouldn't be right because it would hurt the family. Right?"

"Right." Now he sounded glum and sulky.

"Ronnie, this isn't an age in which anyone gives much for romantic love. If it happens that you fall for someone of the right class, at the right time, then fine. But most people don't. Petris and I served on the same ships and never allowed ourselves to notice that we loved each other: it would have been bad for the ship. Grown-ups have values outside their own skins."

"And you're saying I'm not a grown-up yet?"

"No. You are—you've grown a lot in the time I've known you, and frankly you've surprised me. But this last lingering bit of adolescence is hanging on, right where it usually does."

He gave a rueful laugh. "I suppose you think I'm silly."

"Not at all. Nor do I think your situation with Raffa will last forever, especially not if you set out to change it."

"How?"

Heris was tempted to say, You're a grown-up; you figure it out, but she had never seen Ronnie as a master of strategy.

Brave, yes. Bright enough in limited circumstances, yes. But not a strategist. "Two things. You either need to change the overall situation so that your parents' quarrel with your aunt no longer imperils your inheritance and your parents' political and economic allies, or you need to change your situation in relation to your parents. Ideally, both."

"Both! That's impossible." Ronnie began to stride around the small office, exactly like a nervous colt in a small box stall. Heris expected him to bump his nose into a wall and rear at any moment. "I can't make Aunt Cecelia change her mind; nobody's *ever* made Aunt Cecelia change her mind. And I can't make my parents be someone else. Not unless I repudiate them and change my name or something. How will disinheriting myself help convince Raffa?"

Just as she'd thought, no strategic sense at all. "Ronnie, look at what you've told me you want. You want to marry Raffa, but I assume this means you also want a long, happy, profitable life and you don't want to harm either her family or yours."

"Well . . . yes."

"You also want the best for your Aunt Cecelia, don't you?"

"Yes, but I can't do all that at once."

"Not if you don't look at it. You know my background; well, a consistent mistake I've seen commanders make is defining the mission too narrowly. Did you ever study the Patchcock Incursion in the Royals?"

"Uh . . . yes. It got kind of complicated. . . ."

"It was complicated from the beginning, and an oversimplified mission statement made it worse. Military commanders like to see neat, tidy problems . . . well, I suppose everyone does. The dog is howling: shoot the dog. The contract colonists are rioting: shoot the colonists. The contract corporation reneged on its contract to provide medical services: shoot the corporation CEO. The Council told Fleet Command they wanted no more rioting on Patchcock. They *didn't* tell Fleet Command that a two-month interruption in shipments of ore would bankrupt Gleisco Metals, with cascading effects through its parent corporation into half a dozen Chairholders. They didn't tell Fleet that a two-month interruption in ore shipments would mean cutting off the food supply not only to Patchcock but also to Derrien and Slidell. They didn't tell Fleet that Gleisco Metals had refused to provide services agreed on, and then altered the contracts to reflect that. So Fleet went in to sit on some malcontents, and ended up responsible for the deaths by starvation of several thousand people, the deaths by direct action of thousands more, and—if you care to look at it that way, which the then king did, the suicides of eighteen members of high-ranking families, including five of the six Chairholders most closely connected to Gleisco. The other one was murdered by his own sister."

"I didn't know all that," Ronnie said. He looked very uncomfortable. "They told us about it as an example of a commander losing control of troops in a battlefield situation."

"Hushed it up," Heris said. "I thought they might have done it, even after the trials at the time." She grinned, without humor. Her family had been involved in that one, too. "My point is that if you want something to happen, you must specify that something with great care and as much completeness as possible. Then, and only then, can you devise a strategy to accomplish what you really want—all of it—and not some little bit that turns out to be meaningless when everything else falls apart."

He didn't answer at once, a good sign. When the silence had become uncomfortably long (for Heris had chores to do) she tried to divert him to another topic.

"What are they going to do with the Royal Aerospace Service, now that the king has abdicated?" she asked.

"Hmm? Oh . . . I don't know. I'm not—I was told I was not required to report, which really meant they didn't want me. That's one reason I thought I'd do better with Aunt Cecelia, staying out of trouble."

That didn't sound good. The rich young men who made up the officer corps of the Royal Aerospace Service might cause trouble in a lump while on duty, but would surely cause trouble if suddenly turned out, idle and feckless, into the streets of the capital. Someone wasn't thinking clearly, not for the first time.

"That's good for you," she said crisply. "You are free to do something else, something that will convince Raffaele's parents that you are a mature, responsible, independent young man. Ideal husband material."

"But what?" he asked. What indeed? Then it came to her.

"Go talk to Lord Thornbuckle," she said. "I'm sure he can find a mission for you. Don't tell him about Raffa— just ask what you can do to help."

When he'd left, she put her head in her hands for a moment. She wanted to get away before someone else had a crisis for her to deal with. If only Cecelia would quit fuming about her family, they could leave for somewhere— anywhere—and be out of reach of everyone's family problems.

CHAPTER THREE

"What is it, another little problem?" Cecelia was scowling into a viewscreen. "Bad hocks," she muttered, before Heris said anything.

"Where?"

"This excuse for a hunter stallion—look at it!" Heris came around the end of the desk and looked at the shiny black horse on the viewscreen. It trotted back and forth, looking sound enough to her. Cecelia froze the picture, and pointed. "Here—this is the problem. Those hocks should be much bigger—"

"It's the feet that always look too small to me," Heris said. No use trying to get Cecelia's mind shifted to the crew until she'd worked her way through the horse business. "Why are the hocks too small?"

The answer took longer than Heris had expected, because Cecelia insisted on bringing up video files on a dozen or so horses, as well as an animated skeletal model. And when Heris dismissed it, at the end, with "I see—just like ankles, as you said—ankles sprain more often than knees or hips," Cecelia threw up her hands.

"You are ridiculous! It's the same joint, but it's not the same stresses. I give up. What was it you came about?"

Heris had hoped to soothe Cecelia, but since that hadn't worked, she tried for a bland, quick summary of her reasons for wanting a quick departure. "Arash Livadhi, who saved our skins as you recall, has asked me a favor; he wants me to transport one of his crew, who needs to be . . . er . . . out of touch for a while."

"Why?"

"He didn't say, exactly. It has something to do with the mess we were all in, and something the person overheard. He's a communications tech."

Cecelia scowled at her. "Is this a way of sneaking in another ex-military crewmember?"

"No." Heris didn't explain further; it wouldn't help.

"I don't like it," Cecelia said.

"Arash's medical teams saved Sirkin's life," Heris pointed out. "And yours. We owe him, both of us. He got us back here, past potential enemies, in time for the Grand Council."

Cecelia's expression didn't soften. Inspiration hit. "You don't have to consider this person a crewmember, if you wish. Since it's technically my ship, consider him my guest."

"You—!" Cecelia's face went white, then red in patches, then she burst into laughter. "You *stinker*! I almost wish I'd known you when you were all military. You must have been—"

"Difficult," Heris said demurely. "Difficult is what they called it."

"Brilliant on occasion, I've no doubt. If you were my age, I'd thrash you, but considering—I'll just put some interesting problems in your next riding lesson."

It was Heris's turn to stare. "You can't mean that—you think I'm going on with riding?"

"It would exercise something besides your ingenuity," Cecelia said. "And you never know when physical fitness will come in handy. You and Petris, for instance—"

Heris felt the heat in her face. She and Petris indeed. She struggled for something, anything, to say, and blurted it out before her internal editor had a chance at it. "We have other ways of maintaining physical fitness. . . ."

"I'll bet you have," Cecelia said, and smirked. Heris glared.

"Other than *that*." But she had to chuckle; she had done it to herself. "I don't know why I thought you'd mellow after rejuvenation."

"I don't either," Cecelia said. "And I didn't. Mellow was never my virtue. But we've had even honors on this one; I won't say any more about that man's crewman, whatever he is."

"Thank you," Heris said. "May I ask why you were looking at that stallion whose hocks you didn't like?"

"Rotterdam," Cecelia said. "Those people did a lot for me; they're old friends, of course, but . . . I want to do something for them. Of course I can share the bloodstock I have there—but I've been doing that for years. What I'm looking for is some outcross lines that will broaden their base, that they couldn't possibly afford on their own."

"Is that all the planet does, raise horses?"

"Almost." Cecelia touched her screen, and brought up a graphic montage. "It's a combination of climate, terrain, and the accidents of discovery and development. Horses are useful in a variety of ways in colonization: self-replicating farm power, for instance. Pack animals in difficult terrain. Personal transportation. But they're displaced if industrialization provides alternatives. So usually you have poor planets with horses—workhorses—and room to breed but no recreational bloodstock. Then you have industrial planets with a demand for recreational horses, but those horses squeezed into less and less land. Rotterdam was settled as an agricultural world, complete with draft horses. But its climate is far better suited to permanent pasturage than grain farming. Someone apparently obtained some bloodstock semen and began breeding recreational horses. . . ."

"How did they market them?" Heris asked. Horses, she remembered, shipped badly aboard spacecraft.

"With great difficulty. But somehow they got a colt nominated for a famous stakes race, and got him there alive and capable of running. More than capable. That was Buccinator—it was one of his descendants that I rode at Bunny's. I bought into his syndicate as a young woman—"

This made no sense to Heris, but the general plan did. "So you're going to find additional semen or whatever for your friends on Rotterdam. . . ."

"Right. I've got a dozen cubes to review—ordered them from bloodstock agents—and then we'll go take a look. So far most of Rotterdam's produce is semen and embryos. It's too far off the main shipways, and very rarely can a group get together to haul mature animals someplace. When I first set up my stud there, I'd planned to work on that . . . but things changed. . . . Anyway, if they have the quality, the money will follow. And provide transport."

"Have you decided where to go first?"

"Wherrin Horse Trials. I've missed two of them—no reason to miss this time. I should pick up more ideas there, breeders not yet with bloodstock agents, that sort of thing."

"I'd like to leave as soon as Koutsoudas is aboard," Heris said. "He's not the only problem—I know you talked to your nephew—and you know that Lord Thornbuckle has asked me to take on Brun."

"I'm willing," Cecelia said. "The lawyers can handle my suit just as well without me. Better perhaps. They say I interfere. . . . I didn't know it would affect Ronnie and Raffaele."

Heris thought of saying what she thought about the lawsuit, but considering her own family relations she decided against it. She was hardly one to preach reconciliation with relatives.

Brigdis Sirkin hated being back on Rockhouse Major. Over on Minor, she had been able to pretend that they weren't in the same system where Amalie died. Here, every shop window, every bar, every slideway and bounce tube reminded her of Amalie. Here she had died, and into this station's recycler her physical cells had gone, to become the elements of something else . . . even this meal. She shoved it away, disgusted suddenly by the rich aroma of stew and bread.

"What's wrong, hon?" Meharry leaned across the crowded table. "Got a bug or something?"

She didn't want to answer. Meharry and the others had been so careful of her since the shooting, so sorry they'd believed a former shipmate and condemned her. They had organized that revenge on Amalie's counselor in hopes of cheering her up; they had enjoyed it a lot more than she did. She was tired of it, tired of having to be kind in return. What she really wanted, she thought, was to be somewhere else, with someone else, someone who wasn't part of the original mess. A face flickered in her memory a moment, the rich girl who had been Lady Cecelia's friend and pretended to be hers as well.

She scolded herself into a deeper depression. Probably she wouldn't see Brun again. Why would a girl like that want to be around her? It was silly to keep looking at the presents Brun had bought, as part of their pretense of courtship.

"Hi, there!" Sirkin looked up, startled. Meharry scowled, and Oblo grunted. Brun in the flesh, clearly excited and happy, in a soft blue silk jumpsuit that must have cost a fortune and brought out the blue of her eyes. Brun squeezed in next to Sirkin, with a chair she snagged from the next table. "We have to talk," she said.

Sirkin felt her face going hot. There was no need for this; that other game was long over.

"And how did you find our humble eatery?" Meharry asked, with a bite to her voice.

Brun smiled, smugly. "I asked where the *Sweet Delight*'s crew usually ate. Since I'm now in the crew—"

"You're not!" Oblo stared at her wide-eyed, then shook his head. "I wonder what the captain's thinking of."

"My father," Brun said, and reached for a hunk of bread. "He thinks I need seasoning before I'm turned loose on an unsuspecting universe, and he thinks Captain Serrano is the right person to provide it. And you, of course." She grinned around the table. The others all stared at Brun, and Sirkin hoped no one would notice how fast her own pulse was beating. She didn't know yet if she was happy about this or not, but she couldn't be indifferent.

"I hope you're ready to go aboard and start working," Meharry said. "Captain's told us to be ready to ship out at a half-shift notice."

"Fine with me," Brun said. "I've already put my stuff aboard."

"It's called 'duffel,'" Meharry said.

"Duffel." Brun smiled at her, blue eyes wide. "Are you really angry, or just pretending? Because I'm not really an idiot—I actually have some ship time."

"On what?" Oblo said quickly, hushing Meharry. Brun's grin widened.

"On a shit-shoveler," she said. "Caring for critters."

Oblo snorted. "That's not ship time . . . that's just work. Proves you can work, but—we'll see about you and the ship."

Sirkin watched the others watching Brun, and wondered. She felt less alone now, less the one being watched. And Brun still gave her a good feeling, as if they might really be friends.

✳ ✳ ✳

Esteban Koutsoudas arrived at the shipline in a plain gray jumpsuit with a *Sweet Delight* arm patch already on it. That didn't surprise Heris. What did surprise her, a little, was that he'd made it here alive if Livadhi was right about how much danger he was in. Surely it would have been easier to take him on the station than on her ship. If not—she didn't want to think about that.

"Esteban Koutsoudas, sir," the man said. He carried an ordinary kitbag slung over his shoulder, and a couple of handcarries. She would have passed him in the concourse without a second thought—just another traveler, neither rich nor broke, with an intelligent but unremarkable face. Until he smiled, when his eyebrows went up in peaks.

"Glad to have you aboard," Heris said, though she still wasn't sure of that. "Mr. Petris will show you your quarters," Heris said, by way of taking up a moment of time.

"Commander Livadhi sent you this," Koutsoudas said, handing over a datacube. "And he said I was to assist you any way you liked."

Right. Turn a superb longscan communications tech loose on her equipment . . . could she trust this man? Yet she lusted for his expertise; she had suspected for years that Koutsoudas was the secret of Livadhi's success in more than one engagement.

"When you've stowed your gear," she said, "Mr. Petris will introduce you to the crew. Then we'll see." She left a message for Lady Cecelia, who had gone off to talk to her lawyers again. Heris could believe they wanted her out of touch, at least for a while. She had been angry with her own family—she still was, if she thought about it—but it had never occurred to her to sue them. The rich are different, she reminded herself, as she notified Traffic Control that she would need a place in the outbound stack.

Maneuvering in and out of Rockhouse Major had begun to seem routine; Heris found her mind wandering even as she recited the checklist and spoke to the captain of the tug that snared the yacht's bustle. They were leaving behind the problems of the new government, Cecelia's family, Ronnie's romantic problems, and whatever had been chasing Koutsoudas. Ahead—ahead, the frivolity of horse trials, though she dared not call it frivolity to Lady Cecelia.

Her ownership of the yacht had begun to sink past surface knowledge . . . having to pay the docking fees and the tug fees out of her own account certainly made an impression. True, Lady Cecelia had prepaid the charter fee to the Wherrin Trials, but still—Heris hoped she understood how to calculate what to charge.

They had an uneventful system transit, and the jump transition went smoothly as well. Day by day, Sirkin seemed brighter; she and Brun hung around together when they were off-shift. Heris hoped this would last, at least through the voyage. She didn't want to have to deal with young passions unrequited, not with her own relationship going through a difficult period. She and Petris still found it awkward to get together aboard the ship; the intellectual knowledge that their situation was now different could not quite eradicate the habit of years.

She had expected Koutsoudas to be an unsettling presence, but oddly enough, he turned out to be very incurious about his shipmates. Did he already know (or think he knew) everything, or did he not care? Heris found it difficult to believe he didn't care. Was he focussed only on the mechanical, on ship identities? Unlikely: she knew from rumor that he carried with him an analysis of opposing commanders. Perhaps he was here not to be kept out of someone's eye, but to keep her under someone else's. No, that was paranoia. She hoped. She wished her paranoia button had a "half on" setting, just in case.

Brun scowled over the maintenance manual for ship circuitry. "I wasn't fond of ohms and volts two years ago, and they aren't any friendlier now."

Sirkin looked up from her own reading, a year's worth of *Current Issues in Navigation* on cube. "You didn't realize you'd have to learn what you were doing?"

"I didn't on that shit-shoveler. Just put the output into the intake with a tool that's been around since humans had domestic animals."

"This is different." Sirkin prodded Brun with her toe. "Captain Serrano wants her crew to be cross-trained and above-average in skills."

"I know, I know." Brun punched up the background reference again. "It's just that electricity has never made sense to me. I keep wanting to know *why* it does what it does, and all my instructors insisted I should memorize it and not worry about the theory." She entered the values she needed for the problem set. "And these names! How far back in the dark ages was it when they named these things? Volt, ohm, ampere: might as well be biff, baff, boff, for all the sense it makes."

Sirkin opened her mouth to lecture Brun, then saw that the screen had lit with the colored flashes meant to cheer on the successful student. "You got them all correct," she said.

"Of course." Brun didn't look up; she was entering her solutions to the next series of problems. "I'm not stupid; I just don't like this stuff."

Sirkin watched the angle of jaw, the cheekbone, the droop of eyelid as Brun looked down at the reference. She had heard Amalie complain so often about her classwork, but Amalie had had real trouble with it. She had not imagined that someone who could race through the material would still dislike it, and say so.

"You're good at it," she said, feeling her way. "So why don't you like it?"

Brun looked up as if startled, and gave Sirkin a sober look that quickly turned to a mischievous grin. "I'm good at lots of things I don't like," she said. "I was bred to be good at things; that's part of being a Registered Embryo."

"But how do you know what to do? What speciality to pursue?" Sirkin remembered clearly the aptitude tests she'd had, year after year, that had aimed her at her present career with more and more precision.

Brun turned completely around, and set down her stylus. "I never thought about it," she said frankly. "No one expects us to specialize, unless we have an overwhelming talent." That seemed incredible to Sirkin, and her expression must have shown that, for Brun wrinkled her own nose and went on. "There's general stuff we all have to know: economics, and management, and whatever is done by our family interests. You know."

"No." Sirkin didn't know, and she had a vague feeling of irritation. She had never wondered much about the children of the very rich, how they were educated, what they did. But this sounded too flabby, too shapeless, to be worth anything. "I don't see how you can expect to learn anything useful if you study only generalities."

"We don't." Brun, she saw, had picked up that irritation, and chose not to reflect it. "We have a lot of specifics, too— things we'll need—"

"Which fork," Sirkin interrupted. Brun waved that away.

"Trivial. Children learn that by the time they start school, just from eating at tables with a range of flatware. No, there's a lot of background information, on our own families and the other Chairholders. Some of it we pick up, but a lot has to be learnt, formally. To vote my shares intelligently, for instance, I have to know that certain families will not invest in any phase of pork production on religious grounds."

"Shares of what?" Sirkin asked, forgetting her pique in genuine interest.

"Family companies. You know, the things our family invests in, products and processes . . ." Sirkin shook her head. "Do you know how investment works?"

"Not . . . exactly." Not at all, really. She had started her own savings account in the Navigators' Guild; she knew vaguely that they "invested" in something to keep that private bank going, but she had no idea how or what.

The process, when Brun finally got it across to her, she found appalling. She had thought that money—some real substance—sat in the Navigators' Guild vaults. She had thought that some real substance lay behind the ubiquitous credit cubes and credit slips which she used in everyday transactions.

"Not anymore," Brun said cheerfully. "It's all a tissue of lies, really, but it works, and that's all that matters." That didn't sound right, but Sirkin was past asking questions. "It's whether people believe the credit cubes are any good that matters, and they define 'good' by the exchange rate."

"I'm lost," Sirkin said.

"No, you're not." Brun squirmed into the nest of pillows at one end of the bunk and began waving those long arms. "Look—what's the smallest unit of money in the Familias?"

"A fee." At least she knew that much. In rural districts, on more backward planets, you could still find vending machines that took fees, little disks of metal with designs stamped into them.

"And what can you buy with a fee?"

"It depends," Sirkin said. Not much anywhere, she knew that, but something that cost ten fees in one town might cost fifteen somewhere else. She said that; she did not add that already she was beginning to believe in the worth of Brun's education, however unusual.

"Exactly. So a fee is worth what someone will give you for it. The same with all our monetary units."

"But that's not the same as saying they're no good if someone says so. . . ."

"Brig, think a moment. Suppose we're on a station some-where: I run a restaurant, and you want a meal. You hand me your credit cube . . . why would I take that in exchange? I have to believe that with the credits I take off your cube, I can buy things I want or need—like the food I'm going to cook to make your meal."

"But of course you can—"

"As long as we all agree on the same lies, yes. But if we don't—if I suspect you'll eat the food, but the grocer won't accept credit for the raw foods—"

"What else could they want?" It made no sense; every-one used credit cubes, and only a stupid person would refuse them.

"Something of hard value . . . you know, barter. Surely you had friends you traded around with? You know, you liked her scarf and she liked an earring you had, and you just traded."

"Well, of course, but that's not like buying it—"

"It is, really. Look—you might have seen her scarf, and said 'What'll you take for that?' and it wasn't a close friend, so she wouldn't give it to you, and you'd pay a few fees. And then a week later, she spotted your earring, and bought it from you. Only difference is, if you have the things there, you can just trade. . . ."

"Seems more honest, that way," Sirkin said.

"As long as you know how to judge the value of everything—but it wouldn't work overall. I mean, an employer can't keep a warehouse full of everything every employee might like, and let you rummage for a day's worth of goods."

"I see that," Sirkin said. "But I still think money has to be real somehow. Solid. Stored someplace. They talk in the news about depositories as if they had something in them."

"They do, but it's mostly to keep counterfeiters from

running down the value—" Brun stopped, aware that she was only confusing things. "Sorry. Look—this is sort of my field. For all of the Chairholders, I mean. I've explained it badly; I should have started slower."

"I'm not stupid." Sirkin turned away.

"No, and that's not what I meant." Brun waited, but Sirkin said nothing. She sighed, and went on. "Look, if you're determined to be angry, I can't stop you. Lots of people hate the rich. That's understandable. We go bouncing around having fun, and even when we are working it doesn't look like what you do."

"That's not it," Sirkin said, still looking away.

"Are you sure? If not, what is it?"

"It's—not that you have more money. That you can buy things." Sirkin was looking down at her hands now, her fingers moving as if on a control board. "It's that you seem to live in a different universe. Larger. You're so smart, in everything. You've had all this education, in everything. Maybe I know more about navigation, and ten days ago I knew more about this electronic system . . . but you learn so *fast*. I always thought I was smart—I *was* smart; I had perfect scores. And you come waltzing in and learn it without trying, it seems like." Her head dropped lower. "I feel like . . . like you're going to read me, learn me, as fast as you have everything else, and then I'll be just a bit of experience that enriches your life." Sirkin tried to copy Brun's accent. "'Oh, yes, I had a woman lover once; she was a nice girl but rather limited.' That's what's bothering me. I don't want to be your adventure with gender orientation."

"Oh."

"Which is what Meharry says you're doing," Sirkin said, getting it all out in a rush. "She says you're an R.E., and R.E.s are all made hetero, because your families want you to marry—"

"Meharry was supposed to be playing a role," Brun said savagely, slamming her fist into one of the pillows. She didn't want to be talking about this now, and especially not after Meharry had taken the high ground. "And besides she's wrong."

"About what, Registered Embryos in general, or you in particular?"

Brun waited a long moment, gathering her thoughts.

"When I was in that cave, I realized that I didn't want to be anyone's designated blonde. So I understand that you don't want to be my fling with sexual experimentation, a sort of bauble on the necklace of my life story. But that's not how I've seen it, Sirkin. I admired you, and the way Captain Serrano talked about you . . . if it hadn't been for you, they wouldn't have come after us in time. Then we met, and . . . and I liked it."

"But do you love men or women?"

Brun stirred uneasily. "I don't know. I like both—to have as friends, I mean. I never really thought about it, because it didn't matter a lot. Until now."

"How can you not think about it!" More accusation than question. "You have to think about it."

"I didn't." She had assumed, growing up in her family, knowing she was a Registered Embryo, that she would eventually marry and have children, most if not all of them also Registered Embryos. Being an R.E. determined your destiny; only the freelofs could choose. But on Sirkin's face was an angry look that didn't want to hear about complications. She had to try, anyway. "You know about genetic engineering—"

"Of course. What does that have to do with—oh."

"I am a Registered Embryo, Brig. You knew that before Meharry said it; I told you early on. She's right—at least, I thought it meant I wouldn't love women, just because . . . because it's so expensive."

"Expensive?" Sirkin's brow wrinkled. "Loving women?"

"No, being an R.E. They're tough enough to produce with well-mapped sets—and we're fourth-generation R.E., so all our stuff's on file except any new mutations. Because of that, we're all set to be heteros—so the work that goes into each of us will be available for the next generation."

"There's always A.I." Sirkin said. Brun realized she didn't know how Registered Embryos were made. Most people didn't.

"A.I. is already part of it," she said. "Harvesting of ova and sperm, in vitro fertilization and then splicing . . ."

"Then what does it matter what orientation the Registered Embryos have?" Sirkin asked. "If the whole reproductive bit is handled outside?"

"Prudence," Brun said. "In the . . ." she hesitated, trying to think of a polite way to say "important families." There wasn't, so she plunged on to the second level of reasoning she'd been told about years before. "If things go wrong—if something happened to the Registered Embryo program, the families would still need children. We'd have to provide them the . . . er . . . old way. And they'd want us to want to. At least, not to want *not* to."

"Oh." Sirkin reflected on that a moment. "So it's to protect the family against the loss of childbearing capacity if the medical infrastructure fails?"

"Right." Brun frowned. "My mother said that even then the orientation of women wasn't critical—in some cultures, women can be forced to bear children no matter what their wishes—but our culture thought that was unethical. Although it seems odd, that they would consider it ethical to determine our orientation so that it wouldn't be overruled later. But formal bioethics always seemed full of loopholes to me, anyway."

"I still think you have to know what you love, though."

Brun threw up her hands. "I love *lots* of things, Brig. I'm that sort . . . I'm sorry, but that's the truth. That's what got me into that fast crowd at school, really. I want to try everything, do everything, be everything. Logically, that's not possible, but . . . it would be such *fun*."

"And fun is what matters?"

Brun winced. "Not all that matters, no. But—I'm trying to be honest with you, Brig, so please try to understand. I don't think it's being rich that did this. I think some people are like me, rich or not, R.E. or not. When we were trying to think how to get Lady Cecelia out of that horrible place, *I'm* the one who thought of the hot air balloon. And one reason it worked was that it was so utterly ridiculous. Impossible. Crazy. I loved that about it—the very outrageousness of it. New things—different things—they draw me. I asked Dad—I thought maybe the R.E. process had fouled up with me—and he said they'd asked for an extra dollop of some set of multi-named neurochemicals that produce my sort of person. They'd opted for conservative intelligence with the older ones; he said they wanted a little sparkle in me."

"I think we are too different," Sirkin said. "Maybe it's your genes, and maybe it's your background, but we aren't enough alike—"

"Not for a permanent sexual relationship, no. But I don't see why we can't enjoy each other now and be lifetime friends. I like you; I admire you. Doesn't that help?"

"Yes. I just wish—"

"You need a long-term lover. I understand that. And if you want Meharry instead of me—"

"No!"

"I thought you liked her. She's angry enough at me that I thought you two had some kind of—"

"We don't have any kind of anything," Sirkin said. "I mean, I like her, as a sort of big sister, but like any big sister she tries to run my life too much. And she's hard."

"That's being ex-military, probably."

"I still don't like it. She makes me feel like a fluffy helpless kitten, and I don't like feeling helpless."

"But fluffy?" Brun cocked an eyebrow at her.

"Well . . . I have to admit I've enjoyed shopping with you. I was brought up to be practical, of course. But it's—it's kind of fun to dress up."

"So . . . even if you think fun isn't enough—even if you think I'm just a spoiled rich brat with more money than sense—you could have fun sometimes."

"With you, you mean," Sirkin said. It wasn't fair, the way Brun could coil an argument into a trap. "You think I should just relax and enjoy you, and forget the future?"

"Forget it? Never. But right now you can't go hunting a better partner; I understand that you'll want to, when you leave this ship. If you choose, we can be friends—I'd really like that, because I like you, and the friendship can last beyond this voyage. Lovers? Again, that's up to you. I don't want to hurt you, though I may have already—" Brun frowned, thinking about it. "I'd like to help you, if I knew how."

Sirkin looked at her, at the body she now realized had been carefully engineered for health and beauty and even sexuality, at the mind behind the eyes which had also been engineered for intelligence and whatever the genetic specialists meant by "sparkle." She couldn't help admiring Brun; she suspected that that, too, had been built in, as ineradicable as the choice of height and coloring. In one way it seemed weak to admire, to love, someone engineered to be admirable and lovable—it gave her the queasy feeling that she was being manipulated by the genetic engineers. Yet Brun had been the material of their manipulations; she was even less free than Sirkin. She couldn't help being who she was, any more than Sirkin could help being attracted.

"I would like to be friends," she said, after a long pause. "I don't know if it will work, in the long run, but—I do like you, and it's fun having another young woman to talk to. But not more than friends. I could fall for you, Brun, and if there's no chance for permanence, I don't want to risk it."

"Fair enough," Brun said. A faint flush reddened her face, then faded. "Now—if we can go back a bit—I'd like some help with the navigation sets our beloved captain sent down for me."

"You're going to end up better at navigation than I am," Sirkin grumbled.

"Not so. I'll pass the test, that's all. Didn't you ever know anyone who could pass tests but flunked real life?" The tension of the past conversation shattered, and Sirkin found herself laughing, not quite in control, but content to be so.

CHAPTER FOUR

Heris could not define the concern she felt. Cecelia looked healthy, strong, and sane; she spent several hours a day on her riding simulator, but that was normal for Cecelia. Now she didn't need the massage lounger after each ride; she showed no stiffness or soreness. Her appetite was good, her spirits high—so Heris told herself. What was wrong? Was it her own imagination, perhaps her own envy of someone with so much privilege getting even more?

At dinner that very night, Cecelia brought that up herself. "It's indecent, in a way . . . to be so lucky. I try to tell myself it's fair payment for the hell Lorenza put me through, but that's a lie. I've had such good luck nearly all my life, and for the year I lost have been given back forty—not a bad bargain."

Heris wondered how much she believed that. "Would you go through it again for another forty years?"

"No." It came out reflexively; her face stiffened. "It's not the same; it couldn't be. I didn't know how long—or that it would end this way—" Her breath came short.

"I'm sorry," Heris said. "That was a tactless question; of course no one would choose that year. I guess I thought you were making too light of it—"

"Too light! No . . . I don't think so. I'm trying not to let it rule the rest of my life . . . put it behind me." The tension in her shoulders suggested that it still weighed on her.

"Does it bother you that you're not competing?" Heris asked.

"Of course not!" It came almost too quickly, with a flush and fade of color on Cecelia's cheeks. "It's been thirty years; it would be ridiculous."

"Still—"

"No. I just want to see it. I might—someday—think about going back."

Zenebra's orbital station carried an astonishing amount of traffic for an agricultural world. Heris had had to wait two days for a docking assignment, and had eased the yacht in among many others. On the station itself she found the kind of expensive shops she remembered from Rockhouse Major. Cecelia had called ahead, purchasing tickets for the Senior Trials, all venues. Heris saw the prices posted in the orbital station's brochure, and winced. She hadn't realized it could cost as much to watch other people ride horses as to own them. Or so she assumed. She also hadn't realized that Cecelia expected her to come along—that she had bought two sets of tickets. Heris didn't quite groan.

On the shuttle ride down to the planet she heard nothing but horse talk. At least Cecelia's coaching had given her the vocabulary to understand most of what she heard. Stifles and hocks, quarter-cracks and navicular, stocking up and cooling down, all made sense now . . . what it didn't make, she thought to herself, was interesting conversation. The talk about particular riders and trainers made no sense at all— she didn't know why, for instance, "riding with Falkhome" was said with such scorn, or "another Maalinson" seemed to be a compliment. But any notion that Cecelia had no equal in fixation on horses quickly disappeared—the universe, or at least that shuttle, was full of people with equally one-track minds.

Zenebra's shuttle port had a huge bronze-and-stained-glass sculpture of a horse taking a fence in its lobby. The groundcars had horse motifs painted on the side. Along the road to the hotel, a grassy strip served as an exercise area for the horses—all sizes, all colors—that pranced along it. The hotel itself, jammed with enthusiasts, buzzed with the same colorful slang. Heris began to feel that she'd fallen into very strange company indeed—these people were far more intense than the foxhunters at Bunny's.

Heris had by this time seen dozens of cubes of the

Wherrin Horse Trials, both complete versions of the years Cecelia had competed, and extracts of the years since. She recognized the view from the hotel room window—the famous double ditch of Senior Course A, and the hedge beyond. Although modeled on the famous traditional venues of Old Earth, the trials had made use of the peculiarities of Zenebra's terrain, climate, and vegetation. One advantage of laying out courses on planets during colonization was the sheer space available. At Wherrin, the Senior Division alone had four separate permanent courses, which made it possible to rotate them as needed for recovery of the turf, or for the weather conditions at the time of the Trials.

Up close, the Wherrin Trials Fields looked more like the holocubes than real land with real obstacles. Bright green grass plushy underfoot, bright paint on the viewing stands, the course markers, some of the fences. Clumps of green trees. Bright blue sky, beds of brilliant pink and yellow flowers. Heris blinked at all the brilliance, reminding herself that Zenebra's sun provided more light than the original Terran sun, and waited for Cecelia to get back from wherever she'd run off to. They had agreed to meet at this refreshment stand for a break, and Cecelia was late. Then Heris saw her, hurrying through the crowds.

"Heris—you'll never guess!" Cecelia was flushed. She looked happy, but with a faint touch of embarrassment. Heris couldn't guess, and said so. "I've got a ride," Cecelia went on. Heris fumbled through her list of meanings . . . a ride back to the hotel? A ride to her chosen observation spot on the course? "A *ride*," Cecelia said. "Corry Manion, who was going to ride Ari D'amerosia's young mare, got hurt in a flitter crash last night. A mild concussion, they said, but they won't put him in the regen tanks for at least forty-eight hours, and by then it will be too late. Ari was telling me all this and then she *asked* me—I didn't say a word, Heris, I promise—she *asked* me if I would consider riding for her. I know I said I didn't mean to compete again, but—"

"But you want to," Heris said. From the cubes alone, and from her brief experience of foxhunting, she had had a vague notion that way herself, but one look at the real obstacles had changed her mind. "Of course you do. Can I help?"

"You don't think I'm crazy?" Cecelia asked. "An old woman?"

Heris did think she was crazy; she thought they were all crazy, but Cecelia was no worse than the others. "You aren't an old woman anymore," Heris said. "You've been working out on the simulator. You've got a lifetime of skills and new strength—and it's your neck."

"Come on, then," Cecelia said. "I'll get you an ID tag so you can come in with me—you have to see this mare."

Heris didn't have to see the mare; she had only to see the look on Cecelia's face, and remember that less than a year ago Cecelia had been flat in bed, paralyzed and blind.

As with the foxhunting, more went on behind the scenes than Heris would have guessed from the entertainment cubes she'd seen. The Trials organization had its own security procedures; Heris and Cecelia both needed ID tags, and Cecelia had to have the complete array of numbers that she would wear during competition. Cecelia spent half an hour at the tailor's getting measurements taken for her competition clothes.

"I have all this somewhere, probably in a trunk back on Rotterdam," Cecelia said. "Maybe even somewhere in the yacht, though we didn't move everything back aboard. I don't remember, really, because it had been so long since I needed it."

"Why so many changes of clothes?" Heris asked. She had wondered about that even with the foxhunters. Why not simply design comfortable riding clothes that would work, and then wear them for all occasions?

"Tradition," Cecelia said, wrinkling her nose. "And I'd like to know what a shad is, so I'd know why this looks anything like its belly." She gestured at her image in the mirror; Heris shook her head. "Yet that's what this kind of jacket is called."

Heris followed her from the tailor's to the saddler's, where Cecelia picked out various straps that looked, to Heris, like all the others. "Reins are just reins, aren't they?" she said finally, when Cecelia had been shifting from one to another pair for what seemed like hours. Cecelia grimaced.

"Not when you're coming down a drop in the rain," she said. "And by the way, see if somebody can dig my saddles out of storage and put them on the next shuttle. I'd rather not break in a new saddle on course." Heris found a public combooth and relayed the request; Brun promised to bring the saddles herself if Heris would give permission to leave the ship.

"Fine," Heris said, and anticipated her next request. "And why not bring Sirkin down, too? She's probably never seen anything like this."

Finally they arrived at one of the long stable rows. Ari D'amerosia had four horses in the trials, two in the Senior Trials and one each in Training and Intermediate. Grooms in light blue shirts bustled about, carrying buckets and tack, pushing barrows of straw, bales of hay, sacks of feed. Ari herself, a tall woman with thick gray-streaked hair, was bent over inspecting a horse's hoof when Cecelia came up with Heris.

"Tim, we're going to need the vet again. Cold soak until the vet comes— Oh, hi Cece. Have your rider's registration yet?"

"Yes—and this is Heris, who's hunted with the Greens at Bunny's." Nothing at all, Heris noted wryly, about her main occupation as a ship's captain.

"Ah—then you can ride. Ever event?" The woman straightened up and offered a hand hastily wiped on her jeans. She was a head taller than Cecelia.

"No," Heris said. "I came to riding a bit late for that."

"It's never too late," Ari said, with the enthusiasm of one who would convert any handy victim. "Start with something easy—you'd love it."

"Not this year," Heris said. "I'm just here to help Cecelia."

"Next year," Ari said, and without waiting for an answer turned to Cecelia. "Now. I've had the groom warm her up for you—we've got two hours in the dressage complex, ring fifteen. Get to know her, feel her out—she may buck a few times, she usually does."

"Where can I change?" Cecelia asked.

"Might as well use her stall—your friend—Heris?—can hang on to your other stuff until we clear out Corry's locker."

Cecelia ducked into the stall and reappeared in breeches, boots, and pullover; Heris took the clothes she'd been wearing, rolled them into Cecelia's duffel, and felt uncomfortably like a lady's maid. She followed Cecelia down the

long row of stalls and utility areas, past grooms washing
horses, walking horses, feeding and mucking out, around
the end of the stable rows to the exercise rings.

"The great thing about Wherrin," Cecelia said, "is there's
no shortage of space. You don't have to make do with a
few practice rings, a single warmup ring . . ." So it appeared.
A vast field, broken into a long row of dressage rings
separated by ten-meter alleys, and another long row of larger
rings with two or three jumps each. Everywhere horses and
riders and trainers.

At the far end, Heris saw the number fifteen. A bright
bay mare strode around the outside, ridden by a groom in
the light blue shirt of Ari's stable. Cecelia showed her
competitor's pass, and the groom hopped down to give her
a leg up. Heris stood back. She thought the horse looked
different from those Cecelia usually praised, but she couldn't
define the difference. Taller? Thinner? In the next ring, a
stocky chestnut was clearly shorter and thicker, but looked
lumpish to her.

She didn't understand most of what Cecelia was doing,
that first session. That it would lead to a dressage test
the day after next, yes, but not how Cecelia's choice of
gait and pattern aimed at that goal. Cecelia's expression
gave her no clue, and her comments and questions to the
groom, and then Ari, didn't clear things up. Heris felt
uncomfortable, not only because of the hot sun. If anyone had asked her, she thought it was a silly thing to
do in the first place, trying to get horses over those
obstacles. And for Cecelia, at her age, when she hadn't
done it for thirty years—and on a horse she didn't know—
it was worse than silly. But no one asked her, and she
kept her opinion to herself, through the few hours of
training that Cecelia had before the event began.

When Brun and Sirkin arrived with Cecelia's saddle (which
looked just like all the other saddles, to Heris's eye), she
noticed that Sirkin reacted as she did, while Brun clearly
belonged with the equestrian-enthused. Before the day was
out, Brun had convinced Ari to let her work with the
horses—for no pay, of course. Sirkin, having been stepped
on by the first horse led past her, had even less enthusiasm than Heris.

✳   ✳   ✳

Early in the morning two days later, Heris found herself perched on a hard seat in the viewing stands of the dressage arena. Cecelia, already dressed for her own appearance, sat with her at first to explain the routine. A big gray, paired with a rider who had won the Wherrin twice before, moved smoothly through the test. Cecelia explained why the judges nitpicked; Heris thought it was silly to worry about one loop of a serpentine being flatter than another. It seemed an archaic concern, like continuing to practice drill formations never used in real military actions.

Then Cecelia left, to warm up her own mount. Heris worried. She still couldn't reconcile the old Cecelia, well into her eighties, with the vigorous woman who seemed a few years younger than herself. She kept expecting that appearance to crack, as if it were only a shell over the old one.

She was thoroughly bored by the time Cecelia appeared. All the horses did exactly the same thing—or tried to. Some made obvious mistakes—obvious to the crowd, that is, whose sighs and mutters let Heris know that something had gone wrong. One went into a fit of bucking, which was at least exciting, if disastrous to its score. But most simply went around and around, trot and canter, slower or faster, until Heris fought back one yawn after another.

Cecelia and the bay mare did the same, not as badly as some and not as well as the best. Heris tried to be interested, but she really couldn't tell how the judges scored any of it; the numbers posted afterwards meant nothing to her. She climbed out of the stands after Cecelia's round, sure her backside would have been happier somewhere else.

To her surprise, Cecelia said hardly anything, shrugging off Heris's attempt at compliments with a brusque "That's over with—now for tomorrow." Tomorrow being the cross-country phase, Heris knew, with four sections that tested the horse's endurance, speed, and jumping ability. "That's the fun part," Cecelia said. Heris had more than doubts, but at least she wouldn't have to sit through all of it. She could watch on monitors, or walk from one obstacle to another.

Heris watched the start on the monitor, trying not to listen to the announcer's babble. He had already said too much, she thought, about Cecelia being the oldest rider in the event, on the youngest horse. Cecelia had the mare gathered up in a coil, ready to explode, and when the starter waved, she sent the mare out at a powerful canter. The first fence, invariably described as inviting, didn't look it to Heris: the egg cases of the native saurids glittered bronze in the sun and their narrow ends, pointed up, looked too much like missiles on a rack.

"We used to use the whole eggs," someone said in her ear; she glanced around and saw that it was another of Ari's people. "But someone crashed into them one year, and the stench was so bad none of the other horses would go near the fence. Ruined the scoring, completely upset everyone. Now they have to weight the bottoms of them, but at least there's no stink."

Cecelia and the mare were safely over the first fence, and Heris decided to walk across the course to the water complex. Cecelia had said it would be a good place to watch.

Cecelia grinned into the wind. The mare had calmed down on the steeplechase, where she could run freely, and she met all the fences squarely, with the attitude of a horse that knows it can jump. Of course, most horses would jump on the steeplechase course, with its open grassy terrain and its clearly defined fences. The problems would come in the cross-country phase. During roads and tracks, Cecelia tried to feel out how the mare felt about different surfaces, about dark patches of shade and reflections from water. The mare didn't like sudden changes in light, but she would go on if supported by the rider. She paid no heed to the loose dog that suddenly yapped at her heels—a good omen because the crowds in the event course often had dogs, and at least one always got loose.

On the big course, Cecelia continued to feel her way into the mare's reflexes. So far, she was amazed at how easy it all seemed. Her own reflexes had come back as if the thirty years since her last big season had never been. They had cleared that first easy fence. The second fence was another straightforward, well-defined obstacle, made of the intertwined trunks of a stickass thicket. The mare flowed over it.

Now the course ran toward the ridge for which it was named, the grade gentle up to a scary but jumpable set of rails over a big ditch. The mare looked at the ditch, but jumped without real hesitation when Cecelia sat tight. Next came the Saurus Steps, a staircase arrangement that required the horse to bounce up a series of ledges, then take one stride and jump a drop fence. Here Cecelia thought the mare was going to run out of impulsion on the last bounce, and legged her hard into the stride at the top. The mare stretched and almost crashed the fence, but caught herself and landed without falling.

My mistake, Cecelia thought. Too much pushing, too much delight in being here again. But there was no time to reride it in her head; she was already entering the switchbacks that led to the ridgetop, with trappy obstacles at each turn. Two of them required a trot approach; the others could be cantered if the horse didn't pull too badly. The mare pulled like a tractor, fighting the down transitions, snaking her head. On the second trot fence, the mare charged straight ahead past the fence and ran out past the flag.

"Settle down," Cecelia said, as much to herself as to the mare. She was still pushing too hard, abusing the fragile, two-day relationship. The mare switched her tail and backed up, kicking out finally before Cecelia got her lined up for the jump. She jumped willingly once aimed straight at the fence, and didn't charge the next fence. "Finesse," Cecelia muttered. "It's easier if you don't fight the course." Or the rider, but it wouldn't help to tell the horse that. She had to convey that with her body, all the mare would understand.

Now they were on the ridge, headed back to the east, roughly parallel to the early part of the course but higher. Here the obstacles were built to take advantage of natural stone formations. Horses had to jump into depressions, leap back up and over the ridgeline, twisting and turning, changing leads and stride length between each obstacle.

Cecelia had always enjoyed this demanding part of the course. On a good day, it had a compelling, syncopated rhythm, very satisfying to mind and body. On a bad day it was a bone-jarring, breath-eating nightmare of near catastrophe. This mare continued her headstrong, stiff-sided refusal to bend left, but Cecelia kept her on course, regaining her own confidence with every successful jump. Perhaps she was out of practice, but—she hauled the mare around a stone pillar and got her lined up for the next—she could still handle a difficult horse on a difficult course. She felt more alive than she had in years. She knew the tapes would show a wide grin on her face.

The most dangerous part of the course lay downhill to the water complex. From above it could look all too inviting, a long sweep of green to the tiny red-and-white decorations at the water's edge, tempting horse and rider alike to set off down the slope at full speed. But on the way down were two punishing obstacles, a drop fence and a large bank with a ditch below. Cecelia had seen many a rider come to grief here; she had done it herself. She took a firm hold of the mare, and eased her over the drop fence.

Below it, the mare picked up speed. She wanted to charge at the bank, fly off the top. Cecelia wrestled her down to a rough trot, paused briefly at the top and thought she had the mare ready for the slide and jump below. Suddenly the mare swung sideways on the steep slope, reared, plunged, and fell, rolling over into the ditch. Cecelia flung herself off on the upslope side as the mare went down.

"You idiot," she said, without heat. She meant both of them. This finished the round as far as scores went. Completion was the best she could hope for now, and one more refusal would eliminate them. She knew this debacle would be featured on the annual cube; she could imagine the commentator's remarks about her age. At least she hadn't been wearing a camera herself.

The mare lay upside down for a moment, legs thrashing, then heaved herself over and up, clambering out of the muck with more power than grace. She seemed unhurt as Cecelia led her away from the course and checked her legs. Cecelia looked at the saddle, now well-greased with mud, and accepted a leg up into the slippery mess with the resignation of experience. The mare was sound; the best thing to do was keep going and finish the course.

If she could. The water complex was next, offering a serious challenge even to riders with dry saddles and steerable horses. Cecelia decided on the straight route, mostly because the mare's mistakes had all been steering problems. With that in mind, she eased the mare around the one sharp turn on the approach, and legged her at the first fence. The mare jumped clean, sailing into the water with the enthusiasm of youth and a tremendous splash. She cantered gaily through the stream, leapt out the far side, and over the bounce, as if she'd been doing it all her life.

On the far side of the water complex, the course made a circuit of a large open area, with obstacles spaced along it, rewarding horses that liked to gallop on. Here the mare had no problems, attacking one jump after another with undiminished verve. Cecelia put the problems behind her and enjoyed the ride. This was what she loved; this was what she had dreamed of, in those months of blind paralysis. The warm, live, powerful body beneath her, the thudding hooves, the wind in her face, the vivid colors, the way her body moved with the horse, pumping her own breath in and out. Even the sharp bite of fear that made the successful jumps individual spurts of relief and delight.

At the finish, the mare galloped through the posts with her ears still forward and her legs intact. Cecelia felt that if she'd had mobile ears, hers would have been forward too.

"Sorry about the problems," she said to Ari, when she dismounted. "I think I was too rough with her on the stairsteps, and that's why she fought with me later." She didn't really want to talk about it; Ari, after a few perfunctory questions, seemed to realize that and led the mare away. Cecelia wanted to be alone to savor the feelings, the joy that thrust so deep it hurt. She was back where she belonged; she could still do it. Common sense be damned; she didn't have to give it up yet.

Heris, familiar with the cubes of Cecelia's great rides of the past, couldn't help thinking that this had been a disaster. The horse had refused one fence; the horse had fallen upside down in a ditch, and Cecelia was lucky not to have been squashed underneath. Mud from the fall caked Cecelia's breeches.

"Not too shabby," was Cecelia's comment on her own ride. "The mare and I needed more time together." She caught sight of herself in the mirror. "Whoosh! What a mess. I've got to get cleaned up. An old friend asked me to dinner."

"But tomorrow—"

"Tomorrow's just the jumping, and she's going to be a pain to truck around that course. We'll probably have a few rails down. But it's worth it—I can't tell you how much fun it's been." Fun. Heris opened her mouth and shut it again. Her memory reminded her that she had once thought foxhunting was stupid, and had found it fun herself. Maybe this was fun, if you were good enough. She wasn't, and she told herself she never intended to be.

The next morning, Heris was back in the stands, this time with a cushion she'd brought. Since competitors rode in reverse order of standings, Cecelia's show jumping round came early. Most of the horses with more faults had not completed the course and would not be jumping. Heris watched the mare shift and stamp as Cecelia checked the girth and mounted. The horse showed no signs of the previous day's efforts; her bright bay coat gleamed, clean of the mud from the ditch.

The jump course required not only jumping ability but a level of steering that this mare hadn't attained. Heris could see that Cecelia was trying to give the mare the easiest route through the maze, with sweeping turns that set her up at a good distance from the next obstacle. The mare resisted, trying to cut the round corners and charge at any fence that caught her eye. That she went over the fences in the right order seemed a minor miracle; the large one was that she didn't fall or crack Cecelia's head against either of the large trees in the ring. She still had two fences down, one of them in a scatter of rails that made Heris wince—she could almost feel the bruises on her own shins.

By the end of the day's performances, Heris understood a bit more about the sport, but she had no intention of risking her own neck that way. People who craved that much danger should be firefighters, or some other job that accomplished something worthwhile to balance the danger. Cecelia was flushed and happy, eager to talk now about today's winner (someone she'd known as a junior competitor) and the number of Rejuvenants competing. Of the five top placings, three were Rejuvenants.

"Does that mean you'll go back to competition—if other Rejuvenants are doing it?"

"I might," Cecelia said. "I'm not sure. Pedar—my friend that I went out with last night—wants to talk to me about Rejuvenant politics." She made a face, then grinned. "I'll listen to him—but I can't think of myself as a person whose interests have changed just because I'm going to live longer."

"Perhaps not," Heris said. "But if three of the top five

riders are Rejuvenants, where does that leave the young-sters just starting? Experience counts." She was sure Cecelia would compete again; she was far too happy to give it up. She couldn't help wondering what that would mean for her and the *Sweet Delight*.

"And some Rejuvenants don't place," Cecelia said, laugh-ing. "I certainly didn't." But she looked thoughtful.

Cecelia had recognized the face but at first had not known whether this was Pedar himself, a son, or a grandson. The long, bony, dark-skinned face looked all of thirty. Had Pedar taken rejuvenation? How many times? He wore a full-sleeved white shirt with lace at the collar over tight gray trousers . . . he had always, she recalled, favored a romantic image. He had been the first man she knew to wear earrings . . . though now he wore three small platinum ones, in place of the great gold pirate hoop of his flamboyant youth.

"My dear Cecelia," he said, holding her hand a long moment. "You look . . . lovely."

"I look fortyish," Cecelia said, with some asperity. "And I was never lovely."

"You were, but you didn't like to hear it," he said. "And yes, I'm Pedar himself." He tilted his head; his rings flashed in his ear. "I notice you aren't wearing any—are you trying to pass?"

"Pass?" Now she was completely bewildered.

"As your apparent age, I meant. Perhaps you are planning to compete seriously again, and—"

Rage tore through her. "I am *not* trying to be anything but myself. I never did."

"Sorry," he said. "I seem to have hit a sore point. It's just that you aren't wearing any earrings—"

"I don't follow fads in jewelry," Cecelia said, biting each word off. "I prefer quality." She glared, but he didn't flinch. Of course, he hadn't flinched much when they were both in their twenties and she'd glared at him. Now, he shook his head, and chuckled. She had always liked his chuckle; for some reason it made her feel safe.

"Forgive me," he said. "I should not laugh, but it is so like you to be unaware of the code. You're right, Cecelia: you never paid attention to fads, or tried to be anything but what you are. Let me explain." Without waiting for her reaction, he went on. "Those of us who've experienced the Ramhoff-Inikin rejuvenation process several times found that we were confusing some of the people we'd always known. Even within the family we might be taken for our own descendants. We didn't want to wear large signs saying 'I am Pedar Orrigiemos, the original,' or anything like that. We wanted some discreet signal, and—" he touched the rings in his left ear, "—this is what we use."

"Earrings?" Cecelia asked. It seemed a silly choice. She tried to remember how many earrings she'd seen lately, and whether Lorenza had worn them.

Pedar laughed. "They aren't just earrings. The first serial rejuvenations were all done under special license, with very close monitoring. They wore implanted platinum/ceramic disks encoded with all the necessary medical information, from their baseline data to the dosages. Someone—I forget who—objected to the disk, and asked if it could be made more decorative. Next thing you know—rings. Now we use them to indicate how many rejuvenations we've had, which is a clue—though not really precise—to our full age."

"But why would you want to?" Cecelia said, intrigued in spite of herself. "I can see what you mean about families— although there's no young woman in mine who resembles me that closely. But surely they could learn—"

"Oh, I suppose so. It's handy in business, though, when associates know that the youngish man with the three earrings is the CEO, while the one with the single earring is his son, merely a division vice-president."

"Ross never sneaks in another earring?" asked Cecelia, remembering Ross very well. She had never liked him.

"Not while I'm in the same system," Pedar said. "I suppose he could, but then he'd have to sustain conversations with any of my friends—and he couldn't. Which brings up the other issue, perhaps the main one. Haven't you discovered yet how boring the young are?"

"I have not," said Cecelia. She was in no mood to agree with Pedar about anything.

"You will." His face twisted into the wry expression she had once found so fascinating. "Having a young body is one thing—I like it, and I'm sure you do too. No more aches and pains, no more flab and stiffness. Vivid tastes and smells, a digestive tract with renewed ability to cope with all the culinary delights of a hundred worlds. You can ride a competitive course again, if you want. But—will you want to?"

"I just did," Cecelia pointed out.

"True, but that was—survival euphoria, perhaps, after your ordeal. Will you continue to compete?" When she didn't answer immediately, he went on. "The physical sensations you enjoyed, those are strong again, just as I swim in big surf, which I always loved. You will always ride, perhaps. But you may not always want to compete. One reason is the constant contact with the young. There's nothing *wrong* with the young—they will grow up to be old—but you have already solved the problems they find so distressing. Just as, when you were originally forty, you found adolescents boring—and don't tell me you didn't, because I remember what you said about Ross when he was in school."

That was Ross, Cecelia thought to herself. Ross had been boring because all he thought about was Ross. Although, come to think of it, that description fit most of the adolescents she'd known. Certainly Ronnie had been like that.

"Take your average forty-year-old," Pedar said. Cecelia immediately thought of Heris. Heris wasn't average, but she didn't like average anyway. "Your average forty-something is worrying about a personal relationship, and if not rejuved, is having concerns about the first signs of physical aging." Well, that was true. She could not have missed the tension between Heris and Petris, and both of them were making a fetish out of using the gym. "More than half the things you know directly, they know only by hearsay—from their education, which includes only what educators think is important. Nothing of the little things that you and I remember effortlessly. Remember the craze for sinopods?"

Cecelia laughed. She hadn't thought about that for years, a fashion so peculiar it had penetrated even her horse-focussed mind. She had had a sinopod herself, a red and yellow one.

Pedar nodded at her expression. "You see? If sinopods are mentioned anywhere outside obscure biology texts, it's in some terminally boring treatise on the economic impact of fads for biologicals on the ecology of frontier worlds. You and I—the others our age, with our background—we remember the sinopods themselves, and even if we can't explain the attraction, we remember the ones we had."

"I wonder whatever happened to them?" she asked; she remembered that she had even named her sinopod, though she couldn't recall the name. Pedar laughed outright.

"Cecelia, you have a genius for getting off the subject. If you really care about sinopods, look it up. My point is that people in the same generation share experiences—know things—that others cannot know directly. Long ago, people who wanted to pretend they weren't aging tried mingling with those younger—hoping the youth would rub off, I suppose. We don't have to do that. We can have the best of youth—the healthy bodies—and the best of age—the experience."

"So you wear rings in your ears." She hated to admit it—she would *not* admit it aloud—but Pedar made sense. She remembered her exasperation with Heris as far back as that insane adventure on the island. To waffle around like that, about whether or not she loved Petris—she herself would not have been so baffled, and she had straightened the younger woman out. Heris had been wrong again about Sirkin, and again her own age and experience told. But Heris wasn't boring. Ronnie, maybe.

"A ring like this—" Pedar tapped his rings, "simply tells us—those who have had multiple rejuvenations—that you have had one, and how many. We choose to stabilize at different ages, so you have to do a little calculation. The commercial version gives about twenty years per treatment, so if you combine the appearance and the number of rings, you can come close to the actual age." He grinned again, a challenging grin this time. "Or, you can wear no ring and simply pretend to be forty. Talk to other forties, live among them, and become like them. . . ."

"No," Cecelia said firmly. "I have no intention of pretending to be younger than I am. That's why I never wanted rejuvenation in the first place."

"Then wear the ring," Pedar said. "It will save you a lot of trouble."

Restlessness, too much energy . . . was it all because she hadn't had the chance to confront Lorenza directly? She had confronted Berenice directly enough, and that hadn't satisfied her.

Something bothered her about Pedar's advice, about Pedar's

complacency. She had deliberately refused to think about the implications of rejuvenation. It complicated things; she wanted to go on with her life and not worry about it. But his attitude suggested that this wouldn't work, that others would always be assessing her, looking for correspondence or conflict between her visible age and her real self.

Exactly why she hadn't wanted to do it. Better than being blind or having to use optical implants, certainly. She wanted to be healthy, whole, able to do what she wanted to do. But she didn't want to waste her time wondering if she was confusing people or what they thought.

And he implied a whole subculture of rejuvenated old-sters, a subculture she hadn't even noticed. How many serial Rejuvenants were there? She began to wonder, began to think of looking for the telltale rings.

They weren't always in ears, but once she looked, they were on more people than she had expected. Discreet blue-and-silver enamel rings on fingers, in ears, in noses, occasionally in jewelry but most often attached to the body. She began to suspect that where they were worn signaled something else Pedar hadn't told her. Certainly when she saw couples wearing them, they were usually in the same site. She wondered if anyone outside the Rejuvenant subculture had caught on, if some of the rings were faked. She had had no idea so many people had been rejuvenated at all, let alone more than once.

Cecelia pulled out her medical file from the Guerni Republic, something she'd stashed in the yacht's safe without another glance. Sure enough, a little blue-and-silver ring slid out of the packet, and the attached card explained that it contained the medical coding necessary for a rejuvenation technician to correct any imbalance. Odd. Why not just implant a record strip, as was done all the time for people with investigational diseases?

She sat frowning, rolling the ring from one hand to another. Did she want to identify herself to others as one of the subculture? She wished she knew more about it. She disliked even that much concern . . . and yet . . . she couldn't deny that Pedar was right about the callowness of the young.

CHAPTER FIVE

Heris left Cecelia onplanet and went back up to the yacht where, she hoped, she could have ten consecutive minutes in which no one mentioned horses or anything connected with them. She found Sirkin making the same complaint to the rest of the crew about Brun. She herself had had to remind Brun firmly that she was a crewmember, not a rich girl on vacation, and order her back to the ship.

"All she talks about is horses. And she knows a lot of other things, but from the minute she unpacked Lady Cecelia's saddle, everything else went out of her mind."

"Everything?" Meharry asked.

Sirkin reddened. "Well . . . you know what I mean."

Heris cleared her throat and they all straightened. "Any messages?" she asked.

"Yes, Captain." Meharry could be formal when she chose. "All disclaimed urgency when we offered to transfer them down to your hotel, but you do have a stack."

"I'll get back to work then. I have no idea how long Lady Cecelia will stay—the Trials are over, but she's meeting old friends. However, we should be prepared to depart in a day or so." She glanced around. "Where is Brun?"

"Probably watching Trials cubes," Sirkin said. "Again." Everyone laughed, including Heris.

"How's the installation coming?" She had finally decided to let Koutsoudas install his pet equipment on their own scans, with Oblo to ensure that nothing went wrong.

"It's done, Captain." Koutsoudas looked at Oblo, and Oblo

looked back; Heris recognized the expression from years in the Fleet.

"And just what have you gentlemen been up to with it? Looking into the yachts of the rich and famous?"

"Something like that," Oblo said, scratching his head. "But nothing too . . . damaging. They all seem to be down on the planet playing with horses."

In her office, she found most of the messages to be routine queries, including some from travel agents who wondered when she would be free for bookings. She hadn't thought of having any client but Lady Cecelia—but if Cecelia stayed here too long, she'd have to find another charter. And that meant hiring service staff as well . . . she felt her shoulders tensing. She hated the thought of dealing with service staff; she was a commander, not a . . . whatever you called it.

She had gone through the messages in order of time, the usual way, so the one headed "Serrano Family: request meeting" came last. It had arrived days ago, but she saw by the comments that whoever it was had refused several offers to forward the message. She stared at it, breathing carefully: in, out. Which of her many relatives could it be? And why? Only one way to find out; she posted a message to the station address and waited for the response. It came almost at once: request for meeting, and a suggested location, the dock outside the yacht's access tube.

The dark compact form in uniform looked vaguely familiar. Heris paused, suddenly wary. Upright, as only the military youth were, and ensign's insignia. Who? Then the young man turned and met her eyes; she felt that look as a blow to the gut. "Barin!"

"Captain Serrano." His formality steadied her. Her own distant cousin, and he gave her her title.

"What is it?" she asked then. "Would you prefer to talk in my quarters?"

"If—if you don't mind." He waited for her answer in that contained, measured posture she knew so well. He would wait for a day if she chose to make him.

"Come along, then." She led the way; her neck itched with his gaze on it. She felt vulnerable, as she had not for a long time. He could kill her easily, be gone before anyone knew . . . no, that was ridiculous. Why would he?

They passed no one, and neither of them spoke. When they reached her quarters, she preceded him through the door, and went around behind her desk. "Have a seat," she offered, but he stood before her desk like any junior officer called before her. His eyes, after one quick flicker around the room, settled on her face. She waited, wondering if she must prompt him with a question, but he spoke before her patience ran out.

"I came to offer you formal apologies on behalf of the family," he said, stopping there as if he had run into a wall.

"You?" Her mind raced. Formal apology? If they had wanted to apologize, if this were genuine, they'd have sent someone more senior. Not one of the admirals Serrano, of course, but someone her former rank or above.

Barin flushed at her tone. "Captain Serrano, I admit I— perhaps I overstated my authority." That had the phrasing learned in the classroom.

"Go on," she said. In her voice she heard authority and wariness mingled.

He did not answer at once, and she let her gaze sharpen. What had he done, gone AWOL? But his answer, when it came, seemed just possible. "My grandmother—your aunt, Admiral Vida Serrano—asked me to find you. With apologies: no one more senior could be spared, under the circumstances."

"The circumstances being?" All her old instincts had come alert.

"The unsettled state of things in the Familias, that is. All leaves canceled, all active-duty personnel called in—"

"I know what all leaves canceled means," Heris said, dryly. "But I also know they released all the Royal junior officers and dispersed the onplanet regiment on Rockhouse—"

"Things have . . . changed," Barin said. "Glenis and I were the only ones old enough, that didn't have other assignments. She went up-axis and I went down—they weren't sure where and when we'd catch up with you, you see."

"But the point is . . . apology? And for what?" As if she didn't know; as if her heart didn't burn with it.

"For not backing you when you were under investigation," Barin said. In his young voice, it sounded innocent enough; she wondered if he understood what had happened, if his elders had explained it to him. "I was told to say that your aunt the Admiral Serrano was not informed until too late of the situation you were in, and would certainly have given you assistance had she known."

Her aunt the admiral. It was just possible that she had not known, until after Heris's resignation, if no one had thought to inform her. But she should have been told. She was then the most distant high-ranking family member, but not the only one. Other admirals Serrano had been closer, must have known about it. Why hadn't one of them done something?

Barin went on then, as if he had been reading her thoughts. "I—I didn't know any of this before, sir. Ma'am."

That bobble made Heris grin before she thought. "I wouldn't expect you would have," she said.

"I mean, the admiral said there was some kind of trouble in the family, something she hadn't anticipated. Not what-ever it was with you, but—"

Heris felt her brows rising. "You mean you don't know what happened to me? Whatever's happened to the grape-vine? It's been long enough I'd expect it to be all over every prep school with a single Fleet brat in it."

He flushed. "There've been rumors—"

"I would hope so. What's a lifetime of experience for, if not to make rumors fly? Let me straighten out a few things for you, young man." She paused, thinking how best to put it. Honesty first, and tact second, but without bitterness if she could manage it. "What happened was that I accom-plished my assigned mission, but not in the way I'd been told to do it. My way saved lives, but it made an admiral look stupid—Lepescu, if you ever heard of him."

"Uh . . . no, I haven't."

"Bloodthirsty bastard," Heris said. "He liked wasting troops. I killed him—"

"What!" He looked as if the sky had just fallen; she almost laughed. Had she ever been that innocently certain that everyone followed the rules, that hierarchies never tumbled?

"Not *then*. Sorry; I got out of sequence. Let's see. He was furious that I had not won the battle his way, and swore he'd get revenge. There was a Board of Inquiry, of course. Evidence had . . . disappeared." She didn't really want to tell him how; it was too complicated, and involved too many names he might know. "I was offered immunity for my crew if I would resign my commission," she went on. "Otherwise, courts-martial for all. Considering Lepescu's position—the Rules of Engagement—and the fact that no one from the family spoke for me, I decided to resign and save my crew."

He stared at her; clearly he hadn't heard this before. "But—but why didn't—?"

"I don't know why someone didn't do something. Let me finish." More bite got through than she intended; he flinched. It wasn't his fault, she reminded herself, and tried to breathe slowly. "What I didn't know was that after I resigned, after I was gone from his sector, Lepescu charged my crew. Most were convicted of serious breaches of regulation and were dispersed to various Fleet prisons. Some—" The old rage blanked her vision for a moment and she had to force another deep breath to continue. "Some he took to a private hunting reserve and hunted."

"Hunted . . . you mean . . . like animals?"

"Precisely. With friends of his who liked the same thing." She didn't mention the prince; his death had earned her silence.

"How did you . . . how did you find out?" That had not been the first question he thought of; she answered what she thought it had been.

"I killed him when I found him, which was—luckily for me—in the process of that hunting trip, when his guilt was not in question. My crew—the survivors—were rehabilitated and given the choice of remaining in Fleet or taking a settlement and going civilian. Some of them are here, with me."

"Couldn't you have gone back?" He looked puzzled.

"Of course. But—" Heris wondered how much to explain to this young man—this mere child, as he seemed to her. Could he understand that it wasn't merely pique? She'd already explained more than he was likely to absorb. He knew no world but Fleet; he could imagine no other choice than returning to it. "So," she said, changing direction. "That's what my side of the trouble was like. Now—what did the admiral want me to know?"

He looked confused a moment, then got back to it. "She didn't explain much, really. She wanted you to know she hadn't known about your trouble in time, and I think she blames some of the others in the family." As well she might. "Uh . . . your parents among them . . ."

"It's not my problem now," Heris said crisply. She wasn't about to discuss her parents with him.

"No . . . but she'd like to talk to you, the next time you're anywhere near."

Which was likely to be a long time from now. "Did she give you an itinerary?" Already her mind had moved beyond this to how she was going to ease this young relation off the ship and on his way.

"Yes—here." He fished in his pocket and came up with a small datacube. "It's compressed format—she sent an adapter in case you don't have a reader with the right interface."

"Thanks," Heris said. She wasn't going to tell him that she had a couple of experts who could strip the data out of virtually any storage device. Whatever her aunt the admiral was up to, she would keep her own secrets.

Someone tapped at the door. Barin looked around, and Heris called, "Come on in."

Brun opened the door. "Captain, the new installations are ready for inspection."

"Thank you; I'll be along shortly." Heris repressed a grin. Brun definitely had the right touch, timing and tone both impeccable. Brun nodded and withdrew.

"I'll—I'll be going," Barin said, with a hint of nervousness.

"Yes—I'm sorry, but I do have some ship work under way. Tell you what—why not have dinner with me this evening? You can bring me up-to-date on your sibs and cousins."

"Do you really—? Grandmother said not to waste your time. Just give you the message, and the cube, and get out of your way."

Heris laughed. "She must think I've grown to be quite an ogre," she said. *That* Admiral Serrano would know how ogres were grown. Perversely, Heris was now determined to be cordial to the youngster. "Are you scheduled out of here?"

"No—not yet."

"Fine—then you can meet me at the Captains Guild for dinner. They use a screwball clock setting here—five shifts in the day and five hours in each shift, and it starts at what we'd call mainday or first shift. So make it third and one."

"Yes, sir." This time he didn't change it to the civilian usage.

"I'll guide you out." He could find his own way on such a tiny ship, but she wouldn't let even a relative wander around unescorted.

The cube contained substantially more than the admiral's itinerary for the next year or so. Heris had suspected it would when she turned it over to Meharry.

"Video, audio, and an almighty big chunk of encrypted stuff. Does your family have its own code scheme?"

"More than one," Heris said. "I suppose she wonders if I kept the key."

"I should have known," Meharry said sourly. "You great families—"

"As if you didn't have something of the same sort," Heris retorted. "What I'm really concerned about is any kind of ghost or vampire, or even an owl." Anything that might compromise their own information systems.

Meharry shook her head. "No hooters at all, and nothing that my spook catchers notice. Want me to let Esteban have a look?"

"No." That came out with more force than Heris intended, and she calmed herself. "No, I trust your judgment on this. Let's see if my key works on the encrypted stuff."

She didn't bother to explain the key. As with the rendezvous protocols cooked up by young officers and elaborated over the years to an intricate but precise interpersonal code, family encryption keys were combinations of predictable and unpredictable private data. Events important to the family as a whole, to individuals within it, might form part of the key, along with informal rules for making changes. Heris didn't so much have a key, as a procedure for finding the key, a procedure which functioned as part of the key.

Video came up. "She looks like you on a bad day," Meharry blurted. Then, "Sorry, Captain."

"It's our classic bone structure," Heris murmured. "Plus thirty or forty years—I forget how old she'd be by now. Anyway she's taller." Her aunt the admiral had silver hair now, even more striking against her dark face. She still had the Algestin accent, as she identified herself and suggested that Heris watch the rest in private.

"How'd she know I was here?" asked Meharry suspiciously. "Is this going to have a compulsion component in it?"

"I doubt that. Family matters, mostly. Stay, if you want; I'm not sensitive to dirty laundry at the moment."

"No thanks. I don't want more than one Serrano mad at me." Meharry stalked out, very much like a cat twitching its tail after being sprinkled with water. Heris didn't laugh.

Instead, she started the datastream again. Her aunt the admiral . . . someone she had dreamed about being, as a girl. Someone she had hoped to impress, as a young officer. Someone she had thought of as a mentor, and even a friend.

Someone who had not come to her rescue when she needed it desperately.

Now that dark face with the silver aureole wasted no time in apology. "Heris: I trust that you will hear me out, no matter how bitter you are. This is critical material, and it may be my only chance to brief you. I am still not sure who kept me from finding out about your trouble, and at the moment that's no longer a priority item. The future of the Familias Regnant and the Regular Space Service is—"

A full hour later, Heris sat back and drew a long breath. In the same organized, concise way that had earned her an admiral's stars two years ahead of anyone else in her cohort, her aunt had laid out what she knew of the factional disputes within the Regular Space Service, and where the present political stress might rupture the Fleet. She had been given her aunt's best guess on which family members to trust, which senior officers to trust, where certain fragrant bones were buried . . . assuming that she could trust her aunt.

The memory of the last moments of the cube came back full force. Admirals apologized rarely; her aunt had once explained, at a family party when Heris was still a student and her own stars were years in the future, that that was because they planned ahead and had no need to. But the good ones could and did, her aunt had said, when they must. She had believed her aunt was a good admiral . . . her aunt, who had apologized for her own and the family's betrayal.

"I love you, Heris," her aunt had said at the last. "I hope you believe that, if nothing else. With the trouble coming . . . I want you to know that I consider you one of the best Serranos of your generation. And one of the best young officers we had, too."

It would take a long time to digest everything in the cube.

If it was true . . . but she felt that it was true. It felt right, and she'd always had good intuitions about that. And if true, then she thought she understood some things Livadhi had not told her.

The sooner they were off this station the better. Deep space was going to be a lot safer for everyone for a while.

The Captains Guild dining room on Zenebra Station had the usual quiet, respectable atmosphere, not quite as stultifying as the Senior Officers' Club at a sector headquarters, but almost. Two tables away, a merchant captain in the uniform of a major line dined alone, without looking up; across the room, a quiet group of officers from another line chatted while waiting to be served.

Barin had recoiled from the menu's prices at first. "I'm treating you," Heris said. "Have something you like."

"It's all so . . . fancy."

"Not really. Only a step up from any ordinary restaurant on dockside. You've been eating Academy chow too long. If you want to see fancy, you should see Lady Cecelia's tables. I couldn't believe it when I first went to work for her. She thinks every meal should be a work of art."

He wavered, uncertain. Heris took a guess, from his eye movements, and ordered for him, waving away his objections. "Maybe it *is* just curiosity, but if you don't like it you can always get yourself a basic cube of processed goo afterwards."

"But Lassaferan snailfish?"

"You wanted it; I could tell. You might like it; I do."

He relaxed, bit by bit, as he worked his way into the food with youthful appetite. Heris asked no questions, letting him tell her what he would about himself. Jerd and Gesta's oldest son, normal Fleet childhood—which meant in and out of service creches. Academy prep school: he had graduated fifth in his class there. Academy: he had been second to a brilliant daughter of an admiral, who'd been killed in her first assignment when a glitch in a powerplant readout turned out to be a real problem in the powerplant, not the readout. Heris wondered about that, after her aunt's report. *Top Fleet officers are losing too many of their children—the best ones—in accidents in the first two years out of the Academy.* Of course those were the dangerous years. Youngsters full

Elizabeth Moon

of book knowledge, eager to prove themselves—they got into trouble. So had she. But someone had been there to get her out, and if her aunt was right, there were fewer rescues these days.

This boy, though—he was bright enough, and good enough. She liked the way he described his first tour, as ensign on a cruiser. He didn't reveal anything he shouldn't—even though she was a family member and former Fleet officer—and yet he didn't appear to be holding back.

"Communications," she mused, when he ran down. "You know, when I was commissioned, we didn't have FTL communications except from planetary platforms. I was on *Boarhound* when they mounted the first shipboard ansible, and at first it was only one-way, from the planet to us. That was still pretty exciting. Then they worked out how to get enough power for transmission."

"It's still not unlimited," he said, and flushed.

"No, I know that." She didn't tell him how. He didn't know about Koutsoudas and didn't need to. "But someday I expect they'll figure out ways to give us realtime communication in all situations. Something in jumpspace would be a real help." An understatement. A way to communicate in and out of jumpspace would radically change space warfare. "But that's beside the point—you're going back to see the admiral?"

"Yes, sir. Ma'am."

Heris chuckled. "Either will do. Tell her from me that I don't entirely understand, but I have heard what she's saying. Can you do that?"

"Of course, sir."

"Good. And tell her—tell her I love her."

He flushed again, but nodded. Heris was almost glad to see that embarrassment; an honest young man would be embarrassed to repeat such a message, but he would do it. Coming from him directly, it would have the effect she wanted.

She looked at the chronometer on the wall. "Sorry to leave you, but I've work scheduled. If there's anything I can do to assist, feel free to call on me." He pushed back his chair, with a last glance at a dessert guaranteed to cause heart failure in anyone over twenty, but Heris waved him down. "No—finish that, don't waste it. I'll take care of everything on the way out. Give my regards to family." Meaning everyone but the aunt admiral; he could interpret that how he liked. But, polite to the end, he stood until Heris had left the dining room. She hoped he would sit back down and finish that dessert. He had earned it.

The next day, Cecelia arrived without warning. "I had to take a standby seat on the shuttle," she explained. "People are leaving in droves, of course." Heris had noticed that; half the ships docked when they arrived had already left. "But I wanted to talk to you."

"Here, or en route to your next destination?" Heris asked. "If you want to leave, I need to file with the Stationmaster."

"Here for now. I might even go back down once more, to talk to Ari." Cecelia paused, and gave Heris a sharp look. "What's happened? Did you and Petris have a fight? You look upset about something."

"It's not Petris," Heris said, annoyed to feel the heat rising in her face. "It's my family . . . they sent someone to talk to me."

"About time." Cecelia kicked off her boots and wiggled her toes luxuriously. "Ahhh. I was standing in line for two hours. Standing in line is a lot worse than walking."

"Agreed," Heris said. She hoped Cecelia would stay on another topic, but that was too much to expect.

"Your family sent someone," she said. "I hope whoever it was crawled on his or her belly and licked your toes."

"Cecelia!" Despite herself, Heris couldn't help laughing. "What a disgusting thought! No, it was a very nice young man, just out of the Academy, my aunt admiral's grandson."

"Apologetic," Cecelia said.

"In a way. Not personally, but on behalf of. And she sent a datacube herself. It's just—I'm still not sure I understand."

"I know I don't understand. Why didn't she help you?"

"She says she didn't know in time. She wants to talk to me about it, if it's convenient."

"And you?"

"I want to think it over," Heris said.

"Heris, I want to ask you something."

"Of course." Heris seemed relaxed and alert at once, no tension in her face.

"Do I seem different since my rejuvenation? I don't mean the obvious . . . something else."

Heris took a sip of coffee before answering. "The obvious—your body, your hair color. I'm not sure about the rest. A young person is supposed to have more energy, so I presume that along with a younger body, a healthier body, you have more intrinsic energy. Is that right?"

"Yes, but that's not exactly—"

"No . . . I'm feeling my way. You are different, in behavior as well as body, but I'm not sure which caused which. You were never . . . ah . . . passive." Cecelia snorted at that attempt to be tactful. Heris grinned at her. "Look, even as an old lady, you were energetic, feisty, and stubborn. Now your body's younger, and you're even more energetic, feisty, and stubborn. High-tempered. But I didn't know you when you were this age the first time around, so I can't say if you're changed."

That was the crux of it, right there. Heris hadn't been born when she had been forty. What she was right now wasn't really forty—it was eighty-seven in a forty-year-old mask. "I'm not really forty, Heris," she said, trying not to sound as frustrated and annoyed as she was. "I have all the experience of the next forty-seven years. All of it. What I need to know is whether the treatment changed me—the person I am—and sent me off on a new course."

"Mmm. I would say that it had to. The course of a life without rejuvenation, for someone your age—you were preparing to detach, to relinquish your grip on life itself—"

"Not *yet!*" Cecelia said. "I was only eighty-four; I'd have had another twenty years—"

"But you'd given up competitive riding; you'd gradually reduced your social contacts. All signs that you accepted, however reluctantly, the evidence of age. You expected to enjoy your remaining years, but you weren't pushing toward anything new."

"True, I suppose." She didn't like to hear that analysis, but she could not deny the evidence.

"Now you've been put back, physically at least, to your most productive period. You have twenty to thirty years of vigorous activity before you begin the decline again—unless you renew the process. That has to change your course—you could not fail to act differently now than three years ago."

"I had a visitor, that man—"

"Yes." Heris's voice chilled; clearly she didn't like Pedar.

"He's a multiple Rejuvenant. He thinks I should . . . identify myself with them."

"Who?"

"Those who have rejuvenated with the new procedures; those who expect to renew their rejuvenations. They have adopted customs for identification, for interaction. Given the age of the procedure itself, most of those who have used it are my age or younger."

"I thought it had been around for eighty years or so," Heris said.

"It has. But remember that it competed at first with the old procedure, which had proven its safety." Heris couldn't remember, of course. She herself just remembered a discussion of the new procedure, then far more expensive than the standard. By the time she was thirty, it had gained some ground. But it was incompatible with the earlier procedure. No one who had the Stochaster could then have the Ramhoff-Inikin. Lorenza had been one of the first to test—illegally, at the time—the safety of repeated rejuvenation with the new procedure. Cecelia had been nearly fifty when the laws forbidding serial rejuvenation were changed. She explained this, aware of the gaps in her own knowledge. She had been so sure she wouldn't choose rejuvenation that she had ignored most of the arguments about it.

"There's always been age stratification," Heris said slowly. "Particularly those who have attained prestige or power— the older they are, the more they hold. But if there's a sizable group now which is . . . immortal . . ." Cecelia could tell from the pause that the word bothered her. "I see the potential for more rigid stratification, even alienation."

"That's what bothers me," Cecelia said. "I've always been rich; I've always known that my life wasn't anything like the average. I've enjoyed my wealth, but felt that it was fair because I was going to die someday and someone else would have everything I had owned. True, most of it would go to other rich people—my family—but I wasn't trying to hang on to it. From what Pedar said, I'd suspect that others are. Lorenza certainly was. And I feel my own ambition stirring, along with the changes in my body. I won the All-Union championship before; I could do it again."

"How many times?" Heris asked.

"I don't know. I never tired of it when I could still do it; the feel of riding a great course is like nothing else. Mind and body together—stupid riders, no matter how athletic, don't survive, and clumsy smart ones don't either. Yet, in the field I care most about, the prizes are limited. I've won Wherrin, I've won Scatlin, I've won Patchcock—"

"Patchcock!" Heris stared at her. Cecelia had not wanted her train of thought interrupted, and glared back.

"Yes, Patchcock. It's not the equestrian center Wherrin is; it's uglier, for one thing. Not really an ag world. But they have a circuit of five or six major events, in the uplands, and—"

"Patchcock is politically unstable," Heris said.

"That's since my time," Cecelia said, and shrugged. She had not been back since winning the Patchcock Circuit Trophy twice in a row and then losing to Roddy Carnover, after the fall that broke her leg in several places. That had been . . . had been over forty years before. She took a breath and went on.

"My point is, I've achieved all the goals that attract event riders in the Familias. I could compete in the Guerni Republic, I suppose, or even beyond, though the travel times get to be fierce. But why? Suppose I did win the All-Union title forty years in a row—and then rejuved again and won it forty times more. I can't see that, even though I love riding and want to keep doing it."

"And this Pedar—"

"My goals," Cecelia said, "have always been limited. I did learn to manage my own investments, after my parents died, but only so that I had plenty of money to pursue my real interest—the horses. I didn't really care about gaining power in those organizations, running them—there's not time, you see. And horse people have always had more contact with other social strata . . . you can't compete with horses unless you're active in the stable as well. Not mucking out all the stalls, no—again, there's no time—but you aren't likely to be stupidly contemptuous of those who do. Horses are natural levelers, and not only when they dump you in the mud."

"But equestrians have always been rich. . . ." Heris said.

"Yes, and no. The really good ones from poor families get

corporate sponsorship, just as really good singers and dancers and actors get sponsorship. While those of us who do it think of riding as recreational, its position in the economy is actually entertainment . . . the recreation of the audience, not the participant. So there's been access for the equestrian with less talent." Cecelia frowned, remembering that she had told Heris about her own misuse of power and money against a talented junior. Best get that over with. . . . "Of course there are abuses. I did it myself, as you know. But in general, there are openings."

"Don't you think the other Rejuvenants will get as tired of chasing their prizes as you say you will become of chasing eventing titles?"

"I'm not sure—I'm afraid not. By the nature of the system, an equestrian's goals are limited. But someone whose joy is gaining economic or political power . . . what will stop him?"

"I . . . see."

"Lorenza, for instance. Where would she have stopped? Had her ambition any limits? And the more benign Rejuvenant, someone like Pedar—" Though, even to herself, she had trouble with that label. Pedar benign? Better than Ross, but still.

"If the ambition has no natural saturation, then the split between generations gets worse. I see your point. The logical answer is expansion, opening new opportunities. . . ."

"And the Familias Regnant has never been an expansive system," Cecelia said.

"No, but we both know who is." Heris looked worried enough now. "Just how long do you suppose the Benignity has had this process? And did they think of the implications back at the first?"

"It's like training," Cecelia said. Heris looked confused. "The inexperienced or incompetent trainer attempts to control everything through the horse. The good trainer controls *herself*."

"That sounds like something Admiral Feiruss used to say," Heris said. "You can't control anyone else until you can control yourself—"

"Not only until, but only by means of," Cecelia said, glad to have found common ground at last. "It is your control of your own body that allows you to give the signals needed, and notice if they're understood. The bad rider flounders around, blaming the horse that 'isn't paying attention' when he's given so many signals that the horse is confused."

"I've had instructors like that," Heris said with a grin. "I remember one—always yelling at us to pay attention to him, then telling us to concentrate on something else, then yelling again—I couldn't tell if it was more important to watch him or the demonstration."

"What I'm afraid of, with this group Pedar talks of, is that they'll try to control everything else before themselves." Cecelia wasn't going to let Heris wander off on side roads of memory. "I don't want to be around people like that."

It had been easy to say that, but in real life—in practical terms—she wondered what difference it might make. Cecelia clipped the blue-and-silver ring to her ear and grimaced into the mirror. It felt like the first time she had worn a competition number, all those decades ago: she was declaring herself part of something she didn't understand. Although she had a much better idea of what competitive riders were like than she had of her fellow Rejuvenants. She didn't know what kind of reception she would get—if anyone else would notice.

"Ah . . . Lady Cecelia." The bank officer's gaze had snagged briefly on the ring; she noticed that he had two, one in each ear. "And how may we assist you today?"

"I'm going to be traveling to agricultural research worlds, picking up equine samples for my breeding farm on Rotterdam," Cecelia said. "I may be out of touch for extended periods, and I wanted to be sure that there were no problems with my line of credit."

"I wouldn't expect any," the man said. "So far the political situation has had no effect on commerce; certainly our institution is stable—"

"I wasn't doubting it. Only my travel advisors pointed out that some of the worlds I want to visit are served only by ansible, for anything beyond a system transfer."

"Ah . . . do you have a list of these worlds?"

"Yes—" Cecelia handed it over. "Ordinarily, I could deal with an agency that specializes in equine genetics, but I'm looking for something I can't really define. I'll know it when I see it—"

"Yes . . ." He didn't sound interested; he probably wasn't. Then he looked up. "I think the best thing would be a batch dump to the local systems' registered financial institutions. That way, they'd have your references when you arrived, and your line of credit would be established at both ends. Can you estimate your needs?"

Cecelia had that information as well, and he fed it into his desktop. "We're leaving Zenebra shortly," she said, as she waited. "Can you give me an estimate of clearance times?"

"Unless your yacht is faster than anything I ever heard of, your local approvals will all be waiting days before you arrive, milady. And—may I say it's good to see you back in competition. I hope you find the right mount for next year's trials."

The assumptions took her breath away, but she merely nodded her thanks and returned to the ship. The ring in her ear felt huge, heavy with responsibilities she didn't want.

CHAPTER SIX

Castle Rock

Ronnie knew perfectly well he'd been dismissed. His aunt wouldn't listen to him; Heris Serrano, while she might have had good advice, wouldn't help him directly. And Raffa wouldn't answer his calls. He went to George, and poured out his troubles. George's solution, which would have been adequate a year before, now seemed childish.

"I don't *want* to make Raffa jealous," he said. "I don't care about singers, or dancers, or . . . or anything else."

"Then take the bold captain's advice and go do something brave and wonderful, and impress Raffa. She'll come around." That in the confident voice of a young man whose heart had never been shaken.

"It's easy for you," muttered Ronnie. George was perilously near to odiousness again. As far as he was concerned, he had been plucked from life's tree to lie sodden in the gutter, a dead leaf.

"Tell you what," George said. "I'll go with you. It *is* dull, with no more Royals to play games, with no regimental ditties for dancing. Let's go explain to Bunny and my father how useful we can be, if they'll just give us the appropriate errand for two handsome, talented, brave young men."

"You're ridiculous," Ronnie said, but his heart lifted a little, a dead leaf still, but one that might blow where the wind sent it. He let George make the call, and the appointment.

"And don't tell your parents," George said after he had

named the day and hour. "It's all their fault, remember, and you're furious with them."

He wasn't, really. It wasn't their fault; they had tried, and Aunt Cecelia had simply gone off like fireworks. But he understood George's point. It was hard enough to have them lurking around trying to cheer him up about Raffa; if they knew he was about to go do something, they'd hover even more.

Ronnie let George explain that they both felt they could be of use to the new government—that they had unique talents which should be exploited. He halfway expected Lord Thornbuckle and George's father to laugh at them and send them away. But instead, they exchanged significant looks.

"You're serious," Lord Thornbuckle said. "You would be willing to go anywhere and do anything?"

"Well . . ." George looked at Ronnie. "Perhaps not *quite* anything. I mean, if you had in mind sweeping streets in some benighted mining village, I'd rather not. Be a waste of our abilities, anyway."

"And you see your abilities as?"

"Discreet, loyal young gentlemen of the world, able to take care of themselves, strong, healthy, the usual. Intelligent enough, ingenious—" That did get a laugh, from George's father.

"Ingenious, yes. That's how you nearly got yourself killed, wasn't it? But we might have something suitable for two young wastrels, at that."

"It's fairly complicated," Lord Thornbuckle said. "And it's extremely confidential. If you were still on active service, we could not possibly share this with you." That sounded serious enough. Ronnie tried for an expression of intelligent interest. To his surprise, Lord Thornbuckle started by talking about rejuvenation.

"Most people now use the Ramhoff-Inikin method, which allows serial rejuvenations—"

"Up to how many?" George asked.

"I don't know," Lord Thornbuckle said. "Anyway, the pharmaceuticals used in this process are manufactured in the Guerni Republic, or under their license in a few other places. Most are imported from the Guernesi, simply because of their known quality. They developed the process; they know it best. And, of course, it was originally illegal in the Familias, so people had to go there to have it done."

"Why was it illegal?" George asked.

"It's a long story that doesn't concern you," Lord Thornbuckle said. "It's not illegal now, but most of our supply still comes that way. Now. You know that Lorenza was involved in the distribution of illicit pharmaceuticals, right?"

"Like what happened to George and the prince," Ronnie said, nodding.

"Yes. And others—some we know, and some we suspect. Lady Cecelia's medical reports suggest that some of these drugs are very similar to variants of the rejuvenation drugs. We are concerned that our supply of Ramhoff-Inikin drugs might be adulterated at some point between the manufacturer and the user. The Guernesi ship by commercial carrier, and something Heris Serrano said made us wonder about the security of those shipments. If the Compassionate Hand wanted to cause us real trouble, adulterating those drugs— perhaps contaminating them with mind-altering components— would be a good start."

"So," Kevil Mahoney said, before George could interrupt, "it would be very useful to us if you could take a sample of these drugs back to the Guerni Republic and have them analyzed. Are they still what we paid for? If not, what would be the effects of using them in the rejuvenation procedure? What symptoms should we look for in multiple Rejuvenants that suggest a misuse of the drugs?"

"You want us to go—with some drug samples?" George sounded insulted.

"It would be helpful, yes. And the data we've collected so far. We'd been wondering whom we could trust to hand-carry these things; it's not something we want to risk to ordinary shipping."

"You've got perfect cover," Mahoney pointed out. "Young men, rich and fun-loving, the sort who would ordinarily be running off to distant places for the fun of it. Everyone knows Ronnie and Raffaele Forrester-Saenz broke up; everyone suspects the reasons. What's more natural than fleeing from the constraints of home? Especially since your aunt had been there, and you might have legitimate questions about her medical treatment."

"I might?" Ronnie felt humiliated enough to hear older men discussing his lack-of-love life.

"Of course. She came back and sued your parents; you might be questioning whether her rejuvenation—which did not involve suspect drugs, since it was done there—had influenced her mind, or whether the original attack did."

"Oh."

"How are we going to keep the samples from being stolen?" asked George. They had adjourned to George's suite at his father's house, where they could be reasonably sure they were free of intrusive recorders.

"Why would they be? If no one knows we're carrying them—"

"But if someone suspects—"

"Look—you heard what they said. I've got the perfect excuse for going to the Guerni Republic. My aunt was rejuvenated there, and her doctors asked for clarification of the records—"

"They won't let you look at her records!"

"How do you know? They have different laws—maybe their laws don't say anything about medical confidentiality. Besides, I can ask—they don't have to answer."

"I suppose that makes sense." George reached out and took a handful of tawny grapes. "These are good—I wish we were traveling with your Aunt Cecelia. I've never forgotten the food her gardeners and cooks put on the table."

"Which brings up how we will travel. It will be too obvious if we take a private yacht."

"We're going *commercial*?"

"Yes, and not even a major line. Your father suggested a mixed-cargo vessel."

George wrinkled his nose. "Blast him. He's afraid we'll get into trouble on a big passenger liner. He should know better by now."

Ronnie shrugged. "Well, unless you want to pop for the ticket yourself, we haven't much choice." His parents, faced with a lawsuit from his aunt, were busily divesting themselves of assets, trying to lessen the blow. That meant his usual generous credit line had been pared down, if not to the bone at least well beneath its usual cushion.

"No. My father says this is no time for us to show off

our wealth, and I'm not in the Royals anymore, so I don't need that size allowance. I think he's trying to get me to go *do* something with my life. You know?"

"I know." Ronnie stared at the wall, took a deep breath, and intoned, "It's time you made something of yourself young man, and when I was your age I had already—that speech."

"He doesn't say it like that, but he's hinting. At least he's not pushing me to take classes at the University."

"Brun had fun on a mixed-cargo ship," Ronnie said. "We should be able to survive."

Survival won out over fun, when they discovered that there were no—absolute zero—eligible girls on the *Sekkor Vil*. No eligible anythings, in fact; the other passengers were bored middle-aged middle managers on business trips. Once they discovered that Ronnie and George were Chairholders' sons, and not active in any corporation, they went back to their handcomps and ignored them. Ronnie spent hours with the Guernesi language tapes, because it was better than listening to George complain about the way the cards fell when they tried to play a hand.

Finally they arrived in the Guerni Republic and transferred to a local line for the run to Music. At last there were other passengers, not only Guernesi, and not all over forty. Ronnie had no trouble enacting the rich young man, and although he missed Raffa, he had to admit that evenings spent dancing in the passenger lounge were more restorative than those spent lying in the bunk wishing she were there.

On Music, they delivered their samples, and the datacubes, to the pharmaceutical industry's combined quality control laboratory. "We'll have the preliminary results in a day or so," the director said. "But you'll want more precise tests, if anything shows up. If these were not manufactured here, for instance, I presume you would like some idea where else they might have been made."

"Well . . . yes." Ronnie hadn't known that was possible.

"You're not a chemist or pharmacist," the man said. It wasn't a question at all.

"No," he said. He hated to admit he was nothing but an ignorant errand boy, but that was the truth.

"I understood that you had the . . . er . . . confidence of

your new prime minister or whatever you call him." That with a doubtful look, as if he might have fabricated the whole thing.

"Yes . . . that is, he's a good friend of our family."

"Mmm. Well . . . we'll be in touch. If you'll just give me your local address." Clearly a dismissal. Ronnie looked at George and shrugged. Whatever the man thought, they *were* the Familias in this matter, and when he viewed the cube he would probably feel differently about it. In the meantime, they had a world to explore.

Naturally, they spent that evening discovering the many ways in which young people of the city amused themselves.

"Let's not stay too long anywhere," George said, as he watched two stunning women stroll out of the bar they were just entering.

"Mmm. No." Ronnie, with Raffa at the back of his mind, was more interested in music. He had chosen this bar not quite at random, from the music drifting out when the door opened. "Come on, George—we still haven't eaten yet."

"That's not what I meant," George said, but he settled at the table Ronnie chose, and punched up the table's menu. "Ah—I'm hungry too, and they have an illustrated menu. Makes up for their incomprehensible language." George, having declined to "waste any time" with the Guernesi language tapes, was finding it difficult without his usual audience for repartee. Ronnie, who had known he had no aptitude for language learning, now had a serviceable set of travelers' phrases, although he suspected his accent was atrocious. Ronnie leaned back and looked at the musicians clumped on a tiny stage. He saw two instruments new to him, one with strings and one that he guessed was a woodwind. His gaze drifted toward the bar itself . . . and he grabbed George's arm.

"George—look over there. Who's that remind you of?"

"Who—good lord, it is. Gerel. But he's dead—your aunt said he died on her yacht."

"Well, *that's* not dead. If it's not Gerel, it must be a clone. Do you suppose the Guernesi did it?" Through Ronnie's mind ran all the grisly possibilities he'd ever heard of, mostly from wild adventure yarns. Clones developed from the cells of dead men, raised to seek vengeance on murderers and the like.

"It hasn't been that long—I thought they took years to grow." George, clearly, was thinking of the same stories.

"We'd better find out," said Ronnie. "Suppose Aunt Cecelia was wrong? Someone ought to know." Memory tugged at him with that phrase. Who'd said that, with disastrous results? He watched the prince—or his clone—take a long swallow of something in a tankard. It had to be the prince. That way of holding his head, the way his shoulders moved when he drank—it couldn't be anyone else.

"Wait for me," he said. "I've got to check this out." Without hearing whatever George tried to say, he moved closer, his awareness narrowing to the young man at the bar as if he were a hunter stalking prey. When he was close enough, he cleared his throat; the young man looked around, the very picture of slightly bored courtesy.

"Excuse me," Ronnie said. "I believe we met—you're Gerel—"

"You're mistaken," the young man said, interrupting. "My name is Gerald Andres Smith, but we've never met." His eyes had betrayed him, with a moment of fear now shuttered in caution.

"Ah," said Ronnie, who had no idea what to say next. This close, the young man looked exactly like the prince, but a prince not as stupefied as he had been in the last few years. Even the little scar on the temple, from the time he'd fallen against a goalpost playing soccer. "I'm . . . sorry to bother you," Ronnie went on. "But you remind me very much of someone I grew up with. Extraordinary resemblance."

"I'm sorry," the young man said, with what appeared to be genuine sorrow. "But I think we need not continue this conversation. Under the circumstances."

"But—" Ronnie felt a little nudge under his pocket and glanced down. Something glinted there, something his mind recognized, refused, and recognized again.

"I'm sorry," the young man said again. "But I'm not going back."

"But I didn't mean—" Ronnie got that out as fast as he could. The young man's eyes, Gerel's eyes, met his.

"Whatever you meant, it's trouble for me. I don't want trouble. I want to live here, and be left alone. My treatments are almost finished."

"Ronnie—what's wrong?" That was George, finally aware that Ronnie was in trouble. But he was in danger too. Ronnie couldn't think what to do or say. Then he glanced beyond George, and saw another prince—or clone—or whatever they were.

"We need to go outside," said the one whose weapon nudged his ribs. "Don't we?"

Anti-terrorism lectures had instructed Ronnie that going with an abductor made things worse—resist in place, he'd been told. But the lectures hadn't told him about the sudden hollow feeling under his breastbone, or the way his knees would tremble, when he thought about the weapon pressed to his side. And he was sure this was Gerel, whom he'd known all his life. Gerel might want to have their postponed duel at last, but he was honorable . . . wasn't he?

"Are you planning to kill us outside?" he asked, just to be sure.

"I very much hope not," the young man said. "But it's imperative that we talk without witnesses, and I don't intend to argue with you."

Much more decision than Gerel had shown in years, but Ronnie felt vaguely comforted. "All right," he said. "Don't hurt George. He went through enough last time."

The young man's mouth twitched. "I know. But we can't talk about it here. Come on."

George, who had been stopped from an outburst by the same surprise as Ronnie, said plaintively, "But who *are* you?"

The two identical young men gave each other quick, amused glances. "Gerald Smith," they said in unison.

Herded between the two Geralds, Ronnie and George found themselves moving along a crowded street, then into a less crowded one, and finally into a tiny tavern opening on a square with a fountain.

"I didn't know there were places like this here," George said, looking around. It was empty except for an aproned woman behind the bar, and the four of them. "Until now, the Guernesi have been entirely too practical for my taste—everything modern and convenient." Ronnie wondered if his unconcerned tone fooled the Geralds—it didn't fool him.

"This is modern and convenient," one Gerald said. "The Guernesi simply have a different style of modern and convenient. They like small gathering places that cater to particular clients."

"Like clones?" George said, as if determined to make a point of it.

"Clones aren't illegal in the Guerni Republic," the same Gerald said. "In fact, clone work groups are common, even preferred for some occupations."

"Like abducting people?" George said. Ronnie wanted to throttle him—hadn't he learned his lesson on the island? Did he still think he was invincible?

"The odious George," said the other Gerald, almost affectionately. "You haven't changed a bit."

"You are the prince's clones," Ronnie said. He hardly believed it, even now. They looked steadily back at him, then sighed in unison. It was eerie.

"Yes," one of them said. "We are. Illegally created, in the Familias Regnant, to be the prince's doubles when necessary. No one was supposed to know about us, except the necessary few." The other one snorted, a knowing snort, and Ronnie looked at him.

"A secret kept by a couple of doctors, implant-tape technicians, the odd crown minister, the king's immediate family, and who knows what other oddments can hardly be called a secret."

"Did Gerel know about you?" asked Ronnie.

"Oh, yes. He thought it was some kind of game. He wished we could all be together like brothers—he missed his brothers a lot, I think—but of course that was impossible. The only times we were together, in that sense, was when we underwent the matching programming."

"Which is?" George asked.

"Conditioning tapes shared among us, so that we all knew what the public persona was supposed to know, and anything of Gerel's that they felt we needed. Cosmetic alterations to match appearance, following any trauma." The clones touched the matching scars that had convinced Ronnie they had to be Gerel himself. "And no, that didn't hurt. They were humane, our controllers, if you look at it that way."

"I don't think I do," said George. "It doesn't seem fair—"

They both shrugged. "No one chooses a birth," the one

on the left said. "It was a better life than many. Privilege, wealth, an endless party in a way. You know that."

"Yes." Ronnie found it hard to remember clearly how he had thought two years ago—it was embarrassing, really— but he knew he, like the prince, had assumed limitless privilege, boundless wealth, and constant entertainment were his birthright.

"I owe you an apology, really," said the one on the right.

"For threatening me?"

"No . . . for causing trouble between you and the prince. The quarrel was really my fault," the clone said. He traced designs on the tabletop with the condensation from his beer mug. "Gerel Prime had lost interest in that singer months before, but I hadn't. Her voice—I don't know what you did in your time with her, but I was learning opera, you see. She thought it was touching that the prince really cared about music. I prolonged the relationship, so it overlapped with yours. You were jealous, I think—and she certainly found you a better bed partner than I, who cared only for her voice."

"If you'll excuse my mentioning it," George said, "you seem to be . . . er . . . brighter than the prince was toward the end."

"We're clones, but we're not the same person he was. We can't be. Identical twins—bionatural clones—were like that too. Each an individual person, even if outsiders couldn't tell them apart. We have similarities built into the genome, but we're not determined. I happen to love old-fashioned opera; the prince himself had an ear for music, but preferred instrumental."

"And that's *that* Gerald," the other said. "I too have the inborn ear for music, but my preference is far more popular; since I've been here I've discovered *casanegra*, which they tell me is descended from an entirely different Old Terran tradition than opera."

Ronnie glanced from one to the other. "I can't deal with this Gerald A. and Gerald B.," he said. "If you don't help me out, I swear I'll give you nicknames, both rude."

"You forget," the clone said, "that we're armed and dangerous."

"So shoot me," Ronnie said. "But I'm not going to struggle with it." The clones looked at each other, and finally nodded.

The one on the left spoke first. "I'm Andres and he's Borhes. Borhes and opera; Andres and casanegra, if you can keep that straight."

"I don't see why, if you're clones, you're not identical mentally as well," George said. "What's the use if you're not?"

"Identity is more than genes," Andres said. "I didn't understand it all myself, until the medical experts here explained it as they tried to figure out which of us was which. I always knew who *I* was, even when others got us confused. And Bor knew, and . . . and the others, whatever names they might have chosen, if they'd had the chance. And Gerel I suppose."

"When he wasn't so confused he didn't know day from night," Borhes put in. "And in case you wondered, apparently we never got the full dose of the drugs used on Gerel. They tell us we're normal. But even though we're identical at the genetic level, developmentally there are always minute differences in brain structure resulting from exactly which neurons connect with which in what order."

"But why didn't you tell Captain Serrano which was which when she came to take the prince for medical treatment? Or at least explain once you were here? It might have saved—"

"I don't see why we should care," Andres said. "They had us made for their own selfish reasons—yes, we enjoyed a life that was mostly pleasurable, but we had no freedom. Why should we risk anything to help them?"

"I suppose I thought you were a gentleman," said George. Andres laughed unkindly.

"Gentlemen? Clones? I suppose in the historical sense we are, if you think it's all in the blood, but otherwise absolutely not. Not if you mean some ridiculous code of behavior—"

"Which, after all, our Prime didn't adhere to, as you know very well." Borhes grinned at Ronnie. "I don't know what Gerel would have been if he hadn't been drugged, but on the whole he was as little bound by notions of duty as anyone I ever knew. You at your worst were a paragon of dedication beside him."

George flushed, and turned to Ronnie. "I thought your aunt said they were nice young men."

"She also said she was sure that the one who was killed was Gerel himself. A fool, but a noble fool." Ronnie took another direction. "Look—you remember Captain Serrano."

The clones exchanged glances. Andres finally answered. "Of course. An . . . unusual person, we thought."

Undoubtedly. Ronnie wondered if she'd treated them to any of the special methods she'd used on him. "What did you think of her?"

Again the quick exchange of glances; this time Borhes spoke. "Well . . . unusual, as Andres said. Intelligent, perhaps a bit stuffy the way Fleet officers often are."

"And my Aunt Cecelia? I know she talked to all of you."

Borhes looked thoughtful. "She's your aunt? I didn't realize that. She's the one who told the king our Prime was not normal, wasn't she?"

"Yes." Ronnie said no more. They seemed willing enough to rattle on; let them rattle.

"I liked her," Borhes said. It sounded real. "She told us we shouldn't go back; she told us we could make a better life here."

"And she was right," Andres said. "The Guernesi have given us limited citizenship—we can get full rights in five years if we're employed and have a clean legal record. Clones are not only legal, but valued. We'd be crazy to go back."

"I wouldn't ask you to go back," Ronnie said. Had they thought he might? Had that been the core of their resistance? "My aunt would skin me if I did." They grinned at him. "But in your position you might have heard things—things we need to know now, that might help us hold the alliances together. That's what I'd like to ask you about."

Borhes shook his head. "We're a lot safer if we don't know anything—if we did know, did remember, and told you, then the next person who wanted to know mightn't be so friendly. Surely you can see that."

He could. He could imagine a whole series of people who would think the clones must certainly know . . . some of them very rough indeed.

"But we wouldn't have to tell anyone where we got the information," George said.

The clones merely looked at him. Of course that wasn't

enough. Of course they wouldn't trust that. Would they trust anything?

The clones' apartment, when they reached it, was a decent-sized three-rooms-with-bath in an area they said housed many students. Ronnie had tried to convince himself to bolt on the way there—surely the clones wouldn't *really* kill them. If nothing else it would interfere with their citizenship application. But the Gerel who had thrown himself on the gas grenade on Sirialis was dead, from another gallant act: these were only clones, who had already made it clear their ethics did not match Gerel's.

"We'll think of something," Andres said that first night. "We would prefer not to kill you; we're not experienced at this sort of thing and we might botch disposing of your bodies. That way you'd cause us even more trouble. Maybe we can get hold of some drugs to alter your memories or something. In the meantime—" In the meantime meant uncomfortable positions, tethered back to back.

The next morning, Borhes raided their pockets. "Sorry," he said. "But we don't have enough money to feed you and us, and I presume you're hungry."

"We are expected back at the Institute," George said.

"Thanks for reminding us," Andres said, grinning. "I think you need to send a message saying you went somewhere and won't be back for a few decads, at least. Let's see . . . what might two wealthy young men do on this planet besides hang around here? Bor, pick up a travel cube, why don't you?"

With the threat of imminent death, Ronnie found he was quite willing to contact the hotel and explain that they had decided on a tour—no, hold their luggage, they were going horse-packing and would have to buy the survival gear they needed closer to the trailhead. George grimaced when Ronnie got through. "I don't know why you wouldn't go for that cruise," he said. "If anyone asks, Andres, they'll know it wasn't us. Ronnie and me riding horses in the mountains?"

"The cruise ship has constant contact with the shore; it would be easy enough to transfer a query. We inquired, and this tour company offers a real wilderness experience. No comsets at all." Andres smiled. "No one from the Familias is going to try—if they call the hotel, they'll be told you're out of the city, touring. It costs too much, and takes too long, to have a realtime conversation."

* * *

Over the next few days, George kept after the clones whenever he was awake, pointing out repeatedly that they had no plan, that they couldn't hold prisoners in an apartment forever, that someone would eventually find out.

"We could kill you," Andres said finally, in a temper. "At least we wouldn't have to listen to you, even in prison."

"You don't want to kill us," George said. "You know that; you've said that. What you want is decent anonymity, right?"

"Of course."

"Then get plastic surgery." The clones looked at each other, then back at George.

"We like being clones; we're used to it."

"Fine. I'm not asking you to change that . . . but get enough change so that you don't look like Gerel to any casual tourist from the Familias who might happen into a taverna and see you. You can kill us, of course, and you may be right that my father wouldn't be able to find you or extradite you, but if Familias visitors start dying off, the Guernesi are going to notice."

"And you already told us they have a very efficient law-enforcement system," Ronnie added.

The clones looked at each other again. "We're used to looking like this," Borhes said.

"You're also used to being mistaken for Gerel," George said. "But you don't like it. Just a little change—enough that the Familias crown prince isn't the first person that pops into mind when you're seen. Then you could be a normal clone pair here, and no one would ever know."

"Except you two," Andres said.

"And my Aunt Cecelia, and Captain Serrano," Ronnie said. "They haven't spread it around—why do you think we would?"

Andres laughed unpleasantly. "Ronnie—I know you too well. Remember the Royals?"

Ronnie felt himself flushing. "I was a silly young ass then."

"And you are suddenly a wise old graybeard?"

"No. But if I couldn't be discreet, I'd never have gotten my aunt out of that nursing home."

"She didn't tell us that." Were they interested, or just pretending? It didn't matter; Ronnie was more than willing to keep talking if it gave him a chance to live longer.

He spun the tale out, emphasizing everyone's role: George spreading the rumors about a "drop-in" party at the facility that had created the confusion, Brun with her hot air balloon modified with unobtrusive steering apparatus, and the scramble to get his aunt into it. He hadn't told even George all the details, his mingled terror and disgust as he unhooked Cecelia from her medical monitors and dressed her.

"And what did you do then?" asked Andres when he had gotten as far, in the story, as leaving the parking lot at the facility.

"Went home, got out my parasail, and joined our crowd for a party at the beach." The police had found him there sometime after midnight, with witnesses to say he'd been there since late afternoon. And the facility staff had checked him out as he left there, alone. "They knew she hadn't walked off by herself, and they suspected that she'd been—abducted was the word they used—during the Festival, when so many balloons were around. But they couldn't prove anything against me. I kept expecting the attendant who had set up the tape loop to accuse me, but he disappeared. They claimed they had no tape records of any of the patients for that day—that something had happened to them—and Mother threatened to sue them for negligence. I was afraid if she did they'd search harder and find them. Perhaps the attendant ran off with them when he realized Cecelia was gone and his job was forfeit."

"And you didn't confide in anyone?"

"No. It was too dangerous. George knew or suspected that I had something to do with it, but all he'd been told beforehand was to spread those rumors. I knew Brun was going to take Cecelia out in the balloon, but not where—I could guess it was to her family's private shuttle, but from there—I didn't know."

"You would claim this proves your ability to keep secrets?"

"Well . . . yes. Doesn't it?"

"Not really. You just told us, presumably because you're scared. What if someone scared you about us?"

Ronnie sagged, and glanced at George hoping he had a bright idea. But George had gone to sleep, to snore in the irregular, creative way that made sleeping in the same room with him so impossible.

CHAPTER SEVEN

"Raffaele . . ." Her mother's expression hovered between anxiety and annoyance. Raffa blinked. Her mind had drifted again, and the direction it had drifted did no one any good, and would infuriate her mother if she knew.

"Yes?" she asked, trying for a more mature boredom.

"You're thinking about that boy," her mother said. It was entirely unfair that mothers could, breaking all physical laws, practice telepathy.

"He's not a boy," Raffa said, in a counterattack she knew was useless.

"You agreed—" her mother began. Raffa pushed away the untouched breakfast which had no doubt given her mother the evidence needed, and stared out the long windows at the formal garden with its glittering statuary. *The Lady of Willful Mien* gazing scornfully past *The Sorrowful Suitor*. *Boy with Serpent* (she had hidden childish treasures in the serpent's coils) in the midst of the herbs with snake in their names— a silly conceit, Raffa thought now. The group *Musicians* in the shade of the one informal tree (since no one could prune a weeping cassawood into a formal shape) and the line of bronze *Dancers* frolicking down the sunlit stone path toward the unheard music. She pulled her mind back from the memory that led straight from a child fondling the dancers' bronze skirts, to the feel of Ronnie's hand on her arm.

"I agreed to break the engagement. I agreed not to marry him secretly. I did not agree never to think of him again. It would have been a ridiculous agreement."

"Well." Her mother looked pointedly at the congealed remains of an omelet, and then at Raffa. "It will do no good to starve yourself."

"Hardly," Raffa said. She lifted her arms, demonstrating the snug fit of the velvet tunic that had been loose several weeks before.

"Still." Parents never quit, Raffa thought. She wondered if she would have the energy for that when she was a parent herself. Assuming she became one. She supposed she would. Eventually. If Ronnie came back, and his parents quit quarreling with her parents, and so on. In the meantime, she was supposed to look busy and happy. Busy she could manage. She stood up, while her mother still groped for the next opening, and forced a smile.

"I've got to get to the board meeting. Remember that Aunt Marta asked me to keep an eye on her subsidiaries for her?"

"You don't have to go in every day, Raffaele—"

"But I'm learning," Raffa said. That was true. She had known vaguely what sorts of holdings her family had, had understood that whenever certain products changed hands, money flowed into the family coffers, but she had paid far more attention to what she spent her allowance on, than where it came from. "It's actually kind of interesting."

"I should hope so." Delphina Kore had managed her own inherited corporations for years; of course she thought it was interesting. "I just meant—you have plenty of time to learn."

"You used to say, 'when I was your age, I was running DeLinster Elements singlehanded—' " Raffa reminded her.

"Yes, but that was before—when everyone knew rejuv was a one-time thing. Now you have plenty of time—as much as you want."

And parents would live forever, the most effective glass ceiling of all. She would have rejuv herself, when the time came, but she didn't look forward to a long, long lifetime of being the good daughter.

"We might get tired of running things," her mother said, surprising her. Had she been that obvious? Her mother chuckled. "You'll have your turn, and it won't be as far ahead as you fear."

She didn't argue. She rarely argued. She thought about it, calmly and thoroughly, as she did most things.

Brun had wanted to be an adventurer. At least that's what she'd said. Raffa wondered. All those years as a practical joker, a fluffhead party girl . . . had she really changed? Raffa remembered the island adventure well enough. She had been scared; she had killed someone; she had nearly died. She had done well enough, when you looked at the evidence— no panic, effective action—but she wouldn't have chosen that way to maturity, if what she had now was maturity. She had always been the quiet one of the bunch, the one who got the drunks to bed, the injured to the clinic, the doors relocked, and the evidence hidden. She had imagined herself moving happily into an ordinary adult life—ordinary *rich* adult life, she reminded herself. She liked privilege and comfort; she had no overwhelming desire to test herself.

Now . . . Raffa looked at the serious face in the mirror and wondered why she was bothering. Brun, yes—not only her wildness, but her family's flair, if that's what you wanted to call it. Her own family had had no flair, not for generations. Steady hard work, her parents had always told her, made its own luck. Do it right and you won't have to do it over. Think ahead and you won't need good luck.

But Ronnie. Logic had nothing to do with that. She had argued with herself, but her mind had argued back: he was eligible on all counts except that right now his parents and her parents were on opposite sides, politically and economically. Otherwise—they were both R.E., they were both rich, they had grown up together. AND she loved him.

Word had spread that she and Ronnie were no longer an item. She suspected her mother, but it was not something they could discuss, not now. With the Royal Aerospace Service on something like permanent leave, there were more rich young men lounging around, lining the walls at social events, than she had ever known. Cas Burkburnet, who danced superbly and whose parents had something to do with the management of Arkwright Mining. Vo Pellin, a great lumbering bear who could hardly dance at all, but made everyone laugh. Anhera Vaslin and his brothers, all darkly handsome and eager to find wives to take back home. She knew better than that; Chokny Sulet had been a reluctant annexation to the Familias, and the women who went home with its young men were never seen offplanet again.

She had all the dancing, dining, and partying that she

could absorb. If she had been a storycube heroine, it would have defined social success. And like a storycube heroine, she felt stifled by it all. She scolded herself for being self-ish and silly, for remembering the feel of Ronnie's head in her lap—his cold, muddy, unconscious head in her lap—when she was dancing with Cas. She had expected to hear about Ronnie from George Mahoney, who gossiped freely about everyone, no matter which side of a political divide you or they were on, but George had disappeared from social functions at the same time as Ronnie. No one seemed to know where they were, and Raffa couldn't ask pointed questions without brows being raised and word getting back to her mother.

She was delighted, therefore, to get a call from George's father Kevil, who asked her to meet with him and Lord Thornbuckle. She had not been in the Council complex since the king's resignation. But she had grown up hearing about Kevil and Bunny, contemporaries of her parents, long before she had realized that they were important people. Now, as they settled her in a comfortable leather chair and offered her something to drink, she felt an odd combination of maturity and childishness. She was being admitted to adult councils in a way that made her feel even younger than she was.

"Ronnie and George went on a mission for us," Lord Thornbuckle said, after she had accepted coffee and refused thinly sliced nutbread. Raffa clenched her hand on the saucer and set it down before it shook and rattled the cup. Ronnie and George? They had sent those two out together?

"We thought they'd help each other," Kevil Mahoney said. Raffa held her tongue. No use arguing with a lawyer of that class. "It may have been a mistake," he admitted, after a short silence.

"We thought of asking another of their friends—someone from the Royal Aerospace Service—but things are rather . . . delicate at the moment."

"Delicate?"

The two men looked at each other. Raffa felt like scream-ing, but didn't. What good would it do?

"They've disappeared," Lord Thornbuckle said. "And we don't know whom we can trust, in the old administra-tion. We don't know if the reason they've disappeared has something to do with their mission, with something else entirely, or with communications failures. There've been problems recently, as I'm sure you're aware."

Everyone was. The interruption of commercial transfers, even for so brief a period, had panicked the public.

"At the moment, we're dealing with a crisis—more than one, in fact, though you don't need to know all of them. We can't go. We need the information we sent them to get, and we need to know what happened to them. If we send more young men, especially those who've been in the military, it will be noticed in the wrong way."

"You want me to go." Neither of them met her eyes at first. Raffa felt her temper rising. This was ridiculous; they didn't live back on Old Earth, in prehistoric times. "You want me to find Ronnie or George, and you think whoever's up to mischief will believe I'm chasing after Ronnie because of romance."

"That was the idea," said Lord Thornbuckle.

"It's ridiculous," Raffa said. She let herself glare at him. "It's out of a storycube or something. Lovesick girl goes haring after handsome young man in need of rescue. What do you want me to do, wear a silver bodysuit and carry some impressive-looking weapon?" Even as she said it, she realized she would look stunning in a silver bodysuit, and she imagined herself carrying one of the rifles from the island. No. It was still ridiculous.

"People do," Kevil Mahoney said, peering at his fingertips as if they had microprint on them. "People *do* do ridiculous illogical things. Even for love."

Raffa felt herself going red. "Not me," she said. "I'm the sensible one." It sounded priggish, said like that in this quiet room. She opened her mouth to tell Lord Thornbuckle about the times she'd saved Brun from official retribution, and shut it again. That was the past, and didn't matter. "Where?" she asked, surprising herself.

"The Guerni Republic," Lord Thornbuckle said. "Some planet called Music."

"It would be," Raffa said. She felt trapped, on the one hand, and on the other there was a suspiciously happy flutter in her chest. Trapped? No . . . out from under Mother at last, and with a good cause. She was not going out there to be silly with Ronnie, of course not, but . . . "I'll go," she said, as ungraciously as possible, but also quickly. Before she thought about it. Because, underneath it all, she wanted to go. She wanted a chance to get away from her mother, away from everyone, and think. And she wanted to see Ronnie alone, very far away, and make up her own mind.

Traveling alone on a major liner was not an adventure, she told herself firmly. It was nothing like Brun's mad dash across space, working in the depths of livestock freighters and what all. She didn't want that, anyway. She ate exquisitely prepared meals in the first-class dining room, worked out in the first-class gymnasium, flirted appropriately with the younger stewards, and pushed away the occasional desire to measure herself against Brun.

She pored over the tourist information on the Guerni Republic. Her Aunt Marta's holdings included small interests in several Guernesi corporations, inherited through marriage a couple of generations back. Raffa was surprised to find that one of them had its corporate headquarters on Music—handy, but odd. She'd thought it manufactured something used in agriculture—and Lord Thornbuckle had said that planet specialized in medicine. But the headquarters were on the tourist cube as "an example of post-modern business architecture, vaguely reminiscent of the Jal-Oplin style favored in the Cartlandt System two millennia ago." The visual showed an elaborate fountain surrounded by vast staircases that seemed to exist just to create interesting shadows.

Raffa peered at it several ways, and gave up. It didn't really matter what it looked like. She could reasonably visit, as the near relative of a stockholder from the Familias. She composed a short message, and put it in the mail queue. Then she called up the language tutor for another session of Guernesi. She had always enjoyed learning new languages, and Guernesi seemed fairly close to one she'd studied before, the "native" language of Casopayne.

Raffa settled into her rooms at the hotel her travel agent had recommended. She found the Guernesi accent captivating rather than confusing, and her shipboard study had made her comfortable with many routine phrases. She had no idea where Ronnie and George would be staying, but it shouldn't be too hard to find out. The Travelers' Directory listed visitors by homeworld.

The Familias Regnant section had more names than she had expected—and for a moment she let herself wonder what Venezia Glendower-Morreline se Vahtigos was doing there; that redoubtable old lady should have been driving her numerous family crazy at the annual plastic arts festival on Goucault, where she insisted on exhibiting her own creations. Raffa had been at school with one of her nieces, who had had to display a particularly hideous vase and a mask that looked like dripping wax in order to pacify the family artiste. She hadn't thought about Ottala Morreline for a couple of years, at least—she'd wondered at the time if living with her aunt's artwork had warped her mind. But never mind—where was Ronnie?

She found his name, finally, listed as "traveling" rather than at a fixed address. Communications could be left with the Travelers' Directory, the listing said. Great. Ronnie and George had run off somewhere for a little unauthorized fun, and she had no idea when they'd be back. She felt angry, and was annoyed with herself. They didn't know she was coming; it wasn't deliberate. Perhaps a good meal would help. She called up the hotel directory, and decided on the smallest of the dining rooms, described as "quiet, intimate, and refined, yet casual."

The Guernesi definition of quiet, intimate, refined, and casual had tables set into mirrored alcoves. Each alcove was divided from the main room by an arch of greenery from which graceful sprays of fragrant orchids swayed. Once ensconced in her alcove, Raffa discovered that the mirrors reflected only the greenery and the delicate curves of the chandelier . . . not the diners. She glanced casually into other alcoves, just to check—and wondered briefly how the mirrors worked.

She had worked her way through most of her meal, when someone passed in a flamboyant trail of scarlet ruffles that caught her eye. A tall, black-haired woman whose walk expressed absolute confidence in her ability to attract attention. The red dress left the elegant line of her back to no one's imagination, and a drip of diamonds down her spine only emphasized its perfection. Two men in formal dress followed her, one tall, with a mane of red hair, and the other short and stout. Raffa leaned forward, excited despite herself. It had to be Madame Maran, who had toured in the Familias Regnant, though she lived here. Raffa fiddled with the table controls, cut off the sound damping for her alcove so that she could hear the open center of the room.

"Madame—" she heard someone—probably the waiter—say.

Then "Esarah, I *still* think—" and the privacy screen of the other alcove covered the rest. No matter. She had seen the famous diva hardly an arm's length away. She would check the entertainment listings. Perhaps there would be a performance while she was here. She hoped it would be *Gertrude and Lida,* but she would happily listen to Maran sing a grocery list.

She glanced around the tables she could see. And there he was.

The last person she had expected to see was the Familias' former king, but there he sat, spooning up the cold fish soup as if he were at home back on Castle Rock. Raffa blinked and looked down at her own meal. It couldn't be the king. Former king. Former chair of the Grand Council. Wherever he was, he wouldn't be here in the Guerni Republic. Rumor had it that his wife had moved out after his resignation, and returned to her family's estates. Everyone had said he was "helping with administrative matters."

She blinked, but the shape of his face, his way of holding the spoon, did not change. He paused, pressed his hands to his temples a moment, in a gesture she had known from childhood. It had to be the king. It could not be the king.

She lingered over dessert, sneaking furtive glances at the man now placidly working his way through some kind of meat wrapped in pastry. It still looked like the king. Her parents' age, or a little older, but that was hard to tell after a rejuv or so. He held himself like someone used to being served. Anyone would, who stayed in this hotel, and ate in this dining room. He ate quickly, neatly, and refused dessert with a gesture. When he rose, and turned to leave, Raffa looked down, wondered why she didn't smile and greet him.

It was the king. It could not be the king. She would go to bed and think about it tomorrow.

The next morning, the Directory reported no response from

Ronnie or George. Raffa delivered the samples Lord Thornbuckle had given her to the Neurosciences Institute. Then she took a tour of the city's botanic gardens, and discovered that the orchids in the hotel dining room were only one of 5,492 species cultivated on Music. The guide explained more about orchids than anyone on the tour wanted to know, and seemed to think tourists were responsible for the unwanted information. "And *how* many species have been adapted for the production of neuroactive chemicals?" the guide said at the end. No one could answer, and the guide pouted. Raffa looked at the available tours for that afternoon, and decided to work on her Guernesi language cubes.

Traveling alone with the intent to have no adventures continued to be more boring than Raffa had expected. After three days of sensible sightseeing and language practice, with no word from Ronnie and George, she was ready for a change. She was used to having someone to keep out of trouble, which also meant someone to talk to. She had seen the ex-king, and she had no one to tell. Her growing facility with the Guernesi language allowed her to make small talk with hotel employees and tour guides, but she missed the late-night discussions of the day's events. Even her mother, she thought, would be preferable to this empty room with its bland blue, gray, and beige color scheme. It didn't make her feel rested and sleepy; it made her feel like going out to find some color and excitement.

Color and excitement, as the tourist brochures made clear, could be found in the Old City, which was actually newer than the New City, but had been rebuilt to look older. Raffa had found this sort of reasoning on other planets, where war or economic clearances had suggested the profitability of nostalgia. She headed for the Old City, after a discussion with the concierge, who agreed that it was safe at this early hour of the evening.

The New City became the Old City at a dramatic arch. Beyond, the street itself narrowed, but expanded in irregular bays to each side, marked off by changes in paving, colorful plants in decorative tubs, and even the occasional row of formally clipped trees.

Most of the color and excitement aimed at tourists involved displays of Guernesi dancing to music from antique instruments. Raffa wandered into several courtyards, where male dancers in full-sleeved shirts, tight trousers, and boots whirled and stamped, and the musicians plucked the strings of melon-bellied wooden instruments. But this wasn't what she had in mind, she realized. She didn't want to be one of the young women tourists ogling the dancers. Nor did she want to join the tourists in other courtyards ogling buxom female dancers in low-cut blouses and ruffles. From somewhere down the street, a curl of brass slid through the pervasive strumming and lured her on. She almost recognized the melody, but with the competition of clattering boots and the occasional ritual shout "Hey-YA" she couldn't put a name to it.

It came, she discovered, from an open door, not a courtyard. Inside, tables crowded around a low stage. By then the music was over—or interrupted, because she saw the horn player, trumpet tucked under his arm, leaning over to talk to another musician with an instrument she recognized, a violin, on his lap. Two more string players were stretching as they chatted.

"Dama?" When she smiled and nodded, the waiter led her to a table halfway between stage and wall.

She set her elbows on the table and peered at the napkin which, besides suggesting in four languages that the appropriate tip was twenty percent, gave the name of the players. If her Guernesi was sufficient, they were the "Blithe Grasshoppers." Tati Velikos on the "tromp" which had to be trumpet. Sorel Velikos, Kaskar Basconi, Ouranda Basconi, Luriesa Sola. She amused herself during their break by trying to figure out who was who.

The musicians readied themselves again, and Raffa blinked at them. If Tati was the trumpeter, then Sorel must be a twin brother: he looked identical, tall, lean, and dark-haired. And the two Basconis—she assumed the other pair of twins, the women, were the Basconis. They were dark too, though not quite as tall and decidedly bosomy. She had thought Kaskar was a male name . . . Kaskar Aldozina had been one of the historical figures in Guernesi history, and she remembered that the pronoun reference had been male.

She glanced around, suddenly uncomfortable for no reason she could define, and it hit her. At least half those watching came in pairs, triplets, quads—all identical. Another Velikos (she was sure) reached over to hand the musicians some music. Most of the identicals were pairs—twins?—but a few tables away four identical blonde women chatted with three identical blond men—and when Raffa took a second look, she realized that the men and women were, but for differences in hairstyle, dress, and cleavage, identical with each other. Seven faces alike; she shivered. These must be clones. She had heard of them, but never seen them. They were illegal in the Familias space, she knew that much.

The string players began, a sprightly lilting melody Raffa did not know. She looked at them more closely. Were they all clones? They didn't look as much alike as the seven blondes, but there was a family resemblance, even in the fifth player. Raffa tried to tell herself that it was just a matter of different customs; there was nothing *wrong* with clones, and she wasn't in danger or anything. And she liked the music . . . it flirted from violin to cello, tripped into the bass, and then the trumpet plucked it away and flung it out across the room, past all the talk and clink of dishes.

When the music ended, knotted into a tight pattern of chords that left no opening for more variation, Raffa found herself wondering where clone designers found their patterns. That man she had been so sure was the ex-king, for instance . . . could that have been a clone, perhaps? Surely a neighboring government wouldn't make clones of its neighbors' political leaders . . . or would it? Speculation bothered her; she didn't want to wonder about that or anything else.

She had an appointment at the corporate headquarters of Atot Viel the next day. In real life, the arrangement of fountain and stairways made sense; the structure was built into a slope, and the stairs offered open air communication from level to level. Raffa noted that without pausing, and followed the markers set alight by the button that had come with her appointment notice.

The young woman who met her at the reception area seemed to find Raffa's presence entirely understandable. She said, "We'll take you on the usual tour, and then you tell me what else you'd like to see. Your aunt's never visited us herself, but we understood that was for health reasons—"

Raffa, unprepared for that opening, said the first conventional thing that came into her head. "I'm so sorry; I wouldn't know."

"Of course, you can't tell us. We've established no need to know. But if it *is* health, you might want to investigate the medical facilities. Recently one of your prominent citizens benefited from the expertise of the Neurosciences Institute; I'm sure they'd give you references."

"Lady Cecelia," said Raffa, automatically.

"Oh, you know her? Good. We really do welcome stockholder participation, you see, and if your aunt could travel, we would very much enjoy the benefit of her expertise."

Raffa wondered. Aunt Marta's expertise, as far as she had known, consisted of an instinctive grasp of what to sell and what to buy. She never involved herself with management, preferring to live in relaxed comfort, pursuing her hobbies. As for health, she always seemed hale enough to go for month-long camping trips in the mountains behind her main residence. An early experience of Aunt Marta and Lady Cecelia's had convinced Raffa that old ladies were anything but dull and passive, a hope she clung to when surrounded by the senior set at Castle Rock.

Now she followed the young woman along gleaming corridors, wishing she had the foggiest notions what questions to ask. By the time she'd had the usual tour, and collected an armful of glossy brochures, she was ready to quit for the day.

"But you'll come again, I hope," her guide said. "Your aunt's is one of the few licensed facilities using our process." Raffa still wasn't sure what process, but she knew she would have to find out. It would keep her mind off Ronnie.

She had not seen the man who resembled the king for days; she had not forgotten him, but he was no longer part of her anticipation. But the next morning, he appeared again, striding along the carpeted corridor toward the lobby with the firm stride of someone who knows where he's going. Raffa put down the storycube she had just picked up, and watched him. He paused by the concierge's desk, then headed for the doors. Inexplicably, Raffa felt drawn to follow.

"Later," she said to the clerk, and darted through the gift-shop door. The man had already disappeared through the front doors; Raffa stretched her legs and followed. There he was, outside, chatting with the doorman, waiting for a car, no doubt. One of the sleek electric cabs pulled up, and he got in. Raffa waited until it began to move, then went out to the street. The cab moved smoothly away.

"You can't keep us here forever," George said. "Eventually someone will come looking, and you'll have accomplished just what you want to avoid. People who are likely to know you by sight on your trail."

The clone on guard looked at him, an unfriendly stare. "It won't help you."

"But why are you angry with us?" George persisted.

"Remember the commissioning banquet?" the clone asked. George flushed.

"Surely you don't hold that against me—I thought you were him—the prince, I mean."

"I know who you mean," the clone said. "Why does that matter? You were willing to do that—"

"Everyone gets drunk at the commissioning banquet," George said, glancing at Ronnie for support. Ronnie lay back on the bed, eyes shut, but George was sure he wasn't asleep. He couldn't possibly sleep so much. "And after—and the pranks are all traditional—"

"Are you going to try to convince me you drew my name—excuse me, *his* name—from a hat?" The clone made a display of cleaning his fingernails with the stiletto. Over-dramatic, George thought; the bathroom had modern facilities. Then he thought about lying; how could the clone know the name he had really drawn?

"No . . ." he said at last, choosing honesty for no reason he could name. "I drew someone else's, but—I thought I had a grudge."

"Have you ever been glued into your underwear?" The tone was light, but the menace of that blade needed no threatening voice.

"As a matter of fact, yes," George said. "At camp one summer, when I was twelve. Ronnie and I both."

"They were trying to toughen us up, they said," Ronnie said, without opening his eyes. "They'd found out that I liked the wrong kind of music—that I even *played* music." He opened his eyes, and a slow grin spread across his face. "They glued us back to back; we must've looked really silly.

Took video cubes, the whole thing. The counselors finally trashed the cubes, after they'd watched them and snickered for a day or so. George and I spent the time in the infirmary, growing new skin."

"Oh." The clone seemed taken aback. "I—we weren't active then."

"That's why I diluted the mix," George said. "You weren't nearly as stuck as I was."

"What did you do to them?" the clone asked, seeming to be truly interested.

"Nothing . . . really." Ronnie had closed his eyes again. George admired the tone he achieved and waited. Let Ronnie tell it. "There was another boy, not even an R.E., but smarter than all of us put together. He could bypass the read-only safety locks on entertainment cubes."

"You trashed their cubes?"

"Not just that. We replaced their music with . . . other things." Ronnie heaved a satisfied sigh. "Remember, George, how mad that cousin of mine was, Stavi Bellinveau?"

"Yes. And Buttons, too—it was before his stuffy stage," he said to the clone. "He wasn't at all stuffy at fourteen."

"I blame myself," Ronnie said, putting a hand over his heart. "I think it was having to spend the next three weeks listening to an endless loop of all the *Pomp and Circumstance* marches. I should have put at least one waltz on that cube."

The clone glared. "If you're trying to make it clear that you and George share a life I never knew except secondhand, you've succeeded. It doesn't make me like you better."

"No . . . I can see that. But it's not our fault you're what you are. If we'd known, we might have made things easier for you, or harder . . . depends. We were all kids, with kids' idiocies. Rich kids . . . we could be idiots longer than some. It wasn't until my aunt's new yacht captain straightened me out that I began to grow up."

"Heris Serrano," the clone said.

"Yes. You met her—you understand."

CHAPTER EIGHT

Aboard the *Sweet Delight*

Lady Cecelia had debated for several days where to go first after Zenebra. Heris left her to it. She had spent enough time thinking about horses. Now, as the yacht worked its way out of the crowded traffic patterns of Zenebra's system, she concentrated on the crew's training. Koutsoudas worried her, especially in light of her aunt's message. No one but Livadhi knew what he could really accomplish with two bent pins and a discarded chip. An undetectable hyperlight tightbeam comlink, for instance. Cecelia's concern that she could not see clearly where Fleet personnel were concerned warred in her mind with her aunt's trust in her judgment. She would like to believe her aunt, but if she did that, she might as well believe her aunt on everything. Her mind shied away from the implications like a green horse from a spooky fence . . . and that image brought her back to Cecelia.

Inspection. It was more than time for an inspection. Heris checked the set of her uniform before she headed down the passage to crew quarters. As she would have anticipated, the ex-military crew kept their quarters tidy, almost bare of personal identity. The programmable displays that other crew left showing tropical reefs, mountain valleys, or other scenery had been blanked.

Heris continued into the working areas of the ship. The new inspection stickers—real ones, not fakes—made bright patches on the gleaming bulkheads. She checked every readout, every telltale, the routine soothing her mind. Even the memories of violence on the ship—here Iklind had died, from hydrogen sulfide poisoning, and down this passage his distant relative Skoterin had nearly killed Brig Sirkin and Lady Cecelia. Redecoration had removed any trace of corrosive gases, of blood. The memory of faces and bodies that floated along with her were no different from those that haunted any captain's days.

In the 'ponics sections, she found Brun replanting trays, a dirty job that always fell to the lowest-level mole.

"What are you growing this round?" she asked.

Brun grinned. "Halobeets," she said. "I hadn't realized how much sulfur uptake ship 'ponics need."

"There's a ship rhyme about it," Heris said. "Eat it, excrete it, then halobeet it. And it's always confused me that we call the sulfur-sucking beets halobeets . . . you'd think they sopped up the halocarbons, but they don't. How are you getting along with Lady Cecelia's gardener?" Lady Cecelia's gardener produced the ship's fresh vegetables. Ship's crew produced only the vegetation needed to normalize the atmosphere. Brun wrinkled her muddy nose.

"I think he worries that I'll steal his methods for Dad's staff. You know I'm supposed to check the oxygen/carbon dioxide levels on his compartments, but he hovers over me as if I were after industrial secrets."

"Are you telling me you're never tempted to sneak a tomato?" Heris asked.

"Well . . . perhaps." Brun's wide grin was hardly contrite.

Heris left Brun to the tedious work, and continued her inspection. She was not surprised to find Arkady Ginese on his own tour of inspection, checking the weapons controls interlocks. The yacht had once had spacious storage bays, far larger than it needed for the transportation of a single passenger. Now those bays were stuffed with weaponry and its supporting control and guidance systems, with the jamming and other countermeasures that Heris hoped would serve as well as shields if someone were shooting back. They had not had the volume to mount both effective weapons and strong shields; Heris hoped she'd made the right choice.

"All's well, Captain," Ginese said. "I did want to ask you—Koutsoudas says there's a new wrinkle in ECM that we could probably rig onto what we have, if you wanted." *If you really trust Koutsoudas* hung in his words.

Heris thought a moment. "Do you understand it? Does it make sense to you?"

"Yes—it's a reasonable extension of the technology. I don't see why it wouldn't work."

"And how do you feel about Koutsoudas?"

Ginese looked around. "Well—"

"Of course he may have ears everywhere—the better to hear the truth, Arkady. He's smart—he has to know we don't completely trust someone from Livadhi. How do you feel?"

"I—like him more than I thought I would. He's like all scan techs, clever and sneaky. But he doesn't give me that bad feeling . . . then again, I missed Skoterin."

"So did we all," Heris said. "But I think all our sensitivities are flapping in the breeze now. Let's go on and make that change—send my desk a complete description, and I'll file it. If anything comes up—"

"Of course, Captain." Ginese looked happier, and Heris went on to complete her inspection.

By the time she reached the bridge again, Lady Cecelia had sent a message—she had chosen their destination, a planet called Xavier. Sirkin already had the charts up on display for Heris, with a recommended course.

"Looks good so far," Heris said. "I'll want to check—some of those intermediate jump points may have restriction codes on them—"

"Yes, ma'am, they do," Sirkin said. "Four of them are heavy traffic; we'd have to file here before we jump for clearance through them. Xavier itself is in the frontier zone; we have to file with the R.S.S., a letter of intent. I've done a preliminary file, in case—and there's an alternate course that doesn't use any restricted jump points, though it will add sixteen days."

Sixteen additional days times the daily requirements for food, water, oxygen . . . Heris ran the numbers in her mind before checking them on the computer. "We can do it, but it's already a long trip, especially counting the long insystem drop at Xavier. You're right, Sirkin, that short course is the best. What's the maximum flux transit you've plotted?" That, too, was within acceptable limits; Heris reminded herself again that Sirkin had not made the mistakes she'd been blamed for. On her own she had always done superb work.

"Fine—complete that application for the restricted jump points, file the letter of intent as agricultural products purchase, wholesale, and tell me when you anticipate we'll start the sequence. Good work." It was, too. Most navigators would still be setting up a single course.

"Thank you, ma'am." Sirkin might have been her old self, the bright, vibrant girl Heris had first met, but there was still the wariness of old injuries in her eyes. That was maturity, Heris told herself, and nothing to regret. Nobody stayed as young as Sirkin had been and lived to grow old.

Xavier, when they arrived at its orbital station, looked like the uncrowded agricultural world it was. Its main export was genetic variability for large domestic animals too inbred in other populations. A variety of habitats and temperature ranges allowed relatively easy culture of equids, bovids, and less common domestics for many purposes. Cecelia had been there before; she knew most of the horse breeders, and planned to spend several weeks with those most likely to have what she wanted.

"Captain Serrano . . . could I speak to you on a secure line, please?" That request got through; Heris had been wondering how long exactly Cecelia meant to stay, and what the daily docking charges would run to. Some of these outworld stations tried to squeeze every visitor, because they had so few.

"Of course," she said. She wondered what was wrong; they hadn't popped a hatch yet.

"I'm the Stationmaster," the face on the screen said. Heris hadn't doubted it, but she nodded politely.

"I've been authorized to ask this . . . and if it's an offense, please excuse me . . . but are you related to the . . . er . . . *Fleet* Serranos?"

That again. Heris hoped her reaction didn't show. "Yes, I am," she said. "In fact, I was Fleet myself."

"That's what we hoped," the Stationmaster said. "Lady Cecelia said—but I had to make sure."

"Why?" Heris asked. The Stationmaster seemed the sort

to pussyfoot around the point for hours, and she didn't want to wait for it.

"We really need your help, Captain Serrano. Your expertise, if you will. I've been authorized to invite you to a briefing, with our Senior Captain Vassilos, who commands the planetary defense."

Heris felt a prickle run down her backbone. "Planetary defense? Is there a . . . problem?" She would have Koutsoudas for lunch if they had dropped into a shooting war without his noticing.

"Not now, Captain. At the moment. But if you would come, if you would consider helping . . . just advice, I mean; you don't have a warship, we know that." He sounded more desperate than he should if they were in no imminent danger. Heris paused, considering her answer. Behind her, she heard a stir, and glanced around. Cecelia.

"I told them you'd be glad to help," Cecelia said, as if she had the right to dispose of Heris's time and effort. Heris glared at her, then turned back to the screen.

"I'll attend a briefing," she said. "At this point, without knowing what you want—my responsibilities to my ship must, you understand, take precedence."

"Oh, of course. If you'll—when you're ready, there will be a shuttle at your disposal. I'll just tell Captain Vassilos." And he cut the link. Heris turned back to Cecelia.

"Just what did you think you were doing?"

She didn't understand or she wouldn't. "I didn't see any harm in it. They asked about your name; I told them you were ex-Fleet; they started babbling about some kind of problem and needing expert guidance. You don't mind, do you?"

Mind was not the right word. Heris took a deep steadying breath, and told herself that she did, after all, care about the security of the outer worlds . . . and that clouting one's charter across the room was no way to run a chartered yacht.

On the shuttle down, she read through the scanty briefing material she'd been handed, and tried to explain to Cecelia why she should stick to horses and leave defense to the military.

"I know that," Cecelia said, unrepentant. "That's why I said you should take care of it, whatever it is. I know it's your specialty—"

"Used to be my specialty," said Heris between clenched

teeth. "You were the one who pointed out so firmly that I am a civilian now."

"I know." For an instant, Cecelia's expression might even have been contrite, or as close as that arrogant bony face ever came. They rode the rest of the way in unrestful silence.

The little military band in its bright uniforms, buttons and ornaments glittering, played some jaunty march which Heris could have sworn she knew. Across the sunburnt grass, the music practically strutted, as if the notes themselves were proud.

"It's—charming," said Cecelia beside her. Under the clear blue sky of Xavier, her cheeks were flushed, more with excitement than sunburn.

"It's ridiculous," muttered Heris. "If this is their protection—"

"But it's so . . . it makes me feel good."

"That's what it's for, but feeling good because you've got a decent bandmaster won't save your life if you don't have some armament, and I don't see anything here that could take care of a good-sized riot."

"Maybe they don't have riots," Cecelia said. She sounded cross.

"Then they've had no practice, as well as having no armament," Heris said. She knew she was cross. Damn Livadhi and his specialist. Damn her family name, which at the moment was pure embarrassment. Without that, she'd have been comfortably ensconced in the yacht, while Cecelia visited horse farms. Instead, her fame had preceded her, and produced a fervent appeal for help—help which Cecelia had generously offered, on her behalf.

The band switched from one tune to another, this one even more bouncy than the last. Her toes wanted to tap; her whole body wanted to march along a road with a band of brave and loyal friends. A double crash of cymbals and drums, and the music stopped, leaving its ghost in her ears. Trumpets blew a little fanfare, and someone left the group to approach them.

"Lady Cecelia . . . Captain Serrano . . ." He wore a uniform that had been tailored for a slimmer man; it bunched and pulled around the spare tire fifteen years had given him.

"I'm Senior Captain Vassilos. Thank you for your willingness to help."

"You're very welcome," Cecelia said. Heris nodded, silently, and waited to see what would come next.

"I presume you'd like to know more about the problem?"

"Quite," said Heris, before Cecelia could say anything.

"If you'll come this way, then." He led them to a brightly polished groundcar with a big boxy rear end and a little open cab for the driver. Heris had never seen anything like it. She and Cecelia and Senior Captain Vassilos sat in back on tufted velvet; the compartment would have held four or five more in comfort.

"We've had trouble from the Compassionate Hand from time to time—as you know, milady—" He turned to Cecelia, who nodded. "But we don't believe these are the same people. For one thing, the survivors report nothing like the discipline we associate with Compassionate Hand raids. For another, the entry vectors are all wrong. I know: the Black Scratch could be using a roundabout jump sequence. But they'd almost have to trail past an R.S.S. picket line that way, and Fleet keeps telling us there's nothing in the records. Any of them. Of course, they think we're overreacting—at least, that's the message I've had from them. They're stretched thin on this frontier—"

"On all," Heris said. And would be thinner yet, if the government fell. She hoped fervently that Lord Thornbuckle would cobble something together before that happened.

"We used to get a patrol ship in here at least yearly; that kept the vermin away. But in the past eight years or so, it's been less than that, and in the past two years we haven't had a patrol closer than Margate." Margate, two stars away. That wouldn't help. "Frankly, I don't know why the Compassionate Hand hasn't been at us again."

Heris thought they had, but were being circumspect just in case the lack of patrol activity was a trap. Instead of mentioning that, she asked, "Has anyone ever gotten an ID on the raiders?"

"Here." He loaded the cube reader and began pointing to items in the display. "Last time, they knocked out the scanners and the records at the orbital station, but a farmer down here in the south happened to catch a bit—his oldest daughter's crazy for space and handbuilt a scanner of her own. But it was at the extreme of her range, and we don't know how valid the data are."

"We'll have—our expert—look at it, if you don't mind." Heris just caught herself from saying Koutsoudas's name.

"No, that's fine. If you can make anything of it, so much the better."

They had better make something of it. After a look at the files, Heris realized that a farmer's brat's homemade scanner had the only possible data of any importance.

"What sort of defense do you have?" She thought she knew, but better to ask and be sure.

"Well, it's always been Fleet policy that planets didn't need their own heavy ships, as you know." Heris nodded. It was always easier to keep the peace if the peaceful weren't too well armed. "We had two Desmoiselle class escorts forty years ago, but one of them was badly damaged in a Compassionate Hand raid and we cannibalized her to get parts for the other." Heris winced. The Desmoiselle class had been obsolete for decades; it mounted no more weaponry than the yacht, and handled worse. Designed initially to protect commercial haulers from incompetent piracy in the crowded conditions of the Cleonic moons, it had been someone's poor choice for a situation like this.

"And your remaining ship?"

"Well . . . it's not really operational, and we haven't the expertise locally to fix it. Nor the money to send it somewhere." He flushed. "I know that must sound like we want to be sitting ducks, but it's not really that. We keep *Grogon* hanging around with her weapons lit up, hoping to scare off trouble, but the pirates have figured out she has neither legs nor teeth."

"What's the problem?"

"She was underpowered to start with, and she needs her tubes relined, at a minimum. She makes only seventy percent of the acceleration she had when she came, but there's no shipyard nearer than Grand Junction or Tay-Fal. And the cost—"

"Let's see if my engineers can suggest something," Heris said, making a note on her compad. She had to have something as backup, if it were only a shuttle with a single missile tube and a lot of electronic fakery. If this *Grogon* could move in space at all, it was better than nothing. "Anything else?"

"We *did* have a fixed orbital battery, but they got that on the last raid. Then one of the shuttles—" There were only three, as Heris already knew. "We took two of the phase cannons off the other escort—"

Heris blinked. They had mounted *phase cannon* in a shuttle? "Have you ever fired them?" she asked.

"Not yet. But we think it will work."

"I think perhaps my engineers should take a look." Quickly. Before anyone tried it and tore the shuttle apart.

"Of course, Captain Serrano." The man beamed as if she were conferring a great favor. "Does this mean you'll take the commission?"

"Let me confer with my . . . er . . . staff," Heris said. "And if you have any engineering specs on those vessels—?"

"Right away, Captain," he said.

Koutsoudas received the scan cassette with a curl of his lip that made Heris want to smack him. Oblo, she saw, had a sulky look. Fine. Let Oblo work it off on Koutsoudas.

An hour later, Koutsoudas called her with no sneer at all in his voice. "Good data, Captain. The kid knew what she was doing, whoever she is. Recruit her."

Heris had already asked. Regret edged her voice: "Can't, I'm afraid. She died a year back, of some local disease. So what do you have?" She didn't mention the younger sister she'd been told about, who seemed to have similar talents. Time enough for that later.

"Aethar's World, but I think the ship ID's falsified. It'll be Aethar's World, just from the flavor of it, but not that number. It's in the commercial sequence, probably midsize trader . . . too bad that girl didn't build a wide-band detector as well."

"I'll ask," Heris said. "Maybe she did. But only one ship?"

"So far. I'll let you know."

Heris put in a call to Petris, who had gone to take a look at the cannon-loaded shuttle.

"Just got here," he said. "But you were right. They assumed that only the mass mattered. They've got them bolted into the frame—the unreinforced frame—with homemade ports cut in the hull plates." He sounded less contemptuous than she expected as he went on. "Quite a job, really—they put some thought into it. Pity they didn't know more about phase cannon. To make this thing operational, we'll have to dismount them, reinforce, and remount. At best, that's five weeks of work with the equipment available—"

"Downside or orbital?" Heris asked.

"Downside—they've no orbital facilities at all. Anyway, that'd give you a slow shuttle that could fire a couple of bolts every five minutes or so. Not worth it, unless we're desperate."

"That will depend on how bad the old escort is."

All along Heris had wondered who crewed the two escorts. When she swam aboard the remaining Desmoiselle, she found out. Anyone who wanted, it seemed. Oldsters retired from space, youngsters desperate to get above atmosphere, balancing a complete lack of proper training with intimate knowledge of their single ship.

"*Grogon*'s not a bad ship," its elderly captain told her. "She takes a bit of easing along, that's all. . . ." Petris raised his brows but said nothing; he'd explain later. Heris could see for herself most of its problems.

Back with Captain Vassilos, Heris showed him the recommendations of her engineering staff. "Can you tell me why you think the raider's due?"

"It's more a guess than anything else," he said. "It's come twice before in our springtime, and now it's late spring. It feels like the right time."

Heris had heard worse reasons. "Those phase cannon in the shuttle can't be used as they are—and five weeks of downtime, if your planet-side yards can do the work, still give you only a very minimal weapons platform. If you have the resources to start that work, go ahead, but don't count on it to do much. I do have another suggestion. . . ."

"It's a little thing, whatever it is." Esteban Koutsoudas and Meharry bent over the displays. "Let me just tinker a bit here—ahhh." He signaled Meharry with one stubby finger. "That cube I had—put it in here—" Another screen came alive with numbers that scrolled so rapidly Heris couldn't see anything but lines. Then it froze, with one line highlighted.

"Hull constructed at Yaeger, registered with Aethar's World

as a medium trader . . . but Aethar's traders are everyone else's raiders."

That much any of her own crew could have gotten, but Koutsoudas wasn't through. The screen wavered and steadied on a new display: the other ship's design details, shown in three-dimensional display. Colored tags marked deviations from the listed criteria. Where *Sweet Delight*'s other detectors merely showed blots of warning red for weapons on active status, this one showed the placement and support systems for weapons not otherwise detected as live.

"Where'd you get this stuff?" Meharry asked, her voice expressing her lust for that equipment.

"You know how it is," Koutsoudas said without taking his eyes off the display. "A bit of this, a bit of that. It's not exactly standard, so I can't mount it in any Fleet craft—"

"But you can't *get* that resolution that far away," Meharry said. "Thermal distortion alone—"

"You need an almighty big database," Koutsoudas said. He sounded almost apologetic, as he tweaked the display again and an enlarged view of the distant vessel's portside weapons appeared, with little numbered comments. "I've been sort of . . . collecting this . . . for a long time." He tapped the cube reader. "Had to design new storage algorithms too. And the transforms for the functions that do the actual work . . ."

"Magic," Meharry said. Koutsoudas grinned at her.

"That's it. Got to have my secrets, don't I? If I teach you everything, who's going to care about my neck?"

"Nobody cares about your neck now, Esteban. Other parts of you—"

"Are off limits," he said. "Besides, that ship's no good."

"Can you tell what it's getting?" Heris asked.

"It won't have us now," Koutsoudas said confidently. "Not with the last batch of little doodads Oblo and Meharry and I installed. We're in no danger, and we can sit here and read their mail if we want to."

"Not and let them run amok in this system," Heris said. "Not if we can stop them, that is."

"Oh, we can stop them." Koutsoudas pointed to his display. "Their weapons look impressive on scan—or will, when they go active and light up the station's warning system. But this is old tech, slow and stupid stuff. Good for scaring the average civilian, though I'll bet they never take on any of the big commercial carriers. And when they refitted that hull with new engines, they made a big mistake." He brought up a highlighted schematic, and Heris saw it herself. They'd wanted more performance, and they'd mounted more powerful drives . . . but without reinforcing the hull or mounts. If they used those engines flat out, they'd collapse either hull or mount. Even worse, they could do structural damage by combining a lower drive setting with missile firing.

"I'd bet they never have fired many shots in anger," Heris said. "At least, not while under any significant acceleration. That's a beginner's mistake." If only she had a real Fleet warship, she'd simply chase them into their own fireball.

"With any luck, they won't live long enough to learn better," Meharry said.

"Not luck," Koutsoudas said. "Skill. Knowledge."

Heris wasn't sure if that was an attempt to flatter her, or to brag about his own ability. "How long before you can strip the rest you want off them?"

"Twelve to fourteen standard hours, Captain," he said. "With the captain's permission, I'll put one of the juniors on scan, and plan to be on the bridge in four hours for a check, and then in ten hours—"

"Of course," Heris said. "We'll use the Fleet scheduling for this. Firsts, give me your interim schedules, and make sure you are offshift enough for real rest before then."

Koutsoudas smiled. "I didn't know if we'd have the crew for that—"

"Not quite, but better than they have, I expect. As long as we don't let them get past us—or get the first shot—we'll do very well."

After she had the schedules for the next twelve standard hours, Heris went to see Cecelia.

"I don't know how that man does what he does, but we're damn lucky Livadhi wanted me to run off with him. With my people, I'd have a lot less margin to play with."

"So we're going to fight again?" Cecelia looked as if she were trying to project eagerness. But she would be remembering that other battle, in which she was trapped in her aged and disabled body, unable even to speak clearly. She had to be scared.

"Yes, we'll fight—but it won't be anything like the time before. They won't have detected us—and they're unlikely to do so until we blow them away." She used Cecelia's desk display to diagram what they intended to do.

"It's not very sporting, is it?" Cecelia asked.

"It's not 'sporting' at all. It's not a game," Heris said. "Lepescu made that mistake; I don't. This is a band of ruffians who have terrorized this system repeatedly, and I'm going to destroy them. True, their homeworld may send more—I can't help that. But if Koutsoudas is right, Aethar's World may have more to worry about than a missing allied pirate. These people will have months—maybe years—of peace and a chance to develop their own effective defense. So yes, I'm going to destroy them with the least possible risk to us."

"How can you be sure they're the right ones? What if you're about to blow up an innocent ship?" She didn't sound really worried about it, but Heris considered the question seriously.

"By the time we do it, we'll know what brand of dental cleanser they use," she said. "Right now we know they are running with a falsified ID beacon—which doesn't necessarily mean criminal intent; we had one. But they've also got a whopping load of armament. And they're from Aethar's World, which is always suspicious. About the only time those barbarians leave home, it's to cause trouble for someone. They fit the profile of the trouble your friends have been having. . . ."

With the enemy ship only a light-second away, Koutsoudas continued to pour out a torrent of information about it. "Not only Aethar's World, but one of the Brotherhood chiefs. Svenik the Bold, I think—certainly he had this particular ship a while back, and this sort of raid is his specialty."

"I'm surprised he's lasted this long with that hull/engine combination," Petris said.

"So am I," Koutsoudas said. "But he hasn't been up against anything that made him redline it. Yet." He grinned at Heris. "I know you want to do this the quick way, Captain, but I wish we could push him to it."

"Not worth it," Heris said. "I know—it would be fun, but none of our friends can match our scan capability, and if we made a mistake—or he got lucky—"

"He's gone hot," Arkady Ginese, on weapons, did not look up for anyone else's conversations.

"It's not us," Koutsoudas said. "He isn't side-scanning—that's just preparation for hitting the station. He should be transmitting his demands—yes—there it goes—"

"Go ahead, Mr. Ginese," said Heris, feeling that familiar sensation in her belly. Plan, plan, and plan again, but at the moment, there was always one cold thrust of fear. Arkady and Meharry both touched their boards, and their own displays lit. Now, if the raider were looking, they could be seen. The weapons boards flickered through the preparatory displays, then steadied on green, with the red row at the top showing all the weapons ready. It had definitely been worth it to get that fast-warm capability, though it cost half again as much. Or would have, if Ginese and Meharry hadn't done the conversion themselves.

They had the raider now, though he didn't know it and might not before he died. They had calculated their ideal moment to attack, but from here on, the conclusion wasn't really in doubt.

"Screens warm," Heris said. Their puny screens wouldn't deflect much, but better a little protection than none. Second by second they closed.

"Second scan," Koutsoudas said suddenly. "Jump insertion, low velocity. Preliminary says it's a medium-size cargo hull; weapons minimal."

It had always been a possibility that the raider would have a companion. Or rival.

"Koutsoudas on the new one; Meharry, you take main scan on the raider. Ginese?"

"Any time, Captain."

"It's hours out," Koutsoudas said. "And it's not in any hurry. Could be tramp cargo—I'm just getting the beacon ID—but the timing's suspicious."

"That's why we have backup. Meharry, give me a replay of the raider's transmission to the station." The station, as agreed, had rebroadcast that narrowbeam transmission in omni, which allowed the *Sweet Delight* to pick it up—and enter it in the log, for evidence. It was about what she'd expected, the wording varying only slightly from the previous raids. Koutsoudas glanced up briefly.

"That's Svenik the Bold. I recognize his voice; it was one

of our voice-screen samples on file. Want a verification?"
Heris nodded. He reached over to Meharry's board, and
flicked a switch on the module he'd added.

"Transmit our authorization," Heris said. Koutsoudas
grinned, and hit another switch.

Half a light-second; the raiders should be startled to receive
a transmission from a source they hadn't spotted, giving them
official notification that they were unwanted and about to
be fired upon. The question was, what would they do next?

"There's *Grogon*," said Ginese. "Right on time." The old
escort had been given a special set of electronics and now
lit up the scans as if she were studded with more armament than the yacht. Positioned as she was, on the far side
of the intruder's path, she limited its possible maneuvers.
He would have to assume a coordinated attack plan.

"Now," Heris said to Ginese. He ran his thumb down the
firing controls, and the green telltales flicked to red, the red
ready lights to yellow. The *Sweet Delight* shuddered at launch,
even though the missiles were shoved out of the tubes at
low velocity, to light outside. Red to orange to yellow to
green, as the weapons reloaded automatically, and the red
row at the top reappeared.

Meanwhile, Ginese and Meharry tracked the launches.
"Five—eight—all lit," Meharry reported. Half a light-second
still left over 90,000 miles between the two vessels, though
that distance was closing as the raider approached. Certainly
it was enough time for them to maneuver. But which way?
They should be worrying about the old escort; they should
be wondering what other weapons she would launch.

"Koutsoudas?" Heris watched the back of his head. "What's
our friend up to?"

"Dumping vee. With the lag, still a safe distance out. Very
interesting ID, Captain."

"Yes?"

"In the FR registry as an independent hauler, crew-owned.
But I've got a flag on her in the Fleet database for suspicious activities, and a personal flag . . . she's been in the
same system, but remote, during raids by Aethar's World
pirates and by the Jenniky gang." He cleared his throat. "My
guess is she's either a spotter or a paymaster. Maybe both.
Not in her own right, of course, but for someone else. My
guess there is the Black Scratch; she claims to trade with

Xolheim and Fiduc, and you know the Benignity has a strong presence there."

"Agreed. Keep an eye on her, then. Arkady?"

"Nothing—there. They've launched at us, and kicked up another ten gees acceleration. It's within our pattern, and I could stop their salvo with my bare hands, just about. Old stuff."

"A rock in the head will kill you just as dead," Heris quoted; Ginese laughed.

"Yes, Captain, but Aethar's prefers bang to finesse . . . look at my scans." Already the *Sweet Delight*'s elegant ECM had confused the enemy missiles; Heris would need to order no evasive maneuvers at all. She worried more about the old escort, with her novice crew and her faked signatures. If they fired anything much at her . . . but the raider seemed intent on getting away.

"A lot of screaming on their bridge," Meharry said. "I can't understand their ugly language, but it's loud."

"Let me—" Koutsoudas switched back to that channel, and then grinned. "Svenik cussing out his scan tech for not seeing us first . . . someone's left the main speaker open; the station should be getting all this too. Handy for court, if we ever want to pursue it." If there was any court to pursue it in, Heris thought.

The *Sweet Delight*'s missiles carried guidance systems normally found only in military weaponry. Whatever ECM the pirate vessel had didn't affect them; on Koutsoudas's enhanced scans, the missiles closed inexorably. Heris wondered if Svenik's ship had shields of any quality, or if he'd try to outrun them. She almost hoped he would; if he redlined his ship and blew it himself, it wouldn't be her fault. That was thinking like a civilian, though.

"Got him." Koutsoudas, who had seen the inevitable an instant before any of the rest. The pirate ship and the missiles merged, and exploded.

"Easiest kill I ever saw," Oblo said, as if affronted.

"I don't trust it," Heris said. "What's that other doing?"

"It'll be a while before they get it on their scans," Koutsoudas said. "They're still dumping . . . ask me again in a couple of minutes."

"Just tell me, 'Steban," Heris said. She felt itchy all over; like Oblo, she was almost irritated that it had been that easy.

It felt unreal, like a training exercise. Something picked at her memory. The raider had been there before—that same raider—destroying things but doing less damage than such raiders could. So they'd expected the raider, and they'd gotten the raider . . . and all this time the second ship hung out there and watched. "Weapons off," she said abruptly. Meharry gave her a startled look, but shut her board down. "'Steban, signal *Grogon* on tightbeam—shutdown, as dark as possible."

"You want me to put us back in hiding?"

"Not until there's a natural obstacle between us and that other ship. I think we just did something stupid."

"Stupid?" Meharry stared at her.

"We expected an Aethar's World raider, and that's what we got. The same raider. Why?"

"Because the Bloodhorde are stupid," Meharry said impatiently. "They do things like that."

"For a profit, yes. For honor, if you can figure out what they mean by it. But here—look, we were told they've had raiders several times, but they didn't actually blow the station—"

"They wanted to milk the cow, not kill it," Oblo said. But he had a worried look on his scarred face.

"The Bloodhorde always figure there's another cow down the road," Heris said. "I thought maybe—this is so far from their usual range—they were just skimming on the way home from something else. But suppose they weren't. And suppose they weren't on their own business."

"The Black Scratch," Koutsoudas said, without looking away from his scans. "Hired 'em, maybe, or offered Svenik backing against Kjellak—that might do it. Send him in on feints at irregular intervals, see what happens. Likely Svenik didn't know he had a trailer."

"Right. And nothing much happens once, twice, and then we show up out of nowhere, and sparkle all over their scans with stuff no civilian vessel could have. Blow Svenik without a scratch on us—no contest—" Heris paused, wishing she had the faintest idea where the nearest Fleet communications node was.

"He's boosting," Koutsoudas said. "Must have just caught the fight, and he's not wasting time. Wonder why he doesn't just jump? He's far enough from anything massive. . . ."

"Anything we know about," Heris said. She felt little cold prickles down her back. "No, most likely he wants to see what we'll do. If he can get us into a chase. Let's pretend we don't see him. Suck all you can, but don't react."

"And we're not going back on the stealth gear because you hope they'll think we popped out from behind a rock?" Meharry's tone expressed her doubts.

"I think they'll wonder. We're small, and it's a messy system—it wouldn't take a big rock to hide us. If we went back in the sack now, they'd know for sure there was a ship with that capacity."

The distant ship vanished into FTL six hours later; Heris trusted Koutsoudas's scans enough to return to the orbital station then and confer with the Xavierans. They were, she thought, entirely too jubilant, and in no mood for warnings.

CHAPTER NINE

"We want to honor you," Senior Captain Vassilos kept saying when she tried to get her point across.

"There's nothing to honor, yet," Heris said for the tenth time. "You may well have worse trouble coming."

"You must understand, Captain Serrano, that this is the first time in years that we have been able to resist successfully. I shouldn't say *we*, since you did it. But we must celebrate this victory—it will put heart in the troops."

"They mean it," muttered Cecelia from the corner of the office. "Remember that band? That's how they are—you must let them celebrate."

"Very well," Heris said, with as much grace as she could muster. "But I'm still worried—I would very much like to have a serious discussion—"

"Of course! Of course, Captain Serrano. The General Secretary wants to meet you—the entire government wishes to thank you. After the parade—" Heris tried not to let her eyes roll up at this. Cecelia, out of pickup range, was grinning at her wickedly. "And just a few speeches, nothing really fancy—" She could imagine.

As it happened, she couldn't have imagined.

"Aren't you glad I taught you to ride?" Cecelia asked. She sat the stocky white horse with the flowing mane as if she'd grown out of its back. After the first block, Heris had had enough of the rhythmic bouncing trot of her matching white horse. So it was in time to the music—so her legs hurt.

She knew she didn't look as good as Cecelia. She was sure her uniform jacket over riding breeches looked particularly silly. Hard to believe that real soldiers had once ridden into battle.

"I'm glad this is a small city," Heris said. "I bounce too much."

"Open your joints and relax," Cecelia said. "This is fun."

Fun for someone who had been born with calloused thighs, maybe. Fun for someone who had ridden in front of crowds much of her adult life. Heris would rather have celebrated victory by floating for a few hours in some body of warm water. But duty was duty.

By the time they arrived at the site of the celebration, Heris wondered if she'd ever get off the horse without help. Cecelia wasn't sympathetic.

"I told you to spend more hours on the simulator," she said.

"I had other things to do," Heris said. It wasn't an excuse she'd have accepted from anyone else, but she still couldn't see that riding horses was a necessary skill for a ship captain.

"Captain—?" That was a young man in the colorful uniform of the Civil Guard. Heris sighed, and managed to dismount without either groaning or kicking him in the head. She was going to be more than sore for a few days. Cecelia, already down, looked eager and happy. Heris moved over to stand beside her. She had no idea what this world would consider an appropriate celebration, certainly not what might come after a parade on horseback.

The same little band she had first seen on the wide plain of the spaceport (she recognized the conductor's exuberant moustache) struck up another of those jaunty marches. Despite herself, she felt a prickle of excitement run up her spine.

"Up here, Captain," said her escort. Up here was atop a stone platform that resembled every reviewing stand she had ever seen except its being solid stone instead of slightly quivery metal and plastic. Rows of chairs, each with a bright blue cushion on it—that was different—and a little railing painted brilliant white. Behind the chairs, the flags of Armitage, Xavier, Roualt, and the Familias Regnant swung gently in the light breeze. In front of them, the wide field where the parade was coming apart into its constituent elements. Some of them reformed into obvious military units, and some (the children on ponies) milled around until the Civil Guard shooed them away.

Heris sat where she was bidden, and found herself looking down on the heads of the band. Directly beneath her the coiled shape of some kind of horn gleamed in the sun, and it produced substantial deep blats from its great bell. In front of that row were the horns held up and facing outward, and in front of them the little dark and silver cylinders . . . she wished she knew more about musical instruments. The required music appreciation classes long ago had left a residue of tangled facts: some things had strings, and some had tubes you blew through or tubes with holes in them you blew across. Which left that thing on the end there: it looked like an inflated pillow with sticks coming out. Whatever it was, it made a sound she had never heard before, as if something alive were being strangled inside.

As she watched, its player stepped smartly out in front of the band, revolved in place, and faced the reviewing stand. Now she could hear the discordant squeals and gurgles clearly; the rest of the band had stopped in mid-phrase (if music had phrases) to allow it a solo turn.

"Our top piper," her escort said. Heris smiled politely. At least now she had a label for it. Piper.

"You'll see the massed pipes, too," he said, as if that were a treat in store. A mass of these squealers? Heris thought longingly of earplugs. She looked beyond the band. Now the near side of the field was almost empty, and a crowd had formed on the far side. A couple of dogs ran in circles, chasing each other. "I'm sorry for the delay," her escort murmured. "We wanted to get everyone here—"

"Quite all right," Cecelia said, before Heris could think past the piper's screeches to what she might politely say.

"But here they are—" A horse-drawn vehicle rolled across the field, to distant cheers from the crowd. One of the dogs fled; the other ran yapping after the horses, who ignored this familiar accompaniment. So did the elegant spotted dog sitting upright beside the driver.

"The General Secretary, the Mayor and Council," her escort said. "I hope it accords with your etiquette; in ours, the greater honor goes to the one who arrives first." He stood, and Heris took the hint. The little band began something that made her want to sway from foot to foot—not a march, but almost a waltz. The General Secretary, resplendent in a long cape edged with silver braid, bowed to the reviewing stand. Heris had no idea what was required; Cecelia, she noticed, stood still. The Mayor's cape had bright red braid; the Council, in various bright-colored outfits, all glittering with braid, buttons, or other adornment, descended one by one from the carriage and bowed before climbing the steps. When the last was seated, the solo piper let out a resounding screech. Heris was delighted to see that the horses hitched to the vehicle flattened their ears and tried to shy. The driver lifted the reins and they exploded into a fast trot.

No one on the platform said a word; if they had, no one could have heard it, Heris was sure. With a final tweedle and squeal, the piper spun around, and the little band snapped to attention, and marched away. Now what?

Now the General Secretary, it seemed, had something to say. Long experience of political speeches had Heris ready for long-winded platitudes.

"We're here to honor our old friend Lady Cecelia, and our new heroes," the General Secretary. "You saw Captain Serrano in the parade; we now consider her a friend of the same status as Lady Cecelia." The General Secretary turned to Heris. "Please accept this as a token of our esteem," he said. "Wear it when you visit us, if you will." It was a small silver button, stamped with the design of a leaping horse.

"Thank you," Heris said. Before she could finish with the requisite reminder that she had done nothing of herself, but only with the help of others, the General Secretary was interrupting.

"And now, let's show our visitors and friends the pride of our people." And he sat down abruptly, leaving Heris no choice but to do the same.

Heris blinked. Short, and not particularly graceful—not at all what she expected. But it wasn't her place to expect. Now at the far end of the field, a thin sound like the strangling of dozens of geese . . . "The massed pipes," her escort confirmed. Suddenly they were in motion, and with them an array of drums.

"I'm . . . not familiar with the instrument," Heris said, hoping for a diversion. Her escort beamed.

"Not that many worlds have preserved them," he said with evident pride. She could understand that; suppression seemed more reasonable than preservation. "Here we have not only preserved, but developed, the four main varieties of pipe that survived the Great Dispersal. For marching bands, we prefer the purely acoustic, though there is an amplified variety with a portable powerpack."

"They seem quite loud enough," Heris said.

"Oh, but they were battlefield instruments at one time. We find them very effective in riot control."

She could imagine that. An amplified piper—or, worse, a mass of amplified pipers—could send the average rioter into acoustic shock. Most security services had acoustic weapons, but none that looked or sounded like this.

Cecelia leaned past the escort between them. "Isn't it thrilling? I've always loved pipes."

Heris was saved the necessity of answering by the pipes themselves, now close enough to make a wall of sound. The pipers marched with a characteristic strut, the drums thundered behind them, and despite herself her toes began to move in rhythm inside her shoes. The pipes when playing a quick melody sounded much more musical, she thought, dancing from note to note above the rattling drums. Behind this group marched what must be, she realized, the entire planetary militia, each unit in its own colors. Each, as it passed the reviewing stand, turned heads sharply, and shouted out its origin (so her escort explained). She had no idea where "Onslow" and "Pedigrate" were, but the pride certainly showed. Far to their right, the massed pipes wheeled and marched back, this time nearer the crowd.

To Heris's relief, they returned through the town in the gleaming cars of their first visit. She had not looked forward to climbing back on a horse.

"I could get addicted to this," Cecelia said. They had the closed compartment to themselves. Her cheeks had reddened with the unaccustomed sun, but her eyes were bright. A few rose petals clung incongruously to her red hair, and one lay for a moment on her shoulder until the errant breeze lifted it off.

"Addicted to what, riding in parades?" Heris asked.

"That and . . . being the conquering hero. Knowing I did something really worthwhile."

Heris refrained from pointing out that Cecelia herself hadn't done that much. She'd volunteered her—well, their—yacht and crew, but she herself had not fired a weapon. Still, she had been in danger with them. And in all honesty, Heris herself had enjoyed the cheering crowds, even the roses and ribbons. "This is the easy part," she said.

"I know," Cecelia said. "But then I always did like victory celebrations. I never thought I'd have another one—not like the old days."

"Didn't you get any satisfaction out of your return to Rockhouse?" Heris asked.

For the first time, Cecelia looked ready to answer that. "Not really. The king resigned—I had no chance to talk to him first. And Lorenza—she escaped. Even if she died—and I agree she must have—she escaped *me*. I wanted to slap her smug face myself. Then I found out the yacht wasn't mine anymore—I couldn't even take off on my own—"

"But we did—"

"Yes . . . we did. Out of your courtesy; it was no longer my *right*." Cecelia sighed. "I'm sorry, Heris. It must sound silly to you. But all the way back from the Guerni Republic, I fantasized such a gorgeous, impressive homecoming— storming in and confounding everyone. The feeling we've had today—that's what I had in mind. Bands playing, flags waving, my family all in a heap of contrition. Admissions of guilt, begging of forgiveness. Instead—with the king's resignation, everything seemed to fall apart. My affairs didn't matter that much compared to the change in government; I wasn't a hero after all. Very annoying, actually, especially when Berenice had the nerve to say that if I was going to get rejuvenation, I should have spent a little more and gotten some remodelling—"

"What!" Heris had not heard this before.

"Oh, yes. After all, I didn't have to live the same selfish life as before, and if I'd bother to try, I could look quite nice and perhaps marry—I swear, Heris, it was at that moment I decided to sue them for their idiocy. Before that I had been annoyed, but that did it. Not a scrap of remorse for the hell she'd put me through in that damned nursing home, but the same old superior attitude about my looks and my duty to the family. I'll show her duty, I thought."

Heris had wondered more than once why Cecelia was so determined to sue the family; now she was caught between sympathy and laughter. "It wasn't very tactful of her," she said, trying for middle ground.

"She never was tactful," Cecelia said. "No small child is— one reason I don't like small children—but she was remarkable even for a child. She told me once 'You may be famous, but I'm pretty, and you never will be.' It was true, of course, but it hurt anyway."

"So that's why you've sued them?"

"Yes . . . mostly. I suppose. They keep thinking I'm nothing—handy to do their chores, when they wanted Ronnie off Rockhouse for a year, handy for loans when they want to expand their holdings, handy for a joke whenever they want to feel elegant and so on . . . and I just got tired of it."

Heris said, "It's Tommy this and Tommy that and Tommy take a walk. . . ."

"What?"

"I thought perhaps you might know Kipling. One of his poems that will live as long as military organizations, because that's how the military's always treated. Despised until needed, then cozened into things—blamed for whatever goes wrong, and praised—when it gets praise—for the wrong things."

"Exactly. Though I suppose my life hasn't been that bad, really." Heris watched the flicker of amusement in Cecelia's eyes. Just when she'd given up, the woman would show that wry self-assessment, that ability to keep things in balance. They rode another few blocks in companionable silence. Then Cecelia shifted to face Heris directly. "What's worrying you? You were as tense as on the island today, and it wasn't all saddle sores."

"We're celebrating too early," Heris said. "There's something wrong with that raid—we won too easily, and we may have made things worse by winning. I'm half-expecting Koutsoudas to call and say there's an entire fleet of enemy ships coming in."

"That's ridiculous," Cecelia said. "Here? What are they going to steal, horses and cattle and antelopes and sheep? And what enemy?"

"There are mining colonies on the gas giants' moons," Heris said.

"Piddly," Cecelia said. "They're hardly two decades old, and just now beginning to break even. Nothing unusual, and most of it will be processed in this system, developing an industrial base to allow bulk mining later."

"A slow payback on the investment," Heris said, just to make a comment. To her surprise, Cecelia looked startled.

"You're right—it hadn't occurred to me, but—I wonder if that's going to be an effect of Rejuvenant political influence?"

"What?" Heris was still trying to think why some enemy would make Xavier a target. As Cecelia had said, horses and cattle weren't usually of great interest to aggressive political entities. Shipyards, manufacturing centers, things like that.

"Well . . . Rejuvenants can afford the years to develop slow-growth industries—things that would have been marginal at best for non-rejuvenated individuals. Projects that families can carry out only if they convince successive generations to support them."

"Mmm." Heris filed that away to think about later. At the moment, she was more interested in what had really happened with the raid, and what she could say to the Xavieran government. Such as it was.

Once at the party, the General Secretary bowed over her hand and murmured, "I understand you are worried and need to talk. Give us an hour or so, eh? And then we'll find you. People just want to say thanks." Unlike Senior Captain Vassilos, who had seemed almost theatrical in his military posture, the General Secretary looked like an amiable bear. Graying brown hair, bright brown eyes . . . Heris had not really looked at him before, but now she liked what she saw. She smiled, nodded, and let herself be passed on down the reception line.

Beyond the line, her faithful escort showed her to a comfortable, softly padded seat. A waiter appeared with a tray of drinks, and another with a tray of finger foods. Heris chose a sunset-colored juice, and found it tangy and refreshing; the crisp shapes on the plate at her side turned out to be bite-sized pastries filled with meat or cheese. None of the people who came up to her seemed to think she looked funny, and after a while she quit thinking about the riding boots and breeches. Especially when she saw half a dozen others wearing them.

"Heris—these are the Carmody sisters," Cecelia said, appearing at her side with three rangy women as tall as herself. "They own one of the breeding farms I'll be visiting."

"Cecelia says you ride," said the youngest of the sisters— or the one who looked youngest—Heris suddenly noticed a blue-and-silver ring like Cecelia's, only higher on the woman's left ear. Then it sank in—another horse enthusiast.

"Only a little," Heris said. "In the parade, for instance."

"But she said you rode to hounds," the woman said. "Tell me—does Bunny still have that fierce trainer—what was his name?" Heris couldn't believe it. Did they know anything but horses? Did they think this reception was about horses?

"Yes, he does, and you're supposed to be thanking Heris for knocking off that raider," said Cecelia. Heris felt her irritation subsiding.

"Well, of course. But Davin said all that, I thought. Now that it's over—"

"I'm really not an expert on horses," Heris said, as gently as she could manage. "Lady Cecelia has very kindly tutored me, but I'm already out of my depth."

"Oh. Well . . . Cecelia, suppose you give us some idea what you're looking for?" Heris would have laughed if she hadn't been trapped by her stiffening body into a corner that soon filled with all the horsey set on Xavier . . . breeders, mostly, whom Cecelia introduced. Most of them just managed to remember why Heris was being honored before they launched into anecdotes about horses, arguments about breeding strategies and training methods, and plain unmistakable brags. By the time the General Secretary's assistant came to suggest that she might like to meet with him and a few others in the library, she was feeling very grumpy indeed.

"If I understood Captain Vassilos correctly, you believe there were more ships in the system, observing your battle with the raider. If that is so, can you explain why it bothered you? I may as well mention that none of our scan technicians found a trace of such a ship, even when they went back over the recorded scans."

Heris chose her words carefully. "Sir, let me take the last

point first. Your scan techs are working with civilian-level scans, and old ones at that. We happen to have more up-to-date scans on the yacht, which means that we can see farther and detect smaller disturbances."

"You have military-grade equipment?" asked Vassilos.

"I . . . prefer not to specify the equipment we have," Heris said. "Not to impugn the integrity of anyone in this room, but—it may be that our ability to detect trouble at a range where trouble believes itself undetectable will save lives."

"I see." The General Secretary went back to his first point. "And you believe there were other ships in the system, observing . . . how many ships?"

"We detected one," Heris said. The General Secretary nodded; he had caught the implication. "It may, of course, have been an innocent vessel with a very cautious captain . . . but its arrival, its response to the battle, and its departure, suggest something else. My scan tech has been working on the data we got; there is some indication that the ship has a history of traversing systems just as raids are going on. A paymaster, perhaps."

"But who would be doing that? Even when they trashed our orbital station, they got little for it—we couldn't figure out then what they really wanted."

"To see if the Fleet would come clean house, I suspect," Heris said. "When you got so little response from Fleet, they came back—as much to test that hypothesis as anything else."

"But why? We have no great wealth—we are not on the direct route to anywhere else, as I'm sure you noticed."

"To be honest, I have not yet had time for a serious consideration of what may lie behind what we saw. But I am sure that another ship observed our handling of the raider, and that it was there precisely to observe your defensive capability. That suggests some plan for an attack. From whom, or why, I cannot say at this point." She suspected, but she did not want to commit herself yet.

"What should we do?"

"Send an urgent message to Fleet, of course. I'm sure you're aware that things are . . . unsettled . . . in places. They have other problems. Still, we can draft a report that should elicit some response. Even sending such a report may help out; I would expect those watching your situation to know of such a request. They would probably delay any action until they ascertained whether Fleet responded in force." Or they would attack all the faster. If they were nearly ready. Heris wished she had more knowledge, and less intuitive sense of time ticking away.

"You were not . . . sent here? As a sort of . . . representative of Fleet?"

"No," Heris said, making it very firm. From the tone, they wanted her to be a covert presence; they wanted the reassurance that Fleet had not forgotten them. Remote worlds often felt neglected, and some were. "I am not now in the Regular Space Service. I'm a civilian, hired by Lady Cecelia to take her where she wishes . . . in this case, here, to look for bloodstock."

"I thought it was her yacht," someone down the table said. A third secretary to the defense council, Heris remembered.

"It was, but through a legal tangle when she was in a coma last year, it became mine. She will probably tell you the whole thing if you ask her." Heris didn't want to; she realized that someone who wanted to see her arrival with the *Sweet Delight* as more than providential could find other reasons for the change of ownership.

"As long as you *are* here," the General Secretary said, "could we beg your assistance, your advice? I quite understand that you are not, as you say, now in Fleet . . . but you have more experience in these matters than anyone else here. If you could suggest how we should think about this menace you spoke of, or how we could prepare to meet it . . ."

Prepare to die, she could have said honestly enough. With one cranky old escort, underpowered and lightly armed, with no bulk transport to get its population away to someplace safe, Xavier would be no more a match for a serious invasion than the raider had been for *Sweet Delight*. But for all their bright, perky music, their colorful impractical uniforms, their screeching massed pipes—yes, and even the number of horse enthusiasts—Heris liked these people. She liked the careful way a farmer's daughter had documented the raider's characteristics with her homemade scan equipment. The stubborn determination to resist and keep resisting that had led them to mount phase cannon in an atmospheric shuttle. The surprising competence of the old escort's crew . . . even the length of the General Secretary's speech at the parade ground . . . all went into the equation.

"While we're here," she said finally, into the silence, "I will be glad to give you what advice I can. But whether it does any good—that I can't know."

"Of course not. And we will show our gratitude by taking your first advice, to send word to the Regular arm of Fleet—" He reddened. "Sorry—I mean to Fleet Sector HQ."

"I'll get back up to my ship, and see what we've got in our records," Heris said. "Lady Cecelia brought her things down—she plans to visit various breeders here. So, if you can tell me about the next shuttle—"

"You won't stay the night?"

"No—to be honest, I'll be more comfortable up there, in direct contact with our scan techs."

"Quite so. Then if it's agreeable, we'll plan to confer with you on the station in the next few days. And there'll be a shuttle ready—when, Captain Vassilos?"

"Three hours," Vassilos said. "It's fuelling now."

"Thank you," Heris said. She started to stand up, and winced. "Lady Cecelia's right," she said. "I really should practice more on her simulator."

"Never mind," the General Secretary said. "It's not your equestrian expertise we need now."

"All the better, since I haven't any," said Heris; they all laughed.

Back aboard *Sweet Delight*, she called up the data they had gathered and came up with the answers—or answers that made sense. The Xavierans considered themselves remote, far from any population or power center. They were remote from the center of any political entity, but not so remote from frontiers. After all, she had had to file a letter of intent with the R.S.S. to visit Xavier, because it was in a frontier zone.

"Location, location, location," she reminded herself. The Familias Regnant had grown by accretion, expanding along trade routes through unclaimed space, until it bumped into resistance. The neat "spheres of influence" predicted by earlier planners existed only for small political units. Larger entities looked more like multidimensional models of complex organic molecules. Although this meant a larger "surface" to protect for the volume included, the advantage of an outlying lobe that included vital jump points more than compensated for the extra defensive exposure.

Castle Rock, with its massive stations Rockhouse Major and Minor, lay more or less at the center of Familias Regnant space—at least in three major axes. But those axes were not equal. The longest dimension was five or six times the shortest, including two fat tentacles or pseudopods extending toward Compassionate Hand territory. The interface between the Familias and its neighbors resembled that of an enzyme and its protein companion: star by star, the competing entities had fit themselves together in a way that increased the defensive difficulties by making the contact surface vast. Most of the time, this surface was merely a potential one: in spaces far too large to garrison, contact existed only sporadically, and along the usual mapped routes of travel.

Heris knew from experience that the ability to visualize the spatial interactions required both innate talent and practice. The visual representation she took to the next meeting with the General Secretary and his staff was far simpler than the one she and Petris and Koutsoudas would use. Even so, the General Secretary had trouble with it.

"What's this little skinny thing out here?" he asked.

"Us." Heris grinned at his shocked expression. "I know— you thought we were closer to the interior because Xavier is a short jump from Byerly and Neugarten and Shiva. But they're all strung out along one jump route, with an even smaller twig for Neverfall." She pointed. "There's Rockhouse. And there's Rotterdam—" Rotterdam, on its own slender twig, three jump points from Xavier because of the need to go around the saddle-shaped Compassionate Hand intrusion.

As the General Secretary stared at the color-coded visual, Heris added the icons that were Koutsoudas's best guess for the locations of Fleet and Compassionate Hand warships. The Compassionate Hand maintained major bases in the saddle between the lobes where Xavier and Rotterdam lay. Logical—so did the R.S.S. When this survey had been taken, they had had two battle groups at Partis, and one at Vashnagul.

Heris explained what that meant, trying to keep it simple. "The Compassionate Hand intends its battle groups to be more than just space fighters. Each battle group deploys units capable of invading and occupying fixed positions such as space stations and satellite defense systems. On a sparsely settled planet without good defenses, such teams could even take control of the entire world. More commonly, they would 'scorch' the population from space—blow the population centers, perhaps with tactical nukes. Then they'd land their own construction teams and equipment."

"They'd just—kill everyone, for no reason?"

"From their point of view, there's a reason. They don't care about people they don't need, and if they've chosen Xavier for a forward base, they won't want to waste time converting your population."

"And they might choose us because—"

"Because of the jump point access Xavier provides. Although the direct route in is straightforward, there are more alternatives from here than from Rotterdam. It's still tricky— look—" Heris pointed out the difficulties the Compassionate Hand would face. "The point of coming through here is surprise, so if they lose surprise here they've expended effort for no gain. That means they'll try to interrupt communications as soon as—even before—they attack. Do you have daily ansible traffic?"

"No . . . in fact, the charges are high enough that we usually store and batch it. Once a week at most."

"So no one outside would notice if you didn't send a batch for a week or so."

"That's right—oh. I see. Then I suppose they could fabricate a message—"

"If they needed to. My point being, Xavier is most valuable in the early stages of a war, then its value drops until they can get their defenses up, when it becomes valuable again simply because it denies those jump points to Fleet."

"And our strategy?"

"Tell Fleet what we think, and keep telling them until they listen—and don't let ourselves be surprised by an invasion force we weren't expecting." And hope that the enemy had not already intercepted their messages. But Heris kept that grim thought to herself.

CHAPTER TEN

On the planet Music

Raffa wandered around the street market, but caught no sight of the king, or clone, or whoever that had been. She couldn't see far anyway, past the colorful awnings and dwarf flowering trees, the little clusters of booths strung with banners. Finally, when her stomach informed her it was lunchtime, she followed her nose to a booth where a deft-fingered man wrapped spirals of meat and bread dough on sticks, and grilled them. Next to that booth, another sold fruit punches; Raffa picked something called omberri, which she had never had before.

She chose a bench under one of the nonflowering trees—she had noticed the bees humming among flowers—and worked her way down the meat and bread spirals. Her omberri punch had tartness enough to be refreshing on this warm day, without puckering her mouth. When she was through, she sat a few minutes with her legs stretched, watching the crowds of noontime shoppers. She had seen several booths she'd like to visit—shell jewelry, ribbon weaving worked into striking belts and vests—along with displays of native crafts that didn't interest her. Even some pottery as ghastly as that made by Ottala Morreline's crazy aunt.

Now that she'd lost track of the king, and had no idea where Ronnie and George were, she might as well spend the afternoon shopping. With that cheering thought, she worked her way through the booths, back to the one with the shell jewelry.

Then she saw the young man with the familiar way of carrying his head. It couldn't be. Raffa ducked among the people, working her way closer. From behind, he still looked familiar. She edged her way around a booth to get a side view, and caught sight of his profile just an instant before he turned and looked her way. It *was*. Raffa opened her mouth to call out, just as he focussed on her and paled. He spun on his heel and darted away.

Raffa, startled, didn't move until someone touched her arm and pointed out that she was blocking the whole aisle. "Sorry," she said, still feeling blank. It had to be the prince. It had to be Gerel, who was supposed to be dead, and he was afraid to see her.

In one flash she saw the whole pattern of deceit. Gerel wasn't dead; the man she had seen *was* the king, and he had come here to meet Gerel. King and prince . . . the phrase "government in exile" came to mind from her history studies. Lord Thornbuckle and Kevil Mahoney only *thought* they'd defeated the king—he was planning an insurrection.

Which meant that Ronnie and George, if they were still alive, were in mortal danger. Her skin tingled; she felt as preternaturally alert as she had that first night on the island. Did they know? Or were they about to walk into a conspiracy?

She set off slowly in the direction Gerel had fled. She didn't expect to find him—she didn't even want to find him—but she wanted to see what that part of the city was like.

Behind the street market, the streets resumed their normal, sedate appearance. Raffa noted that she was now on Bedrich, just crossing Cole. This was a residential area, five-story apartments lining both sides of the street, each with its own distinct facade. She saw a woman with three identical children in blue smocks . . . tried not to let herself think "clone." They were children—and when they grinned up at her with identical sticky smiles, she couldn't help grinning back. A yellow and white cat leapt off a window ledge in front of her, paraded to the curb with its tail in the air, and then sat to lick its paws.

This would get her nowhere but farther from the hotel.

Gerel had been scared; he wouldn't come back to see if she was in the neighborhood. Raffa slowed at the next street and glanced at the sign. Hari . . . and her tourist handcomp told her she would find nothing scenic if she kept going the same way. Just sore legs on the way back. She glanced around, and finally shrugged to herself. She might as well go back to the hotel, see if any messages had come in from the Institute about the pharmaceutical samples she'd turned in.

"These were not manufactured here. They were manufactured in modern equipment, using a process similar to, but not identical to, the one we developed. I can show you— here—" Raffa stared at the squiggly lines, and wished she had paid more attention to chemistry. "They've used an alternate synthetic route which we don't like because it produces more waste. In addition, the isotope fractions suggest that the raw materials came from a source we don't use. Although we do have one old sample that parallels it— from a mine in your territory. Do you know the Patchcock system?"

Raffa shook her head. "Not except for that mess when there was a war or something." She realized that didn't sound very intelligent, but after all she hadn't been old enough to pay much attention.

"Well, before that we used to import a little from one of the planets there, and we still have reference samples. It's not definitive, by any means, but the Patchcock system could be a source of the raw materials. I do know that there's a sizeable pharmaceutical industry on Patchcock itself. The Morrelines, I believe, are major investors."

Raffa wondered if those were the same Morrelines whose daughter Ottala had been such a pain at school. She and Brun had never liked Ottala that much—well, to be honest, at all—but she supposed she could look Ottala up when she got back to Familias space. "And the drugs themselves? Are they complying with your standards?"

"Aside from the fact that they're breaking the licensing agreement by using an alternate process, those in the first sample submitted do meet our standards. The second sample, however, is subtly different. Do you read chromatographs?"

"No . . . I'm sorry."

"Never mind. I'll give you the complete analysis and references, of course . . . it's important for your neurologists to have this, and understand the effects. In essence, the changes in the ring structures—the substitutions—are going to affect the quality of the rejuvenation, and this degradation will accumulate with repeated rejuvenations. It's not as bad as the old method, and it should be reversible, but if your specialists have noticed some deterioration in memory and cognitive ability in some patients, this may explain it."

"I know there's concern," Raffa said, without specifying whose concern.

"Frankly, I'm not surprised. It's possible that this is merely sloppy quality control in manufacturing—if for instance the reaction in the fourteenth step is poisoned, it's possible for that ring substitution to occur. But you must also consider industrial sabotage. Either a deliberate intent to adulterate the drugs to manipulate someone, or deliberate carelessness with the intent to maximize profits. Especially with the alternate process being used, it would be expensive to maintain the kind of quality we demand; the biologicals used to clean up the unreacted substrate can be difficult to extract."

This was all gobbledygook to Raffa, except the part about sabotage and profit margins . . . she could see possibilities either way, and so, she was sure, could Lord Thornbuckle. "I think this is too important to depend on one messenger," she said. She dug out the authorization card Lord Thornbuckle had given her. "Here's the account number—"

Kemtre Lord Altmann, the former king of the Familias Regnant, limped slightly. His legs ached. He had walked more kilometers in the past week than in the year before. The Neurosciences Institute had refused to give him his sons' address, had said they would not violate the privacy of their patients. When he tried to insist that he was their father, he had rights, they pointed out that under his law the clones had no legal identity at all.

"Here, they are eligible for full citizenship. The biological relationship is irrelevant, especially for clones derived not from division in the embryo but from tissue culture of an older individual. To the extent that these persons have a parent, it is the donor individual—their prime, as they called him."

"But I was his father, too," the king protested.

"And how many biological children did you father?"

"Three boys," the king said.

"And what happened to them?" He could tell by the tone of the question that the interviewer already knew the answers.

"They're dead," he said, after a pause.

"All three. Somehow that doesn't recommend you as a father."

He wanted to say *It's not my fault,* but he knew the other man thought it was.

"What we will do," the man said, "is send word to the young men that you are here, and want to contact them. It is then their decision whether or not to seek you out."

"But—but that's not fair," the king said. "What am I supposed to do if they won't see me?"

"Go back to the Familias," the man said, as if it were obvious.

"I can't do that. I really want—I must see them. If I can only talk to them, I'm sure I can make them understand."

The other man's frown told him he had gone too far. "I rather doubt that—you haven't convinced me. We will do as I said—tell them you are here, and let them decide. They are adults under our law; they've applied for full citizenship. They have the legal right to decide for themselves . . . and I should warn you that you have no legal right to harass them."

He could hardly harass them when he couldn't find them. He knew their alias, at least the one they had been given, and he had started with the Smiths in the city directory. The name was not so common here as in the Familias, but it was common enough. He had met Smiths who were bakers, who were attorneys, who worked in the city's utility repair division, who were midwives and machinists. At least half of them were clones; he learned quickly not to explain his search. None would help him, not even to eliminate their clonesibs from the pattern. At this rate, it would take him years to find all the Smiths on this single planet.

✳ ✳ ✳

"It's not just your girlfriend," Borhes said. "There's some strange man looking for Smiths. Claims to be the king." He took a gulp of his drink. "I didn't dare get close enough to find out. If he saw me—"

"You should have changed your name," George said helpfully. "At least you know that the Neurosciences people are keeping your secret."

"There are lots of Smiths," Borhes said. "And we didn't really think anyone would come looking for us."

"Surprise," murmured George. Ronnie cocked an eye at him. Was George going to be odious again? Here? It was a bad time, he thought, eyeing the tension in every line of the clones' bodies.

"Shut *up*," said Andres. "I didn't like you before, and I don't like your idea of jokes."

"We're even," George said. "I don't like your idea of hospitality. This is silly, you know. Holding us like this doesn't accomplish anything you want. You need new identities, so your father—sorry, Gerel's father—doesn't find you. You need to be free to move around; you need friends who will steer the king away from you, warn you when he's near, all that. Instead, you have tied yourself down, and us up; you're isolated, you don't have friends—"

"I said, shut up!" Andres hit George, then looked at Borhes for his reaction. Borhes shrugged; Andres looked away.

"You could go on and kill us," George said, undeterred by the blow that reddened his face. Ronnie felt a sneaking sympathy with Andres. "—But that wouldn't help, either. You'd have to get rid of two fairly large, heavy corpses. Someone might see you, and although the Guernesi have been cooperative so far, I suspect that murdering us would strain their sympathy. It would certainly upset Raffaele, and since you don't know her as well as I do, I warn you that she is likely to stick on Ronnie's trail until she finds him, dead or alive."

Ronnie felt himself blushing. "George, shut up!" he said. "You're not helping."

"Neither are you," George said. "We've tried being nice. We've tried being polite, helpful, entertaining, amusing . . . and they're still being idiots. Probably enough of that stupidity drug still in their systems—"

"It is not!" Borhes, this time, loomed over George with his hand raised.

In a tone of sweet reason that would have enraged angels, George persisted. "So I thought perhaps a bit of aggravation might make them wake up and think. If they can. Or listen to wiser minds, if they can't."

"We are not stupid!" That was both clones together, almost shouting.

"Right. Raise your voices. Yell and scream, and someone may call the police or whatever the Guernesi call them."

"The Gard," Borhes said, but more softly.

"Whatever. Listen, Borhes, this has gone on long enough. Raffa saw you—she's going to start thinking and doing, a very dangerous combination. She probably thinks you're Gerel, and if she knows the king's here, she's going to think it's a conspiracy to regain the throne—"

"What? That's crazy!"

"No crazier than what you've done. It's what any person would think, believing that Gerel, who's supposed to be dead, and the king are in the same place. She's going to put that alongside our disappearance, and think we're either dead or being held by the king and Gerel—or their supporters."

"I haven't seen her again," Borhes said. George shrugged as well as he could.

"She's not stupid, Bor. She can recognize danger when she sees it. And she can act. So the smartest thing for you to do is enlist us as allies—let us run some interference for you."

"As if we could trust you!" Andres and Borhes exchanged glances and glared at their captives.

"It's probably hard for clones to trust anyone outside the clone cluster," George said. "Especially with the life you had. But someday you'll have to, and you know us better than anyone else so far."

"So what do you suggest?"

"What I said before. Get new identities. Simple disguises to start with, maybe, but probably plastic surgery or biosculpts later. Change your names legally. I'm sure the Neurosciences people will help."

"But—we can't go out until—"

"Oh, come now! This isn't an adventure cube thriller. Wait until dark. Take a private cab. Call the Institute from here and make arrangements." The clones looked at each other but said nothing. Ronnie held his breath. Would this work? "Or," George began, and Ronnie wanted to smack him. Why couldn't he be still a little longer? "Or, you could let one of us out to arrange disguises, transportation, even check at the Institute and make sure the king isn't hanging around the front door. Find the back door."

The clones laughed. "I don't think so," Andres said. "The other—perhaps you're right; it does make sense to disguise ourselves and take other names. One of our therapists at the Institute did suggest that, but it seemed unnecessary then."

"One thing to consider," George said. "The king may not be the only one who wants to find you. If someone did want to set up a contender for a future throne, your tissues would be helpful. With or without your cooperation."

"Well, we certainly can't trust *you*," Andres said. Then he pulled Borhes to the far side of the room, where they whispered in rapid Guernesi.

The outside felt large and dangerous; Ronnie was surprised to find himself flinching away from the bustling crowd on the sidewalk. He had loathed that small cramped room while he was in it, but now it seemed a safe haven. He understood why the clones were reluctant to go back out.

When he came to the street market, he half-hoped to see Raffa there. He bought himself a fruit pastry with the last coin in his pocket and ate it as he walked. No one seemed to notice him; no Raffa appeared, nor did the king. He wondered if Raffa had come across the king—he hoped not. That would really confuse things.

At a public combooth, he stripped his messages at the Travelers' Directory. Eleven from Raffa, all with a reply code. He punched it in, and listened to a series of unmelodious buzzes and hisses, until a message came on: "Please leave a message," followed by the three bleeps the Guernesi used to signal readiness to record.

Ronnie cleared his throat and tried to sound casual. "Hi, Raffa—it's Ronnie. What are you doing here? Did your parents change their mind about the engagement? I'll call again later." He hoped he would. He hoped anyone intercepting that message would hear only a young man in love. He hoped she was all right.

Some dim memory of spy adventure stories suggested that he shouldn't use the same booth for all the calls he planned to make. He walked across the street to another one, and called the Neurosciences Institute. The clones had told him which extension to ask for. The name they'd given him was out to lunch, though. He could leave a message or call later, he was told. He chose to call back. In the meantime, he could find out if the king was using his own name.

Raffa threw her packages on the table, and started to stretch out for a nap—then saw the blinking light on the comconsole. A message? Could it possibly be Ronnie and George? Her heart pounded; she took a breath and told herself to be calm. When she flicked REPLAY and heard Ronnie's voice, her vision dimmed for a moment and her heart pounded. The message was almost over by the time her vision cleared . . . and the idiot hadn't left a reply code. Rage replaced whatever strong emotion had just swept her— she didn't stop to think about it. The comconsole could capture the calling number and display its location; she looked at that, at the time the message had been left, and forgot about the nap.

She was two blocks away when it occurred to her that this might not be a wise move. Perhaps Ronnie hadn't left a reply code because there were problems. Perhaps—she kept walking. Perhaps if she was quick enough, he would still be there.

The booth he'd called from, on the corner of Osip and Dixha, contained a thin woman and three active preschoolers, clearly a triad. Raffa looked around, ignoring the crafts, the food booths, and spotted another cluster of combooths on the far side of the market.

And there he was. Unharmed. Angled away from her, talking—his free arm moved, gesturing—and she was suddenly angry enough to wring that handsome neck. She strode across the market, ignoring everything, until she was right behind him. She could hear nothing—the Guernesi combooths had enviable privacy shields—but he had not blanked the booth visually. Raffa moved around until she could see his face . . . she wanted to see his face very badly, especially when he caught sight of her.

He turned paper white and grabbed at the booth rail. His

lips shaped her name, then he held up a hand. He glanced away briefly, as if something said to him required a change in attention, then ended the connection and shot out of the booth as if kicked. "Raffa! How did you—I mean—Raffa!"

She had been prepared to give him a stony glare and a crisp demand for information, but his hug was more frantic than possessive. And it felt good.

"I was so worried," she said, feeling her anger leak away, to be replaced by first relief than a wave of pure physical passion. Her legs felt odd; the ground seemed very far away. "I was afraid you were in trouble—you'll never guess what I've seen."

"Oh?" He was looking past her now, scanning the crowd as if he expected someone.

"Where's George?" Raffa asked. "We need to warn him—did you know the ex-king was here?"

"Uh . . ."

"And the prince. Gerel, who was supposed to be dead? He's not. I saw him. I think the king is in league with his son to take over the government again."

"The king is not in league with his son. Gerel is dead."

"But I saw him—and he recognized me and took off—"

"That wasn't Gerel." He was still looking beyond her, as if he expected to see someone he recognized.

"It was. I'm not blind, Ronnie—don't think you can treat me like a little idiot." She wanted to grab his chin and make him look at her, but a lifetime of prudence prevented her.

"You're not blind, but that wasn't Gerel." Now he looked at her, but not with the look she wanted. "Think, Raffa—what have you seen since you've been here?"

"Clones," Raffa said. "Gerel's clone? Has the king come here to get another son, take over the government?"

"Not with them—him—" Ronnie smacked himself on the forehead. "Blast it . . . I've already screwed up. No, it's not the king, or not exactly. The clones are from before, when Gerel was still alive. They doubled for him."

"But that's—" Illegal, she started to say, but with so much illegality going on, why not?

"And they don't want to have anything to do with the Familias now," Ronnie said. "They want to get on with their lives, here in a place where clones are normal, where they can be full citizens."

"You've seen—you've *talked* to them. Is that where you've been?"

"Raffa, I can't talk about it now. We have to get them some help, before the king finds them. I was just talking to the Neurosciences Institute; they'll help them get new identities, but we have to help them get there without the king noticing. The Institute says he's made a pest of himself, and they suspect he's having the place watched." He was scanning the crowd again; she could feel the tension in his arm.

"Let's go, then. Take me to them."

"I can't do that!"

"Why not? You don't think I'm going to let you walk back into trouble, do you? So that I can sit here and worry? Forget that." She realized that she had clenched her hand on his arm; her voice had risen, and a few people were glancing their way. She let go and turned away, furious again.

"Raffa, I—I don't want to take chances." With you, he meant.

"And did I survive on the island just as well as you, or not?"

"You did, but—"

"But you're afraid for me now. Who do you think will hurt me? Gerel's clones?"

"They're not quite . . . stable."

"No, but I presume they've had a good upbringing." She gave him another long look, noticing the shadows under his eyes, the tight-drawn skin. "You look hungry—who's been feeding you?"

"They have—but they had to use our money too, and it's been short."

"Well, then. That's my cue." Raffa took his hand again and led him into the market. "I'll be the traditional lady, the loaf bringer. Buttered toast does more than music to soothe the savage beast." She was aware of butchering several traditional quotes, but in the meantime—she led Ronnie from one booth to another, loading his arms with sacks of pastries, loaves of bread, a fat round cheese, and a sausage of indecent length and girth. "Fruit," she muttered then, and carried away a sack of bright gold pebbly-skinned fruits and a basket of dark purple berries. Ronnie quit arguing after she stuck a cheese-filled pastry in his mouth, and when she asked he led her away, to the far side of the market.

"Along this street," he said finally. "You know you're risking a lot."

"Not my sanity, though," Raffa said. "And that was about to disappear right along with you. This is much better. Besides, I have news about your original mission."

"You do?"

"Yes, but I won't tell you until we're there. So hurry up."

Ronnie led her up the narrow stairs, half-hoping the clones would be out, and George would let them in. Instead, Borhes opened the door. His eyes widened. "You promised!" he muttered. "I thought we could trust *you*." Then he recognized the sacks for what they were. He swallowed.

"She found me," Ronnie said. "I swear it—and she bought the food. You'd better let us in."

If Borhes had had any other thought, Raffa made sure he didn't act on it; she pushed her way through the door with her nose on Ronnie's back. George, still tied up, looked around and his eyes lighted.

"Raffa!"

She ignored him for the moment, but gave both clones a long look that brought a flush to their cheeks. "Well, gentlemen. Ronnie tells me you aren't Gerel, either one of you. I presume you have names: may I know them?"

"I'm Andres; he's Borhes." Andres seemed shaken; Ronnie felt an unexpected pang of sympathy. He would not have seen Raffa on the island; he probably thought of her as a frivoler, like the old Bubbles.

"I thought you might like something fresh to eat," Raffa said, and began unpacking the food. When Borhes reached for a pastry, she stopped him with a glance. "Untie George," she said.

"Good for you, Raffa," said George, gleefully.

"Shut up, George," she said, in much the same tone. "I expect you were being odious again. It's not the time." George got up, when Borhes had freed him, and came to the table stiffly, rubbing his wrists.

"Are you going to let us eat?" he asked.

"Yes," Raffa said. "In the faint hope that hunger is what's been dimming your collective wits." Whatever protests they might have made were lost in the descent on the food. Raffa nibbled a few of the purple berries while she watched the food disappear. When the rate of disappearance slowed, she tapped the table with the knife Borhes had used on the sausage. They looked up with the guilty expressions of little boys who have hogged the birthday cake.

"Sorry, Raffa," George said. "We were just so hungry—"

"I'm not complaining about that," she said. "But it's time to start thinking again." When she paused, they said nothing, jaws still chomping busily. Raffa sighed. "All right. Ronnie told me that the Institute is quite willing to help you acquire new identities, but the former king has been badgering them, and they think he may be having the Institute watched."

"And these two—and now you—know about us," Andres said, picking his teeth inelegantly.

Raffa ignored the rudeness. "We're no threat, sir—Andres or Borhes or whichever you are. Ronnie and I have nothing more in mind than living in peace as far from our families as we can get." Ronnie sat up straight; he hadn't realized that she had made up her mind on that as well. "Even George, I'm sure, has better things to do than make your lives miserable."

"Many better things," George said, in the tone of earnestness with which the salesman assures you the item in question is worth twice its price, and only the serious illness of his grandmother allows him to consider such a sacrifice as the present sale.

"Shut up, George," said Raffa again, this time with no sting in it. "So we can help you get to the Institute—and once inside, you know the king can't bother you. He has no authority here."

"But what about the—" Ronnie began; he stopped short as Raffa's glance landed on him like a brick on the head.

"Once we've helped these gentlemen," Raffa said, "then we can discuss the matters you and I still have to discuss."

"It sounds to me as if you'd settled them all," said Andres without sarcasm, as if he were describing the movements of an alien creature.

"Within the limits possible, yes." Raffa made no apologies. "Now, about getting you safely to the Institute—what sort of hours did they mention, Ronnie?"

"They said any time, and I thought in the dark—"

"Would be the obvious time to pick. Have another pastry.

May I suggest lunchtime? Few fugitives choose midday to move around, and the king likes his meals. He wanders around in both morning and afternoon—and goes out in the evenings—but at lunch he's sitting in the hotel, eating. And—as soon as possible. Tomorrow, for instance. If he has people looking for two copies of Gerel, we'll give them something else—a group of young people, none of them exactly like Gerel. Surely you two can do simple disguises?"

"Of course," said Borhes. He looked at Andres. "It might work."

"It will," said Raffa. "Tomorrow, late morning—I'll come here alone. Be ready." She got up to leave, and then laid a sheaf of the local currency on the table. "And here—be sure to eat a good supper."

Late the next morning, Raffa found four alert young men, eyeing each other with some suspicion but no open hostility. Two of them looked like brothers, but not clones. Something had changed in their hair color, the bones of their faces, their way of moving. She didn't stop to analyze it. "Come on," she said. "The king's back in the hotel—I waited to leave until he'd gone into the dining room. Ronnie, George—put your stuff in these packsacks."

"Shouldn't we be less . . . conspicuous?" Andres asked. He was eyeing her cherry-colored tunic, and the sheaf of bright flowers she carried, along with a basket of pastries.

"We can't really be inconspicuous," Raffa said. "What we can be is conspicuously something other than they expect. Students . . . whatever. Anything but two scared clones. If you'll just chatter along like normal people—or eat . . ."

They trooped downstairs as casually as if they were going to a party. George started an anecdote that had nothing to do with anything; Ronnie munched a cheese pastry, and the clones looked a bit dazed.

"I don't see why you didn't bring a private car," Borhes said, under cover of George's story about the girl who had painted her brother's feet purple.

"That would have been conspicuous," Raffa said. "How often do hire-cars come to this neighborhood? Come on—just through the market." The market, bustling with the lunchtime crowd, all more interested in food and drink than a girl with a bunch of flowers and her four companions.

At the transit stop, a loose clump of people waited, most of them eating. Raffa had begun to relax when someone called to her.

"Raffaele Forrester-Saenz!" Raffa jumped as if she'd been poked with a pin, then tried to pretend nothing had happened. All four young men had gone rigid; the clones looked as if they might faint. "Raffaele!" came the voice, louder yet. Through the noise of her heart beating, Raffa could now tell that it was an old lady's quavery disapproval—certainly not the king. She turned around, and found herself face-to-face with Ottala's aunt.

"Yes?" she said, as casually as she could while impaled on that indignant gaze. Ottala's aunt, draped in shades of mauve, with a knitted purple cap adorned with droopy knitted flowers in pink and beige . . . Raffa had to struggle not to burst out laughing.

"Don't pretend you don't know me," Ottala's aunt said. "You were at school with my niece Ottala. You ought to be ashamed of yourself! Your parents will hear about this!"

"About what?" Raffa said. Beside her, Ronnie's arm twitched, but he and the other young men were steadfastly not looking that direction.

"Running off to carouse in foreign parts with a young man! And not just one of them!" Ottala's aunt shook a ring-covered finger under Raffa's nose. "Everyone knows your family doesn't want you to marry Ronald Carruthers, and here you are—" Her head shot forward, like a turtle's from its shell, as she peered at the back of four young male heads. "You needn't hide, young man. I saw you across the market, laughing and chatting as if you had nothing better to do. And who are the others, if you please?" Ronnie sighed and turned around; the others still pretended not to hear.

None of your business was what Raffa wanted to say to the question, but practicality as well as manners prevented her. Old ladies like this didn't quit bothering you just because you were rude; they had dealt with more rudeness already than the average youth could think up. Raffa tried to think if anything would help, and glanced past Ottala's aunt to the person behind her. He was pushing a barrow, and on the barrow were . . . pottery pieces of incredible ugliness. Half-melted graceless shapes in colors that made her stomach turn. Recognition and counterattack came together.

"Those pots," she began. Ottala's aunt turned one of the colors on them, an ugly puce.

"You wouldn't understand," she began. "They aren't just pots, they're . . ."

"I understood that you yourself were quite an artist in pottery," Raffa said, with emphasis. "You gave some to Ottala; she had them at school. I noticed, when I was in the market the other day, how much the local wares resembled them. Perhaps—"

"Great artists derive inspiration from many sources," Ottala's aunt muttered. Her dark little eyes peered up at Raffa.

"And lesser artists plagiarize," Raffa said, with no softening. "Sometimes those who aren't artists simply—"

Ottala's aunt held up her hand, and Raffa stopped. "All right. I—I couldn't make enough pots on my own—my family kept asking for more, and more, and more. Finally I got someone to make a few for me—and then a few more—"

"But why such ugly ones?" Raffa said, shocking herself. Ottala's aunt shook her head, as if she hadn't heard right, and then smiled sadly.

"I kept hoping they'd quit asking—you know, if I made them uglier and uglier." After a pause, she went on. "I really can't explain how everyone in the family has such bad taste—it seems the worse the product, the more they want."

"Why didn't you just tell them you were tired of making pots?"

"My dear, you aren't old enough to understand." The old lady leaned forward, confiding. "Someday, when you're grown, and you're enjoying things, your relatives will start complaining. 'You never finish anything you start,' they'll say. 'You pick up one hobby after another—you're just wasting time and money with all these enthusiasms.' 'You should stick to one thing and learn to do it really well.'" Ottala's aunt sniffed. "It doesn't matter what it is. I expect that Ronald's aunt, Cecelia de Marktos, heard the same thing about her horses."

"That's true," Ronnie put in. "It's one reason Aunt Cecelia's so angry with my parents; they kept telling her that her riding was just a hobby, and not worth all the time she put into it."

"You see?" Ottala's aunt looked triumphant. "I think my

family wanted to make sure I stuck to pottery, and that's why they kept asking for more. And to be honest, my dear, I did want to quit. They were right."

"Still . . ." began Raffa, who wanted to get the conversation back to the covert negotiation she had started. "About these pots . . . and Ronnie . . ."

"Oh, all right," Ottala's aunt huffed. "I won't tell on you, if you don't tell on me. But I still think young girls have no business running around in foreign lands with *four young men*. One was quite enough for me, in my young days." As the tram came in, and Raffa moved to board it with the others, Ottala's aunt called, "And don't think I don't recognize young George Mahoney there, with his ears the color of ripe plums. . . ."

The rest of the trip to the Institute passed without incident.

CHAPTER ELEVEN

"We have more troubles than getting the clones to safety," Raffa said, when they met again. Ronnie and George, fresh from showers, in clean clothes, had their usual glossy surface. "Some of the rejuvenation drugs have been adulterated, and none of the samples we brought—yours or mine—were manufactured here."

"None?"

"None. They did an isotopic analysis, and in their database—which they admit isn't all-inclusive—there's a match with Patchcock." Ronnie and George looked at each other, startled, over her head. "What?"

"Nothing," they both said in the tone of voice that means Something.

"Tell me." Raffa was not about to take any more nonsense.

"Ottala Morreline disappeared on Patchcock. I don't know any more; I'm not supposed to know that much, but I always could read upside down and backwards." George smirked. Raffa could have smacked him, but she wouldn't let herself be distracted.

"Is that why Lord Thornbuckle sent Brun off with Captain Serrano?"

"Maybe. Probably. Just in case someone's out to get the daughters of wealthy families."

"And they sent me *here*." Raffa was seriously annoyed with Lord Thornbuckle and her own parents, but on mutually exclusive grounds. She didn't like being thought incompetent enough to need to be sent away, and she didn't like being thought negligible enough to be sent from Castle Rock to the Guerni Republic alone. If anyone had wanted to harm her, she'd have been unprotected.

Ronnie seemed to have read her thoughts. "You're trustworthy, Raffa—you wouldn't get into trouble. Brun would poke her nose into every stinging nettle she could find. Ottala was the same. . . ."

"She was not," Raffa said. "Ottala was a mean-minded snitch. Brun got into mischief for the fun of it; Ottala poked into things to get other people in trouble."

"I'll never understand the way women pick at each other," George said in his most sanctimonious tone.

"You would if you'd been in school with Ottala," Raffa said. "She nearly got Brun expelled. Besides, I've heard you talk about your schoolmates."

"It's different. None of us were the sweet flower of young womanhood—OUCH!" George recoiled and glared at her. "You hit me."

"And will again if you don't behave," said Raffa. She winked at Ronnie. "Be odious to someone else for a change."

"It's odd about Patchcock," Ronnie said. "It keeps showing up in all this—Captain Serrano told me about the Patchcock Incursion, and Ottala disappeared—"

"That can't be connected," George said. "Those riots were years ago—we were infants or something."

"And now this, about the drugs. It ought to make sense some way, and it doesn't." Ronnie frowned. "It would be great if we could wrap the whole thing up for them. Go to Patchcock, find out what happened to Ottala, find out if the Morrelines are adulterating the drugs on purpose, or just chasing profits. They might not even understand what could go wrong."

"I don't think we can," Raffa said. "We need to take this evidence back to Lord Thornbuckle first, and—"

"He needs it, I agree. But we can't add anything to it. None of us are chemists; we don't understand this stuff." He patted the hardcopy. "If we sent it—by several routes, to be sure it got through—that should be enough."

"Certainly Ottala's friends are more likely to figure out where she's hiding than someone who doesn't even know her," George said. "Not that we're friends, exactly—even I thought she was an awful prig sometimes."

"Besides, we have a flair for it," Ronnie said. "Look at what we accomplished here. It could have been a very sticky situation indeed, even dangerous, but we all came out of it with what we needed to know and no damage done."

Raffa had her doubts about that. Those two unhappy young clones would have more trouble than they thought adjusting to life as independents. Their new faces—whatever they were—would not change their natures. A fragment of poetry her Aunt Marta quoted swam into her mind. "No thing, neither cunning fox nor roaring lion, can change the nature born in its blood," she said.

George looked startled, but Ronnie grinned at her. "Exactly. You and I—and George of course—are good at this sort of thing. Besides, think what will happen if we go back home. We'll all be wrapped away in protective familial swaddlings. Whereas, if we solve the whole rejuvenation problem for them—well, the drug part anyway—they'll have to recognize that we really are adults, and let us make our own decisions."

"I don't know, Ronnie," George said. "Raffa's not enthusiastic about this, and if it's dangerous . . . she shouldn't go, perhaps. She can explain to Lord Thornbuckle what we're up to, in case we need backup or something." In his tone, Raffa heard *She's not Brun*. And he thought Ottala was priggish; did he think the same of her?

"Don't be ridiculous," she heard herself saying. "If you'll remember, I did quite well on the island. Just because I can be prudent doesn't mean I'm timid."

The com chimed; Raffa, who was nearest, answered it. "Dama—a Venezia Glendower-Morreline se Vahtigos wishes to speak with you."

"Oh—of course." Raffa held up her hand for silence, then said, "It's Ottala's Aunt Venezia again." Ronnie and George nodded, and settled back into their chairs with the clear intention of letting Raffa deal with it.

"Raffaele—" That was Venezia. "My dear, it just occurred to me—there's something you could do to help me."

"Yes?" Raffa was not about to commit herself.

"It's Ottala. You were her friend in school, I know." Raffa tried to stop that train of thought.

"Not a close friend, really."

"Well, I remember your name." In auntian logic, that seemed to be enough. "I'm worried about her," Venezia went on. "She missed her brother's *seegrin*, and her parents keep telling me not to worry, that she's a wild girl still under the influence of schoolmates such as yourself, my dear, and that blonde girl—Bubbles or whatever her name was. Do you know where she is?"

"No," said Raffa, leaning heavily on her minimal knowledge of sophistry. She didn't know where Ottala was, even though George had seen something which reported that Ottala had gone missing on Patchcock. Perhaps George had misread it, or the report was wrong, or she wasn't still there.

"I *thought* she told me she was going to visit Patchcock, such a silly idea because there's nothing to see, but her parents insist that I misunderstood, that I must have had my head in the kiln. Of course they don't know that I don't do that anymore, and I couldn't explain—" She paused. Raffa could think of nothing to say; she had to clench her teeth to keep her jaw from dropping open. "I wanted to go look for her," Venezia went on, "but they made it quite clear that I was not welcome to do so. Silly, really, because I own enough stock in the company that I should be able to do what I want. I had to help Oscar and Bertie out a while back, and they repaid me in shares. Not that I care, you understand, but . . . anyway, whatever they say, I think that's where she went and she should have come back by now. I thought that you—that perhaps you, having gone off with a young man, might know if that's what happened to Ottala. Because if it is what happened, then I could tell the family and they'd quit worrying."

Raffa found her attention caught by details that bobbed past in the torrent of words . . . that connected with other details from the earlier conversation. Suddenly the somewhat scatty aunt who created—or faked creating—the ugliest pottery *objets d'art* she had ever seen began to look like someone else—like the investor, perhaps even the major stockholder, who was being kept away from the business while nefarious activities went on. What if Ottala had suspected as much?

"If I could just come up and talk to you," Venezia said. "A bright young girl like you . . . and with a young man like Ronald Carruthers, you couldn't come to any harm."

"Harm?" Raffa managed to say past the whirling in her brain.

"Could I? We could have tea, or—" The thought of tea with Venezia made for a quick decision.

"Not tea," Raffa said firmly. "Why don't you just come up and we'll chat."

"Wonderful," said Venezia, and before Raffa could mention that she had other visitors as well, the connection blanked. Quickly, in breathless phrases, she told the other two what she had heard.

"And so, if *she* wants us to go to Patchcock, it gives us the perfect excuse."

"To be thrown out by her family," Ronnie said glumly. "I suppose she's going to tag along, too, just for decency's sake."

He was interrupted by a tap on the door. Venezia, looking more auntlike than ever, floated in on ripples of sheer lavender that seemed to drape her from head to heel. Scarves competed for space on her shoulders, and strips of lace fluttered in her wake.

"Ah, my dear Raffaele. So like your dear Aunt Marta. She used to wear just that color—"

"You know Aunt Marta?" Raffaele asked, only slightly startled.

"Long ago," Venezia said. "She was more serious—she even took a doctorate in synthetic chemistry, did you know that?" Raffa hadn't; while she digested this surprising fact about her favorite aunt, Venezia looked around. "Ronald—George—where are the other two?" Ronnie's attempt at a smile froze into position. Raffa leapt in.

"Other two—oh, the young men at the tram stop? Just some boys Ronnie and George met in a bar one night."

"Locals?" asked Venezia, but without waiting for an answer she launched into her plan. "I'm glad they're not here, dear, because I would not wish to discuss family business in front of strangers. I know I can trust all of you." She favored them all with a bright little smile that made Raffa's teeth ache. "Have you explained about Ottala?"

"Not . . . really. I thought you—" With that, Venezia interrupted to go over the whole thing again, this time with additional commentary on Ottala's scholastic record, the errors in judgment that had made it necessary for Bertie and Oscar to ask for her financial assistance, her opinion of men in general and her family in particular . . . on and on, until Raffa felt that she would doze off in sheer self-defense.

"And what you would like us to do—" she said, in one of the rare brief pauses for breath.

"Oh. Well. What I'd like you to do is go to Patchcock and find Ottala. If, as I suspect, she's living some kind of adolescent fantasy of being a hero of the working masses or something, let me know that she's safe. I'm quite willing to pay your expenses—" She slowed here, eyeing George in particular as if his expenses might well run over budget.

"We couldn't possibly ask that of you," Raffa said, with all the charm she could muster. "Besides, suppose your family noticed something. We all have ample allowances; it's really no problem." Ronnie stirred; she ignored that. If they were going to be partners for life, he would have to learn to use her resources as she intended to use his.

"I insist," said Venezia, with a touch of color to her cheeks. "At least the tickets there."

"All right," Raffa said. "But we must make our own reservations. In case your family is hiding something from you, it will be easier if they don't make the connection."

Passenger service to the Patchcock system routed through Vardiel and Sostos. Vardiel, Raffa remembered, was the ancient seat of the Morrelines. Ronnie, poring over the display in his copy of *The Investor's Guide to Familias Regnant Territories* (a guidecube purchased in the Guerni Republic), commented that it was a roundabout approach. "I'll bet they don't ship freight that way," he said. "If this is accurate, there are two near jump points, with easy vectors to Brot, Vesli, Tambour. And Tambour's a direct to Rockhouse."

"Morrelines like control," George said. "But why not? It's their investment base." He glanced around their cabin and shrugged elaborately. Raffa glared. If they were being monitored, his glance and shrug would look as stagey to anyone else as it did to her. They had agreed not to discuss their plans once on board the ship to Patchcock. The system itself, yes, since none of them had been there.

The other passengers were all on business transfers, older men and women whose conversation was full of technical detail. Raffa strained her ears and memory to interpret them, but the veneer of chemical knowledge she'd picked up on

Music didn't help her penetrate the dense thickets of jargon. They had dropped into the Patchcock system before any of the other passengers spoke to the young people.

"Are you in Bioset or Synthesis?" an older woman asked Raffa in the lounge. Raffa noticed that the nearest group of older people paused in their conversation.

"Neither," Raffa said. "I don't even know what they are. I'm just a tourist, really."

"Ah." A little pause, during which Raffa could almost see the cascades of decision points in the other's mind. Then, "You're with a Family?"

Though the words were polite, Raffa heard the faint sneer that meant "rich, spoiled, idle." But that was the most harmless hypothesis, so she didn't react. "Yes," she said. "My aunt's trying to get me involved in business, and I told her I needed to travel more. I'm hoping to visit some of the pharmaceutical facilities here."

"Here? Where did you hear about them?"

Raffa tried for the offhand tone that would disarm suspicion. "I went to school with Ottala—Ottala Morreline."

"Were you planning to visit her?"

"Is she here?" Raffa raised her brows. "I thought she lived on Vardiel—at least when she was in school we visited there—"

"No—I mean, yes, she still lives with her family, the last I heard. I just wondered why you were *here*."

"Well, Ottala bragged about the facilities—my aunt, you see, has investments in pharmaceuticals, so I told her I'd like to see these—and others—"

"A good excuse for traveling, then?"

Raffa smiled, and leaned closer, confiding. "Yes . . . and you see, my family doesn't approve of . . . of Ronnie. This way they think I'm traveling on business for Aunt Marta; Ronnie and I met a long way from the capital."

"And the other young man?"

"Ronnie's friend George. Well, of course I know George, too. But everyone knows Ronnie and George travel together, so it's less obvious that I—you know."

The older woman smiled. "I think it's incredible that you Family people go through all these maneuvers . . . why not just take your shares and go live with the boy, if that's what you want?"

"I couldn't do that," Raffa said. "It's just not—not done."
She had never thought of it. The idea sat in her mind staring
back at her; she forced herself to ignore it.

The Guernesi tourist cube had an account of the Patchcock
Incursion (under "investors' warnings: possible political
instability") far more extensive than what Raffa remembered
vaguely from school. Ronnie read the section and nodded.
"Captain Serrano told me about that. I wonder how the
Guernesi found out about the terms of the Gleisco contract?"

"They said they'd bought raw materials from the Patchcock system," Raffa said. "They probably had agents of
their own poking around."

"I suppose—in the aftermath of the incursion—it would've
been easier to start manufacturing the drugs here—retooling
the lines wouldn't be as obvious if they needed complete
rebuilding anyway."

"How are we going to approach this?"

"Didn't you hear what I told those people in the lounge?
My Aunt Marta has pharmaceutical investments; she's asked
me to gather background . . . she *has*," Raffa said, as the
two looked at her in disbelief. "I was in the Guerni Republic,
and heard about Patchcock . . . that's all I have to say. We'll
see where it goes from there."

"Something's going on," George said. He had finally seen
Raffa's point about the way Venezia's family treated her. "I'm
just not sure Ottala's aunt is as stupid as she pretends to
be."

"I don't think she's stupid at all," Raffa said. "But she
may be baffled by the family. And if they're manufacturing illegal pharmaceuticals, perhaps they're even drugging
her."

"If they could do that, they could get their shares
back—"

"Wait—" George looked excited suddenly. "It's—it's all
about the rejuvenation process. And the legal changes—what
do you want to bet that Ottala's aunt hasn't had the new
one? Maybe none at all, but if she did, it was the Stochaster."

"How do you figure that?"

"Because it changed the inheritance laws, and it's going
to change the laws about cognitive competence. The ones
that caused your aunt so much trouble, Ronnie."

"Huh?" Ronnie looked confused. "I don't see how the kind of rejuvenation someone has matters that much."

"Weren't you listening to them at all? Because the Stochaster procedure couldn't be repeated—but people kept trying it and going bonkers. First they made it illegal to do repeats, and then they changed the laws so that a crazy senior couldn't tie up a family's assets forever."

"Yes, but now it's not illegal. The new procedures—"

"Can now be legally repeated, yes. And we have laws about how competency affects inheritance, but no laws dealing with indefinitely extended lives. Think, Ronnie. Suppose your father, or mine, lives . . . well, hundreds of years, if not forever. Those of our class who've been expecting to inherit a tidy living will wait . . . having our own rejuvenations . . . until they finally die."

"But nobody's going to live that long," Ronnie said, frowning.

"Are you sure? I'm not. The oldest serial Rejuvenants are now in their nineties—the oldest people now alive used the Stochaster, which they can't repeat. In the next decade or so, the balance will shift, until all the Rejuvenants are repeats. Maybe the first generation of them will be content with only a few rejuvenations . . . but someone's going to want to live a lot longer. Will your father give up his position in the family business just because he hits eighty, or a hundred, or a hundred and twenty? I doubt it. And the law is set up to test competency, not age."

"But—but no one is . . ." Raffa's voice trailed off.

"And if the Morrelines think they have a corner on the process, they're not going to want a nosy old aunt—whom they cannot control, because she can't rejuv anyway—poking around in their business backyard."

"Even if they're manufacturing the drugs illegally," Raffa said, "does this mean they're adulterating them? I don't see that it follows. . . ."

"Perhaps not," said George. "But if you wanted to control a good bit more than one end of the pharmaceutical industry, wouldn't you be tempted to slip a few attitude adjustments into the mix? Lorenza certainly did."

"We are going to be very careful on Patchcock," Raffa said slowly. "Very, *very* careful."

✳ ✳ ✳

Patchcock would never qualify as one of the beauties of empire, Raffa thought as she watched the dull gray-green brush slide past the windows of the commuter train from the shuttle port. Vagaries of geology and terraforming had resulted in low-relief landmasses and a monotonous climate. Irrigation freshened the vast fields of staple grains and root crops that fed the planet's work force, but beyond the fields— whose bright greens and yellows seemed almost garish— the vegetation consisted of many varieties of thorny scrub between three and six meters high. When the wind blew, which it usually did, the sky hazed with grit; when it rained, erosion scoured the thin, loose soil into twisting arroyos. The train racketed across a bridge over one of these, and Raffa noticed a pile of construction waste that looked as if someone had thought of damming the dry watercourse. It hadn't worked; a deeper channel cut around one end of the pile.

Twoville, almost as dull as its name, was a low-built compact city on the coast itself. Raffa had arranged rooms at the one real hotel. Ronnie and George would share a room in a hostel for transient workers. They were in the car behind her, carefully separate.

When she reached the hotel address, she was startled to find herself facing a small one-story cube with a single solid door. Had someone made a mistake?

Inside, she realized she was at the top of a well, looking down into the hotel. Across the gap, a waterfall poured over a tiled edge to fall . . . she felt dizzy when she looked over the edge.

"It takes most newcomers that way," said a voice behind her. She looked around to see a respectable-looking older man in business clothes. "Especially if they didn't know anything about how Patchcock was built. Bet you thought this was a mighty small hotel."

"Yes." Raffa tried to get her breath back.

"Patchcock's mostly underground," the man said. "There's not much scenery topside, or a climate to brag about, and fierce storms off the ocean. Everything's dug in, just shafts and warehouses on the surface."

"But aren't you too close to the ocean? Doesn't it seep in?"

"Flood would be more like it, except that there's a Tiegman field generator holding a barrier on it."

This meant little to Raffa, who had no idea what a Tiegman field generator was. She did have a clear memory of the perpetually damp sublevels in a seaside resort, resulting from percolation of seawater through porous soil. Patchcock soil certainly looked porous. She wished the building had windows to the outside—she wanted to know exactly how far below the water they would be.

Her nervousness must have shown, for the man went on. "It's quite safe, I assure you. The Tiegman field is absolutely impermeable, and the field shape has been designed to enclose all the sublevels—"

"It must take a lot of energy," Raffa said.

"Not once it's on. Starting it up, now . . . that took half a Patchcock year, and every bit of power they could find. But it's stable once it's on and locked."

"Excuse me, madam." That was the doorman, with her luggage on a trolley. "Would you prefer to glide down, or take the lift?"

"The lift," Raffa said. It would have comforting walls and doors. The hotel registration desk also seemed ordinary, as long as she could pretend it was on ground level, and the great open shaft with the waterfall went that far up in the air.

Her rooms opened onto a private terrace lush with flowering plants. Between the thick vines and bushes, she caught glimpses of what looked like distant green meadows under a twilight sky. Concealed lights produced the illusion of sunlight, shifting with the hours, on her terrace. If not for the EVACUATION PROCEDURES display on the reverse of the door, with the critical data highlighted in red, she'd never have suspected that she was twenty-seven meters below mean sea level, far out of sight of Patchcock's real sky and sun.

It was perfectly dry, with no smell of the sea. She felt the carpet surreptitiously; no hint of dampness. It didn't really make her feel safe. That it was dry now didn't mean it would stay dry. She looked around at her small domain. A bedroom and sitting room, both opening onto the terrace, and a large bathroom with every variety of plumbing she'd encountered before. Handsome furniture, fresh flowers, a cooler stocked with a dozen or so bottles and cans . . . she recognized only a few of the brands. Amazing what money could do . . . she would not have guessed that Patchcock had such amenities. Then she noticed the table lamp.

Puce and turquoise, with an uneven streak of mustard yellow down one side, as ugly as any of Venezia's pots. Raffa eyed it suspiciously. It might have been a pot once. So might the bedside lamp, garish pink splotched with a funguslike pattern of blue-gray. Above the cooler hung a decorative object that reminded her of the mask on Ottala's wall at school. When she looked at the terrace plantings more carefully, the graceful ferns and brilliant flowers were rooted in odd-shaped pots of astounding ugliness.

So—was this what happened to Venezia's output? Were the ceramics her family claimed to prize stuck away in the obscurity of Patchcock? She wondered how many other places in Twoville had been given the dubious honor of showing off Ottala's aunt's presumed talent.

She flicked on the comconsole. Again the emergency procedures, this time requiring her to thumb-sign an affidavit that she had read and understood them. She glanced over to the open closet, making sure that a p-suit hung there, as advertised. Then a string of advertisements for local tour guides and recreational facilities. None looked inviting. ("See the unique sea life on Patchcock's nearest barrier reef," one offered, but the unique sea life in the display was all small and dull-colored. She had not come all this way to see odd-shaped beige and gray blobs no bigger than her hand.)

What she needed was a business directory. There: on the menu after the obligatory tourist advertisements. The list of businesses by type. Vertical integration seemed to be the guiding philosophy here, of industry as well as architecture. Her experience in her aunt's affairs helped her recognize the components of a complete pharmaceutical industry . . . raw materials used to manufacture unit and bulk packaging, labelling, and all the rest, the manufacturing stages for everything from intravenous solution containers to the foam that cushioned the final shipping containers. By the time she called the numbers she thought most likely, she felt she would understand whatever they might say.

"You're who?" the voice said. Raffa repeated what she had begun to think of as pedigree and show experience: her family name, her sept, her aunt's authorization to act as her agent. She rather hoped Aunt Marta didn't ever know how far her authorization had been stretched.

"I went to school with Ottala Morreline," Raffa added. Surely it couldn't hurt to claim (honestly) acquaintance with a daughter of the CEO of the company that owned Patchcock.

"You *what?*" This time the voice fairly squeaked. Raffa frowned. While she doubted that Ottala's friends visited here frequently, surely being a friend wouldn't create that level of upset.

"We went to school together," Raffa said. "The Campbell Academy." Silly name, really—neither its founders nor anyone else involved had been named Campbell; apparently someone a century or so back had simply liked the name Campbell.

"Ah . . . I see. Well, I suppose—there's a tour we give visiting . . . er . . . executives. You'd have to present your credentials—"

"I suppose," Raffa said, with ill-concealed sarcasm, "you're often annoyed by people impersonating Ottala's school friends."

"Pharmaceuticals," Raffa said, trying to sound vague and ignorant to the bright young man assigned as her tour guide. She had met him in the corporate branch office, where she noticed a large, ungainly, ceramic piece in purples and oranges in the reception area, and a small one full of desk accessories on the receptionist's desk. Now they were descending into the bowels of a factory, and even here, in odd corners, she'd noticed signs of Venezia's work. She still thought of it as that, even though she suspected that everything here came from Venezia's sources in the Guerni Republic. "But there's lots of kinds, aren't there?" That sounded really stupid; she wasn't surprised that her guide gave her a sharp look. "I mean," she said, trying to make up for it, "I know there's antibiotics, antivirals, neuroleptics, contraceptives, but the other companies my aunt invested in usually stick to one or two chemical classes. Vertical integration, she says, is very important, from the substrate to the finished product. So 'pharmaceuticals' seemed vague."

"I can't discuss specific processes, you understand," her guide said.

"Of course. But in general?"

"Er . . ." He paused, then spouted a long string of chemical syllables that Raffa suspected were faked. She caught "indole" and "pyrimadine" and "something-something-ergic-acid" but none of it sounded like the quick course she'd had from the Guernesi.

"I see," she said, allowing herself to sound as confused as she felt. "I guess that's what I'll tell Aunt Marta, though I never heard of that before."

"Your aunt's planning to invest?" he asked, as if surprised.

"Didn't they tell you, from the head office?" she asked. "I explained—that's why they sent me on this tour."

"But this is a family business. The Morrelines—"

"Apparently some family member's died, and she thought of picking up anything that might be on the market—" Raffa stopped; her guide's face had gone paper white.

"Died? Who died?"

Raffa shrugged. "I don't know." Especially since she'd made it up. The Morrelines were a large family; surely *someone* had died recently. "Probably a distant cousin or something," she said. "Aunt Marta didn't say. She just sent me here to look into things." That with a bright smile that was supposed to disarm suspicion. But her guide looked away, tension in every line of face and neck.

CHAPTER TWELVE

Sweet Delight, Xavier System

The more Heris worked with the local government, the more she knew about local resources, the more threatening the situation appeared. The mining colonies, most of them concentrated on the second largest satellite of the larger gas giant, Zalbod, had no defenses at all. Rock-hounds, miners who worked the smaller chunks of debris, used little two-to-six-person pods for transportation; nothing could be mounted on them which would affect a ship with shields. There was one antiquated ore-hauler, large enough to mount both screens and weapons if they had had screens and weapons to mount, or if it had had enough powerplant to do more than crawl slowly from one orbital base to another.

"We have to hope someone's listening back at Sector HQ," Heris said. She could hope it, but she also knew, from experience, how civilian reports of trouble could end up at the bottom of someone's stack. She didn't have the current override codes that might have bumped their report up.

"Where's Lady Cecelia?" Petris asked.

"At another horse farm, of course. I have no idea how it can take so long to pick out what she wants—particularly since there are genetic surgeons who specialize in equine design—she told me that. But now she's visiting somebody she calls 'Marcia and Poots,' which sounds faintly obscene. She says she expects to be there several weeks,

and I'm not to worry. Then she sent all these pictures—"
Heris flicked through them on the display. "They're just
horses. Here we are in real danger, and she's worrying
about whether this one's hocks are wiggly. I love the
woman, but really!"

"Captain—" That was Koutsoudas, from the bridge. Heris
leapt up.

"Coming now," she said.

When she arrived, all the ex-military crew were clustered
there, around Koutsoudas's screen. They moved over so that
she could see.

"It's ours," Koutsoudas said. He didn't have to; Heris
recognized the drive signature herself; she had commanded
just such a cruiser. "And . . . another . . ." That, too, was
familiar; although cruisers patrolled alone, this would not
be a routine patrol. She expected three, cruiser and two
patrol ships, and the final signature appeared even as she
thought it. A ragged shift out of jump, or appropriate
caution, depending on how much trouble the commander
had expected to find.

"Find out who's commanding, when you can," Heris said.
"I'll let the Xavierans know—" She turned to her own board,
and tapped in the code. They'd be relieved to know that
the Fleet had finally listened, that help had arrived, that
their survival didn't depend on one armed yacht and its
ex-military captain. And if they weren't relieved enough, she
herself was . . . those had been anxious days, wondering who
would get here first. She knew her limits, even after roses
and bagpipe parades.

"Captain, it's Commander Garrivay." Koutsoudas's expression, which Heris was learning to read, gave some signal
she couldn't yet decode. She tried to remember a Garrivay,
and couldn't dredge up anything but the vague impression
of the name on a promotion list years back.

"Which Garrivay?" Maybe the first name would mean
something.

"Dekan Garrivay . . . Captain Livadhi had . . . uh . . . served
on the same ship with him when they were both jigs. Sir."
Heris gave Koutsoudas a long stare, intended to remind him
that she was now his captain, and this was no time to
withhold loyalty. Koutsoudas sighed. "Right, Captain Serrano.

Dekan Garrivay, in the opinion of Captain Livadhi, would require divine intervention to achieve the moral stature of a child rapist."

"Even for Arash, that's strong," Heris said. More importantly, while Arash had colorful opinions of many officers, he didn't usually—to her knowledge—share them with his enlisted crew.

"It wasn't just that once, either; Captain Livadhi didn't say much about the details of that cruise, but Garrivay was in the same battle group we were during that mess on Patchcock. Sonovabitch blew the second reactor station *after* the cease-fire, and it was only because the rebels came back with heavy stuff that he got away with it. Nobody noticed because they knocked out the command ship, and they had the scores—"

"But you had your own pet scans?" This was something that hadn't made it into the briefings.

"Yes—I did, and Captain Livadhi wanted to make something of it, but the scan data were tricky . . . I'd just figured out how to—to boost the definition, and it was nonstandard. And he wasn't commanding then, of course; he wasn't sure how his captain would take it."

"I don't suppose you know where Garrivay has been stationed lately?" Heris watched the incoming scan data, but let her mind roll fantasy dice . . . the probability of a bad captain being in command of a strike group here, at such a time, the probability that she, and Koutsoudas, would be here to notice. . . . "Livadhi suspected this, didn't he?" she asked, before Koutsoudas had answered the first question. She didn't look at him, but made a private bet on whether he would answer, and if so in what order.

"He thought something would blow, yes." Koutsoudas wasn't looking at her, either; out of her peripheral vision she saw his profile, intent on the displays in front of him. "It's true that I was in some danger; my modifications of scan technology had become a bit too famous. But he said you were the lightning rod, and you'd need some help— unobtrusive help. I don't think he thought Garrivay, in particular. Garrivay *was* attached to Third Ward, Inner Systems." Third Ward, Inner, where Lepescu had been for eight years before taking over the combat position that had cost Heris her commission.

Heris had the prickling feeling all down her back that usually preceded battle. "I am a lightning rod?"

"Serranos in general, he said, and you in particular. Your aunt the admiral told him—"

"My *aunt*!" Now the prickling sensation shifted to anger, pure and white-hot. "What was she talking to Arash for— DAMMIT!" Her vision blurred a moment, then she felt the long habit of control settling back into her mind like a rider on a fractious horse. She glanced around the bridge; none of her crew were staring. They knew better. Koutsoudas met her eye for a moment, as if checking to see if she was about to hit him, then looked away. "Never mind," Heris said, to no one in particular. "I never have been able to predict Aunt Vida. Sorry, 'Steban. If you have any aunts, you'll understand."

"My Aunt Estrellita," Koutsoudas said promptly. "Actually a great-aunt, on my mother's side. She's not in Fleet, or she'd drive me crazy . . . every time I'm home on leave, she's promoting an alliance with yet another second or third cousin twice removed. She runs the whole family, except for my cousin Juil, who's just as pigheaded as she is."

Heris wondered if he really had an aunt like that, or if he just made her up on the spot. It didn't really matter. What did matter was that someone—Livadhi, or her aunt, or both—had expected her to be in trouble, and had provided Koutsoudas, presumably to help her out—or get rid of her, a dark thought intruded. She shoved it back; no time to worry about that. Instead, she could worry about the choice of Garrivay for such duty as this.

Her worry translated into a discreet request to be included in the invitation to senior administrative personnel to meet the new military commander of Xavier's defense. That amounted to a reception and meeting to follow, on the orbital station. Heris, who had met all but Garrivay before, mingled easily and worked her way to the back of the group as she heard the unmistakable click of approaching boots.

A large man introduced himself to the General Secretary as Commodore Garrivay, commanding a battle group. Heris did not let her eyebrows rise at that but wondered why he was trying to impress. True, commodore was the correct term for someone commanding a battle group, but a battle group was defined as a formation comprising at least two heavy cruisers. Commonly, battle groups had two heavy cruisers, a light cruiser, and three to five patrol ships. One cruiser and a couple of patrol ships could be a battle group only if you'd just lost the others in combat.

Garrivay had a strong-boned face well padded with flesh; if he had been a horse (she grinned to herself for picking up Cecelia's habits of thought) he would have been considered to show a coarse, coldblood influence. She noticed that his gaze locked on the person to whom he spoke, a fervent intensity that, in other people, she had found to accompany both the ability and willingness to lie convincingly.

Still, his first questions to the General Secretary were reasonable, as he asked for clarification of the message that had brought him, and the raider's attack. He listened to the somewhat rambling report the General Secretary's aide gave—Heris winced at some of the inaccuracies which Garrivay patiently dissected—and then commended the Xavierans on their successful response.

"Captain Serrano helped us out when the raider attacked," the General Secretary said. Heris wished he'd left her out of it.

"Serrano . . ." Garrivay seemed to consider, then his eyes narrowed. "*Heris* Serrano?"

"Yes, that's the name."

"You *were* lucky." The emphasis could be taken either way; Heris waited to see how he would shade it. He still did not look at her, as if he had not noticed her among the others. "I never had the honor of serving in the same organization with Captain Serrano, but I believe she had a . . . er . . . distinguished record." Again, an emphasis that might be taken more than one way; the pause suggested that another adjective had come to mind before "distinguished." His gaze raked the assembly and snagged only briefly on hers before passing on. So he did recognize her. And had no intention of acknowledging her at this meeting.

"She blew that raider neatly enough." A challenging tone from someone who recognized the ambiguity of Garrivay's . . . Heris didn't recognize the voice and dared not peer down the room.

"I daresay," Garrivay said carelessly. "From what you've

said, a cobbled-up mismatch of weaponry and hull . . . not much threat, really, though I understand your being anxious for the station. Even a gap-toothed wolf can bite."

Heris blinked. They weren't going to like that, neither the words nor the tone, not after the previous raids they'd suffered. And where had he heard about the raider's design flaws? She didn't think her crew had gossiped about that among the stationers—though she'd ask, before making the obvious connection. Sure enough, the General Secretary had puffed up like a rooster.

"I hardly think a raider capable of blowing our main station out of the sky could be called a gap-toothed wolf, Commodore." He glanced around for support, and got it in the expressions of the others. "Those raiders have been at us for a decade, during which no one from the R.S.S. has seen fit—"

"But it didn't blow your station, did it? Not this time, nor any other. So why do you think it could? Because Captain . . . er . . . Serrano told you so?"

She could feel the stubbornness as if it were a visible pall hanging smoglike over their heads. Surely Garrivay knew how they'd react. Why would he want them to react like this, stiffening into dislike of him? With a war looming, he should be doing what he could to rally the civilians behind him. Perhaps he was one of those officers who thought civilians were all fools, good only for providing the money to keep the Fleet going. Perhaps he assumed that if he dismissed their fear of the raider, they would then believe him when he told them something else was a threat. Whatever his intent, she knew it was a mistake.

When the meeting broke up, he made a point of coming to her side.

"Well, Captain Serrano . . . I never had the pleasure of meeting you before." This close, the strong face with its bright green eyes had a raffish charm. His skin was a shade lighter than her own; his hair, clipped short, might have been any shade of brown. "My misfortune, I must say. Of course I heard—your family has branches everywhere, it seems."

Heris decided there was no advantage to be gained by pretense. "Isn't calling one cruiser and two patrols a battle group a bit much?" His eyes widened a moment, then narrowed as he grinned, squeezing the light from their green until they looked almost black.

"Surely you don't feel an obligation to explain," he began. Heris said nothing. "I thought it would reassure the locals," he went on. "Convince them they weren't forgotten. There's not likely to be anything much here—certainly nothing to justify a *real* battle group—and if this satisfies them—"

Heris shrugged as if she didn't care, and glanced around the compartment. "I merely commented. If there were veterans here, for instance . . . they might say something."

"Barring you, I don't expect to find any veterans. Xavier apparently sent few recruits to Fleet, and those old enough to retire chose more populous worlds. Not that I blame them."

"It's not a bad place," Heris said, more to draw him out than in serious argument. She found it more than interesting that he had bothered to check on Xavier's recruitment to Fleet, and where its veterans went.

"You think not?" Garrivay's mobile face drew itself into a knot of distaste. "I hate ag worlds, myself. Dirty, backward, half of them free-birthers whose discontented spawn scrabble for a way offplanet and clog the ranks of unskilled labor hanging around spaceports. I like to eat as much as anyone, but we could subsist quite well without them."

His venom surprised her; she wondered what had given him a dislike for ag worlds. Had he come from one? "It has strategic importance, at least," she said.

"If the Black Scratch is crazy enough to attack through here, I'm not going to be able to stop them," Garrivay said. "Surely you don't think they will? It would be a very inefficient approach—"

"There's the Spinner jump point," Heris said. She had trouble keeping the edge out of her voice; he was treating her as if she were a combination of crazy and crony.

"That!" He waved his hand. "Fleet's got a couple of battle groups on the other side—the Black Scratch can't take it, and they must know that."

Heris opened her mouth to protest this obvious idiocy and stopped. Why reveal herself? "I suppose," she said, and added, as if without thought, "They used to have just a single cruiser—"

He relaxed a little; she recognized the shift in his facial muscles. "Ah . . . no wonder you worried. Of course you wouldn't know the current dispositions." That had a half-heard question mark on it, which she ignored.

"So you're just here to show the flag, as it were?"

"Something like that. Perhaps snag another raider." He grinned at her. He had a good grin, one she might have liked if she hadn't known all the rest. "By the way, I didn't mean to slight your accomplishment in there. Going after a raider—even a shoddy thing like that—with a rich lady's yacht took guts. And you couldn't know how incompetent the raider was until afterwards. . . ." Again, the hint of a question. Heris smiled blandly.

"No . . . to tell you the truth, I was more than half expecting to be blown away myself. The only advantage of being small is that you're hard to detect in the first place, and hard to hit in the second."

"Lucky for you the raider had no decent weaponry. Did he get off even one shot?"

"A couple," Heris said, sticking to the facts that would have been reported by the distant watcher. "But inaccurate—as you say, he had no decent weaponry. He just looked dangerous."

"And these poor sods have been paying tribute to that sort of trash. Well, I can take care of *that*. Tell me, how long do you plan to be in the system?"

"I don't know." Heris frowned as if it bothered her. "Lady Cecelia is visiting bloodstock farms; I think she expects to find the perfect horse genes somewhere and go back into eventing."

"And you have to hang around until your owner is through? Lucky you. It's almost like being back in Fleet, isn't it?" He didn't wait for her to answer. "Hanging around waiting on someone else's bright ideas. Of course, your owner's a Rejuvenant . . . *she* has plenty of time."

Interesting. He didn't know she owned the ship herself. It wouldn't have been big news, not with everything else going on, but he might have picked it out of the datanet if he'd looked for it. Would she, in his place? Of course. On the other hand, never assume the enemy is stupid . . . perhaps he was just sounding her out. "I suppose so . . . but so are many admirals, aren't they?"

"True enough." He sighed. "I don't suppose you could

lend me your onboard weaponry . . . beef up this old clunker they've got here, use it as a decoy or something . . . ?"

"Sorry," Heris said, not sorry at all. "It's not much, and you'd have to take the hull apart to get it out anyway—you can't imagine what it took to get it installed in the first place. Anyway, since Lady Cecelia paid for it, I suppose it's really hers. Of course you could confiscate the whole ship, if it's really an emergency. . . ."

"Oh no, nothing like that. Although if your employer is nervous, I would advise you to get her out of here."

"I'll speak to her," Heris said. That pleased him; his eyelid flickered. He wanted her gone; he wanted her weapons gone. What was he up to? She itched to get back to Koutsoudas and his scans; she was ready to throw roses all over her aunt admiral and even Arash Livadhi. With any luck—and Koutsoudas made his own—he would have the probes in place and she would soon have an ear in this fellow's private counsels.

"There's never been a suspicion of treason," Koutsoudas said when she told him about the conversation. "Over-zealousness, misinterpretation of orders allowing him more leeway . . . but nothing to harm the Familias."

"Adding to the mess at Patchcock harmed the Familias," Heris said. "There's more than one way to cause trouble."

"I . . . hadn't thought of that." Koutsoudas looked taken aback; Heris grinned to herself. She had begun to wonder if the man was a genius at everything.

"We're one of the logical places for the Benignity to strike. You're sure there was a watcher out there when we took that raider—" Something that had bothered her while talking to Garrivay now surfaced. "And he called them the Black Scratch."

Koutsoudas's eyebrows went up. "So? Everybody knows that nickname."

"Everybody knows it, but . . . think, 'Steban. Did you ever hear Arash use it during a briefing? I know I never did. It's slang, and this may be war."

"Now that you mention it . . . no. Commander Livadhi always said the Benignity, or the Compassionate Hand." And Koutsoudas, for the first time, referred to Livadhi by his rank, not his position as captain. Interesting.

"You think he's turned," Petris said. It was not a question.

"I think . . . yes. I do. And I have no proof, and no one to tell . . . not within any range that would help."

"Does he know what you think?"

"No. He shouldn't. I played stupid for all I was worth. Accepted his judgment that the raider was almost harmless—" Ginese growled something incomprehensible at that, and Heris let herself chuckle. "Oh yes, he did. He knew about the mismatched drive/hull fit, too, which none of us told him."

"That counts," Koutsoudas said. "He couldn't have found out about that any other way—unless it was in your report to Sector HQ."

"No, it wasn't. They had no need, and I supposed—I suppose I was looking for something like this. If this is what I think." She didn't want to think that. "It all boils down to data," Heris said. "His . . . ours . . . if any of it's trustworthy. How much of it's compromised. If he knows who you are, what you are, then we're in even worse trouble."

Heris was working her way through routine reports when Koutsoudas called her to the bridge again.

"Captain, you must hear this—it's what Garrivay and his senior officers have said—"

Heris touched the control. Amazing sound quality; she still wished she knew how Koutsoudas did what he did. Garrivay, sounding as pompous among his own people as with her. She was glad to know she hadn't been given special treatment. It will work, he was saying. That Serrano bitch doesn't know anything; she's negligible. One of the others questioned that—a Serrano negligible? Garrivay laughed in a tone that made Heris want to smash all his teeth down his fleshy throat. As they talked on, their plan appeared much as she had expected. The Benignity ships would arrive to find a blown station and helpless planet. Garrivay would exit to another place to do much the same thing. Where else? Rotterdam . . . *Rotterdam*. Cecelia's friends, that lovely place she had wanted to revisit . . .

"Not likely," she muttered. Koutsoudas started, and she realized she had put into that all the frustration and anger she felt at the whole situation. She looked at the others. "We have to stop them."

"Stop them! What—Garrivay, or the invasion?"

"Both, ideally. Garrivay first, of course."

"How?" That was Meharry, blunt as always. "We couldn't breach his shields if we put everything we have into his flanks sitting next to him in dock."

"Actually we might," Ginese said, looking thoughtful. "Of course, his return would vaporize us *and* the station."

"There's nothing in this system that can take Garrivay's ships," Heris said. "Except wits."

"Wits?" Now it was Koutsoudas who gave her a startled glance. "You're planning to trick him out of his ships? How— at the gambling table, perhaps?"

"No. I'm not going to gamble with his notions of honor. We will have to capture his ships, and since frontal assault won't do, it will take wits."

"You're planning to walk onto his ships and just take over?" Meharry asked. "Just say 'Please, Commodore, I think you're a traitor, and I'm taking over'?"

"Something like that," Heris said with a grin.

"And you expect him to agree?"

"I expect him to die," Heris said. A silence fell, as her crew digested that. She went on. "He's not going to sur- render and risk court-martial—neither he nor his fellow captains. The only way to get those ships is by *coup de main*—and then great good luck and the Serrano name."

"I was going to mention," said Meharry, "that most crews don't take kindly to someone murdering the captain and taking over."

"You do realize the legal side of what you're doing?" Petris gave her a dark, slanted glance.

"Yes. I'm proposing treasonous piracy, if you look at it that way, and some people will. A civilian stealing not one but three R.S.S. combat vessels in what will be time of war."

"You won't get all three," Ginese said. "One, maybe. Two if you're very lucky. Not all three."

"That may be. I will certainly try to get all three, because if I don't, I may have to destroy one." She had faced that, in her mind. She could not leave a ship loose in this sys- tem committed to helping the Benignity invasion.

"If you're wrong about any of it," Petris said, "you'll have no alternatives. If the Benignity doesn't invade through here, if Garrivay is just a detestable bully, but not a traitor, if you're not able to get the ships—"

"Then I'm dead," Heris said. "I've thought of that. It means you're dead as well, which is bothersome—"

"Oh, it's not that, Captain," Meharry said. "I wouldn't miss this for anything, and it's a novel way to die, after all. Trying to steal one of our own ships for a good cause. More fun than jumping that yacht out of nearspace."

"If you try it and aren't killed," Petris said, "you'll be an outlaw . . . you can't stay in Familias space."

Heris stared at him; he did not look down. "Petris, if you think I can't do it, say so. If you think I shouldn't do it— if you think I'm working with bad data or logic, say so. But trust that I can do elementary risk analysis, will you?"

He didn't smile. "I know you can. But I also know how much you want to set foot on a cruiser bridge again. Have you factored that into your analysis?"

"Yes." Despite herself, her voice tightened. She forced herself to take a long breath. "Petris, I do miss—have missed—that command. You're right about that, and it is a factor. But I'm not about to risk our lives, and the lives of everyone in this system, crews and landborn alike, to satisfy my whims. There's something I haven't shared with you." Before anyone could comment, she flicked on the cube reader; she had already selected the passage.

Her Aunt Vida's face, an older version of her own Serrano features, stared out at them. She spoke. "I have complete confidence in your judgment," her aunt said. "In any difficulty. You may depend upon my support for any action you find necessary to preserve the honor and safety of the Familias Regnant in these troubled times."

"I don't think my aunt admiral anticipated pirating Fleet warships," Heris said. "But it gives me a shred of legitimacy, and I intend to weave that into something more than a tissue of lies."

"How?" Petris asked bluntly. "Not that I don't believe you, and not that I'm opposed, but—how?"

In the pause that followed, while Heris was trying to work out why Petris was being so antagonistic, Oblo spoke. "What it really is, Captain, is that we never had a chance to be this close while you were planning before. We enjoyed the result, but we never got to see the process."

Petris grinned. "All right, Oblo. You're partly right. It still seems impossible to me that she's going to take over three warships all by herself—well, we'll help, but it's not much. The peashooters we have on this thing wouldn't hurt those ships, and they'd blow us away before we could get a shot off anyway. There's no way to sneak aboard, and even if we could, I don't see how the four of us could seize control of the ship against resistance. She can't just stroll over and say 'By the way, Garrivay, I'll be the new captain as of today.' " He made the last a singsong parody of the traditional chanty.

The delay had given Heris time to come up with the outline of a plan. "Like this," she said. "You're half right, Petris. We're going to walk in peacefully, invited guests—"

"They'll scan us for weapons—" Ginese warned.

Heris grinned. "What is the most dangerous weapon in the universe?" A blank pause, then they all grinned, and repeated the gesture with which generations of basic instructors had taunted their recruits. "That's right. What's between your ears can't be scanned . . . and you're all exceptional unarmed fighters."

"So we stroll in for afternoon tea, or whatever—" Meharry prompted.

"Properly meek and mild, yes." Heris batted her eyelashes, and they broke into snorts of laughter.

"Begging the captain's pardon, but if you did that at me, I'd think you were having a seizure." Oblo, of course.

"And then we jump Garrivay and kill him? It's going to take all of us, and no one's going to notice?"

"Petris, for a bloodthirsty pirate, you're being ridiculously cautious. No, we're going to walk into as many of the traitors as we can find gathered with Garrivay—Koutsoudas's ongoing sound tap will help us there—and kill all of them. You notice that they like to gather and gab—Koutsoudas has them on three separate occasions already. I'd like to take out all three ship captains, but I doubt we'll find them *all* together. Four or five traitorous officers, though, will reduce the resistance we face. Admiral Serrano's reputation will do the rest. Or not, as the case may be."

"Everyone knows you're not in Fleet anymore," Meharry said.

"Yes . . . officially. But suppose the whole thing was a

feint—suppose I'm on special assignment." They stared at her, this time shocked into silence.

"You're . . . not . . . really, are you?" asked Ginese finally.

"See?" Heris grinned at them. "If *you* can think that, even for a moment—after what we've been through—then it can work."

"But seriously—you didn't resign because your aunt—" Ginese continued to stare at her with an expression blank of all emotion.

"No! I resigned—stupidly, I now admit—for the reasons I told you, and without hearing a word from my sainted aunt. But if she *had* intended something like this, no one would know. It is plausible—just—with the Serrano reputation. And it's our chance. A slim one, but a chance."

"I've seen fatter chances die of starvation," Petris said, but his tone approved. He sighed, then stretched. "One thing about it, Heris . . . Captain . . . it's never dull shipping with Serranos." She ignored that.

"So now for the details. It's tricky enough, so we'll have rehearsals—and hope we're not still rehearsing when the Benignity arrives."

CHAPTER THIRTEEN

Xavier, Fairhollow Farm

Cecelia felt a certain tension as she entered the stable office. Nothing she could put her finger on—dear Marcia smiling so amiably, and Poots with an even more foolish grin. Slangsby, the head groom, with no grin at all but something twinkling in the depth of his little blue eyes. Were they upset, perhaps, because she had visited two other breeding farms before coming here? They hadn't been that sensitive in years past.

"Such a fortunate escape," Marcia said. "We've heard all about it."

Now what did that mean? Lorenza's attack, or something else entirely? "I'm surprised such a minor matter stayed on the news this far out," Cecelia said. "With the king's resignation—"

"As if you didn't have something to do with that!" Poots sounded almost annoyed with her. Cecelia blinked, assessing the undercurrents.

"I think perhaps my influence was considerably exaggerated," she said. "Of course, I was at the Grand Council meeting, but—"

"Never mind, then." Marcia's smile vanished, replaced by her more usual expression, which had always reminded Cecelia of one of those toys with a spring-controlled lid that snapped tight. "If you don't want to trust your oldest, dearest friends—"

So that was it. Plain jealousy, and feeling left out. None of the honest replies that sprang quickly to mind would work, because, though true, they were insulting. Marcia and Poots were so far from being old and dear friends that they made the phrase ridiculous. Yes, they were rich, in the same class as those who played with the titles of vanished aristocracies. Yes, they considered themselves the equal of anyone. But half of that was the fraternity of horsemen, who allow no rank but that earned in the saddle. She had known them for years, ridden with them, bought and sold horses in the same markets . . . friends? No. Cecelia tried to think of something placating, but Marcia was already in spate again.

"I suppose you're upset that we didn't come at once to help you," she said. Cecelia had not thought of that, and now resented the suggestion that she might have held such a foolish hope. "I'm sure we *would* have," Marcia said, "except that we didn't even find out for months and months, and by then it seemed—and it was foaling time anyway— and it would have taken us months to get there, because as you know we don't have a private yacht. . . ." The explanation, like most explanations, simply dug a deeper and muckier hole in the claimed relationship. If they could "know all about it" so soon after the king's resignation, then they should have known about her collapse that soon too. Foaling season was a weak excuse; no one would have expected them to load up a ship full of pregnant mares, and it had been years since Marcia attended foalings herself. As for "don't have a private yacht," that was, strictly, true. Their *Fortune's Darling* was well out of the yacht class, and might have served as the flagship of a small shipping company.

Cecelia reminded herself that she had not expected help from them, and wasn't (despite the clumsy excuses) upset that they hadn't provided it. "Never mind," she said, trying to drag the conversation back to her reason for being there. "All I'm really interested in is your bloodstock. Mac said you still had some of that Singularity sperm available?"

"What are you doing, restocking the royal—excuse me, formerly royal—stables for yourself?"

That was too much. Cecelia felt her neck get hot, and didn't really care what her face looked like. "Not at all," she said with icy restraint. "I am trying to do a favor for some friends who saved my life and assisted my recovery. Since you are, as you say, old and dear friends—" The accent she put on "friends" would have sliced through a ship's hull plating. "—I had hoped to purchase both sperm and time-locked embryos from you. However, it seems that other suppliers might be more convenient."

Marcia turned red; Poots, as usual, looked as if he might cry. Slangsby now had the grin the others had discarded.

"I didn't—you don't have to take it that way—"

"What way?" Cecelia considered herself a reasonable person, and she could put no friendly interpretation on Marcia's words. But, as a reasonable person, she would let Marcia try to wriggle out of this. It might even be interesting, in a purely zoological way, to watch the wriggling.

Marcia tried a giggle that cracked in midstream. "Cecelia, my dear, you take everything so seriously. I was just teasing. Honestly, my dear, that rejuvenation seems to have affected your temper." But the oyster-gray eyes were wary, watchful, entirely unlike the frank tone of the voice.

Cecelia let her eyebrows rise of themselves. "Really?"

"All right; I'm sorry." Marcia didn't sound sorry; she sounded very grumpy indeed. "If you want Singularity genes, we've got 'em. Sperm and embryos both. I suppose you're thinking of the Buccinator line you favored so?"

Buccinator, Cecelia thought to herself, had only been the most prepotent sire of the past three decades for performance horses. Minimal tweaking of the frozen sperm gave breeders options for speed on the flat or substance for jumping; Buccinator had been almost a sport, but his genome had enough variety for that. But Marcia had refused to jump on that fad, as she'd called it, and out here in the boonies she had produced, after decades of work, one horse not more than fifteen percent worse than Buccinator. Singularity's sperm would offer genetic diversity, but she intended to have top equine geneticists do some editing before she turned it over to her friends.

"Perhaps," she said, "you'd be kind enough to show me what you've got available. I'd like to see the breeding stock, then the ones in training, then the gene maps."

Slangsby twinkled at her, but she distrusted that twinkle. Marcia and Poots said nothing, and simply led her out into the aisle of the great barn. Cecelia looked up. Marcia's pigheadedness about Buccinator aside, she had excellent judgment elsewhere, and this barn proved it. Local wood, used as logs, so that even the most irate equine couldn't kick through the walls. Good insulation, too. Wide aisles, perfect ventilation for this climate, utilities laid safely underground—no exposed pipes or wiring—and kept immaculate by the workers Slangsby supervised. Tools properly hung out of traffic, the only barrow in sight in active use . . . and down the long aisle, one sleek head after another looking over the stall doors. The horses were under roof in the daytime to avoid the assaults of local insectlike parasites, who lived lives too short to learn that horse blood wouldn't nourish them. The bites—otherwise harmless—were painful and made horses nervous.

"The oldest live-bred Singularity daughter," Marcia said proudly. Cecelia had seen the mare before; her infallible memory for horses overlaid her memory of the four-year-old being shown in the ring with this matronly mare only a month from foaling. Star, crooked stripe, snip, all against a background of seal brown. Common coloring for Singularity offspring, because Marcia (like too many people) had a fancy for color. Predictably, she now said, "We sell the loud-colored ones." Buccinator's gorgeous copper color had been one of the things she didn't like about him, Cecelia knew. She also knew that basic coat color was the easiest thing to tweak in the equine genome; if Marcia had wanted all dark foals she could have had them. But other people wanted variety, and she produced brighter ones in order to increase her sales.

"Lovely," Cecelia murmured. She was, too, a good solid mare who had produced both ova and live foals. "I'm surprised you're still using her to produce live—isn't it a bit risky at her age?"

Marcia's face creased in a real grin. "I keep telling you genetic wizard types that if you breed live, you get real soundness, long-term soundness. Of course we've stripped her ova a few times, because it's so hard to transport the mature horses, but the proof of the value of live breeding is right there: an eighteen-year-old mare who can withstand pregnancy and deliver a live foal."

Cecelia kept her face straight with an effort. Given the right pelvic conformation and good legs, any mare could do that. And any mare could get in trouble in any foaling, too. She preferred to use nurse mares of larger breeds for any of her own bloodstock. She moved to the next stall, and the next. Marcia's idea of perfect conformation hadn't changed since her last visit. Sound, yes, but sacrificing elegance for it. They all looked a bit stubby to her, heavier in the neck and chunkier in the body than necessary.

"And this is our pride," Marcia said. They had passed under the dome at the crossing of the aisles, and were now in the stallion end of the barn. Marcia's pride was, of course, the closest thing to Singularity she had been able to produce. He certainly looked like his famous grandsire, Cecelia thought. Dark brown with the merest whisker of white on his brow, a powerful, well-muscled body, and the arrogance of any stallion who comes first in the barn hierarchy.

"Very much like," Cecelia said.

"He's double-line bred," Marcia said.

"What's his outcross line?" Cecelia asked. She thought she could guess, but waited.

"Consequential," Marcia said, and Cecelia congratulated herself. Consequential had passed a curious whorl on the neck to his progeny, and this stallion had it. And trust Marcia to talk about the stallion side of the outcross line.

"He's a real bargain," Marcia said, and named a price per straw of frozen semen that Cecelia didn't think was a bargain at all. Not for an inbred chunk with all his grandsire's faults and probably few of his virtues.

To check that, she asked, "What's his speed?"

Not to her surprise, Marcia's smile vanished again. "He's far too valuable to risk on the track, Cecelia. His breeding alone, his conformation, show his quality. We wouldn't take the chance of injury." Of proving him racing sound, of proving that his grandsire's unlikely speed and agility had come through along with a pretty brown coat and a thick neck. Cecelia couldn't tell for sure, but even from this angle she suspected that his hocks were not sufficient for his build.

"What's your price for Singularity straws?" Cecelia asked. "They must be getting rare now."

"Well, they are, of course. And we must reserve a certain supply for our own program." As if they didn't already have all that influence they needed. "But I could let you have fifty straws for forty thousand. Each, of course."

Cecelia bit back the "Nonsense!" that wanted to burst out. That was only the asking price, which no one dealing in horses ever paid unless they were novices, in which case it was the price of their education. "Umm," she said instead. It meant she wasn't stupid enough to take the asking price, but might bargain later.

"So you see what a bargain this one is," Marcia went on. "Sixty-two percent Singularity—"

Cecelia had run into this before, the ardent preserver of ancient breeds convinced that concentrating bloodlines would somehow overcome the limitations of time and restore the glories of Terran genetics. Cecelia doubted they had been glories anyway (well, perhaps those pretty beasts with the odd number of vertebrae). From the remaining video chips, most of the breeds had been minor variations on a few themes—large and massive, tall and fast, short and hardy— with serious improvement written out of possibility by restrictive breed registries. Half a dozen breeds supposedly intended for racing, for instance, never raced each other and weren't allowed to interbreed . . . stupid.

"Perhaps I could see this fellow moving a bit?" Cecelia said.

Marcia's smile returned. "Of course. Slangsby, put him in the front ring."

Cecelia stepped back to watch. Disposition mattered, as far as she was concerned. Slangsby clipped a lead to the stallion's halter before he opened the stall door, and ran the chain over the nose and back through the mouth. So. Not a quiet one. With that restraint, however, the dark horse stepped demurely from his stall with an air of innocence that Cecelia didn't believe for a moment. He did not dance, which might have been considered unmannerly, but he walked as if on eggs, as if any moment he *might* dance. Marcia urged Cecelia on, but Cecelia hung back. She wanted to see those hocks close up.

"He can be a bit fresh, when he's been in the stall this long," Marcia said, now pulling Cecelia back. Cecelia ignored this; she was farther back than the longest-legged horse could strike. She closed her ears to Marcia's earnest twaddle, and watched the hocks closely. The stallion swaggered a bit; stallions did that. So the sway of the rump might be swagger, and there would be, from swagger alone, a slight sideways jut of the hock as the weight came over it. But here, as she'd expected, was the real problem. From footfall to footlift, the hock described a crooked circle as weight came onto that leg, and the leg pushed the weight forward. She had seen—had even owned—lanky horses whose hocks moved like that, and they'd been sound. But the chunky, muscley horses, those were the ones to watch; those were the ones who needed rock-solid hocks.

The joint narrowed too quickly, too, more trapezoidal than rectangular, flowing into the lower leg too smoothly. Cecelia liked a hock that resembled a box, flat on either side and cleanly marked off above and below. In action, with weight on, it should flex in one plane only, not wobble like this one. She knew she wouldn't buy a straw of this one's semen; she might as well tell Marcia now . . . but that wasn't how the game was played. She strolled on, and took one of the comfortable padded seats just outside the display ring.

Slangsby unlooped the chain, and clipped on a longe line instead of the short lead. The stallion moved out on the line, circled Slangsby at a mincing trot, and exploded suddenly in a flurry of hooves and tail, storming around in a gallop, then flinging himself in the air, bucking. Slangsby growled something at him, and he quieted to a tight canter, then to a trot, slightly more relaxed than before.

"So athletic," said Marcia. "So balanced." Cecelia said nothing, watching the hind legs swing forward, back, forward, back . . . never quite reaching under as far as she liked. Of course he was not under saddle; he might never have been taught. That kind of explosiveness, she knew, came from a preponderance of fast-twitch muscle fibers, something jumpers and event horses needed, along with the slow-twitch fibers that let them gallop miles without tiring. But she didn't want the rest of that genome, at least not the way it was.

She began to think what it would cost to fiddle the Singularity sperm along. She'd need top equine gene sculptors, and the best were in the Guerni Republic, where a healthy racing industry supported them. It might be simpler to go there in the first place, and not bother with Marcia's overmuscled stock, but the Guernesi concentrated on lighter-boned flat racers. Attempts to sculpt more bone into those had foundered on the difficulty of defining the ideal bone mass for each developing limb at each stage.

The rest of the afternoon, as she watched one horse after another, half her mind was wandering off to Rotterdam and the Guerni Republic. That brought up the last discussion she'd had with her doctors.

"You are physically a young woman again," they'd said. "Your body is in peak condition. But rejuvenation doesn't make your mind forget all it's learned. You are not in your early thirties: you are, in your experience, between eighty and ninety. You will find you want to use your new body in ways that satisfy your mature mind."

She had not imagined what that might mean. What was she to do with the abundant energy that now made her restless? The Wherrin Trials had shown that she could be competitive; she was sure she could regain the championship. She had swum easily against the strongest current the yacht's pool provided, refreshed and not tired by an hour's swim. Pedar's revelations of a Rejuvenant clique didn't attract her, except when younger people were being especially tiresome . . . but they were more tiresome now than when her aging body had left her with less energy to express her irritation.

She considered her family: would young Ronnie have been so feckless if his parents had not been Rejuvenants? Parents who knew they would live forever didn't want competition from their children . . . might be glad if the children were "too immature" at twenty or even thirty to be given responsibility. Were the Rejuvenants heading for a society in which the young would have no opportunity to develop mature judgment? The youngsters had done well enough when they had to—when they had the chance, like Brun, to demonstrate the maturity they should have.

"Would you like to try out some of his get?" asked Marcia. Cecelia yanked herself back to the present, where the chestnut stallion posed in the ring, showing off his muscles. The Singularity line, whatever its structural faults, had never been short of showy personality.

Would she like to ride one? She thought of Marcia's past, and her past, and the way she always felt on a horse. No contest. It was never any contest. She always wanted to ride a live horse, even a bad horse.

An hour later she felt that even the Singularity line had its virtues. True, they didn't have the extension she liked. True, they had trouble with lateral flexion of their stubby bodies. But they provided both springy comfort in collection, and explosive leaps over fences. Cecelia dismounted at last, feeling almost smug. She had seen, in the look on Slangsby's face, that he had not expected her to be that good. And Marcia, who had surely rejuved more than once, must not have expected it either—they both looked slightly stunned.

It might be worth it to have one just for fun—just for herself. Not to breed—she still didn't like the structure—but to ride. An embryo transfer to Rotterdam, brought out of one of the big old mares Meredith kept for the purpose. In a few years, she could play with it—hard to believe she had those years now, could look that far ahead.

It did change the decision points.

"Let's talk about this," she said to Marcia. She was very glad she'd taken care to see her bankers before coming out here; Marcia had made everyone on the circuit uncomfortable about money years ago, and that sort of stinginess didn't change.

Aboard the *Vigilance*, docked at Xavier Station

"Excuse me, Commander, but Captain Serrano asked if she could come aboard. She'd like to speak to you personally." It was past half, in the second shift, a time when attention blurred toward dinner. A time when, according to Koutsoudas and his instruments, Garrivay gathered with his conspirators for a daily conference. The guard at the access, crisply efficient in his spotless uniform, watched Heris and the others closely as he spoke into the intercom. A pause, during which Heris tried not to hold her breath visibly. He must want her to come; it would make things so much easier for him. A Serrano with an armed yacht was the only menace he faced; if the mouse walked into the cat's parlor, it saved the trouble of hunting it down. He had to be smart enough to figure that out. If only Koutsoudas's genius had included mind probes . . .

"Oh, very well." The reply was easily loud enough for her to hear. Then, in a more cordial tone. "Yes, yes—do bring her aboard, and any of her crew that came along. Delighted . . ."

Delighted. She let no hint of her own delight at setting foot on a cruiser deck again slip past her guard. She was the renegade, the outcast who hadn't dared come back in the Fleet. She was a coward who hadn't yet admitted it; she let herself shiver as Garrivay's security patted her down, as if it bothered her.

None of her weapons would show. Behind her, her crew submitted as well. She had worried some about Meharry, who had been a bit too eager to come along, but Meharry said nothing untoward. They were all in obviously civilian shipsuits with Cecelia's family name stenciled (a few hours before) on the chest. Heris had not known how Garrivay would react to this many crew—she had alternate plans for different possibilities—but they were led to his office in a clump.

"Ah . . . Captain . . . or may I call you Heris?" Garrivay, expansive in his own ship, eyed her up and down with the clear intent of discovering any lingering scrap of backbone. As she had hoped, he had not dismissed the other officers. She had suspected he would prefer to humiliate her before an audience.

Heris drooped as submissively as she could, giving a nervous laugh. She scarcely glanced at the other officers in the compartment. They would all have been junior to her, if she were still in; they were all junior to Garrivay. And they were all conspirators. She hoped Koutsoudas was right about that. She had enough innocent blood on her conscience.

"You're the commodore," she said. Would this be too much? But no, he accepted that as his due.

"Right," he said. "I am. You know, I really wish you had left here with your rich lady, your owner. I might have to confiscate that ship if there *is* an emergency."

"I know," Heris said, heaving a dramatic sigh. "She just wouldn't listen. She doesn't understand things; she doesn't believe it can happen to her." Koutsoudas had assured her that Garrivay could not have intercepted the messages between her and Cecelia supposedly discussing that possibility; she hoped not, because all the messages had been fakes. Cecelia had gone blissfully into that horse farm and had yet to emerge. The safest place she could be, right now. "I suppose you'd install your own crew?" she asked, aiming for wistfulness.

"Do *you* want the job?" he asked.

Heris shook her head, looking down as if ashamed. She was afraid she couldn't control the expression in her eyes. "No, I—you know I—had the chance to go back in Fleet."

"And got out while the going was good, eh? Well, probably wise. And your crew—ex-Fleet as well—I don't suppose any of them want a berth on a real fighting ship again?"

"No, sir," said Meharry. *Shut up*, Heris thought at her. *Don't ruin this.* "I got more'n enough scars, sir." Meharry at her best didn't sound entirely respectful, and at the moment she sounded downright sullen.

"I hope we won't have to impress you, then," Garrivay said, in a voice that enjoyed the threat. "If there is trouble, and we run short of . . . whatever your specialty was . . ." He waited, but Meharry didn't enlighten him. Heris stared at the carpet, waiting, feeling the others at her back. Garrivay chuckled suddenly, and she looked up, as he would have expected. "Don't look so worried, Heris. I'm not planning to run off with your owner's ship and your crew unless I have to. You'll never have to fight another battle. Now . . . what was it you wanted to talk to me about?"

"Well . . . Commodore . . ." He liked the title; she could see him swelling up like a dampened sponge. "It's partly my owner and partly the local government. You see, before you arrived, they kind of got to asking me things. . . ." She went off into a long, complicated tale she had thought up, something that kept offering Garrivay hints of intrigue and possibly profit, but entangled in enough detail that he had to listen carefully. She had rehearsed it repeatedly, adding even more complicated sections so that it took up enough time. It had an ending, if needed, but within the next anecdote or so Koutsoudas should—

"Sir—an urgent signal—" There it was; the prearranged distractor, one of Koutsoudas's elegant fakeries. A bobble on the ship's scans that might be incoming ships, something the bridge crew would have to report and Garrivay would have to acknowledge.

"Yes?" Garrivay turned away, reaching for his desk controls; his officers, for that instant, looked where he looked.

No one needed a signal. Heris threw herself forward and sideways, in a roll-and-kick combination that caught Garrivay on the angle of the jaw. His hands flew wide; before he could recover, she was on him, the edge of her hand smashing his larynx. Her other hand had reached the com button, preventing its automatic alarm at the sudden loss of contact. Garrivay, heaving as he tried to suck air and got none, thrashed against his desk and fell to the deck. From his earplug came the tinny squeak of someone reporting the surprise Koutsoudas had created for their sensors.

She looked up, to meet four triumphant grins. Too early for those; they had just started. She leaned over and removed Garrivay's earplug, inserting it in her own ear.

"—it's moving insystem at half insertion velocity, while the other—" She listened, only half hearing what she already knew, but aware of a little bubble of delight at being once more connected to a real ship's command center. Even if it wasn't her ship. Though it was—or would be—if the rest of this worked.

Already the others were stripping the bodies of their uniforms. Oblo looked up and waved something, a data strip it looked like. Heris leaned again to Garrivay, now unconscious, his body twitching with oxygen deprivation, and unpinned his insignia. Her nose wrinkled involuntarily at the unpleasant stench; she ignored the source and pinned the insignia to her own uniform. Thank goodness she had a uniform that could pass for Fleet in a pinch . . . because this was a pinch indeed.

"I can wear this," Petris said doubtfully, nodding at the uniform he'd removed from someone with major's rings.

"No," Heris said. "It won't really convince them, and once they discover where the uniforms came from they'll worry again. I'm the key: if they accept me, they'll accept you." Otherwise, of course, they were all dead. In her ear, the flow of information stopped. She hit the com button twice, the usual signal of a busy captain that the message had been received.

From Garrivay's inside pocket—no more twitches now—Heris took the thin wand that gave access to captain's command switches. From here out, it would get more dangerous. Murder was one thing. Piracy, treason, and mutiny were . . . she didn't think about it.

The wand slid into the desk slot easily. The hard part came next. To forestall just such coups as they had accomplished, the use of the captain's wand triggered a demand for an identity check.

"Serrano, Heris," Heris said, adding her identification numbers and rank, mentally crossing more fingers than she owned . . . *if* Koutsoudas was right, her aunt admiral might have managed to leave a back door in the Fleet database.

Lights flared on the captain's desk, and the computer demanded a reason why Serrano, Heris, Commander was using Garrivay, Dekan Sostratos, Commander's wand.

"Emergency," she said. Then, with a deep breath, took her aunt's name in vain. "On the orders of Admiral Vida Serrano."

The computer paused. "Authorization number?" A sticky one. The only number her aunt had shared with her recently was the Serrano encryption code on that datacube. Would aunt admiral have risked putting her family code into the database, hiding it in plain sight, as it were? Right now Heris believed her aunt admiral might have done anything. She found another mental finger to cross, and gave that number. After the second group, the computer blinked all the lights. "Authorization accepted." So . . . aunt admiral had had more in mind than an apology, had she? And had she known Heris would be in this sort of trouble? Koutsoudas's remark about "lightning rods" flashed through her mind. Interesting—infuriating—but she had no time to sort it out.

Now a touch on the desk opened the service functions. She picked up the command headset and settled it on her hair.

"You don't want the combat helmet?" Petris asked.

"No. If we can do this at all, we can do it this way. We cannot take the whole ship by force, if everyone's turned." She could, with the command wand, destroy it and everyone on it—and, in the process, the station to which they were docked. But she hoped very much that her string of good guesses would continue to hold. "They need to see my face. I'm legitimate, remember? The computer accepts me; my aunt is an admiral." On the desk, she keyed up the status displays. Personnel . . . there were fifteen more known traitors on this ship, and four on one of the patrol craft. Koutsoudas thought he knew which fifteen, and she located them . . . on duty, six . . . one on the bridge, and five elsewhere about the ship.

"You can't take the bridge alone," Petris said.

"No . . . but I can isolate the compartments." She touched the control panels. Now each was blocked from communication with the others, and if she could get control of the bridge crew, if they believed her, there was a chance of capturing the other traitors without a major fight in the ship.

The first thing was to establish her authority with even one legitimate onboard officer. Now on the bridge was a major Koutsoudas thought unlikely to be a traitor. Again, he had better be right. She selected his personal comcode from the officers list.

"Major Svatek, report to the captain's office."

"Yes, sir." He had a voice that gave nothing away; she felt no intuitive nudge of like or dislike. Heris nodded to her crew; they placed themselves on either side of the door and waited.

The major came in without really looking, and by the time he had registered the bodies on the floor and the stranger behind the captain's desk, Petris and Meharry had him covered.

"Sorry about this, Major," Heris said. He looked stunned, and then angry, but not particularly frightened. "It is necessary that you listen to what I have to say, and there was no safe way to do this on the bridge without imperiling the ship."

"Who . . . are you?" The expletives deleted by caution left a pause in that.

"I'm Commander Heris Serrano," she said. It was not an officer she had ever seen before, but he had to know that name. "I'm on special assignment."

"But—" The major's eyes shifted from her to Petris to the bodies and back to her. Recognition; that was good. For once Heris didn't mind having the family face. "But you were— I heard—"

Heris smiled. "You heard correctly. I resigned my commission and took employment as a civilian . . . in anticipation of recent crises."

"Oh." The blank look cleared slowly. "You mean it was all—all faked?"

"Well . . . not uncovering Lepescu's plot," Heris said cheerfully. Everyone knew about Lepescu, she was sure. "That wasn't faked at all."

"But—what are you doing *here*?" This time his glance at the bodies had been longer. His first anger was leaving him, and she saw a twitch of fear, quickly controlled.

"Right now, I'm taking command of this ship, as ordered."

"You—are?" The major's gears were trying to mesh, but achieved only useless spinning; Heris could almost hear the loose rattle. "As ordered?"

"You're aware that this system will shortly be under attack by the Benignity of the Compassionate Hand?" Giving it the full title added weight, Heris thought, to the claim.

"Uh . . . no . . . uh . . . Captain." Victory. The major didn't know it yet, perhaps, but he had accepted Heris in command.

"They scouted it, sent a fake raider in to check out the defenses—"

"That raider we heard about?"

"Yes. With a surveillance ship in the distance. This group was then dispatched . . . but not by the R.S.S. command."

"But—but what are you saying?"

"That your former captain, Dekan Garrivay, was a traitor, in the pay of the Benignity. That certain of his officers were also traitors, that the purpose of this mission was to strip Xavier of any defenses, including me—since I had killed the raider—and open it to the Benignity."

"But—but how do you—" Disbelief and avid curiosity warred in the major's expression.

"You may recall that I have an Aunt Vida . . . Admiral Vida, that is."

Comprehension swept across the major's face, and he sagged. An aunt admiral, a secret mission . . . it was all right. Behind the major, Petris relaxed a fraction. Heris didn't.

"Now," Heris said, "my people need uniforms; they've had to wear those miserable civilian things too long." She paused a moment, wondering if she dared promote her associates to officers. She needed all the loyal officers she could find . . . but instinct said that even the smallest additional lie could topple the major's fragile belief in her story. If he stopped to think, if he doubted, she would become a common murderer again, not a legitimate officer who had been operating under cover. She gave them their original ranks instead, and watched the major's response. He might not know it, but he could still be dead any moment. "And you'll need to get someone up to tape the scene for forensics, put the bodies on ice, and clean up this office afterwards. We strongly suspect that one or more are carrying discreet CH ID markings. And the following personnel must be located and put under guard." She handed him Koutsoudas's list. Making it all up as she went along, she realized, was a lot more fun.

"Yes, sir." A long pause. "Anything else, sir?"

"No," Heris said. "I'll be on the bridge, speaking to the crew."

"But you've got Cydin on your list, and she's on the bridge now," the major said.

"Thank you," Heris said, as if she hadn't known that. "Then I'll take Mr. Vissisuan with me—" Oblo was almost as well known in the Fleet as Koutsoudas. "Who's bridge officer at this time?"

"Lieutenant Milcini," Major Svatek said.

"And the M.P. watch commander?"

"Lieutenant Ginese—" Svatek looked at Arkady Ginese, startled. Ginese smiled.

"That's probably my Uncle Slava's oldest boy. I'd heard he'd been commissioned." Another thin layer added to the skin of belief; Heris could see Svatek processing this. Not only the famous Serrano name, but someone related to the ship's own security personnel.

"Mr. Ginese, you'll accompany me as well," Heris said. "Let's go."

CHAPTER FOURTEEN

The corridors of Garrivay's ship—no, *her* ship—were as familiar as the shapes of her own fingers. Command Deck, dockside corridor, aft of the captain's office. A passing ensign saluted her insignia without appearing to notice anything; his eyes widened at her escort. She wished they'd been able to wait for uniforms, but the scanty tradition behind her acts emphasized the need for immediate action.

Ahead, the hatch leading to the bridge, just where she'd left it, as if she had walked back onto her own ship. This *was* her ship, she reminded herself. A marine pivot stood at ease by the hatch, snapping to attention at the sight of her insignia.

"Sir!" Then his expression wavered, as if he weren't sure.

"Pivot." She snapped a salute. "These personnel are with me." Before he reacted, they were past; she came through into her own kingdom, home at last.

She took the three steps forward, paused while the bridge officer caught sight of her.

"Sir—uh . . . Commander . . . ?"

"Commander Heris Serrano, special assignment." She pitched her voice to carry through the whole compartment. "As I've explained to Major Svatek, I have taken command of this vessel. You are Lieutenant Milcini, is that correct—?" She was aware of heads turning, the pressure of many startled looks. One of the officers on the bridge was Cydin. Heris didn't worry about that;

898

Ginese and Oblo would be watching for her. More important now was the reaction of the loyal crew. So far astonishment held them.

The lieutenant found his voice again. "Captain Garrivay—?"

"Commander Garrivay has been relieved." Heris held up the command wand. "The computer has accepted my authorization code."

"Liar!" There. Lieutenant Cydin, a rangy redhead who reminded her inexorably of Cecelia. "She's a traitor—don't listen to her! She was cashiered—she's not Fleet!"

Heads turned back and forth, uneasy. Lieutenant Milcini started to reach out but froze in a parody of indecision when Heris looked at him.

"Lieutenant Cydin, you are hereby charged with treason," Heris said steadily. "Evidence in possession of Fleet—" Koutsoudas, after all, was legitimately Fleet, even if presently on a yacht "—shows that you conspired with Commander Garrivay and others to yield Xavier to the Benignity of the Compassionate Hand."

"What!" Cydin's face went paper white.

"Recordings of conversations with Commander Garrivay . . ." Heris said. "You are hereby relieved of your duties and will be held in confinement until such time as a Board can be convened—" The familiar phrases rolled out of her mouth as if she herself had never felt their impact on her own life. Necessary, she knew; such formality, such familiarity with tradition, was another proof of her own legitimacy. "Mr. Ginese, Mr. Vissisuan—" She nodded, and they moved around her. Lieutenant Cydin looked around for support she did not get.

"No! I'm not a traitor—*she* is! Ask her what happened to our captain! It's all lies!" But around her was a subtle withdrawing. "Look at her—that's not a Fleet uniform! Those men—they're in civvie shipsuits!"

"*I* know her," someone said. Heris looked for the voice, and found a face she vaguely remembered from several ships back. Her mental name file revolved.

"Petty-light Salverson," she said. "But you've had a promotion—congratulations, Chief."

"I never believed you'd been thrown out," Salverson said. She was a pleasant-faced brunette that Heris remembered best for a difficult emergency repair during combat. "So it was all special ops?"

"I'm not at liberty to say," Heris said; Salverson grinned, and those nearest her—people she would have known well—grinned too.

"You *fools!*" Cydin yelled. "She'll get you killed, all of you." Then, with a glance at Ginese and Oblo, who were almost to her side, she gave Heris a final, furious glare. "You won't win," she said. "You can't—even if you get the ship—" And she slumped where she stood. Those nearest tried to catch her, but failed; her head hit the decking with a resonant thump.

Heris felt a chill pang she had not felt when she killed Garrivay. Cydin seemed so young; she could have outlived her mistakes if she'd wanted to. She had no time for more regrets. "We'll need an autopsy," she said to Lieutenant Milcini. "Until all my people are back in uniform, we'd better have someone else convey the body to sickbay."

"Yes . . . Captain." She left him to arrange it; she had more pressing duties. He had forgotten, in his confusion, to transfer bridge command, but she could never forget that.

She moved to the command desk. "I have the bridge," she said. "Let me explain the situation briefly. I expect communications from the admiralty, and possible hostile action from the Benignity. This action may be imminent; unless we find details in Commander Garrivay's private notes, we must assume that it could come any time."

Silence, attentive now rather than confused. Confront a fighting vessel with an enemy and confusion yielded to training. She had counted on that reaction. Heris went on.

"Officers not involved in the treasonous plot to yield Xavier will be briefed as soon as the ships are secure. In the meantime, all scans will be fully manned all shifts; record in battle code from this hour—" The scan positions, after a last glance at her, erupted in a brief flurry of activity. Garrivay had had them shut down, probably to prevent the operators from noticing when the CH ships arrived.

"Captain—" A light on the command desk, a voice in her ear.

"Yes?"

"Lieutenant Ginese, watch commander. I have just been advised by Major Svatek to take certain persons into custody, and among them a Lieutenant Cydin who is on the bridge—"

"Was on the bridge. She killed herself rather than accept arrest."

"I see. May I ask the captain's authorization for actions taken in relieving Commander Garrivay of his duties?" Deftly put, Heris thought.

"Admiral Serrano," Heris said. "It was a special assignment."

"So I gathered." Like her own Arkady, this Ginese had a healthy lack of awe for officers. After a long moment, the honorific appeared. "Sir. Does the captain have other orders?"

"Secure the ship," Heris said. "No station liberty, no leaves, no offship communications without my express orders. That list is almost certainly incomplete, and as we'll be in combat shortly—" Not too shortly, she hoped, but it couldn't be long enough.

"Yes, sir. Those personnel on the list have been secured under guard, although—we can't maintain a suicide watch with all of them separately confined *and* do the rest of it. Would the captain clarify the priorities?"

"Ship first, of course. If they kill themselves, it's regrettable—the other could be fatal." He shouldn't need to be told that, but she realized he was still feeling his way, not quite sure she was trustworthy.

"Major Svatek said a relative of mine was with you— would that be Vladi?" Despite the casual tone, Heris knew this was a trick question. She had never heard of a Vladi Ginese.

"Arkady," Heris said. "Would you like to speak with him?"

"No—just checking. Sorry, sir. It's my—"

"Job, I know. Now if you'll excuse me, I have other duties myself." As have you, went unsaid but clearly understood. Heris unlocked the inship communications, and keyed for an all-stations announcement. If there were other traitors— or even highstrung overreactors—this would flush them out.

"Attention all personnel. This is Commander Heris Sunier Serrano, now acting captain of this vessel. We are in a state of emergency, expecting the arrival of a hostile force from the Benignity. Your executive officer, Major Svatek, has been informed of the nature of the emergency, and of the reasons for a change of command. Those of you who have served with me before know that I will give full explanations when there's time." A calculated risk, but surely there were others who had been with her before, who would explain to their anxious fellows what kind of commander Heris was. "Some of you will have heard that I resigned my commission and am no longer a Fleet officer; in fact I was on special assignment, and my authorization code is still active, as the ship's computer recognized. This is an unusual situation; I understand that many of you will be confused, but at the moment we have more pressing problems. The Benignity wants this system as a base for invasion; we're going to defend it."

From the expressions of the bridge crew, relief outweighed anxiety. Garrivay could not have been the sort of commander who inspired confidence.

"I want all division heads in my office in one hour," Heris went on. "I notice some discrepancies in the status lists that we'll have to address in order to complete our mission. In the meantime, I'll expect you all to bring all systems to readiness." Which made it sound as if she had an official mission. "Captain out."

She grinned at Lieutenant Milcini. "I'll post the hardcopy of my orders when I get them from *Sweet Delight*. Considering the secrecy, I couldn't bring them aboard with me at first." Certain phrases from the cube her aunt had sent her could, with the proper surrounding verbiage, be taken as orders. Oblo had produced a surprisingly realistic document.

"Yes, sir. Uh—you'll be taking over the captain's quarters?"

"Of course." Implicit in that was her transfer to the *Vigilance* as her primary vessel; the *Sweet Delight* was no longer hers in the same way. And who would captain the yacht? She might need it in the fight. No, first the very dangerous patrol ships.

She had the cruiser . . . maybe. If they captured the other traitors aboard before they could arrange a mutiny. If the other two craft didn't try to blow the cruiser.

"Who's our communications first, Lieutenant Milcini?" Heris asked.

"Lieutenant Granath, sir."

"Have Lieutenant Granath hail the *Sweet Delight*, civilian band four, and route the response to my set."

"Sir."

Moments later, Sirkin's voice answered for the yacht. *"Sweet Delight*, Nav First Sirkin."

"Sirkin, it's Captain Serrano. I've taken over here. How's the longscan look?"

"Captain, there's something far out, Kou—our scan tech says. Very faint, just a ripple."

"I'm having communications here hold an open line. If there's a change, let me know." What she said and did not say fit the prearranged code; Koutsoudas would remove the block he'd put on communications out of the cruiser. Now for the patrol ships. *Paradox*'s captain had died with Garrivay in the captain's cabin; *Paradox*'s executive officer might or might not be loyal. He had not shown up on any of Koutsoudas's scans, but he had been with the traitor captain for two years. The more distant *Despite* had as its captain an officer definitely disloyal. Koutsoudas had recorded her during a conference aboard the cruiser. Heris expected that the crews of both ships were predominantly loyal; she had not forgotten Skoterin, but still believed traitors were rare. If the exec of *Paradox* accepted her . . . that left only *Despite*. Would that captain betray herself? The patrol craft could be lethal, especially if any distractions arose on the cruiser.

"Major Tinsi, I am Commander Heris Serrano, acting captain of the *Vigilance*. You are hereby confirmed as acting captain of the patrol craft *Paradox*."

"What?" The face onscreen matched the database holo of Major Tinsi. "What's—where's Captain Ardos? Who *are* you?"

"Commander Serrano," Heris repeated. "Heris Serrano. I've been on special assignment for the admiralty, investigating irregularities." Such a handy word, irregularities. She was a little shocked at how easily the lie now rolled off her tongue.

"But you're not—and where's Commodore Garrivay? What's going on over there?"

"Commander Garrivay has been relieved of his command," Heris said. "I'm sorry to say that he and your Captain Ardos were involved in these . . . er . . . irregularities." She held up a packet within pickup range. "We have recordings implicating both of them, and some other officers. We assume that officers not implicated are innocent—and that includes yourself, although the investigation will continue. May I take it that you are not in the pay of the Benignity?"

"Of course I'm not—what? The *Benignity*? Captain *Ardos*?" Captain Ardos, Heris reflected, must have been relieved to have so dense an executive officer. No wonder he had kept the man around for two years even though he couldn't confide in him. No better camouflage than honest stupidity, ready to swear he had seen, heard, and suspected nothing.

Heris waved the packet, and Tinsi shut up. "Apparently several officers on each ship were involved. I suggest you take immediate steps to secure your position, in case there are more traitors aboard. We expect hostile forces in this system shortly; you will prepare your ship for combat, Captain Tinsi."

"But I—but—"

"Or, if you feel yourself unequal to command, I can relieve you and assign another officer," Heris said. Tinsi stiffened as if she'd filled his spinal column with a steel rod.

"No, sir . . . Commander . . . Commodore . . ."

"Commander will do. Now. I have a list of possible traitors aboard *Paradox*. These are not confirmed, but you might want to take precautions." She transmitted the names in a burst of code. "You will maintain a shielded link to *Vigilance*, while I make contact with *Despite*."

"Captain—*Despite*'s moving." That was Koutsoudas, not waiting for Sirkin to transmit the call. "Pretty good delta vee, outbound toward the border."

At least it wasn't an attack on the station or her ships. Yet. "Weapons, bring us to readiness."

"Sir."

"*Paradox*, you are authorized to bring your weapons to full readiness." What was *Despite* doing out there? Not simply running away; that would be too easy. Going to feint a retreat and then come back? Going to meet someone? And had she any chance to stop them? "We need to transfer gear and personnel from the yacht *Sweet Delight* to this ship—see to it—" she said to Major Svatek, who had reappeared on the bridge just before she called *Paradox*.

"Yes, sir. How many personnel, sir?" A good question. She

still wanted to crew the yacht, in case they needed it. But right now she wanted Koutsoudas back at the boards of a Fleet ship, with direct access to the onboard databases, and to her. If it cost her a chance at *Despite*, so be it.

"Two," she said. "The gear will be for myself and the personnel who came aboard with me—not much, a little less than standard officer duffel." Already packed, it lay in the access hatch.

"Any problem with them going through the station? Do you mind if the civs know about it?"

"No—that's fine." It would be much easier, both now and when she assigned a crew to the yacht.

"*Despite*, hold your station. Hold your station. This is Commander Serrano, acting captain of the *Vigilance* . . . hold your station or—"

"Or what?" The display flickered as the signal stretched with the other craft's acceleration and the comunit's logic struggled to reassemble it, but Heris could see the face clearly enough. Lt. Commander Kiansa Hearne, not that much different from the days when she and Heris had shared a compartment in the junior officers' warren aboard *Acclaim*. "I don't know what you've done, but you have no authority. You're a civilian now, Heris."

"No," said Heris. "Special assignment, Lt. Commander." She would not use the old name. Kia had been a difficult young woman, but not yet a traitor. Heris had left the *Acclaim* thinking she had made a friend, proud of herself for the effort she'd put into it. "Surely you don't think I was out here by accident."

"I . . . think you're bluffing."

"I think *you* are. We have recordings from Garrivay's office."

"Blast." Hearne's face sagged. "That bastard. I finally get a ship of my own, and the next thing I know—" That had been Kia's problem all along; she always had someone to blame for her failures.

"You've got a shipful of innocent crew," Heris said. "Turn command over to your exec, or another loyal officer, and I'll see what I can do—"

"I'm not stupid, Heris." Hearne scowled. "If you've got real evidence, I'm dead meat anyway. Under the circumstances,

I think a strategic withdrawal is in my best interest. You'd have a tough time catching me—especially if you're crazy enough to stick around and try to stop the Benignity."

"Your crew—" Heris began.

"My crew will have to take care of themselves," Hearne said. "You understand that—*yours* did."

The old rage and grief broke over Heris like a wave; she fought her way out of it in seconds, but made no more effort to convince Hearne.

"Captain, we have a statement from one of the officers on the list." That was Oblo.

"Go ahead," Heris said.

"Seems he was recruited by a Benignity agent about four years ago, and hasn't done a thing for them since. Claims he didn't know about the plan to surrender this system, but after he heard the recording he changed his tune and said he was coerced."

"Well, it's evidence," Heris said. "I assume Lieutenant Ginese knows about this?"

"Yes, sir. And they've got uniforms for us now—"

"Good. You know what to do. Koutsoudas and your duffel will be aboard shortly. I'll be contacting the Xavierans now."

The General Secretary and the Stationmaster were side by side in the screen, looking grumpy until they saw who it was, then relieved. That relief wouldn't last long, not with what she must tell them.

"I've taken command of the Fleet units operating here," Heris said. "The former commander was removed for treason."

"I wondered!" The General Secretary looked angry, ready to pound someone. "Well, you'll have our backing, such as it is. What can we do?"

"Sir, you need to prepare for assault. We have no idea now how many ships are coming—we'll tell you when we can—but delay is the best we can do. Remember what we talked about before. Get your people downside into the best shelters you can find—scattered far away from recognizable population centers, ready to live rough for some months. If you have deep caves, out in the mountains or something, that would be best." She hoped the horse farm

Cecelia was on was far enough out; she reminded herself to find out.

"But our militia—" Heris remembered the proud troops in their colorful uniforms, marching to the music of that jaunty band. How could she save their pride without costing them their existence? "I can't recommend resistance; they'll have trained troops and plenty of them—but if you can hide out for a few months, Fleet should be back in here. Your militia will be best used keeping order on the way, and while you're in exile."

"We can't evacuate?"

"Where?" Heris paused, then went on. "You don't have enough hulls in the system to take everyone, or time to load them. You have only the one station, and they'll blow it. They'll install their own, rather than risk yours being boobytrapped. Get everyone out of the station, downside, and get away from your cities and towns. It'll still be nasty, but that will save the most lives."

This wasn't what they had wanted to hear, even though she had said much the same thing before Garrivay arrived. They tried to talk her into some other solutions. Heris held firm. She would do her best but she could not promise to save the planet from direct attack. And she would need control of every space-capable hull they had, once they'd evacuated the station.

"But you can't hope to fight with shuttles!" the stationmaster said. "They don't have shields worth speaking of."

"No—but we can sow some traps with them. Then we can extract the crews, onto one of the warships."

"And the shuttles?"

"They'll be lost, one way or another. But with any luck, they'll have made things tougher for the invaders."

The General Secretary agreed to have the empty upbound shuttles loaded with readily available explosives. Those waiting for evacuation were kept busy shifting incoming cargo from the shuttles. A few, who had experience with explosives, helped manufacture them into crude mines.

Then she thought of Sirkin and Brun. She had realized that Sirkin, intelligent and hardworking as she was, lacked precisely what Brun had—the flair or whatever it was that picked the right choice when things got hairy. She needed to get Sirkin to such safety as was available, which meant downside, and underground. She had no safe place to stash Brun. What would her father want, given the options? His assumption that Brun would be safer with her now seemed utter folly. She was taking ships into battle against great odds, and very likely the planet would be scorched. Brun, as usual, had her own opinions, and interrupted the transmission from *Sweet Delight*.

"Captain Serrano, please—give me a chance. 'Steban, just a minute—please let me come with you."

Lord Thornbuckle's daughter on a warship? Not likely. "Why?" she asked.

"I know I'm not Fleet, and I know I'd be in the way, but it's better than going downside. Surely there's something simple I could do, so that someone else could help fight."

"There may be, but you can do it onplanet. I want someone I trust with Lady Cecelia. You and Sirkin can keep an eye on her. It's going to be rough down there when the shooting starts." Particularly since Cecelia would be thinking more about horses than the war, she was sure.

"But—"

"I don't have time to argue, Brun. This is one time you'll just do what I say. Besides, you can represent the Grand Council to the General Secretary—assure him that Xavier won't be forgotten." She cut that connection, and found herself faced with a choice of five others. The stationmaster wanted to know what she would do about the small mining settlements on the second satellite of Blueyes, the smaller gas giant. She could do nothing but send them word of what was happening; she had no time to think of anything else. The General Secretary wanted to know if she could use elements of the local militia. (Yes, if they volunteered.) Experienced shuttle pilots? (Yes.) A local news program wanted to interview her. (No. The General Secretary's staff would handle news.) The station's own medical team—doctors, medics, nannies and all—volunteered to come along on one of the ships, because they were certified in space medicine. (Yes!) And what about the breakdown in the financial ansible? And . . .

* * *

Koutsoudas had come aboard with his kitbag of gadgets, and installed them while the other techs gave him startled looks.

"Some of you," Heris said, "may have met Commander Livadhi's senior scan tech, Esteban Koutsoudas. He's been assisting the admiralty in this investigation." By their reaction, they might have waited years for a chance to watch the legendary Koutsoudas in action. "By the way, someone find him a uniform—you would prefer a real uniform, wouldn't you, 'Steban?"

"Mmm? Oh—yes, Captain. Although right now I just want to get these things installed and running." Everyone chuckled; Heris grinned. Better and better. She noticed that Koutsoudas managed to keep a hand or his head between the watchers and what he was actually doing, most of the time. Then his scan lit, obviously sharper than the ones on either side.

"How'd you *do* that?" one of the youngest techs asked.

"Don't ask," Koutsoudas said. His fingers danced across the plain surfaces of his add-ons. Heris never had figured out how he operated them. His display changed color slightly, showing the departing *Despite* in a vivid arc of color that zoomed suddenly closer. Heris flinched, even though she knew it was Koutsoudas, and not the patrol craft. Along one side of the display, three sets of numbers scrolled past. "There—eighty-seven percent of her maximum acceleration, but she's got a bobble in the insystem drive. Sloppy . . . it's cutting their output. Weapons still cold. That's odd. Shields . . . there goes the pre-jump shield check."

"I never believed it," said someone at the margin of Weapons. "I heard about him but I didn't believe—"

"It's impossible," said someone else.

"Cut the chatter." That was the grizzled senior chief poised behind Koutsoudas's shoulder, absorbing what he could.

"Send a tightbeam," Koutsoudas said, and gave the vector. Showoff, Heris thought. Worth it, in what he could do for you, but a showoff all the same.

"There they are." Now his display zoomed to another vector, where three . . . five . . . seven . . . scarlet dots burned. "Tag 'em—" Beside each one, a code appeared.

"Range?" Heris asked. She leaned forward, as if she could

pry more information out of the display. Numbers flickered along both edges of the screen.

"They're in the cone," Koutsoudas said, answering her next question first. "They'll get whatever *Despite* sent—and the range is still affected by downjump turbulence. I won't have it to any precision for an hour, Captain."

"Three to four hours for me, Captain," said the scan-second promptly.

"But they're at the system edge," Koutsoudas said. "It's a cautious approach—very cautious. They won't spot us for another several hours at least, even with boosted long scan; they're blinded by their own downjump turbulence."

"What's *Despite* doing?"

"Running fast," Koutsoudas said, flicking back over that ship's departing signature. "Considering scan lag, I'll bet she's already gone into jump."

Cecelia arrived at the shuttle port in a foul temper. It had taken forever to get a groundcar out to Marcia's place, and she hadn't been about to take any favors from Marcia. Not after that insult—as if she had ever failed to pay her bills! So she had endured a long, bumpy, dusty trip in to the shuttle port. Traffic crowded the road going the other way. It must be some local holiday, with early closing. But once in town, clogged streets delayed them, and she was afraid the shuttle port would be just as bad. She had tried to call Heris, but Sirkin was uncharacteristically vague about where she was, only saying she wasn't on the yacht. Cecelia didn't care where she was, she just wanted to be sure they could leave when she reached the station. Marcia's last words rankled . . . "It is not our habit to haggle, Cecelia," said with injured innocence. Stupid people. Stupid breeders of inferior horses; she would get some Singularity genes from a gene catalog if she wanted, and be damned to them. She forced a smile at the ticketing clerk, glad to find that she wasn't at the tail of a long line.

"Any room on the up shuttle?"

The clerk looked surprised and worried both, but clerks often did. His problems were his problems; she had room in her mind for only one thing—leaving Xavier far, far behind. "Yes, ma'am, but—"

"Fine. First class if you have it, but anything will do." What she really wanted was a long shower, a cooling drink, and a good supper. Depending on how long she had to wait for the shuttle, she might eat here, although she didn't remember the shuttle port having anything but machine dispensers.

"But ma'am—you don't want to go up right now," the clerk said earnestly, as if speaking to a willful child.

Cecelia glared at him. "Yes, I *do* want to go up right now. I have a ship; we're leaving."

"Oh." He looked confused now. "You're leaving the system from the station?"

"Yes." She was in no mood for this nonsense. What business was it of his? "I'm Cecelia de Marktos, and my ship, the *Sweet Delight*, is at the station; we'll be leaving for Rotterdam as soon as I arrive."

"Oh. Well, in that case—let me see your ID, please." Cecelia stared around the terminal as she waited for the clerk to process her ID and credit cube. Beyond the windows, a shuttle streaked by, landing. She had timed it perfectly. She glanced at the clerk; he was talking busily into a handset. Checking her out? Fine. Let him. She was sick of this place.

The shuttle came into view again, taxiing to the terminal. A ground crew swarmed out to it. Cecelia peered down the corridor to the arrival lounge. Finally a door opened, and people started coming out, a hurrying stream of them. More and more . . . more than she had thought the usual shuttle held.

When they got closer, she realized they looked scared. Had the raider shown up again? Was that why Heris didn't answer? But the clerk tapped her on the arm.

"Lady Cecelia—here—first-class ticket up to the station, but I've been advised to tell you that you really should reconsider. I can't sell you a round trip; if you change your mind, you may not be able to come back down. There's an alert. This is the last shuttle flight; they're evacuating—"

"I'm not planning to stay there," she said, accepting the ticket. "When's departure?"

"As soon as they refuel and turn her around," the clerk said. "You may board right away. And I'm afraid you'll have to hand-carry your luggage."

"Not a problem." She hadn't brought much; she could carry it easily. She heaved her duffel onto her shoulder and started down the corridor. She noticed that no one else joined her.

In the first-class cabin, the crew were scurrying around picking up trash. The seats had been laid flat; she wondered if people had been crammed in side-by-side on them. One of the crew looked up, startled.

"What are you—you have a ticket? A ticket *up*? Are you crazy?"

"I'm going to meet my ship, which is departing," Cecelia said. "Don't worry about me." She unlatched a seat back and pulled it upright herself, then stowed her gear on the seat next to her. If she was to be the only passenger, she saw no reason to worry about regulations. Then she heard other footsteps coming, and started to move her duffel. But it wasn't passengers. Instead, a line of men in some kind of uniform formed down the aisle, and began passing canisters and boxes covered with warning labels hand to hand. Cecelia leaned out to look down the aisle and see where they were being put, and nearly got clonked in the head.

"Excuse us, ma'am . . . if you'll just keep out of the way," said the nearest. Cecelia sat back, wondering what the labels meant—she vaguely remembered seeing markings like that on the things Heris had installed in her yacht.

"If you could just move that," said someone else, and handed her duffel over. She sat with it on her lap, and began to wonder just what was going on. On the seat where her duffel had been, one of the men placed a heavily padded container labelled FUSES DANGER DO NOT DROP and strapped it in as carefully as if it were human. "Don't bump that," he said to Cecelia, with a smile. She smiled back automatically, before she could wonder why or ask anything. Someone yelled, outside, and the men turned and began filing out. She heard the hatch thud closed, and felt the familiar shift in air pressure as the shuttle's circulation system came on. A crewman came back from the front of the shuttle and smiled at her.

"All set? You might want to set your stuff on the floor. It might be a bit rough. Last chance to leave, if you're having second thoughts."

She was having third, fourth, and fifth thoughts, but she still didn't want to get off the shuttle and go back to Marcia and Poots. Or anywhere else on this benighted planet. Surely, when she got to the station, Heris could get her out of whatever problem was developing locally. Besides, it would look damn silly to back out now.

"I'm fine," she said. "Thank you. I suppose it is permissible to use the facilities?"

"Yes—but we aren't carrying any meals on this trip. If you need water—"

"I know where the galley is," Cecelia said. "I can serve myself—or you, if you want."

"Great. Stay down until we're well clear." She felt the rumble-bump of the wheels on the runway even as he turned away from her . . . whatever it was, they were in an almighty hurry. The shuttle hesitated only briefly when it turned at the end of the runway, then screamed into the sky . . . she supposed, since the usual visual display in the first-class cabin wasn't on, and the heat shields covering the portholes wouldn't slide back until they were out of the atmosphere.

Nothing happened on the trip; she used the facilities, found the ice water, and a bag of melting ice, offered the pilots water (which they refused) and foil-wrapped packets of cookies, which they accepted. She rummaged in the lockers, finding a whole box of the cookie packets jammed into a corner, and a card with *Meet you at Willie's tomorrow night, 2310* on it in swirly flourishes of green ink. In the top left-hand locker, a pile of coffee filters tumbled out, and she gave up the search for anything more interesting. She shoved the coffee filters back behind their door, and opened a cookie packet. They could call it "Special Deluxe Appetizing Biscuit" if they wanted, but it tasted like the residue of stale crumbs in the bottom of a tin. Cecelia decided she wasn't that hungry.

CHAPTER FIFTEEN

A line of passengers crammed the corridor as she came out; most of them gaped at her. She tried to remember which was the shortest way around to *Sweet Delight*. Then she heard someone calling her.

"Lady Cecelia!" Brun, waving a frantic hand. Sirkin was with her.

"Brun—whatever are you doing there? Why aren't you on the yacht?"

"Don't you know about it?"

"What?"

"The invasion. The Benignity is coming. With a fleet or something. Captain Serrano doesn't think she can hold them off; they're evacuating this station and telling people planetside to go into shelter. Underground if possible."

Across her mind scrolled the broad acres of Marcia and Poots's studfarm, the great log barns, the handsome paddocks, the gleaming horses . . . admittedly horses with conformational faults, but still horses.

"You're serious?"

"Yes—Captain Serrano told Sirkin and me to go downside, find you, and take care of you. She's having a military team crew the yacht—"

"Where is *she*?"

"On the cruiser," said Brun. "Wait—I'll explain—but you have to get into this line. You have to come with us—downside—"

"I don't want to go back down there," Cecelia said, aware

914

even as she said it that it sounded foolish. "I've been there. I want to be on my ship."

"Come on," said Brun. "You can't do that—there's no crew, and when there is a crew it won't be people you know—come on, get in line with us."

Cecelia wavered. "Well . . ."

"Come on." Brun stepped back, making room, but as Cecelia started toward the gap, angry voices rose.

"Hey! No cutting in front—you got no right—"

Brun turned on them. "She's an old lady; she's my mother's friend—"

Another voice louder than the others. "A Rejuvenant! I'm not losing my chance to get home safe for any damned Rejuvenant!" People shoved forward, slamming into Brun and Sirkin, who could not help slamming into those ahead.

"Damn you!"

"Stop it!"

"No shoving there . . . keep order, keep order . . ." That was two harried-looking station militia. "What's this now?"

Voices erupted, accusing, explaining, demanding. Finally things were quiet enough for explanation.

"I'm sorry, ma'am, but we don't have even one space left on the down shuttles. One's filling now—hauling maximum mass—and the one you came in on will be the last down. You bought a one-way; you assured the clerk you were bound outsystem on your own ship—"

"That's right," said Cecelia. "But I can't just abandon these two—" She nodded at Brun and Sirkin. "They're friends' children—"

"Sorry, ma'am . . . the clerk did try to warn you. As it is we don't have shuttle capacity for everyone. Some's got to stay and risk it—"

"I'm staying," Brun said, swinging a long leg over the rope that kept them all in line.

"Brun, no!" Cecelia said. "If there's real danger, I want you safe."

"There's always danger," Brun said. "And Captain Serrano said to keep *you* safe. I can't do that from down there—" She jerked her head in the direction of the planet. The line had closed in behind her, without a word but with absolute determination.

"Brun—" Sirkin turned, started to move.

"No!" Brun and Cecelia spoke as one. "No," Brun said a moment later. "Not you."

"Yes, me." Sirkin too stepped over the rope. "I'm a navigator; I'm good for something in space, and nothing much onplanet. I know I don't have your kind of flair, Brun, but I can free someone else by doing my own work."

Over her head, Cecelia met Brun's eyes. Nice child, Cecelia thought, and if we get out of this alive I will find her a safe berth on some quiet commercial line. Surely I have that much influence. She smiled at the station militia.

"Then you now have two more places for those who thought they must stay," she said. "Do you need these tickets?"

"No, ma'am. Thank you." One of the militia jogged toward the head of the line, and the other nodded to them.

"Well," said Cecelia. "Come along, before the yacht vanishes into space and we're left up here wondering how to run a space station."

"It's a lot like a ship," Brun said. "I've been talking to the people who work here, and met this man who's in charge of—"

"Fine," said Cecelia. "Then if we're stuck we have a chance of survival, but in the meantime, let's catch a ship."

No one was aboard the *Sweet Delight*. Brun and Sirkin both knew the dockside access codes, and the hatches opened for them. Cecelia lugged her gear to her own suite, and activated her desk. A stack of messages had accumulated since the last time she'd retrieved them, including one from Commerce Bank & Trust which informed her that her balance was more than adequate to purchase all the Singularity straws she wanted. She unpacked her duffel, and decided to shower. Whatever emergency was coming, she might as well meet it clean, in comfortable clothes. She stuffed her dirty clothes in the wash hamper, and turned the shower to full pulse.

She was finally feeling clean, all the travel grime and irritation out of her system, when the lights blinked off and back on so fast that her new panic in darkness didn't have time to reach full strength. She elbowed the shower controls, from water pulse to radiant heat and blow dry. Her pulse slowed, as the lights stayed on, and the fan whirred steadily. She turned, running her fingers through her hair to let the warm air reach her scalp. Then she saw the shadow beyond the shower door, a moving shadow.

"What the hell—!" A male voice, a strange one. The door opened, yanked hard from outside, and Cecelia found herself face-to-face with a uniformed man armed with one of her own hunting rifles, the expensive ones Heris had bought for her back on Sirialis. At second glance he looked more like a boy dressed up to play soldier—a fresh-faced youth who couldn't have been over twenty. "Who are *you*?" he demanded.

"Kindly hand me my robe," Cecelia said, not bothering to hide what he'd already seen. It wasn't her problem anyway, even if he was turning an unnatural red around the collar. She felt wickedly glad that he was seeing her younger body, not the eighty-six-year-old version. When he didn't move to comply, she lifted her chin. "It's drafty— and my robe is right there, beside you on the warming rack."

"Uh . . . yes, ma'am." Without looking away, he reached out and snagged the robe, fingering the pockets quickly. Cecelia's brows rose, then she realized he thought she might have weapons concealed in it, and her brows rose higher. Weapons? In a bathrobe? Her? He handed it over, and she shrugged into it, tied it around her waist.

"I'm coming out," she said, when he showed no inclination to move, and he stepped back, giving her room. Without haste, she picked up one of the towels on the warming rack and finished drying her feet, then took another and toweled the rest of the dampness out of her hair. She moved to the mirrors, and picked up the comb on the shelf. "I'm Cecelia de Marktos," she said into the mirror as she shaped her hair with the comb. "This was my yacht . . . it's technically Heris Serrano's now, but I've hired it. And who are you?"

"Pivot Major Osala . . . from the R.S.S. cruiser *Vigilance*. Ma'am."

"And what are you doing on my ship?" Her hair was fluffing into an untidy brush after the shower; it needed trimming. Her lips felt dry; station and ship air was so much drier than the humid surface of Xavier. She spread a protective gloss on her lips and glanced at the soldier in the mirror. He was looking at her as if she were something else—a monster of some sort, a freak.

"Commander Serrano said—is that the same person you called Heris Serrano?"

"I suppose," Cecelia said, turning to face him directly. "Heris Serrano, formerly an R.S.S. officer, and now my captain. She told you to come aboard? I suppose it's all right then."

"Commander Serrano . . . she's taken command of the *Vigilance*." He sounded unsure.

"She has? Good for her. Even though she did kill a raider with this yacht, if there's trouble coming, she'd much better have a cruiser to fight with."

"But ma'am . . . aren't you scared at all? Of . . . of *me*?" The confusion on his young face almost made her laugh. "I have a *weapon*—"

Cecelia snorted. She couldn't help herself, even if it was cruel, but she suppressed the laughter that wanted to follow. "Young man . . . pivot major is it? . . . didn't Commander Serrano tell you about me?"

"Uh . . . no, ma'am. The ship was supposed to be empty, only we found the entry hatch open, and Jig Faroe went to the bridge with the rest of the crew except me and Hugh, we were supposed to look for stragglers."

"Well, young man, if you ask Commander Serrano, she will explain that I'm a very old lady who has been rejuvenated, and I've been face-to-face with more firearms than you might think. You can kill me, but you are unlikely to scare me."

"Oh . . . are you . . . are you an undercover, too? Like Commander Serrano was?"

What was this? Undercover? Heris? A luxuriant vine of suspicion began unfurling in her mind, extending tendrils in all directions . . . Bunny . . . that vicious weasel Lepescu . . . the coincidences . . . and hadn't Heris mentioned some relatives who were admirals? Could Heris possibly have been fooling her all along? While that ran through her mind, she simply stared at the young soldier, until he looked away. "If I were undercover, would I tell you?" she asked finally. "I don't know what your security clearance is."

"Uh . . . no, ma'am. I mean, you don't . . . you wouldn't . . . but I still have to tell them you're here."

"Of course you do," she said reasonably. "Tell Commander

Serrano I'd like to speak with her at her earliest convenience. When I'm dressed." She headed for her bedroom, and the muzzle of his weapon wavered, then fell away. Idiot, she thought to herself. Suppose I *were* a spy or whatever he suspected. I could have an arsenal under my pillows.

She pulled open drawers, rummaging through the clothes she'd left in the ship when she went down. She felt something practical was called for, rather than grand-ladyish. The cream silk pullover, the brown twill slacks, the low boots with padded ankles. When she glanced in the mirror, the soldier had disappeared, no doubt to report her existence. Idiot, she thought again. Heris would have something to say to him about that.

Her desk chimed from the outer room, and she strode out to answer it. There was the young man, looking embarrassed, by the door to the corridor. Another stood with him. Cecelia gave them a distracted smile and touched her control panel.

"Cecelia, what are you doing on that yacht?" Heris, sounding impatient. Cecelia queried for video, but found that the signal carried no video.

"I got fed up with Marcia and Poots, and came back; I was going to ask you to take me to Rotterdam."

"And no one told you about the emergency?"

She didn't feel like explaining why she hadn't heard what she'd been told, not on an all-audio link. "I didn't know, until I arrived at the station, on the last up-shuttle, which was going to be overfull going down." A pause. Heris said nothing. "I found Brun and Sirkin," Cecelia added. "We're all safe." The next pause was eloquent; Cecelia could easily imagine Heris searching for a telling phrase.

"You're not *safe*," Heris said finally. "You're square in the midst of a military action. This system is under attack by the Benignity; their ships are in the outer system now, and I need that yacht and its weapons . . . not three useless civilians who were *supposed* to be down on the surface digging in."

Anger flared. "Civilians aren't *always* useless. If you can remember that far back, one of them saved your life on Sirialis."

"True. I'm sorry. It just . . . the question is, what now? I can't get you to safety onplanet . . . if that's safe."

"So quit worrying about it. Do you think I'm worried about dying?"

"I . . . you just got rejuved."

"So I did. It didn't eliminate my eighty-odd years of experience, or make me timid. If I die, I die . . . but in the meantime, why not let me help?"

A chuckle. She could imagine Heris's face. "Lady Cecelia, you are inimitable. Get yourself up to the bridge; someone will find you a place. Jig Faroe's in command. I'll let him know you're coming."

"Good hunting, Heris," Cecelia said. She felt a pleasant tingle of anticipation.

Even in more normal conditions of war, when Heris had had time to make plans and go over them with her crew, the last hours before combat always seemed to telescope, accelerating toward them in a way that the physicists said didn't make sense. This was far worse. A change of command so close to battle was tricky at best, when it resulted from a captain's sudden illness or other emergency. She had not had time to gain the crew's confidence; she had not had time to assess their competence, their readiness for combat.

The normal thing to do—the textbook thing to do—was get out fast and get help. She had no orders to defend Xavier. She was clearly outnumbered; the loyalty of her crews was questionable. Or, if she chose to stay, it would be prudent to send the yacht, with its civilians . . . it could reach a safe jump radius in time to get away, long before an attack could reach it, and go back to a Fleet sector headquarters and report.

If the Benignity invaders hadn't mined the nearest jump point insertions. They could have, and that could be the reason for the gap in the financial ansible's transmissions. Many communications nodes for ansible transmission were located near jump points, for ease of maintenance and repair. She had an uneasy feeling about the jump points.

I have complete confidence in your judgment. Her aunt admiral had said that, her aunt who had not commented on her performance since the Academy. What did "complete confidence" mean in a situation like this? Would her aunt back whatever decision she made, or did her aunt really think she had some special ability to choose the best course of action?

She could not let any of these thoughts interfere with her concentration. The only plans she had were hasty improvisations: very well, that beat no plans at all. As far as her officers could tell, her plans came down from the admiralty. That the plans were in direct defiance of common sense wouldn't bother them overmuch—it wasn't their judgment on the line. If the message capsule she'd sent reached the Fleet relay ansible—if no one was suppressing such messages—someone would, eventually, consider her judgment, her decision to stay, her choice of tactics. With luck they might even get help before the Benignity blew them away.

"What we've got," she told her more senior officers, "is a very unorthodox force for defending an inhabited planet." They knew that, but they needed to hear the obvious from her, at least at the beginning. "One cruiser, one patrol craft, one armed yacht, one very ancient Desmoiselle-class escort, three atmospheric shuttles, one of them armed with phase cannon—inadequately mounted, but perhaps good for a single round, assuming a suicidal crew."

"Phase cannon in a *shuttle*?" Major Svatek looked as shocked as Heris had felt when she first heard.

"It's what they had," she said. "It's never been fired—of course. We've warned them. It would take weeks of refitting to strengthen the mounts, and we don't have that time. *Grogon* is supposedly hyper-capable, but I don't trust its FTL generator, and neither did my engineers when they inspected it. The yacht is, of course, and it's carrying substantial weaponry for its hull—" She pulled up the display and pointed it out. "But the tradeoff there was on shields—she has only her light-duty civilian screen shields. Nothing else in the system is hyper-capable; the mining colonies have little shuttles and one ore-carrier. It's a big hull, but it's underpowered. And no weapons."

"So—what's our plan?" That was Major Tinsi, on the tightbeam from *Paradox*.

"Harassment with deception," Heris said. "We won't have real surprise, because of Hearne on *Despite*, but she didn't know about everything. Unless we're extremely lucky, we won't destroy the incoming ships—or even deflect them permanently—but we probably can delay their attack on the

planet itself, by making them unsure how many of us there
are. Even if they never use the phase cannon, for instance,
they'll light up someone's weapons scans. So will old
Grogon." Something else nagged at her memory, and finally
broke through. She called Koutsoudas into the conference
line.

"Did Livadhi falsify his ID at the commercial level that
time when he hailed us with the wrong name?"

"You saw through it," Koutsoudas said.

"Yes, but we had military scan, as you know. I didn't
bother to check what a commercial scan would have shown.
How did you do it, how long does it take, and could you
have falsified your beacon to military scanning?"

"It's pretty simple," Koutsoudas said. "It's all in knowing how; it takes maybe an hour or two, that's all. Yeah,
you could do it for both kinds of beacon transmissions . . .
of course it *is* illegal." He said that in a pious tone that
made Heris chuckle. "Captain Livadhi didn't want anyone
in Fleet to mistake him."

"I'm sure," Heris said, with deliberate irony. "Could you
do it for this ship?"

"Well . . . yes. Why?"

"Oblo has installed two different fake beacon IDs in the
yacht. If we could patch something up for this ship, and
Paradox, we could give the Benignity something to think
about."

"We still have only two real warships—"

"But they don't know that. They know *Despite* said that,
running away, which can't have been the plan. They were
expecting Garrivay and friends to be here, welcoming them
in. They probably had a name, possibly even a familiar contact. They drop out of FTL and find one of their expected
allies fleeing, telling them not to worry there's only a single
cruiser and patrol. Would *you* believe that, if you were a
CH captain?"

"No . . ." Koutsoudas looked thoughtful. "I wouldn't. I'd
think double-cross. The conspirators discovered . . . betrayal.
Something like that, anyway."

"Right. Is this a hands-on patch, or can you explain to
Paradox how to change their beacon too? I want both ships
to be able to switch back and forth—"

"It's doable, but it doesn't change the basic scan—nothing's going to convince them that there's more ships, if the beacon data on a masspoint suddenly changes."

"Don't worry about that," Heris said. "Just get hold of Oblo, and the two of you give us some fake identities that would hold up to Fleet standards. I have an idea." She had more than one; ideas flickered through her mind almost too fast to see.

Off to one side, she imagined the Benignity formation commander—he would be one of their Elder Sons, equivalent to the R.S.S. admiral minor. Hearne's message would make him bunch his formation, counting on its weight of weapons and numerical superiority as long as he found what he expected: a cruiser smaller than any of his ships, a patrol ship, a lightly armed yacht, and a slow-moving, nearly toothless scow. But if the scan data didn't fit—or worse, if it was inconsistent, suggesting that Hearne had lied—he would hesitate, pause behind his screening barrage, and prepare for a more extended combat. He might even be unwise enough to detach a ship or so.

If each of her three ships could appear to be one or two other ships—and if she could use the Benignity's barrage as a screen for her own movements—

"We could fake some beacons, as well—launch them—" That was Tinsi, over on *Paradox*. Heris nodded; she hadn't expected him to show that much imagination.

"No mass readings," Koutsoudas said. "It won't fool them more than a few seconds—"

"If we could get mass?" Another glimmer of an idea. Xavier's system wasn't overly full of handy rocks the right size, but those shuttles, loaded with anything massive from the station, and with faked beacons, might distract the CH commander.

"You and Oblo get on it," Heris said to Koutsoudas. "We need it done before their scans clear from jump insert."

"Yes, sir."

Heris looked around at the others, and saw thoughtful looks, only the reasonable amount of tension. "Let's get going," she said.

When she reached the bridge, Koutsoudas called her over. He had the first reasonably detailed scans of the arriving force.

"They're sticking to normal tactics," Koutsoudas said.

"Throwing out a screening barrage on jump exit . . . it'll have tags keyed to their IDs. Coming on in a clump—"

"When will they have scan return?" Heris asked.

"Normally—a solid twelve hours after jump exit, and that's with efficient boosts. They exited eight to nine hours ago, so that means we have three blind hours for certain. But with *Despite*'s signal, if they picked it up—"

"They'll have a lot more detail than the best scans would give them. Current ship IDs. But not everything." That was less comforting than it might have been.

"I'm getting some separation in that clump, though," Koutsoudas went on. "Looks like one or two may be trailing back a bit farther than normal."

"Jump-exit error?"

"Could be. I'll stay on it."

Sweet Delight

Cecelia strolled into the bridge compartment trailed by the two young soldiers. Sirkin sat at the navigation console, looking scared. Brun perched where Petris usually sat, looking excited. Cecelia could not tell who was in charge, and was annoyed with herself for not knowing what all the insignia and markings were.

Cecelia had had no direct experience with the military until she hired Heris. Now she watched as the young man with two comma-shaped bits of metal on his collar organized his crew and set about carrying out Heris's orders. He looked to be Ronnie's age, or perhaps a few years older— she couldn't tell—but he had a hard-edged quality unlike her nephew's. Not courage, exactly—Ronnie was brave—but a definition, a focus, as if he were carved out of a single hard material by a sharp tool. So were the rest. She had noticed that with Heris's old crew, but assumed it was the result of the ordeals they'd been through as a result of Lepescu. And they had been cordial to her, once they knew her. Even Oblo. Of course, she'd never seen them in anything but civilian shipsuits. These all wore R.S.S. gray, with sleeve and shoulder patches and marks that meant something to them and nothing to her. Most seemed very young, but the one sitting where she remembered Oblo had a grizzled fringe around the margin of his bald head.

"You're Lady Cecelia," the young man in charge said. "I'm Junior-Lieutenant Faroe. Jig Faroe is the more common way to say it. Commander Serrano says you offered to help out—"

Cecelia grinned at him. "I presented her with a dilemma, is what you and she both mean. There's bound to be something simple that you need done. Watching gauges or something."

His expression suggested that that had been a stupid idea. "I wish I knew her better—how she thinks. What she thinks you might do—"

"That I can help you with," Cecelia said briskly. "I've worked with her for a couple of years now—" She admitted to herself that the time she spent in an apparent coma wasn't exactly "working with" Heris, but the start of a war was no time for long explanations. And she certainly knew more about Heris's thought processes than this young man. One had only to see someone ride across country to know more about their character than any dozen psychological analyses, no matter what the experts said.

"Oh—you were part of her . . . uh . . . cover?" He looked both eager and embarrassed, someone who wanted desperately to ask what he knew he should not.

"I don't think I should discuss it," said Cecelia. Especially when she hadn't the faintest idea what Heris had actually said and done.

"Oh—no, sir—of course not. Sorry." He dithered visibly, in the way Cecelia found so amusing in the young, and finally blurted, "But feel free, ma'am, to . . . to advise me whenever you have any insight into Commander Serrano's wishes."

"I will," Cecelia said, sorting rapidly through the little she had heard or read about covert operations and Fleet procedures. If Heris had been fooling her, then what would this youngster think she was? All that came to mind was the explanation for the officer's misuse of "sir"—in the military, officers of both sexes were called sir. Which meant that for some reason he thought she was an officer. Odd: surely he would have some sort of list which proved she wasn't. But his mistake could be useful. "For one thing, I can tell you that Commander Serrano found Brigdis Sirkin a most accomplished navigator. She said often that Sirkin should've been Fleet."

"Yes, sir; she told us. Says Sirkin has special knowledge of this ship's capabilities."

"So does Brun," Cecelia added. Should she mention that Brun was Thornbuckle's daughter? Probably not. It wouldn't add anything to the mix at this point. "She's been working with Meharry, I believe it is, and Oblo."

The bald man turned to face her. "That civilian *kid* has been working with Methlin Meharry? And Ginese? And Oblo?"

What was that about? She had expected them to know Heris's name, but the others, as far as she knew, had been enlisted. Enlightenment came just before she made a fool of herself. Foxhunters knew foxhunters, and stud grooms knew stud grooms—of *course* Heris's top people would have their own fame.

"Meharry," said Cecelia, as if pondering. "Tallish woman, blonde, green eyes? Yes. Brun, didn't you tell me she'd . . . er . . . prodded you through some level of weapons certification?"

"Yes, Lady Cecelia," Brun said. Her eyes sparkled; whatever else happened, Brun was having a marvelous time.

"What level?" growled the bald man to Brun.

"Spec third," Brun said promptly. Cecelia had no idea what that meant.

"And what did Oblo have you doing?"

"Well . . . we only got up to second, on account of Captain Serrano asked me to spend more time with Arkady."

A short nod, and a glance at Jig Faroe, who was almost prancing from foot to foot.

The communications board lit, and the bald man touched the controls, then moved back to clear the pickups for the captain. Koutsoudas appeared on screen, with Oblo behind him. "Let me speak to Sirkin and Brun, please, Captain Faroe."

"Right away." He sidled along the arc of the bridge, making room for Sirkin and Brun to squeeze past, into range of the pickups.

"We need to enable the alternate beacon IDs," Oblo began. "Brun, you remember how I showed you the lockout sequences?"

"Yes—you—"

"You'll want them all in readiness; you'll be switching them at your captain's order. Is Cesar there?"

"Yo, Oblo!" That was the bald man, leaning toward the pickups now.

"She doesn't know how to set up that kind of switching, so give her a hand. Quick learner, and she does know the lockouts cold."

Cesar nodded. "Right. Priority?"

"Yesterday. Now—Sirkin—"

"Yes?"

Koutsoudas took over. "Brigdis, Serrano wants you as primary nav for the yacht, because you know the . . . uh . . . special capabilities for FTL insertions and exits. As well, do you remember that little packet I gave you to take downside?"

"Yes, I have it."

"Good. Set it beside your main nav board, right under the shift control. It is not—repeat NOT—to be activated by anyone but yourself, and that is Commander Serrano's direct order. Is that clear?" A chorus of sirs, of which Sirkin's was the weakest. Koutsoudas glared out of the screen. "It's keyed to you anyway, but just in case one of those others gets too curious, it can blow the entire navigation board if you upset it. Hands off." A long pause. "You do remember the activation code, don't you?"

"Yes, it's—"

"Don't repeat it—just use it when it's time."

Cecelia could see that this mysteriousness gave Brun and Sirkin more prestige with the military, but why? Then Koutsoudas appeared to see her for the first time. "Oh! Sorry, sir—didn't recognize you for a moment." As if anyone else would be wearing a silk pullover shirt; as if anyone else could be mistaken for her, with that red hair and plain face. And he knew perfectly well she wasn't a "sir"—she was the civilian who hadn't even wanted him aboard. "Lady Cecelia . . . I believe Commander Serrano would like to speak to you."

Again? But Heris was there now, looking at her with an expression half-concerned and half-gleeful. Damn the woman, she was looking forward to this battle. "Lady Cecelia." She said the name in audible quotes, implying that it was a pseudonym. "Captain Faroe has been instructed to give you every consideration. You have my authorization for the necessary decisions."

What necessary decisions, Cecelia wanted to ask, but she could tell that this was not the time. If she was a Fleet officer who had been pretending to be a civilian, she should know that already.

"Thank you, Captain Serrano," she said with what she hoped was appropriate military formality. Then she ventured further. "I presume that our primary objective remains . . . ?"

"As it was," Heris said, with a look that refused any more inquiries. "When the time comes for you to jump out of the system, don't hesitate." Cecelia blinked. Was Heris telling them to run away and leave her stranded? Not a chance.

"Should that be necessary," Cecelia said, stressing the unlikelihood, "I'll have a word with your aunt."

"You do that," Heris said. "Now I need to speak with Captain Faroe.

"Let Sirkin show you the critical jump distances," Heris told Faroe. "We've put her into jump much closer than the usual: it's part of the nonstandard equipment aboard. You've got the information from Ginese and Meharry on weapons capability?"

"Yes, sir."

"Remember to change beacon IDs based on your determination of the situation, once the CH splits up. Give them as many different vectors as you can—"

"Yes, sir. I understand." Cecelia could tell that Heris wished she had her own hands on the controls. She herself wished she could see Heris on the bridge of the cruiser—it must, she thought, be a sight. But the woman couldn't ride two horses at once; she had to let go the reins of this one. She moved back into pickup range.

"We'll do fine, Captain Serrano. I have every confidence in Captain Faroe." For some reason, that made Heris look bug-eyed for a moment. Then she regained her calm.

"Well, then. I'll expect acknowledgment when the last orders go out." And the beam cut off.

"Do you have any idea what Heris is up to?" Brun whispered a few minutes later. Captain Faroe had insisted that they were off duty for the next six hours, and they'd gone back to Cecelia's suite to relax.

"Aside from fighting off an invading fleet, not a clue in

this world." Cecelia rubbed her temples. "I'm so far behind I can't even hear the hounds. I didn't even know that an R.S.S. battle group was here, let alone that she'd taken command of it. I was down there touring breeding farms and getting into a row with Marcia and Poots—paid no attention to the news, except when the financial ansible went *pfft* and convinced Marcia that I'd gone broke. Idiot fools. I told her to check her own balances, and she had the gall to tell me she didn't need to, she knew her standing, and that's when I stormed out and came back."

Brun was trembling, but with suppressed giggles. "Lady Cecelia, you're incredible! Didn't they tell you at the shuttle port?"

"I suppose the man tried. He kept talking about no round-trip tickets, but of course I didn't *want* a round-trip ticket. I kept telling him I had a ship here, and would be leaving the system. Would you please explain?"

Brun laughed aloud. "Ronnie's so lucky to have an aunt like you. Well, briefly, our Captain Serrano discovered that the captain of the cruiser and some of the others were traitors, planning to help the Benignity take the Xavier system. And she and Petris figured out that they had to get command of the ships, so they got invited aboard—"

"How?"

"I don't know. But I know she took Petris, Methlin, Arkady, and Oblo with her, and the next thing we heard, she was in command. Koutsoudas told me, before he transferred to the cruiser, that the traitors were dead. The cruiser's command computer accepted her—"

"But she's not in Fleet anymore. How could she—?"

"I don't know, I said. She and her old crew had their heads together—sent Brig and me away, said we shouldn't be party to it, so we couldn't be blamed later. She meant us to go downside and take care of you—" Cecelia snorted and Brig grinned. "I know, that bit was silly. You don't need taking care of. But that's why we don't know what she did, exactly. I think I can find out—there's a couple of these new people that will let it slip if I hang out with them."

"I'm sure they will," Cecelia said. "And meantime I'll try to be inscrutable." Inscrutability came easier when she really did know nothing.

CHAPTER SIXTEEN

Part of Heris's strategy needed no explanation. Cecelia could see for herself the advantage in having the yacht able to switch beacon IDs, and the importance of timing was obvious as well. She cut short Faroe's attempt to explain with a curt, "Yes, I can see that it's best to change when we're not in their scan. My question was, are they still clumped up behind their barrage screen?"

"It won't really screen our change," he said again.

Cecelia closed her eyes a moment and gave him a stare that had shriveled young men years before this one was born. He gulped and froze in place, as she intended. "I. Know. That." She had picked it up from the conversations, but he didn't have to know how new her understanding was. "What I'm interested in is whether *we* can tell where *they* are, and whether they're still clumped. When the prey scatters—"

"But—they're hunting *us*," he said. Cecelia felt sorry for Heris. If this was the best she could find to send back to the yacht, she must be working with a real handicap on the cruiser. She should have let one of her own have it.

"So they think," she said, and watched Faroe's face wrap itself around that concept. "I don't believe Commander Serrano looks at it that way." She paused again, waiting for his wits to waken. When she saw a glimmer of intelligence, she went on. "You see, in my experience, Commander Serrano considers *herself* the hunter."

"Oh."

"And it is our responsibility, as I see it, to . . . er . . . herd the prey into . . ." Into what? she wondered in midphrase. You herded domestic animals, not hunting prey. She shook her hand, as if it were obvious, and rushed on. "—Or lure them, confuse them—you see my point."

"But this is a defensive action," he said. He didn't sound convinced.

Cecelia gave him another, but less wounding, haughty look. Even aged civilian aunts knew better than that. "Come, Captain Faroe: what does the textbook say about defensive actions?"

He brightened. "Attack on defense . . ."

"Very well. Which makes us—" What *could* she use as an example. If Heris was the main pack, were they terriers? One terrier? Somehow the image of the yacht as a terrier digging into some vermin's hole simply didn't work. Then that ridiculous exhibit of Marcia's came to her. "Cowhorses," she said. He looked blank. Damn the boy, didn't he have any ability to switch metaphors in midstream? "Riding . . ." What was the term now? "Drag," she said. "Or flank, or something like that. We keep the stragglers from getting away." She risked a glance around the bridge and intercepted some dubious expressions from the rest of the crew, expressions quickly wiped to blank respect. That would have to change. She grinned at them all, until she got answering smiles, however weak. "I'm a scatty old woman," she said. "Don't let my gorgeous red hair fool you—I'm a Rejuvenant, and it's all fake. And sometimes I lose the words I want . . . the brain's stuffed too full of too many damn disciplines."

Cesar chuckled aloud. "It's all right, sir. It's just we never heard a spaceship compared to a cowhorse before . . . or the Benignity as cows."

"I spent the last fifty-eight days at bloodstock farms," Cecelia said. "Horses are my passion, and I've spent all that time with other horse fanciers. Came back up with my head full of bloodlines and genetic analyses, instead of technical data for ships." As if her head had ever been full of technical data. But they didn't have to know.

"And you really think Commander Serrano is planning to do more than just hold them off?" asked Cesar, with a quick glance around.

"Yes. And so do you." That made Faroe straighten up.
"But Commander Garrivay said—"

"Commander Garrivay's dead. Heris is commanding. It's a new hunt."

As the hours passed, Cecelia decided that only inexperience kept Faroe from being a reasonably good young officer. He kept tripping over his former captain's negatives: "Captain Garrivay said no one could . . ." this and "Captain Garrivay said never . . ." that. She had the impression, from him and the others, that Garrivay had wanted no more initiative in his officers than it took to wipe themselves, and he'd have preferred to have them do that on command. But with Cecelia behind him, Faroe began to think of some things for himself. He would glance at her fearfully each time; she discovered that a smile and nod seemed to increase his intelligence by ten points. Success breeds confidence; she knew that from riding. She still wished Heris had sent Petris or Ginese to command, but she realized that it wouldn't have worked. The real military—the military she had always avoided, and especially the military as molded by Garrivay's command—had its own unbreakable rules, and Heris had bent them as far as they would go.

And Faroe's judgment, when he actually got up his nerve to make decisions, was sound. He accepted Sirkin's expertise, and they made their FTL hop on her mark. The first switch of beacon IDs went without a hitch, and then they were tucked in behind Oreson's rings, Sirkin having managed to drop the extra velocity of the FTL jump in some clever way that let them crawl into cover with, as Faroe put it, just enough skirt trailing.

"Which satellite has the mining colony?" Cecelia asked.

"That one." Faroe pointed it out. "But they've got nothing useful."

"For now." The image of terriers still danced in her head. "Who knows . . . if we asked them, they might be able to help."

"I'm not sure I have the authority to talk to civilians at a time like this," Faroe said, looking worried again.

"I do," Cecelia said. What that authority was, she wasn't sure, but her instinct said it was time to form a pack.

* * *

Aboard the Benignity cruiser *Paganini*

Admiral Straosi glared at his subordinate. "What do you mean, *Zamfir* is out of action? There has been no action."

It could be the Chairman. It could be the Chairman's way of punishing him for that foolish jest in the Boardroom, to make sure a problem ship came along. Easy enough to do. Not easy to handle. He could hardly go back and complain. And he wondered if the Chairman had any other surprises for him.

"A drive problem," the younger man said. He looked nervous, as well he might. "A failure of synchronization in the FTL generator, with resultant surge damage on downshift."

A real problem, although it usually resulted from poor maintenance. In safe situations, the best solution was complete shutdown of both drives, with a cold start of the sublight drive, once the residual magnetics had diminished to a safe level, but that left the ship passive, unable to maneuver at all. Straosi had his doubts, though. He could not verify the problem from here, and he didn't trust the Chairman's great-nephew.

Admiral Straosi was glad to have a target for his temper. "You are telling me that you did not adequately inspect your ship before starting off on this mission?"

A pause. "Sir, the admiral knows we were assigned to this mission only fourteen hours before launch—"

"The admiral also knows the entire fleet has been on alert—all ships to be ready to depart at one hour's notice. Had you slacked off, Captain?" Of course they had; everyone did, on extended high alert. But now, with the results of that slack endangering his mission, and his own life, he was not about to be lenient.

"Er . . . no, Admiral. It wasn't that, it was just—"

"Just that you somehow failed to notice a problem that any first-year fresh out of school could see . . . Captain. Let me put it this way—" That was ritual introduction of a mortal challenge. "Either you get your ship back into formation, or we leave you. I am not risking this mission for someone too stupid and lazy to do the job for which he was overpaid."

"The Benignity commands." That was the only possible

answer. The admiral grunted, and watched the scans. *Zamfir* continued to lag . . . the lag widened. By the estimate of the senior engineer aboard the *Paganini*, the other cruiser's insystem drive had lost thirty percent of its power.

"If the R.S.S. ship was right, their cruiser might be able to take *Zamfir*," an aide murmured.

"If they want to waste their time attacking our stragglers, they have my blessing," the admiral said. "Let them trade salvos with *Zamfir*; Paulo might actually blow them away and regain my respect, and at least they'd be out of our way. Our objective is the Xavier system, to prepare it for the use of the entire fleet. We don't care what happens to *Zamfir*."

"And *Cusp*?" The admiral considered. The little killer-ship now flanking *Zamfir* had been intended as rear guard and as messenger both. Had the damaged cruiser been where it should, *Cusp* would have been the tail of the formation.

"Bring *Cusp* to its normal position," he said. He was almost glad to leave *Zamfir* out there unprotected. Paulo's carelessness was going to cause trouble no matter what happened; he was the Chairman's great-nephew. He was supposed to come out of this a hero. Instead, he had already caused trouble. He stared at the scans, waiting for *Cusp* to close up. Nothing happened; the two ships dropped still farther behind.

"What is his problem?" the admiral asked. Then he remembered. The captain of *Cusp* was Paulo's brother-in-law. They had always been close. Well, fine. Let them both hang back, and maybe the Familias commander would think it was some new tactic, and engage them. Together they should be an easy match for an R.S.S. cruiser. Perhaps this would work out after all. Of course it was bad for discipline . . . but he could rescind the order. "I've changed my mind," he said. "Order *Cusp* to hold position, and engage the enemy at will. We have sufficient margin of superiority; we can afford to test new tactics."

Heris tried to think herself into the enemy's mind. Assuming that Hearne had told the truth as she saw it, the Benignity commander believed there were three hyper-capable ships near Xavier, and an obsolete defense escort with no FTL drive. A cruiser: the most dangerous, commanded by a Serrano, a name they should know. A patrol craft, whose new captain was far enough down the table of officers that he might not even be listed in the CH database—certainly there was no combat command listing for him. And an armed yacht, whose real capabilities Heris had screened from Garrivay's personnel. She had told Hearne that she expected a Benignity attack "in a few days, certainly within ten local days." In other words, the Benignity commander would expect them to be looking for trouble, but not necessarily on full alert yet, particularly not after a hostile takeover of the ships. Hearne would have transmitted her assessment of the situation, but her main concern had been to escape. She certainly hadn't stayed around to answer questions.

On the bridge, four clocks were running countdowns: Koutsoudas's estimate of when the CH ships could get reliable scan on them, Koutsoudas's estimate of when standard Fleet scans would have shown the CH jump point exit, the scan-delay display, and the realtime clock which her own crew would use for its timing of maneuvers and firing.

"She's jumped," Koutsoudas said, pointing at the yacht's icon. "You know, I thought Livadhi would pass out when you jumped her that close to Naverrn. What did you *do* to that hull?"

"Ask me no questions," Heris said. At some level below current processing, she was distantly aware of other gears ticking into alignment. Amazing how all those unauthorized and illegal changes to *Sweet Delight* now made sense, in light of her pretense to have been on undercover assignment. She was going to be really angry if it turned out her aunt admiral had diddled with her memory and she only *thought* she'd been forced to resign.

"I always knew Oblo was a genius," Koutsoudas went on. "Him and Ginese . . . and Kinvinnard . . ."

"And you. Don't be greedy. I envied Livadhi for years."

"It was mutual. Ah—she's back. Her . . . er . . . third incarnation, it is. The one from the Guernesi."

"Speaking of geniuses. I think Oblo would emigrate in a flash if they didn't have such stringent rules on personal weaponry." Heris watched the screen. The old *Grogon* now occupied the approximate volume of space where the yacht had been, and its beacon reported that it was the yacht. Although of different shapes, they had similar mass.

Light-hours away, the yacht curved around the largest chunk of rock in this section of the "rockring"—the remains of a small planetoid that had come apart eons before. It still showed on *Vigilance*'s scans, but from the angle of the CH flotilla, it should have appeared briefly, as if it had darted out to get a clean scan or tightbeam message, and then gone back into hiding.

Vigilance itself bored out at half the maximum insystem drive acceleration, as if in cautious pursuit of *Despite*.

"We would be cautious, because we would worry if *Despite* had an ally out there, something Garrivay didn't chart. He didn't even drop temporary mines, did he?"

"No, sir." That was her new Weapons First. "He said there was no need to cause a problem for incoming commercial traffic. It would cost too much to clear later."

"And no beacon leeches, either," said Communications. "That's standard, but we just thought he was in a snit to be sent out here away from Third Ward HQ, when all the excitement was going on."

"He didn't want any clever amateurs on Xavier to pick up a warning," Heris said, wondering what excitement that had been. Something else she didn't have time to pursue.

"They might have us," Koutsoudas said, meaning the enemy. "Another hour, and we have to assume they do." The Benignity flotilla, knowing exactly what to look for and where, would see them as soon as the limits of their technology made it possible. The FR vessels could be presumed to divide their attention in more directions. They might not notice the distant flotilla at first if they were looking elsewhere.

"How's our angle?"

"Well . . . it's close, sir. If they believe that we believe *Despite* is leading us straight to them, then we could miss a signal . . . for a while . . . but the normal cone would pick it up as a primary signal.

"And their insertion barrage?"

"There's nothing between us to cause detonations before we run into it, and the drives should be off by now, realtime."

Time passed. Heris had walked most of the ship by now, letting the crew see her . . . dangerous but necessary. If they were going to fight well, they had to know who commanded them, one of the textbook rules that actually seemed to work in the real world. They were busy; she had told her officers to use whatever training drills they could to get the crew up to peak efficiency. That included rest and food; she herself had left the bridge for a hot meal and a short nap in the captain's quarters, with Ginese keeping watch outside. Now she was back on the bridge, restless as always in the last minutes before action.

"We should be noticing them now," Koutsoudas said. Heris glanced over, and his screen flared as something blew. The enemy icons rippled, their confidence-limit markers spreading out.

"Damn!" Koutsoudas hunched lower. "They blew some of their own barrage screen—they *really* want us to see them."

"The Benignity hates uncertainty," Heris said. "It must have been driving their commander crazy when we didn't seem to notice them."

The *Vigilance*'s screens flicked on at full power, as Heris had planned, and Weapons brought all boards hot. Heris said nothing; she had given the orders hours ago, and so far all was going as planned. They were far enough from Xavier now to jump safely; the cruiser popped in and out, a standard maneuver, slipping back out with a lower relative velocity—*not* a standard maneuver. The low-vee exit on a very short jump meant minimal blurring of scans on exit.

"Got 'em again." Now the scan lag, with Koutsoudas's special black boxes, was less than ten minutes. "Captain, they've brought the heavies with 'em."

"So we expected," said Heris. "Let me see the data." The CH ships had their beacons live; they were not pretending to be anything but what they were, an invading force, and they were in more danger from each other if they went blank. Heris recognized the classes, but not the individual ships, whose names meant little to her. She knew the composer class was usually named for composers—and she knew Paganini—but who was Dylan? Or Zamfir? Not that it mattered. The Benignity cruiser was a third again the mass of *Vigilance*, and thus could mount more weapons. Three cruisers meant impossible odds. Assault carriers held atmospheric shuttles, assault troops for groundside action if needed, and the components for an orbital station that would serve a larger fleet later. Two of these were more than adequate for assault on a planet with Xavier's population and defenses. And the final two ships, much smaller killer-escorts, had the maneuverability the others lacked, along with the firepower of an R.S.S. patrol ship. Which meant Heris's meagre force would have been outgunned even if *Despite* had stayed. Which meant staying was suicidal. The best she could hope to do was delay the invasion long enough for the R.S.S. to defend the jump points exiting this system. So much for "complete confidence" in her decisions.

She could still run. Legally, logically . . . but not as Heris Serrano.

"Those two we thought were lagging are farther behind," Koutsoudas said suddenly. "Not their usual formation."

"A new trick?" Someone across the bridge laughed. The Benignity weren't known for minor innovations like trailing a ship or so from a standard formation. When they changed, they changed radically, usually because new technology provided new opportunities.

"A precaution," Heris murmured. "What class?"

"One cruiser, one killer-escort. The cruiser's really dropping back. It must've come out of FTL with low relative velocity."

"Got to be a feint," Svatek said. "I wish we could eavesdrop."

"Admiral Straosi, the drive continues unstable. If the admiral wishes, it can be confirmed—" Straosi didn't want to hear this.

"What do you want to do about it?"

"We're still losing power. If it drops much more we can't support the weapons—" In other words, they would be slow, unarmed, helpless. Fat sheep in the path of wolves. Admiral Straosi allowed himself a moment of gloating: he hadn't wanted Paulo along, and this whole mess was, ultimately, the fault of the Chairman. But experience suggested that the Chairman would not be the one whose neck felt the noose, whose liver danced on the tip of a blade. At the least, he must conceal his gloating.

"Captain, I apologize for my earlier remarks." That would

go on the records. "I am sure you would not have missed such a major problem in your drive. Have you considered sabotage?"

"I—yes, sir, I have."

"There are those who opposed this mission, Captain. I will make sure that no blame accrues to you for your ship's failure to participate in this action . . . and I'm sorry, Captain, but I cannot jeopardize the invasion for your ship alone."

"Of course not, sir." As he'd expected, Paulo didn't want to appear cowardly. Perhaps he wasn't.

"As one man of honor to another, may I suggest that you could do us great service by conserving power for your weaponry, even though that places your ship in greater danger. . . ." It was not a question, and not quite an order. They both would understand. *Zamfir* was doomed, but it might kill a Familias ship with its death.

"It would be my honor, Admiral Straosi. If the Admiral has specific suggestions—"

"I trust your judgment, Captain." And that was that. Let the boy figure it out for himself, and if he killed that pesky Serrano, Straosi wouldn't mind a bit recommending him for a posthumous medal.

"We'll drop a few buckets of nails on their road," Heris said. She and the weapons crews had already discussed the fusing and arming options. They hadn't nearly the number of mines she really needed, but the more of the enemy, the greater the chance of a hit. She presumed the enemy would see them drop the clusters, and that would provoke some kind of maneuver. "And immediate course change, getting us the vector for jumps two, three, and five."

The trailing pair of enemy ships, cruiser and killer-escort, worried her. Why *were* they hanging back? If the rest of the Benignity formation reacted normally, flaring away from the mines, how would that final pair react? Too much to hope they were back there because they were scan blind or something, and would just sweep on majestically into the mine cluster.

That thought, however unlikely, brought a grin to her face. She had not anticipated how happy she would be, back on the bridge of an R.S.S. cruiser. It was ridiculous, under the circumstances: she had come back only to find herself in a worse tactical mess than any she'd experienced. She had less chance of surviving—let alone winning—this engagement than she had had with the Board of Inquiry. But that didn't sober her. This was where she belonged, and she felt fully alive, fully awake, for the first time since she'd left. Not that she regretted the experience of the past years, but—but this was home.

And *Vigilance* answered her joy with its own. Every hour she could sense the lift in crew morale; they believed in her, they accepted her. From their reactions alone, she learned things about Garrivay that erased the last doubts she'd had. A man might be a traitor to the Familias, and a good leader for his own people, but Garrivay had been a user, someone who abused power.

If they'd had time to prepare, even ten or fifteen days, she'd have had a reasonable chance, she was sure. Now—she didn't even bother to calculate it. Either luck—and whatever training Garrivay had done—would be with them, or it wouldn't. She intended to give luck all the help she could. While she wouldn't mind dying in action, it wasn't fair to the people of Xavier.

Space combat had a leisurely, surreal phase in which nothing seemed to happen . . . weapons had been launched, to find targets or not minutes to hours hence, and the enemy's weapons were on their way, with scan trying desperately to find and track them before maneuvering. No one used LOS, line-of-sight weapons, at this distance, despite their lightspeed advantage; what the best scans "saw" was far behind the enemy's location.

"They're starring," Koutsoudas said. "Avoiding our mines." That was the usual Benignity move; she'd expected it.

"Jump two," Heris said. She had laid out a series of microjumps, options ready to take depending on the enemy's reaction to the mines. This had been the most likely, the starburst dispersal . . . if she had kept on course, she'd have gone down the throat of the bell they made: easy meat. Instead, the course change and microjump popped them out—

"Targeting—" said Weapons First. "On target."

"Engage." —Popped them out in position to fire their

forward LOS weapons at the flank of the massive assault carrier they'd chosen, as it clawed its way into a shallow curve away from its former course. Four light-seconds away, an easy solution for the computers. A roar punctuated with crashes burst from the speakers.

"Turn that down!" Heris had never quite believed the theory that said humans needed to hear the fights they got into. Ground combat had been so noisy it drove men insane—so why had psychologists insisted on programming fake noises for combat in space? "Keep it below ten," she said. It couldn't be turned off completely, but it didn't have to rupture eardrums.

"Sir."

She had had a captain once who had reprogrammed the sounds to be musical . . . he had had other, stranger, hobbies, which eventually led to early retirement, but she had never quite forgotten the ascending major and minor scales he had chosen for outbound LOS weapons. If they hit their targets, the system then chimed the appropriate chord. It had enabled everyone, even the doubting Jig she had been then, to tell whether it was the port (major) or starboard (minor) weapons firing, and from which end of the ship. Forward batteries sounded like flutes, and the aft ones like bassoons, with the intermediate woodwinds ranged down the sides. She'd never attempted anything like it on her own ship.

"Jump six, then eight." On their new vector, a microjump that put them safely away from the probable response of the Benignity's cruisers. If she guessed right. Another immediate microjump following, that brought them out at an angle to another part of the starburst. Another quick targeting solution, another burst with LOS, then back into jumpspace, this time long enough to open a twenty-minute gap, while Koutsoudas and the other scan techs reran the scans of the targeting runs.

The first run confirmed the starburst, and the mass classes of the vessels involved. Seven of them, three heavy cruisers carrying half-again *Vigilance*'s weaponry, two assault carriers massing three times the cruisers, and two killer-escorts. One cruiser and one killer-escort lagging well behind. The second run scans confirmed a hit on the assault carrier, partly buffered by its screens.

"They do have good screen technology," Heris said, scowling at the scan data. They had hit with both of the cruiser's forward LOS, but one ablated against the screens. The second had penetrated, but hadn't breached the ship . . . the screens appeared to be weakened, perhaps down, and the infrared showed substantial heat, but no atmosphere.

The enemy's starburst had modified after the attack, with one side of the starburst rolling over—but slowly, with those massive ships—to regroup along the axis of the original attack. Also quite visible on the second scan was the trace of weapons that had narrowly missed *Vigilance* when she jumped after the attack.

"Damn good shooting," Ginese commented. "From one of the cruisers—their command cruiser probably. We weren't onscan a total of eight seconds, and they nearly got us. It would have been glancing, and the shields would have held, but . . . whoever it is over there is sharp."

"How long did it take us to get our shots off?"

"Six seconds." Long. On her old ship, they had drilled until they could pop out of a microjump and fire within four. No wonder they were almost fried.

"We'll do better," she said, with a confidence she didn't feel. She couldn't move her old crew into every critical position—she hadn't enough of them, and besides, she needed to get this crew working. In a long fight—and she had to hope this would be a long fight—shift after shift would have to fight with peak efficiency.

From twenty light-minutes away, she could not follow the *Paradox*'s attack in realtime, even though Koutsoudas bought her a little advantage with his boosted scans. Tinsi, having the advantage of the postscans of her own attack, had chosen to have another run at the possibly wounded assault carrier. But he took ten seconds to come out of jumpspace, locate his target, and shoot. The assault cruiser's shields failed, but he himself was under attack, and he scorched the Benignity ship without breaching it. He jumped just in time, and Heris wondered if he would follow up his attack or simply microjump his way to a safe jump point.

She had not been sure he would attack at all; he had reported having two serious fights aboard after taking command. Although he had seemed slow, even stupid, when she first talked to him, clearly he had plenty of command ability. His ship not only obeyed orders, but had survived a live engagement.

In any case, it was time for *Vigilance* to re-enter the fray. Another pair of microjumps brought them in behind the laggards. This time Heris chose ballistic weapons, half of them heat-targeting, and the other half fitted with the "kill me, target you" guidance systems that converted scrambling countermeasures into secondary guidance. They might hit the trailing pair; even if they missed, their overrun might bring them up on the other CH ships. *Vigilance* launched all its weapons within six seconds, and was safely back into microjump without being touched.

"There's *Paradox*," said Koutsoudas, as soon as they'd jumped back again; he was replaying the scan of their attack. The patrol ship had come across the bottom of the CH formation, this time firing within three seconds of their jump exit. CH response didn't come close.

"Of course, they'll start microjumping soon," Heris said. "They're going to be highly peeved with us." She glanced at the clocks. "Take us over to Blueyes now." Blueyes was the second-largest gas giant in the system, with its own set of rings and satellites to hide in. It was a considerable distance away, but if she could lure them into pursuing her over there, all the better for Xavier. The jump lasted just long enough for Koutsoudas to switch the beacon ID—the ship that went into jump at point A was not, apparently, the same one that emerged from jump at B.

Redlining the insystem drive to get a tight swing around the gas giant—and then out on a new vector, a longish run on insystem drive to let the enemy get a good look at them while their own scans scooped data.

The CH ships had regrouped, snugging in again and boosting toward Xavier itself. All but the laggards . . . which had vanished, leaving behind roiled traces that indicated either badly tuned microjumps or explosions.

"A lot of infrared," Koutsoudas said. "Lots and lots of infrared, and interesting spectra—not quite what I'd expect if they blew, but definitely not normal jump insertion."

The scans looked messier, cluttered with the probable courses of ballistic weapons that had not hit their targets and the extended lines of LOS weapons. As dangerous as enemy fire, in an extended battle, were the hundreds of armed missiles heading off in all directions. As the ships maneuvered, especially with microjumps, they could find themselves in the midst of these hazards, being blown away by their own or enemy weapons. Long microjumps even offered the possibility for inept commanders to shoot themselves down with their own LOS beams.

"If they've got a new way of foxing our scans, that might explain why they were hanging back," Heris said.

"Dammit," Ginese said, watching the main clump continue steadily toward Xavier, "you'd think they'd have the guts to chase us—"

"Too smart," Heris said. "They know we're outgunned. Well, no one said this would be easy. Is that another one lagging?" The icon indicated that it was the other killer-escort.

"They've slowed," Koutsoudas said. "Gives them more maneuverability."

"And more options for microjumps," Heris said. "Wait— I see only four now."

"Their killer-ship is missing . . . no . . . there it is, sneaking over to—oh, shit."

Over to the yacht's hiding place, and it would be coming in on their blind side. Its commander probably didn't know the yacht was there, Heris thought. He hoped to conceal his ship in the rings, to catch them on the flank. But instead of ambushing a fox, he was going to scare a rabbit out of the brush.

It was already too late to help; their scan data's lag meant that whatever was going to happen, had. Heris said nothing, waiting for the disaster she expected.

When the flare came, it wasn't the yacht.

"They laid their own mines," Ginese said, in a tone that matched her own surprise. *"Faroe* thought of that—"

"Kill," Koutsoudas said, unnecessarily. That size flare had to be a kill, and the spectra matched the reference patterns. "Detonated their onboard stuff—I hope the yacht wasn't too close."

Heris felt a little jolt of satisfaction. She had picked the right junior officer to captain the yacht after all—and whatever effect Lady Cecelia had had on him, he'd managed to kill a bigger, more powerful ship. And the enemy's advantage was eroding . . . from seven ships, any of them a match for hers, the Benignity commander was down to four, one with severely damaged shields.

Assuming the two that had vanished weren't hiding cleverly somewhere. Instinct told her no, that they had either been destroyed, or had fled, damaged, into FTL. Not smart. Ships that entered FTL with major damage rarely emerged on the other end.

If only she'd been able to lay a proper array of mines around Xavier, she'd have a chance to win outright, with all her own ships intact. The sparse ring the shuttles had spread in equatorial orbit would only annoy the ships—might injure the assault carrier whose shields were down, but no more.

Still, they'd done better than she'd expected. In the long hours that remained of the inward traverse, they would have several more chances for the quick, darting attacks that gave her ships the best chance. Especially since the CH formation no longer had killer-ships to duel with them.

"We can't let them alone long enough to repair their shields," she said. "I want to change shifts now—" Two standard hours early. "We need the freshest reflexes we have." She herself had been up and running too long. She didn't even want to think how long it had been since she assembled the small group that had taken over the *Vigilance*. "I'm taking four hours, myself. You have your orders, Svatek."

CHAPTER SEVENTEEN

When Heris woke, she saw that the CH group had not wavered from its course; they had drawn back into a tight cluster where shields could reinforce each other, with the damaged assault carrier in the middle, and they could shrug off the fast, brief attacks. *Paradox* had missed sixty percent of its shots; Heris sent them a tightbeam ordering them to jump a safe distance away and rest for six hours. Faroe, on the yacht, offered to come help harry the enemy. Heris decided against it; the yacht's weak shields and relatively light armament meant that it could be little help, but easy prey. If it bumped into any of the stray weapons now cluttering the scene, it would have no chance. Instead, the yacht could flit in microjumps, reappearing with different beacon IDs, distracting the CH crews from the real attacks, tempting them to waste shots on it. That was dangerous enough. And, in the end, the yacht should run as fast as possible to spill its scan records at the nearest Fleet base. She warned Faroe that one or more nearby jump points might be mined.

For the next six hours, Heris sent *Vigilance* in and out of FTL, harrying the CH group. With every run, the mess on scan worsened, until it was almost impossible to find a safe place to shoot from. Although her ship escaped damage, it inflicted nothing beyond temporary ablation of the enemy shields, and the CH group did not maneuver at all in response to the attacks. Typical of the CH approach: they expected to bull their way through to their goal. If she'd had their mass and firepower, she'd have done the same.

* * *

"Return no more fire," Admiral Straosi said. "They're trying to make us waste it—"

"We have plenty," one of his subordinates said.

"If that traitor told the truth, and there are no more Familias ships to fight. We cannot count on that." He admired the discipline of the enemy ships; they had wasted little of their capacity. Even the misses were close enough to give everyone a scare. His crews were exhausted; they were not used to such sustained fighting, and the loss of *Zamfir* and *Cusp* had shaken them. And then *Snare* . . . he still had no idea what had happened to *Snare*. It could have been as simple as miscalculating the location of ring components, but if that tiny little ship—yacht, the traitor had called it—was capable of blowing a killer-escort, then he had to be wary of it. At least he had not been fooled by the beacon changes, after the first few times.

"If we don't return fire, they'll just come in closer and closer until our shields fail."

"To come that close, they'll have to be in realspace longer. *Then* we return fire." Then we blow them away, he thought with satisfaction. "They are gnats . . . mosquitoes . . . annoying, but not really dangerous. When they get greedy and sit still, we swat them." They were dangerous, and he knew it, but even so he had no other options. Xavier was his target; he could not waste time chasing a Serrano around the system.

He did hope that Serrano hadn't managed to find a way to lay mine-drifts out here somewhere. Or around that miserable planet.

"So—do we close in now?" asked Svatek after they'd made two attack runs with no return fire.

"No." Heris munched on a sandwich. "He's just conserving his weapons—he's not helpless. He must wonder if we've got more ships coming."

"If only *Despite*—" Heris shook her head at him, and he said no more. They had all debated the chance that *Despite*'s crew might mutiny and come back to help them—assuming that most of the crew, like the crews of *Vigilance* and *Paradox*, were loyal. But the hours had passed, with no sign of return.

"If our packet made it out, someone should be getting a poke about now," Heris said. "That still means hours—more likely days—before other ships could arrive." If some traitor at the other end didn't suppress it. If a battle group or wave was ready to set off when the message arrived. She wondered again about her aunt. How much had she guessed of the enemy's intention? Was there a worse problem somewhere else, that she committed so little resources to this likely target?

"At best—we have to hold them off the planet for—"

"Hours and hours," Heris said. "Forever, basically. We don't know how far behind this group their main invasion force is." Far behind, she hoped. Benignity policy usually required an attack force to report back before the supporting force arrived.

They continued their darting attacks, run after run, as much to keep the Benignity crews tired as anything else. And the enemy closed on Xavier, braking in perfect formation.

Xavier Station died in a burst of coherent radiation that fried its way through the station and on into the planet's atmosphere, where its degrading beam wreaked havoc on communications and finally on the surface. The station reactors, as they blew, sent pulses of EMC that destroyed surface-based computers. "I wonder how many were left aboard." Heris glanced at the speaker, one of the enlisted working the engineering boards.

"Supposedly they were all evacuated," she said. "I hope the General Secretary got people into shelters downside. With any luck, everyone was off the station. . . ." But she knew a few wouldn't have been—the last shuttles had been overloaded, according to Cecelia, with near riots as they left.

But planets are large, and spaceships, however large, are small in comparison. It takes time to scorch a planet so that it can be garrisoned shortly afterward—easier to flame it, but that makes it hard to install the kind of military base the Benignity was planning. Heris had counted on that, on their need to be careful, precise. Now that it was five to three—the injured assault carrier's weapons weren't functioning, and the weapons it carried for installation would be stowed away—she might just pull it off.

The CH ships took up equatorial orbits, spacing themselves around the planet where their scans and weapons could reach the entire surface, the two cruisers higher and the two assault carriers slightly lower. The assault carriers would soon crack their bays and start disgorging drop shuttles and equipment drones. The damaged one wouldn't even wait for the cruisers to turn the attacks.

"Damn—I thought we made it clear where to lay the mines," Ginese said, when the data on the orbits sharpened. "Those assault carriers are low enough—or almost—"

"Maybe they went for the lowest orbits—to catch the drop shuttles on the way down. They don't have diddly for shielding—"

"Mmm. And they don't have to stick to equatorial transits, either. Idiots. If they'd done what we told them—"

"Captain, there's a big ship behind us—"

"*Behind* us?" An icy breath ran down her spine.

"It's—it's that ore carrier." Miners. They'd had a big hull, she remembered.

"Weapons?"

"Nothing." It seemed to wallow, even on the screens, a huge hull massing considerably more than anything but the assault carriers. Neither weapons nor screens colored its display.

"What—do they think they're doing?" Heris asked the silence.

"Helping us?"

"With no weapons? Ha. At least, if it has no weapons, it can't shoot us." What had made the miners think they could fight with a bare hull, however large? And why now? Heris forced herself to ignore that enigma and went back to the battle at hand.

So far they'd been lucky. The destruction of the killer-escorts had removed the only enemy hulls that could match them in maneuvering at speed. Now, if they were to save Xavier's population, she had to bring her ships out of hiding and engage in a slugfest. Not her kind of fight, but she saw no alternative. At least, the CH ships were also limited in their options, committed to orbital positions and unable to combine their fire as effectively.

With near-perfect precision, *Vigilance* and *Paradox* exited from microjumps in the positions Heris had selected: within a tenth of a light-second of their targets. Heris had chosen to take on one of the CH cruisers; *Paradox* would hit the weakened assault carrier; and Faroe, on the yacht, would seem to be a new menace to the other cruiser.

The computers fired before even Koutsoudas could have reacted. By the time the scans had steadied, they picked up the results of that salvo, even as Heris emptied another into the nearest cruiser, and sent a raft of ballistics at the ships to either side of her. Her target had suffered shield damage, and the hull flared, hot but unbroken.

"Ouch," said Petris, as their own shields shimmered and the status lights went yellow. The cruiser had returned fire before their second salvo, and now poured a stream of LOS and ballistics both at them. Shield saturation rose steadily, then levelled off. Their scans wavered, unable to see through the blinding fury outside even at close range.

"Faroe fired something," Koutsoudas said. "I can't see if it hit—and he's jumped again." That was good news.

"Both flanks engaged," said Ginese. One of those was the undamaged assault carrier, now clawing its way up from its lower orbit.

Then one entire board turned red, and the alarms snarled. "Portside aft, the missile—" CRUMP. A blow she felt from heel to head, as *Vigilance* bucked to the explosion of her own missile battery. Before Heris could say anything, Helm rolled *Vigilance* on its long axis, so that unbreached shields faced the cruiser that had raked them.

"Good job, Major," Heris said. Around her, she heard the proper responses, as medical, engineering, damage control, environmental, all answered the alarms. Her concern was that damaged flank, now turned to the less-armed but still dangerous assault carrier.

She kept her eye on Weapons, but her crew needed no prodding; they were throwing everything they had at the enemy. The weapons boards shifted color constantly, as discharge and recharge alternated in the LOS circuits, as crews below reloaded missile tubes.

"Captain—portside battery's breached—casualties—" So it was as bad as that.

"Compartment reports!" That was Milcini, doing much better than she'd expected.

The reports matched the displays Heris could see. Several LOS beams at once had degraded their shields, and then fried a hole in the hull and the warheads of missiles in storage. These had blown, ripping a larger hole in their flank. Lost with it were a third of the portside maneuvering pods. Lost, too, were the crews of the batteries on either side of the storage compartment, and a still uncertain number of casualties in neighboring compartments.

Only Koutsoudas's boosted scan still penetrated their own screens and the maelstrom of debris and weaponry beyond them. He hunched over his board, transferring position and ship ID data to Weapons, shunting other data to other stations. He stiffened.

"We got the *Dylan*," Koutsoudas said. Its trace on his screen fuzzed, then split into many smaller ones; its icon changed from red to gray. "There's the reactor, that hot bit there." That hot bit, which would, on its present trajectory, fry in the atmosphere on its way down, shedding a spray of active isotopes. Couldn't be helped, and the nukes already launched were worse. Their scans blurred completely, as the last burst of *Dylan*'s attack hit their shields. Lights dimmed; the blowers changed speed. Then the lights came back up.

"Shields held," someone said, unnecessarily.

The scans cleared slowly. Heris ignored them for the moment to look at the inboard status screens. The breach hadn't progressed, and hadn't compromised major systems. The lockoffs held, and would if not damaged further. Slowly, from the spacesuited medics and repair crew working their way aft, Heris learned more. The hole in the hull couldn't be repaired now—perhaps not at all—but somehow some of the stored missiles had *not* exploded. The force of the explosion had gone outward through the hull breach, and the heat flash in the compartment hadn't been enough to overcome the failsafes on those racked inboard. Some had broken loose, and were probably, the petty chief said, out there ready to blow up if the CH would only be so kind as to hit them. Thirty-eight were still racked, and—if they could get airlocks rigged to the nearest cross-corridor—could be transferred to the surviving batteries.

Engineering reported that the ablated shields could be reset when they'd rerouted some damaged cable. Fifteen to twenty minutes . . . if they had fifteen minutes. Heris forbore to hurry them; it would take as long as it took. She checked again with sickbay: most of the casualties were dead, as expected, but there were eighteen listed as serious, and another five as moderate, out of duty for at least twenty-four hours.

Three to two now. If her two ships had been undamaged, if they had had plenty of weapons left—but *Paradox*, though undamaged, had run out of missiles, and its LOS beams were discharged. In another five or six hours—hours they didn't have—it could support her with beam weapons. Now, though—an undamaged cruiser a third again the size of hers stalked her. Encumbered as it was with a crippled assault carrier it must shelter, how would it choose to fight? The other assault carrier still had more firepower than *Vigilance*, but it was far less maneuverable.

"There's something jumping in," Koutsoudas reported. "Something big—lots—DAMN!"

Heris said nothing. She couldn't help whatever it was, and snapping at 'Steban wouldn't get her the data any faster.

"And skip-jumping. They know exactly what they're coming into." Which meant the Benignity, probably. She had small hope that her own message, sent on the station's equipment, had gotten through.

"It's *Despite*," Koutsoudas said. He didn't sound as if he believed it. Heris certainly didn't. Hearne changed her mind? Hearne led the Benignity fleet in herself? With Hearne, it could be either. Koutsoudas leaned over his screen as if that would help. "The distant ones—it'll be hours before I can get an ID, unless they skip their way into closer range."

"And here's the other cruiser," said another scan tech. "*Paganini*, their admiral's flagship."

"Well," said Heris, "I suppose it's time to face that music." A moment of blank silence, then a groan from half the bridge crew; she grinned at them.

Benignity cruiser *Paganini*

"That patrol craft has quit attacking," the captain pointed out. Admiral Straosi grunted. That patrol craft had almost hulled an assault carrier by itself, and that should not have been possible. If only the damn things weren't so maneuverable.

"What about the others?"

"There's a big cargo vessel moving very slowly in from the gas giant—it could even be an ore-hauler with no communications capacity, possibly unmanned. It's no threat. The cruiser's damaged; *Dylan* and *Augustus* have it bracketed and it won't last long—"

"Sir—" A scan tech, his face paper white. "It's *Dylan*—it's gone!"

"Nonsense."

"It is—and that damnable Serrano is still there."

Straosi's blood seemed to take fire. The bitch had ruined his attack, and his career. The Benignity would have not only his neck, but his family's fortune. "Enough!" he roared. "First we kill that patrol—we show her! Then her. All ships—" The assault carriers could keep her busy while he blew the patrol ship, and then—then all three of them would blast that stupid, stubborn woman right out of this world.

R.S.S. patrol craft *Despite*

Jig Esmay Suiza had survived the battle for control of *Despite*, and after Major Dovir finally died, she ranked all the others—the small band of ensigns and junior lieutenants who had been the nucleus of the loyalists. Now she faced the grizzled, balding senior NCO, Master Chief Vesec, who had just called her "Captain" and asked for orders.

She managed not to say, "Me?" and instead said, "Dovir's dead, then?"

"Yes, Captain Suiza." There had been a time when she dreamed of hearing that . . . of coming aboard her first command, of being congratulated. Now she stared back, her mind foggy with fatigue. Vesec stood in front of her, a stocky man her father's age, with her father's air of impatience with youthful indecision. She was captain. She had to know what to do. She wanted to burst into tears. She didn't.

"Position?" she heard herself ask, in a voice steadier than it had been five minutes before.

"Three minutes from FTL exit through jump point Balrog." That didn't give her much time.

"Balrog has a Fleet relay," she said.

"Yes, sir. Also there's usually a manned station." A wave of relief washed over her. Help. Someone senior who would tell her what to do.

"We'll drop a packet," she said.

"If the captain permits—" he said.

"Yes?"

"It might be wise to take precautions. Sometimes when the Benignity attacks, they've mined nearby jump points."

She hadn't thought of that. She hadn't known about that. "And what would Captain—what's a good way of being careful?" Graceless, but the sense got across. He rewarded her with a careful smile.

"Low relative vee insertion. Shields hot as we come out. Wait for scans to recover."

"Very well," she said. "Then make it so."

"Yes, sir." A ghost of a twinkle as he turned away. She saw covert glances from others on the bridge. Peli, only six months junior, who had proved more than once he was better at things than she was. He stared at her, then his lips moved. She read them easily. Oh—yes. The captain's formal announcement of command. She moved over to the command position and picked up the command wand Dovir had given her after he was shot. She couldn't sit—the command chair still stank of blood and guts—and she had to lean down to insert it in the slot.

"Attention all posts." They had had to memorize this, back in the Academy, and she remembered saying it to the mirror, to her roomies, to the shower wall. "This is Lieutenant Junior Grade Esmay Suiza, assuming command of the patrol craft *Despite*, upon the deaths of all officers senior in the chain of command." She had never commanded anything bigger than a training shuttle, and now—she wouldn't think of it. The computer requested her serial number; she gave it automatically. Then it was over, and she was formally and finally in command. Her vision wavered.

Peli came closer. "Captain," he said formally. The challenge she usually saw in his eyes was missing. "Captain, we're not going back, are we?"

"Back?" She hadn't thought that far; it had been Dovir's decision to run for help, to call in Fleet. Now it was hers; she shook her head. "We're coming out of jump to make our report, Peli. What we do next depends on what we find."

Jump exit brought a ripple of light to the blanked scan screens. Gradually, the ripples steadied, and became points of light, icons tagged with ID numbers, colored lines defining traffic lanes in the Balrog system. Debris sparkled in a ragged shell around the jump point.

"Debris," Master Chief Vesec confirmed her guess. "One thing about it, whoever got blown took most of the mines with him." Esmay felt cold. That could have been their ship, coming out of jump with high vee, fleeing trouble.

"The Fleet picket?" she asked. None of the icons showed a Fleet ID; she could see that for herself. All were far away, days or weeks of travel at normal insystem velocities, and all were civilian.

"We'll hope not," Vesec said.

"Launch that packet," Esmay said, as steadily as she could. "Estimate time to a Fleet node with live pickup."

"Three or four days, sir." Add to that the response time, and it meant that those two ships back at Xavier would be sparkling debris in someone else's scan by the time help arrived. The juniors had discussed that, in the hours before someone appeared to offer them a place in the mutiny.

She didn't want to go back. She had no combat experience. She knew nothing about commanding this size ship on a routine voyage, let alone in combat. She could get them all killed without helping Serrano at all. The smart thing to do was go on, take the jump sequences as fast as possible, back to the central zones, and find an admiral with a battle group ready to go.

She had been a very green ensign, shy, afraid that everyone could see through her shiny insignia and new uniform to the fear—and she had stumbled and dropped her duffel right at the feet of a couple of senior officers waiting to enter the lift. One of them had laughed, and said, "They get younger every year." The other had picked up her scattered datacubes, and said, "Ah—your specialty's scan technology? Good—we've got an excellent Chief. You'll like him."

She had never forgotten that face. She had gotten in a disgraceful (so her commander said) fight with another Jig when Heris Serrano left the Fleet, defending her. And she had seen that face again, trying to talk Hearne into turning around . . . Dovir had played the tape for any doubters among the mutineers.

"We're going back," she said. Vesec looked startled, but didn't argue. "I want the fastest possible transit back into Xavier. They can't wait." She still didn't want to go back, any more than she'd wanted to be part of a mutiny, to have Dovir's blood and organs splashed into her face, to have this command. But it was her ship now, and she would do what she had to.

"Prepare for battle," she said, when they were back in jumpspace. No one argued. No one bothered her at all. She still had no idea how she was going to fight, but she would.

Aboard the R.S.S. *Vigilance*

"They're after *Paradox*," Koutsoudas said.

"And she's out of darts," Heris said. "Dammit, Tinsi, get her out of there!" But the patrol ship was too close to the planet to risk jump, and at these distances its maneuvering advantage disappeared. Scan showed acceleration, but the need to keep the screens on full combat strength held it well below maximum. Then the rising curve took *Paradox* out of their line of sight, behind the planet. She would have to go closer to *Paganini* before she could pull away. If she could.

Vigilance couldn't help. Their flank screens were still down, though the engineers kept saying, "Just another minute or two," and the damaged assault carrier lobbed enough missiles at them to keep them busy, shifting so that those which broke through met solid shields.

"It's not Hearne, on *Despite*," Koutsoudas said a few minutes later. "Someone named Suiza."

A moment later, someone said, "By the crew list, that's a Jig. What'd they have, a mutiny?"

"Must have." Heris had other things to worry about than who had killed whom on *Despite*. "But why are they here *now*?"

"They're coming almighty fast," Koutsoudas said. Their scan icon had the bright blue edge meaning a relative vee in major fractions of lightspeed. "Came out fast, and haven't slowed. Their scans will be useless."

"They're running on maps," Heris said. "Can they slow that thing by Xavier, or are they going to blow by?"

"Wait—there it is—they are braking—by timelag, that's two hours back—" The scan fragmented, as the incoming ship's relativistic motion skewed all the data. When it steadied again, *Despite* was only hours away. Now the audio broke up, until finally Heris could hear a very young voice announcing their arrival.

"Regular Space Service patrol craft *Despite*, Esmay Suiza commanding . . . in advance of a Familias Regnant force—" She probably hoped that would scare off the Benignity ships; Heris knew it wouldn't. They had lost too much; they would fight to the death now, having no alternative.

"At least her weapons are hot," Ginese said, as the newcomer lit up the scan screens like fireworks.

"No Jig can fight an admiral of the Compassionate Hand on his own flagship," Oblo said. "He's no fool. . . ."

Despite had arrived with too much relative velocity, and now she swung wide of Xavier, still trying to brake. "Fire now!" Ginese pleaded. "Dammit—microjump into position—do something—" But *Despite* rolled on.

A moment later, just as *Paradox* came back into line of sight, clawing its way up, its shields flared.

"Damn," Heris said. "He's going to lose them—" Now they could see the enemy cruiser, in the textbook position for killing smaller, faster ships. Its greater firepower had full weight now; the shields flared again and again, each time a little more. Heris wanted to close her eyes, but forced herself to watch. Toward the end, Tinsi must have realized his position was hopeless. Suddenly *Paradox* accelerated, full power—

"He cut the shields," breathed Ginese. "He's going to ram—"

"He's too far away." Koutsoudas was right; the Benignity commander hadn't let *Paradox* get close enough for that. Instead, a final round of fire poured into the unprotected ship, and *Paradox* blew. The enemy cruiser's shields sparkled briefly as it fended off debris. One thousand, eight hundred, twenty-three, Heris thought . . . no one was going to survive that blast.

"Well." Koutsoudas looked up a moment, and rubbed his eyes. "Dammit—if that idiot on *Despite* had done something—anything—to distract that admiral . . ."

"Later," Heris said. If they had a later. Even with *Despite*, the odds were no better than before, and she could not count on an inexperienced captain. Three to one, she faced—and here came the cruiser, and the other assault carrier.

"Shields are up," said an engineering rating.

"Good," said Heris. It didn't make that much difference. They'd lost over half their remaining missiles; they were outgunned and too close to the planet to go into jump. But shields would help—at least delay the end.

The end came first to one of the assault carriers, the one with damaged shields. Heris, concentrating on the enemy cruiser, had no idea why the carrier suddenly burst and spewed its load of vehicles and personnel and heavy equipment into space. No one did, until afterward, when the sole survivor of the shuttle that had used its phase cannon told them. At the time, she assumed that *Despite* had gotten off a lucky shot.

The captain of the other assault carrier reacted by taking his ship down—trying to cut beneath *Vigilance* and perhaps also release his load. He paid for this mistake when he hit a drift of mines so crudely made that they neither showed on his sensors nor responded to countermeasures intended to make mines blow prematurely. Individually, or clustered at any distance, they could not have damaged the ship, but enough of them in direct contact, lodged in the many crevices a deep-space ship offered, blew a sizeable hole in the hull. The carrier immediately launched its drop shuttles, only to have most of them blown by other orbiting mines on the way down.

Heris had no leisure to enjoy his plight, for the remaining cruiser attacked with all its force. *Vigilance* faced the same problems as *Paradox*; its shields bled power from the drive, and kept them from using their superior speed and maneuverability. Through the maelstrom that combat made of their scans, no one could find *Despite*.

"If she'd only come up his rear," Ginese said. "She couldn't blow him, but she could distract him—take a little of the heat off us—"

Then the *Paganini* blew, a burst of debris and radiation that completely blanked their screens. "Ouch," said Koutsoudas. Heris said nothing. She didn't quite believe it. She would have pinched herself if a dozen people hadn't been staring at her, their faces full of her own disbelief.

When the scans cleared at last, *Despite* hung steady, a light-second away, with a very nervous-looking young Jig on a tightbeam link to *Vigilance*.

The extra signals Koutsoudas had noted when *Despite* first blew into the system belonged to Regular Space Service ships:

cruisers, patrols, escorts, battle platforms, and the supply and service ships needed to keep them going—tankers, minelayers, minesweepers, troop carriers.

"The question is," Heris said, "whether they're with us or against us." She felt drained; what she saw in the faces of her crew was the same exhaustion. "Considering the last multiple arrivals—"

"More likely they're answering your signals." Koutsoudas fiddled with his scans, and grunted as if surprised. "Well, Captain—it's family, whether that pleases you or not. That's the *Harrier*, Admiral Vida Serrano's flagship. Signalling admiral aboard, too."

"At us, or in general?"

"In general. They won't have us on scan yet." Even after so long, even with exhaustion dragging the flesh below his eyes into dark pockets, he still had that smug tone about his scans. And deserved to.

"Fine," Heris said. "Then continue our present broadcast, and I want this shift bridge crew to go down for six hours."

"We're as rested as the others," Ginese protested.

"Which is not rested at all. I want my mainshift crew rested first, then the others in rotation. Tabs for all. Oh— and add a timetag to that broadcast, with the end-of-battle-all-secured code. That way they won't have conniptions if they come roaring in and find out I'm asleep." They would anyway, but she would tell the next shift to wake her, once she'd gotten this gaggle off to their racks.

The second shift, called back, looked no worse than the ones they relieved. Heris waited to be sure the young major understood what to do, then headed for her quarters. She had to be awake and alert for the coming confrontation with her aunt. She remembered to put in a call to *Despite*, telling them to get some rest, then fell into dreamless sleep.

She woke feeling entirely too rested, and a glance at the chronometer told her why. Nine solid hours? She would rip the hide off someone, just as soon as she quit yawning. A shower woke her the rest of the way and she came back into the compartment wishing she had a clean uniform. The one she had worn for days looked almost as bad as it smelled.

In that brief interval, someone had made her bunk.

Someone had also laid out a clean uniform. She could see where other insignia had been hastily removed, and the right number of rings sewn on. She tried it on; although it was a bit loose and slightly longer than she preferred, it would do. As she fastened the collar, the com chimed. She grinned. Of course they knew.

"Yes?"

"Captain, if that uniform fits, we can have a complete set ready in a few hours." She didn't recognize the voice; it wasn't any of her former crew.

"Thank you," she said. "It's fine. Whom may I thank for the loan of it?"

"Lieutenant Harrell is pleased to be of service, sir."

"I'm most grateful," Heris said. She noted the name on her personal pad, and headed for the bridge. The familiar uniform felt so comforting—it was going to be hard to take strips off a crew that took such good care of her.

The bridge officer, Milcini again, looked guilty when she glared at him. "He said to let you sleep," he said. "I thought it was your orders, sir."

"He who?" Heris asked.

"Me, sir." Major Svatek, bleary-eyed and haggard. "I know what you said, but we haven't had any urgent messages, and the incoming group hasn't changed course. It's continuing to decelerate. The senior surgeon recommended that all shifts take a full eight hours—"

"You haven't," Heris pointed out. "Does this mean second shift's just going off?"

"No, sir. If the captain recalls, second and third had been on a four-hour rollover standby, while first was on that last long watch. First went out, and after four hours I sent second down, and brought in third. First had eight hours off, six in full assisted sleep; second's been down for five hours, and third's just gone down. In another three hours, second will have had its eight hours, and by the time they're off—"

"Makes sense," Heris said. It wasn't what she'd ordered, but it was what she would have ordered if she'd been thinking clearly. "Good decision. Now—why are *you* still on the bridge?"

He grinned. "Because, Captain, I'm the one whose neck you could wring if you wanted to."

"Better decision." She had to admire that. "Now—take yourself off to bed and don't come back until you've slept it out. At least eight hours. And this time, obey orders." She put no sting in that last.

"Yes, sir." A pause, then, "If I could make a suggestion, Captain?"

"Of course."

"The galleys are back in operation. I'm sure they'd be glad to send something up."

Heris felt her mouth curling into a grin. "What are you, my medical advisor? No—never mind—you're right. I presume first shift ate on the way up?"

"Yes, sir."

"Good. Go on now—don't hover." He smiled and left the bridge. Heris looked around, checking each position. Everything seemed normal, as normal as it could be with a hole in the side of the ship and a civilian very illegally in command of it. She checked the status of the casualties in sickbay, the progress of repairs, and realized that Svatek was right. She needed food.

"I'm going to my office," she said to Milcini. "You have the bridge."

CHAPTER EIGHTEEN

In her office, she looked around a moment. She had hardly seen it since it had been Garrivay's, since she had killed him. Nothing showed in its surfaces, no stains on the rug, no scrapes on the furniture. She sent for a meal—anything hot—and began working through the message stack. *Despite* reported some garbled transmissions from the planet's surface. They had also carried out the orbital damage survey. The Benignity commander, intending to put down his own troops, had used less toxic weapons than he might have. Although the two small cities had been flattened, and wildfires burned across the grasslands and forests near them, the rest of the planet wasn't damaged. It would remain liveable. Heris thought of the pretty little city she had ridden through, with its white stone buildings now blasted to rubble, its colorful gardens blackened . . . it could have been worse, but that didn't make it good.

She ate the food when it came without noticing what it was. One group of miners wanted to know if it was safe to go back to their domed colony. Another claimed salvage rights on the destroyed killer-escort and asked permission to start cutting it up. She suspected it had already started doing so. Those in the ore-carrier, without any explanation of what they'd been doing, announced that they were going back.

Heris called the bridge, and asked for tightbeams to both *Despite* and *Sweet Delight*. The young captain of *Despite* wanted to explain the mutiny, but Heris cut her off. "That's for a Board of Inquiry," she said. "Right now I need to know what you've picked up from the planet."

"We have no estimate of the number of survivors," Suiza said. "We've picked up two transmitters, but one may be an automatic distress beacon. It's repeating the same message over and over. The other seems to be trying to contact the first, not us."

"Ah. They probably don't know who won up here, and they're trying to collect their forces on the ground. A good sign, though it may be tricky for our people to land if they're going to be mistaken for hostiles."

A light blinked on her console. "Excuse me, Captain," she said; the youngster started, as if she were surprised at the formality. "I'll get back to you," she promised. This time it was Jig Faroe on *Sweet Delight*.

"Come on back," she said, only then remembering that she'd told him to keep his distance until called. "We'll need to get those civilians off the yacht, or you off the yacht, I'm not sure which."

"Yes, sir." He seemed much older than the other Jig— but then he hadn't been through a mutiny, and the command of a yacht was well within his ability. Heris still had to find out how Suiza had ended up in command, and how she'd destroyed a Benignity heavy cruiser. "Uh—a couple of them aren't aboard."

"Aren't aboard? What do you mean?"

"Well . . . Lady Cecelia said it was a good idea. Brun's acting as our liaison with the miners."

"Oh. Well, make sure someone brings her in." Another blinking light. This one must be the admiral's call. "Be sure we know your ETA," she said, and clicked off.

"Captain—tightbeam from the admiral—"

"Coming." Heris left for the bridge, very glad of the clean uniform. She nodded to Milcini and sat in the command chair. She hadn't actually sat down in it before; she'd been too busy running a warship in combat, when she always thought better on her feet. Now she put on its headset and enabled the screen. There on the display was her Aunt Vida, admiral's stars winking on her shoulders.

"Captain . . . Serrano." That pause could be signal stretch, an artifact of their relative positions and velocities, but it felt like something else.

"Sir," Heris said. She was aware of a grim satisfaction in the steadiness of her voice. Defiance tempted her, the urge to say something reckless. She fought it down, along with the questions she could ask only in private.

"Situation?" That was regulation enough; it might mean any of several things, including the straightforward need for information.

"No present hostilities," she said, back in the groove of training and habit. "Xavier system was attacked by a Benignity force, which destroyed its orbital station and did major damage to both population centers. Damage estimates for the planet and its population are incomplete; we have not established communication with survivors. There are at least two functional transmitters. The population did have some warning, and the local government tried to evacuate to wilderness areas."

"And Commander Garrivay?"

"Is dead. May I have the admiral's permission to send an encrypted sidebar packet?"

"Go ahead." Heris had prepared an account of her actions, and the background to them; now she handed this to a communications tech, with instructions.

"Status of Regular Space Service vessels?" her aunt went on.

"*Paradox* was lost in combat, no survivors known. *Vigilance* has structural damage to an aft missile bay from a blowout. Engineering advises that it would not be safe to attempt FTL at this time. *Despite* is jump-capable, and essentially undamaged, but extremely short-crewed."

"How dirty is the system?" In other words, how many loose missiles with proximity fuses were wandering around on the last heading they'd followed.

"Still dirty," Heris said. "And we laid orbital mines around Xavier, nonstandard ones improvised with local explosives. None of those are fissionables, but they're potent."

"Very well. Hold your position until further orders. We'll send the sweepers ahead; we're laying additional mines in the jump-exit corridors and closing this system to commercial traffic until the new station is up and operating." A long pause, then, "Good job, Captain Serrano. Please inform your command of the admiralty's satisfaction."

"Thank you, sir." Heris could not believe it was ending

like this. Of course there were reasons an admiral wouldn't get into all the issues even on a tightbeam transmission, but she had expected something, some demand for explanation . . . something.

"Well," she said to her bridge crew. "Admiral Serrano thinks we did a good job." A chuckle went around the bridge. "I think we already knew that. Now let's get things in order for the admiral's inspection, because if I know anything about admirals, she'll be aboard as soon as *Harrier's* in orbit."

Brun woke slowly, in fits and starts. It was dark. It was cold. She couldn't quite remember where she was, and when she reached for covers, she discovered that she was quite naked. The movement itself set up competing fluctuations in her head and belly. She gagged, gulped, and came all the way awake in a sudden terror that slicked her cold skin with sweat.

After uncountable moments of heart-pounding fear, Brun wrestled her panic to a dead stop. She wasn't dead. She hung on to that with mental fingernails. In twenty minutes, maybe, or two hours, or a day, she might be dead . . . but not now. So now was the time she had to figure something out.

You wanted adventure, she reminded herself. You could have been sitting in a nice, warm, safe room surrounded by every luxury, but . . . no, no time to think that, either. Only time for the realities, the most basic of basics.

Air. She was breathing, so she must have air of a sort. She didn't even feel breathless, though her heart was pounding . . . that was probably fear. She wouldn't let herself call it panic. She felt around her . . . finding nothing, at first, in the darkness. Nearly zero gravity, she thought. And air, and not freezing, or she'd be dead. Her stomach wanted to crawl out her mouth, but she told it no. She'd already gagged once; her belly was empty. Dry heaves would only waste energy, she told herself, and hoped that she hadn't already compromised the ventilation system with vomit.

Still, even if she had air now, she might not always. She had to get somewhere and find out where she was and how long she had. She tried to remember what she'd been taught about zero gravity maneuvers. If you were stuck in the middle of a compartment, someone had said (who? was her memory going too?), you could put yourself into a spin and hope to bump into something. A slow spin, or you'd throw up. And how to spin? She twisted, experimentally, and then drew up her legs while extending her arms.

Something brushed her leg. She grabbed for it, automatically; her hand found nothing, but nausea grabbed her, proving that she'd tumbled. She flung out arms and legs both, to slow the rotation, and felt something brush her left elbow. Maddening—she couldn't tell what it was. Slowly, she tried to reach across with her right hand. Whatever it was slid along her arm; she was moving again. On her shoulder, down her back . . . it was hard not to grab, but she waited . . . something linear, like a rope or length of tubing. Smooth, not rough. Cool.

Her head hit a surface, hard; she saw sparkles in the darkness for a moment, then her vision settled. Cautiously, she moved her hand up, found the surface, knobbly with switches. Some were rocker switches, smooth curves of plastic. Others were little metal toggles. A few were round, flat buttons with incised lettering—she could feel that, but not what the letters were. A control panel, but on what? She tried to remember what she'd seen before everything went wrong.

The image that came to her was grinning faces, mouths open, singing. A party. It had been a party, loud and happy— the rest of the memory burst over her. The ore-hauler, stuffed like an egg carton with the little four-person pods: the miners had their own plans for dealing with Benignity invaders. Faroe had been horrified—he knew they couldn't survive a fight with the big ships. She had offered to go talk to them; he'd agreed. Then, against Faroe's expectation (though she had never doubted it) Heris Serrano had defeated the Benignity ships. And Fleet had arrived: they were safe. The resulting celebration involved mysterious liquids far more potent than the fine wines and liquors her father served, even more potent than the illicit brews at school. The last she remembered was sinking peacefully into a bunk while a group of miners sang the forty-second verse of "Down by the Bottom of the Shaft." Or perhaps the twenty-first verse the second time around. It had a fairly repetitive form, minor variations on the same few innuendoes, and she hadn't exactly been paying close attention.

Which meant she was probably in one of the personnel pods, which meant she had seen the control panels before. She didn't want to push any of the flat buttons. They were all critical; one of them, she remembered, was the airlock main control.

She had drifted closer to the control panel; her knee bumped something with an edge (the desks below or the storage shelf above? It didn't really matter) and she felt cautiously around with her foot until she was sure she had the foot hooked under that edge. She felt carefully with both hands until she had the little metal tip of a toggle pinched in either hand. Now she was anchored, if she didn't lose her grip. Her feet defined "down" for the moment. She let the other foot wave slowly until her toes found the same edge and crawled under it. Both feet hooked in . . . now she could release one hand and feel around in a more organized way.

Out to the right . . . the switches ended in a smooth cool surface. That made sense with her memories. Carefully, forcing herself not to rush and break loose, she moved her right hand back, caught hold of the toggle, and slid her left hand across the switches there.

Should she push this switch? Any switch? Panic shook her again, as if some great beast had its jaws around her chest. Think. What would happen if she didn't? She'd be here, naked in the dark, until she died, and she would have no idea when that might be. Was that what she wanted? No.

The first switch she pushed produced no detectable change. Nor did the second. She hesitated before pushing another. If the electrical system was off, none of the switches would do anything. But if the electrical system was off, the air wouldn't be circulating, and that tiny draft on the small of her back suggested that it was, though perhaps on a standby system.

Where had the electrical system controls been? On the left-hand side of the consoles . . . if she was right-side up. Now she could think of that, and how to tell. Below the consoles a kneehole space accommodated the person working them; above was the storage shelf with netting. Her toes wiggled down, and found themselves snagged in something tangled. Netting, she hoped. That meant—her mind struggled.

It was surprisingly hard to think upside down in the dark . . . the lower left console would now be . . . up *here*. She felt over it, slowly. The main lighting control should be about halfway up—perhaps this big rocker switch? She pushed it.

Light stabbed at her; she squinted. She was indeed upside down; her stomach lurched, and she fought back the nausea. It wasn't really upside down, not in zero G, just *relatively* upside down. That thought didn't help. Move slowly, Ginese had told her repeatedly. Now, as she tried to turn her head and look across the tiny compartment, one foot came unhooked and she lost her grip on the toggle. Don't panic, Ginese always said. Just drift, if you have to . . . she drifted, held by her right toes clenched on the shelf's retracted netting. Light was definitely better. She could put up a hand to fend off the stool that tumbled slowly before her (was that what she'd kicked before?) and she could see that what she'd first felt was indeed a length of tubing, perhaps two or three meters of it. She had no idea what it was for.

After a long struggle, she finally twisted and coiled herself into an "upright" position, with her feet under the consoles. With a firm grip on the edge, she rested and tried to think more clearly. She was, as she'd thought, naked. She saw no sign of a spacesuit, but across the compartment were personnel lockers. Perhaps in there she could find something. Meanwhile . . . with the lights on, she could identify most of the switches. She pushed DISPLAYS ON and the smooth screens to either side of the consoles lit up. For a moment they blurred into fuzzy rainbows as tears rose, but she blinked hard. She could cry later, if she had to. For now, first things first. Air: she had air, more than a hundred hours at present usage. She had electrical power keeping the internal temperature high enough for survival—calories, in that limited sense. Water? She found none listed, but that didn't mean much; she might find juice in one of the lockers.

Slowly, carefully, she worked her way around checking the lockers. Two plastic flasks with zero G nipples full of clear liquid—the first she tried gave her a fiery drop of the same stuff drunk at the party. She grimaced and pinched the nipple shut. The other was water, pleasantly cool. The next locker was half full of concentrate bars, sticky-taped to the racks. Better and better: food as well as water. Brun alternated sips of water with bites of concentrate.

She still didn't know why she was in a pod in zero G. Was it someone's idea of a joke? A political move, an attempt to use her as a pawn in play against her father, or Heris?

"I don't think so," muttered Brun. She felt much better even without clothes on, now that a bar of concentrate was doing its work in her belly. She looked at the exterior scans again. The miners had explained their reference system; she could locate Xavier, Oreson, Blueyes, Zadoc. Rock-blips were supposed to be one color, and ship-blips another, which meant—if she was right about it—that there were a lot of ships out there. One of them would be the *Sweet Delight*, and one would be *Vigilance*, with Koutsoudas on scan. Somebody should be able to see the pod—if they bothered to look, with the battle over. And there were lots of little blips going by, some of them marked by the scans as thermally active. Thermally active rocks? Brun frowned. Weren't thermally active rocks found in volcanoes? She'd never heard of volcanoes on anything smaller than a planet.

Ahead, a drift of blips slid across the screen, thickening. She was moving too fast, she realized, relative to those rocks. Pods were tough, but not that tough. It took her a few moments to locate the thruster controls, and confirm the full fuel tanks. Then she began maneuvering, using short bursts, as she remembered someone telling her, trying to work away from the thickest clumps of blips.

"She's *what*!" Heris struggled to keep her voice under control. Faroe looked miserable enough, and he wasn't the one who'd done it.

"She volunteered to go talk to the miners aboard the ore-hauler, to convince them to go back into hiding. I was going to pick her up before our final jump out. When we—you—won, I sent word . . . and apparently they had this party."

Heris could imagine. An ore-hauler full of drunken miners who had just learned that they weren't going to commit suicide by attacking warships with pods . . . they'd have been crazy to start with, and the party hadn't helped.

"—And apparently she passed out, and someone threw up on her, and they cleaned her up and put her in a pod to sleep it off, only someone hit the jettison control by mistake hours later—"

And now Brun was out there in a little personnel pod, unconscious or sicker than sin if she was awake, in space thoroughly contaminated with spent weapons from days of fighting.

"Why didn't they go after her?" Heris asked.

"They *said* that whoever hit the jettison control was so drunk he didn't realize he'd done it—they only realized the pod was gone when they went to give her some clean clothes."

Great. She was not only unconscious, but naked. Heris could imagine explaining this to Lord Thornbuckle: sorry, sir, but I let your daughter experience war in the company of drunken miners and they dumped her into a pod, unconscious and naked, and shoved her out into the debris of battle. . . . No. Not a good plan. Something had to be done. "Do they have any kind of location on the pod?" she asked.

"No, sir." Faroe looked miserable, as well he might. "I've had our scan techs on it since I heard, of course, but there's so much—"

"Captain, you won't believe this." It was Koutsoudas, from across the bridge. Heris looked up. "Some idiot rockjumper is trying to collect weaponry with a personnel pod." He pointed to an icon that darted into a drift and then back out. "At least he's got some sense, but—"

" 'Steban, put a lock on that pod. Can you do a retro analysis—could that have come from the ore-hauler four or five hours ago?"

"It only turned its beacon on a few minutes ago, but let's see if I can get any kind of trace on the recordings. Hmm. Yes, it could've. Why?"

"Because it's Brun," Heris said. Only Brun could be that lucky, although her luck could run out any moment. "You're going to have to guide *Sweet Delight* to it for a pickup. Faroe, are you getting this?"

"Yes . . ." He sounded less confident than she felt. He hadn't been around Brun that long. "It's pretty thick stuff to take the yacht in. . . ."

"You're right." Heris thought a moment. "What we need is in the incoming formations. If we can help her stay alive that long . . . I need a tightbeam to the *Harrier*," she said.

* * *

Brun had forgotten everything but the scans that told her where the rocks were thickest. She had once thought it must be fun to pilot a pod like this in the rings of a gas giant; now she understood the look she'd gotten when she said so to the miners. And although she'd read that rocks usually drifted along together, all moving about the same vector and velocity, these rocks didn't act that way at all. She was constantly having to dodge rocks coming in at different angles, different speeds. She was almost glad she hadn't found any clothes, since she was dripping with sweat.

When the control panel suddenly spoke to her, in a scratchy simulation of a voice she knew, she didn't notice until it repeated her name the third or fourth time. "Brun! Brun! Can you hear us? Brun!"

Communications. Now where was that switch? She groped around until she found it and another little screen lit up to say that her transmitter had full power. "I hear you, but I'm busy," she said, flicking the starboard thruster on again. One thing about it, she was getting better at this all the time.

"Brun, is that you?"

"Yes, it's Brun. There's a lot of rocks out here." Then curiosity got past her concentration. "Who is this?" she asked.

"Koutsoudas," she heard. "Brun, you need to let me give you some guidance; someone's going to pick you up."

"Why can't you just give me a vector over to *Sweet Delight*?"

"Won't work," Koutsoudas said. "And I doubt you've the fuel for it." Brun glanced at the fuel display and was shocked at how much she'd already used. She'd been trying to do short adjustments but— "Give me a tenth-second burp starboard," Koutsoudas said, before she could think about it. "Now port." Something slid by in the scan, long and narrow with a thermally active tip.

"I don't understand all these thermally active rocks," she said to Koutsoudas. "I thought volcanoes had to be on planets."

"They aren't rocks," he said. While she was thinking about that, he gave her more directions. Now the scan blips thinned out.

"But they're not ships . . ." Brun said. She could see the ships clearly. These things were a lot closer.

"No," Koutsoudas said. "They're weapons."

"You mean—someone was shooting at me? Why?"

"No, you were crossing drifts of misses—missiles that didn't hit their target. You're almost out of it now—"

Brun realized she was shaking. It was stupid; she was almost out of it now.

"Is there a suit aboard?" Koutsoudas asked. "You've got ten minutes before your next drift, if you can find a suit—"

She found an EVA suit, a drab utilitarian model nothing like her custom suit. Its owner had been shorter; Brun felt the pressure all along her spinal column once she'd struggled into it. But the locks did fasten, and the internal gauges did turn green. It was fully charged with air, water, and power. Best of all, the suit boots had gripper feet; she now had a solid *down*.

She worked her way back to the control panel and discovered that it was just possible to handle the switches in gloves. She plugged in the suit com to the pod's com, and told Koutsoudas she was suited.

"Just in case," he said, in the same calm voice he'd used all along. "Now—what's your fuel situation?"

"Down to ten percent." And she didn't know what ten percent was, in terms of use. She didn't even know how long she'd been using it.

"Then give me one-half second, thrusters seven and four." She could see the fuel display sag at that, and she said so.

"Not much longer," Koutsoudas said.

When the blow came, it took her by surprise, and slammed her against the adjacent lockers. The suit's padding protected her, but the boots came unstuck from the deck, and she tumbled. Another blow to the pod sent her tumbling in another direction. The pod rang with noise: clangs, scrapes, piercing squeals. Finally it was still. Brun put out a cautious foot and it stuck. She could hear nothing; the end of the communication cable waved around, making it clear that she'd come unplugged. She moved slowly back to the control panel, and plugged it in. A patient voice was calling her, not Koutsoudas but someone else.

"Brun—Brun—Brun—"

"I'm here," she said. "Just shaken up."

"Good," the voice said. "You're now locked onto the R.S.S. minesweeper *Bulldog*, en route to the *Harrier*. Remain in your spacesuit; do not attempt to leave your vessel until docking is complete and you have received notification." And that was the end of that; her comlink cut off and would not reopen.

It seemed like a long time later that a gentler series of bumps woke her from a nap. The comlink hissed gently, live again, then another voice spoke to her.

"Brun?"

"Yes," she said, feeling grumpy. "I'm here." Where else would she be?

"Your pod is aboard our ship—it's the R.S.S. *Julian Child*—"

"I thought I was going to something called *Harrier*," Brun said.

A chuckle. "Oh, you are. But *Harrier* has no facilities for docking like this, and the admiral thought it would be safer to transport you by shuttle, not make you swim tubes."

"Oh. Thanks." Admiral. What admiral? Where was Heris? Where, for that matter, was Lady Cecelia?

"We understand you're in a vacuum-capable suit . . . if you'll open your hatch—it's the left-hand flat button—"

"That says exterior hatch, caution. Yes, I know."

"That will put you in our number six docking bay. It's not aired up—if you have any concerns about your suit air, please tell me now. There's an airlock to ship-normal air about six meters to your left, as you exit, and suited personnel will be there to help you."

Outside the pod, Brun saw a vast cargo bay open to space; craft she had no name for were parked along the sides, and her pod filled the open middle. Beyond the lip of the bay, she could see the hull of another ship, a shape so odd she wasn't at first sure it *was* a ship. She stared until someone touched her suited arm, took the dangling cable of her comunit, and plugged it into his own suit.

"It's a minesweeper," she heard. "Odd beast, isn't it? Nothing else could go in after you."

Then they guided her to the airlock, and on into the ship, where she had a chance to change into a gray Fleet shipsuit before her shuttle flight left for the *Harrier*.

"Some party," the admiral said, without preamble, when Brun had arrived in her office.

"I—don't remember most of it," Brun said. The admiral looked familiar, though she didn't think she'd met admirals before. Not this one, anyway.

"My niece tells me you once wanted to run away and join the service," the admiral said. Niece. Aunt. Brun looked at the admiral again. Graying hair, but the same evenly chiseled dark features, the same compact body, the same confidence.

"You're Heris's aunt," she blurted.

"Yes. And you're Lord Thornbuckle's daughter. Tell me— are you cured of your desire for adventure?"

Brun thought a moment, even though she didn't need to think. "Not really," she said. "I mean, I'm still alive."

The admiral nodded, as if she'd expected that answer. "Do you now understand why my niece and her crew insisted that you learn all those boring bits you complained about?"

Brun laughed, which startled the admiral, then she smiled too. "I always understood," Brun said. "I didn't realize the complaining bothered them. Doesn't everyone gripe?"

Admiral Serrano—she supposed they had the same surname as well as the same genes—tipped her head as if to inspect Brun more closely. "You are a remarkable young woman," she said. "My niece thought so, and you just proved it again. Will you eat with me?"

Brun had no idea what meal might show up, but her stomach was ready for any of them. Any two or three of them. "Thank you," she said, hoping that the admiral would ignore the far less mannerly answer her stomach gave at the thought of food. "I'd be honored."

"She's safe aboard the *Harrier*," Koutsoudas said. "If that's safe . . . they won't let me talk to her."

"I don't think my aunt eats girls for breakfast," Heris said. "Not even that one. Who, I'm sure, is cheerful and bright-eyed and ready to tell an admiral everything she thinks she knows about everything she's heard."

Heris put in a call to *Sweet Delight*, to reassure Cecelia that Brun had survived. Cecelia, relieved of that anxiety, had a long string of other topics to discuss. Heris really didn't care, at that moment, about the fate of the breeding farms she'd visited, the status of the financial ansible, or what might happen to the miners who had thrown the party. She would have been far more annoyed with Cecelia, if the conversation had not included an inquiry about each of the former *Sweet Delight* crew. Cecelia might have her batty side, but she did care about people. She even cared about the present crew, especially Jig Faroe, whom she praised until Heris finally cut her off. She could almost feel his embarrassment through the intervening thousands of kilometers of vacuum.

"You know," Ginese said, without looking around, "it's going to be very interesting when your aunt and Lady Cecelia get together."

Heris had not thought of that. "Oh . . . my," she said. Those of the bridge crew who had been on *Sweet Delight* had the same expression she felt on her own face.

CHAPTER NINETEEN

Castle Rock, Rockhouse System

"Patchcock? What are they doing on Patchcock?" Kevil Mahoney dropped the faceted paperweight and stared at Lord Thornbuckle.

"I haven't the faintest idea." Bunny stared out the window at a day that suddenly seemed less sunny. "It probably has something to do with the technical data on the rejuvenation drugs that they sent us . . . but it'll take me hours to wade through that. And in the meantime—Patchcock! Of all places in the universe."

"It's not a good sign," Kevil said. "Things have gone wrong with this from the beginning. D'you suppose Kemtre had this sort of feeling—that everything was suddenly coated with grease and slipping away in all directions?"

"I don't know, but *I* do. First the financial ansibles in the distant sectors go offline for a few days, and then some crazy admiral demands authorization to take a whole wave on a live-fire maneuver out to the frontier, 'just in case there's trouble. . . .' "

"And you gave it," Kevil reminded him.

"Well . . . they were already gone by the time it actually crossed my desk. And they claimed it involved Heris Serrano, that she was in some kind of trouble—"

"It's probably George's fault," Kevil said. When Bunny looked confused, he said, "Not that, the Patchcock thing. Whatever you don't want George to see, he sees. Whatever

976

you hope he doesn't know, he knows. Some evil instinct told him that there was one place we didn't want our children to go, and he headed for it like a bee to its hive."

"From the Guerni Republic?"

"I know, it's unlikely. But so is George. I wish he'd realize what his talents are, and use them profitably. He—" Kevil broke off as Bunny's desk chimed at them.

"Yes?" Bunny glared at the desk; he'd told Poisson that he didn't want to be interrupted.

"A Marta Katerina Saenz, milord. Says she's going to talk to you."

"I'm—" But the door was opening already.

Raffa's Aunt Marta had the dark, leathery face of someone who spent most of her days outside. On her, the coloring and features that made Raffa look like a Gypsy princess had matured into those of a wisewoman. She wore clothes that layered improbable color combinations to give an overall effect of archaic flamboyance. Bunny had never met her before, since she preferred to live in the mountains of her own planet, but he had no doubt who she was.

"Where is my niece?" she asked.

"You are naturally concerned," Kevil began.

She gave him a look that stopped the words in his mouth. Bunny felt his own mouth going dry. "Don't try your honey tongue on me, Kevil Mahoney," she said. "You've the charm of a horse dealer, but I'm not buying. You sent Raffaele off somewhere, and now you've lost her. Isn't that so?"

"She's not exactly lost," Bunny said, wondering why his collar suddenly felt so tight. He had aunts of his own, formidable aunts, whom he had learned to work with or around, as needs must. But this— "They're on Patchcock," he blurted, surprising himself. He had not meant to tell her.

"They . . ." she said, meditatively. "I presume Ronald Carruthers is one of 'them.' "

"And my son George is the other. She should be safe enough—"

Her dark eyebrows rose alarmingly to the iron-gray hair above. "Did you not hear me before? Your son George, indeed. I've heard about your George." Then, before Kevil could answer, she waved a hand. "I'm sorry. That was uncalled for. Your son's not a bad young man, and what

I heard is years old by now. Just that he had a clever tongue in his head, inherited no doubt from you."

"Quite," Kevil said. Bunny glanced at him, glad to see the flush receding from his neck. Kevil's profession required him to keep his temper, but no man was at his calmest with his son under fire.

"So—you sent Raffaele somewhere with Ronald and George—"

"Not precisely," Bunny said. When cornered by an aunt of this caliber, the best plan was complete disclosure. "We sent Ronnie and George to—on a—to do something for us. And they didn't report in—"

"I'm not surprised," she said, this time with no softening. "And you sent Raffaele to rescue them? I suppose it made sense from your viewpoint."

"Not exactly rescue. We wouldn't—I mean, we assumed they'd just gotten . . . er . . . sidetracked, as it were."

"And because Raffaele loved Ronald, she would seek him out as the stag seeks the doe—though it's backwards in this case—and put them back on track?"

It sounded ridiculous, put like that, and he had realized how ridiculous weeks before. "Something like that," he said, in a tone of voice that admitted the foolishness. She didn't pursue that, but came back to the current problem.

"So now she's on Patchcock, with Ronald and George, and—what's wrong now?"

Kevil spoke up, his famous voice completely under control, its power blunted. "They didn't know that Ottala Morreline disappeared there months ago, after disguising herself as a worker and infiltrating a workers' organization. We are fairly sure she was found out, and killed. We hadn't told them, because we didn't have any idea they would suddenly hare off to Patchcock from the Guerni Republic— it's hardly on the direct route."

"Raffaele," her aunt said, "always had a nose like a bloodhound. Give her a sniff of intrigue, and she would follow it through any amount of boring coverup."

"Really?" Bunny asked. "I hadn't known that."

"She's not your niece. And I'm not sure she knows it herself. But it's one reason I asked her to start going through my files, to test my hypothesis. And sure enough, she discovered one little fiddle after another—spooked the accountants concerned, and delighted me. So if she headed for Patchcock from the Guerni Republic, then whatever you sent them there for is connected to Patchcock."

"But it couldn't be—unless—"

"You might as well explain," Aunt Marta said, "because I'm not leaving until you do." She looked about as moveable as a block of granite, and while technically they could call Security to haul her away, neither of them was willing to get in that much trouble.

"Let's see," Kevil said. "We have now involved five or six major families—"

"At least," said Aunt Marta. "Don't stop now." She sounded dangerously cheerful.

Bunny shrugged. "All right. It's the rejuvenation drugs. And others. Lorenza—" He paused to be sure she knew which Lorenza; she nodded. "—Lorenza had been dealing illegal neuroactive drugs through the upper crust, and we suspect she might have been involved in tampering with rejuvenation drugs. When we looked into it, our supplies are supposed to be manufactured in the Guerni Republic. But they're shipped on a route that could allow the Compassionate Hand—whom we know Lorenza was working for—to get access to some or all of them."

"Not healthy," Aunt Marta commented. "I'm glad I manufacture my own."

"You *what?*"

"Well, not personally. But if you think I'm going to put things into my body that have been manufactured by people who might be my enemies, think again. You know I have pharmaceuticals—"

"Yes, but you can't—but no one in the Familias is licensed—"

"By the Familias. Don't be stuffy, Bunny. We're over near the border; I have a valid license from Guerni, and we manufacture a small supply. Enough for me and my people, and a small . . . er . . . export."

"You smuggle," Kevil said flatly. Her eyes went wide.

"Me? Smuggle? Surely you jest. I do international trade with the Guernesi, who the last time I heard weren't enemies."

Kevil opened his mouth and shut it again. Bunny would have been amused if he hadn't been worried—he had never seen Kevil at a loss for words. Perhaps he didn't have an aunt of his own, and wasn't familiar with their unique abilities.

"I wish we'd known that," Bunny said, hoping to regain control of the situation. It wouldn't work, but he could try it. "We needed reference samples—that's why we sent Ronnie and George. We could have simply asked you."

"Assuming that my starting materials haven't been adulterated. If I remember correctly, the starting materials come from several sources. Come to think of it, quite a bit used to come from Patchcock, before that unfortunate incident."

"The Patchcock Incursion," Bunny said, just to make sure they were talking about the same thing.

"Yes. Once the Morrelines took over, exports dropped; I assume the damage to the infrastructure limited production. And perhaps they found other markets; I don't think I've seen quotes on their production when we've been in the market for materials."

"That's odd," Bunny and Kevil said at the same time, and looked at each other. Raffa's aunt looked thoughtful.

"You're right. It's been years—they should have everything back up to speed. The Morrelines have been gaining in the Index." She blinked, and a slow grin spread across her face. "I wouldn't be surprised if that's what Raffa found out— where the materials are going."

"If they were going to the Guerni Republic, why would she care?" Kevil drummed his fingers on the desk. "And besides, raw materials are raw materials. They may have found something else to make with the same starting material, something more profitable."

"Than rejuvenating drugs? You jest." Marta pursed her lips. "I hate to tell you this, if you don't already know, but the profit margin is . . . ample. Quality control is a bitch—you have to have really good chemists keeping an eye on it, because the lazy ones keep thinking they've found a shortcut. The Guernesi warned me about that—there's an alternate synthesis that looks good but is much more sensitive to minor variations in processing. I've had a research team on it for twenty years now, and we haven't found a way to improve the Guernesi process."

"So . . . you can't think of anything more profitable to do with the substrate?"

"Not unless they've discovered an alchemical stone that

lets them transmute it to whatever's highest at market. No— if it's being produced in the quantities it was, the only thing more profitable than selling to me and to the Guernesi would be vertical integration. Produce it themselves."

"And Raffa could have figured that out." It was not quite a question; Marta nodded.

"If not in detail, enough to follow the lead. Especially if the samples you provided gave the Guernesi any clue— isotopic analysis or something like that."

"Are you a chemist?" Bunny asked bluntly. One did not usually inquire into the formal training of Family Chairholders, who were presumed to be broadly educated. But Marta seemed more comfortable with this than he had ever been with the food chemistry that underlay part of his family's fortune.

She grinned. "As a matter of fact, yes. It was a way of avoiding something my parents wanted me to do, so I completed a doctorate. Then I did post-doc work at Sherwood Labs—not that it would interest you, the details. In the long run, it was more fun to be a rich dabbler with time for other interests than a full-bore researcher, though I may spend a rejuv or so going back to it someday."

"It's all very interesting," Kevil said, "but we've got three young people headed into far more trouble than they anticipate, and I don't see any way to warn them—or help them."

"I shall go, of course," Marta said. "It is, after all, my niece. And I understand the chemical side. But I shall need assistance."

"Yes. Of course." Bunny looked at Kevil, who looked back. Neither of them could leave.

"You won't want to involve Fleet directly," Marta said. "Not after what happened last time. But don't you have a tame Fleet veteran—that woman Cecelia de Marktos hired? Raffa told me about her, how she helped with that mess on your planet—"

Bunny choked at the thought of anyone considering Heris Serrano "tame." Still, it was a better idea than the nothing he'd had. If only Brun weren't with her . . . he really didn't want Brun on Patchcock, along with her old cronies. Rejuvenation would fix the gray hairs, but not the fatal heart attack he felt coming on.

"I suppose—yes. Possible. She's a long way off, but we can signal—" If something else hadn't happened to the ansibles, which had only been back up for a day; messages were backed up and only emergency traffic could get through with its usual speed.

"I will make my own way to Patchcock," Marta said. "Rather than wait—it may take me longer anyway. You will contact this person?"

"Yes," Bunny said, not letting himself think of the difficulties. "Yes, I will. And I'm—" He couldn't think of the right word. Sorry to have dragged her niece into this? Sorry she found out before he got it fixed? Sorry that Kemtre had let this whole mess get started? "I'm glad you came," he found himself saying, and meaning, to his own surprise.

"Secrecy," Marta said, "is usually a bad idea." Then she swept out, with a flourish of her cape.

"That," said Kevil after a pause, "is a very dangerous woman. But did you ever see such bones?"

"Not my type," Bunny said, with more caution than honesty. He opened his mouth to say more, but Poisson came in with an expression that meant trouble.

"It's Fleet," he said. Bunny froze inside, thinking *mutiny*, but the next words relieved him. "They've successfully fought a Benignity incursion—"

"Where?"

"Xavier. It's a fairly isolated system out—"

"I know where it is," Bunny said. "What happened?"

Poisson gave a crisp precis of the action as reported through Fleet channels. "All enemy ships destroyed, and a substantial reinforcement of Regular Space Service in place. And apparently there's a personal message to you—from the admiral."

Bunny took the cube with its encrypted recording, fitted it into the desk, and inserted the earplug. "Lord Thornbuckle," a woman's voice said. "This is Admiral Vida Serrano. I'm glad to be able to tell you that your daughter Brun is alive and well. So is Lady Cecelia de Marktos, whom I understand is a friend of yours. We need to confer at your earliest convenience. The Rockhouse Major Base Commandant can arrange a secure ansible link. Thank you." Bunny pulled the plug from his ear and stared at Poisson.

"Had you heard this?"

"No, milord. It's encrypted."

"It's—I need to speak to the Rockhouse Major base commander; please set up a tightlink for me."

"At once," Poisson said, and went out. Kevil raised his brows.

"Well?"

"Apparently Brun was in the middle of a battle for Xavier—which means that Cecelia and Heris Serrano were, too. And the admiral wants to speak to me . . . says we must talk. Brun's on her ship, I gather. I don't like that at all."

Xavier System, aboard the *Vigilance*

"You have to do something," Cecelia said. Heris had run out of things to say in answer; she just looked at Cecelia and waited. "You have to," Cecelia went on. "Surely you care!"

"Of course I care," Heris said. "But surely you see my problem. I can't just leave—"

"Why not? You're not in the military anymore. You're a civilian; you assured me all that talk about a secret mission was just something you made up in an emergency. You can just walk away, take my—your—yacht, and go find out what's wrong."

"Lady Cecelia, it's not that simple. I am . . . not free to go."

"You mean you don't want to. It's more fun to play soldier—"

Heris's temper snapped. "I was not playing, Lady Cecelia; people *died*, in battle and as a direct result of my actions. Whatever you think about the military, you personally and everyone you know on Xavier would be dead without us. If you want to talk playing, how about a grown woman so fixated on horses that she can't tell a game from war?" The moment the words were out she would have snatched them back, but entropy prevailed. Cecelia glared, speechless . . . but only, Heris was sure, for a moment.

"If I could interrupt." That was a voice more used to command than either of theirs. Heris glanced up and saw her aunt, Admiral Serrano, in the doorway. She started to stand, but the admiral waved her down. "At ease, Captain.

I have things to say to both of you." Cecelia had whirled, still angry and ready to attack, but Vida Serrano seemed not to notice as she came in and took the other chair across Heris's desk. "Lady Cecelia," she began, "I am glad to finally meet the person my niece so respected."

Cecelia's expression stiffened even more. "Not much respect, if you ask me."

"As a matter of fact, I'm not asking. I'm commenting on an observation anyone might make. Now—I understand you've had an upsetting communication from a relative on Patchcock. I was unaware that your family had interests there."

"We don't," Cecelia said. Her face flushed unbecomingly as her anger shifted focus. "I have no idea what Ronnie is doing there, or why Raffa is with him—they had both agreed to her parents' request that they avoid each other for a while. But I don't see what business it is of yours."

Admiral Serrano ran one hand over her short silver hair. "As the commander of this battle group, I have a natural interest in anyone trying to suborn one of my commanders—"

"Suborn!" said Cecelia.

"Commanders!" said Heris. Admiral Serrano's lips twitched.

"The two of you are a well-matched pair. Lady Cecelia: by whatever means she obtained it, Captain Serrano now commands an R.S.S. cruiser. She commanded it in battle, against an enemy of the Familias trying to invade. Now that I'm here, and since I outrank her, I am in command—and she is one of my subordinates."

"I see that," Cecelia said irritably, "but she's not really military anymore. She's a civilian. She assured me—"

Admiral Serrano tilted her head slightly. Heris felt a pang of sympathy for Cecelia . . . everyone in the Fleet knew what that head tilt meant, the final pause before the prey was impaled. "Lady Cecelia, you tell me: if you put a cow's horns on a horse and hung a placard with COW on it, would that make the horse into a cow?"

"Of course not!"

"Very good." Admiral Serrano might have been praising a slow student in some class. "Captain Serrano was bred and trained as a military commander. She functioned as a military commander for twenty-odd years. Do you really think a couple of years running your yacht could change what she is?"

"But I *like* her," Cecelia said. "And I don't—"

"Like the military. Sorry about that. It's always happening, you know—people who think they know what we're like, and then actually meet one of us and discover we're human."

"You're patronizing me," Cecelia said. "I'm not as young as I look."

Admiral Serrano laughed. "I know that. Regulations forbid us to wear them, but . . . I was one of the first multiple Rejuvenants in the Familias. I would have three rings. A volunteer to study the effects, in fact. I would bet our birthdays aren't that far apart."

"You look older," Cecelia said.

"Admirals must have a certain maturity of presence," Admiral Serrano said. "I chose to combine other therapies with my rejuvenations, so that I look old enough to scare young cadets, and can still outrun most field-grade officers." Admiral Serrano waited to see if Cecelia would comment, but she didn't. The admiral went on. "You should know that I, too, have had communications about Patchcock. Lord Thornbuckle is concerned about the situation there. He wanted Captain Serrano to take the yacht and find out what's happening to the young people."

"That's what I said—she should go, and—"

"Lady Cecelia, I can't leave without—"

The admiral raised her hand, a teacher to unruly children, and they both fell silent.

"You want her to go to Patchcock and she won't; she correctly considers herself under orders . . . there's a solution, you know."

Heris realized what her aunt meant a long moment before Cecelia did. Cecelia looked up, startled. "You mean . . . you?"

Admiral Serrano shrugged. "I can order her—" She turned to Heris, "And you had better go, if I do."

"If? Why if? Why not just do it?" Cecelia looked ready to leap out of her seat. Admiral Serrano turned to Heris.

"Captain—what would your orders be, if you were the admiral?"

"I wouldn't send R.S.S. warships to Patchcock," Heris said promptly. "It's likely to make things worse."

"So?"

"So . . . if I could insert a small, nonthreatening civilian ship, with some specialists to . . . find out what's happened, rescue personnel if necessary—" If they weren't already dead.

"Good choices. I was going to relieve you as captain of the _Vigilance_ anyway—you don't need to waste your time shepherding her to a repair dock. _Despite_ is too big for this job, and too small for anything else. You're not officially on the List, even if you are . . . mmm . . . tucked away in a corner of the database. I don't have to notify anyone at Personnel about your transfer. Whom do you want on that yacht?"

"You want me to go on _Sweet Delight_?"

"It's the right ship—small, fast, civilian, and full of specialists—or it will be when you select the right crew for this. Covert, remember."

"Yes . . . sir." Was this really an order? Would she really have the authority to pull out the crew she wanted?

"Actually this will simplify things for me," the admiral went on. "I have some loose ends to tidy before you come back in the Regs—assuming that's what you want—?" She looked at Heris, and nodded before Heris could get the words out. "Yes—I thought so. It's almost time—this little chore will fit in nicely."

"I'm coming," Cecelia said, with a touch of defiance, as if she expected to be refused.

"Of course," the admiral said. "It's your ship and your nephew. Now about that girl—"

"She stays," Lady Cecelia and Heris said together. The admiral raised her brows.

"That's what her father said. What's your reason?"

"She's stretched her luck well past its elastic limit," Heris said. "And she's too valuable as a hostage. She'll be happy enough here if you let her soak up practical matters from your specialists."

"She already is," Admiral Serrano said. "When her father wanted to speak to her, she was down in Environmental, learning to tear down a scrubber and fascinating the Chief at the same time. This afternoon, she was deep in the hull specifications for minesweepers. I hope I'll still be in command of this wave when you've finished on Patchcock." She didn't sound worried. Heris suspected that she'd enjoy Brun as much as the young woman would enjoy a few weeks aboard the flagship.

"Well, then," Cecelia said. "If that's decided, I'll go back to *Sweet Delight*. . . . I expect you two have a lot to talk about." She nodded to Admiral Serrano; Heris called someone to escort her back to the other ship.

"We do need to talk," Admiral Serrano said. "But this isn't the best time. I'll see you after Patchcock."

"There'll have to be a Board," Heris murmured. The thought—the word—sent shivers down her spine.

"Of course." Her aunt looked at her. "It worries you? It shouldn't. There's ample evidence—just in what you've sent me so far, and in what Suiza sent from *Despite*—to support your actions. Not even counting the battle itself. You're in no danger, Heris, not this time. You've done well." She paused, then went on. "You're coming home, Heris. Back where you belong, back with those who love you."

But did they? She could not doubt her aunt, not faced with the warmth in those eyes. But others . . . she would have to know why they had ignored her before. She kept herself busy the rest of that day, visiting the sickbay, arranging the change of command, choosing the crew to go with her in the yacht.

She was choosing the crew for Patchcock—the same familiar faces: Oblo, Meharry, Ginese, Koutsoudas, Petris. Petris. She looked at him with no less affection than before, yet it was different. How many days had it been . . . and she hadn't missed that part, not really.

When all the transfers had been done, when she was back on the familiar (but *tiny!*) bridge of *Sweet Delight*, with the familiar crew around her and Lady Cecelia simmering in her suite like a kettle on the hearth, she realized that the trip to Patchcock would not be peaceful for one person at least.

"I've missed you," he said, slipping into bed beside her. He was warm and smooth, the shape her hands had wanted without knowing it. And yet—even before Xavier, neither of them had taken up the many opportunities. She thought she knew what it meant for her; what did it mean for him?

"I'm just not comfortable aboard ship," Heris said. She rolled her head sideways, facing what must be faced, but Petris merely looked thoughtful.

"I'm not either, if you want the truth of it. I love you; I loved you for years, and getting to be with you was wonderful. But—it doesn't feel right aboard ship, and it's not just the memory of those damnable cockroaches." Heris began to chuckle helplessly, and in a moment his mouth quirked. "Really. I swear."

"I know." Her chuckles subsided. "But we do have a dilemma, especially if you feel the same way. I love you; I want to be around you. And I love being in space—"

"Me, too," Petris said.

"But not in bed in space." She frowned, hardly realizing it until his finger began smoothing her forehead.

"We are grown-ups," Petris said. "We can take our pleasures serially instead of binging. It's fine with me if we put this part of our life aside when we're aboard. For one thing, we won't be waiting for some crisis to interrupt."

"Thank you," Heris said. She sighed.

"I almost wish—" Petris stopped that with a sudden lurch. "Sorry. Nothing."

"Wish what?" Heris pushed herself up on one elbow to look at him. The sight of his brows, pulled together in a knot of concentration, almost undid the previous agreement.

"Nothing we can change. Not about you, is what I mean."

"Petris!"

"It's just—we don't have anything to *do.* This little ship is a beauty, and it was fun fitting her out with some decent equipment and weaponry, but—we don't get to do anything with it. *Vigilance,* now—while I was scared out of my skull shift-and-shift, I felt needed. Competent."

"I know." Heris rolled all the way over and buried her chin in the mat of black hair on his chest. "And that's why I'm going back in, Petris. And I want you to come back too."

"I thought so." He took a deep breath that lifted her head to an uncomfortable angle. "Then we can't—"

"Yes. We can. We're not going to waste what we do have. Either you'll end up with a commission from all this, or we'll simply use common sense—confine it to times we aren't aboard."

"Is that an order, ma'am?" he asked.

"Sir," she corrected, and set about undoing the pact they had just made.

Later, before they were quite asleep, Petris said, "Lady Cecelia would have made a good admiral."

"Mmm. I'm not sure. She might have been booted out down the line; she's got a difficult streak."

"And you don't?" He tickled her extensively, but nothing came of it then but giggles. Finally Heris batted his hand away.

"I admit it; I'm difficult too. But my difficultness is the kind Fleet recognizes and knows how to deal with. And so's yours. And we will work it out—for all of us—and that's a promise."

"Fine with me," Petris said. "I trust you." She lay awake longer than he, stricken again by the weight of all those who trusted her.

CHAPTER TWENTY

Patchcock System

"I don't like it, letting Raffa go off by herself like this," Ronnie said. He slapped at a tickfly, and hit it, which left an itchy wet spot on his arm and a mess on his hand.

"She'll be all right," George said. "She's inside, isn't she? Not out here being eaten up by these . . . *things*." He flapped the gray-green cloth hanging down from his hat and swung his arms in a sort of uncoordinated dance. He had draped himself in the recommended insect-proof veil for their trek along the shore, only to discover that tickflies could crawl up the arms . . . and once inside the veil, they couldn't get back out. Even satiated with blood, they still whined around inside the veil with annoying persistence.

Ronnie looked seaward, where sullen waves lifted murky brown backs; they rolled sluggishly landward and slapped the crumbling shore with spiteful warm hands. Far out, a line of dirty white might mark the reefs he'd seen mentioned in the tourist brochure. Landward, the low boxy shapes of Twoville's monotonous architecture cast uninteresting shadows as square as the buildings. He hadn't seen the hotel, but in the transient workers' hostel, the cramped room smelled of disinfectant and the ventilation fans squeaked monotonously.

"It's not exactly . . . exotic," he said. "Not even the planet itself."

"No." George kicked at a mound of crumbly stuff, and

jumped back as a horde of many-legged, shiny-backed things ran out. He backed up a couple of steps. "Look at that—what d'you suppose . . ."

"Stingtails," said a voice. They both looked up, to find a tall, lean individual with a slouch hat and long, white, perfectly pointed moustaches grinning at them in a way that emphasized their ignorance. "If I were you," the man said, "I'd move farther away. Stingtails know the scent of their nest on the critter that kicked it—" George, who had been fascinated by the fast-moving swarm, backed up again and watched as the swarm continued to move toward him. When he shifted sideways, the front end followed his path, but the swarm kinked in the middle as some of the followers caught the scent and cut the corner.

"Dammit!" George backed away faster. "Now what?"

"Hop," the man advised. "Big hops. When you're twenty meters away, they'll lose track."

George hopped, looking ridiculous with his veil bouncing up and down; Ronnie jogged along, keeping wide of the swarm just in case, and the stranger strolled at ease, hands in his pockets. When they halted again, George breathless and disheveled, Ronnie took a longer look at the stranger.

Despite the old battered hat, with odd decorations stuck in its band (a tiny horseshoe? a fish-hook with feathers? a long, curling quill from some exotic bird? a blue rosette?), the man was otherwise tidily, even foppishly, dressed in crisp khaki slacks and shirt, the pleats pressed to a knife edge. A tiny pink flower in his buttonhole, a perfectly folded white handkerchief peeking from one pleated pocket. Stout low boots of fawn leather. And those moustaches . . . which matched bushy white eyebrows over bright blue eyes.

"You boys must have let Marshall at the station tell you what to buy," he said. Ronnie would have been annoyed, but he was already hot, sweaty, and bug-bitten. "I can smell the Fly-B-Gone from here . . . but of course it doesn't repel tickflies. Marshall got it by mistake three years ago, and none of us will buy it—he has to foist it off on tourists." Another pause; Ronnie slapped at his neck, and missed that tickfly. "Not that we get many tourists," the old man said. "Certainly not your sort."

"And what is our sort?" asked George, whose grumpiness always found voice.

"Rich young idiots," the man said. "More money than sense. I mean, we'd heard the Royals were disbanding, letting loose a plague of your sort, but I thought Patchcock was too far away and too boring to attract any. . . ." His friendly smile mitigated, but did not negate, the sting of that. "And that veil will only trap the tickflies inside," he said to George. "Besides making you hotter."

George tore off the veil and glared. "I know that. I was just about to take it off, when—"

"When you kicked a stingtail nest. And now you're angry with me. I understand." Ronnie had the odd feeling that he did. In fact, he liked the old fellow, and he hoped George wouldn't say anything too rude.

"I'm Ronnie Carruthers," he said, putting his hand out. "And this is George Mahoney."

The old man looked at his hand, and Ronnie realized it was smeared with blood and tickfly juice. "Sorry," he said, pulling it back to wipe on his slacks.

"No offense," the man said. "I'm Hubert de Vries Michaelson. Retired neurosynthetic chemist. Let me tell you what I already know, before you tell me something else. Truth between gentlemen, y'know."

"Ah . . . yes." Ronnie slapped another tickfly, and swiped his damp hand surreptitiously on his shirt.

"I wouldn't do that, by the way. Won't come out in the wash." Hubert grinned, showing a row of very white, very strong teeth. "Now—Ronald Vortigern Carruthers and George Starbuck Mahoney. Arrived yesterday, in company of a pretty young girl named Raffaele Forrester-Saenz. Right so far?"

"Yes, but—"

"You'd traveled together from the Guerni Republic, specifically from the planet Music. Kept to yourselves, but the girl let it be known that she and you, Mr. Carruthers, were traveling together in blatant disregard of her family's wishes." The old man peered at him, blue eyes suddenly frosty. "I hope that was a cover story."

Ronnie felt his ears going hot. "Well, sir . . . not exactly. That is, we didn't start to—it just happened that we—and anyway, it wasn't like that—"

"I see." The blue glare didn't give a millimeter. "Going to marry the girl, are you?"

Ronnie's spine straightened before he realized it. "Of

course!" Then, more calmly, he tried to explain. "We didn't start out together. George and I were on—we had something to do in the Guerni Republic." That sounded weak; he rushed on to the part he could tell strangers. "When Raffa showed up alone—"

"You decided she needed an escort—protection?"

"More or less," said Ronnie. He was not about to explain to this old fellow that the protection had gone the other way. The bright blue eyes blinked, then Hubert grinned.

"Well, well. Young blood. Still runs hot, I see. In that case, young man, you've made a serious mistake."

"What?"

"Letting her go unchaperoned here, of all places."

Ronnie looked around, but saw no particular menace. Besides, Raffa was safely inside.

"You should have registered with her," Hubert said. "The people at the hotel think she's alone."

That had been the idea. Ronnie fumbled for an explanation and came up with partial truth. "The fact is, sir, that hotel—it's the only one fit for her, but—but I couldn't quite—"

"Ah. Funds low, eh? What is it, boy, gambling or chemicals? Give it up, boy. Girl like that is worth it."

"It's not that," Ronnie said, feeling that his ears must be glowing now. "It's . . . it's family." He didn't want to drag Aunt Cecelia into this, and anyway it wouldn't make sense to anyone outside.

"It's his aunt," George said. George never suffered from this sort of embarrassment. "His aunt's suing his parents, and that's why Raffa's parents wanted her to drop him— because his aunt's in the mood to put his parents in the poorhouse, and Ronnie along with them."

"Never mind, George," Ronnie said. "It's not quite right, anyway—Aunt Cecelia isn't vindictive, not really."

"Cecelia . . ." Hubert said.

"Cecelia de Marktos," George said. Helpful, that was George. Ronnie wanted to smack him. "Rides horses. Red hair."

"Ah." Hubert looked Ronnie up and down again. "*That* Cecelia?"

"You know her?"

"Never met her. Never heard of her. Now I know." He

shook his head. "You have a problem, boy. Your young lady may be in serious trouble."

Now Ronnie felt cold. "What? Why do you think that?"

"Because Patchcock in general, and Twoville in particular, are not that friendly to strangers. Especially strangers with a mission." He gave them that toothy grin again. "And no one is going to believe you sneaked off to Patchcock to enjoy the beautiful scenery together."

"I've got to get back." Ronnie turned, and took a long stride without looking. This time it was his boot that smashed into a stingtail mound.

"Look out!" Hubert and George yelled together; Ronnie jumped back from the angry writhing swarm of stingtails that poured out of the hole.

"Not so fast," Hubert said, grabbing his arm. "Here—this way—walk through these—" He led Ronnie a few meters farther from the shore, onto matted rust-brown vegetation that crunched underfoot and released a sharp, garlicky scent. "Now settle down—getting yourself eaten up by stingtails isn't going to help your young lady."

"Eaten up?" George asked. He looked back at the mound, now covered with stingtails.

"Of course. Didn't Marshall tell you? They swarm on you, and start stinging—somewhere between fifty and a hundred stings paralyzes the average human. Unfortunately, it doesn't numb the rest of the stings . . . we lost quite a few settlers at first, people who thought stingtails were no worse than ordinary ants. Luckily, they can't follow a scent across stinkfoil."

"And you didn't tell me!" George glared. "You had me hopping down the shore like an idiot—"

"It worked," Hubert said. "Got your attention, too. Now. Enough flabbery-dabbery. Your young lady."

"She was taking a tour today," Ronnie said. "Her Aunt Marta, you see, sent her here—"

The old man's expression so clearly said *Pull the other one; it's got bells on* that he didn't have to open his mouth.

"I know she was taking a tour. The operative question is, did she come back?" Ronnie felt a sinking inside; he could easily imagine his heart having turned to iron, slowly plunging through his guts to the center of the planet.

"We're supposed to meet tonight," he said. "At someplace called Black Andy's, for dinner."

The blue eyes rolled up. "Oh, dear. Black Andy's is it? Not wise, not wise at all. Let me tell you what to do. You go back to your digs, get cleaned up. Go by her hotel and see if she's back. If she is, stay with her—eat there—and you'll hear from me tomorrow. If she's not, give me a call—" He fished out an immaculate business card, and handed it over with a flourish. "And do be careful on the way back. No more stingtails."

"Can't we just walk on the . . . er . . . stinkfoil?" asked George.

"Not advisable; it's a bit corrosive—if you'll look at your bootsoles—" George lifted a foot and winced at the lines etched in the sole. "It would probably eat through before you reached town. If you're careful along the shore, you shouldn't have too much trouble. I can't go with you— wouldn't be advisable at all, you see." Ronnie didn't see, exactly, but he was ready to run the whole distance back to their lodgings, if only it would help Raffa.

"Thank you, sir," he said. "We'll—we'll be in touch."

By the time they got back to their lodgings, they were both hot, sweaty, and reeking of stinkfoil. The one-armed man at the desk glared at them. "Tourists!" he said. "Didn't have no more sense than to go dancing on stinkfoil—you'll smell up the whole place." He got up and shuffled around the desk. "Might as well throw the boots away; you'll never get the smell out."

"But—"

"We don't like that stink in here—" Two large, beefy individuals had come out of the door to the right, and another from the door to the left. "We don't really like *your* stink in here."

A half hour later, Ronnie and George limped barefoot back to their room, where someone had been kind enough to ransack their luggage and sprinkle it with cloying perfume.

"I don't think they're friendly," George said. Their assailants had done no real damage, beyond bundling them into a smelly blanket, wrapping it with sticky repair tape, and then manhandling them downstairs into a storage closet. It had been locked, once they worked their way out of the blanket and tape, but it was a flimsy lock.

"I wish I knew if Raffa's back," Ronnie said. The room's comunit would be no help; he could see the severed cable from here.

"We'll have to go find out," George said. He pawed through the piles of clothes on the floor. "I hope they left us some shoes."

They had left shoes, filled with something that looked and smelled like rancid cottage cheese. "Not friendly at all," George went on, in a tone of voice that made Ronnie forget all about Raffa for a moment. He remembered that tone, and the smile that went with it.

"George—" he started.

"No," George said. "These were my best pair of Millington-Cranz split-lizard, custom-dyed . . . how petty of them. Truly, truly petty."

"George, you aren't—"

"I have some sense," George said. Ronnie doubted it, in that tone of voice. "Priorities, Ronnie. Great minds always keep their priorities straight. First things first, and all that."

"Yes?" Ronnie hoped to encourage that trend, providing they could agree on the priorities.

"Raffa first; as a gentleman, I fully agree that her safety must come first."

"Good. Then suppose we clean up, and—"

"Just how do you suggest we clean up?" George's expression suggested that Ronnie had just lost his senses. "Are you planning to go down that hall, and into those showers, assuming that ordinary decency prevails and you will come back clean and all at peace with the world? While nothing happens to your belongings here?"

"Well . . ." Ronnie had thought, in the brief intervals available while struggling with three very strong men, with the blanket and tape, with the locked door, that a nice hot shower would be next on his list. Followed by clean clothes. Followed by Raffa. He realized now that George had a point—someone, if not the same men, might be lurking in the halls, or in the showers. The clothes on the floor weren't clean anymore. "I guess I thought we could be ready—"

"No." George shook out a cream silk shirt, sniffed it, and

shuddered. "No, we'll simply have to wear these things, producing an olfactory melange that should certainly confuse any stingtails we meet, and hope that Raffa doesn't pretend she never saw us before."

Glumly, Ronnie agreed. He found a green knit shirt slightly less fragrant than the rest, poured the odoriferous slimy goo out of his own brown shoes, and watched as George put the gritty stained towels to use wiping out his.

"I think," George said, holding one up for inspection, "that it may be salvageable. Good shoes are tougher than they thought. Here—" He tossed the remaining dry towel to Ronnie.

On their way out, the desk clerk said, "Have fun, boys," without looking up. George waited until he was outside to mutter.

"Schoolboys. That's what it is, really. They didn't steal anything; they didn't take our money or papers. Taking revenge on good clothes just because we have them . . . like those ticks in the fourth-floor end dormitory—"

Ronnie was seized with an unnatural desire to be fair. "We did put cake batter in their things first, George."

"Not in their *good* things. In their sports clothes. I have never in my life desecrated a pair of Millington-Cranz shoes, and I cannot imagine sinking so low." He stalked on, in silence, through the hot dusk that ended a Patchcock day. Ronnie, aware of an unpleasant dampness between his toes, followed him gingerly.

The hotel's doorman looked them up and down, sniffing ostentatiously. George stared straight ahead; Ronnie gave Raffa's name and smiled. The doorman pointed to the public comunit in the upper lobby.

"What a hole," George said, as they made their way around the open shaft.

"Yes . . . just a moment." Ronnie called the desk, who transferred his call to Raffa's room. It bleeped repeatedly, and just when he was sure she had been kidnapped by vicious thugs who would stake her out over a stingtail nest, the receiver clicked.

"Hello?"

"Raffa! It's Ronnie!"

"Oh—I was in the shower." His mind drifted into a

fantasy of Raffa in the shower—of himself in the shower—
of both of them—until recalled by her impatient "Ronnie!"

"Yes, sorry. We had a few problems, and I was
wondering—could we come down?"

"Here?" She sounded almost as prim as her mother. "I
mean—why? We weren't going to be seen together—"

"It's too late, Raffa." He took a deep breath and told her
about Hubert, and the men at the transient barracks, as fast
as he could. "And we need to use a shower, and get some
clean clothes. . . ."

"I suppose," she said. "Or—wait—I'll come up. If you're
that raggedy, they might not let you come down."

He and George leaned their elbows on the railing of the
open shaft, watching the waterfall and ignoring the disapproving glare of the doorman that periodically scorched their
backs. Raffa was safe. That's what mattered.

Raffa emerged from the lift looking clean, cool, and
confident. She handed them each a plastic strip. "Here. You
can't go back there—not to stay, anyway—so I went ahead
and got rooms for you here. I'd be delighted to have you
in mine, but there's not enough space. I've got things spread
all over."

"Angelic Raffaele," George said. "Are you sure it's Ronnie
you want to marry?"

"Absolutely," said Raffa. She gave Ronnie a look. "Don't
worry. I don't mind about the smell."

She led them to the lift, smiling brilliantly at the doorman, whose dour expression finally shifted. He shrugged,
hands out, and gave the boys a friendly nod. "My mistake,
sirs."

"You're on ten," Raffa said. "Adjoining singles—I thought
you might prefer that, in case—" In case of what, she didn't
say. It meant two showers, anyway. And, in this hotel,
modern clothes-freshers. By the time Ronnie had showered,
his clothes held no trace of the flowery perfume. His shoes
still reeked faintly, but at least they were completely dry.

Dinner, in the hotel's dining room, completed his cure,
he thought. Raffa in the cherry-colored backless dress with
the full sleeves, the waterfall cascading behind her . . . good
food . . . he could live with that. He was not sure he could
live with George, who was giving his own version of their
day. Finally even Raffa had had enough.

"All right, George. I understand—you had a horrible day and found out nothing useful except that there's a retired neurosynthetic chemist who wants to meet us. Let me tell you about mine." She described a tour of a pharmaceutical plant, a vast production line where gleaming robots ground and mixed chemicals, where the resulting paste, forced into molds, popped out as pills, to be coated with colored liquid that dried hard and shiny. Thence through pill counters, into boxes, past inspectors . . . boring, Ronnie thought. It made his feet ache to think of it.

"But the funniest thing—when I said Aunt Marta was interested in investing here because someone had died in the Morreline family, he turned absolutely white."

"Who?" Ronnie asked.

"My guide. And hustled me back to the corporate offices. You'd think I'd just insulted the CEO or something. I just made it up, really; someone's always dying in big families."

"Ottala!" George said. "It's Ottala who died." The shock hit Ronnie with the same unpleasant thump of reality as the bullies' fists. That made sense of a lot of things.

The disadvantage of a good hotel is that there is no way for guests to sneak out unobserved. Someone is always on duty by the public exits. And Twoville offered no nightlife of the sort to attract three wealthy young tourists . . . not after that afternoon. Raffa had suggested a walk along the shore, but Ronnie explained about stingtails and tickflies. They ended up in Raffa's suite by default; she had a sitting room.

"But if Ottala was killed here—if she was in one of the factories—"

"We're not here to solve Ottala's murder," George said. He paced around the room, peering at everything, before settling into a chair. "Dear heavens, what an ugly lamp! We're here to find out about the rejuvenation drugs—"

"Aren't you forgetting Ottala's Aunt Venezia?" Raffa asked. "She would want us to find out about Ottala's murder."

"Not if it included getting killed," George said, then added hastily, "and even if it did, I personally don't want to get killed finding out. I want to go back to civilization, which this isn't, and let Patchcock stew in its own mess." His shoes, unlike Ronnie's, had peeled in the automated shoe cleaner.

The only footwear in the hotel gift shop were sandals, iridescent lime-green straps over black soles.

"It can't all be the same villains," Raffa said. "The Morrelines making Ottala's aunt do those hideous pots so that she won't have time to interfere in the business is one thing. But they wouldn't have killed Ottala. Whoever killed Ottala had another reason."

"They hated her because she was rich," George said gloomily, staring at his ruined shoes.

"It had to be more than that," Raffa said. "We're all rich, and no one's killed us yet."

"Not for want of trying," George said. "Look at the past few years: we all got shot at on Sirialis. Someone shot Sarah, thinking she was Brun. Ronnie and I were kidnapped by the clones."

"That wasn't because we were rich," Ronnie said. "It was because we knew something someone didn't want us to know—they thought we were dangerous."

"So you think Ottala knew something she wasn't supposed to know? And if we can find out—" Raffa kicked off her shoes and curled her legs under her.

"What if she found out her family were making rejuvenation drugs illegally—would they kill her then?"

"What if she found out someone was adulterating the drugs—maybe not her family, maybe someone else?"

"But why?" Raffa bounced a little, on the couch. "What could anyone gain by adulterating rejuvenation drugs?"

Ronnie thought about it. "Well . . . if people don't like the whole process—if they think it's wrong—then they might do something to make it not work . . . or something." He had no idea how that might be done.

"If I were an ordinary person," George said, in the tone of one who knows he will never be ordinary, "I would resent rejuvenation. There are all these rich people, who are going to live forever, and then there's me—the ordinary person making pills, say—who's never going to get anywhere. It used to be that even rich people died, sometimes inconveniently, and fortunes shifted around—there were opportunities—but now—"

"Even rich people could resent it," Ronnie said. "Take my father . . . he's rejuved only once, but he will again, I'm sure. They want me to be grown up and responsible, but not enough to challenge him. I could be eighty or ninety myself before I have a chance to run a business. Even older."

"And we're always making snide remarks about free-birthers, but if people died off soon enough, there wouldn't be any worry about overpopulation. Not even on ships." George nodded, as if he'd said something profound, then his gaze sharpened. "Free-birthers!"

"What?"

"Logical group to oppose rejuvenation technology. Raffa, where's the work force from? Originally?"

"They're Finnvardians, mostly. Why?"

George sat up abruptly and reached for the comunit. "Let me check the database. I'll bet you they're free-birthers, and now they're having to make rejuvenation drugs, and—" His voice dropped as he scanned the reference files. "Drat. We need a better database."

"You need to mind your own business." That was the leader of four men in hotel livery, who appeared in the doorway to Raffa's bedroom. Another disadvantage of a good hotel is that anyone in the right uniform can go anywhere without being noticed. All were tall, pale-skinned, blue-eyed. "However, since you didn't, I'm afraid you're going to have an unfortunate accident." He had a weapon; Ronnie stared at the black bore of it with the sick certainty that he was going to die. George had paused with his hand poised over the comunit keypad; Raffa simply sat there, looking like Raffa.

"It won't work," George said. "Someone will investigate."

"A major industrial accident? Of course they will. But not your deaths individually. The failure of a field generator explains so much."

Now Raffa moved, a convulsive twitch and a frantic glance at the p-suit hanging from its hook behind the door. The leader laughed, pure glee at her fear. Ronnie wanted to smash his face.

"Not a chance, rich girl. You and your gallant lovers will all die together, just like in a storytape."

"You killed Ottala," Raffa said. Calmly, Ronnie noticed, as if she were commenting on someone's garden. You raise roses, don't you? You killed Ottala, didn't you?

"With great pleasure," the leader said. "Would you like to know how?" His voice promised horrors; he longed to tell them.

"Not really," Raffa said. "I'm sure it wasn't a failure of the field generator."

"I think you should know," the leader said, with a nasty whine in his voice. Ronnie prayed to unnamed gods for a miracle. Raffa should not have to die hearing horrors.

"*You're* not Finnvardian," George said suddenly. Everyone's attention shifted to him. He was looking at the comunit screen, and he read it aloud. " 'Finnvardians, dolicephalic, males generally between 1.8 and 2 meters in height, skin color index M1X1, eye color index blue/gray. Religious objections to contraception, plastic surgery for other than reconstruction after trauma'—but *you've* had plastic surgery, and you're wearing contact lenses." Now that George had said it, Ronnie could see that the leader's eyes were a different blue, darker, intense.

"Nonsense," the leader said. But two of his followers looked at him with obvious suspicion. "Not all of any human stock have blue eyes; they're recessive."

"The reference says, 'Alone of human stocks, the severely inbred Finnvardians have eliminated dark eyes; the light blue or gray eye color has been stable for seventy generations, with the usual medical sequelae. Finnvardians therefore prefer to work and live underground, away from ultraviolet radiation that hastens blindness.' Your eyes are dark," George pointed out. "Your colored lenses make them dark blue, not Finnvardian blue. Furthermore, a Finnvardian should know that all Finnvardians have light blue eyes."

"Is this true, Sikar?" asked one of the others. "You are one of us, aren't you?" All three were looking at him now, light blue eyes narrowed, lips tight. The leader's forehead gleamed in the light.

"Of course I'm one of you," he said. "Who else can speak your obscure language—?" He stopped short, and flushed.

There was a short, uncomfortable silence. Ronnie wondered which deity he now owed for that miracle. If it was a miracle.

"*Your* language," said the man to the leader's right, thoughtfully. He glanced around the leader to one of the others. "Sounds good to me," he said. The man on the left nodded, his hand slipping into a pocket of his uniform.

"No!" the leader said. "Take care of them first—then we'll talk—"

"Talk is talk," the man on his right said. And then he said something Ronnie couldn't understand, Finnvardian apparently, and flung himself on the leader, who shot him. The shot didn't make much noise, but the man yelled. Raffa rolled over the back of the couch, out of sight of the struggle. Another shot rang out. The struggling figures staggered across the room, screaming incomprehensible insults. Ronnie dodged the row, found Raffa behind the couch, and began to crawl cautiously toward the outer door. Maybe they would forget—

"Stop!" yelled someone. He stopped. Someone—perhaps *that* someone—had a weapon.

"No you don't," George said from the other side of the room; Ronnie looked up just in time to see the entire comunit, screen and all, hurtling toward the man with the gun, who shot it. A tremendous crash followed, spraying the whole room with broken glass and plastic. Water gushed from the ceiling, where something had hit a sprinkler control. Ronnie leapt up just in time to catch a blow to his head, but he was already in motion, and his head connected with someone's stomach. That person grunted, and slid down; Ronnie stepped firmly where it would do the most good, ignoring the shriek of pain, and fended off another man's assault with a bit of unarmed combat he'd learned in the Royals. George, he saw, was doing his best to bludgeon one of the attackers with the desk the comunit had been on.

Raffa took care of the last one, with the lamp off the end table. "I didn't think a little more mess would matter," she said. "And it *was* an ugly lamp." And then she was in Ronnie's arms, sobbing a little. He picked her up and carried her into the hall before she could cut her bare feet on the broken glass.

In the distance, he could hear alarms clanging and angry voices. George limped out into the hall, water dripping from his hair.

"He really isn't a Finnvardian," George said. "I have his lenses—look." There on his palm were two contact lenses, bright blue.

"Is he dead?" asked Ronnie. "What about the weapon?"

"He's dead," said George. "One of the others stabbed him. I think it was a ceremonial Finnvardian gelding knife. His weapon's right here—" He pulled it from his trousers pocket.

"Hold it right there!" From the end of the hall, two men in uniform pointed guns at them. "Drop that weapon! Get on the floor! Move!"

"But—but *they* did it," George said.

"DROP THAT GUN! NOW!" George dropped the gun, shrugging at Ronnie. "GET ON THE FLOOR. FACEDOWN. NOW."

"You don't understand," Ronnie said. "There are . . . spies or something in our room—in Raffa's room. They attacked us. They did something to the field generator, and—"

"GET DOWN NOW!"

Raffa slipped out of his arms. "We might as well," she said. "They aren't going to listen until we do."

In the event, they didn't listen at all. Two dead men, in hotel uniforms, and two unconscious men in hotel uniforms . . . and the guests involved were rich young tourists from the inner worlds?

"How much did you offer them to have sex with you?" the policeman said, leaning over Ronnie.

CHAPTER TWENTY-ONE

Patchcock Station

"Cecelia—so glad to see you!" The tall dark woman in swirling reds and purples reminded Heris of someone—she couldn't think who.

"Marta! It's been years!" Cecelia turned to Heris. "Raffaele's aunt . . . Marta Saenz. So—they called you, too?"

"Not exactly." Marta made a face. "Raffa sent me a message saying she was going to Patchcock with Ronnie and George, to follow up a mission for Bunny. I landed on Bunny, because as far as I'm concerned he had no business risking Raffa on any harebrained missions—and frankly, my dear, he was already scared out of his wits, because of Ottala— you did know about Ottala?"

"Yes."

"And so I said I'd come here, but I wanted help, and he said he'd get your Captain Serrano—whom I presume is you?" She turned to Heris.

"Yes," said Heris, not quite sure how to address Raffa's Aunt Marta. She was clearly someone of importance, if she could pressure Lord Thornbuckle to ask favors of her aunt admiral, but did she use a title?

"I just got off the commercial flight a few hours ago, and saw that your yacht was listed as incoming, so I waited— I haven't tried to call yet. I thought I'd see what Captain Serrano advised." Her glance at Heris combined deference and command.

"No harm in calling, I wouldn't think," Heris said carefully. Two aunts! Three, if you counted aunt admiral. She felt outnumbered and very much outgunned.

"I'll do it," Marta said. They followed her to a row of combooths, and waited while she made her call. Heris wondered again if she should have brought along some of her crew, and reminded herself again that she and Cecelia had booked the last two seats on the next down shuttle. When Marta opened the door of the booth, her face had a dangerous expression that erased all musings from Heris's mind.

"You won't believe this," she began. "They're under arrest."

"What?"

"For murder and attempted sexual assault."

"Ronnie? George? Raffa?"

"According to the hotel security chief, they tried to get four hotel employees to engage in—and I quote—'unnatural and lascivious acts against their will.' Then tried to beat them into submission, and then shot two of them. George, apparently, had the gun."

"George is Kevil Mahoney's son," Cecelia said. "If he *had* shot someone, he wouldn't be caught holding the weapon."

"We'll see about this," Marta said grimly. "They're not holding my niece—"

"Or my nephew—"

"Or George," said Heris, purely for symmetry. If George had had an aunt, she would have said it.

The waiting lounge for the down shuttle was decorated with the ugliest ceramics Heris had ever seen. It filled slowly, though it didn't seem to hold a full shuttle load. Perhaps they had small shuttles here, or perhaps there was a heavy cargo load. Cecelia and Marta paced back and forth; Heris sat and watched them. The time for scheduled departure came and went. People began to grumble. Grumbles mounted as time passed.

"We always have to wait if *they're* coming," she heard. "It's got to be family—it's always family."

Heris kept an eye out along the corridor, and soon spotted the likeliest candidate, a short, bunchy, gray-haired woman swathed in layers of uneven soft colors. Behind her, a harried-looking man trundled a dolly loaded with boxes and soft luggage. Sure enough, when she entered the lounge, the signal light came on for boarding. Heris picked up her own duffel, and caught Cecelia's eye.

But Cecelia and Marta were staring at the newcomer. They pounced before she could move past the others, in the lane cleared for her by flight attendants.

"Venezia!"

She turned, her wrinkled face lighting up. "Cecelia! Marta! How lovely to see you—I didn't know you were coming."

"Why did you—"

"Your idiot police—" Their voices had collided; they both stopped, and into the brief silence Heris spoke.

"Let's get aboard first." She grabbed Cecelia's elbow and pushed. Cecelia snorted, but let herself be guided into the clear lane behind Venezia; Marta closed in behind Heris.

The shuttle was full only because Venezia had reserved an entire section. Cecelia and Marta followed her into it as by right, settling into the wide padded seats; Heris noticed that the attendants didn't challenge them. She wished she could call the yacht and slip a couple of her crew into the seats she and Cecelia would have used, but she could not delay the shuttle now.

The shuttle had not cleared the station before Cecelia attacked again. "Venezia, my nephew is down there on your planet being accused of murder that he didn't do—"

"And my niece," Marta said. "Locked up in your filthy police station—"

"What do you know about this?" demanded Cecelia.

"Yes, what?" Marta glared.

Venezia shivered, as if she were a leaf dancing in stormwinds. "I—I don't know anything. I just got here from Guerni. When I asked Raffa to come here and investigate, I had no idea—"

"*You* asked her!" Venezia flinched from that tone as if Marta had hit her.

"I just—it seemed—nobody would tell me anything about Ottala, and I thought maybe she'd done something foolish, like a girl might do, and Raffa being young, maybe she'd figure it out—"

"You sent her into danger—my niece—!"

"And my nephew," Cecelia said, with no less heat.

"I didn't know it was dangerous," Venezia pleaded. "I thought—I thought Ottala had just run away. Perhaps fallen in love with an unsuitable young man, the way Raffaele did—"

"Ronnie," said Cecelia stiffly, "is not unsuitable."

"Raffa," said Marta, "did not run away."

"And I still want to know what happened to Ottala," Venezia said. Silence fell; Marta and Cecelia looked at each other, then at Heris, then at Venezia. "You know, don't you?" she asked.

"Not for sure," Heris said. "But—what is known is that she infiltrated a workers' organization, after having skinsculpting to match her appearance to the Finnvardian workers on Patchcock. Then she disappeared. If she were discovered—"

"Then she's dead." Venezia's chin quivered.

"And the same people could have killed Raffa," Marta said. "And the others."

"Only now they're in jail," Cecelia said, "for crimes they certainly did not commit. And it wouldn't have happened if it hadn't been for you."

The rest of the trip to the surface passed in very uncomfortable silence.

"I want to see my nephew," Cecelia said.

"I want to see my niece," Marta said.

"I want to see whoever's in charge," Venezia said. Heris said nothing. The three older women had charged off the shuttle like a commando team, every action coordinated for maximum efficiency. Venezia made the three necessary calls—to the police, the hotel, and the local corporate headquarters. Marta arranged ground transportation. Cecelia gathered everyone's luggage and dealt with local customs. Heris wondered how they'd worked that out when they hadn't said a word after that first confrontation. She was supposed to be the military expert, but she felt like a young ensign on a first live-fire maneuver.

The groundcar driver, after a look at Venezia's ID, had driven as if they not only owned the road but had proprietary rights to a sizable volume of space above and on either side of it. The three older women stared at each other in grim silence; Heris, after looking out the window to see two battered trucks diving for the nearest ditch, looked at the back of the driver's neck.

When they arrived in the scruffy little town, and pulled

up at the police station, Venezia led the group inside. Now they were lined up in front of a long gray desk.

The uniformed officer behind the desk blinked. The mirage didn't go away. Three angry women—three *old* angry women, the young-looking one wore a Rejuvenant ring—loomed over him like harpies on a cliff. Behind them was a younger but no less formidable woman, who had the unmistakable carriage of a military officer.

"And your name, ma'am?" the man said, trying to stick to ordinary rules.

"I am Lady Cecelia de Marktos, and my nephew is Ronald Vortigern Carruthers." She leaned over as he reached for one of the pencils in a particularly gruesome pottery jar that leaned drunkenly to one side. As he began to write out the names laboriously in longhand, she growled, "Use your computer, idiot, and hurry up."

"What's the problem out here?" That was the captain, languid and unshaven after a night of interrogating the most infuriating prisoners he'd seen in years. "Let's not have any rowdy behavior, ladies, please." Then he blinked at Venezia. "Uh—sorry, Madame Glendower-Morreline—we weren't expecting you."

"You should have been," Venezia said. "I sent a message from the orbital station, and the shuttle port."

"It's here somewhere, sir," the first policeman said, waving his hand at a desk littered with scraps of paper. "The computer's down again."

The captain muttered a curse, in deference to ladies, and then scowled at them. "Your relatives murdered two hotel employees, and beat up two others. They discharged firearms in a public hostelry; they destroyed hotel property; they falsified records—"

"They did not!" Cecelia said.

"And they're being held without bail, pending charges, which will be filed as soon as we have all the data."

"I found madam's message, sir," the desk officer said.

"Forget that. She's here now." The captain wavered, aware of his disheveled appearance and the weight of wealth before him. "Look—as a special favor, I'll let you speak to your relatives—one at a time, in the interview room, with an officer present. But that's all." A disgruntled silence fell. Finally Cecelia and Marta nodded.

* * *

"I didn't do it, Aunt Cecelia. None of us did." Ronnie looked exhausted, but not guilty. Cecelia had seen him guilty.

"I know, dear, but what did happen?"

"I told them—"

"Yes, but they haven't let us see the transcripts yet. I need to know."

Ronnie went over it again. "And I'm sure they weren't really hotel employees—the uniforms didn't really fit—but the important thing is the leader wasn't Finnvardian, and George proved it, and the others jumped him."

"Who has the contact lenses?"

"The police, I suppose. George had them, but they took them away from him."

"They've got it all wrong, Aunt Marta." Raffa's hair hung in lank strings, and the cherry-colored dress had been torn somewhere along the line. "Ronnie and George didn't do it." She gave Marta her view of things. "And if you could possibly bring me some clothes—"

"I'm going to bring you a way out of here," Marta said, "or rip this place up by its foundations."

Raffa turned even paler. "I forgot! They said something about sabotaging the field generator, the one that holds back the sea—"

"I'll tell them. Don't worry, Raffa."

But the captain shrugged off her mention of the field generator. "It's a red herring," he said. "No amateur could sabotage a field generator." Marta glared at him, recognized invincible ignorance, and made a strategic withdrawal to the hotel.

Their descent on the hotel was almost as startling as their descent on the police station. The doorman . . . the hotel manager . . . the concierge . . . all bowed and scraped and fawned and disclaimed all intent to cause trouble for them or any member of their illustrious families. Only . . . there was this matter of shots being fired, and bodies on the floor. . . .

"Were they your employees?" Cecelia asked, when the gush of apologies and explanations ended.

"The dead men? Well, no. They were in our uniform, so

at first we thought, of course, that they were, but they weren't. Perhaps they wore the uniforms to provide some . . . er . . . excitement. The police said—"

"My niece," Marta said with icy emphasis, "does not get sexual kicks from playing with men in hotel uniforms."

"No—of course not, madam." The manager attempted, unsuccessfully, to find an expression which made it clear that he had not thought any such thing.

"Nor does my nephew," Cecelia said. "He is, after all, engaged to her niece."

"Yes, madam. Of course, madam."

"And since they weren't your employees, isn't it possible that they wore those uniforms to gain access to Raffa's rooms without being detected—that they did in fact initiate the attack?"

"I suppose so, madam." This with a dubious look, and an exchange of glances from manager to concierge and back. "But that is a matter for the police to decide. And there is still the damage to hotel property. Valuable communications equipment—lamp—sprinkler system—"

"Insurance," said Cecelia and Marta together.

"Never mind that," Venezia said. "*We* own the hotel." She had been glaring at the masks on the walls and the vases holding floral displays, muttering something about "execrable decorations" since she arrived; Heris wondered why she cared so much about bad pottery, but perhaps she felt responsible for all the details of a family property. She fixed the manager with a steely eye. "It will not be a billing item."

"No, madam."

"Excuse me, ladies." Heris looked around and saw an elderly man who held his hat in his hand. Bright blue eyes peered out from under bushy white eyebrows; his white moustache had been waxed to perfect points. He wore a fresh pink rosebud in the lapel of his gray suit, and his shiny black shoes were covered with white—spats, she finally remembered, was the right word for them. Cecelia, Marta, and Venezia were momentarily speechless.

"I understand the young people have had a spot of trouble. I tried to warn them yesterday—the young men, I mean."

"You talked to Ronnie and George?" Cecelia asked.

"Yes—I'm Hubert de Vries Michaelson, by the way, and from his description you must be his Aunt Cecelia."

"Yes—"

"I'm retired—formerly a neurosynthetic chemist here. Never quite made enough to retire offworld—"

"Can you recommend an attorney, Mr. Michaelson?" Cecelia asked.

"No . . . but I can help you, if you'll let me. I believe I have evidence that may convince the police someone else is involved."

"What concerns me most is this field generator Raffa mentioned," Marta said. "Apparently one of the men said something about arranging a failure. The police wouldn't listen—"

The hotel manager broke in. "They said *what*? About the field generator?"

"Raffa said one of the men claimed it would fail—that their deaths would be blamed on its failure."

"It would destroy this entire structure," the hotel manager said. "And most of Twoville within days or weeks, as the seawater infiltrated." He looked frightened enough. "Should I evacuate now, or—?"

"Of course with one of them dead, and the others injured, maybe there's no danger," Cecelia said. Heris looked at her and wondered if she should get into this discussion. If they were talking about a Tiegman field generator, "danger" was too mild a word for the risk of collapse. Had the threat been serious, or just an attempt to panic the youngsters?

"I think someone had better interview the survivors—I presume they're under medical care?" Marta looked around as if expecting them to be rolled out in their beds, for inspection.

"They're at the clinic," the hotel manager said.

But the survivors had disappeared from the local clinic, to the annoyance of the nursing staff. Their annoyance paled beside that of the aunts, who had walked from the hotel to the clinic at a pace that made Heris breathless.

"They *what*?" demanded the aunts, almost in concert.

"Have you notified the police?" Hubert asked. He had joined their parade, where he formed a decorative accent.

"No. They weren't charged with anything—" That was the nursing supervisor, who had begun with a complaint about the missing patients, as if that were Venezia's fault.

"They will be," Cecelia and Marta said together. "Call the police *now*." The nursing supervisor looked stubborn a moment, but then reached for the com.

"The field generator," Heris said, bringing up the topic which had not left her mind. "If they're loose, and well enough, they could still sabotage it. Who's in charge of the Tiegman maintenance? Where's the power supply?" She wished she had her Fleet uniform, her Fleet authority, and most of all her own expert people who would know how to recognize a problem if they saw it. The thought of someone playing games with a Tiegman field made her feel queasy. She knew a way to knock out a Tiegman field generator with only a few kilograms of explosive, placed accurately for the field configuration. Granted that the calculations were difficult for anything but a spherical field, they were still at the mercy of the saboteur's incompetence. She wasn't at all sure Cecelia and the other older women understood how bad it could be if the field blew.

"Ah—there I can help you out," Hubert said. "I've played cards with the Chief Engineer out at the control station every week for years." He beamed at Heris, and she wanted to smack him. He was no substitute for Petris or Oblo. "If you'll excuse me, ladies," Hubert said. "I think a word with the Chief Engineer is necessary at this point. Perhaps he can be persuaded to take precautions—at least be ready to divert all power to the field—"

"Go ahead," said Venezia, dismissing him with a wave. "Take care of it. We're going back to the police." She marched out. Heris wondered if she ought to go with the dapper little man—how reliable could someone in spats be?— but Cecelia beckoned to her.

"I know it's dangerous," Cecelia murmured to Heris. "I saw your expression. But we can't do anything about it, and if this field-whatever doesn't kill us, Venezia can do something about the worse problem which made this threat possible." That made sense, though Heris wasn't happy to be left out of the action.

By the time they made it back to the police station, both the hotel manager and the clinic had reported. In addition, a perspiring manager from the local corporate headquarters, bearing a bunch of flowers for Venezia. They began a low-voiced conversation while the others approached the front desk. The captain, still bleary-eyed but now depilated and in a clean shirt, glowered at them. "You're complicating a very simple case," he said. "I understand family feeling, but even the best families have bad apples—"

Heris could have told him this was the wrong approach.

"It *would* be a simple case, if you would listen to your prisoners," Marta said.

"When my niece Ottala disappeared," Venezia put in, looking away from the manager, "you found nothing."

"There was nothing to find; there was no evidence." Heris doubted that he had ever looked for any; the rapidity with which the young people had run into trouble argued for a superfluity of evidence somewhere nearby.

"I asked that girl Raffa to come here, to find out what happened to Ottala. I thought a girl could find a girl better than some man. And she did find out what happened, and it nearly happened to her, and now you're ignoring it." Venezia, who had seemed the most insignificant of the older ladies, now had the intensity Heris associated with weapons-grade lasers. Quite unlike the incandescent flash that was Cecelia's anger, Venezia's steady rancor seemed ready to cut its way through any obstacle.

"Just because someone is not Finnvardian, and not really a hotel employee, does not make them a spy or a murderer. Wearing contact lenses is not a crime—"

Stupid captain, Heris thought. He should back down now, before she cleaves him along a flaw he doesn't recognize.

"Ah, so you *now* agree that one of the men was not Finnvardian," Marta said, taking over from Venezia. Heris had to admire the tactic, and the way in which they passed the turn without any prior planning. "Do you know what he was?" The captain looked down. "Well?"

"He appears to have been a citizen of the Benignity of the Compassionate Hand," the captain said, with understandable reluctance.

"A Benignity agent? Here?"

"I have no evidence that he was an *agent*. Merely a citizen—"

"A registered alien?"

"Well . . . no. He had been working in the factory for about three years—"

"Illegally," Heris murmured; heads turned to look at her

and she smiled. "I would consider that a Benignity citizen in disguise, not registered as an alien, and working in a critical industry for three years, was almost certainly an agent."

"Everyone thought he was Finnvardian," the captain muttered.

"Apparently," Heris said.

"But he was murdered," the captain said.

"By Finnvardians who discovered that he wasn't. Who thought, perhaps, he was leading them astray."

"George Mahoney had a gun in his hand—"

"And did that man die of gunshot wounds?"

"Well . . . no. He was stabbed. But there's no evidence that the other individuals under arrest could not have stabbed him."

"And I might have sung grand opera while hanging upside down in zero G," Heris said, to no one in particular. "But I didn't, despite the lack of evidence exonerating me."

"What about the ones who ran away from the clinic," Cecelia said. "Doesn't that convince you they're guilty?"

"Of pretending to be hotel employees, yes. But that's hardly a major crime."

"And the field generator?" Marta brought that up; Heris had been about to ask.

"Hasn't failed yet. Won't fail. Can't fail. It's—" The lights dimmed, flared again, and went out. In the darkness, Heris heard curses and cries, and between them the utter silence that meant no ventilation fans were turning, no compressors working, nothing electrical functioning at all. After too long a wait, dim orange emergency lights came on, and the reflective arrows painted on the floor to indicate the way out glowed against the dimness.

"Possible," Heris said.

"It's not—it's something else—" But the captain was clearly shaken. Sirens began to hoot outside. The company manager stammered apologies, shook himself loose from Venezia, and bolted for the door.

"Let's go," Heris said to Cecelia.

"I'm not leaving without Ronnie," Cecelia said. "No matter what."

"Sir, we've got to evacuate the lower levels—" That was someone from the back; Heris couldn't see the face.

"Very well," the captain said. "Go on now—we'll be

bringing them all outside, just be patient." But Cecelia and Marta and Venezia—and Heris—stood their ground until the prisoners came up, until they were sure that Raffa and Ronnie and George were safely above ground.

Outside, in the hot afternoon, the streets were full of sullen frightened people, more and more of them pouring out the entrances to all the buildings. Heris noticed a lot of pale, light-eyed Finnvardians. The police, after a despairing look at the aunts, gave up any pretense of guarding their young prisoners, and began moderately effective crowd-control efforts. At least they kept people moving away from the shore, away from the police station and hotel. Ronnie and George leaned against the wall, and Raffa leaned against Ronnie; the aunts pursed their lips but said nothing.

"Are all the factories underground?" Heris asked Venezia.

"I suppose," Venezia said. "I know some of them are. I never really—that is, my brothers were in charge, you see, after Papa died. They never wanted to talk to me about business. And of course if you *do* have underground facilities, Finnvardians are an efficient work force."

"I hope that nice little man in the suit didn't get hurt," Cecelia said.

"I hope that nice little man in the suit wasn't a mad bomber," muttered Heris. The rosebud and spats had done nothing to reassure her. The main field hadn't blown, or they'd all be dead, but something had gone very wrong. A misplaced charge could cause sudden loss of power, then field fluctuation and restabilization in another configuration. She could easily imagine Michaelson in the role of inept saboteur or not-quite-rescuer.

Suddenly the floor trembled. Heris eyed the nearby wall. "Out in the street," she said. "Now!" They all scuttled into the middle of the street, as the shaking worsened and bits of plaster fell off the walls. Luckily, Heris thought, these were all one-story buildings. Then a bouncing lurch sent them all to their knees, and the trembling died away, a fading rumble in the distance.

"Field's back on," Heris said as she clambered up, dusting herself off.

"Why did it shake?" asked Cecelia, pale but determined to be calm.

"Reconfiguration," Heris said. "My guess would be that

the saboteur miscalculated the placement of the charge. With power, the field's inertia would damp the fluctuations—that's why the lights went out; the field bled power off the supply net—but it didn't find enough power to regain its former geometry. So it collapsed toward a sphere. What that means to the structures, we won't know until we look."

"Is it—safe now?" asked Marta.

"If someone doesn't tweak it again. We're lucky. If it had blown completely, we wouldn't be here to worry about it."

"I don't want to be here at all," Raffa said shakily.

"We'll go home soon," Marta said.

"No. I don't want to go home. I want to go with Ronnie."

Marta's brows went up, but whatever she might have said was interrupted by a blast from loudspeakers as electrical power returned.

"—Disperse! Go to your quarters! Danger is over; the Tiegman field has been restored. Shift Two, report to your supervisors in Level One. All Shift Two, report—"

"Let's see about the hotel," Cecelia said. "If it's not full of water, maybe we can get something cool to drink."

No one interfered as they made their way back to the hotel entrance. Heris noticed that the local manager trailed along behind, the now-disheveled bouquet still in hand. Venezia ignored him. The doorman, shaken but willing, opened the door. Inside, the lights were on, and the waterfall still plunged over the lip of the central well. The hotel manager scurried to meet them. "Ladies— gentlemen—I'm sorry but our facilities are not back to full operation yet—"

"I want to sit down," Cecelia said firmly. "On something soft. In a cool, shady place. With something to drink—and I really don't care what, as long as it's cool and wet."

"The same," Marta said.

The hovering manager tried again to present his bouquet to Venezia, and she turned on him. "I will be in your office in one hour," she said. "And I will then expect a complete disclosure of your role in this fiasco."

Heris wondered which fiasco Venezia meant. From the look on the manager's face, he might have had more than one to conceal. Venezia finished her first tall glass, called for another, and then spoke to them all.

"You don't have to come with me—I expect it will be a long, tedious afternoon—"

"I wouldn't miss it," Marta said. "If you'll allow a rival into your files, that is—"

"Where I'm thinking of, that's no problem. Cecelia, will you join us, or would you rather babysit the youngsters?" Heris blinked. She still had trouble connecting the dumpy little woman she had first seen with this regal personage who seemed to know exactly what she was doing.

"Let Heris go," Cecelia said. "She can represent the government, if necessary. And it'll be good experience for her."

Great. Something Cecelia didn't want to do, and thought Heris would learn from. Tedious, Venezia had said. Files. Heris groaned inwardly; she could see it now. She was going to spend a hot, miserable afternoon cooped up in an office going through boring files that she knew nothing about.

In the event, Heris found the afternoon far from tedious. When they arrived at the corporate offices, Venezia brushed past the little receiving line the manager had put together, and stormed through the reception area so fast that Heris got only a glimpse of elegant charcoal-gray carpet and oyster-gray leather upholstery, a serene vision marred only by the unfortunate puce pottery statuette displayed on a stand.

The serenity of the front office vanished behind the first glass partition, where *kicked anthill* better fit the level and pattern of activity. Actual filing cabinets stuffed with papers, which scurrying minions shifted from drawer to drawer, with frantic looks when they recognized intruders. Other workers hunched over deskcomps, fingers flickering as they did something . . . Heris could not tell what, at the speed with which Venezia led them along. Where was she going? How did she know where to go? Behind her, the manager bleated occasional cautions, apologies, pleas, but Venezia ignored him. Marta followed Venezia, and Heris followed Marta, and the manager crowded Heris but lacked the force to push past her.

Along a hall, up a flight of stairs, along another hall. Clearly, this was executive territory, still carpeted, with offices opening off the passage and a larger one at the end. That would be the manager's office, Heris was sure; as they neared it, she could read the engraved nameplate.

The manager's office, when they arrived, had been cleared for Venezia, fresh flowers in a hot turquoise and green pot in the middle of the desk. Venezia snorted, and went straight to his assistant's office next door. There, piled in a heap on a side table, was everything that must have been on the manager's desk, including a family portrait. Here Venezia paused, and here the hapless manager caught up.

"Please, madam . . . my office is the best we have; it will suit you, I'm sure." He waved toward the door.

"Later," Venezia said. She prowled the room, eyeing the side table of files, cubes, loose papers. The manager's assistant broke out in a fine sheen, as if someone had sprayed him with oil. His gaze flickered back and forth between her and the screen of his deskcomp. He reached out a trembling hand.

"No!" Venezia said. She had not seemed to be watching the assistant, but her command stopped his hand in midair. "No—get up now, and go out."

"Out—?"

Venezia glared at him; he ducked his head and hunched aside, almost stumbling out of his chair. She moved into his chair herself.

"I'm going to assume that the enabling codes specified in the Morreline Codex are still active," Venezia said, without looking at the manager. Heris, watching him, saw a flush rise up his face, followed by pallor.

"Uh . . . yes, madam, but there are . . . other . . ."

"Give them to me." Heris had heard admirals in battle with less command presence. Stuttering, protesting, the manager finally gave Venezia the codes.

"But it will all be so confusing, madam," he said. "And I have prepared a precis—"

"Good," Venezia said. "If I become confused, I can look at it." She glanced at Marta. "You're the biochemist—what do you want to look at?"

"You're going to give me open access to your technical files?"

"I don't have time to worry about it," Venezia said. "It's an emergency; you're the only independent expert—tell you what, I'll hire you, put you on retainer, and then you'll have to give me a loyalty bond. What's your consultant rate?"

"You always were smarter than you looked," Marta said, and named a figure that Heris compared to a large fraction of her own yearly salary. "Contract accepted. I'll need comp access."

Venezia looked at the manager, who had faded to a depressing shade of gray. "In here, madam," he said softly, and Marta followed him into his own office.

Venezia glanced at Heris. "How are you with personnel files, Captain Serrano?"

Heris wondered what she meant. How was she with personnel files doing what? Her face must have been as blank as her mind, because Venezia sighed heavily. "Export/import ratios?" That made more sense, but Venezia shook her head. "No. Just be ready to keep the interruptions away, if you would." Heris felt silly, demoted from partner to door watch. She said nothing, looking around the room instead. An ordinary office room, large and cluttered. More actual paper than she'd seen in years, including bulky metal files to keep it in. Cube files as well, cube readers, wall display units, schedules with colored lines all over them.

Venezia, when she looked back at her, was hunched over the deskcomp, murmuring something Heris couldn't follow. Heris could just see the flicker of rapidly changing screens, lines of text and blocks of numbers scrolling past much faster than she would have cared to read. Did this old woman really know what she was doing? Cecelia was sharp enough—at least about horses, and her own investments— but Venezia had not yet impressed Heris with her intelligence. She had seemed far more scatterbrained than Cecelia or Marta; she had kept muttering about pottery. What *was* she reading so fast?

"Aha," Venezia said in the midst of this musing. "He's sharpened the blade for his own throat this time!"

"What?" asked Heris.

Venezia glanced up at her. "It's a mistake to assume that people with artistic hobbies can't think," she said. Heris blinked; this was exactly the sort of statement she would have expected from Venezia eight hours before. "Or won't notice," Venezia went on, stabbing at the controls. She had bright patches of color on her cheeks, and Heris realized she was in a considerable rage.

Was it better to say nothing, or show an interest? Heris had opted for saying nothing when Venezia spoke again. "My brothers," she said. "Did you have brothers, my dear?"

"Only one, and he died," Heris said. She had never really known him; she had been only five when he died, and he had been adult.

"Friends tell me they can be human," Venezia said. "But I always doubted it. My brothers—well, most of it doesn't matter now, except as background for not trusting them. But they've overreached themselves this time, and I'm not going to back down." She pushed back her chair and went to the door of the other office. "Marta— anything critical?"

Heris craned her neck to look. Raffa's aunt didn't glance up from the deskcomp she was using, but she answered. "Only if you want your product to meet contract specs. This is very strange, Venezia. Some of the problem is just your biochemists trying for a cheap way around a difficult synthesis, but some of it is . . . could almost be . . . deliberate sabotage. I'm not sure how these changes will function biologically."

"Product liability problems?"

"Unquestionably. You'll have to track the shipments to see how bad it is. And retainer or not, there's no way I can keep quiet about some of this."

"I don't want you to. We're going to have to close this facility down anyway, at least for some time."

"What will your brothers say? Can you convince them?"

The grin on Venezia's face reminded Heris of her aunt admiral on the trail of a feckless ship's captain. "I can do more than convince them, Marta. I can destroy them." Her grin widened. "I have the shares."

"I'm impressed," Marta said. "Then why did you let them get into this mess?"

"I was busy elsewhere." Venezia shifted from foot to foot. "I know that's no excuse, really. It's my money. My responsibility. I should have been keeping track of them, but Oscar . . . he's so difficult. It was easier to stay away. You're going to say I should have known."

"No need," Marta said, still not looking up. "You already know that. What can I do to help?"

"Be sure you bring along any evidence you'll need; I'll try to secure these files, but you can see how it is . . . these people will try to protect themselves."

Heris thought of something she could do. "If it would

help—" she began tentatively. Both the older women turned to look at her.

"Yes?"

"If they think I'm an official Fleet representative, perhaps that will make them think twice about destroying things. Or, if it would help, I've got a really good scan tech who could probably put military-grade encryptions on them. And someone who could watch the door while he does it."

"Perfect," Venezia said. "How long before you can get your people down here?"

"I don't know the shuttle schedule," Heris said. She refrained from telling Venezia that it was her presence on the other shuttle that had kept them aloft. "It shouldn't take long for the little equipment he'll need."

"There will be a shuttle," Venezia said. "I'll order one." Heris was only mildly surprised at the efficiency with which Venezia ordered a shuttle, arranged a secure comlink for Heris to the *Sweet Delight,* and arranged ground transportation for Heris's personnel when they landed. Some officers didn't look as formidable as they were; Venezia must be that sort. And Bunny, she remembered, had had that uncanny ability to change gears from foolish, horse-besotted idle rich, to the very effective Lord Thornbuckle. She wondered what it would feel like to do that. And was it something that came with money and power, or with age? Or all of the above? If age was part of it, the increasing number of Rejuvenants were going to affect society even more than she'd thought.

Marta and Venezia continued to unearth more problems, and discuss them—a discussion that went far beyond Heris's comprehension—until Koutsoudas, Oblo, and Meharry showed up. Heris explained what Venezia wanted.

"No problem, Captain," Oblo said. He looked around the offices. "Just how much trouble do we expect?"

"Not much, really. The damage is done; it's just a matter of protecting the evidence. And they know I represent Fleet. Unofficially, of course."

"Of course." Meharry grinned. She had brought some of the lethal weaponry Heris had bought on the first voyage, and the lightweight body armor under her shipsuit was obvious to the instructed eye. So was the military bearing of all three. Koutsoudas, busy at the computer terminal, had attached some of his pet boxes.

"I've secured the database," he said, in far less time than even Heris expected. "It'll snag and log any attempts to delete or alter anything, and lock the guilty terminal."

"And I'll just go around and put out a few scanners," Oblo said. He waggled the duffel he carried.

"Good," Heris said. The two older women looked pleased, and she let herself enjoy it. At least she didn't feel like a useless idiot next to them . . . although she was beginning to suspect they might not need even this help.

"I'm thinking of dinner," Venezia said, turning to lead the way back out of the building. "Did we ever have anything for lunch?"

All the way back to the hotel, Venezia and Marta discussed the culinary possibilities of the local cuisine, as if all they cared about was food.

CHAPTER TWENTY-TWO

They were all relaxing after a leisurely dinner, waiting for dessert to be served, when a deferential waiter brought Venezia a comunit and plugged it in for her. "A call, madam. From madam's brothers."

Venezia scowled. "Good. I have something to say to them."

But she didn't get the first word. Heris could hear the angry, "Venezia, you stupid cow, what are you trying to do!" from where she sat. Venezia did not click on the privacy screen. The angry male voice ranted on. "You're ruining us! It's all your fault!"

"No." Venezia grinned, an unpleasant grin full of teeth. "I am not the problem, Oscar. You are. I know about Ottala. I know about the drugs—"

"Venezia, no! Not on an open line!"

"I have called an emergency stockholders' meeting—" Heris wondered when she had had time to do that. "And you can either resign now or be thrown out."

"Venezia, you don't understand." Now the angry voice had turned conciliatory, pleading. "It's your artistic temperament; I understand that. Someone's upset you—"

"*You* have upset me." Venezia snorted. "Artistic temperament, my left little toe! Do you think I haven't seen what you did with those ceramics you said you appreciated so much? I even found one on the desk in the *police* station!" She cut off an apology. "Never mind. *I* haven't made a pot in years. I bought them wholesale in the Guerni Republic, just to keep you boys off my back so I could do what *I*

1024

wanted to do, and you never even noticed that I kept picking uglier and uglier ones, hoping you'd quit asking—" She ran out of breath, and panted a moment, her cheeks flushed.

"You just don't understand, Venezia . . . it was for your own good—"

"Ottala's death was not for my own good! She would never have been killed if you hadn't been involved in this mess with rejuvenation—if you hadn't ignored the workers' complaints—"

"Workers always complain!"

"You were forcing Finnvardians to manufacture rejuvenation drugs, and you tried to coerce them to use contraceptives," Venezia said. "Didn't you bother to find out anything about Finnvardians?"

"They're tough, hard workers, and they like living underground," her brother said.

"They're also fanatic about free birth and plastic surgery," Venezia said. "You remember when you wanted my investment in the expansion, I asked you then if you understood what a Finnvardian work force meant, and you said 'Never mind, Venezia, let us boys handle it.' I should have known better," she said bitterly. She looked as if she might cry.

Marta reached for the comunit, identified herself, and went on. "Lord Thornbuckle is personally interested in these matters," she said. "The supply of contaminated, adulterated, and illegal rejuvenation chemicals concerns the highest level of government. I think Venezia's right—resignation's your best option."

"But—but she's never managed any—"

"She has the shares, doesn't she? Besides, it's not a secret monopoly anymore. Your profit margin just collapsed. You'll be lucky if you're not held personally responsible for damages under the product liability laws."

Cecelia went next. "And if there's any evidence of pharmaceuticals from here getting into the hands of that conniving Minister's sister—Lorenza—you know whom I mean—then I personally will sue you for the damages she did me."

Heris decided to join the party. "And while Fleet chose not to act openly, in recognition of the difficulties remaining since the Patchcock Incursion, I should tell you that I have a brief from my admiral to report on the situation here and determine if it poses a threat to the security of the Familias."

"But—but you're just a lot of stupid old ladies!" Oscar blurted.

"Wrong, Oscar," Venezia said, calm again. She looked at each of her allies and winked. "We're a lot of rich, powerful, *smart* old ladies. And as you know, I've never had any rejuv procedure—so I can take the Ramhoff-Inikin and repeat it as often as I like." She paused, but Oscar said nothing, at least nothing Heris could hear. "I'll always be there, Oscar," Venezia went on. "Older, richer, stronger, smarter. Live with it." She cut the connection and grinned at the others. Marta and Cecelia nodded.

"To aunts," Heris said, raising her glass. "Including mine."

Hubert de Vries Michaelson reappeared, this time in a formal black dinner jacket, with one arm in a black silk sling, just as the waiter brought their desserts. Graciously, they invited him to join them, and he eased himself into a chair, careful of his arm.

As Heris expected, he was glad to explain his role. He had tried to warn management of the danger of manufacturing Rejuvenant drugs with Finnvardian workers, he said—and he had argued against the cost-cutting synthesis that sometimes degraded the product—but he'd been forcibly retired, with not enough money in his account to go offplanet. So he had worked alone, gathering evidence as he could.

"It's a wonder they didn't just kill you," Heris said. She thought the black silk sling was a bit overdone. He couldn't be badly hurt—if he was hurt at all—and he didn't need that kind of fancy dress anymore.

"They would have," Hubert admitted, "if I hadn't made such a ridiculous figure. That's why I dressed so formally all the time." His shoulders shifted, emphasizing the well-cut dinner jacket. Heris had to admit it suited him. He twinkled at them, and went on. "They couldn't believe anyone with creases and rosebuds and spats and so on would be a menace. They let me alone, mostly, though I couldn't get access to open communication." His smile widened to a cheerful grin. "I was *very* glad to see you ladies . . . I'm not getting any younger, you know, and I was afraid my evidence would be lost when I died."

"And of course they wouldn't let you have rejuvenation." Venezia looked angry, her plump cheeks flushed again.

He shook his head. "Of course not. Although with what I knew about the production shortcuts here, I'm not sure I'd have wanted it. Now the field generator—I just wish I'd been faster. The Chief Engineer didn't want to believe me, and I couldn't get him to go look—"

"But the field didn't collapse." Heris was not sure how far to pursue this. She still did not know—and wanted to know—if the charge had been improperly calculated, or if Michaelson really had saved them all. Did he even know?

"No." Hubert paused to sip from his glass. "We were lucky, I suspect. Anyway, after the Chief Engineer threw me out of his office, I hung around the control room—I know a lot of the workers there—and was ready to throw the switch diverting all power to the field generator when the explosion came."

"And your arm?" Heris asked. Someone had to.

"I tripped," Hubert said cheerfully. "I'm not as spry as I was, you know. Someone tried to pull me away from the controls; I fell over a chair, couldn't catch myself— and there it was. A simple fracture. A couple of hours in the regen tank, and all that's left is the soreness. They wanted to keep me overnight in the clinic, but I wanted to find you ladies—" Again that roguish twinkle.

"That's very gallant of you." Cecelia, Heris noticed, had a speculative look in her eyes. So did Marta and Venezia. They needed no help, she realized, in seeing Hubert for what he was: a minor player who wished very much to have a starring role on the strength of one decisive action.

"I was hoping we could celebrate together," he said, giving each of them a bright-blue-eyed smile.

"I think the company owes you a rejuvenation, Mr. Michaelson," Venezia said earnestly. "And I will have someone review your retirement folder; a senior scientist should certainly have had enough in his account to travel offplanet. Of course we are all grateful that you were able to do something about the field generator and prevent worse trouble. Unfortunately, while we certainly have cause for celebration, and I personally appreciate your help, we've all been traveling a long time, and would really rather go to bed."

"Oh." To his credit, his cheerful face did not lose its bright expression. "Well, in that case, I thank you for your interest, madam, and hope you have a very restful night." He bowed slightly and walked off, jaunty as ever. Heris found herself unexpectedly sympathetic, now that she was sure her gaggle of aunts was safe. He had been helpful, courteous, brave . . . she hoped he would find someone to celebrate with. With that twinkle, he probably would.

Morning brought more changes. A message had arrived from the police station that all charges against the young people had been dropped. Heris noticed pale bare patches on the wall where the ugliest pottery decorations had hung, and passed one hotel employee hastily tacking up a framed picture of flowers over another. The young people, with the resilience of youth, were attacking a huge breakfast in the hotel dining room when Heris got there; they waved her over.

"Wait till you hear," George said. "Ronnie and Raffa are going to elope."

"Not exactly elope," Raffa said. "But we are going to marry." Ronnie swallowed an entire muffin in one mouthful, and grinned at Heris.

"Aunt Cecelia has decided to drop her suit against my parents." He reached for another muffin. "She says if you are going back in Fleet, and can put up with your aunt the admiral, she can put up with Mother."

"And we're leaving this godforsaken hole," George said. He alone looked gloomy. "I suppose I have to go home—"

Cecelia chose that moment to arrive at the table. "We're *all* going home," she said. "Heris, we have to straighten out the yacht's title—"

"It's yours," Heris said. "It always was, and it still is—"

"Because I'm thinking of selling it." That stopped conversation for a moment as everyone stared at her.

Heris finally said, "Sell it? Why?"

"Because I don't really like living on it. Yes, it's nice to be able to travel when and where I want, but most of the time I want to be on a planet. With horses." She stared at the wall a moment, and turned to Heris. "And to tell you the truth, Heris Serrano, I don't want to travel on that yacht with any other captain but you—and I don't want you anyplace but where you belong. In Fleet." Heris could think of nothing to say. The moment lengthened uncomfortably, until George knocked over the sugar.

They were days from Patchcock, well on their way to Rockhouse Major, when Heris thought of an adequate answer. She looked across Cecelia's study and saw her employer frowning over a hardcopy of equine genetics studies.

"There's another way to travel freely, you know," she said.

"Hmm? Oh—don't worry about it."

"Seriously. You could use a smaller, faster hull than this. It wouldn't be as luxurious, but it would be too small to allow for many—even any—guests."

"I couldn't get stuck with Ronnie," Cecelia said, the beginnings of a grin quirking her mouth. "Although I have to admit that had good consequences as well as bad . . . and I realize I made some of Venezia's mistakes, letting myself be alienated from my family." So it was more than dropping the lawsuit. Cecelia was going home with more than her body healed, this time.

"Yes, but rescuing one nephew is enough," Heris said. She ticked off the other advantages on her fingers. "Faster—less time in transit—so you wouldn't miss the amenities. If you learned to pilot it yourself—"

"What!" Shock in the tone, but Cecelia's eyes sparkled.

"Would you rather ride or be driven?" Heris asked. "You're more than bright; you've gained enough time in your rejuvenation—as we now understand it—that the time taken to qualify for a civilian license would hardly dent what's left. I think you'd enjoy it; your psychological profile certainly fits." She watched as Cecelia's face ran its gamut from surprise to anticipation. "Your own ship under your own control—of course you'd need crew, a few, because it's not safe to solo at the distances you travel. But a small crew, and you yourself in charge—" That would be the real lure; Cecelia's lack of political ambition sprang from no contempt for power itself.

"How long would it take?" Cecelia asked. Ah. She would talk herself into it. Heris relaxed.

"Depends if you go full-time or part," Heris said. "Brun has all the current standards—she's planning to qualify too.

As you Rejuvenants are discovering, there are no limits to learning new skills."

Cecelia had a faint flush on her cheeks, more excitement than anything else, Heris thought.

"I can't seem to get used to it—the idea that we could keep living for centuries . . . forever—"

"Maybe you can't. Maybe there are limits. But you will certainly have time to learn to pilot your own craft, if you want."

"I'd like that," Cecelia said. "I really would. And you?"

"Me? I go back in Fleet, of course—and, while you've been very courteous in not asking, that includes my former crew. Petris as well. We have . . . an understanding."

"Good," Cecelia said. "I'd hate to have you lose what you gained, there. And your family?"

That brought a knot to her stomach. "My family . . . well. My aunt the admiral said we'd talk. I'll do what I have to."

"It will be better than that," Cecelia said. She looked as if she wanted to say more, but Heris was in no mood to listen to auntly platitudes from someone who had taken her own family to court. Perhaps Cecelia recognized that; instead of going on, she asked about Sirkin's plans.

"There's someone you should talk to," Lord Thornbuckle said. He opened the door, and Heris managed by the slightest margin to keep her jaw from hitting the floor. She had not expected to meet her aunt *here*. Lord Thornbuckle nodded at Admiral Serrano, and went out, closing the door behind him.

"Good to see you again, Heris."

"Sir." Formality always worked; Heris fled into it as into a thicket.

"We're off duty, both of us. You can call me Aunt Vida, or Aunt Admiral . . . but not sir."

"Yes, sir—Aunt. Vida."

"Better." Vida took one of the big leather chairs and leaned back comfortably. "You did a remarkable job in Xavier, as you well know."

"Thank you." Heris eyed her aunt, wondering what was coming.

"And on Patchcock."

"That wasn't really my doing, sir—Aunt. Lady Cecelia and the others—"

"Nonetheless. I'm very pleased with your performance. You have more than justified my confidence."

"Thank you." Heris decided there was no use not asking the question that had burned in her mind for all the time since Xavier. "You *did* put that keyhole into the database—"

"Of course." Vida grinned. "If you were smart enough to figure it out, you were smart enough to need it."

That didn't compute, in Heris's mind, but she had no time to think it over.

"I want to talk to you about the family." Vida wasn't smiling now. Heris shifted uneasily in her chair. The old anger and confusion rose like a foul tide.

"I don't," she said shortly. "If they wanted to contact me, they could have easily enough. They haven't."

Vida shook her head. "Heris, your parents made a mistake. They didn't come to your assistance instantly. I do not know their reasons; I have not asked. The only person who really needs to know is you."

"I don't—"

"Perhaps not. If you can accept that they made the wrong decision, without rancor, then you don't need to know. But if not you, then no one. You are still angry; you are still hurt. You should ask them."

"It doesn't matter," Heris said. She had no intention of asking them. She didn't care what their reasons had been. The lump in her throat grew to choking size. She tried not to look at Vida's face, or anything else.

Her aunt sighed. "If you're going to be terminally angry with anyone, be angry with me."

"Why? You're the only one who ever contacted me, who ever bothered—"

"On my orders." A flat statement, no possibility of error. Heris stared at her, seeing nothing in that face she could understand.

"What?"

"On my orders, once you had resigned." Vida paused, and gave Heris another long stare from those remarkable eyes. "You know, that surprised us all. Your resignation, coming so fast."

"Surely Admiral Sorkangh told you—"

"Afterwards, yes. Not at the time of the Board. I would

not have expected that—I would have expected you to fight back—"

Rage exploded in her head like ships in combat, vast flowering shapes of colored light. "By *myself*? With no one from the family coming to my aid? With Sorkangh against me? You weren't *there*—no one was there for me—" The fury came out of her mouth, the debris of her hopes, her career. When she ran down, shaking with rage and sorrow, her aunt sat as quietly as before.

"Heris, you're still suffering, but you aren't yet seeing clearly . . . you did not *ask* any of us. Most of us didn't know until afterwards—I didn't—and you did not ask anyone directly for help. Did you?"

She had not. She had not thought she had to. She had expected them to come to her side without being asked.

"No . . . I didn't." Had that been wrong? She had never wanted to depend on the family connection, overuse it.

"No. And of course we taught you that, early on. That was our fault, perhaps. We wanted all you youngsters to be competent in your own right, not to lean on the family name. All: not just you, Heris."

"But—"

"But you still think someone should have come. I think so, myself. Your parents could have reacted faster. As I said, I don't know why they didn't."

"If I had asked, would they have come?" Heris asked.

"I don't know that, either. Until this mess, I had no reason to suspect them of being any less committed to you than you to them. Had you?"

"No . . . we hadn't seen much of each other for some years, what with assignments, but I thought everything was fine." Heris struggled for calm, getting her voice back under control.

"You're aware that Lord Thornbuckle has some antagonism to our family?"

"Yes—he mentioned it on Sirialis, and I never did find out more."

"Did you ask?" This was becoming monotonous.

"No," Heris said.

"Ah. You know, Heris, someone who wants senior command should cultivate a lively curiosity. Technical competence, even tactical competence, isn't enough. Strategy depends on intelligence, and that depends on asking the right questions."

Heris grimaced. "I felt—uneasy. I didn't want to seem—" Her voice trailed away; she couldn't define now how she'd felt that far back.

"Disloyal?" Her aunt did not smile. "You were angry, bitter, hurt, and yet you didn't want an outsider to think you were disloyal to the family?"

"I suppose."

"You always were an idealist . . . it's one of the things I liked about you. Well, it's time you knew where all that came from." Vida took a long swallow from the drink at her side. "This gets complicated. Every family has its black sheep, or at least its less competent members. Serranos are no exception. One entire branch left the military—flunked out of the Academy, one after another—and went into business. I suppose the best way to put it is that they conducted their business affairs with the same flair as the rest of us conduct wars."

"I never knew that."

"No—like most families, we don't advertise our black sheep. Sometimes we can't even agree on who they are. But I suspect it's this branch which taught Lord Thornbuckle to distrust the name. At any rate, back to your parents—"

"It's still not right."

Now the famous tilt of the head. "Are you telling me you never made mistakes?"

"No—of course I did, but—"

"No personal mistakes, nothing that would look bad if everyone knew—" Sarcasm, when she least deserved it.

Heris glared at her aunt, hoping to shock her. "I have a lover—he was enlisted, one of my crew that was hunted by Lepescu—and when we found each other again, we—"

"Good for you," Vida said. "The burden of perfection ruins more people than you'd think. He's with the yacht?"

"Yes. Of course we haven't—"

"Of course." Vida grimaced. "Heris, I'd hoped you'd learned how to be human—how to forgive yourself for being human. Do you love him?"

"Yes . . . I do . . . but not . . ." It was going to sound crass, but she found herself unwilling to lie to this aunt, so much like Cecelia in some ways, so much like herself in others. "But not more than Fleet," she finished.

"Ah. Yes. A Serrano problem, not unique to you. When you talk to your parents again, perhaps you'll notice how little time *they've* had together in the past fifty years. One solution, it seems to me, is to encourage your friend to take a commission."

"A commission?" She had said that to Petris, but she hadn't thought it would really be possible.

"Yes, you idiot. Did it not occur to you that there's a lot of good cess to spread around after your defense of Xavier? Commissioning a civilian—even a civilian who used to be enlisted—will cause no difficulty." Vida grinned. "And I for one want to meet this paragon who overcame your resistance."

Her aunt had insisted that she must make the contact. Would they answer? And if they did, what would they say? She hoped to find that they were outsystem somewhere, a safe distance. Instead, the directory listed them not only insystem, but on the base itself. Aunt Vida's meddling, no doubt. Heris left her message in both stacks, and waited. Tried not to query her own stack every five minutes.

Finally she made herself go to lunch, then to the tailor's, for a new set of uniforms. When she came back, her desk's telltale blinked. Someone had left messages. Her heart thundered; she could hear nothing past the pulse in her ears. A long breath. She touched the controls. And there it was: a formal request for a personal meeting. Her breath caught in her throat. She couldn't. She had to.

"Heris." Her mother and father stood side by side, formally, their faces as wary as hers must be.

"Come in," she said. She couldn't bring herself to call them by name.

"Thank you for seeing us." That was her mother, as usual the spokesperson.

"I . . . talked to Aunt Vida."

A quick look passed between them, the kind of sidelong glance Heris remembered so well. Her father spoke at last. "Heris, I won't try to explain—"

She wanted to say something, but couldn't. The silence stretched, until she felt that her bones were drawn out thin as wires.

"I will," her mother said finally. "I'm not a born Serrano; I don't have to play this game." Her mother, the bronze eldest of a bronze clan, the Sunier-Lucchesi, whose roots went as far back in Fleet as any. "We heard it; we didn't believe it; we expected you to come and tell us what you wanted us to do."

"So it's my fault?" Heris managed to say it calmly.

"No," her mother said. "It is not your fault. It was our fault, for listening to the wrong advice, and for not realizing that you would not come. And saying we're sorry doesn't change it. If you want to stay angry, you can."

"That's true," said Heris. But she didn't feel angry; she felt tired. "What do you mean, wrong advice?"

"Admiral Sorkangh. He called your father, and said you were determined to work your own way out of it—that if you needed help, you'd call. We didn't know until afterwards that he'd turned."

"And then you listened to Aunt Vida, who said let me alone?"

Her father grimaced. "No, then I tried to figure out some way of killing Sorkangh without getting caught, or hurting anyone else. I told him—never mind what I told him; it's on both our records now. And I called in every family member I could find. Your Aunt Vida came up with a plan— I didn't like it, but she pointed out that I had made a royal mess already."

Heris could almost smile. She could imagine her Aunt Vida making them all squirm. She was glad.

"Did she tell you about it?" her mother asked.

"She told me that she'd ordered everyone to avoid contact once I'd resigned my commission."

"Did she tell you why?"

"No—but I guessed some of it. A Serrano she believed loyal, in a perfect position to strain blackmailers and enemy agents out of the stream . . ."

"Something like that. When you got Lepescu, she felt she'd proved her point. I didn't." Her mother grimaced. "I thought that should be the end of it; you'd earned it. But your Aunt Vida—"

Heris felt tired. "I wish—" She couldn't finish; she didn't know what she wished, except that none of this had happened.

"I'm sorry," her mother said again. "But I hope you'll forgive us, in time. If not now."

If not now, when? A family saying intended to spur reluctant youngsters to try the difficult, to achieve the impossible. Forgiveness was impossible, looked at one way—the pain was still pain, the loss was still loss. In another way . . . it had been too long already. She could tell that they had suffered too; she was not alone in that.

"I missed you," Heris said, and reached out for them. "I missed you so much—"

Vida Serrano, in uniform, behind her own desk, was back to being the admiral, full of advice for younger officers.

"If you get your mind straightened out—if you learn to ask the right questions—you'll be an admiral yourself, in a few years. As for now—you did well enough with *Vigilance* and *Paradox*. We'll see what you can do with a real battle group. I'll expect you to be ready to ship out as soon as you get *Vigilance* back out of the yards."

A battle group. *Vigilance?* A real—? She looked at her aunt, and Vida grinned, a wicked grin of delight at her niece's surprise. "You've earned that much; I can't get you a star yet, but if you handle the group the way I expect, it'll come. You'll be going straight into trouble, of course—"

"What about personnel?"

"Your lover?"

"All of them," Heris said, persisting.

"I thought I'd give you Arash Livadhi as second in command," her aunt said, ignoring her question. "That should make an interesting combination, you and Arash."

"He's senior." Heris had her doubts about Arash, even now.

"He was. You're getting a promotion, remember?"

What was the right question? Did you trust me? Did you care? Heris fumbled around in her memories of the past few years, trying to untangle what she burned to know from what her aunt would consider strategic thinking.

"How did I get that first job, with Lady Cecelia?"

"Good girl." Vida's grin widened, pure approval this time.

"That took a bit of pressure on the employment agency. I wanted you to have flexibility, a ship with decent legs, a wealthy employer with an irregular schedule. Lady Cecelia was the first one to meet those qualifications."

"Did you know her?"

"Not really. We'd met years back at a function she probably doesn't remember. That didn't matter. The other things did. And, since you're now on the right track, I won't make you drag the rest out piecemeal. Yes, it was more than blind good luck or your talented scavenger's native ability that put certain items in his way when you needed them—those military grade scans, that weapons-control upgrade. You'd earned that when you got Lepescu. I made sure Livadhi got the assignment to carry the prince, rather than Sorkangh's grandson. And yes, Koutsoudas was planted on you—and a good thing, too. Not that we didn't need to get him away from the trouble he'd brewed before it cost us his life and Livadhi's ship. You don't know yet how ticklish things were in Fleet after the abdication. Or how many holes I had to try to plug with too few resources."

"You're going to explain?" Heris said, doing her best not to let sarcasm edge her voice.

Vida smiled, and ignored the question. "As for the yacht, you can tell Lady Cecelia that the Fleet would be delighted to purchase it from her at a good price—we can always use ships like that on covert ops, and I really admire the beacon switch your technicians put in her."

"Uh . . . yes, sir." Admiral Vida Serrano was back to being entirely admiral.

"Welcome home," the admiral said, with just enough softening. "Welcome home and good hunting."

"No, I'm not 'trying to copy that Thornbuckle girl' as you put it." Raffa stared her mother down. "I don't have her flair. I don't even want her flair. But I do want my own life, and that life is with Ronnie Carruthers."

"I suppose you'll do it whatever I say," her mother said.

"Yes." Raffa waited while her mother worked it all out.

"Where are you going?"

"We're going to migrate over to the Polandre Group and take up an investor's claim."

"But Raffa—dear—you don't have to do that. It's all right about Ronnie; now that his parents and his aunt aren't feuding—"

"We want to do that. It's nothing to do with his parents or his aunt—we want our own lives, and we can have it out on the new lands." She hoped she didn't sound bitter; she wasn't bitter. Not really. But she wanted her children to have a chance to advance, without a layer of Rejuvenants over their heads, smothering them. She thought of the specs she'd seen, and found herself grinning. "It's not like it used to be," she said to her mother. "Pioneers these days have it much easier." Never mind that she and Ronnie had already decided to spend most of their money on a bigger grant, and fewer amenities. By the time her parents found out— if they ever did—she and Ronnie would have it all straightened out.

Her mother gave her a long, straight look. "You must have more of your Aunt Marta in you than I thought. Well, just be sure to keep a little back for escape if things go haywire. Your father and I didn't stay on Buriel—"

"*You* pioneered?"

"Not exactly. We tried to go out and run a subsidiary by ourselves—"

"And you think *I* take after Aunt Marta!" Raffa laughed. "Mother, you're a fraud."

"I don't want you to make our mistakes," her mother said, primly.

"We'll make our own," Raffa said.

"Keep a little back," her mother said. "But—I hope you never need it." She sounded almost wistful. "You will let us give you a good wedding, won't you?"

"As long as it's in the sculpture garden," Raffa said. "And I get to choose my own dress."

George stared moodily at the ceiling. It wasn't fair. Ronnie and Raffa running off to play pioneer over in the Polandres. Brun being mysterious and busy and having no time for old friends. Captain Serrano suddenly restored to her former rank and commanding a battle group, with no interest in helping a former Royal Aerospace Service officer transfer his commission to the regs. The clones off wherever they were. Nobody to play with.

"Moping?" George jumped; he hadn't heard his father come in.

"I feel left out," he said, and wished he hadn't. His father had that knack of extracting what you least wanted to say, fatal for many a witness.

His father came around and looked at him; he realized that his father looked older and more worn than he had seen him before. "Time to grow up, George. They have."

"It was fun," George said. He didn't like the petulance in his own voice.

"Yes. But it's over. If you want to enjoy the rest of your life, you'll have to find another way." That famous voice, which could sting like acid in a cut, or croon like a lover, spoke to him without sarcasm or contempt or anything but plain reason. He could have defended himself better against the sting or the croon.

"I don't know what to do," George said. "I'm not like Ronnie—I don't have Raffa, and Brun isn't the girl I grew up with anymore."

"You're not that boy, either, though you don't seem to know it yet. George, tell me—why didn't the clones kill you?"

George snorted. "I think I talked them to death, nearly, and it confused their circuits."

"And back on Sirialis—you influenced the men who captured you—"

"Not well enough. I got shot in the gut anyway." He shivered; whatever the experts said about the impossibility of remembering pain, he would never forget his.

"Well, then—what do you really like to do?"

"Talk," George said promptly, surprising himself. Then, more slowly, "Talk, and . . . and make people do things. Just by talking at them. Sometimes it backfires."

"Yes," his father said. "Sometimes it does, but when it works . . . you know you've just described my career."

"Law?! I wouldn't be any good at that!"

"Because you're lazy, self-indulgent, and sometimes drive people crazy?"

"That's not how I'd have put it, but yes."

"George, you've defined yourself in relation to Ronnie and Buttons and their friends for years. Rich, idle, spoiled, all that. But you're not, really. That's why they find you odious. Not because you are idle and spoiled, but because you pretend to be, and they scent it like hounds scent blood. For instance—suppose you tell me about Varioster Limited versus Transgene."

George scowled, and hesitated. It had popped into his head, but he didn't like where his father was headed. He gave a precis of the case, then said, "The only reason I know about it is that you left the brief out one time when I was trying to find your signature pad so I could get a signed excuse for class."

His father grinned. "George, most kids who want to forge a signature simply use a copy algorithm in their notepads. They don't wade through thousand-page briefs, and remember them well enough to give a cogent precis twelve years later."

"Was it that far back?" It surprised him; he'd thought it was only seven or eight, and said so.

"Not quite," his father said. "So you remember that as well, do you?" Tricked again. At least it had been by an expert. "You might not find it as boring as you think, George. After all, you've been sneaking looks at my work for years— has it been that bad?"

"Well . . . no." But law school would be. He could just imagine day after day with a cube reader.

"The thing is," his father said, "when you're in law, everyone assumes the odiousness comes from that. And you can save most of it for the courtroom."

"Law school . . ." he muttered.

"Law school is where I met your mother," his father said. "It's not all cube readers."

The ginger-haired girl he vaguely remembered from that Hunt Ball grinned at him from across the room when he went in to take the placement exam. She had certainly grown up, he thought. He had enjoyed that evening, but he hadn't seen her since he'd left Sirialis. Now—she winked at him and he winked back. *She'd* never called him odious. He looked at the exam, and realized it was full of things he actually knew something about.

Brigdis Sirkin reported to the crew lounge of the great liner, hoping her luck had changed. Lady Cecelia had found her this berth. She had said goodbye to Brun and Meharry

and the rest the day before, over in the Regular Space Service section of Rockhouse Major. Now she was committed to a civilian life. She had few regrets.

"Brigdis Sirkin?" That was the third mate, checking crew aboard. "Welcome aboard! We've heard about you; we're all glad to have you on our ship."

Here they found her exotic. Her adventures convinced them she was extraordinary, someone of exceptional courage and wit. As the weeks passed, Sirkin relaxed, finding new friends and a lot less tension. She found it hard to define the difference; the crew were all highly competent, and the standard of courtesy was as high. But the great ship had polish without an edge, like a ceremonial, a work of art and not a weapon. She liked that. She was glad to have known Meharry and Brun and the others, glad to know what protected her and her crewmates . . . but even more glad that she was no longer trying to live up to that standard.

The curtained alcove gave them privacy; the cooks gave them the best food for light-years around. They ate slowly taking the time to savor every nuance of flavor. Their tabl conversation lingered on the antics of favorite relatives: niec and nephews, for the most part. The waiter, carrying aw the remains of the fish course, commented to the kitch worker who received the tray, "It's so nice to see real qual Ladies who appreciate good food, who take the time to courteous to the staff. Just sitting there talking about t families without a care in the world. Reminds me of own auntie." Later, when they were giggling over some he didn't understand, he reported again. "Perhaps tipsy—all that champagne, you know—but they're r sweet, if you know what I mean. Perfectly harmles

The End